BAY AREA DUET SERIES COMPLETE COLLECTION

USA TODAY BESTSELLING AUTHOR

PERSEPHONE AUTUMN

BETWEEN WORDS PUBLISHING LLC

Books by Persephone Autumn

<u>Lake Lavender Series</u>

Depths Awakened

One Night Forsaken

Every Thought Taken

<u>Devotion Series</u>

Distorted Devotion

Undying Devotion

Beloved Devotion

Darkest Devotion

Sweetest Devotion

<u>Bay Area Duet Series</u>

<u>Click Duet</u>

Through the Lens

Time Exposure

<u>Inked Duet</u>

Fine Line

Love Buzz

<u>Insomniac Duet</u>

Restless Night

A Love So Bright

<u>Artist Duet</u>

Blank Canvas

Abstract Passion

<u>Novellas</u>

Reese

Penny

<u>Stone Bay Series</u>

Broken Sky—Prequel

Shattered Sun

Fractured Night

<u>**Standalone Romance Novels**</u>

Sweet Tooth

Transcendental

<u>**Poetry Collections**</u>

Ink Veins

Broken Metronome

Slipping From Existence

PUBLISHED UNDER P. AUTUMN

<u>**Standalone Non-Romance Novels**</u>

By Dawn

contents

Through the Lens

CLICK DUET
BOOK ONE

<h1 style="text-align:center">through the lens</h1>

Photography term.

Through-the-lens (TTL) metering refers to a feature of cameras whereby the intensity of light reflected from the scene is measured through the lens; as opposed to using a separate metering window or external hand-held light meter.

one

CORA

Is this real? This cannot be real.

I ball my fingers into loose fists, rub my eyes, and look ahead once more. Yep, still there. Still strutting around like a peacock fanning its tail feathers. How fortunate are we to bear witness to this monumental event? An event we could all live another day without seeing. An event I pray never repeats itself.

For the love of all that is good in this world, please make it end.

On the compact stage of our favorite bar and grill, a seventy-something grandpa wears an eighties rock band muscle tank top, ripped jeans, and faded black Converse high-tops that have seen better days. He holds the mic to his mouth, tips his head back, and belts out the words to Def Leppard's "Pour Some Sugar on Me." Some might say, *what's the big deal. Let the old man enjoy life.* And I would probably agree.

But singing is not all he is doing. Nope. Karaoke grandpa has added a little "show" to his rendition. Giving the crowd something to remember. For life.

Not ten seconds ago, he picked up his full glass of water, tipped his head back, and poured it down his chest, driving us all down wet T-shirt contest lane. The crowd whistles and eggs him on, and he eats up every cheer given. Flaunts his man chest through the wet tank. But wait, it keeps getting better. Now… Some dumbass walked up to the stage and just handed him a soft-serve ice cream cone. Since when did the bar serve…

What the hell is he…

Oh. My. God!

No he isn't. Please tell me he did not just…

My hands fly up and mask my gaping mouth. My eyes unable to do anything except stare. I shake my head, barely noticeable to anyone not at my table.

How is this happening? How is it I am here right now? This will undoubtedly be scarred into my cerebral cortex for the rest of my life. Marked in my mental scrapbook for years of reference. A tale told to grandchildren to make them laugh at their grandfather.

Not only is grandpa up on the makeshift stage, singing to the world like he is fifty years younger. Not only has he ripped off his wet T-shirt and flashed his elderly man-boobs to the cat-calling natives. Now he has taken his soft-serve vanilla and is smearing it all over his now exposed nipples. But that is not the worst of it. Nope. Not even close. Because he just brought the dripping cone to his lips and is sucking on the dairy confection as if his life depends on it.

Gag!

Somehow, I manage to break my eyes away from the geriatric porn in front of me and glance over at Shelly and Jonas. When I see that both of their expressions are equally as awestruck as mine, all I do is laugh. I have yet to figure out if we are fortunate to have seen this. Or if we are being punished for something. It's a crapshoot.

"Are you two seeing what I'm seeing?" I ask, already knowing the answer. To be honest, I want to hear their interpretation of it all. There is no way I can be the only one thinking this is nutty as hell. Karaoke Grandpa has definitely fallen off his rocker.

"I think I need to go home and bleach my eyes. Some things cannot be unseen. Some things should never *be* seen," Shelly says on a chuckle.

"Mad props to the old-timer. One, such as myself, can only hope I'm that fucking cool when I'm his age," Jonas states, an echo of pride in his voice. I giggle as he sits taller on his stool.

And when he glances my way, his sweet smile lights up his face. The one that makes the dimple on his left cheek pop. The dimple that makes me question why we are only friends. Why does that damn dimple exist? Ugh.

But deep down, I know the answer. Or at least I believe I know the answer.

Jonas and I have been friends for most of my adult life. Close to ten years. He is sexy as hell and has a heart of gold. And I know he would be there for me in a heartbeat if I needed him. But I am not so sure if he is long-term relationship material. He has had girlfriends in the past, but most of his relationships only stick for a month or two. And I want more in life than a couple months of good times.

I wish I could be one of those women. The ones who have a couple months of great sex and move on. Just go with the wind. But I am not engineered that way. Never have been, never will be.

Sometimes, I wonder why his relationships have never made it past the two-month mark. Is there an asshole side to Jonas I don't know about? Or is it the women who are assholes to him? Does the fun fizzle out at two months? Does he get bored with them? As badly as I want to ask him, I can't do that. It is none of my business, unless he wants to divulge. But still, I wonder. Often.

I laugh at Shelly and Jonas, slapping my hand on the table for good measure. "Tonight will not be forgotten anytime soon. I guarantee it."

"Word," Jonas adds.

His knee brushes mine under the table and I suddenly hear my pulse. Heat flushes my skin and dampens my palms. As much as I know I shouldn't be in a relationship with Jonas, I can't ignore the way he causes my heart to beat a little faster. The way my breathing turns a bit ragged. There is something about him. Something I have yet to pin down, but maybe one day I will figure it out. Maybe one day, my heart won't be overruled by my past.

A change of topic is needed, especially since sticky, sweet grandpa has now left the stage after his standing ovation. Bringing the brown bottle with the label peeling at the corners to my lips, I peer over at Shelly and ponder over the neutral things we can discuss. But I don't have to worry for long because she comes to my rescue.

"So, anything new or exciting happening with work?" she prompts.

Definite neutral ground. Bless you, my friend. Bless you.

"Yeah. I wrapped up a project for the parks department the other day. It was awesome to visit all the county parks and shoot pictures. I didn't realize how many parks we have in the area. Anyway, they're publishing a magazine next month and hoping to get people outdoors more."

"And why didn't you ask either of us to tag along while you were taking said photos?" Jonas shoots me with faux guilt. There is that damn dimple again.

Why am I choosing to not date him? The more I am near him, the more interaction we share, the more I ask this question. If only I had a legitimate answer before getting admitted to a psych ward.

"Next time," I mutter. "My next shoot is on Clearwater Beach, for the most part. It's an advertisement for beach attire—on the beach and off—including accessories. It will be the first time I've worked with Global Beach Magazine, which will be an amazing addition to my resume and portfolio. I'd invite you to watch, but that might be awkward. Not like visiting the park."

Jonas rests his hand over mine for the count of three, two, one. *Breathe, Cora. Breathe.*

"When does that start?" he asks as he lifts his hand and rests it beside mine.

"Next week. The first of April. The shoot is spread out over a week. Some indoors, but most on the beach. A few also taken in Dunedin. I'm excited and freaking out at the same time."

Shelly sets her fruity, pink drink on the table, but twirls the blue drink umbrella. "Why are you freaking out?"

"I have no idea. Every time I think of the shoot, I get this weird twinge in my gut. It's strange. I've never felt this way before a shoot. Maybe it's because my name will be plastered in a national magazine next to some pretty boy's face." I wince and shrug.

Snatching my beer from the table, I chug the rest and hold my bottle up, signaling to the waitress for another round. She catches my request and nods.

"But I thought you were hot for the pretty boys," Shelly teases.

I bat my eyelashes at her. "Damn! You got me."

And then we are all laughing. Yet another reason why I love hanging with Jonas and Shelly. We can say the stupidest shit and there is no judgment. We love each other for who we are and would never want anything different. That is how friendship should be—unconditional acceptance. Quirks and all.

The waitress drops off another round of drinks and I request an order of tortilla chips with salsa and guacamole. Might as well get comfortable, seeing as karaoke night started with a bang. One can only hope the next act is equally awesome. And by awesome, I mean not another rendition of geriatric porn.

"You guys want to hang tomorrow?" Shelly pipes up. "Maybe we can hit Putt-Putt and go-karts at Celebration Station. I'm feeling the need to speed past some prepubescent punks." She laughs then sips her fresh cocktail.

"I'm in," Jonas answers.

"Definitely," I say. "I'm always up for putting punks in their place."

Just as Shelly is about to screech with excitement, karaoke grandpa's competitor jumps onstage. Let's just say she is trying to up his show and is making a valiant effort. The unmistakable intro and beat of "Baby Got Back" by Sir Mix-A-Lot pours from the speaker. Every possible body part on her body is jiggling as she attempts to shake her ass.

Maybe I shouldn't have ordered food.

Dear Lord, someone save us from the hell we are being subjected to this evening. Shelly and Jonas simultaneously gape at the stage before turning to stare at me. All of us thinking the exact same thing.

"You guys want to head out?" I ask, praying one of them will relieve us all from this new form of torture.

"It's like you read my mind," Jonas states. "You want to hang somewhere else?"

It was still early in the evening and I had only had a couple drinks. I wasn't quite ready to say good night to my friends. "Yes. You want to go to another bar? Or we could hang at the house. Whichever you prefer."

Shelly pipes up. "Let's go to your place. We can stop and grab drinks on the way. Maybe watch a comedy on Netflix."

"Cool with me," I tell them both.

Bringing my beer to my lips, I swallow the remaining liquid and signal the server. When she steps up to the table, I ask her to pack my appetizer in a takeout box and bring us the check.

One more glance up at granny and I contemplate stopping at the grocery store across the street and raiding the cleaning products aisle. Is it a full moon? A new moon? Whatever celestial event is happening, it has definitely brought out the crazies tonight.

Will my eyes ever be wiped of this night? No. No they won't.

Three beers and two shots in me later, and the three of us are laughing our asses off to *Sausage Party* on Netflix. It is a toss-up between Shelly and me on who is drunker. I would suggest we flip a coin, but I don't think that will work out so well. We may have consumed equal amounts of alcohol, but her tolerance is higher than mine. Sometimes I envy her that. Either way, our inebriation is in full swing and life is good.

My eyes grow heavy and I lean more into Jonas's body with each passing second. The warmth of his skin on my bicep adds a new flush to my skin. Like the sensation of a fresh sunburn. Hot, but not unbearable.

It would be easy. Tipping my head, a little more to the right, I could kiss him. Just like that. And I want to. I really want to. But even in my tipsy/borderline drunken state, I still hesitate. I still resist the urge.

Why do I always keep us in the friend zone? What the hell is wrong with me?

Pressing more weight into his side, I inhale deeply and absorb the scent that is pure Jonas. A strange blend of sunscreen and gasoline and grease. His scent so familiar and somehow appealing. Pleasant and comforting and—

"Cora?" he cuts off my thoughts, my name spoken like a prayer on his lips.

Tipping my head back into the couch pillows, my eyes wobble to his as I half-ass smile. "Jonas?"

The air grows heavy between us. The room quieter than I remember from thirty seconds ago. It is one-hundred-percent possible Shelly fell asleep on the blankets near my feet. But I can't see her face, so there is no way to be certain.

"What are you doing?" His simple question comes out breathy.

My brows pinch together as I study his eyes. "What?"

He leans in closer, his lips inches from mine. "What are you doing?"

Was I doing something? I don't remember anything from a couple minutes ago. Having him this close, though, makes me dizzy. Dizzy with desire. Dizzy for more than his lips a breath away from mine. But I also think the alcohol is working some serious voodoo on my organs right now.

A light sheen of sweat breaks out over my skin as my stomach gurgles. I scoot forward on the couch and take a slow, measured breath. My gut groans at me again and I have a feeling everything is about to head south really quick. Or would it be north?

"I don't feel so good," I tell Jonas.

The back of his hand brushes over my forehead and I catch a blip of relief before he removes it. "Cora, you're kind of pale and clammy." He rises from the couch and extends his hand out to me. "Let me walk you to your bed. I'll grab you a cool cloth."

Slipping my hand into his, he walks me the short distance to my bedroom. As I go to sit on the bed, nausea rolls through my core and I bolt up and run for the bathroom. This will not be pretty.

Thank the angel watching over me for allowing me to make it to the porcelain throne in time. Besides the fact that I am expelling the contents of my stomach, the one takeaway from this moment… Jonas is by my side, rubbing my back and holding my hair. He really is a great guy.

two

Why can I not walk through this fucking airport without people smacking into me?

Flying is bad enough. Mix that in with LAX during the early morning and my life is a new version of hell. Some woman with a stroller smacks into my arm while the child who should be in said stroller hangs limp at her side. Literally hanging. Under normal circumstances, I might tell the woman her little girl is adorable. But circumstances aren't normal because the little girl is shrieking like a banshee. Limbs thrashing and kicking anything within reach. No doubt the entire terminal hears this girl.

Could the mom not just move out of the way and deal with her kid? Seriously. Why drag your kid around and make a show out of it? If it were my child, I would be embarrassed as hell.

"Gavin? Did you hear what I said?" Alyson asks through the phone pressed to my ear as I am about to knock some twenty-year-old prick out of the way. This whole situation is already shit. Is it everyone-get-in-Gavin's-way day?

"Can you repeat that, Alyson? There're more dicks than normal in the airport today." I speak louder than necessary, hoping the dipshit hears me and gets out of my fucking way. He peers over his shoulder, catches my expression and hustles to get out of my way.

Thank fuck.

"You should be landing in Tampa around six fifteen p.m., eastern time. I emailed the hotel details to you. Please be on your best behavior. My flight leaves in the morning tomorrow, so I'll meet up with you for dinner and we can get caught up on your itinerary."

Of all the things that come along with this crazy job, I am glad it includes Alyson. I never realized how amazing it would be to have a personal assistant/agent. When I first started this gig, I thought it would be as easy as pose, click, done. Good looks should have made it simple. Boy, was I wrong.

Dead wrong.

It has taken years, but I have finally mastered the art of angles and lighting. Knowing which way to face in different lighting. How to dip or lift my chin. How to stand so the right muscles pop for the photo. Nothing is ever as easy as it seems. But with great mentors and years of practice, confidence is on my side.

After checking my luggage, I head to the terminal for my flight. I have about twenty minutes before they allow us to begin boarding. So, while I wait, I decide to hit one of the eateries and grab a quick bite and a drink.

The moment the airline calls for us to board, my palms break out in a cold sweat. I finish off the drink and the coolness calms me a fraction as I head for the gate.

Just breathe, dude.

I have flown enough times in the last eight years to be a pro. Have racked up so many airline miles I can't redeem them quick enough. My job has taken me to some of the most amazing places, within the states and beyond. Not once have I been so nerve-wracked before boarding a plane.

So why now? What is so different about this trip?

The Bay Area is just another sunny oasis with hot chicks and tourists for days. Minus some of the landscape, it's not all that different from California. I honestly don't know why people prefer one oasis over the other. Guess it depends on if you prefer elevation or not.

I board the plane and locate my seat, throwing my carry-on in the overhead compartment. Staring out the window, my eyes zoom in on the wing of the plane, when the person I will sit beside for the next six hours bumps my elbow. I roll my eyes and shake my head.

Can people just stop knocking into me today? For the love of…

I turn to see who sits beside me and my breath catches a second. A sexy as sin blonde shifts, trying to wrangle her purse strap over her head, which seems to be caught on her necklace. What a perfect setup.

"May I?" I gesture toward her neck, offering to help separate the two.

"Please," she huffs, obviously frustrated and embarrassed with the state of what is happening.

Aiding her with the strand and strap, we free her from the entanglement. She tips her head back against the seat, inhales deeply and takes a moment to calm down. After a sigh, she turns in her seat to better face me.

"Thanks for that. As cute as this purse is, I think I'm going to get rid of it. That wasn't my first rodeo in the tangled department." She shakes her head and laughs.

"Sure thing. Glad I could help," I offer. I extend my hand to her. "I'm Gavin."

"Brandy. Nice to meet you," she says and shakes my hand. "Business or pleasure?"

"Sorry?" The way the word pleasure rolls off her tongue has me thinking of several ways I can give her exactly that. Blonde isn't generally my type, but when it's just for fun, does it really matter?

"Your trip. Is it for business or pleasure?"

Ah, yes. Generic question, generic conversation. I should be used to having meaningless conversations by now. Not like my job requires me to engage in deep, life-changing chats. Would be a nice change, though. Whatever. At least I get to sit next to someone who isn't painful on the eyes. Could be much worse.

"Business. You?"

"Pleasure. I'm meeting up with my boyfriend and a couple friends in Brandon. I was out here visiting family."

"Cool."

Nothing else comes to mind to say after learning she has a boyfriend. Automatic buzzkill. Sure, I could ask how her visit with her family went, but we don't know each other and it is none of my business. So, I don't dig.

At the mention of friends, I wonder if I will see anyone besides Micah from my teen years while I am on this trip. It will be nice to hang with Micah and catch up. I haven't been back to this part of Florida since my mom received a promotion thirteen years ago. A promotion that had us moving out of the Sunshine state and across the country to the Golden state. A move that changed my life in more ways than one.

Maybe that is what has me so on edge. The possibility.

Brandy retrieves her phone and plugs in her earbuds, essentially talk-blocking me for the entire flight. So much for having a cute blonde to distract me. Generic conversation would have been better than nothing at all. This flight will last longer than the actual flight time.

I retrieve my phone from my back pocket, open up my Spotify app and hit play, looping the playlist. Leaning my head back against the seat, I gaze out the window and let my eyes lose focus on the skyline.

Ten days. I will only be there for ten days. A week and a half. It will fly by.

What is the likelihood I will run into anyone? Run into her? Slim. One in a million.

Majority of my time there will be wrapped up in photo shoots and dinners with Alyson and the photographer. There won't be any time to do anything else. And besides, I am sure everyone has moved away. I mean, who stays in the same place they grew up? As soon as they come of age, most people move away.

But a part of me begs the universe to let me see her again. Even from a distance. See how she is. If she is with someone. Happy. What she looks like. Has she changed from the girl I knew? God, I hope there is no animosity after all these years. After everything, I hope she doesn't hate me.

The plane taxis down the runway and we are off the ground seconds later. I pinch my eyes shut and focus on the music blaring in my ears. The music blankets the roar of the engine just barely, but does nothing to mask the vibration. Or the queasiness in my gut.

Just breathe, dude. The chances are slim.

three

CORA

"Where do you want me to put this?" Erin asks as she holds up the soft umbrella reflector.

I point over to the left of a small side table. "You can set it there. The stand should be ready, if you could put it on there for me."

"You got it, boss," she jokes.

The first day Erin and I worked together, she called me boss. I told her to never dub me with such a title again. Although she has worked as my assistant, we had known each other beforehand. Erin is my friend, who just so happens to help me with my job and I compensate her. We work well together and there is no sense in ruining a good thing.

But since that first day, when our friendship added business partners, she lives to mess with me. To keep our relationship light and fun and not so work-y. So, calling me boss is her work version of sarcasm. And I love all her witty and sarcastic tendencies.

Erin fumbles with setting up the lighting while I do some test shots with my camera. I point the camera off in the distance, catching sight of a few passersby and pressing the shutter release. Pulling the camera away from my eye, I glance down at the LCD screen and view the image. The lighting is sufficient, as is the image. Hopefully, we get all the shots in before the lighting from the windows shifts and adds unnecessary shadows. Not like I can't Photoshop them out, but the less I have to adjust, the better.

As I shoot a few more test shots, the door to the banquet room opens. I continue taking a few more test shots, not looking to see the model or his agent as they shuffle into the room. I don't know much about the shoot. Just that it's a male model and he is an up-and-comer in the fashion industry.

Snap. Shot of the framed art on the wall.

I make a couple adjustments and take the same shot again. Perfect.

Setting the camera down on the table loaded with my equipment, I school my expression and put on my professional face. Just as I prepare to turn and meet my clients, a familiar voice echoes in my ears and I freeze.

A voice I haven't heard since I was sixteen-years-old.

A voice that hasn't changed in the thirteen years since I last heard it.

A voice that tortured me in my dreams for almost a decade.

Sucking in a deep breath, I turn with a huge smile plastered across my face and greet my newest client. *Should I act as if I remember him? Or not?* I am baffled as to how I should respond. I haven't dealt with a similar situation yet.

I extend my hand to the agent first, seeing as she is the reason I work with her client in the first place. "Cora Davies. It's a pleasure to meet you." My smile as tight as a fresh facelift.

"Alyson Jameson." Her overly manicured hand slides into mine, shaking it with no strength. "This is my client, Gavin Hunt."

When Alyson drops her hand from mine, I focus my attention on Gavin, offering my hand. His dark brows pinch together for half a second. Most people wouldn't catch the twitch, but I do. Not only because I am a photographer and part of my job depends on seeing beyond the superficial. But also, because I know Gavin. Intimately. And this shoot just became awkward with a capital A.

He shakes my hand, the rough contours of his skin tingle against my smooth palm. I study him a moment, our hands still connected. Not much has changed since I last saw him. Same height. Same brown-black hair, the style new—buzzed short from the base of his skull to a couple inches above his ear, the remaining hair seven or so inches long and swept to his right. His body, though… time and hard work show as evidence in the taut fabric pressed against his muscular frame. His shoulders seem broader than I remember. And his throat… I swallow just looking at it.

It is difficult to not speak with him like I knew him for years, but I do my best to maintain my businesslike persona. To present myself as the photographer the magazine chose. This is a job. Nothing more.

"Gavin, it's great to see you again. It has been far too long."

Too long didn't even begin to cover it. But no one else in the room needs to know the meaning behind my words. Or the hurt that pairs with them. I pray I have mastered my poker face by now. Because inside, I am seething. And weeping.

All of a sudden, a million questions run a marathon in my head. Except this marathon isn't on city streets, but on an old-school track. Circle after circle after circle. It makes me dizzy and breathless. My heart thumps erratically and beats against my ribcage harder than necessary. Of all the people I would be okay with not seeing again, Gavin ranked in the top three.

"Cora…" he drawls. My name, four simple letters, spills off his lips soft and wickedly. A smile kicks up the corners of his mouth, and it looks like something he flashes with frequency. It is not a personal smile and doesn't touch his eyes. Not the smile I was once overly familiar with. The smile I memorized for more than a year. Those must be reserved or nonexistent. This smile is forced and pretentious and ugly. I don't know this Gavin. Not really sure I want to, either. "Feels like it's been forever. A lifetime. I didn't know you were a photographer."

His words weren't meant to insult me, but they do. They literally feel like a slap to the cheek. *How would he know what I have been up to?* You would have to communicate with someone to know what is happening in their life. Am I right? I am tempted to say exactly that, but I somehow restrain myself. I need this shoot to go off without a hitch. The paycheck would be a great boost to my savings.

"And I didn't know you were a model. So many things have changed for us both, I'm sure." As much as I try to restrain my sarcasm, it pours out of me with ease. When it comes to Gavin, it is difficult to restrain my true feelings. With anyone else, I easily mask my emotions and go about my business. But with him, it just spills out of me. Always has.

The air around us is thick and heavy with our history. A history his agent and my assistant are unfamiliar with. A history I should put on the back burner while I am the photographer and he is the model. This is not the time or place to bring up the past. And if I am lucky, there won't be a time while he is here.

I can be the skilled photographer and focus on the task at hand. Can silence my emotions. And ignore the flutter circulating in my chest at the sight of him. Ignore the hunger building in my core at the resonance of his voice. Ignore the flashes of our past that float through my mind.

A glowing smirk lifts a corner of his lips, as if he knows he has gotten to me. As if he can read me like he did all those years ago. But he doesn't know me anymore. Doesn't know what I went through after he left. Doesn't know how much I have changed. And two can play his game.

"Mr. Hunt—" I cut the silence. "If you could please move over to the backdrop near the windows."

He cocks an eyebrow in challenge and his smirk deepens. "Sure thing, *Ms.* Davies." His emphasis on the prefix doesn't go unnoticed. Figures he would assume I am still single. Maybe I kept my name for my business. He doesn't know one way or the other. But it is irrelevant, because his assumption is correct. And that pisses me off further.

Prick.

He saunters to where I directed him and turns when his feet land on the fabric. "How do you want me?" he asks with a sultry rasp to his voice.

"Have a seat on the stool. We'll start with some headshots displaying the clothes and watch."

His smile bumps up a notch and the faint glimpse of his dimples appear. "You know, I always loved it when you bossed me around." This time, when he smiles wider, it touches his eyes. But it reeks of mischief versus genuineness.

If my eyes roll any farther back in my head, I will see the inside sutures of my skull. This is going to be a long week.

~

Three hours later, after endless banter and flirting from Gavin, I am ready to go home and drink away any thought ever including him. Drink away memories skirting on the edge of my mind. Drink myself into a stupor. Today was only three hours. But there are several days listed for the shoot, plus dinners.

Can I just request a drink from the hotel bar now?

There is no denying Gavin is gorgeous. Even more than the last time I saw him. Time has treated him kindly. Wish I could say the same for myself.

Seeing him today has stirred up so many festering emotions, bringing them to the surface. Pain and hurt I thought no longer existed or held me hostage. But the second I heard his voice; it was as if my prince returned and kissed his sleeping princess. My body stirred back to life and my heart resumed its rhythm. Hope flickered for the briefest moment for the first time in years.

But I shut that shit down. Reminding myself what he had done thirteen years earlier. Reminding myself how I felt after what he did thirteen years ago. And there is no way in hell I plan to relive that anytime soon.

Minutes ago, he and his agent strolled out and left Erin and me to clean up in awkward silence. But not before he managed to make things a little more confusing between us. He doesn't need to say or do much, just his presence put me on edge. Being close to him wasn't always like this. There wasn't always this looming tension hovering over us. But now, how can there not be?

I have this inkling to explain myself to Erin. To share fragments of my past to help her understand my behavior today. The way I acted when he came in the room is out of character for me. On more than one occasion, Erin stared at me with shock in her eyes. I maintained my expert smile and kept my voice as neutral as possible. But the tension could be cut with a knife.

But I keep my cards close. If Erin broaches the subject, I will spill my heart out to her. Until she asks, though, I won't say a word. Until she asks, I will process it all and devise a plan on how to work with him for a week. Gavin is just one of those topics I hate bringing up.

As if she can hear my thoughts.

"So… what was up with all that?" She gestures to the doors, waving her hand aimlessly.

"What do you mean?" I play coy.

She freezes and glares at me as if to say *you're shitting me, right?* Silence stretches between the two of us for minutes—her glaring at me, me ignoring her penetrating gaze. A game of cat and mouse. But the longer we stand here, the more I come to realize she is not caving until I answer. *Damnit.*

"Ugh. Gavin and I knew each other in high school," I mutter.

"And…" She draws out the single syllable and leaves it hanging like bait on a hook. She is relentless and won't give in until I hand her more information. Only I don't know how much information I want to give up. Not that I am scared to share history with my close friends. More like I am scared of what will happen to *me* when I dredge everything up.

"And we dated for years."

There, I have said it. Got it out in the open. The sour taste on my tongue turns bitter.

I haven't discussed anything relating to Gavin in so long, I am not sure if I am being relieved of a burden or gaining a new one. Shelly, and her brother Micah, are the only two people in my current life, other than my parents, who know about me and Gavin. They also know not to mention him around me.

"You know I'm going to need more to go on. Spill," Erin coaxes.

But I am not surrendering everything I have worked so hard to forget in one sitting. I don't mind sharing with her, but will do so at my own pace. And now is definitely not the time.

"Maybe later. Right now, my head is pounding. I just want to gather up all the equipment, shove it in the car, and head home. Perhaps drink enough to pass out, but not so much I will have a hangover tomorrow. Since we'll be in the blinding sun for hours."

Erin nods and collects equipment from around the room, placing it in the appropriate storage crates. A few minutes pass as we break down the set in silence. Just as I think how great it is of her to stop playing twenty questions with me, she speaks up.

"I'll drop the subject for today. But tomorrow…" She pauses for a breath. "You're catching me up on this whole Gavin-Cora history. We can do it at your place or out somewhere. Either way, you're giving it up."

I stop and stare at her, realizing she is more than just an assistant. Erin is a bestie. One I am proud to have at my side. My team. All the years of not sharing this part of me, it was for selfish reasons. All because I didn't want to rehash old wounds. Or cut new ones when hope sparkled in my eyes at remembering him.

Wounds heal, right? Sure, some leave scars. But scars don't define you; they mend you. Give you thicker skin. Show you different paths.

I am more than that small, worried, heartbroken girl. Now, I am a woman. A woman who takes no shit. Or allows anyone to trample over her heart. And gives no fucks to someone such as Gavin Hunt—a selfish asshole who didn't have the decency to try and keep his word and what we had.

He doesn't know it yet, but because of him… no one can ever knock me down. No one can take my heart captive.

No one. Not even him.

four
GAVIN

The last few hours of the shoot were a blur of confusion. I did my best to focus, but my head was all over the place. Every time Cora held the camera to her eye and peered through the lens, my skin flamed. Yes, she was doing her job, but it felt like so much more.

Thirteen years have passed since I last saw Cora. Thirteen years since I last spoke with her. And somehow, it feels like thirteen years is about to catch up with us in no time.

Just as Alyson and I prepare to leave, I ask Alyson to give me a moment. She checks her watch and nods with slight annoyance. Not sure if it is directed at me personally or the fact I am derailing her schedule. She lives and dies by schedules, but we have nothing planned after the shoot. Sure, she is just tired. It has definitely been a long day.

I walk over to Cora, her hands fidgeting with her equipment. As I step close to her, she stops but doesn't look up. Funny—or cruel—reality, we have always sensed each other's proximity. From the day I met Cora, her energy danced with mine. Her energy is my energy.

"It was good seeing you again," I mutter. For some reason, I feel the need to keep this conversation quiet from the other sets of ears in the room. Alyson knows nothing about Cora, and I don't know if Cora's assistant knows of me.

She sets the camera on the table, takes a breath, then turns to face me. A softness hazes her green eyes. "You, too." Something resides beneath her exterior. Something she doesn't want me to see. And the notion bothers me.

"You want to grab dinner? We can catch up."

Her brow furrows a moment. Eyes twitch before working to right themselves. Lips pinch then loosen. Pain dances over her face for a breath and it stabs me straight in the heart. "Maybe another time. I'm tired and I think I'll just head home for the night."

Her rejection hits me harder than I care to admit. I blink away the sting behind my eyes. "Another time," I mumble, walking away and out of the room with Alyson on my heels.

I am so fucked.

Alyson drones on about today's shoot. Talking to me as if I had never stood in front of a camera before and had millions of photos taken. Telling me which shots she thinks will be the money makers and which I could have improved. I fucking hate it when she talks to me as if I am a goddamn child. How many years have I been doing this now? A decade, or close to it. I may not hold any *Man of the Year* awards, but people know me. People respect me.

When she gets like this, I zone out. Same conversation, new shoot.

While she carries on, we step into the elevator and ride up, away from the banquet room where Cora remains. Alyson gets props for hooking me up at a luxury hotel on Clearwater Beach. This place sits on the water and I have an unobstructed view of the beach and when the sun sets. Sunsets are the ideal end to my day. Hopefully not my life.

The elevator dings and the doors slide open. We step out and walk toward my room. Alyson yammers on beside me, saying how this shoot is somewhat of a new concept for me. How the majority of my work has been modeling for romance novel covers or risqué images. Personally, I enjoy the latter.

Today started a new journey for me. I stepped foot into the world of designer clothing modeling. Modeling clothing isn't foreign to me, but it has never been for an internationally known fashion designer. This contract could take me to the next level. This contract could open up so many future opportunities.

I hold my key card against the door lock and push through the door a second later. Alyson continues sharing what the company is looking for from the week-long shoot. At this point, I listen to her. This information I need to absorb. We talk back and forth as we sit on the couch in my suite. Strategizing how to maximize this shoot.

Click. Click. I recall the camera shutter sounds from hours ago when we stepped into the banquet room.

I shake my head in an attempt to dissolve the trickling memories of earlier and try to focus on what Alyson is saying. But it is no use. An impossibility.

The moment I was within twenty feet of Cora, a hum I haven't felt in years buzzed in my veins. A buzz only one woman created. When I glanced up to locate the source, I was rendered immobile. Confusion trickled through me as my chest tightened. All I kept thinking was *I know that black hair and slender frame.*

"Gavin, are you hearing a word I'm telling you?" Alyson asks as she grabs a bottled water from the mini-fridge.

"Yeah, I'm listening." Lie. I haven't heard a damn word she has said in the last ten minutes.

The second Alyson drones on about the contract, I zone out again.

Cora's forced, tight smile flashes in my head. The way it lit up her face, but wasn't exactly how I remembered it. And I never forgot her face. Never. It may not look the same as it did all those years ago—now a touch fuller and more woman than girl—but I would know it anywhere. Know *her* anywhere. Without question.

And her demeanor. Parts of her seemed so artificial now. From the fake smile to the handshake. I expected her to shake Alyson's hand, but mine… I don't know why, but part of me hoped to hug her. Begged to feel her petite frame pressed to mine. But we are here for business, so I suppose hugs would be inappropriate. With my career, I am not one to cross certain lines, but this is Cora. It is different. We are different.

Or so I thought…

But in front of my agent and her assistant, she put on a front that we were old friends, united once again. I know things between us ended in a shitty way, but let's get real. Once upon a time, we were way more than friends. We were… everything.

And suddenly, my wallet rests much heavier in my back pocket, knowing what I have kept under my license all these years. Something not another soul knows about. Something sacred.

Throughout the shoot, I messed with her. A little banter here. A dose of flirting there. Every chance I had to say her name, I swirled it over my tongue and plastered on a smile all women swoon over. At times, it amazes me what I have gotten out of using that smile. But that smile doesn't faze Cora. Not in the slightest.

Seeing as we haven't spoken in more than a decade, I'm sure I know very little about her anymore. Even when I chat with Micah from time to time, he hasn't said much about her.

Micah is one of my closest friends. We have known each other since I was eleven and him thirteen. He also happens to be the older brother of Cora's best friend, Shelly. Not sure how close Micah is with Cora, but seeing as he never spoke about her with me, I assume not close at all. Either that or he makes sure he doesn't broach a subject as sticky as me and Cora.

Even with the time and distance apart, Cora gave me a ration of shit as if we had seen each other days ago. A few times, it was easy to think she was flirting back. Her smirk. The way she peeked around the camera a little longer than typical. The occasional cock of her brow.

She is kind of feisty now. And the thought of provoking her further turns me on.

But each time she schooled her expression, flipping her photographer persona on, all I wanted to do is fuck with her more. And she made it way too easy. Like she was secretly enjoying it. Who knows, maybe she was.

As much as I feared the possibility of seeing her during my time here, feared her reaction and my own, a new burst of excitement courses through me. Every time our eyes met, I put on a snide, panty-dropping smile, and waited for her to direct me. It was better to be a distraction than own how I really felt. Because if I own my true feelings with her eyes on me, she will know. Without a doubt, she will read every wish and regret I own.

"Mr. Hunt, if you could please move over to the backdrop near the windows."

She was all business. But I was, and am, determined to challenge her.

I used her name like a weapon, shooting it off my tongue in slow motion.

"Earth to Gavin?" Alyson waves in front of my face.

"Huh?" *Shit.* It is blatantly obvious she has caught me ignoring her. Probably didn't miss anything noteworthy. "What did you say?"

She shakes her head at me. "I said you'd better not mess this up with whatever is going on with you and the photographer."

Alyson isn't being a bitch, but the way she said *the photographer* pisses me off. As if she doesn't know or remember her name. Makes me want to grab her shoulders and shake them. Get in her face and hiss Cora's name. But I don't.

"I won't," I promise. And I mean it.

As much fun as it is messing with Cora, I won't jeopardize my contract with the magazine. It has taken me years to get to this point in my career. No way I will ruin it overnight.

But I would be a liar if I said this shoot won't be a challenge. Without a doubt, it will be the most difficult shoot of my career. It will push me to the edge mentally. Have me second-guessing my every move. Have me wondering if I am being crazy. And I have done some crazy shit.

All the back and forth between us today, I had to have made a dent in her fortress. Chipped at her armor.

"Don't make me babysit you," Alyson threatens. "I don't like being that kind of agent."

"Yeah, yeah." I hold up three fingers. "Scout's honor."

Alyson rises from the couch, smoothing her skirt. "Also, I booked a shoot with you and Layla. It's a week after we fly back to Los Angeles. Okay? I'll leave you alone for the night. Be good." She points a finger at me. "And I'll see you in the morning."

I salute her. "Yes, ma'am."

She shakes her head at me and walks out the door, taking her cloud of tension with her.

As soon as she is gone, I collapse on the couch. This week will be tough, but I don't have a choice. I made a commitment. One I have no intention of backing out on. One that will take me to the next level. Cora is an unexpected surprise, but one I can handle. I just need to apply the techniques taught to us in school. Meditation. Shaking off self-doubt. Being my own cheerleader. Clearing my thoughts of everything not pertaining to the moment.

At times, it can be taxing to separate reality from the portrayal of who you are in an advertisement. Like an actor, I have to be whoever the people want me to be. Look the part. Play the role. Make the men want to mimic me. Make the women want to date me. And with Cora being around, I suspect I will be acting a lot.

And the most straining part of this shoot—not staring at her. *Fuck.* It is incomprehensible how much I have missed her. Beyond wrong to sit there and have absolute silence between us. A lot can be said in silence, but we were not those people years ago.

But isn't that how most shoots go? The only talking occurs when the photographer gives direction or I give feedback. With her, though, it is different. The silence a heavy burden crushing my windpipe.

Click. Click.

The shutter snap will repeat in my sleep tonight. The click sounded so many times today. More than I recall from other shoots. She must have taken enough photos to fill a terabyte of memory. And if honest, I hope she keeps the photos somewhere sacred after I leave.

I wish I had current photos of her. Maybe I will snag one—or a few—before I leave. There has to be a way to sneak in a photo with my phone.

Tomorrow, we will be on the pristine sands of Clearwater Beach. The beach is one of the best parts of this trip. The sand, the sunsets, the salty air. And after everything today, I don't want to be holed up in my hotel room. I need to get out of here. As enticing as the beach is, I need some other form of release.

Reaching for my cell, I type out a new message.

> Hey bro, want to grab a bite?

MICAH

> I'm down. Where?

We pick a bar between the beach and his place and agree to meet in an hour. I riffle through my suitcase, toss the designer's pieces in the box they came out of, and head for the shower.

As the hot spray rains between my shoulder blades, I hang my head and wonder how I am going to survive after my time here. Leaving the first time was hard enough. Leaving again will be hell.

five
CORA

My purse hits the floor with a loud thump, startling Luna as she weaves between my legs. "Sorry, pretty girl."

I bend down and run a hand over her soft, black fur and she purrs in return. Scooping both hands under her belly, I lift and flip her belly-side up, doting kisses on her. She is the sweetest cat I have owned, never wanting to leave my side. She also serves as the world's best cuddle buddy.

As I land on the couch with her snuggled in my arms, my phone rings from my abandoned purse. *Ugh.* I just want to unwind and get some sleep before tomorrow. No rest for the weary.

I set Luna down and kiss her head before I snag my phone from my purse. Shelly.

"Hey, girl," I answer.

"You sound beat. Want me to let you go?"

"Long day, and no. What's up?"

"You'll never guess who's in town," she says in a rush. If we were on FaceTime right now, I would see her jumping up and down, hands flailing. That's just Shelly. A big ball of unending enthusiasm.

"Bet I can." I burst her bubble of excitement.

"Wait, wha—?" she stumbles. "How did you know?" She actually sounds bummed to not break the news to me.

I huff into the phone, wishing to escape all things related to Gavin Hunt. But as usual, everything cycles back to him. "Because he's the model I'm currently shooting."

A shriek tears through the line and I hold the phone away from my face until she stops. "Shut the fuck up. Are you serious? How weird. Or maybe not. Is it weird?"

What is she talking about? "Huh?" It is all I can say.

"You know it's not his fault he moved to California years ago. Maybe fate has found a way to bring you back together," she says, words all dreamy.

Although she has been single for some time, Shelly is adamant about the topic of love and fate and how everything happens for a reason. I have lost count of how many times she has told me I will find my Prince Charming one day soon.

While she can't see me, I roll my eyes. Fate. *What a load of bullshit.* If fate existed, things between Gavin and I wouldn't have ended how they did. He would have done more. Would have at least tried.

"I know it wasn't his fault, but he didn't even try for long. It's like he gave up or caved or moved on. Like I no longer mattered. It…" I will not fucking cry. Nope, I refuse to shed another tear over Gavin Hunt. I tip my head back and blink in rapid succession. I inhale deep and continue. "It hurt seeing him today. He acted as if nothing existed between us before. He's not the same Gavin I once knew."

"Yeah, I get that. I'm sorry if him being here is digging up old memories. But you know something?" Shelly's voice escalates in pitch the more she talks.

"What?"

"I love you," she croons, wrapping me in a virtual hug. "And we should go out and grab dinner and a couple drinks. You should be celebrating your new contract. Not worrying over Gavin or the past."

As much as I would love to lay in bed, watch reruns of *Supernatural* and eat left-over Chinese food with Luna at my side, how can I say no to Shelly. Still somewhat early, it would be nice to chat with her about how I am in emotional overload right now. Shelly's the only person who knows everything there is to know about me. She is the one person I can pour my heart out to and she won't judge me.

"I can never say no to you. Where should we go? No karaoke. I'm still having strange dreams from the last one."

Her laughter pierces the air, one I would recognize in a room full of strangers. "We can hit that Thai and sushi restaurant on Patricia. I've been craving green curry for days."

Now it is my turn to laugh. Not only does my best friend know me well, she also caters to my hankering for Asian food. I also believe I have made her as equally addicted, which warms my heart.

"Sounds good. I'll meet you there in thirty."

"Thirty," she agrees and disconnects the call.

The server sets down a plate of Pad See-Ew with tofu in front of me and I lean over and breathe deep. My mouth waters at the sweet and savory aroma and I can't wait to dive in. What is it about Asian food that makes me so damn happy? No one knows the answer—not even me—and I will die happily oblivious. Years ago, Shelly joked I must have been Asian in a former life. When she suggested it, I shrugged and continued shoveling udon noodles in my mouth.

After the server walks off, I finish my last spring roll while Shelly begins attacking her rice and chicken with green curry. A moan rips from her throat and I laugh at her lack of shame. It is one of her many qualities that makes me love her. Shelly is just one of those humans who is one-hundred-percent herself. Her candid nature refreshing.

"Good?" I inquire with a layer of sarcasm.

"Mmm. You have no idea," she mumbles around the food in her mouth.

All I can do is shake my head and laugh again. It is at the exact moment when I am shoving my noodle-packed chopsticks between my teeth that Shelly decides to ask me a question. Is that a secret rule at the dinner table? To ask people questions when it is most inconvenient? Seems the case.

"So, what was it like seeing him again?" Her question is innocent, but I almost choke on my noodles when she asks.

What was it like?

Like thirteen years vanished and I saw the first guy I fell in love with standing in front of me. My heart beat behind my rib cage as if I had locked it in a coffin and tossed the key. My heart has never thumped and thrashed so hard, so loud, so uncontrollably in my chest. I broke out in a sweat, nervous to be near him. Nervous to know if he missed me in all the ways I missed him. Nervous to know if he ever thought about me as often as I did—do—him. It was—is—terrifying.

"It was strange," I lull. I want to own my truths, but I don't know what they all are yet. How can I express emotions I don't quite understand right now? How can I express the cacophony of feelings when they're a cyclone in my skull?

Was I ecstatic? Without a doubt. Did I freak out? Definitely. I still am. Did every memory of him come sprinting to the forefront? Most of them. My favorite memories, anyway.

But it has been several years since we have seen or spoken to each other. He may look the same—with the exception of some added muscles and a semi-different hairstyle—but we are poles apart from who we once were. I can't speak for Gavin, but our breakup broke me. The loss of him made me view relationships differently.

Shelly regards me a minute, looking in my eyes and trying to read the deeper meaning I avoid speaking aloud. "No doubt. How many days is he here?"

"Not sure," I tell her. Because it is true. I have no idea how long he will stay. Part of me wants and doesn't want to know when he leaves. "But the shoot ends in seven days. Each shoot is a different location in the area. There's also a rest day scheduled. How long he's here after… I'm not asking."

She shovels a forkful of meat and rice into her mouth, nodding. When she finishes chewing, her eyes meet mine and she has her protective mask on. "Do you need me to hang around more? While you're doing the shoot, that is. Kind of like reinforcement, in case he's being an ass or you need a minute."

My heart melts at her sentiment. I have no idea what I did to garner such an amazing friend, but I love Shelly hard. No one comes to my rescue as much as she does. She protects my heart as if it were her own. And she knows I would reciprocate in a heartbeat, if need be.

"Nah. I'll be alright. I just need to keep my focus and not let my mind drift to the *what ifs* like it has before." Too often, I have thought over every possible what if. And it does nothing but give me anxiety.

"Fine. But the first time he fucks shit up, I'm kicking his ass."

Her face is dead serious, but all I respond with is a laugh. One that starts in my belly and rises quickly in my throat. The hearty laugh cathartic and exactly what I need after today. There is my Shelly. The best sidekick a friend could ask for.

"I know you will." I reach over the table and pat her shoulder. "I know you will."

People. Are. Everywhere. Surrounding and trapping me. Bodies rub against mine. Music blares so loud, hearing will be a challenge in the morning. Micah picked some bar and restaurant on North Indian Rocks Beach. I don't remember the name, nor do I care. All that matters is being out of that hotel.

What I *do* care about is personal space. And these fucking people don't seem to understand the concept. Claustrophobia has never come up as an issue, but in the last couple of days it has consumed me. I just like personal boundaries. And it seems as if everyone has forgotten what they are. Seems as if everyone is in on some massive joke to crowd me.

"You alright, man?" Micah asks when he notices me tense on my stool.

"Just a little crowded in here."

"Sorry about that. You know how it is this time of year. Spring break seems to go on till the end of April. You want to head somewhere else?"

Dragging in a breath, I answer, "No. Crowds tend to freak me out more now. You think I'd be used to crowds with my job and people doing whatever they can to catch my attention. But nope. Still don't want people in my perimeter." I draw an imaginary bubble around my body for emphasis.

Micah slaps me on the back and adds a laugh for good measure. "Some things never change." He pauses to take a swig from his beer. "How've you been, man? It's been a while since I've heard from you."

Guilt rushes through me. It had been close to six months since I last spoke with Micah. Time escaped me as life got busier. But I had known for a few months I was returning to the area. So why hadn't I messaged or called him to let him know? The answer hits me like a bulldozer and I know exactly why I didn't tell him.

Cora.

Although Micah's connection to Cora is weak at best, his sister *is* best friends with her. So, if I had told Micah, he might have shared with his sister without thinking and so on. Things would have been much worse than they were today. And the potential for Cora backing out of the magazine shoot early on was higher. Although neither of us knew we would be working together, she would have put two and two together if Micah started talking.

"Yeah, I apologize. Things have been mad busy with work. Every time I thought to reach out to you, I was in the middle of something. By the time I was free, I'd forgotten. Time got away from me." I give him a sheepish shrug.

"It's all good. Just don't do it again," he teases.

For the next two hours, we sit on stools and drink beers and share chicken wings. We catch up on what has been happening outside our work lives. At all costs, we both do a damn fine job of avoiding the topic of Cora. And although it is still early, we both agree to leave. In the time since we have come in, the bar has gone from packed to overflowing and I am at my whit's end.

Micah offers to drive me back to my hotel, rather than let me wait for an Uber. No doubt they are probably bombarded this time of year on the beach. On the short drive, we discuss getting together another few times before I leave. When he drops me at the hotel, we agree to go out night after tomorrow. And as Micah drives off, I vow to be a better friend to my best friend. Thousands of miles may divide our houses, but calls and texts and airplanes can solve those problems and I need to put in more effort.

The elevator ride is brief. Although I took a shower earlier, the sea of sweaty bodies from the bar has me jumping in the shower again.

The hot water hits my back and I brace my hands on the white tile wall in front of me and hang my head. My breath comes heavy and fast. My mind running overtime as it scans its memory bank for images of Cora. It doesn't take long. Never has. One of my favorites pops up. An image I have plucked from my memory bank numerous times when shit has gotten bad.

Her onyx black hair hugged her face like an embrace. A smile lit up her lips and curved the corners of her pale green eyes. Eyes that stole my breath every time she looked at me. Every time she got serious and told me she loved me. That she would love me forever, no matter what.

That blip in time was the week before my mom received a promotion and was transferred from Florida to California. I had only been given two weeks before my life would become something polar opposite. And like an asshole, I waited until a week before we had to leave to tell Cora. It was selfish of me, but I didn't want to ruin the last bit of time with her. I didn't want to spend our last weeks together like one of us was on our death bed and trying to complete some bucket list.

Does that still hold true? Does she still love me? After the separation—the rift—is it possible there is still a part of her that loves me? Even if the tiniest of slivers, a micro-blip in the cosmos, I will accept whatever she offers.

Does that make me a fool? Desperate? Probably. Fuck if I care.

Her face flashes across the backs of my eyelids like a movie. The way she used to smile at me and press her lips to mine. Heat radiates in my chest and I press a hand against my breastbone, suppressing the ache that slowly builds every time I allow myself to fantasize about her. And after thirteen years, the ache burns fresh.

I remember the first time she laid beneath me, her bare flesh warm and trembling against mine. I had asked her why she was shaking and she had said *because I love you so much*. I clutch my chest harder as the backs of my eyes sting.

We were so many firsts for each other. Relationship. Kiss. Love. Sexual partner. And heartbreak.

And even though I broke her heart, even though I broke every promise I made her, I will kill any man who does the same.

～

Shoving back the curtains and sliding the balcony door open, I stare out at the beach and notice how quiet it is this time of the morning. The waves break at the shoreline. Salt and a hint of shea butter linger in the air, sticking to my skin. The horizon still somewhat dark with a tinge of peach skirting between the water and sky.

Silent. Peaceful. And the perfect start to my day.

Couples holding hands. Single people with their dog. Majority of the people walking through the sand at this hour are probably residents, enjoying the beach before it is littered with tourists.

I plan to do the same.

Slipping on a pair of board shorts and a plain T-shirt, I step into my flip-flops and head for the beach. The moment my feet hit the sand, I take off my shoes and wiggle the fine grains between my toes. Beaches in California are different than those in Florida. People flock to the beach in California, but not like they do in Florida. Out west, the sand is course and damp. The water cold, even during the hottest part of the year.

But not in West Florida. Here, the sand is fine like fairy dust and as warm as a lasting hug. I rake my toes in the grains before walking to the edge of the surf. Stare at the horizon and soak in the view. *God, I have missed this place.* The warmth and smells and sounds and vibrance.

I walk along the shoreline, lost in my own head for an hour, before heading back to my room and dressing in the beach gear for today's shoot. Basically, I trade one pair of board shorts for another. The same with my shirt and shoes. Stupid, but it pays the bills.

As I walk out of my room, my phone chimes and I check to see a text from Alyson.

> Good morning. I won't be at the shoot today. Think I caught something on the plane. In bed & not doing so well.

> Sorry you feel like shit. Need me to get you anything?

> No. I called room service and they're bringing me the works. Thanks.

> Okay. Let me know if you need me to get you anything later.

> All I need is for you to take awesome photos & be on your best behavior.

> Aren't I always?

Our texts end when she sends me an eye-rolling emoji. She knows me too well. But Alyson also knows I won't ruin this for any of us. Personally, there is no doubt she loves messing with me as much as I do her. Probably the reason we work so well together.

And although Alyson lies in bed sick, an over-stretched smile tightens my cheeks. Knowing I will see Cora in less than ten minutes has my synapsis firing double time. We are scheduled to meet on the beach by the gate for the hotel patrons. If lucky, maybe today I can convince her to have dinner with me. Just me and her. Some good food and conversation. No promises. Just two people with history catching up with each other.

At least that is what I try to convince myself.

seven
CORA

It might be completely out of my way, but I leave my house early and drive to my favorite juice place in Dunedin. When I step inside, the owner is busy making an açai bowl for the only other person. I walk over to the cooler across from the bar top seating and grab my favorite juice from the shelf.

The owner promises she will be with me in a minute and I nod. I sit at the long dining table and look at the cute bohemian décor along the walls and tables. There is a small couch, chairs, and coffee table opposite the dining table. A couple times, I have come in and sat at this very table and done photo edits while enjoying one of their bowls. It can be noisy at times, but it doesn't bother me when I get in the zone.

The woman before me pays and leaves. I head for the register and am surprised when I spot my favorite bowl packed into a container and waiting for me. Setting my juice down, she bags everything and I pay.

"Thanks for remembering," I tell her. Perhaps I visit more than I realize. Guess there are worse addictions to have.

"You're welcome. Have a great one," she says and waves as I go.

I decide to drive along Edgewater and am glad I do. The sun is barely in the sky, so the hues are soft and muted and it makes for a beautiful morning and backdrop to wake up to. For me, to love photography is to love getting lost in everything. Landscape and architecture and strangers. Everything and everyone has its own beauty. My job is to locate that one angle or profile or perfect lighting and accentuate it. The job is equal parts challenging and artistic. Keeps my blood pumping and my mind churning.

I glimpse the skyline as I drive over the Memorial Causeway. If it remains a little cloudy, it will be perfect for taking photos. One less piece of equipment to lug on the beach.

Arriving at the hotel thirty minutes earlier than necessary, I park and take my breakfast to a bench by the sand. I sit and watch the surf, enjoying the quiet before all the bodies fill in the empty sand. I am two bites away from finishing when I see a familiar silhouette walking toward the hotel's guest gate on and off the beach.

Gavin.

For the love of all that is holy in this world. Some divine intervention needs to swoop down and rescue me from this man. As hard as I work to keep him at arm's length, failure takes residence in my veins. Gavin has been—and probably will always be—my one weakness. The boy who captured my heart, held it prisoner, and took it with him when he left.

Last night, for the first time in years, my sleep was shit. My mind cycled through every moment we were together. Remembering the way my skin heated when his fingers painted over my flesh. How he always found a way to touch me, even if it was only him tucking my hair behind my ear. The way his eyes held mine. As if nothing else mattered or ever would. And his smell… an odd mix of beach and pine. Nothing compared to Gavin's hypnotic scent.

All night, memories of him and us flickered through my head like an old black and white movie. And no matter how hard I tried, no matter what I did, the flashbacks wouldn't shut off. Eventually, exhaustion overtook me and I fell asleep. This was four hours ago.

Seeing him now, when he is himself and oblivious to my voyeurism, has my stomach doing somersaults. How much of Gavin is real and how much is for show? Working in an industry where you're in the limelight hardens you. Changes fragments and splinters of who you are. But in the end, how much of Gavin is still inside?

The Gavin I knew, those two perfect years, is not the same as the man walking inside the hotel. Yes, they are spitting images—time has been kind to him—but when it comes to personality… current Gavin is a douchebag. He has got an ego bigger than the state of Florida. And his general attitude could use a little love.

Parts of me want to believe it is forced; all for show. Yes, he was a bit confident when we were together, but he never displayed it in front of others like a badge of honor. Is he like this with his family? The day he acts like a dick in front of his parents is the day lightning strikes me down.

I finish the last of my bowl and toss my container and utensil in the recycling bin. Walking back to the car, I spot Erin pulling in and give her a wave. She parks near me and we start hauling equipment from our cars and into a collapsible buggy. We lock up and start walking to where we told Gavin to meet us.

Erin glances at me from the corner of her eye and her inspection weighs heavy. It is way too early for this. Too early for inquisitions and judgment. *Please don't let this be how my entire day goes.*

"Yes?"

"Nothing." She is quick to respond. "You look a little tired is all."

"Your assessment would be accurate. I had trouble sleeping last night."

If possible, she studies me harder. Her eyes narrow and her head tilts as she assesses me like a mother. "Any particular reason why?"

And seeing as I am fueled on three hours of sleep and the breakfast I just consumed, I fire off, "Oh, you know. Just another asshole I have to take pictures of." *Damn, I am feisty already.*

She stops walking and gasps, her hand flying over her mouth. "Did you just say that? Or am I hearing things?"

"Depends," I say. "What did you hear?"

She repeats my words and I hear the surprise in her tone. Yeah, today will suck. Challenging enough to be near the man who swore we would be together forever, let alone doing so on zero sleep. And zero sleep means my brain to mouth functionality does its own thing.

Fuck my life.

We approach the gate and spot Gavin. Erin waves his way and I give him a half-hearted smile. The action brief and cold and says *don't fuck with me today*. If he is able to still read me like he used to, I hope he reads me loud and clear. I don't have the time or patience for games or bullshit today.

He rises from the chair and offers to help us wheel the equipment to the beach. I happily forfeit my cart and follow in his wake as we go through the gate. After a minute of trudging through the sand, reality catches up to me.

"Hey." I tap his shoulder. "Where's your agent? Alyson, right?"

"Alyson," he confirms. "She said she's not feeling good. Thinks she caught a bug on the plane or something. She locked herself in her room and will only open the door for room service."

"That sucks. Is she okay with us still doing the shoot today?" I don't need to step on any toes. Or not follow a specific itinerary she set. In a single day, I learned the type of woman Alyson is—regimented. Organization isn't a bad quality. Just one I don't want to fuck with. Not with this shoot.

He peeks at me over his shoulder, a small, sweet smile touching his lips. A different smile than those he gave me yesterday. A smile that wakes me up further and quickens my pulse. *Fuck.*

"Yeah, it's fine. Most of the time, she stands there and hovers, checking emails and text messages. She feels obligated to be present in case something happens."

In case something happens? What does that mean?

"Like what?" I ask, my curiosity getting the best of me. If I had gotten better sleep, I probably wouldn't have asked. Maybe. Who really knows at this point.

He laughs, his body shaking from the extent of it. "One of her previous clients got a little too *involved* with things during the shoot. So now she's always on set with her clients. Either that or someone within the company."

I am still confused. I should have bought an espresso with my breakfast. "A little too involved?"

His smile glows brighter than the rising sun. "Yes. As in, unprofessional things occurred during the shoot. They were mutual, but it later caused issues."

Light bulb moment. One of her clients slept with a photographer. While they were supposed to be doing the shoot. Woah. Seriously unethical.

"Well, she doesn't have to worry about that with us," I blurt out, mentally slapping the side of my head when I realize I had spoken the words aloud and not in my head. Foot meet mouth.

When I meet his eyes, an odd sadness lingers. I don't think the solemnity shadows him because I said we won't have sex while in the middle of working. No, I assume the actual reason digs deeper. The expansive roots wrapped tightly around one another. I shake off the thought and try to focus on where to take photos.

"Here," I belt out, then apologize for my volume. "Let's work from here."

Gavin nods and walks off for a minute, his hands resting on top of his head, fingers laced together. He walks ten, twenty, thirty feet down the beach before he stops and stares out at the vacant water. His eyes don't avert. His body a sand sculpture. And for a moment, I see the Gavin I knew all those years ago. Without armor or ego. Just the man.

Erin softly touches my shoulder and startles me. "Sorry," she says. "You okay?"

I meet her eyes a second, nod and return to watching Gavin. "I'll be okay." *I hope I will be okay. Please let me be okay.*

"If you need anything at all, say the word. Even if it's a breather."

My eyes fall back on her. Erin is such a great friend and I am beyond lucky to be surrounded by so many wonderful people. I place my hand over hers. "Thanks for always being here for me. I don't say thank you often enough."

She swats the air between us. "Some things don't have to be said, but I appreciate it nonetheless."

After Gavin walks back, we discuss the various images the brand is seeking and the photos we will shoot today. I recognize the moment when Gavin slips into model-mode—the shift in his expression, his body language more exposed, the wall he erects to protect the deeper parts of himself. The way he carries himself in model-mode, it is obvious he is not a model only for the attention or the paycheck. He enjoys the end result as well as what comes along with it.

He may have been a cocky prick yesterday. He may have pressed every button under my skin. But today, Gavin flaunts an unexpected side of himself. One rawer and more appealing. One he should show more frequently when working. A side most photographers would drool over.

Is it because of Alyson's absence? Does she smother this side of him?

We take numerous shots with him in the board shorts, shirt, and flip-flops. We scroll through several of the images, hemming and hawing. After he and I are satisfied with what has been taken, we move to the next feature. Gavin in board shorts only.

Yes, I have seen Gavin naked. Yes, I understand Gavin will not be naked for the shoot. But does that halt the rapid flutter of butterflies beneath my breastbone? Nope, not one bit. Does the idea cause my breath to hitch? One-hundred-percent. Like a damn teenager again.

He kicks the shoes off, flinging them toward the cart. A small laugh erupts from his chest as he catches me ogling him, my eyes averting and coming back faster than a ping-pong ball. In my semi-awake state, there is no point in resisting what I want. Like alcohol, sleeplessness drops your inhibitions. Makes you do things your rational mind would lecture you on.

Erin giggles under her breath and I give her a *shut up* look. But as I turn to face Gavin again, he peels his shirt overhead with his back to me. As the cotton rises further up his back, I gasp and am certain he can hear it plain as day.

A tattoo inked into the flesh rests between his shoulder blades. Guessing, I would estimate it is six or seven inches wide and a foot tall. My shock isn't over the fact that Gavin has a tattoo. Not by a longshot. Really isn't too surprising, to be honest. What has me sucking in a breath is the art he selected to permanently etch into his skin.

When we were together, one of the things he always picked on me for was my love for *Lord of the Rings*. He would joke with me and tell me I couldn't watch it anymore because I knew every line and scene. I would rebut and tell him he was just jealous and wished he could be as cool as me. A nonstop banterfest over my adoration of the movies.

Now… I stare at the back of his torso, my jaw slack, tongue tasting the salty air. I rub my eyes for good measure, to check if what I am seeing is real. To make sure I'm not still sleeping. I drag my hands away and stare at his back. Yep, still there.

There it rests, in all its glory. A tattoo of the tree of Gondor, seven stars hovering above the limbs, a word in elvish above and below the tree.

As for me, I have no words.

Before I turn to see her reaction, I hear her gasp. An obvious reaction because she sees my tattoo. But I am also curious if her elvish is as good as it once was. When I peek over my shoulder and see she works to decipher the words, a smirk kicks up my lips. *She doesn't remember. Good.* It will give her something to work on while I am here.

She catches me studying her and stutters. "Wha… are you… y-you had…"

This moment will definitely get stored in my memory bank. Her lack of speech and wide-eyed ogle is absolutely adorable. "Use your words, Cora," I tease as I turn to face her.

"Shut up," she retorts. "Since when do *you* love the *Lord of the Rings* that much?" Her eyes dance obsessively over my skin and I love the fire it stirs inside of me. A flickering flame swelling to an inferno. Will she stare at me longer if I don't answer her immediately?

I shrug. "Someone I know watches it a lot. Guess it kind of stuck with me."

Like you did. I long to say the words, but resist the temptation. Not speaking my mind with her is the hardest challenge I have faced in years. Almost all of my life-challenging moments revolve around Cora. But I won't tell her that. For starters, she probably wouldn't believe me.

Her eyes dance back and forth between mine like she is reading between the lines of my soul, seeking clues to hundreds of unanswered questions. I would love nothing more than to profess my feelings to her. Tell her I never stopped loving her. Share with her the reason I didn't call or write after her last letter. A million words rest on the tip of my tongue, but I won't say them. Not now.

Because now is not the time.

When the timing is right, I will know. And when the time arrives, I will tell her everything. Confess all the fractured pieces of my soul. Spill my heart on the pavement.

As for now, I watch her and wait. Wait for her eyes to unlock from mine. For her to look down my body and absorb me. The temptation is there. Just below the surface. But her actions remain guarded and unsure. She wants to scan me head to toe, but doesn't want me to watch her observation in action.

Too fucking bad, tu es les étoiles de ma lune. We aren't kids anymore. And I enjoy as each second passes and her eyes linger. As they fight against the tide.

We are at a standoff. Pure, undiluted energy spills off her in waves. Anxious and molten and a touch of exasperation. As much as I hate making her this way, frustrating her more than turns me on.

The waves crash along the shore. Children scream in delight, ordering their parents to join them in the water. A dog barks nearby, excited for its owner to play with them.

Meanwhile, clouds pass, dimming and brightening the sky around us. Cora refuses to cave, but she forgets how well I know her. Forgets, regardless of the amount of time we have spent apart, that I can read her body like Braille. I know her tells. Know what each arch and bow and breath and flush means. Know her stubbornness and passion and strength. But I also know her weakness. A commonality we share.

When you are acquainted with another person like I am Cora, you don't forget those little snippets. They are rare gems and get tucked away for safekeeping. She may not be the woman from thirteen years ago, but some traits never vanish. They adjust with the journey.

She tries to disguise it, but I know she sighs. Know she is throwing in the towel.

Her eyes fall to my lips, lingering for a moment. Her tongue sweeps out and brushes across her lower lip. The sight sends a pang to my groin, but I control my actions and don't let her see how it affects me. How it makes me want her more.

When she leaves my lips, her eyes trace my throat in no hurry. Skirting from one shoulder, across my collarbones, and landing on the other. Her eyes drop and her body jerks in shock as a brief smirk pops on my lips.

"Like what you see?" I rasp, my voice thick with the desire my body masks.

Her eyes shoot back to mine as her mouth opens and closes and opens again. "When did you…" She points to my chest, unable to finish the question.

"Get my nipples pierced?" I finish what I assume she was going to ask.

"Yes," she sputters. "When did you do that?"

How cute is it that she flushes a scarlet resembling her cherry lips? How cute is it that she is embarrassed to ask about my nipple piercings? "A few years back."

"Oh. Huh. Well, I'm not sure how to compliment them," she mumbles.

"The same way you compliment anything else." I put on my best impression of her voice. "*Hey, Gavin. Those nipple piercings are hot.*" I bite my lip to resist laughing.

She smacks my chest, hard. "Shut up, asshole."

"Ow. I think that's going to leave a mark," I tease.

"Shit! I'm sorry. Damnit. Now we'll have to wait. Can't have red handprints on your chest in the photos." She places a finger over her lips. "Although, I could just Photoshop it out." She shrugs, noncommittal.

"You're the one running the show. If you want to take handprint photos, then that's what we'll do."

She cocks her head to the side, a curious look about her. I may be able to still read her, but she has lost that finesse with me. I have had years to learn how to plaster on a different face. To pretend to be someone I am not. That is the thing with actors and models, we are taught how to be someone else. To be whoever the camera or customer is supposed to see. We live different lives and portray different personalities daily.

We are a façade.

"Since the light has shifted, let's move over there." She points over to a patch of seagrass. "Different light, different background, different reach."

"You're the boss." In more ways than one.

Time becomes this nonexistent entity when I am near Cora. Hours pass as if time is a delusion. Tons of pictures get taken in various places along this stretch of the beach. As nervous as I originally was for this campaign, posing for the camera while Cora looks through the lens gives me an ease I haven't felt in a long time. Being in her presence has never felt more right.

Like coming home. *My home.*

I help her and Erin put everything in their carts, hauling Cora's to her car after. Everything gets unloaded into the cars and we wave goodbye to Erin as she drives away. Erin is a sweet girl—timid but a devoted friend to Cora. And for a time today, I forgot she was on the beach with us. Obviously, she assists Cora with her shoots, but most of the time she hangs on the sidelines, quiet.

After she drives out of the lot, I face Cora and my fingers brush against hers. Flickers spark from our minor touch and I feel compelled to touch her again. More. Trace my fingers along her forearm, her bicep, her collarbone. My eyes flit to her throat as she swallows hard. I finish the ascent, her eyes riveted to mine.

Our eyes have a silent standoff. Questions appear as quickly as they disappear.

"Have dinner with me," I state.

Last time I asked, she said no. Now I want it more like a command, but not in a *you must do this* way. More of a *just agree with me* way. I want her to want to say yes.

The motion is subtle, but she shakes her head as she drops her chin and breaks eye contact. "I can't. You know I can't. It goes against the contract we've both signed."

I stare down at my feet and hers, shaking my head. "Bullshit," I mutter.

My irritation isn't directed at her, more the situation. But I bet she takes it as the former. The last thing I am is upset with her. She has to know this. Right?

"You know we can't," she whispers, refusing to look at me.

But I need to see her eyes. Need to know what she is really thinking. Her eyes will tell me all the words her mouth refuses to speak.

Tucking a finger under her chin, I lift and bring her eyes back to mine. She has told me no twice, but her eyes tell another story. They speak of her hesitation and fear. Worried if she says yes that I will hurt her again. And I want to reassure her that will never happen again, but how can I? Words are useless. Especially with our past. Only my actions will supersede my words.

Plus, the evidence is stacked against us.

She lives here. I live thousands of miles across the country. Her life is here. My life is out west.

With reluctance, I lean in close to her ear and whisper, "True, but you don't know how much I want to."

And with that, I step back, drop my hand, and walk back to the hotel. To my empty hotel room. My soundless existence. My life without her.

nine
CORA

Sleeplessness has become a plague since Gavin walked through those banquet doors two days ago. When my head hit the pillow last night, my body melted against the sheets as exhaustion radiated in my bones. Luna curled up beside me, her purr fading as she drifted to sleep.

With heavy eyes, my lids closed. Just as my body began hitting solid sleep, my phone wailed on my dresser. I shot up as worry flooded me. My *Do Not Disturb* mode set and only select people could break through the function.

When I answered the phone in a groggy voice, Shelly instantly apologized. She had called on a whim, wanting to hang out but not knowing I had gone to bed early. I asked her why she really called and she told me we could talk about it in the morning.

But I was exhausted and angry and allowed my frustrations to sneak out and snap at her. Two minutes of apology later—and zero information as to why she called—and we agreed to talk tomorrow. Several times, she had done this to me and the conversation consisted of nothing significant. But I was a good friend and I let it slide.

Unfortunate for me, sleep didn't creep up as easily after as it did before her disruption.

I laid in my bed until two-thirty in the morning, thinking about the rough texture of Gavin's hands when they were on me earlier. And the words he whispered to me, I listened to them on a loop in my head, trying to decipher what exactly he was saying.

Were his words genuine? Did he just say those things to get into my pants? Or is it all a load of bullshit?

I felt clueless, and the lack of sleep didn't help the situation. There had to be some hidden meaning behind it. There just had to be. In the wee hours of the morning, I convinced myself Gavin had an ulterior motive.

After hours of watching the ceiling fan spin circles above me, my body relaxed enough and I fell asleep.

My alarm startles me awake at six forty-five and I slap the beast, groaning and cursing the universe. A little more than four hours of sleep won't get me far today. Not after having five and a half the night before.

I cannot live like this. Anyone glancing my way today will surely do a double take—because my resemblance to a zombie will be uncanny—and whisper behind my back. Honestly, I give no fucks.

Luna paws at my face, meowing and purring. "At least one of us gets sleep," I grumble as I run a hand over her soft fur.

She rubs her face along my cheek, silently asking me to get up and give her breakfast. Shoving the comforter to my waist, I huff and scoot up to a sitting position. Luna meows her excitement, jumps off the bed, and trots out of the bedroom. I follow behind her, walking half alert to the kitchen. Thankfully, this part of the morning routine requires no brainpower.

One scoop of food and a few pets later, Luna purrs like a champ while she eats. I wish my morning could be so simple. Wake up whenever, disturb my parental, make them feed me, then go about my day. If only…

I head for the bathroom and jerk back when I see myself in the mirror.

Hot. Fucking. Mess.

A hot shower and a smear of makeup can only do so much. By the looks of it, I need a couple bottles of concealer. Fingers crossed I can perform miracles and mask the dark half-moons under my eyes. *Lord, help me.*

After my shower, I dress and do my makeup, adding more concealer than normal. Not two bottles worth, but enough to feel like I now have three additional layers of skin. I snag my phone from the charger and sift through my notifications while I eat a quick breakfast.

One of the first alerts I see… an email from Alyson Jameson, Gavin's agent. Emails in the middle of a shoot gives me hives. Especially after the comment Gavin made yesterday about one of Alyson's prior clients.

My finger taps on the notification and my email opens. Eyes scanning the email, I read the message twice, making sure I read and decipher it accurately.

Ms. Davies,

I would like to extend a personal thank you for your time. Sorry I missed yesterday's photo shoot due to circumstances I couldn't prevent. Today is a new day.

Tonight, we would like to sit down with you and talk about the remaining days. Please join us for dinner at the Island Way Grill at six thirty p.m.

Cordially,
Alyson Jameson

Why is she calling a dinner meeting to discuss the photo shoot? Seems odd. The itinerary is written and has been reviewed countless times before this week. By myself, the agent, and the company.

Shit.

Did she see me and Gavin last night in the parking lot? Not that there was anything noteworthy. Nothing inappropriate or unprofessional occurred. But that is the only possible reason I can think of as to why she is requesting I meet with them for dinner.

Taking my remaining breakfast to the garbage can, I scrape the last few bites into the bag. At least I had eaten the majority of the food before the taste turned bitter on my tongue. As long as it stays down, everything will be alright.

I do a few last-minute checks in the house before grabbing my purse and heading to my car. My head in a fog, a list of scenarios running rampant in my head as to why we are having a dinner meeting. The distraction gets the best of me and before I realize what is happening, I trip over an uneven paver and fall face-first into the grass. I turn my head and grimace at the paver I have been meaning to fix for months but have ignored.

"Shit," I curse into the wind.

It is my fault, I recognize this. But it doesn't make it hurt less.

What I need to do is focus. Quit worrying over *what if* and pay attention to *what is.* And right now, my sole focus is this photo shoot. Not the man whose picture I take this week. This is my job, my livelihood. The only thing that will remain constant when he leaves again. Because he will leave again.

~

Thirty minutes later, I wind through the two-lane road inside Sand Key Park. The sun hasn't been up long, which is why the park remains quiet. None of the locals, or spring breakers, have arrived yet. But within an hour or two, this place will be inundated with exposed flesh and sunscreen.

Driving past a few covered shelters, I glimpse the birds and squirrels as they peck at the semi-scraped BBQ grills in hopes they will find a morsel. Half a minute later, the road winds left and I near more shelters, restrooms, and the beach access parking. This park is the perfect mix of park-life and beach-life. And makes an excellent backdrop for any outdoor photo shoot in the area.

I park the car and feed the meter station. Leaving my equipment in the car, I walk down the path leading to the beach and look for potential places to work today. Sitting on a boulder-sized rock, I stare out at the water and get lost for a moment.

Although my job takes me to various locations, I never have the time to stop and enjoy where I am. The beach is great at times—in the early morning or late evening. But I love wandering in the parks and nature preserves. There is something magical about being in the thick of nature. Disconnecting from life and reconnecting with yourself. Forgetting about social media or texts or all the distractions and simply focusing on you.

And in my zoned-out mindset, I recall the occasions when Gavin and I would play-bicker over the beach versus the park. How he stated the beach was superior because of sunsets (on our coast) and sunrises (the east coast). My rebuttal consisted of how the sunlight filtered through the trees and the connection with the earth. We debated over it for hours before deciding it didn't matter.

Spotting a few places, I head back to the car and wait for Erin to arrive. As I take out the last few things I will need, I hear a car and look up. Erin waves at me as she parks in the space beside me.

"Morning," she hollers as she gets out of the car. "Present!"

I am momentarily confused until I see her retrieve and then hand me an oversized iced coconut milk matcha latte and a chocolate croissant from a local bakery.

Swooning at the treats, I kiss her cheek and snatch them from her. "Have I told you how much I love you?" I ask as I bite into the sweet pastry and moan.

Two seconds later, I regret that moan. Because that is the exact moment Gavin walks up behind me, rests his hands on my hips, and scares the shit out of me.

"That's a sound I haven't heard in years," he says then smirks.

Almost dropping my drink, I whip around and glare at him. "JFC, Gavin. You scared the bejesus out of me."

He laughs before asking, "JFC?"

Erin shakes her head and answers his question, noticing how I am hunched over and still trying to catch my breath. "It stands for Jesus fucking Christ. She uses the acronym in public, so she doesn't offend anyone."

"Ah," he lilts. "Still so considerate of everyone else. Good to see the good qualities haven't changed."

Briefly, I want to ask what other qualities he remembers. Or consider good? But I opt not to. The last thing I need after a second night of shitty sleep is a trip down memory lane. Because memory lane when you're not altogether there is a dangerous setup.

Once I locate my voice, I scold him. "Don't do that again! You know how much I don't like people sneaking up on me."

His smile is subtle, falling away as quickly as it appears. His actions were intentional and got the result he was hoping for, that much I read from his smirk. "I can't make any promises, but I'll try." Great, now Gavin plans to use my quirks against me.

I look around the lot, expecting to see Alyson. Although she spends a great deal of time on her phone, she seems the type to be involved. Especially after receiving her email earlier. But she is nowhere in sight. "Where's your agent?"

Gavin gazes out toward the beach, his sunglasses shielding his eyes from mine. "She'll be here soon. After yesterday, she's taking her time waking up today. Says she may have had a twenty-four-hour bug or food poisoning. She's not sure, but doesn't want to run full force this morning."

I let Erin know the three places I want to be sure we shoot today. We take a few minutes to prioritize the order, guaranteeing the best shots with the least amount of beachgoers, and how to use the natural lighting to our advantage in each spot.

When we finish talking strategy, I glance around the lot again and something dawns on me. "Gavin, how did you get here?"

"I walked," he replies flatly. As if it should be obvious. But for all I know, he could have gotten an Uber and let them drop him off at the entrance of the park.

"*Over the bridge?* The walk is long enough, but that incline is ridiculous." Walking the distance probably wasn't too bad. It was maybe three miles. But with the traffic, the tourists, and the bridge incline, I would have fallen over by now. Not to mention the mix of humidity and sweat.

As if he can hear my thoughts, a smile perches on his lips. "I've hiked worse trails in Cali. I didn't even break a sweat. Should give it a try sometime."

Shrugging him off, I face Erin as we toss everything in one cart today. Today's shoot should be easier and less obstructed than yesterday.

As I reach for the cart handle, Gavin does also. Our fingers touch for two breaths, and that old familiar current buzzes up my arms and slithers directly to my chest. Warm and comforting and libidinous. I yank mine away and try not to think about why my body is reacting to his. After everything that happened and how much time has passed, no part of me should be thrilled or eager or accepting. If anything, his touch should garner loss and heartbreak and depression.

He laughs at me, gestures with his other hand in front of him. "Lead the way, boss."

"Shouldn't we wait for Alyson?" I ask. Definitely don't need his agent pissed because we didn't wait for her arrival.

"When we get to wherever, I'll text her. Don't worry about it," Gavin says breezily.

But therein lies the problem... I am worried about it.

Ten
GAVIN

Being near Cora intoxicates me. After so many years apart, and seeing her for hours each day since I arrived, it has been a challenge to feign my feelings. If I thought leaving her the first time was difficult, this time will be a hundred times worse. If not more.

But what if it didn't have to be that way? What if we didn't have to go our separate ways after the photo shoot?

Both our careers allow flexibility. And I am sure she travels for work as much as I do. So why couldn't things be different now? Our circumstances are not what they were thirteen years ago. We are no longer children, forced to go where our family takes us. We are adults, and we decide how to run our lives.

So why can we not make this work? Why can we not give *us* another shot?

I want to tell her this. Tell her I would like—after this shoot is over—to try and get back to where we were. Although we are no longer the same people we once were, my feelings for her have never waned. If anything, they have only amplified over time, not revealing themselves until I prepared to board that plane in Los Angeles.

We stand near a jetty of rocks. Cora and Erin mess with cameras and equipment as they prep for the shoot. Knowing they don't need assistance from me, I wander toward the water. Silent and deep in thought.

"You okay?" Cora asks before I step out of earshot.

I peek over my shoulder at her, subtly smile, and nod. "Yeah, I'm good."

After about fifteen feet, I stop and stare out at the Gulf. The water crashes against the rocks and sand in choppy, small waves. Salt absorbs the humidity and dampens my skin. Seaweed and the earthy scent of sand permeate my nose. The rising sun warms my exposed arms and legs. And I am thankful this time of year isn't scorching, but the heat will be here soon enough. That is one thing I don't miss —the heat. Sure, California gets hot, but it's not equivalent to Florida and neither is the humidity.

I get lost in my thoughts, working to clear my head, when flip-flops smack in the sand behind me. But I don't turn toward the sound. Instead, I close my eyes and imagine what it would be like to be here with her without our jobs in the mix. To slip my fingers between hers and walk hand in hand down the beach. To watch the sunset together and talk about everything we have missed about each other. And kiss her lips for the first time in forever. To simply just exist with her at my side.

Absolute perfection.

Warm, delicate fingers brush down my bicep, stopping at my elbow. I stop breathing.

"Gavin," she whispers. "We're ready when you are. Take your time."

I glance over my shoulder at her and give a small smile. "I'll be just a second," I rasp, my voice rattled with emotion. I swallow, aiming to moisten my suddenly dry throat. As much moisture as there is in the air, you would think there is no possible way to be parched.

She nods and I watch as she walks back over to where Erin stands. They talk quietly and I am unable to hear them over the waves hitting the rocks. When I start walking their way, I catch how Cora peeks up at me then looks away. A step later, Erin mimics her. Interesting.

I conclude with this minor detail they're talking about me. And as soon as I reach them, they both fall silent. Yep, they were most definitely gossiping about me. The idea does strange things to me. Twists my stomach in heart-shaped knots. Alters my breathing pattern into an odd staccato. Adds a new layer of sweat beneath my salty, humid skin. Makes my fingers fidget enough that I want to shove them in my pockets. Pockets I don't have today.

Cora's eyes refuse to meet mine. If honest with myself, I would venture to guess she is avoiding eye contact on purpose. But her avoidance isn't cold. It's as if she donned a new suit of armor, the type designed for the sole purpose of protecting one's heart. Her heart. The same heart I shattered into a million shards. And another blade stabs me for what I did to her. What I could have fixed if I had the balls to do it.

My heart beats so violently, as if it's trying to rip its way out of my chest. But the pericardium encasing my heart holds it back, restrains me, as hers does the same. I have to keep reminding myself, I am the reason for her walls. I am the reason she keeps telling me no. But I also hope to be the reason those walls come down.

We are ten minutes into the shoot when Alyson approaches. For someone who said she was on death's door yesterday, she looks a few shades tanner. Maybe it's the white summer apparel she wears, making her skin pop against the stark color. Or maybe she wanted to enjoy a little downtime while here, knowing she could trust me to do the right thing.

No matter. Neither scenario bothers me. Just glad she is okay. Alyson may be the bridezilla version of a talent agent, but I have known her years and still care about her as a person.

We finish up shooting near the rocks, then spend an hour snapping photos by seagrasses. The shoot wraps after we take numerous photos on a path resembling a pier in the sand. Cora takes photos from several different angles and I honestly cannot wait to see the end results.

Erin packs a few things into the cart when I approach Cora. "So, I'll see you at six-thirty?"

She checks her watch, noting our dinner is a little more than three hours from now. "Yes, I'll be there. I let Alyson know earlier."

Right, Alyson. I ignore the idea of Alyson disrupting dinner and change the topic.

"Do you need help?" I point to the cart.

"No, I'm good. Thanks, though."

We all shuffle back to the cars. And although I walked here this morning, the temperature is much warmer now and I don't want to spend over an hour with the heat beating down on me. I ask Alyson for a ride back. She concedes and we hop in the rental after saying goodbye to Cora and Erin.

We are out of the park and turning off the bridge when Alyson turns down the radio, muting the local rock station. "So, what's the plan for tonight?"

I peer over at her, her eyes glued to the road as she watches for pedestrians. "Not sure I understand the question," I answer. I have an idea of where this is headed, but I won't put words in her mouth or give her fuel for the fire.

Stopped at a red light for Hamden Drive, she faces me a second and then returns her eyes to the street. "The dinner *meeting*." I don't miss the way she emphasizes the word meeting. Her tone mirroring a bad taste on her tongue. Yep. Just as I suspected.

"I thought we already discussed this. I really don't feel like repeating myself," I clip.

She turns onto Hamden and we wade through traffic for the next twenty minutes. Not another word passes between us and the silence leans more toward uncomfortable than not.

Once she parks the car, we head into the hotel. I press the call button for the elevator and notice her slight fidget as we wait.

Is she nervous? Why the hell would she be nervous?

"You okay?" I ask as the elevator car arrives and we step in.

We press the buttons for our respective floors and the doors close. Once we are in the confines of the elevator, she answers, "I'm fine. Just…"

I hold up a hand, stopping her from continuing. Already aware of what she is going to say. She is warning me. Telling me to *be on my best behavior*. As if I am a fucking child. As if I am her former client who liked to stick his dick in anything with a hole. I understand her role in our business relationship, but she needs to give me some slack. She needs to trust me.

The elevator pings for her floor and she hesitates a moment. A second later, she steps out and faces me. "Enjoy your dinner, Gavin."

I nod, a snide smile on my face. *Thanks, I will.*

~

Searching through my memory, I cannot recall a time I remember being as nervous as I am right now. It has been ten minutes since the host seated me. Eight minutes since the server came to the table, pouring two glasses of ice water and asking if I would prefer something else to drink. Five minutes since I picked up the menu, scanned the options but didn't read a single word of it.

But none of that matters. None of it.

As I twist and untwist the cloth napkin in my lap, the only thing that matters is standing at the host podium. She is utter perfection. And I am second-guessing this whole situation I masterminded.

While she waits for the host to return and direct her to the table, I sit in silence and watch her. Her silky, straight hair grazes the tops of her shoulders. The inky black strands parted off-center, the side with less hair tucked behind her ear. The other side hangs straight and blankets half of her cheek.

God, I miss running my fingers through her hair.

She bounces from one leg to the other as she waits, her bare calves accentuated by the black chunky-heeled Mary Jane's she wears. My eyes stroll up the length of her body, pausing and relishing on the dress that stops just above her knees. It hugs her body like a glove. Matching her hair and shoes, it's black in color but embellished with large rivets.

This is my Cora. The girl I knew all those years ago. The girl I fell in love with. The woman I still love.

Regardless of how much time has passed, she still manages to keep the root of who she is alive. And although she dresses as expected for her career, she hasn't abandoned who she is at heart.

The host returns to the podium and they exchange words, her smile lighting up the room before he turns to walk her to the table. Should I keep my eyes on her? Or should I avert my gaze and play it cool? As if I wait for her arrival disinterested.

The napkin rubs against my palms as I wring the cloth tighter. When she sees me—and only me—her brows scrunch in question. She stands ten feet from the table when a bead of sweat rolls down the side of my neck. Five feet when I swallow the boulder in my throat.

I can do this.

"Hey," I stammer as she sits, the host unfolding her napkin and offering to place it in her lap.

Once the host walks away, she looks around the room before circling back to me. "Hi," she says. "Where's Alyson?"

I don't want to lie to her, but I fear what she will do when I tell her the truth. If I ever want anything more with her again, I can't lie. Honesty is essential. No matter the consequences.

"Not sure. She's doing her own thing. Exploring the area and whatnot."

I mentally prepare for the backlash. The anger. For her to get up and stomp off and not talk to me again. Because she has to be upset at the fact that I coordinated a dinner with her and made her believe it was a meeting.

My eyes dart between hers, watching her expression and waiting for the fire that is bound to blaze at any moment. But I don't see anger. Confusion still paints lines on her forehead, her eyes pinching at the corners.

"So, there's no meeting?"

"Sorry to disappoint," I tell her.

Her shoulders drop as she exhales a deep breath. *Was the idea of having a meeting a concern for her?* I hadn't read the email Alyson sent Cora, but I told her to make certain it was vague. Had it been so vague she was concerned for her job? *Shit.*

"You okay?" I ask.

"Yeah. I've just been pondering over why we were having a meeting. Everything has been laid out since the beginning, so I wasn't sure if something had changed. I'm relieved everything's good." She takes a sip of her water, sets the glass down, and then points her finger at me. "You, on the other hand, I'm a little peeved at."

I knew I wouldn't be let off the hook so easily, but I feign innocence for shiggles. "Me? What did I do?" I press a hand against my chest and pop my mouth open in mock horror.

"Please," she drawls out the word, lacing it with sarcasm and making me smile. "You've asked me to have dinner with you twice. Both times I've told you no. So instead of hearing a third rejection, you tell your *I'll-kiss-your-ass-every-day-of-the-week* agent to orchestrate a phony dinner meeting and not be at said meeting. Am I missing anything?"

Her spunk and tenacity spark a thrill in my chest, a fire I haven't felt in years. If anything, her spunk seems to have grown. I would give up everything to keep our fire burning. To keep her.

"You kept saying no. How else am I supposed to get you to have dinner with me?" I joke.

She rolls her eyes. "I don't know, maybe ask another time or two. I would've caved."

That's an admission I wasn't expecting. *She would have given in? She would have said yes?* This adds a whole new layer to our already complicated situation. I open my mouth to respond, but have absolutely no idea what to say. So, I close my mouth and simply stare at her awestruck.

"Yes. Eventually I would have said yes," she admits.

Wait… what? "Did I just say that out loud?"

"If you mean, *she would have said yes?* Then yes, you said it out loud."

Fuck my head for not operating at full capacity.

"Well, I'm humiliated," I tell her, heat crawling up my neck and scorching my face. I pick up my water and down half the glass.

"Gavin…" she says my name like it's her favorite, and not, at the same time. "I need this contract. This is huge for me." Her words are a plea for understanding. "I can't risk messing it up. This shoot will be the most valuable item on my future resume. When future clients see that I've done a shoot for Global Beach Magazine, it'll push me to the next level. Open doors I've dreamed about for years."

I stare at the empty white plate in front of me, nodding in realization. Me asking her to dinner could royally screw her career. The contract we each signed explicitly stated no fraternization between the model and photographer. And my selfishness could fuck that up for her. "Sorry," I whisper.

She reaches over and places her hand on mine. The heat from her skin penetrates mine, sending a ripple of emotions from my fingertips to my core. I have no idea how I survived the last thirteen years without her. Without her touch, without her embrace, without her lips on mine.

"Don't apologize. I just need you to understand. This career is my life and I have to be careful not to jeopardize it," Cora states as her forehead scrunches.

"I get it. Things are somewhat the same for me. Sure, I could justify us having dinner together as being old friends, but I know it's more than that. At least it is for me."

Cora opens her mouth to respond, but is cut off when the server sidles up beside the table and asks for our drink orders. We order drinks, telling the server we need a few more minutes before ordering our meals.

The moment he walks away, I catch her watching me. Her green eyes soft and caring. She doesn't say a word. Doesn't have to. We lock eyes for twenty rapid beats of my heart before my eyes break away first.

I am so fucked.

"We should probably decide what we're eating before the server returns," I tell her.

With a nod, she removes her hand from mine and picks up her menu. The heat she ignited minutes ago… it evaporates the second her skin leaves mine.

And now, I will do whatever necessary to have it again.

After the server takes our dinner order, Gavin and I fall into comfortable conversation. Although we had once known everything about each other, there is so much we don't know now. We spend the time, before our dinner arrives, playing twenty questions.

I ask him about California. What he likes and dislikes. His favorite places there. Where else he has traveled for work. What he does when he isn't working.

As challenging as it is, I do my best to steer clear of the topic of him leaving. The first time as well as the next time. It's inevitable he will leave again. And as much as I hate the idea of him leaving, I remind myself of this regularly. His home is thousands of miles from here. Everything he has is there—family, career, friends— waiting for him to return.

Another topic I dare not mention… relationship status. His or my own.

The way he has acted around me, I am unsure how to digest it all. Is it just old feelings coming to the surface because he is here again? Does he act like this with other women photographers? Or women of interest in general? Is he a player? Is he playing me?

But the biggest of them all… does he have someone waiting in California for his return?

After all these years, there is no way Gavin is single. It isn't possible. Yes, he is busy with his career. But a busy career doesn't equal single status. Not with his good looks.

My endless mental list of questions is disrupted when the server sets a plate of coconut shrimp and coconut almond rice in front of me. I lean over the plate and inhale the delicious aroma, moaning my delight.

Gavin laughs, "Now that's a sound I haven't heard in a long time. Not quite the same as your breakfast today." He gazes at me with a tenderness I haven't seen in a long time. A tenderness I am all too familiar with. Hummingbirds take flight in my chest, flapping their wings beneath my sternum and causing palpitations.

I play it off and swat him with my napkin. "Shut up," I say with a giggle.

We eat and laugh and share great conversation over dinner. Being here with Gavin feels normal. Natural. When we finish eating, he asks if I will meet him at an ice cream shop across from his hotel. Without hesitation, I tell him yes.

Tonight has been fun. It has been a long time since I have been this relaxed and more myself. As if a part of me has returned with Gavin here. I miss that part of myself. The carefree, jubilant, and eccentric girl. He has been the only person who loved every side of me. And the only person I have exposed so much of myself to.

When he moved away, a slice of me went with him. The piece of me reserved only for him. The piece that feels as if it has returned home.

We stroll down Mandalay Avenue, hands clasped while he eats a cone topped with cookie dough ice cream and mine topped with mint avalanche. Our hands swing between us, our lips silent as we consume our confections.

Simple moments like this are ones I will never forget. Memories stashed away for the days when he is gone. Memories of all the wonderful times we have shared.

We don't need to say anything. We don't have to do anything. As long as it is just us, everything in life is perfect. Our time apart resides in some nether region of the universe.

At a crosswalk, we wait for the traffic to stop and move to the beachside of the street. He leads us down one of the small side streets and toward a public access point for the beach. As he pops the last of his cone in his mouth, he bends and begins removing his shoes.

"Will you walk with me?" he asks as he stands upright. His love for the beach hasn't vanished over the years. He was lucky his mom's promotion led them to another coastal state. If Gavin didn't have the beach, I don't think he would be whole. Not sure if it's the sand or the water or the salty air, but Gavin was born to be near a beach.

Part of me wants to give him a hard time and say *isn't that what we've been doing?* But I stop myself. It's one thing to weave in and out of people on a busy, pedestrian-loaded street. It is completely different to step onto the fine-grained beach, barefoot, and walk in the dark along the surf holding someone's hand. Though the beach may not be pitch black, it's dark enough to make the level of intimacy go from zero to one hundred in seconds.

He studies my face, waiting for me to answer. I take the last bite of my cone, buying myself a few more seconds. I reach forward and take his hand again, squeeze it gently and nod. Before I bend down to remove my shoes, I catch a glimpse of the smile I remember. The smile that flashes in my memories. The smile that lured me in when I was fourteen.

∾

I park in my driveway and grab my purse and shoes from the passenger seat before getting out. My thoughts swim and swirl and blend together. Old memories of Gavin and me. Happy memories. Memories I will never forget.

Once inside, I add food to Luna's bowl and pet her a few times before heading for my bedroom. I toss my shoes in the closet and strip off my dress, heading for the shower. The walk on the beach with Gavin was wonderful, but I need to wash the sticky beach air and sand off my skin.

With a towel wrapped around my torso, I dig through my dresser and grab a pair of boy shorts and a tank top. Clad in my nightwear, I plop down on my bed and flick on the television, scanning Netflix for something to watch. I pick a random movie, which ends up becoming background noise to my racing mind.

A pair of warm hands cover my eyes, too large to belong to any girl I know. His hot breath on my ear sends a chill down my spine. My breath hitches and my heart beats as if it will never have the chance after today.

"Guess who…" his whisper like sun and thunder and a bolt of lightning to my heart.

"Hmm…" I toy with him. "I can't be sure. Jake?" I tease.

His hands rip from my eyes, the bright light instantly returns and makes me squint. "Who?" He spins me around and hugs me so tight I can't speak.

"Nope, not Jake," I joke again.

"Who the hell is Jake?" he asks, defensive.

I love it when he becomes possessive. "I don't know. Just made up the name to mess with you. Of course I knew it was you." Pushing up onto my tiptoes, I press a kiss on the corner of his mouth. "Don't be mad."

"I'm not mad," he mumbles, but the grumpy doesn't leave his face. We are about to turn the corner in the hallway when he lifts me up and hoists me over his shoulder, fireman-style. Everyone at their lockers starts laughing at the spectacle. And it is most definitely a spectacle.

Because as he is walking down the hall with me over his shoulder, I am smacking his ass and kicking my feet in the air, begging for him to put me down. It wouldn't shock me if this scene floods the internet once it ends.

As we walk out the double doors, his stride grows faster and more urgent. He stops next to a big oak—our tree—and sets me on the ground, smacking my ass for good measure.

"Gavin! Why did you do that? That was so embarrassing." It was beyond embarrassing, yet I loved every second of it. Loved that he didn't care who was watching.

He takes a step closer to me, eliminating the empty space between us. I suck in a breath, my body straightening and my breasts brushing against his chest. His hands dance along my jawline before his fingers lace in my hair and he brings his mouth to mine.

He kisses me with such intensity, I forget how to breathe. His tongue traces over my lower lip and I open for him. Our tongues begin this wild dance, fevered and needy. Wolf whistles erupt around us, but we ignore every one of them. It is just me and Gavin as the world disappears. And as quickly as the kiss began, it ends.

I grab hold of his biceps, dragging in ragged breaths while trying to calm my heart.

"You are forgiven," I tell him when my lungs settle.

He presses a sweet kiss to the center of my lips. "Thanks."

When he pulls away from our embrace, he looks over at the tree beside us. My eyes shift to see what he is looking at, and my jaw falls to the ground.

"When? How? Did you?" I fumble over what I am trying to ask him.

"This morning. With the pocket knife I snuck into school. And yes, I did."

My fingers brush over the chipped away bark. On the trunk of the tree, he has carved "C+G tu es les étoiles de ma lune." He had been taking French for the last three years, but I'd chosen Spanish and had no idea what this said.

"What does it mean?" I ask, my fingers still caressing each of the indentations he had made. Must have taken him a while.

He brushes the back of his index finger along my jawline to my chin. "It says 'the stars to my moon,'" he whispers, although I'm the only person close enough to hear.

My face hurts from the smile he has given me. "I love you, too."

A tear rolls down my cheek and I wonder if that tree—inside the confines of our high school—still displays our initials. Or if the bark has grown and covered it over the years. The younger, lovestruck part of me wants to visit the tree again. The tree where it all began. Our tree.

Luna curls up beside me, purring with vigor as I stroke her soft fur. And after a few minutes pass, I drift off to a deep sleep where I dream about trees and love and the starry skies above.

Today is the fourth day of the shoot and I am nervous as to how it will go.

Last night was one of the best times I have had in a while. We didn't do anything extravagant—a nice dinner, an ice cream cone, and a walk on the beach. Breezy conversation and a comfort that only comes with familiarity. It was better than any other night I have shared with a woman. And there is only one reason.

Cora.

Being near her again is like learning how to breathe for the first time in years. Sure, breathing happened while we were apart, but it was merely to exist until I found my way back to her. And it feels as if I have finally rediscovered her. I only hope she has managed to do the same.

During today's shoot, we are supposed to be strolling through parts of downtown Dunedin. Me in some hoity-toity outfit while Cora walks five to ten paces behind me, snapping photos of me "looking casual" on the street. Looking casual in my world translates into walking along the sidewalk and turning to look at something with your profile or whole face toward the camera. But don't look at the camera. Because looking at the camera is not natural, or so they say. Whatever.

It's all ridiculous if you ask me. But that's what the companies and consumers love. At least for this particular brand. The shoots for romance novels and risqué, they want your hungry eyes straight on. They want the consumer to feel as if you're reaching out and luring them in.

So, after my morning walk on the beach and a shower, I dress in a linen short-sleeve, white button-up, a pair of khaki cargo shorts with more pockets than I'd ever fill and a pair of boat-style shoes. And don't forget the chunky watch and dark-tint sunglasses. Each shoot's ensemble hangs in plastic wardrobe bags in my closet, labeled, courtesy of my wonderful agent.

The only part of this whole ensemble I would use again is probably the sunglasses. They mask the sun better than any pair I have owned in recent years. Lucky for me, I get to keep everything from the shoot.

Alyson and I meet in the lobby and walk to her rental car, sliding in and driving off the beach. The shoot doesn't start for a little more than an hour, so we agreed to grab breakfast nearby.

Once we are seated and place our breakfast orders, Alyson chimes in and starts asking about last night. I expect nothing less from her.

"So, how was dinner? Anything I need to be concerned over?" A look of genuine worry pinches her brow line.

"Dinner was good. She was worried at first, because she didn't see you. But after we talked for a few, everything went well."

"And I'll ask again. Anything I need to be concerned over?" Alyson persists.

"Nope. Just two old friends, eating together and sharing good conversation." Maybe if I say it enough times, I will start believing it myself. Because Cora and I will always be more than "old friends."

"And there were no flashes going off anywhere? From your phone or anyone else's?"

"I didn't catch any. No one around here knows me as a model. The only people who know me are the few friends I have still living here." If anyone recognizes me as a model while I'm here, shocked wouldn't begin to cover it. Yes, celebrities live in the area. But this isn't Los Angeles, and people aren't stalking celebrities. Not that I consider myself one. For the most part, when people spot celebrities here, they just whisper and go on with life.

She spins her fork in a circle on her napkin. "I hope you're right."

We finish breakfast in silence, and I take the time to do a self-evaluation of how I feel.

Being around Cora stirs up loads of memories and emotions I suppressed for years. But I can't ignore how I feel when near her. The way my heart rattles my ribcage. Or how my stomach quivers with excitement. Of course, I plan to follow etiquette and maintain a professional appearance while working, but once "off the clock" I cannot speak for my actions. I also won't resist what is right in front of me.

Because each moment I have with Cora, I intend to take full advantage. This shoot could be complete happenstance. Or maybe it is kismet. Personally, I believe in the latter.

After Alyson and I leave the restaurant, we stop at the juice place up the street. Cora had one of their juices the other day, so I Googled the business. Once I buy something for each of us, even grabbing a duplicate of Cora's drink for Erin, we jump back in the car and drive up the street to the main hub of downtown.

It is eight-thirty in the morning on a Thursday, and the streets already have people walking and bicycling everywhere. Downtown Dunedin is a quaint place. I hadn't come here much when I lived in the area, but I can see I missed out.

Restaurants and boutiques and eclectic shops line the streets. People bustle along the sidewalk, going from one shop to the next. Some people just sit on benches under trees and chat about what a nice day it is outside. And as busy as it is, it's not busy at the same time. Everyone is friendly as smiles are shared amongst complete strangers.

It's pieces of home like this that make me want to return.

Don't get me wrong. There are many stretches of California I love. Forests and mountains and waterfalls. Many I would love to show to Cora, knowing her love for the wilderness. But I haven't been anywhere resembling this. The happy town with ever happier residents. Everyone shares warm greetings and pleasant words and exchanges hugs. It makes me homesick for a place I haven't called home in a long time.

Alyson parks the car in a small lot near the epicenter of downtown and we walk over to the outdoor trail, standing in the shade. Cyclists whip past us, waving and smiling. Dogs sniff the grass as they walk alongside their owner. People window shop the storefronts nearby.

"She emailed me early this morning and said for us to meet her here," Alyson tells me.

A moment later, Cora and Erin pull into the parking lot at the same time and park beside Alyson's rental car. My eyes remain fixed on Cora behind my sunglasses as she gets out of the car and strolls to the back hatch, opening it and taking out her camera bag.

"Check yourself, Hunt," Alyson chirps behind me.

"Did I do something, *Miss Jameson*?" I curl my lip at her. She is really starting to piss me off.

"First, remember that you hired me to do exactly what it is I am doing. Second, don't take that tone with me. You will respect me." Alyson stares at me like a mother scolding a child. In some respects, she is correct. I did hire her to keep me "in line."

But she also needs to remember her place in the grand scheme of things.

"I know what I hired you to do. And since I'm the one signing your paycheck, I suggest *you* check yourself. I'm fully aware of my boundaries. And if I want to cross them, it'll be when the shoot is done. Which, by the way, is only a few days from now." I pause and lower my voice since Cora and Erin are walking our way. "I'll be here a few days after the shoot ends, I intend on enjoying that time however I see fit."

Alyson purses her lips. "You're the boss."

Damn right I am. Best you remember.

Cora and Erin step up and I hand them the juices I bought them. "Good morning, ladies. Just something to help keep you going today."

Cora's lips curve up at the corners while Erin blushes at the gift. It's just juice, not a bundle of flowers. Maybe Erin is naturally timid and the rosiness comes easily. Or there is the possibility she knows about the "meeting" last night. Whatever, it doesn't bother me either way.

∼

I glance down at the chunky watch on my wrist to see it is just after one when we wrap up for the day. This shoot dragged out longer due to the amount of pedestrian traffic we had to avoid for photos. It's challenging to capture someone's face, and their attire, when people walk all around you.

Erin heads to her car, and Alyson to the rental. I tug on Cora's hand and keep the two of us by the trail for a minute, giving us a fraction of privacy while we talk.

"What's up?" she asks, her tone casual and light.

"Just wanted to say thanks again. For not walking away from me last night. And for hanging out. Was nice to see you outside of all this." I wave my hand around us.

"It was nice," she says as a smile softens her features. "Do you want to go out with everyone tomorrow? We're going bowling."

"I'd love to. Who's everyone?"

"Me, Erin, Shelly, and Jonas. We can ask Micah, too. If you want."

All but one of those names is familiar. "I'll text Micah and see if he wants to go. Who's Jonas?" Because I really want to know. Jonas is not the name of any female I have ever met. Micah would have told me if Shelly has a boyfriend. And Erin seems too innocent to be dating—although, I could be way off base with her.

"Jonas is a friend. He helped me try to fix my old car years ago. It had so many problems and I was a frequent shopper at the mechanic shop he works at and we just became friends. He's a nice guy. I think you'll like him."

A furnace boils in my veins as I try tapering my emotions before I say something harsh. It is not my place to play the jealous anything. I lost that privilege years before she met this Jonas person. And I know absolutely nothing about him.

But that doesn't stop my truths from surfacing.

Am I still in love with Cora? Absolutely. There is not a day of my future I foresee not loving her.

Does that give me the right to dictate who she hangs around? Nope, not one bit. If she tells me she and this Jonas character are just friends, I believe her.

So, I suck it up like a trooper and put on the smile I have been trained to use. "If you think so, I'm sure it's true." I relax my forced expression, only because she is looking at me as if she can see right through it. "Will you give me your number?"

She shakes her head for a few beats. "Why? Don't misunderstand me," she says as she jerks her head toward Alyson. Her teeth tug on her lip as she regards Alyson's eyes on us. But I don't give a fuck. Alyson can take her sinister stares and fly them back to California.

"So I can text you after I talk with Micah." That's a perfectly sufficient reason to need her number, seeing as she asked me to join them.

"Okay." She nods and I pull out my phone.

I open up a new text and she prattles off her cell to me. When she finishes, I type a message and send it to her. Her phone chimes in her back pocket and a smile dons my face as my heart beats a little faster.

I glance up and see Alyson drilling holes through me with her eyes. Her irritation is raking my nerves. "I should head out," I tell Cora, although it's the last thing I want to do. If anything, I would love to spend the rest of the day wandering downtown, holding her hand and chatting more.

"Me, too. I'll see you tomorrow."

"See you tomorrow." I lean into her, wrap my arms around her midsection and inhale her scent. She smells so much better than I remember. The perfect blend of frankincense and gardenia. Against every fibrous desire in my body, I release her and head to the car, giving her a small wave after I get in.

Once we are out of the lot and driving back toward the hotel, Alyson decides it is time to give me her two cents. "I get that you think you know what you're doing, but please be careful. There are only two days left for the shoot. All I'm saying is to be mindful."

I opt to not respond, and the drive back to Clearwater Beach takes twice as long. But during the entire ride, Alyson's words repeat in my head.

Be mindful.

thirteen

CORA

The fifth day of the shoot comes and goes and remains uneventful. Which boggles my mind.

The shoot was on the beachside of the hotel, this time in the water. Normally, a shoot like this would be classified as simple, easy. The model is out in the water, playing amongst the waves, posing on occasion and I snap the shot. Easy peasy lemon squeezy.

But, of course, with Gavin it is the complete opposite.

The shots weren't difficult to capture. My breath, on the other hand, seemed to get lost in the breeze. My racing heart chasing on its heels.

Sitting cross-legged on my bed, I pick up my camera and remove the SD card. After inserting it in the card reader, I plug it into my laptop and download the photos. A few minutes later, my eyes are inundated with thousands of photos of Gavin in the surf. I scroll through the tiled photos, clicking on this one and that one. Some appear the same with maybe a slight angle change with his chin or eyes. Others are noticeably different.

My finger taps the trackpad and the next photo fills the screen, corner to corner. I suck in a breath at the sight before me, my eyes glued to the screen and glazing over. I can't look away. Can't stop the category five hurricane wreaking havoc on my insides.

Today's shoot started earlier than the previous days. We needed to have Gavin in the water with no one nearby. In order to do that, he was in the water as soon as the sun started rising behind us in the east. The lighting was just enough to see him and the shorts hanging low on his hips.

The photo in front of me left me speechless.

Gavin stood in the water, the surface a few inches below the waistband of the shorts. His torso slightly twisted, palms resting on top of the water outstretched, his profile staring south into the distance. The dim morning light just enough to outline his silhouette. The length of his hair hiding parts of his profile. His contours defined with glimpses of curves and valleys and sinew, and droplets of water beaded on his skin. And the sharp edge of his stubble-covered jawline.

"Wow," I whisper-gasp to myself.

This photo… consider me stunned.

Stunned by his gorgeous features, the relaxed muscles peaking and dipping and contouring in all the right places. Breathless by his form and posture in the light. Shocked by the way my chest heats and thumps vigorously at the sight of him like this. In his element and one-hundred-percent himself.

Flashes of his love for the beach wake from my memory. Not for the fine, white sands or the warm, salty water. But for the serenity it provides him. The occasional stillness mixing with absolute chaos. How the sun dips below the horizon and lights the sky in breathtaking pinks and oranges. We watched so many sunsets together before he left. No two the same. And each time, I watched him from the corner of my eye, captivated by his tranquility.

This is him. Pure and uninhibited.

And this photo may not be what the brand is looking for, but it is something I will never let go of. A piece of him. The real him. The Gavin I fell in love with all those years ago.

My finger strokes over the photo, the outline of his triceps and forearm. I sigh and drop my hand from the screen.

I am fucking hopeless. And screwed.

I save the photos to my external drive and shut down the computer. My head still in the clouds as I dream of Gavin in my life in ways he never has been. Jumping up from the bed, I startle Luna in the process.

"Sorry, Luna. Momma's head is somewhere in la-la-land right now."

I head for the bathroom and crank the hot water in the shower, praying the spray will snap me out of my thoughts. Thoughts which will more than likely lead down a fresh path of sadness and heartache. I should be trying to erase the daydreams running circles in my head, right? Erase them and replace them with Gavin's inevitable departure. The more days that pass, the closer it gets to the end of the shoot. And the sooner this dream will fade away. Because that is all this is. A dream.

The parking lot of the bowling alley is packed. I wind up and down the rows in search of a vacant space, finally parking after I hit the fourth row. Jogging up to the entrance, I spot Shelly and Micah and slow when I notice they are in a heated conversation.

As I approach, Micah notices me and stops speaking, an artificial smile marking his face.

Great. I must have been the topic they were arguing politely about.

"Hey, Micah," I say, laying the sweetness on a little thick. "Long time no see."

Shelly bounds over to me and squeezes me as if I'm her lifeblood. Micah watches us, a smirk pulling at the corner of his mouth as he mumbles something unintelligible.

What the hell is his problem?

"Just ignore him. He's pissed because he thinks you and Gavin will ruin his night of fun," Shelly tells me before sticking her tongue out at her brother.

Not quite sure how he thinks us bowling together is going to disrupt his good time. And if I'm honest, I don't really care about his feelings. I have seen Micah a couple times over the last year. About the same number of times I see him every year. And usually that is because I attend gatherings with Shelly where he happens to be also.

Whatever. He can suck it up like the thirty-one-year-old big boy he is.

"Micah," I say, snagging his attention from the parking lot. "The only person that can ruin your night is you. So…"

In all his my-best-friends-big-brother glory, he salutes me with his middle finger. Asshole. And so immature. An outsider would peg him as the youngest out of all of us.

I loop my arm in Shelly's and we skip into the bowling alley, ignoring the dipshit standing outside. We head over to the check-in counter, pay for shoes and receive our lane number. I shoot a text to Erin and Jonas, letting them know Shelly and I are inside and which lane number we are at.

Shoes laced up, Shelly and I go in search of the perfect bowling ball. When we return to the lane, Jonas is there and swapping his steel-toe boots for the snappy red and blue bowling shoes. He notices us step into the bowling circle and lifts his head up, a megawatt smile spreading his lips. I have missed his face this week.

"Hey, ladies. What time does galactic bowling begin?"

I wrap my arms around him, hugging him as hard as I normally do. "In about fifteen minutes."

Just as I release him of the hug, I hear footsteps thunder behind me. I turn to see Micah and Gavin, and before I can greet Gavin, I stop myself. The relaxed and soothing demeanor Gavin has displayed toward me all week is nowhere to be seen. Instead, it has been replaced with ego and rage and maybe a hint of jealousy.

He needs to chill the fuck out.

"Gavin," I sing, "this is Jonas. Jonas, this is Gavin."

I wait for one of them to be the bigger man and offer their hand to shake. An eternity passes before Jonas rises from the plastic bucket-style seat and offers his hand. How did I know he would be the one to extend the olive branch? Maybe because he and I don't share the same sort of history Gavin and I do.

"Hey, man. Nice to meet you. Cora's told me a little about you."

Gavin shakes his hand, his eyes sizing up Jonas in the process. "Has she now? And what, pray tell, has she told you about me?" His voice laden with sarcasm and authority and ownership.

For fuck's sake. Put your dick away, Gavin. This is not the time or place.

"Just that you guys dated in high school and she hasn't seen you in years. Until this week, of course. She said the shoot has been great, though." Jonas's tone is calm and collected. But his choice of words is meant to inflict guilt and envy.

Seriously? I do not want to be the center of some stupid pissing match. Why is it so difficult to be friends with men?

Gavin's eyes narrow and I almost see the witty comeback he works hard to deliver. Everything inside me just wants this to stop, so we can have a few drinks, eat some greasy pizza, and play hours of black light bowling.

And just when I think Gavin might keep his mouth shut, he proves me wrong.

"It has been great. Nothing like spending several hours of the day with a beautiful woman. And an evening too."

That's it. I have had it. I shove against Gavin's chest. Hard. "Okay, okay. We all get it. You both have dicks. Could you stop being one so we can have a good time? I don't plan to spend my evening defending myself against testosterone."

I watch as he stares at Jonas, jaw clenched, before he softens his features and shifts to look at me. "Sure thing. Let's have some fun."

And before I realize what is happening, he bends down and kisses the corner of my mouth. I don't respond. No flinch. No kiss in return. Nothing.

Instead, fire ignites in my chest and radiates through every molecule in my body. Fire from feeling his lips on me again. But also because he did it to use me as a pawn. And I am no one's pawn. How can desire and anger be so in unison? I don't have the answer, but they both flood my veins like the Nile. Fuel my indignation. And slowly steal every bit of happiness I had about having a night out with friends.

I stare up into his eyes, his face a look of victory. But I am ready to slap it right off his pretty little lips.

Pressing up on my toes and leaning toward his ear, I whisper-hiss, "If you ever try to use me like I'm some sort of prize again, you'll wish you'd never returned here."

I step back and set my expression to a level so frigid he shivers. We stare at each other a minute. His eyes never leave mine. They ask me a million questions regarding me and Jonas and him. But I hold my ground. Jonas is my friend and I made that abundantly clear to him when I invited him. If he can't handle me having other men in my life, then this second chance at whatever will end faster than it began.

He nods and his lips move without sound, *I'm sorry.*

I give him a tight smile and return to my friends. Erin joined us sometime during that whole showdown. Sitting between Jonas and Erin, I watch as Shelly types names on the screen—giving each of us an alternate identity.

I have been dubbed "The Raven." Shelly "The Queen." Jonas landed "The Machine." Erin bows at "The Peacekeeper." Micah gets "The Asshole." Because that is what happens when your sister picks your name. And Gavin receives "The Dreamer."

Everyone except me questions their names and tells her to change them. The raven suits me on many levels, and the temporary nickname perks my lips. First and foremost, black is life. Second, intelligence. No doubt there are plenty more sufficient reasons, but I will just stick with those two.

Once everyone stops antagonizing Shelly about name changes, bowling balls are chosen and the game begins. Five minutes into the first game, the bright fluorescent bulbs go out and are replaced with black lights and flashing party lights. A DJ belts out of the speakers and prattles on about people coming to the booth for music requests.

The first of many remixed or electronic songs comes on and I start bopping in my seat. Erin currently rolls her ball down the lane, a sad puppy expression on her face when she turns after only knocking one pin down. My hand comes up in a *rock on* gesture and I smile at her in encouragement. Her next ball yields seven more pins and she walks away with a smile.

"That's my girl," I holler. Her beaming smile is the best response and I put my hand up for a high five.

Frames are played and pitchers of beer and greasy pizza get ordered as laughter and goofiness ensue. For the next two hours, everything goes well. No testosterone battles. No bitching. It almost feels like old times.

Until one minor touch.

I grab my ball from the return, shift into the approach area and line my feet where I typically set them. Lifting the ball, I hold it steady and study the pins in front of me. When ready, I take a left-right-left, followed by a swing back and release as I swing forward. Normally, the ball would glide off my fingers and spin down the lane, the marble pattern hypnotizing on its path to the pins.

But that is not what happens.

What actually occurs is left-right-left, swing back, a smack to the leg and a twist of the ankle as the ball flies backward. It hurts like a son of a bitch and I cry out as I crumple to the floor.

Within seconds, Jonas is at my side, asking if I am okay. When I let him know I will be fine and I just need to sit a minute, he offers to help me up. Up to this point, everything is okay and I realize this because Gavin and Micah had walked off to get more beer.

The moment I stand upright, Jonas steadies me with both his hands resting on my shoulders, his eyes scrutinizing my face. "You sure you're good?"

"Yeah. Thanks for helping me up."

And that is when it happens. When the shit hits the fan.

Jonas brings his hand to my cheek, brushing his thumb along my cheekbone and down to my jaw. He tugs lightly on strands of my hair before swiping them behind my ear. The gesture is tender and sweet and is taken away the second Gavin is within eyeshot.

"What the fuck do you think you're doing?" Gavin rages, his hands balled into fists at his sides.

"What's your deal, man? She just hurt herself and I was helping," Jonas charges back.

Gavin takes two steps closer. "I can see you helping. Keep your fucking hands to yourself, asshole."

What the actual fuck?

"Gavin," I soothe. "Jonas was helping me. I hit my leg with the ball and fell. He was making sure I was okay and helped me stand back up. You'd know that if you were here." My voice transitions from soothing to bold to anger in a flash.

Who does he think he is? He has no hold over me. He has no right to step in and assume the role he is taking right now. That role was extinguished when he stopped calling and writing. That role was extinguished the day he abandoned me.

He steps up to me, looks me square in the eyes, ignoring the fact that Jonas is less than two feet away. His eyes bounce back and forth between mine as he searches my face for answers. Answers to questions he has been dying to ask me, but is scared to know the truth. If he wants the truth, he will need to man up and ask what he is so desperate to know.

"Please," I beg then close my eyes. As much as I would like to continue staring into his mesmerizing eyes, I can't focus when I do. I continue speaking with my vision shielded. My voice just above a whisper. "Please stop doing this. You can't do this. You can't come back after thirteen years and act as if nothing has changed. *Everything has changed.*"

"Look at me," he whispers.

I pinch my eyes tighter a moment before opening them and refocusing on his face. His face is inches from mine, and it is both exhilarating and unnerving. In my periphery, I notice everyone has moved away from us. Even Jonas.

The music morphs to one song then another, and we stand in silence. His eyes hypnotize me more with each passing beat and I swear he is figuring out a way to imprint his soul onto mine. Little does he know, he already has.

And when his finger traces the line of my jaw, I stop breathing. My eyes close and I wish on every star I have ever seen in the night sky that he will kiss me. But he doesn't.

He leans forward, his stubbled cheek lightly scrapes against mine, and whispers in my ear. "Not everything has changed. At least not for me."

He doesn't pull away from me. His warm, cotton-covered chest presses against mine and I feel the acceleration of his breathing—on my chest and at my ear. Calloused fingers traipse, with the slightest pressure, from my upper bicep down to my elbow and follow the lines of my forearm until he reaches the tips of my fingers. His fingers leave a trail of sparks everywhere he touches me and I can't ignore the swirl of energy erupting in my body.

"Gavin…" *Fuck*, I can't breathe. Can't think.

His breath is hot on my ear. "I won't come out and say it, but my feelings for you… if anything, they've only gotten stronger."

No. No, no, no, no. He can't do this. Not now. Not after all this time.

My brain jumbles into a fog of confusion. How can this be happening? It took me years to get over him. Years. To accept that he was never coming back. To accept I would never have the same connection with another person like I did him. Accept that I would exist among my friends and become some old cat lady.

And then he waltzes back into town—although it was his job that brought him and no other reason—and acts as if it is okay to resume his role beside me. It is *not* so simple.

It sounds strange, but I mourned his loss. Literally mourned him. Laid in my bed for weeks, aside from school, and cried until the tears would no longer fall. I lost sleep over him, far too many hours to track. This went on for months. So many months it was almost a year before I stopped crying for him. But the crying wasn't the end of it. It got replaced with well-disguised depression. Depression that still lingers to this day.

I won't let myself be that girl again. He can't do this. Make me fall in love with him again and then hop on a plane and fly back to the other coast. I won't survive. Not again.

Coolness replaces the heat of his breath at my ear, but I know he hasn't shifted far because his chest still rises and falls against mine. Not knowing what I will see, I take a chance and open my eyes and am met with the softest gaze. His grays spill into me. Plead with me. Implore me. Their silky silence calls to my heart and begs me to be something more. Begs me to be vulnerable for him again. And it hurts that I want to. So much.

"You can't say that. Not to me." The harsh scrape of my own words is an unfamiliar sound to my ears.

His eyes hold mine as he weaves his fingers between my own. "Why?"

"Because you can't say things like that and then leave me," I blurt, my body trembling. "The last time you left." My voice breaks. "It took me a really long time to find myself again. And even after I did, there were still days I lapsed. If it happens again…"

His eyes darken as he studies me. If he moves two inches closer, his lips will be on mine. And as much as I long to know how it would feel again, I fear the consequences my heart will endure.

"I'm sorry how things happened last time. You *know* I had no control in that scenario. But now…" He takes my chin between his thumb and first finger. "You and I have all the control."

"Do we?" I counter. "We live almost three thousand miles apart. How do we have control?"

The pad of his thumb brushes over my lower lip, causing me to close my eyes and suck in a breath. Blood whooshes loudly in my ear. My fingers tighten around his. Adrenaline parades throughout my body as flutters swarm beneath my sternum.

"What if we didn't live so far apart?"

Red and yellow lights spin circles around us when my eyes bolt open. Hundreds of people hurl globes of plastic-resin along oil-slicked hardwood in the hopes of knocking over wooden pins. Music wails from speakers and I have zero clue as to what is playing. Our friends resumed bowling without us, presumably playing our turns when they came around.

"What?" I stumble. The question is twofold. One—did I hear him correctly? Two—is he suggesting what I think he is suggesting? That one of us moves?

"It's something I've thought about for a while now. The only reason I moved away was because I *had* to. That's not a sufficient enough reason for me to be there anymore."

My mind dizzies with his confession. Part of me is ecstatic at the possibility of him moving back to Florida. Another part of me is wary. Wary things can never go back to how they were, regardless of how either of us feels.

"But how? Your job. Friends. Life," I ramble.

His thumb strokes my lip again and he moves a breath closer. "I can do my job from anywhere. As it is, I'm almost never home. I fly somewhere new every week or two. But I've stockpiled and I can lessen how much I work. As well as be pickier about the shoots I do. The few friends I have there will understand. Believe me. And my life? It has never been in Cali. I may live there, but my life is here. Always has been."

This is too much information all at once. My free hand comes up to his bicep and I brace myself against his weight. *I can't get my hopes up. Not again. Not after last time.*

"I need to sit down," I tell him.

He helps me to a seat and squats down in front of me. The look in his eyes says three words I haven't said to another soul since he left. And right now, it is way too much.

"Tell me what you're thinking," he stammers.

I memorize his expression and then drop my head in my hands. "I'm thinking this is going to slay me in the end. That I'll wither and crumble."

His fingers play with the strands of my hair that cover my hands. It is a balm to the conflicting emotions that spiral around my heart. And I temporarily relish in the feel of such an intimate gesture.

"I won't let that happen," he promises.

My head jerks up. "How can you be certain? How can you make such a colossal vow?"

His eyes lock on mine, assurance backing his words. "Because it's the only thing I've wanted since I was forced to leave you. Cora…" he says as he strokes a hand down the side of my face. "You are everything to me. You are the reason I breathe."

I drop my head back into my hands, hiding my face from the world and convincing myself not to cry. After a few minutes, I inhale deeply and force myself upright. When I check the time, I realize an hour has passed and guilt washes over me at how I have abandoned my friends.

"We need to continue this conversation, but not now. Right now, I need to drink more and throw a ten-pound ball. I need to hang out with my friends. Okay?"

He nods and stands up in front of me. "Okay," he whispers as he kisses the top of my head.

We turn back to the group and talk with everyone. The night has morphed into an awkward ball of tension. No one is sure how they should act or what to say. But I do my best to ignore the weirdness and continue bowling and drinking.

But when the night ends, everyone is quick to leave. Too quick. And, unfortunate for me, I am too inebriated to drive and Gavin is the only person standing beside me.

Fuck. My. Life.

fourteen

GAVIN

Since I took an Uber to the bowling alley, I assumed I would leave with Micah. Assumed he and I would hang after. But that is not how things happened. Instead, Micah changed his shoes and headed out without a word. When I shot him a text to check on him, his response was lackluster.

> We'll catch up another time bro.

Lame. But after the whole debacle in the bowling alley, I don't blame him. And I am a shitty friend for ignoring him most of the night. Something I need to correct. But not now.

Because now I am driving Cora's car and following her slurred directions. Toward her house. Just me and her. Alone. And my nerves zap like live wires.

Not so sure this is the best idea. But there was no way in hell I would let her get behind the wheel when she consumed close to a pitcher of beer after our talk. Erin or Shelly could have driven her home, but then she would have had to worry about her car tomorrow.

It is easier for me to drop her home and catch an Uber back to the hotel. To make sure she gets home safely. To make sure she gets inside and locks the door. At least that is what I keep telling myself.

She slurs from the passenger seat as she points like a madwoman at the exit sign. "Take exit Drew. Snot so much traffic," she snorts. "I said snot."

I shake my head and laugh at her. The last time I saw her, we were too young to drink. Not that age stops people from drinking alcohol, but we didn't back then. Seeing her like this, I'm not quite sure how I feel about it.

Is this a normal thing for her? Going out with her friends and getting hammered. Does she drink heavily and drive after? Does she get wasted with that Jonas prick around? My blood boils at the idea. Has he tried to make a move on her while she was tipsy or drunk?

Fuck.

Just the thought of her with another guy pisses me off. Not like I expected her to not move on or see other people after everything. Hell, I did my best to soothe my crippled heart. Had meaningless sex with countless women. Tried to date. None of it stuck, though.

But seeing another man near Cora—his interest in her far beyond friendship—was a smack in the face. My blood turned molten and I was pumped and ready to kick his ass. If she hadn't been there to stop me, I probably would have and regretted it later.

What intrigues me most is how Cora thinks this Jonas prick only wants to be friends with her. Is she blind to the way he looks at her? Or how eager he is to touch her? Their hug earlier… the way he stroked her cheek and hair after she fell… *Fuck.* Either she is oblivious or doesn't want to believe.

I can't let these thoughts fester inside me. I need to know what sort of relationship exists between Cora and this Jonas guy. She doesn't owe me anything, and I would be shocked if she answers me, but I have to ask.

"Hey," I start, and she looks over at me. "What's up with you and this Jonas guy?"

She tilts her head to the side and remains silent in the passenger seat. After a minute, she starts laughing. At first, it is her typical laugh, but then it morphs into hysterics and snort-laughing. And then she laughs at her own snort-laughing. It's kind of cute.

This goes on for another minute until she tells me to turn left at the next light. We take a left and another left a couple blocks later. Less than a quarter mile later and we are parked in her driveway.

She still hasn't answered my question and I wonder if she even remembers I asked it. We sit in silence after I cut the engine and neither of us moves to get out.

"He's just a friend," she whispers into the quiet, her voice somber. "I know he wants to be more than friends, and it's crossed my mind on occasion, but we've been friends too long to ruin it. At least that's my opinion."

She sounds more sober than she did fifteen minutes ago and I wonder if it is the topic at hand or if she wasn't that drunk to begin with. I don't plan on asking her. But if she will keep talking, I will probe for more.

"If he asked you," I hesitate, unsure if I want to know her truth. I search her eyes, wondering if she can read me in the darkness of the car. Her eyes used to read me like a book. She knew all my answers before I did. Knew all my tells. "If he asked you, would you guys be together?"

Her silhouette is all I see in the car as a light on the back of her house casts an aura around her. I am unable to see what she thinks, but I *feel* her eyes scan over every part of my face. Look into the windows of my soul. Wonder what would provoke me to ask her. Memorize the curves along my cheekbones in search for a twitch or indication of doubt. She studies the line of my jaw and waits for me to speak more. I may not be able to see her face, but with the angle of the light I know she sees mine.

She reaches toward me, finds my hand in the dark and wraps it in hers. "I... I don't think so," she whispers, her words clear. "He's a great guy and has been a good friend. It's just..." She shakes her head. "Relationships and me haven't had the best of luck in my adult life. So, I just do the friend thing with sporadic dating. But never the same guy for more than one date."

Shit. Did I do this to her? Did I ruin love for her? God, I hope she is not like this because of me. The selfish part of me jumps up and down in victory. But the selfless part of me, he stands in the corner with a baseball bat, beating the shit out of himself.

"I'm sorry," I say the words before I stop myself.

"For what? Ruining me for every other man in the world. Don't be sorry. I don't want or need your pity. If I wanted to, I could have dated more and been in a solid relationship. But I get to decide. Is it such a bad thing to be picky? Especially after your soul has been crushed by the one person who was supposed to protect it."

Slap. Fuck, that stings. But I sure as shit deserve it.

"Can I walk you in?" I ask, wanting to steer us away from talking about this now. Not when I know she's not sober. Not when we can't discuss what happened rationally.

"What? That's it? You're done talking about it, so conversation over?"

She shoves her door open and gets out, slamming the door behind her. I rush to get out, to catch up to her before she gets inside. Halfway to her back door, I catch her wrist in my grip.

"No. That's not it at all. I just don't think we should be having this discussion when you're not one-hundred-percent coherent."

She huffs, trying to yank her arm from my hand. "You're ridiculous. You bring up the topic of discussion, but when it gets too thick… conversation done. It makes me dizzy."

She sways and I want to tell her it's not the conversation making her dizzy. But I don't because she is already pissed at me. Yanking her arm, I release her wrist and she wobbles to the door, me on her heels.

I hand her the key ring with three keys and she unlocks the door. As she steps through the door, I go to follow her and she stops.

"What are you doing?"

"It's late. Can I sleep on your couch? I won't bother you and I'll leave in the morning. If not, I'll find a ride."

Her eyes wobble a little as she studies my face. After a few breaths, she nods. "Couch." It's all she says as she walks toward a door I can only assume is her bedroom.

"Thanks," I whisper into the darkness.

Walking slowly through her quaint house, I locate the couch and kick off my shoes. I check my watch and realize it is really fucking late. Or is it really fucking early at this point? Whatever. Thank God tomorrow is an off day for the shoot. Because both of us would be fucked if it wasn't.

I stretch out on the couch, situating pillows and a blanket around me. Shifting my hips and my neck until I get comfortable. Am I really in her house? Or is this all just some bizarre dream? It all seems so surreal. Seeing her again. Touching her again. Smelling her again. Fuck, how I have missed everything about her. Even the way she says my name.

Her adorable smile. The subtle fragrance she wears. How she peers up at me. The way her body reacts to mine. As if no time has passed.

But it has. And I fucked up. Big time.

Staring up at the ceiling, my eyes lose focus as the moonlight casts shadows from the tree outside the window. Shadows of limbs and leaves dance and entertain me. Tonight, so many things have happened and changed. It's overwhelming to think of how life and our relationship could possibly shift in the future. Shift in a positive way.

The future… something I always dreamed I would have with Cora, but wasn't sure would happen. I wasn't sure I would ever see her again, but wished for it often. Wished on every star in the night sky. Wished with every penny I threw in a fountain. And wished every time I blew out a birthday candle.

When I boarded the plane in Los Angeles, the possibility of seeing her seemed minuscule. So outlandish. So impossible.

But fate intervened. Slapping us together and giving us the opportunity to discover each other again. To learn about all the years we missed out on. Learn how much we have changed yet remained the same. And now that things are lining up for both of us in our respective careers, the possibility of a future with her has greater potential. If a future with me is what she wants.

Please let it be what she wants.

If she would be willing to try with me again—if she gave me a chance to explain—I would move my life back here again. Back home. To her. For her. In a heartbeat. Regardless of my life and family and friends back in California, I would leave it all behind if I knew we stood a chance.

The day I was forced to tell her my mom received a promotion and we were moving out of state was the day my life started falling apart. One speck at a time. When my mom told me the news, I hesitated to tell Cora. Not because I didn't want to, but because when I did tell her, reality would hit hard. And when I shared the news with her, expressing the pain and anguish I felt at leaving, she held me and soothed me. She was the strong one, telling me we would be apart for less than two years. That we would see each other during breaks and summer. Less than two years and we could be by each other's side again.

We had it all mapped out.

Unfortunately for us, it didn't work that way. Within ten days of being in California, my life was utter chaos. Upset and angry, I lashed out. Got in fights and provoked anyone near me. I think a part of me thought if I acted out, I would be able to return to where I wanted to be most. Where I belonged. With Cora.

But it didn't work that way and I shut down. To my family and Cora. I allowed my anger and frustration and sadness to consume me until numbness took over. A numbness that pushed me forward, but I lost every real part of who I had been. Including Cora.

It may have taken thirteen years for me to return—by complete accident—but I am here. And I plan to do whatever it takes to regain all I have lost. I will make up for every tear she cried. Every sadness she suffered. I will make up for every pain and absence of love she has endured since I left. She deserves nothing less from me.

I surveil the shadows as they continue to sway and, within minutes, I drift off and hope I dream about the most incredible woman I have ever loved. The woman who sleeps less than twenty feet from me. The woman I hope will forgive me in the end. And somehow, love me again.

Fifteen years ago

I jump out of the bus and land on the concrete sidewalk of my new school. *High school. I am in the big leagues now.* No stopping me.

Freshman year holds so much promise. Making new friends. Meeting new people. Hot new females. Life couldn't possibly get any better.

I toss my backpack over one shoulder and head for the class where my home-room is said to be. The first day is usually full of chaos, and today is no exception. Even though it is corny as hell, I am glad my mom forced me to come to orientation so I at least got a lay of the land. The last thing I need is to look like a dope wandering the halls while staring at a map.

Navigating the hall, I locate the correct room and find a desk in the back row. There is still another six minutes until the bell, so I pull out my notebook and begin doodling while I wait. Stomps and thuds and soft pitter-patters echo off the sterile white walls as everyone files into the room. I ignore all their steps and continue my artwork, the buzzing of the bell causing me to stop.

When I peer up at the front of the room, a raven-haired girl walks through the door, huffing and bending at the waist as she tries to catch her breath. Her skin is pale as cream, her onyx hair as bold of a contrast as her bloodred lips. She reminds me of a modern-day, punk rock version of Snow White, except with shorter hair. And I immediately like everything about her.

When her breath catches enough, she stands and wanders through the rows of desks, picking an available seat two over from me. I try not to stare at her, but can't help how she has caught my eye. Surely, she has caught the eye of many others as well. And not just because of her entrance. Everything about her is bewitching.

I avert my gaze when the teacher introduces himself and begins going over some of the basic school rules and hands out paperwork for our parents, the code of conduct, and our class schedules. Typical first day of school stuff. I scan over my class schedule, check I was assigned all the appropriate classes, and then wonder what classes the raven-haired girl has. Hopeful we will have at least one or more classes together.

The bell sounds and I sidle up beside her, trying to spark a conversation.

"Hey," I say with a wave. "I'm Gavin. Crazy morning?"

She glances over at me, confused. "Hi," she mumbles. "Cora. And yes."

Maybe she isn't a morning person? Or maybe she is not having the best morn-ing. Whatever.

"Sorry to hear. Anything I can do to help?" Why not offer, right? No harm, no foul.

"Gavin, is it?" I nod. "Thanks, but I'm good," she says with a brush-off.

But I don't back down so easily. Something about her begs me to keep trying. "Well, let me know," I offer with a smile.

When she walks away, I check to see which class I head to first and make my way to the science wing. Honestly, who thinks it is a good idea for people to learn science this early in the morning?

~

Slap.

My geometry book closes too loud in the room and several sets of eyes stare at me like I am their next meal. *Sorry.* Why does everyone seem so touchy today? *Just brush it off, man.* No one likes the first day of school. Actually, no one cares for school on any day. But no one needs to bite my head off.

I shoulder my backpack and head to the cafeteria. After I load up a tray of random crap food, I head out to the tables in the sun. The summer heat still blazes, but I would rather be outside than in the dank cafeteria. The cafeteria feels claustrophobic and I question the cleanliness.

When I step out and search for a good place to sit, I spot her. The raven-haired girl with bright red lips. Cora. She sits under a tree, eating a sandwich and reading a book. Before I realize what I am doing, I trudge over and stop in front of her. She ignores me for a few seconds, bookmarks her page, and finally looks up.

Shielding her eyes with her hands, she squints and tilts her head to the side. "Can I help you with something?"

"Mind if I sit with you?"

"Gavin… right?" I nod at her. "Well, Gavin, I'm kind of a loner."

It is not a denial, only a statement meant to scare me away. But it won't work on me. If anything, the attempt at a brush-off has me wanting to sit with her more. Cora… what a fascinating creature.

"We don't have to talk. I'm just here for the tree," I joke.

She shakes her head in disbelief, a subtle laugh under her breath as she gestures to the landscape beside her. "It's not my tree."

I squat down and manage to sit cross-legged without dropping anything from my tray. *Thanks to whoever is looking out for me so I don't embarrass myself in front of this girl.*

We sit in companionable silence—me munching on the cafeteria's mystery casserole and her eating a banana while reading *Wuthering Heights*. The book tattered and well-loved—cover curling and faded, multiple pages dog-eared.

Part of me wonders if she is reading the book for school or pleasure. My bet is on the latter considering the appearance of the novel. Can't say I have ever read the book. I'm sure it is good, but reading isn't much of a priority for me. Haven't heard of anything noteworthy.

After finishing the semi-decent casserole, I finish off my bottled water. Although our silence under the tree has been enjoyable, I itch to talk with this girl. Spark some form of conversation. Get to know the girl with the bright red lips. But she doesn't seem like the type of person who fills space with meaningless conversation. Part of me is intimidated by this. Another part of me enchanted. What do I say to someone like her?

So, I aim for obvious.

"Good book?" I ask, smacking myself upside the head internally.

Of course it is a good book, dumbass! Otherwise, it wouldn't look like she has read it a hundred times. Idiot.

She finishes the sentence or paragraph she is reading and faces me, a slight hint of annoyance on her face. It both frightens and intrigues me. "Yes." It is all she says before turning back to the book and ignoring me again.

Okay…

I stay under the tree with her for a few more minutes before rising to take my tray back to the cafeteria. After I dump the trash and deposit the tray in the bin, I turn to catch one more glimpse of her before heading to my next class. But the moment I look, she is no longer there. A strange sadness takes hold, but I brush it off.

"I'll try again tomorrow," I mumble to myself.

The art quad is located at the back of campus, on the farthest outskirts. As if sketching and paints and clays need their own world away from the books and projectors and regimented studies. As odd as it is to be isolated at the back of the school, I enjoy the fact I won't hear anything else on campus while in this class.

Walking into the large and open classroom, I scan all the various projects the teacher has kept throughout the years. Oils and watercolors, charcoals and pencil. Each unique on their own. The air rich with canvas and pencil shavings and earth. As my eyes follow around the room, they stop when they spot a head of black-as-night hair.

Cora sits at one of a dozen long, rectangular tables. Her head down as her fingers draw vigorously on a sketch pad. Almost like the artist version of a mad scientist. No one sits beside her, so I gather myself and head for the table. Of all the classes I could share with her, art feels beyond perfect. A way to express yourself without speaking.

When I sit down beside her, my wooden stool squeaking against the linoleum floor, she doesn't move. Doesn't lift her head or greet me. She is so focused on what is in front of her, it's as if the rest of the world isn't really here. And a part of me kind of digs her level of concentration.

Seconds pass and her head remains down, hovering six inches above the table. I peer around her hunched body and sneak a peek at what she sketches, my eyes widening and breath falling short as I see it come to life.

The trunk of a tree. Shade and foliage hovering above. A raven-haired girl, her face hidden by an open book. And a boy. Taller than her, lean in stature. He watches her from the corner of his eye, a timid smile on his face.

It's her. *And me.*

A strange contentment washes over me. Although the image is nowhere near done—no shading or fine lines and details—the outlines are all in black and white. She abandoned the tree early to come draw the two of us beneath it. My stomach is sort of queasy, and I don't think it is from the mystery casserole.

How has she put this on paper so quickly?

And it occurs to me. Maybe she had previously drawn herself alone under a tree. She did say she was a loner. Five minutes was definitely not enough time to have this much detail on paper. Not even by the best.

The bell rings and I inspect another twenty bodies in the room, all seated at the other tables. Footsteps tick on the tile and the teacher walks to the front of the room. But I don't look at the five foot, four inch red-haired woman at the head of the room introducing herself as the art teacher.

Because just as the teacher begins speaking, Cora lifts her head and realizes I'm sitting beside her. And that I have seen her drawing. Her face is stoic and as unreadable as a professional poker player.

A smile breaches my lips and I face the teacher at the head of the room. Beside me, I hear the sketchbook close and a soft sigh. A sigh I will remember for the rest of my days.

sixteen

GAVIN

The sun wakes me up just before seven, although sections of the house remain somewhat dark. Cora still sleeps and the house is quiet. Too quiet. As if no noise exists here. Seems odd to have no noise. No cars driving by. No people talking outside. Not even the chirp of birds in the early morning light.

I should leave. The last thing I need is for Cora to wake up, find me in her house and not remember why I am here in the first place. All it would do is freak her out and set us back. When it comes to Cora, I need all the forward momentum possible.

Rising from the couch, I stretch out my limbs then fold the blanket and drape it over the couch. I tiptoe through the house in search of the bathroom. After I relieve myself, I wash up and tiptoe back out.

Finding a piece of paper and pen on the desk nestled between the living and dining area, I write a quick note. As I set the pen back in its place, I bump the corner of her open laptop and the screen lights up.

Shit.

Snagging the note, I go to close the lid of the laptop and hide its bright light. But just as I begin to push the top down, I see a photo from one of our shoots this week. A photo she left open. A photo of me.

Confusion flickers in my veins. Rapid-fire questions pop up left and right. Was the photo left open because of work and editing? Or was it left open for other reasons?

A strange, woozy sensation floats in my chest at the possibility of her ogling a photo of me. Of her sitting in this very spot and gawking at my images. But I shut down the idea, not wanting my hopes to get the best of me.

I ignore the laptop and leave it open since it will return to sleep mode within minutes.

Walking over to her bedroom door, I stand in front of it and close my eyes. Do I go in and leave the note where I know she will find it? Or should I slip it under the door? This isn't my house. And technically, Cora isn't my girl.

My internal battle continues a minute before I choose the obvious path.

I slowly twist the knob and am thankful the door stays silent as it opens. Padding through the room darkened by black-out curtains, I walk toward her bed and set the note on top of her phone. A place I know she will find it.

Before turning to leave, I stare down at her a moment. Although I should leave now, the selfish part of me stays to observe Cora without distraction. To take in the woman who has held my heart captive most of my life.

And for a moment, I study the lines of her face as she sleeps. How her brows arch up, not in the middle but closer to a lateral point. The way her long lashes fan across the purple half-moons beneath her eyes. How her black strands splay across the dark gray cotton pillowcase.

A red tank covers her chest, but rises up her midriff to unintentionally display her navel. A small locket rests atop her shirt, and I remember it as the one her mom gave her. The sheet bunches near the thick band of her underwear. Her body askew on the mattress, taking up half of the queen-size space like a giant starfish.

A contented sigh leaves my lips as I pivot to leave the room. As much as I would like to stay, now is not the day. After closing the door behind me, I retrieve my phone from the living room and head for the door. I lock the handle as I step out the back. Scanning the street, I try to orient myself and figure out where I am.

Across the street from Cora's house is a large, open park. Honestly, doesn't surprise me she purchased a home within fifty-feet of a park. I cross the street, land on a small paved path and wander through the greenery in the faint morning light.

It is peaceful here. Most of this side of the park is filled with lush oak trees and a pathway for leisurely strolls. No wonder it was so quiet in her house.

I stand near the edge of a pond in the center of the park and watch a raft of ducks as they splash and quack and say good morning to each other. Squirrels dig at the earth in search of hidden food. A gentle breeze blows off the water, cuts the morning heat and rustles the leaves. A few people pass by with dogs and wave as if I live in the neighborhood. Everything about this place is quaint and chill and absolutely perfect.

After fifteen minutes of wandering the park and collecting my thoughts, I locate a bench on the outskirts and request an Uber. I pluck a twig from the ground, twirl it between my fingers and zone out while I wait.

Thank God I have today to myself. After everything last night, I need the time. To think and map out what happens next. Because after last night, I won't deny myself or Cora. Not again.

seventeen

CORA

Something wet scrapes over my nose. My cheek. My eye. It stops after a minute, but starts up again. My eyebrow. The corner of my mouth. Then my ear. Argh! *What the hell is that?* I swat at the air and come in contact with a bulky body of fur.

Luna.

She paws my face, a sweet and pleading meow only inches from my ear. When I don't respond, she paws me again and meows louder. It is a scratchy-whiny meow. One that tells me it is past time to wake up. One that tells me I need to pay her attention.

Grr… I shove her to the side and scoot to sit up. Luna rubs the side of her body against my arm, doing a figure eight and coming back for more, a noticeable purr echoing in the darkness. Giving her a light pat and a few pets, I creep out from under the sheet.

"Come on pretty girl. Let's get you some breakfast." As soon as the word breakfast is said, her cries morph into a frenzy as if I never feed her. Ridiculous, but adorable.

When she hops off the bed, I reach for my phone and pick up a piece of paper resting atop it. I pinch my eyes together in the darkness and see it is a note from Gavin.

> *C,*
>
> *I didn't want to wake you. Or disturb your morning. Or make things awkward when you woke up and I was still here.*
>
> *See you tomorrow. Enjoy your day off.*
>
> *G*

I flip the paper over as if looking for more. Or him. But find neither. No more words. No Gavin.

After drinking far too much last night, things are a bit foggy. I walk to the kitchen and pour some food into Luna's bowl before grabbing a glass of water. His note still in my hand, I walk over to the couch and plop down, a waft of his beachy pine scent hits my nose and I close my eyes as I inhale deeply.

I am so very fucked.

I reread the note a few times, trying to find some hidden meaning in his words. But nothing stands out. There is no hidden agenda. No secret meaning. It is just Gavin being Gavin.

I tip my head back and stare at the ceiling. Stare at the minor imperfections and connect them like constellations. Which makes me think of stars and night skies and sunsets. *Ugh.*

No way I can sit in this house all day. If I stare at the walls, my mind will keep venturing off into uncharted waters. Waters that always circle back to Gavin. I need to get out and do something. Anything. Maybe have a girl's day with Shelly. Watch some memorable karaoke and eat fried foods with her and Jonas. Like we always do.

Rising from the couch, I go snag my phone from the charger and shoot a text to Shelly.

> Got plans today?

Not sure what her work schedule is since it fluctuates week to week, but fingers crossed we can hang today. I just need to get out of my head. And in order to do that, I need distractions and meaningless conversation.

> Off work soon. What's up?

> Hang out when you're done?

> I'm down. 2:00ish good?

> I'll be ready. See you soon.

Happy to have a planned distraction, I eat a yogurt with granola before heading to the shower. As I wash away everything that happened last night—professed feelings back out in the open and slapped across my friends' faces—I make a vow to myself.

I will not fall in love with Gavin Hunt. *Again.* I will not. Or at least that is what I keep telling myself.

~

"How's it look?" Shelly asks through the fitting room door.

I stare at myself in the wide, full-length mirror and wonder what the hell I am doing. *Being a goddamn idiot is what I'm doing.*

My fingers toy with the black lacy boy short underwear, my eyes glued to the bra—also lacy, but resembling that of a leather cage. If I really want to, I can snap a few clips and the two undergarments connect and resemble a vixen-like leotard.

"Uh… I like it. I think."

Actually, I love it. Shelly doesn't need to know that, though. But why the hell would I need to buy lingerie like this? Not as if I have someone to wear it for. And I haven't stepped foot in a club in years—the only other place I might wear something like this.

I stare at myself in the mirror as I fiddle with the lace under my fingertips.

Not as if I need clarity to strike, but let's be honest. I know why I want to buy this. Want to wear it. The exact reason. The one person who has infiltrated my thoughts since the beginning of the week is said reason. Gavin. I picked up this sexy-as-hell lingerie set because I was thinking about him when we walked past the table. Part of me snatched it because it is black and punk and risqué. Another part of me is optimistic I will have a reason to wear it.

Many women wear sexy lingerie because it provides an air of power. Even if no one else sees it, they come alive with the provocative attire on their skin.

"You think? How can you not know? Let me see," Shelly insists. And before I realize what is happening, the fitting room door opens and she steps in.

"What are you doing?" I whisper-yell.

"If you didn't want me coming in, you should've locked the door."

"Lesson learned," I mumble.

Shelly's eyes sweep over the racy ensemble before a low whistle leaves her lips.

Her scrutiny isn't uncomfortable or awkward. Neither is the fact that she stands in a five-by-five dressing room with me while I wear next to nothing and she ogles my semi-naked body. We have been friends long enough to have more of a sister bond than anything else. That is not to say we didn't share the curiosity phase in our younger years. But that was all it was for both of us, curiosity.

"He'll love it." She claps her hands together, a wicked gleam dancing on her face.

"Who?" Confusion laces my tone as I cock my head and stare at my best friend.

"Gavin," she says, looking at me as if I have two heads for questioning her comment. "He *is* the reason you're trying this on. Right? I mean, I know you're unique in many ways, but no woman tries on lingerie like this unless she has a reason."

Of course she is right, but I will not admit it. Not to her and not aloud. Geez. When did I become such a hot mess of confusion? Oh, I know. Since the moment I heard his voice drift into that banquet room. The logical side of me gets up in my face and screams. She tells me to finish this shoot and act as if he never stepped foot back in Florida.

But the rest of me… she is off traipsing along the beach, holding hands with the only person she has ever loved. The only person who stripped her bare and shattered her to pieces.

No, I refuse to be that lost, melancholy girl again. Downright refuse.

"Get out," I mutter. "I need to change."

Shelly registers the shift in my demeanor and steps out of the fitting room. When the door clicks shut, I take one last look at the siren lingerie on my body before stripping it off and tossing it to the side. After I redress, I leave the room and hand the lingerie to the attendant, thanking her.

"Not buying it?" Shelly asks, a sorrowful look aimed my way.

"No. I have no reason to."

And that sad, lonely truth hits me harder with each step as we exit the store.

Fifteen years ago

Three weeks have passed since the first time Gavin sat next to me under the oak tree at school. Three weeks and we had become friends. Good friends. So good, we spend time together outside of school.

Gavin has even become a close runner up in the best friend department. Shelly will always take the lead. But after the first day, after he saw me adding his frame to my loner girl drawing, it had been nothing except uphill.

Besides hanging at lunch, we saw each other in art and English. Our conversations started off basic, discussing our family life and what we liked doing outside of school. Gavin seems to love art as much as I do, but swears his talents are nowhere as amazing as mine. Only time will tell that truth. We also like similar genres of movies.

By the end of the first week of school, I learned about his love for fish tacos, the beach, music, and sunsets. He told me a great day involved all four and the thought makes me smile at how easily they could be done together.

I lean against the wide trunk of the oak tree. *Our tree.* Retrieving the baby carrots and hummus from my bag, I start snacking as I flip through my book and wait for Gavin to join me. A page and a half later, he sits beside me and grumbles under his breath.

"You okay?" I ask and pause reading my book when I notice the firm pout on his face. His pouty face is kind of cute.

"Yeah. Just a little turned off by this tuna noodle casserole they're serving today. It's gnarly looking." His pouty face resumes and I bite my lip to stop myself from laughing.

"News flash, Gavin. All the cafeteria food is gnarly looking. Why do you think I bring my own food?"

He pokes his fork at the pale, goopy casserole and pushes it to all corners of the tray. As if spreading it out will magically make it more appealing.

"I might have to start waking up ten minutes earlier, so I can make something. Or…" He peeks over at me with a shit-eating grin. "You could always make lunch for both of us. I'll pay you instead of the school."

I toss a carrot at him. "I'm not your mama, boy," I tease.

He catches the carrot, sets his tray on the ground, and pops the snack in his mouth. But what I don't expect is when he starts reaching for more of my food, play fighting with me as I try to push him away. This happens for a couple minutes —him trying to steal my food, me defending my territory. We both laugh and taunt each other.

But then something shifts.

His playfulness stops when he knocks me to the ground and hovers inches above me. Carrots forgotten. Steely-gray eyes pierce mine and my breath hitches. If he lowers himself a few more inches, his lips would touch mine. And this fact heats parts of me I didn't know existed. Like I have a new organ named Gavin.

I want him to kiss me.

Only two boys have kissed me before. Greg Barton and Jeremy Ashford. Greg, two years ago. And Jeremy last school year.

Greg Barton is a year older than me and I thought kissing him would be life-altering. And it was, just not in the way I had hoped. It actually grossed me out. He had kissed me sloppily, his saliva-coated lips and tongue painting my mouth like they had no idea *where* my mouth was. I never kissed him back because the thought terrified me.

Jeremy Ashford went to middle school with me and was the most popular boy in the school. I was so nervous just before we kissed. Probably because we were at a friend's party playing truth or dare. He was dared to kiss me. Poor guy. I still feel bad for him and the bite I'd given his tongue when he pushed it between my lips.

Needless to say, after my most recent experience, rumors spread about how I didn't know how to kiss or make out. And everyone consoled Jeremy and his marred tongue. Whatever. He was a douche. Besides, I always did better on my own. Loner girl and all.

But looking into Gavin's eyes above mine, his lips separated just enough for him to draw in breath, I know kissing him would be different. Not another awkward kiss to add to the list of strange life experiences. But maybe on another list. One where you write down all the things you never want to forget because nothing else will compare.

We may have only met three weeks ago, but Gavin is not like every other guy. And I don't know how that makes me feel.

His body presses heavier into my belly and chest, his lips a breath from mine. I close my eyes, sending a message to the gods above and thanking them for whatever is happening. My breath hitches again in anticipation and then he is gone. His weight removed from my body and the warm breeze blowing my hair in my face.

My eyes fly open and glance over to where he sits up, a gleam of pure joy smeared across his face as he pops a carrot in his mouth.

Did he only want the stupid carrot? Or did he want to kiss me too?

Rising up from the ground, I tackle him and reach for my stolen lunch. It's not long before we share my food and his tray of scary casserole is long forgotten. We munch on veggies and hummus, and I share half of my cashew butter and banana sandwich with him. We share jokes and laugh. And I promise to make him lunch every day, as long as he foots the cost.

But when we walk away from our tree today, a new sensation flutters inside me. A new wish to be fulfilled. A desire to be kissed by the boy walking beside me.

nineteen
CORA

"Another round?" the server asks as she deposits loaded fries, onion rings, and our specified burgers on the table.

"Please," I tell her as I stuff the veggie burger between my lips.

I glance over at the stage and wish karaoke grandpa was doing his number up there. Could really use the laugh. Instead, I am forced to watch some fifty-something guy going through a midlife crisis. He practically makes out with the microphone—*I hope someone sanitizes that thing before anyone else uses it*—while he sings "Every Rose Has Its Thorns" by Poison.

...and I think his tongue just grazed the mic. Ew!

Our table is momentarily quiet as the four of us scarf down our burgers, occasionally snatching an onion ring or fry. When I come up for air, I notice I have three sets of eyes on me. Erin, Shelly, and Jonas each drill their own hole into my skull, mining for details of why I am acting off. Their weighted stares like an unannounced party in my head. Shelly and I spent the afternoon together, so her matched stares can take a pill.

Personally, I always think I'm strange. So, I don't know what their deal is.

"I wish you would've invited me shopping earlier," Erin speaks up, bringing conversation back to the table.

"Sorry," I confess. "I didn't purposely exclude you. Just wasn't thinking straight. Guess my brain was still a little foggy from drinking too much last night." Amongst other things. But I am not announcing that to the table.

To be honest, my day out with Shelly didn't clear any of the fog either. Not like I hoped it would. Every store we passed, something caught my eye and sent my thought train Gavin's direction. It's only been a matter of days, yet he consumes every part of my day. Even now, while I sit with three of my friends and try to have a night of fun.

"It's okay. Next time," she indicates.

"Next time," I promise.

Another round of silence ensues as the woe-is-me guy leaves the karaoke stage. I cross my fingers under the table, hoping the next person is better and more upbeat. And as I watch a pair of ladies walk up to the stage, each grabbing a mic and whispering to each other before the music kicks in, I hope my prayers will be answered.

Seconds later, "Bootylicious" by Destiny's Child crackles in the air and the two begin singing. They aren't horrible, but also not great. But at least the way they are shaking their asses onstage is entertaining. I laugh lightly and keep my eyes on the stage.

"You make it home okay last night?" Jonas's voice breaks my trance on the singing duo. And when I peer over at him to speak, guilt riddles me at the concern stretched over his face. Normal me would have let him know I made it home safely. Normal me was absent last night.

Since the day Jonas and I met, there has always been an easy way about us. Jonas is a great guy. Genuine and thoughtful and kindhearted. He knows how to have fun and make people laugh. And there is no denying I like him. But nothing more could ever happen between us. It wouldn't be fair to him if I couldn't be all in. That and his former relationship statuses.

"Yeah," I mumble. "Gavin drove me home in my car."

He nods, slow and steady, as his eyes stay fixed on his plate. Although his head is down, I notice the twitches in his expression. The flickers of emotion he doesn't want on display. And it's a stab to the heart that he doesn't want me to know what he feels or thinks.

Please look at me. Don't shut me out. That is what I *want* to say to him, but I stop myself. I don't want to send him mixed messages. Say words that mean one thing but could be interpreted in some misconstrued way.

Jonas and I have been friends for years now. I don't have many male friends or acquaintances—not on purpose—and I can't imagine having a better guy friend than him. Things with Jonas... nothing is complicated or artificial. What you see is what you get. And that is not a bad thing. I never have to question our friendship or who he is or what his motives are.

He is sweet and funny and would go out of his way to help a stranger. Having him in my company has never been weird. And although I know things have shifted a little between us, he would do anything for me. As I would for him. Like a true friend.

"Can I ask you something?" Jonas asks. Erin and Shelly sit across from us, chatting separately.

"You know you can," I tell him. Because it's true. I don't hide who I am from people I trust.

"What's going on with you and Gavin?" His face serious. More serious than I have seen it over the years.

"Not sure what you mean. He's the model I'm shooting right now."

In actuality, I know exactly what he means. Where his question is directed. He wants to know the history between us, and how that affects things now. I have no intention of lying to Jonas, but I don't want to spew word vomit and overshare information he doesn't want to hear. There is no need to dredge up things better left behind.

He cocks his head and studies my face a moment. "You know that's not what I mean. There's something else going on between the two of you. Am I right?"

I have no clue. God, I wish I knew the answer. The seesaw of emotions makes me nauseous. "Maybe. But I don't know," I say with a shrug.

His bluish-hazel eyes bore into mine as he tries to read the words left unsaid. Under the table, his knee brushes against my leg and I close my eyes as the contact sends a rush of jitters through my chest. There is no use in denying my attraction to Jonas. After all, he is easy on the eyes and looks at me as if no other woman walks the earth.

What woman doesn't want a man like that? Someone who only sees her.

The music fades into the background as his knee stays pressed against me. My eyes remain closed and my food forgotten. His weight shifts against me, his knee sliding higher up the outside of my thigh as I feel him lean into me. My breathing picks up as his rough stubble grazes against my cheek. *What is he doing?* I might just have a heart attack in the middle of the bar.

His breath is hot on my ear and I stop breathing altogether. "I hope not," he whispers. "Because that wouldn't bode well for me." And then he kisses me below the ear, trailing two more below it before pulling away.

Damnit. I am so royally fucked.

My heart hammers against my rib cage while my lungs try to remember how to work. His knee slides back to where it was moments earlier, but still touches me. The three spots where his lips touched my skin singe and sting, as if branding me with his essence.

The idea of opening my eyes scares the hell out of me. I'm scared of what I will see and feel and possibly realize. The overwhelming sensation has crept into my veins many times, but I purposely shove it down. Emotions and thoughts that tell me it is okay to like Jonas more than a friend. That it's okay to want someone other than the boy—now man—who holds my heart prisoner.

God, what do Shelly and Erin think of me right now? As I sit on this stool and fight the urge to kiss a man I have thought about kissing countless times, but stopped myself because my heart steps up to the plate.

I take a deep breath and harness every ounce of bravery inside me as I open my eyes. Jonas's link to mine immediately. Something different resides within them, though. Fire. Passion. Desires he has kept smoldering for years. Has all this come to life because Gavin is here? Is he finally acting on how he feels for me because he fears his chances are fading?

Or has jealousy brought them to the forefront? I don't want jealousy to be the reason he chooses to make a move. Jealousy isn't the right reason to tell someone you care for them.

Looking across the table, I realize Erin and Shelly are absent. "Where are…" I trail off.

"They went to the bathroom before stepping outside to make a call," he informs me.

"Together?" I ask, the absurdity of it layering my tone.

"I guess so. They got up at the same time and went the same way." His eyes never leave me. "Does that bother you? That they left us alone."

My eyes dart between his and I suddenly see him a little different than I did ten minutes ago. "No. Don't be silly. Of course it doesn't bother me." I snatch an onion ring to occupy my mouth before I ramble any further.

"Good." His arm inches closer to me and his warm hand rests atop my bopping knee. "Because I'd hate to think you're nervous to be around me now."

It is not that I'm nervous per se to be around Jonas. More like I don't want history repeating itself. The last guy I loved—who had also been my best friend beforehand—moved across the country. Granted, it wasn't his choice to do so, but he made zero effort to return. I put in all the effort and he just didn't. The only reason Gavin is here now is because his work brought him here. Not me.

If this shoot hadn't come up, would he have returned?

I have asked myself this question too many times this week. Have questioned if he ever had intentions of returning. Even if I ask Gavin, would he tell me the truth? Or only what I want to hear? Would he sugarcoat the reason it took him more than a decade to come back here? To me. If he is doing so well in his career, if he still loves me the way he claims, why didn't he return sooner? This whole situation frustrates me on so many levels. I don't know which way is up anymore.

God, it feels as if I'm in the middle of an epic battle. The battle for my affection. And somehow, I became the prize. Against my own volition. What if I want things to stay how they are? What if I don't want a relationship—other than friendship— with either one of them? Do I get a say in the matter? Of all the people in this situation, I should get the biggest say in the outcome. My heart is the one on the line, after all.

"I'm not nervous to be around you," I say after a long stretch of silence. "More worried, I guess."

"Worried?" He is quick to ask.

"Yes. I don't want things to change. And whether intentional or not, relationships change the dynamic between people and friendships. This" —I point between the two of us— "is perfect right now. What if us being more than what we are changes that? I can't lose you as a friend, Jonas. It would crush me."

Jonas's fingers trace small circles above my knee, the gentle motion is soothing and worrisome. I have always enjoyed Jonas's company. Always smiled and laughed and had a good time when we were together. A time here and there, I thought maybe he wanted more than friendship, but he never made a move or asked me on a date. So I brushed it off and assumed I read him wrong.

Ninety-nine percent of our outings include Shelly and/or Erin. It isn't me not wanting to spend individual time with him. More like the thought never occurred to me for us to hang out alone. Jonas is my friend, and I usually do friend stuff in group settings. Things have always been that way. And only occasionally veer off.

"Believe me, I know exactly where you're coming from. That's the reason I've never said anything. Never put myself out there to you. Because I'd be broken without you," he confesses then pauses, taking a breath before locking eyes with me. "But now... it seems like if I wait to tell you how I feel, I'll miss the opportunity. Or I could lose you. He's had your heart once before. If he's lucky enough to have it again, I..."

He doesn't finish his thought as he drops his chin, but I know what he would have said. *I wouldn't stand a chance.* Is he right? If Gavin somehow won my heart again, would I cave and be with him? Part of me instantly says yes—the part that has longed for him for years. Another part of me says no—that being the logical, rational side. The side that reminds me of the painful days, the loneliness and the heartache from before. All the tears and cold nights and nightmares.

I lay my hand over Jonas's and his eyes jerk up to meet mine. "I know," I tell him. "But no matter what, you'll always be a part of me."

Seconds later, Shelly and Erin plop back on their stools and look over at the woman singing karaoke. My thoughts run on high speed, and I have no clue what song is playing, nor do I care. All I know is, below the wooden grain of this tall tabletop, Jonas hasn't removed his hand, and neither have I.

Fifteen years ago

One more hour and Thanksgiving break starts. Nine glorious days of not getting up before the sun. Of sleeping in and zero required reading or assignments. But those aren't the best parts of time off school. Not by a long shot.

What I'm really over the moon about is having uninterrupted time with Cora.

Sure, I see her throughout the week at school. And sporadically we see each other on the weekend to "study." But we are never really alone. When we are "studying," it is in her living room or mine, our parents not far away. One of us on the couch, the other between their legs on the floor.

On occasion, I catch myself playing with a strand of her hair while she sits in front of me, arms warm against the inside of my calves. Or I lean into her legs when I'm cross-legged on the floor. She never brushes me off or acts as if the gesture makes her uncomfortable. And every once in a while, the light brushing of her fingertips draws on the skin of my neck. When she does this, I have to remember how to breathe. How to think.

We have preplanned a couple days of Thanksgiving break. Meeting with friends, hanging out and playing Putt-Putt or bowling. But I hope she will want to spend more time together, just the pair of us. Within a week of school starting, she easily slipped into friend—if not best friend—territory. A week after that, I craved to see her as much as possible and had an inkling she would always be more. At least to me. And I hope she reciprocates.

The bell rings and cheers can be heard throughout the school. Cheers of a week of freedom and sleep and no schedule. Cheers to less supervision and good times with friends. Closing my textbook, I stuff it and my notebook into my backpack. I slide out of my seat with a smile plastered on my face and head out the door. This week will be perfect.

~

Through the dark lenses on my sunglasses, I stare out at the water and watch Cora as she splashes Shelly in the shallows. Although it is late November, the sun beats down mild temperatures ranging from the low eighties to the high seventies in this part of Florida. The Gulf is still warm, but will cool in the next couple of weeks.

Micah, Shelly's older brother and my best friend for the last few years, sits next to me and doesn't hide the fact he ogles women ten-plus years his senior. But I'm cool with him being distracted. It disguises the fact I can't seem to remove my eyes from Cora's creamy white skin. The pallor similar to the snow I saw last winter when my parents took us on a road trip during winter break.

Hair black as coal, skin white as cotton, lips red as fresh cherries. Her smile bright as the sun on a summer day and her laugh a sound that sings to my heart-strings the moment I hear it.

Everything about her stunning. Spellbinding. Hypnotizing.

It's not until Micah backhands my bicep that I realize he has been talking to me and I have no clue what he said. "Sorry, man. What?" And I will my eyes to leave Cora to look over at Micah.

"I said we picked the perfect day to come out here. Lots of oil-slicked beauties out today," he states, brows waggling. Today is one of those days when Micah behaves like the typical horny teenage boy. Both annoying and not. But he is my best friend and I tolerate his ways.

There is only one person I have an interest in looking at, but for the sake of not being razzed, I nod and add, "Definitely a perfect day." I leave my response generic, hoping he won't press further.

But Micah isn't the type of guy to leave things unsaid. I have only known him a short time, but it hasn't taken long to learn how outgoing he is. "Anyone catching your eye? You've been a little zoned out."

Only one person has caught my eye, but I have no intention of divulging this tidbit. Not now. "No one in particular. You?"

"There's a trio of blondes at three o'clock I've been watching for a few. Think I might go say hello. You want to go with?"

"Nah. Think I'll cool off in the water for a bit."

I would rather be inches away from the magnetic girl sporting a black two-piece with curves in all the right places.

Micah rises from the blanket, brushes sand off his legs and board shorts, and straightens his spine. I'm half tempted to tell him it doesn't matter if you have sand on you, dipshit, you're at the beach. We are surrounded by sand. But I opt to refrain from jabbing him.

In a few quick strides, he walks away from me and makes a beeline for the females who I hope will occupy his time a while. After I'm certain he is not turning back, I scoot to the edge of the blanket and stare out at the water a moment. Cora and Shelly tread water just deep enough to reach the edge of their shoulders. They talk about something, Shelly's hand animating above the water every five seconds. Cora watches her studiously behind the dark tint of her sunglasses and smiles here and there.

Deep breath in, I stand from our reserved spot on the beach and trek fifty feet toward the water's edge. The small waves break over my shins as I shuffle into the water. Once I stand waist deep in the salty surf, I sink in the water, and wet my hair before swimming to Cora and Shelly.

As I approach them, I hear them talking about seeing a movie later. Intrigued, I wonder if I will be invited to said movie. Who cares what plays on the screen, I would love to just sit beside Cora for two hours in the dim-lit theater. Would I even be able to focus on the movie? Probably not.

"Hey," Cora says, breathless. I tread water on her right until I realize I can reach the sand below, planting my feet but keeping my body the same height as the two of them. "Tired of tanning yourself." A teasing smile lights her face.

"Ha-ha. Micah walked off to hit on some chicks and I was getting toasty on the blanket. Thought I'd see what you two were up to."

"We were just talking about seeing a movie later," Shelly chimes in. "Not sure what's playing, but we could pick whatever. Usually, there's always something good at the theater around the holidays."

"I'm in, if that's okay with you guys," I tell them both.

"Cool," Shelly pants, her body winded from treading water so long. "I'm gonna head back to the blanket, tan for a little, and see if anyone else wants to join us."

Before either of us says another word, Shelly swims to shore and leaves me alone with Cora. Exactly what I was hoping for.

In the anonymity of the water, my hands itch to reach forward and grab hold of her waist. I stare at her dark lenses through mine, neither of us uttering a word. We have never needed to fill time with meaningless conversation. By some unknown universal connection, we can read each other without ever speaking a word.

As if she hears my thoughts, as if she knows the urge building inside me, she swims closer and stops inches from my frame. The water surrounding me ebbs and flows with her arm and leg movements as she continues to tread. I stop fighting my instinct. Stop resisting what is in front of me.

The moment my hands grasp the curves of her waist, her arms and legs still. To anyone looking from the shore, nothing has changed except for her lack of distance. Our bodies hidden in the wide open. It is exhilarating. Not that I care if anyone sees us together. If anything, it would be heaven to tell the world my feelings for Cora. Feelings that have been growing stronger by the minute.

One hand holds her steady while the other begins to trace lines along the side of her torso. Up and down. Bikini top to bikini bottom. Her lips part just enough to see past the bold red rouge.

Under the water, her chest expands and contracts under my touch. She doesn't stop me, but I have to know if she is okay with me touching her like this. As much as it would devastate me to hear her say no, I would never press her for something she had no desire to pursue. I don't want to ruin what we have.

Leaning forward, my face an inch or two from hers, I whisper, "Is this okay?"

Her breath hitches, and I wonder if her eyes are closed behind her heavy-tinted lenses. She nods, her voice breathy when she speaks. "Yes."

Her fingertips brush over my chest, startling me. "Sorry," I mutter. "Just unexpected."

She doesn't say anything in response, her fingers exploring my chest as we bob in the water. Minutes pass, the sounds of other beachgoers fade away. All that exists is her and me and our bodies growing closer and closer as we explore each other's skin.

My eyes drop from her frames, focusing on her lips and wondering what it would be like to kiss her. I have dreamed of kissing a few girls before, but that is all. Just dreams. But I think if I kiss Cora, I will never want to kiss another person in my life. My eyes pop back up to hers, wishing I could see her bold green irises. See what she is thinking. What she is feeling. If they hold the same questions or possibility mine do.

Without thinking, I close the last inches between us. My head tilting, lips hovering breathless above hers, waiting to see if she backs away. When she doesn't draw back, I take the gesture as invitation and seal my lips to hers.

Warm, soft lips press against mine, her hands breaching the water's surface and wrapping around my neck. I pull her impossibly closer to me, swiping the tip of my tongue over her lips and relishing in the sensation when she parts them and lets me in.

Her mouth is sweet and hungry on mine. And when a small whimper echoes in her chest, I am a goner. My hands roam her body under the security blanket of the water, kneading and caressing her hips. We stay like this, the measure of time nonexistent.

But when I feel her legs wrap around my waist, her strength locking us together at the hips, I break my mouth from hers, gasping. At this rate, things will progress much quicker than either of us is prepared to handle. In public, no less.

"Why'd you stop?" she asks, confusion lacing her voice.

"Because we have forever. And I don't want to rush anything with you."

She leans into me, pressing a sweet, brief kiss to my lips. "I like the sound of that."

Present

"I don't understand the issue, man," Micah harps from the driver's seat. "I may not grasp what's going on between the two of you. Honestly, I never have. But you got to do what's best for you."

Why is it so hard to talk about women and relationships with guy friends? Unless they are in a relationship, everything comes out piggish.

Over the years, I've had several female friends. One of my best friends in Cali is female. We could talk about anything. Have in-depth conversations, no matter the topic, and come out feeling resolute. None of that is happening right now. Maybe because Micah has never been in my position. Never felt torn or anguished or helpless because of someone else.

"That's the problem. I'm not sure I know what's best for me anymore," I groan. "Before my mom took the promotion and moved us across the country, I had everything mapped out. Things changed days after we landed in California. Not only was my life turned upside down, everything I thought I'd have was ripped away from me." I pause, taking a swig of water before continuing. "Over the last decade-plus, she's always been the one thing I held on to. Even if I was the only one who knew. And now…"

Music blares from the speakers, masking the silence between us. Micah has no comprehension of what I am going through. My inner turmoil. A waging war roaring inside me. One side says I should head back to California when this shoot ends, leave her behind and allow her to resume the life she has built without me. The other side screams at me to return to California, sell my shit, strategize my future gigs and return to Cora's side. Sensible versus senseless.

The decision is one only I can make, but I was hoping for some form of support. Maybe some strong words of advice. Or just some *if I were in your shoes* talk. And unfortunately for me, Micah is no help whatsoever.

"And now, someone else is trying to step up to the plate," Micah states over the music. He states the obvious and my blood runs cold. I shiver at the thought of Cora being with someone. Someone who isn't me. Yes, I am a selfish ass for even thinking that way. But I left my heart with her all those years ago. I refuse to let an outsider stomp his steel-toes on it and whisk away my girl.

He steers the car into a parking lot, finding a spot amongst the crowd. We step out of the car and head for the entrance. Music blares loud and obnoxious every time the doors swing open. As we climb the few steps, I slap the back of his shoulder. "Thanks for bringing me out tonight. And thanks for listening."

"I'd be a dick if I didn't."

The whole situation with me and Cora is the furthest thing from what Micah wants to discuss, but he has always been a good friend. If anything, he probably just wants us to get things figured out—whichever way it turns out—and be done with all this back and forth shit.

We walk through the doors and the music hits me like a wall. Micah gestures to the bar when he steps up to the hostess stand and she signals us to head over. Both of us park on a stool and order a beer when the bartender comes over. After she deposits them in front of us, we each take a sip before sparking more conversation.

Micah and I catch up on life, avoiding all subject matter that could lead to Cora. He relays how the nightclub he manages is going. I suggest he brings me out there before I leave. He talks about an older woman, Rochelle, he dated for a little over a year. How serious his and Rochelle's relationship was until he found her fucking another guy. A guy ten years younger than Micah, and twenty-three years younger than Rochelle. Many heated words were exchanged between the two of them, but Micah said he would never be able to trust her again.

Since the relationship with Rochelle, Micah hasn't committed to anyone. He no longer sees the value in devoting yourself to one person. In his words, "setting yourself up for pain and heartbreak." Now, over the last year since they broke up, he is a proud manwhore. And when he tells me this, a pang of guilt hits me over the manwhore moments I have had myself.

Because over the last thirteen years, I have never wanted a relationship with anyone other than Cora. Although, I have gone on dates. Fucked a sea of women. Never once feeling guilt over suppressing the loneliness inside me. But now that I am back here. Now that I am within proximity of her. Everything is changing.

Micah prattles on about themed nights they do at the club, and I zone out while my eyes wander around the bar. The place is packed, which isn't abnormal for a Friday night anywhere. Bodies dancing on a makeshift dance floor. Tall tabletops littered with brown bottles, fried foods, and pint glassware. Horrible, screechy voices up on an eight-by-eight stage attempting to sing lyrics on a prompter. No matter where you are in the States, bars are bars. The only thing different is the accents and clothing.

As I make a final visual circuit of the bar, I freeze when I hit a tabletop close to the corner of the room.

Rage gushes in my bloodstream. My heart bashing against my ribcage like a boxer to a punching bag. Everything inside me molten lava and I am ready to beat the shit out of someone. Specifically, the brown-haired motherfucker touching my girl.

I kick back the stool, hitting the person behind me and causing Micah's head to swing my way. "Dude, you okay?" he asks.

My eyes fix across the room, hands balled into fists at my sides, breath heaving in my chest. Micah touches my arm and I flinch at the contact. When I don't answer him, he follows my line of sight and mutters *fuck me* under his breath.

"Let's just go, man. They're friends."

I hear his words, but can't take my eyes off *his* hand on *her* thigh. *Friends, my ass.* They may be *friends*, but he definitely wants to be more than her friend. And I am not having it.

Yanking my wallet out, I drop a twenty on the bar and storm off, half my beer forgotten. As I weave my way through the crowded bar, I hear Micah yelling for me, telling me to just leave it alone. But there is no chance in hell I am walking out of here and ignoring the two of them together. No fucking way.

I am ten feet and three bodies away from them when Cora looks up, her eyes going wide and her body scooting off the stool. She reaches me before I can get close enough to the table. Close enough to beat the shit out of this guy.

"Gavin!" she yells at me over the music. My eyes lock on his, and the self-assured smile he throws at me has me trying to push Cora aside. But her hand comes to my face and instantly stops me. "Gavin!" she yells again. This time I look down at her, noticing the fear in her soft green eyes.

We stare at each other a minute, her eyes trying to tell me that everything is not as it appears. I want to believe her. God, how I want to believe her. I have no reason to doubt her or her truths. But my insecurities sit on my shoulder, mocking me and whispering falsehoods into my ear. Telling me I will never have her again. Reminding me how I lost her once and how I will lose her again.

"It's not what you think," she whispers, and I have to read her lips over the noise.

"And what was I thinking?" I prompt.

"That we're on a date. That we're more than friends." Her voice grows loud enough to break the volume barrier, but not loud enough for others to hear us.

"His hand looked quite cozy on your thigh. For someone who's *just a friend*," I sneer.

Her hand runs down my chest and squeezes my hand. "Come outside with me." And then she pushes past me, towing me out of the bar and away from *him*.

We weave through the crowd, exit the front and continue walking until she stops us beside her car in the back of the lot. When she spins around, she drops my hand and hits me with years of anger and frustration.

"What the hell, Gavin!"

"Sorry I interrupted your date with mister auto shop," I jab, laying the sarcasm on thick. "I thought you two were just friends. Looks like he seems to think otherwise. Maybe I should go back inside and reiterate the definition for him."

"First of all" —she points her finger in my face— "you have no say in regards to who I date and who I don't. Second, why do you suddenly think you're all high and mighty? What… you stroll back into town and think the whole place stopped existing when you left. That everything is exactly as it was when you left. Newsflash, asshole. Nothing is how you left it. Nothing."

"I can see that," I seethe, stepping closer into her space. "If it was how I left it, this conversation wouldn't ever happen. We'd be…" I bite my tongue.

"What? What exactly would we be doing, Gavin?"

God, she is gorgeous when she gets angry. Dangerously so. And before I can form a rational response in my head, I reach for her face and drag her into me, crushing my lips to hers. Her hands shove and beat against my chest, her lips trying to pull away. But I strengthen my grip and get lost in the feel of her. The warmth. Her taste.

In two breaths, her will caves and she melts into me. Her hands fist my shirt as she kisses me with a fervor I have never known. I wrap one arm around her waist while the other hand skims up her back and gets lost in the length of her strands.

The kiss is packed with anger and frustration, fear and worry, happiness and pain. But most of all, it shares the depth of our deprivation. How neither of us has been complete since the day my mother put me on a plane and flew me thousands of miles away. How we have gone about life, but had forgotten what it was like to live.

She breaks the kiss, gasping for air as she tries to come back down to earth. When both of our bodies have calmed, she peeks up at me. "Gavin…" My name a blessing and a curse on her tongue. "Please. Please don't hurt me again. I can't..." she pleads. Begs me not to put her through the heartache she suffered thirteen years ago.

I yank her impossibly close to my chest, my arms cocooning her frail frame. "Shh. I know, baby. I know." The ease with which the term of endearment slips out isn't lost on me. It also doesn't appear to bother Cora. We stand like this—her clutching me and me pressing her to my chest, rocking her—for minutes, maybe hours. Letting her go isn't an option I am comfortable with, so I hold her and wait for her to break the connection. Praying she never will.

"Can we go somewhere to talk? I really don't want to stand in this parking lot all night," she whispers.

"Yeah. Wherever you want to go, baby."

$\sim$

Somehow, we land on the beach. Of all the places we could have gone, not quite sure why she picked the beach. The park across the street from her house is more her style. But maybe she chose the beach because it is mine. Or maybe she chose the beach because that is where everything evolved for us. Where everything went from friends to something words can't describe.

Either way, she is with me now and it is the only thing I focus on.

When we arrive at the beach, she pays a meter and we stroll north. After separating from the busier section of the beach, everything around us grows quieter and calmer. The only sounds are the crunch of sand under our shoes and the choppy water breaking on the shore. The air thick with humidity and salty on our skin. This part of the beach darker with the lack of businesses to illuminate it. A few residents out for a late-night walk.

Her hand presses softly against mine as she stops us from walking any further in the soft sand. Plopping down, our fingers still woven together, we sit on the beach and face the darkness of the Gulf. Neither of us says a word. We simply sit in silence and lean into each other for a while. Her ink-black hair whips across her face and mine.

The ease I have with Cora has never been replicated with any other person. Over the years, I tried dating. Tried putting myself out there and moving on, certain Cora was doing the same. And over time, I learned I would never find someone else who I'd want to be in a long-term relationship with. So, I shifted my ways. Became the polar opposite of how everyone knew me. Morphed into a slut. Because slutting around was easier than finding someone else and losing the one person you really wanted all along.

Because regardless of how things go between us now, Cora is it for me. The one soul on this planet, packed with eight billion others, meant for me. I have known it since the first day I saw her in high school, when she bolted into homeroom out of breath, making me out of breath. Confirmed it when we kissed for the first time, a beach not many miles from this one, and my soul sighed while my heart soared. I will never experience that with another person.

Nor do I want to.

"Gavin," she whispers into the darkness, breaking me from my introspection.

I turn and kiss her temple. "What, baby?"

She rests her chin on my shoulder, the waning moonlight illuminating her enough to where I can make out the soft lines and strong features of her face. Eyes a muted green in the shadows. Skin seemingly paler. Lips red and full and inviting. "How can this possibly work?" Her question weighs heavy and is full of doubt.

How can I reassure her everything will work out? That I have the capability to move closer to her. How I don't have to be located on the other side of the country to work. I know she should know this, with what she does for work. But there is only one way she will believe it all. Proof. And I have to give it to her.

My eyes hone in on hers. "I want to move back. The sooner, the better," I admit.

She straightens her back, stiffening at my admission. A thick strand of her ebony hair whips across her face, hiding her eyes from me. She doesn't move to swipe the hairs aside, and I force myself to keep my hands rooted in place, as challenging as it is. Minutes pass, the wind shifts and brushes the hair away. As desperate as she is to school her expressions, I read her like a book. Always have.

Curiosity. Speculation. Doubt. Fear. Elation. It is all written there in an ink only my eyes see.

I grab hold of the elation and press it close to my chest. Of all the emotions swirling in her eyes, it is the one that raises my hope for us. That we can find our way back to each other.

"But how?" Her question as wispy as the wind.

Cupping her left cheek, I brush my thumb over her plump lower lip. *God, I want to kiss her again.* But I must wait. Wait until she is certain that I am still what she wants. As much as it guts me to think of her with another guy, it isn't right of me to assume she will come back to me as easily. I hurt her.

"Baby, I can live anywhere and do my job. With what you do, you have to know this."

"But what about your life out there? Your parents? How can I ask you to leave everything you've built out there? It isn't fair for me to do that."

Her question about my parents strikes a chord in my chest. I'm not ready to update her on what has happened in that part of my life. Not until I know she is open to exploring *us* again. "You don't need to worry about that. Since the day we set foot in California, my mom has heard nothing except my orchestrated plans to leave. And you may believe it isn't fair for you to ask me to come back here. Back to you." I reach forward and press my palm against her sternum. "But this is where I belong. This is where I have always belonged. You are all that matters. All that has ever mattered."

She sucks in a breath as her eyes pool with unshed tears. In the shadowed night of the beach, everything is heightened and intensified. As if being in the darkness provides a blanket of security and you feel safe enough to expose your heart. There is something to be said about the darkness and its allure. Not just the darkness of night, but the yin in all things. That is what she is… my yin. The strong, feminine cosmic force who took hold of my heart and molded it with hers. Without her, I am a pointless yang. No balance, no life, no love.

Soft, thin fingers rest atop mine, encompassing my hand in the warmth of her skin. Below my palm, her heart beats wildly. Irrationally. While her heart tells me tales of excitement and joy, her eyes shed tears of insecurity and apprehension. Both of which I understand.

But a glint of something else resides there. Hope. A belief there is truth behind my words. That I am not just saying these things to taunt or mislead her. That there is an actual chance for us to rekindle something that never should have been diffused in the first place. A new opportunity to share the undeniable magnetism we have always had for each other. Hope for a new version of us. A better version.

"How?" The single word a question that rests heavy on her lips.

"I've been talking about moving back home for years. And now that my career has a better base, I can live anywhere. I don't have to be in the thick of Hollywood for people to find me. It was different in the beginning. Being out there helped get my foot in the door. Got me in front of the right people. But now… now I can be wherever. Alyson deals with all the contractual and legal aspects. She lets me know when someone is interested in hiring me. Sure, me living out there makes life easier for her. But she can still be my agent no matter where I am. Technology allows people to be on opposite sides of the world and still work together."

Beside me, Cora's body softens and relaxes into my side once more. And it feels so fucking good to have her body pressed against mine. Her warmth and energy radiating into me. Soothing me. Revitalizing me. Like being home again. She rests her head on my shoulder and I rest mine on hers, closing my eyes and breathing in this moment.

Waves crash along the shoreline, cars rev and honk in the distance, wind whips our hair and I can't tell where hers stops and mine begins. But neither of us moves. Both of us in a strange limbo of emotions and confessions. Our hearts thrown on the line, praying to not suffer the same pain as before. Promises exposed and hanging on the line as we breathe the same air for the first time in years.

But one truth holds absolute. I could sit with her on this beach for hours, not a soul around us, and feel nothing except bliss for the rest of my days. Everything about this moment is perfect. Everything about this moment is us.

Time evades us and I get lost in thoughts of what could be, causing me to almost miss when she speaks again.

"When?"

I am half tempted to tease her regarding the singular worded questions, but I bite my tongue. Now isn't the time to tease and play.

"When the shoot ends, I'll obviously need to go back. Alyson set up another shoot for me, but it should only be a day or two. And even though I don't have to do it in person, I need to go talk with my mom. Tell her I plan to move back as soon as possible. She is the only person, besides Alyson, who needs to know."

She lifts her head, stopping me. "What about your dad?" she asks, confused at why I only mentioned my mom.

I didn't want tonight to be when I brought this to light, but it looks as though I will have to tell her now. I take a deep breath and hold her gaze. The only set of eyes to ever provide me solace. "My dad passed away a couple years ago. Heart attack."

Instantly, her arms pull me into an embrace, lips at my ears softly whispering through light sobs. "Gavin, I'm so sorry. I didn't know."

Instinctively, my arms curl around her frame and I bring her closer to me. Within seconds, her legs straddle my lap and lock together at my backside. Yin and Yang. She weeps for me and my family. And I allow myself this moment to be raw, shedding tears for a man who was my role model for so many years. A man I have grieved for and thought I would eventually find peace after his passing. Until now.

Sharing this with Cora makes the loss of him more potent and noteworthy. More real and closer to my heart.

Part of me forgot my mom and I weren't the only people to lose him. When Cora and I started dating, my parents became hers too. After so many years apart, it never dawned on me to let her know sooner of his passing. Especially since we hadn't spoken for more than a decade.

When the tears quiet, she doesn't remove herself from our embrace. As if she knows the power it holds. As if she isn't ready to let it float off with the tide.

"Thank you," I whisper into her hair, my hands stroking lazy trails up and down her back.

"For what?" she asks, head tucked in the crook of my neck.

"For saying the right words. And just being you. Everyone I've told says or shows me pity. Or walks on eggshells when we're in the same room. As if I'm this fragile creature who will crumple. So, thank you. You've always known how to say just enough to convey the right thing."

I press a kiss to her temple and her arms and legs squeeze me tighter. We sit like this a little while longer before I make a suggestion to check the time. She pulls her phone from her back pocket, lighting the screen and mutters *shit*.

"Must be late," I assume. We have been here a while. Felt like hours. But when emotions are heightened, time has a tendency to not measure the same way clocks do.

"Almost two. We should go. We have to be at Honeymoon Island by ten. Somewhere in there, both of us need to sleep and eat and whatever else."

I laugh at her slight state of panic. "It'll be fine." I stand us up, her legs tightening around my waist, arms circling my neck. "Let me walk you back to your car."

After a few strides, she unhooks her ankles and drops her feet to the sand. Once she is upright, I weave my fingers with hers and we trudge through the powdery sand and back to her car. Every six or seven steps, I glance down at her and happiness floods my heart. Warmth and love and everything right in the world.

Fuck, I have missed her.

We reach her car ten minutes later. She offers to drive me the quarter mile back to my hotel, but I decline, wanting to walk back and reminisce over tonight. She slips into the driver's seat, starts the car and rolls down the front windows. Her hair whips across her face and steals my view of her perfect, soft green irises.

Bending down, I tuck the strands behind her ear and relish the way she leans into my touch. "I'll see you in the morning." *Fuck, I want to kiss her again.* My thumb brushes over her lower lip and she shudders, eyes slipping shut. How easy would it be to kiss her right now? But I don't. I won't. From now on, she needs to lead me. She needs to let me know she wants this as much as I do. I cannot be the only one putting myself out there. The only one pressing for this. For us.

When her eyes open, they smolder and I feel it deep in my groin. "See you soon," she mumbles, releasing a deep breath.

I step back from the window, internally cursing myself for not taking what I want. But I know I am doing the right thing. All good things come to those who wait. Right? She pulls out of the parking space, gives me a brief wave and drives down the road. Taking a chunk of me with her into the night.

Fourteen years ago

Thank God it is the last day of school. I have never really been one to not like school, in fact I have always been eager to be there. But I am counting down the minutes, psyched to have the summer off and spending more time with Gavin. This school year is one to go down as a year worth remembering. So much has happened, and it is unimaginable that I am dating my best friend.

Weekdays seem to snail along, with the exception of when Gavin and I are together. Most weeknights we study together. And by study, I mean finish homework between make-out sessions. Not that I have another person to compare it to, but Gavin really knows how to kiss a girl senseless. It is ironic we are both each other's firsts. First real relationship. First kiss. Those two kisses before Gavin don't count since neither guy knew what they were doing either.

Oftentimes, I wonder what other firsts we will share. Perhaps we will be the first people, besides our family, we say *I love you* to. Just thinking about him makes me want to scream it to the world. Let everyone know he belongs to me. And I belong to him. But I want to wait for the perfect time. To say the words to him when everything feels perfect.

Another first that has crossed my mind is sex. I know neither of us is quite ready yet.

We have been friends since the beginning of the school year, which turned into best friends within weeks. But we have only been girlfriend and boyfriend for six and a half months. Plus, we are only fifteen. Isn't sex something you wait to do when you are closer to adulthood? At least that is what all the adults tell you. But who knows when it's actually okay.

Any day now, it wouldn't surprise me if Mom and Dad have "the talk" with me. The talk is just a load of crap they tell you so you will stay focused on whatever it is they want you to focus on. Parents think having sex equals not doing anything else in life. I wonder if my parents dreaded the infamous talk. By now, everyone the same age as me has had at least one or two sex-ed classes—we aren't stupid. And we all have access to the internet.

But now… as I sit here in my English honors class, I'm not focused on the teacher—who yammers on about what books we should be reading over summer break. Nope. Instead, my mind swims with thoughts of me and Gavin and summer break and making out and sex. Anyone glancing my way would certainly notice the flush spreading along my face and neck.

From head to toe, I am hot. And it has nothing to do with the stifling outdoor temperatures.

Sex isn't a topic either of us has broached while together. But the thought has probably crossed his mind if it has crossed mine. How could it not? Don't guys think about sex more often than girls? That is what everyone says. Is he sitting in class right now thinking about it? Probably not. Geometry and sex aren't two subjects that pair well. Then again, I'm ignoring everything my teacher says and thinking about it. What's to say Gavin isn't doing the same. If I think about sex every other minute of the day, is Gavin constantly thinking about it?

Sex, sex, sex.

I shake my head, trying to clear my thoughts and catch Ms. Winters' final thoughts on summer reading. "Everyone, be sure to pick up a copy of the summer reading list from my desk before you go," she says a minute before the bell rings. "The sheet also has a few minor assignments you can earn extra credit on from your sophomore English teacher when school resumes." Thank God everything she just told us is on paper.

The bell buzzes for the final time of my freshman year and cheers erupt from every classroom in the quad. Twenty-three of us rise from our desks, gather our belongings and head for the door. I grab a copy of the printout and wish Ms. Winters a happy summer break. She gives me a brief smile on my way to the door and returns the sentiment.

When I step out into the summer sun, I take a deep breath and tilt my chin to the sky, closing my eyes. I stand there a moment, hundreds of bodies moving around me like the running of the bulls. Summer fever is in the air and everyone is excited to not be here for months. Me included.

Strong, warm arms circle around my waist, tugging me back until I make contact with the body behind me. *Gavin.* I would know him anywhere. Even if I couldn't see him, I would know he was there. That is just the connection we have with each other. An inexplicable bond fusing us together. Like a form of symbiosis.

I twist in his arms and turn enough to see his radiant smile in the sunlight. "Hey," I say.

He kisses me sweetly on the lips before responding. "Hey. You ready to get out of here?"

"Definitely. Want to grab something to eat? I think a bunch of people are headed to the sub shop."

"Yeah. Micah and Shelly are going. He said he'd give us a ride after if we went," Gavin states.

"Cool. Anything you want to do after?"

"I thought maybe we could hang and watch your favorite movies on repeat."

Like a five-year-old, I start jumping up and down like a fool. "Seriously?!" I plant a quick kiss on his lips. "You really are the best boyfriend ever."

His returning smile and hug tells me he knows.

∿

We are curled up on the couch, my back to Gavin's front, as *Lord of the Rings* plays on the television. We have just reached the part where Arwen is trying to help save Frodo's life because he had the ring on too long. Gavin stretches behind me, adjusting his arm as we spoon in the dim living room of my house.

His finger slowly skims up and down the side of my torso, repeating the circuit over and over. Since we started dating, he has touched me like this countless times. The soft strokes are sweet and soothing and stir flutters in my chest. But today, his touch feels different. My skin hotter. My body needier. Breath heavier. Heart more anxious. Only I'm not sure if it is just me feeling it.

God, I hope it isn't just me feeling it.

My parents won't be home from work for at least another two hours. And the realization of this tidbit causes perspiration to break free across my skin. My heart thump, thump, thumps louder in my chest. A tight pinch in my lungs as I try to breathe normal and not start panting. His fingers light a frenzy under my skin everywhere he touches.

When his fingers graze over the curve of my hip, my eyes roll back and I close my lids. A deep breath later and I roll over to face him. Once I resituate, his fingers continue their slow, sensual tease of my opposite side. I study his face, the light from the screen dimming and brightening with the scene and hiding his face every few seconds.

"You don't want to watch the movie?" he asks, confused.

I swallow hard and want to laugh at his question. Want to ask if he is joking. He knows I have seen this a hundred plus times. I have most of the lines memorized. Have backup DVDs in case one gets scratched. But he knows how much I love it, so I don't laugh. He watches them over and over with me because of how he feels for me. If that isn't some form of love, I don't know what is.

Reaching up, I thread my fingers through his hair and lean forward, bringing my lips to his. My top leg wiggles between his as he throws his over my hip, pulling me closer. We have made out on the couch before—at my house and his— but today feels different. More heated. More intense. A desire to go further. To take the next step.

His hand dips under my shirt and he grazes my navel with the tops of his short nails. The stroke has me drawing back and gasping. A second later, I bring my lips back to his in a frenzy. My hands roam his face, his neck, his chest through the cotton rock band tee. When I reach his waist, my fingertips tickle along the skin there, eliciting a hiss from his lips.

The urge to take it further lingers in the gravity surrounding us. Weighs us down. Both of us greedy. The fire. The hunger. The raw intensity of lust and desire. It drives us forward. As much as I have thought about waiting until we are a little older, I can't deny how much I want him in this moment. And if I want him like this, I can only imagine what he must be feeling.

But he breaks the kiss. Our breaths panting, hearts hammering. And neither one of us can shift our eyes from the other.

"Do you not want to…" I leave the question unfinished, unsure if this is something he wants. He has as much of a choice to make as I do.

He catches the worry on my face and his answer is immediate. "I do. Believe me, I do. It's just… what if your parents come home? That'd be a moment no one would ever forget. Plus" —he sweeps a few straggler hairs aside— "I'd like our first time to be more special than the couch while watching a movie. Not that we have to plan it, but it's a big deal. For both of us."

He makes a valid point. But I can't help the rapid-fire pulse banging in my chest right now. Or the intense craving that grows low in my belly. "I guess you're right. But can we keep making out? I was enjoying myself immensely."

His laugh is loud and throaty and vibrates against my chest as he brings me closer to him. "Sorry I cut you off, baby."

And then he leans down, brings my mouth back to his and we get lost in each other for the remainder of the movie. Arms and legs, hands and fingers, feet in tangles, skin touching skin. It's hot and needy and all-consuming. When the credits scroll up the screen, we have to tear ourselves away from each other. Gasping and overheated.

Everything is perfect. Everything is wonderful. And I pray it will be like this forever.

twenty-three

CORA

Present

Can exhaustion and jubilation go hand in hand? Most days I would answer with a resolute no. Absolutely not.

But today, after only five hours of sleep, I haven't stopped smiling since my eyes opened. It was the first reaction I had when my alarm sounded. Made brushing my teeth a bit more challenging. Even Luna noticed the difference in my demeanor when I poured kibble into her bowl, her furry little body weaving between my legs and purring loudly. If her mama is happy, she is happy.

The young woman behind the counter at the juice bar hands me my coffee and a small brown bag containing my coconut bowl. I sip the delicious brew before exiting and hopping back in my car. Before starting up the engine, I steal a quick bite of my bowl and relish in the creaminess.

The drive from Main Street to Causeway Boulevard is brief, loaded with sights and people. Runners and cyclists and families. Parks and playgrounds and golfers. One of my favorite parts of Dunedin is the small-town vibe. Everyone here is friendly. The town bursts with energy. Events pop up every weekend, if not more frequently. Not every city has the same community atmosphere. It is invigorating and refreshing to know places like this still exist.

The line to get into the state park is long, as is typical on a beautiful day like today. I pay the attendant and drive into the park, heading for the agreed-upon meeting location. Blue skies with sparse clouds make up the view as a gentle breeze blows through my rolled down windows. The trees lining the road inside the park sway and glow under the beaming sunlight. This time of year is when my slice of Florida is perfect. A slight coolness with a ghost of the summer to come.

Parking under a small, rare patch of shade with my car backed in, I scan the lot for Alyson's rental. When I don't see it, I retrieve my bowl and enjoy my breakfast while waiting for her and Gavin to arrive. Rock music vibrates through the speakers around me. Five bites from finishing and three songs later, Alyson and Gavin drive through the lot in search of a space.

Dark sunglasses mask Gavin's eyes from the world, his head pressed against the headrest. I imagine he is as tired as I am. No doubt his eyes are closed behind the lenses. We have exhausted each other, but are taking things in stride this week. I wouldn't change any of it. More than happy to have exhaustion bleeding through my veins if things between us will shift for the better. Head back down the path we once traveled.

"God, I missed him," I whisper to myself.

Although I haven't dreamed it for two or three years, envisioning Gavin in my arms again has been something I never let go of. How could I let him go completely? How could I wipe away what we had? Our history… we didn't just share the best two years of my teenage life. Two years that tattooed every perfect moment and emotion on my heart. Every important exchange between two people in a relationship, we had every single of those experiences together. First legitimate relationship. First real kiss. And sex... no one ever forgets their first. He was mine and I his. And no one can change any of that. No one can rewrite our firsts.

When he left, I was certain he would come back as soon as he could. We had it all planned out. Down to the very last detail. Or so we thought. But when you're young, and can't pay to travel across the country, plans change. Promises slip through the cracks. People fade into the background.

Alyson parks three spaces down and across from me. I sit in my car a minute longer, watching from the driver's seat as Gavin gets out of the car and scans the parking lot, a hand hovering above his sunglasses. The moment he spots my car, his shaded eyes landing on mine, a monumental smile stretches across his face.

"Damn," I whisper on a sigh.

I have only seen this smile a few times from him, including the one he gifts me now. It echoes off him, bounces through the atmosphere, and hits me with a force that knocks me breathless. My lips part as I suck in a breath, his eyes not missing the effect he has on me—even fifty feet away—causing his smile to brighten further.

Walking with a bounce in his stride, he sidles up to my door and pokes his head through the open window. "Good morning, baby." His lips warm against my neck as he imprints his lips on the skin below my ear.

An audible sigh exhales from my chest as my eyes roll back before my lids shut out the world around us. Heat fires in my chest; surging, rising, spreading to every nerve ending in my body. His lips and tongue travel a path along the curve of my neck. All coherent thoughts vanish and I melt into a puddle in my car.

A cough from behind him interrupts the moment and snaps us both back to the reason why we are here. My eyes flick to Gavin's, his happiness reflecting my beaming smile. "Good morning," I say, breathless.

"Shouldn't we get started?" Alyson gripes, a hint of irritation in her voice.

"Yes. Sorry," I apologize, rolling up my windows and stepping out of the car. "Let me grab my equipment from the back and then we can start."

She nods, then asks, "Where's your assistant? Do we need to wait for her too?" Her tone transitions from irritation to annoyance in point-five seconds.

What crawled up her ass and died?

"Erin won't be here today. Minimal equipment is necessary for today's shoot. Plus, she had a prior engagement." My tone is courteous, when all I want is to give her the same level of shit she dishes out to me. But, as always, I take the higher ground.

She starts walking toward her car, speaking over her shoulder at us. "I'm grabbing my bag from the car. Be ready when I walk back over."

As soon as she is out of earshot, I glance up at Gavin, silently asking why the hell Alyson is being a top-notch bitch to me today. Lifting the hatch on the back, I grab the cameras I plan to use today, hooking the straps over my head.

Seconds pass before he speaks up, his voice raspy and low. "She's upset with me. This morning, I broke the news to her that I plan to move back to Florida. She knows I still want her as my agent, but isn't thrilled with the idea of doing the job from the other side of the country."

Hanging my head, I mumble, "So, this is also about me. Her frustration isn't just with you, but also with me. Am I right?" I hate that us being together will cause a rift in his career.

He brushes my hair behind my ear and follows the gesture with his eyes. "I didn't mention you when I spoke with her earlier. But I'm sure she put two and two together with my greeting you. None of that matters, though. I'll talk with her. Explain things she knows nothing about."

My chest tightens as guilt riddles me. I don't want animosity—between him and his agent or me, by proxy. "Okay. But, Gavin…" I pause and he locks his gaze on mine. "Please don't make me the sole reason you return."

He cocks his head and studies me a minute. His eyes narrow then relax behind his sunglasses as he starts to shake his head. "You don't get it, do you?"

"Get what?" I furrow my brows, obviously unaware. A small piece of my heart tells me I know the answer. Whispers it softly in my ear. But the gut-wrenching memories step out of the shadows and remind me to never assume. Assumptions kill dreams and crush hearts.

"It has always been about you. It always will be."

"Gavin…" He can't say things like that. Not unless he is prepared to back every sentiment. And not with more words or promises, but with actions. Actions are what I need.

His fingers brush along my jawline, from my temple to my chin. "You don't get it, baby. I have missed you every day since the moment my mom packed our life up and moved us away. It's been four thousand six hundred and ninety-eight days, Cora. And until I'm back here, with you beside me again, I won't stop counting. Because it's the only thing that gives me hope."

My throat squeezes at his words, making it hard to swallow the lump building from emotional overload. Making it difficult to breathe. How do I follow up after he confesses facts so heavy? Anything I say after seems minuscule. But not responding makes me an asshole. Just as I am about to formulate a response, about to use my words, Alyson steps up to us and huffs.

"You two ready? The day won't last forever," Alyson snaps.

"Yep," I snap in return. "Just discussing things while we waited for you." I am over her shit already. It is too damn early to be bitter, but my lack of sleep is making me grouchier than usual. "Follow me," I command, turning and walking away, not looking to see if either of them follows.

I understand her pissy state—I do. But being a bitch because someone chooses their happiness over yours is just plain shitty. Yeah, her job won't be as easy going forward, but it's manageable. Several professions nowadays don't require people to reside in the same city, let alone state.

We walk a while, maybe thirty minutes. None of us mutters a word. The silence between the three of us borders on awkward. But the quiet gives me time to replay Gavin's earlier confession. To come to the realization that he has missed me more than I previously suspected. But if he has pined for me all these years, why has he not done anything to remedy it? Why didn't he reach out to me? He should have at least tried to explain what changed. It makes no sense. In the beginning, sure. Neither of us had the means to visit each other. But if he has wanted to return so badly, what has stopped him? His job? His mom? Maybe someone else?

The thought of another woman being the reason has my stomach churning. No doubt Gavin spent time with or dated other women over the last thirteen years. I'd be shocked if he hadn't. But the idea of him being in a relationship *now* has bile coating my throat. So, I shove it aside and file it in the *ask Gavin later* part of my mind.

A quarter mile down the trail, I stop in my tracks, and Gavin runs into my backside.

"Sorry," I mutter. "I should've said something to let you know we were here."

"It's okay, baby." He kisses my temple before correcting his stance.

Behind us, I hear Alyson huff and mumble something under her breath. Honestly, if she doesn't chill the hell out, I am going to open my mouth and bark out things I cannot take back. I won't regret a single word, but they will reflect poorly on my professionalism. And today is not the day to test my sanity.

Alyson slides a collapsible chair from a bag, opens it and plops down. After a minute, her focus shifts from me and Gavin to her incessantly dinging cell phone. Whatever keeps her attention focused elsewhere is good with me. Because every ounce of my rational side prays she remains silent the entire shoot. For her sake and mine.

This section of the trail is near the water, so we have the ability to get photos in the greenery, near the water, and a combination of both. The location is absolutely perfect. Not only for the scenery, but also because today's shoot entails more skin. More skin than I typically shoot. More skin than I have probably seen on another guy in years. And not just any skin, but Gavin's skin.

Please, powers that be, let me make it through today without doing or saying something stupid. Please.

Hence the need for partial seclusion. Alyson is nearby, but not close enough to see us in clear view. Let alone, hear us.

Don't get me wrong, I have taken intimate pictures before. Couples who wanted to capture special moments such as pregnancy. Women—and men—who wanted to do something special for their significant other such as boudoir sessions. Boudoir sessions are the extent of the raciness in my portfolio. And they were saucy, steamy, and intimate as hell, but very different from this.

Because this is Gavin. The only guy I have loved. The only person I have imagined having a future with. And the one guy who ran away with my heart thirteen years ago and held it hostage.

The first shots are simplistic. Him in board shorts against the foliage backdrop. Some with the waterfront at his backside. All reflecting the strength of his chest and arms without flaunting it. The shorts rest low on his hips, the definition of his lower abdominals peeking at the front of the waistband. I swallow and do my best to maintain composure. After I'm satisfied with the number of shots taken with all backdrops, we prep for the next set of photos.

When he drops his shorts, and I glimpse the thick-banded boxer briefs hugging his toned gluts and upper quads, I swallow. Hard. My insides swirl with a new thread of desire. My thighs clench together as I gawk at the outline of him in the branded underwear. And for a moment, I forget I am here to do a job.

I am so fucked.

When my eyes come back to his, a teasing smile occupies his face. Not only was I checking out the lines and definitions of his body, but I was caught doing so. And he is eating it up.

Should I be embarrassed? Normally, the answer would be one-hundred-percent yes. If it were any other client, I would be apologizing endlessly. But with Gavin, I wear my ogling with pride. It's difficult not to smile back at him. And let's get real, Gavin is hot as hell.

Bringing the camera to my eye, I flush as I stare through the lens. He is enjoying this way too much. It is written all over him—how he flexes his muscles and contorts his body, how he eats me alive with his eyes, and how the prideful smirk refuses to leave his lips. I inhale deep, realizing I have had the camera pressed to my face for more than a minute without taking a single photo.

And he knows it.

"See something you like, baby?" His smugness penetrates the air and drifts my way.

Don't answer him. Stay strong. Keep your mouth shut. Don't...

"Maybe," I tease. "Still up for debate."

His laugh pierces the silence of the pathway and echoes through the trees and out to the water. While not posing, I hold down the shutter and capture Gavin in his natural state. Candid photos have always been my favorite, although most of them are kept in my own private collection. The shots just taken will more than likely never leave my laptop. And I will enjoy them for years to come.

After we capture enough shots along the path, we walk to the small section of beach. Some poses on the sand before he enters the water. Several poses while he is in the water, the waistband and a couple inches of the cotton below it visible. And then he strolls out of the water, prepared for the shots of him lying wet in the sand near the surf.

In this moment, three things hit me with complete clarity.

1. Gavin is wearing white underwear.
2. The fabric isn't as thick as I originally thought.
3. Gavin is hard as steel as he walks toward me with a shit-eating grin on his face.

I can't breathe. Can't speak. Am rendered immobile. My face is hot, and not from the sun beaming down on us for hours. My limbs have forgotten how to function and my jaw is stuck in the open position.

Breathe, Cora. Inhale... Exhale... You can do this.

I can't do this.

Shit. Fuck. Damn.

The camera hangs suspended in my hand, just below my rosy face, as my sole focus is on his body. Yes, my eyes are zeroed in on the girth below the now see-through cotton. But my periphery catches the ripples of his lower abdomen, his V more visible and pointing directly at his pot of gold at the end of the rainbow.

It's not as if this is the first time I have seen Gavin in all his glory. But the last time I saw him anywhere remotely close to naked, we were sixteen and his body looked nothing like the one before me. The Gavin from my memories is good-looking and desirable and made my heart sing.

But this older version of Gavin...

Heat rises in my chest, trickling throughout my torso and seeping into my limbs. It isn't as simple as me being turned on by his appearance—I have seen numerous attractive men over the years that never sparked this incendiary feeling inside me. Part of it is visual, but another part is the knowledge that he only has eyes for me. That he only wants me. That every part of him is reserved for me.

"You okay, baby? You look a little heated," he teases then adds a soft chuckle. "We can take a break. Grab some water."

I stick my tongue out at him as if we are kids again, following it up with a goofy face. Bringing the camera to my eye, I drag in a deep breath.

This is work, Cora. Focus on the work aspect.

"Nope. I'm good," I tell him, coughing to clear my throat. "Although, I'm not sure how many of these shots will be usable."

Through the lens, I see his head cock to the side as his brows pinch together. The shutter closes at a rapid-fire pace, photo after photo taken and stored on the SD card. He steps closer and closer as I try to focus the lens higher and higher.

A hundred or so frames later, Gavin speaks up. "Why?"

For a moment, I am confused by his question. Not sure what he is asking about. "Why what?"

"Why won't some of the shots be usable?"

I continue shooting as I speak, not taking my eye away from the viewfinder. "Well, from what I've been told, this shoot is for magazines everywhere. An ad campaign for the clothing and accessories."

He nods. "Yeah. So?"

"And I think it's meant to reach a wide age range, starting with teens."

"Okay…"

He is not picking up on this. Not one bit. And damnit, I am going to have to come right out and say it. Internally, my hand slaps my forehead. *Just say it. We are both adults, for fuck's sake.*

"Gavin, parents won't want their teenage kids looking at an ad where the model has an erection, which is one-hundred-percent visible through the wet material. Many of the older female population may enjoy it, maybe some men too, but that won't be the only eyes on the ad."

His laugh is throaty, his abs contracting in ways that coil my insides tight. I continue taking photo after photo, capturing more candid shots. When he finishes laughing, he walks the small distance to me. My camera still glued to my face as he approaches, snapping as many photos as possible. He slowly pushes the camera aside and tips my chin up so we are eye to eye.

"Do you know how *hard* it is to stand practically naked in front of you? Knowing your job is to look at me. To take photos of me. Your visual assessment has me hungrier for you with each press of the shutter release."

I swallow hard, the sound from the action echoes loud in my head and I wonder if he hears it too. His pupils dilate more, his steely-gray irises darkening with each passing second. If he believes it is challenging to be in front of the camera, he has no idea how difficult it is to be on the other side. To view him through the lens and attempt to keep every thought I have as practiced as possible. To remind myself I am working and to be on my best behavior.

"It's not so easy from where I'm standing either. Having to maintain complete photographer-client idiosyncrasies while I snap photos of the one person who incinerates my insides. When—right now—the only thing I want to do is trace my fingers over every line of your body."

Neither of us looks away. His chest rises and falls faster with each breath he takes. The friction of his chest brushing against my nipples builds a delicious, insatiable heat between my legs. Right here, on the white sands of the small beachfront, I want him to kiss me. Want to feel the heat of his lips brush against mine. Against my skin, down my throat and…

A cough rings out behind me, and I snap out of my fantasy. Gavin peeks over my head, his smile faltering when he sees who stands there. Only one possible person could be there. Alyson. And from the scene she walked in on, I would not be shocked if she policed the rest of the shoot.

Gavin's eyes come back to mine before he bends to press a soft kiss on my lips. "I'll try to think about something else so we can wrap this up."

I nod, blurting, "shitty diapers."

He tips his head in question. "Shitty diapers…" he says, dragging out the words.

"Yeah. Think about that and it'll solve the current *setback*."

He walks backward, a hearty laugh bellowing from his chest. "You always know the right thing to say."

We hike back to the cars, Alyson leading the way twenty feet ahead of us and griping over how bloodthirsty the insects are in Florida. Gavin falls in step beside me, his fingers wrapped around mine and clutching me as if I might slip away. Not a single word is spoken for ten minutes as we follow the trail.

When we reach the opening, I hear Alyson mutter *thank God* under her breath. Gavin laughs loud enough for only me to hear, shaking his head at her bitching. Obviously, the mosquito population isn't as predominant in California. Seeing as summer exists the majority of the year in Florida, I would not be shocked if mosquitos were dubbed the state insect one day.

Once we are back in the lot, Alyson walks over to her rental, but not before sending a knowing look to Gavin. A look that says she understands, but also not to push her boundaries. What those boundaries are, I am not privy to.

I press the unlock button on my key fob, lifting the hatch and tucking my cameras into the bags under the cover. Gavin stands inches away as his gaze sears me. After everything is in its rightful place, I step back and close the hatch. When I turn to face Gavin, my eyes roam his body. Starting at the waistband of his board shorts—which barely hang on his hips—trailing up the grooves and curves of his abdomen, falling on his pecs—where my mouth waters at the sight of the barbells through his nipples—rising up his throat. I watch his Adam's apple bob as my eyes scrape over his stubble and lips, and eventually land on eyes that want to devour me.

Fuck me.

His expression says everything his mouth is not. The way his tongue jets out and swipes along his bottom lip before he clamps it between his teeth. The slight smirk that follows. How his irises shift from steel to pewter. A slight rise and fall of his shoulders as his breath comes faster. How his pulse noticeably pumps harder in that spot just below his ear.

Not only does he want to kiss me. He wants to peel away my shorts and tank. But he also aches to run his fingers through my hair, ball them into fists and yank the strands taught against my scalp. To see my body bow and plead for his touch, his mouth, his tongue. Along every inch of my skin, rebranding and rememorizing all the places he has been once before.

Both of us stand stock-still. Not touching. Not speaking. Sharing a bond our bodies and hearts have never forgotten. The void between us grows less dark and vacant with each passing second.

He flings the shirt he's been holding over his shoulder, sliding his sunglasses down and shielding his eyes from the sun. "Have dinner with me tonight," he states. It is not a question, but also not a command.

Every coherent thought in my mind screams at me to tell him no. That we shouldn't be doing things together as if we are a couple. At least not until this shoot is over and I know I'm not throwing my heart on the line. My brain fights with my heart—battles with my soul—and tells me to be rational, to think this through and understand the repercussions if something goes amiss.

But I ignore my brain. Tell it to shut the hell up and let me live in the moment. Because it has been so long since I have lived in the moment. Or lived life to its fullest. And I am tired of hiding—who I am and what I want. Tired of missing out on life and love.

"Yes." It's all I say. Because I don't trust myself to say anything else right now. If I open my mouth, I may say words I said once before but should wait to say again.

His body comes alive and his expression mirrors a jubilance I have not seen in ages. It rolls off him in waves, piercing my aura and infecting me with a dose. I cannot help but smile at his behavior, his energy, his life force.

"Any requests? I'm open to whatever," he says.

Feigning indecision, I tap a finger against my lips. If Gavin remembers anything about me at all, he would know my answer. But for good measure, I drag out my supposed thinking. When I feel I have sufficiently tortured him enough, I answer.

"Maybe we could grab some Asian," I suggest, biting my lower lip.

A laugh rips from his throat as he shakes from head to toe. "I should have known that would be your answer," he chuckles out. "Anywhere in particular you'd like to go?"

"How about I figure that part out, seeing as I'm more familiar with the area. Want me to pick you up?"

"It wouldn't be a proper date if you're the one picking me up. How about I meet you at your place and we drive from there?"

"Seriously? We're almost thirty and it's the twenty-first century. Women can pick up men for a date."

He nods, his laugh sparking back to life. "I realize what era we live in, baby. Doesn't mean I can't try to be somewhat of a gentleman. Even if I don't have my car with me. But I'll find a way to get there, then you can take the helm."

I walk to the driver's side door, Gavin a step behind me with his hand on my hip. Opening the door, I toss my phone on the seat before turning to face him and say goodbye. When I turn, his face is a breath from mine. His lips hovering danger-ously close and his eyes locked with determination. As he leans closer, my eyes close, my body ready and waiting to feel his lips on mine. Just as warmth paints my lips, Alyson honks the rental's horn.

"Let's go!" she hollers.

And just like that, she has plucked my last nerve today. I swallow it down and don't let it ruin the moment.

Reluctantly, we pull apart. Our bodies now separated by feet rather than inches. But the vibrating energy between us remains. Almost like when we were teens and our parents walked in the room.

His hand squeezes my hip. "I'll see you later, baby. Is five thirty okay?"

"That's fine. See you then," I say as he releases my hip and walks away.

Immobile, I watch as he gets into the car and Alyson backs out. He gives me a sweet half smile as they drive past me. The car leaves the lot, drives on the paved two-lane road and heads for the exit. It's not until the car is out of sight that I slide into my car, start the engine and roll down the windows. And as I drive out of the park, my mind drifts over all the possibilities of what tonight means. For us. For our future.

This is really happening. The only person I have ever truly loved is back in my life. And he has promised to return to me. To stay with me. To keep me forever.

Fuck if I am not excited about tonight. About the possibility of a future with the one person who has been tattooed on my heart for more than a decade. The one person I never want to be apart from again. The one person I cannot wait to spend every day of forever with.

The entire way back to the hotel, Alyson chews me a new asshole. Bitching and moaning about how I need to be more mindful in regards to my actions. Scolding me worse than any occasion my parents did. And how I better not forget I am under contract—with her, the clothing designer and the magazine. As if I need reminding. As if this is my first shoot.

I let her have her moment. Allow her to complain and reiterate the same shit on repeat. Spew the same garbage she has since the first day of the shoot. But when she finishes, I take it as a sign that I finally get a chance to speak. To tell her what is on my mind. To shut down her tirade.

"Alyson, you know how much I value your opinion and expertise. But there are a few parts of my life that are *not* what *I* pay *you* to handle. My love life is not part of your job and most definitely will never be a part of your pay grade. Do you understand?"

There is no plainer way to express this to her. I only hope she gets where I am coming from. That I am not trying to be a dick and just laying the basics out there. She needs to understand me being with Cora is permanent. She needs to get used to us being together and me living my life how I want.

We drive south on Edgewater, not far from the Dunedin-Clearwater border. "Of course, I understand. But you pay me to make decisions that will impact the future of your career. And this" —she gestures behind us— "her, will impact your future. In more ways than one."

That is what I am hoping.

"I realize she'll change my future. It's what I'm hoping for. The one thing I've wanted for years. And now I have the ability of returning to her." I pause a moment and ponder over my next words. "This will make things different with our relationship, but you can either represent me from afar or I can find someone else. The choice is yours."

I hate to throw ultimatums on the table, but I will not have her or anyone else hindering my return. Not Alyson. Not my mother. No one. Although, a small part of me thinks my mom may be happy for me. After our move to Cali, I witnessed how sad she was for me. How guilty she felt for removing me from my friends and girlfriend. It hurt me, and her by proxy.

"Well, aside from your plan to move—" she says hesitantly, then continues. "—don't forget about the shoot you have booked with Layla. And speaking of Layla, how will all of that work out if you move across the country?"

I shoot her a pointed look, but she doesn't catch it with her eyes on the road. "I'll talk with her. She'll understand. Besides, she's good now."

"I hope you're right."

"What's that supposed to mean?" I question, fire building in my chest. I am so over Alyson, her selfishness and her annoyance with me living my life how I choose.

"Nothing. All it means is I hope it doesn't ruin you or her."

"It won't," I snap. Alyson is grasping at straws. Trying to make something of nothing. Trying to rile me up. But I won't feed into her line of bullshit.

The remainder of our drive is quiet. Alyson churning my words in her head, realizing she has an important decision to make. She is either on board or she isn't. And trying to throw bullshit about Layla in the mix—it is a low blow, even for Alyson. I have been working for years to get to this point. To return to Cora. And now that I am able, nothing will stop me. Nothing will take this away from me. From us.

～

The Uber driver dropped me off in front of Cora's house five minutes ago. So why am I standing out front? My feet locked in place on the rustic paver pathway leading to her front stoop. I stare at the gray siding, black shutters, and black-framed glass door, taking my first, true assessment of her home.

A large oak tree shadows most of the yard with lush ferns growing around the base of the trunk. Two ducks waddle away from the ferns and cross the street to head for the park's pond. A brick chimney painted dark gray crawls up the eastern wall of the house—and although fireplaces aren't used often in Florida, I bet she uses it every chance she gets. Small flowered plants encompass the border of the house—pops of yellow and red and purple in the foliage—white rocks at their base. Large windows take up the majority of the exterior walls and allow for hours of natural light. Strands of starry lights dangle from the roof over the stoop. Every-thing about this house screams her style. Simple. Clean-cut. Monochromatic. With the exception of the colorful plants.

I remain rooted another minute before dragging in a deep breath. The reality of us coming back together hits me like a lead weight. A burning tightness takes residence in my chest, building and expanding with every breath. It consumes every molecule of oxygen, every drop of blood, every fiber and jolts me back to life.

This is my future. She is my future.

God, I have dreamed about this moment for so long. Dreamed of her in my arms again. Imagined what life would be like waking up in the same bed every day. Moving around each other in the kitchen while making breakfast. Spooning on the couch as we watch movies in the dark. Discussing our day over dinner. Laughing together with friends. Creating a family and growing old together.

She is it for me. Always has been. Always will be. Not a single day has passed where I haven't thought of Cora. Wondered what she was doing. How she fit into the world now. If she still thought of me. If she would be able to love me again.

Fuck, I love her so much.

The front door opens and Cora stands in the doorway looking at me with ques-tions in her eyes. "You okay?" she asks, doubt in her voice. No doubt she has seen me standing out here. Hopefully not for too long.

"Yeah. Sorry." I stride up the path and stop in front of her. I plant a kiss on her forehead and inhale deeply, filling my nose with the scent that is one-hundred-percent her. "Was just admiring your house. You've done so well for yourself. And it suits you so much."

"Thank you," she says, a timid smile pushing up her cheeks. "You coming in? Or do you plan to stand out here until we leave?"

I step past her, seeing the inside of her house in a new light. The interior isn't overly spacious, but it is enough for her. *For us.* I love how easily I picture our future. Our road may have had major detours, but we are finally coming back to the path we belong on. *Together.*

To the right, the living room—maybe twelve square-feet—showcases the fireplace from the eastern wall with a charcoal and gray fabric couch opposite. A resin-coated wood slice coffee table rests between the two, decorated with a wide bowl of succulents. To the left is the kitchen and dining area. The kitchen is small yet vast. A large fridge at one end, the range near the other end. On the small island sitting between the kitchen and dining is a farmhouse sink and enough space for a few people to sit on stools and eat at the bar. Planked wood and riveted steel make up the dining table with four seats attached that swing underneath. Along the far wall of the dining area is her desk—a restored piece with distressed black paint and two shallow drawers. Simplistic art decorates the walls while minimal pieces adorn the furniture. With a tall vaulted ceiling, the cozy house is more spacious than it would appear from the outside.

I smile as I take it all in. There is not one part of this house that doesn't have a piece of her in its grain or plaster or beams. Without a doubt, I would recognize this place as hers in a heartbeat. Her style screams from every nook and cranny. Her predilection for minimalism and simplicity shine from every corner, wall, and piece of décor.

"I was almost finished getting ready when I saw you outside. Give me a minute and then we can go."

"Take all the time you need, baby. I'll be out here waiting," I say as I sit on the couch.

Seconds after I sit, an all-black cat jumps up beside me, purring and rubbing its head on my arm. I scratch and pet the cat as it takes a liking to me. *Glad you like me because I will be around quite often.*

"And that would be Luna," Cora shares. "She's a lover and will probably coat you in her fur before we leave. Good thing I own several lint rollers."

I laugh as I pet Luna and she loves on me further. As I stroke her soft fur, the thought of her one day being *my* Luna brings a smile to my face. Since becoming a model, I have never owned a pet. As much as I wanted one, the thought of leaving a dog or cat behind for weeks on end doesn't sit well with me. It would be unfair to them, and me, to have someone pet sit and me not spend time with them. They may not be human, but they are your children all the same.

Cora breaks my introspection when she walks back into the room. "Ready when you are. Unless you'd rather spend date night with Luna," she says and giggles, a sound I haven't heard in so long. I almost forgot how musical her laugh is. Almost.

Patting Luna's backside, I whisper my apologies to her before rising from the couch. "Lead the way, baby."

We head out the back door, get in her car and drive to dinner. A little over thirty minutes later, we pull into a small parking lot beside an Asian vegan restaurant.

She leads us inside and I love it immediately. The restaurant is small and simple, low-key. Absolutely perfect.

Once we are seated, we look over the menu and choose a few appetizers as well as our meals. We talk about life and key things that have happened to us over the last thirteen years. And as awkward as it is, we discuss relationships we have had. Funny enough, neither of us has had a relationship that lasted more than a few months. Neither of us finding someone who fulfilled us in the same way we do each other. And to me, that speaks volumes.

I share with her my plan to move back after the shoot in Cali and how I will still be able to work being out here. She points out why she is skeptical it will work— not us, but me working. That I won't have the same connections as I do now. But I beg to differ. Since I have been working in the industry for the last ten years, I have developed several contacts and am able to find work whenever and wherever I choose. And moving to Florida, I will end up discovering a whole new array of connections. Ones I would never have in California. Tampa, Orlando, and Miami are major cities picking up steam in the modeling industry.

The rest of dinner goes by seamlessly. Conversations about both of our work lives cease. We pack up our leftovers and I pay the bill. Soon thereafter, we are on our way back to her house. The drive back absent of conversation as we listen to music and enjoy the feel of our fingers laced together. And when we park in her driveway, the atmosphere between us grows heavy. With questions. With uncertainty. And most of all... desire.

twenty-five

GAVIN

Thirteen and a half years ago

As dorky as it sounds, I can't wait to celebrate our one-year anniversary together. Although we have been best friends for the last year and a half, we weren't dubbed "official" until this time last year. Most people assume it is only the girl who gets excited about these moments. But I am buzzing with the thrill and ready to celebrate with the one person who means the world to me.

Brakes squeak as Cora parks in the driveway, the new-to-her Toyota a little rumbly. Her parents bought her the used car a couple weeks ago after she officially got her license. It has been great to be able to do our own thing, within reason, and not be subjected to our parents taking us places or annoying older friends with cars.

I run out the front door, yelling to my parents that I will be home by curfew. Swinging open the passenger door with a bit more oomph than expected, I slip into the seat, lean over the center console and kiss my girl breathless. When we come up for air, I stare at the hazy expression on her face. It is a dash of euphoria mixed with the soft lines of her angelic face. And I never tire of seeing her this way. Happy.

"You can't do that," she whispers, her eyes hidden behind her lids.

Leaning back into her space, my lips hover a breath from hers. "Can't do what, baby?"

"Kiss me like that and expect me to be able to function afterward."

I press a soft, chaste kiss to her lips. "How can I not kiss you like you hold the other half of my soul?"

Her eyes flick open, her green irises shimmering in the fading light of the day. Darting back and forth between mine, her eyes expressive in their desire to know how we could both feel the way we do. We idle in the driveway another minute, the car vibrating beneath us, as so many things are said without a single word spoken. How is it I know everything she is thinking without her even telling me?

The answer is simple really. Cora is my home. She is the one place where I feel most at ease. The one person I can be myself around and never feel a sense of shame or reservation or judgment. She makes my breathing spike and my heart soar. And her fingers on me… her touch is lightning in my veins.

There is no other person I could imagine spending my life with. I may be only fifteen—almost sixteen—and less experienced with life, but this fact is etched in my bones. Carved since the day I was born. Not just for me, but for her as well.

After a moment, she drags in a breath and faces the steering wheel. "You ready?" she asks, her voice unsteady.

"As ready as I'll ever be."

Rock music spills out of the speakers as we drive toward Indian Rocks Beach. For our one-year anniversary, we decided to go to a small Italian restaurant between the beach and intercoastal. Asian food is Cora's version of crack, but she wanted to do something different tonight. And as many times as I told her we could go to our favorite Thai or Japanese restaurant, she gracefully suggested we go somewhere new.

To create a new memory for this milestone moment. A memory we will never forget. I wanted to tell her there is no way I would ever forget any minute involving her.

Pulling into the parking lot, she finds a space and parks. We get out of the car and it is the first time tonight I get the opportunity to see what she wears. Part of me is shocked, while another part of me is turned on.

For the first time ever, Cora is in a dress. Her usual denim bottoms and cotton graphic tee are nowhere to be found. But this dress suits her. In more ways than one. The fabric clings to her like a second skin, accentuating all the curves lying beneath. Curves I have touched, but not really seen altogether. Nestled in the black material are small shapes I can't make out from where I stand. As I inch closer to her, looping her arm in mine, I see the shapes are cat faces. From afar, anyone could misconstrue them as polka dots. Her dress is the perfect mix of black, rock and Cora.

"You look beautiful," I tell her, planting a kiss at her temple.

"Thank you. You're looking pretty good yourself."

To be honest, I feel underdressed next to her. In a pair of black jeans and a navy button-down with the cuffs rolled to my elbows, this is the most dressed up I have been since I was little and my mom dressed me for special occasions. It isn't that I don't look nice, but Cora is stunning.

The hostess walks us to our table, a flickering votive candle and a small vase holding two red roses rest in the center. Our server greets and informs us of the specials for the evening, then takes our drink orders and disappears. We are both silent as we look over the menu, my mouth watering at all the delicious options. In my periphery, I catch Cora setting her menu down.

"Do you know what you're having?" I inquire.

"Yeah. I was tossed up between the spaghetti carbonara and the gnocchi a la Villa Gallace. They both sound amazing, but I think I'll get the carbonara. You want to share the Caesar salad for two?"

"Caesar sounds good. I'm still on the fence. Lasagna or rigatoni Bolognese?" I look to her for guidance.

"Ooh, that's a tough call," she says, tapping a finger against her pushed out lips. "Layers or tubes, layers or tubes." She bobs her head side to side as she tries to help me decide. "Tubes," she exclaims. "That's what I would choose."

"Tubes for the win!" I belt out a little too loud, mouthing my apologies to the other patrons when they look at me. "Oops," I whisper, both of us laughing with hands over our mouths.

Our server returns, setting our drinks and a basket of bread with garlic and herb oil on the table, then takes our order. When he walks away, we simply gaze at one another. In the time since Cora and I first met, we have learned we don't need to fill time by talking about things that don't hold value to us. We have a bond, a language all our own. Words don't need to be spoken. *We just know.* I stretch my hand across the table and she places hers in mine. Connected. Everything is always better when we are connected.

Our dinner arrives and we dive right in. On the small bread plates, we each portion our dish and pass it to the other. As we eat, we talk about school and friends and our plans during the summer. When we finish, I pay the bill and we leave the restaurant.

Cora drives the car to a beach access parking lot on the other side of the two-lane street. This time of day is generally busy and it can be challenging to find a space, but we land one and make our way to the sand. Just before we step onto the beach, both of us slip our shoes off and carry them as we stroll onto the warmed, soft grains.

After walking for five minutes, we locate a spot where no one obstructs the view in front of us. Plopping down on the sand, Cora leans into me as we watch the sunset. We had timed dinner perfectly so we wouldn't miss this moment. If you have never watched the sunset along the water's horizon, you have been deprived.

The sunset was a favorite of mine. Sharing it with my girl made it more special.

Right now, the sun radiates a hot orange glow like the sphere of fire it is. The sky surrounding it shifts from a soft blue to a light yellow. And the lower the sun drops on the horizon, the more brilliant the colors. Yellow morphs into faint and then bold oranges. A mixture of orange and pink spark next, filtering between the clouds. Shadows and hints of purple edge the stratocumulus clouds floating above as the sun slowly descends.

When the sun dips below the horizon, the sky still dances with colors and clouds. The visual is magical and I am so lucky I get to share it with someone I love.

I shift and turn to face Cora more, her head lifting from my shoulder. One arm still wrapped around her waist, I bring the other to her face and cup her jaw, brushing my thumb over her lips. "I love you," I whisper.

Just now, it is the first time those words have been said in our relationship, but I mean them with every fiber in my soul. Whether or not she reciprocates doesn't matter. Something inside me yearned to release the sentiment. Like a ticking time-bomb would detonate inside me if I held it in any longer.

Her eyes hold mine—unmoving, welling. She kisses my thumb that continues to stroke her lips. "I love you, too." The second those words leave her lips, every single molecule inside me radiates warmth. My soul is complete, whole.

Under the brilliance of the setting sun, I lean in and kiss the hell out of the only person in this world that matters to me. The only girl I will ever say those three miraculous words to. My Cora. My love.

~

We stumble into Cora's house, giddy as school girls. After our proclamations, we left the beach and headed back to her house to watch a movie since I have a few hours until curfew. No doubt it would be *Lord of the Rings* again. But I don't care, as long as she is beside me. In my arms.

When I notice all the lights are off, I prompt, "Where are your parents?"

"At some charity function in Tampa. They probably won't be home till close to midnight, if it's anything like last year."

A sudden rush of anxiety trickles up my spine, spreads through my limbs, and explodes beneath my sternum. Today is our anniversary. We are alone. After professing our love for each other. And she is looking at me like she has no desire to watch a movie, but perhaps do something else. Something more.

She stalks closer, locks eyes with me and stops when her chest brushes mine. Her fingers reach out and draw lines down my bicep, my forearm, interlocking our fingers. Heat expands and contracts like a breathing organism in my chest. My breath comes in quick, short bursts as she inches closer and closer. And when she pushes up on her toes and kisses me, I forget how to breathe altogether.

The kiss starts off tender and gentle. She slides her hands back up my arms and laces them behind my neck, toying with the edges of my hair. Her tongue darts out and swipes a slow and sinful line over my lower lip, and I moan at the sensation as I part my lips and invite her in. My arms snake around her waist and draw her impossibly closer. Within seconds, the kiss elevates into more. More heated. More passionate. And I can't get enough of her. Her lips, her warmth, her taste.

We start moving, but I don't open my eyes as she slowly guides us. It seems as if we have been walking for hours when her body weight shifts and we settle in place. Our lips break for a moment, which is exactly when I realize we are in her bedroom. Next to her bed. Dim moonlight illuminates the space between the slats of her blinds. And the sudden proximity to her—in the darkness, in her bedroom— amplifies everything I feel for her.

Standing tall, I gaze down at her as she lies back on the bed, elbows propping her up. I want this—want her—but I need to know she feels the same. That she doesn't feel a sense of obligation to take us to the next level. That she wants to do this of her own volition. I would never pressure her into doing something she isn't ready for. Never.

"Cora…" I rasp, my voice thick with emotion as I draw out her name.

She reaches out her hand, her eyes telling me to take it. Wrapping her fingers with mine, she drags me closer. My knees bump the edge of the bed and sweat breaks out across my skin. "Yes, Gavin."

Yes? As in she is responding to me. Or yes, she wants to do this? Wants to take the next step. Sex. What exactly is she saying yes to?

"Are you sure?" I ask, reluctance in my tone. I don't want her saying yes because she thinks it's what I want her to say. "Because we don't have to if you're not ready."

Her brilliant green eyes pierce mine, her voice steady and firm when she speaks. "I am sure. I don't think I've ever felt more ready in my life." She gives my hand a gentle tug, signaling me to join her on the bed.

This exact moment has infiltrated my dreams for months. I never knew when it would happen, but the fantasy of it was a regular occurrence. Now that it is happening, I am not sure what to do. My feet remain rooted to the floor as I look down at her on the bed. She wants me as much as I want her, although it may be a bit lopsided in my favor. Am I ready for this? To share this once-in-a-lifetime moment with her? Yes, I have never been more ready. So, why am I not moving? Why can I not put my knee on the bed and crawl my way up her body?

"Gavin?" She peers up at me, confusion furrowing her brow. "Are you okay?"

"Yeah, I'm okay. Just give me a second."

"If you're not—"

I cut her off. "I am. It's just… you don't know how long I've waited for this moment. And now that it's here…" I trail off, not knowing how to explain how overwhelmed and buoyant and in love with her I feel right now.

She rises on the bed, perching up on her knees on the mattress edge. "We can go slow. Maybe just fool around with clothes on. Go from there."

I nod, inhale deeply and focus on her eyes. The way they glimmer in the dim light in her room. Her lips. And how soft they feel when I press mine against them.

The warmth of her hands as she frames my face and leans forward, her breath teasing my lips. Her frankincense and gardenia scent wafts around me and entices me further. Makes my pulse throb in my ears and my heart pound in my chest. Has my breaths coming faster, dizzyingly. And when I lean in to kiss her, we melt together.

Our kiss starts off slow, two sets of soft lips brushing together. Her hands slide down my neck and onto my chest as her delicate fingers separate buttons from fabric. I break out in goose bumps when she spreads the cotton, pushes it down my arms, leaves it to dangle from my waist and exposes my skin. A new form of hunger surges beneath my ribcage and in my groin. The kiss morphs, growing in intensity and becoming more animalistic when her nails scratch light lines down the backside of my torso. I tip my head back and gasp.

She takes hold of my hips and starts to crawl backward on her knees, pulling me on the bed. And this time, I don't stop her. Every part of me is desperate for her. Lips, mouth, tongue, hands… more.

Our kiss never falters as she lies back on the mattress and brings me with her. A frenzy erupts between us, and the urge to taste more of her grows stronger with each passing second.

Breaking the kiss, I paint my lips along her jaw, her ear, down the curve of her neck. Her breath ragged beneath me as her chest rises and falls faster with each taste as I consume every inch of her. Running my hands down the sides of her dress, I slide down her body and begin kissing her ankles, her calves, her thighs. When I reach her dress, I slip my fingers under the hem—warranting a gasp from her—and scoot the material up her body. Cora sits up, helping me lift the tight, stretchy fabric and yanking it off her body.

As her body lands on the mattress again, my dick jolts at the sight of her. Matching black lace covers her breasts and the junction of her thighs, the material sheer enough to see her pert nipples and a thin patch of curls. *Holy shit.*

She wrenches me down, and we are all mouths and tongues and roaming hands. Minutes later, she tosses my shirt away as she unbuttons my jeans and shoves them down my legs. The second my pants hit the floor, my lips move down her chest and explore. My tongue lavishes her nipples before licking its way down her navel and hovering above her panties.

My eyes lock with hers, asking permission. She nods, running her fingers through my hair and tugging. Slipping my thumbs under the elastic, I slide the lacy triangle down her thighs and to the floor. When I come back to her body, I taste her for the first time. Her addictive flavor a blend of salty and sweetness on my tongue. A moan rips from her throat as I melt into her, my dick throbbing between my legs.

"Oh, god…" she garbles.

She is sweeter than any confection I have ever tasted or imagined. But when I kiss my way up her body, and our tongues collide again, I become even hungrier for her. Her hips grind against me, begging for me to give her more.

Rising from the bed, I reach for my pants and remove my wallet, taking the condom out of the hidden pocket. Holding it between my teeth, I shove down my underwear, tear the package open and roll the condom in place.

Hovering above her on the mattress, I hold her gaze. Neither of us moves. Neither of us says a word. We stay like this a minute, letting the reality of what we are about to do settle in. Then, I press a soft kiss to her lips. I kiss her slow. I kiss her as if no one else exists.

"I love you, baby."

"I love you, too."

And then I learn about heaven.

twenty-six

CORA

Present

Why does it feel like this is our first date? The passion and heat and uncertainty. Will he kiss me? Will he stay the night? What will happen once we exit the car? Should I invite him inside?

Why the hell am I so nervous? This is Gavin.

I find it funny that I feel all these things because we have done this once before. Every. Single. Part. Of course, the experience is different when you are sixteen and your hormones are on a one-way track to Sex Town. The excitement and lust are tenfold because the experience is new. But as an adult, it all just feels… different.

My heart and mind no longer ruled by my hormones. Not that I discount them because I know they lurk in the shadows. But as a woman… if Gavin and I go there. If we do this again—us—and it doesn't work out, I won't recover. Us trying to reignite what we once were, our history has been magnified times a thousand. Every memory is amplified and with more definition. Each new touch is layered with a newer meaning, a promise of forever. Something we thought we understood all those years ago, but couldn't quite grasp the magnitude.

But now… we comprehend it all. And spending forever with someone you love resonates in a whole new light.

We get out of the car and walk to the back door off of the driveway. He walks me inside and goes to the couch, Luna jumping on his lap the second he sits down. *Traitor.* But in the same breath, it melts my heart that my faithful companion has taken such an easy liking to him.

"Do you want to watch a movie?" I ask, hoping to break the pressure mounting between us. No doubt he feels it too.

"Sure. Whatever you'd like."

I kick off my shoes and settle in on the couch beside him, Luna looking at me as if I am invisible. *Double traitor.* Grabbing the remotes, I turn on the soundbar and Apple TV. After scrolling through my movie library, I click on *Hunger Games.*

Gavin wraps his arm around me and I lean into his chest, my head resting just below his shoulder. When the weight of his head rests atop mine, I sigh at the closeness we share. It has been a long time since I have had this connection. A bond that never goes away, never breaks. Something I have longed to have again, but came up empty-handed in every search.

For a brief time, I had thought maybe Jonas and I shared such a bond. But the more I tried with him, the more it felt forced and inappropriate. An imitation in a nice package. The only feelings I have for Jonas are strictly platonic. All I can hope is for his understanding. As my relationship with Gavin progresses, my relationship with Jonas will taper. Yes, I will always be his friend and he mine. But the boundary lines must be firmly drawn.

Luna purrs in Gavin's lap as the three of us cuddle on the couch. This is the closest I have felt to home in thirteen years. Warm and comfortable. As if the stars have realigned and everything is as it should be. And I pray I get to feel it every day going forward. The day Gavin left; a void took over the part of my heart reserved for him. A black hole. Life no longer functioned quite the same. The only thing that kept me going was knowing we would see each other again.

I secluded myself from friends and family. Found comfort in nothing as I sat thoughtlessly in my room, day after day. Went to school as required, but lost all sense of focus or determination. I ate less and slept more. Never left the house unless mandatory. Was forced to bathe and put on something other than pajamas or pieces of Gavin's clothes. Clothes which I refused to wash.

When minutes became hours and hours became days, days turning into weeks and months, a light inside me died. A light I thought would never burn bright again. Sure, the world wasn't quite as dim as the years became a decade and more. But now… now there is a flicker.

I wake wrapped in Gavin's arms, my body curled and pressing against his chest. Snuggling into him further, I inhale his beachy pine scent before he lays me on my bed and pulls the comforter over me. Beneath the covers, I undo my jeans, sliding them off and tossing them to the floor. He plants a kiss on my forehead and starts for the door.

"Stay." It is all I tell him. All I croak out in the darkness.

He spins around and his eyes search mine. Indecision highlights his face. So, I fold back the comforter on the other side of the bed and pat the sheet. I have no idea what the time is, but it is late and he has to be tired. No need for him to request an Uber at this late/early hour when he can just stay here.

"Are you sure?" His voice is riddled with insecurity.

"I'm tired. You're tired. We both need to sleep. So, just come lay down and get some sleep."

My words sound simple enough, but is the notion of sleeping in bed with Gavin really so simple? Sex is the furthest thing from my mind. His arms around me, though…

He hesitates a minute, watching me with an unreadable expression. Soon, his will caves and a thump hits the floor as he toes off his shoes. A second later, he tugs his shirt over his head and drops his jeans to the floor. The bed dips under his weight, the comforter shifting as he gets situated. When he stills, I roll to my side and snuggle close to him. Into him.

Oh god, how I have missed this.

For a solid minute, I swear he stops breathing. I lay my hand to the left of his sternum and feel his heart beating a vicious rhythm beneath my palm. *Is he nervous? Why on earth would he be nervous?*

"Gavin, is this okay? Me being this close," I whisper against his skin.

As his breath returns, his hand covers mine and holds it in place. His other arm snakes around my shoulders and hauls me closer. "Yes, better than okay. It's just been a long time."

I press my lips to his chest and settle against him, cocooned in his embrace. "Good night, Gavin."

"Night, baby."

〰

My body is hot. Like I have been tanning in the sun for countless hours during mid-August slathered in tanning oil. Every inch consumed by heat and sweat. The sweltering heat inescapable and becoming far beyond unbearable. I may suffer heatstroke any second.

On the cusp of sleep and awake, I shift between the sheets and kick a leg out, hoping to cool my body. As I scoot closer to the edge, pushing the comforter down to my waist, the bed shifts beside me as a hand crawls across my belly.

In a matter of seconds, I go from foggy and semi-alert to eyes wide open and body hyper-aware.

A groan rumbles next to me, a weighted thigh draping over my waist, the calf falling down my leg. The black-out curtains in my room make it close to impossible to see anything in my room. Under normal circumstances, I would be ecstatic not to see a single thing in my room. But that doesn't apply in the current situation.

Moving as slow as humanly possible, I turn my head and look to my side. Next to me, Gavin lies asleep. His face relaxed and flaunting the soft yet masculine lines of his face. I take this quiet moment, the one where he isn't studying my every observation or movement, and absorb all the parts of him I have missed over the years.

With my eyes, I trace the thick curves of his brow. Drift down and get lost in the feather of his long, dark lashes. Follow the line and curve of his nose to the philtrum above his upper lip, the small indentation masked by a day's worth of dark stubble. Stubble I want against my soft skin. And then resting on his full pink lips.

Seconds become minutes and I can't seem to locate the strength to look away from his mouth. My own mouth waters at the sight, the temptation to lean forward and wake him with my lips pressed against his grows with every beat of my heart. But as much as I want this man—this beautiful and enigmatic man—part of me screams to keep my heart protected. Memories flash in my head like old photographs, providing me with glimpses of the past and how I crumbled when he left. How impossible it was to breathe without him here.

With every cell inside my body, I want to believe what he tells me. That he is moving back. That he has never stopped thinking of me or us or the future we always wanted. And that his only desire is to be with me again. Believing those words, those sentiments, is all I have longed for with him. All I need. I want to breathe again.

But listening to your heart and protecting it don't always go hand in hand. They are two different plates on the scale and weighed separately. And I need to make a choice on which matters most. Giving in to what my heart desires or shielding my heart from future pain.

"Good morning, baby," Gavin rasps, my body jumping at the sound.

My eyes bolt to his as if I have been caught doing something forbidden. The top length of his dark hair sits partially on the pillow and his forehead. I gaze into his steely-gray eyes, the irises a thin outline of his dilated pupils—which are immersed in me. His fixation on me is possessive and powerful. And as captivated as I am, I am also fearful and nervous.

What if we do this and we find out we are not who we used to be?

What if the affection is one-sided? Or too lopsided to make things work?

What if he moves back and it negatively impacts his career—or both of ours—

and he resents me? Can we continue a happy and healthy relationship in that instance?

What if we get back together and everything is perfect?

I allow the last question to tumble through my thought processes for a moment. Allow myself to believe that us coming back together is nothing short of amazing and perfect. Allow myself to believe this is our chance at a happily ever after. One can only hope we are fortunate enough for life to ebb and flow with ease and bliss.

"I can practically hear the cogs in your head cranking. What could require so much thought this early in the morning?" Gavin's eyes bore into mine, a light-hearted act meant to bring my thoughts to life.

"It is early." Closing the gap between us, I give him a chaste kiss before continuing. "And way too early for in-depth conversations. Maybe after we have some coffee and breakfast."

His fingertips trail along my cheekbone, tracing to my ear and leaving a current in its wake as he tucks my hair behind my ear. "Breakfast sounds fantastic. Here or out?"

"I think I have everything needed here, so let's stay in. Plus, I think Luna is upset with me and the lack of attention I've been giving her over the last week. She needs a little mom time and affection."

Gavin groans as he closes his eyes, his arm drawing me in closer to his warm body. He caresses the tip of his nose over the flesh of my collarbone, skimming up the front of my throat and inhaling deep below my ear. When he speaks, his words reverberate from his chest to mine and dampen my panties.

"Mmm, I can understand the need for time and affection. If I purr and rub on your leg, will I get something in exchange?"

My breath hitches as intensity and hunger bloom between my legs. As much as I want to play-shove him, I ache to bring him impossibly closer. To tear off the remaining clothes on our bodies and rememorize every freckle and scar and curvature that has changed over the years.

But I am not ready for us to take that step yet. At least that is what I keep telling myself. Maybe if I repeat it enough times, I will believe it.

"You know you're making it really difficult to leave this bed," I whine.

"Maybe we can have a different form of breakfast," he coaxes.

"As tempting as that is, I'm going to vote we do the real food thing. I'm not sure I'm ready..." I trail off.

His thumb brushes over my cheek, eyes sweet and conveying his agreement. "Baby, I will wait forever for you. It feels as if I already have. When you're ready" —he kisses me tenderly— "that's when I'll be ready."

Although I am not ready to voice the words aloud again, all I can think about is how much I love this man. How I have always loved him, even when I had found a way to shove every memory of him and us into some desolate corner of my mind. He is my foundation, cracked or whole.

"Thank you." The words barely audible.

"For you—" he says. "Anything."

And without a care in the world, our lips and tongues do a dance as old as time.

twenty-seven

This view will never get old.

After a half hour of lips sucking and tongues tasting and hands groping, we finally decided it was best for us to get out of the bed. Not that a bed is required for the many things I want to do with her. Although we have already had sex, that time of our lives was different. Back then, everything was awkward and new and questionable.

But now…

Our time apart is not something I relish, but it does give both of us a different vantage point. For me, I respect people and life on a whole new level. Everything has a fresher perspective, is more eye-opening. That is not to say I don't do stupid shit from time to time—because don't we all. Just that I now know, understand, and am willing to deal with the consequences of my actions. Whatever they may be.

Right now, I refuse to disguise my ogling of Cora's body. She moves around the kitchen—her back facing me—in a black cotton ribbed tank top. The hem clings to her hips while the bust line accentuates the curvature of her tits and shows a hint of natural cleavage. I know she isn't wearing a bra beneath the tank as evidenced by the occasional visual of her firm nipples against the fabric. Below the tank, cherry red low-cut boy short panties cover most of her round ass cheeks.

Watching her—I groan internally—has my dick hardening and my mouth watering. Her body is not the only part of her I love, but it is a nice bonus. The last time I got such an intimate view of her body, we were teenagers and our bodies still had a year or two of developing to go. Cora's body is as curvaceous now as it was then, but not quite the same. She has taken care of herself—diet, exercise, enjoying life as best she can—and it shows.

Cora moves around the kitchen—slicing strawberries and apples, adding them to a bowl with blueberries and squeezing a lemon over top. Stirring a large frying pan loaded with shredded potatoes, chopped onions, oil, herbs and spices. Flipping a few "sausage" links—I learned this morning Cora is slowly eliminating meat from her diet. And occasionally checking the time on her Instant Pot, where she cooks a batch of cinnamon steel-cut oatmeal.

When she told me she was removing meat from her diet, I rattled off twenty questions asking why. I also questioned whether or not the food she was making would be any good. But the savory aroma of garlic and the sweetness of maple and cinnamon flitting through the air has me hungrier than ever. The true test will be when I taste it all. Honestly, the links are the only thing I am questioning. Everything else is somewhat normal.

The Instant Pot signals it is done cooking the oatmeal as she flips the potatoes one last time. One thing I remember from our breakfast excursions years ago, Cora likes her hash browns dark with a crispy crust and tends to pile them high on her plate. And it looks as if nothing has changed in that department.

She heads to the cabinet holding the dishware, grabbing two plates and mugs. Setting the plates beside the stovetop, she pops a K-Cup in the Keurig and presses the large brew button after her mug is under the drip. When it finishes, she repeats the process for me.

Everything about this blip in time is perfect. This is how my life should be. Our life. We ebb and flow in synchronization. Natural. Comfortable. Synergistically.

As much as I tried, I never found another person who made me feel more myself than Cora. Being with her… everything just fits in place. Nothing is forced. It just… is.

"Would you like anything in your coffee? Sugar? Creamer?" she asks, breaking me from my endless one-sided staring contest.

"Creamer. Dare I ask what my options are?" I give her my best goofy-scary face.

"I only have one and it's coconut milk-based. It's good. You'll like it," she states with confidence.

I nod. "Then that's what I'll have," I tease.

Cora adds creamer to both cups and a small spoonful of sugar to hers. She sets my cup in front of me, then turns back to the stove and begins plating the food. Before I can offer to help, she sets a plate and bowl in front of me. Within seconds, she adds maple syrup, a jar of cinnamon and a jar of garlic between our place settings. A smile perks up the corners of my mouth at the sight.

My love for maple and cinnamon.

Her indescribable love and obsession for garlic.

When we were younger, Waffle House was a regular occurrence—as it is with most teens and partiers. But she always ordered a triple portion of hash browns—scattered and smothered—and brought her own container of garlic powder. The small jar an additional accessory in her purse. I had gotten used to seeing it for the almost two years we were together. It was second nature. But seeing it today has me laughing at the fact she still has the habit.

"What are you laughing at?"

Rather than saying it, I simply point to the jar before spearing a sliced strawberry with my fork.

"There is no shame in loving garlic. If I knew you loved it, I would have added it to the hash browns. Normally, when I make my own, I add at least three or four cloves of garlic. The more, the merrier."

Shock registers in my expression. "Three or four? In a single serving? That's a lot of damn garlic, baby. You worried about vampire attacks?" I joke.

"Ha-ha," she deadpans. "No, goofball. With anything else, you build a tolerance level over time. What would be a potent level of garlic to some, I barely taste. What can I say—it's not just my favorite food, but it is also good for you." She shrugs off her response as if it should be public knowledge.

"Next time, just add the garlic in with the potatoes. I'm a big boy. I can handle it."

"Alright, big shot. As long as you promise not to bitch about it," she prompts me.

I hold up my right hand. "I swear I won't complain—" I hesitate, but continue. "Much."

She sticks her tongue out at me, crossing her eyes and cocking her head to the side. And I fall a little harder.

～

We spend the work-free day driving all over. She takes me to downtown St. Petersburg, where we stroll along Beach Drive, check out some of the storefronts and visit the Dali Museum. So much of downtown has changed and it is as if I am in a whole new version of an old city.

The St. Petersburg Pier is no longer there. Cora tells me it was torn down about five or six years ago. Now, a large outdoor area has taken its place. A restaurant sits closer inland and the pier is more outdoor activity focused. It is kind of weird to wander around here and not see the old inverted pyramid building. I had so much fun there as a kid. Hopefully the city builds something that adds more flare to the current structure, which seems blah in comparison.

The Dali has also been relocated and looks nothing like the original. Now it resembles a piece of art and is amazing without even stepping foot inside. But we do walk through the exhibit. Dali's work has always fascinated me, with all the droopy clocks and ants or distorted images of his wife. One of my favorites is the *Geopoliticus Child*. It just reaches me on some strange level; intrigues me.

When we leave the Dali, we opt to leave Cora's car in the garage we parked in earlier. Hand in hand, we stroll along the waterfront near the marina and eventually walk toward the shops and restaurants. After about ten minutes, we are trekking down First Avenue North.

As we head for the entrance of a restaurant to grab lunch, I push out a quiet laugh at her choice of location. No matter how much time has passed, some things about her will always be predictable. And I love that those parts of her remain. That time hasn't changed her completely. She is still the same girl I fell in love with. Only now, she is one-hundred-percent woman.

"Are you laughing at me?" she insinuates.

I squeeze her fingers with mine. "You're joking, right? I mean, I should have guessed we'd be having Asian for lunch," I tease.

"Why mess with a good thing." It is all she says, her shoulders shrugging as if eating what you love should be a given. I suppose she is right.

The hostess seats us at a table, handing us menus and letting us know our server will be with us soon. As my eyes dance over the options—sushi and non-sushi alike—I am a bit overwhelmed at the options available.

"Do you know what you're getting?" I ask Cora, praying her order will guide me in some direction.

She taps a finger to her lip. "We're about to see what you really think about me," she states, her words cryptic and confusing the hell out of me.

"Huh?"

Laughter bursts from her lips, dying quickly before she rambles off her intended order. "Here we go... I'm getting an order of spring rolls, seaweed salad, the vegetable ramen—which comes with a salad—and a yam yam sushi roll minus the eel sauce."

My gaze locks in place, the sight of her blurring. *Is she going to actually eat all of that?*

"Um. Is there something you're not telling me? That's a lot of food for just one person."

Cora just shakes her head at me. "Nope. I like ordering a lot so I have leftovers to take home. I won't eat it all while we're here. Swear," she states with a giggle.

Thank fuck. I was seriously worried some other reason had her ordering enough food for two.

"Maybe I won't need to order anything if you're getting so much," I taunt.

"Makes no difference to me. But you should get whatever you want to eat." Then she smiles and I forget what to do. I snap out of my Cora-fog and shake my head, internally laughing at myself and how easily she sidetracks me.

I scan the menu one last time as the server approaches. Gesturing for her to order first, she prattles off her mile-long lunch order. When the server looks to me, I feel like a pussy for only ordering a shrimp tempura appetizer and a Tampa roll. As if we reversed roles in the food consumption department and my masculinity has been knocked down a couple notches.

We chat while we wait for our food. And once everything is spread out on the table before us, to say I am overwhelmed would be an understatement. Everything has its own dish and there are currently seven dishes on our tiny two-person table. Seven. But I'm intrigued to see how much she actually does eat.

Bite after bite, the food begins to vanish. Needless to say, I am done eating before Cora, and all I can do is sit back and enjoy the entertainment before me. She pops a piece of her sushi in her mouth, moaning around the tempura fried sweet potato and rice. The sound stirs me up. Has me dying to hear that moan—and all other delicious sounds—with me hovering above her.

When we were younger, we'd had sex a number of times before my mother shipped us off to California. In the beginning, things were awkward and uncoordinated—as it is for anyone having sex for the first time. But the six months that followed our first time, we learned and explored many things with each other. One thing I never remember Cora doing was groaning in pleasure. It's not that she didn't enjoy sex or that she wasn't orgasming—she was just a quiet lover.

And so many parts of me want to know if that little fact still holds true.

Today has been one of the best days I have experienced in a long time.

Gavin and I walked around downtown St. Petersburg for hours and had a great lunch, although he teased me endlessly about the amount of food I ordered and ate. What can I say? I love my Asian food and I love it more when I can enjoy it a second go-around.

After eating lunch, we strolled a few blocks before turning around and heading back to the parking garage. We blared music from my Spotify playlist through the speakers and drove with the windows down, the wind whipping our hair everywhere on the short stretch of interstate and highway driving. Close to an hour later, I drove over the backed up Memorial Causeway and on to popular Clearwater Beach.

As I pulled into the parking lot, Gavin spoke up for the first time since we had gotten in the car. "Come up with me."

Once I found a place to park, I looked over at Gavin, unsure of what to say.

"Come up with me," he repeats, soft-spoken.

Should I? Everything about us is molding back into place. Him asking me to come up to his room could be completely innocent. After all, he did say he would wait until I was ready before we took things further. And I believe him.

"Okay," I stammer. "Yes, I'll come up."

We hold hands from the parking lot to the bank of elevators, my bag of leftovers in his other hand. No words or sentiments are exchanged, not that they need to be. His body language and expressions tell me everything I need to know.

How much he cares for me.

How excited he is for us to be together again.

How nervous he is, his palm clammy against mine.

But most of all, how much he loves me.

Neither of us has broached the infamous *L* word, but it is there, dangling in front of us both. A few times I have almost let it slip from my lips. But I caught myself and battened down the hatches.

It's not that I don't want to tell him I love him. The complete opposite, actually. But if I allow myself to say the word, to convey the enormous level of emotion that partners up with confessing such a sentiment, it may change everything. And right now, I have no idea if the change would be for the better or worse. The way he has been around me—calling me *baby* like he did years ago—leads me to believe it would be the former.

And if I muster up the courage to profess my love for him—again—will he do the same? I can't put my heart on the line, not if I am unsure he will do the same. Not enough time has passed since his return. Not enough to know whether or not he will run off again.

The elevator pings when we reach his floor and we step out. Retrieving his wallet from his back pocket, he unlocks the door and ushers me in. With a loud thump, the door closes and he wanders over to the kitchenette, placing my food in the refrigerator. I stand in the entryway, staring at the room and how messy it looks. It is obvious he has told the maid service to ignore his room, which makes me want to laugh.

Thirty minutes later, we sit cuddled on a small loveseat, laughing at an episode of *Lucifer* on Netflix. We munch on chips and candy he had purchased on his first night here. The episode is almost over when a knock sounds at the door.

We both look at each other, confused. Before we started watching the show, we talked about grabbing dinner after, but not from room service. Maybe the maid was upset over not being able to clean his room for more than a week.

Gavin rises from the couch, kissing me on the crown of my head. "Probably someone knocking on the wrong door. I'll be back in a sec."

His bare feet pad across the floor as he disappears from my direct line of sight. The loud clunk of the deadbolt disengaging echoes in the room, followed by a slight creak of hinges. When he got up to leave the couch, he had paused the show and created a vacant silence in the room. Right now, that silence is deafening.

Mumbled voices come from where Gavin went to open the door. A door which has yet to be closed. Which means whoever is at the door is either lost or is someone Gavin knows. My stomach suddenly constricts, a heavy sickness settling in my core.

Is it Alyson? Is she giving him more shit regarding us?

Curious as to what is taking Gavin so long to return, I rise from the couch and walk toward the door, my stride quiet and slow. The closer I get, the clearer I hear the conversation. A woman's voice chirps from the hall, her words sweet and her tone casual. And I determine by their exchange she is someone Gavin knows. And knows well. And it isn't Alyson.

When I take a few more steps, I hear Gavin muttering under his breath, anger seeping into his voice. A couple more steps and I can see the door. Can see Gavin's back and the slightest bit of wavy, blonde locks. His words to her are venomous as he tries to make her leave. But when he shifts to his left an inch or so, she catches sight of me and a devilish smile takes over her features.

Who the hell is this woman?

Thirteen years ago

"What do you mean you're moving?" I ask, tears welling in my eyes and threatening to spill at any second.

He runs his fingers through his hair, grabbing hold at the roots and yanking as he bows his head. "My mom. She got transferred; promoted. Whatever. But her new position is in California. So, we have to move." He tugs his hair harder before releasing it from his grip and looking at me with bloodshot eyes.

I have no clue what to say. Or what to do. How to react. In this situation, is there really anything I can do? There is no way I can stop his mom from accepting the promotion she rightfully deserves. Nor can I stop her from taking the only person I care about to the other side of the country, almost three thousand miles away. If we were older, maybe we would have a say.

Covering my face with my hands, I mumble, "When?" Although, I am terrified to know the answer.

"She said we're leaving next week," he says, his voice cracking at the end.

"Next week?" I whisper. "But what about school? And us?" My voice shrinking the more I speak.

A vignette darkens the edges of my vision. My world slowly closing in on itself. Nausea roils in my belly and crawls up my throat.

He wraps his arms around me, enveloping me in a tight embrace. His warmth is pure comfort, and I close my eyes and allow myself a moment to get lost in the feel of him. Breathe in his scent, the earthy beach smell that only Gavin has. Hear the sound of his erratic heartbeat beneath my ear on his chest. My head shifting with the rise and fall of his lungs.

He can't leave. He just can't. Gavin is home. Where I belong. And I am where he belongs.

One of his hands caresses the back of my head as his lips pepper small kisses on the crown while he shushes me. Our bodies rock back and forth, the movement subtle. And I squeeze him as tight as humanly possible, my body trembling as I am wracked with sobs. Maybe if I hold him tight enough, he won't leave.

"We'll figure something out, baby. This is just as painful for me as it is you. I don't want to leave," he confesses. "Not you. Not here. You are my home, Cora." He echoes my internal sentiment.

"You're my home, too," I reply as tears flood my cheeks. "If you're not here, I'll be so lost."

He wraps me more securely in his arms as if he is trying to prevent the eventual departure we both know we have no control over. I wish it were that simple. I wish we had a say in the matter. A voice. But we don't and that hurts even more.

He withdraws from me, bringing his fingers to my chin and tipping my head back. Our tear-stained, puffy red eyes hold each other's. The pain in my chest swells more with each passing second. My lungs burn as I refuse to breathe in this form of reality. This cannot be happening. This cannot be real. If I don't believe it, maybe it won't happen. Maybe he won't leave.

"I will find a way back to you, baby. It may not be right away. But never doubt that I will return. The only place I want to be is beside you. Forever."

A heavy sigh escapes my lips. *Why could this have not waited another two years? When he could stay behind.*

"I love you, Gavin," I tell him, and it reaches deeper than the hundreds of times I have told him before.

He brushes a cluster of stray hairs from my face, tucking them behind my ear. "And I love you, Cora. More than anything else in existence."

I sniffle back my tears and congested nasal phlegm, the sound and motion very unladylike. We both laugh at me. But when we stop, both our faces locked in serious expressions, I whisper-rasp, "Happy Birthday, Gavin."

And seconds later he has me wrapped in his arms again.

I help Gavin put the last of his things in a cardboard box, closing the flaps and sealing it with tape. Grabbing the Sharpie on the floor, I write *Gavin's room* on the box and proceed to doodle a quick image of a beach beside it. If having a small drawing by my hand on cardboard is the only piece of me he can take with him, I will draw on every box possible.

"Thanks," he mutters, his mood growing infinitely more sour as we packed up his life here. I don't blame him. If our roles were reversed, I would behave the same.

"You're welcome."

Looking around his room, I take in the bare blue walls. Before he was required to pack everything he owned, the walls had been littered with rock band posters and concert flyers. Images of surfers and the beach and us as well as our friends. Now, all those pieces rest in boxes or tubes, waiting to be added to new walls. In a new house. Thousands of miles from here.

The built-in bookshelf is now coated in a layer of dust after his collection of magazines and books got tucked away and packed inside the large moving truck outside. All the furniture had been taken out of his room a few hours ago. The carpet depressed from the feet of the bed and dresser, and outlined with the faded color where the sunlight couldn't reach.

His room now a skeleton of a space I once deemed comforting and warm. His room as hollow as the hole growing in my chest.

He lifts the box from the floor and heads for the door. The last box. And the last time we would be in his room. I carry the packing tape and marker, trudging down the hall and blindly following his footsteps.

With each step we take, the world as I know it slips further and further away. No more lunches at school or meetups before or after. No more laughter or teasing. And no more movie nights or walks on the beach or sunsets. Or holding hands, embraces, or lips against mine. No more Gavin. And no more us.

By the time we reach the moving truck, tears flow like rivers down my cheeks. I do my best to make no sounds, but the restraint it requires is fading fast. It feels as if I am intentionally giving the love of my life away. Shoving everything he owns into this truck and saying goodbye forever. Packing him up and shipping him off to who knows where.

Over the last week, we spent every possible moment together. Not a moment wasted. Yes, he had to pack up his life. But he tried to do that after curfew so we could have as much us time as possible. Yet it feels as if we had no time at all. It feels as if every moment we have shared for the last two years is being ripped away and shredded into a million pieces.

As soon as he gets to California, I bet I won't hear from him often. He will be busy unpacking and adjusting to a new school just before the year ends. It isn't only a major adjustment for me, but more so for him. Not only is he losing me— losing us—he is also being thrown into a foreign place with zero friends. The only people there to comfort him are his parents. The people upending his life.

He sets the box in the truck, taking the tape and marker from my hands and placing them beside it.

Before I can think of a single word to say, he yanks me close and holds me as if his life depends on it. On me. My sobs come faster and harder. His chest shakes around me with his own turmoil. Anguish and heartache leak from both of us and there isn't a damn thing we can do about it.

Minutes later, his dad taps on his shoulder and tells him it is time for them to leave.

After a few labored breaths, he pulls back with hesitancy. His eyes swollen and red as he looks into mine. "I love you, baby. Hopefully, I can come back during the summer." He kisses me and steals my breath, my pulse soaring in my veins.

"I love you, too, Gavin. Call me when you land."

We exchange one last kiss and embrace, and then he is whisked away. My legs giving out as I collapse to the ground, where I cry for the next three hours. Alone. In the front yard of the boy I love. The boy who just left.

Present

When I open the door, I am beyond shocked to see Layla in the hall.

"Hey," she singsongs, waving a hand at me.

"What are you *doing* here?" I whisper-yell. "And how did you know where my room is?"

Her bright smile fades as her brows furrow in confusion. "I had a shoot in Miami. Just thought I'd surprise you on my way home. Alyson adjusted my flight for me, so I'm here till tomorrow morning. She told me which room you were in and suggested you might want to grab dinner."

What. The. Actual. Fuck. Alyson?

She knows Cora and I have been working on mending our relationship. And she also knows I have every intention of moving back to Florida as soon as I can sort out the details. Is this her play on keeping me in California? Sending Layla to my door and having her attempt to swoon me over dinner.

Not that Layla could ever hold my attention in that way.

Now I have got some choice words for Alyson the next time we talk. And they won't be pleasant. In fact, they will be downright ugly.

"That was nice of her, but I already have plans for the evening," I tell her as I start closing the door.

Her hand comes up, preventing the door from moving any farther into the frame. "What the hell, Gavin? So, *you have plans* and now I'm no longer good enough to be around?"

I really wish she would lower her fucking voice. Not only do I not want Cora hearing her, but I also don't need the people staying in the other rooms to hear her flipping her shit. I give her a pointed look, telling her to quiet down. She huffs and rolls her eyes like she gives two shits what anyone else thinks. After all, Layla is quite the attention whore.

"It's not that. I have plans with someone else. Plain and simple. Please don't try to peg me as the bad guy here. If you would've called or texted me and told me you were coming, I could have made different plans," I press, my body heating and becoming more anxious with each passing second I am away from Cora. As it is, I have been at the door far too long for it to be a wrong room situation.

"Why are you being such a dick?"

"Me? You randomly show up and expect me to drop whatever it is I am doing because you're here. Sorry. Doesn't work that way."

She needs to fucking leave. Now.

"You're different," she accuses. "Alyson was right."

"What the fuck does *that* mean?" Now Alyson is talking shit behind my back. I groan as I picture Alyson calling Layla in for interference. And at this point, pissed doesn't even begin to cover how I feel.

"Don't worry, she didn't go into any specific details with me. But she told me you've changed since being out here. That you plan to make bigger changes, too."

Tomorrow, Alyson and I are going to sit down and have a very detailed conversation about keeping her mouth shut and her nose out of other people's business. One—I pay her. Two—her job is to do what's best for me, not her. And in no way is this benefiting me. This is all about her. I cannot believe she brought Layla here, purposely changed her flight and gave her my room number. What sort of game does she think she is playing? Does she seriously think this will sway my decision? My privacy is more invaded than ever now and a newfound rage builds inside me. A rage neither Alyson nor Layla will enjoy.

"Not that it is any of your business, but yes. I plan on moving back to Florida after I get a few things situated in California."

"You cannot be serious. How will you work from here? What is so goddamn alluring about this place?"

I shift my weight, her questions irritating me. This conversation is done. And I'm done. With her and Alyson.

Just as I am about to shut the door again, a wicked grin lights up Layla's face. A grin I know all too well. One that tells me she is about to do something spiteful and vindictive. Her eyes look past me, over my shoulder and into the room.

The hair on the back of my neck stands at attention. A boulder sinks in my gut. Before I even turn around, I know Cora is standing behind me. I *feel* her. More than likely, she was curious as to what was taking me so long to return. She has no idea who Layla is, but Layla knows about her. Not her name, but that the one person I cared about most lives here. Right now, I am one-hundred-percent certain she knows this is her. And I know her well enough to know she is about to fuck everything up.

Before I turn to face Cora, I give Layla a glare of warning. Wordlessly telling her to keep her mouth shut and leave. But her smile grows wider and I know nothing good will come of this.

"Gavin—" Cora calls out behind me. "Is everything okay?"

I school my expression and turn to face her. "Everything is fine." I want to add more, but I am at a loss for what to say.

"Hi," Layla speaks up, my body going rigid at the sound. "I'm Layla. And you are?"

Layla extends her hand in Cora's direction, but I step in front of her and block their possible connection. I don't want her touching Cora, let alone getting within arm's length.

"And you need to leave," I tell her over my shoulder, trying once more to close the door.

"Why are you being so rude, Gavin?" Layla says, her pitch an octave higher and she reaches out and touches my bicep. I cringe away from her and start pushing the door closed, only to be met with Layla's boot.

"Gavin, what's going on?" Cora asks, hundreds of questions skittering across her face.

"Yeah, Gavin, what's going on?" Layla's tone becomes venomous and shrill.

I stand between the two of them, hoping this nightmare will end. Praying I fell asleep while Cora and I were watching television and this is all one huge, fucked-up dream. But somewhere in the back of my mind, I know it isn't. And Layla is really standing here. And I am about to lose Cora all over again. Because what other plausible reason would Alyson have for bringing Layla here? None. Not a single one. And I don't know which emotion holds more power over me in this moment—fear or fury.

The silence in the room has every nerve in my body on edge. My heart slams against my ribcage, grabbing the bones and rattling like a madman. I can't breathe. Can't speak. The light at the end of a very long tunnel slowly dims and fades. I have no idea what to do. Where to be. How to function. But just as I am about to spew out something, Layla shatters the silence in the room. Along with everything that matters in my life.

"Well, since no one else is speaking, I guess I'll take the stage." Layla steps closer to me, her hands clasping around my arm. "Like I said, I'm Layla. Gavin's fiancée."

Fuuuuck…

Time Exposure

CLICK DUET
BOOK TWO

exposure

Photography term.

Exposure is the total amount of light that hits the sensor for one frame or shot. It is determined by the exposure triangle settings (ISO, aperture and shutter speed).

How much light is captured depends on three things: aperture size in the lens, ISO sensitivity on your camera's sensor, and the length of *time* you leave the shutter open.

one

"Like I said, I'm Layla. Gavin's fiancée."

Fuck, fuck, fuck…

Why the hell is she doing this? What does Layla stand to gain by doing this? By ruining the one chance I have at getting Cora back. What did Alyson offer her in return?

Cora's eyes grow impossibly wide as her soft green irises darken and tears pool in the corners. Her jaw drops as she stands stoic, eyes bouncing between me and Layla. For a moment, she doesn't move a muscle or utter a single word. And her stillness scares the shit out of me.

When her synapsis fire again, Cora takes a few cautious steps forward, bends over and picks her shoes up from the floor. I stand helpless, less than five feet away, and observe her as she squats down to sit on the floor and slides the sneakers on. Her movements are slow and measured. She makes it a point to make zero eye contact with me as she ties her laces with precision. The longer she keeps her head down, focusing on the task, the less I breathe.

Every moment we shared over the last week just nose-dived off my balcony. Every word I said, every promise I made, she will now perceive as a lie. After all this time, after everything we have endured, our second chance at forever will be ruined at the hands of two petty, jealous, greedy bitches.

But not if I get a say in the matter.

I rip my arm from Layla's grip and jerk away from her. Heat and anger boil my blood and explode from my pores as I turn to face Layla. "Fucking leave. Now!" My voice is venomous and louder than she expects and she startles. Her momentary wide eyes twitch before she yanks on her bitter bitch mask.

"What the fuck, Gavin?" Layla bites back. "You don't want your *soul mate* to know about us?" The way she rolls soul mate over her tongue is dangerous. Poisonous. Vile.

What the fuck is Layla's deal? She has never been like this. Never stepped up and blocked me from what I want. Acting like a jealous girlfriend. Or a straight-up bitch. This is a whole new side and it disgusts me.

"There is no *us*," I snap. "Your need for attention has no bounds, does it? Get the fuck away from me. Your little arrangement… done. I'm done."

I shove Layla out the door and her eyes widen once more before I slam the door in her face. Not sure what provoked her to act vindictively, but as soon as I fix things with Cora, I will settle things with Layla.

Bitch.

I walk over to where Cora sits on the floor and hesitantly kneel in front of her. Lowering my head, I try to get her to look up at me. Her head hangs low as her eyes hone in on her shoes. Slowly, she loops and ties them, but doesn't peek up. I desperately want to reach forward, slip my fingers under her chin and tip her head back so she will look at me. But I don't. Because it scares the shit out of me to see what is in her eyes right now.

"Cora? Baby? Look at me," I whisper. My voice is gruff and dry, and I don't recognize the pitch with my own ears.

Her chin pops up and her eyes snap to mine. "Don't you dare," she seethes as she scoots away from me with a finger pointed at my face.

"What?" I ask, confused. "Don't what, baby?" This won't be good, but I need her to tell me what she is thinking. What she is feeling. Because fuck, I am scared shitless.

Cora unsteadily rises to her feet and locks eyes with me as I stand. I take a step in her direction and she steps back before lifting her hands to stop me. Tears well in her eyes. Her exposed skin painted in red blotchy patterns. Eyes narrow and straighten over and over as she assesses me. Pain etches the lines of her forehead as her chin starts to quiver.

And fuck if I am not losing my goddamn mind because she won't let me get any closer to her. Won't let me touch her. Won't let me connect with and soothe her. The once-old stab wound in my heart slices wide open and the pain of this whole situation lances me.

I cannot lose her. Not again.

"Don't call me *baby*." My term of endearment for her spits out like acid on her tongue. "Not after some woman you've never mentioned tells me she's your fiancée. What the actual fuck, Gavin?" With each word Cora speaks, her volume goes from soft to livid in a matter of seconds.

Cora isn't just angry with me or this situation, she is fucking furious. Can't say I blame her, but I wish there was an abbreviated way to explain it. One where she would understand. One where the nightmare we are currently stuck in will transition into your average dream.

Unfortunately, this nightmare is very real. And it won't go away with the blink of an eye.

Just out of arm's reach, her frame shakes as she clenches her fists so tight her knuckles whiten. Her jaw tightens as she stares at me and subtly shakes her head. Eyes glassy, but the tears have yet to spill down her cheeks.

I take another step forward and she steps back again. Each step she takes away from me is a knife twisting my heart. Raw and painful and a reminder of the suffering we both endured thirteen years ago. A pain neither of us will survive again.

Holding my hands up in surrender, I gaze into her wet, red eyes. "Baby," I say, cringing when she grinds her teeth. "Please, let me explain. It's not what you think. Layla is just a friend. We aren't actually engaged."

Cora cocks her head and glares at me, unbelieving. Her eyes lock on mine and study them as if I just asked her to read my palm. She scrutinizes them a moment before eyeing the lines of my face and finally dropping to stare at my lips. I know what she is doing. Because Cora and I don't have to speak for reality to be stated. So, instead of asking me more questions, she tries to read the truth through my expressions and body language.

And god I hope she sees the truth in my words. Because they are nothing but real.

Layla has never been anything other than a friend. Our relationship has never skirted any line other than friendship. And Layla stating she is my fiancée... there is more to the story than meets the eye. A story privy to me, Layla, and Alyson. A story I hope Cora gives me a chance to explain.

Just when I spot a glimmer of hope, Cora speaks. And her words are far from what I expect to come out of her mouth.

"This can't happen, Gavin." She gestures between us. "This is too much. Even if you are telling me the truth now, I can't deal with bullshit drama like this. Women claiming ownership over you. Women saying vicious things to steal you from me. Why would you hide something like this from me? Because you thought it would never be an issue between us?" She pauses to catch her breath. "I knew this was a mistake. I need to leave."

No. No, no, no. This cannot be happening. This cannot be fucking happening. I cannot lose her. Not again. And not over this.

She swipes her purse from the table and starts for the door. I freeze momentarily, not wanting to believe this is my reality. That I am losing her again after finally getting her back. It's like I am sixteen all over again. Like I don't have a say in the matter. Like what I want doesn't count and won't be taken into consideration.

I refuse to let this be how we end. Downright refuse.

The heavy hotel room door slams shut and snaps me back to reality. *No!*

I bolt to the door and yank it open. Stepping out into the hall, I look left then right before spotting Cora. She isn't running, but her feet trek along the carpet faster than a steady walk. I sprint after her, giving no fucks that I have just locked myself out of my room.

"Cora," I yell. "Wait. Please, let me fix this."

She stands in front of the elevator banks and religiously mashes the down button like her life depends on it. Her teary eyes glance my way and it rips open every suture in my stitched-up heart.

I did this to her. I hurt her. Again.

The elevator car arrives and she steps in, the doors closing just as I approach. *Damnit.* I smash the down button, hopeful the elevator car she stepped in reopens. Seconds later, the other set of doors opens and I jump in and hit the button for the bottom floor. The car pings as it passes each floor, my heart wrenching tighter and tighter with each second I spend away from her. Not knowing if she has already reached the lobby and is darting out the doors to her car.

When the doors slide open, I dash out and scan the lobby for Cora. My eyes land on her as she weaves between people in the full reception area and I race toward her. As long as she remains in my line of sight, I will catch her. I will not let her go this easily. Not after the strides we have made this week. Not after I got back the only person who matters.

"Cora," I yell. Instantly, every set of eyes on the ground floor whips my way. "Please wait."

She peers over her shoulder, tears trailing down her cheeks, and makes a beeline for the exit. Just as she makes it to the door, I catch up to her and grab hold of her arm. As badly as I want to haul her into me, to wrap my arms around her and pin her to my chest, I stop myself. Now is not the time. Although I won't let her leave without a fight, I won't be the man who doesn't give her a choice. After everything we have endured, she deserves to choose what happens next.

"Let me go, Gavin," she spits out as she tries to yank her arm from my grasp.

"No, baby. Please, let's talk about this," I beg. "Please let me explain everything. I wasn't intentionally keeping this from you. And, like I said, it's not real."

Her soft, sad bloodshot eyes stare up at me, pleading with me to let her go as nonstop tears spill down her cheeks.

This pain, her pain… what she is experiencing in this very moment. If it is even remotely close to what she felt when I left thirteen years ago, I hate myself. I hate myself for doing this to her. For letting her experience such heartbreaking emotions. Again. No one should have to undergo this form of torture—once, let alone twice.

"Please, Gavin," she mumbles, her eyes darting around the room. Embarrassment creases her brow as she squeezes her eyes shut. "Please just let me go." When she opens her eyes, a new emotion paints her expression. Disparity and numbness. An emptiness that has me stumbling back, physically and mentally. "Can't you see?"

See what? That I have inflicted the worst pain on the sole person I live and breathe for. Yes, I see it. I hate that I see it. But something twists in my gut and stabs at my heart. And I have a feeling her words have an ulterior meaning. Definition unbeknownst to me.

"See what, baby?" I ask, terrified to know the answer. Terrified of what she will say next.

I ache to touch her. Yearn to embrace her and pepper kisses on her hair, her temples, her forehead. But I fear the worst. That she will pull away. Reject me. And her rejection would sting worse than any words. So, I keep my hands at my sides and imagine all the ways I wish to right my wrongs.

"Isn't it obvious?" she asks, not waiting for me to answer before she continues. "It's like the universe is trying to tell us something."

Cocking my head, I narrow my eyes in confusion. Is she suggesting what I think she is? That we don't belong together. That as much as we love each other, we aren't meant to have each other.

How could something so perfect not be meant to exist?

The universe isn't trying to tell us shit. And if for some nonsensical reason she believes fate is telling us we don't belong together; I will grab fate by the balls until it comprehends the truth. That Cora and I belong together. Always have and always will.

And until I fix this, nothing else matters.

"Baby, I have no idea what you're thinking, but it better not be anything along the lines that we aren't meant to be together. Because that's bullshit and you know it."

Cora turns away from me and walks out the exit with me hot on her heels. Her pace picks up and I jog to keep up with her. She darts past the valet and heads for the lot where she parked her car.

I will not suffocate her. She needs time to mull things over. But she has to know things between us won't get better if we don't discuss them. She needs to hear the whole story.

When she reaches her car, her hands dive in her purse and shove stuff left to right as she searches for her keys. She pulls out the fob and unlocks her car as I jog up to her.

"Baby, please don't leave. Let's go back up to my room and talk about this." We need to talk, that is the only way to resolve this.

"No, Gavin. As much as I want this, as much as I want us to be together, it feels like the world is against us. And I can't do it. I can't fight anymore. I fought for so many years. Cried a million tears until my eyes couldn't do it anymore. And it's happening all over again. My heart fell in love with you all over again and I let it. *Stupid, stupid girl.* As soon as I allowed myself to be vulnerable, I got crushed. I feel like the earth is swallowing me whole, like it's clawing at my insides and eating me alive. And I can't deal with it. Can't deal with you. Not now."

Her words paralyze me. Make my limbs numb and my heart hollow. Pain spills out of her and infiltrates me like liquid poison. Slithers in my veins and takes up residence. And it doesn't just hurt. It kills.

The first time we were separated, it was against what I wanted. Against what either of us wanted. But I had no say or power to stop my parents from moving us across the country for my mom's promotion. Although I was older, I was still just a child.

Now, I may no longer be a child, but I inflict her with the same heartache and torture. Except this time around, our emotional state has evolved. We understand love and hope and pain and anguish. We grasp fear and hopelessness and sorrow and dejection. And in the blink of an hour, I have given all of them to her.

I have never hated myself as much as I do right now.

I step into her, a tear slipping down my cheek as she steps back and bumps into her car. But I ignore her retreat and reach up, framing her face in my hands. This will not be the last time I see her; I won't let it be. This is not how our story ends.

"I fucked up, and I'm so sorry. So, so sorry. But I will fix this. I swear to you, I will fix this. And when I do, I'm coming back for you. You can count on it. Because, Cora" —I pause, pinching my eyes shut— "you and I belong together. No matter what obstacles come at us, we belong together. I love you. And I will always love you. Until my last breath. Until my dying day."

I lean down, press my lips to hers and kiss her softly. Our tears blend at our joined lips and I don't know which are hers and which are mine. When I break the kiss, I lick our tears from my lips and step away. She stares at me a second as hundreds of thoughts invade her mind. Then she rushes to get in her car, starts the engine and drives away.

Away from me. Away from us.

I will give her time, but I won't go down without a fight. Not this time. Never again.

I can't breathe. Literally.

A block from Gavin's hotel, I turn onto a small side street and shift my car into park. The engine idles quietly as I rest my forehead against the steering wheel. Tears flood my eyes and blur the world around me. Violent sobs wrack my body as I lose all sense of composure. With every breath I try to inhale, the emotional boulder in my throat grows larger and heavier.

He said it isn't real. That this supposed engagement is a farce. A fallacy. Said *she* is only a friend. Just a friend. Nothing more. But if all of what he said is true, why do I feel like this? Empty. Broken. Shattered. Desolate.

Why do I feel as if I have just lost the one person who makes me whole? The one person who soothes the ache. Makes me smile. Mends the wounds once created from his loss. A loss he had zero control over.

I replay snippets of the conversation in my head, trying to find truth in Gavin's words. Trying to *listen* to what he said. Really listen. Because the moment she announced their supposed relationship, the world spun off its axis. I wobbled. Stumbled backward in time. Back to a time when vows were made. To the day he left and promised to return, but abandoned me for more than a decade.

He swears he and this other woman are not in a relationship. That he and this other woman are not betrothed. That they are just friends. Only friends. But why would Gavin's friend say such things? Cruel words meant to inflict pain. To make me suffer.

As is, my memory is one huge blob of confusion right now. It mixes in words and visuals from various conversations. Mingles them like partygoers. And I hate it. Hate that I don't know what is real and what is artifice. I have no way of knowing what memory is fact or fable.

So how can I decipher what to believe and what to disregard? And how the hell will I handle what happens next? I just don't know. Can't think past what just happened or the laceration in my heart.

The one thing I do know with absolute certainty is I cannot sit on this beach another minute, crying my eyes out. Sooner or later, a cop will tell me to move along. Tell me I cannot be parked here because I don't have a permit. Who cares if I cry so hard I risk an accident. Who cares if I have a meltdown and can't feel my limbs.

And with that, another round of sobs takes hold. I let it out, fishing a napkin from my glove compartment to blow my nose and dry some of the tears. When my cries slightly settle and I can breathe a little, I decide going home isn't the best option.

I grab my purse from the passenger seat and dig out my cell phone. With shaky hands, I unlock the phone and call Shelly. The ringing blares in my ear while I attempt to stop crying altogether. On the third ring, Shelly answers.

"Hey, girl. How's it going?" Shelly cajoles.

I don't answer right away as I still work to control my tears and breathing. But it is no use and I start blubbering like a baby. The semi-composed state I was in moments ago vanishes.

"Cora?" she beckons, panic edging her voice. "Cora, are you okay? What's wrong?"

"I… I'm… Shelly…" I fumble, my words a mess of inconsistency. Just like my head. Just like my heart. "Shelly, can I… can I come over?" I manage to frame the question around my sobs.

"Oh my god! Are you okay, Cora? What's happening?"

She still hasn't answered my question. *Please just tell me to come over. Just tell me it is okay.* Not that I really need an invitation to her house, but I don't want to intrude if she has plans.

"Shelly, please. Please can I come over?" I plead through my incessant tears and sobs. I wish the blubbering would just stop. It hurts. Every muscle and bone and organ just hurts.

"Yes, of course you can. Are you okay to drive? I can pick you up."

As tempting as her offer is, if I leave my car on the beach it will get impounded. And that is a whole separate nightmare I don't need. Bad enough my heart is in shambles, I don't need to have automobile and financial issues too. Shelly lives in a small one-bedroom in Largo, and I should be able to make it there in twenty minutes. If I collect myself mentally, driving to her house shouldn't be an issue. It won't take long. Then I can let it all go again.

"You don't need to come and get me. I'm leaving Clearwater Beach. Should be there in twenty to thirty, depending on the traffic."

"Cora, you've got me worried. Did something happen? Are you okay? Is Gavin okay?"

Just hearing his name brings about a new bout of tears. My chest caves in on itself as my heart shrivels and lungs forget how to function. *Breathe Cora.*

"I'll tell you when I get to your house. See you soon."

And before she can say or ask anything else, I disconnect the call. If I plan to make it to her house in one piece, I need to clear my head as much as possible. Her infinite questions won't help matters. She can ask them all when I get to her place.

I sit unmoving in the car another couple minutes, taking deep breaths and attempting to refocus on physical objects.

A man walks his dog on the sidewalk. The neon signs across the street promote beer and pizza and a live band. A child swings wildly between her parents as they head into a seafood restaurant. *Breathe in. Breathe out. Just remember to breathe, Cora.* The flash of the pedestrian crossing sign lights up. An older woman rides by on a tricycle with colorful lights.

Once calm enough to drive, I turn the car around, drive off the beach and head in the direction of Shelly's place.

A couple blocks down, I crank up the radio and play loud, upbeat music. Then I roll down the windows and let the wind pelt my skin and whip my hair. Minutes later, I no longer smell the salty beach air and am hit with the occasional scent of fast food or well water. But right now, I would rather smell the foul odor of greasy meat and sulfur than the beach.

Because no matter how much time passes, the sight, smell and feel of the beach will always remind me of Gavin. Always.

After weaving down a couple streets, I park my car in front of Shelly's apartment building. As I get out of the car, I spot Shelly running down the stairs and heading in my direction. She slams into me and wraps her arms around me, squeezing me with boa constrictor strength. And I don't pry her off me. I simply cry into her shoulder. Soaking her hair and shirt. Couldn't tell you if anyone passed by us. I honestly don't give a damn.

We stand like this for a while before she breaks the hug. "Come on, let's go inside."

I don't say a word, stumbling beside her with my arm hooked in hers. She guides us inside, takes my keys and purse and sets them on the coffee table. We plop down on the couch and she hugs me close again, stroking my hair. She lets me cry and sob until my body can no longer do either anymore. Shelly knows exactly what I need and doesn't bother trying to ask more questions. Not yet, anyway.

When my sobs recede, Shelly assumes I have reached the max quota for tears in one day. She leans away from me and ducks her head to look me in the eyes. "You want to talk about it?"

And for the first time since I arrived, our eyes finally meet and hold. Her expression a heaping pile of concern as she regards me. My eyes feel ten times bigger than normal and sting from crying for the last hour straight. No doubt they are bloodshot and lifeless.

Lifeless. Exactly how I feel right now.

"It's Gavin," I say as I stare at my fumbling hands in my lap. If I look back up and see sadness in Shelly's eyes, I will lose it again. And I am so tired of crying. So very tired. It hurts too fucking much.

Shelly rubs my back with gentle, endearing strokes. "What about Gavin?"

I swallow, not wanting to speak about the fiasco that happened tonight, but knowing full well I need to get it off my chest. To tell someone. To get insight from someone I trust.

Gavin told me none of it was true. That they were only friends. But if they were only friends and not actually engaged, why would he hide all of it from me? He never mentioned her as being one of his friends. Or a fellow model. Actually, he hasn't mentioned anyone he knows in California aside from his mom. And something about that doesn't sit well with me.

Does he not want me to know about his life the last thirteen years? Does he have something to hide?

Inhaling deeply, I prepare to recant the evening before I called. *Deep breaths, Cora. You need to let it all out.*

"Gavin and I went back to his hotel after spending the day together. He invited me up to his room and I obliged. Everything was good. Perfect, actually. We cuddled on the couch and started watching Netflix. Halfway through the show, someone knocked on the door. We were both confused by it, but Gavin said it was probably someone at the wrong room and he'd send them away."

I stop talking. Stare at my fumbling fingers in my lap. Pick at a loose thread along the hem of my shirt. Bite the inside of my cheek and try my best not to start crying. Again.

If what Gavin said was true, why is this so hard to say? Why is it so hard for me to believe? To believe he is telling me nothing except the truth. Once upon a time, I never doubted a single word Gavin spoke. So, why do I doubt him now?

And although the answer lingers at the edge of my thoughts, I don't dare voice it. Not now. Not yet.

"Take your time, Cora. Do you want some water?"

I nod as I wring my shirt between my hands. She returns seconds later and hands me a glass. I drink the water and thank her. After I place the glass on the table, I rip the bandage from the wound in my chest and continue.

"When Gavin didn't come right back to the couch, I wondered who was at the door and what was taking so long. I headed for the door and heard him arguing with a woman. At first, I couldn't make out what they were saying, but could tell they knew each other. For a moment, I thought maybe it was his agent. When I was close enough to hear them talking, I heard Gavin tell the woman he was planning to move back to Florida. At that point, I knew it wasn't his agent because they'd already discussed him moving back. The woman seemed pissed and asked what was so great about being here. Just as she asked him, she caught sight of me."

Shelly gasps and slaps a hand over her mouth as her eyes widen. And suddenly, it seems I don't need to tell her what happens next, because she already knows. She may not know the pertinent details, but she has a vague idea. And I plan to tell her everything. To get it all off my chest. I need to. Because bottling this up will kill me.

"The second her eyes landed on me; an evil smile lit up her face. Like she knew who I was. Like what would happen next would hurt me and Gavin, but she didn't give a shit. Anyway, after she saw me, she became sweet and formal. She introduced herself—"

"What's her name?" Shelly interrupts.

"Layla."

For a minute, Shelly lifts her eyes to the ceiling and studies the popcorn as if it is art. She searches her memory bank for anyone with the name Layla. But her search will yield no results. Because if Gavin didn't mention her to me, I am positive he didn't mention her to anyone else. Not even Micah. Why would he?

"Don't know her," Shelly confirms.

"Me either. She's one of his California friends. After she introduced herself, she asked who I was. Seconds after, Gavin tried to make her leave. More than once. But she was insistent on staying and butting in. After no one spoke for a moment, she smiled big again and tells me she's Gavin's fiancée."

Shelly's jaw drops to the floor as she stares at me. As her mouth closes, she narrows her eyes. "I'm sorry, what? I must have misheard you. Did you just say this bitch is his fiancée?"

I nod as a fresh round of tears escapes and spills down my cheeks. "But he swears it's not true. He wanted to *explain* it to me, but I bolted. And after he chased me down the hall and through the lobby and to my car, I didn't want to hear any of it. Because even if what he says is true, why didn't he tell me? We've talked so much over the last week. So why not explain it to me then? Why hide something like this if it means nothing?"

And that is the biggest question of them all. If what Gavin told me is correct—that he and Layla are not together—why not tell me about her from the get-go? If there is nothing to hide, he should have been forthcoming. Not let me find out later or in some roundabout way.

Shelly nods as she sits immobile. Her eyes fog over as her brain works double time. I stare at her as she sorts through all the details and tries to devise possible reasons why Gavin left this one piece of information out. Layla isn't some minor tidbit. Not equivalent to admitting you have a dog that may not get along with my cat. No, Layla is a huge bomb to leave unattended. A bomb that blew up in both our faces.

As it stands right now, my heart feels like it has been run over by a semitruck. Then it backed up and squashed me a second time for good measure. My head hurts—from the endless tears I keep crying and the thought that Gavin lied to me. Yes, it was a lie of omission. But he could have just told me and purposely chose not to.

And that hurts more than anything.

With his line of thinking, I have no doubt he planned to fly back to California and cut ties with whatever "fake engagement" he and this Layla woman have. Then, I would be none the wiser. Right? But I am a firm believer in the old adage "everything happens for a reason." There is a reason Gavin never brought her up. Perhaps he thought it would be pointless. Maybe he thought the two of us would never meet and didn't see why it was pertinent to disclose that part of his past. Or maybe he couldn't figure out a way to tell me without hurting me. I have no clue. The only question rolling around in my head now is why did I need to know? What do I gain from this?

Do I only want to know because it is a piece of Gavin? A part of his past that doesn't include me. A gap filled by another person. Another woman. A woman who he claims is just a friend after she flaunted their familiarity.

Is this me punishing myself? Pushing him away so he doesn't break my heart again? Although, fragments are chipping from the edges and falling to my feet.

"I don't want you driving home tonight," Shelly says as she sweeps a few stray hairs from my face and tucks them behind my ear.

And the last thing I want tonight is to be alone. Shelly probably knows this—twenty-plus years of friendship teaches you these things. Plus, going home would entail me stripping the sheets from my bed. Sheets that smell of Gavin and me and the two of us tangled together this morning. Sheets full of memories of his lips on mine, his hands on my skin, his body fit perfectly against mine.

"You're okay with me staying?"

"As if you have to ask." She leans forward and wraps her arms around me. "You are always welcome in my home. No matter what."

I hug her as if it was our last. Shelly is a great friend. The best a girl could ask for. And I am thankful every day I have her in my life. To have her big heart and warm hugs.

After the couch transitions to my makeshift bed for the night, Shelly gives me one last hug before going to her room. I turn off the tall floor lamp across the room and slip under the blanket. The moment my eyes close, flashes of Gavin spill from my memory.

Memories of us as teenagers—at school, under our tree, walking the beach at sunset, our first kiss—and memories of the last week—his cocksure smile, how easily we slipped back into old habits, the way he *looked* at me, how he held me, kissed me, promised me the future.

And I am crippled by the pain that spins a vicious web throughout my body. It twists and spirals and weaves itself around my organs and engulfs me with an unfamiliar force. The gravity of it all crushes my heart ten times more aggressively than it did thirteen years ago. Knocks the breath from my lungs. Blinds me.

I draw my knees to my chest and wrap my arms around them as another wave of tears bleeds from my eyes. As my body tremors more violent than the earth ever could.

How could I let this happen again? How could I get in this deep? Let myself fall in love with Gavin Hunt a second time?

The answer is simple. Always has been. I belong to Gavin. But does he belong to me?

Thirteen years ago

The plane jolts forward as the wheels touch down. A shriek from the brakes echoes in my ears and I wince. I stare out the window and take in the landscape surrounding the airport as we taxi to our gate. I haven't stepped off the plane yet and I already hate this place. Hate everything it represents. Hate everything it stole from me.

I reach around to my back pocket and grab my phone. After switching off airplane mode, I open the text screen and type out a message to Cora.

> Just landed. It's only been hours, but I miss you already. So much.

My phone jingles and pings with notifications as it catches up from being offline the last six hours. Seconds later, Cora responds. Her notification the only one I check.

> I miss you too. Text or call when you get to your new house.

House is the operative word in her message. Because where my parents are moving us to is a house. Not a home. There is only one place I will ever call home. Wherever Cora is. She will always be my home.

> I will. Hopefully we'll get there soon.

"Let's go, Gavin." Dad nudges me and tilts his head toward the plane's exit.

I swipe my backpack from under the seat in front of me and shuffle out of the cramped seating. Once we deplane, I hang ten feet back from my parents. Let the throng of people separate us on occasion. Although my mom's promotion is a good thing for her career and our family, I am beyond irritated with this whole situation. The only way to express my anger and frustration is to ignore them.

Is my logic juvenile? Yes. Do I give a fuck? No.

As we walk through the airport, Mom and Dad take turns peering over their shoulder every other minute. They have concerns, I get it. But where the hell am I going to go? Not like I can jump on a plane and leave. I have no clue where I am. Nor do I know anyone here. All my friends live in Florida. Every part of my life exists on the opposite side of the country. The one person that matters most, the one I left my heart with, is thousands of miles from here.

I grind my teeth so hard my jaw aches. The thought of making new friends sends a fresh wave of irritation through my veins. Feels as if I am entering kindergarten all over again. The new kid. In the middle of high school. Just before the school year ends.

Complete and utter bullshit.

We reach the baggage claim and wait like fish for bait. The metal carousel circles around a continuous loop. I lean against a far wall and watch as my parents patiently wait for our two pieces of luggage. Normally, I would wait beside them. Offer to help. But seeing as I hate this whole situation, I choose to stand here and go through my notifications.

Micah sent a text while we were in the air.

> Let me know when you land bro. Can't believe your gone.
> Who am I going to do stupid shit with now?

> Right? At least you know other people there. I'm a loner here. Fucking hate it.

My parents step up to me, but I keep my eyes on my phone as if unaware. How long can I avoid eye contact with them? At this rate, weeks seem probable. If I piss them off enough, would they let me go back to Florida? Maybe, but I highly doubt it. Micah's parents would probably let me stay with them if we asked nice enough.

"Gavin, we're leaving. Put your phone away. You can text your friends later," Mom snaps.

Is she pissed at me? Good. Maybe a dose of her own medicine will do her some good. Because pissed is all I have felt since she told me we were moving to this shit-hole. Since the moment she told me I didn't have a choice—or voice—in the matter. She didn't even give me a chance to protest. Her word was the final say.

Fucking bullshit.

I follow in my parents' wake as we exit the airport and my Dad hails a cab. After our luggage is crammed into the trunk, I slide in front beside the driver rather than sit with one of my parents. I have no animosity with Dad, but it seems only fair I treat them equally. After all, they are a team. And they made this decision together. Without me. Without taking any part of my life into account.

We drive away from the airport and I lean against the window, staring at nothing. I don't care if this place holds good qualities. Mountains or celebrities or monuments. None of it matters. Because I don't want to be here. An hour later, the cabbie parks in "our driveway." He helps Dad get the luggage from the trunk before driving away a minute later.

I stay rooted at the end of the driveway and stare at the house I will never call home. A desert-colored Spanish-style house with vines growing up one side of the exterior. Large, grassy plants rest along the front edges of the structure; red rocks fill in the plant bed. The grass mowed with perfect precision. Sporadic large windows fill the walls with the occasional extended half-round window. A small iron gate encloses the driveway from the house to the set-back garage.

Nothing about this house resembles the home we left behind in Florida. This place feels like something to flaunt. A dollar sign. A pretentious badge of honor. Nothing about it could ever be homey. The core of it too frigid and formal. Too "look at me and the salary increase I just earned."

My stomach roils at the idea of my family becoming snotty or ostentatious. Of throwing black-tie parties and drinking with our pinkies out and tilting our noses higher.

When did my parents become these people?

Several minutes pass before I decide to go inside. My parents nowhere in sight when I enter. No doubt they are wandering the property and making sure there is no damage. I scan the bare interior, the moving truck not arriving until the day after tomorrow. *Fucking bullshit.* We have to sleep on the damn floor until our shit arrives. Could we not even get air mattresses?

I walk down a hall and find the room Mom said would be mine. Once inside, I shut the door and lay on the tan carpet. No matter how many photos or posters I add to the walls, this room will never be mine. At most, I will only live here the next two years and then fly back to Florida. Back to Cora and Micah and everything I love.

I crawl over to the suitcase deposited in my room—probably by Dad. Unzipping the case, I riffle through the contents until I locate what I search for. Tucked between my jeans is a small wooden box. I trace my fingertips over the lightly stained grain, a tear slipping from my eye as I stare at my most prized possession. My favorite birthday present from my favorite person.

The box is about the size of a novel, but deeper. Cora used a wood burning tool and inscribed our names on the top surface as well as the date when we became official. Then she got artsy and added a beach sunset.

I brush my fingers over our names and the tears spill heavier. Not even a full day has passed and I can't breathe. The constant warmth I once felt beneath my sternum is now cold and sunken and empty. Without Cora nearby, the world wobbles off-kilter. Revolves slower. Shifts to an endless night.

Flipping the small latch, I open the box and stare at the contents. Lose focus as the one person who means more to me than anyone else is just a memory in a fucking box. One by one, I pull each item from the box. One by one, I cry a little more. So many photos. Of us together—laughing, kissing, watching television. Of Cora by herself—some posed, some candid. Goofy faces, serious faces, expressions she reserved only for me. Drawings she did on napkins, scrap pieces of paper and other random types of paper. Some folded, some small enough to sit open in the box. Most she doesn't even know I possess. Small tokens of her I kept since the day we met.

Pieces of her. Pieces of *us*.

I set the drawings on the fluffy carpet and spread them out so I have an unobstructed view of them all at the same time. Once I have them all spread, I go back to the box and take out the next items. Photos.

Polaroids and regular four-by-six printed images. Cora almost always had a camera with her everywhere we went. She kept it stashed in her purse or backpack, taking it out whenever an opportunity presented itself. Most of the photos on her camera—an older, thirty-five-millimeter film Nikon—were of places, things or other people. Every once in a while, I would snatch her camera and shoot pictures of her. And every once in a while, we were able to get someone else to take a photo of us together.

Sifting through the photos, I land on one of my two favorites. The photo is just of Cora. We were wandering along the trail in Walsingham Park and I had been holding her camera for a bit after she stopped to use the restroom. At the time, I had been walking ten feet behind her. Her eyes drifted up to the trees, searching for birds or squirrels. Or maybe she was simply admiring the trees—she did that sometimes, got lost staring at the trees. I lifted the camera to my eye and snapped the shutter, capturing her profile with the sunbeams haloing around her. She looked like a peaceful angel. My peaceful angel.

When she printed the black and whites, she teased me and asked why I took the picture. My response to her was "you just looked so peaceful and in your element. I wanted to capture the moment." All she did was nod and smile.

My second favorite photo was of the two of us. More like our silhouettes. In the photo, we stood side by side with an arm around each other. A friendly guy on the beach snapped the photo as the sun set behind us. It wasn't noticeable to most people who glanced at the photo, but we were both smiling like idiots. Giddy after dating each other for six months. Just looking at the photo now makes me smile like a fool. A fool madly in love with his soul mate.

I set the two photos beside each other and stare at them a while. Go back to the time they were taken. Remember how I felt those days. How the sight of her made my heart swell and breath vanish. Tears drip from my chin and splatter on the photos. I trace my finger over Cora in each of the pictures.

Fuck. Two years away from Cora will feel like an eternity.

"Gavin?" Mom bellows from somewhere outside the four walls that will now be my room.

I ignore her call a minute as I continue going through the box. Get lost in the drawings and photos as tears continue to fall. But the moment doesn't last long.

Knock, knock, knock.

"Gavin, didn't you hear me calling you?" Mom asks. In my periphery, she stands in the doorway with her hands on her hips, staring at my profile and the scattered images.

After a moment, I lift my tear-stained eyes to hers. *Yeah, I heard you. But I don't fucking care.* That is what I want to say to her. But I don't. Instead, I lie.

"Nope."

I don't elaborate. Don't give her anything to expand on. Because I don't want to look at her. Don't want to speak to her. And a second later, I go back to staring at the items in front of me. But she interrupts me again and I groan.

"Well, Dad and I were thinking we should go out and grab something to eat. Maybe see what's near here too. Sound good?"

She is doing her best in a shitty situation she is aware upsets me. And I guess I should reciprocate and try not to be too much of a dick. I mean, is it really such a bad thing that she is good at what she does? That her boss deemed her better than others in her field. A good son would be happy for his mom. A good son would be proud. But every time I try to be happy for her, all I think about is how I drew the short end of the stick in this whole situation. How I had no say or alternative.

I may be sixteen, but shouldn't my voice count in matters like this? Shouldn't I have a say?

"Yeah, Mom. Can you give me a few minutes? I want to call Cora before it's too late for her."

Something new to deal with. Fucking time zone differences. Bad enough I don't get to see her or speak to her regularly. Now I have to fight with the fact that our lives exist with a three-hour time disruption.

"Sure thing. Ten minutes. And then we'll go."

"Thanks, Mom."

She gives me a sad smile then closes my door and walks off. Once she has been gone a few seconds, I call Cora.

She answers on the first ring. The moment I hear her voice, every live wire inside of me calms. Almost three thousand miles away and Cora still holds the balm to my heart. We talk nonstop for ten minutes—her more than me. She talks about Shelly hanging out with her and staying over at her house. How they have been watching *Lord of the Rings* on repeat and Shelly wants to kill her. This makes me laugh for the first time in weeks.

And then Cora becomes quiet. So quiet I wonder if she fell asleep. I close my eyes for a minute and picture her sleeping with me curled up behind her. Our bodies flush and my arms wrapped around her waist. Before I ask if she is still awake, she whispers into the phone.

"It hasn't even been a whole day and I already miss you so much." Her voice trembles over the line and I know she is holding back tears. I won't tell her, but I saw her collapse outside my house as we drove away. She may have thought we were far enough away, but we weren't. And the sight of her on the ground crying crushed me. The fact I couldn't turn the car around and go to her, scoop her up in my arms and rock her to soothe the pain, kills me.

"Me too, baby."

"I'm getting a job soon. Save up money so I can fly out to see you. Maybe by our anniversary."

Hope filters through her words and spreads from her phone to mine. With it, I sense her warmth and a hint of gladness. Maybe that's what I should do too. Find a job and save money. Teens don't make much money, but earning something is better than nothing at all. Maybe I will call it my Cora fund. Both of us can save up to fly back and forth.

"That's a good idea. I'll do that too."

Just as Cora starts talking again, Dad walks into the room and signals it is time to go. I nod and hold up a finger. He taps his watch and walks out, leaving the door open. Door open equals time is up.

"Gavin?"

"I'm still here, baby. Mom and Dad said I need to get off the phone. We're going out to dinner."

"Okay." Her voice drops so low I barely hear her. And I wouldn't be surprised if the second we hang up, she starts crying all over again. I will too. Because this situation is annoying and heartbreaking and fucked up. And I hate that I can't hold her right now. Can't press her against my chest and rub a hand up and down her back. Can't promise her everything will be alright. Although, the prospect of getting a job and saving to see her again lights a fire inside me.

"I wish I didn't have to."

"I know. I love you."

"I love you, too. I'll call you in the morning."

Seconds later, and with much reluctance, the call ends. As sad and frustrated as I am with being stuck in a situation I can't reverse, hope flares anew for us. And we both hold on to that hope with every breath we take. Because hope is all we have.

But little do we know, things don't always go according to plan. And life has a way of throwing curveballs. Curveballs that batter and bruise hearts.

four
GAVIN

Present

Something jabs me in the ribs as I roll from my side onto my back. I swipe my hand behind me in an attempt to remove said object. I pat and swipe and wave my arm. Whatever it is, it's still there. What the hell? I dig near my ribs and after no success locating the source, I flop over, land on my back and groan. Not only am I being stabbed by some invisible foreign object, but my body is on fire.

I open my eyes and squint, feeling disoriented for a moment.

Never-ending blue, puffy white clouds and the morning sun brighten the sky directly above. In my left periphery is a tall oak tree, the limbs hang overhead while the leaves flutter in the slight breeze. To my right is a row of bushy grass plants. The smell of grass and earth and something floral hits my nose. Birds chirp all around. Squirrels scamper past me. And I swear I hear ducks quacking nearby.

When I roll to sit up, every muscle in my body reacts. My back stiff, neck throbbing, shoulders sore, eyes swollen. Like I partied all night and missed all the good parts.

Once I reorient myself and attempt to work the pain from my muscles, I squint at my surroundings. Adjust to the brightness and focus on what is in front of me. Gray siding, black trim and window treatments, and bushy shrubs.

Cora's house. More accurate—Cora's back patio.

I glance over to the driveway and notice her car is still missing. And the fact that she hasn't been at home all night worries me in more ways than one. She was so upset when she left my side last night. She tried to fight it, but I could tell the dam was about to burst the second she left. I only hope wherever she is, she arrived safe.

If anything happened to her, if she got into a car wreck, I would never forgive myself. Wouldn't be able to live with myself.

"Fuck…" I mutter as I stretch my neck and back.

I walk over to the stoop by her back door and make myself comfortable. There is no way I am leaving until I know she is home and she is safe. Even if that means I sit here for hours. She may not want to talk to me right now, which I completely understand, but I won't let her run away from this. From us.

Not when I just got her back. Not after all the strides we have made. The rekindling we have done. The love I saw in her eyes when she looked into mine. I refuse to lose her.

No matter what it takes, I will fight for her. For me. For us. No chance in hell I am letting this slip through the cracks. And although it took me far too long to come back to her—and under the wrong circumstances—I won't throw in the towel now. Not happening. I won't let her give up so easily either. Our lives may be in different places now, but one fact remains one-hundred-percent unchanged.

We love each other. Plain and simple.

And nothing or no one will steal the love we share from us. Never again.

~

I pull my phone from my pocket—again—and check the time. Ten thirty-five. Not only have I been awake and sitting by Cora's back door for over two hours, I have been at her house for close to twelve hours. And she hasn't.

Luna is probably freaking out inside looking for her Mom and her breakfast.

Slowly but surely, I start to freak out a bit too. By now, I thought she would be home. The fact that she isn't, has me worrying more—about where she is and why she hasn't come home. Elbows resting on my knees, I drop my head in my hands and groan. *Please let her be okay.* Not in some hospital getting treated for injuries because she couldn't focus enough to drive.

But another thought crosses my mind. A thought that boils my blood and chills me to the bone simultaneously.

Who is she with? After our argument last night, would she go running into another man's arms? And not just any man, but a man she trusts. A man she is comfortable with and confides in. *Jonas.*

Would she go to him to be consoled? Would she use her friendship with him to punish me? God, I hope not. The Cora I know doesn't seem the type to do such petty or callous things. But the Cora I know isn't the Cora that exists today. And that scrap of knowledge stings more than anything.

Even if Cora refuses to see it, it is more than obvious Jonas likes her. Hell, any man who looks at a woman the way he looks at Cora doesn't just want to be friends. He may even love her.

At the thought, my skin prickles. He could be soothing her right now. Wiping her tears away. Holding her in his arms. Shushing her cries over another man. A man who claims to love her, but supposedly has a fiancée. A fake fiancée.

And suddenly it feels as if I just handed over the love of my life to another man. "What the fuck was I thinking?"

I wasn't thinking. That much is now obvious. My reaction to a friend's unfortunate situation was simple. Or so I thought at the time. My friend needed help and I offered up my solution. To make people believe we were engaged. An easy, straightforward way to improve her life. No big deal, right?

Wrong. Evidently.

But it isn't real. And Layla damn well knows nothing about our engagement is tangible. There will never be a wedding or vows or permanency. No flowers or additional jewelry or change of name.

So why the show? Why the hell did she act like a catty bitch last night? I saw the wicked gleam in her eye, the vicious curl of her lip. Why did she intentionally try to hurt the one person who matters most to me? I don't get it. Don't understand her motive. What does Layla stand to gain by ruining what Cora and I have? If Layla really was my friend, if she really cared about me as a person, she would have cheered me on. Not shattered my dreams.

So many questions need answering, but they will have to wait until later. Right now, I need to focus on fixing my relationship with Cora. It will take time to mend our relationship, but she needs to know the truth. From my lips. A truth I should have told her from the get-go.

Once I fly back to California, circumstances will change. Life will change. And unfortunately for those in my line of fire, the people stepping on my toes with stiletto heels, they will wish they never fucked me over.

It is one thing to fuck with me, individually. But it is a whole new ball game when you involve people I love.

My internal tirade gets disrupted when I hear a car pull into Cora's driveway. When I lift my head from my hands, I catch her profile behind the tint. But she is so focused on parking the car, I don't think she has spotted me yet. Not like most people survey their house the second they get home.

So, I choose to stay seated on the stoop and let her see me when she is ready.

My eyes remain glued on her as she opens the car door and steps out. As she swipes her fingers under her eyes and sniffles. As she steps around the front of her car and starts for her back door. Her eyes swollen and red. Cheeks blotchy and wet. Hair windblown. Clothes the same she wore last night. Posture defeated. And the second she notices me on her back stoop, I catch the break in her stride as she stumbles a little and takes a step back.

"Gavin?" she asks as if it is impossible for me to be here. Her voice gruff and scratchy and parched. "What are you doing here?"

I rise, roll my neck and shoulders, and take a few tentative steps toward her. But when I do, she steps back again and keeps the distance between us. There may be ten feet between us, but it feels like ten miles. And she wants this distance because I hurt her. Again.

"Hey, baby. I was worried about you after you left last night. You were so upset. A little after you left, I got a ride here to make sure you were okay. When I saw your car wasn't here, I worried. So I stayed, wanting to be here when you got home. I needed to know you were safe and knew you wouldn't answer if I called or texted. And at some point, I must've fallen asleep."

We stand there and stare at each other. She doesn't say a word while I study her more in-depth. Her eyes are bloodshot, her green irises more opaque. Dark half-moons paint the pale skin below her dark lashes. Lines crease her forehead and the small space just above her nose pinches her brows together. She bites the inside of her cheek as she looks everywhere but at me. The blotchy patches on her cheeks spread down her neck and onto her chest.

It has only been one night and she already looks like she hasn't slept for weeks. And I am the sole reason. If she looks like this now—after just one night—how will she look for the several days I am gone? How did she look for the *years* I was gone?

A red hot poker scalds my heart at the pain I have caused her. The pain evident in her eyes and her posture and the way she reacts to me. How she purposely backs away when I try to get close. When I try to repair the shifting fault lines in her heart.

But I refuse to let everything we have gained get thrown aside like last week's leftovers. Our relationship isn't garbage and neither is how we feel about each other. Last night's debacle with Layla was just another rift. But we will get past this. We will flourish. Together.

"Gavin, I think you need to leave."

"Baby, please—"

"No," she yells. "You don't get to call me that anymore. You don't get to be smooth and sweet and all *baby* this or *baby* that. Not after what just happened. It's time for you to leave. I'm exhausted and Luna is probably crying for me. So, please. Just. Go."

"If you'd just let me explain—"

"No, Gavin. The time for explanations has passed. You should've told me about her a week ago when we were catching each other up on life. I haven't withheld anything pertinent from you. And I'd thought you'd done the same. But I guess that's what I get for thinking." She stops for a moment, chest heaving and fists clenched at her sides. When she speaks again, her voice drops and I have to fight to hear what she says. "So, *please*, I beg of you. Please leave."

I don't want to stand out here and argue with her. Cause a scene and have her neighbors come check to see if she is okay. If anything, I want to walk her inside and wrap her in my arms and tell her everything will be okay. That I will fix the problem I created. That I will right my wrongs. And that I will return to her again.

But actions speak louder than words. And right now, she needs actions. Actions that tell her I won't break my promises. Not again. Actions that prove Layla is what I say she is. That she is a friend I did a favor for and nothing else.

I take a step toward her, and this time she doesn't back away. Her frame wilts like a sad flower, I know it's due to hurt and sleep deprivation. When I stand an arm's length from her, I reach for her hand. She doesn't stop me, but closes her eyes and hangs her head in defeat. She is tired and hurt and needs time to think. But I need her to not give up. Not on me and not on us.

Taking advantage of her non-retreat, I hold her hand for a beat. "Baby," I whisper. "I know you're upset with me. I would be, too. But I promise you, I will make this right. You and me—I am not giving up. It's not my style. Never has been. My initial reason for returning may have been for work, but once I laid eyes on you again... it was as if I could finally breathe for the first time in thirteen years. As if I became whole again. I screwed up. Big. I own this mistake. Am punishing myself for it. But when I fly back to Cali tomorrow, they won't know what hit them." With my other hand, I lift her chin so her swollen eyes meet mine. "Once I've fixed my mistakes there, I will be back. And then, I will fix what I've messed up here."

Her chin trembles in my grip. She tucks her lips between her teeth to keep from breaking down in front of me. Tears pool in her eyes as they dart between mine. She wants to believe me—I see a tinge of hope just beneath the surface—but doesn't know if she can. When all is said and done, I will be the man she deserves. The man she can believe and count on. No matter what.

"I love you, baby," I choke out as a tear rolls down my cheek. Because I won't leave here without her knowing how I feel. We may have only reconnected a week ago, but I have loved Cora half of my life. No use in denying it. "And I will be home soon. Before my birthday."

And before I can stop myself, I lean forward and place a tender kiss on her lips. Our lips may touch for less than two breaths, but those two breaths are equivalent to forever. And as difficult as it is, I back away and drop my hands from her. I grant her the space she needs.

Without another word, I step around her and walk toward the park across from her house. But just before I get out of earshot, I overhear her wails as they bounce off the trees and wisp away in the wind. Her cries for us. And for herself. And the love that binds us together like nothing else. A love that brought us together, shredded us, and will unite us again.

The second my feet touch the grassy park property, tears stream down my face. I stare back at the house briefly, and although I cannot see her, I *feel* her. Feel her anguish. And I vow to never be the reason she cries like that again. Vow to wipe away all her pain.

five

Once I make it inside, I throw my purse to the floor and go feed Luna. From the back door to her food bowl, she weaves between my legs and meows her love for me. At least I have someone who will give me her undying love. All she wants in return is the occasional scoop of food, water, a clean litterbox and my affection.

If only human relationships were so simple.

I scoop Luna some food and pet her a few times while she eats and purrs simultaneously. Once she is sated, I head to the bathroom and do my business. A moment later, I swap out my clothes for a tank top and undies then crawl into my bed. Since I left the door cracked for Luna, I fetch my eye mask from my nightstand and block out any semblance of daylight.

Even if it's just a few hours, I need some sleep. Because no matter how much I tried to fall asleep on Shelly's comfy couch, it never happened. My mind ran vicious circles in the dark. And the muffled tears never let up.

One moment, my mind was trying to rationalize the reasons he would be in a fake relationship with someone. Why he would let the world think they were engaged. What would Gavin gain from a setup like that? Especially if he professes to love me the way he does. But instead of coming up with viable answers, all I did was cry more. And I prayed that Shelly couldn't hear me sobbing into the pillow.

A few minutes later, Luna jumps onto the bed and curls up beside me. Her purrs soothe in a way nothing else does. As if she senses my forlorn demeanor, she inches her way up to my shoulder and nestles in the crook of my neck, purring stronger. I tug the sheet higher and get hit with Gavin's smell on the cotton. Upset as I am, his beachy-pine scent soothes me. Settles my soul. And within minutes, I fall asleep.

I jolt awake to the sound of my phone ringing. As badly as I want to ignore it, I can't. It could be someone other than Gavin calling me. When you work for yourself, you never get a day off.

Rolling over, I slap my hand over the surface of my bedside table until I come into contact with my phone. Not removing my eye cover, I manage to answer the call. "Hello?" My voice is raspier than a grizzly bear.

"Cora, it's Mom. Did I wake you, sweetie?"

I push the mask up to my forehead and hold the phone away from my ear a second, checking the time. *Holy shit.* It's just after three in the afternoon. I am more than thankful for the sleep, but most of the day has withered away. But it's not as if I had plans, so whatever.

"Yeah, but it's okay Mom. Is everything alright?"

A second later, a knock raps at my back door. I bolt upright and hold my breath as my heart hammers a vicious rhythm in my chest. *Shit.* Did Gavin come back? Please, please, please don't let that be him. I don't think I can deal with him—or us—right now. I just need more time to process everything.

I shove the covers from my legs and plant my feet on the floor, reluctant to move. The knock comes again as I pad down the small hall to the back door. Unfortunately for me, the back door is solid and I'm unable to see who stands on the other side—unlike my front door. I really should invest in a peephole or one of those video doorbells for the back.

As I stand at the door, hand on the knob, reluctant to turn it, my mom speaks up. "Cora, it's me. I'm the one knocking on your door."

Relief hits and I remember how to breathe again when I discover Gavin isn't the person outside my house. In the last two minutes, I somehow forgot I'd been holding the phone to my ear and my mom was on the other end. Probably because the moment there was a knock at the door, Mom stopped speaking. If she would have just told me it was her outside, I wouldn't be tiptoeing through my own house and she'd be inside already.

I twist the knob and swing the door open. I shield my eyes as the bright afternoon sun temporarily blinds me.

Stepping off to the side, I let Mom pass and then shut the door. I follow her into the kitchen and notice she's putting food in my fridge. "What's all that?" I ask.

"I stopped at the Patch and picked up a few things for you. Figured you wouldn't be in the mood to go anywhere." Her tone casual and body language easygoing. As if today is just another day.

She pulls out a couple pans and pots and starts chopping vegetables on the cutting board. Then she fills a pot with water and turns on a burner. I follow her movements for a few minutes while she busies herself in my kitchen. She moves as if she has cooked here hundreds of times, when it is quite the opposite. Of the countless times Mom has been in my home, never once has she cooked here. So watching her right now is peculiar. It isn't an anomaly to see my mom in the kitchen. But to see her in *my* kitchen, bustling around like she cooks here every day, is weird.

"Mom?"

Lifting her eyes from the cutting board, she peeks up at me. "Yeah, sweetie."

"What made you think I might not be in the mood to go anywhere?"

I have a sneaking suspicion what the answer is, but I need to know for certain before making assumptions. Before opening my mouth and spilling all the juicy details of my wretched love life.

"When Shelly came into the shop this morning, she looked a bit rough. I asked her why and she said you were at her apartment last night. She said you were upset, but didn't tell me why."

And thankfully Mom isn't one to pry, but I have no doubt she wants to know why her twenty-nine-year-old daughter spent the night at her friend's house. Pretty sure she also wants to know the source behind why I was so upset. Because why would a grown woman, who owns her own home and lives alone, go to her friend's place and spend the night? Adult friends don't generally have sleepovers on purpose.

Does Mom know Gavin is in town? Mom was friends with Gavin's mother, but I have no idea if they have kept in touch. Does she know that he was the model I photographed all week? It wouldn't be surprising if Shelly told her everything, but maybe my best friend kept this news to herself. Shelly picks and chooses what to share with Mom. She doesn't want to be the gossip mill, but she also wants to look out for me.

"Yeah, it was a rough night," I say.

Mom nods then throws noodles in the boiling water before heating up the other pan. Once the pan is hot, she adds the chopped veggies to the pan and tosses them. And right now, I love Mom more than ever.

Shelly may not have told her the reason why I am upset, but she must have indicated it was pretty bad. And what did my mom do? She left work early and went to the store, buying me groceries and comfort foods. And now, she stands in my kitchen and cooks me stir-fry. She may not know the extent of what has me upset, but she knows I need her comfort more than anything.

When the pasta finishes, she scoops it out of the water and adds it to the veggies. Then she pours in a sweetened soy sauce from my fridge. After it all comes together, she portions us both out a plateful and we go to the couch.

A few bites into the delicious meal, Mom speaks up. "So, you want to talk about it?"

She doesn't make it uncomfortable. And when I glance up from my plate, she's digging around in her plate with her chopsticks. Mom has always had a finesse with conversations. Something I never had. Not with anyone except Gavin. And even that was questionable over the last week.

Conversations with Mom have never been awkward—not even the period and sex talks when I was younger. She always has this gentleness about her. One which could console the most anxious soul. And right now, her tranquility is the exact balm I need.

Thinking back, the past week had been great. Or so I thought. Until *she* showed up last night. Until some "fake" relationship they had was used as a weapon against me. The smile she threw after she spotted me in the room, that was nothing short of malicious. She knew her words would hurt me. Hurt us. And she tossed them like landmines and waited for the fallout.

Without further ado, the tears start back up and I immediately hate my stupid emotions and bodily functions. Can I not cry for a few non-sleeping hours? Is that too much to ask?

After I get my tear ducts under control, I peek up at my mom. "How much do you know about this past week? Besides me telling you I had a photo shoot on the beach."

She sets her plate on the table, half her food forgotten. "Shelly said Gavin was your model for the shoot."

I nod. "Did she say anything else?"

"Only that she was worried about you. But she gave me no specifics."

I set my plate beside hers, mine hardly touched. Eating is the last thing I want to do, but I appreciate that Mom isn't pushing the topic. For a moment, I stare at the fireplace as flashes of the past week flicker through my mind. Next thing, I cover my face with my hands and start crying. If Gavin leaving thirteen years ago is any indication of what is to come, I may as well just throw in the towel. Trying to be "okay" is getting old. And I am so tired of pretending to be something I am not.

Normal. Happy. Thrilled with my life.

"I let him in again, Mom. I let him wiggle his way into my heart and he broke it all over again." I stop, unable to contain the torrent spilling from my eyes.

Mom leans into me and wraps her arms around me. She shushes me while she strokes my hair and murmurs unheard words into my ear. Her hand runs slow circuits up and down my back, soothing me like only a mother can. The occasional kiss to my crown as she squeezes me closer. The extra squeeze in her hug every once in a while.

"I've got you, sweetie. No matter what, I've got you."

I sniffle between sobs. "Thanks, Mom. I love you so much."

"I love you, too. And if you want to talk about it more, I'm here. Okay?"

I squeeze her tighter and nod into her neck. "Maybe another day. I just need a day without tears."

~

When I told Mom I needed a day without tears, I didn't mean today. I had already cried thousands of tears today and was okay shedding more.

But shortly after Mom left, Shelly called. As if the two of them were playing telephone tag and I was the name they passed back and forth. Shelly told me she was bringing Erin and Jonas over tonight. That we would watch movies and eat junk food and just hang out together.

The first thing I wanted to tell her was not to come over. That I wanted more alone time. Honestly, the only thing I want to do is sleep. Sleep for days or weeks or months. Sleep an eternity and erase all the bad memories. I just want everything that happened to fade away. Out of my mind. Out of my heart. Gavin. Layla. The whole thing. I want it all gone. Forgotten.

But there is no chance in hell Shelly will ever let that happen. She is determined to keep me from drowning. To keep my head above water as I gasp for breath. For life.

And that would be why my living room resembles something from our preteen years—blankets and pillows and snacks strewn across the floor. The television plays some movie from Netflix. To be honest, I have no clue what we are watching. Since the movie started, my eyes have been glazed over. My mind in a fog.

All four of us lay on the floor. Shelly on my left, Erin on her other side, and Jonas on my right. The only source of light spills from the screen. Occasionally, the room goes dark. I relish those scenes the most. The ones that give me a semblance of solitude. A breath of privacy.

Currently, Shelly's fingers play with my hair as her eyes remain glued to the television. Erin is out of my line of sight, but I assume she's focused on the movie. And although my eyes aren't absorbing a single minute of the movie, I am fully aware that Jonas has been staring at me for the last five minutes.

And I don't know how that makes me feel.

I glance over at him—to confirm—and catch him before he can look away. His eyes crinkle at the corners and his sadness for me weighs heavier than I can bear. When he turns back to the movie, he scoots down and lays flatter. And something inside me flips. Begs for his comfort.

Shelly and Erin bring me solace, but it isn't the same. Women experience emotion different than men. They also console in other ways.

I roll onto my side and snuggle against Jonas's frame. Without hesitation, he wraps his arm around me and draws me closer. His heat warming my cool skin. But the second he places a kiss on the crown of my head, I lose it. The flood gates open once again and I cry into his shirt. Soak the cotton. With each round of tears, he holds me tighter, strokes my hair softer, shushes my cries more, and I clench his shirt in my fists harder.

We lay like this for hours—me curled into his side and him cradling me. The first movie ends and a new movie starts right after. I have no idea what plays, nor do I care. I just want to lay here and cry my eyes out. Cry until I have no more tears. Cry until I pass out.

After my tears subside a while, I sit up and notice Erin and Shelly fell asleep at some point. I envy how peaceful they both look. And I pray to whatever power resides over me, *please let me sleep tonight.* I need a deep, dreamless sleep. Just one solid night.

Jonas sits up and tenderly tucks my hair behind my ears. I don't doubt I look a hot mess right now. Hair a rat's nest. Pajamas still on from earlier when Mom was here. Eyes puffy and bloodshot. Lips cracked. But the way Jonas stares at me right now, I feel the exact opposite. His swirly blue-hazels are gentle as he searches my face.

"You want to go lay down? Maybe try to get some sleep? I'll tuck you in."

God, I hate myself and the fact I was never able to be anything but friends with Jonas. He is such a good man. A family man. Is someone I depend on. Someone I trust. Someone I care about. He likes me on a much deeper level than friendship. In the back of my mind, I think I have always been privy to this. I just shoved it away. Smothered it. Because my stupid brain has never been able to let go of Gavin.

But after everything that has happened, maybe I should let myself try again. Let myself find love with someone else. Someone who won't abandon me. Someone who will do anything for me.

"Yeah, okay," I say.

Jonas stands and extends his hand out to me. I take it and rise from the floor. He walks me toward my bedroom with his arm around my shoulders. A sudden nervousness hits me when we walk into my bedroom. It's like nothing I have experienced with Jonas. Like a hurricane swirls beneath my ribcage.

I slip under my covers and he slides them up to my chin before sitting beside me on the bed. He gazes at me with an expression very un-Jonas. His forehead bunches and straightens and bunches again. When he reaches forward and brushes his knuckles across my cheek, the gentle touch trips a live wire inside me. I lean into his touch and close my eyes momentarily. The pent-up emotions I have ignored with Jonas detonate with ferocity.

I study his blue-rimmed hazels as they hone in on my lips. His eyes perplexed and loaded with indecision. Then his tongue darts out and wets his lips. Adam's apple bobs in his throat. But after a second, I catch a slight shake of his head. The indiscernible gesture probably wasn't meant to be seen, but I am the body language detector and pick up on the smallest of signals.

"How are you?" Jonas asks, voice soft and endearing. And something tells me that wasn't what he wanted to say. But I shove the thought aside.

When most people ask me this question, I tell them I am fine. That everything is okay, although I silently scream in my head. Although I am slowly shattering inside. But there are a select few people I am straightforward with, Jonas being one of them. Shelly, Erin, and my mom being the others. I talk with Dad, but we discuss different stuff—less of the emotional, more of the rest.

"I don't know. Feels like I'm falling apart. Like someone took a chisel and hammer to my heart and started chipping it away all over again. It took so long to somewhat heal from the first time. Jonas, I don't think I'll survive this time." As the final words slip from my lips, tears roll down the sides of my face and spill to the pillow.

Jonas scoots closer, gently plants his hands on either side of my face, and leans over me. He hovers there a moment, inches from my face. From my lips. "You will get through this, Cora. I won't let it be any other way." He lifts one hand from the bed, brushes my hair from my face, and wipes away my tears. His calloused fingers so tender on my temples. "This time will not be the same," he says, huskily.

"How can you be so sure?" I ask, needing some form of reassurance.

"Because you have me and Shelly and Erin and so many others. We're all here for you. On your team. And no matter what happens, we'll be here for you."

I nod, not knowing how else to respond. But the truth in his words erases some of the chill in my bones.

"Try to get some sleep. If you need me, I'll be on the couch. And we'll all be here when you wake up in the morning."

Jonas leans in and I hold my breath as he presses his lips to my forehead. His lips are soft and warm. I close my eyes and allow myself to feel something other than sadness for a brief moment in time. To envision what life could be like if I gave Jonas a chance. If I set my heart free from the cage it has been in for far too long. Because life with Jonas would be good. Filled with smiles and laughter and warmth and love. I don't have to experience it to know it.

When he slowly lifts his lips from my skin, I shift below him and move my lips closer to his. And for a split second, our lips touch. The air crackles and steals my breath. But as quickly as our lips make contact, he breaks away.

"No, Cora." He rears back and scoots farther away from me, his eyes closed and head shaking.

Rejection hits me with incomparable force. Tears sting the backs of my eyes as I press a hand to my lips.

He doesn't want me? How could I be so stupid? What the hell was I thinking?

"I'm sorry. I just thought..." I stumble over my own words as I fight crying in front of him.

When he opens his eyes, glassy hazels stare back at me. "Please don't apologize. Believe me, I have wanted this—us—for so long. But after seeing you around Gavin this past week, it's quite clear where your heart lies. He hurt you, but you wouldn't be this devastated if you didn't still love him."

"I don't love—"

Jonas holds up his hand to stop me. "You're upset right now, and I understand why you're saying that. But you can't run from the truth, Cora. And as much as I care about you, I don't want to be the runner-up. For a long time, I thought I had a chance. But after seeing you two together, and seeing how devastated you are right now... you never fell out of love with him. And that's okay. If us just being friends is the only way I get to have you in my life, so be it. At least I get to have you."

Jonas said he cares about me. That he would be with me, if I could give him my whole heart. Although he didn't outright say he loves me, part of me deep down knows he does. But our love isn't the type to stop time. The type that consumes every breath and thought and cell. And that's okay. Because at least I still have him. Even if it isn't the way he wants. And that speaks volumes to the type of man he is.

I nod. "Okay. Thank you."

His brow knits in the middle as he tilts his head. "Why are you thanking me?"

"Because I'm so lucky to have you in my life. Lucky I met you. Our friendship is like none I've had." I swallow past the emotional lump in my throat and blink back tears. "I wouldn't get through this without you. Wouldn't make it out of this whole without you. You will always have a special place in my heart. Always."

"I know." He leans forward and kisses my cheek, his lips lingering a little longer than friendship warrants before he sits back up. "Ditto. Try to get some sleep. And in the morning, we'll all go out to breakfast."

And before I respond, Jonas gets up and walks out of my bedroom, closing the door behind him. I don't know what I did to deserve a man like Jonas in my life, but I am indebted to whatever power brought us together. Maybe the universe knew I needed someone as tenderhearted as Jonas to help heal my heart. Not completely, but enough to live in the world.

I roll over and hug the other pillow to my chest, catching Gavin's scent. I inhale deeply and, for the first time in twenty-four hours, allow myself to purposely think about Gavin. Flutters echo in the chambers of my heart and I hug the pillow tighter. I imagine my arms wrapped around him as his scent fills each alveolus in my lungs.

Within minutes, my eyes grow heavy and drift shut as I dream about beaches and sunsets and giant evergreen trees.

Six

CORA

Thirteen years ago

Summer was once my favorite time of year. Now it officially sucks.

It has been two weeks since Gavin left and all I feel is hollow. A mere shell of the girl I was weeks ago.

Talking with him on the phone every day relieves some of the anguish in my heart. But it never fully dissipates. The strangest part of it all… Before Gavin, I was this loner girl. Someone who never cared for the company of others—with the exception of Shelly. Before Gavin, it had never been challenging to sit beneath a tree by myself and get lost in a book. To hang out in my room alone and listen to music. To walk in the park and listen to the leaves rustle and the birds chirp.

Now, I don't want to even imagine sitting beneath *our* tree when school starts again. It is bad enough Gavin won't be there, but I also don't have Shelly to hang with since she goes to another school. Listening to music hasn't been the same and I have no desire to step foot outside unless absolutely necessary.

I reach for my sketch pad and pencils and drag them closer. For the next two hours, I get lost in art. At least with art, I create whatever I feel. Art doesn't have to be rainbows or cheeriness or the sunny side of life. It can be anything at any given time. Emotion spilled on paper or canvas and up for interpretation.

When I finish, I dust off the page and take in my drawing. The graphite dons the page in sharp lines and subtle smudges. The scent of pencil shavings pricks my nose. A layer of shiny carbon coats the edges of my palms and several fingertips.

On the page, I drew a beach sunset with a silhouette couple walking hand in hand by the water. In the bottom right corner, I scribble the signature I add to all my art pieces. Before I fold it into thirds, a tear slips from my eye and lands on the page.

I don't wipe it away. I let it stay and bleed through the paper, knowing Gavin will see it when I mail it to him.

On a piece of notebook paper, I start writing a letter to Gavin. Although we talk on the phone regularly, there is something different about sending him drawings or pictures and letters. Like I am sending a physical piece of myself to him. Something for him to hold in his hands when he can't hold me. Something he can look at in the future when he needs me with him. A form of solace in our time apart.

Gavin,

I miss you so much. Sunsets aren't the same without you by my side.

And I'm so tired of everyone asking me if I'm okay. Why would they think I'm okay? My boyfriend, the love of my life, just got shipped off to California. I mean… would they be alright if it happened to them?

I seriously doubt it.

Have you gotten your room situated yet? I know it'll never be like your room here, but maybe you can make it as close as possible.

Thanks for sending me the picture of the California sunset. It's definitely a different view than anywhere here. I hope we can share the sunsets there together sometime. More to add to our memories.

Have I mentioned how Shelly has been following me around all summer like a lost puppy? It's annoying as fuck.

I know she means well, but is it wrong for me to not want to be around anyone else right now?

Whatever. I don't really care what anyone else thinks. All I know is this sucks.

It's like I'm hyperventilating all the time. I'm never able to catch my breath. And it's like my heart is literally missing. If I thumped on my chest, I wouldn't be surprised if it sounded like tapping on a watermelon.

Anyway. The point of these letters isn't to depress you. You miss me as much as I miss you. I just wish I could hug you. You give the best hugs. Did I ever tell you that? No other hug on earth compares to yours. It's warmth and peace and home all wrapped up in the perfect package.

Fuck! I'm crying again. I am sick and tired of crying. My eyes hurt. They're always red and puffy and I have to hide them behind big sunglasses everywhere I go.

This really fucking sucks!

I really hope you're able to come home sometime during the summer. Even if it's just for a long weekend. I'm not picky and will take whatever I get.

Okay, I'll wrap this up. In a few hours, you'll call me and we'll talk until we're forced to hang up. But I never want to hang up. Ever.

I love you so much!

Cora

I trifold the letter and stuff it in an envelope, along with the drawing. After I address it, I ask Mom for a stamp and then walk it out to the mailbox. I place it in the mailbox like it's my most prized possession. And for good measure, I press my palm over the envelope and send a piece of myself with the envelope to Gavin.

When I walk back inside, Mom tries to lure me into the kitchen. "Want to make cookies with me?"

Do I look like I'm five and I want to lick the dough from the mixer blades? But I don't say that because I know she is only trying to lift my spirits. She has been trying since Gavin told me they were moving. And more so since the day his parents put him on the plane. I am grateful to have her as my mom, but her love will never be the same as what I give and receive from Gavin.

She means well, and I love her greatly for that, but I just don't see how making cookies will make up for losing someone.

"No thanks, Mom."

I walk back to my bedroom, lay on my bed and curl into a fetal position. I hug my phone to my chest and close my eyes. It won't be long before Gavin calls, but until then I just want to sleep. Sleep away all the minutes and hours and days between when I get to talk with him again. Sleep away every tick of the clock until I get to see him again. And hopefully that day arrives soon.

seven

GAVIN

Present

Is this what dying feels like?

All the years spent apart from Cora and I never felt as horrible as I do now. Did I miss her every goddamn day? Hell yes, I did. Seconds felt like years and years felt like centuries. Did I want to kick myself in the balls for the choices I made? More often than not. Do I regret my idiocy? More than ever.

But the past cannot be changed. It is what it is. No use dwelling on what has come to pass. The future… now that is something I have more control over. Or at least I hope I do.

My stomach churns as I picture her on the ground crying. I stop breathing. Clutch my chest because it feels like I am having a fucking heart attack. Fear rips through me and shreds my insides. And I let the feeling consume me. Let it slither through my veins and take me over. Let the pain settle in my bones. Because seeing Cora in that state was like having someone throw mace-coated sand in your eyes. And I deserve to suffer for not sharing everything with her.

I will accept my punishment. Will let it weigh me down temporarily. Because our relationship can only go up from here.

Since leaving her house yesterday, I have made a new best friend. The porcelain throne in my suite and I have spent quite a bit of time together. I keep telling her I want to see other people, but she is a persistent bitch. As is my stomach, which has kept nothing down.

I press a loose fist to my mouth as I stand beside the bed. I close my eyes and take a deep breath. For the love of all that is holy, please do not let me throw up again. One—I don't like it. I loathe it with a passion. Two—my body cannot handle much more of this. My head hurts from all the dry heaving. Lips are dry as fuck and starting to crack. Throat feels as if a carpenter scraped a layer of tissue off with sandpaper.

I take a few more deep, methodical breaths and am thankful when my stomach finally calms.

I resume packing my suitcase, but the whole act is robotic. Pull from hanger. Fold clothing into a shape other than a ball. Put in suitcase. Repeat. Shoes set inside. Brush. Toothpaste. Toothbrush. Razor. Hygiene products zipped in a bag.

After everything from the closet, dresser, and bathroom are packed up, I walk around the remainder of the room and do a small search. Inspect the kitchen area and small living space. When I get to the couch and table, I lift the cushions like I usually do when I travel. All it takes is one time losing something to develop weird habits like this. And when I hold the seat cushion up, something shiny catches my attention.

I reach for it and discover the shiny object is a hair clip. One that had been in Cora's hair earlier and she took out when we got to my hotel room. She must have slipped it in her pocket and it fell out when we were watching television.

I turn the small clip over in my hand again and again, studying the intricate design. It's nothing girly. Just a simple metal clip with a simple purpose. But it belongs to her.

Cora has never been a girly-girl. But she has never been a complete tomboy either. She resides somewhere in the middle and is absolutely perfect. A girl... A woman not afraid to sweat or get her hands dirty or belch around her friends. A woman who gives as good as she gets and isn't afraid to speak her mind and sees the world as a piece of art. A stunning woman that still puts on a dash of makeup and occasionally wears dresses and fixes her hair with hair clips.

I stare at the clip—a mix of girly and punk rock and hard rock. One-hundred-percent Cora.

I tuck the clip in the pocket of my jeans in the suitcase. When I get home, I will add it to our box. A box that isn't as full as it would have been if we had kept in contact over the years. If *I* had kept in contact with her.

Once my temporary life in Clearwater is packed up, I roll my suitcase to the elevator and press the down button. I step into the car and head for the ground floor. I walk past the front desk and give a courtesy wave on my way to the exit. This is it. After I walk out this door, I am headed back to California.

But not for long.

"Did you already schedule a ride, sir?" the valet asks.

"Yeah. They should be here soon."

"Very well, sir. Have a safe trip home." My body recoils a little at the word *home*.

"Thanks," I tell him, not wanting to be impolite.

When I return to Cora, I will be home. We will be home once I fix my mess and we are together again. Because Cora is home. Always has been. Always will be. Nothing can change that.

The Uber driver picks me up and heads for the Tampa airport. He shoots the shit with me during the entire ride. More than once, I want to tell him I would prefer a quiet drive. But I don't. It's not this guy's fault I am in a foul mood. It's not his fault I left out important details of a favor I did for a friend. And it's not his fault that my so-called friend took said favor and used it as a weapon, attempting to kill the best thing in my life for her own selfish reasons.

Unforgettable. Unforgivable.

When he pulls over at the airport drop-off, I thank the driver after he hands me my suitcase. The doors whoosh open and a wall of cool air hits me as I enter the airport. Weaving through the sea of bodies, I head to the baggage check area. Once I finish checking my luggage, I head upstairs to the gates and TSA checkpoint.

Thirty minutes later, I slip my shoes back on and walk toward the gate. I stop at one of the restaurants and order something small to eat. While I wait, I open the text history between me and Cora. Does this make me a glutton for punishment? Probably, but I don't fucking care.

I have messaged her several times since she got in her car and drove away from me on the beach two nights ago. Most of them say the same thing. *I'm sorry. How are you? I miss you. I love you.*

But she never responds to a single one of them. Not that I really expect her to. If our roles were reversed, I wouldn't do anything different.

Regardless of her lack of response, I type out another text to her. And I will type out many more between now and when I return. Because I will return.

> Just wanted to let you know I'm at the airport. When I get back to Cali, I'm fixing all this. All of it. Then I'll be back. I love you. I miss you.

My food arrives and I eat it, not really tasting it. But I repeatedly tell my stomach to keep it down. At least until I land in Los Angeles.

Minutes later, the airport announcement over the intercom says my plane has started boarding. I file into the boarding line and shuffle onto the plane. Once in my seat, I put my earbuds in and shut my eyes. My stomach twists and my palms break out in sweat, but for very different reasons than when I left Los Angeles. This time, the panic forms out of fear.

Fear that I won't be able to fix my mistakes when I land in California. Fear that I won't be able to return to Cora like I desperately want to. And worst of all, fear that she won't take me back when I do return to Florida. Because no matter what happens, I am coming back. Even if it means I have nothing.

~

The moment I deplane in California, I am a man on a mission. After I text Cora and let her know I landed safely, I bolt from the terminal and head for the baggage claim. As per usual, the airport is a madhouse.

When people bump me along the way, I am more vocal about my irritation than usual. "Fucking asshole" leaves my lips far more often than not. People need to learn some damn etiquette—like moving aside if you plan to text or check apps on your phone. *For the love of God, show some fucking respect.*

And the second I step foot outside the airport, for the first time in years, Los Angeles feels nothing like home. Like the very first time I arrived. If anything, now it feels like a cesspool of hungry and desperate people. A façade disguising itself as reality. And I have no desire to be a part of it.

I was brought here out of obligation, but why did I stay so long? This question has cycled through my head countless times over the last week. Haunted me every waking minute.

Why?

I have been financially secure for years. So why didn't I leave then? Why didn't I pack up everything I own and move back to Florida when I could have? Moving would have been easy. Too easy.

But I hadn't moved for several reasons.

Until a week and a half ago, I hadn't spoken with Cora in years. It wasn't to intentionally hurt her. More like I thought I was doing the right thing when I couldn't see me making it back to her. So, I was doing right by her. At least that is what I told myself. I was letting her go. Letting her move on and find love again.

Only I didn't share that with her. I made the decision all on my own. Because I figured a clean break was the best way. For obvious reasons, I am an idiot. Live and learn, I suppose.

When I get in the Uber, I tell the driver I would like some quiet. I need time to think, to strategize. And I can't do that while a bored driver shoots the shit with me. Thankfully, he respects my request.

After battling late-day traffic, the driver pulls into Mom's driveway on the outskirts of Burbank. I thank the driver, grab my luggage and walk up to the house. Mom's house looks much the same as it did thirteen years ago when we moved to California. The only difference is the paint has faded slightly, the plants have been swapped for more colorful versions, and the tree in the front yard is a little taller and bushier.

Although I have adjusted to Mom living here, this house has still never felt like home. Just a layover until my path realigned.

Maybe I should have messaged Mom before just showing up on her doorstep. She will probably think me crazy. Question me endlessly. Popping up here is nowhere near my norm. Whatever. Perhaps I am going crazy. But if being crazy equals being happy, consider me certifiable.

I punch my code into the door lock and step inside. The moment I pass the threshold, the scent of curry and bell peppers and grilled chicken attacks my nose. A second later, my stomach growls in response. Obviously, the airport food didn't hold me over long.

"Mom?" I call out.

"Gavin, is that you?"

Every time she asks that, it makes me laugh. Does she have other children I am unaware of? Better yet, is there another guy in her life that could be walking through the door? The latter never crossed my mind until now. I wouldn't expect my mom to remain celibate after Dad passed, but she still wears her wedding jewelry. Wonder if I need to give her the okay to move on? If I need to tell her it is okay to find love again. That I am okay with her loving someone besides Dad.

Maybe another time.

"Yeah, Mom. Are you in the kitchen?" I ask as I walk in that direction. I figure I will ask a stupid question in return. With all the deliciousness floating through the air, she is either cooking or just sitting down to eat.

The second I round the corner and the kitchen comes into view, the grilled peppers and spices hit me full force. My stomach bellows out and constricts, and I pat my abdomen. *Calm down, we will eat soon.*

"Hey, honey. What are you doing here?" She smiles, wraps me in her embrace, and I squeeze her a little harder than usual. "Is everything okay?" Concern laces her voice since I have yet to let her go.

I give her one last squeeze, take a deep breath, then let her go. She steps back to the stove, but has her eyes on me. "No, everything's not okay. I just flew back from Clearwater."

In front of me, Mom freezes with the spoon mid-air above the pan. Her eyes search mine, looking for clues as to what I am thinking, before pinching tightly with sadness. "Oh, Gavin. Was that where your shoot was?"

"Yeah. I didn't think I'd see her. But I was so far off base. Mom… she was the photographer for my shoot."

Mom sets the spoon on the rest and comes to stand beside me. She rubs my back, trying to soothe away my pain. She remembers, all too well, my rebellious days after we moved to California. The torment I endured and inflicted on everyone around me.

"What can I do?"

I turn to her and hug her again. When I release her, I relay my plan to her. And I tell her what happened in Clearwater with Alyson and Layla. How both of them behaved as if their needs and desires supersede mine—even with me in the epicenter.

The fire in Mom's eyes is like nothing I have seen before. Even with all the shit I put her through, she never showed this side. At least not to me. Her cheeks burn bright red as she balls her fingers into tight fists at her side. Right now, Mom is as livid as I am. If not more.

"I'm moving back, Mom. But I have a lot of work ahead of me."

The fire leaves her eyes and is replaced with a gentle smile. "Please tell me what I can do to help. Of course, I'll miss you, but I understand. Your heart never left Florida, honey. Not once."

Since Dad passed away two years ago, Mom and I have grown much closer. For a little while, I let go of the anger and resentment I held toward her. Once I understood she had no choice—take the promotion or possibly lose her job—my forgiveness was easier to dole out.

"True. But I messed up, Mom. I don't know if she'll forgive me."

Mom walks over to the stove and turns off the burner. She grabs two bowls from the cabinet and portions us both some food. We walk over to the small, four-seater dining table and sit. She sets a bowl in front of me before speaking.

When her eyes meet mine, they are serious and determined. "Gavin... Don't stay away and wonder what if this or what if that. If there is one thing losing your father taught me, it's that life is much shorter than we give it credit for. You have to do things now, while you still can. There are so many things your father and I didn't get to do together. Things I will never get to do with him. And I'm fully aware he'd want me to keep living my life. To find someone else who brings me happiness. But I'm not ready for that. It's too soon. Maybe one day..."

I reach across the table and take her hand. "When you're ready, Mom. It's okay if that doesn't happen for many years to come. Or if it happens sooner than you expect. Anyone who says otherwise is an asshole."

"Gavin," Mom scolds. I shrug her off. "Anyway. You and Cora are young. You have what looks like a lifetime ahead of you. But I thought the same with your father. So, I chose to work hard and save for us to do everything after retirement. But we can't predict the future. I never thought I'd be spending my retirement without your father. It's a hard pill to swallow. And it's not something I want for you. To live in regret. So whatever I can do to help you, let me know. Because your happiness matters more than anything else in my world."

I give her hand a gentle squeeze. "Thanks, Mom. You always say what I need to hear. And after I sort out all the details tomorrow, I'll let you know."

Silence rings around us a moment, but soon Mom and I fall into easy conversation. She talks about work and some new software they are developing to detect specific heart defects in the womb. Some new, experimental noninvasive technology. I listen to every word she says, but a lot of what she tells me is gibberish. A strange blend of medical terminology and techie talk. But it's my mom, so I pay attention to every detail. I smile at her excitement.

When she finishes her story, I tell her about the shoot in Clearwater for Global Beach Magazine. How the magazine will reach major cities across the world. I also let her know I have no doubts about finding a new agent, especially after this shoot. Then I share the last shoot I plan to do here. That it involves Layla. Alyson hasn't told me what the shoot is for yet, but I can only assume it's something to do with couples. If that happens to be the case, I will be speaking with that photographer the moment I arrive on set.

After we finish eating, Mom drives me to my house. We exchange hugs and promises to keep in contact throughout the week. I unlock the front door and wave at Mom as she backs out of the driveway. I stand in the darkness a moment and breathe in the stale air and vacancy around me. When I flip the light on, I scan the empty and soulless house I have lived in for the last eight years.

Then I drop to my knees and cry. "I'm finally going home."

The sun burns fiery as it collides with the horizon.

Over the last week, I have visited the beach every evening. Sat in the same exact spot and nestled my feet in the warm sand. Watched the sun plummet into the water and fizzle into darkness. Smelled the mustiness of the dampened earth. Felt the salty breeze brush against my skin and whip my hair across my face.

Every night is different. The way the sun glows, how the sky changes colors, the scents in the air and on my skin, the sounds of the waves crashing or people chatting, how the breeze fluctuates. All of it. One night, I sat here in the rain. Actually, it was a downpour. But I refused to leave. If anything, I compared the changes in the atmosphere to the temperance of my mood. Like Mother Earth was going through mood swings and taking me on the journey. And I plan to embrace every leg of said journey.

A half hour after the sun is no longer visible, I rise from the sand and walk back toward my car. The drive home is forgotten, and at times I am surprised I make it home in one piece. I recall getting in my car and parking in the driveway, but nothing in between. Every day is the same.

I unlock the back door and flip on the lights. The scent of daily flower deliveries dying on my kitchen counter permeates the air. For the last five days, a new bouquet of flowers has arrived on my front doorstep. Red roses. White roses. Yellow roses. A mixed variety of roses. And a mixed variety of non-roses.

Each bouquet from my mom and Shelly's florist shop. Each bouquet sent with a small note. And I read each one of them. Absorb all the words. Unlike the text messages I continue to get from Gavin.

The notes sweet and short.

I miss you, baby.

Sunsets are never the same without you.

Tu es les étoiles de ma lune.

Can we watch Lord of the Rings on repeat for a week straight?

Soon, baby. Soon.

Surely, my mom and Shelly are enjoying Gavin's whole charade a little more than most people. And as bad as my house started smelling yesterday, I can't throw any of the flowers away. I just can't. Maybe I should dry them. Drying them would at least eliminate the funk in the air.

Luna weaves figure eights between my legs, purring and mewling as we head toward her bowl. After I give her a scoop of food and a few pets, I head to my room to change clothes. I love the scent of the beach—it conjures up so many wonderful memories—but I don't enjoy the constant sand on my skin. Beach sand is nature's equivalent to glitter.

A few days ago, Shelly stated we were going out. There was no asking and I wasn't allowed to refuse. Everyone was going and we were visiting the nightclub Micah works at in Tampa. Although I didn't want to go, I had no energy to fight Shelly. So I caved. It wasn't worth the argument.

I riffle through my closet and grab a pair of black skinny jeans and an equally black short-sleeve top. On a normal night, I would brush my hair and make myself look presentable. But since I currently give no fucks... I drag my hair up, combing it with my fingers, and securing it with an elastic band. It's sloppy and tired looking and I don't give a shit. If Shelly wants to force me to go out, she will suffer the consequences of my appearance.

Undoubtedly, Shelly will give me a ration of shit, but whatever. She can suck it up like I am.

Minutes later, a knock raps at the door. "It's open," I scream, louder than necessary.

The door opens and three pairs of feet trample across my wood floor. I remain on the couch, staring at the unlit fireplace. Visually tracing the rough grain of the chopped raw wood in the firebox. Pondering if I will ever get to light a fire and snuggle close to Gavin. I briefly close my eyes and take a deep breath. Nowadays, no breaths seem deep enough.

"Why the hell is your back door unlocked?" Shelly asks in her best motherly tone.

And I don't want to listen to her lecture me, just because it is all I have heard for days. If she felt an inkling of what I do, she wouldn't bother with such frivolity. "Because I've only been home for fifteen minutes and knew you guys would be here soon."

Shelly walks over to me and points her finger in my face, her other hand on her hip. "That's no excuse. Lock your freaking door."

I shake my head at her. "Yeah, sure thing *Mom*."

Erin and Jonas walk over and stand beside Shelly. I scan them head to toe. Everyone looks great. Hair, attire, overall presence. Me? Looks like I rolled out of bed five seconds ago. But I am not out to impress anyone, so who cares. If people stare, let them.

"You ready to go?" Jonas asks, voice soft with a hint of concern.

"Yeah, let me *lock up* and we can go." I smirk at Shelly and rise from the couch. I give Luna a couple pets and kisses, then we head out.

The drive to Tampa is a blur. Traffic is busy as usual, but I just stare at the lights along the highway. Shelly, Erin, and Jonas try to include me in more than one conversation, but I wiggle my way out of each one. Nothing I have to say matters right now, so it is better just to stay silent and stare out the window.

After we find a place to park, we walk down the sidewalk to the club. Music shakes the walls of the surrounding buildings. Car exhaust floats in the air. Bright headlights blind us as we head to the club's entrance. And I am numb to it all.

Once inside, we find a tall tabletop with stools near the bar. Jonas goes to the bar and buys us all a round. When he returns with our drinks, I practically chug the entire beer. Tonight will be a long night. One of many, unfortunately.

Forty-five minutes and three more beers later, I am somewhere between tipsy and drunk. And for the first time since we arrived, I listen to the music playing. Some electronic dance music I haven't heard before. The beat holds my attention while the bass resonates in my bones. If I wasn't in loner mode, I would head out to the dance floor and give everyone the show of their life. But thankfully, some microscopic piece of logic still resides inside me.

Micah comes over to the table and shoots the shit with Jonas for a few minutes. Moments later, Jonas, Shelly, and Erin get up and go out to the dance floor. Leaving me alone with Micah. Who has hated me since Shelly and I became friends in the third grade. But the way he regards me right now is different. A sort of sympathy residing in the lines of his face. Sympathy he has never directed at me a day in his life.

"How are you?" Micah leans over and asks.

I bring the bottle to my mouth and finish off my beer. "Tired of people asking me how I am. You?"

"I've been better." I catch him glancing over at a woman behind the bar. She's pretty—simple makeup, darker blonde hair piled high on top of her head, a smile that would light up the night sky.

"Who is she?" I openly point at the woman behind the bar.

"Could you please stop pointing?" A few seconds after I comply, he continues. "That's Peyton. She's the new bartender."

"And how long have you been in love with her?"

If Micah had a drink, he would have spit it across the room. Did I hit the nail on the head or what?

"I'm sorry, what? She's only been working here for a couple weeks."

"The length of time she's worked here and how you feel about her are irrelevant. How long have you been in love with her?"

He stares at me like I have two heads. "You're right, it's irrelevant. But you know what isn't? You and Gavin."

I roll my eyes. Nice change of subject. One I cannot ignore or evade. "Ugh, can you please not join the *Save Cora and Gavin* party? If someone isn't talking to me about it every day, the daily flower deliveries are. Isn't it okay for me to just want to go bury myself in blankets and darkness?"

"Seems you are," he states, lifting his chin toward my hair. "Your hair looks like it hasn't seen a brush in weeks. And I know you love rocking the black, but not every day is a funeral."

"You don't get to judge me," I say, pointing my finger in his face. "Black is life. And maybe I feel like death every day. Why do you fucking care?"

He sighs and slumps forward. "Normally, I wouldn't care. But since I talk to Gavin every single goddamn day now, it seems caring is my new middle name." He cocks his head and plasters on a pissy smile.

Gavin and Micah are speaking to each other every day. What the hell are they talking about? Me? Us? There is no us. There hasn't been an "us" in thirteen years. And especially when he decided to stop returning my calls or responding to my letters shortly after he moved away. No matter how much time has passed, those memories still sting. Burn. Char.

"You guys talk that often?" I mumble, staring down at my beer bottle.

"Yeah. He's got a lot happening all at once. Cora…" I glance up at Micah when he says my name. His expression shifts to something more sullen. "He hurt you, I get it. Believe me. But you two need to talk. Really talk. If you don't want to speak to him on the phone, at least respond to one of the million texts he's sent you. Of all people, I figured you'd be the first person to listen. You don't need to explain anything to me, but don't shut him out. Not when he's doing everything within his power to make things right. Not when he's doing everything to come back to you."

Over and over, Gavin told me he would fix this. Told me he would come back to me. But I had heard those words before. Granted, we were kids and didn't have the means to follow through. But like I told Gavin before, actions were what I needed. Lies are made up of words just like truths. And other than flowers, love notes, and his constant reaching out to me, I haven't actually *seen* his actions.

"I'll think about it. But I make no guarantees. I've been dealing with a lot on my end too."

"Like I said, I get it. I've been burned in the past."

And that is the most personal thing Micah has ever shared with me. This whole conversation is surreal. Maybe whoever burned Micah made him realize that being a dick wasn't all it is cracked up to be. Hallelujah!

Shelly, Erin, and Jonas return to the table. They laugh about something, sweat shining on their skin under the multicolored lights. Seconds after their return, Micah slips away. Goes back behind the bar and wistfully side-eyes the new bartender.

I repeat Micah's words in my head. Gavin is fixing things. Gavin is doing everything to come back.

To Florida.

To me.

And the light that snuffed out in my heart a week and a half ago, it flickers for a second. A blip. But sometimes, a blip is all it takes. Sometimes, a blip is what turns darkness into light.

nine

Thirteen years ago

"I'm sorry, Gavin. We just don't have the money to let you fly back to Florida right now," Mom says with a sad smile.

Although she is trying to empathize with me, she has no idea how I feel. And I don't know what upsets me more—the fact I can't fly back to see Cora or that Mom plays the *I understand* card. "But you promised, Mom," I yell across the room, nails biting my palms.

"Don't you take that tone with me. And I never *promised* you'd be able to fly back this summer. I said we would see. And it's not possible right now. I'm sorry."

I storm off to my bedroom, slam the door behind me and lock the handle. "I hate you!" I scream at the walls as I fist my hands in my hair.

"Gavin! Come back out here and apologize to your mother! Now!" Dad stands on the other side of the door, banging.

"Fuck you! Both of you!"

I pick up my desk chair and throw it across the room. One of the legs shatters on impact and I stare at the rubble. A moment later, I punch a hole in the wall beside my bed. Then I collapse on the bed and cry into the comforter.

I lay on my side and draw my legs to my chest. Hours pass and all I can do is lie here and cry. Cry until my eyes burn and my throat numbs. This is utter bullshit. They promised me I would be able to fly back to Florida during the summer. They promised I would be able to see Cora soon after we settled.

But their promises are lies.

It has been a fucking month. We are pretty fucking settled. Although, I don't think I will ever settle here. Everything about this place feels like a death sentence. A prison cell keeping me away from the one person I want more than anything. And why did they make a promise they never had any intention of fulfilling? Just to pacify me? If that's the case, I am more pissed.

Grabbing my phone from my back pocket, I call Cora. Hearing her will settle the anger inside me. Cora has always held the elixir to my soul.

"Hey, Gavin." Her voice perky and happy when she answers. This is exactly what I need right now. Just her.

"Hey, baby. I miss you."

"I miss you, too. Did you talk to your parents? Are you flying back soon?"

The hope in her voice echoes through the line. And I hate that I am about to destroy it. Well, my parents are destroying it. But I am the bearer of the bad news, and I hate it more than anything. Hate that I can't give her—us—better news.

"Yeah, I talked to them."

"And?"

"And they said we don't have the money right now. That there's no way I can fly back this summer."

"Oh," she whispers. And the disappointment is evident in that single word. "Oh. Well, that sucks."

"That's putting it nicely. I told them I fucking hate them."

We stay on the phone—silent—for a moment. She tries to muffle the sound, but I hear her crying. And my heart shatters further because there is not a goddamn thing I can do to make this better. I hate that I can't be there with her. I hate how helpless I feel. That I have no way to console her. To hug her close and kiss her hair. Rub a hand up and down her back, over the back of her head as I press her to my chest. This whole situation is such fucking bullshit.

"Gavin?"

"Yeah, baby?"

"Please don't hate your parents. It's your mom's job that did this, not her specifically. Your Mom would never intentionally hurt you or us." She chokes out the words and I hate that she is fighting her tears to say nice things about my parents.

But she is right and I know it. Though, I don't know who else to blame for us moving so far away. I am drowning and no one is jumping in to save me. No one tosses me a life preserver.

"I don't really hate them. It's this whole situation that I hate. But I have no other way to express how it's making me feel."

Silence steals the air between us again. But the silence is not uncomfortable. Never has been with Cora. If anything, it calms me. Settles my soul. Gives a peace only she provides.

"Can we talk about something else? Anything else? I don't care what it is," she says. "Have you been to the beach out there yet?"

I love how she knows my favorite place on earth. How she knows it is the one place where I feel solace, other than with her. How she understands my love for the water, the sand, the comfort.

"We went to the beach for the first time a few days ago. It's not the same as the beaches at home."

"How so?"

"The sand grains are bigger. And the water is fucking cold, even in the middle of summer. I didn't get in past my knees. And even that only lasted a few minutes."

"Did you get to stay and watch the sunset?"

God, I love her. Love how she knows me, inside and out. Love how she soothes me so easily. Sunsets are the best, but they will never be the same without her. If I never saw another sunset, but was able to see her again, I would be one-hundred-percent okay with that. Without her, a sunset is just a ball of fire disappearing from sight. Sunsets hold no magic without Cora at my side.

"No, baby. My parents didn't want to stay that late. But maybe we'll get to watch a California sunset together one day."

"We *will* get to watch one together. More than one." The optimism in her voice spreads warmth from the center of my chest to the tips of my fingers and toes.

"One day. Until that day comes though, you watch the sunsets there for me. And I'll watch them here. But I'd rather wait until you're with me."

"Me too."

For the next hour, we talk about random things. Places we went together. Things that made us laugh. And it's not until I hear her yawn that I realize it is past midnight in Florida. Another shitty side effect of this move—the three-hour time zone difference. I would stay up all night and talk with her. But we are both tired, more mentally and emotionally than physically.

"I should let you go to bed, baby."

"As sweet as that is, it doesn't matter much. I only sleep a couple hours a night now. But I guess you're right."

I don't want to hang up the phone. Even if we sit here and say nothing for hours on end, just hearing her breathe on the other end makes me feel at home.

As if she can read my mind, even with several states and thousands of miles between us, she says, "Maybe we can just lay down and set our phones on our pillows. We can pretend that we're side by side."

"That sounds like the best idea I've heard in days," I tell her as I fight the tears stinging the backs of my eyes.

And for the next two hours, I listen to her sleep. Listen to her soft breaths and occasional sleep-spoken words. Words like *love* and *soon* and *forever*.

ten

GAVIN

This shoot with Layla is exactly what I thought it would be. A shit show to flaunt our "relationship." Well I hope she is prepared for said relationship—as well as our friendship—to end. Because the line has been drawn and this is definitely over. Hope she enjoyed riding in my wake while it lasted.

The photographer directs us here and there and I follow through as if nothing has changed. But everything has changed. And in about fifteen minutes, Layla and Alyson are about to find out exactly how much it has changed. In less than a minute, everything in their world will tip on its axis. As it did mine.

They shouldn't have pushed me here. They should have let me pursue my relationship with Cora. Live my life how I want. But neither of them seemed capable of handling life when I wasn't improving theirs. Now… now there is no other option. They did this and now they will pay the consequences.

A few more clicks of the camera and the photographer announces the shoot is a wrap. As soon as those words are spoken, I distance myself from Layla. And she notices immediately.

"You okay?" Layla asks as she approaches me.

I slip a hoodie over my head before chugging my water dry. During the whole process, Layla stands a foot away and regards my lack of speech and eye contact. Good. I hope it makes her sweat. Hope it makes her question why I have been so standoffish. Hope it unsettles and worries her. It should.

But she won't have to question much of anything in a moment. Shit… meet fan.

Out of the corner of my eye, I spy Alyson walking toward us. I drag in a deep breath and prepare for what will happen next. If I know these two women well enough, one will go into hysterics while the other throws a rage fit. Not that I care, but let's see how right I am.

"Gavin. Layla. Great job out there today," Alyson chirps. Her whole demeanor is as it was before we ever went to Florida. Chipper and smiley and completely artificial. Since she has been my agent, I always sensed her artifice. But I passed it off as being out in Los Angeles, and that is how most of the population is. Now, I see things differently. Now, I see she only cares about me for one reason. My signature on her paycheck.

Alyson starts scrolling through her phone and ignoring Layla and me. As she has done a thousand times prior. So, I steel myself and start the inevitable.

"Alyson. Layla. We need to talk."

Layla stares at me, her amber resin eyes asking me question after question. But I ignore her and stare at Alyson, who has yet to look up from her phone. With each passing second, the fact that she continues to ignore me pisses me off further. So to grab her attention, I opt to snap my fingers in her face.

When she finally looks up from her still lit-up phone screen, irritation rests on her face. Irritation for me disrupting her. But I don't give a fuck.

Welcome to the club of pissed-off people, my name is Gavin.

"Gavin, I was just reading an email for another shoot. If you would've waited another—" Alyson attempts to hold the floor, but I cut her off.

"Stop," I shout. My voice bounces around the small studio. The eyes of crew members still in the room look our way. But I don't give a shit. I am over this. More than over it. "As I said a moment ago, we need to talk. The three of us."

"I heard you, Gavin. Can it not wait? I have other appointments I need to get to." As she says the words, she flicks her wrist and glances down at the gold and diamond watch on her arm. This irritates me more.

"No, Alyson. It cannot wait," I seethe.

She locks her phone and rests her hands on her hips. She purses her lips and regards me as if I am behaving like a stubborn child. Obviously, she has forgotten her place in this world. Has forgotten the fact that she only has a paycheck because I grant her such a privilege. Sure, she has other clients, but none of them are as big as I am or as fruitful to her bank account. If anything, she should be vying for my attention. Doing whatever makes me happy.

"Well, spit it out. As I said, I have other appointments to get to."

Beside me, Layla starts biting her fingernails. It is such a disgusting habit. One I tried to help her curb time after time. By the time I finish, she probably won't have any nails left.

My eyes dart between the two of them—one worried, the other annoyed. "You're fired," I state firmly, not an ounce of regret in my voice.

Alyson blinks a few times before taking a step back. Confusion mars her face for a beat as she lifts a hand to her chest. "Sorry, I think I may have misheard you. What did you just say?"

I want to laugh and shake my head, but bite my lip and resist the urge. She heard me loud and clear. Just doesn't want to believe it. "You heard me just fine. But if it needs repeating… You. Are. Fired." She jerks her head away as if I slapped her. But before she says another word, I face Layla next. "And you… I don't ever want to see you again. We're done. No more fake engagement. No more friendship. I hope you enjoyed the ride because it's time to exit."

Layla goes wide-eyed and stands speechless. She stares at me slack-jawed as her eyes glaze over. A million thoughts and questions flit across her face, but she remains stoic. After a moment, she finally locates her voice. "This is because of *her*, isn't it?"

I don't owe either of them an explanation after the shit they have put me through, but I answer her anyway. "If I'm being honest, it's not just because of Cora. But yes, Layla, she is the shift that has made this happen. It was a long time coming, and she gave me the push I'd been missing for years."

"You can't do this!" Alyson yells, not caring who heard her outburst. She points her French-manicured nail in my face. "We have a contract." Her eyes light up, hoping she caught me in some loophole I forgot about.

But I didn't forget about our contract. She must have me pegged as an idiot. Joke is on her.

"Actually, I can do this. We *did* have a contract. A contract I had my attorney look over when I told him I wanted to seek a new agent. After some light reading —" I smirk "—it was determined that our contract period ended almost two years ago. But seeing as we had been doing so well together, neither of us paid much attention to that fact. Too bad for you."

Alyson is a deer in the headlights. She has no comeback for the truth I just laid on the table. No rebuttal for the fact that we carried on for an additional two years without signing a new contract. This hiccup is a win for me, and a major loss for her. If she would have continued looking out for my best interests, our business relationship may have continued. But greed took hold. And greed loses in the long run.

While Alyson marinates in the loss of being my agent, I turn and speak to Layla. "You know, we had a great friendship. One I never questioned. We were always there for each other. Had each other's back. But your ego surpassed your morality not too long ago. And the stunt you pulled in Florida... it's unforgivable."

A lone tear rolls down her cheek, her perfect stage makeup not smearing or running. Sadness hits when I question if I should believe this tear or not. As a model, Layla is an actor. She knows how to put on a show for the camera and crowd. Knows how to make people believe what she is selling. So how can I believe this lone tear is real? That it comes from somewhere genuine.

The answer is simple—I can't.

"Gavin," she chokes out and sniffles. "I'm sorry. It's just... Alyson called me and told me what was going on. That you planned to move back to Florida. And I just reacted. I freaked."

I shake my head. "You *just reacted*? You *freaked*?" I laugh at her, incredulous. "No. What you did was behave like a child who didn't get her way. Because if I moved away from you, you wouldn't get to ride my coattails anymore. But instead of talking with me, you chose a different tactic. Chose to be bitter and selfish and vindictive. Too bad it didn't work in your favor."

Her tears flow a little more steadily now. Maybe they are real, but no chance in hell am I letting my guard down enough to question their validity. If my guard goes down, she will push her guilt on me to appease herself.

"Gavin, please," Layla begs. "If our years of friendship mean anything to you—"

"No," I shout. "You don't get to pull the friendship card to manipulate me. After the stunt you pulled, knowing full well what it would do, there is no friendship card anymore. It expired the moment you used me as a pawn in some game to keep me. You know what she means to me, and you used that knowledge as a weapon. Friends don't do shit like that, Layla. Friends congratulate each other when good things happen."

In my periphery, Alyson unlocks her phone and begins to frantically go from screen to screen. I told my attorney I planned to speak with Alyson and Layla after the shoot ended, and gave him an estimated time as to when that would be. By now, he has emailed the termination paperwork to Alyson. A few seconds later, my thoughts are validated when Alyson slaps her hand to her mouth and gasps. As if she did not believe me.

My work here is done. And I have other obligations to attend to. So, without another word, I turn my back on them and walk away. Both women try to garner my attention as I head for the exit, but I ignore them as I push through the door. Already, a major weight lifts from my chest and I breathe a little easier.

～

Studio lights blind me as a man attaches a small microphone to my shirt. "Mr. Hunt, could you please say a few words so we can test the mic?"

I have the sudden urge to behave like a child with a toy microphone. I tap the mic clipped to my shirt a few times. "Testing. Testing. One, two, three. Can you hear me?"

A woman behind a soundboard with headphones over her ears gives a thumbs up. The man beside me returns the gesture then fidgets with the mic a little more, trying to disguise it behind my shirt. A moment later, he walks off and leaves me to sit on the studio stage alone.

Before I have too much time to ponder how long I will sit here alone, Janet Maverick sits in the plush armchair beside me. Janet Maverick—one of Holly-wood's top reporters. When she talks to a crowd, people listen. And that is the exact reason I came to her. So my story will be heard by the masses.

"Hey, Gavin. How are you today?" Janet asks, genuinely interested.

"Oh, you know. Things aren't so hot. But I'm hoping this interview will be the fresh start to things getting better."

She nods. "I'm sure everything will work out. Just stay positive."

A moment later, the stage crew crowd around us. We are asked to get in position on set. Janet and I are asked to say a few last things for a final check of our mics. Then a woman behind one of several cameras begins counting down with her fingers before pointing at Janet.

"Good evening, Los Angeles. If this is your first time tuning in, I'm Janet Maver-ick. And you're watching The Heart of Hollywood. Tonight, I am honored to have Gavin Hunt on stage with me." Janet faces me and gives a warm smile. "Welcome, Gavin."

I have been in front of a camera hundreds of times, but in this moment an over-whelming sense of stage fright consumes me. "Thank you, Janet. It's great to be here," I stumble then cough. A stagehand points to a bottle of water beside me, signaling me to drink. Glad someone is looking out for me.

Janet carries on as if there is no reason to panic. As if millions of people aren't flipping on their televisions to watch this very moment. Right now, I envy her this.

"For those of you who aren't familiar with the man beside me… First of all, shame on you," she jokes. "Seriously. Mister Gavin Hunt is a model. You may have seen his work in a magazine or twenty. He has also appeared on the cover of several romance novels. Ladies, check those book covers."

Someone behind the soundboard presses a button and some previously recorded laughter echoes around us.

"But let's get down to the nitty-gritty," Janet says. "Gavin, you just returned from a photo shoot in Florida. How did it go?"

I hold Janet's gaze, doing my best to ignore the cameras and crew focused on us. After a quick inhale, I answer. "The photo shoot was phenomenal. It was nice to return to Florida after being away for so many years."

Janet perks up at this. "Return to Florida? Is that where you're originally from, Gavin?"

"It is. I moved out to California when I was sixteen after my mom received a promotion. This past trip was the first time I'd been back."

She nods, her face studious over my response. "So, what can we look forward to seeing after this shoot?"

"I was doing a shoot for Beach Global Magazine. There will be several images with a new line I'm helping them promote. Casual wear for the beach and city. As well as swimwear and undergarments," I say, waggling my brows.

Janet lays her hand over her heart before fanning herself. "Gavin, you can't just say things like that. Now I'm blushing on national television." She swats me with a small pad of paper.

"The magazine is set to release at the beginning of summer. Make sure you get your copy. I guarantee you won't be disappointed." I wink at her.

"Ladies, you heard it here. Keep your eye on the magazine stands." Janet takes a sip of water, then switches tactics. "Other than work, Gavin, how is life treating you?"

This is why I came here. To expose my life to the masses. Tell my story—the truth as well as the web of lies. I need the façade of what Layla and I had to be uncovered. For all the stories of our perfect "engagement" to be brought out in the light and diminished.

"Well, Janet, things are a bit rough right now," I say.

"Aw, I'm sorry to hear this. What's going on?"

"My trip to Florida ended up becoming more than just a work trip. For the first time in thirteen years, I ran into the love of my life."

Janet gasps and slaps a hand over her mouth, eyes awestruck. "Oh my, Gavin. I don't know what to say. Why has it been so long since you've seen this woman? And wait… what about your engagement?"

The perfect segue into clearing the air. Thank you very much. "That's part of the reason I'm here tonight, Janet. I want to clear the air about a few things. The first thing being my engagement to Layla Hendricks. After running into my high school sweetheart, many things were put into perspective. One of those things being said engagement. An engagement that was done purely for business reasons."

"Well, you are just full of surprises tonight," Janet states.

I nod. "Indeed. Layla and I have been friends since I moved to California. But that's all. My heart has always been in Florida. As my career took off, Layla struggled. Our agent got her shoots with several well-known photographers, but nothing boosted her career. After a year, our agent suggested we pretend to get engaged. That my soaring career would lift hers. So, I agreed. Layla was my friend, and I wanted to help her. But while I was in Florida, that favor and my friendship was taken advantage of. As of today, I have cut all business ties with my agent and Layla. And have also severed my friendship with Ms. Hendricks."

Janet and I sit in silence for several long seconds. Now that I have said my part —gotten the falsehoods of my engagement to Layla off my chest and told the world I am in love with someone else—relief rushes through my veins. A weight that has anchored me in place for years instantly lightens. With such a simple action, I feel a hundred pounds lighter. Now, I need to repair things between me and Cora. And with my level of determination, I will fix us.

"Wow, Gavin. I'm not even sure where to begin. If you don't mind sharing with us, what happened in Florida that sparked this dramatic change? Other than seeing this mystery woman."

I hadn't been given permission to mention Cora's name, so keeping her anonymity is vital. Although, Hollywood will figure out who she is eventually. But until that day arrives, my lips remain sealed.

"Janet, there aren't adequate words to explain what seeing this woman did to me. It's as if my heart started beating again." At my words, Janet and a few of the female crewmembers swoon. The visual adds a smile to my face. "When I was younger, I didn't have a say in my family moving to California. But now, I make all my decisions. And that's why I have chosen to move back to Florida."

Saying the words aloud, announcing them to millions of viewers, sets my pulse to a wild gallop beneath my sternum. But after seeing Cora, after being in the same space as her for a week, there is no possible chance of me staying away. Not anymore. Cora is everything I always wanted. A breath of fresh air. The only person to soothe and satiate my soul. Moving back to Florida is something I should have done years ago. For too long, the flashing lights and starry eyes distracted me. But I have no doubts this is the right choice. Cora has always been the right choice.

"Well, Gavin. I'm not sure I know what else to say. California will miss you. I will miss you," she says, smiling wide.

"You haven't seen the last of me, Janet. I'm not leaving the industry. Just making some personal changes. But you'll still get to glance at my pretty face," I tease.

"Whew. That's good news. I'm not sure how my life would continue if I didn't see you around the city." She pauses, reaching across the space between us and resting her hand on mine. "Thank you for sitting with me today. It was wonderful to see you. Keep us posted on how things go with this mystery woman."

"Will do, Janet. Thank you for having me."

As Janet says her parting words into the camera, I review all the things I need to do in my mental checklist.

Fire Alyson. Check.

Give Layla the boot. Check.

Review my new agent's contract. Still need to do.

Call Micah. Still need to do.

Deal with the house. Work in progress.

As I walk off the stage, my phone dings in my pocket. When I retrieve it, there is a message from the realtor I contacted yesterday. Her timing couldn't be more perfect. And I take it as a sign everything will work out as planned. At least that is what I hope.

～

"Of course, you can stay with me, man. I'd never leave you on the streets. When do you think you'll get here?" Micah asks.

Not sure why I was worried, but I am so relieved he said yes to me staying at his place until I buy a new house. Micah and I have known each other almost twenty years, but I had my doubts about him agreeing to let me stay. He may be my best and longtime friend, but how he acted around Cora while I was in Florida had me antsy to hear his response. The fact he said yes alleviates another concern.

"Maybe in the next few days or so. The house is under contract and I'll know more tomorrow or the next day. Is it cool if I ship some boxes and my car to your place?"

"Sure thing. Whatever you need. Mi casa es su casa. Just let me know when they'll be here, so I'm home when they arrive."

The sale of my California house is moving much quicker than anticipated. And I took it as yet another sign. The cosmos are rooting for me—for me and Cora. The stars aligning invigorates me, has me doing things at maximum speed. If the forward momentum continues at this pace, I will be back in Florida within a week. Hopefully sooner. Fixing things with Cora can't happen fast enough. Being with her again, especially.

"Thanks, bro. I'll shoot you a text with the shipping info. For now, I'm only sending clothes and necessities. When I find a place, I'll have everything else shipped."

Micah and I talk for a few more minutes, catching up on other things. After we hang up, I go into beast mode. By the end of the day, ninety percent of my house is packed into boxes. Lucky for me, I have never been a packrat. By no means am I a minimalist, but over the years I had no desire to fill my house with endless knick-knacks. I suppose I always knew I would pack things up.

I call the shipping company and set up a time to have the boxes and my car picked up. After, I set up for the remaining boxes and furniture to be shipped to my mom's house. When I told her how quick things were progressing with the sale of my house, she offered her unused two-car garage as storage space.

Everything came together with ease. How can I not believe in fate? Everything continues to line up for us to be together again. If it isn't divinity, I don't know what it is.

But as I lay awake in bed, I question how I will fix things with Cora. As smooth as things are going, a twinge of doubt lingers in the back of my mind. It taunts me and has uncertainty creeping in my veins.

What if she rejects me? Although the chemistry between us is more than obvious, I hurt her. More than once. Hurt like that doesn't just vanish. What if she doesn't forgive me? The possibility lingers in my thoughts and gnaws at my heart. Because as much as I have done to prove my promise to Cora, the possibility of her not letting me back in still stands. Which begs the question…

What if all this is for nothing?

eleven

News travels fast in the photography and modeling circuit.

Only two days have passed since I sent over the finalized photos from Gavin's shoot to the magazine. Riffling through thousands of images of Gavin wasn't easy by any stretch of the imagination, but eventually I selected my top three from each look the magazine wanted. Most of the images I sent aren't my personal favorites—those I kept all for myself—but they are notable and sales-worthy photographs.

As I sip on a cup of hot caffeine, I read the fifth email from a local company seeking my photography skills. And I am in complete awe. Doing this photo shoot with Gavin has already opened multiple doors for me. Some doors I wish would have remained closed. The doors trapping my heart and memories in the dark corners of my mind.

I keep thinking of Gavin's promise to return to me. His promise to fix past mistakes and explain all the things I didn't understand. But as each day passes, I wonder if he will follow through with his promises. If the perfume from days' worth of flower deliveries was any indication, he plans to return. The only thought constantly rolling around in my head is how we move forward.

So much of our lives has changed. Adulthood changes people. But so much of what we once had remains untouched.

At one point in our lives, Gavin and I shared everything with each other. There were no secrets between us—intentional or by accidental omission. With the latest revelation—his supposed fake engagement to *her*—I wasn't sure I could give Gavin my trust. I want to believe it is possible for us to get back to where we were years ago. The place where I knew every facet of his life and vice versa.

Because the end of us couldn't be *this*—an ugly, painful, heart-wrenching reality.

The way things are now, they are so different from when we were younger. What I thought was pain at age sixteen is nothing compared to this vacant space beneath my breast bone. At least, back then, I experienced sensation where my heart resided in my chest. Now, my heart feels numb and hollow. The organ still beats, still pumps blood through my veins, but it only does so to keep me in existence. There is no life behind the rhythm. No real purpose. Just a machine doing its job.

My phone pings with an incoming text. Reluctantly, I glance at the screen. Although I haven't responded, Gavin continues to text me updates. Last I heard, he fired his agent and broke off his friendship and fake engagement with *her*. That text brought an actual smile to my face. But we still have a long way to go.

SHELLY

You, me, Jonas. Bar. Tonight.

Shelly has always known how to make me smile and laugh. Her simple text does exactly that. Her message short, sweet, and to the point.

As much as I want to be a hermit and hide in my shell of a house, Shelly has the right remedy. A night out with my friends is exactly what I need to boost my mood. To sit amongst the crowd, sip on a beer and listen to people belt out karaoke. The solution to every bad day in history is awkward karaoke.

> Sounds good. What time?

> Six. We need to grab a good table before the crowd arrives.

> See you at six.

I read through the emails again and decide to accept two of the offers. Respectfully declining the others, I tell them to reach out in the future and check my availability. The two I accept are in the Bay Area. One is for the city of St. Petersburg, who has requested for me to do a cityscape with some patrons. The city is looking to update images for tourism since the city has changed so much in the last five years. They want to show off city life and all the wonderful things the area has to offer. The other offer is for boudoir photos of a couple in Tampa. Details are vague, but enough for me to be comfortable and accept.

After I respond to the emails, I make the mistake of opening the file on my laptop titled "DO NOT OPEN." Because, for some reason, I am a glutton for punishment.

For the next hour, I scroll through photo after photo of Gavin. From the photo shoot, and times when he wasn't paying attention. Frame after frame after frame. Years ago, I had photos of us from high school digitized. Those same images were now parked in this folder. And I cannot force myself to look away.

Click. Click. Click.

Cue the tears. And the burn in my nose. Followed by the clog in my throat.

As each image from our younger years passes over the screen, I cry uglier and harder. I tremble from head to toe as my vision blurs and a tight pinch pierces between my lungs. The onslaught of memories set off the full emotional spectrum and it is pure misery. And I welcome every ounce of it.

At least anguish is better than numbness. At least it reminds me I am still alive. Because some days, I wonder if this is one huge nightmare. Some sick, twisted version of hell. Some days, life is hell.

~

I wake up on the couch, the blanket cocooning me and Luna purring on my chest. The light of day dims, but the sun is still up. I give Luna a few pets before cuddling her in my arms. After a moment, I bolt upright and Luna hisses at me before scampering off.

"Sorry, Luna."

Shit. What time is it? I told Shelly I would meet her and Jonas at the bar.

I glance at the clock on the kitchen wall, noting it's five-twenty. Flying off the couch, I head for my room and riffle through my closet. Thank goodness the bar is a short drive from the house, otherwise I would be screwed. After picking out a top and a pair of jeans, I jump in the shower and wash away the pool of sorrow I have been swimming in all day.

Once out and dressed, I feed Luna and grab my keys and wallet. I dash out the door and drive to the bar. Seven minutes later, I park in the lot and step through the bar doors.

I spot Shelly and Jonas at our usual table and walk over to them.

"Hey, you look like shit," Shelly says, not sugarcoating my wayward appearance.

"You really know how to flatter a girl. *Thanks*. I haven't been sleeping much. You're lucky I got a nap in before tonight, otherwise I'd look so much better."

I flip her the middle finger. But she knows I'm teasing her.

"Sorry. You know I call it as I see it," she apologizes with a shrug.

"True. Can we please talk about something else?" I didn't come out to talk about how depressing my life is. Tonight is about having fun and feeling better. If that isn't going to happen, I will just go home and wallow alone.

"Yeah, sorry," Shelly says.

The waitress approaches the table and sets down three beers. Mine is at my lips within a second, half of it down my throat. At this rate, I will be drunk in no time. We order another round and some appetizers.

By the time karaoke starts an hour later, I am somewhere between tipsy and drunk. And it is a nice place to be. In this state, not much of anything matters. Life has no issues. No drama. No life-altering decisions need to be made. It's all rainbows and unicorns and horrible singers on small stages.

As some overly primped woman sings the words to Bon Jovi's "You Give Love a Bad Name", I lean on Jonas. His arm wraps around my shoulder and keeps me from teetering off my stool.

Jonas really is a great guy. I hope he happens upon the right woman one day. As much as we went back and forth, part of me always knew nothing more would evolve between us. Jonas has a big heart and will be perfect for a very lucky lady one day. But that lady won't be me. And I hope he knows Shelly and I will need to approve whoever this future mystery woman will be. She will have a lot to live up to.

Jonas presses a kiss to the top of my head. "Are you okay?" he whisper-asks just loud enough for me to hear.

For a second, I nod. But the nod slowly transitions, and soon I shake my head before turning my face into his shoulder.

God, I am sick and tired of crying. My bloodshot eyes ache and feel as if they are swollen to twice their size. My throat scratches every time I speak and throbs with each breath I take. And honestly, I don't know how much more of this I can handle.

Jonas delicately rubs a hand up and down my back. Says soothing words only I hear. Shushes me and tells me everything will be alright. And his kindness has me on the cusp of crying harder, but I resist. There is only so much my body can handle.

Two lackluster karaoke songs later, we all agree to call it a night. We pay our tab before I stumble out the door. Jonas drives me home in my car and Shelly follows us so she can take Jonas back to his Jeep. The drive is short and filled with low-volume rock music from the radio. Jonas doesn't speak up while I lean against the window with my eyes closed. Minutes later, we park in my driveway and shuffle out. Shelly and Jonas walk me inside, hug me goodnight and disappear out the door.

Once alone, I kick off my shoes and peel off my jeans, crawl into bed and curl into a ball. Luna jumps up on the bed and nudges her head against mine. For a beat, I pet her soft fur and a sense of comfort washes over me as she purrs loudly and professes her unconditional love.

"At least you'll stay by my side, pretty girl," I whisper.

As if she understands me, Luna meows in response. I snuggle her into my chest and fall asleep, waking on and off through the night. Throughout the night, dreams of photos and drawings, hand holding and kisses, goodbyes and love letters haunt me every hour. As they do every night. And probably will for the rest of my life.

Twelve

CORA

Twelve and a half years ago

Today is the most important day of my life. But it doesn't matter. Not anymore.

On this day two years ago, Gavin and I officially started dating. Before he moved to California, we celebrated every possible relationship milestone. One month. Three months. Six months. One year. But today, on our two-year anniversary, I haven't heard a word from him.

His lack of reaching out to me can easily be blamed on time zone differences. The hour is still early in California, and he is probably sleeping. But a sinking suspicion in my gut tells me it has nothing to do with the time zones. This nerve-laden ache has been getting bigger each day we are apart.

Six months has passed since Gavin left Florida. Six very long, dark months. The last four… I haven't heard from Gavin at all. No return phone calls or texts. No response to the numerous letters I have mailed him. As if he vanished from the earth. Poof. At one point, I called and asked Mrs. Hunt if Gavin was still alive. She apologized profusely and told me Gavin was not doing well with the transition.

Neither was I, for that matter.

Since Gavin left, life has been complete and utter shit. My mom is lucky if I get out of bed each day. After weeks of tears and depression, Mom and Dad took me to see a therapist. We talked, she prescribed me anti-depressants and that was all she wrote. But pills will never replace my heart. Pills will never make this ache vanish. Only Gavin can do that. And he is gone.

Poof.

As with Gavin, everything I ever loved disappeared. My love for art has been almost nonexistent. School is going down the drain at a rapid pace. The only thing that kept me attending each day was the opportunity to sit under our tree. To trace my fingertips over the carved wood where our initials reside, along with his words only for me. Under that tree was our spot. Will always be our spot. The only physical piece of him I have a connection to every day.

I call Gavin's house and the phone rings twice before Mr. Hunt answers. "Hello?"

I waited as late as possible, so it isn't too early on the west coast. Currently eight in the morning in California. "Hi, Mr. Hunt. It's Cora. Sorry to call so early. Is Gavin awake?" I pick at the hem of my jeans as I wait, nervous.

"Good morning, sweetheart. It's not too early. But I'm sorry, Gavin isn't home. He stayed over at a friend's house last night."

"Oh," I say, disappointment evident in my tone. "Okay, thank you. I'll try calling his cell phone."

Before I hang up, Mr. Hunt speaks. "Cora? I'm so sorry about everything. I know neither of you is handling this well."

I bite my tongue to avoid crying in the phone. I wonder if he knows how distant Gavin and I have become. Miles and states aren't the only things that separate us now, it is also our lack of connection. Our lack of communication.

Is this what happens when soul mates are ripped apart? They drift and fade and become shells of themselves.

"Thank you, Mr. Hunt," I manage. "Please let Gavin know I called."

"I will, sweetheart. If we don't talk again before, have a happy Thanksgiving," he says.

And I almost lose it on the phone. "You all too." Then I hang up.

I wait a few minutes, gathering my thoughts and emotions. The last thing I want is to call Gavin and cry during our conversation. Although, nowadays I cry more often than not.

Opening Gavin's contact on my phone, I tap the little phone image before bringing the phone to my ear. *First ring.* God, I have missed hearing his voice. *Second ring.* But not more than I have missed his touch. *Third ring.* Or the feel of his lips pressed against mine. *Fourth ring.* And the way he held me close any chance he got. *Voicemail.*

"This is Gavin. Leave me a message. Or don't. I really don't give a shit either way."

Why isn't he answering? By now, it seems as if he purposely avoids me. And I don't know why. Because he won't fucking talk to me.

Beep.

"Hey, Gavin. It's me. Your girlfriend. Although that seems questionable since you haven't spoken to me in four months. Not once. I really miss you. And of all days to not respond to me… guess I should've known you'd find someone else to love. Thanks for having the balls to tell me. Whatever. You probably won't even listen to this. But if you do… Happy anniversary. Hope you have a *great* day."

I hang up and throw my phone across the room, screaming at the top of my lungs. And it's no surprise, no one comes to my room and asks what is wrong. Because Mom and Dad both know. They know what day today is. They know that I have only gotten worse with each passing day. Mom also knows I haven't spoken to Gavin in months. The longer I don't hear from Gavin—let alone see him—the more bitter I become. The more withdrawn I become. Whatever his reason for cutting me off, it would have been nice if he made me privy. As it is, I feel like I have been played.

After screaming a few more times, I rummage through my closet. When I locate my art supplies, I yank them down and cast them across my bedroom floor. For the next few hours, I submerge myself in charcoals and my art pad. My fingertips are coated in black coal, and I am certain my face has streaks from where I scratched my face a couple times.

But it doesn't matter. Nothing fucking matters.

I draw and shade and accentuate. When I finish the first image, I tear it from the pad and start a new piece. This process happens on repeat for hours. By the time I stop, the sun has begun setting. Three finished drawings lay in front of me, another still attached to the pad and left unfinished. I stare at the three images as a tear drips from my chin and splatters on the charcoal.

The first is a replica of the first day I met Gavin. Both of us sitting under our tree, before it was blemished by his pocket knife. Before it was *our* tree. I recall that day and how eager he was to make conversation with me. Continually ignoring him, I read my book and secretly memorized the lines of his face out of the corner of my eye. I listened to his breathing pattern and tried to match mine to it. I glanced down at his hands and watched them fumble as he sat nervously beside me.

The second image is a flashback to two years ago. Of Gavin and me at the beach, in the water, kissing for the first time. That day was pure magic. No other day compares to how I felt when his lips grazed mine for the first time. Like an incinerator ignited low in my belly, heat spreading throughout my body in the cool Gulf. And no matter who was looking, we stayed like that for hours in the water. Tangled limbs and hungry kisses. On that day, he became mine, and I became his. Forever.

And the third image makes me blush. In this piece, we are topless. Lips locked. Bodies crushed together. Hands in the other's hair and groping body parts. This was us. Exposed and vulnerable and losing ourselves in one another. And the night we lost our virginity. A night that will be forever engraved in my memory. Not just the physicality, but also the way his eyes softened and his breath caught and my name rolled off his tongue.

The more I stare at the drawings, the harder the tears fall. Before too many hit the pages, I swipe them away and fold up the pages. The unfinished page stays attached to the pad—a picture of me now. More like a silhouette. Because all I feel is darkness. Nothingness.

Grabbing one of my school notebooks, I open it to a blank page and write a letter to Gavin. One I hope he reads.

Gavin,

Today is our two-year anniversary. And all I want to do is talk to you. But we haven't talked in so long. Now, I am just empty inside. Lifeless. Moving to California wasn't your fault. You hate it. I hate it. And there is nothing we can do about it.

I called your house earlier and your Dad told me you stayed over at a friend's house. I'm happy you've made new friends out there. And I'm happy you seem to be moving on without me.

I won't bore you with my life. Because it's one big shit show on my end. Maybe I'll start my meds again, so at least I experience some form of happiness. Even if it is fake. Fake is better than nothing at all. Right?

Inside this envelope are three drawings of happier times. After this, I may just burn all my art supplies. Because anything worth capturing doesn't exist anymore. Not since you left. Not since you stopped talking with me.

Why? Why have you stopped talking with and writing me? Did you find someone else already? Was I that easy to forget? Am I not even worth friendship?

I hate myself. I hate my life. Hate that I have given you my heart and you've stomped on it until it turned to dust.

Does your heart feel like a black hole? Because mine does. It feels like this dark, hollow place that sucks all the happiness from the world and demolishes it.

It doesn't matter anymore. None of it does. You. Me. Us. Who were we to think we would see each other again? We're fools. Or at least I'm a fool. Because I believed we would. Believed this separation was a temporary blip in our relationship. Something easily fixed after a little patience.

But it seems I was wrong.

Because it feels like you have moved on without me. Left me to rot with the garbage.

And I'm done. Done spending every second of every day wondering what you're doing. If you care or think about me still. It's pretty obvious what the answer is, especially if you never speak to me. This situation sucks, but I never imagined you'd do this to me. Ghost me.

So, goodbye Gavin. It was my privilege to love you. And maybe one day in the future, I will get the chance again. God, I hope so. Because I will never love anyone the way I love you. If I'm honest, I don't ever want to love anyone else. I'd rather die alone, miserable and frail.

I hope you read this and it makes your heart hurt the same as mine. I hope it makes you shed as many tears as I have. And I hope you find it in your heart to come back to me one day.

Because I will always love you. Forever.

Tu es les étoiles de ma lune.

Cora

I fold the paper into thirds and set it with the drawings as I search the house for a large envelope. When I locate one, I shove the drawings and letter inside, addressing it to Gavin and slapping on too many stamps. A minute later, I walk to the mailbox and place the envelope inside, raising the red flag.

As I walk away from the envelope, I settle into my new reality. A reality where Gavin and Cora don't exist. A reality where love dies and hearts shatter into millions of little fragments. And a reality where nothing matters, because what is the point. What. Is. The. Point?

thirteen

GAVIN

Present

I stare off in the distance as my Range Rover is loaded into a freight box with a few boxes of my clothes inside the car. The car should arrive at Micah's house tomorrow evening. My SUV being loaded and shipped has reality setting in. And my nerves zapping like live wires.

This is really happening. I am going home.

> Car with three boxes inside should be at your place tomorrow night.

MICAH

Cool. I'll let you know when it arrives. What time is your flight tomorrow?

> 10am, with a stop in Houston. Should be in Tampa between 7-7:30pm.

If your shit arrives before you land, want me to pick you up?

> Nah. I'll just grab an Uber.

See you tomorrow. Tell your mom I said hi. Fly safe.

After my car is driven off, I go back in the house that no longer belongs to me and breathe deeply. In Los Angeles, houses sell faster than imaginable. At least that is what my realtor said. Regardless of the reason, I am happy to have things coming together. Call it divine intervention or luck of the draw—I don't care—but thank god I was able to check every item off my to-do list.

Scanning the empty house, I sigh. The day I put my house on the market, I also asked every person I knew if they wanted to purchase any of my furniture. A few hours ago, the last piece—my bed—was picked up. With not much furniture in the first place, it wasn't challenging to sell a bed with two nightstands, a couch, loveseat, coffee table, and a dining set. I had buyers lined up on the first day. In less than half a day, each piece was claimed.

Everything kept falling into place. And after each domino fell, I thanked the higher power watching over me. Because obviously someone out there wanted me to repair our broken relationship.

My phone buzzes in my palm, Mom's name and picture flashing on the screen.

"Hey, Mom."

"You ready, honey?"

"Yeah, I just have a couple more boxes for your garage." Yesterday, I took over the majority of what I planned to keep. All I had left was my carry-on for the plane and two small boxes.

"Okay. I'm leaving the house now. We can grab something to eat after I pick you up. See you soon."

"See you soon."

~

Mom and I sit in silence at the dining room table with two open pizza boxes between us. Of all the things to have for dinner on my last night here, Mom suggested our favorite pizza place. Honestly, it didn't matter what we ate. As long as we spent this time together, I was happy. And as much as I dislike California, I will miss Mom terribly.

"I wish you would come back to Florida with me," I tell her.

She sighs before taking a bite of pizza. After she finishes chewing, she says, "Gavin, maybe I will return in the future. But for now, my place is here. Maybe I'll feel different once you're gone, but I won't know until that happens."

I nod, accepting her answer. "Just hate that you'll be out here alone. If Dad was still alive, I'd feel different."

"I'm not alone, Gavin. Believe it or not, I have friends. Lots of them. And we spend time with one another." Mom points her slice of pizza at me and laughs. "Just because I'm a mother and older, doesn't mean I forgot how to enjoy life."

"Ha ha. Fine, I guess I believe you'll make it without me here. But if anything changes..."

"I promise you'll be the first to know."

We finish eating and put the extra pizza in the fridge. Plopping down on the couch, we spend the next two hours laughing at old episodes of *The Simpsons*. The night is the perfect end to my time in Los Angeles. Next to my mom, laughing and spending time together.

And right then, I send a wish to the universe that Mom will want to move back to Florida soon. Because I need her just as much as I do Cora. The only women in my life that matter. The only women who keep me whole and in check. My secret request is selfish, but I don't care. There are some things in life worth being selfish over. Like love.

We rise from the couch around ten thirty, give each other a hug, and head to our respective rooms. I kick off my shoes and tug my shirt over my head before landing on the bed. I stare at the ceiling for a while, counting the plastic, glow-in-the-dark stars I stuck to the ceiling when we first moved here. The stars were a constant reminder of Cora and the French sentiment I once told her. She truly is the stars to my moon. And she illuminates everything important in the world. Everything important to me.

And soon, very soon, I will be near her again. See her again. Breathe her in again. Touch her again. Because we haven't reached the end of our road. Not by a long shot. Anyone who tells me otherwise is a fool.

Shortly after I turn off the lamp, I fall asleep under the same stars I did almost thirteen years ago. Stars that spark my mind to dream of the most beautiful woman. The woman I love. The woman I have to win back. No matter what it takes.

When I wake in the morning, Mom is in the kitchen cooking us breakfast. As I sit at the breakfast bar, she slides a plate of eggs, sausage, and toast in front of me.

The last woman to make me breakfast was Cora. And I laugh, remembering my first taste of meatless sausage.

"What's so funny?" Mom asks.

I share my story with her and she laughs too. So many things have changed over the years, yet one thing remains the same and true. My love for Cora. And no matter how much has changed for either of us, I will love her regardless.

Mom and I finish breakfast, then talk about my new agent and how I plan to stay with Micah until I buy a new house. I help her with the dishes and then we prepare to leave. The drive to the airport goes faster than usual. Before realization sets in, Mom and I hug at the departure drop-off. After someone honks their horn, we break apart.

"Call me when you land, please."

"I will, Mom. I love you."

"I love you too, honey." For a moment, I stand rooted in place and stare as her car exits the airport drop-off.

This is it. The day I have been waiting for. Today, I am going home.

One of the hardest things I have ever done is sit on my ass and do nothing. Literally, nothing. Especially when I could be out there, trying to win back the love of my life.

But somehow, Micah has convinced me to sit in his house and be patient. To bide my time. The only thing keeping me sane is searching the internet for houses. Several nice houses have sparked my attention, but none of them give me a sense of fulfillment. And I think the reason is Cora.

If I buy a new home, I want Cora to be a part of the process. To hear her opinions on the appearance—inside and out. Get her input on which kitchen she likes better. If the house gets enough light or has the right number of trees. Or maybe which house she pictures us growing old in together. Which house she imagines us raising children and grandchildren in, their little feet trampling through a large back yard and playing on swings.

I slap my laptop shut and stop staring at houses. No matter what I do to occupy my time, every piece of my life always circles back to Cora. She is literally in every thought I own—awake and asleep.

Turning on the television, I search for something to watch. When I scroll through the guide and see *Lord of the Rings*, I laugh. If the cosmos aren't trying to tell me something, I don't understand what the hell is happening. One sign after another pops up. From the second I decided to mend my mistakes and our past, fortune has been on my side. And after seeing this, I vow to not spend another day sitting on this couch, bored out of my skull, doing nothing.

Just as I start watching the movie, Micah bursts through the front door. "Guess what?" he asks, a little out of breath.

"Whatever you're dying to tell me must be good if you're out of breath."

Micah flips me off. "Well, I was about to give you the best news since your return yesterday, but now I think I'll wait." He cocks his head and smirks.

Fucker.

"Don't be a dick. I'm sorry if I hurt your feelings." I frown at him for a half second, but the sarcasm doesn't go unnoticed. "What were you going to say?"

He stares at me a minute, tapping a finger against his lips. "A little birdie told me a specific photographer will be out and about tomorrow, taking photos."

At his words, I fly off the couch and grab his face. Practically throttling his skull off his spine. "Where? Tell me where." My voice frantic while my body sings.

"Ah, ah, ah. Not so fast. Tit for tat, my friend." Micah waggles his finger in front of my face.

I drop my hands from his face. "What could I possibly do for you?" At this point, I would do just about anything to see Cora again. Sitting in this house is making me nutty.

"How about you just owe me one in the future? Deal?" Micah asks.

Definitely a deal I can't pass up. "Deal," I say. Micah extends his hand and we shake on it.

A minute later, Micah shares with me all the details Shelly told him about Cora's shoot tomorrow. Shelly knows I have been back in town since yesterday, but Micah asked her to not make Cora aware. But by Shelly knowing I returned home, she and Micah have been secret go-betweens for me. Their sibling bond has never been better and I love how much they are team Gavin-and-Cora-together-again.

Later, when I try to fall asleep on the couch, I spend an hour planning how I will surprise Cora. I have it all mapped out in my head. But the hidden weight in my wallet makes me second-guess what might go down.

My only hope is she doesn't run the opposite direction.

I park my car along Central Avenue, near Fifth Street. After I feed the parking meter, I walk into the nearest coffee shop and order a coconut milk latte.

After I'm slightly caffeinated, I wander for a few blocks. I take in all the sights, categorizing what would be great to photograph. Murals on select buildings. Downtown life. Restaurants and museums and shops to visit. The Sundial. The historical Vinoy hotel. Tampa Bay, from the St. Petersburg side. And that's only downtown. I have dates scheduled to shoot other parts of the city.

Once I make it back to my car, I have over ten different sections of downtown St. Petersburg I plan to photograph. I grab my cameras from the back of my car and head toward the farthest location. As I stroll through the morning crowd, I glance over my shoulder a time or two. Every other storefront, I get this odd feeling someone is following me. Like my intuition is having a light bulb moment. But each time I check, I spot no familiar faces in the crowd.

Starting at First Street, I snap photo after photo. A restaurant here, another there. One storefront after another. Downtown has so many unique shops, it is difficult to choose what to photograph. So, I snap as many as possible. Once I go through the editing process, I will siphon out what stays and what goes.

The closer I get to my car, the more it feels as if someone is following me again. So instead of being obvious and staring up and down the street, I step inside a cafe and order a drink.

Once the young girl behind the counter hands me the drink, I sit one table away from the window and stare outside. Girlfriends flock into shops together, smiling and laughing. A man with a little girl on his shoulders walks by. Minutes pass and I recognize no one on the sidewalk, but the twinge in my gut remains.

Five steps from opening the door, I spot him. Gavin.

He stands across the street, in front of a clothing store, watching me. How long has he been there? Why wasn't I checking across the street too? Clad in a pair of dark gray and black checkered shorts, a form-fitting black T-shirt, and dark sunglasses shielding his eyes.

I don't need to see his eyes to know he has missed just as much sleep as me. Has been in just as much pain as I have been.

We stand staring at one another for a moment. And it isn't until someone else leaves the cafe that I move from where I have been locked in place. As my feet shuffle toward the exit, he raises his hand and waves.

When I step onto the sidewalk, I shift to the side and move out of pedestrian foot traffic. The moment I lock eyes with Gavin again, he starts crossing the street and walking in my direction. When he crosses the double line in the center of the street, I run. And I hear him yelling and running after me.

"Cora!" Gavin screams. "Cora, wait!"

With my arms pinning the cameras to my chest, my run morphs into an awkward jog. I weave in and out of the growing crowd, spotting my car in the spaces one block away.

I will make it before he catches me.

Repeating the mantra with my eyes focused on the driver's side door of my car, I almost jog in front of a moving car. Almost. But Gavin yanks on my bicep just in time to pull me out of the street.

"Oh my god, Cora! Are you okay?" Gavin holds me at arm's length and inspects me head to toe. Once he determines I am unscathed and his breathing settles enough, he speaks up. "You didn't have to run into traffic to get away from me."

Stunned, I stare back at him. Is he really here? Is he back? For good? I shake my head, not wanting to get ahead of myself. One step at a time, Cora. No sense in getting your hopes up when you don't have all the facts.

"I wasn't purposely running into traffic. Just wasn't paying attention. Sorry I scared you," I say. Because it's true. I would never do anything to that extreme.

Gavin bends at the waist, places his hands on his knees and breathes heavily. After a moment, his breathing regulates and he stands up straight. "Why were you running from me?" He studies the lines of my face as his bunch just above the bridge of his nose.

"Don't know. Guess I thought it'd be better than confronting you and losing my shit. The last few weeks have been a clusterfuck. Not sure how much more I can handle," I admit.

He nods and purses his lips before relaxing them again. "I deserve that. Can we please go somewhere and talk? There's a lot I need to tell you. And even more wrongs I need to make right." He shoves his hands in his pockets and teeters back on his heels as he regards me.

We silently stand on the sidewalk for a couple awkward moments while I weigh my options. If I don't grant him time to get everything out in the open, he will continue to pursue me tomorrow and every day thereafter. Plus, I need to know where everything stands with his agent and *her*. And where we stand. But where we stand will depend on what he tells me.

I would like to believe I am capable of forgiving him for the lies. Because deep down, he didn't do it with the intention of hurting me. He simply thought it was something he could resolve without issue.

Only time will tell.

"Yes. Let's find somewhere to get lunch. Then you can tell me whatever it is you need to. But I make no promises about how I'll feel afterward."

He nods. "I accept that. If I were you, I'd feel the same."

Gavin and I walk to my car and I stow my cameras. A few minutes later, we stroll into the Cider Press Cafe and get seated near the window. I peek at him over my menu, waiting to see his expression as he reads the food options. As soon as his gray irises thin and pupils dilate, I laugh. At least eating here will lighten the mood as we discuss some heavy stuff. Because right now, I need a good laugh more than anything.

fifteen

GAVIN

I stand in a sea of suffocating black polyester. Bodies bump against me every five seconds, and the lack of personal space pisses me off. Who the hell organized this damn function? Whoever the fucker is, they should be fired. Because this is nothing short of chaos.

After a few minutes, we are all corralled through a doorway and led out to a spread of plastic folding chairs facing a stage. On the stage is a podium, a table, and several more folding chairs. The principal and other school staff sit on the stage chairs, their robes puffy and sashes colorful. A person stands in the aisle along the student seating, directing us to which row we're to sit in. Not like it matters, we all have our names written on a card that we hand to someone to read.

Once we are all seated, various teachers stand at the podium and share positive words for the future. I choose to ignore their words. The only reason I agreed to do this whole ceremony bullshit is the end result I hope to receive. A trip home to Florida.

The ceremony passes with nothing monumental occurring. When it ends, I walk into a room where we get our actual diploma. The second it is in my hands, elation courses through me. This small rectangle of paper is my ticket back to Cora. My ticket home.

Although we haven't spoken in close to two years, I hope she will forgive me. When I stopped answering her letters, calls and texts, my intention was to do what was best for her, since I had no way to see her. To let her go.

But after that letter and those drawings she sent me, I am nervous as hell about how she will react to seeing me again. I went about things a shitty way, but what else was I supposed to do? We were in a fucked-up situation and I thought what I was doing would mend it all somehow.

But I was wrong. Dead wrong.

I walk out of the back and go in search of my parents. They stand outside, waiting for me with giant smiles plastered on their faces. After a handful of photos are taken, we head to the car and drive to a restaurant for my graduation dinner. In the car, they reminisce over the ceremony and how nice it was. I stare out the window and pray it won't be much longer before I don't see this skyline again.

Once we order food and my parents express their unwavering excitement, I mentally prepare to ask the question I have been waiting to ask for the past two years. Asking is going to burst the joy bubble they are trapped in, but I don't care. My bubble hasn't held joy since I was forced to leave Florida and step foot in this state.

"Mom? Dad? Can we talk about me moving back to Florida?" Straight forward and to the point. No need to beat around the bush. A man on a mission.

Mom tips her head to the side as a frown takes residence on her lips. Dad doesn't move, his expression stoic. Their lack of communication says more than any words ever will. The silence tells me the trip I have longed to make won't be happening. But I refuse to believe it until I hear the actual words. Until they tell me I cannot go.

"Gavin—" Mom starts, but pauses to look at Dad for silent support "—I would love nothing more than for you to be where you want to be. But things have been really tight for us financially. And right now, we just don't have the money to fly you to Florida."

I fucking knew this would happen. Knew it. As soon as we got here, I should have gone to every store and restaurant and applied for a job. Bagboy, stocker, cashier, busboy. Anything. If I had, maybe I would have more than enough money by now to leave. But I was so wrapped up in throwing a pity party for myself, I didn't do shit.

Fuck my life.

"So there's nothing we can do? Didn't you have some college fund for me? If so, cash it in. I have zero plans to go to college, especially here."

"Son, I wish it were that simple," Dad chimes in. "We did have a college fund for you, but we had to cash it in shortly after we moved here. Things have been a little tougher than we suspected. I'm sorry."

You have got to be fucking kidding me. Not only can I not go back to Florida, but college isn't even an option. I may not have wanted to attend college, but they banked on my not mentioning it. Score one for the parentals. Zero for the child. Fucking bullshit.

"Wow. I don't know how to respond to any of this. You both knew my plans after graduation. How could you not say anything to me? You could've suggested I go out and get a job. If only for three or four months. At least I'd have money to fly home."

"This is home, Gavin," Mom says.

"This has never been home, Mom. You know it just as much as I do," I snap.

"Don't speak that way to your mother," Dad states, his voice sharp and stern. "We have had to make tough decisions for our family and I wouldn't change a single one. You may not have liked our choices. You may not like your life here. But you *will* respect us."

Wow. Just wow. So does respect only go one way? The parents *deserve* it, but their children don't? What sort of asinine bullshit is that? Yes, I was underage when we moved and didn't have a say in the matter. I accept it. But to purposely hide this… I am done.

"Sorry, Mom. Sorry, Dad," I seethe. "I respect you. This just fucking sucks! And I can't help but wonder why neither of you said a damn word to me sooner. Oh, I know," I say, holding up a finger and firmly pressing my lips together. "Because you knew this would be my reaction, that's why. Fucking bullshit."

"Watch your mouth, Gavin," Dad snaps.

I shake my head. "It's a little late for that, Dad. You forget, I'm an adult. Like you never swore when you were younger."

Mom and Dad go silent on the opposite side of the table, shutting down the conversation. Our server delivers the food a minute later, but I don't eat a bite. Instead, I open up the photos on my phone and scroll through the folder marked "C+G." With each swipe, my throat swells and the back of my eyes sting.

Fuck.

There is one singular thing I have wanted for the last two years. One thing that provided purpose and gave me hope. To go home to Cora. To see her beautiful face cupped between my hands again. Listen to her laughter as I tickle her in that spot under her ribs only I know about. Wrap my arms around her waist and draw her close to my body as we lay on the couch and watch *Lord of the Rings* for the hundredth time.

But now it seems that won't be happening. Not unless I figure out how to get there on my own. And it looks as though that is my only option. But I will make it happen.

～

My fourth job interview ends like the previous three. With a *"we'll get back to you soon."* Which equals we have no intention of hiring you. Why is it so fucking hard to get a job? Working retail isn't rocket science.

I walk out of the preppy clothing store with my head hung low. *Where the hell will I get a job?* At this point, I am not above selling shit on the streets to get the money I need. Whatever it takes to get me back to Cora. And although I haven't spoken with her in far too long, in my mind's eye, I picture her face lighting up the moment we reconnect. As if we scoured the earth to find each other and succeeded.

There is one more interview on my list today. One more opportunity. And I hope like hell it won't end like the last four. This interview is a long shot, but I have to try. At this point, what do I have to lose?

Two hours later, I walk through the front door of Elite Models. My stomach twists in a knot and a bead of sweat rolls down the back of my neck. When I approach the reception desk, a woman ten years my senior gawks at me head to toe. Her perusal isn't distasteful, but makes me want to curl inward.

"Can I help you?"

I step closer to the counter. "Yes. I have an interview with Sharon and Gus."

The woman peels her eyes away from me and scans her computer screen. A few scrolls and clicks later, she locates whatever she had been looking for and smiles. Her fingers tap the keyboard before she picks up the phone and dials.

"Your next candidate is here," she says. Her eyes pop back to my body and visually rip away my clothes. The act is a total violation and I wonder if this is what girls feel like when men ogle them in public. If so, it is awful and makes me want to cover myself with my arms.

She sets the handset back down, but keeps her eyes trained on me. I want to look away, escape the unease of her gaze, but choose not to. Because who knows how she will visually obsess over me when I turn away.

God, this is awkward.

A set of smoky glass doors open and a man walks out. He could be Dad's age, maybe older, but is layered in makeup and trendy clothes that shave years off his appearance. His hair is styled like a magazine ad—not a single strand out of place. For a moment, inferiority swamps me. *I can't do this.* But I have to do this. Every other option has been tossed away.

"Gavin Hunt?" the trendy man asks and I nod. "Hello, Gavin. Gus." He extends a hand and I shake it. "It's nice to meet you. If you'll follow me, we'll get started."

I follow him through the smoky doors. With each step, I ask myself if doing this is the right thing. If getting sucked into the limelight is how I get back to Cora. The hall we walk down is littered with countless photos. Women, men, people my age, people my parents' age. The images range from luxurious to hobo and everything in between. Each face is beautifully sculpted and emotionally connecting with the onlooker.

How the hell do they do that? How the hell would *I* do that?

There is no way I can do this.

Two hours later, I shake Sharon and Gus's hands. They don't throw me the infamous line I have heard at every other interview. Instead, they tell me what time to return on Monday. Relief courses through my veins.

Finally, an opportunity.

Not only did I land a job. I landed the opportunity of a lifetime. Modeling will not only flood my pockets, it will have me back in Cora's arms sooner than expected. Today ends on a high note and I wish I could share the news with the one person who matters.

Soon. After I get a couple photo shoots under my belt, I will call Cora and let her know the good news. That I will return home.

～

Why is this shit so goddamn difficult?

Every photo I have studied makes modeling seem effortless. Smiles and smirks and deadpan expressions. All in my repertoire. Stand in front of the camera, plaster your face with whatever emotion the photographer seeks and pose. Boom. Photo acquired.

Wrong.

After several failed attempts to appear smoldering, I am asked to put my shirt back on and report to Karen on the third floor. What the fuck is smoldering anyway? If I didn't fear the repercussions of having my phone out, I would search the term online.

Instead, now I sit in a room with five other people. Our chairs in a small circle facing each other. Feels like I am at a group therapy session. My knee bounces and I gnaw on my thumbnail.

A fifty-something woman glides into the room. Yes, glides. For a moment, I wonder if she wears special shoes under her floor-length, flowy dress. She owns the room in one breath. Everyone in the circle equally mesmerized by her appearance. Her finesse. Her ability to instantly garner everyone's attention.

"Good afternoon. I'm Karen, your modeling coach."

Modeling coach? Damnit. Obviously, my modeling skills were zero on a scale of a million. Because this sounds like school. And school hasn't been something I excelled in since moving.

The girl beside me leans in close. "Is it just me? Does this lady make you feel as inadequate as she does me?"

I lean an inch away and glance at her a moment. "Uh, I guess." I shrug. Inadequate wasn't quite the word I would choose. Maybe intimidated.

The girl smiles big at me. Her smile makes me more uncomfortable than Karen's entrance and presence. Not able to pinpoint my discomfort, I opt for niceties and extend my hand to her.

"Hi, I'm Gavin."

She stares at my hand a moment, a few emotions flit across her face but don't linger. Then she takes my hand and shakes it. "Layla." Her eyes ping to mine and she keeps our hands connected. I want to yank it back. Her touch scalds my skin. Not in the way Cora's touch heats every molecule inside me. Rather, Layla's skin on mine is invasive. Parasitic. Wrong.

When she doesn't remove her hand from mine after an uncomfortable five breaths, I slip mine away. The second she looks away from me, I wipe my hand on my jeans. Something about this girl makes me uneasy. The only person I read easily was Cora. So, it confounds me to not figure out why this girl makes me uneasy.

Maybe she is just as upset about being in this class as I am. Maybe she is only trying to be friendly.

I lean back in my chair and listen to Karen prattle on about why we are all here. Honestly, if this class makes me better at modeling, I am all for it. It gets me one more step closer to Cora. The main reason I'm doing this in the first place.

For her. For us. And our future.

Hours later, the class ends. All of us numb from the lessons on facial expressions and how to achieve them. According to Karen, we will be seeing her five days a week for the foreseeable future. Once she determines we are worthy of "graduating," she will pass such information to the appropriate people.

In other words, it may be weeks or months before I model. Weeks or months before I take a decent photo. Weeks or months before I earn a penny.

On the upside, the modeling agency pays for the classes. Only because we are "assets." Calling me an asset is objectifying, but I suck it up. Modeling is just temporary. A stepping stone to get me where I need to be.

As I leave for the day, Layla stops me. "Hey, Gavin. You want to grab something to eat? I could eat a cow after today." She laughs and it sounds forced. Awkward. Exaggerated.

All I want is to go home and crash. But it would be nice to know someone else in this boat. Someone I can talk to when I have a rough day. A friend. "Yeah, sure."

The moment I agree, a rock plummets in my gut. It sinks and settles deep. Nausea threatens and I shove it down. Layla is a nice person—at least that is what I continually tell myself. Our relationship will only consist of friendship. Nothing more.

No one will ever take Cora's place. No one.

GAVIN

Present

The server walks away and I wonder what the hell I just ordered. Some mock version of pulled "pork." Except this place serves no meat. Cora assures me it was a good choice, but I will be the judge.

Cora picks up her water and sips it while staring out the window. Her fingers twist and roll the paper straw while her eyes narrow slightly then go back to their normal shape. Occasionally, she bites the inside of her cheek. Beneath the table, her leg bounces and ghosts against mine every other breath.

Does she feel it each time her skin grazes mine? She is so lost in her thoughts, I doubt it. But I do. Every. Single. Time.

"Cora."

Her eyes dart from the window to mine as she snaps out of her fog. "Huh?"

"Why are you so nervous?"

She rolls her eyes and it is fucking adorable. "Don't be silly, Gavin. I'm not nervous." Her leg bounces faster.

I tilt my head and study her a minute. "You know you can't fool me. So why try?"

Cora huffs and sets her water down. A second later, she tucks her hands under her thighs. We sit in silence a moment, staring at each other. Holding her gaze has never been uncomfortable, whether for five seconds or five minutes.

And then I remember the reason why we are sitting together right now. The reason she's giving me a chance. Because she is waiting to hear my truth. A truth I swore to tell her. That I plan to tell her. I only hope she listens. Truly listens and digests what I say.

"I'm sorry," I say. An apology is the best place to start. Unfortunately, I have far too much to apologize for.

Her leg finally stops bouncing. "Sorry? And what exactly are you sorry for?" Her question slaps me in the face. A slap I more than deserve. A slap I will take like a man.

I reach under the table and rest a hand on her knee. The simple and innocent touch soothes my nervousness and helps me focus. "Where do I begin?" I pause a moment to gather my thoughts. She needs to know everything, but I don't want to bounce from one end to the other and back again.

My question was meant to be rhetorical, but she answers. "How about the beginning. I find that to always be the best place."

Cora's snappy demeanor has me on the cusp of smiling. On the verge of teasing and light sarcasm. But the last thing I need is to piss her off more, so I resist the urge and trudge forward.

"I'm sorry I stopped answering your calls and texts. Sorry I didn't return a single one of them. My parents had thrown every hope I had of getting back to you out the window. So, I thought I was doing the right thing by letting you go. By giving you a chance to move on without me. To have a life and smile and maybe find love again."

A glutton for punishment, I refuse to look away from her. Refuse to not see every emotion she feels as my words set in. As I share the reason why I abandoned her years ago. Even as her eyes brim red and well in the corners. Even as her brow furrows and lips purse. She breaks eye contact and shifts her gaze to the street, not looking at anything specific. She just has difficulty looking at me. A tear rolls down her cheek and she swipes it away with the back of her hand. Her chin quivers as she clamps her lips between her teeth.

I walked into this knowing sour memories would be rehashed. That me spilling my truth, telling her where my head was at, would be hard to hear. But fuck, it hurts to watch her break down in front of me. To see her fighting off emotions as we sit in public and talk about the most painful parts of our past.

After a minute, I give her knee a squeeze. Her soft green bloodshot eyes come back to mine and the emotion in them is raw. It claws at my heart and shreds it in a million pieces. As painful as this is, I did this to her. And I deserve every gut-wrenching second of the pain I feel. Her pain.

"Why didn't you tell me?" she croaks out. "Why didn't you call or text or write and tell me what was happening? We shared everything with each other. Every-thing." She shakes her head. "But you up and decided to make this monumental decision without me." She sucks in a breath and speaks on the exhale. "Gavin, I shut down. Detached from the world and crawled into a hole. All I wanted was to talk with you. My best friend. My everything. And you shut me out."

A fist wraps around my heart and constricts the organ like a squeaky toy. Over and over and over.

How could I have been such a dick? How could I have been so selfish? Every-thing I did was in the hopes of Cora not being in pain. At least that's what I kept telling myself. I thought letting her go was the best option. What other option was there? I had no way to get to her, and my parents did nothing to help. So, in my eyes, letting her live life without restriction seemed like the better option. I didn't want her to feel obligated—to me or the possibility of me.

Obviously, I am a fucking idiot.

"No matter what I say, it'll never make up for what I did. But I'd like to try now. Try to fix what I've done. Will you let me try? Please."

I reach for my wallet and she follows my every move. Behind my license, I retrieve a folded piece of yellowing paper with tattered edges. After a deep breath, I set it on the table and slide it to her.

Cora's red-rimmed eyes study my face. Her eyes dart between mine. Her lips press in a firm line and wobble side to side. And her chin continues to tremor as she reaches for the paper. Fixing this is not enough. I need to make it up to her every day of forever. And I will. I swear I will.

She sniffles and nods. "You know I will. But you have to tell me everything. No more secrets." She holds up the paper. "What's this?"

Before I answer, the server delivers our food to the table and cuts off our conver-sation. Cora tucks the paper in her pocket and I know she will read it when she is alone. Read the last letter she sent me, smudged with her tears and mine.

I stare down at the basket. I have no clue what I am about to eat, but I pick it up and bite down. An odd texture licks my tongue, but tastes weirdly like pulled pork.

I shrug and continue eating while Cora giggles across from me. At least my eating brings a smile to her face. A smile is a smile, and I will call it a step in the right direction.

A few minutes pass before I wipe my hands clean and lean back in my chair. "I sold my house in California. Currently, I'm sleeping on Micah's couch until I find my own place."

Cora sits quietly across from me. Questions flit over her face, but she doesn't ask a single one. Her mouth opens and closes. This happens a few times before she finally speaks. "Oh. What about your mom?"

I love how she worries about my mom, now that I moved away. "She'll be okay. I think she was surprised it took me so long to move back. We argued so much the first two years out there. She expected me to run away and hitchhike back to Florida." The idea was given serious merit, but was ignored after the reality of how far I *wouldn't* get settled.

Cora nods and I continue. "When I got back to California, I sat down with Mom and discussed my plan to move back. Told her about the photo shoot with you. Also told her my time out west should have ended years ago. She was more than understanding and offered to help me in any way possible."

"I miss your mom," Cora says.

I lean forward and lay my hand on her knee under the table again. "She misses you, too. I wouldn't be surprised if she visits soon, now that I've moved away. She'll probably wait until I have a place." I sip my water, allowing a few breaths to pass before I speak again. "Alyson and Layla have been dealt with also."

I don't miss the way Cora flinches when I say Layla's name. The way her lips curl for a split second. But she collects herself and responds as if she had no reaction. "Uh, I'm not sure what to say."

"There's nothing to say. I'm only sorry you were on the receiving end of their jealousy. The moment I got back to California, I reviewed my contracts and sought out a new agent. After I finished my final shoot with Layla, I fired Alyson and told Layla I never wanted to see or hear from her again. It went about as smooth as expected."

"Gavin, you didn't have to do that. Not for me."

Although her words tell me I didn't need to make such a drastic change in my life, I don't miss the way her body sags in relief. The small shift in her demeanor speaks a thousand words her lips won't. Ease slips into her expression and I know what I did was the first step in the right direction.

"Yes, I did. But not just for you, I did it for myself also. Too many nights have passed since I set out to come back to you. When I started modeling, it was to earn as much money as possible so I could fly back to Florida. To you. I hadn't spoken to you in over a year, but not a day went by where my goal changed. Being with you has always been my endgame."

She scoots back in her seat and her knee shifts out of my reach. Her elbows rest on the table as she lays her forearms toward me. Palms up, her hands rest as an open invitation for mine. As eager as I am to lay my hands on hers, to feel her warmth, to connect with her intimately, I don't rush this. I slowly withdraw my hands from under the table and place them in hers. Beneath my palms, her fingers trace steady lines along my skin.

I close my eyes and surrender to my senses. How her soft skin faintly brushes my palms as she trails her fingertips there. Subtle hints of her frankincense and gardenia scent wisp in the air and flutter in my nose. A small hitch in her breathing as she continues to reconnect a bond once severed. The shiver down my spine and fast-growing bloom of heat in my chest as it all swirls together.

God, I want to kiss her. More than anything.

When my eyes reopen, Cora sits across from me slack-jawed. So fucking beautiful.

No matter how much time has passed, she is still the only woman I see. The only woman I want beside me. Today and every day that follows. Cora is it for me. And I assume the same holds true for her. Because she has never moved on from us either. Not fully.

"Gavin, how did *she* go from being your friend to your fiancée?" I don't miss the way Cora says *she* with distaste on her tongue. But I don't blame her. No doubt I would feel equally as disgusted if the situation were reversed.

"Layla wasn't getting as many callbacks or opportunities for shoots. My career, on the other hand, was booming. Alyson sat down with the two of us and threw out the idea of us "being engaged." Of course, it would be strictly for publicity reasons, but I still wasn't keen. Alyson said we would cut it short after Layla was seen enough times with me. But every time I brought it up, Alyson told me to wait another month. That some brand was on the fence of signing Layla. And I obviously bought the lie every time. From the get-go, something didn't sit right with me when it came to Layla, but I ignored it. I'll never be so naïve again."

I curl my fingers into hers and stare at our hands a moment. The reality of my naïveté is a punch to the gut. How much time was stolen from me because of it? Countless months and years. All because I had tunnel vision—Cora standing in the light at the end. Alyson and Layla—both who knew about the woman in Florida, but not who she was—took advantage of me. Of my eagerness to return to her. They played me. And I had been the damn fool falling for every line and promise.

"After my last shoot, I had an interview scheduled with The Heart of Hollywood. Millions of eyes would see or hear my interview. I blasted the truth to everyone. About Alyson and Layla. How my engagement was a ruse to garner attention for Layla and her lackluster modeling career. And then I told millions of people about you. About us. How I ran into the love of my life and instantly decided I was moving home."

Across from me, Cora gasps. For a completely different reason, her eyes pool, soften. Her lips tremble. And I can't take it anymore. No longer able to stay on the opposite side of the table, I rise and slide into the seat beside her. She watches my every move as she bites her lower lip.

"Gavin," she whispers.

I frame her face with my hands and brush away a fallen tear. Leaning into her, my lips a breath from hers, I tell Cora the words only meant for her.

"I love you. Only you. Always."

And as badly as I want to kiss her, I resist the urge. With all the shit I have put Cora through, I won't fuck this up. I want her to want to kiss me. Want her to initiate. Need her to be the one who moves us forward. No matter what, my heart is hers. Always has been. Always will be. But I crushed her heart all those years ago. And I will wait however long it takes for her to be ready for us. For me.

Cora wraps her hands around my forearms and grips them like it's her last breath. Her gaze unwavering as her watery green eyes stare up at me. "I love you, too." She pinches her eyes shut and wetness slips between her lashes to my fingertips. I wipe them away, then lift my lips to her lids and kiss them each with reverence.

"I know it will take time, but I vow to make us whole again. Whatever I need to do to fix us, I will. Without you, nothing else matters."

She attempts to nod, but my hands keep her face hostage. We both laugh a moment, and I am certain we look like lunatics. But as long as Cora is with me, I don't give a damn what people think of me. With her by my side, I can be anyone.

After I drop my hands, I switch to a more serious tone. "Go out with me. On a date. Please?"

Cora reaches up and cups my cheeks, scratching my jawline before her hands fall to my chest and rest over my heart. "What if we go out with everyone? Obviously, you know Micah and Shelly, but I would love for you to get to know Jonas and Erin better. They've been there for me when I needed them. They're family. And I really want you to be comfortable with them."

Hanging out with everyone else isn't exactly what I had in mind for a date with Cora, but I will take every moment she grants me. If this is important to her—Jonas and I being friendly—I will set aside my jealousy. Jealousy over the fact that this guy has spent more years with her than I have. Although their relationship is strictly platonic, I am not blind to the way he looks at her. Maybe time with him is the perfect idea. For both of us.

"Okay, let's go out with everyone. When? Where?"

She claps and fidgets in her seat. "Yay! I'll talk to Shelly and we'll figure everything out. Then you'll be the next to know."

Her happiness is infectious. It lures me in and holds me captive. And I stay willingly, a prisoner of her heart. Whatever it takes to make my girl happy, I plan to do it. Because seeing her smile brightens the darkest skies.

After I pay the bill, we walk back to her car hand in hand. Our stride is leisure. Our voices absent. And it is absolute perfection. When we reach her car, I spin her around and wrap my arms around her. I rest my chin on the crown of her head and gently rock side to side, shutting my eyes and relishing the weight of her body pressed to mine. Her arms snake around my back and squeeze me tight. I don't want to let her go. Not now. Not ever.

I kiss her hair, release my hold on her and run my hands down her biceps. "Call me when you get everything sorted out with Shelly."

She tips her head back and meets my sunglass-covered eyes. "I will. Promise."

I step back and play with a strand of her hair. "I love you. See you soon."

God, I don't want to walk away, but know I need to. Cora needs to have control over what happens with us. What happens next. Unbeknownst to her, I have put my life and the future of us in her hands. My fitful heart and restless soul sit nestled inside her. This time around, she makes all the decisions and I make none.

"I love you, too."

As soon as she says the words, I pivot and walk away. Her eyes singe me as I amble down the sidewalk, away from her and into the unknown. But there is no other place I would rather be.

It feels as if I am in grade school again as I stand outside the entrance of Dave and Busters. Bright orange and yellow paint coat the brick exterior. A large, angular metal awning hangs over the entrance. The automatic doors whoosh open then glide shut. The action mesmerizes me briefly until Shelly comes up behind me, bouncing like an adolescent.

What is it about an arcade that makes you feel twenty years younger? Who knows, but whatever it is, I love it.

Shelly unlocks her phone and scrolls through her text history. A moment later, she assures me everyone should be here in the next ten minutes.

We loiter near the entrance, steering clear of patrons coming or going, and get lost in our cell phones. Shelly zones out in social media land while I check my email. A few minutes later, Erin and Jonas walk up.

We are catching up when I spot Micah and Gavin getting out of an all-black Range Rover. Black paint, pitch-black tint, blacked-out logos. All. Black. Although I only see Micah on occasion, I know this car isn't his. This must be Gavin's car. And the idea of him owning an all-black custom vehicle has me smiling like an idiot.

When they approach us, Micah rolls his eyes at me and I laugh. Micah and I will never share best friend status, but we will always be family. Not only because of my friendship with Shelly, but also because of Gavin. Micah will just have to learn to live with me being around. He is the grumpy big brother I never had and I am the annoying little sister he wished he didn't have.

Gavin steps up and encircles me with his arms, kissing the top of my head. A charm of hummingbirds takes flight in my chest, wings fluttering rapidly and stealing my breath. The more Gavin inserts himself back into my life, the less I want to resist him. Part of me recalls the last time we were in this place—inseparable—and what life was like when he left. That part of me keeps the barrier I have built around my heart upright. Solid. Impenetrable.

Or so I keep telling myself.

When I got home from St. Pete and emptied my pockets, the worn paper mocked me for hours. Until I unfolded the creased edges and saw what he gave me. What he had stashed in his wallet. *My letter*. The last letter I wrote him. On our anniversary, six months after he left.

Seeing that letter again stirred up more than a decade's worth of emotions. But the fact he kept it, tucked it in his wallet, said more than words ever would.

He promises to repair every cut and scrape and rift between us. And I believe him. But I need evidence. And until I see the proof with my own eyes, I still can't expose myself fully. Not yet. Not until I have absolute reassurance he will stay.

After we load up our gaming cards and purchase drinks, we wander through the arcade and scope out all the games. Micah heads over to the virtual reality area while Shelly, Erin, and Jonas go toward the classic arcade games. As soon as Shelly decided we were coming here, my first thought was Skee-Ball. Not only was it my favorite arcade game to play. It also happens to be Gavin's favorite.

"Skee-Ball?" Gavin asks. He cocks a brow up in challenge.

"As if you need to ask."

One of our many rendezvous years ago was to a local arcade. We would play Skee-Ball for hours. Not for tickets, but for bragging rights. Gavin won more times than I did. But when I did win, I rubbed it in his face for weeks. Whatever tickets we won, we handed over to children nearby.

Tonight would be no different. Minus the tickets.

I have been here with Shelly and Jonas several times over the years. And I have broken some high score records. Not that I plan to give this statistical information to Gavin. But my Skee-Ball game is strong. So strong, I am willing to bet money he hasn't played since the last time we played together and can add another Skee-Ball trophy to the shelf. Which works great for me.

We step up to the lanes and swipe our cards. I glance over at him and feel a little cocky. "You ready to get your ass handed to you?"

He throws his head back and laughs, his entire frame shaking. "Who's handing it to me? You?"

"Not sure how good your game is, but I've been practicing." I pop an eyebrow and give a snide smile.

"Have you now?" The balls roll down the chute and clunk together. "What makes you think I haven't been practicing?"

I pick up a ball and shrug. "Call it a hunch." Then I face the lane, swing my arm back and release the wooden ball. It rolls up the lane with perfect precision and flies into the 100-point hole. With pride lighting up my face, I face Gavin again and shrug again. "Whatcha got, Hunt?"

"Oh, it's on, baby." Gavin smirks and lines up to shoot the ball. But I zone out. Molecule by molecule, my body comes alive. Warmth blossoms in my chest, spreading its petals open like the roses Gavin sent me. I get lost in the intimacy of this moment. Of his term of endearment for me. In the banter and ease with which we slip into it like second nature. How being beside him feels right on so many levels.

As much as I want to ease into a life with Gavin, it won't happen. Because that is not how things have ever been between us.

From the first day we met, under our tree, we were destined for more. We slipped into friendship easier than anyone else. Our friendship morphing into best friends was inevitable. We loved spending time together and laughed without effort. Everyone said they knew we would start dating. It was only us who didn't see it happening. Not until that day at the beach over Thanksgiving break.

Our first kiss. The most amazing and memorable kiss of my life. The kiss that started it all.

From that moment forward, I never wanted to kiss another person in my life. My body sang for Gavin. Hummed with hunger and lust and love. No one else has lit my soul on fire like Gavin. And no one else ever will. When one person holds the key to your heart, no other key will ever unlock it. Gavin has always been my key.

Watching Gavin beside me, my heart swells like a hot air balloon—hot and combustible. All the old feelings I buried for thirteen years assault me in the middle of the arcade. Hit me like a hammer to the chest and leave me breathless. I want to yell and cry, cheer and sing, throw myself at him and crush him in my arms. He tosses another ball up the lane, oblivious to my never-ending stare down, and scores another forty points. He glances up at my score and notices it hasn't changed since my first roll.

Gavin rotates his head and drops his gaze to mine. "You okay, baby?" There it is again. The familiar endearment I love rolling off his tongue. And the flutters that come along with it.

Fuck. They're coming. The back of my eyes sting as I nod. I swallow down the expanding boulder in my throat and work to answer him. "Yeah, I'm good."

He sets his ball down and steps up to me, running his fingers through my loose strands. "What's wrong?" Bending his knees, he comes eye level with me. "Talk to me."

I swallow again and tip my head back, batting my lashes. *No crying, Cora. No more tears. Not even happy tears.*

"Just remembering us. This." I gesture to the lanes. "How things were before. How comfortable and easy it is to be with you."

He stands tall and peers down at me, his thumb dusting over my bottom lip. "We've always had this effortless connection. Do you know why that is, baby?"

I fear opening my mouth, fear speaking. Afraid my words will be unintelligible. Garbled. So, I swallow and shake my head.

Gavin presses his palm against my breastbone and locks his steely eyes on mine. "Because I'm here." Then he reaches out, takes my hand, and places it over his heart. Beneath my palm, his heart beats a vicious rhythm. "And you are here. Before we met, we held a piece of each other hostage. It wasn't until we found each other that those pieces reconnected. As if they'd known each other in another lifetime."

I will not fucking cry.

"Cora, you're it for me. No matter how hard I tried to forget about you, no matter what I did over the last thirteen years, you always danced in my dreams and called out to my heart. I may have ignored it for stupid reasons, but it was there nonetheless."

Goddamnit.

He is going to make me cry. He rests his cheek against mine as his lips hover near my ear. My chest rises and falls as I gasp for breath. I pinch my eyes shut. Swallow hard. Curl and uncurl my fingers.

"I love you, Cora. More than anything or anyone in this world. And fuck if I don't want to kiss you in the middle of this arcade, in front of all these people."

My breath comes faster, but I don't say a word. Will he kiss me? I want to kiss him, but still hesitate. Kissing Gavin again will end any chance I have at resistance. We need time. Time to relearn each other. Time to adjust to a newer version of us. A little more time.

Or am I being absurd?

We have spent so much time apart. Days and months and years disconnected. Broken. Hurt. Do I really want to waste more time? Do I really want to keep him at arm's length? No, I don't. And keeping us divided when he has done everything in his power to bring us back together is asinine.

I lean back from Gavin just enough to see his eyes. If I shift an inch to the side, we would kiss. His eyes lock on mine and read every thought passing through them. And I know he knows what I think. He doesn't flinch or veer from his position. A second later, his eyes close and he draws in a labored breath.

This is it. The moment we have been leading up to. The inevitable.

I line my lips up with his, leaving only a shadow between us. Just as I lean in, just as I'm about to give myself over to him, someone brushes my arm and I retreat.

"Hey, man. Sorry to interrupt. Can I talk with you a minute?"

I open my eyes and spot Jonas beside us. His gaze fixed on Gavin, who is staring at me. Gavin's eyes burn with familiar longing. Something I saw every time he looked at me years ago. Something primal and potent and only ours. It resonates in my marrow. Keeps the chambers of my heart beating. Jonas may be inches from us, but we only see each other. Only *feel* each other.

Gavin's eyes still connected with mine, he answers Jonas. "Sure, man. What's up?"

Jonas shifts foot to foot. "Maybe over there." Jonas points to a table ten feet from us.

"Yeah, no problem." Gavin kisses my forehead. "I'll be back in a minute, baby. Finish my game and yours."

I nod and watch as Gavin and Jonas walk over to the empty table and sit down. They sit so neither of them faces me, but I see both their profiles. Jonas starts talking and Gavin listens intently. Seeing as I can't read lips, staring at them will get me nowhere.

So, I go back to the game, tossing ball after ball up my lane and Gavin's. When his game ends, I finish the round on my lane. Occasionally, I peek over my shoulder at them. They don't shift in position. Neither of them appears to be angry or ready to throw down—which is a good sign. Two more rounds pass before Gavin walks back over to me. His expression neutral.

"Hey. What did Jonas want to talk to you about?" I ask.

He wraps his arms around me and squeezes me close. "I'll tell you in a little bit. Are you hungry?" He kisses my forehead then leans back to peer down at me.

I don't argue with him. If Gavin says he will tell me later, he will. "Yeah. Let's find everyone else and grab dinner."

Micah seems a bit perturbed when we disrupt his virtual reality simulation, but agrees to meet us at a table. A moment later, we locate Shelly and Erin playing Dance Dance Revolution—Jonas teasing their dance skills.

We all converge at a table and order drinks and food. Light chatter fills the space between us. The dynamic between Gavin and Jonas has shifted into something unfamiliar. They sit opposite one another, but don't look or speak to each other. I find it very peculiar. I want to ask Gavin what they talked about, but remind myself he will share with me later. So, I ask Shelly and Erin who is winning their DDR showdown.

I never got into DDR. Classic games have always been my thing. Pinball, Skee-Ball, Pac-Man. But I love Shelly and Erin's enthusiasm for DDR. So, like the amazing best friend that I am, I listen as they regale us with colorful accounts of their competitions. And to be honest, they are pretty hardcore. Intimidating. Kind of makes me glad I never got into it.

Micah and Gavin talk quietly beside me. Micah mentions Peyton and I stop listening. It isn't my place to interrupt two guys chatting about a girl. Especially one I don't know. Who knows how much Micah has told Gavin. But if Micah is bringing her up again, one thing is certain. Micah has a major interest in her. Hopefully Gavin can reassure him that it is okay to move on from his ex. She was a real piece of work and it sucks he still harbors feelings for her.

I peer at Jonas and note his eyes glued to me. How long has he been staring? I wiggle in my seat and Gavin places a hand on my thigh. Ease passes through him to me and I relax into his side.

Jonas mouths *you okay?* His eyes pinch at the corners and his lips form a tight line. I smile and nod at him. *Yeah. Perfect.* I mouth back as I rest a hand over Gavin's. Everything is exactly as it should be in this moment. How it should have been for years.

When we finish eating, Jonas, Shelly, and Erin leave. When hugs are exchanged, Jonas whispers in my ear. "Good to see you happy. It suits you."

"Thank you," I whisper back, hugging him a little harder.

Micah tells us he will be back after another game and then be ready to leave. After Micah walks off, I ask Gavin what he and Jonas talked about earlier.

"Jonas was quite forthcoming." Gavin takes my hand and weaves his fingers with mine. "He told me he's been in love with you for years. We spent most of the conversation getting to know more about each other. And now, I know he's a good guy. I also know he won't be more than your friend because he doesn't want to hurt or lose you." Gavin pauses a moment and chuckles. "He also told me if I ever hurt you again, he'd cut my dick off."

"Oh my god," I say, slapping a hand over my mouth.

"Yeah. At least I know he'll protect you if I'm unable to." Gavin lifts my hand to his lips and presses a few soft kisses to my knuckles. Warmth spreads up my limb, weaves its way through my chest and strikes my heart like lightning. "He also wished us luck. Said this, minus the last couple of weeks, is the happiest he's ever seen you. And that's all he wants."

I swear the guys in my life are out to make me cry. There will always be something I love about Jonas. My love for him is more familial, but love nonetheless. How the hell did I get so lucky? How did I end up with so many wonderful people in my life? Family and friends and people I don't want to live a day without.

"Well it sounds like you two had a great talk." And it sounds like they built a bridge and are trying to meet in the middle for me. I hope one day Gavin and Jonas will be good friends. After time passes, I picture them laughing over beers together.

When Micah finishes his game, we decide to leave. We wander through the parking lot and over to my car. Gavin hands his keys to Micah. "I'll be there in a minute." Micah nods and leaves us. We stare after him as he walks to the Range Rover masked in the shadows.

Once Micah slips into the SUV, Gavin takes a strand of my hair between his fingers and plays with it. "Go on a date with me, baby. Just the two of us."

Every muscle in my body screams at me to say yes. But the wall around my heart stands firmly in place and says we need a little more time before it is just the two of us.

Earlier, I almost annihilated that wall by kissing him, but life intervened. And that little disruption made me wonder if it was a sign I was moving forward too fast. Can't be sure. If Gavin loves me, he won't mind if I tell him to have a little more patience. After all, he had the patience of a saint while we were together.

"Don't hate me," I say as I squint. "Is it okay if we hang with everyone again tomorrow night?"

Please be good with this. Please, please, please.

He strokes my hair, grazes his thumb along my jawline, then kisses the tip of my nose. "If that's what you want, baby. As long as I get to spend time with you, I'm happy."

I sag into his touch. "Thank you."

He kisses the crown of my head then hugs me as if he never will again. "For you, anything. I'll see you tomorrow, baby. Drive safe. I love you."

"I love you, too. See you tomorrow."

Gavin breaks our hug and starts toward his car, fingers still in mine until distance separates us. As he gets in his car, I get in mine. He and Micah talk a moment until he puts the car in gear.

I idle in the parking lot a moment, waving to Gavin as he and Micah drive off. He hasn't mentioned it, but tomorrow is Gavin's birthday and I want to surprise him. I want to host a game night. Ask everyone to bring food and drinks and laughter. Maybe decorate the house and have a cake. Make it one of his best birthdays yet.

Gavin and I may have been apart more than a decade, but some dates will be forever engraved in my heart. Including the day Gavin was brought into the world. And Gavin is definitely worth celebrating.

eighteen

GAVIN

Eight years ago

Today is the happiest and saddest day of my life.

November twenty-first.

Mine and Cora's anniversary. If we were still together, today would be our seventh anniversary. If it were a wedding anniversary, I would buy her something made of wool or copper. We would be corny like that, buying gifts according to outdated anniversary traditions. Finding unique ways to celebrate our time together.

But we haven't celebrated an anniversary together in over five years now. Not that I plan to celebrate this date as anything except ours. This day, until the day I die, will be ours.

Fuck.

I want to call her. Am desperate to hear her voice.

Would she still sound the same? Is she happy? Does she miss me like I fucking miss her? Some days, I don't have it in me to breathe, let alone exist in the world. Every time I talk with Micah, I ask vague questions about Shelly in the hopes he will give me a hint of something regarding Cora. But he gives nothing away. And it fucking sucks. He knows I won't come right out and ask, so he dances around my inadvertent questions.

Rather than hunt for a gift I will never give Cora, I opt for something else. Something permanent that will add a piece of her to me. A lifelong reminder—not as if I need one, but somehow this enhances our bond. With things booming in my career, I have gone back and forth for weeks about this. But it is my fucking body and I will do with it what I please.

I walk into the tattoo shop and walk up to the reception area. A young woman with fluorescent green hair peeks up from her magazine. She swivels the lollipop in her mouth from left to right a few times. "What can I do for you?" She pops the lollipop from her lips, licks them, then puts the lollipop back in her mouth. Don't know why, but it annoys the shit out of me.

"I have an appointment with Talon," I say.

She scans the screen before clicking the mouse. "I need a copy of your ID and for you to fill out this paper." She hands me a clipboard. While she makes a copy of my license, I read over, fill out, and sign the form. She hands me back my license. "He'll be with you in a minute. You can have a seat." She points to a leather couch off to the side and goes back to her magazine as if I never walked in.

"Thanks," I mumble.

A few minutes later, a burly man greets me and introduces himself as Talon. His arms are sleeved with a mishmash of tattoos. Muscles twice the size of mine. A bald head with full facial hair. And he towers over me by at least five inches, which is saying something considering I am six-two. Intimidating is definitely an adjective I would associate with this guy.

Talon leads me to a small cubicle with a black leather seat. He tugs a lever and flattens the table. "Have a seat, man. Here's the image you sent me." He slides a paper toward me. "This is what you want, right?"

"Yeah, between my shoulder blades," I reply.

Talon nods. "Is the size good? Or you want it bigger?"

I study the image a moment. Go big or go home, right? "Let's go a little bigger. Whatever you think will look best with the space."

He walks away and I stare around the booth. The short walls are littered with photos of other tattoos Talon has done. They range from intricate to minimal. Symbols and portraits and watercolor and quotes. Some with tons of color, others done with thin lines of black ink. Seeing all these photos—a portfolio of sorts—is reassurance this guy has done enough tattoos to not fuck mine up.

When he walks back into the booth, he shows me the new, larger version of the tattoo. "Look good?"

"Perfect. Thanks, man."

Talon directs me to take off my shirt, lay on the table, and find a comfortable position for my arms. He tells me how long he thinks the tattoo will take and that we will take occasional breaks, if needed. After everything is prepped and ready, he dips the tattoo gun in the ink and presses a peddle. When the buzz erupts next to me, I startle.

"You have any other tattoos, man?" Talon prompts.

"Nope. This is the first."

"Virgin skin," he says with a wicked gleam in his eye and wide grin on his lips. "My favorite."

The buzz cracks again and a sting pricks my skin. I close my eyes and take a deep breath. Sweat breaks out across my skin as adrenaline floods my veins. As he moves the needle over my skin, a blend of pain and thrill courses through me. Each line of ink he impregnates my skin with, I grow one step closer to Cora. She is the only reason I would mar my skin with something so permanent.

An hour into the tattoo, Talon asks me why I am getting a *Lord of the Rings* tattoo.

Not many people in California know Cora's and my history. I have mentioned things about her to Alyson and Layla, but never her name and never too much detail. Cora is my heart. Something I have no intention on spreading like free samples. Even though we have been apart for years, I hug her essence close to my chest and protect it with every breath.

"My soul mate." It's all I say.

But that isn't enough for Talon. He wants more. "You're getting a tattoo for a girl? Shouldn't that be hearts or butterflies? Maybe initials or a date?"

He teases me, knowing I will tell him more. And he is right. "Nah, she's not a hearts and butterflies kind of girl. She is, on the other hand, addicted to *Lord of the Rings*. So, this is fitting and perfect."

Talon teases me further. "Aren't you a sweetheart. Does she have a tattoo for you?"

His question is innocent, but it gets under my skin and stabs at the throbbing organ beneath my sternum. "No, she hasn't gotten any ink yet." At least not that I am aware of. I haven't seen her in years, but I couldn't imagine her getting a tattoo without purpose. Talon doesn't need such information, though.

A few hours pass before the tattoo gun goes silent. He sprays something on a paper towel and swipes it over my newly tattooed skin. Although my skin is slightly numb, the wiping stings. A minute later, he helps me up and hands me a hand mirror. "Use that to check it out on the wall mirror." He points to a floor-length mirror opposite his booth.

I walk over and turn my back to the wall mirror and hold up the one in my hand. Twisting to see from different angles, I glance over the black ink on my back. Absolutely perfect.

"What's it say?" Talon asks as I stare at the mirror. "Elvish, right?"

"Yeah. Above the stars it says *love*. At the roots, it says *forever*. *Lord of the Rings* fan?"

"Only seen them once, but remembered the tree. So, I assumed the writing. Your girl will love it, man. The nipple piercings, too."

"Thanks."

One day, I hope she gets to see it.

nineteen

GAVIN

Present

The stereo blares in the living room. Queen's "Another One Bites The Dust" at a volume way too loud for this early in the morning.

Micah comes up and taps my shoulder. "Get up, brother. Happy motherfucking birthday."

You have got to be fucking kidding me. I groan, roll to face the back of the couch, and smother myself with the pillow over my face. "Go away. It's too fucking early for this bullshit."

"Nope." He yanks the pillow from my hands. "I haven't celebrated a damn birthday with you in years. We're rectifying that right now. Up you go." He tugs the blanket off me and walks away, whistling like a cocky bastard.

"Asshole," I grumble as I sit up. "What time is it?"

Micah walks back into the room, pillow and blanket gone, and tosses a shirt at me. "Almost ten. For us normal folks, early was three hours ago. Uppity up." He steps up beside the couch and waves his hands as if to push me off.

"Since when do you get up early. Don't you mainly work at night? Like late?"

He doesn't respond.

After a minute, I get up and stumble to the bathroom. I crank the shower to scalding and step in. The water slowly washes the sleep off me, and soon I step out.

Once dressed, Micah suggests we go out for breakfast. I agree, but tell him he has to go with me to an appointment after. He directs us to a mom-and-pop restaurant where the line for a table is ten deep. After we get seated, we order breakfast and talk about everyone hanging out later tonight. He tells me he didn't hang around everyone else while I was in California because it felt weird. Supposedly, he has no idea what tonight entails, but I believe he knows more than he lets on.

Micah changes the topic and asks why Jonas pulled me aside last night. Says he checked on us from his spot in the arcade a few times. I smile and relay the conversation. Good to know Micah always has my back, even when I don't know it.

"That's pretty ballsy of him," Micah states. "No lie, he's spent a lot of time with Cora. I'm shocked they've only remained friends all this time."

"Yeah, we touched on that when he admitted he was in love with her."

"And what did he say?"

I chuckle. "He said he's actually tried a couple of times to push for more, but she stopped him. The only time she didn't was when I left, and she was pissed and drunk. She leaned in to kiss him and he cut her off. Told her he didn't want to be a backup option. She told him how sad she was and that she just wanted to feel something again."

When Jonas told me that last tidbit, I cringed. I did that to her. Made her so desperate for affection she was willing to fall into the arms of someone she didn't love. Not romantically, anyway. Hearing the truth was a hundred punches to the gut. I never want her heart to feel such depravity again. Never want her to be desperate for love because she feels she has none.

"Dude, that's some crazy shit. All in all, he's a good guy. He's never done anything horrible to Cora, Shelly, or Erin. Their relationship is odd, but they all have a good time together. I hate to say it, but he helped her smile again."

"Fuck."

"Don't beat yourself up over it. For years, there was nothing you could do about it. And you can't change the past. It's done. So now, you just move forward. She loves you, bro. Always has, always will. He just kept her afloat while you were gone. Be thankful for that. Some of the shit Shelly told me painted a pretty ugly picture. She didn't leave her house for months after you left. Almost flunked school. A lot of people were worried about her."

Although Cora and I stopped talking after a couple months, she was always front and center in my mind. The times we did talk after I moved to California, she never portrayed what Micah tells me now. She masked her pain, and she did it well. Either that or I relieved it when we talked. I can only imagine how it all went to shit when I stopped talking with her altogether. Every time I hear a new snippet about our time apart, the fault line in my heart opens wider.

But I deserve the pain. Deserve to let it tear me apart inside. Every horrible memory. All the sleepless nights and days of depression. Because her pain is my pain. And I pledge to never let her experience such pain again.

Micah and I eat breakfast in silence. Once we finish, we pay and head to my appointment. I crank the radio while we drive, silencing any further conversation. I need to clear my head and music is my favorite form of therapy.

When we pull into the parking lot, Micah laughs loud enough I hear him over the music. After I cut the engine, Micah asks, "So what irreversible decision are you making today?"

"Shut the fuck up." I get out of the car and walk into the tattoo shop, Micah following in my wake.

I go through the normal spiel with the lady at the front counter, filling out the form and providing identification, then sit and wait to be called back. She twirls her pink hair and pops her bubblegum loudly.

Ten minutes later, I sit in a chair with my shirt off. The artist prints the tattoo and Micah is staring at me with a gleam in his eyes.

"Speak your mind," I tell him.

"You're really going to do this?" Micah asks.

"Isn't it rather obvious I'm doing this?"

"You can still back out."

"Backing out is not an option." I shake my head at him.

"But this is different than the other one, bro. And it doesn't get more permanent."

I cock my brow at him. "Actually, other permanent things have also crossed my mind."

Just as Micah is about to give me a ration of shit, the tattoo artist walks back in. He verifies I want the tattoo on my left pec and presses the layout to my skin. A couple minutes later, the tattoo gun is piercing my skin and a new form of euphoria filters through my bloodstream. This is different from the last tattoo. More. Everlasting. And I wouldn't change it for anything.

"So, who's Cora?" the artist asks.

"Girlfriend," I say. Micah makes a face that indicates otherwise. "Although, I'm hoping she'll be more one day." At this, Micah shakes his head.

"Don't we all, man. My old lady and I have been together for years. Can't imagine life without her. Just haven't bucked up the courage to ask her yet. You?"

"Soon."

"Really?" Micah asks in disbelief. "You have got to be shitting me."

I drill holes in his head with my death stare. "Yeah. Why would you think otherwise? She's it for me, bro. Always has been. Just because you turned into a manwhore…"

"Let's not talk about me right now. We'll be here all day. Maybe we should be talking about the fact that you plan to marry Cora. Have you asked her?"

The artist laughs at our banter. "Not yet. But I'm not waiting. When the time comes, it's happening."

"You're ridiculous," Micah says.

"Why? Because I love her? Because I refuse to fuck this shit up again? Nothing will keep me from her now or in the future."

Before Micah chimes in with something snarky, the artist speaks up. "You two whine like a pair of bitches." He laughs, then goes back to the tattoo.

I tip my head back and close my eyes, shutting Micah out and dropping our conversation. He is such a pain in my ass sometimes. When the tattoo is done, I check it in a mirror and pay the artist.

When we get back in the car, Micah speaks up for the first time in an hour. "What's the French line?"

I tell him the line I memorized a lifetime ago. "Tu es les étoiles de ma lune. It translates to *you are the stars to my moon*."

"You really are lost," he says before laughing and cranking the music.

"In the best way. One more stop to make, okay?"

He nods. "Yeah, sure. Where to now?" I don't answer him as we pull onto the street and head south. He shakes his head and shrugs. "Whatever, bro. It's your day."

Damn right it is.

We arrive at Cora's house just before six. In her driveway is her Subaru, a motorcycle and a Beetle. I park behind her car and glance over to the window by the back patio. Through a crack in the curtains, I spot people running around like rapid fire. I squint and shift my head to the side to get a better view, but don't see anything else.

What the hell are they doing in there?

"Don't be upset," Micah says. When I shift to look at him with narrowed eyes, he shrugs. "She wanted to do something for your birthday."

For the first time in years, my birthday isn't an upsetting day. In fact, this is the best birthday I have had since my teens. Heat spreads through me like warm honey. She intentionally planned a gathering for my birthday. Not just so she and I could spend time together, but also so others could celebrate too. God, I missed celebrating birthdays and holidays and monumental occasions with her. They were never elaborate, but she added flare to the day.

"I'm not upset," I say. "Far from it. Best birthday I've had in a while."

We step out of the car and take our time walking to the back door. No doubt Micah texted Shelly as we got closer, so it should be no surprise when we knock. Just as I bring my hand up to knock, the door flies open and Cora stands on the other side. She is all smiles and slightly out of breath.

My girl. *My. Girl.*

"I was beginning to wonder how long you were going to sit in the driveway," she says.

"You knew we were out here?" I ask.

"Yeah. Shelly saw you turn onto the street. Come in, come in." She waves us in and her excitement is infectious.

Micah steps past her and wanders into the house. But I step up to her, my mouth an inch from hers. "Thank you. This is perfect." I wrap my arms around her and kiss her forehead.

"You're welcome. Glad you like it."

"I love it. I love you."

She squeezes me tighter. "I love you, too. Come on, everyone is waiting."

We step into her small house. Once in the open space, I scan the rooms. Added to her normal decor are shiny happy birthday banners and cheesy kid's decor. On one wall is a plastic version of pin the tail on the donkey. The moment I see it, I burst out laughing. She loops her arm in mine and keeps us going forward.

On the kitchen countertop is a small round cake, *Happy Birthday* piped in white over the black icing. Next to the cake is an array of finger foods and alcohol. When I glance over at the dining table, which has a couple chairs added to the ends, I spot a small pile of gifts next to a stack of board and card games.

"I vote food first," I say.

"Second that," Micah chimes in.

And just like that, we all clamber into a line and grab platefuls of finger foods. We clear the games and gifts from the table and gather around to eat. When our plates are almost empty, Shelly pipes up and suggests I choose the first game. I riffle through the choices and go with the adult version of Watch Your Mouth.

For the next thirty minutes, each of us slobbers over semi-dirty phrases that sound absolutely filthy. Cora tries for a solid two minutes to say something no one can translate. While this happens, I pull out my phone and record a video of the whole show. I will definitely be watching that over and over. After we have all laughed our asses off, we opt to take a game break and dish out cake.

Cora and Shelly make a show out of adding twenty-nine candles to the cake and lighting them. The lights go out and everyone sings happy birthday to me as Cora holds the cake between us. The entire time everyone sings, I stare at her. Watch the mini-candle flames flicker on her skin. Take in her smile, remembering how long it has been since I saw her smile like this. Genuine and wide and happily. When the song finishes, I silently wish to spend every day of the rest of my life with Cora, then blow out all twenty-nine candles in one breath.

Cora smiles, then takes the cake in the kitchen. She hands me a big enough piece of cake for two and I take it back to the table while she finishes cutting it.

With a forkful of chocolate cake in my mouth, Shelly shoves the stack of gifts toward me. "Happy Birthday, Gavin."

I thank her after I swallow. "You didn't have to buy me anything." After I shove another bite in my mouth, I unwrap the small box. As soon as I see the package, I spit cake out of my mouth. "What the hell, Shelly?" Thank fuck Cora is still in the kitchen messing with cake. Not sure if she would be embarrassed or giggly or shocked.

I stare down at the one-hundred-count box of condoms and shake my head. When I peek up at Shelly, she shrugs in the same manner Micah does. "Not like you won't use them. Especially if you guys are back together. Plus, they were on sale at Costco."

As discreetly as possible, I wrap the paper around the box again and push it aside. The other two gifts are simple and normal. A gift card and a card with cash. Somehow, I will use the cash and card to buy them all something in return. I don't need gifts as long as I have Cora. She is the greatest gift of all.

For the next two hours, we play cards and shoot the shit with each other. Tonight is the most enjoyable evening and birthday I have had in a long time and I bask in the sentiment. My mom or parents always did nice things for me over the years, but it was never the same as when I was with Cora. Now that she is back in my life, I will never let anything break us apart again.

Erin yawns and it starts a ripple effect throughout the room. Within ten minutes, Erin, Shelly, and Micah pile into Shelly's car, and Jonas hops on his motorcycle. In the blink of an eye, only me and Cora stand in her house. And the solitude is heaven.

I help her clean up a few things that need to be put away now. After, we sit on the couch and simply hold each other. Only with her is silence comforting. I close my eyes and enjoy the warmth radiating off her and soothing me. Reminisce in the affection and warmth we once shared as I dream about what the future holds.

"Do you want to watch a movie?" she whispers into the dim-lit living room.

"Only if you want to. I'm content like this."

She turns into me more and presses her hand over my heart. I suck in a breath when her weight covers a portion of my new tattoo. Her eyes widen at my expression. "Are you okay? What's the matter?"

I sit up a little and kiss her forehead. "Yeah, baby. I'm okay. Just got a new tattoo today."

Cora perks up next to me. "You got a new tattoo? Can I see it?"

Eventually, I knew Cora would see my new tattoo. I just had no idea it would be tonight. Not that I fear her seeing it. Only curious how she will react.

I scoot forward a few inches and tug my shirt over my head, tossing it aside. The moment she sees it, all air leaves the room. "Gavin," she gasps. "I… I don't know what to say."

As I sit back against the cushion, she shifts closer to me. Her fascination with the ink is cute. By the way she studies it, I know she wants to run her fingers over it. "It'll heal over the next week," I inform her.

Her eyes well as she peeks up at me. "You know that's forever, right?"

"You are my forever, Cora. No other name will brand my skin. No other woman will have my heart. It has belonged to you since the first day of high school. The day I joined you under that tree and you drew me beside you on a sketch pad."

Tears spill from her eyes. "You're my forever, too. I tried to move on for so many years. Tried to care for another person. God, how I tried. But it never happened. Even when I tried to force it. Because I could never imagine life with someone other than you. So, I tucked you away for safekeeping in the hopes you would return."

I pinch the ends of her hair and play with it between my fingers. Fuck, I want to kiss her. But I promised I wouldn't kiss her until she initiated the kiss. And fuck if that isn't the most difficult vow to keep right now. Because everything about this day, this moment, cries out for me to lean forward and press my lips to hers.

She brings a hand to my other pec and skims over the flesh. Electricity shoots through every atom, cell, and molecule in my body. I swear to god, if she doesn't kiss me soon, I will break my promise. Because as patient as I am, this is pure torture.

Just as I am ready to cave on my desires, she leans forward and presses her lips to my left pec, an inch above the tattoo. "I love you," she says, breath hot on my skin.

And a switch flips inside me. Fire heats my blood, scorches my skin, has me panting for breath. I become a starved man and Cora is what my body needs to survive.

The moment I kiss Gavin's chest, a ticking time bomb detonates beneath my lips. As if my lips on his skin is the invitation he has been waiting for. The key to solve a riddle.

Before I grasp what is happening, Gavin scoops me up in his arms and walks toward my bedroom. A moment later, he tosses me on the bed and crawls over me. His lips brand my navel as he shoves my shirt up my torso and over my head. Every press of his lips is kindling added to a raging inferno inside me. An inferno that has always been there, but faded with his absence.

He peppers kisses across my collar bone and up my neck, nipping and sucking. His forearms press into the mattress on either side of me and cage me in. I knead the sides of his ribcage and around his backside, digging my nails into his bare flesh.

"Oh god, Gavin," I gasp, tipping my head back.

His lips graze my jawline and finally land on my mouth. Liquid heat swipes across my lower lip and begs me to open up for him. The second his tongue brushes against mine, I lose all coherent thought. Gavin is everywhere. The saltiness of his lips on my skin mingles with my taste buds. His fevered skin heats up every inch of my skin. The piney-beach scent only Gavin has seeps into my senses. Fuck, it's too much.

He hovers above me a second. "I want you, baby. To be inside you."

"God, yes."

As soon as I grant him permission, Gavin's hands travel to my waist and unfasten my jeans. He jostles them down my hips and yanks them to my ankles before depositing them on the floor. The pads of his fingers graze the tips of my toes and slowly descend over the tops of my feet. "Do you know how long I've waited for this?" Heat dances over my ankles and ascends my shin. "How long I've waited to see you?" Tingles play over my knee and tease the distal end of my thigh. "To touch you." Sparks ignite in my quads and I squirm beneath him. "To love you."

His hands reach my hips and I am ready to explode from anticipation. But he remains idle, his fingers toying with the bands of my panties. I pant and wriggle beneath him. "So, what are you waiting for now?" I tease, egging him on.

A smirk tugs at the side of his mouth. "Baby, I'm just reveling in the moment. I won't take you or us or our lives for granted. Never again."

"Gavin…" I whisper into the darkness.

He lowers himself and presses a sweet, earnest kiss to my lips. Packed with intensity and longing and hope. "I love you, Cora. I have loved you for as long as I can remember. And I will love you for the rest of my days." We kiss as if the past thirteen years never happened, as if time was never stolen from us, and the world rights itself again. Stars burn brighter. Planets align. And everything goes back in its rightful place.

As our lungs gasp for air, Gavin breaks the kiss and his lips trace my ear and down my neck. He massages the sides of my torso as he lavishes kisses down my sternum, between my breasts, and stops at my navel. Fingers skirt around my backside and unhook my bra. Heated breaths paint my navel for three unshakable beats before his hands glide out and slip the black barrier from my breasts.

Neither of us moves for a moment. Instead, we lay impossibly still and absorb everything about this experience. The last time Gavin saw this much of my body, I was a sixteen-year-old girl. Although my body hasn't changed drastically over the last thirteen years, I am not the same. And neither is he. Not just our bodies, but also who we are as people. Yes, I am still that girl under the tree in the courtyard who fell desperately in love with Gavin Hunt. A boy who only wanted to share the shady tree with me.

But now, I am the woman who has fallen in love all over again. The woman who is brave enough to give myself over to him, wholeheartedly. As heartbroken and devastated as I was over the last thirteen years, I forgive him for the things he could not control. Things neither of us could control. For all the moments he wanted to come back to me and was unable to. As much as I tried to deny it, Gavin was always here. Tucked away in my heart. Rooted deep in my bones. Flowing through my veins. Hiding in the corners of my mind. Holding me captive. Telling me to be patient and wait for him. I see this now. All these reasons are why I was never able to truly let anyone else into my heart. Because Gavin had it. *Has* it.

And he always will.

"I love you, Gavin," I whisper as I comb my fingers through his hair.

He shudders above me before he feathers a kiss to my navel. The pads of his fingers imprint my back, my sides, my hips. They knead and paw and bruise in the most delicious way. His kisses transition from sweet to hungry and ravenous. I curl my fingers into fists and tug his hair as my back arches off the bed and I gasp at his touch. Gavin nips along the hemline of my underwear until he reaches my hip. He sucks and sucks and sucks, and it is not until a moment later that I realize he is marking me. Claiming me. As his. The notion of his lips and tongue bruising my skin sets me on fire and I moan.

After he is satisfied with his work, he raises enough to peer up at me. "Fuck. The way your soul coos for me, baby. You're my own personal heaven and I never want to leave."

"Never."

"Never," he repeats.

Gavin slips his fingers beneath the band of my panties, grazes the skin below one, two, three times, then hooks the cotton in his grip and peels it away from my body. After he tosses them to the floor, he stands at the foot of the bed and ogles every inch of me. His steely eyes sear my flesh as he takes in every inch of me.

Normally, I would be shy under such scrutiny. But with Gavin, I crave his appraisal. Long for his eyes to drink in every fragment of my wanton body. Beg for his undeniable *need* for me.

Over the years, I never allowed this with the few people I'd been with. Never let them that close to me. Hell, I never removed my clothes. I was good with celibacy.

But with Gavin… I willingly bared every aspect of myself to him. Heart. Soul. The good, bad and ugly. He is the missing piece. My forever. The be-all and end-all. And there will never be anything that stands between us.

My eyes lock on his for three panting breaths before he breaks the connection. His drift down the lines and curves of my body, and mine do the same. Down his neck, across his collar bones, the hollow spot at the base of his throat. When I get to his pecs, I groan as I read my name permanently imprinted on his skin. Who knew something so simple could be the hottest display of affection. My heart is a fierce monster beneath my breast bone—pound, pound, pounding to be set free.

In my periphery, Gavin unbuttons and lowers his shorts. Black boxer briefs barely contain his erection, and I unabashedly stare at his groin. *Was he always that big?* I swallow and know he hears it.

He palms his erection through the cotton. "See something you like, baby?" A hint of sarcasm laces his question.

"You have no idea," I say, brazen.

My eyes pop back to his as he shoves his underwear to the floor. A second later, he presses a knee into the mattress and crawls back up my body. No barriers. No secrets. Just me and Gavin.

He kisses up my stomach, my breast, my neck, and stops when we are eye to eye. "I want nothing between us, Cora. Ever." He inhales deeply and shuts his eyes a second. "I've always used condoms. It's been a while since the last... and I got tested after."

I reach up and lace my fingers behind his neck, draw him down to me and press my lips to his. He doesn't want either of us to admit that we have been with other people since each other. Doesn't want to tell me the ways he filled the void. And neither do I. But this is us. Open. No holds barred. No skeletons.

"Thank you." I kiss him again. "I've been tested, too. And I'm on the pill."

His whole body relaxes. A second later, his lips are on mine as he grinds his length against the apex of my thighs. I lift my hips and add more pressure. And god is it amazing. His pecs squash my breasts as his abdomen slides against my belly. Strong hands frame my face and Gavin worships my mouth with his. I caress his biceps, the sides of his torso and slip my hands around to his lower back. Time has made Gavin's body a work of art. A sculpture. A god-like effigy worthy of worship and devotion.

I grab hold of his ass and paw at the muscular flesh in my palms. His hips rock into mine as his erection coasts up and down my entrance. A moment later, his palm grazes down my side and slips between us. With a lift of his hips, he slips his hand between my thighs and runs a finger over my slit.

"Fuck, baby," he growls. "You are so damn wet."

As his finger toys with my lower lips, I pivot my hips at the perfect time and his digit sinks inside me. It may be only one finger, but it consumes me. A second later, I rock forward again. Back and forth. Faster, faster. Gavin inserts another finger and I moan. His hand pistons as my hips plunge and we form the perfect rhythm.

As I fuck his fingers, he reveres my mouth, my neck, my breasts. He is everywhere. Every molecule. Every fiber. Every beat of my heart and breath in my lungs. Too much and not enough at the same time. Breath and heat and sweat. Friction and passion. While one hand pistons inside me, his other slides into my hair and clutches at the crown. He locks me in place with his grip and his lips and his fingers.

Fire blazes hot in my epicenter. Building faster, hotter. Gavin nips along my jaw and stops at my ear. "So fucking hot, baby," he whisper-growls. Then sucks at the spot just behind my ear. The one only he knows about. The spot that tips me over the edge.

White hot heat detonates low in my belly and ricochets through every muscle. I pinch my eyes shut and stars glow on the backs of my lids. I bow into his body as mine clutches his fingers with every ounce of strength. High pitch gasps for air whine from my lungs and Gavin crashes his mouth to mine. Dizziness warps my vision as I ride the wave of my high.

For a moment, we lay motionless—Gavin hovering above me. Panting as the scent of sex floats in the air. I haven't had an orgasm like that in years. Too many years. And I want more. So much more.

"Gavin?"

"Yeah, baby?" His breaths as labored as my own.

I kiss along his jaw and graze the flesh with my teeth before reaching his lips. Pressing one, two, three kisses to the soft lips I could lose myself in for days on end. When I break the kiss, I frame his face with my hands and lock eyes with him. Then kiss him one last time. "Please, I need you inside me," I whimper.

A growl reverberates low in his diaphragm and ripples into me like a tidal wave. He scoops one arm around the back of my shoulders and the other around my hips. Before I realize what is happening, he flips us over and straddles me over his thighs. All the times we had been together years ago, I never sat atop him. Never had control when we had sex. And now, I feel like a goddess. Like the master of our world. Of Gavin.

"Ride me, baby," he purrs.

His request is gasoline to the fire blazing in my belly, I press my palms flat on his chest, lift myself and position my entrance over his cock. Inhaling deeply, I lower myself onto him slowly. Inch by inch, I take him to the hilt and audibly gasp once I am seated.

Gavin sets his hands on my hips and locks me in place. And for a moment, neither of us moves. We relish in being connected like this once again. Skin to skin. Completely vulnerable. Absolute exposure.

His breathing spikes and I lean down and take his mouth with mine. The kiss starts slow. Sweet, gentle pecks. Then I paint his lower lip with my tongue and he invites me in. Our tongues taste and devour one another for a beat. And then I rock my hips back and slam them forward.

He breaks our kiss, my mouth an inch above his, and hisses. "Fuuuuck…"

I do it again, sinking my nails into the flesh just beneath his pecs. When I roll my hips again, Gavin thrusts up and hits a spot deep inside me, a place only he reaches, and I cry out. One thrust, then another, until we find a rhythmic dance only two lovers know. His hands roam my abdomen and my breasts before he sits up. One, two, three more rocks of my hips and I orgasm a second time.

A second passes and before I catch my breath, Gavin flips us back over and hovers above me. "Wrap your legs around me, baby."

I do as he says, locking my ankles together, and he thrusts hard and fast into me. Gone are the moments of sweet caresses and gentle strokes. Now, the inferno blazing between us is set to atomic levels. And if this burn doesn't get satiated, both of us will implode.

Gavin buries his face in the crook of my neck, lips and tongue sucking my skin. One arm braces my shoulder while the other clutches my hip. He pumps in and out of me—faster, harder, hungrier. His mouth, his cock, his heart, it is almost too much to bear. Almost.

Sweat pulses from our pores and slicks us from head to toe. His breath hot on my neck as his teeth clamp down on the tender skin. Our cries of pleasure mingle in the air and bounce off the walls. And I climb, climb, climb back up the peak once again. "Oh god, Gavin. Don't. Fucking. Stop," I pant out.

His grip on me tightens as his hips buck harder. He grunts into my skin, and I know he resists his own need to come. Resisting so we can prolong this reunion. And that fact sets me off again. Has my walls constricting and my vision fading.

My body a limp noodle as I come down from my orgasm. Gavin brings his lips back to mine, kisses them tenderly, and whispers, "One more, baby." I nod and he pulls out of me, flips me on my belly, and hikes my ass in the air.

With my profile against the sheets, I stretch my arms above my head and clutch the pillows in my fists. He lines himself up with my entrance, but doesn't push inside. Not yet. He leans over me and whispers in my ear. "I love you to the ends of the earth, Cora. Forever." When he lifts off of me, his fingertips dance over my neck before tracing down the length of my spine to the base of my tailbone. It is more than just a touch. It is devotion. Awe. Adulation. Reverence. Intimacy. Worship.

With both hands squeezing my hips, he eases inside of me. Each inch forward is a step closer to heaven. Closer to where Gavin and I will be for all eternity. Together. Connected. Unbreakable. Inseparable.

When he is fully seated inside me, I mewl into the sheets and tighten my fists. He relaxes his hands for a split second before clamping down harder. Tomorrow, my body will artfully display the evidence of our reunion. And I plan to revel in every single line and stroke and strawberry on my skin. Cherish them and create new ones before they fade. Memorize the feel of them and how they came to be.

Gavin doesn't move for a minute and I peer over my shoulder at him. His eyes closed and brow furrowed. Before I open my mouth to ask if everything is okay, a tear rolls down his cheek. I push up so I'm on my hands and knees, ready to spin around and soothe whatever sadness has taken hold. Just as I straighten, he presses a palm flat between my shoulder blades and presses me down to the bed.

"Gavin, are you okay?" I ask, genuinely worried.

His hand rests between my scapulae a beat before gliding back to my hip. "Never better, baby," he chokes out.

"Then why are you crying?"

My eyes still trained on his as he stares down at me. "Because I haven't been this happy in a really long time."

"Happy tears?" I ask because I have to be certain.

"Yes, baby. Happy tears." And then he rocks his hips back and drives forward.

He fills me so fully, I forget how to breathe. How to speak. My eyes roll back and I groan. "Oh fuck…"

In. Out. Stroke after stroke, he brings us both closer to nirvana. His hips slap my ass, balls whack my clit, head of his cock rubs the nerve endings inside my walls. Building. Climbing. Taller. Higher. His tempo increases and I know he is trying to get me there before he lets go. As if confirmation of my thoughts, his hand snakes around my waist and his finger circles my clit. His hips piston faster as our moans consume every lick of empty space in the room.

"Gavin…" I wring the sheets in my fists. "So close. Don't stop."

He adds more pressure to my clit and circles faster as his hips thrust like a well-oiled machine. I clamp my eyes shut as my breath comes in short, staggered whimpers. On the next stroke, the head of his cock strokes perfectly over the nerve cluster in my walls and I detonate. A grunting scream rips from my throat as he continues to slam into me. My vision blanks as I convulse and milk his cock.

My orgasm feels like a never-ending stream of consciousness as Gavin releases inside me. Only when his hips slow and he collapses over top of me, does my body calm down.

"Holy shit," he breathes into my hair.

Gavin rests his head beside mine, arms clutching my breasts and belly, and heaves. No intimacy compares to what Gavin and I share. It isn't just the sex—although sex with Gavin is literal euphoria.

Intimacy with Gavin is so much more. Friendship and love. Sunsets and strolls in the park. Shared whispers and tender kisses. Side glances and subtle smiles. Speaking without words. Acceptance. An incomparable bond. A life force all its own. The promise of forever.

My hips drop to the mattress and I relax more than I have in thirteen years. Gavin lays beside me and I roll to face him. He drags me closer to him, weaves our legs together, and plays with the ends of my hair. Tenderness bleeds from his pores into mine. So pure and true. He leans in and kisses my lips, the tip of my nose, then my forehead.

When our breathing regulates, he traces my cheekbones with his finger, then my lips—his eyes fixed on the movement. One, two, three heartbeats later, his gray eyes lock on mine. Gets lost in them. We lay like this for minutes or hours, entranced with each other. No words are spoken—not that they need to be. We simply breathe each other in. Realign our souls. Remember the feeling of us.

For the next several hours, we memorize every inch of the other's body. Learn all the new lines and curves and dips and scars. And get lost in paradise time and time again.

～

I peek over Gavin's shoulder at the clock and check the time. Five twenty-one. For the last seven-plus hours, we have worshiped one another. And although I would love nothing more than to pass out wrapped in his arms right now, a different idea pops in my head.

I bolt up and fumble through the darkness. "Cora, what are you doing?" His mumble is sweet and inquisitive as he props himself up on his elbows.

"Get dressed. I want to go somewhere."

Gavin glances at the clock, then flops on his back. "Come back to the bed and cuddle with me. We can go later." As adorable as he is in this very moment, I resist the temptation of falling back into the sheets with him.

After stepping into a fresh pair of lacy boy short panties, I slip on a pair of black jeans. "Can't wait. It's time sensitive."

Gavin sits up and stares at me as I yank a shirt from a hanger. In the dark, I have no idea what shirt it is, nor do I care. I tug it over my head then walk over to the bed and grab his hand. He gives in and stands up, pulling me to his chest and kissing me. "Okay, baby. Where are we going?" he asks as he locates his clothes and dresses.

"It's a surprise. But you'll love it. Promise."

While Gavin finishes dressing, I head out to the kitchen, feed and love on Luna, and make us both a large to-go mug of coffee. When he emerges from the bedroom, I hand him a steaming mug and place a kiss on his cheek. We're quiet as we walk out the back door and get into my car. After a little maneuvering around Gavin's car, we get on the road as I speed toward our destination.

Less than thirty minutes later, we land on Central Avenue in downtown St. Petersburg and head toward the water. The streets are still dark, but slowly waking up in the early morning hours. Soon, I park the car, feed a meter on Beach Drive and grab a blanket from the back of the car—one I kept back there to protect my camera equipment when I cart it onto the beach during shoots.

Gavin slips his hand around mine and I guide us near the waterfront. Near the new pier is a small man-made beach. We open up the blanket and spread it out on the sand. Gavin sits with knees up and legs spread, and I sit down between them. He wraps his arms around me and pins me close to his body.

"This is perfect, baby," he whispers, his chin resting on my shoulder as we stare out at the Bay.

I relax into him more. "It's time for a sunrise. Our lives have been filled with countless sunsets. Time to start fresh with new traditions. I want just as many sunrises as sunsets."

Sunrises are the start of something new and invigorating. Although Gavin and I have known each other for what feels like a lifetime, we hit a snafu. A fault we couldn't scale until the time was right. During that time, we grew. Into ourselves and into adulthood. We had the chance to discover who we are without each other. And fate still found a way to reconnect us. Make us whole again. Give us a chance to start anew.

A sunrise after the darkest sunset.

The sky pinks near the horizon and Gavin squeezes me tighter. "I'm sorry it took me so long to get back to you. Believe me when I say, if I had known it'd be this long, I would have done things differently."

I shake my head. "No, Gavin. Everything is how it's meant to be. Was our time apart the most gut-wrenching experience of my life? Yes. There has been no pain worse than losing you. Never will be. But would I change any of it? I don't think I would. It sounds wrong, but I think the years have taught us so much. Taught us how to love. Showed us what we'd miss without one another. Many couples stay together for years and grow unhappy with their relationship. A rift divides them and they fall out of love." I pause, take a deep breath, and collect myself. "If that would've happened between us... as hurt as I was when we lost touch, I never stopped loving you. I suppressed it. Smothered it. Buried it deep in the corners of my heart and packed it tight with dirt. But it has always been there."

Gavin inhales deeply and drags me impossibly closer to him. "I could never not love you, Cora Davies." Everything about his statement is permanent, carved in stone, and I fall inconceivably harder for him.

The light pink sky blooms into a hot pink-orange as the sun edges closer to the horizon. Darkness fades from the sky as a faint blue comes into view. Another couple walks onto the sand and sits fifty feet from us, phone out and snapping images of the glowing scenery.

I lean my head against Gavin and marvel in his warmth behind me. His arms holding me close. His fingers drawing soft patterns on my forearms. I sigh and feel the pain of the last thirteen years lift away. Beautiful colors paint the sky. A few clouds linger and add touches of lavender and gray. Feeling like I can finally breathe for the first time in over a decade, I whisper, "Life is perfect."

Gavin shakes his head beside me, and I turn to glimpse his expression. A smile stretches his face from ear to ear and displays his perfect white teeth. "There's only one thing that could make life perfect."

His steely-gray irises swirl with love and passion and admiration. I get lost in his eyes. Eyes I missed every day. Eyes no camera captured the way my memories did. Momentarily, I forget what he said and shake my head to snap myself out of the temporary fog.

"And what's that?" I ask, matching his smile.

He lifts an arm from my waist, cups my cheek, and brushes his thumb in small circles. I lean into his touch and sigh. His other arm holds me unimaginably closer. Eyes hold mine as he breathes slow and steady. Quiet for a beat, his expression turns intense. Fierce. One-hundred-percent serious. His lips part and I drop my gaze just as he licks them. "If you were my wife."

All air gets sucked from my lungs.

twenty-one

CORA

Three years ago

Women swarm the room, buzzing around like worker bees eager to aid the queen. The queen—actually, the bride—sits on a tall chair, labeled "Bride" in silver letters on the back, and breathes heavily while another woman does her makeup. Her thick, black locks are pinned back partially and curled. Eyelids brushed a soft blush. Lips coated in a neutral gloss. A subtle shimmer added to her skin.

Most brides are so nervous on their wedding day and never remember all the little moments. Like this one in the dressing room of the church. Which is why I am here. To capture the bride with her bridesmaids tending to her. Her mother keeping the bridesmaids—as well as people not in the room—in check. Novelty items such as jewelry and robes and hangers.

I bring the camera to my eye and snap a handful of images. Before anyone stepped foot in here, I walked around the grounds and took several photos of the church, flowers and various displays. The wedding is nowhere near luxurious. Sherrie—the bride—was adamant about keeping the ceremony clean and simple and pristine. Not an overabundance of flowers or decor. Whites and creams and a hint of blush-pink. Very subtle, but utterly breathtaking. The photos of her gown on the hanger will be coveted for years to come.

"Twenty minutes, ladies," a woman shouts from the door before disappearing.

As if that is the cue they have all been waiting for, everyone's pace triples. Bridesmaids zip each other up in their blush-colored gowns before removing the bride's dress from the hanger. Once the makeup artist steps away, the bridesmaids step front and center. I bring the camera back to my eye and snap continuously as they help her into her dress.

When the dress is in place, her maid of honor hands her the bouquet and everyone steps back a moment, allowing me to take some individual photos of her before she leaves the room. After I finish, hair and makeup step back up and double-check to make certain everything is perfect.

She makes such a beautiful bride. Something I will never be.

I shake off the errant thoughts and leave the bridal suite. A moment later, I knock on the door for the groom's suite. A guy with dark hair, gauge-pierced ears, and a wicked smile answers the door. For a moment, I flashback to another guy who had similar features, a guy I once cared about, but push it aside and slip on my professional mask.

I lift my camera and waggle it. "Is everyone decent? I'd like to get some photos of the groom's suite before the ceremony begins."

He peeks over his shoulder then steps aside and gestures me to enter. "Sure, we're dressed. Can't speak for decent," he snickers.

I ignore his insinuation and walk into the room. Snapping a few pictures, I tell the guys to do whatever it is they were doing before I came in. The guys relax and start joking with each other, slapping backs and teasing the groom about how he will only have one piece of ass for the rest of his life. But the groom lights up at the idea and I capture every little tweak in his lips. Every crinkled uptick near his eyes. Every ounce of joy he exudes.

Love is a funny thing. When you see it with your own eyes, it is unbelievable. Unparalleled. Simple touches—the way he tucks your hair behind your ear or toys with the ends of the strands or draws art on your skin with his fingers or holds you close every chance possible. A small upturn of the lips—just enough to let you know he is thinking of you. A slight lean of the body—because he can never be too close or get enough of you. Love sneaks up on you, slithers itself around your heart like vines, blankets you in warmth and security and joy, and blossoms like a field of wildflowers. It is incredible and incomparable and incomprehensible.

And I hope to never feel it again.

I take a few more photos of the groom and groomsmen, excuse myself, and head for the main area of the church. Once there, I walk in and photograph the crowd in the pews. Candid images of family and friends, old and young. People carry on conversations about how the bride and groom met and fell in love instantaneously. They recant how inseparable they are and how they never imagine them apart. After several more clicks of the shutter, I head back to where the bridal party will enter. And thankfully, away from all the puppy-love conversations.

It isn't as if I don't believe in love. Love is real and magical and undeniable. But love is also a rusty, jagged hunting knife in my chest. Twisting and depressing.

The music shifts and I take a deep breath. Ten seconds later, the groomsmen walk through the large wooden doors. I snap photo after photo. The guy who answered the door to the groom's suite passes me and winks. I continue taking photos and don't acknowledge the gesture. If I were any other woman, I would melt into a puddle at his feet. Swoon at the prospect of him asking me to dance later or grab a drink or exchange phone numbers. He is definitely gorgeous, but unfortunately for me, I am far from interested. In anyone. Ever.

I purse my lips, bring the camera to my eye, and continue photographing the wedding. After all the groomsmen pass, the music changes again. The wedding march—a standard, but elegant choice. Once upon a time, this song popped into my head. Impregnated visions of white gowns and black suits and promises of forever. But I was young and naïve then. I am neither of those things anymore. And after my dreams were obliterated, I am quite content becoming an old cat lady. At least as a cat lady, I will receive nothing but unconditional love.

The wedding passes and a million photos are taken. But it is not until the reception when I lose my shit.

Upbeat music fades from the sound system and the deejay speaks up. "This is for all the lovebirds in the room. Grab your guy or lady and head out to the dance floor."

A new song crackles through the speakers. A song I haven't heard in years. One that cracks my heart and cripples me on the spot. The twangy guitar intro to "Better Together" by Jack Johnson floods every available space in the room and drowns me instantly. Tears prick my eyes and, within seconds, roll down my cheeks. An emotional ball the size of a softball lodges in my throat.

I can't breathe.

Fuck. I can't be here. I can't be here.

The groomsman hottie approaches me, a smile plastered on his face until he notices my state. "Hey, you okay?"

I shake my head. It is too much. All of it. The bride, the groom, the promises, the happiness, the music. One big ball of happily ever after. Something I thought I would have. Until my heart got ripped from my chest and annihilated.

"I need to leave," I tell him. "Now."

"Do you need a ride? I can drive you."

As great as the idea sounds, I decline his offer. The last thing I need is to lose my shit with a guy that resembles the reason *why* I am crying. All that would lead to is another hot mess.

After I pack up my camera equipment, I find the bride and groom and apologize for my early departure. Thankfully, all the necessary photos for the wedding have been captured. Now it is just flat out party time. They hug and thank me and then I bolt out the door. Away from the reminder of broken promises.

When I reach my car, I set everything in the back then get in the car and lock the doors. I sit there, alone in the lot, for over thirty minutes, crying in my hands. Sobbing as if I am sixteen all over again.

Over the last decade, I have lost so much in my life. All of that loss wraps around one person.

Gavin Hunt.

Losing Gavin was like cutting out my heart with a spoon and tossing it in the darkest, deepest parts of the ocean. Without him, I had no reason to love. No desire to love. Nothing has changed. Over the years, brick by brick, I slowly built a towering wall around the space where my heart once sat. Reinforced it with steel beams and barbed wire. Hardened myself to everyone. Family. Friends. I would never allow someone to do to me what Gavin Hunt did—crush my heart and run away with my soul.

Right here, in the parking lot of the reception hall, where two lovers celebrate their joyous union, I make a vow to myself. A vow that will never be broken, because I hold the key. I am the gatekeeper of this truth.

"I will never open my heart to anyone ever again. I will never love another person ever again. And I most definitely will never marry anyone."

GAVIN

Present

"Life is perfect," Cora whispers as we stare toward the rising sun.

Now that things are finally back as they should be, now that the stars have realigned and I can breathe, life is pretty great. But I wouldn't say life is perfect. Pretty close, but not quite.

I shake my head and Cora peers over at me. My smile stretches so tight my cheeks hurt. I can't help it. This is what she does to me—shines a light on every shadow, lifts me up, makes me feel alive and whole and worthy. When I am with her, life is worth living. A life with her is worth living.

"There's only one thing that could make life perfect," I tell her. For some reason, I feel as if I should be nervous. Should have sweaty palms or be biting my lip or fidgeting. But I don't have a nervous bone in my body. If anything, I have never felt calmer a day in my life.

Cora studies me intently, her vibrant green eyes glowing in sunrise. She scans my eyes and forehead before dropping to my lips. She is absolutely stunning right now and I make a mental note to see a million more sunrises with her at my side.

As if coming out of a daze, Cora shakes her head and asks, "And what's that?" A hint of teasing lingers on her tongue.

But I am dead serious. More serious than ever. More than any other time in my life. Nothing in my life or this world matters if Cora isn't beside me. And I want her beside me through it all. The good days and bad. Our young days and old. With children and grandchildren. I want it all, and only with her.

I peel one arm away from her waist, frame her cheek in my palm, and swipe my thumb over the soft skin below her cheekbone. As soon as I do, she leans her face into my palm and I scoot closer to her. I stare into her magnificent green irises—a perfect blend of the trees and the sea.

Cora is everything I want in my life. Beauty and charisma and spunk and passion. She holds the key to my heart and is the guardian of my soul. In the last thirteen years, she has never left me—in spirit, anyway. Every woman I looked at was compared to her. And there was no contest. Hands down, Cora is it for me. There is not a single person walking this earth I want more than her. She gives me breath and life and purpose and love. Without her, I wander the earth with no destination.

"If you were my wife," I announce.

Cora gasps and freezes in my arms. For three of my breaths, she doesn't breathe once. And then she inhales deeply. Deeper than I have ever heard another person breathe. "Gavin…" She says my name as if it is her dying breath.

"Cora, I have spent far too much time away from you. Without you, I am a shell of a man. Every second we were apart, I merely existed. It wasn't until I saw you again that I remembered how to breathe. That my heart remembered it had another purpose other than beating. I dreamt of this day, but feared it would never happen. No more. Life is too short to not spend it with the person who matters most." I spin around to face her and prop myself up on one knee. "Cora, I know what life is like without you in it. I never wish to experience pain or darkness like that again. Nor do I want you to. The day my plane touched down here, I somehow knew life would be better. I didn't have the answers, but I felt it in my bones. And I wasn't wrong. How could it not be kismet bringing us back together? I belong to you, Cora. And I would be honored to be your husband. Will you marry me?"

Behind Cora, the other couple on the beach have their camera turned toward us. No doubt they're recording this. Another win in my favor.

Please let her say yes.

When she doesn't say anything for a moment, I remember the box is still in my pocket. Maybe if she sees the ring I bought, she will realize just how serious I am. I fish the soft, black box from my pocket and lift the lid. Nestled inside the box is a two-carat, square-cut black diamond in a tall setting. Along each edge of the black diamond are three smaller white diamonds. Several white diamond chips burrow in the titanium band from top to bottom. Hugging the engagement band is a matching wedding band with larger white diamonds.

Her hands fly to cover her mouth as she gasps. A second later, she lowers them to her chin. "Gavin…" she whispers. "Oh my god." Her glazed green eyes dart to mine and tears spill out, sliding down to her illustrious smile. "Yes. A million times yes." Cora crawls up on her hands and knees and launches herself at me. We fall to the sand and laugh.

I wrap my arms around her body and squeeze her with every ounce of strength I possess. "Fuck, baby. I love you so goddamn much."

After a minute, I sit us up and kiss the hell out of her. She tastes like salt and passion and forever. The best fucking taste in the world. And I am the luckiest man alive because she just said I get to keep her forever.

When the kiss breaks, I scoot back an inch and take the ring out of the box. She juts her left hand toward me and I slip the link to forever on her ring finger. The second it rests in place; the sun brightens the world more. I slam my mouth back on hers and kiss her as if she has already slipped a ring on my finger. The sooner, the better.

Forever will never be long enough with Cora. No matter how many lives we live, we will always find each other. Eternally.

After we dial down our public display, the couple from down the beach walks over and congratulates us. They offer to send us the video they recorded plus a few still pictures and I instantly jump on their offer, thanking them. We talk with them a few minutes before we shake out the blanket, fold it, and walk back to the car.

The second we get in the car, Cora's stomach grumbles and we decide to grab breakfast. As we head back toward Clearwater, I stare at the engagement ring on her finger. She isn't left-handed, but now she proudly drives with her left hand on the wheel. Every time the sun catches her ring just right, a halo flashes on the interior roof of the car.

Like an angel. My angel. My future wife.

After all these years, I wasn't sure if we would find our way back to each other. But we did. And I wasn't sure if I would see this day. This exact day. The day when Cora and I were back together and she wore my ring on her finger.

And now that the day is here, an odd flutter ripples beneath my ribcage. The sensation light and exhilarating and eternal. Does she feel this fluttering right now? The exultation of finally living the life you were destined to live.

We pull into a parking lot and hop out of the car. Although we are both dog tired, there is enough adrenaline coursing through our veins to keep us both up all day. I sidle up to her left and slip my hand in hers, loving the way it feels when the ring grazes my palm. Until it comes to fruition, I imagine no other moment or emotion or experience topping this.

After we eat breakfast, Cora starts driving us back toward her house. As much as I want to lay in bed with her curled in my arms, there is something else I want to do. "Do you mind if we make another stop?" I ask.

She glances over at me a second, then faces the increasing traffic. The wind whips her hair across her profile as I inhale a hint of her frankincense-gardenia scent. "Yeah, sure. Where to?"

"I'll give you directions," I tell her.

I guide her through traffic for four or five miles before telling her to pull into a parking lot. When we park, she peers up at the sign, shakes her head, and laughs. "Really? Again?"

Laughing right alongside her, I shrug. "What can I say? There's just something I need to do before we go home."

Cora cocks a brow at me and I know it is due to my casual reference to *home*. But she won't argue with me. For us, home has never consisted of four walls, a floor and a roof. Home has always been when we are together. "Alright."

We get out of the car and walk up to the storefront. I open the door and Cora's eyes scan every inch of the tattoo shop. Luckily, this shop is open more hours than most due to the number of artists. I walk up to the counter and the woman that looks up at me shakes her head. She is the same woman from yesterday. Hot pink hair, the front half rolled up and pinned close to her scalp, the back half left loose to her shoulders. She blows a bubble from her gum and lets it pop like it's second nature.

"Everything okay?" she asks. No hello or how are you. She must assume something is wrong with the tattoo I got yesterday.

"Everything is fantastic," I say and she rolls her eyes. "I'd like to get another tat."

"Oh," she perks up. "Well, the same artist who worked on you yesterday isn't here right now. You cool with that?"

"That's fine. It's nothing extravagant."

After a few minutes, I fill out the same form again and give her my ID. Once the formalities are out of the way, a woman comes out of the back. Her right arm is decked out in a full sleeve of ink. From what I can tell, it appears to reach her back as well. Her hair is a rich, dark brown and she has it pinned in a messy bun with a folded bandana tied at the top. She has this whole 1950s pinup girl/rockabilly vibe going on.

"Hi, I'm Autumn," she introduces herself and shakes my hand. "Looking for something specific today?"

"Gavin. Nice to meet you. Yeah, I want to get a wedding band tattooed on my ring finger."

Beside me, Cora sucks in a sharp breath. No doubt she wasn't expecting that. "Gavin, you don't need to do that," she says.

"I know, baby," I tell her. "But I want the world to know I belong to you. And no one else. Always."

Cora nods and doesn't utter a sound. The tattoo artist, Autumn, guides us back to her booth and has me sit in the chair. Currently, Cora and I are the only patrons in the building. Not having people coming and going right now is nice and odd at the same time. When the gun sparks, Cora startles next to me. I reach out and she takes my hand.

Twenty minutes later, I stare down at the thick black band at the proximal end of my fourth finger. Tears sting the backs of my eyes as a thick boulder of emotion lodges in my throat.

"What do you think?" Autumn asks.

I clear my throat and croak out, "It's perfect."

Cora stares at me in awe and sheer amazement. Then her eyes flick to Autumn. "Have time for me?" she asks.

"Yeah, sure. Just fill out the paperwork and give me a moment to sanitize the station."

Cora hops up and goes to the woman at the front. I amble behind her. "You don't need to get ink unless you want to, baby."

"I know. And I want to."

I nod and watch as she fills out the consent form and provides her license. Ten minutes later, we are back in the booth and Cora is sitting in the chair. Her shirt is hiked up and rests on her bra. Thankfully, the only skin exposed is what anyone would see if she were in a bathing suit. Otherwise, I might have hovered over her worse than a parent of a teenager.

"You ready?" Autumn asks Cora.

She nods and takes my hand. When Autumn presses the pedal and the gun starts buzzing, Cora jumps a little. I draw circles with my thumb over her hand and try to soothe her nervousness. "It only hurts for a minute. Then it numbs a little from the vibration."

The gun draws black lines on her skin just below her left breast. I sit mesmerized as Cora gets her first tattoo. It isn't just the fact that this is her first tattoo, but what she decided to imprint her skin with. Autumn dips the gun in the ink then comes back to Cora's ribcage.

When Autumn swipes some of the excess ink off, I squeeze Cora's hand a little tighter. Cora peeks up at me, her smile brighter than the sunrise this morning.

"You okay?" she asks.

"I didn't think this day could get any better. But I was definitely wrong."

"Wait until you see what I do next." Cora giggles.

Wait, what? Is she getting another tattoo? Maybe she means something completely unrelated. Something when we leave here.

Another ten minutes pass before the tattoo gun is set down and Autumn is cleaning the tattoo and covering it up. Just beneath Cora's left breast rests my name in a feminine font. I am completely awestruck. It was one thing for me to get her name permanently etched into my skin, but I never expected her to reciprocate.

As I stand dazed, Cora asks me to go to the waiting area. For a moment, I am confused and ask her why.

"It's a surprise. Please," she pleads.

I nod and walk out to the waiting area, plop down onto the couch and grab a magazine. Every time I hear Autumn's tattoo gun spark to life, I peer toward the back of the studio. All I see is Autumn's head hunched over Cora.

What is she getting now?

Forever passes and I haven't heard the tattoo gun spark up in minutes. I toss the magazine to the table and rise from the couch. After I wear a new pattern into the linoleum floor, Cora walks back out to the waiting area. I pay and we walk out the door. The walk to the car is silent and I am dying more than ever to know what else she had done.

Once we are in the car, I ask, "So, what else did you get?" For whatever reason, I am more antsy now than I was when I asked Cora to marry me.

Cora faces me and juts her left hand toward me. On her ring finger, where her engagement ring sat less than twenty minutes ago, is a black band of ink that matches mine. It is slightly thinner, but otherwise mirrors mine. "Baby..." I whisper. "You didn't need to do that. I got you rings."

She nods and smiles. "I know, but I want the world to know I belong to you. No one else. Always." Cora throws my sentiment from earlier back at me. It steals my breath and kick-starts my pulse. Thank god we are in the confines of her car, otherwise I may have hit the ground. When I glance down at her right hand, I notice she has moved her engagement ring to that side. She takes stock of where my eyes focus and answers before I ask. "I'm only wearing it on my right while it heals. Promise."

The fact that she worries if it bothers me her engagement ring sits on her right hand is adorable. Honestly, which hand her ring is on is the furthest thing from my mind. Right now, I want to take her home and make love to her until our bodies give out. Celebrate that we are finally getting the happily ever after we deserve after so many years apart.

Today, Cora permanently gave herself to me as I have her. With each passing second, the day gets better and better.

I nod. "Let's go home, baby. I'm dying to make love to my fiancée."

twenty-three

CORA

November 21 - Seven months later

"Come on, Cora. You do *not* want to be late today," Shelly yells from the living room.

"I'll be out in a second," I yell back at her. I scan the room, checking every surface to make sure I haven't forgotten anything. Satisfied, I grab the two bags on my bed then turn and walk out of the bedroom.

When I enter the living room, I glimpse my best friend who is currently trying to wear a new pattern into the wood floor with her heels. She mumbles under her breath, but stops when she spots me.

"Did you feed Luna?" I ask.

"Yes. Everything is done. You ready to go?"

I glance down and inventory the bags in my hands. "Ready," I answer. "Erin picked up the other totes and food already?"

"Yeah, she left a few minutes ago."

I nod. Shelly and I grab our purses, I give Luna one last pat and kiss, then we head out the door. We deposit the bags in her back seat and jump in the front. Seconds later, we are on the road and driving toward Sand Key park.

I stare out the window, take in the blue skies, fluffy white clouds, and sparkling sunlight, then thank the weather gods for keeping everything perfect today.

The weather has turned cool, but it isn't cold yet. Thanksgiving is right around the corner and this year I am thankful more than any year prior. For destiny and Gavin and the best circle of friends a person could ask for. Too often, we take life and the people we see daily for granted. After losing Gavin and getting him back, I take nothing for granted. Each day, I thank my lucky stars life brought us back together.

Over the last seven months, the emotional scale of our friends was all over the place. One day they loved us. The next, they freaked out. Shelly questioned me for hours once I flaunted my engagement ring. She had seen all my tears. All of them. She experienced my pain. Both times. And she wanted to be sure I wasn't acting on a whim. That I hadn't said yes because I felt pressured by the question or situation.

Everyone thought the engagement and us getting married was too soon. Irrational and foolish. That we should wait. Give it a year or so. Especially after rekindling what we once lost. Spend more time learning the adult versions of each other.

"You can't rely on your feelings from the past, Cora." Shelly had said. And I don't.

What I felt for Gavin in our early teen years is nothing compared to what I feel for him now. Circumstances ripped us apart. Tested our strength and ability to love. Time had been our enemy, but also our saving grace. Without time apart, Gavin and I may have become complacent in our relationship. Grown apart. But time hardened us. Made us see the world and life and love in a different light.

When we each hit a point in our lives of numbness, of not caring about anything aside from daily monotony, fate brought us back together. Showed us how life could be if we gave us another chance. The short road was rocky, but our hearts knew from day one.

Hints of skepticism floated in the air from our friends, but every time they saw us attached at the hip with rosy eyes, their doubts were squandered.

Now when I look at my friends, all I see was happiness. For me. For Gavin. And for what we have together.

In no time, we drive into the park and weave around the outskirts. Shelly drives to the designated location, not far from the beach parking, and parks the car.

Soon, we have all the bags out of the car and in the makeshift dressing room. Shelly attacks me with makeup brushes as soon as my butt hits the chair. I close my eyes and let her do her magic while I go to my happy place—Gavin. As Shelly swipes a soft-bristled brush over my cheek, Erin walks into the tent.

"Hey, ladies. How's it going in here?"

Erin is dressed in a knee-length bloodred lacy dress with a nude underlay. Her curly red locks are pinned up in a loose chignon while a few long strands frame her face. Her makeup is subtle and accentuates her freckled skin. Shelly has her hair pinned in the same fashion. And soon, Shelly will don the same dress when she finishes my makeup. Seeing my best friends like this is surreal. For the longest time, I never thought a day like today would be in my future.

"We are on schedule. How's everything else?" Shelly asks Erin.

Erin gives two thumbs up. "All according to plan." Before I can ask what *according to plan* entails, Erin sneaks out of the tent and leaves.

Shelly continues the task at hand. I follow her hands with my eyes and wish there was a mirror nearby for me to catch a glimpse. Considering I barely wear makeup in the first place, it seems as if she put every product from Ulta on my face. As if she reads my mind, she meets my gaze and smiles.

"You don't need to worry about anything. Today will be perfect. Take a deep breath and let everything happen how it's meant to."

I nod, close my eyes again, and let her work her magic.

One breath in. One breath out.

GAVIN

Standing on the semi-warm sand, I wriggle my toes through the soft grains as I peer over my shoulder at the closed-off tent.

Shelly's car is parked just outside the tent, so I know my girl is inside. What are they doing inside that small tent? Can't be much based on the size. And how much longer will I have to wait to see her? I check my watch. Thirty minutes. Only thirty more minutes and she will stand beside me.

I stroll farther down the beach and out of the view of the tent. Popping my earbuds in, I crank up my music and stare out at the water. Feels like it has taken us a century to reach this exact moment, but the day has finally arrived. Finally.

Fifteen years ago today, my best friend became something greater than I could fathom at the time. Something bigger than my fourteen-year-old brain could comprehend or imagine. She became the love of my life. Honestly, she had been since day one, but I wasn't equipped to understand such things.

If we had been together the whole time, no doubt married before now, we would celebrate our fifteenth anniversary today. But rather than celebrate this day as boyfriend and girlfriend—an antiquated term—today, we will officially become husband and wife.

Cora will be my wife. Mine. Forever.

The second everyone found out we were engaged, the first question that popped up was "Have you set a date?" We hadn't discussed dates, but, funny enough, we both blurted out November 21 at the same time. It was our day. Always will be. Until death do us part, and beyond.

Someone taps my shoulder and I turn to see Mom as I take an earbud out. "Hey, sweetie. You should probably get in position. Things will start soon."

I nod. "Thanks, Mom. Love you." I kiss her cheek.

She kisses the air next to my cheek, careful to not smear her lipstick on me. "Love you, too." After a quick hug, she walks off and joins everyone else not in the tent.

I wander toward the makeshift aisle, arch, and chairs. Cora and I are far from traditional. But our style resonates in every flower arrangement, decor piece, and article of clothing we all wear today. We kept the number of attendees to a minimum—twenty people, including Cora's maid of honor and my best man. On the aisle side of each row of chairs is a small bundle of black calla lilies and red roses—identical flowers to Cora's bouquet and the boutonnière flowers. Although Erin isn't in the wedding party, we got her an identical dress to Shelly since she is taking photos for and with us.

The arch at the end of the aisle is decorated in black and red sheer fabrics and flowers. Cora's mother and Shelly did an awesome job with the floral arrangements. They truly scream us and our style. As does our ensemble for the day. Although I have yet to see her dress, Cora and I are both in black. While Shelly and Micah are in red.

I slip my earbuds in their case and set them, and my phone, with my other clothes.

Before I grasp the gravity of it all, I walk down the aisle, bare feet crunching in the sand and heart jackhammering in my chest. When I reach the arch, I spin and stand in my place. Hands clasped at the front of my waist.

Micah walks up and stands beside me and pats my shoulder. "You nervous, bro?"

I stare down the aisle and shake my head. "I've been waiting for this day my entire life. Just can't wait to call her my wife." Those words hold so much truth.

As soon as the words leave my lips, the music starts. "Back In Black" by AC/DC blares from the setup speakers and echoes off the water. This song has nothing to do with weddings or love, but is one-hundred-percent us.

Gavin and Cora.

And the best fucking song to replace the traditional wedding march.

My breath comes in sharp bursts as I fumble with my fingers, eager to see her. One, two, three heartbeats later, Cora steps around a sand dune and I stop breathing. Dress black as night, several layers of tulle ghost the sand as she grips her father's elbow and walks toward me. The V-line bust of her dress is vintage lace that comes to a point at her solar plexus and also decorates the length of her arms.

And just below the hollow of her throat is the locket her mother gave her years ago. A locket that now holds pictures of us.

"Fuck, she is gorgeous," I mutter and a couple people laugh. But I give no fucks. Cora is absolutely stunning and I refuse to take my eyes off her.

That is my wife. Mrs. Cora Elizabeth Hunt. My best friend. My lover. My life.

CORA

I round the sand dune with Dad on my arm, catch sight of Gavin near the arch, and suck in a breath.

Goddamn. I am one lucky-ass woman.

Gavin stands clad in a long-sleeve black button-down, the top two buttons undone, and black dress slacks. His red rose and black calla lily boutonnière rests above his left breast pocket. A thin layer of stubble accentuates his jawline as his hair kicks up with the occasional breeze. And the second he sees me, he bounces a little in place.

At the end of the aisle, Dad clings to my arm and gives me a quick squeeze. "Ready, pumpkin?"

I peek up at him for a split second, then revert my eyes back to my husband —*husband*—twenty feet away. Am I ready? I have been ready for this moment for as long as I can remember. "Yeah, Daddy. I've been ready."

We both take a deep breath, then Dad slowly guides me down the aisle and closer to Gavin. The love of my life. The man I don't ever wish to live a day without. The other half of my soul.

When we reach Gavin, Dad gives me a kiss on the cheek, unhooks his arm from mine, and goes to sit next to Mom.

Gavin and I lock eyes and the world around us disappears. The only other person in our bubble is the ordained minister. He begins speaking the preplanned speech, but neither of us hears a word of it. We are both well aware we don't have lines to speak for at least another minute. Until then, we drink each other in. Bask in the love we share.

I love you, Gavin mouths.

I love you too, I mouth back.

"Gavin and Cora have prepared their own vows and will read them to each other now. Gavin…" the minister says.

Gavin takes a deep, shuddering breath and keeps his gaze locked on mine. "Cora… We have overcome so many obstacles to get to where we are right now. And I'm so glad we did. All that aside, I remember the first day I fell in love with you. The first day of freshman year. Yeah, we were barely friends that day, but one look at you and I knew you were the one. Under that shady oak tree, our tree, everything changed. And afterward, in art, when I caught you drawing me into a self-portrait, I fell even harder."

The backs of my eyes burn. Tears threatening to break free. My throat closes in on itself as emotion chokes me. My fingers wring the stems of the bouquet as I hold his gaze.

"Months later, on this very day, we became more than friends. We became each other's everything. Every single damn day, I am thankful for you. For the love you give me. To have you at my side. To have you in my life. More than anything, I am thankful you gave me your heart and love in return. I've already experienced life without you, and know that will never happen again. Cora Elizabeth Davies, I give you me. All of me. The good, the bad and all the parts in between. I want to experience every day, for the rest of our lives, with you by my side. Forever."

He plucks the matching wedding band for my engagement ring from his pocket and slips it on my finger, resting it atop the tattoo that matches his own, then slides my engagement band on after. I stare down at our hands and breathe easier than I ever have. Everything about this moment, about Gavin and I joining our lives in every possible way, feels more right than anything.

Feels more at home than ever before.

Gavin finishes his vows and I swap my bouquet with Shelly for a tissue. I dab my eyes and take a deep breath. "Cora…" the minister says.

GAVIN

Cora slips her hands into mine and her fingers tremble beneath mine. Her eyes stained red from the happy tears she cried while I said my vows and slipped her wedding band on her finger. She peeks skyward and bats her lashes a few times before bringing her eyes back to mine. Then she smiles and my heart gallops in my chest.

"Gavin…" My name is a prayer on her lips. "You have brought so much into my life. Laughter and love, strength and beauty. Together, we have been through so much. Time may have been stolen from us, but you can't shake destiny. And that's what you are—my fate. My destiny. Fifteen years ago, you became something greater than my best friend. You became my everything. My first boyfriend. My first real kiss. And some things we won't discuss in front of company."

I burst out in laughter and our audience mimics.

"From that fateful first day during freshman year, the one where you sat beside me and ate the nasty school casserole, I knew we would never only be friends. But friends was the perfect place for us to start. Because through our friendship, we fell madly and deeply in love with each other. Gavin, I never want to experience another day of our lives apart. How can I not believe in kismet when it brought you to me more than once? Gavin Eli Hunt—see, even our parents knew we were two halves of a whole and gave us similar middle names. Life without you isn't one worth living and I am eager to see what the future holds for us. I love you beyond comprehension. Will love you until we both take our last breath. Always."

Cora takes my black titanium band in her nimble fingers and slides it up my ring finger. Nothing has felt as amazing as this moment right here. The moment we seal our lives together and become one. A unit.

My life is her life. And hers is mine. My fucking wife.

Fuck.

The tears are coming and I am about to cry like a bitch. But I don't give a shit. This woman is in my blood. My heart. My every breath. And fuck if I don't want to kiss the hell out of her right now.

The minister starts talking and I work hard to listen. Needless to say, it is a challenge. "Cora, do you take Gavin to be your lawfully wedded husband? Through good times and bad, sickness and health, until death do you part?"

Cora's smile brightens the setting sun. "Hell yes."

"That's my girl." I laugh.

"Gavin, do you take Cora to be your lawfully wedded wife? Through good times and bad, sickness and health, until death do you part?"

"Fuck yeah. And we're never dying, baby."

The crowd roars in laughter as the minister pronounces us husband and wife, and finally gives us permission to kiss. I wrap my *wife* in my arms and kiss the fuck out of her. In front of everyone, I kiss her like no one else exists.

Because no one does. And never will. It is just me and my girl. Forever. Always.

Five years later

"You alright, baby?" I ask Cora as we hit the three-mile marker of a five-mile trail in the redwood forest.

"I need a water break."

We stop on the trail and drink water for a minute. We have been hiking a little more than an hour, but we are more than halfway. Cora has been a trooper during this trip. Nonstop adventure. But we plan to only be in California for a couple weeks and I want to show her all the wonderful parts. The places I knew she would fall in love with.

California is definitely different than Florida with all its monster-sized trees and mountains. The scent of the air and saltiness of the water is different too. As much as I miss the landscape and long list of adventures here, I love our little slice of Florida more.

For our five-year anniversary, Cora suggested we come out to California and visit Mom, but also share some adventures of our own. The redwoods, Yosemite, and some of the obvious tourist spots. Our trip so far has been incredible.

Currently, Mom is watching Clara, our three-year-old daughter. Us visiting California is more than a treat for Mom. Not only does she get to spend time with me and Cora, but she also gets to spoil Clara rotten.

Clara is the most amazing gift Cora has given me, aside from her heart. Until the day Cora told me we were pregnant, I never pictured myself as a father. Not that I didn't want to have children with Cora. More like I was so wrapped up in our bubble, I didn't envision beyond it.

But becoming a parent is one of the most awe-inspiring experiences. From learning we would soon be three instead of two to watching my gorgeous wife's belly grow to seeing my daughter enter the world. As a man, I saw the world one way. As a husband, I saw it another. Now, as a father, I see so much more. More love. More possibility. Just more.

"Ready to finish the back half of the trail?" I ask Cora.

"Ready as I'll ever be."

We continue along the rest of the trail, hand in hand. On occasion, we stop and admire something we see. Plants and trees, animals and streams. Nature and wildlife in California are the polar opposite of Florida, and Cora is in seventh heaven. Being in the middle of the forest is one of her favorite things and, every opportunity we can, we adventure somewhere with forestry.

After we reach the end of the trail, we call Mom's house and talk with both her and Clara. Since we are in northern California, we won't be at Mom's tonight to tuck Clara in. Cora and I are staying at a bed-and-breakfast just outside of San Francisco and enjoying a couple days of our anniversary alone.

"Night, night, Daddy," Clara says. Her voice is the cutest thing I have ever heard in my life. The melody is a sweeter, younger extension of Cora. Part of me wonders if Cora sounded the same when she was Clara's age. Either way, it melts my heart and makes me goo in her little hands.

"Night, pumpkin," I say and make a kissing sound into the phone. "Be good for Nana. I love you and we'll see you tomorrow."

"Love you, Daddy."

"Here's Mommy."

I hand the phone to Cora and she and Clara have an in-depth conversation about which is better—chocolate chip cookies or brownies. Cora tells Clara her favorite is the brookie we buy at the vegan bakery near home. Cora yanks the phone away from her ear as Clara starts yelling "brookie" over and over. Clara and Cora exchange goodnights and I love yous before disconnecting the call.

"I really hope Mom isn't feeding her cookies and brownies. We'll never be able to curb her cravings once we leave," I say and wince.

"Yeah, I hope not either."

I drive us back to the bed-and-breakfast and we get ready to go out for our anniversary date. As Cora puts on her jeans and sweater, I notice the way she stares at her outfit with extra scrutiny.

"Everything okay, baby?" I ask as I pull her into a hug.

She snakes her arms around my waist and squeezes me tight. "Everything's fine. Just wondering if I brought warm enough clothes. The weather here is so much different than home."

"You look beautiful," I admit. "And if you get cold, just say the word and I'll keep you warm." I kiss the top of her head.

Once dressed and ready, we head to the restaurant in the city. Since Cora loves everything Asian, I thought she would love tasting how amazing food is out here. We arrive at the restaurant and are seated right away. After we order drinks, I notice Cora didn't get a glass of wine—her typical choice when we go out and don't have to worry about Clara.

Cora plays with her napkin and then places it in her lap. She stares at her lap a minute before locking her gaze with mine. Teeth capture her bottom lip and worry it.

"Baby, you sure everything is okay? You're worrying me."

She releases her lip. A smile brightens her face as she holds my gaze. "We're pregnant." And just like that, her confession steals my breath.

CORA

"Gavin? Did I break you?"

A minute ago, I told Gavin we were pregnant. Again. I expected his response to be like last time. Screams and cheers and swinging me in the air. Instead, he just sits across from me, frozen. A few minutes ago, he said he was worried. Now it seems to be my turn to worry.

Does he not want more children now?

It's not as if we have done much in the prevention department. We have actually been pretty up-front about children and our future. Especially after we learned

I was pregnant with Clara. Since I don't have much time left to safely carry a baby, we thought trying now for a second baby was better than waiting.

But now, his current state has me not so sure.

Finally, his face relaxes. "You took a test?"

"Yeah, a couple days ago, after a trip to the store with your mom. She doesn't know, though."

"Why didn't you tell me you thought you were pregnant? I hate that you were wondering alone."

I didn't have a logical explanation as to why I hadn't told him yet. Guess I just wanted to give it another day or two before I took a test. Plus, we were going on our trip.

"Sorry I didn't let you know I suspected it. I'll blame it on foggy, pregnancy brain. You're not upset, are you?"

Gavin shakes his head. "No, baby, I'm not upset. The opposite actually. I just wish I could've waited for the positive result next to you. I know it's way too early to know, but I hope Clara gets a little brother."

I roll my eyes and he laughs. "I'm sure Clara will love him or her, no matter what gender they are. You sure you're okay, daddy?" Heat pierces Gavin's eyes and I swallow. The same heat that pops up every time I call him daddy… in my seductress voice.

"You don't need to worry about daddy, baby," he growls across the table. "But let's take the rest of the trip easy. Had I known before today, I wouldn't have taken us on a five-mile hike in the mountains."

"I'm not that fragile, Gavin. Besides, I need to maintain my girlish figure for as long as possible. Soon enough, I'll look like a whale."

Gavin shakes his head. "No, baby. You'll be the most beautiful woman in the world, still. There is nothing sexier than the love of my life carrying my unborn child inside her belly. If anything, you get sexier with each stretch mark."

Heat rises to my cheeks. "Gavin…" I whisper.

Dinner goes by much quicker after the *we're pregnant* conversation. Chinese food in San Francisco is phenomenal. Anytime we eat Asian in Florida now, I will undoubtedly whine and complain. Plus, I think pregnancy makes it taste even better.

We arrive back at the bed-and-breakfast and head to our room. Three breaths after the door closes, Gavin and I frantically rip each other's clothes off. In the last five years, a few things have changed in our relationship.

The addition of Clara.

Our need to kiss and grope and be completely consumed by each other.

How much we love each other.

The last two have multiplied to levels I never knew existed. With each passing day, I don't think I can possibly desire or love Gavin more than I already do. But each day I wake up next to him, his warm skin and beachy-pine wrapped around me, I learn a new truth.

Our love is boundless.

Gavin yanks my shirt over my head and tosses it to the floor before bruising my lips with his. The rest of our clothes hit the floor seconds before we land on the mattress. Everything about us—our life, our love—grows hotter with each passing day. As Gavin kisses down my body, he stops and hovers above my abdomen a moment.

"Hey, little man. Yeah, Daddy is predicting you'll be a boy. Don't let me down, okay? Us guys got to stick together." I laugh and Gavin continues. "Anyway, I can't wait to meet you. And for you to meet me and Mommy and Clara, your big sister." Gavin presses his lips to my belly and kisses me tenderly.

Gavin Hunt. My best friend. My lover. The best husband. And an even better father.

"I love you, Gavin," I whisper.

He crawls up my body and kisses me reverently. "I love you, too, baby. Forever."

"Always."

bonus content

GAVIN

Click. Click. Click.

I peer up from the sink to see Cora standing ten feet away with the viewfinder to her eye. Snapping photos of me. Nude. At least the back of my nude body.

Not that I give a damn.

"What're you doing, baby?"

"Capturing the moment."

Click. Click.

There are several other ways I imagine capturing the moment with my *wife*. Between the sheets. In the pool or jacuzzi. On the beach—although, sand and sex are not favorable when mixed together.

"How about I capture…" I trail off and bolt for her.

The second she realizes my motive, she squeals and dashes to the side. But she isn't quick enough and I catch her, toss her on the mattress and gently set her camera aside. Then I kiss my way up the inside of her bare calf. Nibble from her knee, up her thigh and lick inches from the apex of her thighs.

"Gavin," she whispers as her hand fists my hair. When she gets lost to the sensation, I pick up the camera and snap a few pictures of her. Before I take a third, her eyes fly open and her arms drape over her breasts. "What are you doing?" she all but shrieks.

"Capturing the moment, baby." I set the camera back down, peel her arms away and kiss my way up her midline until I reach her lips. "Don't worry. No one will see them but you and me."

Being on the opposite side of the lens is difficult for Cora, but I want more pictures of her. Of us. Especially from this time. Our honeymoon.

When it came to choosing where to go for our honeymoon, all options were possible. Exotic islands, deserts, mountains. Whatever my wife wanted.

But when it came down to it, we ended up staying local. Chose a beach in south county and booked a reservation at a chic resort. Mom took extra time off around the wedding and we wanted to see her more before she flew back to California.

So, we simply chose another beach to see every morning. And the great thing about south county is easy accessibility to the sunrise and sunset.

"Fine." My eyes must bug out of my head at her response because she laughs. "But *no one* can see these."

I nod like a loon. "As if I'd let anyone else catch a glimpse of my naked wife."

And the moment the word wife leaves my lips, a naughty smile I know and love curves up Cora's lips.

"Hey, husband?"

God, I love the way she calls me husband.

"Yes, wife?"

"Let's capture some more moments… in the bed."

Say no more. Husband… reporting for duty. "Yes ma'am."

And right there, tangled in the cotton sheets—with the sliding glass doors open to the beach, the cool salty air on our skin and the crash of the waves in the background—we create more moments. More memories.

Fine Line

INKED DUET
BOOK ONE

<h1 style="text-align:center">prologue</h1>

JONAS

Fuck, she is beautiful.

My best friend. The woman I have loved for years. The woman walking down a sandy aisle in a stunning black lace wedding dress. To another man. A man she has been in love with since high school. A man I will never compare to in her eyes.

And although he broke her heart at sixteen, she never fell out of love with him. Gavin Hunt. The luckiest fucking man on the planet. The man at the end of the aisle holding his breath as she steps closer.

I close my eyes and duck my head. "Can't watch this," I whisper to myself. Because watching the woman I have loved for nearly ten years marry the love of her life is… painful. No, not painful. Debilitating. Excruciating. Crushing.

Fuck, I can't breathe.

Don't get me wrong, my heart holds so much happiness for Cora. Glad she reconnected with the one person who puts a permanent smile on her face. The person who constantly sparks her laughter. Who fulfills her in a way no one else has been capable of for years. As gut wrenching as it is to admit, Gavin is Cora's soul mate. Her *person.*

Once upon a time, I filled the role. For a phase of her life, I was her person. Was the only guy she leaned on for comfort or support. The one person she laughed with and spilled her heart to.

Cora is my best friend.

But she isn't mine.

And as much as it hurts, she never was.

I dreamed of the possibility, but she always tossed out those "you really are a great friend" lines with such ease. Every time she did, it twisted the knife in my heart a little more. Tore away another piece of my soul that I willingly handed her.

The day I met Gavin, the day we all hung out and I witnessed their chemistry for the first time, I threw in the towel. The energy in the room shifted and I witnessed it ebb and flow and magnetize them closer to each other. Cora and I have an undeniable bond, but it paled in comparison to the connection she and Gavin share.

In her own way, Cora loves me. Just not the way I love her.

But now, I have to let her go. Finally let go of the daydream. Let go of the possibility I stood a chance.

Snapping my attention back to my best friend, I memorize her happy, tear-stained face as she speaks her vows to Gavin. Tells him he was her first everything. *Twist.* Jokes how their middle names are similar—another sign they're meant to be. *Deeper. Twist.* Explains how life isn't worth living without him at her side. *Shattered. Split in two.*

I stop watching. Stop listening. My heart balls into a fist, clenches hard, and crumbles to ash beneath my ribcage.

Fuck, this hurts.

As badly as I want to rise from my seat and walk off, I won't. I will not ruin my best friend's wedding with my own selfishness. Won't squash her happiness with my sorrow. I am not that guy. Not an asshole. Or a prick.

Everyone laughs and cheers. I follow suit, not knowing the reason. My laugh floats off with the Gulf breeze, hollow and empty. Like my heart.

I chance a glimpse at my best friend. Bad timing. The moment I choose to look up, Gavin envelops her in his arms and kisses her the way I have always imagined doing. The way that haunts my dreams often.

The next hour trickles by in a fog. Shelly and Erin hang out with me. I remember to smile and laugh and joke at the right times. I hide the fact I am a withering mess inside. People scurry into the reception hall and tell everyone to prepare for the newlyweds. Reminding us to hoot and holler as they enter the room.

I clutch my stomach. *Think I am going to be sick.*

Cora and Gavin enter the room and everyone erupts in cheers and wolf whistles. I mimic with an empty smile plastered on my face.

An emcee announces the newly married couple before soon inviting everyone to eat. I fall in line with Shelly and Erin. They must sense my mood. Neither of them has said a single word to me. Can't blame them, I am shit company right now.

Shortly after everyone eats, Cora and Gavin share their first dance as husband and wife. I struggle to keep my meal down, but I do. I refuse to make a scene. Refuse to ruin this for her.

Shelly elbows me and I peer over at her. "What's up, Shell?" But the moment I look up at her, I realize why she nudged me.

Cora.

The most stunning bride I have laid eyes on is standing beside me with a glowing smile. "Hey you," Cora says. She extends a hand out to me. "Will you dance with me?"

Fuck. *Fuck, fuck, fuck.*

I swallow and work to dislodge the lump in my throat. "Yeah," I choke out before coughing to clear my throat. "Yeah," I repeat.

She smiles as I take her hand and follow her to the dance floor. At the center of the room, she spins around and holds me like we are at senior prom. All too briefly, serenity blankets me. Cora in my arms has always felt *right.*

But she isn't mine. And I need to continue to remind myself of such facts.

"Are you okay?" she asks as we sway back and forth.

I won't lie to her, but the truth hurts like a motherfucker.

"Not so much." I lock eyes with her. "But I'm working on it. Promise."

"Jonas…" Cora smiles, but it doesn't touch her eyes. "Sorry. I wish…"

She doesn't continue. The way she holds my gaze tells me everything she wants to say, but can't articulate the words. How she wishes things could have been different. How she hopes I find happiness like she has. And how much she loves me. *Like family.*

I shake my head and close my eyes. "You have nothing to apologize for, Cora. Life has happened how it's meant to. You're my best friend," I whisper the last line and she lays her head on my shoulder. Closing my eyes, I soak up her warmth and relish the moment. "And no matter what, that will never change."

"Good." She laughs, but it isn't the unrestrained laughter I have heard countless times. "Because you're stuck with me, mister."

For the first time in months, a genuine smile stretches my cheeks and I chuckle.

"Glad to hear it." I take a deep breath and swallow my pride. "Sorry if I haven't been the best party guest."

She lifts her head from my shoulder and I hide the disappointment threatening to flash across my face. "Jonas, you're here. That's all I care about. I don't give a damn what anyone else thinks. We've been through a lot over the years. If you're sad" —she studies my eyes for a minute— "you're entitled to feel how you feel. I'm sorry if this is hard for you. Being here."

The song changes and we continue to sway around the dance floor. Her sparkly green eyes stay on my hazels. The sweet, earthy floral notes of her perfume float in my nose. I will miss this. Miss the little pieces of her I have familiarized myself with over the years. But I need to do right by her. I need to remove the guilt she holds captive because of our bond.

I need to let her go.

For her. For me. For our future friendship.

Swallowing down the pain, I vow to myself to never let her feel guilt or sadness because of me. If I can't have her any way except for friendship, I need to accept it. Accept it and move on. Accept it and allow her to be happy.

"Cora…" I stroke my knuckles over her cheek and sigh when she closes her eyes. "It isn't easy." When I remove my hand, her eyes open and lock on mine again. "But I wouldn't miss this day for anything. The day you told the world you found love and grabbed it by the horns." She giggles and my pulse jump-starts. "Glad I could be here to witness this day. I will always be here. Even if we're just friends."

She lays her head on my shoulder again and snuggles closer to me. "My best friend," she whispers. "I love you, Jonas."

My eyes glaze over and I am damn glad she isn't looking at me right now. Glad she won't witness the dam of tears threatening to unleash. I hug her tight. "I love you, too," I croak.

We dance for the rest of the song in silence. When it ends, Gavin walks over. "May I?" he asks. He fucking asks. If I were in his shoes, I would probably yank Cora out of my arms. But he doesn't because he knows her heart. More than anyone.

I step back and smile. "Yeah, man." I offer Cora's hand to him. As she breaks from my embrace and glides easily into his, I take a deep breath and release her. "Congratulations. Not gonna lie, I'm envious as hell. But I'm happy for you both."

Gavin glances down at Cora and the smile on his face tells me he knows he is a lucky son of a bitch. And he will never fuck this up with her. He faces me again. "Thanks, man. Means a lot. To me and Cora. Don't give up." I flinch for a second and he registers my confusion. "Hard as it is to believe right now, the right woman is out there waiting for you. You're a good guy. Fate won't fuck you over."

Okay. Wasn't expecting that. And I have no clue how to respond. So, I remain tight-lipped.

Cora lays her hand on my bicep. "How could no one love you." She meant it as a rhetorical, so I don't answer her. "I have a sneaking suspicion you'll meet her soon."

"Her?" I ask.

"Yeah. The one. The girl who will seal all the cracks and make you whole again."

This conversation is one of the most awkward of my life. The woman I have loved for almost a decade, the woman I am trying desperately to let go of, is telling me I will soon find the love of my life. Which is supposedly not her.

I nod. "Hope so. I'm gonna head out." I hug Cora and memorize her one last time. We will see each other again, but it won't be the same. Then I extend my hand to Gavin. He shakes it, then surprises me when he pulls me in for a hug.

"Thanks for taking care of my girl when I didn't," he whispers in my ear. "Don't give up, man. Your girl is out there, waiting."

We break apart and I smile softly. "Congrats again." I turn on my heel and head for the exit, keeping the torrent of emotions at bay.

Outside, I bend at the waist and slap my hands to my knees. *"Your girl is out there, waiting."* Yeah, I don't see how that's possible. I hop in the Jeep, crank it to life, and let the tears fall.

I hope you're right.

one

The flashing yellow arrow torments me as I patiently wait for a break in the oncoming traffic. With everyone and their mother out shopping, on the hunt for the deal of a lifetime, the roads are busier than usual.

Black Friday has never really been my thing. People swarming like agitated bees. Fighting over electronics and shoes and kitchen gadgets. Don't get me wrong, I love shopping. Love buying cute new dresses, fun graphic tees, and endless accessories. But you will never find me throwing punches for *things*.

"Caution" by The Killers spills out the speakers as the traffic breaks. I turn onto the side street and hook a sharp right into the tattoo shop parking lot. Driving to the far rear corner, I back into a space, hop out, and enter through the back door.

"Hey, chicky. Busy?" I ask Penny as I wander over to my booth.

She smacks her strawberry bubble gum and shakes her head. "Nah. But it'll pick up soon. You have a packed schedule today."

Mentally, I throw devil's horns with my hands. A busy schedule equals a kick-ass payday. "Awesome. Thanks, Pen."

"Just doing my part," she says as she ambles over to my booth. Penny gives me the rundown on my appointments as I resanitize my workspace. The distinct smell of disinfectant fills the air as I wipe everything down. For years now, this has been my favorite smell. Most of my appointments today are small jobs. A name here, a symbol there, and a couple photos to etch in ink.

"Well, I appreciate you."

Penny curtsies, tilts her head, and smiles wickedly. She is a freaking nut, which is why we are such great friends—and roommates.

"How was the wedding?" Penny asks.

She met the bride and groom months back when they came in to get tattoos. When they invited me to their wedding, she frowned. Think she was a little butt hurt, especially when I didn't RSVP with a plus-one. She will get over it.

"Gorgeous," I say with a green man on my shoulder. "Lots of black." I laugh. "But mostly beautiful. They're so sweet together. I envy their connection."

The green devil pops back up on my shoulder as I recall Cora dancing with a man other than Gavin. Remember the way he held her. The glints of his profile in the dim, shimmering lights. He held her closer than a typical friend. But the exchange didn't faze Gavin whatsoever.

A balloon swells in my chest as I reminisce over the way he held her. I ache to be wrapped in someone's arms like Cora was his. To feel wanted and loved without effort.

"Yeah, they seemed pretty inseparable when they came in. How does one nail down a guy like that?" Penny asks as she rests her thumb and forefinger against her chin, inquisitive.

"Not sure. If you figure it out, let me know."

I finish organizing my booth and Penny goes back to her seat at reception. Soon, the bell hanging over the door chimes and the bodies flood in. Reznor strolls in and starts cleaning his booth after he throws me a wave. I toss one back before Penny hands me my first client's paperwork.

Name—Sean. Age—eighteen. Tattoo—the name "Nina." Placement—over his heart.

I avert my eyes to the floor and roll them. *Kids...* will they ever learn to not tattoo names on themselves? No. Fingers crossed Nina is his mom. But, deep down, I know it isn't.

My guess? Nina is the bouncy girl on his right, gripping his hand like a vise. The girl smiles at Sean as if he is the reason she breathes. Hope she feels that way for many years to come. Him, too.

"Sean," I call out as I wander over to the couches in reception.

He kisses her knuckles and hops up. "That's me," he says. "Can she watch?"

I nod. "Sure. Come on over." I wave them over to my booth, then point at the chair. "Have a seat." Scanning over the paperwork one last time, I review his tattoo with him and verify the placement. After he agrees on a font, I print "Nina" on the transfer paper, moisturize his young, hair-free chest, and apply the stencil.

The next hour is full of minor flinches and loud hisses. When I set the tattoo gun down, he sucks in a lungful of air. I spray a paper towel and wipe it across the fresh ink as I explain tattoo care to him. He nods at all the right times and smiles feverishly when I hand him a mirror and he stares at the tattoo for the first time.

When he rises from the chair, he wobbles in place. "Be sure to grab a bite to eat when you leave here." I point to who I still assume is Nina. "Please don't let him drive until he eats." She nods and they head over to Penny to pay, leaving me a gracious tip.

The day trickles by much the same as usual.

My next appointment wants an old photo of her grandparents tattooed on her bicep with dates and the single word "forever" underneath. The memorialization is sweet, really. I press the pedal and the gun vibrates to life in my hand.

As I engrave her grandparents into her skin, the woman shares their story. How they met in a hospital during the Vietnam War and her grandmother nursed him back to life. How her grandfather could no longer fight on the front lines because he was too severely wounded to stand with his comrades. How pissed her grandfather was and how quickly he got over it because he saw a "pretty nurse lady" every day.

The way she conveys the love story of her grandparents, there was no doubt she heard their story firsthand hundreds of times.

Far too often, I dream of a love like theirs. One I hug close to my heart and brag to others about. *Maybe one day*, I mentally profess.

Halfway through, the woman closes her eyes with a smile on her face and remains silent for the rest of the session. While she zones out, so do I.

Every time a person sits in my chair or stretches out across my table, I mentally prepare for all or nothing. Clientele come in mixed bags. From nervous to somber to never-ending bursts of energy. Some talk your ear off for days. Others never speak a word. Then you get the ones who do a mix of both. Those who talk because they are nervous or shy, then quiet down once the initial buzz wears off.

I love it. Love my job. Love all the wonderful—and crazy—stories I hear. It's kind of like reading a new book every couple of hours. Living in someone else's shoes for a snippet of time.

When I finish up my second appointment, I clean and prep my station for the next—who Penny said is already here. After I wipe everything down, I pick up the clipboard with his paperwork and scan it.

Great. One of those. Lucky me (insert sarcasm anytime you would like).

My next client—male—wants the word "heaven" inked into his skin. No big deal, right? Sure, if he was getting it in any other location. I roll my eyes and lay out the narrow massage table in my booth. Because my next client is getting "heaven" tattooed an inch or two above the base of his penis.

Dumbass. Arrogant dumbass.

Penny waltzes over and sniggers as I lay paper gowns on the table. "Hope he's hung, otherwise a lot of people will be disappointed when they don't reach heaven as indicated."

I slap her arm and laugh. "Shut. Up." I shake my head. "How am I supposed to concentrate and act professional when you say shit like that?"

Penny shrugs, pops her pink bubblegum, and skips back to the reception area. Halfway across the store and I still hear her giggles.

Walking over to the waiting area, I retrieve Mr. Heaven and bring him to my booth. Without shame, I admit he is hot. Inches taller than me. Tan skin like he just left Clearwater Beach minutes ago. Bulky muscles showcasing his arms and legs.

But as I have learned, not all those qualities add up to "heaven" in the bedroom. I cough into my elbow to cover the laugh bubbling up my throat.

Get it together, Autumn.

"Any particular font you were looking for?" I ask.

He shakes his head. "Maybe old English. Something masculine."

I show him a few variations and he chooses one. Once I have the transfer paper ready, he shoves his sweatpants down until he exposes his hairless skin and I glimpse the base of his penis.

Ugh, this is going to be a long—ha ha—and awkward session.

Mr. Heaven raises his arms and tucks his hands under his head. He has the audacity to smirk at me. Cocky bastard. Can't wait to wipe the smirk from his face when the gun bites his skin.

An hour and a half and an H-E-A-V later, Mr. Heaven isn't as suave as he thought he was. *Ha! Take that!* A sick pleasure floats in my veins each time he jerks or flinches or hisses. *Hope it is worth it, buddy.*

As I am midway through the second E, the bell over the door jingles. When I lift the gun away from Mr. Heaven's skin and wipe the excess ink away, I glance up and spot Penny chatting with the guy who walked in.

I stop breathing. Stop thinking. Stop everything.

"You good?" Mr. Heaven asks.

Snap out of it Autumn. "Yeah, sorry." Mr. Heaven glances to the man up front. "Thought it was a friend of mine," I say to cover up my flounder.

"No worries," he says as I finish working on the end of his tattoo.

Every now and again, I peer up and see the man is still here. Currently, he sits on one of the couches as he flips through the artist's albums. He studies the photos with obvious interest. From my vantage point, I sporadically—and, fingers crossed, inconspicuously—survey him.

He hunches over an album as he flips the pages. His milk chocolate hair sticks out in different directions on top of his head—the underside buzzed short. When he swaps albums, I spot some of the ink between the bottom of his shirt sleeve and his elbow. Sacred geometry. Interesting.

I focus on Mr. Heaven as I finish the last of the N. As soon as I set the gun down and glance over at Penny, album-flipping guy waves at her and walks out the door. All I got was his backside.

But what a glorious backside it was.

Mr. Heaven rises from the table and hobbles over to the floor-to-ceiling mirror and inspects his fresh ink. He smiles like the cocky bastard he is. Penny cashes him out and he tips me well.

"At least Mr. Heaven was good for something," I say with a giggle as Penny heads my way.

"Yeah. But, girl, I'd climb that stairway to heaven." As if on cue, "Stairway to Heaven" by Led Zeppelin plays through the shop's speakers.

We both fall into a fit of laughter as I play slap her arm. "Shut up. You're sick." She shrugs without care. "Who was the guy?" I point to the door as if it explains who I am referencing.

When Penny deciphers who I am talking about, she smiles. "Your final on Wednesday. Hottie, huh?"

"Only saw the top of his head and a few inches of his bicep," I fib and pray she doesn't notice. Now is not the time for me to go into my starry-eyed moment. Fact is, I noticed so much more. But if Penny hears that, she will give me shit until Wednesday.

"Well, he'll be the cherry on your hot fudge sundae." Penny fans herself. "Let me just say it was hard not staring the entire time he was here."

Tell me about it.

"Stop," I tease. Couldn't place it, but something felt oddly familiar about him. "What's his name?"

Penny studies me a moment as I go through my usual sanitizing procedure. *Spray. Wipe. Repeat.* "Jonas. Why?"

I shake my head. "No reason. Just looked familiar. But I don't know a Jonas." I shrug and continue as if unfazed.

"You will," she teases and walks off.

I will. But something tells me I already do.

My last client is quick and easy. A young woman. I tattoo the kanji symbol for fierce on the back of her neck. The entire time I have the gun in my hand, my mind wanders to the tall, chocolate-haired man. His stature and sullen demeanor. Somehow, someway, I know him. Just can't place from where.

In my line of work, I see thousands of faces a year. Is there a possibility I inked his skin before? Maybe. But I would remember him. His broad shoulders and creamy brown locks. His long legs and strong hands. His stare-worthy ass as he strode out the door.

Jonas.

Don't remember a Jonas. And I would *definitely* remember him.

When I finish cleaning up my booth for the night, I walk over to Penny. "See you at home. Drive safe."

"You, too. Love you."

"Love ya, chicky."

I unlock my '57 Bel Air, slip inside, and spark the engine to life. Scanning my music, I tap on a rock playlist and sing along as I roll out of the parking lot. The entire drive home, I sing the songs I have heard hundreds of times, but don't hear now. Because my mind is stuck. Stuck on the future. On Wednesday, and a mysterious man named Jonas.

Consider me screwed.

JONAS

I pick up Spartan's leash and he yaps, running excitedly in circles around the living room. "Come here, nut. Have to put your leash on if you want to see Grandma and Grandpa."

Spartan drops his front legs to the floor—his hindquarters still up as his tail swats the air. I step closer to him and he pivots sideways. We do this a few times, mixed in with more barking. The same game happens every Wednesday when we head to my parents' house for dinner. I grab the leash and my goofy as hell, three-year-old fur-child loses his shit.

At least he brings a smile to my face.

"You want to see Grandma?"

Woof, woof, woof.

"Well, we have to put on your leash." I flick the clasp a few times and he jumps. "Get over here, dude."

Woof, woof, woof.

I rest my hands on my hips and give Spartan the look that says *we are not going anywhere until you put on your leash.* And just like that, he wags his tail, steps forward, and stands tall at my side.

Once I lock his leash in place, we head out the front door and hop in my Wrangler Sahara. When we are both in the cab, I connect his collar to a safety harness in the car. Last thing I need is my little man jumping out of a moving car because he spots a cat. His crazy ass would, too.

Windows down, I drive down the street and head toward my parents' house. Spartan hangs his head out the window with his mouth open as he squints at the oncoming wind. The temperature in our part of Florida is still warm—a toasty eighty-two degrees at four thirty—but you can feel a shift in the air. Not just the cooler days as we transition to Florida's version of winter.

Something else lingers in the air. A new beginning, maybe. Whatever it is, it terrifies and invigorates me.

I stick my arm out the window and shift it up and down in a wave motion. Glancing over at Spartan, I soak up a little of his boisterous energy. Smile at his silliness as he tries to bite the wind. Every time I peek over at him, I am grateful he is in my life. If not for this crazy as hell husky, I would be drowning in alcohol or in a hole somewhere. He keeps me going.

Thirty minutes later, we park along the street at my parents' house in St. Petersburg. I jump out and Spartan barks at me as if I forgot him. Opening his door, I loop the leash around my wrist before unclipping his car harness. Once I do, he flies out of the car and yanks me toward the house. I barely get the car door closed.

"Who's excited to see Grandma?" I announce as Spartan drags me inside.

"Where's my good boy?" Mom calls back. "Where's my Sparty?"

I drop Spartan's leash and he scrambles across the floor in her direction. Mom has her arms open as she squats down and waits to hug Spartan. He bolts into her arms and it is a hugging and licking contest between the two of them. Spartan's the only one doing the licking, obviously.

Wandering into the kitchen, I step up behind my older sister, Jasmine, and peek over her shoulder. She is so focused on stirring the hamburger meat on the stove, she doesn't hear me come in. *Perfect.* Slowly, I bring my hands to her sides before going all in and tickling the hell out of her.

"Ah!" she screams, dropping the spatula. "Stop, stop, stop." I tickle her harder. "Jonas! Please…" She laughs so hard she snorts. "Please."

"Mommy, Mommy, Mommy!" My nephew, Lex, comes barreling around the corner. "I save you from Unkie Jonas." Lex is armed with his favorite stuffed animal and ready to whack me with it.

I drop my hands and step back. "Whoa, buddy." Scooping him off the floor, I twirl him in a circle. "I stopped. Please don't get me."

Lex stares over at Jasmine with the most serious expression I have ever seen on his face. "Okay, Mommy?" Such a protector at two years old.

She ruffles his hair and kisses his forehead. "I am now. Thanks for saving me from Uncle Jonas."

He nods with enthusiasm and I set him back on the tile. "Hey, buddy. Why don't you go play with Grandma and Spartan. I'll help Mommy in the kitchen." Without so much as another glance in my direction, he bolts from the kitchen and calls across the house for Spartan.

"We're making tacos tonight, if you want to dice onions and tomatoes and slice up some lettuce," Jasmine says.

I hug her from behind and kiss the top of her head. "On it." Grabbing the produce from the fridge, I step up to the counter beside the stove and get to work. "Anton here?" I ask.

Anton, my big sister's husband, doesn't always make it to Wednesday night dinners. Depending on his work schedule, sometimes he doesn't beat the Tampa traffic when he leaves work. If he runs too late on Wednesdays, he heads home and Jasmine brings him leftovers. Nine times out of ten, though, he makes it. For the most part, investment banking has a set schedule. Only time his schedule changes is when the firm gets a new client.

"Yeah, he's out back with Dad."

Garlic, peppers, and smoked paprika float in the air and my mouth waters. "Hey, we having grilled onions and peppers?"

"If you cut 'em, I'll cook 'em."

My sister and I work in the kitchen like a well-oiled machine. When we were growing up, oftentimes we cooked dinner for everyone. Dad sometimes got stuck at the shop late, while Mom was wrapping up her latest words of wisdom for the local newspaper's advice column. And sometimes our baby sister, Jillian, got hungry earlier than everyone else. Mom taught us early on how to fend for ourselves and help around the house. We didn't always have to, but we loved giving her a break from the kitchen after a really long day.

I chop up large chunks of onion and bell pepper for Jasmine. She rotates between all the burners on the stove, stirring the taco meat, a pot of beans, another with corn, and now the onions and peppers. On the fifth burner—whoever came up with that idea is brilliant—is Tex-Mex rice. Once I finish with the veggies, I shred a big bowl of cheddar cheese and lug out the other toppings. Just before everything is ready, I lay the taco shells on a tray and toast them in the oven for a minute.

A moment later, I wander to the sliding glass doors that lead to the back patio and pool and poke my head out. "Dinner's ready."

Dad and Anton pop their heads up simultaneously as Dad rubs his hands together. "Perfect timing. I'm famished."

Everyone piles up their plates—Anton helps Lex with his—and we all sit down at the table built for six, but extends out for ten. We all wait to start eating until Jasmine has Lex situated in his booster chair. We have never been a religious family, but Mom always likes to say a few words of gratitude before we eat.

"I'm so glad everyone could be here tonight." Spartan barks in the living room and we all laugh. "You, too," Mom says. "Seriously, though. I'm grateful to have all three of my kids here, plus Anton and my baby boy, Lex. You all are the highlight of my week."

Smiles and *awes* spread throughout the room. Moments like these are my favorite. Of course, we banter. What family doesn't? But these moments are the ones I hold close when I have a bad day. Like watching my nephew make a hot mess of his tacos and hearing my Mom laugh when my dad leans in and whispers in her ear. Truly the best.

"So, what's new with you, oh quiet brother of mine?" Jillian teases.

Jillian was a surprise baby. But she is the best little sister anyone could ever ask for. She keeps me levelheaded with her jokes and nagging. Where Jasmine is two years older than me, Jillian is seven years younger. For a mature young woman, sometimes she still acts like a teenager. She gives me clarity when I am stressed and makes me laugh when I am down.

"Nothing exciting," I answer. "Same stuff, new day. What about you? How's the wild world of fashion?"

She rolls her eyes. "Nice avoidance tactic, big bro. The store is great. Just got a glimpse at the spring line. We're putting in out just before Christmas."

I cock my head and stare at her. "It's not even winter, technically. Why so early?"

"You have so much to learn, dear brother. It's kind of like when car dealers put the next year's model out months before the year begins. Sales tactic." Jillian taps the side of her head as if her brain holds all the secrets.

. Jillian is smart. Not like Mensa-smart, but pretty damn close. Her IQ is stellar. She graduated Salutatorian of her class in high school and graduated two years early—with honors—from college where she studied business and marketing.

At least she went to college. My path has been carved in stone since I picked up a wrench in Dad's garage. You don't need college to be a mechanic, but I did attend a trade/vocational school. I wanted the merits under my belt. Plus, school taught me more of the computerized auto information Dad occasionally searched for online. This way, we both brought something to the table.

And one day, when Dad finally decides it is time to retire his coveralls, I will take over Thompson's Garage and Body Specialists. Dad put a lot of time and energy and grease into our shop. I want him to be proud when I take over.

"I will never understand fashion," I tell her.

"True. And you're still avoiding my question," she repeats and I hang my head. The table goes silent and Jillian leans in closer. "If you don't want to talk about it, just tell me to shut up."

I laugh and she backs away. "You're fine. Just been a rough week. But I'll be okay. And if not, you can tease me more." Off in the living room, Spartan barks. "You, too, buddy," I shout.

The rest of dinner goes by a little quieter. Conversations and laughter still carry on around the table, but the mood has tapered. They all know about Cora. Hell, they have met her and invited her to dinner a few times. They knew we were just friends, but thank god they bit their tongues about more. It has been obvious for years I had feelings for Cora, but no one ever shed light on those feelings. Which makes this whole new awkwardness a little less weird. Only a little, though.

Once everyone finishes eating, I help clear the table. "Hey, Mom?"

"Yeah, honey." She sidles up next to me and wraps her arm around my waist.

"You mind if I head out? Know it's early, but I have an appointment at eight."

She squeezes me harder for a second, then releases me. "Sure thing. What's the appointment?"

"Time to brighten up the canvas," I say with a smile on my face.

It is no secret Mom isn't a fan of tattoos, but she never judges. "Just don't understand the desire to sit in a chair for hours, in pain, while someone paints lines on your skin."

I laugh. "Maybe one day I will better explain it to you, but I need to head out so I'm not late." I kiss her forehead and she hugs me as close as humanly possible.

"See you next week. Love you."

"Love you, too," I tell her.

After I make my rounds, I leash Spartan and drive home to drop him off. Thankfully, the tattoo shop is close to the house. I check the time on the dash as we drive away from Mom and Dad's. Spartan barks his goodbye before resuming his usual car window position.

～

I arrive at the tattoo shop with ten minutes to spare. Perfect amount of time to fill out paperwork and mentally prepare myself for being in the chair for more than an hour.

A bell chimes when I open the door and step inside. The same woman sits behind the counter. Her hot pink hair reminds me of the color candy companies give artificial watermelon. Nothing like the actual color of the fruit. She twirls a finger around the locks on her shoulders while she pops her bubble gum.

All I do is laugh internally. She is a strange mix of pinup girl and grunge princess. Hair to the nines. Clothes casual and baggy. I wonder if she dresses like this outside of the tattoo shop?

I step up to the counter. "Hey," I say, giving a small wave. "Jonas. I have an appointment."

Bubble gum princess peeks up at me and sits a little straighter. "Hey, Jonas." The way she says my name insinuates she holds secrets about me. She grabs a clipboard and hands it to me. "Fill this out and I need to make a copy of your ID."

Fishing my license out of my wallet, I hand it to her before sitting on one of the couches and filling out the standard paperwork. Once I finish, I hand it back to her and she hands me my license with a smirk.

"She'll be with you in a minute, sugar."

While I wait to be called back, I mindlessly stare at the funky art on the walls.

Each drawing and painting has one of the shop's artist's name below with a price tag. Kind of cool the artists put work on display to show their individual talents.

"Jonas?" a soft, cheery voice calls out.

"That's…" I spin around and stop short at the petite brunette staring at me. Clearing my throat, I try again. "Sorry. I'm Jonas."

She smiles and the room brightens instantly. "Autumn. Follow me." I follow in her wake as she leads me to her booth.

Unabashedly, I check her out as she walks in front of me. Autumn is roughly six inches shorter than me, but leggy as hell. In a pair of black and white plaid-like skinny pants which hug every curve and a black top with straps looping around her neck and a dangerous dip at her cleavage. Her hips sway slightly when she walks, and I remind myself to keep my eyes at a gentleman's level—up. As we reach her booth, I notice the bandana in her hair. It matches her pants and is a simple accessory to her pinned-up locks.

"Have a seat," she says, gesturing to the chair in her booth. "Your paperwork says you're wanting to continue one of your half sleeves."

I nod and search for my voice. *Use your words, Thompson.* "Yeah. I brought the drawing with me." I hand over a folded paper.

Autumn takes the paper, unfolds it, and studies the intricate artwork. Artwork I spent weeks drawing. This piece is my right arm. The left is similar in design, but not the same. Only a true enthusiast would detect the dissimilarity.

She examines the lines, dots, and shading on the paper, then peers over at my arm. After several back and forth examinations, I wonder if it would be easier for me to take off my shirt. My shirt sleeves block at least half of the current art on my skin, and she is probably gauging where to start.

"Need me to take off my shirt?" I ask.

Her eyes lift from the paper and meet mine. *Fuck.* The most delectable glass of cognac stares back at me. Dark chocolate rims her irises, softening from brown to a golden, bold orange near her pupils. A light rouge pinks her pale cheeks.

"Um." She swallows. "Probably a good idea," she mumbles. "So I can see what's already done, of course."

Is she nervous? If so, it is adorable as fuck. Seriously, she has to have seen hundreds of people in her line of work. Work in the oddest places and a plethora of designs. I cringe mentally at the idea of her tattooing some asshole in awkward places. But pricks like that exist.

"Of course." I smile and tug my shirt over my head. If possible, her cheeks darken from a gentle blush to the soft petals of a pink rose and a surge of excitement floats beneath my sternum.

She swallows again and blinks rapidly. Her eyes drop back to the paper as she tucks her cherry red lips in her mouth. Is she fighting off a smile? When she keeps her eyes downcast too long for my liking, I lay my shirt over my chest in the hopes she will look up again. I need another shot of her cognac irises.

As soon as my torso is covered, she sighs. *Sighs.* The sound a mix of disappointment and relief. Dear god. This is going to be one of the longest tat sessions in history. And she won't even finish the rest of the design tonight.

Studying the current ink on my skin against the drawing, she bites the corner of her lip. I avert my gaze to the ceiling and pray to someone holier than me.

Please let me get through tonight unscathed. Please let me get through this without the embarrassment of a hard-on. At this rate, there's a high likelihood. I beg you, please.

"Be right back," Autumn says as she rises from her stool and strolls out of the booth. Once again, my eyes wander to her backside until she is out of sight.

I slide my shirt down and expose my skin to the cooler air. Let it temper my overheated skin as I take a few deep breaths.

But the fire Autumn created still burns hot. I love and hate how it simmers in my veins.

What the fuck is happening?

Jonas's eyes scald me as I walk out of the booth. For the first time in years, I enjoy male attention. Jonas's attention. His eyes on me make my blood pump harder, faster.

As I make copies of his design to cut and put on transfer paper, Penny sneaks up from behind. "I was right, he is a hottie."

I jump and slap a hand to my chest. "Jesus, Pen. Don't do that."

"Do what?" She feigns innocence while smacking her bubble gum. Why didn't I hear the distinctive smack of her lips as she came up behind me?

"Scare the shit out of me."

She throws her head back and laughs. I glance over at Jonas—who seems oblivious to Penny's obnoxious chortle—then back at my friend. I narrow my eyes at her and she lifts her hands in surrender. "Sorry, not sorry. But I wasn't lying. He is hot."

I focus on my task—Jonas is a paying client, after all. "Yeah, I guess." A heatwave spreads across my skin.

Penny leans in closer and scrutinizes my every move. "You guess?" Keeping my head down, I peek up at her. She smiles at me with wicked intent. "Girly, you must be blind if you don't recognize a good-looking man when you see one."

The printer finishes and I grab the transfer paper. "I'm not blind. Okay? Just trying to breathe through the next two hours of my night. So" —I point to her chair — "go back to your desk and do what you do. And don't pester me. Last thing I need is to fuck up his tattoo."

She giggles, salutes me, and walks off. "Yes, dear."

I take a deep breath and gather my wits.

You can do this, Autumn. He is just another guy in your chair. A hot guy. Shut up!

When I turn the corner of my booth and glance over at Jonas, I stop breathing. Since I left, he has pushed his shirt down his chest and sits perfectly still with his eyes closed. Is he sleeping? Stepping over to my stool, I set the papers down on the counter. His eyes remain closed as I start prepping for our session.

Part of me wants his eyes open. A big part.

As if I professed it aloud, Jonas opens his eyes just as I glance up at him. My stomach flips and I swallow. I have never seen eyes like his. Such fascinating shades of blue with a burst of sunshine at the center. As if his DNA couldn't decide whether to make his eyes blue or hazel. I prefer the indecision.

"So, I printed off more than what I'll actually work on tonight. Some of what I printed, you already have done. But I did that so I could line it up."

Jonas nods. "No problem. You know what you're doing. I'm not concerned."

He closes his eyes and lays his head back again. My whole body sags at the loss. "I need to shave your forearm. Thankfully" —I trace the corded muscles in his forearms with my fingertips— "most people won't notice the difference." His eyes pop open and lock on mine. I try swallowing the lump in my throat. "Your arms aren't really hairy. It won't look weird when I shave it, is what I mean."

He smiles and a dimple accentuates his left cheek. A dimple I want to kiss.

Shut up, Autumn. He is your client.

"I don't care either way."

When I think he is going to close his eyes again, he surprises me. Instead, his eyes drop to where I lather soap on his arm. I dry off the gloves and pick up a disposable razor. Inch by inch, I swipe the razor over his skin. Finished, I wet a paper towel and wipe away any excess soap.

After I rub a thin layer of natural moisturizer on his skin, I line up the stencil on his forearm and press it in place. I peel back the paper and smile at the purple lines on his skin. On the small rolling table next to my stool, I set his original drawing next to the small ink caps filled with black ink.

Jonas closes his eyes again as I go through the process of opening the sterile needle pack and loading it on my gun. I run through my usual routine and make sure I have everything ready before I start. Once everything is set, I pick up the gun and press the pedal on the floor.

When the gun buzzes to life in my hand, the old familiar joy of why I do this kick-starts my adrenaline.

As a child, I always loved to color and draw. The older I became, the more I honed my craft. I took every possible elective art class in school. Somehow, I also managed to coerce the art teacher during my sophomore year to give me art lessons outside normal class hours. We worked at the school, of course, and she gave me extra credit—which I didn't mind, but also didn't ask for. Through Ms. Gibson's lessons, I learned to love art over everything. She taught me every medium and how to open my imagination beyond what the human eye sees.

I took those lessons and the skills I learned, and eventually discovered my preferred canvas. Skin.

Leaning forward, I stretch the skin near Jonas's elbow and press the buzzing needle forward. He startles, then relaxes. "Okay?" I ask, not looking up.

"Yeah," he answers, voice scratchy. "No matter how many times I've been under the needle, when it first hits my skin, I jump."

I nod but don't look up. "Me too."

For the first ten or fifteen minutes, I work in silence and locate my rhythm. Every person you work on is different. Depending on their age, how often they are in the sun, and how well they take care of themselves determines how easy or difficult it is to work on them. Skin is skin. But at different stages of life, it has different density and elasticity. The older you are, the thinner your skin is. It is a natural progression. Also, the more exposed to the elements—sun, wind, level of humidity, and so on—you are, the more your skin is impacted.

Jonas has nice skin. Slightly tan. Not the type of tan you get from regular visits to the beach. Jonas's tanned skin is from everyday activity—mowing the yard, jogging outdoors, driving with his arm out the window or the top down. For a moment, I picture him in a lush, green yard. Black shirt stretched taut on his broad chest. Khaki cargo shorts hanging low on his hips. A bright smile and that adorable dimple on his face as he pushes a little girl on the swings.

I lift the gun from his skin, turn my face away from him, and cough into my elbow.

Stop it, Autumn.

"Grab some water," Jonas says as I spin back his way.

"I'm good. Just a tickle." I play off the softball-sized lump of emotion in my throat. What I need is a distraction. "So, Jonas…" His eyes shift from my hand dipping the needle in the ink cap to my eyes. "Tell me about yourself."

His Adam's apple bobs in my periphery before he sits a little taller. "What would you like to know?"

I bring the gun back to his arm and spark it to life again. "Girlfriend? Wife? Kids? All the good stuff."

"The good stuff, huh?" He snorts and I peek up at him for a second before refocusing on my work. "I'd laugh, but I don't want to throw you off." Out of the corner of my eye, he points to where I am currently working on a flower of life pattern.

"I appreciate that. No way I'd be able to sleep if I jacked up your tat."

"Good stuff," he mumbles then goes silent for a moment. "No girlfriend or wife." And I can tell—without looking up—his face is turned away. It piques my curiosity. "No kids. Unless fur children count. If that's the case, then I have one. Spartan. He's three."

"Spartan. He a fighter?" I ask.

He laughs, but not enough to jostle his arm. "Nah. He's a big softy. Fifty-seven pounds of pure energy. Loves hugs and barking."

Now it is my turn to laugh. "What kind of dog is he?"

"Husky."

I pause and meet Jonas's eyes. "So, a fur baby. But no fur baby mama?" My retort is meant to be funny, but a gray cloud suddenly masks his joy.

"Nope. No fur baby mama."

I hate how sad he sounds right now. Hate that I wrecked his mood. "Want to talk about it?"

First and foremost, I am no therapist. But far too often, people sit in this chair and spill some of the craziest details of their life history. Some fascinate me. Others… not so much. But I have learned over the years to just go with the flow. If people need to get things off their chest, I let them. Not like I am the gossiping sort.

"Yes. No. I don't know." He looks away and I slump at the obvious discomfort I spurred.

Instead of pestering him, I continue working on his tat. If Jonas wants to divulge whatever is bothering him, he will. A few minutes pass and neither of us says a word. But I feel his eyes on me. Not on my hand as it holds the gun and carves intricate black lines into his skin. No, his eyes are on *me*. A buzz ripples through my body. A buzz that has absolutely nothing to do with the tattoo gun vibrating in my right hand.

"My best friend just got married," he whispers. Voice so soft I almost miss it.

I stop working and gauge his expression. Eyes sad. Smile absent. Shoulders low. Everything in his body language tells me he is upset or disappointed over this marriage. "Not my place to ask, but shouldn't you be happy for him?"

"Her," he corrects.

Ah. There it is. The fine line detail. His female best friend just got married. And he isn't too keen on the idea.

"Shouldn't you be happy for her?"

He nods. "As painful as it is, I am happy for her. She's with the one person she can't live without. They've known each other since high school, but his family moved away when he was in high school. They reunited this past spring."

There is a peculiar familiarity to the story he tells me. Could be sheer coincidence. But it might not be. What are the odds?

"This might be weird." And suddenly, I have his full attention. "But is your best friend Cora?"

His eyes widen at the mention of her name and a ball of jealousy forms beneath my diaphragm. His expression tells me he considered her more than a friend, but she never did. Most women would cringe at the notion. Me? I bask in it.

Bask in the fact he never overstepped his bounds with her. As quickly as my jealousy formed, it melts away.

Over the last seven months, I got to know Cora. Mostly through text and the occasional girls' night, where we had dinner and a movie at her house. She is super sweet. Told me about this guy she had known for years—who she had given the same title. Best friend.

Don't know the dirty details of Jonas's life, but I do know Cora thinks highly of him.

"He just needs to find the right woman, you know. Someone who will make him smile and laugh. Someone who will hug him tight and make every day better than the last."

Her words come back to me from a couple weeks ago at her bachelorette party. I had no clue who she was talking about, but she wanted to make it her life's mission to see her best friend happy.

Now I know why.

He swallows. "Yeah. You know her?"

I lock eyes with him and nod. "Yep. Did her and Gavin's tattoos back in April. We've chatted and hung out here and there. Attended their wedding." His eyes sparkle at this fact. "She never mentioned your name. And, obviously, we never all hung out at the same times."

"Obviously." He averts his gaze and mumbles, "I would definitely remember you."

I smile at the words I am sure he didn't mean for me to hear. "Back atcha."

He faces me again with a soft smile on his lips. "It hasn't been easy seeing her with Gavin, but I keep telling myself everything happens for a reason. Keep reminding myself she was never mine to keep. Not in the way I originally intended."

I continue working on his tattoo. "Sometimes, people come into our life to teach us something. Not necessarily like an actual teacher. In your case, maybe Cora taught you how to open your heart. How to love someone in a nonfamilial way. She may not be the person you're meant to love, but she helped teach you what love *feels* like."

He sits quietly in the chair for a few minutes as I get closer to the center of the flower of life in the middle of his forearm.

Did I say too much? Go too far?

From what Cora told me, her "best friend"—aka Jonas—has crushed on her for years. Several years. Honestly, I lived vicariously through her. The fact she had one man pining over her while she was in love with another... color me jealous and envious and dark, dark green.

Just as I start to apologize for stepping over the line, Jonas speaks up. "I never looked at it like that. Actually puts it in a whole new perspective." He hums. "Not as if it concerns you, but I've been slowly working on letting her go. Not fully. She is my best friend, after all. But I've been trying to disconnect myself from her romantically. See her more like a sister or one of the guys. Know what I mean?"

"I do," I tell him. "But it's easy to say 'you are my friend.' The difficult part is accepting it."

"Yeah. Weeks before the wedding—which I did not see you at, by the way—I repeatedly told myself she was never mine to have. That I needed to find a way to get over her. Move on." I feel his eyes on me again. "I'm getting there," he whispers.

"I'm getting there." What exactly does that mean?

"You think?" I glance at him as I dip the needle into the ink cap.

Eyes locked on mine, the corners of his mouth tip up the slightest bit. "Yes."

Dear God. Please forgive me. But I really want to sin with this man.

I am the last person in the world anyone would consider to be religious. My history could sway the decision either way. But this man makes me want to drop to my knees, hold his gaze, and pray for him to let me make his life better.

I may not be a miracle worker, but I could do many miraculous things to this man.

"W-well that's great," I say with a little too much enthusiasm.

In turn, he laughs. And since I don't have the tattoo gun anywhere near his skin, he laughs harder than earlier. Deeper. Throatier. Louder. So loud, Penny and Rex—another artist in the shop—glance our way. Penny's eyebrows waggle and I roll my eyes at her.

When I sleep tonight, I will dream of his laugh and the way my insides swirl at the sound. The way my body sparks to life.

"Glad you think so," he teases. "Your turn." I cock my head to the side and narrow my eyes. "Tell me about you," he clarifies.

"Ah. Tit for tat, huh?"

He smirks and I realize the innuendo he has created from my words. "If that's what you want to c-call it." I love his slight stutter at the end. His jitters as we tease.

"What would you like to know?" I prompt.

He taps his chin with his free hand. "Boyfriend? Husband? Kids?"

Keeping my face down as I work on him, I stop breathing for a minute.

You can do this, Autumn. Baby steps.

I smile at his arm, but, if he saw my face head-on, he would know the smile is forced. So, I keep my head down. "No boyfriend or husband. Most guys I've dated were grossly immature. Don't get me wrong, I love silliness every once in a while. But some guys don't know when to be serious."

"I hate how I'm automatically lumped into this category because of the extremity between my legs." For a moment, I glance at his groin. No doubt he notices. *Great.* "But I get where you're coming from. I know plenty of guys who act exactly how you're describing them."

"Not trying to harp on the male species. Just noting the history I've had with them. Hasn't really worked in my favor."

I sit up straighter as I wipe excess ink off his arm. When he remains silent for a minute, I meet his gaze. He just… looks at me. Looking at me like no one else has. As if trying to read more into what I say. Tapping into my brain and digging for unanswered questions. Answers I am not ready to divulge yet.

"Sorry to hear. But you shouldn't give up."

I cock a brow at him. "No?"

He shakes his head. "Definitely not."

His words are laced with more. Emotions left unsaid. The sentiment weighs heavy and I blink rapidly to snap myself back to reality.

Is he suggesting what I think he is? When he says I shouldn't give up, is he inviting me to give him a shot? *"Definitely not."* His answer repeats in my head over and over. Unsure how to process it, I change the subject.

"What do you think?" He scrunches his brow. "Your ink? It's done. Well, done for tonight. What do you think?"

I grab a fresh paper towel and the alcohol blend I use to clean it up. Squirting some on the paper towel, I swipe the damp cloth over his skin and clean up the fresh tattoo.

"Perfect," he whispers.

And for a moment, I wonder if he's only referring to the tattoo. When I peek up, his eyes aren't on his forearm. They are on me.

The intensity of his stare sends a shock wave of heat across my flesh. Under the thin material of my bra, my nipples harden. At the apex of my thighs, dampness slicks my skin. I press my legs closer together and pray he doesn't notice. Pray he doesn't call me out. Because if he studies my reaction hard enough—pun intended—he will know exactly where my head is at.

Why has it been so long? Why the hell have I denied myself for so many years? And why has it worked until now?

"Thanks," I whisper back.

The answer to all three questions is simple. Because I have been waiting. For the right guy. For a guy like Jonas.

four

I soak up every line and curve of Autumn's profile as she cleans the new addition to my sleeve. Never thought I would say this about another woman, but damn, she is beautiful.

Autumn has a classic beauty, not one born of facials and layers of makeup. A heart-shaped face with a slender button nose and full lips. Scarlet paints her lips while a thin black wingtip accentuates her eyes. The only additions I note. We may be surrounded by beaches, but her alabaster skin tells me it isn't a place she frequents. A full sleeve of flowers and vines is inked on her right arm. And the style of her clothes and how she has her hair pinned… she reminds me of a modern-day pinup girl.

My pinup girl.

The errant thought catches me off guard, but I don't dismiss it. Not yet.

Autumn is a breath of fresh air. The fresh air I didn't think would filter through my lungs ever again. A new breath of life. Invigorating.

Beside me, she adheres a thin film to the new ink. Lifting her eyes to mine, I hold her swirly cognac gaze as she explains the new product. "Not sure if you've used this yet, but it's called Saniderm." I glance down at the clear film on my skin for a beat. When I shake my head, she continues. "It's a new, breathable way to protect your tattoo while it heals." She goes over the specifics and I get lost in the sound of her voice.

How have I not seen her until now?

The answer sits on the tip of my tongue. I won't say it. Not even in my thoughts. Let's just say I was otherwise distracted.

Now, though… I see clearly. The curtains over my eyes have been shoved to the wayside. The light of a new day shines bright. Has me seeing the world I have ignored for years.

When Autumn stops her spiel on tattoo care—which she knows I am obviously familiar with because of my previous tattoos—she stands and leads me back to the front desk. Call me a pig, but I eat up every inch of her as she walks in front of me. How can I not?

"Hey, Penny," she says, talking to the pink-haired woman behind the front desk. "Will you add Jonas on my schedule for next week. Wednesday or after." Autumn leans on the counter, pops her hip out, and faces me. *Someone rescue me from my depraved thoughts.* "If that works for you."

I nod, not trusting my voice yet. After I swallow a couple times, I pray to not sound like a prepubescent boy. "Yeah." *Thank fuck.* "Thursday might be easier, though."

"It's a date," she says as her face flushes rosy. She tucks both her lips in her mouth and clamps down before releasing them. "See you next week."

"Next week," I reply.

She scurries off to her booth and it's fucking adorable how flustered Autumn is. *Me too,* I want to tell her. Because this is the first time I have felt so immediately enamored by a woman. Although I undoubtedly loved—still love—Cora, my heart never hummed with her. Never galloped. Nor did I forget to breathe around her.

Maybe Autumn was right. Maybe Cora was a lesson. The lesson which taught me nonfamilial love.

Cora was never mine to love. I know this now. She was just a star in the constellation leading me to where I belong. And the constellation shines brighter than any other star in the galaxy now.

My constellation.

Penny cashes me out and I hand her a tip to give Autumn. "I'll make sure she gets it, sugar. What day works best for your next appointment?"

Getting here tonight after the weekly family dinner was cutting it close. I would rather get here a little earlier, so I am not here until ten at night. Although I don't need to be at the garage until eight each morning, I usually arrive between six and seven to help Dad catch up on invoices.

"Is Thursday at six available?"

Penny leans close to the computer monitor, rests her chin on her palm, and clicks the mouse a few times. Her eyes flick across the screen as she scrolls down. She pops her bubble gum once then looks up. "Six is all yours, sugar." Her fingers run across the keyboard. "Probably another two-hour appointment."

I nod. "Thanks. See you next week."

She leans back in her chair, pops her gum, and gives me a spirited wave goodbye.

As I reach the door to leave, I glance over my shoulder toward Autumn's booth. She stands frozen in place, eyes on me, with a new wave of crimson on her cheeks at being caught ogling. A wide smile tugs at my cheeks as I raise a hand and wave her direction. She timidly lifts her hand and returns my smile with one of her own.

I turn just in time to not smack into the door and make a fool out of myself.

Walking out of the shop, I head for the Jeep, hop in, and crank it to life. I sit in the lamplit parking lot for a few minutes and stare at the steering wheel in a fog. Although nothing extraordinary happened over the last two hours, the most mysterious and alluring woman blipped on my radar.

How the hell am I supposed to function for the next week? On a shitload of caffeine and daydreams, that is how.

Daydreams of an exquisite, petite pinup woman named Autumn.

~

The alarm squawks on the bedside table. I roll over and slap the snooze bar as Spartan vaults onto the bed and licks my face.

Swinging my arms in the air, I jerk my face left and right. "Spartan." I laugh at his relentlessness. "Stop, stop, stop." I cover my face with my hands and he starts licking my ear. "Argh! Okay, I'm up."

I wrap my arms around Spartan's belly and wrestle him on the bed for a minute before I slip out of the covers and turn off the alarm clock. He jumps off the bed and bolts for the front door, barking. After a quick trip to the bathroom, I throw on a hoodie, sweatpants, and sneakers, then hook Spartan's leash to his collar.

Out the door, we wander in the dark around the neighborhood. Houses on the street only illuminated by porch lights. Most of the windows still dark as residents continue to sleep.

Spartan sniffs and marks as many patches of grass, bushes, and signposts as possible. Cool air whips through my hair and, for the first time ever, it invigorates me. For years, I gravitated toward all things sunny and warm. Now, I discover a new appreciation for the opposite.

The cool breeze reminds me of fresh starts and new beginnings. Something I am in desperate need of.

"Spartan," I call out. He glances back at me a second, but doesn't stop tugging me forward. "I met someone." Funny enough, he barks.

I laugh. "You'd like her, buddy. Real pretty." He stops, sniffs at something I can't see on the sidewalk, and I run into him. "Whatcha got there?" But before I get close enough to see what caught his attention, he drags me forward again. "Anyway. She's really pretty. Like the women in fashion magazines or something." He barks again and I shush him. Last thing I need is for an angry neighbor to complain my dog woke them up at five in the morning.

So, for the rest of our trip around the neighborhood, I stay quiet while Spartan takes me for a walk.

Once we get back home, I jump in the shower. The instructions for this new tattoo cover say I shower normally with it on, just not to scrub it. Tattoo innovations—gotta love 'em. Out of the shower, I scramble a couple eggs, fry up a few pieces of bacon, and butter some toast. In no time, breakfast fills my stomach.

I secure Spartan in his crate, turn on the radio to our favorite rock station, and head out the door.

It's no surprise Dad is already at the garage when I arrive. Parking my motorcycle behind the building, I stroll into the office and greet him with a thermos of coffee.

"Morning, Dad."

He pops his head up, checks the time on the clock over the door, and smiles at me. "Up early today?"

I set the thermos in front of him and grab his mug from the small dish rack and hand it to him. When Dad bought this garage in 1980, he cleaned it up and changed a few things around before opening. Dad had worked in several mechanic and body shops prior to owning Thompson's Garage. He knew the ins and outs of daily activity. Knew what made a shop dysfunctional and what made it flow with ease. Taking bits and pieces of all the things he loved, he set up this garage.

Thompson's Garage and Body Specialists has four bays total. One bay is used for bodywork, unless we have no bodywork to work on. Each bay is only separated by the occasional pillar and larger machines. Along the back wall of the garage is section after section of chrome and black industrial automotive cabinetry. Every tool we possibly need inside. And if we don't have it, Dad orders it.

He also added a small kitchen dinette and a couch and small table in the office space of the garage. One thing he said bugged him at most shops he worked at was how they didn't have simple necessities—a sink for dishes, a fridge, and a small table for lunch (and breakfast for the early birds). Or a place to sleep on exhausting days. Dad made sure Thompson's had all of those, plus some counter space and a few cabinets.

Our garage was voted top family-owned mechanic of the Bay Area ten times. And we take pride in our work.

"Nah. Just moved faster than usual." I laugh and he joins in. "Best night of sleep in a while, I guess."

He fills his mug with coffee as I grab the creamer from the fridge and sugar on the counter. Setting it down, I pour my own mugful. We both add cream and sugar, and sit in silence a moment as we take the first few sips. Something Dad and I have in common is our morning routine. Maybe it's because I am the only son and I wanted to be just like him growing up. Or I could chalk it up to the fact we both wake up crazy early Monday to Friday and share the same job.

"What changed?" he asks after sufficiently caffeinated. I furrow my brow. "What happened after dinner last night? Said you slept better."

I smile and bring the mug to my lips. He studies me when I don't answer and shakes his head, following it up with a smile that matches my own.

Dad and I, for as long as I can remember, share a secret language. As a child, I dubbed it the *Boys Only Club*. That's how I kept my older sister away. Jillian was a baby during the age of *Boys Only*, so I never worried about her. Over the years, it evolved and I learned Dad and I just shared the same mindset. He is simply an older version of me.

I lift my arm and show him the new addition to my sleeve. "Went to the tattoo shop last night."

"Son, tattoos don't make you smile." He points at me as he shakes his head. "Not like an idiot, anyway."

Slapping a hand to my chest, I gape at him. "You wound me."

"Dumbass." He laughs.

I finish off my mug and set it down. "Met someone. A woman," I clarify. "She works at the tattoo shop."

"And?" Dad drawls out the one-word question.

"And I don't know. Couldn't stop looking at her. Or thinking about her. We talked the two hours I was there. Not sure, but I don't think the feelings are one-sided."

He nods, drinks the last of his coffee, and looks me square in the eyes. "Well, it's nice to see you smile again." Rising from his chair, he goes to the sink and washes out his mug before setting it in the rack. "Time to get to work."

And just like that, the conversation ends. Another great thing about the relationship Dad and I share is how we don't need all the nitty-gritty details. If either of us wants to disclose something, we will.

One day, I hope to have more to share with him.

"Leaving the mall now."

I pin the phone between my shoulder and ear as I fumble through my purse for the keys. "Find anything good?" Penny asks on the other end. In the background, I hear my favorite sound ever. Little girl giggles.

"Show you when I get home. Just need to stop and pick up a few more ingredients for the lasagna. Anything else we need?"

I unlock the door, slide into the car, and toss my bags on the passenger seat. Cranking the ignition, I pull the phone away when the engine lags and rumbles rougher than usual. I shrug as the roar settles in its typical hum.

Bringing the phone back to my ear, Penny rambles on. Who knows what I missed. "And will you grab Twizzlers, popcorn, M&M's, Red Hots, and Mike and Ike's. Oh, and ice cream." God, she probably rattled off twenty other different forms of junk food before I paid attention. Oh well.

"Are we serving sugar comas for dessert," I joke. "We do not need all of that."

"Hey," Penny says in a stern motherly voice. "We *need* them for movie time. Don't be a Debbie Downer, Auti."

I laugh. "Alright, I'm hanging up now. Should only be another thirty minutes. You guys okay?"

More giggles. Tickle-fest giggles. "We're fine. Drive safe and see you soon."

Disconnecting the call, I toss my phone in my purse and back out of the space. Two miles down the road, the car idles high at a red light. I check the gauges and note nothing looks off. No warning lights light up the display. Giving the dash a gentle tap, I tell the car we are almost done for the day.

Inside the grocery store, I snatch up the final missing ingredients for our Sunday night lasagna. Reluctantly, I grab a handful of sugary snacks for movie night per Penny's request. After checking out, I head back to my car, slip inside, and go to start it.

But the engine doesn't turn over.

I crank the key again. Nothing. No ticking or whining. Not a single sound.

"Well shit," I say, slapping my hands against the steering wheel.

Digging my phone out of my purse, I call Penny. "Are they out of Cherry Garcia? Please tell me they aren't."

"Pen, my car won't start."

The television mutes in the background. "Won't start? Does it sound like it's trying?"

I shake my head, then remember she can't see me. "No. It sounded off when I left the mall, but nothing bad. Just louder."

"Need me to come get you?"

Giggles erupt in my ear. "No, stay with her. I'll call for a tow truck. Hopefully it won't take long."

"You at our usual store?"

"Yeah, why?"

When Penny doesn't answer right away, I pull the phone away from my ear to see if the call dropped. Nope, still connected. "Sorry," she says when I bring the phone back to my ear. "Was looking up tow places nearby. Looks like there's one a couple miles away. I'll text you the number."

A second later, my phone pings with an incoming text. "Got it, thanks."

"Sure thing. Keep me posted."

"I will."

After hanging up with Penny, I dial the number she sent to me. A gruff voice answers and I explain my situation and ask if he can tow my car. Thankfully, I am met with a resounding yes. The man tells me he should arrive within thirty minutes.

While waiting for him, I turn the key one click in the ignition and listen to the radio. *At least it's not the battery and I don't have to wait in silence.* Five songs and two commercials later, an older man pulls up behind me with a flatbed.

As I step out of the car, he strolls forward staring at my Betsy and whistles. "Where'd you get a beauty like this?" he asks.

"Long story short, it was my granddad's. He restored it and passed it on to me."

"Well she's a beaut." The man extends his hand my way. "Name's Aaron."

I shake his hand. "Autumn. Thanks for coming to my rescue."

"Tell me what seems to be the problem."

I explain to Aaron what happened earlier when I left the mall and at the traffic light. Then how it wouldn't start when I walked out of the store. Thank goodness I didn't buy any perishables.

"Mind if I give it a try right quick?" Aaron asks.

I shake my head and gesture to the driver's side door. He sits in the car a moment and turns the key a few times, leaning closer to the dash. He listens intently, trying to locate the source of the issue. A minute later, he hops out and closes the door.

"Not sure what's wrong with her, but I'll give it a full rundown at the shop in the morning. Anything you need to grab out of the car before I get it on the flatbed?"

"Just a few bags."

After I collect my bags and purse, Aaron loads Betsy up on the truck. Soon, we are driving down the road toward his shop. A mix of gasoline and pine-scented cardboard trees fills the cab. Aaron whistles along with a country music song on the radio as he taps his fingers on the steering wheel.

I glance over at his profile and can't help but think he looks familiar. Not sure how, but his profile gives me déjà vu. But I shake it off and stop scrutinizing him.

Just as another song starts on the radio, we pull into the parking lot of an auto repair shop. The exterior a bright and bold blue with an oval white sign in the center. Thompson's Garage is swirled in the same blue on the white sign. Several cars are parked on the side of the building, shaded from the afternoon sun by a handful of various trees.

As Aaron circles the lot and starts to back up to one of the white bay doors, it rolls up. I look in the side mirror, but don't see anyone and assume Aaron must have pressed a garage door opener.

When the truck stops fifteen feet from the bay, I glance over at him and he gives me a warm smile. "Time to get your girl inside. Then we'll do paperwork. Do you need a ride home?"

"No, I'll request an Uber. Thank you." We hop out and I hear him talking over the Diesel engine on the opposite side. I walk around the front of the truck, ready to ask him to repeat himself. "What was…"

Words fail me as I round the tow truck and none other than Jonas is eyeing my Betsy with a giddy expression. He says something to Aaron, and I can't quite make it out. He starts to say something else, turns his head to face Aaron, and spots me.

A brilliant smile lights up his face and Aaron notices. "Hey," Jonas says as he walks past Aaron, heading straight for me. "Is this you?" He points up at Betsy.

I nod. "Yeah. She won't start."

"Dad just told me." *Dad?* Now the déjà vu makes sense. Similar profiles because they are from the same gene pool. "Sorry she's being stubborn. We'll fix her up for you."

I smile. "Thanks, I appreciate it."

Aaron sidles up to us. "Jonas, you know this pretty lady?"

Before Jonas answers, I speak up. "We just met. I work at the tattoo shop a few miles down the street." I point to Jonas's forearm. "Worked on his newest addition."

A wide, toothy smile stretches from ear to ear on Aaron's face. "Huh." Aaron glances to Jonas then back to me. "Well you did a great job, sweetheart." He throws a wink my way. "Gonna unload your girl here. Shouldn't be long."

"Thank you." Once Aaron is out of earshot, I face Jonas again. "That's your dad?"

"Yep. And this is our shop."

Oh, wow. Suddenly, I am wondering if there were any photos online of the shop owners when Penny chose this place. Sneaky wench. Not sure if I should hit or thank her.

Not sure what to say, I glance up at the sign on the building. "So, has your dad owned it since eighty?"

Jonas follows my gaze. "Yeah. He'd been saving for years. Worked as many hours as he could to still pay the bills plus save. Lucky for Dad, the bank took over the place from the previous owner and he purchased it cheaper than expected. Kismet, I suppose."

"Kismet," I mumble.

I had never given much thought or energy to the term. Fate. Destiny. Devine providence. Fate had its place in the world, I suppose, but the idea of some outside force steering me this way or that way didn't sit right with me. I liked believing I was in control of my life. That I made the rules and held the power. The notion of being in control, I could apply it to so many scenarios from my past.

No one held power over me.

But the idea of kismet is starting to grow on me. How else could I explain meeting Cora and Gavin, and, by proxy, Jonas? Did they just stumble into a random tattoo shop? Or did some invisible force guide them my way? Not sure I will ever know the true answer. And the more I think about it, the more my head hurts.

What I did know for certain was Jonas walked in. He sat in my chair. And my heart somersaulted like a gymnast for hours. By the way he looks at me right now, I would venture to guess Jonas's heart is flipping and twirling too.

"While Dad unloads your car, we can step into the office and start the paperwork."

"Okay."

Jonas leads us into a spacious room on the south side of the building. As we step inside, I scan the room and see a couple rows of chairs next to a table with a Keurig and coffee fixings. A large window consumes half of the south wall and brightens the room naturally. A rack of magazines sits beside the coffee station and a small flat screen hangs near the ceiling. The large window is partially cut off by a wall, which looks to be an addition to the original structure. That specific wall is painted with a mural of the shop, I assume, when it first opened.

Jonas leads us through a door and into an office, where the large window continues. Two desks sit butted up against one another. There is a small kitchen/dinette area and a plush couch with a coffee table. The walls have a coat of beige paint with several framed photos—which I can't make out without closer inspection. Cozy—for an auto repair shop.

"Have a seat," Jonas says, gesturing to a chair near one of the desks. "Let me just grab the paperwork." He sits at one of the desks and rummages through a drawer. Retrieving a triplicate form, he puts it on a clipboard, grabs a pen, and leans back in his chair. "Just a few questions and then you can head out." Then he glances up from the form. "Do you need a ride? I can take you home, if you want."

I shake my head. "Nah. I'll grab an Uber. Only live a mile or two from here, so shouldn't cost much."

He nods, then prattles off a handful of questions. Name. Address. Phone number. When he asks for my number, I stumble for a moment. *Your phone number is for the paperwork, idiot.* At least that is what I tell myself. He continues the questionnaire as if he fills them out a thousand times a day. Most of it was simple maintenance history on the car.

After all the questions, I sign the bottom and he gives me a copy. "Once we get a look under the hood in the morning, we'll call you and let you know what we found."

"Sounds great." I rise from the chair, grab my purse and shopping bags. Retrieving my phone, I open up the Uber app and request a ride.

"Sure I can't give you a ride?"

I shake my phone in front of him and smile. "Already got one. Thanks, though."

"Mine is better," he teases.

No doubt about that. Heat crawls up my neck and blazes across my cheeks. "What if my Uber driver pulls up in a snappy sports car?" I joke.

He rolls his eyes and laughs. "Mine would still be better."

We wander out of the office and back into the sticky, Florida fall weather. Just outside the building, we pause under an awning. The sun still shines down from above, but is slowly fading as afternoon drifts closer to evening.

Beside me, I *feel* Jonas's eyes on my profile. Tracing the angle of my jaw to my chin with his hypnotic eyes. Skirting them up to my lips and honing in on them. I tuck my lips in my mouth for one, two, three before I pop them back out. And I don't miss the soft groan from him.

"Can I call you?" he asks.

I peek up at him and his eyes are exactly where I knew them to be. "About the car?" I play innocent, but know his question has nothing to do with the car.

In slow motion, he shakes his head and meets my gaze. "You know I'll call about the car." His eyes drop to my lips for a split second before returning back north, and my heart skips. "What I mean is, can I call you" —he pauses and licks his lips— "and take you out sometime?"

Every atom inside my tiny five-foot-five frame jumps up and down like I just won a million dollar lottery. Because Jonas is definitely a prize. A prize any woman would be lucky to hold in her arms. So why am I hesitant? What is stopping me from blurting out *yes, yes, yes* at the top of my lungs. I know the answer to this question. It's a question I have had to answer several times over the years. But it's an answer I keep to myself.

"Jonas… I-I don't know…" His eyes wilt as his shoulders sag. *Damnit.* "It's not that I don't want to."

And just like that, hope glints anew in his eyes.

This is going to be so much harder than I imagined.

six

JONAS

She likes me. I see it in the upward curve of her lips. In the extra sparkle in her eyes. How her breathing changes. The way she automatically leans an inch closer. She likes me, but is afraid to admit it.

"What is it then?" I run my fingers through my hair. "Am I too pretty for you?" I tease.

Autumn throws her head back and laughs. The sound bubbly like a fountain-style cherry cola. "Maybe." She waves her hand up and down my body. "I mean, how's a girl going to compete with this?" Her words are meant as a joke, but they heat me from head to toe.

When I finally get my wits about me again, I say, "Swear I'm not always this pretty."

She laughs again and shakes her head. "You're persistent, aren't you?"

I shrug. "Only with people who count."

At this, her smile softens. Becomes more shy. "Jonas…" She steps closer to me and I pick up hints of vanilla and something fruity—cherry, maybe. "I really would love to talk more and go out sometime, but…"

At the tattoo shop the other day, she said she wasn't seeing anyone. Right? "But?"

"I- I have other obligations."

What does *other obligations* mean?

Maybe she has a sick family member she helps when not at work. Or maybe she works more than one job. I never really took that into consideration. Could be something completely innocent. She could be a volunteer at a shelter or attend school during the day.

But does she have said obligations every day of the week? I wouldn't think so.

"Well, if you ever find yourself free of said obligations for a teeny, tiny minute, I would love to take you out. I'm willing to beg, if necessary." I glance over at Dad who continues to ogle Autumn's car. "Dad would never let me live it down if I got on my knees and groveled. But I'm willing to live with the incessant teasing."

She laughs again, and I press record in my mind. I love the carefree sound and want to play it on repeat. A white SUV pulls into the lot and Autumn glances down at her phone.

"My ride is here." She locks her phone and drops it in her black, white, and red purse which looks strikingly similar to a bowling bag, only smaller. "Let me see your phone."

I glance down at her outstretched palm. Without hesitation, I pull my phone from my back pocket, unlock it, and hand it over. Polished nails matching the rouge on her lips tap with efficiency over the screen. Seconds later, her phone pings in her bag and she hands me back my phone.

"Gotta go." She salutes me. "Talk to you later."

My head drifts in the clouds. I watch as she gets in the SUV and buckles up. I wave as the car drives off and just stand there like an idiot. Hand still up a minute later. Snapping out of my fog, I unlock my phone and stare down at the screen where she messaged herself from my phone.

Can't wait for you to call.

A smile slowly creeps across my face as I fixate on the simple text. *Me either.*

"So, that's her, huh?"

I jump. "Argh! Dad, you scared the shit out of me."

He laughs. "Guess there's a first for everything. She must have you all kinds of twisted up if your old man scared ya."

"Guess so."

He points to my phone. "If my instincts are right—which let's get real, they always are—she's a keeper."

Yeah. But how do you keep something not yet yours? "Couldn't agree more."

After parking my bike near the back of the lot, I enter the pub, wave to the hostess, and weave through the crowd to our usual table. Twenty feet away, I take a deep breath and throw on a smile as I approach Cora, Gavin, and Shelly.

More than a week has passed since Cora and Gavin's wedding. And so much has happened in that small blip of time.

Tonight will be the true test. To see whether or not the love I have had for Cora over the last ten years has changed. If it has really transitioned from romantic to friendship. Most people wouldn't be able to set aside such potent feelings. But when something else—someone else—clicks in place, you see the world a little different.

As I step up to the table, Cora laughs at something Shelly said and I absorb her laughter. Test how it makes me feel. See if it strikes me as it did weeks and months and years ago. It echoes across the table, has the corner of my mouth perking up for a beat, then settles.

The first thing I realize is it doesn't sink in. Her laughter doesn't seep into my pores, bleed through my veins, and root itself in my marrow. It just floats through the air and settles. The only reason I smile is because it's natural. Her happiness makes me happy.

"Hey, man," Gavin says as I settle on a stool next to Shelly.

"Hey." I raise a hand and nod at Chris, the bartender. He throws me a thumbs up. "Any good ones hit the stage yet?"

For years, Cora, Shelly, and I came to this bar at least once a week. The local bar and grill hosted karaoke several nights a week. If it was a slow night on non-karaoke days, the manager would let people go on stage and sing for the hell of it. The more drinks people consume, the more interesting the singing. Definitely some memorable performances.

Cora perks up. "You just missed the Momma Train Gang."

I glance over at her and *see* her for the first time. No doubt, Cora is a beautiful woman. But in a strange twist of events, I no longer see her how I once did. I don't study her eyes or lips or smile with too much depth. Don't feel the urge to stare at her for hours and pine over what I can't have.

The day I met Cora, I remember how her smile made me sweat a little. Made me a little fidgety.

Now when I look at her, a familiarity settles inside me. Still a form of love, but more comparable to what I feel when Jasmine or Jillian are around. Sibling love.

Maybe this is how close friendship should feel. Like family.

"Momma Train Gang? Dear lord, dare I ask?"

Shelly snort-laughs just as a beer is set in front of me on a coaster. "Thought I'd seen it all." She slaps her hand on the table. "Boy, was I wrong."

I glance between the two women, both of which laugh uncontrollably, then to Gavin. "Care to fill me in since these two are obviously incapable."

Gavin tilts his head and eyes me for a beat. Once he satisfies the question in his head, he tells me what I missed. "Four women, probably in their mid-to-late forties, jumped on stage and mutilated 'My Humps' by Black Eyed Peas. Mix the singing with the way they shook their… assets, let's just say it was memorable."

We both take a sip of our beers and shake our heads. "You guys eat yet?" I ask him.

"Nah. Thank god. Might've come back up. Not sure how you guys have been doing this for years. Some of these people make me want to gouge my eyes out."

I throw my head back and laugh. Shelly and Cora join me. "Dude, the first time was a total accident. But it wiped the stress of the day away. So, we kept coming. Call it tradition. Need a good laugh? Come in for karaoke night." Scanning the bar for our server, I spot my oldest friend, Trevor. "Be back in a sec."

Slipping off my stool, I walk over to the bar and sidle up beside him.

"Hey," he says as soon as he notices me. "What're you doing here?"

I point over to the table I just abandoned. "Hanging out. Drinking beer. Listening to shit karaoke. Grabbing a bite. You?"

He stares down at his glass, rounds his shoulders, and sags. "Just broke it off with Christine."

Well, this throws me off. "Seriously, bro? What the hell happened?"

Trevor and Christine have been connected at the hip for the last three years. Went everywhere together. If we had a guy's night without her tagging along, we were lucky. So hearing that they are no longer together shocks the hell out of me.

"Got off work early on Friday. Thought I'd surprise her. Get home before her and make a nice dinner."

"Okay…" I drawl.

"When I parked at the complex and spotted her car home early, I was bummed I couldn't surprise her. But excited she was home early." Trevor pauses to down the last of his drink. Something tells me this tale is about to go south real fast. "I heard it before I unlocked the door." He cringes. "Her screams. The ones she only makes when…"

Fuck. His pain is so out of my element. But like a good friend, I listen and give him a shoulder.

"I walked into the bedroom. Saw *everything*." He taps the bar before peering up at me. "Dude, it's burned into my retinas. I can't unsee it and it pisses me off. So, I'm trying to forget," he says as the bartender sets another Jack and Coke in front of him.

What the hell do I say? How does a friend comfort another when something like this happens? Fuck if I know.

"Wish I could say or do something to make this better, man."

Trevor slaps the back of my shoulder. "You're a good friend, brother. Thanks for that."

I glance back at my friends across the bar and battle internally where I should be. With them? Or Trevor?

Why choose.

"Trev, come hang out with us." I point over to the high top. "We'll help take your mind off things for a bit."

He stares across the bar at the laughing trio and gauges what to do. "I don't know, brother. Not sure I'm in the mood."

"Exactly. Which is why you need to."

I grab hold of his arm and drag him off the stool. He stumbles beside me through the bar.

Fuck, he has had a lot to drink already.

When we reach the table, I plop his ass on a stool and sit next to him. Gavin scrutinizes every visible inch of Trevor then glances over to me with a silent question. Asking if Trevor is good. Subtly, I nod.

"Shelly, Cora, you remember Trevor?"

They chime in with a unified yes, followed by a bout of laughs.

"Trevor, this is Gavin. Cora's husband. Gavin, this is my oldest friend Trevor. We go back to the days of BMX bikes and when boys thought girls were gross."

Gavin laughs and it thins the bubble of intensity surrounding us. "Sometimes," Gavin says as he side-eyes Cora, "girls are still gross."

"Hey!" Cora play slaps him. "Take that back or you'll regret it."

For the next couple of hours, I sit in the middle of a bar surrounded by a group of people I care about. Smiles and laughs and banter bounce back and forth the entire time. Happiness hovers in the periphery when I catch Trevor smile for a moment. Because if anyone can come out on the other side stronger after something shitty like cheating happens, it is Trevor. And I will help him however possible. Maybe lug him to Wednesday night dinners for the foreseeable future.

Whatever it takes.

The only person missing from this semi-perfect moment is a petite brunette with stormy, cognac eyes and scarlet lips. Maybe I will get lucky. Maybe one day, she will sit on the stool beside me.

seven

AUTUMN

Two days. Two days have passed since I pushed past my doubts and insecurities. When I, for the first time in years, handed out my phone number to a guy.

And he hasn't used it. Not once.

What the hell?

Jonas threw out every hint. Practically begged to call me. So why hasn't he?

And why the hell am I being such a *girl* about the fact he hasn't called or texted? This is one reason why I don't put myself out there. Why I haven't dated in years. Because I can't get my hopes up. Not when my heart isn't the only one on the line. Relationships—no matter the type—don't involve just me. Others have to be taken into consideration.

Penny plops down on the couch and lays her head on my shoulder as I sip my coffee. "Whatcha thinking about?" she asks.

I lean my cheek on her crown and shake my head. "Ridiculous nonsense."

Her body vibrates with laughter, but she contains the sound. "Just call him already. Pull a Sadie Hawkins and woman up."

I laugh at her reference. Penny is always so gung ho and dives in headfirst. Her energy and enthusiasm boost the parts of me I squander. Like reaching out to a guy who is seemingly interested in me, but has been radio silent since I gave him permission to call.

"But…"

"But what, Auti? From everything you told me, the guy is interested. So no buts."

I roll my eyes, sit taller, and spin to face her as she falls from my shoulder into the couch cushions. Drama queen. But I wouldn't want her any other way.

"What if I'm reading him wrong?"

"What if you're not?" Penny garbles into the couch cushion before sitting up and swiping her hair out of her face. "I saw the way he looked at you last Wednesday. Girl, you can't fake the way he reacted. He wants you. Probably more than either of you cares to admit."

"Say you're right." Penny waves her hand in the air and rolls her eyes. I ignore her antics and trudge on. "Why hasn't he called me yet? If he is as interested as you suggest, why am I sitting here questioning it?"

Penny crisscrosses her legs and lays her hands on my knees. "Because he's a guy." I shake my head as she continues. "And because he's probably working all day to fix your car."

I hadn't thought about Betsy or the fact Jonas has his hands all over her. Is it weird to suddenly be jealous of a car? That she's getting more action than I have in years. Hope she isn't too broken. Hope it won't cost a fortune either.

"Forgot about Betsy," I admit.

Penny lifts her hands to clutch my shoulders. "Then use Betsy as a reason to call. Ask how things are going with the repairs. Throw out a little charm. No way he'll resist."

I inhale a deep breath and tuck my hair behind my ear. "Say I call. Besides Betsy, what else do I talk about?" I drop my eyes to my lap. Study a nonexistent loose thread on my pants. "You know how long it's been."

"Yeah, I do. And I question your sanity." I go to interject and she holds her hand up to stop me. "Hear me out. I know *why* you haven't dated or gotten close to anyone in years. But it has been *years, Auti.* Enough time has passed. It's okay to do what makes *you* happy. No one will fault you for that." Penny picks up my hands and envelops them in hers. "Give yourself permission to live. To find happiness."

Although I hate to admit it, she is right. But owning the truth in your head is wholly different than speaking it aloud. Because once the truth leaves your lips, you can never rein it back in. The words can never be unsaid.

"How?" I whisper. "How do I *live* when..." I trail off and she squeezes my hands.

"You let us help. Just as we always have. Me, Reznor, Iliana, Rex. We may not be conventional, we may not share the same genetics, but we're family. And family always sticks together. Through thick and thin."

I nod robotically. Times like this, I wish my actual family gave a damn. Wish they actually loved me for who I am, instead of hating me for the choices I made over the years. Choices I wouldn't change if given the opportunity. Because all my choices led me to where I am now. To Penny and my tat family. To happiness and potentially more. To so much love.

I reach for my phone and Penny claps like a lunatic. "You need to leave the room. I can't call him with you sitting in front of me, judging every word or gesture."

Penny sighs like the drama queen she is and rises from the couch. "Fine." She huffs and wanders down the hall. "If you need me, I'll be in the tub, reading and soaking up lavender bubbles. I expect a full rundown after."

"Yeah, yeah."

Once the bathtub faucet cranks on, I bite my lip and scroll through my text history. I tap on the message I sent myself from Jonas's phone and read it for the hundredth time. *Can't wait for you to call.* And it suddenly dawns on me. If I read this as the recipient, it sounds as if *he* is waiting for *me* to call.

Shit. Has he read this message over and over, wondering why *I* haven't called?

I tap the top of the message and stare at the different options below his phone number and blank contact image. My finger hovers over the small phone icon as I suck in a deep breath.

Now or never, Autumn. Just tap the screen.

Swallowing, I press the phone icon and lift the phone to my ear. One ring. Two. Three. Just as I consider hanging up, the line connects.

"Hello?" Jonas's low, throaty voice floats through the line and settles deep in my bones. A flutter stirs in my belly. My tongue suddenly thick. "Hello? Autumn?"

Did he add my name to his contacts? A new wave of excitement washes over me as I clear my throat. "Yeah, sorry," I answer.

"Everything okay?"

No, because I am a complete moron. "Yes. Just calling to check on Betsy." And ask why you haven't called me yet.

"Betsy's doing just fine," he answers with jubilance in his voice and I picture a smile brightening his face. "Should be done with her in time for Thursday."

"Thursday?"

"My appointment." Right, he will be back in my chair in two days. My belly does another flip. "Thought I'd bring the car to you. If that's okay."

I nod, then remember he can't see me. "Yeah, that's fine."

The line goes silent for a moment as I pick at the chipping polish on my finger nails. *Need to repaint them later.*

The longer the silence stretches, the more I wonder why I am so bad at this. Years ago, I never had issues talking to guys. Hell, most of my friends are men. Always have been.

So why am I struggling to find a single thing to say? Why is it so difficult to ask him how he is doing? Or if he would like to hang out sometime. Penny's words from minutes ago repeat in my head. *Give yourself permission to live. To find happiness.*

Is Jonas the happiness I have been missing all these years? Maybe. But I will never know until I put myself out there. Until I ask.

Just as I open my mouth to ask if he would like to get together sometime and get to know each other, a bang on the other end of the line breaks the silence.

"Shit," Jonas mutters. "Sorry, but I need to go. Some people can't be left unattended." He doesn't sound angry. Amused, maybe. "Glad you called."

"You are?" I slap my hand to my forehead and close my eyes.

"Definitely. But I really do need to go before *someone* breaks shit." I pick up on the humor in his voice. "See you on Thursday."

I nod. "See you Thursday."

"And Autumn?"

"Yeah."

He stays silent a moment. "Nothing." I hear his dimpled smile in the single word. "Bye."

"Bye," I whisper as the line disconnects.

I keep the phone at my ear long after Jonas hangs up. What was he going to say? Doesn't he know my mind will spin with endless possibilities until I see him again? Until I ask him.

Holding on to the phone, I drop my hands to my lap and stare at the screen. Stare at the generic contact image and the number beneath it. Tapping the top of the screen, I click on the info icon and add Jonas's contact information. Somehow, I need to figure out a sneaky way to get a picture of him. I hate not having images to associate with my contacts. Just a weird preference.

"Why aren't you in here telling me all the juicy details?" Penny yells from the bathroom.

Rising from the couch, I head down the hall. When I reach the bathroom, I peek in and laugh at Penny as she bobs in the middle of a two-foot tower of bubbles. "You're a freaking nut," I tell her.

"And you're avoiding a conversation. Better luck next time."

I roll my eyes, walk into the bathroom, and plop down on the closed toilet lid. "There's not much to tell. I called him, he was busy at work, there was awkward chitchat about Betsy, then silence, and goodbye."

"You should've been in here with it on speakerphone. Then I could decipher all the things you're leaving out."

Forever wanting all the dirty details. "There was this one thing," I trail off.

She sits up taller in the tub, sloshing water over the sides and flashing me her boobs. I cover my eyes with a hand and she laughs.

"First, you've seen my boobs a million times. No need to be prude now."

"But we weren't talking about guys then."

Penny shrugs and scoops bubbles closer to her chest to appease me. "Anyway. Elaborate. What does *this one thing* mean?"

I huff and lean back on the toilet tank. "There was this one point when it sounded like he wanted to say something. Maybe ask me something. But then he just blew it off and said bye."

During the call with Jonas, that moment of silence dragged out for hours in my head. I filled it with daydreams of my hand cradled in his. Of his cheek pressed to mine as he whispered sweet words in my ear. Of his soft lips brushing mine while his stubble scraped my skin.

Did his mind wander much the same? Did he picture the possibility of us?

Penny shrugs and the bubbles flatten a little in the tub. "Maybe he was going to ask you something, but didn't want to over the phone. Have you ever considered the idea he may be just as nervous as you are?"

Have I given the idea consideration? No. I pictured most men as forward and cocky. Majority of the men I ink represent the notion well. Hundreds have asked for my number. When they do, I just hand over my business card for the shop.

Except for Jonas.

Granted, he has my phone number on an invoice in Thompson's Garage. But I never picture him abusing the privilege. He asked for my number because he was raised to be a gentleman. He asked for my number because he wanted to give me the choice. To say yes or no. When I said yes, I assumed he would use my number sooner rather than later. Most men don't have the patience to sit idle and wait for the woman to make the first move. Obviously, Jonas has many redeeming qualities I have yet to learn.

"Actually, I haven't. Suppose you could be right."

"Could be? Girl, I'm right ninety-nine point nine percent of the time. And you know it."

"Alright, conversation is officially over," I tease as I stand up and head out of the bathroom. "Finish your bath and we'll head out."

"Yes, mother," she teases back. "Be out in a jiff."

I amble into my bedroom and sift through my closet. Tugging a shirt from the hanger, I toss it on the bed and grab a pair of jeans. Mindlessly, I dress and replay Penny's response to Jonas's silence.

Is Jonas nervous? If he is, I am curious as to why. He doesn't come off as timid. At least not to the degree where he would be nervous asking a woman out. In some respects, he already did. So why would he be nervous to ask again? Is it the simple notion of being rejected twice? I hope that is not the case. Because if Jonas asks me again, my answer will be different.

If he asks me again, I will say yes.

I crank the Bel Air to life and smile when it purrs like the beauty it is. Dad wanders over and I roll down the window.

"She sounds good as new." He wipes his hand with a red rag then stuffs it in his coveralls. "Tell Autumn I say hello."

I laugh under my breath. Since Autumn's car arrived at the garage and she went home, Dad has given me a ration of shit every single day. Teases me about wanting another grandchild. Asking me over and over if I called Autumn yet. If I asked her on a date. Sometimes, I swear he is worse than Mom.

And when she called on Tuesday, Dad knocked a fender off the workbench as he snuck closer to eavesdrop. Always lurking about. Hence why I ended the call abruptly with Autumn.

"Will do." Dad taps the roof before I throw the car in reverse.

Since the trip to the tattoo shop from the garage is short, I take the 'scenic' route to listen better to the car. Thankfully, nothing major was wrong with the engine. Just typical wear and tear on easy-to-replace parts. Cars like the Bel Air can be more challenging to repair if it's a major component. Engines just aren't made how they once were. When this car was manufactured, the engine didn't rely on hundreds of little computers and motherboards. They were solid and metal and everlasting. And their parts weren't easy to find nowadays.

Five miles later, I roll into the back parking lot of the tattoo shop. Shutting off the engine, I sit in the car another minute, study the silver and black upholstery, and inhale the peculiar Coke float scent.

Every inch of this car screams Autumn. Fits her personality and the way she carries herself.

Question is, do I? Do I fit into her lifestyle? Who she is and the life she leads.

Because I want to. Desperately.

Other than Cora, I never thought it possible to feel so intensely for a woman. And I never thought I would feel it so soon and easily.

Exiting the car, I lock it up and head for the front entrance. The bell jingles when I walk in and I love the smile on Autumn's face when she peeks up and notices my arrival. Her smile brightens the room instantly. *Hey* I mouth and her cheeks pink.

I wonder if she blushes this much with other men. Hopefully not. I would like to believe she reserves the crimson heat just for yours truly.

After I check in with the Bubble Yum queen, I pace the lobby and stare at the art on the walls. I scan each image but pay closer attention to the artist's names on the bottom. I stop at the third piece and study it intently. The eleven-by-fourteen heavy cream paper penned with millions of small dots. Up close, I spot each pinpointed speck of ink on its own. Stepping back, the dots form the image of two people holding hands and strolling down the sidewalk. Of the two people, you only see their hands and half their forearms. When I glance down at the artist's name, it doesn't shock me when I see Autumn's next to a hefty price tag.

But the art is worth every penny.

A finger tap on my shoulder interrupts my fascination with the art. I spin around to find Autumn. Her smile bright and shy. One-hundred-percent adorable and addicting.

"Nice piece," I say, pointing over my shoulder.

Autumn glances around me and eyes the art. "Thank you. Took months to finish." A fresh blush paints her cheeks and I love her bashful nature more.

"No doubt. Wish I had the patience to create something so priceless."

She tucks her lips in her mouth and bites down to fight against her smile. Then she pops them and I can't look away. Don't want to look away. Her crimson lips an invitation I want to answer with a resounding yes.

"You ready?" she asks.

I nod. "Yeah."

Autumn leads us to her booth, and I don't miss the way Bubble Yum winks and smiles as we pass. Interesting.

I sit in the chair while Autumn preps everything. In no time, she places the stencil on my forearm. After it's in place, I remember I still have her keys and pull them from my pocket. I set them on my lap and chance a look at her. She has been quiet. Too quiet.

"Sorry I didn't hand over the keys before you gloved up."

"No biggie," she says and shrugs. "Why was Betsy being temperamental?"

I love how she refers to her car as a person with an ill temper. Yet another quality to add under the adorable category. An ever-growing list.

"Just needed to replace the starter and a couple other small parts."

Autumn slumps and sighs before meeting my eyes. Her brows pinch slightly and accentuate her swirly cognacs. "Sounds pricey."

General automotive repair racks up over time. Certain parts and repairs costing more. But repairing Autumn's car was simple. Easier than most newer cars. The beauty of older cars is how spread out the engines are. How you don't have to remove half or more of the engine to get to one part. Whenever Dad and I get to work on older vehicles, we savor it. Drool like idiots. Take our time to have it around longer.

"Not at all, actually."

She perks up at that. "Great. Let me know how much I owe you, and we can settle up when we're done."

After Dad and I finished up Autumn's car earlier, he followed me into the office and closed the door. As I finalized the paperwork for Autumn's car, jotting down what repairs we had done, Dad walked over and slapped his hand on top of the invoice. "*No charge,*" he'd said. He looked me in the eyes and shook his head. His decision was final and not up for debate.

Honestly, I was happy to not charge Autumn. But I didn't have the final say in waiving payment. Dad still holds the power where Thompson's Garage finances are concerned.

"Not a dime," I tell her. "Dad insists. He says hello, by the way."

Autumn slouches and pouts.

Fuck me running. If I don't look away now, I will embarrass the hell out of myself. Nothing like sitting in a chair next to a beautiful woman with a hard-on while her eyes focus less than six inches away.

Think, think, think.

Images of my sisters pop in my head and is exactly what I need. Nothing like siblings to kill any sort of mood.

"Well, I'll have to repay him. Bake him a cake or brownies or cookies. Does he like any of those?" she asks.

"All of the above. He's not picky and will love whatever you make. Thanks."

"For what?"

For existing, I want to say, but bite my tongue. "It's a generous thing to do. Most wouldn't."

She nods. "Well, I'm not most people."

This much I have figured out.

For the next twenty minutes, I close my eyes and lay back while she starts on my tattoo. For the first time, I don't enjoy the silence. I want to talk to Autumn. Ask about her life. What she does for fun. What she does when she isn't working. Ask her to have dinner with me. Or do something she enjoys.

For obvious reasons, I haven't had an actual girlfriend in years. I tried. Tried to date other women while I pined over Cora. But it never worked out. Never got past the first kiss on the doorstep after our date. Because I never wanted it to.

But now… I want it more than anything.

Want to take her out and share a meal together. The food or restaurant doesn't have to be fancy as long as Autumn is there. I want to hang out with friends and have her hooked on my arm. Feel her warmth against my skin and bask in her sweet perfume and infectious laughter.

I peel my eyes open, lift my head, and glance down at her. Hunched over my forearm, she shifts my skin and runs the gun over the purple lines. I study her every move. The way she cocks her head when she scrutinizes her own work. How she leans back to see the tattoo from farther away. The way she tucks her lips in her mouth when hesitant—like she is right now.

"What are you thinking about?" I croak.

She sits up straighter and meets my gaze. Her eyes tell the tale of struggle. Struggle to do one thing versus another. A battle of wills.

Her lips pop out and I swallow. "What were you going to ask me the other day?"

I furrow my brow and tilt my head to the side. "When?"

"On the phone. Sounded like you were going to ask me something, and you didn't."

Ah, yes. Because I did have a question on the tip of my tongue. Until I caught Dad snooping. The plan was to ask if I could take her to dinner. But I chickened out when I spotted Dad ten feet away with his head leaning in close as he picked up the fender.

"Um." I rub the back of my neck with my free hand. "Was going to ask if you wanted to maybe grab dinner sometime."

I get drunk on her cognac irises as she doesn't blink or look away. Sweat a little from the intensity of her gaze. Stop breathing when she doesn't utter a single word in response.

A guy such as myself would strike gold if Autumn agreed to go on a date. I still have so much to learn about her, but from what I have seen so far, she is a rare gem. Sparkling in the sunlight and stealing your breath.

She parts her lips to respond, but snaps them shut a moment later. When she does it again—and again—I perk up at her speechlessness. Before I have the chance to tell her to not worry about it, she dips the gun in the ink cap and works on my arm again.

Rejection washes over me—for a second time—as I slump in the chair.

What exactly stops her from saying yes? This is the single, most important—and frustrating—question rattling inside my brain right now. The one that makes me question her bashfulness and blushing and frequent eye contact. The reason must be huge. Has to be. Because the chemistry between us is off the charts. At least it feels off the charts from where I sit. And there is no way this attraction is one-sided. Can't be.

As I lean back and rest my head against the chair, I get a quick glimpse of her smile and a blush smattering her cheeks. I close my eyes and smile like a fool—not giving a damn who sees. She may not respond verbally, but her body language gives so much away.

The next hour breezes by as I daydream of taking Autumn on a date. Where we would go. What we would do afterward. Her warm, slender fingers woven with mine. My arms holding her close as I hug her good night. Her sweet perfume swathing me in a cocoon as I lean in to press my lips to hers.

A chill snaps me out of my daydream as Autumn cleans my finished tattoo.

"So jumpy," she teases. "Might start to think you're a virgin." Autumn laughs, then stops once she realizes what she said. "Sorry," she mutters. "That was inappropriate."

Tattoo virgin is what she meant. Not a virgin in the sex department. My virginity had been surrendered long ago in both areas. For obvious reasons, she knew I wasn't a tattoo virgin. But Autumn had no clue about my sexual history—which isn't extensive, but exists.

Which is the exact reason her cheeks are currently one shade lighter than her rouge-painted lips. And I love how the intimacy of this conversation makes her squirm. Her semi-shy nature is not something often seen nowadays.

"Would that be a bad thing?" I mean the question as a joke. But a joke she isn't privy to yet.

She tucks her lips in her mouth and clamps down. I want to reach forward and release her lips from their prison. But I stop myself. We don't know each other well enough for me to do such things.

"Um, no," she answers softly.

Although my tattoo is as clean as it will get right now, she continues wiping it to avert her eyes. "Autumn…"

"Yeah?" she says, eyes still laser focused on my distal forearm.

"Look at me," I whisper.

She licks her lips. "Mmhm?" Slowly, she lifts her gaze and locks it with mine.

"There's no need to be embarrassed." The desire to touch her expands like a hot air balloon in my chest. And I don't want to deny myself any longer. I reach forward with my free hand and graze the skin of her forearm near the black glove edge. Her momentary gasp trips my heart. I swallow and say, "Was only kidding." The corner of my mouth kicks up as I draw circles over her skin with my thumb.

"You were?" she asks, voice cracking.

I nod and she exhales. Her bashful nature continually takes me by surprise, but I love how flustered she gets when we are near. Because she has my stomach flipping on a trampoline nonstop. "About being a virgin, yes." She snorts quietly. "But not about wanting to ask you out."

Autumn peels off her gloves and tosses them in the trash. She rises from the stool and stretches. I study her a beat before standing up on stiff legs. Taking a moment, I stretch my limbs and arch my back, working out the kinks.

Please tell me I didn't scare her away.

She steps in front of me and moves to exit the booth, then stops and spins to face me. Tipping her head back slightly, she homes in on my lips. When I lick them, her lips quirk up at the corners as she nods.

"Yes," she whispers. "I would love to."

What? I stop myself from sticking my fingers in my ears and wiggling them. "Yes?"

She nods slowly as her nervous smile grows bolder and brighter. "I need to check my schedule, but yes. Can I call or text you later?"

I want to jump on the chair and scream *hell yes you can*. But like the proper gentleman my parents raised me to be, I keep my feet planted firmly on the floor and answer her as levelheaded as possible. "Of course. Wednesday is family dinner night, just so you know."

"Cool."

"Cool," I repeat and suddenly feel as if I am fifteen all over again. "Talk to you later."

She bites the inside of her cheek and nods. "Later." After a cute wave, she spins on her heel and wanders back into her booth with a little extra sway in her hips.

After I pay at the desk, I walk out the door and smile when the bell jingles. Who cares if I need to walk two-plus miles back to the garage to get my bike. Who cares if I forgot to bring a hoodie to the shop. Winter is still a few weeks away—not that the first official day of winter equals cool weather in Florida.

The only thing I *do* care about is the fact Autumn said yes to a date. And the promise of a date with Autumn is enough to keep me warm and has me walking faster. Has me smiling like an imbecile. Makes my heart beat faster and my breath stutter.

Today marks one of the happiest days of my life. A day I will never forget.

Jonas leaves the shop and I stand like a fool staring at the door for who knows how long. Staring at the place he last stood. Imagining him walking back in for no other reason than to see me.

I agreed to go on a date with Jonas. Me. A date. An actual doll-yourself-up-for-a-guy date.

Oh my fucking god.

I want to cheer and scream and jump and puke all at once.

When was the last time I was on an actual date? I would have to consult a 2013 calendar to determine the answer. And that little fact makes my stomach ball into a fist and squeeze tight. I may have sequestered myself for all the right reasons, but in doing so, I lost part of who I am. A spontaneous and vivacious woman.

Not as if those elements aren't still inside me. But now they have been tamped down by other qualities. Traits which currently reside in the spotlight for good reason.

"What just happened?" Penny asks as she skips into my booth.

I snap out of my daze and start cleaning my workstation. "Not sure what you're talking about," I reply, working hard to hide the smile painfully stretching my cheeks.

"Don't toy with my emotions, Auti. Spill. I know something happened."

After I drop the needles in the red bin, I peer up at her and shrug my shoulders. She widens her eyes when I hesitate and torture her a little longer. When she grunts, I decide to alleviate the torment. Because if I don't, Penny will make a scene.

"Jonas asked me on a date."

"And?" Penny steps closer, claps her hands in prayer position, and bats her eyelashes. Utterly ridiculous.

"And…" I drag the word out and count to five before continuing. Last thing I need is Penny strangling me because I am not forthcoming. "I said yes."

She gasps and leans back. Slaps a hand over her heart. "You said yes," she says in disbelief, voice decibels higher than normal. "Did I hear you correctly?"

I ball up the paper towel in my hand and toss it at her face. "Shut up." I laugh. "You heard what I said. Don't be a doofus."

"A doofus? Really? You sound like a five-year-old." Penny puckers her lips and cocks a brow. "Whatever." She blows a bubble and pops the pink gum with a loud smack. "So, where's he taking you?"

Her question has reality setting in a little more and a buzz hums low in my belly. *Jonas is taking me on a date.* A real date. Out in the world. Where other people exist. Where other people sit together and eat meals and laugh.

Holy shit.

"Not sure," I whisper before clearing my throat and finding my voice. "Told him I needed to check my schedule and I'd call or text him."

Penny rolls her eyes. "Check your schedule? Girl, you make your own schedule."

"True. But I'd be an asshole if I told him a day and someone was booked on my schedule already. Not cool. Someone would end up disappointed, and you know how I feel about that."

She nods. "Guess you're right. So..." She drags the single syllable into a ten-letter word. "What are you going to wear?"

Her question stops me in my tracks. For the first time in almost a decade, restlessness blankets me. Any other day of the week, this question wouldn't bother me. Could prattle off my ensemble in the blink of an eye. But something about dressing myself when I know it's for a set purpose—what I imagine will be the most amazing date of my life—has me stumbling in my tracks.

Jonas makes me stammer. For all the right reasons.

"I have no clue." I stare at Penny dumbstruck.

Stepping closer, she lays her hands on my shoulders and shakes me. "Snap out of it. That's what you have me for." I nod. "Okay, you finish cleaning up. I'll check your schedule for the next week and then we can game plan. Sound good?"

"Yes." I still can't believe this is real.

"Auti, I'm so excited for you."

I glance up at her and soak up her sunshine of a smile. Her enthusiasm has me smiling back. "Thanks. Pen?" She lifts her brows in question. "I'm going on a date," I squeal.

Reznor pops his head up from his client and smiles. "You know we all need to approve of him. Right?"

Stepping up to the wall between our booths, I prop my elbows on the ledge. "Yes, big brother. But let me have a date or two first. Before you and Rex scare him away."

Reznor dips the needle in an ink cap and leans back over his client's posterior ribcage. "Sure, little sis." He smiles and returns his focus to his work.

Once my booth is sanitized, I sidle up next to Penny. It surprises me when she tells me my Saturday night is free. Saturday is generally a busy day at the shop. Although not everyone works Monday to Friday, nine to five, majority of our clientele comes in on Friday and Saturday nights. So it blows my mind when she says my Saturday is bare.

When I question it, she winks conspiratorially and tells me all my other days are jam-packed. I narrow my eyes, but don't push the topic. Penny has been dying for me to get out in the world for years. She accepts why I haven't, but reminds me to live my life. *"How can you ever be happy if you never live outside the same four walls?"* Her words from over the years float through my thoughts.

Penny and I get home an hour later. Iliana is stretched out on the couch, asleep. *Gilmore Girls* plays quietly on the television. When there is nothing new to watch, we watch *Gilmore Girls*. Might be up to our seventh visit to Stars Hollow now. Never gets old.

I pick up the remote and press mute before sitting down next to her. Laying a hand on her forearm, I gently jostle her. "Ili. Wake up," I mumble.

She groans and squints. "What time is it?"

"Little after ten. Everything go okay tonight?" I ask.

"An angel, as always." Iliana scoots herself upright. "You guys finish up early?"

"Yeah. Rez still had someone in his chair, but said he'd be cool if we headed out."

Penny comes up behind me and rests her chin on my shoulder. "Auti has a date."

Iliana's jaw drops. "I'm sorry, but did you just say she has a date?"

Dear, god. Will I ever hear the end of their mockery? In short, no. No, I won't. My two closest friends will surely poke fun at me for quite some time. But I don't care. Wouldn't want them any other way.

"Well, more like the promise of a date. The actual day hasn't been determined yet. Although" —I turn and face Penny for a second— "my Saturday schedule is magically vacant."

"People must be out holiday shopping," Penny tosses out. "Can't help where people go to spend their money."

"Whatever." I roll my eyes, then refocus on Iliana. "I have to reach out to him and let him know what days I don't work."

Iliana leans forward, wraps her arms around me, and surprises me with a hug. "So happy for you," she whispers in my ear. Before I can squeeze her back, she releases me and rises from the couch. "I'm gonna head out."

"You're welcome to crash on the couch if you're still tired."

She smiles. "Thanks, but I'll make it home okay. Rather sleep in my bed, no offense."

After we exchange hugs and goodbyes, Iliana heads home. A second after the lock clicks in place, Penny hauls me to the couch and plops us down. She stares at me, expressionless, until I squirm under her scrutiny.

Why is she looking at me like that? Like a stern mother. Or a perturbed friend. She almost looks… bored. God, she confuses the hell out of me.

"What?"

"Auti," she says, more earnest than ever. "This is very serious."

My brows bunch together and I try to decode what the hell she is talking about. "What is, Pen?"

"Him. Jonas."

I nod. "Yeah," I whisper.

"I can't begin to tell you how excited I am for you." She glances at the hallway, down toward our bedrooms. "But this is big. Not just for you."

"Why do you think I haven't dated in years? Not like I've never wanted to. Believe me, I *miss* it. But, over the years, I made the right choice."

She nods. "You did."

Solemnity settles between us for a few minutes as we sit quietly on the couch. It isn't just the fact I haven't sat across from a good-looking man and shared a meal in several years that weighs heavy. But also the emotions and expectations which usually come with said scenarios. Emotions and expectations I have no idea if I am ready to handle.

The occasional blip on my radar isn't love. Love takes time. Is substantial and messy. Swallows you whole and never lets you leave.

Thirst is what currently consumes me. Thirst and hunger. My years without companionship have left me starved. Practically emaciated. But my attraction to Jonas isn't some attempt to fatten the ravenous fiend living inside me. My attraction to him is pure and mystical. Makes the organ beneath my breastbone swell and gallop wildly. Has my lungs burning for breath and my stomach topsy-turvy.

Never have I experienced the sensations Jonas induces. Emotions and energy and a gravity that hauls me into his atmosphere.

"Enough with the heavy," Penny announces quietly. "We have more important things to discuss."

"We do?"

She nods. "Like what you'll wear. How you'll fix your hair. What color you plan to paint your nails. The important stuff."

Eyes meeting hers, I pucker my lips and wiggle them side to side. "Oh my god, Pen," I whisper-scream. "Oh. My. God. I have a date."

"What about…?" Penny glances down the hall.

I peek over my shoulder and follow her gaze. "Can you? Please?"

A smile kicks up the corners of her mouth. "I got you covered."

"Thanks, Pen."

Penny and I gossip and giggle on the couch for another half hour before she heads to bed. She mothers me and suggests which top I should pair with which bottoms. What shoes I should wear. How to pin up my hair. I cut her off when she tells me to paint my nails a different color besides my typical cherry red. Polish and lip colors don't get messed with. Ever.

When I hear her bedroom door click shut, I dig my phone out of my purse. Opening up the text history between Jonas and I—where I texted myself from his phone—my fingers hover over the keyboard. Where to begin?

I check the time on the top of the screen and realize how late it is. Almost midnight. He is probably in bed already. No doubt the garage opens early.

I will send a quick message. If he doesn't answer, we can talk tomorrow. If he does answer, well… we shall see where it leads.

> Hey. You still up?

My finger hovers over the arrow to the right of my message. *Press send, Autumn. Just. Press. Send.*

I drop my finger and slump into the couch when the blue bubble populates the screen and it says *delivered* beneath. To my surprise, a small bubble hovers on the lower left side of the screen. Three tiny dots dancing as he types a response. My stomach dances alongside the dots.

> Still up. Too wired to sleep.

Is he ramped up from the adrenaline of getting new ink? Most people find it difficult to sleep shortly after getting a new tattoo. The adrenaline keeps them buzzed for hours afterward. Or is he riled up because I agreed to go on a date with him?

Hopefully it's the latter.

> Me too.

> You just finish work?

I smile. Why does him asking about work make me smile?

No. You were my last victim. Pen and I got home an hour ago.

You guys live together? Must be interesting.

This makes me laugh, and I slap a hand over my mouth. He barely knows Penny, yet has already deemed her a fascinating creature. Which is more than true. Penny is a sassy diamond in the rough.

She keeps life interesting.

I bet. You get to check your schedule?

Eager. I love it. More than I thought possible.

I did. Somehow, the gods have shined down on me and I have Saturday free.

Perfect. Would it be okay if I pick you up?

Yes.

My cheeks sting from the broad, permanent smile plastered on my face. Why can I not stop smiling?

Six?

Can't wait.

Although he could dig it up from my paperwork at the garage, Jonas asks for my address. I give it without hesitation. He bids me good night with the promise of picking me up at six on Saturday. Less than two days from now.

I hug my phone to my chest like a preteen. After I swim in the sea of serenity a moment, I rise from the couch, flick off the light, and head down the hall.

Slipping into my bedroom, I quietly change into a tank top and boy shorts. I peel back the covers and ease into bed. Head on the pillow, I follow the moonlight as it dances on the wall and ceiling through the blinds.

I fall asleep with a smile on my face and gentle, sweet snores beside me.

Ten

JONAS

I change my shirt for the seventh time.

Somehow, going on a date with Autumn has turned me prepubescent again. I have never cared so much about my clothes or hair a day in my life. Never lifted my arms so many times to check if I put on deodorant. In the last thirty minutes, I have probably sniffed my pits more times than in the last three months.

Someone send help.

I decide on a long-sleeve, black Henley, jeans, and my leather boots. Staring at my reflection in the bathroom mirror, I brush my hair left, then back again. Regardless of my efforts, the few inches of hair atop my head stays a mess. So I give up, comb my fingers through it, and abandon my reflection.

Spartan barks and zooms around the kitchen island like a bewildered maniac.

"Come on, nut. Let's get you dinner before I leave."

He barks in approval and drops on his haunches in front of his bowl. I scoop a cup of food into his bowl and make him wait with a hand signal. For a spaz, he obeys every command I give without hesitancy. Thank you obedience classes for all you do.

While Spartan vacuums down his dinner, I fetch my keys, wallet, phone, a couple blankets and my leather jacket.

Done with his dinner, Spartan runs up to me and barks. I shuffle my hand back and forth over his head, roughing up his fur. "Good boy. Let's go outside really quick. Then Dad has to go."

I open up the door to the back yard and let him loose. He runs the perimeter, finds several patches of grass he hasn't marked as his, then runs back into the house. I secure him in his kennel, turn on the radio, and head out the front door.

After stowing the blankets in the back, I crank the Jeep's engine and set the heat to low. Yesterday's cold front finally brought cooler temps to our part of the state. The air isn't frigid, but for us natives, it is on the cooler side. Especially once the sun goes down.

A second after I park the Wrangler in front of Autumn's apartment, her front door opens and she steps out. I swallow and all but choke on my own saliva.

How the hell am I supposed to focus all night?

Autumn stands in front of her door in a dress hugging every curve beneath her bust to her knees. The dress bolsters a snug but loose red top and a slim-fit black skirt. The sweetheart neckline accentuated with a small black bow. Her dark, rich locks frame her face in soft waves.

I swallow again and remind myself to breathe. Remind myself to not be an idiot or say the wrong thing.

Cutting the headlights, I step out of the Jeep and we meet in the middle. A jacket drapes over one of her arms while a small black purse hangs on the other.

"Hi," I rasp. "You look… wow."

She giggles. "Hi. And thank you." Reaching forward, she traces her fingers over my bicep. "You look great too."

The corner of my mouth kicks up. "No one will give me the time of day with you in the room." She peeks up at me from beneath her lashes. "Shall we?" I gesture toward the Jeep and resist the urge to lay my hand on her lower back.

Not yet. Soon, but not yet.

Both of us buckled in, I flip the headlights back on and drive. We sit in the dark cab with only the low volume of my rock playlist floating around us. The air weighted with thrill and anxiety as neither of us speak. And for once, the silence kills me.

"Are you warm enough?" I ask to break the constant quiet.

Out of the corner of my eye, she swivels to face me slightly. "Yes, thank you. Where are we going?"

"Well…" I glance at her a second before returning my eyes to the road. Damn, she robs my every thought. "Wasn't quite sure what you liked to eat, so I aimed for variety. Hope that's okay."

"For future reference, I eat just about everything. Well, at least everything I've tried."

I don't miss the start of her words. *"For future reference."* Three simple words have me soaring high as a kite on a summer day.

"Good to know." I tuck away the new information for safekeeping. "Hope you're hungry. You'll want one of everything. Guaranteed."

"Now I'm intrigued." I hear the smile in her voice and wish I could take my eyes off the road.

Minutes later, I park and help Autumn out. This time I don't resist the urge to rest my hand on her lower back as I steer us to the front door of the restaurant. We may be at the start, but the simple touch feels more than natural. Right. The second we step inside; it feels as if we stepped back in time. Back to the 1950s.

Black-and-white tiles checker the floor. Pops of red and chrome accent backless stools and the lengthy diner counter. Fountains line the counter like keg taps in a bar. The back wall loaded with vintage metal signs for cola and floats and items more popular during a different era. Shelves packed with glassware for milkshakes and sundaes and banana splits. Red and black vinyl booths line the windowed walls, while small two-seater tables sit nestled between the booths and fountain counter. Each booth has its own jukebox. A handful rest on the counter for patrons who sit near the fountains.

A young woman seats us at a booth, hands us menus, prattles off the evening specials and reminds us breakfast is served all day.

"How did I not know this place existed?" Autumn asks and I shrug. Her eyes float around the room. Awe and delight twinkle in her eyes as she takes it all in. "I think I'm in love."

When her eyes circle back and land on me, she tucks her lips in that cute way she does. A flush paints her cheeks. And I bite back the urge to say what is on my mind.

Me too.

"Wait until you taste the food. This is nothing," I say as I wave around the bustling mom-and-pop diner.

Silence falls over us as we study the menu. After a beat, the server returns to take our order. Autumn orders first and I bite the inside of my cheek at the amount of food she orders. She is either really hungry or had difficulty deciding. Either way, the notion is adorable.

Once both of us order and the server leaves, I laugh.

"What's so funny?" Eyes trained on my face, her brows lift incrementally.

"Hungry?"

My new favorite shade of red tints her cheeks. "There were a hundred different things on the menu I wanted. You're lucky I only ordered what I did."

"Autumn, if you wanted to order the whole menu, I wouldn't care."

And I didn't. As long as I get to sit with her, talk with her, have her in my presence, consider me a happy man. I believe in the simple things. That life doesn't need to be full of miracles, money, and endless *stuff* to discover true happiness. Moments matter more than material possessions. Moments can't be taken away.

"Well, damn. I should've ordered more." She laughs and I join in. "So, Jonas..."

"So, Autumn..."

"Tell me all there is to know about you." She leans forward, sets her elbows on the table, and rests her chin in her palms.

Damn, she is lovable. I mentally shake my head. Shake off the ease at which I fall so easily for a woman I barely know. Am I fortunate or cursed? Fate has yet to decide.

"All of it?" I tease.

"Don't leave anything out."

If possible, I would share my entire life with her in a split second. But light speeds aren't possible when it comes to relationships. The good ones built over time—marinate. Any great relationship starts with friendship. And friendships start with details and trust.

"Alright. Let's see how much I can spew before our food arrives." Just as the words leave my lips, the server drops off my cherry cola—a newfound favorite— and Autumn's vanilla milkshake. She plucks the cherry off the whipped cream and pops it in her mouth. "Uh, where to start..."

Her lips wrap around the cherry as she pops the stem off. Liquid cognac and red lips swirl my vision. The bright lights, bopping music, and bustle of the restaurant fade in the background as I stare at her mouth. How the hell am I supposed to speak basic vocabulary when she inadvertently teases me.

As if unaware of her influence, she suggests, "Tell me about your family. I already met your dad."

Family. A safe place to start, I suppose. I sip my soda to wet my throat and start somewhere near the beginning.

"Dad and I are a lot alike. I don't know if it's because I inherited more from him than Mom. Or if it's because I'm the only male child."

Autumn sits up straighter and sips on her milkshake. "So you have sisters?"

I nod. "Yep. Two. Jasmine and Jillian." She giggles and the sound spreads warmth in my chest. "What?"

"Do your parents have a thing for the letter J?"

"Never asked, but often wondered myself. Maybe it's because of Grandpa and Uncle John on Mom's side. Not sure."

She leans forward and resumes her position with her chin on her hands. "Continue, please."

"Jasmine and I are two years apart—she's older. But Jillian is seven years younger than me. And because Jasmine and I had more years together before Jillian was born, we're closer. We're all close, though. Mom made sure of it. Hence our weekly family dinners."

Across from me, Autumn sits back against the booth and sighs. Her bright spirit from seconds ago fades as she speaks. "Wish my family mirrored yours. I'd give anything for a close-knit, kind family."

Something in her tone stings when matched with her words. At times, my family annoys the heck out of me. Always in my business or making suggestions on how I handle this or that. As if they know what is best for my life. But I wouldn't trade them for anything in the world. And honestly, I might be lost without them.

"Want to talk about it?" I ask. Because I don't want to pry something out of her that she isn't ready to share.

She shakes her head. "Not tonight. Too heavy for a first date." A smile curves the corners of her mouth, but it doesn't reach her eyes. This moment is the most solemn I have seen her.

And I don't like it. One bit.

"Well, maybe sometime you can meet the rest of my family." Her eyes widen and I fear I have just sunk the evening deep at sea. "If that's something you'd like. Eventually."

The more I correct myself, the bigger her smile gets. "I'd like that."

The server stops in front of our table and sets the tray on a stand. Plate after plate, I laugh as the server keeps setting dishes on our table. When finished, she glances between the both of us and winces. "Anything else I can get you right now?"

I want to laugh because I know she is just doing her job. After looking at Autumn, I shake my head and relieve the poor girl. "Nah, we're good." When she walks off, I stare at the five plates in front of Autumn and laugh. "This will be interesting."

"Don't worry, I plan to have leftovers."

"Good to know. Because I don't imagine *I* could even scarf down mozzarella sticks, a plate of onion rings, potato skins, a double cheeseburger with all the fixings, fries, and coleslaw. Plus a milkshake."

She giggles and it vibrates across my skin and warms me more than the summer sun. "I plan to sample it all. But I have to save room for dessert, too."

"Dessert? Dear god, woman. How can you even think about dessert already?"

With a shake of her head, she says, "Dessert is the first thing I think about."

Something about the way she eyes me as she says the word dessert has me wanting to box everything up and leave. But Mom would smack me across the back of my head if I did. Lecture me until her voice scratched and my ears fell off.

I eat my BBQ-style double cheeseburger and fries while watching Autumn in awe. Surprisingly, she demolishes a third of the food without breaking a sweat. We ask the server for a couple to-go boxes before Autumn orders a banana split made with toasted marshmallow and Smurf-flavored ice creams.

When her dessert arrives, I gape at the heaping mound of sugary cream and fruit. Blue and white ice cream sits sandwiched at the base between a split banana and under a mountain of whipped cream, sliced strawberries, pineapple nibs, chocolate syrup, colorful jimmies, and three maraschino cherries.

"Holy shit," I spit out. "Are you going to eat all that?" Jesus. What is that, a thousand calories?

"Nope." I blink away from the mammoth-sized dessert to catch her expression. "You're going to help."

"I am?"

She slowly nods. Picking up one of the spoons, she scoops some of the confection up and brings it to her lips. I follow the spoon with my eyes and swallow when it disappears between her lips. She closes her eyes and hums. The sounds go straight to my groin.

"Here," she says as her eyes pop back open and she scoops more on the spoon. "You need to taste this."

My gaze locks on to her lips and I imagine better ways to taste dessert. More intimate ways. She holds the spoon inches from my mouth. The whipped cream and blue ice cream melt together as a piece of strawberry dips slowly in the middle. I lean forward, lift my eyes to hers, and open my mouth as she feeds me dessert. I haven't even tasted it yet, but know it is—and forever will be—the best damn dessert to hit my tongue.

The sweet confection melts over my tastebuds and I moan. As messy and funky as it seemed, it tastes damn good.

"Was I right?" she asks. All I do is nod.

We take turns feeding each other until we have scraped every last bit of dessert out of the small glass boat. It is the most innocent and provocative meal I have eaten. A meal I won't soon forget. After I pay the check, we walk out to the Jeep and I start it up.

"Is it okay if we are doing something else, too?" I ask.

As much as I don't want the evening to be over, I don't know how she feels after eating half her weight in food. Not that I could tell when she stood from the table.

"I'd love to. What'd you have in mind?"

I tap my temple and smile. "Top secret."

"Fine," she huffs out and rolls her eyes. "Take me on your top secret adventure."

I laugh and put the Jeep in gear. Music floats in the cab and Autumn asks if she can change it. I hand her my phone and tell her the code to unlock it. "Sure. The app should be open already."

Out of the corner of my eye, I see her gawking in my direction. I want to ask why, but I think it's because I just gave her the code to my phone. If something so simple surprises her, it breaks my heart. But I have nothing to hide. Hell, I already told her about Cora the first day we met. The only skeleton I had in my closet has come out.

Trust is a big deal in every relationship. As of now, I have absolutely no reason to not trust her. I don't know much about her, but I hope to change that. Hope whatever keeps her from opening up—her avoidance on discussing her past—can be ripped to shreds. But everyone exposes themselves in their own time, and I need to give her the space to do it at her own pace.

She scrolls through the app and selects a song. An upbeat rock tune spills from the speakers and I can't help but bop to the sound. After the next song, I pull into a parking lot and weave through the rows until I locate a spot.

"The park?" she asks.

I cut the engine and glance over at her in the dark. "Yep. Tonight is *Movies In The Park* night." She bites her lip and shrugs. "Every two weeks, the park hosts a movie night after the park closes to foot traffic. You bring your own blanket or chair and they supply the movie."

"Really?" There is a lightness to her voice. A level of wonderment. And I love that I put it there.

"Really."

I slip out of the Jeep, open the back door to grab the blankets and my jacket, and round the back to help her out. A man in a bright orange vest wielding a flashlight approaches and directs us down the path for the movie. We walk across the lawn in silence, weaving between the people already set up and waiting for the movie to begin. Twenty feet on the lawn, my knuckles graze hers and a jolt of energy zings me head to boot. My pulse whooshes behind my ears and I remind myself to breathe.

If she affects me this easily from a single graze of the hand, it's unimaginable how I will feel when we kiss.

"How about there?" Autumn points to an open spot on the lawn since I have obviously stopped focusing.

"Perfect."

We weave between more blankets and finally reach the vacancy. I ask her to hold the extra blanket and my jacket while I spread the one for us to sit on. Once set up, we plop down and kick off our shoes.

"What movie are we seeing?"

"Not sure. I didn't look up the schedule. Mom and Dad have come to a few of these. That's how I knew about them."

"Fun. I like surprises."

You are the best surprise of them all.

A few minutes later, the movie flickers on the temporary screen. One I haven't seen.

"Oh god."

"What?" I ask.

"I'm going to cry."

Shit. Is this bad? Should we leave? "We don't have to stay," I suggest. Although every atom in my body screams to stay put.

"No." She presses her hand to my chest and I stop breathing. "It's a good movie."

About five minutes in, the title *A Star Is Born* pops up in red on the screen. Now I understand why she said she will cry. Jasmine told me she and Anton saw this in the theater and she bawled like a baby, but it was worth every tear.

We slip on our jackets as the movie rolls on. I lay back on my forearms while Autumn sits up, leaning back on her hands. My attention shifts between Bradley Cooper and Lady Gaga to Autumn. I follow the lines of her profile as her eyes remain glued to the screen. The slim line of her nose. The voluptuous curves of her lips. Down to the slight dip in her chin. I would rather watch her for two hours than this movie, but I force myself to alternate between the two.

Halfway through the movie, she shivers beside me. "Cold?" She nods. "Here." I unfold the second blanket and go to wrap it around her.

"What about you?" she asks as she mimics my position.

"I'll be fine."

She shakes her head and sits back up. "Sit up."

"What? Why?" She gives me a pointed look. "Fine."

When I sit up, she cocoons us both with the wool blanket. My mind thinks a hundred different ungentlemanly thoughts and I tell myself to shut up. Slowly, she starts to lie down and I get the hint.

We lay on the blanket—my front to her back—and I stop watching the movie altogether. All I can focus on is the way her body molds to mine. How she pulled my upper arm down and wrapped it around her waist and laid hers over top. How her fruity, vanilla scent wafts from her hair into my nose. And how perfect she feels in my arms. Like she belongs there. Like she has always belonged there.

With Autumn in my arms, I close my eyes and get lost in my imagination. Lost in the fantasy of what kissing her will be like when it finally happens. Because it will happen.

I keep my eyes closed as I splay my fingers on her belly and she weaves hers between mine. Everything about this moment, about us, continually comes together with comfort and ease. Without difficulty, I envision Autumn in my arms often. Imagine her lips pressed to mine daily. Believe this rhythmic rush beneath my sternum will only get stronger the more I see her. Spend time with her. Hold her.

Hopefully, she believes and feels the same. That she reciprocates this unfamiliar rush of emotions.

Before long, the movie ends. I mentally whine at the fact I have to unravel her from my arms. But I do. We fold up the blankets, hop in the Jeep, and head back to her apartment. The entire ride back, neither of us says a word. The silence isn't uncomfortable, but seems like a missed opportunity to learn more about each other. Soon, too soon, I park in front of her apartment and cut the engine.

We sit in the dark a moment before I finally open the door and walk around to her side. Out of the Jeep, we take slow, measured steps to her front door. Not that I have a professional dating degree, but if I am reading the signs correctly, neither of us wants tonight to be over.

When we reach her front door, she spins to face me. But she doesn't look up. Not yet.

"I had a really nice time," she whispers into the darkness.

Lightly, I brush my knuckles from her temple down to the angle of her jaw. "Me too," I whisper. Her gaze lifts to meet mine. "Can I kiss you?" Her eyes dart between mine for a moment before she subtly nods.

Thank fuck.

I lift my other hand and frame her face with my palms. She sucks in a breath as I lean down, but doesn't exhale. The red cotton covering her breasts brushes against my chest and my heart bangs its fists against my ribcage. Less than an inch from her lips, she closes her eyes just before I do the same.

And then my lips press to hers and nothing else exists.

The faint porch light fades away. The occasional roar of a car engine or pitter-patter of an animal scurrying across the grass in the dark disappears. I lick her lower lip and she opens up like a flower blooms. Every sense I own homes in on her.

The residual taste of ice cream on her tongue. Her sweet perfume in my nose. How warm her body is as it presses flush with mine. The small whimper from her lips when I break the kiss. How her cognac eyes slowly open and beg for more. And how I *know* this will not be the last time our lips meet.

I lean in for one last peck and love how she whimpers again when our lips separate.

"Thank you," she whispers. "Best date ever."

I hold her gaze. "Hopefully I can top it next time."

"No doubt about it." I step back from her and a slight frown mars her face. I brush my thumb over her cheek. "Good night, Jonas."

"'Night, Autumn."

eleven

AUTUMN

Jonas walks back to his Jeep, and I want to run after him. I press my fingers to my lips and reminisce in the fire he set moments ago. A fire I don't want extinguishing.

"Wait," I holler then jog out and meet him by his car door. "Please don't think I don't want you to come inside."

Although he never made such a suggestion, part of me feels the need to confess this aloud. To share what I desire, but am not ready to explore. For him to hear it from my lips—not only the words, but the subtle message behind my tone.

"Autumn, I would never assume anything." He caresses my cheek with his knuckles again and I melt into his touch as emotion dances like carbonation in my chest. "Much as I would love for you to invite me in, I don't think either of us is ready for that step. Not yet." He inches forward, the proximity of him hot on my skin. "I will wait until you're ready."

I peek up at Jonas from under my lashes and wonder where the hell he has been all my life. Why I hadn't met him sooner. A man with endless patience and unshakable kindness. A man that looks at me with gentleness and ardor.

"Jonas…"

Another shuffle forward, his lips now a breath away from grazing my own. Oh, how I want to taste him again.

"Please don't feel like you owe me an explanation. Because you don't."

Our eyes meet and my throat goes dry as I soak up the intensity of his gaze. The magnificent swirl of blue and green and gold, but a hint darker. They remind me of an incoming rainstorm at sunset. Not a storm worthy of fear, but one that lures you outdoors and begs you to get lost in it. To dance in the rain rather than try to escape the waterfall.

God, how I want to kiss him again. More than I want to breathe.

"Thank you. For telling me I don't owe you anything." My eyes drop to his lips and I tell myself to look back up. To focus on what I should say. To use my words. "There is so much I want to tell you. So much. But I need things between us to go slow. Not because I don't want you. I do, believe me." *You're rambling, Autumn.* Rambling aside, Jonas gives me his smile. One full of contentment with a dash of humor. "But my past has roots. Roots I need time to dig up. And it may take time."

He frames my face in his hands. "Hey." When he knows my attention is solely on him, he continues. "Like I said, we go at your pace. I'm not in any rush. I'm not going anywhere."

I really hope his words hold truth. Because what I haven't told him could be the one thing which scares him away. Jonas doesn't seem the type to scare easily, but it is best not to assume. Some people surprise you.

"You're the first person I've dated in a really long time," I confess. He cocks his head, toys with a strand of hair, and waits for me to continue. "Years ago, I dated this guy who swore he'd always be there for me. But" —I swallow and hang my head— "when things got more serious than he wanted, he bailed. It threw a wrench in everything. With my parents and my sister, and other parts of my personal life."

I glance over my shoulder at the front door. Picture who is on the other side. "If it weren't for Penny and everyone else at the shop, I would've stayed on the street."

Jonas drops his hands from my face and the immediate loss sends a chill across my cheeks. But before I dwell on the absence of his touch, he slips his arms around my waist and envelops me in a hug so potent, emotion stings the back of my eyes. He holds me close to his chest, shushes the tears threatening to fall, and whispers how everything is fine now because he is here.

And I believe him. Right here, right now, I believe him. Regardless of how little I know Jonas, some facts are undeniable. Jonas is a good man. A good man raised by another good man.

I sense it when he hesitates to do things other men would assume is normal and acceptable. Like resting his hand on my back or taking my hand in his. Like asking for my phone number or address when he had the means to get it without my consent. Or when he asked, only minutes ago, permission to kiss me. Most men don't ask, they just take.

Jonas isn't like most men. He is levels above.

Not sure which of us initiates, but we slowly pull back from each other. Jonas lifts his hands back to my face and swipes his thumbs over my cheeks before leaning in and pressing a sweet, chaste kiss to my lips. "Although I don't like why you were crying, you look more beautiful than ever."

I close my eyes and get lost in the gyroscope of emotion spinning in my chest. Before Jonas, no man ever had me so tongue-tied and wobbly. Although I have walked on my own two feet for years, with Jonas I feel as if I am truly learning how they work. How they will carry me where I need to go. Toward him.

"Only you would think I look beautiful with mascara staining my cheeks."

He shakes his head. "You don't get it." No, I don't. Though, I won't admit such things aloud. "It's not that you have tear-stained makeup. It's the reason why. That you're exposing a piece of yourself and letting me see the parts no one else gets to."

When he explains it like this, I understand better. Little did I realize, I unintentionally opened myself up to him. I let him in when I never let anyone else in. With the exception of Penny. Reznor, Rex, and Iliana know minor, rough-around-the-edges details, but they don't know anything with depth. Penny, on the other hand, knows everything. Not because I favor her over the rest of my tattoo family, but because we live together and there is no possible way around it.

I drop my gaze from his eyes to his lips again. He won't make me ask permission, but I want to taste him one more time before we say good night again. Taste the sweetness of our shared dessert mixed with a flavor I define as distinctly Jonas. When my eyes remain on his lips, he makes my wish come true.

He leans forward and the space between us disappears. I close my eyes and fist his shirt as his lips press mine with unprecedented tenderness. He kisses me once. Twice. On the third kiss, I sweep the tip of my tongue along the seam of his lips. A low groan rumbles in his chest. I tighten my grip on the cotton as he slips his fingers into my hair and opens up to let me in.

Then I taste him again. Hot and sweet and addictive on my taste buds. The heat of his tongue tangling with mine is a shock wave throughout my body, waking all the parts once dormant. Loosening my hold, my hands trail up his chest, cup his cheeks and revel in the gruff grain against my soft palms.

He groans at my touch, drops his hands to my hips, and draws me impossibly closer. Close enough for the bulge beneath his zipper to brush my abdomen. The temptation to invite him in multiplies tenfold seconds before he breaks the kiss.

"You might be the death of me. But it'd be a good way to go," he says, gasping.

"Back atcha."

"As much as I don't want to leave, I should go."

I fight the urge to disagree, and nod. "Yeah," I whisper. "Will you call or text me?"

"Better believe it."

I smile and peek up at him. "Good night, Jonas."

He sweeps a stray hair out of my face, tucking it behind my ear. "Good night, Autumn."

As I walk back to the front door, he gets in the Jeep and starts it. We keep our eyes on each other until he backs out and drives away. For a moment, I stare at the space where I last saw his taillights. Absorb every moment of the evening, now that I am alone. Well, alone for a minute longer.

I take a deep breath and dig for the house key in my purse. Just as I go to insert the key in the lock, the door swings open and an overzealous Penny yanks me inside.

"I want details. Now."

I stumble over my own two feet as she closes the door and drags me over to the couch. "Pen." I laugh and plop down on the middle cushion.

"Don't you *Pen* me. And don't pretend like you weren't just outside kissing a hot-as-fuck man. Twice."

Biting the inside of my cheek, I fight the smile and laughter dying to burst free. But I lose the battle.

"Do you want a complete rundown of the evening? Cause I promise the entire date wasn't like what you witnessed out front, Peeping Tom."

"Girl, you better tell me everything. Beginning to end. And don't you dare leave a single detail out."

I kick off my shoes and tuck my feet beneath my butt. Penny draws her legs to her chest, rests her chin on her knees, and listens to every intricate detail about my date with Jonas. From the cutest retro diner I ever set foot in to the movie in the park where he held me close and I stopped paying attention to the screen and focused solely on his warm body curled behind mine. How his fingers splayed my belly and held me close. How I never wanted to miss a single moment of his breath on the back of my neck. She already witnessed the two separate kisses out front.

As I tell Penny how I broke the barrier and told Jonas a little about my past, she slaps a hand over her mouth. Me explaining an ounce of my past to anyone—no matter how big or small the detail—is a huge step. Penny knows I wouldn't tell just anyone. Which means I believe Jonas and I could become far more than just two people dating for the sake of dating.

"Auti, I'm so happy for you." I give her a half smile. "Seriously. It is way past time you did something for yourself. Be a little selfish for a change. Be happy. It looks good on you."

"Thanks, Pen." I yawn.

Although I have been awake much later than this countless times, the exhilaration from the evening is slowly fading and exhaustion is taking over.

"Go." Penny throws a thumb over her shoulder toward the hall. "Wash up and go to bed. We'll go out for breakfast in the morning. My treat."

I squint at her and she shakes her head. Rising up from the couch, I snatch my shoes off the floor and kiss the crown of Penny's head. "Thanks for always being the best. Don't know where I'd be without you."

"Love you too, Auti. Sleep tight."

After stowing the leftovers in the fridge, I go about my normal nightly routine before bed. As I brush my teeth, I zone out and replay my evening with Jonas. Recall the buzz zapping every inch of my skin and the hum deep in my belly as he laid behind me and pressed his palm to my lower abdomen. Jonas encasing me in his arms… I never felt more at home.

Flipping off the bathroom light, I tiptoe into the bedroom, change into my pajamas, and quietly slip between the sheets. I curl onto my side and face the opposite side of the bed. Face the angelic form beside me. Chest steadily rising and falling in the darkened room.

"I'm not going anywhere." Jonas's words creep back in from earlier. And as I take in the most important person in my world, the little girl less than a foot away, I pray his words stick when I tell him.

twelve

JONAS

I lay awake in bed, eyes on the ceiling but not really seeing it. Spartan twitches and dream barks at the foot of the bed. For once, it doesn't bother me. Nothing could right now.

When was the last time I felt like this? Lighter. Carefree. Happy. Like the future has a million possibilities and I can't wait to explore them all.

Easy. I haven't.

Date night with Autumn was literally one of the best in my life. Hell, I spent all day yesterday smiling like a goddamn idiot. I never enjoyed doing housework so much. Never enjoyed tearing up the back yard to landscape it like I did yesterday. Spartan ran around the yard, barking incessantly at squirrels and hunting for lizards. But it didn't irritate me as per usual.

The alarm blares on the bedside table and I slap the snooze button to shut it up. Spartan pops his head up from the mattress and yips.

"'Morning, buddy."

He yips again. I like to call it his quiet voice. As if he knows it's too early to use his full bark yet. Either way, it's adorable how quiet he is until I get out of bed. Then his typical, boisterous bark commences.

We get out of bed and ready for our morning walk. Once we step out the door, Spartan leads us down the street and along our usual morning path. Glad he can focus and lead the way because mentally I am still standing in front of Autumn's apartment, kissing her.

Lost in my daydream, it seems as if only a few minutes pass before we arrive back home. After filling Spartan's bowl with kibble, I go about my morning routine. I slip on a Thompson's Garage shirt and a pair of jeans before heading into the kitchen to make breakfast. Belly full, I slip on boots, secure Spartan in his kennel, and head out the door. A moment later, I zip through Clearwater on my bike, relishing the sharp sting of wind on my cheeks, and arrive at the garage early again.

When I walk into the office, Dad glances up from the stack of papers in front of him to the clock and shakes his head. "You keep this up and I might start setting your schedule earlier."

"Ha ha, old man." I brew a fresh pot of coffee before sifting through the invoices on my desk. "Looks like a busy day."

Dad doesn't say anything for a moment and I wonder if he didn't hear what I said. When I glance over at his desk, he stares at me with the biggest shit-eating grin on his face. The type you see when people know something you don't. I cock a brow and he shakes his head.

"Interesting," he says, cryptically.

"What?" I drop my head and scan my shirt to see if my breakfast is still hanging around. Nope.

"How was your weekend, son?"

My weekend? Why the hell would Dad ask about my weekend. Not that we never chat about how we spend our time apart, but it isn't an automatic Monday question. I think back and try to remember if I told him I was going on a date with Autumn.

Think, think, think.

No, don't think it ever came up. Especially after his snooping while I was on the phone. He means well, has a good heart, but it suddenly feels as if I'm a teenager all over again.

"Great. Why?"

His grin widens further. "Great, huh? What'd ya do?"

What the hell is this? Twenty questions of obscurity? Dad isn't the type to be evasive. At least, not from past experiences. Then again, I have never openly discussed my interest in someone. Does he know what I did this weekend? I mentally shake my head. Not possible.

"Went out. Did stuff around the house. Why?"

"Where'd you go?"

Okay, game over. Between him skirting around what he wants to say and the devious smile on his lips, I am about to explode from curiosity. "Why don't you just spit it out, old man."

He tips his head back and laughs. A full belly laugh. Similar to the thousands I have heard over the years. He's yanking my chain and he full well knows it. Even enjoys the slow torment with a wicked gleam in his eye.

"Back at ya, son." He points to my face. "Only reason I'm giving you a hard time is that."

"What?" I swipe my palms over my face and feel for the evidence he refers to. But I don't find it.

"Your permanent smile." My cheeks heat. "Don't be embarrassed, son. The smile suits you." He gets up, walks to the coffee pot, and pours us each a cup. "Plus, a smile like that could be good for business."

"Alright." I laugh. "That's enough from you, old man."

He hands me a mug while he fishes the creamer out of the fridge. After he pours some in his coffee, he passes it my way.

"In all seriousness, it's really great to see you happy, son. And if a certain female car owner has anything to do with it, then I approve."

I pour cream in my cup then spoon in a little sugar. "Thanks, Dad. Means a lot."

We drink our coffee and work for the next hour in silence. But it isn't awkward or filled with the expectation to spill more details. Although, if I keep dating Autumn—which I have every intention of doing—Dad will dig for more. And I won't hold back.

The Thompson family is an open family. We don't hide anything from each other. We were all raised—Mom and Dad included—with the belief it is better to be open and honest from the get-go. Just saves from stirring up future problems.

After I finish paperwork in the office, I head to the garage bays and start on the first clients of the day. As of now, most of the morning is filled with appointments for routine maintenance. I step up to an SUV and match the vehicle to the invoice then get started on the oil change.

As I wipe my hands clean after finishing, my phone pings in my pocket. Pulling it out of my coveralls, I smile down at the screen. Two bays down, Dad laughs and points between my face and my phone. *Yeah, yeah, old man.*

AUTUMN

Morning. Hope the rest of your weekend was good.

Her text has me smiling for two reasons. One—she sent me a text. How can I not be happy over that small fact? Getting a text means the other person was thinking of you. Two—her actual text. The message is sweet, but also makes me think she had no idea what to say. She simply wanted to text me, but didn't know how to initiate conversation. It reminds me how she said she hadn't dated in years. She didn't go into great detail, but someone probably didn't treat her right.

Good morning. Best weekend in years.

Yeah. What made it so great?

Is this Autumn subtly flirting? And why does every single word from her lips— and her fingers, I guess—make my cheeks sting? Heat me head to toe. Make my mind wander to places it never has. Places which include her in every facet.

Oh, you know. A night on the town with a beautiful woman. Being domestic at home.

Domestic, huh? *screenshots for future reference*

And there it is again. *Future reference.* The term sinks deeper into my marrow every time I hear—see—it. I love how she sees us beyond a single date or moment in time. How she wants more between us, even if she doesn't openly say it. Little indicators such as saving something I say for *future reference* means more to me than imaginable.

What can I say... My parents raised me to be self-sufficient. Want to know a secret?

steeples fingers and leans in close Dish it out already.

I laugh as my fingers fly over the screen.

Mom taught me how to sew buttons when I was 5. Said every man should know how.

And now I'm in love with your mom.

A small tornado swirls in my chest—flipping things upside down and causing my heart to beat violently. *Don't take it out of context.* Her text is meant to be funny or cute. That she loves my mom because she taught me things the general populous deems a female activity. But Dad taught my sisters how to change their own oil and swap out a flat tire. It's just how the Thompson family rolled. Being self-sufficient is a life skill, not a gender skill.

Is it too soon for me to tell her that? She might replace me
with you. The third daughter she never had.

Did that come out wrong? I reread my text and mentally wipe my brow with the
back of my hand. *Whew.* For a second there, I thought maybe I insinuated something else. That our relationship would lead her to becoming my mother's daughter
—in a sense.

Aaron already knows me. Wouldn't bother me if you told
your parents we are dating.

Dating. Not "went on a date." I glance up and across the garage. Dad leans
against a silver pickup with a knowing smile on his face as he watches me text
Autumn. Time to wrap this up, otherwise Dad will tease me until the end of time.

Hate to cut this short. Dad's giving me the side-eye.

Sorry 😞 I'll bring him cookies later.

No need to apologize. And sprinkles are his favorite.

Sprinkles. Check. See you in a bit?

I'll be here.

I tuck my phone back in my pocket and look over at Dad. "What're you smiling
at, old man?"

"Ah, to be young and in love again," he says and I stop breathing.

Autumn is gorgeous and funny and downright lovable, but I never indicated I
was *in love* with her. Did I? I mean, Jesus, I have only known her just shy of two
weeks.

"Dad…" I warn. But he just waves me off. "By the way, since you wouldn't let
Autumn pay for the repairs, she's bringing you cookies later."

"Really?" I nod and his grin brightens. "Well, son, I approve."

An hour later, I hear the telltale sounds of a classic car. Rolling out from under
the sedan I currently work on, I sit up and swallow at the woman walking toward
the bays with a bag in her hand.

Autumn strolls up in an off-the-shoulder, black-and-white striped top under
dark denim overalls folded up to land just below the knee. Her black-brown locks
are pinned up high on the back of her head while a folded bandana loops from the
base of her skull up into a bow at her crown. Lips painted scarlet, as are her nails.
And today she wears dark-tinted, black-framed, wingtip sunglasses.

I swallow harder with each step she takes in my direction. This woman will be
the death of me. No doubt about it. Dad steps out of the bay next to me and meets
Autumn five feet away from where I still sit on the ground.

"Hey there, sweetie. My son tells me I get cookies for being a nice guy."

Autumn slides her sunglasses up to rest on top of her head. "And I hear you
love sprinkles."

Dad smiles down at me before meeting Autumn's gaze again. "You hear correct. Honestly, haven't met a cookie I don't love. Sprinkles just make them fun."

She laughs and hands Dad the bag. "Well, I didn't have time to bake. But there's lots of sprinkles plus some other flavors, in case anyone else wants cookies."

Without asking permission, Dad leans forward and side hugs Autumn. Doesn't seem to bother her one bit. "Very generous of you." Dad hands me the bag and I rise from the ground. "Son, why don't you take lunch and put these cookies in the office."

It's a suggestion, and one I appreciate. "Yeah, sure."

Walking over to a shelf, I set the cookies down and slip out of my coveralls. And I don't miss, in my periphery, the way Autumn ogles me as I disrobe. Although I am fully clothed beneath, she looks me up and down as if I stripped bare.

"Hungry," I croak out as I lead us into the office and set the bag of cookies on my desk.

"Starved," she whispers. But her response seems weighed down with so much more.

A foot between us, I keep my arms tucked at my sides and hold her fiery, cognac gaze. "Wish I had more than an hour for lunch."

Autumn steps closer, leaving a breath between us. "Any amount of time is better than none at all."

I nod and take a deep breath. My time with her now is limited. Lunch dates are not the same as dinner and a movie and her lips pressed to mine. Lunch dates are time crunched and light conversation and hugs until next time.

"C'mon. There's a sub shop up the street. My treat."

We walk out of the office and into the lot. "Well, if you're buying, I'm driving."

"I have no qualms about riding shotgun. Besides, I rode my bike to work."

"You own a motorcycle?" I nod as I slip inside the car and she cranks the engine. "Never been on a motorcycle before. Maybe sometime soon."

What is it about Autumn that lights my soul on fire? With a simple suggestion, my chest swells and my stomach ties knots faster than a sailor. Hell yes, she turns heads everywhere she goes. But her heart-shaped face and curvy body are just the tip of the iceberg. Autumn is so much more than the physical sum of her parts. All her remarks about the future, I ink them into my memory for later reference.

"I'd love to take you for a ride. Early morning works best on the weekends. Less traffic."

A couple miles down the road, I point out the sub shop and she pulls in. We head inside, order, and sit at a table while we wait for our sandwiches. I tell Autumn about some of my favorite places to ride during the early hours of the day. On a few occasions, I left town earlier than I leave the house for work and drove north. An hour or two north, the roads have fewer commuters and there are several small towns with attractive scenery. If the opportunity ever presents itself, I would love to take Autumn on one of those day trips.

"It'd be nice to visit these places you're telling me about."

"Well, if you're ever up for it, let me know."

A man deposits lunch on the table and walks off with the numbered plastic tent. We dig into our sandwiches and eat in silence for a minute. For some reason, a weird vibe bounces off Autumn. Not sure if it is because I mentioned going out of town on the bike or if it's something else altogether. She never mentioned how the rest of her weekend went.

"Sorry I didn't get to ask earlier, but how was the rest of your weekend?"

She finishes chewing the bite in her mouth, but still covers her mouth with her hand when she speaks. "Good. Went out for breakfast yesterday. Then binged on snacks and Netflix. I was definitely not productive." She laughs and it is music to my ears.

"Love those kinds of days. I try to have one at least once a month. Spartan and I spent most of the day digging up old flower beds in the back yard. Previous owners had a thing for cementing pavers together. Was probably a great idea thirty-plus years ago, but now it's just horrible."

The rest of lunch goes by way too fast, and before I know it, we have to head back to the garage.

At the traffic light two blocks before the garage, I lean my back against the passenger window and soak up every inch of Autumn. I want to kiss her again. Soon.

"Are you busy tomorrow night?" I ask.

She peeks up at the red light then over to me. "Haven't checked my schedule for work yet. Why?"

"I'm meeting friends at the bowling alley. Cora should be there. We get together at least once a week. Tomorrow, we're bowling. Wanted to know if you'd care to join."

She tucks her lips between her teeth and I want to reach over and pop them out. But I don't.

"When I get to work, I'll check my schedule. What time is everyone meeting up?"

"Seven. We usually bowl a couple games and call it a night."

"I'll tentatively say yes, but let you know if there's a schedule conflict."

She steers the car into the garage lot and stops parallel to the storefront. I unbuckle my belt and lean toward her. Her eyes drop to my lips and I take it as a sign of permission to kiss her.

The moment my lips graze hers, the cooler December temperatures vanish. Our slow and sweet kiss ends far too soon. "I'll text you the details for tomorrow night when I'm off work."

Our lips a breath apart, her eyes shift back and forth between mine. "Look forward to it," she says, voice drug laced and lips parted.

One last chaste kiss and I force myself to exit the car. "See you tomorrow." She nods, and I love how I struck her speechless.

I turn on my heel and walk back to the garage bay with an ear-to-ear smile. Dad spots me. "Good lunch?"

Best damn lunch in the history of lunches.

thirteen

Is this a mistake?

I turn into the parking lot of the bowling alley. Since when are bowling alleys this busy on a Tuesday night? Sure, it has been forever and a day since I have set foot in one, but it was always a weekend day. And every place is busy on the weekend.

Winding through the lot, I park Betsy and cut the engine. Facing the entrance of the bowling alley, I scan the sea of faces standing outside. Among them is Jonas. With his messy chocolate strands, broad shoulders, and booming laughter, I will always be able to pinpoint him in a crowd.

He stands with two other women—a dirty-blonde nearly as tall as him and a curly redhead closer to my height. For a moment, I observe how he interacts with them. By the ease at which they interact, it's evident they all know one another. They smile and laugh and look completely comfortable with one another. When the blonde pushes at Jonas's chest and the trio laughs in unison, the little green monster perks up on my shoulder as a rush of jealousy spikes my bloodstream.

"Get it together," I chide myself. "Men and women have non-romantic relation-ships all the time."

Nothing but truth. After all, the same can be said about some of my male friends. Then why does seeing Jonas so casual and relaxed with two other women make my jaw clench? More than likely, it is the result of not dating or being in a committed relationship for years.

Taking a deep breath, I open the door and exit the car. Seven steps forward and Jonas homes in on my presence. Locks eyes with me. Stops listening to the two women at his side. Smiles so wide, the dimple I love makes an appearance. Pushes off the wall and walks my direction. Meets me a few feet from the paved walkway around the building.

"Hey," he says as he steps into my space.

"Hi."

When he drops his lips to mine, I don't stop him. If anything, I encourage him to give me more. His tongue sweeps over mine and I moan. He tastes of cherry cola and desire. Far too soon, he breaks the kiss and chuckles under his breath as I lean into him.

"If we keep this up, we'll never see the inside of the bowling alley." *Sounds good to me.* He laces his fingers with mine. "C'mon. Let me introduce you to Shelly and Erin."

Hand in hand, we walk back to where he stood earlier. Where the two women he chatted with stand. "'Kay," I whisper.

A few strides forward, he pauses. "Everything alright?"

I nod and tighten my hold on his hand. "Yeah. Just nervous. Don't hang with new people often."

He drops my hand and I pout until he frames my face with his palms. "It'll be okay. Promise. Everyone is pretty chill. Plus, Cora and Gavin will be here too." He plants a chaste kiss on my lips and I silently beg for another.

We step up to the two women and I paste on a polite smile. If I thought they were attractive from a distance, I was sorely mistaken. Attractive isn't the proper term. Because up close, they captivate and hold my attention more. And the wicked green monster pops up on my shoulder again, swinging its legs and whistling. *Shut up.*

"Shelly" —Jonas gestures to the blonde, then the redhead— "Erin, this is Autumn. Autumn, this is Shelly and Erin. Shelly and Cora have been friends since boys were gross. And Erin works with Cora."

I extend my hand to each of them. "Nice to meet you both."

Shelly performs a quick scan. "You are fucking cute." I laugh and peek up at Jonas who chuckles under his breath. "Really dig your vibe."

"Thanks." Although we just met, it's easy to see Shelly is a hoot.

Jonas wraps his arm around my shoulders. "Ladies, let's head inside and grab lanes. Everyone else should be here soon."

We stroll through the automatic doors and are immediately hit with the cacophony of Tuesday nights at the bowling alley. Colorful globes of resin clash against wooden pins. Upbeat dance music booms from the overhead speakers. Patrons hoot and holler and cheer each other on. Claps and whistles. Middle-age adults jumping off the floor when they manage to knock all the pins down.

The energy is boisterous and infectious.

We pay for shoes and get assigned two lanes. On our way to the lane, we pass the bowling alley's food bar. Melted cheese and baked bread and cinnamon sugar waft up my nose. My stride falters and Jonas pauses beside me.

"You okay?"

I point over at the neon lights highlighting every party food known to man. "Yep. Just swallowing down my hunger."

He laughs. "After we get everything set up, we'll order food."

After swapping out our shoes, Shelly, Erin, and I venture off to find a ball. Can't remember the last time I bowled, let alone what weight ball I used when I played. Once I decide on a lime green, eight-pound ball, I head back to the lane where more bodies have congregated.

Cora and Gavin stand near the seats of the left lane we rented. Arms wrapped around each other; she looks up at him as if no one else is here. Maybe it holds true for them. Their happiness makes me smile and spreads warmth in my chest.

I set my ball down and sidle up to Jonas. He curls his arm around my waist. "Everyone else is here. Let me introduce you." I nod and bite the inside of my cheek. "Hey guys." Six sets of eyes glance over at us. "This is Autumn." Although I have met four of the six, the attention from all of them makes me wilt into Jonas's side. "Autumn, this is Cora, Gavin, Shelly, Erin, Micah, and Trevor." With each name Jonas prattles off, he points to each person.

Lifting a hand, I wave to the obviously tight-knit group as heat crawls up my neck and lands on my cheeks. "Hey everyone. Nice to meet you." I am not necessarily a shy person. Hell, sometimes I am pretty outgoing. Just don't prefer the spotlight. Especially around new faces.

"Let's order food while everyone finishes getting ready," Jonas suggests.

Three pizzas, two pretzels, a basket of loaded fries, and two churros ordered later, we head back to the lanes with two pitchers of beer and glasses. The young girl at the counter told us they would bring the food to our lane soon.

We settle in the chairs at the lane. Jonas places an arm around my shoulder and inches closer to me while I snack on the churros. As we wait for Trevor and Gavin to come back with a ball, I people watch the group Jonas calls family.

The dynamic between all of them is fascinating. If I had to guess—strictly by appearances and the way they interact—Shelly and Micah must be siblings. Same dark blonde hair. Same dark blue eyes. And they tease each other in a way only brothers and sisters do. When Gavin winds his way back over to us, I follow his every move until he sits down next to Cora. Who is staring at me. With piqued intensity.

Nothing in the way she watches me feels malicious or worrisome. If anything, she studies me with intrigue. Beside me, Jonas talks to Trevor—who I hadn't real-ized returned—with his arm still around my shoulders. A small smile perks up the corners of Cora's mouth. But her smile amplifies when Jonas stops talking to Trevor and he presses his lips to my temple.

Cora is happy for me. For Jonas. And her silent interest says more than any words could express.

Jonas drops his lips lower and his breath heats the shell of my ear. "Ready to bowl?"

You have no idea. "Yes."

One by one, we roll our ball down the oil-slicked lane and occasionally knock down pins. Early on, I learn Jonas, Shelly, and Trevor play a decent game. The rest of us are mediocre. The first game ends and I land a whopping seventy-eight points. Thankfully, I don't stand alone in my meh score. And I didn't score the lowest.

I snag a third slice of pizza and laugh when Jonas catches me scarfing it down. "What?" I ask around a mouthful of dough, cheese, ham, and pineapple.

He steps up to me, rests his hands on my hips, and draws me close. "Nothing. You're just so damn cute." I swallow my bite just before he leans down and kisses me.

Not sure if it's because we are surrounded by hundreds of people—and a handful of Jonas's close friends—but this kiss feels different. Loaded. Intense. Powerful.

Jonas brings both his hands to my cheeks and holds me reverently as our lips move in time and his tongue dips inside my mouth. I reach forward and grip the hem of his shirt, bringing him closer. Warmth radiates off his chest and seeps into every one of my pores. Heats every molecule in my body and fevers my skin. The cacophony surrounding us vanishes. Bursts of red and orange splash the backs of my eyelids like fireworks in the night sky. The pericardium encasing my heart swells and constricts with each frenzied swipe of his tongue against mine.

I drag him impossibly closer. Deepen the kiss. Sink my nails in his hips. Moan against his lips.

Until someone coughs behind Jonas and dumps a bucket of ice water over us.

"Sorry to interrupt, man. You're up," an embarrassed Gavin says.

If anyone should be embarrassed, it sure as hell shouldn't be him. It should be me. He wasn't making out in the middle of the bowling alley like a hormonal teenager. Nope, that was most definitely me.

Jonas inches back and meets my eyes. His palms still pressed to my cheeks; I swelter beneath the swirl of his irises. Like two thermal hot springs, they smolder as the blue and gold and orange devour me. I can't look away. Won't look away.

He places one last, all too brief kiss on my lips. I visibly pout when he retreats and he chuckles. "Be right back."

Stepping up to the ball return, he picks up his ball, positions himself, and follows through. The ball whirls down the lane and knocks all the pins down with a loud *whack*. He returns to my side and kisses my temple.

"You're up," he whispers against my skin.

I bowl my turn and knock down nine—which is better than most of the frames in the first game—and slap a few high fives on my way back to Jonas. A few more frames pass with *ooh*s and *aw man*s. The laughter is nonstop and I quickly love this group of people. They remind me of my tat family. Not conventional by any means, but everyone cares about each other. How real family should be.

As Jonas refills his beer, my phone vibrates in my pocket. I tug it out, glance at the screen, and let Jonas know I will be right back.

Stepping away from the lane, I head near the entrance where it is somewhat quieter. Covering my left ear with my palm, I lift the phone to my right. "Hello?"

"Hey, someone wants to say good night," Penny says.

I step a little farther from the noise. On the other end, the phone changes hands and a sweet voice filters through the speaker. "Hi, Mama. Are you having fun?"

"Hey, pumpkin. I am. Are you and Auntie Penny having fun?"

"Yep. We watched *The Nightmare Before Christmas* again."

I laugh internally. Penny groans every time Clementine wants to watch it. Probably because she has seen it a hundred times. "Was it good?"

"Better than last time," she announces. "What time will you be home?"

"In a little bit. My friends and I are almost done playing our game. Then I'll be home."

"Okay, Mama. I love you."

I smile into the phone. "Love you too. I'll kiss you when I get home."

"M'kay. Night night."

"Good night."

As I disconnect the call, I look up and spot a confused Jonas a few feet away. *Shit.*

Is there ever a good time to tell someone you're dating you have a seven-year-old daughter? Nope. Because no matter the reason, Jonas will be upset I haven't told him about her. Which will end in one of two results. One—he will drop me faster than a hot pan. Or two—we will stay together, but his trust in me will diminish for a bit until I can prove myself again.

Either way, it sucks.

"Who was that?" Jonas asks, pointing to my phone.

I want to tell him. Want to let him in on this part of my life. But it's too soon. We still have so much to learn about each other before I let him know this other part of my world exists. And I don't let many people know Clementine exists for one reason. Hurt.

If Jonas decides to stop seeing me because I have a daughter, I can suck up the pain that will undoubtedly consume me with his absence. But my daughter, she doesn't need to feel hurt or pain or sadness. It's horrible enough her own father has never been around. Never seen her face or heard her precious laughter. I don't need Clementine to suffer the loss of a pseudo-father.

"Penny called," I say.

He purses his lips and breaks eye contact. "Does she often call for a *love you* and *good night*?" His tone isn't angry or spiteful. But he knows I am not telling him the whole truth. And this is not the right time or place.

But before the end of the night, I will have to tell Jonas about Clementine. Hopefully afterward, he won't hate me for keeping the biggest secret from him.

Am I an asshole? Because right now it is difficult to tell.

A minute ago, I heard Autumn tell whoever she was talking to that she loved them, would kiss them when she got home, and wished them a good night. When I asked her who she was talking to, she said Penny called. Is her relationship with Penny more than friends? Because I didn't sign up for that.

But here I am, lipping off like a douchebag. Throwing accusations at my girl-friend when I haven't given her the chance to explain anything. Going against everything my parents taught me—which is to never assume. All assumptions do is cause harm and way too much stress.

Yep. Official asshole.

We walk back to the lane in silence. Usually, silence with Autumn is easy. Comfortable. Pleasant.

This new version of silence sucks.

Every few steps, I peek over at her out of the corner of my eye and berate myself mentally. Autumn hangs her head—not sure if she is embarrassed, angry or upset. Regardless, I hate how I put her in a foul mood. How I am the reason she went from enjoying a night out with me and my friends to probably wishing she wasn't here.

Before I buck up the courage to apologize, we reach the lane. She lifts her head, smiles, and pretends like the last few minutes never happened.

For the next five frames, neither of us speaks. We don't whisper to each other, kiss or remotely touch. And I hate every single second. It sears my heart like a branding iron. Except this brand doesn't mark me as hers, it just keeps pressing on and scalds until I black out from the pain.

When the game ends, Cora sidles up beside me as Autumn puts her ball back on the rack.

"Everything okay?" she asks.

This is beyond awkward. The woman I thought was the only person I wanted, who recently married the love of her life, is asking me about the woman I have been dating for almost no time at all. Funny thing is, it feels as if I have known Autumn for years. As if she has always been mine. What Cora and Gavin have, I get it now.

"Not sure." I glance toward the wall with the ball racks and spot Autumn chatting with Shelly. A smile sits on her face, but it isn't genuine. I have seen the genuine smile. "She was on the phone earlier and I overheard part of the call. Then I said something dickish."

Cora smiles subtly. "Your relationship with her is still very new, Jonas. But the way you both look at each other… it's deep. You guys need time. Don't rush it. Get to know each other. Autumn is a sweet woman. But we all have history and baggage. The older we get, the more we have."

I stare at my best friend straight-faced. "When did you become so wise?"

She slaps my arm and laughs. "Jerk. I've always been wise." Another laugh. "It just takes everyone else way too long to realize it and catch up."

"Ouch," I say, and it has nothing to do with the playful smack a moment ago.

Autumn walks up to us with a shy smile on her face. Without permission or announcement, Cora hugs Autumn. Cora squeezes her tight and whispers something in Autumn's ear. Too quiet for me to hear. When Cora lets her go, she braces her hands on Autumn's shoulders and gives her a pointed look. Autumn's lips curve up and she nods.

"Have a good night. See you next time," Cora says to Autumn before turning to me. She gives me a hug and whispers in my ear next. "Assumptions are the death of relationships. Ask, but be patient. Because I love the way she makes you come to life."

Before Cora pulls away, I whisper *thank you* in her ear.

Everyone else leaves before me and Autumn. As if they wanted to give us privacy to talk. To hash out whatever changed both our temperaments three-quarters of the way through our night out.

On the way out of the bowling alley, I desperately want to wrap Autumn's hand in mine. But I don't. I feel as if I don't deserve her hand right now. Not after how I behaved earlier. How I accused her of being dishonest.

It was super shitty and I wish there was a way I could take it all back. Take it back and say something different. Or not say anything at all.

But instead of giving her time to slowly divulge her past to me, I ripped the proverbial bandage off and basically forced her to explain herself. My parents would be pissed with my juvenile behavior. I am.

Her conversation could have been completely innocent. But instead of allowing her the opportunity to tell me in her own time, I snooped and jumped to conclusions. Mom always taught my sisters and I that snooping never accomplished anything except for causing more problems. And I have learned, over the years, Mom always steered me down the correct path.

A couple cars from Autumn's, I reach for her hand and she lets me take it. *Thank goodness.*

"Hey" —I halt us at the back of her car— "I'm really sorry about earlier. I shouldn't have been such an ass."

Autumn closes her eyes and essentially cuts me off from her sweet, addictive cognac irises. And the loss of her eyes on me sends a sharp pain through my chest. Slow, yet steady and debilitating. I don't like it.

"Jonas…" She says my name as if it causes her pain. The ice pick in my heart twists and deepens. "Please don't make me choose."

I shake my head, confused. "Choose?"

She opens her eyes and my pulse silences for one, two, three beats. "Jonas, I…" She swallows and peeks up at me. Tears stand on the ledge of her eyes, thinking of jumping. And I hate how I have put her in this place.

"What is it, Autumn? Please tell me. I… I hate that I did this. I hate that I upset you." I wipe away a tear that escapes and rolls down her cheek. "That I made you cry. I will never forgive myself."

She leans into my touch and I take it as a good sign. "Thank you. But, Jonas…" Autumn kisses my palm, then stands straighter. "I need to tell you something."

I bend at the knees and lower myself to her height so we stand eye to eye. "You can tell me anything," I say.

Her eyes dart between mine. She swallows and nods. "Jonas, I have a daughter." Her confession comes out barely audible.

What did she just say? Did I hear her correctly? Did Autumn just tell me she has a daughter?

Dumbstruck, I have no clue how to respond to her confession. Does it bother me that she has a daughter? A child? No. But the only thing I know about kids I have learned from being around my nephew. Which isn't often enough to say I have knowledge. He is cute and fun and says the craziest shit sometimes, but I don't spend long periods of time with him.

"Jonas?" Autumn asks after I don't say anything for far too long.

"Sorry. I'm just…"

"Terrified?"

I shake my head at her. "No. But I don't know what to say or do next." Her phone call earlier makes perfect sense now. And I hate how I reacted. Ugh, I am such a prick.

"There's nothing to do," she says. And the way she says the words adds a new wound. But this one feels different. Deeper. Harsher. One which will leave a vicious scar. "I think we should take a break."

Shaking my head and pinching my brow, I stumble back from her. "Wait, what? Why?"

Is she really doing this? Breaking up with me before we even begin. I can't fucking breathe. Can't hear anything except buzzing white noise. Can't see anything except Autumn's face slowly fading in the darkness.

Please tell me I misheard her. Please tell me this is all a farce.

"This is why I never dated, Jonas. Because it just gets in the way."

Seriously? How on earth is this reality? Two hours ago—hell, even an hour ago—everything was perfect. We were perfect. And now…

"Is that what I am, Autumn? In the way?" Anger seeps into my veins and coats the hurt residing there. Because anger is easier to manage than heartache. Heartache and I seem to be besties nowadays.

"Jonas, that didn't come out right."

I throw my hands in the air, ready to go to battle. Hours ago, I would fight to the death for Autumn's happiness. But this stubborn rejection she tosses at me for shits and giggles… it's bullshit.

"Then please, clear it up for me. Explain it so I understand."

She rolls her eyes. "Please don't make this harder than it is."

I laugh without humor. "Why? Because you like me? Because I like you? Breaking up a relationship shouldn't be easy, Autumn. Not when both parties feel the way we do." Part of me wants to drop to my knees and grovel. But I won't. Not here. Not tonight.

"It's just easier this way."

"For who? You? Me?" I step within an inch of her face and lock eyes with her. "Losing you will never be easy," I whisper. "Never."

Autumn closes her eyes as if it pains her to look into mine. Good. It should hurt. Breaking off what we have, what we could have, should hurt. Nothing has ever crippled me like hearing Autumn tell me she no longer wants me.

A tear rolls down her cheek and, this time, I don't reach for it. Don't swipe it away with my thumb while muttering sweet reassurances. Words which tell her everything will work out. That we will be okay. That we will survive this.

Because I don't believe it myself. How can I?

"As great as we are… were…" Tears spill from her eyes more easily now. Pain floods every line and curve and dimple of her face, but she won't admit the pain this causes her. Not aloud. Not when she believes being alone for her daughter is the right thing to do. "I can't do this, Jonas. It wasn't a good idea."

I bite the inside of my cheek to prevent myself from saying something I will later regret. As determined as Autumn is, I will find a way to make this better. I have to.

"If that's how you feel," I say before swallowing down the wad of cotton in my throat. "If this is what you want, I guess there's nothing I can do to change your mind."

I take a step backward. Then another. And another.

With each falter back, the pain on her face intensifies. Each move away from her, she flinches. But I refuse to be a punching bag for someone. Refuse to stand on the sidelines while she lives her life as if I don't matter to her. Because I do. I do fucking matter.

She won't admit it to herself, but she cares. Maybe a little too much. And perhaps therein lies the problem.

"Jonas," she mumbles.

I take another step away from her. And another. Then I spin around and stride toward my bike. After I slip on my helmet, I rev the engine louder than appropriate. I am in no condition to ride, but I can't be here any longer. Not after everything that has happened here tonight.

How do I go from being on the cusp of slipping the infamous *L*-word to breaking up with the one woman I can't imagine life without?

Fuck.

I smack the handlebar as I fly down the highway. As I ugly cry for a woman for the first time in my life. As I feel my life crumbling into a pile of ash.

Jonas revs his motorcycle louder than polite several spaces down from me. Still standing at the back of my car, I stare glassy-eyed at him as he backs the bike out of the space then zips out of the parking lot and onto the highway faster than safe.

And the moment I no longer see him, when I no longer hear the angry growls of the bike engine, I start shaking head to toe. My heart hammers in my ribcage. My breath coming in short bursts.

What have I done?

I reach behind me and brace myself on the car. Slowly, I guide myself to the driver's side door as a torrent of tears spills down my cheeks. I fumble through my purse—frustrated as hell with my oversized bag—until I locate my keys. Drop the keys from my trembling fingers as I try to unlock the door.

Once I finally get the door unlocked, I fall into the seat and slam the door shut. Tossing my purse on the passenger seat, I white-knuckle the steering wheel as I rest my forehead on top.

My chest wrenches violently as the sobs continue to come. I can't catch my breath. Can't think clearly. And there is an ever-expanding hollowness beneath my breastbone.

It fucking hurts. Hurts more than anything I have ever known. The exponential pain unbearable.

I lean back into the seat with my grip still firmly on the wheel and scream at the top of my lungs. Slightly cathartic, it only serves to exacerbate the emptiness taking over my heart.

"Why," I scream at the windshield. "Why did I do this to myself? Why did I do this when I knew it would be a bad idea? When I knew it would end badly."

Simple. When your heart is involved, your brain no longer makes rational decisions.

And Jonas was definitely in my heart. Still is.

But doing this, breaking things off, before either of us becomes too heavily invested, is for the best. At least that is what I keep telling myself.

How could it be for the best if it hurts this much?

Shouldn't I be relieved? Now I don't have to worry about the awkwardness of being a single parent and trying to fit another person into my life. Don't have to worry about my daughter becoming attached to a man who won't stick around. Don't have to worry about her little heart being crushed by losing another person in her life.

I should be relieved, but I am far from it.

Minutes tick by as I work to cease the dam of tears spilling from my eyes. Once they subside enough for me to see clearly, I pop the key in the ignition and start the car. I ease out of the space and exit the lot.

The drive home is a blur. Not because I can't see, but because I go from point A to point B on autopilot. No music to distract me. No visual stimulation to spark my brain back to life. And somehow, I make it home safely.

After I cut the engine, I sit in the dark for a moment and try to compose myself.

Surely, I look like shit. There will be no hiding what happened tonight from Penny. Nothing except time will erase the pain on my face and in my heart. Quite a bit of time.

I suck in a deep breath and tug the handle to open the door. Each step toward the front door feels like a step closer to my demise. Where I will have to relive everything all over again. A vicious cycle of hurt on repeat.

As I unlock the front door, the television mutes inside. When I swing the door wide and Penny sees my face, her smile vanishes as she bolts from the couch.

"Oh my god, Auti. What's wrong?"

And I lose it. Again.

Penny wraps her arms around me and holds me in a death grip hug. I cry into her neck. On her shoulder. And she gently strokes my hair and shushes me, telling me everything will be okay.

Before I realize it, Penny has walked us to the couch and is sitting us down. She lets me cry until I am ready to stop. Doesn't ask any questions and just lets me sob uncontrollably.

When I finally compose myself enough to speak, everything comes out broken and stilted. "I broke up with Jonas." A new torrent floods my eyes. Penny rises from the couch, disappears down the hall, and returns with a box of tissues. She pops one from the box and hands it to me before settling the box on the couch in front of me.

Penny brushes fallen strands of my hair out of my face as I swipe my eyes dry. "Want to talk about it?" she asks, her tone soft and cajoling.

I blow my nose and try to rein in my sobs so I can explain how everything unfolded at the bowling alley. When the tears settle to a lesser flow and the sobs quit wracking my body so heavily, I dive headfirst into how everything went from fantastic to shit in the blink of an eye.

"Let me start by saying, the night had been perfect up until your phone call."

Penny scrunches her brow. "My call?"

Nodding, I continue. "We bowled. Ate all the junk food from the food bar. Had some beer. Shared smiles and laughs with his friends." I suck in a breath. Futz with tissue between my fingers. "He kissed me in front of everyone like no one else existed. It was perfect," I whisper. "And then a couple of frames later, you called and I stepped away."

She reaches forward, takes my hands in hers, and gives them a little squeeze. Encouragement to continue, but also to remind me she is here. That no matter what she says, she has my back.

"I guess he saw me walk off and followed. But I had no idea. He overheard part of my conversation with Clementine. After I hung up and saw him watching me… Pen, you should've seen the look on his face. It's like he didn't trust me. He asked who I was talking to and I told him you had called."

Penny snorts and shakes her head. "Truth and not."

I nod. "Yeah. Well, I guess he heard me tell Clementine I love her and that I'd kiss her when I got home. I never said her name. And when I told him you'd called, he flipped on me. Got upset and thought I was lying. Asked if you called for a good night often. I'd backed myself into a corner and had no idea how to get out."

"You should've told him about her then."

"I know," I say as I hang my head. "But he was acting like such a jerk. And I didn't have the energy to go into explanation right then. Plus, his friends were all waiting on us to return. When we did, they all knew something was off."

I go on to tell Penny how we finished the rest of the game in the thickest cloud of tension. How I got more and more frustrated with each passing moment. How I decided, when the night was over, that I would break things off with Jonas because it seemed like the right thing to do. To just cut out the heartache now. To eliminate the need to skirt around the truth. That I had a daughter and she was my world. Clementine would always stand front and center in my life, no matter how much I cared for someone else.

"When we got ready to leave, Cora came over to me and gave me a hug."

"Cora? As in Gavin and Cora, Cora?"

"Yep. She and Jonas have been friends for years. He supposedly had the hots for her."

"Had?"

"Until he met me," I whisper.

Penny stares at me wide-eyed. "Wow."

"Yeah. Well, when Cora hugged me, she whispered something to me."

"What?" Penny asks, leaning in closer, hungry for all the details.

"She told me she'd never seen Jonas so happy. And she hoped he made me happy too. When she pulled out of the hug, all I could do was nod. Because I knew I was about to rip it all away."

A new onslaught of tears pours down my cheeks as Penny tugs me forward into her arms. God, I have never cried this much in my life. And it fucking sucks.

I thought getting this all off my chest, spilling all my pain out, would help. That talking with Penny would alleviate some of the devastation coursing through my veins. Bring a sense of comfort and slowly wash away the heartache I know will reside in me for days or weeks or months to come. But it isn't. If anything, it only serves to amplify it. Spark it with new life.

Penny eases her embrace and leans back to swipe at my tears. "Auti, do you really think what you did was the right thing?"

What? Why is she asking me this? Of all the people who I assumed would be Team Autumn, I pegged Penny at the top of the list.

"What kind of question is that?"

She shakes her head as she cups both my cheeks and locks eyes with me. "Don't be upset. It's a fair question. If you thought breaking up with Jonas was the right thing to do, you wouldn't be crying like this. Not after dating for such a short period of time. Neither of you knows much about the other. Your relationship is, was, still in the beginning stages. You're getting to know one another. Finding the quirks and kinks. Learning about pasts as well as likes and dislikes." She drops her hands from my face and leans back slightly. "Please don't take this the wrong way, Auti, but you didn't even give him a chance."

I narrow my eyes at her. Did she really just say that? Or did I mishear her?

"Let me clarify," she says.

"Please do."

"Auti, you left him high and dry not explaining the phone call. Then, when you finally do go into explanation, when you finally tell him about Clementine, you break it off with him. You never gave him a chance to register any of what you told him. You never gave him a minute to comprehend what you'd just told him. To grasp the fact you are a mom. It's a lot to process. I hate to say it, but it isn't fair to him. It isn't fair for you to have dropped a major bomb and then run for the hills."

When she says it like that, it dawns on me how much of a jerk *I am*. She has a point. Without considering Jonas's feelings, I dropped a whopper of a bomb and then told him we would be better off apart. A knee-jerk reaction, but now I am slowly seeing the error of my ways.

Since my pregnancy with Clementine, all I wanted was to do what was right for my daughter. Give her a good home. Shower her in love and smiles and laughter. And have good people around her. Her father and my family may have severed ties with us, but she has never felt unloved or unwanted a day in her life.

"How do I fix this?" I whisper-ask as fresh tears spill from my eyes.

"Give him a little time. And then, reach out to him again. Spill your heart out to him. Let him know you're sorry. Grovel, if necessary." I laugh at the last bit. "Just don't wait too long, Auti. Because men like Jonas only come around once."

Shit, shit, shit.

Did I royally screw myself by jumping the gun? I made a decision in the heat of the moment without really thinking things through. I made a decision based on the people of my past and how they hurt me and, by proxy, Clementine. But Jonas isn't like Clementine's father. Nor is he like my own mother and father, who disowned me.

Jonas is this sweet and wholesome guy. One who holds your hand and sets your body on fire at the same time. Who kisses me breathless as if I hold the key to a life he never thought he would possess. Who looked at me as if no one else existed.

What have I done?

Penny rises from the couch and kisses the top of my head. "I'm headed to bed. Try to get some sleep. It'll all work out, Auti. Just believe it will and it will."

"Thanks, Pen. Love you."

"Love you too. Night."

"Night," I whisper as she walks to her room.

I turn off the television and the light before heading to the bathroom. When I flip on the bathroom light and see my reflection in the mirror, I immediately flick the light off.

Looks as if I have been at a funeral for ten days straight. My eyes are veiny and angry, red and puffy. My cheeks and throat blotchy. And the mascara streaks down my face could double as clown makeup.

After I finish my nighttime routine in the dark, I slip into bed and kiss Clementine on the forehead. Turning so I face away from her, I cry silently into my pillow.

Cry for the loss of a good man. Cry for the mistake I made in assuming he would no longer want me once he found out I am a single mom. And cry for myself. For the throbbing ache in the center of my chest. The ache which only grows stronger with each passing second. The ache I deserve after what I did tonight.

But I will make this right. I have to. Not just for selfish reasons. Also because I need Jonas. More than I thought possible after such a short period.

I only hope he still wants me when I crawl back and beg for forgiveness.

sixteen

The entire day at work sucks.

I slept for shit last night. No matter which way I had lain in bed, sleep was impossible. I tried counting backward from one hundred. That only lasted to eighty-five, when my brain sidetracked and I had to start all over again. Tried listening to calming music, but it only fired me up more. Even tried a meditation app I downloaded at three this morning. Nothing.

Dad knows something is wrong. He sees the complete one-eighty in my demeanor. But he won't ask what has me on edge. When I feel ready to tell him, he knows I will. Our entire lives, that's how he and I operated.

So, he will wait patiently for me to explain why I can't focus on one goddamn thing. Why I have yelled and cursed more times today than I have in the last decade. Why I slam the tools down instead of carefully put them in their place. Why I have stormed out of the garage and into the office more than a dozen times in the last three hours.

It might be a while before I mention anything to Dad, though. My ego is littered with bruises while my heart lies scattered in bits.

She didn't even give me a chance. Not having a chance stings the worst.

Last night's conversation in the parking lot cycles through my mind for the thousandth time. Each time I recall what she told me, a new wave of emotion rolls through me. Anywhere from anger to frustration to agony to understanding. And then it starts all over again.

Autumn broke things off with me for one reason. Well, maybe two. To protect herself. And to protect her *daughter*.

Still blows my mind Autumn is a mother. Not because it was inconceivable to picture her with a small bundle in her arms. Picturing her that way is actually quite believable. But because she thought hiding a major piece of herself was the right choice. She once told me she hadn't dated in years. Is her lack of dating because she is a single mother?

Another stab to the heart.

I only got a small glimpse at life with Autumn on my arm. With her lips on mine. And I miss every second of it.

The hurt on her face last night flashes in my memory. She didn't want our evening to end the way it did. She didn't want *us* to end. But she did it anyway. To protect the only life she has known. To shelter her heart and the heart of her daughter.

How do I fix this? Fix us?

Because I refuse to believe there isn't still an us. I refuse to believe what we have is beyond repair. All I have to do is figure out how to go about it.

Minor relief washes over me when the Harley-Davidson clock in the garage reads five and I can call it quits for the day. But the day is far from over. Because today is Wednesday. Family dinner night. And family dinner night equals several sets of eyes and ears homed in on me. No doubt Dad will go home and tell Mom something is up. If my sisters arrive before me, the *what's-wrong-with-Jonas* gang will be in full effect upon my arrival.

Might be a good night to hang on the back patio with Anton.

When I get home from work and let Spartan out of his kennel, he mauls me as if I have been gone days and not hours. He licks my face and jumps excitedly around the living room.

"Well, I'm glad to see someone is happy to have me around," I tell him as I rough up the fur on his head. "You ready to see Grandma tonight."

Woof, woof.

I love how Spartan answers me as if we are having a genuine conversation. He has always been this way. Makes me laugh at times. Who knows, maybe he does actually understand what I say. Never underestimate the intelligence of your fur-child.

We go out in the back yard for a little bit. Spartan trots along the fence line and sniffs every possible tuft of grass to make sure no one else has marked his territory. I sit on the small outdoor couch set up on a paver patio I laid months ago. The L-shaped couch can easily seat five and has a matching lounger and two chairs. A canopy spans the entire patio and shades the seating while protecting the gas fire table set up in the middle.

Occasionally, I will sit out here and get lost in a book or the flicker of the fire. Being out here is a great place to unwind after a long day. Plus, Spartan gets extra outside time when I hang out here.

After Spartan alleviates a tenth of his energy, we hop into the Jeep and drive over to Mom and Dad's. I watch Spartan as he finds happiness in the little things—such as riding in the car or biting the wind or barking at a passing car—and do my best to soak up some happiness of my own.

The moment we walk in the door, Spartan runs off and Mom is on me as if I am three years old and fell from the treehouse again.

"How's my baby?" She frames my face and twists it left and right as she examines me.

"Fine, Mom," I say as she hauls me against her for a hug. I wrap my arms around her, close my eyes, and soak up her hug more than normal. Mom has always been a great hugger. Warm and giving and soothing.

"Don't you lie to me. Your father says you've been in a sour mood all day."

She releases me from the hug and holds me at arm's length. Her scrutiny is somewhat unsettling, but I know it comes from a heartfelt place. Even when I felt sad about all that happened with Cora, my parents never reacted this way. They checked in more often, but otherwise let me be.

"Well, he wouldn't be wrong. But I don't want to talk about it right now."

Her eyes scan every fine line and detail of my face. Judge my eyes and lack of smile. "Just don't keep it bottled up. Okay? Never solves a thing if you keep it to yourself."

I raise my right hand and press it over my heart. "Promise."

In a flash, she grabs my hand and drags me into the kitchen. "Now that that's out of the way, let's make dinner." And just like that, Mom makes me laugh.

Joining Jasmine and Jillian in the kitchen, Mom and I chop potatoes for cooking and mashing, and vegetables for salad. Garlic, garden-fresh rosemary and lemon waft through the kitchen, and it isn't hard to guess we are having Jillian's favorite

—lemon and herb roasted chicken. We all work in synchronicity until dinner is ready.

As much as I wanted to seclude myself to the back patio earlier, it was better being in the kitchen with my sisters and mom. We worked as a unit and nothing needed to be said as we went about our individual tasks. Without a word, the women in my life helped lift me up. And I love them more for it.

Dinner went on much like it normally did. Lex flung bits of salad at my dad as he tickled the bottoms of his feet. Jasmine scolded Dad and told him to quit teaching Lex food was a toy instead of something you eat. Anton laughed with Dad and egged him on. Mom asked Jillian about work and when the next batch of new fashions would hit the racks.

The only exception to the usual conversation was me. I sat quiet and shuffled the cut pieces of chicken around my plate. Stirred the mashed potatoes more than ate them.

As plates emptied, Mom went into the kitchen and grabbed dessert. Apple cobbler and vanilla bean ice cream. My favorite.

Dad must have called her during the day and forewarned her of my mood. Because the cobbler would've had to be in the oven long before the chicken. Plus, she would've had to shop for the missing ingredients I know weren't always in the house.

Jasmine scoops out a helping of cobbler. "What's the special occasion, Mom?"

She glances at me briefly before peering at my sister. "No special occasion. Just thought it'd be nice to have. Been a while." Shock must register on my face when Mom looks back at me because her eyes widen. All I do is smile in return.

Neither Mom nor Dad told Jasmine or Jillian about today. About my adult-sized temper tantrum. They really do love me. If my sisters don't know the nitty-gritty details, my parents get how bothered and upset I am.

After we all have our fair share of cobbler, my sisters and I go out on the back patio while Anton and my parents stay inside with Lex. We sit on the poolside loungers in silence for a few minutes and enjoy the soft glow from the twinkling lights around the yard. A breeze kicks up and Jillian shivers in the lounger on my right.

"Want my jacket?"

"Nah, big brother. But thanks."

"So, what's up with you?" Jasmine asks a moment later. I know she isn't asking Jillian, but I play coy anyway.

"Me?"

"Yes, you. You've been acting *off* all night."

Jillian sits up and spins to face both of us. "You do seem more bummed than usual."

Great. Mom and Dad may not have said anything to my sisters, but they are more intuitive than I give them credit for.

Maybe talking with them—two women I trust, and from different ages—will help. Fingers crossed.

"I recently started dating someone…" I trail off, trying to figure out what else to say.

"And?" Jillian drawls out the single-worded question.

"Jesus. Give me a minute." I pause and stare up at the stars. "Last night, she told me she has a daughter." To my left, Jasmine gasps. "Then she said we need to take a break."

"What? Why?" Jasmine asks.

As I continue to stare at the stars, I secretly hope I get the opportunity to sit under a starry sky with Autumn in my arms. Somewhere far from the city, where there is less light pollution and only the stars brighten the night sky. Where we can point out different clusters and tell each other what we see.

"Not really sure. I think she's just scared to let anyone in. She's a single mom. And from what I know, it's been that way for a while. She told me I was the first person she's dated in years."

Now Jasmine sits up and faces me. It feels as if I am stuck in a sisterly vise. Except they won't squeeze the life out of me. They will just pump me full of advice. But their words of wisdom may be exactly what I need.

"Brother, if you're the first person she's dated in years—possibly the only person she's dated since her daughter was born—she had to have broken it off because she's scared. Letting someone in is probably huge for her."

I lift my head from the lounger and turn to my left. "Yeah, I get it, Jas. But why would she let me in to drop me five seconds later?"

"Easy," Jillian says, and I turn to face her. "She wants to see if you're worthy."

"If I'm worthy? What does that mean?"

"It means" —I turn back to Jasmine, almost dizzy sitting between my sisters— "she wants to see if you'll just let her go. Or if you'll step up and fight for her."

Okay. If I thought women were complicated before, now the ideal has been solidified. Women are the most complex and confusing creatures on the planet. They say one thing and want something completely opposite. How is any man supposed to grasp this concept? Or know when they are doing something right or wrong?

"And how am I supposed to do that? How do I fight?"

"Little things," Jillian says. "Leave notes where you know she'll find them. Send her flowers. Nothing major, just small tokens to let her know you're still thinking about her. As complex as we seem, big bro, we are simple creatures. Those little things add up over time. Women are more sentimental. Sure, we all love gifts. But when it comes down to it, we want the reason behind the gift, not just the trinket."

At the word trinket, I run my fingers over the Eisenhower dollar in my pocket. A token I have carried with me for years. Something Grandpa John gave me just before I started kindergarten. *"Keep this close by and it'll always give you luck."* Since he slipped the large coin into my small palm, I never left home without it. It was either in my pocket or my wallet or somewhere close by. It wasn't only special because Grandpa said it was a good luck charm, but also because it was a gift from him.

"So, if you were in my position, what would you do?" I ask them both.

"This all went south last night?" Jasmine asks and I nod. "Give her a couple days to breathe. Give her time to process everything. She asked for a break so she could think clearly about how you fit into her world. And her daughter's world, too. If you don't give her the time she needs, she'll push harder."

"Okay, I get that. But how much time is enough?"

"Maybe wait until the weekend. I like Jillian's idea with the notes," Jasmine states.

"Thank you." Jillian tips her head in gratitude.

"Write her a note. Tell her how you're feeling. It's easier to say things when you're not face to face. Then leave it somewhere she'll find it."

This is something I can get on board with. Writing her notes. Love letters. Something short and sweet which lets her know she is still on my mind. But for how long?

"How long would you suggest I do this?"

"Forever," Jillian says at the same time Jasmine says, "Until your hand falls off." We all laugh.

"Seriously, big bro. If things pan out with her, keep doing it. She'll love it."

Good to know. But it still doesn't answer my initial question. Maybe I need to rephrase.

"Okay. When do I take the next step? When do I move from letters to something more?"

Jasmine shrugs. "Whenever it feels right to you. If you leave her the first note and she reaches out to you, angry, back off. Otherwise, use your best judgment. Women like to be wooed. All of us. Woo her."

Woo her. Notes and flowers and standing on her front porch singing old love ballads. I got this. Maybe.

My sisters pile on top and hug the hell out of me. For a moment, I fake cough as their weight presses down. But as they lift off me, I wrap my arms around them and hug them tighter.

"Thank you both. I love you."

"Love you, big brother."

"Me too. Now make things right. Cause I want to meet her."

I laugh and sit up. "On it."

We all wander inside the house and exchange hugs before heading out for the night. Although I was hesitant to be here tonight. To deal with my family as they breathed advice down my neck. Being here was exactly what I needed. To be reset back to what matters. To get clarity only my family delivers.

As I head out the door with Spartan on my heels, Mom hands me a container of leftovers. "Extra cobbler." A gentle smile lifts the corners of her lips.

"Thanks, Mom. Love you." I hug her again.

"Love you too. See you next week."

The ride home has me thinking nonstop. Of what messages I want to write Autumn. Of what else I want to do to show her how much I care. A small list fills out in my head and I am excited to begin.

Once home, I get to work. Writing notes. Whipping out my sketchpad and my pencils, I draw for hours. Get lost in the notion of wooing Autumn. Of getting her to see I still want her, even if I have to share her.

AUTUMN

The last week has been miserable. Well, not completely miserable, but not really good either.

I miss Jonas. A lot. How the hell do you miss someone you barely know? But how do you not miss someone who walked off with a chunk of your heart? Because Jonas definitely took a piece of me with him on the back of his motorcycle. Hopefully bits of my heart aren't strewn all over the highway.

Although I have a feeling he would never do such a thing.

Clementine asked to set up the Christmas tree and decorate the apartment. The temporary distraction was needed, but only lasted for a few hours. In no time, the tree was up and littered with a mix of homemade and store-bought ornaments. Stockings hung from the far side of the breakfast bar we never sit at. Sporadic glittery Santa's and elves and snowflakes were spread throughout the living space.

Everywhere you look, there is a splash of holiday cheer. The apartment oozed festive and fun.

Difficult as it has been, I kept a smile plastered on my face. The last thing I want or need is Clementine wondering why or what has me upset. To ask questions I don't know how to answer. The timing isn't right. Not yet.

Over the last five days, when I left the shop, I discovered a folded piece of paper under my driver's side windshield wiper. At first, I was leery. I'd heard stories about criminals who place things on cars to distract the owner before attacking them. With Reznor and Rex close enough to hear my screams, I scanned the lot, took a breath, and plucked each paper from the wiper blade. Then, I unfolded the page and saw who it was from. Warmth instantly spread through my limbs to my chest when I read it.

The first note, on Thursday, was short.

Autumn,
I'm sorry. I miss you.
Jonas

The note said so much with only a few words. Not just an apology. Not just to say he missed me. But to remind me he was still there. And he was thinking about me after everything that happened.

On Friday, the paper on my windshield was bigger, the stock heavier. When I unfolded it, I gasped. Jonas had drawn what I assume was the two of us, curled up on a blanket in the park, watching a movie on the makeshift theater screen. His arm around my waist and body snug against mine. When I showed it to Penny, all she said was *"He's got it bad."*

Saturday, Sunday, and yesterday each ended with another note. Typically, I had two days off during the week. Plus, the shop closed on Sunday. But with everything that happened last Tuesday between me and Jonas, I came into work on my days off. Worked some. Hung out mostly. Even brought Clementine with me on Sunday while I worked on two desperate clients. Although the shop was closed, it was better than sitting at home. Chores only distracted so much of my time.

The other notes were much the same, but each got a little longer. Sweeter. Made me miss him more.

> *Autumn,*
>
> *No matter what it takes. No matter how long it takes. I will fix us.*
> *Jonas*

> *Autumn,*
>
> *The first time I saw you, I forgot how to breathe. How to speak. How to function. But then you smiled and the world righted itself again. Because you make the world, my world, a better place.*
> *Jonas*

> *Autumn,*
>
> *On our first date, I constantly wanted to hold your hand. Touch your skin. Kiss your lips. But I was raised a gentleman. Raised to respect women and wait until they're ready.*
>
> *When I kissed your lips for the first time... I never want to kiss another woman. Never want to taste anyone other than you. Because you're the perfect mix of everything I have ever wanted. Breathtaking and genuine and funny.*
> *Jonas*

I may not have seen Jonas in a week, but he still held my heart in his clutches. Don't think he will ever let it go. Not that I want him to. If anything, I want him to hold it closer. Longer. More tenderly. I want to hear him whisper the words on these pages —the ones secured in my purse, that go everywhere I go—in my ear. To say all these sweet words with his warm breath on my skin.

With each note I receive, Penny cradles her heart and coos. Begs me to call or text him. Give him another chance. And I want to. God, do I want to. I want his arms around me again. Want his lips on mine again.

But after how I behaved last week, I'm terrified to show my face again. How do I begin to fix this? Fix us. I harbor most of the blame with why we aren't together. Past insecurities gnaw at my happiness. Tell me romantic relationships aren't in the cards. So, how do I let Jonas in? How do I introduce Clementine into the mix? This is all so new to me—dating as a grown woman and single parent. The idea of us not working out, of Clementine getting hurt, terrifies me to no end.

Twenty minutes in with my current client—an eighteen-year-old getting her first tattoo—the front door jingles. Automatically, I peek up to see who walks in. The blonde from the bowling alley—Shelly, I think—ambles in with a cheery smile on her face. She glances over at me and her smile glows lumens brighter.

But it isn't her or her smile that surprises me. No, it would be the bouquet in her hands which has me stunned. Because I know who the arrangement is for and who sent it. Shelly delivers the bouquet to Penny and hangs out at the front desk until I finish the small script tattoo.

After I clean up the girl's tattoo and give her instructions for aftercare, she pays and leaves.

Now I have to deal with Penny *and* Shelly. Yay me—insert sarcasm.

"What's this?" I ask, feigning ignorance.

Penny rests a hand on her hip, pops it out, and cocks her head. "Really, Auti. Gonna play stupid?"

"You know what they say about assuming." I laugh and both of them stare at me as if they don't know. "It makes an ass out of you and me. Please tell me you both have heard that saying before."

Penny rolls her eyes and Shelly laughs. "Yes, dippy. I've heard the saying. And you know what I meant."

I ignore Penny and look up at Shelly. "Jonas?"

She nods slowly. "He's a mess, Autumn. I've never seen him like this. *Ever.* Not sure what happened last week, and I don't expect you to tell me. But please talk to him. Give him a chance. Give your relationship a chance." I subtly nod. "You make him smile. Like really smile. And I miss seeing his smile."

I miss seeing his smile, too.

I take in the arrangement. Unique and beautiful. A handful of soft pink roses. A vine of pale pink and white orchids. Small white flowers at the base. Light green and lavender succulent buds. Pulled together with curly willow and blue thistle. A blend of rustic and opulent.

Not too flashy. Not a typical floral arrangement. Perfect.

"Thank you, Shelly," I whisper.

Out of nowhere, Shelly hugs me. "See you soon," she says so only I hear her. Then, she releases me, pivots away, and walks out the door.

Penny tips her head toward the front door. "One of his friends?"

"Yeah. She was at the bowling alley last week."

I pick up the arrangement, turn on my heel, and head back to my booth. Attached to the bouquet is another note, and I would prefer to read it without Penny hovering over my shoulder. Not like I won't show it to her later, but I want to read it on my own first.

Leaning forward, I inhale the subtle perfume from the flowers. Understated and delicate, yet exemplary. I pluck the note from the plastic tong in the center and unfold it. Taking a deep breath, I scan the page and absorb each of his words.

Autumn,

There is something so classic about your beauty. You ravish me. Without doing anything extraordinary, you shine. Brighten the darkest night sky. Ignite a fire inside me. And without you, the fire has extin-

guished. My true north has vanished, and I'm wandering alone in the dark.

If you can find a place for me in your heart, I would love another chance. A chance to show you more than one person can love you. And when you're ready, I would be honored to meet the little girl who holds your heart captive. Because if she is anything like her mom, I already know how I will feel about her.

Please give me—us—another chance. I will do whatever, give whatever, you need. Time. Patience. As long as you are in my life. All I ask is that you call me. Talk to me. Let me back in.

Yours always,

Jonas

I read the letter again. And again. Then crush it against my chest and start crying. Reznor glances over the wall separating our booths, then over at Penny. Seconds later, Penny is in my booth and trying to snatch the letter from my arms. I fight her tooth and nail.

"If you won't let me see the letter, then you better start talking. I've seen enough tears from you over the last week to last a lifetime," Penny says, frustration lacing her tone.

"Pen, it isn't bad. Quite the opposite, actually. So, stop mothering me."

She extends her hand between us, flexing her fingers in a *give-me* motion. "If it isn't bad, let me see it."

"Can I have just this one to myself? Please."

Tilting her head to the side, she gives me a sad smile. "I guess. But if he makes you cry again, I'm cutting his balls off."

"Ouch," Reznor says. "Little extreme, don't you think, Pen?"

She shrugs. "Just telling it like it is." Reznor shakes his head and continues working on the guy face down in his booth.

I fold the letter up and tuck it away in my shirt—close to my heart and where Penny can't reach it easily. She harrumphs and leaves my booth. In a slight fog, I clean my workstation up and prep for the next person on my schedule.

Two more clients and then I am done for the day. Two more clients and I can leave work and call Jonas. Hear his voice again for the first time in a week. Although, with every note he has left me, I have read them with his voice in my head. Heard each and every word in his low baritone. Felt comfort with each letter. With the fact he was still nearby. Seeking me out.

The next three hours go by slower than any other time in my life. It didn't help that both my clients had no idea what they wanted inked in their skin. But it didn't shock me to find out they came in together. Eventually, the first decided on a rose. And although the second could have figured out her tattoo while number one was getting hers, it took her fifteen minutes past her session start time to realize she wanted the exact same thing. And it wasn't as if they had never gotten a tattoo before. Hell, they had them everywhere.

Finally, I finish up the night. Clean my workspace faster than any previous shift. Shoulder my purse, cradle the bouquet in my arms, and bolt for the back door. Once alone in the confines of my car, I inhale the gentle bouquet perfume one more time before setting it on the passenger seat. Then I dig my phone from my purse and open up Jonas's contact info.

The screen illuminates my face in the dark as my finger hovers over the call button. I suck in a deep breath and tap the screen.

Shelly called me hours ago and said she delivered the flower arrangement and note to Autumn. I have been on pins and needles since. Yes, I realize she was working when the delivery arrived. But I really hoped I would have heard from her already.

Either Autumn has been crazy busy with work. Or she is avoiding me. Hopefully, it is the former.

Spartan noses my elbow and whimpers before running to the door which leads to the back yard. I ignore him the first two times. When he noses my elbow a third and barks at me for good measure, I rise from the couch, grab my phone off the coffee table, and head for the door.

As soon as I open the back door, Spartan bolts down the three short steps and races through the grass toward the back fence. His energy is off the charts and I wish I had a fraction of it.

"Ya freaking whacko," I call after him.

Sitting on the lounger on the patio, I light the fire bowl and lean back. Eyes closed and head against the cushion, I absorb the world around me. The still night air—cool and crisp. Perfect for the second official day of winter. The soft hum of an airplane as it flies overhead toward Tampa. The flames flicker in the rock-filled fire bowl, a faint smell of propane floats through the air. Spartan trots nearby, his coat brushing against my elbow as he passes me to scavenge in another section of the yard.

I love this small slice of heaven I created. But it isn't quite perfect. Not yet. And only one thing could make it perfect.

Autumn. And the echoes of young laughter and pitter-patter of small feet.

A wad of cotton clogs my throat and strips it dry as I daydream—well, night dream—of a future I hope happens. So strange, but I never imagined the future so in depth until Autumn. Sure, I wanted to land the woman of my dreams and build a life with her. But until Autumn, I never had vivid pictures in my head of the end result. Small Kodak moments captured in time, printed on matte photo paper, and wedged between glass and wood.

But I see it all so clearly now. See her beside me, for years to come.

My cell phone rings in my pocket and startles me from my fantasy. I bolt upright, fumble to get it out of my pocket and answer it just before it goes to voice mail.

A half second glance at the screen has me smiling from ear to ear. "Autumn?"

"Hi." Her voice wispy and muted. I melt back into the lounger and close my eyes.

Just the soft resonance of her voice settles every anxiety I have endured over the last week. Every questionable minute where I wondered if she would give us another chance.

"Hi," I say back. "How are you?"

As much as I don't wish Autumn to feel any sort of anguish, I secretly hope the last week has been as equally challenging for her as it has been for me. Although I only flaunted my emotions the day after, they ate away at me the entire week. With each note I wrote, I took pause. Stared at the paper for hours with pen in hand. How do you express yourself with so few words? How do you not slip up and say the words you feel will scare someone away?

I loved writing her the notes and letters, but they weren't so simple.

The drawing, on the other hand, was easy. Like extracting a strip of movie reel from my memory and scrawling it across paper with pencil. I could have drawn us together with my eyes closed. The subtle curves of Autumn's body as she lay on the blanket, her back to my front. My arm around her waist. Her warmth heating every inch of me.

I swallow and shake off the real-life fantasy floating in my thoughts.

"Okay, I guess." She says the words, tries to believe them, but the slight crack in her voice tells me she doesn't. Pain pierces my chest and I pinch my eyes tightly as she continues. "Thank you. For the notes and the d-drawing" —she sniffles— "and the flowers. They're all so beautiful."

Her heartache bounces through the air and smacks me like a bullseye in the chest. Settles deep. Liquifies and sheathes the rapid pulsing organ between my lungs. I clench my hand into a fist and press it over the sensation robbing me of breath.

"You're welcome," I croak out. "Meant every word. Every line and smudge."

On the other end, Autumn goes silent. The only indication the call hasn't dropped is her occasional sniffle in my ear.

What is going through her head? Why is she so quiet? Is she battling what to do next? Where we go from here?

God, I hope she wants to try us again. Give us another chance. With her biggest skeleton out in the open, and me still fighting for her, she has to know where I stand. That I still want her. Want more with her. Want more of us.

She has been silently sniffling on the other end for minutes now. But I don't break the silence. As many questions as I want to ask her, as much as I want to pour my heart out, I stay tight-lipped and give her however much time she needs. Time to formulate whatever it is she wants to say to me. Because I will wait as long as she needs me to.

"I miss you," she whispers. Three simple words. But how they swallow me whole and hug me fiercely. "A lot."

I inhale deeply, hold the air in my lungs for one, two, three before exhaling. Opening my eyes, I stare up at the inky night sky and land on the brightest star. Hold it in my sight and watch it brighten and dim as if pulsing.

"Me too. So damn much."

During the last week, Spartan has even grown frustrated with my temperament. Since he sees every side of me, he has sat grumpy beside me on the couch. Curled up with me at night. Groaned when I didn't want to throw his ball in the back yard. And licked my face when I spent too much time in bed or on the couch.

"Jonas…" My name leaves her lips as a plea.

My pulse kicks into fifth gear. "Yes?"

"I…" she starts, then pauses briefly. I don't dare interrupt her silence. Don't push her to say the words waiting in limbo. When she speaks again, it's not what I expect. "I'm sorry."

Why is she apologizing? If anyone should be apologizing, it should be me. I was the one who misconstrued things. Got frustrated with her evasion and lost my cool.

I was in the wrong. She was merely protecting her daughter. She has every right to protect her daughter.

"Autumn, please don't apologize. It should be me saying sorry, not you."

"Maybe we were both in the wrong. I could have been more honest about the call when you asked. But I was scared. It still scares me."

"Will you tell me why? Help me understand."

She remains silent for a beat, then sniffles again. "Jonas, I haven't dated anyone since Clementine's father."

Clementine. How charming and sweet and totally Autumn. I wonder if Clementine is anything like her mother? Beautiful, charming, and someone I always want close. If so, consider me double screwed.

"How old is Clementine?" Not that it matters in my eyes, but I am curious how long Autumn has deprived herself of happiness. How long she has dedicated herself solely to this little girl. Not that I assume her daughter doesn't bring her joy.

"Seven."

To be honest, I am glad we aren't having this conversation face to face right now. Because seven was not what I expected to hear. Maybe a number closer to three. Not seven. Seven years is a *really* long time to not have any sort of romantic relationship. I understand her desire to be dedicated to her daughter, but as a woman—hell, as a grown human being—she has needs. Not necessarily sexual, but basic human desires. Companionship. Love. Having an intimate relationship—sexual or not—is basic human nature.

"Wow," I whisper. She starts to speak, but I cut her off. "Autumn, seven years is a really long time to rob yourself of love. Love other than the one you share with Clementine."

"Well," she starts. I picture her tucking her lips between her teeth a moment. "Her father and I separated before she was born. Being a parent wasn't in the cards for him."

In the blink of an eye, red pricks the backs of my eyes as I close them and grind my jaw. *Piece of shit. Fucking asshole.* I take a minute to simmer my boiling blood. Not only did this douchebag leave her, he left her high and dry when she needed someone most. Not to mention the prick abandoned his child. No wonder she has steered away from a relationship.

Breathing deep, I exhale and speak as calmly as possible. "Autumn, I'm so sorry. Can't imagine what that must've been like for you."

"Everything happens for a reason, right?" She says it with such nonchalance.

"Guess so." She has a point, though. Because if she was still with him, we might not have met. Might not be having this conversation. Might not have the possibility of getting to know one another and growing close.

"Can we save this topic for another time?"

"Of course."

"Jonas, will you forgive me?"

Her request renders me speechless for a moment. She is asking *me* to forgive *her.* The concept seems backward. Wrong. Just because Autumn had yet to tell me about her daughter, she wasn't the one out of turn. Protecting your child is never wrong.

"Only if you'll do the same. I shouldn't have been so harsh. Shouldn't have lost my temper. Should have let you tell me when you were ready. It was wrong of me to be upset over something so private."

"It's done then. All is forgiven." For the first time during this conversation, Autumn has a sliver of happiness in her voice. "Jonas?"

"Yeah?"

"I want to see you."

I sit up on the lounger and Spartan glances up at me from his spot on the patio. *She wants to see me?*

This is good. Really good. Because, fuck, I miss her. Her sweet smile and laughter that settle in the left chamber of my heart. Her fiery cognac irises which have me drunk in seconds. The warmth of her touch that fevers every molecule in my veins.

"Yes," I answer, too dumbstruck to form a proper response. "Would love to see you. More than anything."

She giggles and my chest swells in delight. "Glad to hear. Wasn't sure you would."

"Autumn, do you know how difficult it was to slip notes under your windshield wiper and not walk in the shop to see you? To sneak a peek at you through the windows? Walking away each night got more and more punishing. A couple times, I wanted to wait by your car and hand the note to you personally. But I knew it wouldn't be received the same. So, I left. As difficult as it was, I walked away and gave you time to think."

The first three nights I left notes and the drawing for Autumn, I stood next to her car for at least ten minutes. Stared at the driver's seat and pictured her behind the wheel. Imagined opening the door and her stepping out. Dreamed of her in my arms again. Of my lips on hers.

"Thank you," she whispers. "For giving me time to sort this out. To sort us out."

Us. Hope soars in my chest. "I got some sisterly advice," I confess.

"Well, your sisters are wise women." She giggles again. Each musical note of it lightens the weight I have felt over the last week. "Jonas, if you're open to it, I'd like you to meet Clementine."

Wow. This shocks me more than anything. Only because she has protected her daughter so fiercely over the last seven-plus years. Because she has forfeited her own happiness to make sure her daughter doesn't get hurt. Has dedicated her life to her daughter so she doesn't feel any less loved because her father abandoned her long before she took her first breath.

"Autumn…" My voice is barely audible. "I would like that very much. But only if you're comfortable with it."

"Wouldn't suggest it if I wasn't. But Jonas?"

"Yeah?"

"This is a really big deal for me. Me introducing you to Clementine… this has never happened before. I wasn't kidding when I told you I haven't dated."

The gravity of her repeated confession strikes me in the solar plexus. The words engulf me. Tell me how much I mean to her without actually expressing them in the terms most do. This is Autumn's way of saying she wants me more than a fling. Wants permanence. A life.

"Don't know what to say. I feel like an idiot."

"You're not an idiot. Just let me know you grasp how big this is for me."

"I do. Honestly, it's a big deal for me too. Just for a different reason."

For a moment, neither of us says anything. We sit in comfortable silence as the magnitude of what is happening between us evolves. Autumn wants to introduce me to her daughter. Wants me to meet her. And for her to know me. This isn't a baby step. It's a leap. A headfirst dive into uncharted waters. It invigorates me and scares the hell out of me in equal measure.

"Is Thursday okay?" she asks. "Or do you have plans with your family?"

I want to remind her Wednesday is when I have family dinners. But then it hits me. This is Christmas week. And Thursday is Christmas Eve. A day when most families gather and celebrate traditions other than exchanging gifts. Now that my sisters and I are grown, we don't get together until Christmas evening. So my oldest sister can celebrate with her husband and son however they choose.

"Thursday is perfect."

"How do you feel about pizza and a G-rated movie?"

I laugh. Never has greasy cheese-coated dough and animation sounded so wonderful. "Well, I've never met a pizza I didn't like. And I watch G-rated movies with my nephew now and again, so I'm up for it."

"Awesome," she says with enthusiasm. "If it's okay with you, I'll figure out the where and when and what to see then text you."

In this aspect of her life, Autumn needs full control. And I will happily give it all to her. Give her whatever she needs so long as I get to be by her side.

"Sounds great. Can't wait to see you. And to meet Clementine. Thank you."

"Why are you thanking me?"

How in depth do I go? How do I tell her I am just thankful for another chance with her? The answer has so many layers, and tonight isn't the time to unravel them all. "Because you deserve it. Because you didn't completely dismiss me or my silly notes."

"They're not silly," she whispers.

"No, they aren't. But I've never written notes to anyone, and I felt like a teenager again. Felt like I was asking the girl stuck in my head if she likes me or not."

"Well, this girl likes you very much."

"Good to know." My cheeks sting from smiling. Only Autumn makes me this way. Happy like this.

"I should go. Been sitting in the parking lot behind the shop this whole time. Kind of need to head home."

"Head home. Sorry I kept you so long."

"No worries. I'll text you. See you Thursday."

"Thursday. Good night, Autumn."

"'Night, Jonas."

The call disconnects and I fall back against the lounger again. Spartan pops up on all fours and nudges my elbow. But I ignore him for a minute as I stare up at the night sky. As the stars stare back at me with more twinkle.

I get to see her again. Hold her. And meet the little lady who is the most precious part of her existence. Hopefully that little girl approves of me too.

nineteen

AUTUMN

"Ready, pumpkin?"

"Yeah, Mama." Clementine picks up her small red purse and tosses the strap over her shoulder like any other day. Like any other night out for pizza and milkshakes.

Yesterday morning, while we sat down for breakfast, I told Clementine about Jonas. About the man who was a friend, but who I like more than a friend. The whole conversation with my seven-year-old daughter was awkward to say the least. Honestly, it felt like I was the child and she was the adult. I only imagine how weird and uncomfortable it will be to have the birds and bees conversation with her.

Although Clementine acts older than her age at times, she still holds so much innocence inside. And I take the blame as well as pride. Nowadays, too many kids grow up too soon. At every turn, I try to give my daughter a chance to remain a kid. To be spirited and not worry about things children shouldn't be burdened by— including my love life. Past or present. Most girls her age go out and do things I didn't until my preteen/early teen years. But I have done well at preserving her innocence as long as possible. Every once in a while, her sassy, trying to be older side comes out. Most of the time, though, she acts like seven-year-olds did before tablets, computers, cell phones, and online games stole their attention—and I am grateful.

We only get eighteen years to be a child. Adulting lasts three or more times longer.

When I asked Clementine if it was okay to share pizza and watch a movie with Jonas, her excitement shocked me. She jumped off the couch and started dancing. I bet it was a happy dance for pizza and a movie, but at least she wasn't perturbed by meeting Jonas.

"Let's go." We shuffle out the front door and soon buckle up in the Bel Air.

Part of me is happy Penny is at work, while part of me wishes she was home. Her constant attention would be both annoying and desirable. Her dating words of wisdom. Her constant nagging and mothering. Asking if I have my lipstick in my purse. If I put on deodorant. Reminding me to spritz perfume on my clothes and not my skin, in case Jonas kisses me. The little things which drive me crazy on a normal day, but would love tonight.

I back out of the space and drive toward the Italian restaurant we agreed to meet at. It butts up against the movie theater and makes pizza-movie night easy whenever I take Clementine.

In the passenger seat, Clementine bops to the song on the radio. Singing the lyrics she knows and humming the ones she doesn't. As on edge as I am about Jonas meeting Clementine, seeing her so at ease with the whole evening tapers the anxiety a smidge. I bask in her carefree existence. Her lack of fear or worry. Use that spirit to calm my nerves with each passing minute.

A few songs later, I steer the car into the lot. For a Thursday evening, the lot is fuller than expected. Granted, school is on break right now and parents are probably trying to find ways to amuse their children, so the crowd isn't a shock.

As I search for a place to park, I spot Jonas on his motorcycle in the next row. I swallow and clamp down on my lips. Clementine continues to sing, completely oblivious to the sudden panic attack creeping through my veins.

I pull into a spot and throw the car in park, but leave the engine and heat running. Clementine unbuckles her belt, but doesn't go to open the door. She knows if the car is still on, she stays inside.

When I glance in the direction of where I saw Jonas on his bike, he is no longer there. Instead, he slowly walks toward the car. I close my eyes and take a deep breath. *You've got this. Don't chicken out now. Not yet.*

"Mama? Are you okay?" Clementine rests her hand on my forearm and I open my eyes.

"Yeah, pumpkin. Will you please stay in the car a minute? I want to speak with Jonas before you meet him."

She nods. "Can you leave the radio on?" I love how something as simple as leaving the radio on will keep her happy.

"You bet. Stay here. I'll be back in a second."

"Okay, Mama."

Now or never, Autumn.

I open the door and step out. Jonas is a few cars away. I step around the front of the car and meet him at the rear of the car parked in front of me. Clementine still within sight, but far enough away she doesn't hear anything. Just want to gauge Jonas's mood before I open the floodgates.

God, he steals every practiced word from my lips and renders me speechless every time he is near. We haven't seen each other in nine days, but those days feel like months. Years. How is it possible he looks a hundred times more appealing? Taller. Broader. More handsome.

Two more strides and he stands inches from my touch. "Hey," he whispers. As if speaking too loudly will shatter our reunion.

"Hey." I lock on to his magnetic hazel eyes and swallow. Before I formulate what to say next, Jonas steps into me and wraps his arms around my center.

I melt into his embrace. Inhale deeply and pull in the scent of him—a distinct blend of sunscreen, gasoline, and the smell of Thompson's Garage. Bask in the warmth and strength of his arms snug around my waist. I would stay in Jonas's arms forever if given the opportunity.

Far too soon, he slips his hands to my hips and breaks the hug. But before I can pout, he dips down and presses his lips to mine. Shock registers for a split second, then slips away as my lips move with his.

Every anxiety-ridden minute I have suffered since we last saw each other vanishes. His lips brush against mine, slow and measured. Each move calculated and perfect. He swipes the tip of his tongue against my lower lip and I open up for him. His hands snake up the sides of my torso and frame my face as we memorize each other again. Memorize our individual tastes. The way our bodies curve in exactly the right places against each other. And the way we cannot get enough of the other.

Lost in the feel of Jonas pressed against me, in his taste, I audibly pout when he breaks the kiss. He chuckles and presses a chaste kiss to my lips again. "You have no idea how much I love it when you pout."

I fist his shirt, tug him closer, and rest my forehead in the crook of his neck. "Well, I missed you."

"Missed you too." Jonas slips his arms back around my waist and holds me close. His embrace is the most at home I have felt in a long time. He kisses the crown of my head. "Are you nervous?"

I nod into the collar of his leather jacket. "Definitely."

"Me too," he whispers. "But also thrilled."

I lean away, tip my head back, and take in his expression. He smiles, but his dimple I love so much doesn't pop up. His eyes are as soft and brilliant as always, but his pupils are dilated. And every few seconds, he looks toward my car. Where Clementine sits patiently, singing songs.

Taking a step back, I slip my hand down to his and lace my fingers between his. I lock eyes with him and smile. "You ready?" He nods but doesn't say anything.

Slowly, we walk hand in hand toward my car. Jonas's fingers squeeze mine slightly every other step forward. I weave us over to the driver's side. When we stop, I give him another kiss before opening the door and ducking my head inside. "Hey, pumpkin. Thank you for waiting."

"You're welcome, Mama."

Behind me, Jonas's fingers tighten around mine. I give him a gentle squeeze of reassurance. I reach in, cut the engine, and pull the keys from the ignition. "Grab your purse and crawl across the seat. Let's go get some pizza."

"Yay, pizza!" She slides her purse on her shoulder, locks her door, and crawls across the seat to exit through my door.

As Clementine steps out of the car, Jonas inches away from me. Not in fear. More like he doesn't want to give Clementine the wrong impression. But Jonas doesn't realize Clementine doesn't have any set impressions of anyone or relationships. Unfortunately, she hasn't witnessed many. Penny never brings dates home per my request. Just so Clementine doesn't feel uncomfortable with a stranger in her home.

"Pumpkin, this is Jonas." I glance up from my daughter to look into Jonas's eyes. "Mommy's boyfriend." Jonas tightens his grip on mine as a cute smile pops up on Clementine's face. "Jonas, this is my daughter, Clementine."

He squats down to her height and smiles so bright. "Hi, Clementine." Jonas extends his hand to her. "It's nice to meet you."

She looks at his hand as her brows bunch together. Jonas meets my gaze and I shrug. And then Clementine launches forward and hugs him. When he loosens his grip from mine, I let him. I let him hug her back as I smile like a fool. I forgot to warn him Clementine is a hugger.

When she lets him go, she smiles at him. "Nice to meet ya." She glances up at me. "Can we get pizza now? I'm hungry."

And just like that, the awkward stage of the evening ends.

Jonas walks on my right, Clementine on my left. All of us connected. We stroll through the lot toward the pizza shop, Clementine swinging our connected hands and talking animatedly about all the holiday décor on the buildings. The sparkling reindeer and glowing lights and shimmering tinsel.

She asks Jonas if he has a Christmas tree up at his house. If he has cookies and milk for Santa and the special sparkly oats for the reindeer. I shrug and let him answer on his own. Clementine knows not everyone celebrates Christmas, but can't help her own enthusiasm for her favorite holiday.

"I don't have a tree up at home. Spartan would knock it down and eat the ornaments," he answers.

We arrive at the entrance of the packed restaurant. Jonas gives his name and our party info. A high school–age boy hands him a buzzer and lets him know it will be a ten-to-fifteen-minute wait.

The three of us sit on a bench just outside and bundle up close. "Who is Spartan?" Clementine asks.

"Spartan is my dog."

Clementine bolts up from the bench and stares at Jonas with wide eyes. "You have a dog?" Jonas nods and chuckles. Clementine turns her attention in my direction. "Mama, can we meet Spartan sometime?"

One thing you learn about children, especially younger children, is they speak their mind. It isn't until we grow older—somewhere around puberty—that we learn to taper our reactions and the words we say. Hopefully, I can continue to teach Clementine to voice her thoughts, but just be mindful of how she says things so as not to hurt anyone's feelings.

"We'll see, pumpkin."

Jonas leans closer to me, his breath hot on my ear. "He's good with kids. Licks my nephew to death." I hear what he says, but my brain won't react. Can't with his lips so close to my skin. As if he senses my debacle, he kisses the soft skin beneath my ear and sits up. "So, Clementine, what's your favorite part of Christmas?"

I shake my head and snigger. "You asked for it," I mumble.

Until the buzzer goes off, Clementine prattles on about her favorite parts of Christmas. All with hand gestures and full exaggeration. About her love of decorating trees and hanging the stockings. Squishing her fingers in the sugar cookie dough, licking the extras off the spoon, and frosting them after they cool. But most of all, she loves Christmas movies. *The Polar Express* and *The Nightmare Before Christmas*.

Jonas play-argues with her for a bit. Debating whether or not *The Nightmare Before Christmas* is a Halloween or Christmas movie. Clementine cocks her head as her brows pinch at the middle, settling the debate with a resounding "both."

As we walk to the table and sit in the booth—Jonas and I on one side, Clementine across from us—I can't help how *normal* this feels. How wonderful it all is. How jovial my daughter is in the company of Jonas. More so than I expected. But it warms my heart. Fills me more than I ever thought it could. To have my daughter happy in the company of someone I am growing more and more fond of with each passing day.

How could life possibly get any better? I don't see how it can.

Mini-Autumn—aka Clementine—is the cutest little girl I have ever laid eyes on.

Not only is she a spitting image of Autumn—hair, eyes, ensemble—but she has an addictive personality. With her little hands flailing in the air as she tells me about the sparkly snowflakes her class made before the holiday break. And that she has never seen real snow before.

Part of me itched to tell her I would take her and Autumn to see snow one day. But I bit my tongue and listened to all her stories. Tales about her schoolmates— and the one boy who seems sad all the time, but who she makes laugh.

The more she says, the more I fall for Autumn and her mini, Clementine. God, even her name is fucking adorable.

We order pizza—a mini cheese for Clementine, while Autumn and I split a medium; ham and pineapple for Autumn, and supreme on my half. Nothing about sitting in this pizza shop with Autumn and Clementine—surrounded by several other parents and children—feels wrong. If anything, nothing has ever felt so *right*.

Autumn rests her hand on my thigh and I set mine over hers. I haven't dated a lot of women. Most were one-night stands. Only there to fulfill a primal need while I pined for another woman. A woman whose heart belonged to someone else. Until Autumn, I didn't comprehend the connection Cora and Gavin share. Now, I get it.

When Gavin first flew in from Los Angeles to work, he had no clue he would see Cora. Actually, hoped he wouldn't because of how he left things with Cora. But the moment they saw each other again, it was like they never parted. That's how bonded they are. When Cora tried to explain it to me, I couldn't grasp how she still wanted him. How it was possible to be in love with him after so many years apart. After what he had done.

But now, I recognize the bond. Their constant need to be near each other. Because I feel the same thing with Autumn. Clementine is an added bonus. The little girl I never knew or saw coming, but has filled some gap in my heart in less than an hour.

Autumn rests her head on my shoulder and sighs. "How ya holding up?"

I turn and press a kiss to her forehead. "Fantastic. She's perfect, Autumn. You've done so good with her." She smiles into my neck. "Seriously. She is the cutest thing ever."

"Cuter than me?"

I chuckle and shake my head. "No. No one will ever be cuter than you." I kiss her forehead again and note the flush pinking her cheeks. "But since she is a mirror image of you, she takes second place."

The pizza arrives and we all go quiet as we scarf down our pieces. Clementine starts talking with pizza in her mouth, and I laugh when Autumn corrects her. Citing why it isn't ladylike to talk with her mouth full of food. Where most kids, including my nephew, would argue, she doesn't. She simply finishes chewing then picks up where she left off.

When we finish eating, I pay the bill and we head toward the movie theater. But stop short when we see the ticket line a mile long.

"How set are you on watching this movie?" I ask.

Autumn tucks her lips in her mouth a minute then releases them as she squats down in front of Clementine. "Hey, pumpkin. There's a really long line to get into the movie. Can we do something else instead?"

Clementine glances between the two of us. "Like what?"

"I have an idea," I say as Autumn stands up. "What about the arcade down near Park?"

"The Fun Center?" Autumn asks and I nod. "That might work. Pumpkin, what if we go to the arcade. We can play all kinds of games and win tickets for prizes."

Clementine claps rapidly. "Yay! Prizes. Let's go." She grabs Autumn's hand and starts dragging her toward the parking lot. But Autumn digs her heels in.

"Hold on a minute, pumpkin." Autumn spins to face me. "Want to ride together?"

I shake my head. "Nah. I'd rather not leave my bike here. It's okay, we can meet there. Only five or so minutes up the road. Let me walk you to the car."

We all walk hand in hand back to Autumn's car. After Clementine gets in and her door is shut, I walk around to the driver's side with Autumn. Before she gets in, I draw her in close and kiss her. Deeper and slower than the kiss we shared earlier. She tastes sweet and salty and something distinctly Autumn. When she fists my jacket lapels and moans into my mouth, I reluctantly break the kiss.

"We're like horny teenagers," I say against her lips.

She giggles. "I really like kissing you. Will that be an issue?"

"Nope. Not at all."

"Good." She inches back. "We should get going if we want to get there before closing time."

"See you in a few." I kiss her again before jogging over to my bike.

I spark up the bike and put my helmet on. Glancing over my shoulder, I see Autumn back out of the space and drive away. Rolling the bike back, I fall in line behind her. We roll down the street and a sense of serenity fills me.

I may not be in the car with her, but I have never felt closer to her.

And Clementine… she is a hoot. I was so nervous to meet this little girl. God, I don't ever remember being that nervous before. Where I was completely riddled with anxiety. Meeting Clementine felt more powerful than meeting parents. That little girl's approval could have possibly made or broken our relationship.

But from how everything went over dinner, I am positive Clementine approves of me and my relationship with Autumn. That little girl's approval means the world—not just to me, but also Autumn.

We pull into the parking lot at the Fun Center and I park the bike next to Autumn's car. When Clementine gets out of the car, she runs up to me and spreads her arms wide.

"You have a motorcycle?" she asks with wide eyes. "That's so cool!"

I laugh and squat down in front of her. "Maybe one day, you can sit on it with me." Autumn stares at me wide-eyed and mouth agape. "But only if it's okay with your mom." I stand back up and lean into Autumn, whispering so only she can hear. "The bike would be parked. No actual riding until adulthood."

"Thank god. I was freaking out for a minute there."

I want to tell her it was written all over her face, but I don't. "No need to panic." I kiss her temple. "Believe it or not, I know better."

She hums. "But I still want to ride on your bike."

In an instant, I picture Autumn snug behind me on the seat, her legs clamped around mine. Her arms wrapped around my waist. Hands under my shirt and grazing my abdomen. The trail of fire her touch would leave on my skin.

Fuck, I need to stop thinking about that right now. *Focus, Thompson.*

"Let's head inside and play some games. Clementine, have you played arcade games before?"

She shakes her little head. "Nope, just the games on Mama's phone. But not a lot."

"Well, you're in for a treat. Because arcade games are way more fun than games on the phone. Plus, you get tickets when you play. Then you turn in your tickets for a prize."

"What kind of prizes are there?"

We walk through the front door, music blares around us as kids run left and right to different games. Heading over to the check-in counter, I swap out twenty dollars for tokens. The girl behind the counter hands us each a small cup to carry our tokens and tickets in.

After we step back and organize our tokens, I show Clementine the various display cases and huge wall with prizes pinned to them. Anything from plastic vampire teeth to nail stickers to stuffed animals and everything in between. She oohs and awes over each item she sees.

She points to a small makeup set. "I want to win *that.*"

"Okay, well let's go find what game we want to play so we can earn tickets."

Clementine bounces in place on her toes. "Let's do this," she announces and Autumn and I both laugh.

For the next hour, we play various video games, but Pac-Man seems to be her favorite. Autumn and I try our hand at Skee-Ball and the basketball game. Both of us trying to find easy games for us to win as many tickets as possible.

When we tally up all of our tickets, we don't have enough for Clementine to get the makeup kit—which Autumn doesn't seem too upset over. But Autumn and I both still have tokens. So, we pass our tokens on to Clementine and follow her around as she tries different games.

By the time all the tokens run out, we have hundreds of tickets. I walk us over to the ticket feeder to redeem them in for a receipt. Clementine laughs when she feeds the long strip of tickets into the machine and it sounds as if it's chomping them up. Like a monster lives inside the ticket machine.

With her tickets, she chooses a stuffed animal. A rainbow unicorn with shimmering hair. She hugs it close to her chest and it warms my heart.

As we stroll out to Autumn's car and my bike, Clementine stops us in our tracks. "Mama, can we meet Mr. Jonas's doggy tonight?"

I smile, but keep my eyes straight ahead. Kids are the cutest creatures in the world. They say whatever pops in their head. Whether it be wanting to meet a dog or if they don't like someone's clothes or talking about body parts. They literally have no filter and I love it. I wish that little piece of humanity existed among all ages. But somewhere along the line, we are taught certain things are inappropriate to say in front of other people. Although, once you find your circle of people, that filter slips away.

"Not tonight, pumpkin. But I'm sure we can meet Jonas's doggy soon."

"Really?" she asks, hopeful.

"Promise, pumpkin."

We reach the car and Autumn unlocks it and starts it. I squat down in front of Clementine. "It was really nice to meet you, Miss Clementine. See you again soon."

She wraps her little arms around my neck and squeezes me as if I might run away. *Never*, I think to myself. "'Night, Mr. Jonas." I want to kiss her head, but don't. It's too soon.

Clementine hops in the car and slides over to her seat, buckling her seat belt without being asked.

"Thank you for tonight," Autumn says. "I had a really nice time."

"Me too." I step into her, rest my hands on her hips, and bring her flush to me. "Can't wait to see you again."

"Soon," she whispers a breath from my lips.

I close the space between us and press my lips to hers. Warm and sweet and inviting. She instantly opens up for me, and I brush my tongue against hers. When she moans against my mouth, I deepen the kiss. I could kiss her for hours and not tire from it.

Her lips on mine intoxicates me. Makes me drunker than her cognac eyes. The more I kiss her, the harder I fall. Fall for this astonishing woman. A woman I never saw coming. A woman I don't want a day without.

We kiss in the parking lot, against the side of her car, as if no one else exists. I frame her face in my palms. Draw her into me. Press my hips to her belly. Her hands slip beneath my jacket. Under my shirt. Graze the skin just above the waistband of my jeans.

I hiss and break the kiss. My lips still hovering a fraction above hers. "Autumn…" Her name a plea. A prayer. An urge for more. But I know there is nothing more we can do right now. Not in the middle of a parking lot, out in the open, with Clementine less than five feet from where we stand.

"Jonas," she moans. My name painful, but not in a bad way. More like she wants me just as badly as I want her, but knows this moment won't go much further than where it is now.

I lean my forehead against hers and breathe in her cherry vanilla scent. It inebriates and soothes me in equal measure. Settles every anxiety or fear I have experienced. Soothes me more than any other person ever has.

No doubt about it, Autumn is my balm. The remedy to any ailment I possess. As if made for me.

"Much as I want to stand in this parking lot all night and kiss the hell out of you, we should probably leave."

God, I don't want to let go of her. Don't want to stop kissing her. Or stop touching her. More than anything, I don't want her to stop touching me. Her fingertips on my skin elicits the most exhilarating sensation. Leaving a trail of sparks wherever she touches. Embers burning in their wake.

"Probably. But I don't want to," she confesses. "I wish I could invite you back to my place."

Me too. But even if Autumn offered for me to join her, I would be the gentleman. I would tell her it's too soon. All good things come to those who wait. At least that is what everyone says.

So why does that old adage feel like a line of crap right now?

All I want is to hold her in my arms all night. Sex would be great, but neither of us is ready for sex yet. Not mentally or emotionally, anyway.

"Yeah. But not tonight. Baby steps. Tonight was a big leap. For all of us. Let's ease into the rest of it. We have time."

She nods. "Lots of time." And I love the way the words leave her lips. Like more than a promise. A commitment.

I pocket her commitment and seal it away for safekeeping. Hold it close to my heart. Let it warm my bones.

Taking a deep breath, I slowly inch away from her. Give us both room to breathe. To cool off in the chilled winter air.

I open her door for her, peek my head inside, and look over at a singing Clementine. "'Night, Miss Clementine. Be good for your mom."

She waves at me. "'Night. I will." She draws an X over her heart. "Promise."

Autumn slides into her car, but doesn't shut the door immediately. I lean down and kiss her innocently. With Clementine's eyes on us both, I won't do more. A sense of inappropriateness washes over me like a cold shower.

"Night, Autumn. Text me when you get home so I know you made it okay."

The corner of her mouth kicks up. "I will. 'Night."

Reluctantly, I step back and close her door, tapping the roof. I walk over and straddle my bike, watching as she backs out. Clementine waves and I return the gesture with a smile.

As soon as they disappear from sight, I stare up at the night sky and smile at the brightly lit dark backdrop. Tonight, more stars appear in the skyline. Each moment with Autumn seems to add another star. Hopefully one day, the night sky will glow so bright, I won't need additional light.

The entire ride home goes by in a blur. A slideshow of memories of the evening. Memories I will never forget. And what I pray is the start of a million more memories. After I park the bike in the garage, I step into the house and tell Spartan all about Clementine. The little girl who will win his heart faster than she won mine.

The past two weeks has been nothing short of bliss.

Jonas and I have seen each other several nights a week. Dinner at his house or my apartment. Although, Clementine prefers going to Jonas's. The second she laid eyes on Spartan; my daughter forgot I existed.

I didn't take offense to it. In fact, I found it downright adorable how the two of them hung out together. Clementine would hug or pet him. Talk with him— because yes, Spartan barked back when you spoke to him. They were like a dynamic duo.

Each time we had dinner at Jonas's house and had to leave, Clementine wrapped her small arms around Spartan and hugged him tight. Kissed his head and wished him a good night. Adorable didn't even begin to cover how they interacted together.

When dinner happens at the apartment, Clementine asks if Jonas will bring Spartan along. Bless his heart, he always finds a valid excuse as to why he can't come along. Tired. Grumpy. Had a bad day. As the list grows, it makes me laugh harder.

On a few occasions, Penny joined us for dinner. But for the most part, she goes and hangs with friends or chills in her room.

I told her it was cool if she hung with us, but she laughed it off and said, "It's pretty much a date, Auti. I will not be a third wheel." She makes a valid statement.

A couple nights ago, we watched a movie after dinner. Our nights together have been some of the best moments of my adult life, but they were also a strain. The more Jonas and I see each other, the less time I spent at the shop, and the more I considered it wise to shift my work schedule. Honestly, I don't know why I didn't do it sooner. It works better with Clementine's school schedule. Now, I work fewer hours in the evening and she spends less time with a sitter. It's a win win. More time with Clementine and Jonas.

And although we have been seeing each other almost nonstop for the last two weeks, we have yet to do anything beyond some serious kissing and light petting. Not that either of us doesn't want to do more. The perfect opportunity just hasn't presented itself yet. But it feels fast approaching.

Tonight, we are having dinner at Jonas's house. Clementine is bringing her favorite movie with her for us to watch afterward. This tends to be the trend with each dinner we share. The only night we don't see each other is when he goes to his parent's house for their weekly family dinner. It gives us both a night apart to do anything we want.

I park in Jonas's driveway and cut the engine. As soon as I do, Clementine unbuckles, grabs her purse with the movie tucked inside, and hops out of the car.

"Sparty," she hollers as she runs for the door. "I'm here, Sparty."

Her enthusiasm to see Spartan cracks me up. But what's even funnier is Spartan on the other side. Jonas has told me each time we pull up, after our first visit here, Spartan sits at the door and whimpers until Clementine walks in. Their instant connection is so freaking precious.

Clementine bolts up the three steps and turns the door handle, walking into Jonas's house as if she lives there. I laugh and shake my head.

As I step up to the front door, Jonas greets me with a chuckle. Both of us bewildered by his fur-child and my human one. "Hey, scarlet," he says, kissing the hell out of me as I shut the door.

Sometime over the last two weeks, Jonas started calling me scarlet. The first time he said it, I cocked my head in question. Wasn't sure if he was calling me someone else? Then, he explained between my lipstick, nail color, and my overall fashion sense, it fit. It didn't bother me. If anything, I loved it. Quite a bit. The term of endearment made my cheeks heat. Scarlet, of course. And since, he says it more often.

When he breaks the kiss—because let's be honest, I will never break our kisses—I sigh and lean into him. "Hey. What's for dinner?"

We wander from the living room—where Clementine and Spartan sit on the couch and cuddle together as Clementine tells him about her day—to the kitchen. I could easily stare at the two of them for hours and not tire of how darling they are. Two peas in the cutest pod.

"Thought we'd have homemade chicken tenders with macaroni and cheese and corn on the cob."

"You really are domestic," I tease as I hug his middle and stare into the large pot of cheesy noodles. A girl could really get used to this. Her guy cooking dinner nightly. And if I get lucky, he will let me help with the dishes.

"My momma taught me right. Wanted to make sure we were all self-sufficient. Either that or so we could pull our weight in a relationship."

When I get the opportunity to meet Jonas's mom, I plan to thank her. She raised a wonderful man. No doubt his sisters are equally amazing. From what he has told me, during their weekly dinners, Jonas and his sisters usually make most of the meal. The only exception is when they have something which takes more time to cook.

"Look forward to meeting her," I say.

He stops stirring the pasta and I stop breathing. Did I go too far? Suggest meeting the parents a little too soon. Meeting Jonas's mom—since already meeting his dad—seems inevitable, but I don't expect it by any specific time.

Jonas sets the spoon on the rest and spins to face me. He clasps my hands and wraps them around his waist, drawing me near. My hips press to his upper thighs. He sweeps my long flowing hair off my cheek and tucks it behind my ear before cupping both my cheeks in his palms. Slowly, he closes the space between us and kisses me.

Fevered and intense. Lips smacking. Tongues tangling. Hips grinding. Moan emitting.

His fingers slip into my hair and curl in my locks. He draws me closer. Kisses me deeper. Kisses me as if I am his oxygen.

Over the last two weeks, I learned to wear my hair down more with Jonas. Otherwise, it ended up looking like a hot mess in less than an hour. At least with my hair down, I didn't spend every five minutes trying to fix it. And Jonas really loved my hair down. A lot. Oftentimes, his fingers toyed with the strands. While we cooked dinner. During movie time, while we spooned on the couch. Every possible chance he got.

When he breaks the kiss, I gasp and work to catch my breath. He rests his forehead against mine, eyes closed. We stand absolutely still for a moment, absorbing our exchange.

"Can't wait for you to meet her, and my sisters, too. Think they'll love you and Clementine. Plus, Clementine can play with Lex and Spartan. Whenever you're ready, of course."

I nod. "We should talk about it. Everything you've told me about them, it feels as if I already know them."

An angry beeping fills the room as the timer on the stove interrupts our little moment. In the living room, I hear Clementine tell Spartan dinner is ready. And just like every other time she says this to him, he yips and bounces around the house. Because Spartan is trained to know the word dinner equals food. Same goes for breakfast. Clementine giggles every time she says it and Spartan flips out.

Jonas presses the buzzer and shuts it off. Then removes the lightly breaded chicken strips from the oven and sets the tray on trivets. After they cool a minute, we portion our plates then feed Spartan.

Just like we have several times over the last two weeks, we sit at the breakfast bar and eat our meal. When we finish, we settle on the couch and watch Clementine's movie. She lies on the end of the couch with a chaise—Spartan sprawled at her feet and facing the television. Jonas and I lay on the longer section of the sofa. Him behind me, his front to my back. Hand on my abdomen, toying with the hemline of my shirt. Knuckles brushing back and forth across my skin just beneath my navel. His breath hot on my neck below my ear. On occasion, he lightly kisses the sensitive skin there.

And every time he does, I groan as quietly as possible while grinding back against him.

As big a fan of foreplay as I am, this level of teasing may soon be my demise. Weeks of titillating torture. I love it and hate it at the same time. All I know is, is when we eventually have sex, it will be mind blowing.

Slowly, I turn around so Jonas and I lie face-to-face. I brush his fallen hair off his forehead and lean into him. As I weave my upper leg between his, he draws me closer and throws his leg over my hip.

Weeks ago, it would have freaked me out to do this with Clementine in the room. But now, things have become more comfortable with all of us. One, her eyes are on the movie as she combs her fingers through Spartan's fur. Two, she has seen Jonas and I kiss so many times now, it is normal. Natural. Nothing to bat an eye at.

I brush my lips over his then retreat. "God, I want you," I confess. His hand on my lower back holds me in place as he slowly rocks his hips forward. My eyes roll back then close.

"Right there with you, scarlet. Not tonight, though," he whispers. "But soon."

I nod and bring my lips back to his. For the remainder of the movie, we make out like teenagers. Jonas tucks his hand between us and explores my skin beneath my shirt. He doesn't dip beneath my bra or push it to the side. And hell if I don't have lady blue balls by the time the movie ends.

As the credits scroll up the screen, neither of us moves. Clementine doesn't say a word about the movie being over, which means she recently fell asleep. But the moment we move, she will wake. It happens every time.

So, we stay right where we are. Cuddled in each other's arms. Lips locked and tongues a tangled mess. Hands traveling the others' body. Squeezing and groping. Taunting and teasing.

When Jonas's fingertips graze the elastic band of my panties, I gasp and tip my head back. He trails his lips and tongue down the column of my neck. I rock into him, needing to feel him against me. Even if we are both still completely clothed, I need the friction.

"Oh god," I whisper-moan.

Jonas's hands are in a frenzy—kneading my hips harder, driving us together over and over. He sucks at my skin, at the dip below my collarbone—from sternum to shoulder—nipping my skin when he reaches the end point. He rocks our hips together, again and again. The friction rubs me in all the right places. Sparks fire beneath my skin. A light sheen of sweat coats my skin. Energy swirls throughout my body, like a river from head to toe, and slowly converges beneath my navel.

His lips travel up my neck, across the line of my jaw, then return to mine. He devours me as if I am his last meal. Hips rocking in time together as his hand trails along my abdomen and lightly scrapes my flesh.

I moan against his lips, fist the fabric of his shirt, just before my body stutters and releases. He sucks on my lower lip as my orgasm consumes me. Swallows me whole.

"Fuck, that was sexy as hell," he whispers against my lips.

Clementine groans and I stop breathing. "Mama," she says, her voice thick with sleep.

"Yeah, pumpkin," I answer, hoping I don't sound too far off from normal. Jonas smiles wickedly in front of me and I resist the urge to slap him.

"Are we going home soon?"

"Soon, pumpkin."

She doesn't say anything else for a minute and I wonder if she dozed back off. When I lift up and glance over at her, her eyes are closed but her fingers are moving in Spartan's fur again.

"I feel bad," I tell Jonas.

He furrows his brow. "Why?"

Glancing down between us, I rock my hips against him and hear him groan. "Because I can't return the favor now."

He nods and kisses the tip of my nose. "Please don't worry about that. I'm a saint in the patience department."

"Still feel bad."

A wide, toothy smile spreads across his lips and his dimple makes an appearance. "Just remember it for when you *can* make it up to me."

I lean back in and kiss him, but he breaks his lips away far too soon and leaves me wanting. "Fine. Guess I better go. Not that I want to."

Jonas softly brushes his knuckles over my cheek. "More than anything, I want you to stay. But not tonight."

Pushing out my lip, I pout and laugh when Jonas drops his face in the crook of my neck and grunts. "Please stop pouting. You have no idea what that does to me."

"Oh really..." I kick the corner of my mouth up in a devilish smile. "Note to self. Pouting is my weapon."

"Yeah, that may be true. But I'm sure I have a few up my sleeve too."

I narrow my eyes at him and he laughs quietly. When he doesn't budge or say anything else, I shift to roll off the couch, but Jonas stops my momentum. Rolls me back to him and proceeds to tickle the sides of my abdomen. I shriek and twitch beneath his hands. Clementine wakes up more at the other end of the couch and sits up, watching as Jonas tickles me.

"Tickle Mama party!" she announces, way more awake than she was a minute ago.

And then Clementine crawls over and drops on top of us both. Her little fingers dig in near my belly and wiggle around. Jonas laughs as he and Clementine continue to torture me.

"Stop," I shriek. "P-please. Pr-pretty please." No matter how hard I try, I can't stop laughing.

Eventually, Jonas stops tickling me and suggests they *give Mama a break to breathe*. As much as the whole tickle fest made my abdomen sore and my throat dry, I wouldn't trade out this moment for anything. Jonas and my daughter tag-teaming me in the name of fun. Joining forces to make me laugh. Seeing Clementine jumping in the game with Jonas, it jolts something in the center of my chest.

My little girl has a father-type figure in her life. Someone she is fond of and loves spending time with. As this realization hits me, I stare at the man lying in front of me. Really look at him. Study the kindness in his gaze. The way he looks at me. And the way he looks at my little girl. How thoughtful and generous he is toward us both.

And at this exact moment in time, reality dawns brighter than ever. A truth I can no longer ignore. But a truth I am not ready to confess aloud.

I am in love with Jonas Thompson. Madly.

Leaning back in, my eyes open and locked on his, I kiss him tenderly. He closes his eyes briefly and exhilaration bleeds from his lips to mine. The surge amplifies and pulses through my veins. Wakes every nerve ending and lights me on fire. Spreads from my lips to limbs and comes back to center where it fuses together and forms a life all its own.

My pulse goes into overdrive and I breathe shallowly. When Jonas breaks the kiss, his eyes pop back open and he sees it. The intense emotion alive between us. What I feel. What I know he feels too. But we both stay quiet.

This is not the time or place. But soon, without a doubt, I will tell him.

"Mama, is it time to go home?"

My eyes don't leave Jonas's. "Why don't you pick up what you brought over. We'll go in a moment." But my eyes tell Jonas leaving is the last thing I want to do. A slow nod of his head, he then kisses the tip of my nose.

Reluctantly, I sit up and fetch my shoes. In less than five minutes, Clementine and I are ready to go. I wish for a valid excuse to stay longer, but it's late and Clementine is tired. And I should do what is best for her.

We walk out the front door. I unlock the car and start it up so the heat will warm the cabin. "Give me just a minute." Clementine rests her head against the door and nods. She will be out before we get home.

I close the door and turn to Jonas. We don't say a word. He holds my face in his palms and leans in closer. When his lips touch mine, he is so tender. More tender than I have ever felt before and I mold my body to his. Thread my fingers through the loops of his jeans and pull him against my waist. Hold him flush to me as we express all the emotions we aren't saying aloud.

Because Jonas feels it too—how deeply I have fallen—and matches the emotion.

When he breaks the kiss all too soon, he swipes both his thumbs over my cheeks and places one last kiss on my lips. "Drive safe, scarlet," he says, soft and gruffly.

"I will. And I'll text once we're home." The sentiment—those three words—almost slips from my lips, but I catch it. Catch it and remind myself now is not the time. Soon.

"If you really meant it when you said you'd like to meet my family, I can see if they have room for two more on Wednesday."

Placing one last kiss on his lips, I smile. "Yes, I would love to."

"I'll double-check. Not that I think it'll be an issue." He kisses my forehead. "'Night, scarlet. Get little C in bed."

"Night." I get in the car and back out of Jonas's driveway. On the drive home, with my baby girl in the passenger seat passed out, I recall my eureka moment. The exact moment in time when I realized I am in love with Jonas.

Sure, we haven't been dating very long. Maybe a month altogether. But does love have rules? Is there some hidden decree which dictates how long you have to know someone before you can realize the depth of your affection for them? No. Because love has no rules. Never has. Never will.

Society may deem it odd to do or say or feel certain things in a relationship when it is still new. But societal rules were made by people who feared being vulnerable. And love is one of the most vulnerable emotions in existence.

Now, I just have to find the right time to tell Jonas of my revelation. And be ready to hear it in return. Because I see it in his eyes. Jonas Thompson loves me. Unconditionally.

After talking with Mom—who I knew would freak out in the best way—I open my text history with Autumn to let her know Wednesday is a go. I also mentally prepare her for the onslaught of questions she will get. Because as much as I love my mother and sisters, they are curious women. Especially since I have never brought a woman home. Ever.

The moment I get off the phone with my mom Saturday morning, I text Autumn.

> Mom is way too excited to meet you. Haven't said anything to my sisters yet, but I'm sure they know.

Oh god. Should I be worried?

> Nah. They're harmless. But be ready.

Don't think I've ever been this scared. lol

> I'll protect you.

My hero.

Autumn and I chat a little longer. She and Clementine are going to the park with Penny and Rex, from the tattoo shop. From everything Autumn has shared with me so far, everyone in the shop is pretty close. More like family. When she first mentioned it to me, but didn't say anything about her actual family, I tucked that little tidbit away for the future. A conversation for down the road when Autumn is ready to tell me more about her past.

Reluctantly, I let her go so they can enjoy the park. Spartan and I head out to the back yard where I work on the flower beds more. Spartan lays in the grass and soaks up the sunshine for a while.

I add new fertilizer to the beds in the area I work on and plant the small shrubs and flowers I had Clementine help me choose. Last weekend, I told her I needed her help to make my back yard pretty. She stood tall, more than willing to assist.

We walked around the home improvement store for an hour and stared at rows and rows of options. We narrowed down her twenty choices to four, for now. When we got back to the house, she helped me plant the first flower plant. I told her I would do most of the rest and make the flower beds pretty for her to look at when we were outside.

In a matter of no time at all, this little girl abducted my heart. And honestly, I don't care if she never gives it back. She is the sweetest little human I have ever known. Mom, Jasmine, and Jillian will have a field day with her. And without a doubt, they will fall in love with her just as quickly. As well as with Autumn.

Halfway through planting, my phone rings in my pocket. When I pull it from my pants, I roll my eyes and answer. "Hey, Jas. What's up?"

"Mom says you're bringing your girlfriend and her daughter to dinner Wednesday."

Her words are a statement and leave it wide open for me to mess with her. "Do you have an actual question for me?"

"Don't be a jerk, Jonas. Anything you want to tell me before Wednesday?"

What? "Uh… I don't understand what you're asking. Is this a trick question?"

"Sorry, bro. Just didn't know if there's anything I shouldn't bring up. Never been in this situation before."

Alright, my sister is being dramatic. I roll my eyes and laugh. "Jas, she's not an outcast or something. She's a wonderful person. I really like her. She really likes me. And it just so happens she has a daughter. But you'll love her too. Both of them."

"Okay, brother. Just elbow me if I start acting weird."

I laugh. "Can I elbow you no matter what?"

"You're an ass."

"Love you too. See you Wednesday."

"Bye."

The call disconnects and I shake my head. Of my two sisters, I knew Jasmine would be the one to freak out more. Jillian has always been more laid back about life. Sure, she will ask questions, but it won't feel the same as when Mom and Jasmine do.

I finish putting the last of the plants in the soil and head back into the house. After washing up, I plop down on the couch and lay where Autumn and I do every time she visits. The fabric smells like her. Like vanilla and cherry and the distinct scent of Autumn.

Like a weirdo, I press my face into the cushions and inhale deeply. Only a few more hours and I will see her for dinner. I set an alarm on my phone and take a nap with my nose against the cushion where her scent is strongest. Fuck, I love her….

⌢

Autumn wanders around her apartment in search of a specific bandana she wants to wear in her hair. I offer to help, but stop after a minute when it seems I am only in the way. Clementine tries to tell her the last place she saw it, but steers clear of Autumn while she scours the apartment.

Five minutes later, the bandana is secure in her hair. But she fidgets more. Bites her lips frequently. Checks her hair. Questions what she wears. And I can't help but adore how nervous she is about meeting my family.

Her anxiety says more than any words. Says how much she cares—not just about me, but also wanting my family to like her. And Clementine.

I step up to her and rest my hands on her hips. "Autumn." She stops for a minute and stares up into my eyes. "It'll be okay." Her eyes dart between mine and don't calm down. At this rate, there is only one way she will calm down. So, I dip down and kiss her. Kiss her so deeply, I steal her breath.

When I break the kiss, she stares up at me as her body sags. "Thank you."

"Any time." I scan down the length of her. "You look great. Ready to head out?"

She stares down her front, then meets my gaze again with a sigh. "As ready as

I'm going to be." Spinning away from me, she calls down the hallway. "Clementine, time to leave."

The cutest girl in the world comes barreling down the hallway with Spartan as her sidekick. I swear he has never been so loyal to a person before. Not even me. But any time Clementine is near, he switches to this whole new dog. Yes, he is still silly and wild, but he is also gentle and attentive with her. The two of them in the same room is the strangest and most interesting sight to witness.

When Clementine and Spartan stand a few feet away, I cock my head and take in the new accessory around his neck. A bright red bandana, folded into a triangle, and hanging proudly around his neck. And no joke, I swear Spartan smiles.

I bite the inside of my cheek. The last thing I want to do is laugh and let Clementine think it's about her. But I do want to laugh at Spartan's new attire. Especially since I tried to make him wear several similar items over the last three years and have failed. Put him in a room with Clementine for five-plus minutes and bam. Done.

"Spartan." He jerks his head my way. "Ready to go see Grandma?"

Woof, woof, woof.

"That is hilarious and cute as heck," Autumn says.

"Just wait, it'll get better when we get there."

The ride from Autumn's apartment to my parent's house passes quickly. Autumn bounces her knee in the passenger seat more often than not. Each time it bobs, I give her thigh a gentle squeeze to reassure her everything will be fine. Then again, can't say I have ever been in her shoes.

Sure, I have hung out with friends' families several times over the years. But meeting them was different. Cora is the only friend whose parents I met that made me semi-nervous. But they were hosting a Memorial Day BBQ and invited everyone. But she was the only person whom I ever had a romantic interest in as an adult where anxiety would apply.

It surprises me, though, how not nervous I am about tonight. Will my mom and sisters probably probe Autumn with a hundred awkward questions? I hope not, but wouldn't be shocked if they did. But I am driving the two most important people in my life right now to my parents' house—to our weekly family dinner— and I have never been calmer in my life.

Huh. No doubt this could be psychoanalyzed for days.

When I turn onto Mom and Dad's street, Autumn grips my forearm. And when I park the Jeep in the driveway, she practically digs her nails into my pulse point.

Spartan barks like the lunatic he is, dying to get out and run for the door. Clementine bounces in her seat with obvious excitement. While Autumn stares at my parent's four-bedroom house with lips tucked between her teeth and eyes scanning every flower and shrub along the exterior.

I lean over and kiss the soft spot beneath her ear. "Hey." Slowly, she rotates her head to face me. Our mouths a breath apart. "Breathe. There is absolutely nothing to be nervous about."

"Says you," she whispers.

"Promise I'll keep you safe. Just stick by my side." I close the space between us and kiss her sweetly. "Okay?"

She nods. "Yeah."

Both of us hop out of the Jeep. I fetch Spartan from the back, while Autumn helps Clementine down. As soon as we are close enough to the door, I let go of Spartan's leash and he bolts. Before he can bark for Mom to open up, the door flies open and he leaps into her waiting arms.

"Who's my favorite grandpup?" Mom asks Spartan. His responding bark makes me laugh per usual.

"Mom, he's your only grandpup," I say.

She rises back to her normal height and looks me square in the eyes. "True, but he doesn't know that."

I laugh as we step up onto the porch. "Mom, this is Autumn and her daughter, Clementine. Ladies, this is my mom, Irene."

"Autumn, it's wonderful to meet you." Mom lifts her hands and silently asks permission to hug. When Autumn leans in to reciprocate, I exhale.

"Nice to meet you, Irene." The hug lasts for two breaths, but Autumn relaxes the second Mom's arms wrap around her. "Clementine" —Autumn peers down at her daughter— "say hello to Miss Irene."

Clementine lifts her hand and waves. "Hi, Miss Irene." Then she leaps forward and hugs Mom's midsection. "Nice to meet you."

Mom laughs at Clementine's spunky nature before throwing a smile my way. A smile I have never seen before.

Once Clementine breaks her hold, Mom escorts us into the house. "Your sisters aren't here yet, but we can start prepping dinner now."

We step past the foyer and into the formal living room. The sofa, matching chairs, and table are like new, only because my parents hardly use the room. Usually, we sit in here during Christmas or other big gatherings. Otherwise, we sit in the family room.

I let Autumn know where she can set her purse and tell Mom I'm going to give her a tour before we start dinner. Mom agrees to keep an eye on Clementine, who is currently talking to Spartan. No doubt they will entertain each other most of the evening.

As we wander down the hall, I slip my hand around Autumn's and walk backward so I can face her. "Still nervous?" She has been silent—with the exception of introductions—since we left her apartment.

"Yeah," she says with a nod. "God, I've never been so anxious to impress people."

I lead us into the bedroom at the end of the hall on the right. My old bedroom, now a guest room. Shutting the door behind us, I steer us to the bed and sit us on the edge. "Hey, you don't need to impress anyone here. We don't operate that way."

"You know, I got that vibe from your mom right off the bat. But I think your sisters will be more critical."

Autumn may not know Jasmine and Jillian yet, so I get her concern. But if either of my sisters make Autumn uncomfortable or give her the third degree, I won't be the only person giving them a ration of shit. Mom and Dad would both jump in the ring and defend her too.

"They won't be. If either of them so much as says something off-putting, you'll have three people in your court." She smiles, but it doesn't reach her eyes and falls away as quickly as it appeared. "Hey." I pinch her chin in my thumb and forefinger, lifting her line of sight. "It'll be fine, scarlet. Promise."

She nods, eyes still swirling with apprehension. I hate how her nerves are eating her up. How they hinder the great night to come.

Leaning forward, I lower my mouth to hers. Kiss her slow and sweet. Part her lips with my tongue. Taste her distinct flavor, a flavor I cannot pinpoint but also cannot get enough of. Her hands trace my jawline. Nails scrape my scalp until they reach my longer strands and take hold. Drawing me closer. Deeper.

My hands drop to her hips and fist them as I step back, sit on the bed, and haul her onto my lap. Her legs straddle mine as if they have done it hundreds of times before. We kiss as if another opportunity won't arise. As if our lips won't have contact for days or weeks or months. Our passion is a firestorm. Unrelenting. Building. Flourishing into something primal yet unexplainable.

Autumn rocks her hips against me. Moans down my throat. The bulge beneath my zipper thick and swollen and starving for her. I break the kiss and trail my mouth over the soft line of her jaw, nipping and licking. Down the column of her throat as she throws her head back and gasps, fingers clutching my hair and locking me to her skin.

When I reach her shoulder, I stop and lay my forehead on her. Inhaling her delicious scent, I close my eyes and bask in her weight on my lap. If I keep this up much longer, every adult in the house will know what we are up to. Which will only serve to stir up more discomfort.

Our rapid breathing floats in the room as our pulses slowly settle. I lean back and trail my eyes up her neck until they lock on to her intoxicating irises. So many words pass through her eyes without a single word leaving her lips. And I feel it. Deep down in my bones, I feel all her unspoken thoughts. Because those same words trickle through my every vein and artery like DNA.

Neither of us has brought up the extent of how we feel for the other. But staring into her eyes right now, the way she refuses to look away, it is obvious she is in just as deep as I am.

Some men would be unsettled by this revelation—falling in love. Me? I indulge in it. Take it and tuck it safely inside the cage surrounding my heart.

I brush my fingers from her temple down to her lips. "As much as I'd like to stay in here the next several hours, we should finish the tour and help with dinner."

Autumn kisses my fingers before sliding off my lap. "Suppose you're right. Last thing I need is your family thinking we're in here having sex."

I laugh to cover my sudden choking. She pats my back a few times then laughs too. Rising off the bed, Autumn straightens her shirt and runs her hands down her thighs to smooth her jeans.

Once she finishes, Autumn steps between my legs and combs her fingers through my hair. "If we walk out with your hair like this, everyone will know what we were up to in here." She giggles as I roll my eyes closed and sit perfectly still.

Her touch is the cure to every ailment I will ever have. My remedy. Created for only me.

When she stops fixing my disheveled strands, I open my eyes. "Thanks," I whisper. "Let me show you the rest of the house. Oh" —I wave my hand around the room as I stand— "this was once my room."

"Fitting." She hums and nods.

Taking her hand in mine, I lead us back into the hall. I play tour guide through the rest of the house and finish up the circuit in the kitchen. Which is where my mom and sisters reside.

The moment we step into the room, all three of them look to us. Autumn's grip tightens and I kiss her temple. "Jasmine, Jillian, this is Autumn. Autumn, these are my sisters. Jasmine" —I point to my older sister, then to my baby sister— "and Jillian."

Jasmine picks up a hand towel and wipes her hands before extending one to Autumn. "Wonderful to finally meet you, Autumn. My son, Lex, is playing with Clementine in the family room. She's a doll."

"Nice to meet you. And thank you." Autumn smiles like a proud mom. A smile that warms me throughout.

Jillian steps forward and Autumn extends her hand. But Jillian takes us all by surprise when she hugs Autumn. Not that my family doesn't hug. We just don't generally hug new people. Especially Jillian.

"Wow, Jilli," I say when she releases Autumn. "Feeling extra affectionate today?"

She play-punches my bicep. "Ha ha, big brother. And so what if I am. Can't I be happy and want to hug people?"

"Forget I asked," I say, throwing my hands up in surrender. "Mom, what can we help with?"

Mom directs me to the cutting board to help with the salad. She frequently gives me the task and I wonder if my slicing and chopping skills supersede those of my sisters. While I slice carrots, Mom asks Autumn if she will help her with dessert— magic brookie bars. If there is one thing my mom is master of, it is dessert. And her magic brookie bars are to die for.

The kitchen fills with chatter as everyone catches up. Jasmine tells us how Lex heard someone say the word shit the other day and he won't stop saying it. I laugh, probably harder than I should, because my sister is adamant about raising Lex to be a proper young man. Mom chimes in and tells her about each occasion when we all said our first bad word. It only serves to make me laugh harder.

After Dad and Anton set the table, we all carry out dishes while Mom puts the magic brookies in the oven. We take our seats at the table and start passing around food from one to the next. Beside me, Autumn relaxes more. Clementine is the life of the party. And I spend the entire hour at the dinner table with a wide smile stretching my cheeks.

"Irene, I need this recipe," Autumn says as she chews her last bite of magic brookie bar.

Mom smiles at the other end of the table. "I'll jot it down before you go. Let's clean up and sit out back for a little bit before everyone goes."

And just like that, everyone rises from their seats and shuffles around to clean up. Then we all sit out back on the loungers near the pool while the kids watch a movie on television. Autumn sits between my legs and chats with everyone as if she has been here several times before. Her earlier nerves nowhere to be found.

When I check the time, I suggest we head out so Clementine can get a good night's sleep before school. We collect the goody bag Mom made us, give hug after hug, and say our goodbyes.

Once Clementine and Spartan are secure in the back seat, Spartan lays down and rests his head on Clementine's lap. Autumn and I hop in, and soon we head for Autumn's apartment.

Tonight went better than expected. Mom and my sisters didn't probe Autumn with questions. Thank god. The conversations in the kitchen and around the dinner table flowed naturally. And Autumn smiled often, as did I.

A few miles from the apartment, I stop at a red light and look in the rearview mirror to see Clementine asleep. I nudge my head toward the back seat. "She passed out."

Autumn glances back at Clementine briefly and smiles. "Was a busy night for her. But she had fun."

"Did you enjoy yourself?"

She nods before I face forward again and drive. "Yeah." She reaches across the console and rests her hand on my thigh. I swallow. "Your family is wonderful," she says wistfully.

"They are," I mumble as I envision her and Clementine as part of the family out of nowhere. Crazy how my mind jumps from point A to point Z before stopping at any of the other points in between. But I can't help how Autumn makes me feel. How she makes me long for more. To fall asleep with her in my arms and wake with her curled to my torso and tangled in my limbs.

A block from her apartment complex entrance, I strike up the nerve to propose an idea to her. After double-checking Clementine is still asleep in the back, I take a deep breath and swallow. I reach over the console and rest my hand on her leg.

"Autumn, I want to ask you something. But I don't want you to freak out."

She turns in the seat to face me better. In the process, my hand slides farther north and stops inches from the junction of her thighs. She doesn't lean back or shift it away.

"Okay," she drawls out.

"Keep an open mind and don't shoot me down right away." I glance over at her as I steer us into the complex. "Will you stay at my place?" I park the Jeep and take in Autumn's wide-eyed, frozen state. "Obviously not tonight, but one night soon."

Autumn looks to the back seat out of the corner of her eye. "Jonas, I don't know."

"Think about it. No rush. And Clementine can stay over too. The couch doubles as a bed too."

"Jonas…" I lean toward her, press a finger to her lips, and cut her off.

"All I ask is for you to think about it. No pressure. If you decide it isn't a good idea, I'll understand. But at least give it a day." She slowly nods, and I remove my finger from her lips.

I open and close my door quietly and meet Autumn on the passenger side. Before we open Clementine's door and I carry her in, I cage Autumn against the front passenger door. Her arms wrap around my waist, beneath my shirt. The heat between us wiping away the evening January chill.

Her nails softly dig into my skin as I lean down and press my lips to hers. The kiss starts off slow and steady, but heated. I paint her tongue with mine as soft moans echo in her throat. I deepen the kiss, shifting my hands to the back of her neck and the curve of her hip. My groin presses into her lower abdomen. Unhurried, her hands dance across my skin from back to front. Skimming up the length of my torso with purpose.

I hiss and our lips part for a second. In the darkness of the parking lot, Autumn kisses down the side of my neck. Claws down my chest. All but unmans me against the Jeep. *Sweet fucking Christ.* I drop my other hand to her hip, hold her steady, and rock mine forward.

"Fuck, scarlet," I whisper toward the heavens.

She kisses back up my neck until her lips reach mine again. We stand tongue-tangled like teenagers for I don't know how long. When I'm on the verge of ripping her clothes off in public, I tear my lips from hers. Her pouty lip makes an appearance and I laugh.

"We should stop, I know," she says.

Hesitantly, I step back from her and grunt. "Yeah, we should. Just consider what I said before. About staying over. Promise if you say no, I won't be upset."

"Swear I'll think about it."

After I give my body a moment to cool off, I open Clementine's door slowly, unbuckle her, signaling Spartan to stay while I carry her inside. Once I lay her in bed and slip off her shoes, Autumn walks me out. Kisses me again, but this time more tenderly. Every ounce of affection poured into the gesture before we say our good nights.

On the way home, one constant thought swirls through my mind. The possibility of soon not having to say good night to Autumn as one of us leaves. A man can only hope.

"Earth to Autumn."

I snap my head up to find Penny staring me down, hand on her hip and brow cocked. "What?"

"Said your next appointment is here. I'll let them know you need a few more minutes to get ready." She scrutinizes my expression. "You alright? Haven't been yourself all day."

I sigh heavily and nod. "Yeah." Curling my finger, I beckon her closer. "Jonas asked me to stay the night. Clementine, too."

Penny steps back with the most wicked smile on her face. "And?"

"And nothing. He asked and told me to think about it." Now me spending the night with him is the only thing occupying my mind. My clients are lucky I haven't jacked up their art today.

She plops down on my client chair. "You are going to say yes, right?"

Herein lies the dilemma. Every atom in my body, every firing live wire zapping my skin, tells me to say yes. I *want* to say yes. But one thing still has me hesitant. Not Jonas. He is the best man to enter my life. The piece which has me mulling it over, to death, is Clementine. Not because I would bring her, but the possibility of her getting attached to Jonas.

What if our relationship is all smiles and laughter for a bit, but then something changes and it no longer is? What if Clementine falls in love with the idea of always having Jonas around, and then he isn't? These are the thoughts which have me uncertain. It's one thing for me to hurt, but I never want that for Clementine.

"Pen, I want to. Badly. But…"

"But what, Auti? Jonas is a good man. Everyone sees it. And I know you see it. So what has you second-guessing?"

I huff, hating that this conversation has to happen. Being put on the spot sucks, as does my uncertainty. "What if it doesn't work out with Jonas and Clementine gets close to him?"

Penny tilts her head to the side and pops her gum. "Honestly?" I nod and tuck my lips between my teeth. "Think you're more scared of you and Jonas staying together." My forehead scrunches and she holds up a hand to stop me from rebutting. "Auti, you haven't had the best relationships in the past. Clementine's birth father was the last person you were with, and he was an asshole. Any person who tucks their tail and runs when shit gets serious is a piece of shit. Especially after what went down with your parents."

Wiping down the counter and chair, I nod as Penny continues.

"Jonas is not Leo, Auti." I meet her eyes and she holds strong. "He isn't. And the way Jonas looks at you, the way he looks at Clementine… he wants so much more with you. Tell me you see it. Tell me you *feel* it. He flaunts his heart like a marquee sign."

I do sense the way Jonas cares about me. About both of us. Part of me is scared to take the next step. To get consumed by all that we feel. To open up, share my past, and let Jonas in all the way. Because if I open up, if I give him every little piece of my heart, and he crushes it… there is no coming back from such devastation. And if I fall that hard, that deep, and come out on the other side hurt, I can only imagine how my sweet, innocent little girl would handle it. Clementine should never have to experience such heartache. Not until she is strong enough, old enough, to deal with such anguish.

"Yeah, Pen, I see it." Probably because my heart reflects his. I pop up and glance at Rex and Reznor in the booths next to mine. "Boys?" They both perk up—eyes on their clients, ears on me. "Thoughts? Am I thinking too much into this whole scenario?"

Without a doubt, they have heard the entire conversation between me and Penny. Plus, they are family. Between all of us—Rex, Penny, Reznor, Iliana, and me —there are no secrets. Granted, Penny is the only one who knows every sorted detail about my past, but no one is out of the loop. They know enough I don't have to skirt around topics. Penny and Iliana generally work opposite days or shifts, so Iliana and I aren't as close as me and Penny. But we are all tight.

"Think if you explain it to the little princess the right way—staying over—it shouldn't seem abnormal to her. And yes, I think you should do it." Reznor pauses to dip the needle in the ink cap. "You deserve happiness, A. I love seeing you smile. And he makes you smile. All the time."

As if on cue, a smile perks up the corners of my mouth.

"I'm with Rez," Rex adds. "He seems like a great guy; legit. And if he isn't, your brothers will make it right."

I laugh and shake my head. "Oh god." But Penny gives me a look that says *see, I'm right*. Yeah, yeah. "Alright, let me get back to work before the natives become restless."

The next few hours go by slower than desirable. With each line and dot and shading I etch into skin, I ponder over saying yes to Jonas. To his proposition of staying the night. A constant buzz courses through my body and it has nothing to do with the tattoo gun in my hand.

God, I cannot remember the last time I thought about spending the night with a man. Well, back then, they weren't men. Clementine's father and I had only been together six months when I found out I was pregnant. Pregnant at twenty. A single mother at twenty-one.

Sure, I had spent the night with other guys prior to Clementine's father, but during those days, most of us still lived at home with our parents. Spending the night wasn't so much an option, unless someone's parents were out of town. And that was almost never. At least, in the circle of people I knew then.

As an adult—a woman—this has never come up. That's what happens when you don't date. Seemed like the best decision at the time. Now, I wish maybe I would have given it a try once or twice. Just so I wasn't so inexperienced. Ugh.

When I wrap up with my final scheduled appointment, Penny skips over and watches me clean up. She doesn't speak a word. Just follows me with her eyes and pops her gum. But her gaze is loaded with questions. Questions I will answer, but not until she asks them. So, I continue to wipe everything down and dispose of my trash while she hovers like a grade A helicopter parent.

I laugh under my breath as she studies my every move out of the corner of my eye. Cracks me up how she waits—impatiently—for me to blurt out my decision. Penny has known me for years—I met her and the guys shortly before Clementine was born—and knows I won't freely hand out information. More often than not, someone has to ask for me to answer.

"You know, I thought maybe Jonas would've at least gotten you to be more forward. But it would appear otherwise," she says, narrowing her eyes.

Now I laugh out loud. "Old habits die hard," I answer.

"Well, that's one habit I hope he influences." She gives me a snide smile. "So, did you figure out what to do?"

I nod. "Yep." Penny waits for me to say more, but I stay tight-lipped. It's too much fun dragging it out and torturing the hell out of her.

"And?" She waves her hand frantically as she pops another bubble. "You live to mess with me, don't you?"

Shrugging, I bite the inside of my cheek and try to taper my smile. "It's fun. What can I say?" Her chin juts forward and her eyes widen. "And I decided to say yes."

"Eep!" Penny squeals, a body piercing sound from her throat as she jumps up and down in place. "Oh my god! Oh my god!" She looks between Rex and Reznor. "You guys hear that? She's going to say yes."

Heat creeps up my neck and fills my cheeks. "Penny, shh." Reznor and Rex give me subtle smiles. They are happy for me, but I'm glad they don't shriek and draw all attention my way.

"Whatever," she says. "So, is he coming over for dinner tonight? Should I be the annoying roommate? Or do you want me to act ignorant to all these details? Not clap when you tell him."

Oh Jesus. "Penny, please just be normal. No clapping or screaming or teasing. Please," I beg.

"Fine," she huffs out. "I'll be good." Penny puts on her cutest sulking face. "But when he leaves, I'm freaking out."

I snatch my purse and head for the exit. "I'm good with that. See you at home in a bit."

She waves. "Deuces."

～

I put the salmon fillets in the oven just as there is a knock at the door.

Clementine barrels down the hallway. "Mama, Jonas is here. And Sparty." Her excitement makes me smile.

"Hang on, pumpkin." Although we know who is at the door, I still don't let Clementine answer the door without an adult.

She bounces in front of the door, eager to see Spartan. As soon as I unlock and open up the door, I don't know who is more excited—Clementine or Spartan. He bounds inside and she leads him to the couch. They plop down and she starts telling him all about her day. The project her class has been working on. The icky cafeteria food. Everything. And it is too damn cute.

"Hey," Jonas says as he steps inside and kisses my temple. "How was your day, scarlet?"

His lips on my skin always make me forget whatever I plan to say. The only thought invading my mind now is the heat from his lips spreading across my skin. When I remember how to use my voice again, I speak up. "Long."

He chuckles against my hair, wraps his arm around my waist, and pulls me into him. "Mine too. Glad to be here now, though."

I breathe him in and melt at the scent I classify as one-hundred-percent Jonas. "Me too." I lean back and look up at him. "Want to help me finish up dinner? Pretty much done. Just have to plate it."

We move around the kitchen in symmetry. Yin and yang. Dark and light. Moon and sun. Opposing forces balancing the other out. Ebbing and flowing.

Penny joins us for dinner when she gets home. We each take turns talking about our day, but we all give Clementine more time than the rest of us. She talks animatedly about the seeds the class planted and how they started sprouting today. All of us zero in on every word she says and ask more questions to hear her enthusiasm about growing herbs.

Plates cleared; we load up the dishwasher then head for the couch to watch an episode of *How I Met Your Mother*. Clementine and Spartan sprawl out on a blanket on the floor. I curl into Jonas's side at one end while Penny sits on the opposite end. Halfway through the episode, Penny rises off the couch and fake yawns.

"Gonna head to bed. Night everyone," she says then tosses a wink in my direction.

I roll my eyes. "'Night."

After her door clicks shut, Jonas shifts beside me and finagles so we lay down. I scoot back and snuggle against his front as he splays a hand across my abdomen beneath my shirt. He kisses the spot beneath my ear and I close my eyes. Tingles ripple from his kiss on my neck to where his hand caresses my skin.

Jonas continues to explore my neck and ear with his lips, driving me wild. I lace my fingers with his. Tighten my hold with every other kiss. Breathe heavier with each press of his lips or nip of his teeth.

"Did you think about what I asked last night?" he whispers in my ear just before he takes my lobe between his teeth.

I clamp down on my lips and moan as quietly as possible. "Yes."

His lips pause at the curve of my neck. "Yes, you thought about it? Or yes, you'll stay?"

Chuckling, I spin around in his grip and face him. I lay my palm on his cheek and kiss him. "Both. Yes, I want to stay. For us to stay."

It takes a moment for my words to click into place, but as soon as they do, Jonas's eyes burn brighter. His hand skims up my spine beneath my shirt as he leans forward and presses his lips to mine. Consumes me. Gives me a piece of him.

When he breaks the kiss, I lift my gaze to meet his, and get lost in the intensity. In the volcanic eruption. Hot. Magnetic. Hypnotizing. It draws me closer and dampens my skin.

He glances over my shoulder to Clementine and Spartan on the floor. "Have you?"

I shake my head. "Wanted to tell you first. We can tell her together." He nods.

While the rest of the episode plays, Jonas and I lay facing each other, silent. And I have never been more comfortable in my life. Never more ready to share my life with another person. To let someone in and explore everything love has to offer.

And when we explain having a sleepover with Clementine, she seems nonchalant. Only excited she gets to spend the night with Spartan. It was all so easy. Simple. Perfect.

I hope our life stays exactly like this. Easy and blissful in our perfect little bubble.

Autumn has been to my house before. Has seen every room. Traipsed her fingers on countertops and bookshelves and blankets. Stood at my stove and cooked alongside me. Cuddled with me on the couch and kissed me senseless.

But right now, I dash around the house as if none of that holds weight.

Tossing my clothes in the washer after moving the bedding to the dryer. Washing every cup, plate, and pan immediately after use. Wiping down the counters in the kitchen and bathroom. Scrubbing the toilet. And the shower. Dusting. Vacuuming. Mopping.

I woke before the sun came up. Made breakfast, then realized I needed to clean out the fridge. That very moment is when the manic cleaning marathon started. When I deep cleaned the entire interior of the house from top to bottom.

Spartan watches me with keen interest. Wondering what the hell is wrong with his dad. Tilts his head left then right as I dart from one end of the house to the other. But I don't have time to explain it all to him. Not like he would understand, anyway.

After making the bed and switching my clothes to the dryer around noon, I head outside and mow the yard. Thankfully, enough of my yard is landscaped that I only push the mower and thrust the weed whacker for an hour.

After a quick but thorough shower, I put away the last of the laundry and jot down some last-minute groceries. Out the door and at the store less than ten minutes later, I fill the cart with my normal weekly purchases plus some extras for tonight. During my last couple of grocery trips, I started picking up items specifically for Clementine. Little things such as her favorite juice and mini marshmallows, popcorn, and red licorice. The girl is fond of her movie snacks.

But today I plan to grab extras. Not just for Clementine, but all of us. Extra movie snacks and extra breakfast items.

Two nights ago, when Autumn agreed to stay over, my brain went frantic. I waited until yesterday to ask her what kinds of foods she and Clementine both liked for breakfast. Breakfast. A meal we haven't shared yet. A meal which could consist of hundreds of different options. Of all the meals, breakfast is generally the easiest. But only if you liked the standard breakfast foods.

With each day we spend together, I learn how much Clementine resembles Autumn. Appearance. Personality. And their love for food. I honestly have no idea where they pack it all.

After I check out at the grocery store and head home, the first thing I notice when I walk in the door is the strong blend of multi-purpose cleaner and generic pine. Once I put all the groceries away, I sift through a few cabinets in the utility room and locate a small tote of candles I have collected over the years. Candles I rolled my eyes at during the holidays when my sisters gifted them. Now, I need to remember to thank them during family dinner next week.

I remove the lid from the black candle, bring it to my nose, and inhale. Masculine. A blend of leather and teakwood. I light the wicks and place it as centrally as possible in the open floor plan of the house. Within minutes, the house smells less like a janitorial closet and closer to a men's clothing store.

A few minutes pass as I get lost in the flickering candle flames. Lost in the reality that Autumn and Clementine will be here in a couple hours' time. Since we have been officially seeing each other, shared dinners have happened almost nightly. But she or I always went home at the end of the night. And the thought of her not going home tonight has me unable to focus.

Tonight, Autumn will lay beside me. In my bed. Between my sheets. The heat of her skin pressed to mine.

Spartan barks and I snap out of my daydream. "Thanks, buddy. Time to prep d-i-n-n-e-r and dessert." He barks again. "Mine, not yours."

I get to work in the kitchen and prep the muffin-sized personal pies. Assembled in the pan, I cover and set them in the fridge until it's time to put them in the oven. Then I get to work on the baked macaroni and cheese, coconut chicken bites, and parmesan zucchini fries.

I move around the kitchen with ease and send silent thanks to my mom for teaching me how to cook and bake. Whether it was only for me or me and others, learning how to cook is one of the most valuable gifts she has bestowed upon me.

As I slide the pan of coconut chicken in the oven, Spartan perks his head up from his spot on the couch and barks like a loon. Jumping down, he continues to bark while running in circles. When there is a knock at the door, he practically rips it off the hinges. I laugh as I walk from the kitchen to the front door.

When I open the door, Spartan launches forward and licks every square inch of Clementine's face. She giggles and wraps her little arms around his neck. "Sparty," she giggle-squeals.

"C'mon, buddy. Let them in."

Spartan scoots back. Autumn and Clementine step in and I take a deep breath. We have done this many times before, but it suddenly feels as if this is our first time. Anxiety surges in my belly like a summer storm rolling in off the coast. I step into Autumn and kiss her chastely. And just as quickly as the storm rolled in, her warm lips against mine brings out the sun.

"Hey, scarlet," I croak.

She looks up at me from under her lashes, a shy smile on her lips. "Hey." Lifting the bag in her hand, she asks, "Where should I set this?" Her overnight bag.

This is really happening. Autumn and Clementine are here. And they are staying overnight. Not leaving until tomorrow.

"Let me." I take the bag from her and walk it back to my bedroom, setting it on the bed. When I spin around, Autumn stands in the doorway. Her eyes scan every inch of the room, stopping on me when she finishes.

Is she as nervous as I am? Maybe more. Neither of us has spent the night with another person in a long time. Not like this. Not with hearts out in the open and on the line.

In three short strides, I stand inches from her. Lower my mouth to hers and taste her again. Sweet and addictive. She grips the hem of my shirt and drags me closer. A soft moan spilling from her into me. My hands frame her face as I deepen the kiss. Consume her. Share one of the many ways I need her.

The timer on the stove beeps, letting us know a minute remains. Reluctantly, I break the kiss and inch back. "Help me finish dinner?" Autumn nods and presses her fingers to her lips.

"What're we having?" she asks as we stroll back into the kitchen.

The buzzer rings through the kitchen and I shut off the timer as I open the oven door. "Coconut chicken, baked macaroni and cheese, and zucchini fries," I tell her as I flip the chicken over and add the zucchini fries to the oven.

"Wow. Maybe I need to get cookies for your mom, too." I shake my head. "What? Not only are your parents generous, but your mom made you into every woman's dream man." She waves a hand toward the living room. "You clean. You cook. What other domestic duties do you fulfill?"

I cock a brow and smirk at her. "Hmm… I'll have to show you later." A blush I haven't seen on Autumn's skin in several days makes an appearance. And I love how her mind goes to exactly where I wanted it to.

She licks her lips and tucks them between her teeth a moment. "Later."

Soon, dinner is out of the oven and cool enough to serve. I pop in the muffin pan pies so they finish baking by the time we clear our plates. Autumn fills a plate for Clementine, then herself as I make mine. We sit at the breakfast bar and eat in silence for a few minutes. There is no unease. If anything, eating dinner with both of them feels like the most natural part of my day.

We all grab mini pies and ice cream after dinner and cozy up on the couch. Spartan tries and fails to eat Clementine's dessert, but she giggles each time his snout gets close. "What are we watching tonight?" I ask Clementine.

"Mama bought *The Secret Life of Pets 2* for tonight," she says, dancing in her seat as the movie starts.

I laugh alongside Autumn as we watch the silly animated kid's movie and finish our dessert. An hour later, Clementine softly snores on the chaise section of the couch with Spartan as her pillow. Quietly, I rise from the couch, collect our dishes, and take them to the kitchen.

As I rinse the bowls, Autumn wraps her arms around my waist and kisses over my spine. "She'll be out for the rest of the night," she whispers into my shirt.

Spinning to face her, I glance over her shoulder and take in the sight of Clementine and Spartan cuddling. "Should we leave the light over the stove on? In case she wakes," I ask and Autumn nods.

I take her hand in mine and weave our fingers together. Without a word, I flip the light over the stove on and steer us out of the kitchen. After we turn off the television and drape the throw blanket over Clementine, I lead Autumn down the hall and into the bedroom.

This is it. The moment that will change our relationship. Add more definition. Sharpen the edges. Bring us closer. Closer than I have ever been with any other person. Make us never want to be apart—at least for me.

Autumn closes the door behind us, and I have never heard the latch click so loudly. Facing Autumn, I walk us to the bed, my eyes tracing the curves of her silhouette as we move. The back of my knees hit the mattress and I draw her close. Wrap her in my arms. Feel the tremble of her hands as they snake around my waist and under my shirt.

I drop my chin, bring my lips within a breath of hers. "We don't have to do anything you're not ready for. If you only want to sleep, then I'll happily hold you in my arms all night. Okay?"

She nods and pushes up on her toes. Our lips connect and I roll my eyes closed. Heat swelters in my chest and blooms across every lick of my skin. And the second she paints her tongue across my lower lip, I open for her and deepen the kiss. Her heat matches mine and ignites the kindling simmering low in my groin.

I groan, slip my hands under her ass, lift her up and spin around to toss her on the bed. She thumps against the mattress and I crawl up her body, slamming my mouth back to hers. Our hands fevered. Lips irrational. Breaths erratic.

Autumn slowly peels my shirt up my torso and over my head, then discards it on the floor. She trails her fingers down my pecs, my abdomen, and along the waistband of my jeans. Reading every dip and line and ridge of my skin like braille. I suck in a sharp breath as she charts new territory and memorizes the landscape. Her fingertips sear my skin, leaving a tingling trail of sparks in their wake.

Her fingers wrap around the button above my fly and I stop her. "Slow. There's no rush." I dip down and kiss her sweet mouth. "I want us to savor this. To savor us."

I roll us over and relish the sight of her straddling me, my palms cupping her hips. She strips her shirt off and tosses it in the same direction as mine. In the dim lighting, I make out the scalloped curves of her bra cups and sit up to get a closer look. The dark lace teases me. Taunts me. Sticks out its proverbial tongue and sneers.

I give her hips a quick squeeze before winding my hands to her backside and softly grazing them up the sides of her spine. She arches and presses her breasts closer to my face. And I can no longer resist the urge to taste her skin. Savor her uncharted territory.

Leaning in, I kiss the swell of her breast. Once. Twice. Lick along the lace edge of her bra cup. She rocks her hips against me, and I pin her in place as I grip her waist. Switch to the opposite breast and pay it equal attention. She threads her fingers in my hair, tips her head back, and moans at the ceiling.

As my tongue trails the swell of her breast, I unhook her bra and flatten my palms against her bare back as the lacy material falls between us. For the first time, the heat of her bare skin presses flush with mine. Fevered and damp and absolutely perfect. I stop breathing. Stop kissing her skin. Close my eyes and savor the moment. The heat, the longing, the absolute need for this connection.

After a beat, I roll Autumn to her back again. Kiss her lips. Kiss down the column of her throat. Along her midline to her navel. To her left hip, then her right.

She pants into the darkness as I unbutton her pants and drag the zipper down the teeth. As I peel the denim down her thighs, I spot her matching lace panties and smile. I pause to press my lips to the material. She groans and fists my hair.

I trace a finger along the waistband of her panties. "Did you wear matching bra and panties for me?" I rasp against her skin.

"Yes."

"You'll have to show them to me when the lights are on."

She moans. "Promise."

I kiss her hip and continue peeling away her jeans. Drop them to the floor, followed by my own. Pressing one knee, then the other, into the mattress, I crawl back up her body. Hover above and lock eyes with her. With exception of her panties and my boxer briefs, we are skin to skin. Her eyes swirl like the Great Red Spot of Jupiter. Call out to me. Seduce me.

"Are you sure?"

"Never been more sure," she answers and lifts her lips to mine. Sucks my lower lip. Then clutches the back of my neck and draws me low, low, lower until my weight presses into her.

Her kiss rages and amplifies and turns white hot. Has me sweltering and begging for more. Rocking forward and grinding my erection against the junction of her thighs. Her nails scrape along either side of my spine. I hiss as she tucks them beneath the elastic of my briefs and shoves them toward my ankles.

We fumble and laugh as we maneuver the last scraps of our clothes to the floor. And when they drop away, all laughing stops. I kiss her gently. More tender than any time previous. Trace the curve of her jaw with my lips and pepper kisses down, down, down her body.

When I stop at the junction of her thighs, she sucks in a breath and holds it. I trace up the midline of her body with my eyes and revel in the sight of her. Fuck, she is perfect. "Is this okay?" I ask as it dawns on me that not all women enjoy oral sex.

"God, yes," she moans and I chuckle.

But it's the second she threads her fingers in my hair and thrusts my head between her thighs that I stop laughing. I clutch her hips, run my nose along the thin strip of hair, and inhale. *Fuck.*

As if a light flips on in my head and my primal nature surfaces, I lick up her center and taste her for the first time. Sweet and salty and one-hundred-percent Autumn. Addictive and crucial. God, I could exist solely with the taste of her on my tongue.

I take my time. Devour her. Flick her clit with my tongue and lick up her seam. Insert a finger. Then another. Watch her writhe as I bring her higher and higher. Inhale her pheromones as she edges closer to orgasm. Groan against her skin as her whimpers escalate. Suck and lick her flesh when her release spills around my fingers. *Holy Christ.*

"Jonas…" she whimpers. "I need you. Need to feel you inside me."

I crawl back up her body and kiss her as if I never will again. She moans against my tongue as her hand dips between us and wraps around my erection. I break the kiss and gasp as her hand slides up and down my length.

Shifting closer to the bedside table, I open the drawer and grab a condom. I tear open the foil, slip out the condom and roll it on. Pressing my weight back over her, I line myself up with her entrance and wait.

In this monumental moment between us, there is one thing I want to say to her. Tell her. What this means to me. What *she* means to me. How much I cherish her. How I always will. But it might be too soon for her.

I lower my lips to hers. Kiss her tenderly. Tell her with my lips and not my voice. Sweep my knuckles lightly over her cheek as I slowly rock forward and push inside her. We both gasp into the silence. Lock eyes and hold. Don't flinch as her body adjusts to my invasion.

Her nails bite my upper glutes. "Please, Jonas," she pleas.

I rock back, then forward again. Her nails dig deeper and my eyes roll back. I drop my head into the crook of her neck and find my rhythm with her. Relish in her heat and the vice-like grip her body has on mine. I kiss and nip at the base of her throat. Stroke slowly in and out. Kiss my way back up to her lips and express how much she means to me with my body.

For the first time, Autumn breaks our kiss. Gasps and whimpers as her nails rake up my back. Her body hugs me like a glove. Squeezes. And Jesus fucking Christ... I bite my lip and restrain myself as I wait for her climax to peak. She pants sweet little whimpers into my ear as it hits. Takes her over.

White-hot heat snakes around my spine and fuses in my groin as her body milks mine and I lose all sense of reality. I slam my eyes closed as stars steal my vision. Blind me and help me see clearly for the first time in my life. I clamp down on her shoulder with my teeth and release inside her. My pulse throbs behind my ears. Pounds viciously and creates white noise.

I breathe her in as she strokes her fingers up and down my spine. *I love you.* The words are on the tip of my tongue, but I bite them back. Instead, I lift my head and lock onto her gaze. Drown in her fiery cognac irises. Get drunk in them.

A cluster of loose strands lay haphazardly on her face, and I sweep them away. Kiss her slow and sweet.

"Jonas, I..." She stares up at me with unsaid words on the tip of her tongue. Words I want to tell her too.

I brush my knuckles over her cheek and press another kiss to her lips. "I know. Me too," I whisper.

And without actually saying the words, we have both just said we love each other. The actual words may not have left either of our lips, but it's there. Pumping through the atriums and ventricles of our hearts. Ebbing and flowing with each breath we take. Rooted deep in the confines of our marrow. Consuming us.

After I dispose of the condom, I crawl back into the bed, curl up behind Autumn, and swathe her in my arms. She draws lines with her fingers over my forearms before rolling over to face me. Autumn inches as close as humanly possible and hugs me tight.

"Good night, Jonas." She presses her lips to the hollow point at the base of my throat.

I kiss the crown of her head and secure my arms around her. "'Night, scarlet."

I have no clue what time it is right now. Nor do I care. Only one thing, one person, matters right now. Jonas.

His still sleeping form lays peacefully beneath me. Chest rising and falling in a slow, rhythmic pattern. Disheveled hair I itch to comb my fingers through. Long lashes brushing softly against his sun-kissed skin. A peppering of stubble that makes my mouth water and has my thighs squeezing together.

Thin rays of sunlight dance across his bare chest as I lay with my chin on my hands just over his heart. *Tha-thump. Tha-thump. Tha-thump.* Steady and sure, I study the pattern of his heartbeat and lock it in my memory. A safe place. So any time we are apart, I can rest my hand over mine and imagine his is there with me.

And then the rhythm changes. Picks up speed. Wakes up.

His breathing becomes more noticeable. Not louder, just deeper. His body stirring to life as he leaves the land of dreams.

When his arm shifts and his hand slowly trails up my spine, I hold my breath. Relish in the warmth of his skin skirting over mine. The trail of fire his touch leaves in its wake. Watch as his eyes slowly open and notice me ogling him. The way his incandescent irises swirl with love and hunger and bliss. I lose focus as a soft, radiant smile lifts the corners of his lips. The lips I want to kiss all day. Every day.

He tucks his hands under my arms and slides me up his body. Brings us face to face. And it strikes a match low in my core. Roars into a bonfire. A wildfire.

"'Morning, scarlet," he whispers against my lips. His fingertips dance up and down my spine. Create a buzz in my veins. A hum low in my belly.

I press my lips to his and kiss him as if he is my lifeblood. Breathe him in as our lips break apart. Revel in the flutter swelling in my chest. "'Morning."

He turns his head and glances at the clock on the bedside table. Just after seven. Feels I have been awake hours. "I haven't slept this late in a while."

"Did I wear you out?" I tease.

He groans and brings his lips back to mine. Slips a hand into my hair and presses the other against my lower back. Curls his fingers in my hair as the kiss morphs from wholesome to libidinous. Rolls me over and pins me to the mattress with my hands above my head as he peppers kisses down my throat, my breasts, my belly.

Freeing my hands, he nips and licks a path down to the apex of my thighs. Inhaling deeply before his tongue darts out and sweeps a line up my slit. I bow off the bed, rock my hips into him, and fist his hair.

"Fuck, I love the taste of you."

A moan bubbles in my throat and spills from my lips. With every flick of his tongue, a new flash of euphoria glows in my vision. With each pinch and roll of my nipples, white noise fizzles my hearing. Fever blazes inside me and slicks my skin. Builds. Expands. Then constricts and erupts and renders me senseless.

Slowly, the room comes back into focus.

Jonas is above me on his haunches. He rips open a condom wrapper and rolls it down his length. I lick my lips.

One day, I will taste him on my tongue. Feel his silky hardness against my lips and down my throat.

Without preamble, he lines himself up with my entrance and rocks his hips forward. I tip my head back and gasp. Solid and thick and perfect. When I open my eyes, his are locked on the line of my face. Watching me. Memorizing me.

He slips a hand under my neck and holds me in place as he pulls out to the tip and drives back forward to the hilt. The entire time, his mesmerizing gaze stays locked with mine. An inferno of heaven and earth.

Then he rocks his hips again. And again. Eyes never straying. Speaking volumes all on their own as we make love. As he places a chaste kiss here and there.

And when his lips part, when I know he is close, a new sensation floods my veins. Red and potent and fervent. It fills my vision and expands the thumping organ in my chest. Intensifies. Surmounts every doubt in my heart. I allow it to consume me and hold me captive as I bend to its will.

Then I let go. Release and give in to the glorious vibration swimming in my bloodstream. Savor the ardor dominating Jonas as his body tightens and reddens and empties inside me.

Damn, he is beautiful.

We don't move. Don't look away. Not until our pulses settle and our breathing regulates. And even then, we don't stray far from one another.

Reluctantly, we rise from the bed and dress. I slowly crack open the bedroom door and see Clementine is still curled up with Spartan. I tiptoe to the bathroom and go about my morning routine. Jonas comes in, shuts the door, and does the same. As if we have done this time and again. The way we move around each other feels natural.

When we slip out of the bathroom, Jonas kisses me on the forehead. "Any breakfast requests?"

I shake my head. "Whatever you make will be perfect."

As Jonas heads into the kitchen, I wander over to Clementine and gently wake her. Even though I would love more individual time with Jonas, I don't want to disrupt her routine too much.

Any other time in history I have woken Clementine, she was a grump. But not this morning. And I don't know if it's due to her furry bedtime companion or she slept really well. Either way, I will gladly take the change.

"Can I watch cartoons?" she asks.

"Sure, pumpkin." I flip on the television and let her choose which show she wants to watch. And once Spartan comes back in from doing his morning business outside, he hops back on the couch and watches cartoons with Clementine.

Soon, we all sit on the couch—well, everyone except Spartan—and eat French toast, scrambled eggs, sausage, and hash browns. I peek over at Jonas and sigh. This all just feels so *normal*. Right. Perfect. As if everything in my life is finally falling into place.

In place with Jonas at my side.

Once Jonas loads the last of the dishes into the dishwasher, he suggests we go outdoors and enjoy the day. Although it's mid-January, the temperature hasn't dropped too much. And I packed options and jackets for me and Clementine.

~

The beach in January is an odd place. Odd because there aren't thousands of bodies covering every possible grain of sand. No beach towels stretched out or umbrellas shading patrons. No permanent perfume of shea and coconut floating in the air.

In January, most walk the beach in jeans and sneakers and long sleeves. Couples huddle close to one another for warmth. People sit on collapsible chairs in the sand and listen to the small waves crash along the surf. Occasionally, you spot a snow-bird in shorts and flip-flops. Some in swimwear. One or two dipping their toes in the Gulf.

I shiver at the prospect of getting in the water this time of year. Unless it's in a heated pool or hot tub.

Jonas, Clementine, and I wander hand in hand on the white sands in Sand Key Park. Every fifty feet, Clementine begs us to lift her off the ground and swing her between us. Her resounding fit of giggles each time we do has me hoping she will ask again. Because her giggles match the happiness swimming throughout my body. A happiness I haven't known until now. A happiness I want forever.

Not that I never felt happiness when it was only me and Clementine. My daughter fulfills me in a way I never knew possible. She fills gaps in my heart. Makes me smile when I have a bad day. Gives me purpose when I feel as if I have none. Keeps my feet on solid ground. Makes me see the world in a new light.

But with Jonas, happiness feels different.

Jonas blankets me in warmth. Stirs passion in my soul. Resuscitates me after years of not experiencing a connection with another person. Bonds me to him with his lips and words and skin on mine. Grounds me when life feels off kilter.

For years, I wondered why I never had the urge to date. To spend time with someone romantically. I always told myself it was because of Clementine. Because she needed me, and my attention was best spent focusing on her.

Then Jonas stepped into the picture. With his sad heart and soulful eyes, he stole my breath from the start.

I tried to fight our connection. Tried to deny anything was there. But I knew. Knew I was lying to myself to guard my heart again. Guard it from hurt and heartache and abandonment.

But Jonas will never leave my side. Never.

"Let's go to the playground before we leave," Jonas suggests.

Clementine bounces between us like a kid on a sugar high. "Yay! Jonas, will you push me on the swings?"

He looks down at her and smiles. The way he adores her has me melting into a messy puddle of emotions. "Of course, I will."

For the next twenty minutes, Clementine hauls Jonas around the playground like a rag doll. Asks him to push her on the swings. Join her on the teeter-totter. Spin her on the merry-go-round until she dizzies and can't walk straight. Go down the slide after her.

And he does it all. With a smile on his face and without an ounce of hesitation.

I sit on a bench and warm myself in the sunlight as I watch my daughter and the man I *love* play together. I listen to their banter and laughter as she tries to outrun him and he chases her. Watch her squeal in delight as he catches her, swoops her off the ground, and tickles her into a fit of giggles.

Life couldn't be any more perfect.

All too soon, we hop in the Jeep and drive toward my apartment. The closer we get to my home, the less it feels as if I belong there. Penny and I have shared an apartment since the beginning. Turned housing into a home. But for the first time in my adult life, I don't feel as if I am headed home.

Jonas is home. Wherever he is, that is my home. And after spending the night in his house—in his bed—I don't know how I will sleep any other way.

As if he hears my thoughts, he lays a hand on my thigh and glances my way for a split second. "You okay?" he whisper-asks. "You've been awfully quiet."

I nod. "Yeah. Just thinking."

"About?"

I shift in my seat so I face him more. "How much your house feels like home," I mumble. Although Clementine is happily singing to the radio in the back seat, her little ears pick up so much. I don't need her partially hearing what I say and misinterpreting it.

A smile kicks up the corners of his mouth as he lightly squeezes my thigh. "Honestly, I've been trying to drag out the day. Didn't really want to make the drive back here." He lifts his hand from my leg, and I immediately miss his warmth. But I don't go without it for long as he cups my cheek. "As much as I'd love to drag you back to my house, I don't get to make that decision. My greed isn't what's important. What does matter is what you want for you and her." He nudges his head toward the back seat. "Whatever you decide, that's what I'll go along with."

He drops his hand to mine and lifts it to his lips, kissing my knuckles. Inhaling deeply, I ponder over his words. Smile at how lucky I am to have found such a wonderful man. Revel in the notion of how patient and kind he is, and how he will wait alongside me until I decide where we go from here.

How did I get so damn lucky?

Jonas steers the Jeep into the complex and winds around to my building. As my car comes into view, my heart bottoms out. I swipe at my eyes and squint as if I am not seeing things clearly. But I am. And I think I am going to throw up.

"Why is he here?" I mumble.

Autumn tenses beneath my hand as I park the Jeep.

"Why is he here?" she asks no one in particular. Her eyes shoot daggers toward her car, where a man stands in a suit and tie with a cell phone glued to his ear.

I cut the engine and glance over at her. "Autumn, who is that?" Tears well in her eyes as she shakes her head. "Are you okay?"

She shakes her head again. "No," she whispers.

Leaning across the console, I frame her face in my palms. "Talk to me. You're scaring me."

"Mama, can we get out?" Clementine asks as she unbuckles her seat belt.

"Not yet, pumpkin. In just a minute." Autumn lifts her somber eyes to my concerned ones and I hold my breath. Fear and anguish and panic mar her features. She leans closer so her lips are at my ear. "That's Clementine's birth father," she whispers so only I hear her.

I lean back and stare at her wide-eyed. "What's he doing here?" At this point, Autumn and I talk in hushed tones. The only thing I know about Clementine's father is that he abandoned Autumn before Clementine was born. And that is more than enough to tell me what kind of human he is.

She shrugs. "Haven't seen or heard from him since he left years ago." Autumn shifts her eyes toward Clementine. "She doesn't even know who he is. Not his name or what he looks like. And I'd imagine the same in reverse."

Stroking a thumb over her cheek, I try to soothe away some of the worry Autumn must be experiencing. "Well, let's grab your stuff and go into the apartment. If he wants to talk, he can do it without her present." I nudge my head toward Clementine.

Autumn nods before we both open our doors and get out of the Jeep. She helps Clementine out while I grab their bag from the back seat.

As we meet at the front of the Jeep, the man starts walking toward us. I step in front of Autumn and Clementine and act as a barrier. The sight of him makes me sick, but I swallow it down and guard the two most important people in my world.

"Help you with something?" I ask as he approaches us.

The man does his best to look around me, but I tower over him and shield Autumn and Clementine from his view. "Who the fuck are you?" he bellows. "Autumn! A word. Now."

Who the fuck am I?

Well, asshole, I am about to become your worst fucking nightmare. Especially if you continue to talk to my girls like a dick. No man—or woman—disrespects my girls. No one.

I swing my face back in his line of sight. "Hey," I thunder and wave a hand in his face. "You need to step back. Now." I return his tone with a verbal punch. "Back. Up."

When he steps back, I look over my shoulder and signal Autumn to take Clementine inside. She complies without hesitation. Once Clementine is behind closed doors, once she is out of earshot and Autumn returns to my side, I get in this piece of shit's face.

"Who the *fuck* am I?" I belt out. "None of your damn business. And neither are they. Not since you jumped ship and left them to drown. What kind of man does that? What kind of man abandons his own child? You've got a lot of nerve coming here."

"You done, pretty boy?" He cocks an eyebrow at me. "Who I am and what I did have nothing to do with you. Matter of fact, you can be on your way. Seeing as this doesn't involve you."

I throw my head back and laugh. "Everything to do with them involves me. But you wouldn't understand such a concept. So get back in your car and drive off to wherever it is you came from."

Autumn grips my bicep and stands unified beside me. She hasn't said anything since we exited the car. Honestly, I think she is too afraid to speak. I don't know much about this guy, but from his demeanor I know he is a pompous prick. And if Autumn didn't want me to speak, she would have given me a sign or stopped me when I overstepped. She hasn't done either.

We stand five feet apart, glaring at each other. His clothes may scream money, but his expression yells piece of trash. As does his lack of human decency.

He takes a step back. Then another. Sizes me up with a snarl. Shifts his gaze to Autumn and his snarl turns mocking. As if he has a secret. As if he holds the key to her future.

"Sorry we couldn't have a civil conversation, Autumn. Seems lover boy does all the talking for you now."

"Say what you came here to say, Leo. Then leave and never come back."

The sneer returns to his lips. "Just thought I'd give you a heads-up. Being the nice guy I am."

A chill snakes down my spine that has absolutely nothing to do with the winter temperatures. I glare at this pathetic excuse of a man and try to read the hidden message in his words. But he holds his cards close. Waiting for the perfect moment to throw down.

I glance down at Autumn. She tilts her head as confusion mars her brow. "Quit being cryptic. Heads-up about what?"

My eyes dart back to him as he takes another two steps back. His sneer slithers into a smile that makes me uncomfortable. Autumn clamps on to my arm tighter and sucks in a breath. Both of us waiting for the other shoe to drop.

"I'm filing for sole custody of our daughter. Clementine, right? You should be served tomorrow."

And I can't breathe.

Love Buzz

INKED DUET
BOOK TWO

One

AUTUMN

I can't breathe.

Did Leo just say what I think he said? That he has filed for custody of *my* daughter. Swear to God, I must be hearing things because Leo hasn't spent a day of his pathetic adult life near *my* daughter. Why would he suddenly want to now?

Leo waltzes toward his car, and I lose focus, gripping Jonas's arm tighter.

An evil cackle floats through the air and robs all but my hearing. His wicked laughter will no doubt haunt me for days and weeks and months to come.

All I want is to wake up from this nightmare. Because this has to be my mind playing a sick trick. An attempt to rip away the only true happiness I have in my life.

My vision focuses enough to see Leo slip into a white Mercedes sedan. He starts the car and revs the engine—which is a joke because the car isn't equipped to sound threatening. Then he rolls down the driver's side window as he rolls past us slowly. One corner of his mouth tugged up. Brow cocked. Hoity-toity sunglasses over his eyes.

"Until we see each other again." He throws a flippant wave and drives off.

For the first time in minutes, I breathe fully. But it doesn't last long. My deep, full breaths turn to short gasps. Come faster and faster. Pulse pounding so power-fully, I clutch my chest to smother the pain. Fist my shirt and tug at the cotton.

Then I lose it.

I drop my arm from Jonas's, stammer in place, then tip my face to the sky and scream. Belt out my anger and fear and frustration. I scream for all the bullshit I have dealt with since Leo up and abandoned me. Scream for all the pain and heartache I have endured. And I scream at the universe for doing this. For inflicting me with this level of misery.

What the hell did I do to deserve such duplicity?

From the moment I learned I was pregnant; I have been a good mother. A really good mother. I have given up everything for my daughter. Forfeited every part of life not revolving around her. Sacrificed everything so her life won't feel any less with only one parent. Given up on love—until Jonas.

Yet here I am, still on the receiving end of punishment. And I don't get it. Why? Why me? What past blunder has put me on the chopping block? Haven't I endured enough?

Jonas places a hand on my back—warm and comforting—and draws small circles with his thumb. My anxiety settles down a notch. Just barely. Every nerve ending sparks with unrelenting fury. And I hate it. Hate how easily Leo gets under my skin after so many years apart.

The worst of all… I have been so stuck in my head the last five minutes, I forgot Jonas stood less than a foot away. The man I care deeply for; I mentally abandoned him in a blink. If that doesn't make me a horrible girlfriend, I don't know what does.

Jonas steps closer—close enough, he is all I see—and frames my face in his palms. Brow pinching at the midline, he holds my gaze. His eyes a mix of concern and fear, strength and courage.

"Autumn, what can I do?"

The backs of my eyes sting as I slowly shake my head. "I don't know." Then the first tear spills and slips down my cheek. Jonas swipes it away. "Jonas, I don't understand why he is doing this. Why the sudden interest in her? He didn't care before. Threw us out like trash. So, why now? What triggered this?" As if the first tear granted permission for the others to fall, the floodgates open and flow uninterrupted. My body trembles crown to heel.

Jonas drops his hands to my waist and hauls me closer to him, swathing me in his strong arms. I snake my arms around his waist and cry into his shirt. He shifts one hand to the back of my head, strokes my hair, and shushes me.

"I got you. Just let it out."

We stand near his Jeep for minutes or hours. I cry gallons of tears as I bury my face in his cotton tee. My eyes puff up painfully. I fist Jonas's shirt, push off his chest, and add distance between us. Slowly, I peer up at him. His iridescent hazels hold my gaze and silently ask if I am okay.

No, I am nowhere near okay.

Honestly, I don't know if I will be for some time. But none of my feelings matter right now. Time to put my selfishness on the back burner. Again.

Inside the apartment, there is a little girl whose feelings matter more. Whose will always matter more. And I plan to do whatever it takes to protect that little girl. Protect her from a man who never cared for her or even the idea of her. Protect her heart from the pain this situation may inflict on her.

"We should check on Clementine," I say, emotionless.

Jonas nods then swipes at my cheeks. He studies me with worried eyes. "Yeah. Let's check on her."

I step up to the Jeep and check my reflection in the window. *Jesus, I look like shit.*

Taking a minute, I swipe at my cheeks to clear as much of the trailed mascara off them as I can. Then I slip my sunglasses on and smooth my hair. Not as if Clementine won't notice the difference in my appearance, but if I can make it as subtle as possible, I will. I need to.

Taking a deep breath, I square my shoulders and step back from the Jeep. Jonas wraps his arm around my waist and presses me into his side. Warmth and strength pass from his touch throughout my body. We walk to the apartment door, a couple united.

But in my head, I slowly lose my mind as I question every circumstance in my life. Including my relationship with Jonas.

For now, I shake it off. My focus needs to be on my little girl and no one else. Not myself. And not Jonas.

We walk inside the apartment and shut the door. Penny sits on the couch beside Clementine. Thankfully, Clementine is oblivious to any disturbance as she watches *The Nightmare Before Christmas* at a deafening volume. My guess is Penny turned it up after I brought her inside and she caught the ghostly expression on my face.

Bless you, my friend.

I slide my sunglasses to the top of my head and Penny's eyes widen. "You okay?" she mouths. Subtly, I shake my head and clamp my lips between my teeth to fight the tremor of my chin.

Jonas walks us over to the couch and we sit. For the first time since we strolled through the front door, Clementine peers over at us. Her sweet, innocent face nothing but smiles and love and cheer. She crawls across the small space between us and hugs me. I have no idea why—maybe she senses I need her little arms wrapped around me—but I hug her closer than ever.

When she unhooks her arms, she sits back and smiles up at me. "Mama, who was the man outside?"

In my periphery, Penny cocks her head and scoots closer to the couch edge. She picks up the television remote and turns the volume down. I peek over at her and give a subdued smile.

Inhaling deeply, I prepare for the grocery list of questions Clementine will have after I answer. "No one important, pumpkin. Just someone I knew a long time ago."

Ever the intuitive, Clementine gauges my expression. Studies my face longer than typical. But by some divine miracle, she appears pleased with my response. "Oh, okay. A friend?"

It takes every rational atom inside me to not rebut her terminology. But I remain tight-lipped. "Pumpkin, will you stay here and watch your movie? I need to talk with Jonas and Aunt Penny alone for a minute."

Clementine smiles up at me and nods. I swallow the emotion slowly building in my mouth. Bite back the tears that threaten to fall. And force it all past the boulder in my throat.

"Yeah. Can I turn it back up?"

I love how her sole concern lies in the volume of her movie. That her little seven-year-old mind knows no other worries. "Sure, pumpkin." I hand her the remote. "Stay here. We'll be back out soon."

Glancing at Penny, I tip my head toward the kitchen. The apartment isn't necessarily closed off in the main living spaces, but at least a partial wall blocks the conversation we need to have. Penny, Jonas, and I rise from the couch and head to the kitchen. In the small space, I drag us as far from Clementine's eyes and ears as possible.

"What is going on?" Penny whisper-shouts.

"Leo was by my car when we pulled up." I tuck my lips between my teeth and blink back the tears threatening to make an appearance.

Now is not the time to break down, Autumn.

"What the hell did he want?" Not too often will anyone ever meet a pissed-off Penny. But when she hits that point, people instantly know. Being on Penny's bad side isn't pretty. Not pretty at all.

I tip my head back and stare at the ceiling. For the umpteenth time since I spotted Leo outside, I fight the anger and frustration and fear boiling in my veins.

Hold it together, Autumn. Crying and screaming right now will not help anything. Just say what needs to be said.

Lowering my chin, I level my gaze with hers. "Said he's filing for custody of Clementine. I will be served tomorrow."

Penny slaps a hand over her mouth and slowly shakes her head as her eyes widen. After she marinates on the outlandish news, she opens her mouth. For a moment, she doesn't say anything. She snaps her jaw shut, then opens it again. "This makes no fucking sense. After all this time. After walking away without worry. So, why now?"

"Question of the day." I laugh without humor.

Beside me, Jonas remains silent with his arm around my waist. No doubt he is as baffled with what happens next as I am. His thumb draws lazy circles on my hip, his gentle reminder so I know he is here for whatever I need. That he supports my decision, whatever it may be. That he will be a leaning pillar of strength through this rocky time.

And I love how much he cares. Love how he will do anything for me, even after such a short time together. His level of love speaks volumes and resonates deep in my bones.

Penny continues to shake her head while tapping a finger over her lips. "Why?" she mumbles. The question not directed at anyone or meant to be answered. Just pure curiosity.

The three of us stand in the kitchen, staring at each other and nothing. My mind wanders as I search for some hidden reason or an obvious resolution. And honestly, I have no idea where to begin.

If Leo is filing a lawsuit through the court system, should I obtain legal counsel? Is an attorney my first step in handling this? Not as if I have friends or family who have been through this. Will I be able to afford an attorney? Especially on such short notice. How much does it cost to hire one? Will Leo drag out the matter and slowly drain my savings?

Panic hits my bloodstream anew and a tremor vibrates my body. Not enough for Penny to notice, but Jonas does. His hold on me is stronger as he leans in and kisses my temple.

Why the hell is Leo suddenly so interested in Clementine? After jumping ship close to eight years ago, telling me he had no idea how to be a father—nor did he want to be—why is he so eager to fill the role now? And how does he know where we live? What I named her?

Something had to have provoked his interest. It's the only logical explanation. But what the hell changed?

Then the answer hits me like a wall of summer humidity. Steals my breath and robs my heart. Jonas. Jonas is the only difference in my life after all these years.

What if Leo has secretly kept tabs on me over the years—kept tabs on Clementine—and recently learned Jonas and I started dating? Although he has no desire to be with me or be a father, is this his way of saying, *I don't want them, but no one else can have them either*?

My stomach balls into a knot and twists my gut.

If this holds true... one—this is fucking bullshit. And two—in order to not lose my daughter, I need to do something harsh. Something I may regret for the rest of my life. Something that has me queasy and on the verge of vomiting.

I need to distance myself and Clementine from Jonas. If my being with Jonas prompted this whole debacle, I need to back off. At least until I consult with an attorney and everything clears up.

Bile rises and burns my throat as I pinch my eyes closed. Jesus, I am going to be sick.

As if Jonas senses my dismay, he squeezes my hip and I open my eyes. I peek up at him and every molecule of love I hold for him slumps with sadness and heartache.

I don't want to do this. Can't do this. But what other choice do I have? Leo has dumped my worst nightmare in my lap and I see no other way out of it. Not yet, anyway.

"How am I supposed to handle this?" I whisper more to myself than to Jonas or Penny.

Jonas takes both my hands in his and lifts them to his chest. Beneath my palms, his heart thumps the rhythm I recently memorized. A rhythm I tucked away for safekeeping. And now it seems as if I will be unlocking that vault sooner than expected to play the recorded rhythm.

Because I am about to change everything. I am about to break both of us.

I stare at Jonas's chest as my fingers gently rumple his shirt. He places a finger under my chin and tips it up until our eyes meet. Golden to hazel. In his eyes, I see promise and hope and love. The knife twists harder beneath my diaphragm at seeing his unconditional support.

I will miss him. So goddamn much. Every second and minute and hour. Every day and week and month. I mentally clench my fists and pinch my eyes.

"We will get through this together. Okay?" Voice soft and tender and barely audible. It shreds my heart further. "No matter what happens, as long as we have each other, we will survive this."

The backs of my eyes sting, but I don't dare let the tears break free. Tears may be what gives me away. And me putting distance between us won't happen if he picks up on my plan.

For now, I keep this tidbit to myself. I trudge forward and let him believe everything will be okay with us. I pray, in the end, it will be better than okay. So, I nod and force past the pain piercing my heart.

Regardless of my feelings, I must remain strong. Not just to get through whatever bullshit Leo is about to deliver, but also to protect my daughter. Above any person, Clementine matters most. And since the moment I learned I would be a mother, I swore to do whatever it takes to keep her safe and feeling loved.

Even if that means losing the only other person I have ever loved. Even if that means losing Jonas.

Two

JONAS

The alarm clock wails on my bedside table and, for a moment, I ignore it. Ignore the blaring tone as it changes every ten seconds and becomes more frantic. When Spartan nudges my ribs, I roll my eyes and slap a hand in the general direction of the clock. After a few blind slaps, silence consumes the room again.

Silence and darkness.

After leaving Autumn's apartment last night, I couldn't shake the sudden pain in my chest. This sinking, drowning, I-can't-pull-in-enough-oxygen sensation. No matter how much I assured Autumn I'd be at her side, that we would get through this, a nagging pinch lingered beneath my sternum.

All night, I laid in bed and stared at the ceiling. Studied the minor imperfections in the plaster. On occasion, I drifted off. Only to be woken fifteen, twenty, thirty minutes later.

The pang beneath my ribs didn't exist solely from Clementine's father making an appearance—although he royally pissed me off. The stab persisted because something was off with Autumn. With us.

When Autumn, Penny, and I went to the kitchen to talk, I *felt* the rift start. Our relationship may still be young, we may not know much about each other, but I have never been more hyperaware of anyone. Not even Cora. And seconds after we stepped into the kitchen, something in Autumn changed.

Can't pinpoint exactly what, but the ground shifted beneath us. The tectonic plates holding our hearts started slowly drifting apart. And the crack between us swallows me whole.

The snooze alert booms off the walls and I slap the clock again. As exhausted as I am, sleep evades me. No matter how many times I close my eyes, my mind refuses to shut down and let me sleep. But the energy to leave the bed won't come either.

Spartan noses my elbow and groans. "I'm getting up. Just give me a minute."

I roll over to turn off the clock, inhale Autumn's scent on the other pillowcase, and close my eyes. Fisting the pillow to my nose, I drag in the smell of her. Allow it to lessen the sharp sting between my lungs, if only for a minute.

When I drop the pillow and sit up, the pain throbs anew. This is going to be a long fucking day. I feel it in my bones.

Out of bed, I go about my typical morning routine. Taking Spartan for a walk—thank god he knows our route because I am mentally dead on my feet. Shower faster than usual. Dress for work robotically. As I take out items to make breakfast, I spot Clementine's juice in the fridge.

The knot in my stomach twists tighter. Has me nauseous. I cook half my normal breakfast and barely eat any of it. Before leaving the house, I brew a pot of coffee and fill my work thermos to the brim.

Today is going to snail by.

With Spartan secure in his crate, I turn on the radio for him and head out. I opt to ride the bike today and, since it is still pretty early, drive aimlessly for almost an hour.

The cold air stings my skin as I ride around the city. I welcome the frigid burn. The bite of cold air better than the uncertainty clouding my every thought.

I drive aimlessly. Focus on the road. The vibration of the engine between my legs. The heat from the pipes near my calves. When I need to change gears and steer the bike, I focus on what I can control.

After an hour of aimless riding, I park behind the shop and amble into the office. Dad sits behind his desk, his stack of invoices thin as he peeks up when I enter.

I don't miss how he checks the clock above the door. How he scans my face after noticing I am only thirty minutes early rather than my typical hour-plus early. And I definitely don't miss the brief droop at the corners of his eyes and lowered edges of his lips when he scans my face and notes my sullen demeanor.

I never need to tell Dad something is wrong. He just knows. Until Autumn and I got close, I thought no one would be able to read me better than Dad. His parental superpower is sensing when his children aren't one hundred percent.

And right now, he more than senses something is off.

Giving a wave, I hold up the thermos. "'Morning. Coffee?"

He tilts his head slightly and gauges my stilted greeting. But he doesn't mention it. Doesn't shine a light on it and probe for further explanation.

"Please. Thanks, son."

I nod then turn my back to him, grabbing mugs, creamer, and sugar before parking it all on the desk. Filling the mugs with coffee from my thermos, I hand him his mug without meeting his eyes. Once he adds cream and sugar, I follow suit. It all feels routine... and robotic.

The slowest first ten minutes of my workday tick by. We drink our coffee in silence as Dad wraps up the last of his paperwork and I stare at a framed picture Mom suggested we add to the office. A mountainous landscape at sunset. *"You need more than bare walls and automotive posters in this place."* At least I have something to lose focus on while I sit here. A place to mentally get lost in.

"Want to talk about it?" Dad prompts after he stacks the day's invoices in a wire basket.

Dropping my gaze from the picture, I face him and shake my head. "Not yet."

Dad nods as his chair legs scrape the tile and he stands. Starting for the door, he pauses beside me and lays a hand on my shoulder. "Whenever you're ready, I'm here." Before I respond, he pats my shoulder, strolls out the door and into the garage.

I finish my coffee, wash the mug, and set it in the rack. Grabbing a fresh pair of coveralls, I slip them over my clothes, pick up the thermos, then mosey out to the garage. I survey the roster and see the majority of the schedule is full. A busy day is good. A busy day is exactly the distraction I need.

Three oil changes and a full set of new tires later, I would swear it should be closing time. No such luck. Still another thirty minutes until lunch. Then the back half of the day.

Dad has not so nonchalantly checked on me five times. At minimum. I understand his concern, but his constant overshadowing doesn't make matters better. If anything, it constantly reminds me why my mood is sour.

After I replace a starter, Dad orders me to take lunch. My stomach growls for me to feed it, but my head shoots down the idea. Instead, I lie on the couch in the office and close my eyes. Although I won't sleep, my exhausted body will rejoice at being horizontal.

I jolt awake when Dad nudges my shoulder. "Jonas, you should wake up."

Rubbing my palms over my eyes, I stare up at him. "How long have I been in here?"

Dad glances at the clock on the wall. "Little more than an hour."

Shit. I may have needed sleep, but now I will be the chump not returning on time. The one screwing up everyone else's lunch break. The day just keeps getting better.

"Sorry. Be out in a minute." I drop my feet to the floor and sit up, propping my elbows on my knees as I further rub the sleep from my eyes.

"Take your time, son. Garage has been slow since you been in here. I sent one of the other guys to lunch shortly after you."

I nod. "Thanks, Dad."

Without another word, Dad pats my shoulder then exits the office. Once the door clicks shut, I drop my head in my hands and groan.

Why is it when life is going great, time whizzes by? But when life isn't all it's cracked up to be, time barely ticks. And to reaffirm the statement, I glance up at the clock and see I still have another four hours left to work.

Fuck.

I comb my fingers through my hair, tugging at the ends. "Just get off your ass and get the day over with." Besides, I still have dinner to look forward to. Dinner with my girls. Just the idea of dinner, of seeing Autumn and Clementine, perks me up.

Rising from the couch, I grab a cold bottle of water from the fridge and guzzle half of it before I head back to the garage. I will make the rest of the day better. Even if I have to fake it.

～

Dad and I roll down the bay doors and I sigh. The entire day crept by, but thank fuck all is said and done now. Dad checked on me just as much after lunch as he did before. And as we lock up the shop and head to our vehicles, he surprises me with a hug. Not just any hug, but one of his *I'm always here for you, son* hugs.

"Drive safe, son. See you in the morning."

"You, too. Thanks, Dad."

Dad hops in his truck, cranks the engine, and waves to me as he drives off. Once out of sight, I straddle the bike and pull my phone from my back pocket. As with the last hundred times I have checked my phone today, there are zero notifications. At least none I want to see. Which doesn't help the pang since leaving Autumn's apartment last night.

Inhaling deeply, I open our text history and type out a quick message.

> Hey, scarlet. Still coming over for dinner?

I hold my breath as I stare, stare, stare at the screen. Silently willing Autumn to read my message and respond.

The screen dims and I tap the glass to wake it. Twenty painstaking heartbeats later, the little gray bubble pops up and those three magical dots dance inside it. Finally, I exhale.

Too soon.

> Not tonight. Got served today and I just want alone time with Clementine.

Her rejection hurts, but I understand the reason behind it.

> Want to talk about it?

> Not tonight. Please. But soon.

God, I wish we were face to face. I desperately want to wrap her hand with mine. Want to comfort her and take away the heartache she must be suffering with all this. But I won't thrust myself in her face. Won't annoy her with my anguish. She has enough on her own plate; I shouldn't add to the list of things to worry about.

> Sure. Talk to you later.

> Later.

Can't imagine what Autumn must be feeling right now, but God how I want to hold her. Tuck her snug in my arms and reassure her everything will be fine. That it will all work out, in her favor. It has to. After everything she has endured as a single parent, how can this not end favorably for her?

I tuck my phone away, start the bike, and drive home. Mindlessly, I weave through the evening traffic. See other drivers on the road, but pay them no attention. The trip is a blur of early sunset colors and bright red and white lights.

The second I set foot in the house, Spartan barks incessantly and bounces around as per usual. Once out of his crate, I open the back door and let him roam the yard while I kick off my boots and grab a beer.

The entire day—and now the evening—feels forced. Mechanical. Lifeless.

I feed Spartan dinner and polish off beer number one. Every few seconds, Spartan stops eating to peer over at the door. His heart hopeful a specific small human will walk through the door and shower him with hugs and conversation.

"Not tonight, bud." I rough his fur up as I grab the throw blanket from the couch.

Spartan finishes eating in record time. I snag a fresh beer from the fridge and walk out the back door with him hot on my heels. He bolts past me and scavenges the yard for who knows what.

While he forages for lizards that aren't there, I grab the lighter from the cabinet beneath the fire bowl, crank the gas, and ignite the rocks. Kicking back on the lounger, I sip beer number two and stare up at the black sky.

Tonight, the sky is absent of bright, twinkling lights. No stars to guide me. To lead me in the right direction. To guide me down this new path.

It is just me in the darkness with only man-made fire to light my way. The irony isn't lost on me.

Maybe I should have called Autumn rather than texted her. At least I would have heard her voice. Gotten an idea where her head is after being served. After she read the painful lines on the scariest document. I may be reading the whole situation too deeply, but even her texts felt *off*. Clipped. Glum. Harsh.

God, I just want her in my arms. To be by her side and help make this all vanish. Figure out a way to fix this for her. Make it so she never worries about someone trying to take away the most important person in her world.

Long after I empty my beer, Spartan nudges my elbow. His way of telling me he is bored and wants to go inside. I sit up from the lounger and extinguish the fire. "C'mon, bud. Let's go."

Woof, woof, woof.

Although the muscles in my face have refused to let me smile all day, this dog brings one out of me anyway. Never have I met or owned a dog like Spartan. Wild and crazy and my main man. Perfect.

And with the uncertainty revolving around Autumn, I am grateful to have Spartan to cuddle me when home. To keep me company and drive me up the wall on occasion.

I toss the brown bottle in the recycling bin then heat up a small portion of leftovers. I eat to satisfy my stomach—seeing as I have eaten next to nothing—and not my taste buds. After I clean my plate, I turn off all the lights and go to my room.

I tug my shirt over my head and toss it in the hamper. Then my socks and jeans. Spartan hops on the bed and settles where he normally sleeps when it is just us.

Statically pulling back the comforter and sheet, I slip under the covers. But as soon as I bring them to my chest, a waft of Autumn's scent hits my nose and takes residence. Her cherry vanilla perfume floats up my nose and drowns me.

And all I do is drag the bedding closer to me. Close my eyes and inhale deeper. Picture her in the bed next to me—hair loose and framing her face as she leans in to kiss me. The warmth of her skin as it melds with mine. Her soft lips as they brush mine and take me prisoner.

I groan into the darkness as the throb in my chest expands and I fist the bedding. No matter what it takes, I will make this better. Because, *fuck*, there is no way I can live without her.

three

AUTUMN

How does four days feel like a lifetime?

The whirlwind makes me dizzy. Sick to my stomach. The earth never felt this lopsided. This uneven and unpredictable. My life flipped upside down Sunday and I no longer know which way is up.

The day started out perfect. Full of warmth and love and everything I have missed out on as a woman. Waking up with Jonas beneath me in bed was nothing short of bliss. *God, I miss him.* Miss his heat and heart and whispered affection. His arms wrapped around my waist. We spent the day together like a normal couple. We enjoyed life. Simply being near each other—breathing the same air, sharing blissful smiles, and walking hand in hand.

Every facet of our weekend was sublime.

Then our bliss was stolen. Our bubble popped. Yanked out from beneath our feet and knocking us on our asses.

Leo. Fucking *Leo.*

Never have I been a violent person. Never have I sunk so low as to intentionally hurt someone. Physically, mentally, or emotionally. It isn't in my makeup. Inflicting hate makes me nauseous.

But since *Leo* waltzed back in and threatened my livelihood, threatened my sanity, I have conjured up countless ways to make him disappear from the world. Allowed my mind to adventure into some dark places.

None of the horrible ideas will come to fruition, nor will I speak them aloud, but they continue to pop up like an uninvited guest.

The funniest, nonviolent idea so far… tattooing "commitment issues" on his forehead. Or better yet, instead of his forehead, the best place is just above his dick. So every woman sees it when he strips bare. So every woman questions why. Questions him. No doubt Rex and Reznor would be up for the challenge.

Beside me, Clementine stirs and slowly wakes. And I envy this little girl right now. How she remains oblivious to what's happening with her sperm donor and the obstacle he threw our way. How she continues each day with a smile on her face and love in her heart.

And as long as there is breath in my lungs, I will keep her in oblivion. Keep her safe—physically, mentally, emotionally—from whatever tricks Leo has up his sleeve.

No matter what stresses life hands us, it should be me who loses sleep and worries about the outcome. In time, I will need to share everything with her—who her birth father is and what he is trying to do. But the time hasn't arrived. Not yet. And I plan to keep her life normal and full of the routine she knows.

Her eyes flutter open and peer up at me. "'Morning, Mama."

I love her sleepy voice. Sweet and raspy and innocent. Not a care in the world. A perfect mix of angel and groggy.

"'Morning, pumpkin. Did you sleep good?"

She nods, slow and steady. Then she stretches out her tiny hand and paints small semicircles beneath my eyes with her fingertip. Her lips turn down at the corners and sadness shadows her eyes.

"Mama, why do you look so tired?" My sweet, sweet girl.

Generally, Clementine is happy-go-lucky. Smiles and laughs and goofs off. But she has the biggest, empathetic heart. She may not understand the trials and tribulations adults deal with, but she senses when something is amiss.

"Just didn't sleep well." I bop her nose with my finger. "Nothing you need to worry about, though."

"Okay, Mama." A soft smile plumps her cheeks. "When will we see Sparty again?"

Over the last few days, I have dreaded the moment Clementine would ask about Jonas or Spartan. One of the reasons I didn't want her getting attached. Because if shit hit the fan—which it did, just not the shit I expected—she wouldn't understand why we didn't see each other anymore.

For now, as painful as it is, I just need things between me and Jonas to slow down. Dramatically. As in, press pause. For now, I need to spend all my time with Clementine. Because the possibility of Leo taking her from me seems inevitable.

Not that I will go down without a fight.

"Soon, pumpkin." And I hate how easily I make the promise to her. Hate how I don't know if I can fulfill said promise. "I have to take care of some special Mama-only tasks first. Okay?"

I love and hate how her little golden eyes narrow as she tries to read my mind. To find falsehoods in my words. I pray she doesn't. "Okay. But I really miss Sparty."

"Me too, pumpkin." I bite the inside of my cheek and smile halfheartedly. "Now, though, it's time to get up and get ready for school."

And just like that, conversation over.

Clementine and I go about our morning routine of dressing and styling and eating breakfast. Thankfully, she doesn't mention Spartan again. Before long, we hop in the car and drive toward her school. She bops and sings to the music and I savor every moment from the corner of my eye. Her dark hair in a ponytail with a bandana tied around the elastic. The snug black long-sleeve top with cherry print, loose jeans, and saddle shoes. My sweet girl.

I will not lose her. I refuse to lose her.

After I drop Clementine off and watch her enter the school, I drive to the appointment I have dreaded all week. An appointment with a family law attorney.

After being served Monday morning, I read through the not-so-thin packet of paperwork. Overwhelmed doesn't remotely cover the whirlwind spinning in my head. I am no idiot, but legal jargon is not a language I speak. It was easy enough to decipher Leo requested sole custody of Clementine. The rest of the documentation was jibber-jabber.

Parking in the lot, I stare up at the building and read the large placard on the wall. *Theresa Chang, Esq. Family Law Attorney serving the community for over 20 years.*

Twenty-plus years has to count for something, right? No one flourishes and stays in business if they have no idea what they are doing. God, I hope so.

I double-check I have the folder of documents tucked in my purse, take a deep breath, then exit the car.

After setting an appointment over the phone, the receptionist gave me a rundown of what today's appointment would entail and what I needed to bring. My sole wish is this attorney will be the one to represent me. Time and money are tight. Bad enough I have to shell out thousands of dollars to deal with Leo in the first place. I don't need to waste any of the limited time I have.

The building is a subtle gray with large white pillars along the front, giving an outward appearance of a small courthouse. Two large oak trees shade majority of the building while ferns surround the trunks. An array of colorful flowers planted in large terra-cotta pots sit near the entrance and give an inviting vibe to an otherwise daunting structure. For a law office, it holds enough charm to appear less unnerving.

I fist the strap of my purse tight, take a deep breath, and stroll toward the entrance as I mumble self-assurances to settle my nerves.

Two feet from the door, I freeze and stare at the handle as if the metal will scald my skin. A delusion that holds no truth, but since Sunday evening, most of my thoughts have been a mishmash of chaos. How could they not be? Anyone in my shoes would freak out. Scream and tug at their hair. Ask why this was happening. Hell, plenty of people would behave much worse. Turn physically violent.

But I rein it in. I have to. For Clementine.

I clench my palms then release the tension and stretch my fingers straight again. *You got this. No one will take Clementine from you. No one. Just breathe.*

For days, this has been my mantra. What has kept me moving forward every time I want to crawl in a hole and wither. Fingers crossed this attorney will give me good news. I *need* good news.

Reaching out, I clasp the handle and open the door. *See, Autumn. Nothing to fear.* I step inside and meet the gaze of a young man behind the reception desk. His short blond curls bouncy. Periwinkle button-up undone at the collar. Bright smile on his face as he sits taller and faces me.

"Good morning. How may I help you?"

I step up to the counter. "Good morning. I have an appointment with Ms. Chang. Autumn Rooker."

He reads the computer screen and clicks the mouse a few times. He nods then faces me again. "Yes, Ms. Rooker. If you'll have a seat, Ms. Chang will be with you in a moment. Feel free to grab some water, coffee, or tea."

I thank him and amble over to the waiting area, taking a seat and foregoing the drink. Last thing I need is to fill my bladder then excuse myself in the middle of my appointment. Not only would I embarrass myself, I would probably pay for it—literally—since most attorneys are paid via time put into the case. Every minute counts. Every minute costs.

I weed through a handful of junk emails on my phone before I hear my name called. "Ms. Rooker?"

I lock my phone and shove it in my purse, then look up to meet a petite Asian woman. Her long black strands up off her neck and swirled into a prestigious bun just above the base of her skull. Although she appears of similar height, she stands taller. Fearless. Formidable. Her black pantsuit with an ivory silk top screams *powerful woman* and immediately boosts my confidence. She extends her hand.

"Theresa Chang. Thank you for waiting."

I shake her hand and rise from my seat. "Autumn Rooker. Thank you for seeing me on such short notice."

She guides us down a short hall and steers us into a conference room. At the opposite end of the room, a floor-to-ceiling window illuminates the room. Outside the window, plush green shrubs and colorful flowers add to the view. A hint of shade from one of the oak trees balances the bright morning sunlight. A large, refurbished oak table with a small potted plant in the middle occupies the heart of the conference room. The ivory walls decorated with framed art that has nothing to do with law and everything to do with family. A watercolor of a woman at the park pushing a child on the swings. A photograph of two men side by side, each of them holding a baby. Hand-drawn crayon pictures of stick figure families. And so much more.

My eyes blur. Pulse turns wobbly. Breath comes in jagged bursts.

I chose the right woman for the job.

"Have a seat Ms. Rooker and we'll get started."

Over the next hour, Ms. Chang—who insists I call her Theresa—reviews the documents I received. She asks several questions regarding me, Clementine, and Leo. After our thorough discussion, she addresses the financial end of things—which is hefty, but not as bad as I originally expected. All in all, the appointment wraps up with me less stressed and a strong woman standing at my side. A woman who has every confidence we will walk away from this better than before it began.

After I pay the retainer fee and sign documents to allow Theresa to start the proceedings, I walk out the door and unlock Betsy. I start the car and crank up the heat while I gather myself. For the first time since Sunday with Jonas, I smile. Not one worthy of awards, but a smile nonetheless.

Dealing with this lawsuit won't be easy. Fortunately, I found a woman who will fight to the bitter end beside me. Her confidence the exact boost I needed. And now, it's time to share the good news.

I dig through my purse until I locate my phone. Without giving any thought, I open the text history between me and Jonas and type out a message.

> Spoke with an attorney. She is optimistic I won't run into trouble.

I hit send, tuck my lips between my teeth and stare at the screen, impatiently waiting for Jonas to respond. Glancing at the time, I remind myself he is at work and might not be able to answer. But as the thought crosses my mind, the indicator bubble pops up.

> Glad to hear. How are you?

He doesn't seem upset. Thank god. I have put him through the wringer since this started. And I worried my putting distance between us would upset him. Without a doubt, I'm sure he misses me as much as I miss him.

> Better now, but still a little frazzled. I miss you.

> Miss you too, scarlet.

As soon as the term of endearment flashes on the screen, I audibly exhale. With everything going on, I have been so laser focused on how to handle things with Leo. Meanwhile, I dropped all interaction with Jonas. Granted, I did it because I thought it was the appropriate thing to do. But Theresa told me to live life as we have been. Knowing Jonas still holds me close to his heart is a major relief.

> Can we have dinner tomorrow?

> Definitely. Mine or yours?

> Your house. Clementine misses Spartan. And you.

> See you tomorrow, scarlet.

Four days have passed since I last saw Jonas. Four very long, painstaking days. I miss him on an unhealthy level. A therapist would undoubtedly tell me this. Doesn't matter, though. Can't tell your heart what to feel. It also isn't wise to deny your heart what it wants. Even if what your heart desires may hinder your future.

Theresa told me to live life how I had been. And I want to. More than anything.

But something niggles at my subconscious. Tells me Leo will use my life and how I spend my time as a weapon. Hold it over my head and taunt me.

Sure, several factors of my relationship and history with Clementine weigh in my favor, but Leo—and his family—have money. More money than fathomable. If Leo wants something bad enough, he will have no issue paying the "right" person to get the job done.

I toss my phone back in my purse, grip the steering wheel, and take a deep breath. I stare at the jagged bark on the old oak tree and lose focus. Taking this fraction of time for myself, I let my thoughts roam free.

How do I live life normally? Is there a way to blend how life was before I dated Jonas with us being together? A middle ground.

The last thing I want is to alienate Jonas—and Spartan—from my and Clementine's life. In such a short period, they mean so much to us both. But I also don't want to become complacent. Don't want to rely on the assurances of my attorney—not that she isn't brilliant, but I haven't seen her in action yet—especially when the livelihood and well-being of my daughter is on the line.

Middle ground. At least for now.

Somewhere in the middle is better than nowhere at all. Right?

For the first time all week, the workday doesn't feel forty hours long.

I cash out the final customer of the day, walk them out, and give my practiced business goodbye. Once they drive off, I lock the office door and join Dad in the garage as we close everything up for the night. Currently, we stow one vehicle as we work on extensive repairs, but most of our recent clients have been easy same-day jobs.

As I stash the last of the tools in bay one, Dad coughs to get my attention.

After Monday, I have kept to myself most of the week. Conversations with me have been nonexistent. I arrive at work, spend fifteen or so minutes in the office, work until lunch, sleep on the couch at lunch, then work until the garage closes. I mind my own business and only speak when absolutely necessary. Today may have been the only exception. I probably spoke a few more sentences. And I blame it all on the fact I will see Autumn and Clementine soon.

I glance over my shoulder at Dad but don't say anything. His cough was intended to get my attention. Attention does not equal spoken words.

"How're you holding up?"

I shrug. "Been a rough week. Haven't seen my girls since Sunday night. But they're coming over for dinner tonight, so…" I trail off and finish my task.

Unexpectedly, Dad sidles up to me and hugs my side. "Sorry you're having a rough patch. And I know you don't want to talk about it. But if that changes, you know we're here for you."

The Thompson family unit. Although all adults, we are a tight-knit bunch. We stand by each other no matter what. Mom and Dad instilled that in us. Even at their most annoying stages, Jasmine and Jillian have always been there when I needed them. Have given me the female perspective I sometimes require. And vice versa.

"Yeah, Dad. When Autumn is comfortable with me sharing, I'll explain."

Dad gives me another hug, this one front facing and more constricting than an anaconda. And I let him squeeze the air from my lungs as I revel in the love he passes on. And for a brief moment, I close my eyes and embrace him with equal fervor. Then he pats me on the back and releases me.

"Just keep reminding yourself everything will work out in the end. All you need to do is be there for her, however possible. Now get out of here and go home. I hear you have a date with two special ladies."

A small smile curves up one corner of my mouth. "Thanks, Dad. Tell Mom I say hello. Have a good weekend."

"Will do. You too."

After I strip out of the coveralls, I throw on my jacket, zip it up, and hop on the bike. Helmet on, I spark the engine to life and drive home. The road mild with traffic as the wind whips the exposed skin between my helmet and collar. I don't move to raise my collar and shield my neck. Instead, I let the bite remind me I am alive. Not only alive, but that I also get to see my girls tonight.

My girls.

Fuck, I have missed the hell out of them. Autumn's cognac eyes and natural radiance. Clementine's boisterous tendencies and sweet laughter. The way Autumn holds me close and breathes me in as if she never will again. How Clementine has full-blown conversations with Spartan as if they speak the same language.

Saying I miss them doesn't seem sufficient enough. More like an afterthought or brush-off. No, being apart from them has me missing a piece of myself. A huge piece. An absence. And I will do whatever it takes to have them back. To make us whole.

I park the bike in the garage, set my helmet on a shelf near the door leading into the house, then head inside. Spartan immediately loses his shit the moment I set foot in the house. But this is typical, even if I leave for fifteen minutes. Spazz is his middle name.

"Chill out, I'm coming." I shut off the radio and open the door on his crate. He flies out as if a wasp stung him in the hindquarters. "Wears the fire at, little man. Come on." I point to the door that leads to the backyard. "Let's go outside a minute. Then Dad needs to get to work."

Spartan bolts outside the second I open the door. He locates the perfect blade of grass, lifts his leg, and does his business. Typically, he runs off after, but tonight he dashes back into the house. Like he knows his new best friend is coming over and he needs to prepare himself.

Me too, buddy. Me too.

Back in the house, Spartan goes to the couch and grooms himself. Suppose licking his coat clean is his form of preparation. Whatever. If it keeps him out of my hair while I make dinner, I won't complain.

I get to work on dinner. Tonight's meal will be easier than usual, so I get more time with Autumn. From the freezer, I grab a bag of waffle fries. Then grab the turkey burger patties I set in the fridge to thaw. After setting the temperatures on the oven and stove, I toss the fries on a baking sheet and take the burgers out of the package.

Once both start cooking, I grab the pretzel buns and burger toppings. I slice up tomato, onion, and pickle, then tear up a few leaves of lettuce.

Just as I close the oven door after stirring the fries, Spartan barks like a banshee. *They are here.* I turn down the burner and head to the door. The second I open it, Spartan shoves past me, practically knocking me on my ass, and runs for Clementine.

"Sparty!" Clementine hugs his neck while Spartan licks her like a fiend.

"Let's go inside, pumpkin."

"Sparty, come on. You heard Mama, let's go inside." And just like that, Spartan runs into the house with Clementine on his haunches.

I open the door farther and let Autumn pass. She looks like my girl but exhausted as hell. Maybe more drained than me. The dark half-moons under her eyes appear tattooed like permanent makeup. Her cognac irises more transparent than usual; as if the fire in them almost burned out. And her frame seems thinner, cheeks more hollow, lips less pouty.

Seeing Autumn like this wrecks me. Tears me limb from limb. Going forward, I don't care what the hell is happening, we won't spend this much time apart. Not when it slowly crushes us all.

I shut the door and turn to face Autumn. Before either of us says a word, Autumn steps into me and wraps her arms around my waist. Without hesitation, I snake one arm around her center while the other presses her close to my heart. Resting my cheek on her hair, I inhale deeply and bask in her perfume. One that has slowly faded from my sheets. One that reminded me she was here not so long ago. Time ticks on as we stand unmoving near the door. We shift to inch closer together but don't move otherwise.

Too soon, I lift my cheek from her hair and inch back slightly. Autumn peeks up, her lips a breath away from mine, and I see a hint of the fire returning to her intoxicating irises.

"Hey," I whisper, gaze locked on hers.

"Hi," she whispers back. "Missed you."

"Missed you more."

A small half smile perks up the corner of her mouth before she pushes up on her toes and presses her lips to mine. Warm and soft. Exactly as I remember.

Autumn kisses me sweetly as she curls her fingers in the cotton of my shirt. I frame her face and trace my tongue across the seam of her lips. As if we kissed thousands of times, Autumn opens up for me and tangles her tongue with mine. The kiss is slow and meticulous while we taste each other for the first time in far too long.

Far sooner than preferable, I break the kiss. Autumn slowly opens her eyes and stares up at me with hunger for something other than food. As much as I want to gift her that, now is not the time.

"Come on." I take her hand and start toward the kitchen. "Help me finish dinner."

I flip the burgers one last time and add cheese to each. Autumn gets plates from the cabinet and starts assembling toppings and condiments for everyone. Once the fries come out, we add the patties and fries to the plates and sit down to eat. Spartan whines as I go to sit, reminding me he needs his dinner too.

Over dinner, Clementine shares all the school stories I missed throughout the week. She tells me about one boy who always picks on her—says her clothes are weird or she doesn't have normal hair. I softly chuckle and tell her that is what boys do when they secretly like girls. The face she makes—as if a foul smell sits under her nose—is the cutest thing ever. Oh, how I missed my girls.

Once we finish eating, I set the plates in the sink and tell Autumn to ignore them. Clementine and Spartan get cozy on the chaise as we find a movie to watch. As the intro of *Finding Nemo* lights up the screen, I lie on the couch and create space for Autumn to lie beside me. Rather than lie with her back to my front, she settles in so we are face to face.

Minutes pass and neither of us says a word. We simply lie here and study the patterns of the others' irises. I get lost in the swirl of honey and cognac and love. Memorize the fan of her lashes and arch of her brow. Autumn leans in, lifts her hand to cup my cheek, and I close my eyes a beat before our lips connect.

The kiss is soft. Gentle. A reminder of the connection we share. It isn't lust driven. Not one ounce of it. The root of our bond is incomprehensible. Stardust and luster and vitality. An invisible force of life and love.

I break the kiss and hold her gaze. Although I could keep my lips on hers for days, I also want more than just the physical. I need to know her heart. "How are you?" I whisper-ask.

Her eyes drop to my lips as she swallows. "Better now. Until my appointment yesterday, I couldn't catch my breath. Thought everyone I loved would be stolen from me."

I lift a hand to her cheek and stroke a thumb across her more prominent cheekbone. "Won't let that happen." And I mean it. With every ounce of strength I possess—mentally, emotionally, physically—I will not let anyone hurt Autumn. Or Clementine. Ever.

"How can you be so sure?"

I lower my hand and press my palm to the left of her sternum. For a moment, I stare at my hand as it cradles her heart. "Autumn, you and Clementine mean more to me than anyone. *Anyone*." Her eyes glass over as she tucks her lips between her teeth and swallows. "No matter what obstacles pop up, I will be here to help you, to help us, overcome them."

She releases her lips as a tear rolls over the bridge of her nose and splashes on the couch. "But what if he t-takes her?" she croaks out.

Leaning in, I kiss her forehead. "Between me and you and your attorney, and probably anyone who knows you and Clementine, no one is taking her from you. No one."

"God, I want to believe it. Been telling myself the same thing since Monday morning. But every once in a while, doubt creeps in. With his money, the possibility of him pushing me hard is plausible."

I tuck fallen strands of hair behind her ear. "Scarlet, all things are possible. Even the outcome being in your favor. Although it's difficult, you have to believe you will win. Put the positivity out into the universe. You are a wonderful mother. Have done everything right by Clementine. You may not have an overflowing bank account, but money does not make a good parent. Providing a loving and safe home for them does. Making sure she goes to school and smiles and is happy, those are what matter most."

"But..."

I press a finger to her lips. "No, Autumn." I tip her chin up so her gaze meets mine again. "You are a terrific mother. Please believe it. Tell yourself you are. Make a list of why you are and read it when you doubt yourself."

She nods as her eyes drift back to my lips. I close the space between us and press my lips to hers. They taste salty and sweet like kettle corn at the state fair. I savor the taste and remind myself this sadness is only temporary. A hiccup.

As long as Autumn and I are together, we can get through anything. And we *will* get through this.

Being back in Jonas's arms again is nothing short of bliss. Not even a full week passed and yet it felt as if we spent months apart. With every brush of his lips, the idea of taking our relationship slower becomes more of a challenge. With every calloused caress of his fingers along my skin, I question how I will take a step back.

Then I shut down my inquisitive mind.

We should slow down. I *need* us to slow down. Spending less time with Jonas will be difficult. But fighting to keep my daughter supersedes my personal needs. I only hope I don't let Jonas drift too far and lose him in the process.

Seven-plus years have passed since I last saw or spoke with Leo. The Leo I knew in the past also didn't remotely resemble the Leo I met last weekend.

Thinking back, I don't recall Leo as pretentious and mighty. When we were together, he held a softer side. He had yet to be influenced by the patriarchy of his family. But life changes. Who you surround yourself with alters your perception of the world. And Leo has several larger-than-life people circling him.

What do I have? A group of overprotective tattoo artists, a goofy-ass friend, and a man who will do anything for me. Who will do anything for my daughter.

Is that enough? Is my small, yet consequential, circle of people enough to go up against Leo's army. In all honesty, I don't know.

Before visiting the attorney yesterday, I spent several hours online. Searching for anything and everything on Leo. News articles focusing on him and the business he and his family own. Is business good or bad? Has he been seen with women? His dating status was vital for several reasons.

One… if Clementine did spend time with him, who else would she be spending time with? What is Leo's family like now? In our time together, he never spoke much about them and introductions never happened.

Two… is he in a long term committed relationship or does he play the field? Important because my daughter does not need to be subjected to a revolving door of playmates. And after my history with Leo, I don't picture him committing to one woman for years.

Three… what types of women does he date? Are they bitchy and pretentious? Do they like children?

Ugh!

The questions constantly trickle in. The more research I did, the more questions I scribbled on paper. One photo of him, in particular, continues to throw gasoline on the slow-things-down-with-Jonas fire.

A professional photo of Leo alongside his father and two brothers, all wearing tailored five-piece suits that ooze money, smiling at the camera as they cut the grand opening ribbon on their fortieth luxury hotel in the state. Four-zero.

How do I compete with a family like his? How do I keep the most important person in my life when I have nowhere near the same resources as he does? His net worth is more than I will make in my lifetime.

Jonas runs the tip of his nose along the side of mine before dropping a chaste kiss on my lips. My eyes refocus and lock with his.

"What has you thinking so hard? Your cogs are in overdrive."

A brief glance over my shoulder, I check on Clementine. In her own world, she curls up with Spartan, her head on his belly. Her little fingers wiggle in his fur as she watches the movie. And I take a mental snapshot of the moment. Of her happiness with her new best friend. Of her innocence.

For as long as I am able, I want to shelter her from the case. Shelter her from all the bullshit. The last thing Clementine needs is to stress over a battle she cannot fight. Or worry about a man she has never known.

I roll back to face Jonas again. His fiery hazels lock with mine, studying every move and expression. Gauge every fissure and twitch and almost spoken word, patiently waiting for my response.

God, I have never met someone so patient. Someone who will lie beside me, unspeaking for hours, and wait. Wait for me to find the strength and courage to speak or act in my own time.

How the hell did I get so lucky?

"He's so different from how I remember him," I whisper.

"How so?"

Where do I even begin? A major gap exists between now and then. Suppose the start is as good a place as any. How else can I explain the old versus the new Leo to Jonas? Explain how we met—two people from polar opposite lives.

Taking a deep breath, I dive in headfirst. "Leo and I met at nineteen. Neither of us knew much other than high school and a glimpse of adulthood. We both still lived with our parents. Parents who forced us to attend a fundraiser in Tampa." I pause to lick my lips, small snippets of the evening flashing in my memory. "Even then, Leo had the capability to get whatever he wanted. Always the smooth talker." I roll my eyes. "Mom and Dad insisted I attend the fundraiser with them. The church mentioned the event would raise proceeds to help a fellow member with MS. Each ticket cost a fortune, but the money went to a good cause. But the major influx of money came from auctions."

I close my eyes and take slow, methodical breaths. Jonas trails his knuckles softly over my cheek. "Stop anytime you want. Please don't feel obliged to tell me everything."

Nodding, I take another second to rein in my emotions. Meeting Leo wasn't necessarily all bad—when things were good, they were really good. Plus, Clementine wouldn't be the most astonishing part of my life if not for Leo.

Slowly, I open my eyes and study the staggering man in front of me. A man who wants nothing other than my happiness. My heart. I lean forward and press a tender, quick kiss to Jonas's lips.

"About an hour into the event, Leo approached me and introduced himself. We chatted briefly—two bored teens, forced to attend an event with their parents— before he asked me to dance." I didn't know how but agreed. It was better than sitting at the table with my parents.

"Before the night ended, we exchanged phone numbers. The first few weeks, we texted back and forth. Nothing important. Just idle chitchat. After a month, we went on our first date. He didn't ooze money then, but you could tell by his clothes and car he wanted for nothing. Not that my family was poor, but we didn't have anywhere near the same means."

I take a moment to catch my breath. To settle the bubbling anxiety beneath my diaphragm. "Anyway, we went on a date and really hit it off. One date led to another, and it wasn't long before we'd been together six months. It was close to New Year's, so we decided to celebrate. Although neither of us could buy alcohol, he had access to plenty. The both of us were so drunk, and we forwent a condom."

When I stop to gather myself, Jonas kisses the tip of my nose as his fingers toy with the length of my hair. I love his supportive nature. How he lets me set the pace while he holds me close. And the small gestures and touches to remind me he's still here.

Taking a deep breath, I mentally prepare to trudge through the ugly part of my relationship with Leo.

"A week before my twentieth birthday..." Jonas's eyebrows shoot up, silently asking the date. I chuckle. "Top secret. But I'll tell you soon." He shakes his head, kisses my nose, then gives me a nod to continue.

"A week before, it dawned on me I hadn't gotten my period since mid-December. Needless to say, I freaked out. Went to the store and bought every pregnancy test brand on the shelf, embarrassed as hell." I didn't have a job, unless you counted my measly pay from helping Dad at church, and I still lived at home. College was a bust because my parents convinced me art wasn't a notable major. The thought of becoming a mother with no future made me nauseous.

"Days before my birthday, we went on a date and I broke the news to Leo. At first, he remained quiet. Speechless. He didn't seem mad, except maybe at himself. The rest of the date felt awkward and ended sooner than usual. After that night, I never heard from him again. He either blocked me or got a new phone number. I had never been to his house, so I had no idea where he lived. By the time I pieced together he'd abandoned me—us—I told my parents. Telling them turned into a vicious cycle of one-sided conversations where they told me how disappointed God was with me. So, I packed up what mattered most and left."

As painful as I thought it would be telling Jonas this piece of my past, I harbor no apprehension. If anything, relief enters my veins. A major chunk of burden weighing down my shoulders lifts away. Some of the ghosts from my past vanish as the hurt I subconsciously held on to releases.

"How did you meet Penny and the guys?"

I close my eyes as love blooms beneath my breastbone. Although life hadn't been easy after I left home, I wouldn't change anything. Not even the times when I questioned whether or not I'd be able to eat.

"For a week, I stayed at a shelter for women. They had resources for jobs and provided me with so much love and support. With my love for art, I read over every art-related ad first. An ad for the shop popped up."

Clear as day, I see the ad in my head. *Tattoo shop seeking artist to help draw intricate pieces.* I had never set foot inside a tattoo shop. My parents would probably have a heart attack at the mere thought of it. Which is the exact reason I applied.

"Penny worked the front then too, and I instantly fell for her spunk and I-don't-give-a-fuck mentality. She may be a year younger than me, but even then, she had her shit together. The more we talked, the closer we got. I still lived at the shelter and she found out. From that day forward, we lived together. After Clementine was born, Reznor took me under his wing and taught me how to ink."

As weeks and months passed, everyone at the shop became my family. They cared more for me and Clementine than my actual blood relatives. For a time, this ideal made me sad. But as more time passed and I learned what it's like to care for someone else, the memories of them drifted. The way I see it... their loss.

Jonas holds my gaze. Intrigue and awe and admiration spark his fiery irises. "Wow." He doesn't say another word. Doesn't need to. His wide eyes and slightly parted lips say more than enough. His wonderment has the chambers of my heart working overtime as I fall a little more for the man a breath away.

"Leo made a choice back then. Whether it was out of fear or anger or selfishness, he decided. I shouldn't be punished—again—for his decision. Neither should Clementine. And I plan to do whatever it takes to make sure he doesn't hurt *my* daughter."

Jonas snakes his arms around my waist and draws me into his chest. I fist his shirt, inhale his familiar scent, and sigh as every muscle in my body calms. This man is my mojo. My lucky charm. The only person who soothes my soul just by being in the same room. When Jonas holds me in his arms, nothing else matters.

"He won't take her from you, scarlet. A judge would have to be insane to allow it. Especially with his past taken into account and everything you have done for Clementine. You may not have forty hotels and a couple commas in your bank account, but you are an exemplary parent. You always put her first. Always. And that counts more than anything."

I gather his sentiment, hold it close to my heart, and bask in the heartfelt meaning. Our relationship may still be fresh and young, but I savor every kind word and gesture from Jonas.

During my appointment yesterday, Theresa stated the same. Just using different words. She also emphasized most mothers maintain custody of children unless deemed incompetent. The fact that Leo popped up out of nowhere is suspicious and concerning, and Theresa plans to dig up as much dirt as possible. Plans to see if there is an ulterior motive to his sudden appearance.

I snuggle closer to Jonas and breathe in the peacefulness he exudes. Let it fill my lungs and add life to my veins. With each passing minute, I feel more serene, more at ease. My confidence may not be tipping the scales in my favor, but it certainly weighs heavier on my side now than it did hours ago.

The music indicating the end credits echoes throughout the living room. I sigh heavily as Jonas kisses the crown of my head. The last thing I want right now is the absence of Jonas's arms. Or to go home.

But a voice in my head has me hesitant to stay. Whispering ways Leo will use my relationship with Jonas against me to obtain custody of Clementine.

And how did Leo know where I live? Has he been watching me all this time? Following me? I shiver at the invasion. If that's the case, he more than likely knows where Jonas lives too. Where I work.

My stomach rolls as if I just stepped off the Tilt-A-Whirl. I swallow down the urge to vomit.

Every bone in my body opposes, but I pull away from Jonas and sit up. Rest my elbows on my knees and drop my face in my palms.

Why has this become my life? Why am I the one nauseous over being with someone I care for? Deeply. This is horseshit. I shouldn't be made to feel guilty over wanting companionship and affection. And I shouldn't be punished—nor my daughter—for wanting more out of life.

I take a deep breath. Then another. And another. Jonas softly strokes up and down my spine. Soothes the pain a fraction. Again, I hate that we have to leave. But I suck it up and sit taller.

"Pumpkin, we need to head home."

Clementine snuggles closer to Spartan. "Why can't I stay with Sparty?"

"Not tonight. Maybe we can see Sparty again tomorrow."

Clementine groans and reluctantly slides off the couch. "Fine."

I watch my daughter pout as she puts her shoes on slower than any other time in her life. Occasionally acting as if the shoe doesn't fit her foot. She takes it off, loosens the laces more, then does it all over again. God, if she behaves this dramatically at seven, no telling what nonsense I will deal with when she is a preteen or teenager. Someone better rescue me.

Ten minutes later, Clementine finally has her shoes on and is ready to leave. She hugs Spartan so hard I hear him exhale. But he doesn't seem to mind. Jonas walks us out to the car. After Clementine hops in and buckles up, I start the car. As I shut the door to say good night to Jonas, Clementine mutters something about kissing and I shake my head.

Jonas tugs me close and bands his arms around my waist. "After having you here, I don't want to let you go."

"Me, either."

"Let me know when you get home. Would love to see you tomorrow. We can talk about it in the morning."

I fist the back of his shirt before leaning away and tipping my head back. Without hesitation, Jonas lowers his lips to mine and kisses me breathless.

In the kiss, he tells me how much he cares, how he will be at my side through thick and thin, and how we will get through this together. I match his fervor and pray he is right. Pray this ordeal with Leo ends quickly. That Clementine remains with me and comes out of this whole scenario unscathed.

Our lips break apart and Jonas places one last kiss on my nose. "'Night, scarlet. Talk to you in the morning. We'll plan the day then."

I nod, opening the car door. "'Night. Talk to you in the morning." And I almost slip up. Almost drop the *L*-bomb, but catch myself as I duck into the car.

Jonas closes my door and pats the roof. After buckling my seat belt, I throw the gearshift in reverse and back onto the street. Jonas waves and waits for us to drive off before going into the house.

I thought I should slow our relationship down, but I haven't the slightest idea how. And if I am honest with myself, I don't want to slow down. Quite the opposite, actually. The urge to sprint forward screams from every corner of my mind.

But the dark cloud that is Leo hovers over me with threats of robbing me of my joy. A joy no one can replace.

What the hell am I supposed to do? Standing at the proverbial fork in the road, I ponder which direction to take. As I steer the car left, I pray to whoever listens.

Please let this be the right decision.

six

JONAS

Coldness jabs my elbow. I groan and tuck my elbow more securely to my side. Just as I drift off, wetness replaces the jab. Poke. Nudge. Another round of moisture.

Argh!

I bolt upright, swatting the air. Spartan grumbles when I connect with his furry chest. With each breath in, disorientation fades as reality comes into focus.

I'm in bed. Spartan has been trying to wake me. And I actually slept. Not the best sleep, but sleep nonetheless.

"Give me a minute, bud."

I swipe a hand over my face and widen my eyes a few times. The sun bleeds through the curtains and brightens the room more than usual when I wake. What time is it?

Scooting out of bed, Spartan jumps down alongside me and races out of the bedroom. I grab my phone from the charger and click the side button. A little after eight. Wow. Sleeping past six thirty is a miracle on its own. Spartan doesn't always let me sleep in, but perhaps he knew I needed the extra time.

I set the phone down, shuffle out of the bedroom and over to the door leading to the backyard, where Spartan bounces like a kangaroo. As soon as I open the door, he flies out and whips across the yard. And just as quickly, he runs back in the house and bolts to his bowl, knocking it with his nose.

"You have way too much energy for me today. Maybe we'll get some playtime in later." Adding a scoop of kibble to his bowl, I ruffle his fur. He stops vacuuming his food long enough to glance up and give me his best doggy smile.

I amble back to the bedroom and flop down on the bed after snagging up my phone. I type out a text to Autumn and hit send. Clementine's energy often matches Spartan's, so I doubt she is still asleep.

> Morning, scarlet. Up and ready to plan the day whenever you are.

I head for the bathroom and go about my morning routine. While brushing my teeth, I ponder what to do with my girls today. The cooler air outside may eliminate some options, but there are still plenty of alternatives. Indoor options are endless—movies, arcade, bowling, wandering the mall, trampoline playground.

I swish and spit out mouthwash as my phone pings.

> About to eat breakfast. Give us at least 30 and come by?

> See you soon.

After a quick shower, I let Spartan out and whip up scrambled eggs and toast. Autumn said thirty minutes, but giving her and Clementine extra won't hurt. Finished eating, I wash the dishes then grab my wallet and keys. The second he hears my keys jingle, Spartan bolts inside his crate. I hand him a treat and turn on his radio then head out the door.

I type out a quick text to Autumn to tell her I am on my way.

Cracking the window, I shiver at the breeze blowing inside the Jeep. It should reach the upper sixties today, but with the sun beaming down, it will feel closer to mid-seventies. A day at the park may be an option if my girls are up for it. Perhaps a park Clementine hasn't visited yet.

I park outside Autumn's apartment and all but dash to the door. Seconds after I knock, Clementine squeals on the other side.

"Mama, he's here!"

Clementine's boisterous, joyful nature soothes me in an unimaginable way. Her radiant smile and sweet laughter cause my heart to swell in ways I never thought possible. It's strange. That exact moment you discover you were missing this odd-shaped piece of yourself. Not the piece that completes you as a lover. But the one that makes you whole as a man.

The door swings open and my girls stand a foot away with bright smiles warming their faces. And my heart. "'Morning, girls." I step inside, squat down to hug Clementine, then stand tall and kiss Autumn.

"'Morning, Mr. Jonas. Where are we going?"

Door closed, I reach down to take Autumn's hand in mine and walk us to the couch. The simple gesture warms my skin and jump-starts my heart. This feeling— like the start of a summer rainstorm, when two energies collide and turn electric— will never get old. Will never fade away. Not for me.

"Thought I'd ask if there was anywhere you wanted to go. It's nice outside. The park could be fun."

Clementine bounces in front of us. "Ooh, ooh, ooh. The park, the park. Can we go to the playground?" Seriously, she and Spartan must have taken the same bouncy pill this morning.

Autumn leans into my side and I inhale her cherry vanilla scent. The fragrance hits me, and I close my eyes. Relish the perfume I have memorized. And delight in the way it relaxes every ache in my body.

"The park sounds nice. Let's go to a different one. Okay, pumpkin?"

"Only if there's a playground." Clementine gives Autumn a look that states she is not to be messed with. I bite the inside of my cheek to resist laughing. Last thing I need is to provoke her sassiness, which reminds me of Dad with Lex during Wednesday night dinners.

"Promise we'll find the perfect park, pumpkin. Go grab your jacket, just in case."

Clementine runs down the hall to get her jacket. Autumn spins to face me and smiles. The dark circles under her eyes not as significant today. Like mine. The luster in her cognac irises glows brighter today. Warmer. More inviting and intoxi-cating. Her lips perkier.

All from spending time together. One evening. Nothing extravagant. A small increment of time. Enough to see and touch and hold each other. To breathe life back in our hearts.

I reach up and caress her cheek with my knuckles. The second our skin connects, she closes her eyes, leans into my touch and sighs.

"Missed you. So much," I whisper.

Her eyes slowly open as she nods. "Me too." Autumn twists just enough to press her lips to my palm.

Clementine rushes back into the living room, jacket in her clutches and a bright, toothy smile on her face. She grabs Autumn's hand and attempts to yank her off the couch. "C'mon. Let's go!"

The mini bubble of solitude Autumn and I shared seconds ago pops as we stand. Some people would be upset at the intrusion, but neither of us minds. Every moment with Clementine is a breath of fresh air.

"We were just waiting on you, slowpoke," she says, sticking her tongue out at Clementine as she grabs her purse and jacket.

Their banter continues as we exit the apartment and load up in the Jeep. All I think as they carry on teasing each other is how lucky I am. Lucky to have found this wonderful woman. And luckier that she came with a mini version of herself. Someone who makes us both smile, even on the darkest days.

I drive through Clearwater without direction. Unsure where to go. Until an idea pops in my head and I steer the Jeep toward Safety Harbor.

Clementine bops and sings to the song on the radio in the back seat. Autumn lip syncs the rock lyrics as she looks out the windshield and draws small circles on my upper thigh with her thumb.

Nothing has felt more right than the three of us. Nothing has made my heart thump as wildly than the three of us. Me and my girls.

Twenty minutes later, I maneuver the Jeep into Phillippe Park and drive toward the playground area. As I locate a parking space, Autumn spins in her seat to face Clementine.

"Hey, pumpkin." In the rearview mirror, I see Clementine perk up. "After we play on the playground a bit, I'd like to walk around the park. This park is special and I want to share it with you."

I cut the engine and turn to face the back seat. Clementine's eyes are wide as she stares out the window and looks at the trees.

"Why is it special, Mama?"

"A long time ago, this park belonged to the Native Americans. Their homes were here. They also cherished the earth and sun here, so there's a lot of special energy here."

"Really?" Clementine's brows shoot to her hairline while her jaw slackens. Her amazement is adorable. It makes coming here more memorable and special.

"Yep. We'll look at all the special places after we play at the playground."

We unload from the Jeep and Clementine runs to play. Autumn and I locate a bench in the sun and sit. Clementine climbs the ladder and slips down the slide several times. Then she goes to one of the mini rock-climbing walls and navigates the six-foot venture. Next, she hops on a swing and hurls herself back and forth to dizzying heights.

Autumn leans into my side, loops her arm in mine, and rests her head on my shoulder. Our fingers weave together and we both sigh at the contact. Not a single word exchanged. We simply sit here, in this peaceful place, with our eyes on Clementine.

Faster than anticipated, Clementine declares she is done playing and wants to go see the special part of the park.

The three of us wander hand in hand across a grassy patch. Within minutes, we reach a stairway made of large earth-colored flat stones. The couple dozen steps wide and shaded by moss-covered oak trees. We take the steps leisurely as we observe the park from a different vantage point.

On the landing at the top of the stairs, a large storyboard shares the history of the land with park visitors. We step up to the wooden sign and Autumn reads the story about the Tocobaga Temple Mound. The story of the Native American village that existed here before a conquistador arrived in the early 1500s. For a time, their cultures coexisted, but it wasn't long until European diseases caused their demise.

When Autumn finishes the story, Clementine's lips turn down as her eyes glaze over.

"That's so sad, Mama."

"Yes, it is. But many people say the energy from the Native Americans still lives here. That it gives them strength or soothes them or protects them."

Clementine peeks up at us, the skin between her brow bunching. "How?"

I squat down in front of her. "Well, the Native Americans prayed to the earth and sun and animals. Thanked them for shelter and food and life. Sang special songs to them and asked for their protection. The energy from their spirits is said to still live here."

Clementine stares off at the trees and whispers, "Wow."

Autumn takes Clementine's hand. "Come on, pumpkin. Let's walk around and see it all." Clementine nods, speechless.

We stroll without hurry down another, steeper set of stairs closer to the Bay. Every five to ten steps, Clementine stops and points to something fascinating her. A crooked tree, squirrels, birds. At a few trees, she steps up and places her hand on the bark as if trying to feel the energy. Who knows? Maybe she does. Children are more in tune with energy and the spiritual elements of the world.

When we reach the bottom of the steps, we walk along the waterway and stop to admire the Bay. I see the appeal Odet Phillippe had to owning this land in the mid-1800s. A glorious view of the water and nothing but peace.

My stomach grumbles and I press a loose fist to my belly to quiet it. Beside me, Autumn laughs as she fishes her phone out of her purse and checks the time.

"Might be a good time to grab lunch. It's almost one."

Time flies when with people who make you happiest.

It's like pulling teeth to get Clementine to leave, but she concedes when we promise to bring her back on a different day. We trek back to the Jeep, hop in, and buckle up. Since we aren't far from downtown Safety Harbor, I suggest we find a restaurant there to eat.

Soon, we walk into a pizzeria on Main and get seated. After perusing the menu, we decide to share a Sicilian pizza. But it's no shock when Autumn orders mozzarella sticks, toasted raviolis, and garlic knots for appetizers. Maybe with three of us here, there won't be as many leftovers. But let's face it, who doesn't love leftovers. My girl definitely does.

The second the appetizers hit the table, we each dive in. Surprisingly, three-quarters of the appetizers are demolished before the pizza arrives. Thank goodness we didn't order a large. I see possibly two days of leftovers in the future.

After our bellies are full and half the pizza gets boxed up, we head out and window shop Main Street.

Our county only has a handful of cute downtown districts and Safety Harbor is one of them. Most of the shops and restaurants here are locally owned. Everyone is friendly as they stroll up and down the sidewalks and visit the shops. Trees drape several sections of street and sidewalk, keeping patrons cool on summer days. Some buildings are colorful and grab your attention. Eclectic and unique, as are most of the downtown areas near us.

Clementine walks a few strides ahead of us. Her eyes scanning every storefront, eager to see what's inside.

I lean in and kiss Autumn's temple. "Today has been wonderful. Especially after seeing you last night."

"Agreed. I slept better for the first time in days."

"Would love to do our dinners again. I miss my girls."

"Miss you, too." I hear the dejection in her voice. Catch the minor twitch of her lips.

All day, I considered mentioning the party Cora and Gavin are throwing me for my birthday tomorrow. More than anything, I want to celebrate with Autumn and Clementine. But something keeps me quiet. Autumn's somber mood has me hesitant.

In all seriousness, why would she want to celebrate anything when her life feels as if it's being ripped out beneath her?

So, I don't bring up the party. As long as I get time with my girls—like today—I am happy.

"But?"

She tucks her lips between her teeth and watches Clementine as she stares inside a candy shop. "But I don't know if us being together right now will hinder things. While this case with Leo lingers, I mean. I can't lose her, Jonas," she whispers at the end.

I haul Autumn into my arms, bundle her close, and hold her as if she could slip from my reach. "No one will take her from you. Ever."

"How can you be so sure?" I hate how small her voice sounds. Fragile and vulnerable.

I make a silent vow, once this case ends, to never let her feel this way again. To never let another person make her feel helpless or frightened. No one hurts my girls. No one.

"Call it intuition or instinct or a vibe. You have enough love surrounding the two of you to protect you for a lifetime. No way someone like him will tear it down."

Autumn takes a deep breath and fists my shirt beneath my jacket. "Hope you're right."

Clementine dashes over to us and jumps up and down. "Mama, can we get candy from there?" She points to the shop. The all-window storefront displays hundreds of chocolates and taffy and tons of other confections.

"Sure, pumpkin. But not too many."

"Yay!"

And just like that, we mosey about as if our conversation was background noise since we don't discuss Leo and the case around Clementine. I just pray Autumn doesn't continue to believe shutting herself and Clementine away from the world is the best solution.

I will never leave her side but fear she may try to abandon mine.

seven

Our day has been absolutely wonderful. But also offbeat.

Spending time with Jonas lifts my spirits and eases some of the agony festering in my head. In the same breath, time with Jonas leaves me exposed. Wide open to what-ifs and dreams. Unfortunately, with all the shit Leo is stirring up, I cannot afford to live in the world of what-ifs and dreams.

Jonas parks in front of my apartment. After our conversation outside the candy shop, neither of us has spoken much. He means well and speaks the truth when he says I have a small army of people ready and willing to help me. But how will my family compete against Leo? Against everything his family has to offer? Money may not buy love, but, for the right price, it buys other things—including legalities.

When he cuts the engine, Clementine unbuckles her belt. "Wish we could have dinner at Mr. Jonas's house so I can see Sparty." The blend of sadness and sarcasm in Clementine's voice doesn't go unnoticed.

I twist in my seat and half smile at my daughter. "We'll see Spartan again. Just not tonight, okay?"

She huffs in the back seat and turns away from me. Why is it every time I feel I am making the right choice—not just for me, but also for Clementine—I appear the bad guy? Yes, she has bonded with Jonas and Spartan. Their connection should make me smile like a fool. And it did until Leo popped up. Now, their connection adds another pang in my heart because I have kept them apart.

But how do I tell her it's just until the case concludes? Which, fingers crossed, won't be long. What happens if I throw in the towel? What happens if I live "normally?"

If I live life as I did before Leo made an appearance, I have a sneaking suspicion my and Clementine's relationship with Jonas will be dragged through the mud. Become tainted and damaged. With his money and resources, Leo has the ability to dig up dirt—or create his own. The last thing I want is for me or Jonas to question each other. Our pasts or some fabricated version.

Seems easier to lay low and dial our relationship down until everything passes. Theresa never gave a specific timeline as to when this would end, but the way she explained the process, I foresee it wrapping up sooner rather than later.

Would I miss the hell out of Jonas? Undeniably, yes. In such a short period of time, he has become so much more than the man I date. He has brought me back to life. And with this minor hiccup of time apart, at least we will come out clean on the other side. Or so I hope.

I peer over at Jonas; his fiery hazels stare back at me with questions. Questions I wish I had the answers to. Sentiments I hug close to my heart.

Will you and Clementine come to the house again? What can I do to help? You know you're not in this alone, right? Please, let me help. Please, don't shut me out.

Before I open my mouth and say something undesirable, I twist in my seat and exit the Jeep. As soon as I do, Clementine opens her door. I extend a hand to help her down. She glances at it briefly, ignores it, and shimmies her way down without assistance. "I'm a big girl and can get down by myself. I don't need your help."

Knife to the heart.

Once her feet hit the concrete, I reach for her hand and stop her. "Excuse me, young lady." I drop down in front of her and wait until she looks me in the eye. When she does, I see fire and heartache. "You're upset, I get it. But that is no reason to be lippy with me. Was I mean to you?"

She bites the inside of her cheek. Behind me, Jonas comes around and stands near us. His stance and energy project his agreeance with me. *Thank, god.* He doesn't say a word, but provides me with the strength to hold my ground.

"No, Mama." Clementine hangs her head. "Sorry."

"Thank you for apologizing. Sometimes emotions make us say and do things we normally don't. So, remember to think about other people before you say mean things. Words hurt too, pumpkin."

She sniffles. "I promise to think harder next time."

Rising to stand, I hold my hand out to her and she takes it within seconds. Clementine is frustrated with the wishy-washy too. One week, we see Jonas every night. Then, without warning, I strip it all away. I recognize this wasn't fair of me to do. Maybe with more time and better explanation—not today, but soon—Clementine will understand my reasons.

Inside the apartment, Clementine dashes for the room we share. More than likely, she will be in there until dinner. She apologized for her behavior but now needs solitude to understand it all.

I step into Jonas and wrap my arms around his waist, peering up at him. "Want to help me in the kitchen?" I ask, praying he says yes. My cooking isn't horrible, but Jonas cooks pasta better.

He plants a quick kiss on my nose. "Sure. Have anything in mind?" I shake my head. "Okay. Well, let's go investigate our options."

We head into the kitchen and riffle through the fridge and cabinets. Within minutes, Jonas has chicken, carrots, potatoes, onion, garlic, and green beans on the counter. After I show him where to find the pots, pans, and cutting boards, he gets to work. He puts me in charge of cleaning and cutting the vegetables to roast in the oven. Then he gets to work on cleaning and cutting the chicken into smaller pieces.

Being in the kitchen with Jonas feels routine. Right. A part of who we are. The way we move around each other. How easily life flows when we are together.

In no time, we have a pan loaded with vegetables and olive oil, and a sheet pan covered in barbecue glazed chicken. We pop them in the oven—which I didn't realize Jonas preheated—and start cleaning up. He makes dinner seem so effortless. I would have given up sooner and probably eaten the leftovers from lunch. Or found something that required less preparation.

Once the dishes are clean, Jonas dries his hands, steps into me and draws me close. My hands automatically wind around his backside while his rest on my lower back and shoulders. And for a moment, we stand stock still. Silent. Nothing but our uneven breaths and pitched heartbeats filling the room.

I love being in Jonas's arms more than anything. Love how his warmth blankets me, protects me. Love the erratic tick of his heartbeat beneath my ear as I lay my cheek to his chest. I snuggle into him farther, not wanting this moment to end.

Which is the exact moment the voice of uncertainty in my head whittles at my happiness. Eats away at my smile. Steals the hope and joy in my heart. And I hate that I listen to it. Hate that the moment it creeps in, I drop my arms from Jonas and take a step back. That I let it overpower me. That I let it fill my head with hesitation and doubt.

"You okay?" he asks, lines marring his forehead.

I nod, although my internal voice screams *what the hell are you doing?* "Yeah. Shouldn't we check the food?" My excuse is lame, and Jonas is no fool. Since the day we pulled up to my apartment and spotted Leo, everything between us has been off-kilter.

"Set the timer." He peers around me. "Still have another five minutes before I flip the chicken."

And because I am irritated with my unsure mind, I remain tight-lipped and nod. When Jonas steps up to me again, I don't resist his embrace. But I don't give myself over to it as much as I long to. Don't melt into him. Don't clutch on to him as if my life depends on it—which is partial truth.

Until dinner finishes cooking, we hold each other in an awkward embrace. If I sense how odd the energy in the room is, he does too. But he doesn't say a word. He just holds me; his cheek resting on the crown of my head.

Dinner is quiet. Not even Clementine speaks up. The vibe while we eat is stifling.

Clementine is upset and pouts for good measure. I push food around my plate like a picky child, eyes glued to my fork. But even with my eyes downcast, I *know* Jonas is staring. I feel his gaze deep in my bones. Every other minute, he spears food on his plate in my periphery but does so blindly. When I lift my chin and catch his eyes on me, my assumptions are answered.

Before I open my mouth to stupidly ask what is wrong, Clementine speaks up. "May I be done, please?"

I glance at her plate, which is mostly clear. "Sure, pumpkin. Go pick a movie and we'll be there in a minute."

The moment Clementine is out of earshot, Jonas locks onto my eyes. "Did I do something wrong?" His voice so soft, I barely hear him. But in his tone, I decipher hurt.

Gah! I have been so worried and distracted with Leo and the case, I am already messing this up.

This is why separation—temporarily—is the best idea. Because I am screwing up the best relationship, the best man, in my life. All because I don't know how to balance our time together along with raising my daughter and dealing with an ex who gave zero shits about me or Clementine then suddenly does.

What *is* the right choice here? Feels as if there isn't one.

God, I like Jonas. Considering I almost slipped and said the *L*-word, I more than like him. He possesses every great quality I desire in a partner—kindness, affection, warmth, and he cares for Clementine as if she were his own. No matter how you spin it, I am lucky to have Jonas in my life.

But I can't stop thinking about Leo using Jonas as a weapon. What if he tells the courts I didn't give him a chance to be a father to Clementine because Jonas assumed the role? Although the idea is far-fetched, I wouldn't put it past Leo to say such things. Which is why I need my relationship with Jonas to slow down a bit. Not full-fledge stop, but ease off until I have better reassurances from Theresa.

Could the teeter-totter balance in the middle for just a bit.

"No, you've done nothing wrong. But I need you to understand how torn I am right now."

His chair scrapes against the tile before he rises and takes his and Clementine's plates to the kitchen. I follow in his wake, adding my uneaten food to a leftover container with the rest. Once all the dishes are rinsed and in the dishwasher, he spins to face me again.

"Can you please tell me what has you so divided?"

I take a deep breath and step within inches of Jonas. Reaching forward, I fist his shirt and peer up. "I feel… stuck. Like no matter what decision I make right now, it won't be the right one. If we go about things as if nothing has changed, what if Leo digs up stuff and pins us against each other."

"Autumn, I have told you about my past."

"Romantically, yes. But Leo's family can get dirty when they want something. No doubt he picked up the habit. He may not dig up something bad about either of us in the romance department, but what if you got into a physical altercation before? He may claim to the courts you have a history of violence."

"That isn't true, though."

"Yes, but his money will make it true long enough for him to win. Do you understand where I'm coming from now? Why I have been so tossed up? Jonas, I lo — care about you. A lot. And I don't need Leo ruining your life just for the hell of it."

Jonas closes the space between us and swathes me in his arms. "I care about you a lot too, scarlet." He kisses the crown of my head. "The only way he can ruin my life is to take you away from me."

Knife in the heart, twisting and digging deeper.

"Can we talk about this later? Let's go watch the movie with Clementine."

Jonas kisses the crown of my head again, then releases me. "Sure."

We weave our way into the living room and plop down on the couch. Clementine is a good twenty minutes into *The Nightmare Before Christmas* already. She lays sprawled across pillows and blankets on the floor, twirling the length of her hair around her finger. In no time, Clementine will pass out. She fights sleep by twirling her hair.

And as we do every time a movie plays while we are together, I curl into Jonas. Sometimes we spoon—his front to my back—but tonight I want to nestle into his chest. I burrow my nose where his neck and shoulder meet, and inhale his scent. A blend of working in the garage, sunscreen, and Jonas. My favorite smell.

His arms snake around my backside to press me closer while I hold on to him for dear life. Legs tangle. Breathing spikes little by little. Hearts thump, thump, thump to a vicious rhythm. But we don't move. We remain close, encased in our own little bubble of bliss.

When the familiar jingle plays for the credits, I quietly huff into Jonas's chest before separating us.

"Stay here," he says. "I got her."

I scoot to sit up. Jonas eases off the couch, crouches down, and gingerly scoops a sleeping Clementine off the floor. As he tucks her close to his chest and her little arms cling to him, I melt into the cushions. When he rises from the floor and snuggles her closer to his chest, Clementine reaches for his hair and plays with what her little fingers reach.

I stop breathing. While Jonas walks her down the hall to the bedroom, he whispers in her ear and she hugs him tighter. My heart melts and puddles on the floor. Doesn't matter what he said to her. His whispered words were meant solely for my daughter.

Jonas is so good with her. Cares for Clementine more than I ever imagined possible. More than I pictured any man caring for my daughter.

Which makes my indecisiveness that much more difficult.

A moment later, Jonas returns to the living room empty-handed. He sits on the couch beside me and picks up his shoes with hesitance. Jonas doesn't want to leave. I don't want him to leave. But until we know what type of Leo fire we need to extinguish, us sleeping apart is for the best. At least this is what I continue to tell myself.

When he finishes tying his laces, we rise from the couch as I walk Jonas to the door. We stop a foot away and Jonas closes the space between us. He brings one hand to my cheek, then the other. For a beat, he just holds me there, his gaze locked with mine. His face inches away, I swear he will kiss me any second.

He brushes the tip of his nose along the length of mine, and I close my eyes. Then his lips drop to mine. Warm, soft lips press to mine as I wrap my fingers around his forearms. His lips caress with such tenderness and devotion. Our breaths swirl in the air as we gasp between every other kiss. Then he slowly brushes the tip of his tongue over my lower lip. A shiver ripples through me before I open up and invite him in.

A hand slides into my hair while another drops to my hip and squeezes. I skim my hands up his chest, over the column of his throat, and into his hair, fisting the dark locks. We kiss until we need to come up for air. Even then, I need more of his kisses.

Foreheads pressed together, we work to settle our erratic breathing and hyper heart rates. I wish for this blissful bubble to never burst. Wish me, Jonas, and Clementine could stay in this happy place forever without disruption. But, right now, this wish won't be coming true.

I pinch my eyes closed and wish I felt confident enough to *not* do what I am about to do. Maybe I will get lucky and someone will smack the obvious against my skull. Until then, this is the only way.

"Jonas," I whisper between us. He inches back enough to see my face. To see the worry lines marring my forehead. The pain in my pinched eyes.

"Scarlet, open your eyes." It would be so much easier if I didn't have to *see* his pain when I say this. But I deserve to feel the impact. "Talk to me."

I tuck my lips between my teeth, take a deep breath, and swallow. "Until I get more details from my attorney, about Leo and any possible leverage he may hold, I think it's best we slow down more."

Jonas flinches as if I slapped him. "Slow down more? Yesterday was the first time I saw you in almost a week. After we…"

Now I flinch. I deserve the virtual slap to the face. He was going to say after we made love over the weekend. More than once.

"Please, Jonas. I can't lose her, or you. But I don't know how to navigate down this path. The only person who can guide us safely is the woman I just handed half of my savings to. And she's currently digging to find me answers. Until she does, I shouldn't jeopardize any chance I have of keeping my daughter."

Jonas drops his hands to his sides and steps back. The second step back hurts worse than the first. His eyes dart between mine, looking for any semblance of misunderstanding. When he doesn't find any, he shakes his head and takes another step back. God, why won't he say anything? His speechlessness kills me just as much as the pain smeared across his face.

He pats his back pockets before pulling his keys from the front. "I need to go," he mumbles.

"Jonas, please tell me you understand," I croak.

The longer we stand like this, the more pained Jonas appears. The backs of my eyes sting. I blink and blink, begging my eyes not to betray me while he stands here. Why did I believe this was the only viable solution? I need answers. Now. But all reasonable thought has left the building.

"Wish that was possible, Autumn." He shakes his head. I don't miss how he calls me Autumn instead of scarlet. Twist the knife a little more to the left. "Not like I have a choice. I'll be waiting in the wings. Let me know when I'm allowed to care for you and Clementine again. Hope it's not too long."

He steps around me, opens the door, and storms out. The door hangs open and I follow him with my eyes as he unlocks the Jeep, jumps in, cranks the engine, and whips out of the complex.

What did I just do? What the hell was I thinking? He's gone. Jonas is gone. And I did this.

I shut the door, lean my back against it, and slide down until my butt hits the ground. As soon as it does, a torrent of tears lets loose, soaking my cheeks and shirt.

Don't know how, but I need to resolve this mess. Quickly. I need answers from Theresa. Because this isn't like last weekend when Jonas and I parted. This isn't like after the bowling alley when I told him about Clementine.

No, this is a million times worse. And I fear I permanently messed us up. Ruined the best thing, other than Clementine, to happen to me… all because I am too scared to take a risk. Too scared to let love stand up and fight.

"Did you actually pay attention in body shop class, Ken? Or did you just watch videos on YouTube?"

Ken shrivels under my harsh criticism, but I don't give a fuck. Feels as if it has taken him ten times longer than usual to replace the rear quarter panels on the sedan he's working on.

"Jonas," Dad barks from the door leading into the garage office. "Office. Now." He doesn't wait for me to answer. Just pivots on his heel and heads inside.

I throw the wrench in my hand in the general direction of the toolbox, the metal on metal clangs and echoes off the concrete walls. Just as I open my mouth to snap at Ken again, Dad hollers from the office. "Now, Jonas."

Weaving between the cars in the bays, I head into the office. I shut the door and huff as I cross my arms. "What, Dad?" I bite out.

Dad steps up to me and points a finger in my face. "Don't you take that tone with me, son. You may be a man, but I don't deserve the shit coming out of your mouth."

I flinch, not used to hearing my father speak to me in such a harsh manner. He lowers his finger, then walks over to the couch and sits down. Eyes on me, he doesn't ask me to sit down, but his narrowed lids imply I do so. Taking a deep breath and dropping my arms, I amble over to the couch and sit.

"You need to talk to me, Jonas. I have put up with your foul mood for more than a week now. I've let some things skirt by because you are obviously upset. But yelling at the employees for no reason, I draw the line there."

I rest my elbows on my knees and drop my head in my palms. *Fuck, fuck, fuck.* I am a goddamn mess.

The last time Autumn and I truly spoke was when I left her apartment… ten days ago. After the way we left things, I haven't reached out. She texted once to say she missed me but left it at that. What did I say in return? Nothing. If she still wants to spend time with me, if she still wants our relationship, Autumn needs to be the one to take the leap. She needs to say something more than *I miss you.* Show me some indication she wants to see or spend time together.

"Haven't talked to Autumn in almost two weeks," I groan. "She said things between us needed to go slower because of her ex making an appearance and filing for custody." Beside me, Dad gasps. Not loud, but enough for me to hear. "Autumn thinks if we're together, the ex will use our relationship against her. I don't get her reasoning. And considering the guy ditched her before Clementine was born, I don't think he has a leg to stand on."

Dad pats my shoulder. "For obvious reasons, I didn't go to law school. But after seeing how friends of ours handled divorces and custody battles, I would side with you on this. If the man has never been around, his case probably holds no weight."

I lift my head from my hands and sit up straighter, peering over at Dad. "This is what I've tried to tell her. Even her attorney said to live life as she had before he showed. There has to be something she hasn't told me. Something else about him that scares her. Which bothers me more."

"Son, all you can do is support and be there for her. Even if it's sporadic. If she hired a good lawyer, this will work itself out soon. And although she asked for distance, don't keep hiding in the shadows. Reach out to her. If she doesn't want to talk, she won't."

This has been one of my fears. After this much time apart and no real interaction, will she just shrug me off? She has handled this without me for more than two weeks since it all came to light. Does she need me for anything at this point?

"Dad, if she doesn't want to talk to me… I don't think I'll handle that well. At all. You think the last ten days have been bad?" I shake my head and leave it at that.

"I don't doubt it, son. But stop for a moment and put yourself in Autumn's shoes. Imagine all the stress and uncertainty she has to deal with right now. Until not too long ago, her life was normal and boring. She went to work and spent time with her daughter. Then you came into the picture and stirred things up." I give him the side-eye and he holds his hands up in surrender. "In a good way. But she was still adjusting to a new way of life with you, then her ex blindsides her and threatens to take away her daughter. Son, she went into protection mode. Like any good parent would do. And I attest to doing irrational things while in parent mode."

"Okay. So, how do I insert myself into her life then? I don't want to overwhelm her. But I want to be there. Right now, it feels as if I don't matter. Like she could live without me."

The more days we spend apart, the deeper the ache in my bones. I can't seem to catch my breath. And the pain in my chest grows stronger each day. Worst of all, I get next to no sleep. So, all I have is time to think. And I just want my brain to shut the hell up. Just one night.

"Text or call her. Without too much detail, tell her how you're feeling. Don't make your chat a guilt-trip. Don't make it all about you. Ask her how things are going. If she's gotten any updates." Dad clasps my shoulder. "Son, it's okay to go at her pace. Just don't lose sight of her."

I nod. *Go at her pace, but don't lose sight of her.* Got it.

We sit in the office in silence for a bit. Dad knows I am marinating on his words. Trying to absorb and digest them. Dad may not have a wall full of college degrees or any special initials after his name, but he has always been a good listener and an even better advice giver. He has the patience of a saint. Who wouldn't after dealing with us Thompson kids?

Dad claps my shoulder and stands. "Heading back out to the garage. Stay in here as long as you need. Come back out once you're levelheaded enough."

"Thanks, Dad. Be back out shortly."

Once he exits the office, I fish my phone out from my coveralls. Unlocking the phone, I open my text history with Autumn and read her last message for the millionth time.

I miss you. Same, scarlet.

I take a deep breath and poise myself to type out a text. My fingers tremble above the screen and I close my eyes and take a few more deep breaths before I type.

> Sorry I didn't answer before. Miss you too. Terribly. How are my girls?

After I hit send, I question whether or not it's okay to still call Autumn and Clementine "my girls." But as soon as the three dots dance in the gray bubble, my doubt gets shoved aside.

> Clementine is a grump. Me too. I have another appointment with my attorney Thursday. Hoping for good news.

I don't know much about attorneys and the timetables for legal matters, but two weeks have passed since Autumn last spoke with them. Shouldn't there be updates already?

> Fingers crossed. I'd love to see you. No pressure, though.

Adding the last part was painful. As if I have ever pressured her into spending time together. If anything, I have been more relaxed than most.

> Me too. I promise. Soon. Gotta go - client.

I want to text her back and say more, but I stop myself. She wouldn't see it until later anyway. Maybe I should write her another letter. Her work hours are earlier now, so I would have to either drop it at her apartment or give it to Penny or one of the guys at the shop. Maybe I will just leave it at her door.

In the meantime, I should get all the advice I can right now. With my phone still out, I open up another text history and type.

> Busy tonight?

CORA

No, what's up?

GAVIN

Just watching Lord of the Rings for the 361,722,908,639th time.

CORA

Shush, mister.

> Mind if we hang? Could use some advice.

CORA

Come over when you're done with work. I'll cook.

GAVIN

Eat meat ahead of time, if that's your thing.

I laugh out loud, and it feels good to smile a moment. Although my time with Cora isn't as frequent as it once was, I still remember her no-meat diet.

> Not worried about it. I'll be there a little after 5.

CORA

See you.

GAVIN

It's your stomach. Later, bro.

I stuff my phone back in my coveralls and amble out of the office. Work is the last thing I want to do, but I need to pass the time with distractions. Later, I will ask Cora and Gavin the hundreds of questions brewing in my head. Hopefully, they will have answers.

~

After going home to let Spartan out and feed him early, I ride over to Cora and Gavin's house. At times, I still find it odd calling it *their* place.

Not a full year has passed since Gavin returned to Florida, and yet it feels as if several years have flown by. So much has happened since last April. Most of the monumental moments have occurred in the last two and a half months. In my eyes, anyway. Between Cora and Gavin getting married and me falling for Autumn and Clementine, life has been a whirlwind. And now with the custody case, seems I can't catch my breath.

I pull onto the paved driveway and park my bike behind Cora's car. Kicking the stand out, I rise off the bike and remove my helmet. For a beat, I stare at the small patio area just outside the back door. Most of the decor is small pieces Cora had before Gavin returned, but every now and then I spot new touches. Pieces that reflect Gavin's taste or their combined taste. As similar as the two of them are, I notice the small nuances after knowing my best friend for a decade.

If I get lucky, one day I will see pieces of Autumn in my life.

Taking a deep breath, I head for the back door. Although my family would be more than happy to give me advice with what's happening, my friends are what I need. People who are family, but in a different light. That have no bias because they know my childhood or want to soothe my wounds. Cora and Gavin may not have experienced the same hiccup in their relationship, but they have had hardships.

Just as I lift my hand to knock, the door swings open and a smiling Cora stands on the other side. "Hey." Without warning, she lunges toward me, grabs my hand, and hauls me forward. Her slender arms wrap around me and squeeze with unimaginable strength.

I welcome the embrace and return it. A year ago, Cora's hugs held different meaning. They once held the hope of something beyond friendship. Now, hugging Cora is like hugging Jasmine or Jillian. Full of warmth and tenderness and love, but familial.

"Hey," I say as I peel my arms away.

Gavin steps past Cora and pulls me in for a half hug and shoulder slap. "Hey, man. Come in."

My relationship with Gavin shifted quicker than imaginable. Since our conversation at Dave and Buster's, after he packed up his life in California, Gavin and I developed a slow but great friendship. Until I met Autumn, I remained envious of him. Now, I envy the bond he shares with Cora. A bond I believe lies buried deep between me and Autumn too.

The back door closes and I step farther into the house, Cora and Gavin following in my wake. As I make it past the short hall, hints of basil, garlic, tomato, and an unfamiliar savory scent flit through the air. After I set my helmet in the living room, I join Cora and Gavin near the kitchen on one of the barstools. Cora stands at the counter, slicing up a baguette. I follow her hands as she saws the serrated knife across the crusty bread. Watch as she mixes olive oil, herbs, garlic, and parmesan.

"Want a beer?"

I snap out of my daze and turn toward Gavin. "Yeah, thanks."

He twists the cap off and hands me the brown bottle before resuming his seat beside me. "So, what's going on, man?"

I lift the bottle to my lips and sip the local brew, the flavor more bitter than I'm used to. Setting the bottle down, I pick at the corner of the label. "Did you know Autumn has a daughter?"

Gavin says "no" at the same time Cora says "yes." Well, at least I am not spilling too much if Cora knows. I assume Autumn sharing with Cora would mean it is safe for Gavin to know.

"I haven't met her," Cora states. "But Autumn has mentioned her when we hung out—just her and me."

After another sip, I take a few breaths. "Her name is Clementine, and she is the cutest little girl."

Across the counter, a soft smile perks up Cora's lips. "What a sweet name."

"Yeah," I mutter as I continue to pick at the label. "I hope you meet her soon. You'll both love her."

"Would be great. Is Clementine the reason you need advice?" Gavin asks before sipping his own beer.

I nod. "Not the only reason." Peering up from my bottle, I glance between my friends. "Also regarding Clementine's estranged birth father's return."

Cora's eyes widen at the same time Gavin's jaw drops. *My thoughts exactly.* The timer on the range buzzes and we all jump.

After Cora extracts a hefty pan of lasagna from the oven, she sets it on trivets to cool before returning to the counter. "Are they back together?" Cora asks, hesitant to hear the answer.

"No," I answer with obvious relief. "He jumped ship while Autumn was still pregnant. Now, more than seven years later, out of nowhere, he has filed for sole custody of Clementine."

"Are you serious?" Gavin stares at me with fire in his eyes. The same fire that roars in my veins every time I mull over this whole scenario. "Why the hell would anyone even give his case merit? He hasn't been around."

"Right there with you, man. But Autumn isn't looking at it the same way. She believes his family's money will hold enough ground to take Clementine away from her. So, she's trying to be the supreme model parent. Which includes spending no time with me."

Without a word, Cora rounds the bar top, sidles up next to me, and hugs me. "So sorry, Jonas." She drops her arms and steps back. "How can we help?"

This is my dilemma. I don't know how anyone can help. Autumn is so stuck on thinking Leo will use our relationship as a weapon. I have yet to figure out how. So what if Autumn is in a relationship with someone other than the father of her child. This is not an abnormal occurrence in the world. If I were a piece of shit, then sure, it would make sense for Autumn to be concerned. But I care for my girls like no one else. They mean everything to me.

"Autumn is convinced the more I am in the picture while the case is open, the likelihood of her losing Clementine is greater. But I don't understand why. She needs someone to literally write it out that her ex has no chance of winning. And I don't know where to go from here. Dad tells me to be patient, but I'm losing it."

Cora shuffles back into the kitchen and starts portioning out lasagna for the three of us. "Do you want me to reach out to her? See if I can get a girls' day with her? Maybe she will explain her fears to me differently."

"Give it a try. Not sure she'll spend time away from Clementine, though. You may only get her on the phone."

Cora carries the plates to the dining table while Gavin brings the bread and dipping oil. I slide off my stool and join them at the table.

"I'll send her a text first. Check in. Haven't seen her since bowling, so it wouldn't seem odd for me to ask for updates. I won't mention our conversation."

I nod. "Thanks. Appreciate it."

Scooping a portion of lasagna onto my fork, I let it cool a moment before tasting it. The hot cheese melts over my tongue as I bite into something resembling meat. My brows pinch together as the flavors hit my taste buds.

"What do you think of the lasagna?" Cora poses the question with obvious curiosity.

After I swallow the bite and take a sip of my beer, I answer, "Thought you didn't eat meat?" Across from me, Gavin snickers.

"I don't."

I point my fork at the heaping square of layered pasta on my plate. "Uh, this states otherwise. Not sure if Gavin snuck it in, but there's meat in this." Now, Cora giggles and confuses the hell out of me.

"Nope. No meat. In fact, this lasagna is one-hundred-percent vegan. You like it, don't you?"

I startle with a slight shake of my head. "No denying it, but you better tell me what I'm eating before you expect me to eat more."

Gavin full belly laughs before shoveling another forkful in his mouth. Traitor. Not that I expect anything else. He loves Cora enough to eat whatever she cooks.

"Pasta, red sauce, plant-based meat, and cheese." She says the ingredients as if everyone eats them.

"And how exactly do plants equal meat or cheese?"

For the next half hour, Cora goes into a long drawn-out explanation of plant-based substitutes. Although it's not something I see myself switching to, I don't dismiss it either. If I would have eaten this lasagna anywhere else, I'd have guessed it was traditionally made.

The rest of our night is filled with light conversation and talks about upcoming projects Cora and Gavin have. And when I leave their house after watching something other than *Lord of the Rings*, I feel a little lighter. My relationship with Autumn may not be better, but sharing with my friends has helped. Plus, Cora reaching out to Autumn is perfect. Although Autumn has Penny, sometimes talking with someone outside of the situation makes a difference.

I hope it does. Hope it helps Autumn look at the case and us in a different light. That being with me won't hinder her chances. Hell, it might help.

But most of all, because I need her, maybe more than she needs me.

nine

Swiping the dampness from my cheeks, I slip out of bed and tiptoe out of the room. I have another thirty minutes before Clementine has to be up. I intend to use the time to shower away the tears staining my cheeks.

Steam billows throughout the bathroom as I step under the hot spray. Under the stream, I cry for the umpteenth time since this nightmare began. I cry for my daughter—who has been affected in this whole scheme, although she still has no idea what is happening. I cry for the man who cares more for me than anyone, who cares for my daughter as his own, and who I have sidelined.

Damn, I miss Jonas.

I miss the way he presses me against his chest and holds me close to his heart. Miss the warmth of his lips on mine, kissing me breathless and waking up my soul. Miss the fire in his magnificent eyes and the inferno he creates when we are skin to skin. But most of all, I miss having him beside me. His strength and heart and smile.

I am sick and tired of crying. Sick and tired of being punished for someone else's choice. Why the hell am I the one who suffers in all this? Why do Clementine and Jonas have to suffer? None of us have done anything wrong. I may be far from perfect, but I am a good person. Do good things. Make good choices.

The tears stop flowing as I rinse the suds from my skin. Before the bubbles swirl down the drain, anger replaces the tears. Anger for a man who has no right to disrupt my life. To insert himself after abandoning me and his unborn daughter. Uprooting the life we have built.

I crank the shower to cold and allow the frigid water to diminish the fire boiling beneath my skin. Because I need to remain as levelheaded as possible around Clementine. Even if just for show. Once I cool down to a simmer, I shut off the water and towel dry. Wrapping the towel around my torso, I tiptoe back into the bedroom.

As I tug a shirt over my head, the alarm clock buzzes on the bedside table. Clementine groans, rolls over, and slides under the comforter, as if hiding will make the need to get up vanish. I laugh under my breath as I turn off the alarm.

"Time to wake up, pumpkin," I singsong. "Gotta get ready for school." I rub the comforter where her back is and she wiggles.

"I don't want to get up."

"Neither did I, but we both have things to do today."

"Why can't I stay home from school today?" Clementine never stays home from school unless she feels sick, which is next to never.

"Because you can't stay home unless you're sick. Those are the rules," I remind her.

Beneath the comforter, Clementine starts coughing. "I don't feel so good, Mama," she croaks. *Nice try, kiddo.* I whip the comforter off of her and she yelps. Then, I tickle her. "Stop." Giggle. "Please, Mama. Stop." Snort laugh.

I pause the tickle fest. "Are you going to get up and get ready?"

Who knew a seven-year-old could scowl? Not me. But Clementine scowls for two beats before replacing it with another forced cough. "But I said I don't feel good."

"And you didn't mention not feeling well until I told you it was the only reason to miss school. Plus, you don't have a fever and you wouldn't be laughing if you were sick, even if I tickle you."

In the same fashion as she has for the last couple of weeks, Clementine jerks upright and storms out of the bed. She heads straight for the bathroom without a word. At least I convinced her early on to not slam the doors with Penny sleeping. My daughter may be upset, but she isn't heartless.

Once dressed, she meets me at the table to eat breakfast. I whipped up some quick cheesy eggs and toast. She sits down and eats. After a few bites, she peers up at me.

"When can I see Sparty again? He misses me."

I love how each time Clementine brings up Spartan, she mentions how he misses her and not vice versa. No doubt it holds true, but Clementine misses him more than she cares to admit. And I hate that I have separated them this long.

Yesterday, out of the blue, Cora texted me. When my phone dinged, I half expected it to be Jonas. Especially after he left another note on my car sometime between Tuesday night and yesterday morning. The note simple—*I miss you*. And I have a sneaking suspicion Cora's sudden interest in talking was sparked by Jonas. Either way, I was happy to talk with her. Penny is supportive, but she has too much inside information to give me an outsider's perspective. Which Cora did with perfection.

Our texts weren't anything spectacular, but she started it off with "heard you might need someone to talk with." An hour later and I had spilled my fears to her. In return, she told me I should share the same with Jonas if I hadn't already. Not until the end of our texts did she mention Jonas, and even then it was just that I should talk to him. Cora opted to play the neutral party to help steer us back toward each other.

"I bet he does, pumpkin. After my appointment today, I might stop by Jonas's work to talk with him." Clementine's face lights up. "But no promises." Her face falls again.

For a few minutes, we remain quiet. Clementine scrapes the fork tines across her plate between bites. After she finishes her breakfast, I take our plates to the sink and wash them. While she stomps around the apartment to grab her belongings, I ponder explaining to her why we haven't been to see Jonas and Spartan as often. She may be seven, and her little mind might not grasp all the ins and outs, but she has every right to know why everything has changed so drastically in such a short period of time.

Glancing at the clock on the microwave, I note we don't have to leave the house for another fifteen minutes. I walk into the living room and sit on the couch. Clementine should be out here in a moment with her backpack. And like clockwork, she stomps out and sits to my right.

"Pumpkin, I want to talk to you before we leave. About why we haven't seen Jonas or Spartan as much."

She peeks up with worry lines drawn across her face. "Is Sparty okay?"

"Yeah, pumpkin. He's okay." The lines on her face smooth out as she exhales.

"You remember the day we came home from the beach park with Jonas and there was a man outside?"

She looks up and to the left while bunching her lips. After a moment, she nods. "Kind of."

I take a deep breath and prepare for the most adult conversation with my seven-year-old. "The man who was outside when we came home that day, he is your father." I don't use the term dad because I have always seen a dad as someone who participates and spends time with their children.

"Mama, I don't understand."

"Before you were in my tummy, I met that man. Back then, he was nice. And we spent time together like I have with Jonas now. And after we dated a while, he became my boyfriend. When grown-up people date for long periods of time, they do certain grown-up things to show each other how much they care."

"Like what?" Clementine interjects.

Kind of walked myself into a corner with this one. "Things we will discuss when you're closer to being a grown-up. Anyway, after we showed each other how much we cared, you started to grow in my belly. But your father didn't want to be a daddy, so he stopped being my boyfriend and didn't talk to me anymore."

"He didn't love you?"

My poor sweet girl. Voice so soft and frail. If I tell her he no longer loved me, then she will assume it was her fault.

"Pumpkin, I'm not sure if either one of us really loved each other. We liked each other a whole lot, enough to make a beautiful little girl." I bop her nose. "But there are just some people in the world who don't want to have children, and that's okay. There are still plenty of other people who do."

The skin between her brows bunches. "So how come he was here that day?"

Here is the part I dread telling her, but I need to be open and honest with my little girl. "He said he wants to be your daddy." The confusion still sits on her face as she stares at me with unfocused eyes. "And he wants you to live with him and not me."

At this, Clementine jumps up from the couch and balls her little hands into fists. "He's not my daddy," she screams. "I won't let him be. I hate him." She snatches her backpack and storms to the front door, cutting our conversation off.

Penny comes out of her room, wiping her eyes. "Everything okay?"

"Peachy," I deadpan. "Tell you later." She waves and goes back into her room.

I grab my purse and head for the door. A few feet from Clementine, she unlocks the door and stomps out. Nothing like starting the day with a moody seven-going-on-seventeen-year-old. Can't wait to see her temperament when she actually gets closer to her teens.

The drive to her school lacks conversation, but at least she sings and bops to the music while staring out the window. As soon as we get to the drop-off point in the school car line, she hooks her backpack over her shoulders, grumbles out an *I love you*, and exits the car. I stare after her as she steps on campus and smiles at some of her friends. Sighing, relief fills me that she can at least smile with her friends.

Leaving the school, I steer the car in the direction of the attorney's office. Theresa said she had some updates she wants to discuss, plus a document I need to sign. After dealing with morning traffic for forty minutes, I park in front of Theresa's office. Today, the building isn't as intimidating as on my first visit.

I head inside, wait a few minutes, then am escorted back to the conference room. Over the next hour, Theresa explains how Leo holds no weight in the case. Since he intentionally left before Clementine was born, has never spent time with her or attempted to, and has never contributed to her well-being, the judge will side with us without question. Theresa assures me no amount of money will sway a decision in his favor. There is no justification or evidence to back up such a ruling.

The document I sign is for the court hearing toward the end of the month. *Sooner than expected, thank god.* I sign on the line and Theresa steps out of the room to make me a copy. During the minute of her absence, I go back and forth on an idea I have toyed with. She enters the conference room and I decide to heck with it.

"As I stated at our first meeting, I have no intention of giving up custody of Clementine." Theresa nods. "But I am okay with her meeting Leo's family, if they would like that. Supervised, of course. She would be so scared if I wasn't there."

Theresa smiles. "A kind gesture. Not many would be so nice. Not after everything you've had to deal with on your own."

"I like to offer second chances. We all make mistakes. If Leo's family would like to meet her, it's only fair of me to allow it."

"I will make note of it in your file, but we won't be mentioning this until the hearing. If we bring it up now, they may push for more."

"Sounds good. Thank you for everything you've done so far. Don't know where I'd be without you."

She offers another smile. "I'm here to help you win and relieve you of legal stresses. In the meantime, don't let this wear you down. Enjoy your life. You're an excellent mother and don't deserve any undue strain."

At this, I question my being with Jonas. Now is the perfect time to ask the proper person. "Theresa, I have a personal-ish question."

"Shoot."

"Does it look bad for the case if I am in a relationship with someone other than Clementine's father?"

Theresa cocks her head and studies me a moment. "Why would you think that?"

At this point, I don't know. "Honestly, I wasn't sure how the court would perceive it. Leo's family has money and can no doubt provide for Clementine. I didn't know if me being in a relationship would make me vulnerable. An easy target. If they could say my time is divided and not solely focused on Clementine."

Theresa scoots the paperwork aside, laces her fingers, and sets her hands on the table as she leans in. "Autumn, you are allowed to be in relationships. Long term or short, doesn't matter. You are allowed to continue living. Allowed to be happy, as is your daughter. I encourage you to be in a relationship. Lean on someone. Share the burden of this situation. Don't take it on alone if you have others willing to stand by your side."

Several people tried to tell me the exact thing Theresa said, but an unsettled part of me needed to hear it from her. Someone who knows the outcomes of cases like mine with different variables. In her twenty-plus years of practicing, she has surely seen every possible case out there. Has fought for women with similar circumstances.

"Thank you. You have no idea how much I needed to hear that. Especially from you."

We stand and she walks me out. "Don't worry about a thing. Do what is best for you and your daughter. If that includes you being in a relationship, then you do it."

I give her a quick hug and am a bit surprised when she returns the gesture. Theresa is more than my attorney; she's a friend too. And more than anything, I am grateful to have her fighting my case.

Leaving her office, I drive down the road with a smile on my face. Minus Clementine's outburst this morning, it has been a great day. Better than the previous twelve. And I hope it continues to get better.

I make a quick stop at the sub shop Jonas and I ate at during one of his lunch breaks. After I study the menu, I order us both sandwiches. Even if I didn't remember the correct sub, he won't care. Once the food is ready, I hop back in the car and drive up the street.

As I pull in the lot of Thompson's Garage, my pulse whooshes behind my ears. My breathing morphs from a walk to a sprint. With the car in park, I close my eyes a beat and work to settle my nervous body.

Our texts have been so abrupt—my fault, if I am honest. And he was so upset when he left my apartment a couple weeks back. Will he forgive me for my irrational fears? Will he take me back with open arms?

God, I hope so.

I turn the key until the engine quiets and look over at the bays, spotting Jonas right away. His gaze locked in my direction. I swallow hard, grab the food bag, and exit the car.

Here goes nothing.

Ten

JONAS

A familiar rumble echoes across the lot. The rumble any mechanic would automatically recognize as a classic car. When cars are created different ways, with different components and materials, they just sound *different*. Most newer cars are quieter—unless they have major issues or added upgrades. But classics have this low purr-like roar.

I roll out from under the pickup I work on and scan the lot. Sure enough, a black Bel Air I know all too well is parking near the office.

Rising off of the creeper, I stand, pull the red rag from my coveralls, and wipe my hands. I stare through the windshield at Autumn as she locks eyes with me. Feels as if I haven't seen her in years.

She breaks eye contact when she fetches something on the passenger seat and gets out of the car. Without a side-glance, I toss the ratchet in the general direction of the toolbox. When a loud clang rattles, I give myself a mental high five.

Autumn walks my direction—cute as fuck in a dress that makes concentrating impossible. The navy material V's at her bust, but doesn't dip too low. It hugs all her curves and stops at her knees. Large white buttons start to curve from her left hip to the base of the fabric at her midline. White accents the base of each sleeve, the neckline, and the waist. And like a cherry on a sundae, two houndstooth bows rest near her shoulders.

Not sure if this is her dressy look—since she had an appointment with her attorney—but I love it.

I meet her halfway. "Hey, scarlet," I whisper. "Happy to see you."

She smiles and my heart hiccups. "Brought us food." She swings a bag in the air.

I glance back at Dad and he tips his head toward the office. "Let's go inside." She nods and I direct us to a more private place to talk.

Once we reach the office, I strip out of my coveralls. "Jonas, what…" Before she gets another word out, I wrap my arms around her and breathe her in. She drops her purse and the bags of food to the ground and winds her arms around me, squeezing me as if I may disappear any minute.

We stand like this—unmoving, not a word spoken—for minutes. Autumn presses her ear to my chest and listens to my heartbeat. With one hand around her waist, I stroke the length of her hair with the other. I close my eyes and rest my cheek on the crown of her head. Breathe slow and steady as I reacquaint myself with her perfume, the feel of being in her arms, her warmth. Everything about this moment feels like returning home after years apart. No matter what, there is no way in hell we are spending so much time apart again. I may have said as much last time, but I don't care. She means too much.

"God, I've missed you," I whisper.

Her arms squeeze me tighter as she fists the back of my shirt. "Me, too. So much."

I lean away and she tips her head back, her cognac irises swirl as she soaks me in. Without hesitation, I lower my lips to hers. As soon as our lips meet, I am home again. Every tear, every spit of anger, every hair pulling moment since I last saw her disappears. Wiped away with the press of her lips.

The kiss isn't lusty or intense but expresses every emotion we experienced in our time apart. Deprivation. Anticipation. Hope. Love. It spins in the air, surrounds us, like a gyroscope.

Reluctantly, I break the kiss and press my forehead to hers. "Can we please not torture ourselves like this again?"

Autumn lays her palm on my cheek and strokes her thumb over my stubble. "No more torture. Promise."

I exhale and pull back to look in her eyes. "Thank fuck." I kiss the tip of her nose. "Let's sit down so we can talk and eat."

After picking the food bag up from the floor, I guide us over to the couch. Rummaging through the bag, I note she went to the sub shop I took her to months ago. And she ordered the exact same sandwich I got that day. Either she has a fantastic memory or she made the perfect wild guess. Either way, I smile at the notion.

We unwrap the brown paper from our subs and dig in. After each of us has a few bites, Autumn sets hers down, wipes the hint of mayo off her lips, and faces me.

"I'm sorry for how things have been between us since all this chaos started. It wasn't fair of me to not include you. Thought I was doing right by Clementine."

I reach for her hand and hold it between mine. "You do not need to apologize for loving your daughter. For wanting the best for her. And with her father showing up, neither of us knew what the best looked like."

She nods. "True. But I have a better grasp now." Autumn tucks her lips between her teeth as her jaw wobbles. "Jonas, it has been terrifying. Not knowing what will happen from one minute to the next." Her eyes glaze over. "I had it drilled in my head that if I wasn't the picture-perfect parent—and who knows what that looks like—I would lose Clementine. And although I have always been there for her, done everything to provide for her, I feared me being with a man other than her father would look bad in the court's eyes."

I give her a minute to catch her breath before speaking. "Not to come across in a derogatory way, but why would you think they'd look down on you for being with another man?"

Autumn sighs as her head slumps an inch forward. "I don't want to get into it too much because it rehashes bad memories, but my parents would be the reason." She closes her eyes a moment and swallows. When she opens them, I see the tears ready to spill. "Long story short, my parents don't believe a woman should be with any other man except the father of her children. Most people call my parents extreme. I didn't know any different until my late teens. In their eyes, when I told them I was pregnant, I should have married Leo. Of course, I got lectured several hours a day and handprints on my cheeks for having premarital sex. Until I left."

Just wow.

Yes, I have heard of people behaving like this. Only seeing the world as one way. Expecting or assuming every man and woman lived their life in this way. But I have never personally known anyone with such perceptions. I haven't met Autumn's parents, but if I ever do—after what she just said—I don't imagine the meeting will be pleasant.

"I don't know what to say. Sorry doesn't seem appropriate."

"It's okay. You don't need to say anything. I haven't seen or spoken to them in almost eight years. But every now and again, small tidbits of how they raised me creep in and fill me with doubt or fear. Make me wonder if I made the right choice when I left their house. Eventually, I remind myself why I chose to leave and the questions and uncertainty fade. But when Leo made an appearance, it was the first time since leaving I let all their hurtful words seep back in. Let them overrule every rational thought. And I don't want it to happen again."

I want to assure her it won't happen again. Not with me supporting her. But now is not the time to make such proclamations. Not when the case with Leo still looms over her like an angry thunderstorm.

"You know I'm here for you, right?" Autumn nods. "Good. Nothing will change that. You and Clementine are my world. My girls." A delicate smile tugs at the corners of my mouth. "Just don't shut me out again. Please."

I have never been the type of man to beg or grovel, but I will do whatever it takes to keep Autumn and Clementine close. Being without them for the last couple of weeks has been torture. The sleepless nights and lack of laughter and joy. My purpose had been stolen. Robbed by someone who holds no significance in any of our lives.

Autumn shakes her head. "I won't. It's been hard dealing with all this Leo stuff. When I sat down and really thought it over, dealing with it all without you to support me is harder."

I take the sandwich in my lap and set it on the table, followed by Autumn's sandwich. As soon as they are out of the way, I scoop her into my lap and just hold her. Hold her until my arms grow tired. Hold her until she melts into me and I melt into her. For as long as I live, I will never have my fill of this woman. Of the love she gives.

A soft knock raps at the door. "Come in," I grumble against Autumn's neck, refusing to let her go.

"Sorry to interrupt. We just had a few more clients pull up," Dad informs.

He won't come right out and say he needs my help. But he needs my help. "I'll be out in a minute." Without another word, Dad exits and closes the door.

I groan against Autumn before kissing the spot where her shoulder and neck meet. "Why isn't the workday over yet?" I grumble.

Light laughter shakes Autumn's frame and I lean away from her. She lifts her hands to frame my face and leans in. Her lips close enough to kiss. "Soon." Eyes open, she closes the space between our mouths and presses our lips together.

Her intoxicating eyes locked on mine while we kiss makes me dizzy. In the best way.

"Come over tonight. Have dinner at the house. You and Clementine. Spartan has been a mess without his new favorite person."

Autumn laughs. "Clementine keeps telling me Spartan misses her, and not the other way around. Although I know she misses both of you. And yes, we'll come over tonight."

I grab Autumn's hips and slowly shift to stand, planting her on her feet. Then I kiss the hell out of her. Kiss her like oxygen feeding the flame. Kiss her to make up for all the kisses we have missed ever since this fiasco began. And as much as I don't want to stop kissing her, I do. Because I am at work and she probably needs to go to work too.

"See you tonight, scarlet." I kiss the tip of her nose. "Let me walk you to your car."

We wrap up the rest of our uneaten sandwiches, put mine in the fridge and hers in the bag. Then I walk her out. On the way to her car, I catch Dad smiling as he fakes busywork. Somehow, he knew everything would work out. I had doubts, probably because my emotional scale went from jovial to freaking out in point-five seconds.

Everything is better now. I have my girls back. In my arms. And no one will take them away again. No one.

eleven

AUTUMN

All in all, today has been better than any day in the last few weeks.

When I picked Clementine up from school, her pouty face dwindled slightly when I told her we were going to Jonas's house tonight. She wouldn't show or admit it, but this news made her day better. Knowing she would see Spartan later, that she would get to cuddle with her favorite furry friend, made a smile tug at the corners of her mouth.

The first question out of her mouth was why we couldn't see them before, but can now. I didn't have a short answer for her, so I just told her I needed my friend—meaning Theresa—to assure me everything would be okay. For the first time ever, Clementine rolled her eyes.

And I gave her a one-time pass.

On the drive to Jonas's, I work to wipe away the discontent Clementine has felt through all this. "Blinding Lights" by The Weeknd comes on the radio and I crank up the volume.

Usually, she sings at the top of her lungs and dances in her seat when the song plays. At one point, she tried to convince me to make a TikTok video with her to this song. Didn't happen, of course. I hope to get a little bit of her typical energy going. And she doesn't disappoint. Clementine doesn't belt the lyrics out like usual, but she sings loud enough for me to hear it and dances in her seat slightly.

A small win that I gladly take.

Before long, I park behind Jonas's Jeep. The second we exit the car, Spartan starts yipping from inside the house. *He really has missed Clementine.*

Clementine bolts to the front door as fast as her short legs will take her. "I'm here, Sparty. I'm here." Just as she reaches the door, it flies open and Spartan attacks her with slobbery dog kisses. And my little girl giggles and giggles. The most perfect sound in the world. A sound I missed these last weeks.

When I reach the door, Jonas looks up from the Spartan-Clementine hugfest and smiles. "Hey, scarlet." He takes my hand and tugs me into his chest, hugging me as if we hadn't seen each other earlier. And I welcome every second of it. "Come on, let's go inside."

We head inside and go separate ways—Clementine and Spartan to the couch while Jonas and I go to the kitchen. The simple routine something I more than missed. While Clementine whispers to Spartan on the couch, catching him up on all the stories he hasn't heard over the last two weeks, Jonas and I cook dinner.

"What's on the menu tonight?"

A smile kicks up Jonas's lips. "Thought I'd keep it easy tonight. Pizza."

Across the open floor plan, Clementine hoots. "Yay for pizza!"

"Dad told me about a new take-and-bake place that opened. We'll see how it is. Clementine…" Jonas calls across the room to her and she perks up. "I got you a four cheese pizza. Hope that's okay."

"She loves all cheese," I mention.

Clementine scowls at me a second before looking at Jonas and smiling. "Cheeses is my favorite. Thank you, Mr. Jonas."

"You're welcome, cutie." After Clementine focuses her attention on Spartan again, Jonas turns to me. "What just happened there?"

I purse my lips. "Caught that, did you?"

"Kind of hard not to."

"She's been upset with me for days." Understatement of the decade. Upset doesn't begin to cover how Clementine has acted. I don't blame her, but it also means she has become very much attached to Spartan and Jonas. In some respects, I love the idea of her connecting so easily with them. But I fear the worst if something bad happens. "Today hasn't been as bad since I told her we were coming over."

"Sorry you've had a teenage seven-year-old on your hands." He leans against the counter and pulls me to stand between his legs. "Hopefully the dramatics fade soon, now that we'll see each other more."

"Fingers crossed."

The timer buzzes and Jonas checks the pizzas. As soon as they are out of the oven, the air fills with the delicious scents of cheese, bread, and herbs. After they cool a moment, Jonas cuts the pizzas and sets them on the breakfast bar.

"Time to eat, pumpkin."

Clementine huffs, walks from the couch to the breakfast bar, then pulls out the stool on the far end. She doesn't say a word before she swaps the pizzas—hers and Jonas's. In the past, Clementine sat between us. But she is still upset, and her payback is to not sit next to or acknowledge me unless absolutely necessary.

After Jonas feeds Spartan, we all sit down to eat. Dinner is quieter than any previous time. Part of me worries my former decisions have screwed up my relationship with Jonas. As if he hears my wayward thoughts, he nudges me with his elbow. I peek up from my pizza and meet his gaze. He shakes his head.

"Your thoughts practically scream from your head. Stop. It'll be okay."

"Maybe we should both talk with her after dinner. Since I seem to be the enemy, maybe she'll listen to you."

He nods. "Good idea. Better to nip this in the bud now."

I swoon a little at how effortless it is for Jonas to want to speak with Clementine. How he assumes a fatherly role with her without overstepping. How he wants the best for her—for us—and has no issue doing whatever it takes to make it happen.

We finish eating our pizza in amicable silence. When Clementine finishes, she hops down and runs back to the couch. After Jonas and I clean up our plates, we join her in the living room.

"What movie are we watching, Mr. Jonas?"

"Not sure. Before we watch a movie, your mom and I need to talk with you."

She rolls her eyes and I lose it. Although this entire ordeal has been nothing but painful, I don't deserve to be treated as the villain in all this.

"That's enough, young lady." Clementine's eyes go wide. "The eye rolling stops now. It's rude and disrespectful."

She crosses her arms over her chest. "Well, you haven't been very nice either."

I have to remind myself that Clementine is seven and not an adult. The way she reacts to situations will be different than me or Jonas. Juvenile. All her little mind knows is I took away someone she cared about, and it hurt her feelings. I take a few deep breaths and calm my nerves.

"Yes, I have made some choices that have upset us all. And I apologize."

Jonas rubs his palm over my thigh. "Clementine, your mom did what she thought was best for you at the time. She didn't know another way yet. Now she does and we can be together more. But you have to stop being mean and hurtful. Being that way will only make everyone stay upset longer, and we want to be happy." Jonas's tone is gentle and nurturing.

Clementine looks between me and Jonas, unsure. She wants to believe him. Wants to believe he wouldn't tell her lies. But after all the back and forth over the last few weeks, it's like grasping at air. My poor girl.

I did this to her. Let her get close to someone. Someone I care about deeply. Then I pulled the rug out without warning. Left her in the dark because I didn't want to burden her with topics a young child shouldn't have to worry about. But it still didn't work. I still messed up. My only hope is it won't take long for her to smile at me again.

"But what if that man takes me away?"

Twenty-four hours haven't passed since I went into a better explanation about Leo to Clementine and she is already worried about the outcome of the case. A burden I did not want for her.

I scoot closer to her and, thankfully, she doesn't back away. "You know all those appointments I've been going to, pumpkin?" Clementine nods. "Those are so I can talk to my attorney friend, Theresa. When I saw her today, she gave me good news." At this, Clementine leans an inch closer. Eager to hear more. "She said because I have been such a good mom and your birth father has never seen you, the judge will let you stay with me." Partial truth. Still have to wait until the judge puts his seal of approval on the paperwork. But Clementine doesn't need semantics. "We just have to wait for the special meeting later this month. But Theresa also said it's okay for you and me to be with Jonas and Spartan. Before, I didn't know if spending time with them would make it harder for you to stay with mommy."

All of this is a lot for Clementine to process, but I need for her to understand that I haven't done all these things to be mean. Being apart from Jonas hurt us too. Since seeing him earlier today, after agreeing to not be apart again, the ache I experienced since this whole nightmare started has lessened.

I may not *need* Jonas to get through this, but I want him by my side. Without effort, he makes me whole. Lifts me up and keeps me standing strong. Has my heart beating vigorously. My lungs flooding with oxygen. He gives me life.

After a moment, her eyes dart between me and Jonas. "Okay, Mama. Can we watch a movie now?"

"For a little bit. Not too late. We still have to get up early tomorrow." She nods.

And just like that, the conversation ends. We turn on the television and find something to watch on Netflix.

Jonas and I curl up on the couch facing each other. Neither of us says a word, we just lie there, get lost in each other's eyes, exchanging the occasional touch or kiss. Everything about the moment feels right. Meant to be.

Before long, the show ends and I decide it's time to head out. Not that I want to. More than anything, I want to stay in this house, crawl between Jonas's sheets, and never leave. But not tonight. Probably not tomorrow either. But hopefully soon.

Clementine hugs Spartan and whispers in his ear before letting go. As we walk to the door, a smidge of her sulkiness lingers. But this version is much more tolerable.

Jonas walks us out to the car. After Clementine is in her seat, I start the car and turn the heat on low. "We'll go in just a minute," I tell Clementine. She nods and turns up the radio. Good sign.

With Clementine situated, I close the door and face Jonas. He wraps his arms around me and hugs me tight. "Come over again tomorrow. Feel like we have so much time to make up for." He kisses the crown of my head.

"Yes, we do. And we'll be here."

Jonas brings his hands to either side of my face and holds me as if I am the most precious person in existence. He lowers his lips to mine and lights a fire under my skin as he kisses me senseless. No matter how much time passes, I will never get enough of Jonas. Not his hugs. Not his kisses. Nor his love. Call me addicted, I don't care. All I know is, Jonas is the only person who has completed me. Made me whole. A better version of myself. And I don't want another day without him in my life.

Jonas breaks the kiss and inches back. "Text when you get home."

"I will. See you tomorrow."

"Tomorrow…" And I swear he wants to say more. I see it linger in the air. But he bites his tongue.

Me too, I say to myself. Because I swear Jonas was just about to say he loves me.

"Not sure what happened yesterday, but it's good to see a smile on your face again," Dad says as I stroll into the office early.

For the first night in weeks, I slept without disruption. Yesterday, the stars in my and Autumn's constellation realigned. Everything wasn't back to before Leo made an appearance, but I don't imagine it will be exactly that way again. If I had to guess, I would say our relationship will be better. Stronger. More potent and appreciated.

After our time apart and the heartache we both endured, neither of us will take our relationship for granted. We will cherish it more. Every touch—big or small—will hold more meaning. Every kiss will have deeper sentiment.

"Autumn and I had a lengthy discussion after her appointment at the attorney's office. The attorney gave her the reassurance she needed to be comfortable in our relationship while dealing with her ex."

Dad sets his pen down on a stack of invoices. "Glad to hear things are on the upswing. We all enjoyed meeting her and Clementine. Hope to see them again, when the dust settles."

I brew a pot of coffee and bring the cream and sugar to the desks. "Me too. She loved meeting everyone."

Once the brewer finishes, I pour a mug for us both and sit at my desk. The stack of paperwork on my desk has gotten taller and taller with each day I didn't see or hear from Autumn. Thank goodness I am not in charge of billing, otherwise we would be too far behind. My job is to file away invoices for record keeping. No big shake. Usually finish the prior day's paperwork before the garage opens each morning. But seeing as how I haven't filed paperwork for several days, I may be spending my lunch breaks playing catch up.

I use every minute possible before the garage opens to file invoices. When the time comes to roll up the bay doors, Dad and I head out to the garage.

One after another, customers clamber in with their vehicles. Oil changes. Tire replacements. Dent removal. Windshield replacement. The day whizzes by. The entire time, a painful smile stretches across my cheeks. Nothing can ruin this day.

The back half of the day goes by just as fast as the morning. It boggles my mind how easily my mood changes the pace of the day.

About an hour before closing, I glance up from an engine I'm working on. A familiar white Mercedes drives into the lot and parks near the office.

How can my blood boil and turn to ice simultaneously? I set the ratchet down, grab the red rag from my coveralls, and wipe my hands as I step toward the car.

"Jonas," Dad calls from a bay over. "Everything alright?"

I tip my head toward the car. "Autumn's ex."

Dad sets down the wrench in his hand and steps closer in my direction. "What's he doing here?"

"Hell if I know. Probably stirring up shit. Seems to be his thing."

"You need me with you?"

I subtly shake my head. "No, but stay within earshot in case he causes problems."

Dad pats my shoulder. "I'm here."

Leo steps out of his pricey car wearing an even pricier suit. He scans the garage as if he doesn't see me twenty feet away. When his visual perusal stops on me, a smug grin lights his face. He closes the door and presses the fob, locking it as if someone might steal his precious car with him feet away.

Ten feet from him, I stop. The distance between us intentional. I know next to nothing about this man, but he has done nothing but piss me off and upset my girls. No telling what I will do if I get within a foot or two. So, for now, it is in the best interest of us all if I keep my distance.

"What can I help you with?" I continue wiping the oil and grease from my hands to keep my mind distracted.

He takes another step closer. I don't move. But if he gets much closer, I will have to divert him. Distance from him is best no matter what goes down.

"You need to back off."

I know he refers to my relationship with Autumn and Clementine, but I plan to play coy. "Don't know what you're talking about."

"Maybe you're as dumb as you look."

"Best if you think before you speak."

He cocks his head. "Like I said, you need to back off."

Less than five minutes has passed and I already want to punch him in the face. In my periphery, Dad takes a step forward but doesn't say a word. He will go to bat for me—and the girls—without hesitation. Dad may be a kind and forgiving man, but no one steps on him or his family.

"Well, *Leo*, seems as if you're confused." The skin between his brows bunches then relaxes. "Seeing as you have no claim."

This pisses him off. Within seconds, his posture shifts. He leans in closer. Takes another step forward. Balls his hands into fists at his sides. Curls his upper lip. "Hate to break the news, lowlife. I have more claim than you'll ever have. That little girl… she's mine." His voice climbs an octave. "And if I want Autumn again, she will be mine."

I grind my molars and breathe through my nose. I don't give a fuck what this prick says, he will never get Clementine and he was too chickenshit to stick around for Autumn. His loss. All my gain. And that knowledge alone fuels the beast within.

Throwing my head back, I laugh. When I meet his eyes again, he looks even more pissed. *Good. Asshole.* "You may have donated sperm to the cause, *Leo*, but you have zero claim on that little girl. You lost that privilege when you left her mom high and dry. Pregnant and alone." I point my finger at him and inch closer. "Your money won't win this war. Best if you leave and crawl back in the hole you squirmed out of."

Leo's face turns a brilliant shade of red. The color nothing to do with the sun beaming down on us. He is livid. Furious I called him out in front of other people. Made a mockery of him. He should be angry—at himself. No one but himself put him in this position. He has no one else to blame.

"Best if you watch your back, lowlife. You think money can't win this war? Who knows, maybe you're right. But it sure as hell can make things highly uncomfortable. Unpredictable. Unsafe."

Now I step forward. Resist every urge inside me that says to knock him to the ground. I have to—for Autumn and Clementine. I lean in closer and laugh when he jolts back. "You threatening me? Threatening Autumn? I'd watch what I say next, if I were you."

He takes a step back. Then another. His shitty smile dons his face. "See you around, lowlife." He unlocks his car, gets inside, and drives off a moment later.

Until he is out of sight I don't move, don't breathe. Dad steps up to me and rests his hand on my shoulder, and I inhale for the first time in too long. "Go sit in the office and cool off. I'll close everything up." I close my eyes and nod. When I open them, Dad stands inches to my left. "Everything will be fine. Just keep Autumn and Clementine safe. Keep them front of mind at all times." Dad gives my shoulder one last squeeze and heads back in the garage.

I go to the office and pace. Think over how I will explain this to Autumn. She needs to know her ex is threatening people. Threatening her and Clementine. She needs to inform her attorney. No way this is acceptable or allowable, especially with the case open.

I will tell her. Later. Not yet. Not when my synapses are firing on overdrive. After I calm down and can properly articulate what just happened. Last thing I need to do is freak Autumn out after we have just returned to a better place. Either tonight or tomorrow, once I have had time to let his words simmer and digest.

Until then, though, Autumn and Clementine shouldn't be alone. Not with him tossing threats around like beads at Mardi Gras. Leo is scrawny. But who's to say he won't pay someone else to do the dirty work. Isn't that what people with money do?

I fish my phone out of my coveralls and unlock it. Pulling up the text history with Autumn, I type out a message.

> Hey, scarlet. Almost done at the garage. Any dinner requests?

We may have only just decided to pick things up where they left off, but I have to ease into asking things of Autumn.

> Breakfast sounds fun. Doesn't matter, though.

Breakfast. Perfect segue.

> What if my girls stay over and we can have 2 breakfasts together.

A minute passes while I stare at the screen. She hasn't responded yet. The indicator bubble to tell me she's typing hasn't popped up. Was it too quick for me to jump on the "stay the night" train again? Things have been off, but I don't think she has reservations about staying. Maybe the doubt her parents cause crept back in. The last thing I want is for her to slow things down again.

Before she responds, I send another message.

> No pressure. I'd just love to have my girls stay over. Think about it. I'll see you in a little while.

And with that, I leave the decision up to her. Until she answers, though, I am a live wire. Thank god, I have plenty of stuff to preoccupy my time between now and when Autumn and Clementine arrive at the house. Grocery shopping. Spartan. Dinner/breakfast.

Dad steps into the office and tells me everything is taken care of. After we strip out of our coveralls, we lock up and exit through the back. He gives me a hug and pat on the back. "Just stay levelheaded. It will all work out." I nod. "And if you need me, you better call."

"Thanks, Dad."

"Those girls are family. And Thompson's protect their own."

I love how easily Autumn and Clementine have won the hearts of my family. Even through all the craziness, Dad recognizes what I feel. That the love I have for them won't fade. And that I intend to keep Autumn and Clementine for the long haul.

Penny strolls into my booth and plops down on my chair. "What's up with you? Look like someone just shredded your favorite dress."

In all the madness, I have been a bad friend and roommate to Penny. Between my grumpy antics and Clementine's tantrums, we have to be driving her insane. If so, she hides it well.

"Jonas just asked me and Clementine to stay the night."

Her brows shoot up as she continues to smack her gum. "So, what's the big deal? You stayed over before."

True, but that was before Leo waltzed back in and trampled over my life. "Things have been off since Leo showed up. Do you think it's too soon? Again."

Penny blows a bubble and pops it. "No. You guys have it bad for each other. Plus, your attorney said to do you. Don't let *him* dictate your life, Auti. That isn't fair to you, Clementine or Jonas."

I huff, tossing the wad of paper towels in my hand in the trash bin. Nothing about Leo returning has been fair. From the second I saw him standing next to my car, I knew nothing good would come from his sudden appearance. And no matter how I try to let it go, I continue to question why he materialized out of thin air. After no communication in years, why now?

None of it makes sense. Every sleepless night, my mind orchestrates countless possibilities as to why he wants custody of Clementine. Publicity, perhaps? But giving the appearance of a family man to the media, claiming a little girl as yours when no one has seen her previously, would pose more questions and issues than Leo probably wants. So, why?

"It isn't fair. But I just don't get it, Penny. I don't understand his motivation."

She jumps off my chair and skips around it to stand where I see her better. "Auti, maybe you aren't meant to understand. Not yet. But have patience. You have a kick-ass attorney who will dig. And if she doesn't find anything before the hearing, maybe the judge can pull out his reasoning. You have a right to know, but quit letting the whys and what-ifs rule your life. Don't give him your power."

I shift ink bottles around on the shelf in my station. Organizing the bottles then rearranging them. Anything to keep me busy while I mull over Penny's advice. She stares at me while I stall, but I don't rush my reaction or answer.

Every time the topic of Leo and the custody case comes up, it always cycles back to the same result. Everyone telling me to let the attorney do her job and for me and Clementine to go about our lives. God, am I trying. Some things are easier said than done.

But I don't want to regret missing out on life. Of being happy, of Clementine being happy. Regret will eat at my joy more than Leo.

"Guess you're right."

"Damn straight I am. And as far as staying over at Jonas's house, I say do it. You never know what will happen tomorrow, Auti. Live today, and don't have regrets tomorrow."

I throw my arms around Penny, hugging her close and squishing her more than normal. But she gives as good as she gets and has me tapping out of the hug first.

"Love you, Pen."

"Love you, too." Penny slaps my ass and winks. "Now finish cleaning up and get out of here."

Once I finish wiping my booth down and everything is back in place, I snatch my purse and say bye to the guys. Before leaving, I give Penny one last hug. "Thanks again. See you tomorrow."

When I release the hug, she narrows her eyes before tossing out another wink. "Have a good night," she singsongs.

~

"You ready to go, pumpkin?"

Clementine comes barreling out of the bedroom with a tote bag hooked over her shoulder. Shortly after I got home, and Iliana left, I told Clementine we would stay at Jonas's house tonight. Not a second after the words left my lips, she bolted from one corner of the apartment to the next. When I started packing an overnight bag for us, she asked if she could pack her own.

Mama, I'm a big girl. I want my own bag.

How could I deny her sunshiny smile? Too much time had passed since I last saw that smile. And the fact I stole that from her stabbed me center chest.

"Yep." She pats the overstuffed bag. "Got all the goods."

"What on earth did you put in there? Looks like it weighs more than you."

She purses her lips and narrows her eyes. "My clothes, some movies, and some stuff I want to show Sparty."

I laugh under my breath. Spartan has become her brother, their bond unrivaled. "Okay. If you have everything, let's go. Jonas is making breakfast for dinner."

Clementine's eyes go wide and she scurries for the door. "Come on, Mama. Let's go."

As soon as Clementine learns the dinner menu, she rushes us. Has me shoving our bags in the back and all but snaps her fingers for me to start the car. Thankfully, it's a quick ride to Jonas's house. Music and singing pass the time faster.

I park in Jonas's driveway and cut the engine. Clementine hauls her bag from the back and bolts for the front door. I dash to keep up with her sprint. Before either of us can knock, Jonas opens the door with a wide grin splitting his cheeks. Spartan tackles Clementine with kisses. It all just feels normal.

"Let me take your bags," Jonas offers, taking Clementine's off her shoulder before holding a hand out for mine.

The start of our evening goes much the same as before. Except now, Jonas and I discover every possible moment to touch each other. In the kitchen, while we eat, when we curl into each other on the couch. His fingers sweep stray hairs off my cheek. Arms around me as he demonstrates how to cut the fruit "easier." My knees grazing his over and over as we eat our meals. And now, his fingers splayed on my belly, thumb drawing small circles, reminiscent of the movie night we shared in the park.

The movie plays on the screen, but I don't see or hear any of it.

Eyes closed, I focus on my breathing. His breathing. The rapid uptick in each pattern. From shoulders to toes, our bodies mold as one. Heat radiates off him, burning through layers of clothes, and scorches my skin. And a rhythmic cadence I memorized, one I called to mind several times while we were apart, beats fierce in his chest and thumps between my shoulder blades.

A light sheen of perspiration prickles my skin as Jonas skims his palm higher and higher, slow and steady up my abdomen. When he traces the underwire of my bra, I stop breathing. When he kisses the sensitive skin behind my ear, I grind my hips into him. Jonas exhales a soft growl, his breath hot on my neck.

"Cannot wait for this movie to end," he whisper-growls in my ear.

I open my eyes, peek at the screen before shifting my gaze to Clementine. The movie is almost over, but she is wide awake. Time to offer alternative solutions.

Rolling over to face Jonas, I bring my hand to his cheek and run my palm over the stubble. "She's still awake. Might need to put on another movie to watch, flip the lights off, and we can go to bed." He lifts his head to spot Clementine then nods.

For the last fifteen minutes of movie one, Jonas and I kiss and touch and reacquaint ourselves with simpler contact. When the movie ends, I pop off the couch. "Pumpkin, what other movie do you want to watch? Jonas and I are going to bed, but you can stay up and watch."

The Nightmare Before Christmas." I should have known.

"You got it. Go change into your jammies while I set it up."

She jumps off the couch and bounds down the hall with pajamas in hand. While out of the room, I start up the movie while Jonas sets up the couch for her to sleep. A few minutes later, she plops back on the couch in her movie-themed pajamas with Sally on her limbs and torso. She wiggles her way under the blanket, Spartan curls up beside her, and we kiss her good night.

Jonas and I stroll back to the bedroom, hand in hand. The second the door clicks shut, the energy changes. Grows heavier. Potent. Feverish. I freeze and Jonas steps up to my backside. Hands on my biceps. Fingers traipsing down until they weave with mine. He inches closer. Heat swirls in the air, licks my skin, and blankets me. His breath comes faster, hotter, sweeping across my neck.

He brings one of our joined hands to my abdomen and grazes the skin above the hem of my jeans. Presses me into him. Rocks his hips against my butt. I tip my head back and rest it on his shoulder. A slow moan on my lips.

"Missed you so much," he growls and trails kisses up my neck. Along my jaw. Consuming my lips.

I unweave my fingers from his and spin to face him. "Missed you more."

Pressing my hands to his pecs, I trail my palms down his chest, relishing the dips and ridges beneath my fingertips. When I reach the hem of his shirt, I fist the material and tug up. The cotton hits the floor as I lean forward and press my lips to his skin.

He hisses in the dimly lit room, hands clutching my hips as I navigate the terrain with my lips. Each clavicle, left then right. The dip at the base of his throat. Down his sternum—paying extra attention to the flesh protecting his heart. I kiss my way across his left pec, drawing circles with my tongue around the nipple before pulling it between my teeth. Mimicking the same on the right.

As my lips pop off his flesh, he tugs at my shirt and whips it over my head. Before the fabric hits the floor, his fingers tug at the button and zipper of my jeans.

In a blink, we flip from hungry to famished. Hands pawing, fingers grasping, lips groping.

When the only thing separating us is underwear, Jonas guides me to the bed. Slides me toward the headboard then yanks the comforter down. He crawls up the mattress, hazels locked on my golden irises. Kisses my knee, my thigh, the waistline of my panties before trailing his lips and tongue up my center to the base of my throat. He nips at my jawline as my back bows off the bed.

My bra unfastens as Jonas trails a finger along my spine. I wiggle out of the lacy material and drop it to the floor just as Jonas takes one nipple between his lips, then the next. A firestorm rages beneath my skin. Scorches me from crown to toe. Builds. Faster. Needier.

"Jonas…" I moan, grabbing at the waistband of his underwear. "I need you inside me."

He rocks his hips and grinds his erection against my apex. His lips crash to mine and he devours me as if he will never taste me again. I shove his underwear down his legs, using my feet to push them off completely.

Jonas breaks the kiss and trails his lips down my center again, painfully slow. When he reaches my panties, inch by slow inch, he peels them away. He crawls back up the bed, locks his thermal gaze with mine, and kisses me with reverence. Cherishes me. Worships me. Then rocks his hips forward and fills me. I gasp and knead his firm glutes.

"Fuck." He rears back and rocks forward again. And again. Building a rhythm until my body remembers his girth.

He flips us over, grabs my hips, and guides me up and down his length while I flatten my palms against his chest and ride him. I pick up speed, rock my hips as he meets me thrust for thrust. Energy builds in my chest, hot and heavy and powerful. Trailing down my spine and seating low in my pelvis. It's liquid fire and hunger and lust and love. And as I dig my nails into Jonas's pecs, body rocking to a feverish rhythm, I shatter around him.

In a blink, he flips me on my back, lifts one of my legs over his shoulder and pistons his hips. His lips crash to mine and I weave my fingers through his hair, fisting the strands. He braces one hand at my shoulder while the other holds my hip, pinning me in place, hitting me deeper and deeper with each thrust forward.

And my body climbs up that mountain one more time. My breath coming in short bursts. Heart pounding. Orgasm building. Heat scorching. Body dripping.

Then my body finds oblivion. And Jonas is right there with me. Kissing me. Caressing me. Whispering how beautiful I am. Holding me in his arms. Stirring me back to life. Loving me.

And that's exactly how we fall asleep. In each other's arms. Blissfully replete.

Cherry and vanilla waft around me in a cloud of bliss as I wake from the best sleep in weeks.

On my back with eyes closed, I bask in the heat of Autumn's body draped over mine. Bare skin pressed to my chest and limbs. Cheek nestled between my shoulder and pec. Arm draped across my torso. Leg tangled between mine. Her soft, shallow breaths painting my skin as her chest rises and falls. Heartbeat steady beneath her breast bone pressed to my ribs.

I want to open my eyes, shift an inch or two, and memorize the lines and curves and peaks of her face while she sleeps. In the early morning light, I want to take in the shape of her brows, where they arch and end. Study her lashes as they fan out over the small area just above her cheekbone. Trace my eyes around the edges of her lips until I follow where they join in the center. Navigate the soft edges of her jawline. Regard the movement of her eyes behind her closed lids as she dreams.

But I don't dare move an inch. Don't jostle her awake. Because everything about this moment is as perfect as it should be.

As I listen to the soft cadence of Autumn's breathing, I notice it changes. Takes on a new rhythm. Grows in tempo. Her fingers twitch on my chest. Toes wiggle beneath the sheet. Jaw flexes as she licks her lips. Breasts press against my side. Hips wobble just above mine. Unhurried, she lifts her head to peek up at my face.

When she catches my eyes already on her, a brilliant smile plumps her cheeks. Seeing her like this—not a lick of makeup on her face, hair messy in every direction, lips plump and perky, irises glittery in the morning sun—steals my breath. Jolts the chambers of my heart. Robs me of every rational thought. Has me in a trance.

I return her smile as my fingertips dance up and down her spine. "'Morning."

She wiggles up my body, leans in and presses her lips to mine, slow and sweet. "'Morning. How long have you been awake?"

"Not long." I skirt my fingers up her side, from hip to the curve of her breast.

Her fingertips stroke the stubble along my jaw before she brings her lips to mine again. This kiss hungrier as she lifts her hips and straddles me. Nipples hard, scraping against my pecs. Hands planted on both sides of my face, caging me in. Her hips rock over mine, skimming my erection with her slick lips.

I take hold of her hips. Squeeze them with inexplicable roughness. Match the intensity of our kiss as I rock her core over my erection. A heatwave ripples through my body, scorching every inch of me in its wake. Dampness slickens me from root to crown. The heat converging, pooling, settling in my groin.

I bolt upright, her legs encircle my waist as her hands glide around the back of my neck, into my hair. Curling. Fisting. Tugging at the strands. I scoop my hands under her ass and lift her enough to rock back and glide the crown of my cock against her slick folds. For one, two, three strokes, I tease her entrance. On the next stroke, I lower her on to me with precision and fill her fully.

Autumn tips her head back and gasps at the feel of me inside her. Presses her breasts against my collarbones as she yanks my hair with such force, the ceiling comes into view. I don't move. Not an inch. I wait for her to let me know she is ready. Until she drops her chin, until her addictive cognac irises lock with mine.

Her fingers loosen their grip, just slightly. But I keep my head back. I stare up the column of her throat, lock on to her pulse as it pounds beneath her ear, watch her swallow and drag in a deep breath. Her chin drops lower, lower. Our eyes meet. The tip of her nose brushes the bridge of mine. Lips lock and claim. Licking, sucking, consuming.

Bundling her in my arms, I harden my hold on her and rock my hips. She moans against my tongue, down my throat, and it's a bolt of lightning to my cock.

Her fingers release my hair, ankles unhook behind me, and before I protest, she pushes me down into the mattress. Pins me, fingers digging into my skin. Grinds her hips, moves against and in time with me. Nipples pebbled. Jaw slack as soft whimpers spill from her lips. She tucks her chin, her hair falling forward and framing her face.

I bite my lower lip and groan as every nerve in my body sparks like heat lightning. The electrical current ebbs and flows. Fuses together. Slithers down my spine until it settles in my groin. Expands and pulses with each rock of her hips.

She buries her nails in my flesh as her body constricts. I flip her on to the mattress, lift her legs to rest on my shoulders, grip the back of her neck, and slam into her. Autumn tucks her lips between her teeth before turning her head and biting the pillow. One, two, three more thrusts and my vision hazes as I release. Ringing echoes in my ears as bright lights sparkle behind my lids when I slam them shut.

I release Autumn's legs and press my weight into her. Kiss her fiercely as she combs her fingers through my hair. When I break the kiss, I press my forehead to hers and breathe her in.

"God, I love waking up with you in my arms," I confess.

"Couldn't agree more." She brings a hand to my cheek and strokes her thumb over my stubble. "I don't want to, but we should probably get up. Before Clementine."

I sneak in one last kiss before leaving the comfort of the bed. Autumn sticks out her lower lip, pouting, and it is one of the cutest fucking things I have seen. She rolls on to her belly and groans into the pillow before reluctantly abandoning the bed.

"I want to take my girls out today," I declare as I shrug a shirt on.

"Oh, yeah?"

"Yep. Don't know where. Not sure what we'll do. But we should make today adventurous." Autumn giggles at my proclamation. "And cake should be involved more than once."

"Cake?" Autumn's eyes widen. "Clementine won't disagree with you."

"Lots of cake. We'll call it a belated birthday celebration."

Autumn freezes, hand hovering over the zipper of her jeans. "When was your birthday?" Her question comes out squeaky.

"Couple weeks back." Autumn's face pales as her eyes glaze over. I frame her face in my palms and shake my head. "No, scarlet. No tears. We will have plenty more birthdays to celebrate together. And I'm not upset. Just because we didn't celebrate on the exact day doesn't mean anything."

Autumn works to blink away her tears before taking a deep breath. "I promise to make it up to you."

I lean down and kiss her briefly, tenderly. "You being here, staying with me, has more than made up for missing the day."

Just as Autumn opens her mouth to rebut, the soft sound of little feet padding on the floor, followed by a knock, halts any further conversation. Autumn pats her head in an effort to tame her sex hair before opening the door.

"'Morning, pumpkin. We were just coming out to see if you were awake yet."

Clementine hugs Autumn's waist, then mine. "Sparty needs to go potty," she says as she releases me and walks out of the room.

Just like that, our morning has officially begun. The three of us—plus Spartan—in the same space feels *normal*. And I love every second of it.

~

After our previous visit to Phillippe Park, Clementine immediately suggested us spending the day at a park. Although I love revisiting parks, I asked her permission to go to a different location since we were celebrating my birthday. When she cocked her head and pondered, it was the cutest thing ever. But she agreed with one condition.

We have lots of cake and ice cream.

Sold!

Foraging through the garage, I locate the cooler and carry it inside. Once we are ready to go, I toss the cooler in the back of the Jeep and we all pile in. On the way to the park, we stop at the grocery store and buy subs, drinks, snacks and a small bag of ice. With everything packed in the cooler, I drive us to a nature preserve at the northeast corner of the county.

Clementine kicks her feet while she sings along with the song on the radio. She sports a pair of black wingtip sunglasses and stares out the window at the passing scenery. The closer we get to the preserve, the less buildings we see. In our part of the state, most of the land is packed with streets, malls, shopping plazas, and homes. More concrete than trees. Thankfully, though, some beautiful stretches of land have been preserved.

As I steer the Jeep into the preserve, Clementine sits up straighter. Scans the land with curious eyes. "Is this the park?"

"Yep," I say, turning down the music. "But this park is different than most parks by us."

"Why, Mr. Jonas?" I love it when she calls me Mr. Jonas.

"This park is ginormous. Bigger than any other park close by. With lots of big trees and trails to walk on and a nature center to learn about the animals."

"Will we see animals here?" she asks as her pitch bumps up.

"If we're lucky. We might see some deer or rabbits or other animals."

She gasps and stares into the passing trees. "I hope we see a deer. Would be so cool."

I glance over at Autumn and match her ear-to-ear smile. Seeing her this happy, seeing Clementine this happy, it brings new meaning to love and life and joy. Clementine may not be my daughter, but she is as equally precious to me as

Autumn. *My girls.* I never knew I could be this enamored by a woman and her daughter.

As I park the Jeep, Clementine bounces in her seat, eager to jump out. We hop out and leave the cooler in the back. For the next few hours, we wander through the education center and along the trails of the preserve. The sun beats down on us and keeps us warm in the cool February air. Every once in a while, Clementine has us swing her in the air as we walk.

When our stomachs begin to rumble, I grab the cooler and we sit at a partially shaded picnic table to eat our lunch. For the most part, the preserve has minimal people here. At most, we have seen ten people. During our visit, we see one deer, a few rabbits, several squirrels, and a snake that slithers away. Clementine has been fascinated with it all.

All in all, it's been a peaceful day. Which is exactly what the three of us needed.

With full bellies and tired feet, we decide to head back to the house. But as promised, on the way back, we stop at the store to pick up cake and ice cream.

We stroll into the store and beeline to the bakery. "If I get to pick the cake, you can pick the ice cream," I offer to Clementine.

She taps her lips with a finger and narrows her eyes a moment. How can someone be this adorable? "Deal." Clementine extends her hand and we shake.

After I select a small vanilla and chocolate cake with chocolate frosting, we go to the frozen section. For the next ten minutes, Clementine studies the ice cream selection as if her decision will end a war. Autumn holds her up every other minute so she can see the higher shelves better. I don't rush them.

Instead, I stand back and observe my girls. *My girls.*

Clementine points at a container and Autumn whispers in her ear what the flavor is. Clementine shakes her head and they move down the line. This happens over and over, and yet, it doesn't bother me. Doesn't make me impatient.

If anything, I ask for more time like this. More time to bask in the joy of being a part of their lives. More time to watch the woman I care about dedicate herself to her daughter. To help her with tasks most adults consider menial. To focus on her daughter and forget everything else. Autumn is a phenomenal mother to Clementine. I envy her devotion. Having them in my life… I have never been so lucky.

After Clementine chooses, we check out and leave the store. "Happy birthday, Mr. Jonas."

I peek in the rearview mirror at Clementine. "Thank you. Hope you're ready for cake and ice cream."

She gives a confident nod. "Born ready."

Autumn laughs, slips her hand into mine over the console and squeezes. "Today has been wonderful. And it's still somewhat early."

At the red light, I meet her eyes. "Maybe we can take a nap after cake." I cock a brow. "A nap, huh?"

I simply shrug and focus my eyes on the road again. A few minutes later, I park in the driveway and we all hop out.

In the house, Clementine tells Spartan about the preserve while we dish up cake and ice cream. And after our plates our clean, I mention napping again. Clementine says she will watch a movie with Spartan while Autumn and I take a short nap.

Once we land on my bed, I close my eyes. Although I can't see her, I *feel*

Autumn observe me. "You really wanted to sleep? Interesting. Thought you were using a nap as an excuse for birthday sex."

I laugh and pull her down to the bed. "We can do that later. For now, I just want to lie here and hold you. That okay?"

Autumn snuggles into my side. "Yes, but we should set an alarm. Just in case."

After we set an alarm for forty-five minutes, we just hold each other. And for the first time since yesterday evening, I think of Leo's visit to the garage. I need to tell Autumn what happened. Not just for the sake of telling her, but also because I worry for her and Clementine both. Plus, she should forward the incident to her attorney.

Tonight, I will tell her. After dinner.

"Stay with me again tonight," I whisper against her hair. "I love having you both here."

Autumn stays quiet a moment and I wonder if she fell asleep. Until she gently fists my shirt. "Yes." She lifts her head and rests her chin on my chest. "We love being here."

I sweep a few wayward strands from her brow and tuck them behind her ear. Then lean up to kiss her. We lie in the bed until the alarm buzzes. For the rest of the day, we take it easy. We order Chinese takeout and laugh over fortune cookies, and another helping of cake and ice cream while watching *The Secret Life of Pets.*

When Clementine falls asleep, I extend my hand to Autumn. "Come sit out back with me for a bit." She takes my hand as I lead her to the patio.

I light the fire bowl before sitting on the lounger and nestling Autumn between my legs. We stare at the flames and weave our fingers together. I close my eyes and breathe in her cherry vanilla scent, letting it center and soothe me as I muster up the courage to tell her about yesterday.

Inhale. Hold it. And exhale. I do this a few times. "Autumn," I say softly. "I need to tell you something, but don't want you to freak out."

As the words leave my lips, she locks up. Not moving for ten rapid beats. Then she breathes again and twists to look at me. "What is it?"

I swallow, trying to dampen the sudden dryness in my throat. "Leo stopped by the garage yesterday."

She sits up straighter and spins to face me full-on. "What?" she exclaims, eyes wide with fear. "Why? What did he want? How did he know where you work?"

All questions I wanted answers to as well. Honestly, I think he was looking to start a physical altercation with me to make Autumn appear bad in the court's eyes. Too bad for him, I am not a dumbass.

I relay everything that happened. How Leo flaunted his tail feathers and acted possessive. How I kept my cool but put him in his place. And how Dad stood in my peripheral the entire time and had my back. When I finish, Autumn shakes her head. Not because she doesn't believe me, but more as if she doesn't understand his sudden interest.

"Just let your attorney know as soon as possible. Sometimes, little things add up in the end."

We stay out by the fire a while longer, enjoy the quiet as our minds run wild. When I extinguish the flame, I guide us back in the house and to the bedroom. As soon as we step over the threshold, I pull Autumn into my arms.

"In here, we don't talk about anything but you and me and, occasionally, that little girl in the other room." I trace along Autumn's jaw and tip her chin up. "Okay?"

She nods. "Yes." Pressing up on her toes, she leans in and kisses me. On her next breath, she says, "Let's go to bed." And I let Autumn guide me to the bed as we peel away our clothes.

Jonas snores softly beneath me. His chest rises and falls in a slow, rhythmic pattern under my cheek. Palm over his heart, I fan out my fingers, tempted to draw patterns into his skin with my fingertips. But I lie unmoving, eyes closed, mind unable to shut down.

New questions run wild in my head. Questions asking what Leo aims to accomplish with his relentlessness. What is his endgame in this scenario? What is he out to accomplish? I just don't get it. If he would have stepped back into the picture within the first two years, I might have understood the desire to be a part of Clementine's life easier.

But too much time has passed. Too many circumstances in both our lives have changed. For someone who ditched me—us—without a backward glance, Leo's newfound persistence worries me. His pursuit of sole custody of Clementine is tied up with something. Something just out of my reach. And it twists my insides in a nauseating pretzel.

I *need* to learn what's behind his motivation and soon. I need the truth behind his sudden desire to be a father. Not just for the sake of knowing, but because Clementine's well-being hangs in the balance.

Curling farther into Jonas's side, I work to match my breathing pattern to his. Inhaling his unique scent, my body relaxes more. And before long, I dream about Jonas at my side until we are old and gray.

～

What's better than a great night of sleep? Waking up with Jonas's lips on my skin. God, if every day starts like this, I will never leave this bed.

After he ignites every inch of my skin and liquifies each molecule in me—three times—we stumble out of bed and dress. My legs are noodles walking on gelatin as we exit the bedroom and I slap a hand over my mouth to stifle my laughter.

Clementine lays curled in a semi-fetal position with Spartan as a partial pillow. But it won't be long before she wakes.

Jonas and I step into the bathroom, brush our teeth, and groom enough to not look as if we have spent the last hour trying to yank each other's hair out. I skip putting on makeup and twist my hair into a topknot.

Stepping up behind me, Jonas locks eyes with me in the mirror over the vanity. His hands secure on my hips, lips grazing the shell of my ear. "I love waking up with you in the morning. Seeing you like this." He kisses the spot below my ear, grinds his hips against my low back, then locks his gaze with mine again. "Natural and perfect and more stunning than ever."

I spin around, tip my head back, and lace my fingers at the nape of his neck. "You trying to flatter me, Mr. Thompson?"

His intense, addictive hazels lock me in place and I stop breathing. Heart thrashing against my ribcage. Limbs tingling as heat courses through my veins and sparks new life. Jonas drops his chin an inch, his lips so close I practically taste the peppermint on his tongue. He traces the tip of his nose along the ridge of mine and I stutter an exhale.

"How can I not?" he whispers against my lips. "Hope you let me flatter and compliment and kiss you every day."

I press my lips to his in answer just as a knock on the door disrupts the moment. "Are you almost done? I need to go potty," Clementine states from the hall.

"Just a second, pumpkin." I peek up at Jonas. "As long as you can handle the two of us, you may dote upon me any day of the week."

"Wouldn't want it any other way." He steps back, adjusts himself in his sweatpants, and opens the door with a smile on his face. "'Morning, sunshine."

Clementine narrows her eyes with suspicion. "Why are you both in the bathroom? That's weird."

"We didn't want to wake you while we brushed our teeth," Jonas answers without delay.

And as if his answer needs no further questioning, Clementine shrugs and relaxes her expression. "Okay. Can I go now?" She points toward the toilet.

"Sorry, pumpkin."

We scurry out of the bathroom and leave her be. Heading into the kitchen, we start our morning like a family. Jonas and I take out ingredients to make chocolate chip pancakes, cheesy scrambled eggs, and turkey bacon. We move seamlessly in the small space as if this normal task happens daily. While I whisk the eggs, he ladles batter on a hot skillet and sprinkles it with mini chips. The bacon sizzles in the oven as I pour the eggs into a pan.

Jonas deposits the first batch of pancakes on a plate, butters the skillet again, and adds more batter. Spatula midair, he glances my way. "I don't want this to come out the wrong way, but you and Clementine shouldn't be alone. Not until the case ends."

I stop scraping the eggs from left to right and peer over at him. He means well. Wants to protect me. Protect us. But if I am supposed to live my life normally, that means I will be alone from time to time. Or with only Clementine. How can I not be?

"Jonas, I get where you're coming from. I understand it. But how am I supposed to follow a regular routine—work, school, errands—if I" —I pause and take a deep breath— "we need a bodyguard all the time."

He flips the pancakes, sets the spatula down, and steps closer. I peek over my shoulder and check Clementine isn't eavesdropping. "We'll find a way. Between me, Penny, everyone at the shop, and our friends, we can make it happen. We need to." I roll my eyes and shake my head. Jonas grazes his knuckles down my cheek. "It's only temporary. And if something happens to either of you, I won't be able to live with myself."

I turn the heat on the stove to low and face him fully. His eyes bore into me, glassy and a tinge red. Concern written in the underscoring on his forehead. I snake my arms around his waist and rest my cheek over his heart. Warm arms envelop and hug me with renewed strength. "It won't be easy."

"Doesn't matter," he mumbles into my hair.

"How will we get everyone in on the plan?" A legitimate question, considering not everyone knows the details of my past.

Jonas kisses the crown of my head and releases me, stepping back to the skillet.

"The shop is closed today?" I nod. "Let's invite everyone over for an impromptu cookout. We can use my birthday as the initial excuse."

Not a bad idea. The guys will definitely be down for a gathering if we involve food and drinks. Penny will get Iliana on board. The last time we all did something outside of work was too long ago. Years ago, we'd hang out a Sunday per month. Nothing special, just enjoying life and seeing each other somewhere besides the same four walls.

"Okay. After breakfast, I'll get the ball rolling with everyone from the shop. What time?"

"Is five good? We can chat a bit while I get the grill going. Eat around six."

"Should be fine. Clementine will also get to play with Ashton, Rez's little boy."

Jonas cooks the last of the pancakes while I take the bacon from the oven. We plate up the food and sit at the breakfast bar with Clementine, sharing our plan for the day. A lazy morning, followed by house cleanup and a trip to the grocery store before having friends over. She chimes in with food she wants added to the grocery list and tells Spartan he will meet one of her friends today.

After texting our friends and watching hours of Sunday morning cartoons, we decide to vacate the couch and get to work. The inside of the house sparkles within the hour. A candle lit in the living area wafts the scent of fresh cotton around the house. Jonas goes outside to check the grill, making sure we have enough charcoal.

The trip to the grocery store goes quicker than expected, but we walk out with more than our list of items. Every time Clementine pointed to something and begged, Jonas caved and added it to the cart. Thankfully, she only did this a handful of times. She picked good things, though—s'mores making supplies, a couple movie night candies, and berries to go with our leftover cake.

Back at the house, Jonas marinates chicken and forms burger patties while I cook pasta and potatoes for salads. Clementine digs out colored pencils, crayons, and a coloring book from her stuffed overnight bad. Sneaky girl brought everything.

We finish prepping whatever possible. Every opportunity we get, Jonas and I exchange touches. A forearm graze. A kiss on the cheek as he reaches for a gadget. His front brushing against my back as he moves past me. My fingers tracing his low back as I set the strainer in the sink.

Will it always be like this? The constant need to touch each other. For me to feel his warmth and strength and love. To be near him, to see him, to smile with him. Some may consider our attachment unhealthy. Clingy. I say, when you find the person who connects all the dots perfectly, the person who makes you see the whole constellation and not just a mess of stars, do what makes your heart happy.

Yes, I pushed us apart when Leo made an appearance. But it was maternal instinct to shut everything down and protect my daughter. Little did I know, Jonas was equally willing to go to battle for her to stay. And no matter what is thrown at us going forward, I won't make the same mistake.

The doorbell chimes and snaps my attention to Clementine, who peeks out the window and waves like a loon. "People are here."

That she doesn't mention names has me heading for the window. Glancing out, I spot Cora and Gavin. Walking up the drive is Erin, Shelly, and Micah. "Those are my and Jonas's friends. The ones we went bowling with." Clementine nods.

Jonas opens the door and invites everyone in. I introduce Clementine to everyone and she gives each of them a hug. The guys loiter in the kitchen and catch up while us ladies sit in the living room. Less than five minutes pass before Clementine bolts up from her spot at the coffee table and peeks out the window. The recognizable low rumble of Reznor's car echoes outside.

"They're here," she exclaims, jumping in place. "Can I open the door?"

"Wait until they walk up, so Spartan doesn't run out."

Jonas excuses himself and joins us at the door. Clementine peeps up at me and I nod. She flings the door open and runs up to everyone, giving them hugs. I stare after her a minute, watching as she plays mini hostess. "Come on, guys. Let's go inside." She takes Ashton's hand and helps him up the porch stairs.

Once everyone steps inside, I introduce my tattoo family to everyone already here. Gavin shakes Reznor's hand and gives a more in-depth introduction to Cora. I learn Reznor inked Cora's name on Gavin's chest before I inked bands on their fingers. Small world. Reznor introduces Tatyana—his long-term girlfriend—and Ashton, their son. Before everyone settles, Jonas suggests we head out back and start grilling.

Cora deposits a small cooler on the counter and takes out a few items. When she sees me staring, she explains. "Vegan burger and sides."

"You should've said something. We would've got stuff at the store."

"No worries. Kind of used to bringing stuff when we go places." She hands the patty to Jonas and says to cook it like a normal burger.

Everyone heads out back, Spartan on Jonas's heels, praying for him to drop something. The kids share a lounger and pull up a side table to color. Spartan runs around the yard, sniffing the grass and searching for lizards. I light the fire bowl while Jonas mans the grill. Beforehand, we brought out extra chairs from the garage, and now have more than enough seating for the large group.

The guys shoot the shit by the grill while us ladies talk on the outdoor L-shaped couch. Cora tells me about an upcoming wedding she and Erin are shooting. Erin has slowly transitioned from an assistant to a photographer over the last year. She continues to learn, but Cora is the perfect teacher. Since the change, the two of them have tweaked the business. A fresh name—Hunt-Wallace Enterprises—and new faces. They reach more clients, hired assistants, and have the ability to take time off. Cora says she couldn't do it without Erin, while Erin disagrees.

Shelly talks about the floral industry in ways I have never heard. Quotas and sales and deadlines. Sounds like a nine-to-five corporate office gig. But I suppose all industries have this. I never think of the tattoo industry like this, but I suppose Oscar—the shop owner—does. He pops in once a month to check on us but leaves us be for the most part. He owns several shops in the state but designates a manager for each location to make on-the-spot decisions. That would be Reznor for us. He keeps the shop going with ease.

Penny chimes in on occasion, but otherwise chills beside me with our arms hooked at the elbow.

Once the food is ready, we all gather around the fire bowl and eat. Smiles and laughter and shoulder bumps flow like the beer in our bottles. When people start leaning back and patting their stomachs, I glance up at Jonas and nod.

"Thanks for coming on such short notice, everyone," Jonas announces. "We brought you here under the guise of a makeup birthday celebration. While that's true, there's more to it."

All eyes turn my direction. The men with an air of concern and the women silently questioning what the hell is going on. Penny glances down at my abdomen before meeting my eyes again and I shake my head. She laughs.

"Some of you know," Jonas continues, looking to Penny before scanning the group, "and some of you don't. But Autumn's ex has started stirring up trouble." This causes Rex and Reznor to sit taller. "He filed for sole custody of Clementine and has since made verbal threats to both of us. We have maintained our cool and done everything through the appropriate channels. But it seems he is stepping up his game. So…" Jonas smiles and my favorite dimple appears. "We are enacting Operation Don't-leave-Autumn-and-Clementine-alone."

Everyone nods except the children.

"What does this look like?" Penny asks.

"Basically, someone is with them around the clock. Doesn't matter who. Even together, someone should be with them. Obviously, when here, they'll be with me."

"And with me at the apartment and work," Penny chimes in. "But if our schedules don't align, we'll sort it out ahead of time."

The conversation flows for another hour before people leave. Beforehand, we all exchange phone numbers and sort out tomorrow's schedule for now. Since Penny rode with Reznor, Tatyana, and Ashton, she stays to ride home with me and Clementine.

We clean up the back patio and kitchen. The closer we get to clean, the tighter my stomach twists. After a wonderful weekend with Jonas, I don't want to leave. I want to crawl into bed and snuggle with him. Listen to his soft breaths as he sleeps. Fall asleep to the thumping cadence of his heart beneath my ear. Wake up to the scent of his skin and the warmth of his embrace.

But we aren't there yet. Aren't to the point where we spend several days straight in the same place. Should we be? Would it be odd this early on? Some would say yes while others would suggest there is no correct timeline.

Reluctantly, Clementine and I gather our bags and trod to the door. Penny holds out her hand for my keys. "I'll start the car so you can exchange good nights." After I hand them over, she walks to the car and starts it.

Clementine hugs Jonas around the waist. "'Night, Mr. Jonas."

He hugs her small frame. "'Night, sunshine."

She clings to Spartan a moment. "Night night, Sparty. See you soon. We can have more slumber parties." Giving him one last squeeze, she trots down the drive and gets in the back seat of the car.

"I don't want to leave," I confess, peering up at Jonas.

He pulls me into him, wraps one arm around my waist while he braces the length of my spine with the other, fingers in my hair. "Don't want you to go either. After we figure out schedules, we'll be together more nights. Guaranteed." He kisses the crown of my head.

"Music to my ears."

We inch apart. Jonas frames my face in his palms and drops his lips to mine. He kisses me sweet at first, then traces my lower lip with the tip of his tongue. I deepen the kiss, devouring him as if I won't see him for days again. When he breaks the kiss, I brace myself on his forearms.

"See you tomorrow, scarlet."

"Tomorrow." I give him one last kiss before walking to the car.

I toss my bag in the back, then get behind the wheel. As we back out, Clementine and I wave goodbye.

A block from Jonas's house, Penny twists in her seat to face me. "I foresee needing a new roommate in my future."

I slap her arm without looking. "Shut up," I joke. But I don't fight the painful smile. Nor do I dispute her accusation. Because I see it too.

sixteen

JONAS

Nothing like startling awake to a cold nose and wet tongue in your armpit.

"Argh! What are you doing?" I croak, arms flailing in a desperate attempt to stop Spartan.

Woof, woof, woof.

I peek up at the husky hovering an inch from my face. "You don't behave like this with Clementine," I accuse.

Woof, woof.

"I see how it is. Well, I'll remember this conversation next time you beg for treats."

The alarm buzzes and Spartan jumps off the bed. I slap the clock and roll into Autumn's pillow, smothering myself with her scent. Not quite the same as her in my arms, but it will make due for now.

I fall out of bed, slip on sweatpants and a hoodie, and use the bathroom before clipping Spartan's leash on. We trod out the door and walk our normal route around the neighborhood.

Five houses down, an odd sensation washes over me. A fluttery twitch in my solar plexus. I stare down the sidewalk and across the street but spot nothing out of the ordinary. When Spartan stops to sniff a mailbox, I glance behind us and scan where we came from. Being five in the morning, I don't usually see neighbors during our morning walk. And this morning is no exception as I spot nothing. But the uneasy tremble in my gut begs to differ. The sensation screams at me that I am not alone.

Unable to shake the feeling, I cut our walk short.

Back in the house, I go about my morning weekday routine. After eating a quick breakfast, I pour the pot of coffee in my thermos, grab my wallet and keys, then put Spartan in his crate and turn on his radio.

"Be good. See you later, bud." I ruffle his fur through the grate.

I lock up the house and walk to the Jeep. As I peer up and press the fob to unlock it, I notice a slip of paper pinned beneath my windshield wiper. Approaching the Jeep, I scan up and down the street for signs of anyone but see nothing odd or notable.

Once the paper is within arm's reach, I tug it out. I check the street one last time before unfolding the paper and looking down.

She doesn't belong to you.

What the actual fuck?

My fingers curl as I start to ball up the note. But before I wad the note or rip it to shreds, I take a deep breath and relax my digits. I walk to the end of my driveway and scan the street again as I stuff the note in my pocket.

I scrutinize every car along the street. Peek through the windshields for people or movement. Scan the length of the sidewalk, searching for anyone on foot. Glance up the nearby trees and stare through every shrub within a fifty-foot circumference.

Not a goddamn thing.

"Come at me, motherfucker," I growl. "You won't touch her."

Not sure who this asshole thinks he is, but there isn't a chance in hell he will lay his hands on Autumn. He is damn lucky I restrain myself from beating his ass.

I get in the Jeep and start it. While the engine warms up, I take out my phone and type a message to Autumn.

> Morning. After you drop Clementine at school, please call me.

I send the message, connect my phone to the Jeep, and drive to work.

When I step into the office, I stash away my concerns about the note for now and smile when Dad looks up. He matches it with one of his own. "'Morning, son. Glad to still see a smile on your face. How are the girls?"

"Good. We had a nice weekend together. Created a plan to make sure they're safe."

Dad rises from his desk and walks to the dish rack to grab his mug for coffee. After mixing our morning caffeine, we sit behind our desks. "Glad you're taking care of them. Raised you right," he states with pride in his voice.

Shortly after the garage opens for the day, my phone rings. I wipe my hands and retrieve it from my coveralls. "'Morning, scarlet," I say, walking toward the office.

"Good morning. Everything okay?" Concern laces her words and I hate that I have to deliver more unsavory news.

"Are you driving?"

"No. Penny is. We just dropped Clementine off."

Once I step inside the office and close the door, I tell her about the note. "As I left for work this morning, I noticed a piece of paper under my wiper blade. It was a note." The line goes silent for too long. I check the screen to make sure the call didn't drop and see it hasn't. "Autumn?"

"Yeah, sorry." I picture her with her eyes closed, taking deep breaths. "What did it say?"

I swallow and relay the message. "When I took Spartan for a walk earlier, I felt as if someone was following me. But I never saw anyone."

"This is ridiculous," she mumbles. "Will you take a picture of it and send it to me, please?"

"Of course." At this point, I have no idea what steps we should take. But she should definitely tell someone. "Should you send it to your attorney?"

She huffs into the line, exasperated over the whole scenario. "Probably. I don't know. When we get off the phone, I'll call her."

I don't want to upset Autumn with how I feel right now, but I refuse to hide or run from the stabbing pain in my chest. When it comes to Autumn and Clementine, everything needs to be out in the open. She needs to hear where my head and heart lie. "Autumn, please be safe. Both of you. Keep your eyes open and stay vigilant."

"I will," she whispers. "Promise."

"Thank you." I sigh. In some respects, I am glad Autumn and Clementine didn't stay over last night. They would have been witness to the note this morning and Autumn might not have been able to keep her cool in front of Clementine. Then again, maybe the note wouldn't have been there if they stayed. Who knows? "Call me back when you know more."

"Okay." Her voice travels from miles away, quiet and somber. "Talk to you soon."

The need to tell her I love her hangs from the tip of my tongue now more than ever, but I don't say the words. I want to. God, do I want to. But now feels so far from appropriate. Her thoughts are probably all over the place with worry. I don't want the first time I express my love for her to be during a moment of stress. I don't want it to be over the phone, where I cannot see her face and vice versa. Plus, I don't want her to feel obligated to return the sentiment just because I put it out there.

So I bite my tongue and project my love into the universe in her direction. Send her every ounce of positivity and love she has stirred in my veins.

"Soon. Stay with Penny."

"I will. Bye."

"Bye, scarlet."

The call disconnects and I stand staring at the wall a moment. I zone out, close my eyes, and beg to the heavens for all of this madness to end soon.

Then I remember to take a picture of the note and send it to Autumn. Once she receives it, she texts her thanks.

I stay in the office a moment to drink another mug of coffee. When I head back into the garage, Dad catches my eye and waves me over.

"Everything alright?"

I nod. "Just more drama. Autumn is calling her attorney to figure out what we do next." I tell him about the plan for the girls to not be alone and about the note this morning.

"Keep me up to date."

I agree and amble over to the car I was working on before the call. Picking up the socket wrench, I get back to work. Thankfully, I can work on the engine without one-hundred-percent focus. Because my mind is far from this garage. My arms mentally around Autumn as we navigate through this nightmare.

seventeen

"What's going on?" Penny asks when I get off the phone with Jonas.

I huff and drop my head back on the seat. "Jonas found a note on his car this morning." My phone pings with an incoming text. I open it and see the note. The handwriting too boxy, as if someone put extra effort into disguising their penmanship. "And he just sent a picture of it."

"Can I see?"

"In a minute. Let me call Theresa first."

I scroll through my contacts and tap on the attorney's office, bringing the phone to my ear. On the second ring, the young man at the front desk answers. "Good morning, attorney Theresa Chang's office. How may I assist you?"

"Good morning. This is Autumn Rooker. I need to inform Theresa of some new information regarding my case. It's somewhat urgent."

"Let me check if she's available, Ms. Rooker. I need to place you on a brief hold."

"Thank you." Jazzy café music floats through the phone line while I wait. Not a minute later, Theresa answers.

We exchange pleasantries, then she turns all business. Asking if Clementine and I are okay. Once I assure her we are physically safe, I share the incident of Leo stopping by Jonas's work on Friday afternoon and the note on his car this morning. She asks me to send her the picture, but to get the actual note from Jonas. When I have it, I am to bring it to her after I file a police report.

Not that I didn't foresee this happening, but dizziness starts to swallow me whole. Everything whirls around me in the passenger seat as I take deep, relaxing breaths. Beside me, Penny reaches over and clutches my arm.

"Auti, you good?"

I nod, slow and unsure. Lifting the phone away from my mouth, I whisper, "Go to Jonas's work." She gives me a thumbs up.

Theresa informs me she will spend the day trying to get the hearing moved up in light of this new information. I thank her and promise to see her soon.

"Talk to me," Penny states as soon as I hang up with Theresa.

"The note says *she doesn't belong to you.* Jonas thinks it's about me, but I think it refers to Clementine." I take a deep breath then continue. "We need to get the note from Jonas, go to the police station and file a report, then take the note to the attorney as evidence." I press my palms to my eyes. "How am I supposed to work today? And how am I supposed to get around if you have to work today and I shouldn't be alone?"

"Call Rez. He'll understand. As for me, I'll tote you around as long as possible. My shift doesn't start until noon. Hopefully, we can knock this out in the next couple of hours."

While Penny drives, I call Reznor and explain the situation. He waves off my worry and tells me to take the day off. With everything going on, his empathy is bar none. At least I have one less stressor to bog me down.

Penny parks in front of Thompson's Garage and I jump out. Jonas dashes over to me and we exchange a brief kiss.

"Hate to cut this short, but I need the note to file a police report and take to the attorney's office."

Jonas fishes the note from his jeans pocket beneath his coveralls. When he hands it to me, he kisses my forehead. "Let me know how it goes." He waves at Penny. "And if you need me later when Pen goes to work."

"I will." We exchange one last kiss. "Call you when I know more."

Penny whips out of the parking lot faster than she pulled in. We speed down the road, but I miss the blur of the buildings and trees.

I stare down at my hands in silence. Stare at the ivory paper between my fingers. Rub the vellum with the pads of my thumbs. The subtle roughness familiar, but can't place from where. I unfold the paper with ease, eyes glued to the shaky block letters. Tracing the slight swoops and lines and edges of the letters, I study the print for any indication of who wrote it.

The answer is there. Just out of reach. On the tip of the tongue. But it retreats back into my mind, mimicking a frightened child.

Folding the note back together, I tuck it in my purse before eyeing the road. We are blocks from the police station now. Any other day, I would reprimand Penny for her lead foot. But today, grateful doesn't begin to cover her speediness.

She parks the car in the police station visitor lot and stands at my side the moment we step out of the car. For a beat, I contemplate telling her to wait in the car but know I won't win the battle.

After checking in with a receptionist too bright-eyed and smiley to work in a police station, we sit in the waiting area. With the early hour, I pray we get in and out quickly. Minutes later, the gods answer my request and send an officer to call me back. Since we're in the station, Penny opts to sit in the waiting area while I speak with the officer.

I have never seen the inside of a police station but didn't picture it looking like an open area call center. Cubicle central with low glass walls dividing clusters of desks. Weird.

The female officer directs me to have a seat. Unyielding plastic digs into my hips as I sit down. Minus a few framed photos of her with fellow officers or superiors, her workspace appears as sterile as my booth at the shop.

She extends a hand across the desk and I shake it. "Officer Martinez. I was told you need to file a harassment report."

"Yes. I'm in the middle of a custody suit and my daughter's birth father has begun harassing my boyfriend." Opening my purse with shaky hands, I retrieve the note. "Friday, the birth father went to my boyfriend's place of business and provoked a verbal altercation. This morning, when my boyfriend left for work, he found this on his car." I hand the note to her. "My attorney advised me to come here and file the report before giving her the note."

Officer Martinez takes the note and studies it momentarily. "Bear with me, I need to ask you questions and document everything. Shouldn't take long. Please answer as openly and honestly as possible."

For the next thirty-plus minutes, Officer Martinez prattles off question after question. Some in regards to Jonas, others in reference to Leo. I provide her with as much detail as possible. She scans the note into the digital file and hands it back.

With the note being touched so much this morning, she said the likelihood of lifting prints from someone other than me or Jonas is low. Before she walks me to the front, she prints off a copy of the report and hands it to me along with her business card.

"If anything else pops up, reach out." She points to her contact information on the card. "I may not respond immediately, but will as soon as possible." I nod. "In the meantime, I suggest being vigilant. Stay aware and steer away from any possible interactions unless your attorney is present."

"Thank you, Officer Martinez." We shake hands again.

"You're welcome. Stay safe." With that, she leaves me in the reception area.

Penny peeks up from her phone, locking it and rising when she spots me. "Done?"

"Yeah. Now, to Theresa's office."

I tuck the report and note in my purse on our way to the car. The second I click my seat belt in place, Penny backs out of the parking space. I prattle off the address for the office and direct her where to go. Thank goodness, the drive to Theresa's office takes less than ten minutes.

Inside, Penny does the same as at the police station and waits out front. In the conference room with Theresa, I relay what Officer Martinez said, then hand over the police report and note. An unfortunate side effect of no prints or detectable handwriting, the police cannot point the finger directly at Leo without further evidence.

Theresa keeps the original documentation but makes copies for my records. "I submitted a request for an earlier hearing date. Should receive a response soon. As soon as I do, I'll reach out to you. Meanwhile, steer clear of Leo, if possible. If he approaches you or Jonas, call the police. With a report filed, it will reflect poorly on him if an officer arrives on scene." We rise from our seats, and before leaving the conference room, Theresa gives me a hug. The embrace comforts me and I return it. "We'll get through this. Until then, stay strong and lean on people you trust."

"Thank you," I say, breaking the hug. "Doing my best."

She walks me back to the front and reminds me she will be in touch. Stopping here hasn't wiped away all the anxiety and stress, but knowing I have a team of people on my side helps ease it slightly.

Penny and I stroll out to the car, the adrenaline buzz from the morning fading as it inches closer to midday. We get in the car and sit quietly. Penny doesn't start the car or turn the key to kick the radio on. For a moment, we just breathe in strength and exhale the bullshit.

Until Leo reappeared, life had been low-key and kosher. Yes, my romance life was snore-worthy until Jonas came into the picture, but I had been content with sharing all my time with Clementine. She is the most important person in my world and her happiness is more important than my own. Little did I know, me being in a loving relationship boosted her happiness.

After a deep breath, Penny starts the car and steers us out of the lot. "Don't know about you, but I'm ready for this day to be done."

"Me—" My phone buzzes in my purse and I dig it out. Clementine's school name flashes on the screen. I rush to answer. "Hello?"

"May I speak with Ms. Rooker, please?"

"This is she."

"Hi, Ms. Rooker. This is Daniel in the front office of Clementine's school. We have a gentleman here, not on the approved list, who is trying to take Clementine out of school early. He will not identify himself. We have denied him, of course, but need to notify you."

I stop breathing. *What the fuck is going on?!* I have no clue what the hell is going on in the world, but all the walls are caving in. Seems if it isn't one thing, it's another. Like my and Clementine's life are some big game to toy with.

"Is the man still there?" Penny glances at me, wide-eyed.

"Yes, ma'am. He refuses to leave without Clementine."

I inhale deeply and ball the hand not holding the phone into a fist. My nails bite the skin and I welcome the reality check. "If possible, don't let him leave. I'm on my way. He is *not* to leave with her."

"We will keep him here as long as possible."

"Thank you." I disconnect the call and face Penny. "We need to get to Clementine's school. Now. A man is trying to withdraw her from school."

"What the actual fuck?" Penny belts out as she changes course and speeds toward the elementary school.

"My thoughts exactly."

I scroll through my contacts and tap on Jonas. He answers on the second ring. "Hey, scarlet. That was quicker than expected. Everything go alright?"

For a beat, I stay silent. I clench and relax my fingers a few times. "Jonas, please don't freak out. Because I'm freaking out enough for the both of us."

"You're scaring me. What's going on?"

I pinch my eyes together so tight, a sharp jab shoots from the midline out. After a deep breath, I answer. "Penny is driving me to Clementine's school right now. An unidentified man is trying to withdraw her."

Deafening silence. Then a bang so loud I hold the phone away from my ear. "Motherfucker," Jonas growls. He remains quiet a minute. "Want me to meet you there?"

Part of me wants to say yes. To ask him to meet me there and help protect me and Clementine from all this craziness. But it isn't sensible. More angry tempers will not fix this. And without seeing his face, I *feel* the pain and anger radiating off Jonas. He loves my little girl as much as he does me and is willing to do whatever necessary to protect us both.

"No. We're pulling in now. I'll check in soon. I—" I cut myself off. *Not the time, Autumn.*

"Me too, scarlet."

The call disconnects just before Penny parks the car. I jump out while she waits in the lot. My feet carry me faster than ever before as I run for the office. Daniel from the front desk buzzes me through a locked door and I step inside the warm office.

"Autumn Rooker. You called about a man trying to withdraw my daughter from school."

Daniel smiles as if a stranger wasn't just here trying to steal my child. And it pisses me off. But I bite my tongue and breathe through my anger and frustration.

"Yes. He left a few minutes ago after we wouldn't comply."

"Did you get a name?"

"No, ma'am."

The heater kicks on and ruffles papers on the countertop between us. Daniel's clipped answer bumps my irritation up a notch. The whole situation isn't his fault and I don't want to take my problems out on him, but the fact he seems so nonchalant about this annoys me further.

"Can you tell me what he looked like?"

"A few inches taller than you, gray hair, balding on top. Short-sleeve dress shirt. Khaki pants. Older, but I'm not good with age." He winces. "Until I asked for his identification, he was overly polite."

"Did he say anything else? Besides asking to pick up Clementine?"

He shakes his head. "No, ma'am."

Well, at least my daughter is still here and safe. "Thank you, Daniel. While here, I'd like to review and update who may pick up Clementine."

"Sure thing."

With each tap of the keys on his keyboard, I lose my cool a little more. Why the hell is this my life right now? Why are people trying to steal my daughter? Whoever came to the school today was not Leo. His father, perhaps. No one I know fits the description Daniel provided. Nicely dressed fits Leo's family.

All I want to do is tip my head back and scream at the sky. Scream loud and violently. Scream until my throat becomes sandpaper and my larynx shrivels.

As I update Clementine's approved pickup list to include Jonas—just in case—I decide to withdraw her from school early. At this point, she has less than half the day left. Once she arrives in the office, I take her hand and hold it tighter than usual.

When we walk out of the building, she glances up at me. "Why did you pick me up early, Mama?"

My daughter doesn't need my stress, so I choose to skirt around the truth. "Today has been a crazy day. Just need to have you with me." She hugs my side but doesn't say a word.

I open the back door for her and she hops in. Sitting in the passenger seat, I face Penny. "Not there," I mumble. "Left before we got here. But it wasn't him. Someone older." Parallel lines wrinkle Penny's forehead. "Will you drop us off at Jonas's work? You can keep the car."

"Of course."

In my short-lived life, I have experienced a lot. Not in regards to travel. But actual life experiences. Hope and adoration. Despair and worthlessness. Love and joy.

Today, in this very moment, is the first time I encounter extreme vulnerability. Today is the first time I feel my and my daughter's safety is at risk. And I have no clue where to go from here.

When I plucked the note off my Jeep this morning, fury slithered in my bloodstream. When Autumn stopped here earlier to collect the note to take to the police and her attorney, her red eyes and withered stature nearly crippled me. But when Autumn called forty-three minutes ago to tell me an unknown man was trying to remove Clementine from school, I lost my shit. Literally.

Once our call disconnected, I threw a wrench at the back wall of the garage. Then, stormed into the office, grabbed a pillow off the couch, and screamed into the stuffed material. More than once. Although the action was cathartic, relief didn't follow.

The measures this man takes to hurt Autumn, emotionally more so than physically, blows me away. Disgusts me more than comprehensible. Makes me violent and irrational. I aim my rage at inanimate objects, but it boils beneath the surface, begging to seep out. I remind myself this is probably all a ploy. A way for him to provoke me or Autumn. And as much as I am dying to take my aggression out on him, I won't.

I refuse to stoop to his level and be a lesser man. Money may buy you fancy things, but it doesn't make you a decent human. People choose to be decent. From what I have seen so far, Leo has made his choice and it is nowhere near respectable.

For the last five minutes, I have laid on the creeper and stared at the same oil filter. If today were a good day, I would have removed it four and a half minutes ago. I have yet to lift a finger.

Just as I do, the familiar rumble of Autumn's car garners my attention. I roll out from under the car, point to James and ask him to finish the job. After my outburst earlier, everyone here is on edge. So James nods and shifts his attention. After this is all over, I need to treat the staff to beers and burgers.

I jog over to the car. Autumn and Clementine both get out, opposing expressions on their faces. Autumn looks as if she just went ten rounds in a fight and came out visually unscathed. But I know her insides are pulverized. Clementine is all smiles and sunshine. Obviously, she has no idea what all has happened today. Which is good. Children don't deserve to bear the brunt of adult issues.

With as much enthusiasm as I can muster, I haul both my girls in for a hug. "Hey," I whisper in Autumn's ear. "Been worried about you both."

Autumn squeezes me with more oomph. "Can we stay here until you're off work? I-I don't feel safe going anywhere else right now."

"Don't even have to ask." I unravel my grip on them and squat down in front of Clementine. "Hey, sunshine. Let's go sit in my office for a bit. Is that cool with you?"

Clementine nods and scrunches up her nose. "It smells funny here."

Autumn and I laugh. "Yeah. Sometimes the stuff in car engines smells weird. But I promise the office smells nice." I cup a hand around my mouth and lean into her. "My dad sprays flower air freshener in there sometimes." She giggles and I love how unaware she is of the chaos.

I lead them into the office and tell them to use whatever they need. Before I head out to the garage, I order lunch for the three of us and promise my girls to be in when it arrives.

Back in the garage, Dad wanders over. "Everything okay?" He tips his head toward the office.

There is no use in sugarcoating it. Because shit is definitely *not* okay. "Not really." I relay what happened at Clementine's school. Relay how unsafe Autumn feels. Share how she is doing her best to not let Clementine hear all the nitty-gritty details because it isn't fair to worry her over something she ultimately can do nothing to fix.

Out of nowhere, Dad hauls me in for a hug. "Sorry you're both dealing with this. Let us know if you need help. Even to watch Clementine so you two can run errands or go to appointments."

I nod. "Thanks, Dad."

Taking back over my job, I thank James and work until lunch arrives. Now that Autumn and Clementine are here, I breathe easier. Focus without difficulty. Relax with less effort.

When the food is delivered, Dad tells me to take as much time as I need. I carry the bag into the office and enjoy the next hour with my girls. Clementine has been busy doing schoolwork while Autumn occupied herself with the internet, reading old magazines in the office, and occasionally helping Clementine with her work.

We munch on sandwiches while Clementine tells us about the art project they are doing—a collage made from magazine clippings where each image must represent a letter of their name. Needless to say, her collage will have lots of pictures. While Clementine eats french fries and does a sheet of math equations, I take the opportunity to talk in hushed tones with Autumn.

"Might be a good idea if we update everyone later. We can visit the shop after work, then text everyone not there."

Autumn nods and leans on my bicep while resting her head near my shoulder. "Good plan." I kiss the crown of her head and she closes her eyes. "Just want this to be over."

"Me too. Soon." I take one of her hands between mine in my lap. "Until then, definitely don't want either or both of you alone. Not even at home."

May seem like drastic measures, but when it comes to my girls, no measure is too extreme. I will protect them until my last breath. And that breath won't come anytime soon.

Wetness hits my collarbone, and I tip my chin to look at Autumn. She stares at Clementine with silent tears rolling over the bridge of her nose and down her cheek. I drop a hand from hers to reach up and wipe away her tears. She leans in to my touch and kisses my palm.

Autumn tilts her head on my shoulder, pressing her lips to my neck, my jaw, beneath my ear. My eyes roll back as my jaw falls slack. We have kissed several times with Clementine in the room, but right now, I want to kiss her fiercely. Much stronger than any PG suggested rating.

I cup her jaw and meet her lips in the middle. Warmth and tenderness and intimacy collide as our lips move in time. Soft and gentle at first. But the moment she paints the tip of her tongue across my upper lip, I gasp and tug her closer. Inhale her heady cherry vanilla aroma. Taste the cola on her tongue. Tremble as she adjusts her position and fists my hair. Scoot her closer when she moans down my throat. Groan in return when I brush over her pulse and feel how viciously her heart thumps for me. For us. For this kiss.

When her hands untangle from my hair and drop to my chest, I break the kiss but don't lift my lips from hers. "If she wasn't here right now…"

Autumn presses her lips to mine again. "Same."

Reluctantly, I inch away from her and groan. "I have to get back out there, but only a bit longer. Do you need anything? You can use the computer if you want." She shakes her head. "Be done soon." I kiss the tip of her nose before getting up, adjusting myself as I do.

When I get back to work, Dad and James take their lunch. For a Monday, the garage is slow. Then again, we are caught up on the few labor-intensive jobs we had, which helps other jobs go quicker. While Dad has lunch, I finish a routine oil change James started, plug a tire in no time, and schedule body repair for a crumpled fender.

As a new customer pulls up, Dad exits the office/customer waiting area. I check the wall clock between two of the bay doors. He took twenty, maybe twenty-five minutes for lunch. At minimum, we take thirty. Been that way since day one of Dad buying this place.

After collecting basic information from the customer, I show them to the waiting area while we work on their car. When I walk back into the garage, Dad is gearing up to take over.

"Hey, old man. I got this. You should finish your lunch."

He laughs and shakes his head. "When James gets back, you head out for the day."

What? Although I'm grateful for the offer, I don't want to ditch everyone and overwhelm them. "Why? I can stay longer."

Dad steps closer and rests a hand on my shoulder. "Of course, you *can*. Doesn't mean you *should*." He points his thumb over his shoulder. "They need you more than me right now. And we'll be fine here. Been slow." He taps my shoulder one, two, three times. "Son, there are times when the people you care about are more important than work. You need to recognize those moments and do what's right. And being with them while all this is happening, it's the right choice."

Who knew my dad was philosophical? He is a good man. Always has been. Puts those he cares about above everything else. Which is exactly what he tells me to do now. How can I not be proud of the man who raised me with heart? Hopefully, I meet his expectations when it comes to being a good man. Tough shoes to fill and all.

I pull him in for a hug and hold him longer than our typical hugs. "Thanks, Dad. For everything you've done and always do."

"Love ya, Jonas. Now, stop being all sappy. We have work to get done before you go."

I laugh and slap the back of his shoulder before I release him. We work in sync for almost thirty minutes before James returns. Once he jumps in, I say my goodbyes and collect the girls from the office.

We make a quick stop at my house—which is easier said than done when Clementine and Spartan get together. Once Spartan has done his business, we pile back into the Jeep and drive toward the shop. Autumn has been quiet since we left the garage. More than likely, overwhelmed with everything happening. If my nerves are shot over this whole Leo debacle, I only imagine how crazed she must feel. I just wish there was more for me to do to make it go away.

Monday appears to be an all-around slow business day when I park the Jeep behind the shop. Autumn leads us inside through the back entrance. When we round the front desk where Penny sits, she pops her gum, bolts out of her chair, and hugs Autumn with undeniable strength.

Penny steps back, holding Autumn at arm's length. "Any updates from earlier?" Autumn shakes her head, still silent.

"We thought it might be a good idea to come update you guys in person."

She nods. "Rex should be done in a few. Rez is indisposed."

Autumn walks us over to her booth and plops down on her stool. I pick Clementine up and sit with her in my lap. Understandably, Autumn is upset and frustrated. But since the day we met, I have never seen her like this. One hundred percent in her head. I would give anything to know what she's thinking right now. To help her trudge through all the *what-if*s and *whys* and *where do we go from here* moments. None of us have all the answers, but we will find them easier together.

Rex finishes up and wipes down his booth. Once everyone comes together, we give the simple version of what happened today. Clementine acts as if she isn't listening, but I notice her ear perk up on occasion.

Everyone is on the same page when it comes to Autumn and/or Clementine always being with someone. The only exception is work and school, which happen by default. For the first time since I met her, Penny stopped chewing gum. Her face never more serious.

"Why don't the two of you stay with me until this settles," I suggest.

Autumn turns to me, eyes wide and jaw slack. "Don't you think that's extreme?"

"Quite the opposite."

"Jonas, I love being at your house. But being there nightly, without everything I need, or everything Clementine needs, it's more of a hassle."

Ouch. I see her point—us picking up their belongings frequently—but it still stings. "Can we at least compromise?" Last thing I need to do is give Autumn something else to worry over.

She tucks her lips between her teeth and rocks her jaw side to side. Her cognac irises have dulled today. Darkened. They dart between mine, glassy and indecisive. I hate that she has to make these choices. I hate that she fears stepping foot outside, worried who might be waiting. Hate that she questions every decision about their lives.

"We should do at least two to three nights a week at the apartment." Her decision lacks confidence. She may change her mind. Make it more time at her apartment. Or... possibly more time at the house. Fingers crossed for the latter.

"Whatever you feel most comfortable with, scarlet. You good with Spartan tagging along?"

Clementine bounces up from my lap. "Sparty!" She rushes Autumn. "Please, Mama."

Autumn tucks a strand of Clementine's hair behind her ear. "Sure, pumpkin." She meets my gaze. "Tonight, let's stay at my place."

I lean in and kiss her forehead. "Fine with me. We should grab dinner soon."

The group disburses. After saying our goodbyes, the three of us pile into the Jeep and pick up a quick bite to eat. We stop at my house, feed Spartan, and gather everything we need for the night.

No matter how many trips it takes, no matter how uncomfortable the arrangement, I will protect my girls.

nineteen

AUTUMN

I told Jonas we would alternate between staying at my apartment and staying at his house. That was Monday. Monday, we stayed at my apartment. Now it is Thursday, and we haven't been at my apartment since, with the exception of packing stuff to bring to Jonas's. To be honest, I would more than love to stay here every night. Question is, am I ready?

Two very different voices clamber inside my head. Take up space and want to be heard. One claims to be reason, while the other claims to be reality. Both make me seem certifiable.

Believe it or not, reason is the temperamental one. The loudest and most annoying voice. Reason spews off all the what-if questions. Reason makes me second-guess myself and the choices I have always made. Makes me paranoid and uneasy. Before reason came into play, I never felt this uncomfortable in my own skin or mind.

Now, reality… she sits in the corner. A quiet spectator. She only speaks up when reason gets a little out of hand. But when reality voices her opinion, everyone stops to listen. Reality stands tall and fierce. Is a force to be reckoned with. Reminds me I deserve to live a life full of love and passion and exultation. I deserve to smile and laugh and joke around with people who lift me up and stand strong beside me. I deserve to live the life of my choosing, not what someone else deems fit.

Some days, reality rises above. Other days, reason stomps her foot and knocks reality down a notch.

Since the note and incident at Clementine's school on Monday, nothing else has happened. Seventy-two-plus hours without a peep. I want to be excited, but worry something crazy will happen if I get ahead of myself. Celebration is an invitation for chaos.

Clementine sits beside Spartan on Jonas's couch, reading her book to him as part of her homework assignment. Jonas stirs a pot of pasta sauce on the stove while the noodles boil and meatballs bake in the oven. I offered to help, but he shooed me away.

"Need me to pack anything for you? Seeing as I have nothing to do."

He side-eyes me over his shoulder. "Already packed. You just stay on the stool. It's okay to just be sometimes."

I roll my eyes at him. "Says the man who hasn't sat still in days."

When Clementine and I stayed over on Tuesday, the house looked different. At first, I had difficulty putting my finger on what changed. Wasn't until we headed to bed, walking down the hall, that I noticed more light in the second bedroom on the way to Jonas's room. I never toured the office set up in the room, but the desk grabbed your attention when walking by. Now the desk was gone.

I just stood in the hall and stared into the room. Jonas stepped up behind me, wrapped his arms around me, and told me he hadn't used the desk in a while. So, he donated it. The bookshelf had been moved to the living room, which is what was different.

But that wasn't such a big deal.

Nope.

Not by a long shot.

I rest my elbow on the breakfast bar, chin on my palm, and smile at Jonas—well, his backside. The man who took it upon himself to clear out a room less used. To repurpose it and put it to better use. Not better for him, though. Better for Clementine.

Two nights ago in the hall, he steered me into the second bedroom, closed the door, and flipped on the light. I didn't see the white-framed twin bed in the dark, but with the light on, I saw it perfectly. It wasn't only a frame and mattress. It was so much more. *Is* so much more.

"Do you like it," he had whispered in my ear. "It's for Clementine. So she has her own bed here. But don't tell her yet. I want to surprise her."

When Jonas told me this two nights ago, I cried the happiest tears of my life in his arms. With the exception of the day Clementine was born.

In that moment, when Jonas confessed his selfless act, I fell even harder for him. Me telling him I love him was there. Right there. Ready to dive headfirst off my tongue. But reason slapped me in the moment and I didn't profess anything.

But the resistance in me is fast fading.

Yes, it terrifies the hell out of me to tell Jonas I love him. It terrifies me to cut myself open, expose my heart, and pray he knows how to handle the beating organ with compassion and tenderness. That he won't abandon me when times get rough. That he won't jump ship because something doesn't go according to plan. Since Leo appeared, Jonas has stood strong at my side. Fought for me, even when I pushed him away. But reason whispers doubt in my ear. Tells me different circumstances create different responses. Maybe next time around, whatever pops up will push Jonas over the edge.

"If you think any louder, I may actually hear what's brewing in that head of yours," he teases as he strains the pasta.

"Just thinking about the room." As promised, I have not told Clementine. If I refer to it as *the room*, she won't make the connection if she eavesdrops.

Still, Jonas glances over his shoulder at her. She flips the page of her book and points out a picture on the page to Spartan. Oblivious.

"Anything in particular?"

"No. Just the room itself." I tuck my lips between my teeth. "What might look good in there."

Jonas blends the pasta and sauce together, then takes the meatballs out of the oven. He sets the pan on the stove, then steps my way while they cool. "Throw some ideas my way."

He tosses me a wink. A wink. Have I ever seen him wink in my general direction? Not so much. Smile? Yes. God, I love his smile. Especially when his dimple makes an appearance. But winks are not a Jonas thing.

I narrow my eyes. "What are you up to?"

"Just making dinner," he says, a wide smile plumping his cheeks and displaying my favorite dimple. *Way to distract me—for now.*

We plate up dinner and eat earlier than usual. Spartan crunches on his kibble and tries to get Clementine to sneak him pieces of meatball. Thank goodness, she doesn't give in to his cute whines and grumpy groans at her feet.

Once we finish dinner and clean up, I check my email while Jonas grabs his things. An email from Theresa is the bearer of good news.

"Guess what," I say as Jonas walks back out to the living room.

"What's up?"

"The hearing has been moved up. Monday, the twenty-fourth." I smile, glad to have some form of happy news.

"This month?" I nod and Jonas pulls me in for a hug. "Thank god. That's less than two weeks."

His realization swirls in my head. *Less than two weeks.* Before the end of the month, all this will be over. I hope. *Please, let this be over.*

Maybe the hearing adjustment is the reason for all the quiet. No more signs of Leo. No threats or unannounced appearances. I have no plans on jinxing this, but I will take all the good news and positive energy I can get.

"Come on, let's go."

We file out to our cars. Although Operation Don't-leave-Autumn-and-Clementine-alone is still in full swing, it has been deemed safe for me and Clementine to be in my car if someone in the trusted circle follows us. A smidge more freedom while remaining safe.

At the apartment, we crash on the couch and settle in to watch a movie with Clementine. On the nights we stay at the apartment, Jonas sleeps on the couch. Initially, I protested and said he could sleep in bed with me. The gentleman his father raised him to be, he refused to uproot Clementine's normal bed space. It wasn't fair to her.

In the same breath, he also said if she fell asleep on the couch curled up with Spartan, he may reconsider my offer. I don't believe him.

While Clementine watches the movie, Jonas and I watch each other. He lays on his side—back against the cushions—while I lie on my back. With the softest touch, he slowly traces his fingertip over my skin. Following the motion with his eyes.

Over my collarbone, from shoulder to sternum. Up the column of my throat before brushing my hair aside. Along the sensitive skin beneath my ear. Around the shell of my ear. With each direction change, a shiver rolls through my body. When he reaches my temple, he draws small circles there. Drags his finger down my cheekbone. Encircles my lips, then presses the single digit in the middle before bringing his gaze back to mine.

Have you ever watched your lover as they intimately touch you non-sexually? I have never been so enamored with another person.

Without effort, Jonas loves me. Gives me every non-materialistic gift a woman desires and needs. Worships me. Cares for my daughter as if she were his own.

And he does all this without a single word said. His love is in his actions. The way he cannot keep his eyes off me. How he reveres me as a woman and a mother —strong and capable and exceptional. How he touches me—gentle and rough. The way he kisses me—as if every kiss may be our last. The way he breathes me in and hugs me close.

He leans down and I close my eyes as he presses his lips to mine. Slipping a hand behind my neck, he presses more of his weight into me. I pant when he sucks on my lower lip. Roll my eyes back when he dips his tongue in. Fist his hair when our bodies tangle like wild teenagers.

I really want to take him to bed. Strip him bare. Feel his steely-soft erection between my lips. Taste him on my tongue and swallow every drop when he releases down my throat. Grind my hips against his face and scream his name as I gloss the stumble on his jaw. Kiss him like a savage and taste my saltiness on his skin.

I want to do all of this and more. But not tonight. Not here.

In my apartment, we exchange simple touches. Touches that imprint your skin more than any tattoo ever could. Touches that express our fierce connection in other ways. The emotional and mental and spiritual.

Reason says all things never stay. But reality gives a swift kick in the ass to reason, telling her to shut the hell up. Because Jonas… he will always be around.

As an adult, I have never celebrated Valentine's Day. Not in the sense of buying flowers and chocolates and gifts for a person I care about. My mom and sisters do not count in this equation. I'm strictly thinking of romantic interests. Considering the only other woman I thought of romantically never reciprocated, I never bought her anything.

For the first time, Valentine's Day is a big deal.

After I leave Autumn's apartment, I drop Spartan off at home and head to work. I relay my plan to Dad when I get to work and he tells me to take a half day so I can get everything done in time. I debate with him a moment, but give up after he tells me he will close the garage for the day if I don't.

Twist my arm.

Before arriving at work, I pictured the day going by slow. Excitement has me jittery and on edge. So, when lunchtime rolls around, I freak out. I let everyone take lunch, with plans to leave when they return.

"What if I don't get everything done in time?" I ask Dad.

"Most of the stores are right next to each other. Unless you have no idea what you're getting, you'll do just fine." Dad pats my shoulder. "Proud of you, son. And I'm glad you found someone who makes you happy. You deserve it."

"You trying to make me cry, old man," I tease.

"Would be a beautiful thing if you did. Shows how much they mean to you. Never be ashamed to show how you feel." Dad gives my shoulder another pat. "I'll be done in a bit. Then you get out of here and surprise those girls."

Dad takes his lunch and returns in no time. When I try to protest his twenty-minute break, he shrugs and tells me he ate. Conversation done. I finish the car I'm working on then prep to leave. After the tools are back where they belong, I ditch my coveralls and wash up.

"Sure you're good with me heading out this early?"

Dad shakes his head on a chuckle. "If you don't get out of here, I'll spill your secret plans to Autumn." He reaches for his phone.

The second time I brought Autumn and Clementine over for family dinner night, Dad gave her his number in case she ever needed help and she couldn't reach me. She reciprocated. Not only did the exchange shock me—our relationship still so young—it stirred up new admiration for my father. A man I hope to live up to.

"God. Fine. I'm leaving."

"Enjoy your weekend," Dad shouts as I exit the back of the garage.

"You too. Buy Mom some flowers."

I hop in the Jeep and drive toward the mall. Every store I need to hit is within a mile or two. And since it's still early in the day, traffic is light. Altogether, I have five stops. Only one stop will be challenging. So, I make it the first.

The second I set foot in the store, I question every reason behind the choice. But when a woman walks up to me and asks to help, I breathe a little easier. She asks open-ended questions and lights up when an idea strikes. In less than thirty minutes, I swipe my card as she bags up my purchase.

With an extra bounce in my step, I leave the store and go to the next. Fifteen minutes later, I exit the mall with the hardest part of my shopping done. I am in and out of the next stop faster than either shop in the mall. When I reach stop four, Shelly greets me with a goofy smile.

"Feel like I haven't seen you in years," she teases.

"Were you not just at my house last weekend? I swear you hung out, ate the food I grilled, and chatted with my girl."

A breezy smile kicks up her cheeks. "I love how happy you are."

The last time I remember blushing is middle school. So, the sudden heat on my neck and cheeks comes as a surprise. "Thanks, Shell."

After a quick hug, she slips into business mode. "What can I get for you?"

"Obviously, I'm here for flowers." Shelly rolls her eyes at me. "But I don't know what flowers Autumn likes. Or Clementine. I'd prefer to not get roses."

"Too cliché?" she jokes, but continues. "Do you want to get the same for both of them?"

"No. Think it would be nice for them to have flowers they call their own."

Shelly taps her lips for a beat before her eyes light up. "Wait here."

She dashes around the floral shop so quickly it dizzies me. After stopping at several bins, she meets me back at the counter. One hand overflows with flowers while the other holds greenery. This is why I come here. Because Shelly and Elizabeth, Cora's mom, don't mess around when flowers are involved. I love their passion and how easily they can make an arrangement look like art.

"Blush ranunculus and eucalyptus greens for Autumn," she mumbles, setting them on brown paper. "And red poppies, baby ranunculus, daisies, and kumquats for Clementine." She secures the flowers for Autumn in the brown paper with black ribbon. Clementine's flowers are artfully arranged in a mason jar with the same black ribbon tied around the jar threads. Shelly sets a vase on the counter. "When you get home, add water to the mason jar. After you give Autumn her flowers, put them in this vase and do the same."

Although I am thankful for her step-by-step instructions, she talks to me as if I have never bought my mom or sisters flowers here. I let her do her spiel, though. "Thanks, Shell. They're perfect."

I pay for the deeply discounted flowers and we exchange one last hug before I leave.

Next and final stop before home; the grocery store. I breeze through the aisles, man on a mission, and pick up all the ingredients for the dinner and dessert I have planned. Once I check everything off the list, I load everything on the belt at the register and exchange Valentine's chitchat with the cashier. She tells me my lady friend is a lucky woman. *I consider myself the lucky one.*

Minutes later, I haul everything into the house and let Spartan out. I stow the food and flowers while I set up one of the gifts. Finished, I package up the only other present that didn't have a gift wrap option. I set out several candles and light them before filling out a card I bought for Clementine and writing a love letter to Autumn. Once that task is complete, I straighten up around the house and prep dinner and dessert.

Cutting the last of the strawberries, I check the time. Just after four.

"Whatd'ya say, Spartan. Should I tell the girls they can come over now?"

Woof, woof, woof.

"Will do."

I wipe my hands on a towel, then snag my phone from the counter.

Whenever you're ready, come on over.

Almost done prettying ourselves. Be over soon.

I smile at the screen. Neither of you needs to pretty yourselves, I mumble.

The buzzer on the stove goes off and I take the angel food cake out of the oven. I adjust the temperature of the oven and blend the ingredients for the baked five-cheese macaroni. Sprinkling it with bread crumbs, I place the deep dish on a sheet pan and slide it in the oven.

As I deposit the mojo chicken in the oven, Spartan barks like a loon. Which can mean only one thing… they are here.

I open the door to see my girls walking up and Penny waving behind the wheel of Betsy. My cheeks grow painfully tight as I wave back at Penny. *She's letting Penny take the car.*

Spartan tackles Clementine before they reach the door. "Come on, bud. Let them inside." After another lick or two, he runs back in the house, barking for Clementine to follow.

"Hey," Autumn whispers as she sidles up to me.

I lean down and kiss her. "Hey, scarlet." Another kiss. "I have surprises for you both."

We walk into the house. "Oh yeah…" Her voice trails off the moment she spots the flowers on the breakfast bar. "Jonas." My name rolls softly off her tongue. "You didn't have to buy me flowers." She pivots to face me, a gentle smile on her lips. "You didn't have to buy us anything."

I snake my arms around her waist and draw her closer. "True. But I wanted to." I drop my lips to hers and bring her hips flush to my body. "And there's still more." I step back and weave my fingers through hers, walking her to the bar. "For you." I point to the ranunculus and letter. "For Clementine," I say, pointing to the mason jar of flowers next to a card.

"Thank you." She lifts the flowers to her nose and inhales. "They're beautiful."

"You're welcome. Glad you love them."

"Clementine?"

Her head pops up from the couch where she and Spartan appear to be having a serious conversation. "Yeah, Mama."

"Come see the flowers Jonas got you."

I kiss the crown of her head. "You two enjoy those a moment while I check on dinner."

Autumn and Clementine ogle over the flowers and read the notes I left them. When I peek over my shoulder to see if they are still reading, I spot a tear roll down Autumn's cheek. Normally, I would worry. But the constant smile on her lips tells me the tears are happy ones.

"About ten more minutes until dinner," I announce. Autumn lifts her gaze to mine and I stop breathing. Her cognac irises swirl with admiration and passion and something powerful. Love. *She loves me.* The confession plain as day in her eyes and on her face, but I won't force the words from her lips. She will say the words when she is ready. "In the meantime… Clementine?" She glances up at me from her card. "Would you like your other Valentine's present?"

Her face lights up as she hops off the stool and bounces. "Yes, please."

I walk over to Autumn and lace my fingers with hers. "C'mon, scarlet." She slides off the stool and I lead us to the second bedroom. When I open the door and flip on the light, Autumn gasps and lifts her free hand to her mouth.

"Jonas…" she mumbles.

"Clementine." I squat down and look her in the eye. "This room is for you when you're here. Decorate it however you like. Hang out in here with Spartan. Whatever you want. This is your space."

Her little jaw drops as her eyes widen. "Really?" she asks in disbelief. I nod. She squeals and lunges forward, wrapping her arms around my neck. "Thank you, Mr. Jonas."

She releases the hug and I stand up. "You're welcome. Hope you like it."

She spins around and stares at the oak-framed twin bed. A khaki comforter with a punk version of Alice from *Alice in Wonderland* drapes the mattress. Two matching decorative pillows rest against normal bed pillows. On the floor, a shaggy five-by-seven red rug adds a pop of color to the room. The room still needs more work, but for now, it will do.

"I love it," she exclaims, running and hopping on the bed. "C'mon, Sparty." She pats the bed beside her and he jumps up.

My work here is done.

Autumn and I leave the room and return to the kitchen. She parks on a stool while I check the last of the food cooking.

"You didn't have to do all this," Autumn whispers.

I take what is left in the oven out and set it on trivets before facing her. "Yeah, I did." I circle the bar and step into her. "You and Clementine deserve to be doted on." Leaning down, I kiss her. "And I'm not done yet."

Once dinner is plated up, we call for Clementine. I have a sneaking suspicion we won't see much of her or Spartan, now that Clementine has her own space. While eating, we discuss what movie we should watch tonight. Being Valentine's Day, Clementine suggests a love movie. I laugh at her exaggeration of vowels in the word love.

While I clean up dishes and assemble dessert, I tell my girls to find us a *love* movie to watch. I tote dessert out to the living room and receive oohs and awes from Clementine when she spots my mom's version of chocolate-dipped strawberry shortcake—aka strawberry shortcake with chocolate drizzle. But before either of them reaches for their plates, I hold up my hand.

"Another present. Then dessert." Surprisingly, neither of them says a word. Hands folded in their laps, both smile and bat their lashes. "Actually…" I point to Autumn. "I have two more for you."

I take two velvet bags from my pocket and a small box. Autumn follows every move I make as she tucks her lips between her teeth. I hand the satchel tied with a red ribbon to Clementine. She opens it up and plucks out the silver link chain with a heart charm in the center.

"Look how pretty this is, Mama." Clementine holds up the necklace for Autumn to see. Autumn nods before tipping her head back and blinking rapidly. "Open your presents."

Autumn levels her gaze with mine. "You really didn't have to."

I cup her cheek and nod. "Both of you deserve nothing less."

She clamps down harder on her lips, then swallows. I tip my head at her gifts and she opens them. Inside her satchel is a matching necklace. The linked chain matches a charm bracelet I spotted on her wrist a time or two. I help them both don the necklaces before Autumn opens the final gift. The one I worry over more than the rest.

With trembling fingers, she peels back the paper and removes the lid. The second she sees the key inside the box, she grabs my wrist. Tears flood her eyes and spill down her cheeks.

"I'm not suggesting anything you may or may not be ready for. But I want you to have a key. In case you need to be here when I'm not. Or just to let yourself in. But Autumn…" I wait until she looks up at me. "There is no pressure. Please don't think I'm pressing you to move in. Not that I wouldn't love to have you both here every day."

She gingerly sets the key back in the box and replaces the lid. Leaning forward, she places it on the table without a word. Then she whirls around and hops in my lap, peppering me with kisses. I wrap my arm around her waist and haul her closer.

"Guess this means you're okay with having a key," I joke.

"Best gift ever." She crushes her lips to mine until Clementine pipes up and asks if we can eat dessert yet.

And just like that, life is perfect. Autumn and I scarf down dessert so we can touch and kiss and do anything except watch the movie. When Clementine passes out, I carry her to bed and we tuck her in. Spartan jumps up and lays at the foot, guarding her.

As we walk out, I leave the door cracked. Weaving my fingers with Autumn's, I guide us down the hall to the bedroom. *Our room.*

The moment our door closes, I step into Autumn. Frame her face in my hands. Kiss her without reservation. Her fingers trace up my biceps, along my clavicles, winding up my neck and into my hair.

Without hurry, we strip away our clothes. I guide her onto the bed and crawl up until her cognacs line up with my hazels. Sweeping the hair from her face, I press my lips to hers.

Today has been a whirlwind of adoration. Every glimpse, every touch, every kiss, every word. All of it swirls together in kaleidoscope fashion. A pattern of me and Autumn and Clementine. A life full of exhilaration and laughter and love. One I don't want to live without.

My heart gallops into a full sprint as my breathing spikes. Autumn reaches up, traces her fingers from my temple to my chin. I close my eyes and absorb the tingle she ignites under my skin. The burn that never fades away. The fire she blazes beneath my sternum.

I open my eyes and lock on to hers. Her breathing shifts; grows heavier. She sees it in my eyes. Feels it in my touch. Tastes it on my lips. And I won't keep it in any longer.

"I love you, Autumn." The admission soft and strong on my lips. "More than imaginable."

Her eyes glass over and she lifts her lips to mine. The kiss gentle. Heady. A proclamation. And for the first time, she breaks the kiss.

"I love you, too," she whispers against my lips.

"I love you, too," I whisper against his lips.

Beneath my breastbone, the chambers of my heart contract in a vicious rhythm as the rest of my body catches up to this revelation. I drag in a lungful of air and tremble. Jonas ghosts his lips over mine and I close my eyes. A low-frequency buzz radiates off him and spills into me. I have never felt so completely vulnerable and alive in my life.

"You feel that?" he murmurs against my lips. "The energy vibration between us." I nod as the vibration sparks every nerve in my body to life. "Know what that is?"

"No," I confess, breathy.

"Love buzz." He presses his lips to mine. "The energy of two forces merging into one."

I slide my hands down the sides of his torso, past his waist, until I take hold of his glutes. Lean and muscular. I hold him in place as I gently rock my hips up. "Make love to me, Jonas."

His forearms planted on either side of me, he slowly drops his mouth. The soft caress of his lips on mine incinerates something deeper inside me. Love buzz, as Jonas called it. Deep in my bones. A low-frequency hum simmers in my marrow. Rocks my frame. Jars my strength. Stimulates every nerve ending from head to toe. The sensation starts at the epicenter between my lungs. Radiates until it reaches every possible end point. Then boomerangs back and blooms with fire and zeal and hunger.

I claw my way up Jonas's back. Rock my hips and grind against his length. He trails kisses along my jaw, sucking on my earlobe.

"Wanted to take this slow. Show you how much I love you. But you're making that a bit challenging."

Trailing my hands down his back, I squeeze his ass and press his erection between my thighs. "You do show me. Slow and sweet sex isn't the only way to express love. Sometimes, rough and fast is just as powerful."

"You're going to be the death of me."

"But what a good way to go," I growl in his ear.

Confession. I have never had rough sex. At least not what most people constitute as rough. Considering the last person I had sex with was barely twenty, neither of us had much experience at the time.

With Jonas, though, I don't imagine rough sex being something unenjoyable. I welcome the experience. Welcome the tinge of pain that marries with the pleasure. I may be less experienced in the partner department, but all women have needs. And I have done whatever necessary to satiate those needs over the years. But they don't hold a match to Jonas.

Jonas licks and sucks his way from my ear to my collarbone. Nips and marks my skin. Takes hold of my breast and kneads it in his palm. Drops his mouth to my nipple and sucks with teeth.

The pressure skirts the cusp of pain. Heightens the buzz low in my belly. Has me rocking my hips up, seeking relief. When he doles attention on the other breast, my eyes pinch shut as my back arches off the mattress. I fist his hair and yank. Hard. His responding growl with teeth has my breath coming harder. Faster. Heavier.

He kisses his way down my midline. Sucking and biting and marking me as his. When he drops between my thighs, I clutch his hair like a horse's reins. Rock my hips up to meet his tongue. Mewl as he teases and tastes. Moan as he builds me up and lets me fall.

And when he crawls back up my body, when he hikes my legs over his shoulders and locks me in place, when he clamps down on my neck… I groan.

He enters me slowly. Inch by glorious inch. And his eyes never veer from mine.

"Good, scarlet?"

"God, yes," I moan.

"Hold on. And let me know if we need to stop."

Stop? Holy hell. What did I get myself into?

Jonas leans in closer. Presses my thighs closer to my belly. Knees almost to my face. The position more awkward than uncomfortable. He kisses my calves as he palms my thighs. Then he rocks his hips forward. Fills me fully. And I bite my fist to stifle my cries.

In and out. In and out. Every movement fluid. Pulsing. With each new thrust forward, he picks up speed. Adds more weight. Hits that spot inside me harder. Builds me up and makes me cry louder.

He slides his hand from my throat to cover my mouth. Presses hard but doesn't mask my nose. "Let go, Autumn."

Sweat drips from his chin to my chest. My eyes roll back and I focus on every sensation he creates. The heat from our skin on skin friction. The sweat slickening our flesh. His girth and strength and stamina. His weight pressing down on me, pounding into me. But most of all, I focus on the love we share.

I fist his hair. Bite his palm. Cry out against his skin as my body has him in a viselike grip. And as soon as my muscles relax, he leans back. Drops my legs to the mattress. Peppers kisses wherever his lips reach until he lands on my lips.

And then he moves again. Slower. Measured. His palm caressing my cheek, my temple, my brow. Down my neck, my breast, the side of my belly, my hip. He makes love to me. Unhurried. Every touch and stroke and caress deliberate and tender.

"I love you, Autumn." He rocks forward. "More than I ever thought I could love another person." Forward again. "And I don't want a day without you by my side."

Reaching up, I frame his face in my palms. Meet him stroke for stroke. "I love you, Jonas." My eyes roll back. "Never thought anyone would matter the way you do." I moan as he drops his lips and delivers an evocative kiss.

Our bodies move in synergy. Steady and unyielding. Constant and loving. Building. Blooming. Higher and higher.

"Look at me, scarlet."

I open my eyes and lock on his gaze. The orange near his pupil glows wild. My body on the brink and he knows it. Feels the way my body starts to grip his tighter.

"Love you, Autumn." His admission all I need to set myself free.

I quiver as my body grips him tight. "Love you, too." And Jonas releases inside me. Lips on mine. Our love sealing every crack our hearts ever held.

Jonas shifts to lie beside me, tugging me close. He envelops me in his arms and kisses my forehead, my nose, my lips. His touch adding a new layer of timbre or resonance to the buzz swimming in my veins.

No other time in my life compares to this. Loving Jonas is magical. Sublime. Irreplaceable. Before him, I never pictured myself happy with someone else. My priorities were set in stone and immovable. Or so I thought. Now, I never want to picture a day without Jonas. Without his joy and warm heart in my—and Clementine's—life.

I snuggle farther into Jonas's frame. Grip him tighter. "Good night," I whisper against his chest. "Love you."

He gently strokes my hair before kissing the crown. "'Night, scarlet. Love you, too."

∾

The house is unbelievably quiet when I wake. No snores or tip-tap of dog nails or whispered conversations from a little girl and her dog. Which surprises me with how bright the sun filters through the blinds. Has to be past nine, although I have zero intention of moving to check.

While everyone sleeps, I decide to daydream. Fantasize over what life would be like with Jonas. Dream of sharing a bigger home and maybe the pitter-patter of more little feet. Going to weekly Wednesday night dinners and gaining a family. A family much larger and more loving than my own knew how to be. Affectionate people who love to see me and ask how my life has been. Remarkable people who don't criticize or judge who I am or what I enjoy.

They just care for *me*.

I picture a life with Jonas full of endless smiles and hearty laughter. Of sitting on the patio, cuddled in each other's arms, and listening to the cicadas chirp and fire crackle. Of teaching Clementine—and future children—how to ride a bike or grow gracefully into adulthood. I picture all of this and so much more.

And it stirs me to life. Heats my blood and quickens my pulse. Has me desperate for Jonas. To taste him on my tongue. Feel him skin to skin. Hear the hitch in his breath as he climbs higher and higher.

Without second-guessing, I dip beneath the sheet and wake Jonas with my tongue on his flesh. And I feel it. The moment he rouses from sleep. The moment it dawns on him I have my lips wrapped around him.

The more I lavish him with my tongue, the wetter I get. He swells in my mouth; close to climax. But before he releases down my throat, he hauls me up and positions my hips over his. Just as I start to protest, he lifts his hips and pushes inside me. The most unladylike groan rips from my throat.

I slap my palms to his pecs and rock back. Every thick inch of him stretches my walls. Strokes with precision. Drives me wild.

With his grip firm on my hips, I lift my hands to my breasts and palm them while I ride him. We set a relentless tempo. My fingers pinch and tug my nipples as I tip my head heavenward.

"Fuck, you're bewitching," Jonas grunts out.

Then he sits up, hands still on my hips. I wrap my limbs around him like tentacles and lock him in place. He fists my skin tighter, slams me up and down his length. Paints my skin with his breath. Groans in my ear. Dampens my skin. Presses his forehead to mine and holds my gaze. The room smells of sex and forever.

I weave my fingers in his hair, clamp down, and yank his head back. "I want you dripping down my legs."

He groans louder as his eyes roll back. *Slap, slap, slap.* Our hips collide with violence. His jaw slackens; opens wider. His cock grows impossibly thicker inside me. *Slap, slap, slap.*

Then he lets go. As do I.

Eyes open. Breathing stops. Mouth wide. He wraps his arms around my waist and bear-hugs me. Holds me still as he spurts inside me. Fills me. Marks me—again —as his.

And as our breaths quiet down and our heartbeats resume their normal pace, I imagine what it would be like to spend forever in his arms.

twenty-two

JONAS

I toy with the ends of Autumn's hair as we lie on the lounger in the backyard. She sits nestled between my legs, her back on my chest as we watch Clementine and Spartan run around the backyard.

She sips her coffee before setting it down and twisting in my arms. Chest to chest, she bends her legs at the knee and crosses her ankles in the air while propping her elbows on me and resting her face in her palms. She looks like an old-school pinup girl. *My pinup girl.*

I sweep a few wayward strands from her cheek. She leans into my touch before kissing my palm. "I love sitting out here. It's peaceful."

"Lounging with you makes it a hundred times better than when I sit here alone."

"What, Spartan wasn't a good lazy day companion?" she teases.

I glance over to where Clementine points out flowers to him and tells animated stories. "He's only ever chill with her. Early on, I was worried he would knock her over being a spazz." I shake my head and laugh. "Guess he only reserves that for me."

Autumn smirks. "Maybe."

A week has passed since I redecorated the second bedroom and gave Autumn a key to my house. And not a day since has Autumn slept anywhere other than my bed. *Our bed.* Nothing official has been said regarding the two of them moving in, but the only time we spend apart is during working hours.

The more clothing and personal items Autumn brings of hers and Clementine's, the more like home this house feels. Small touches in the kitchen or living room. Clementine's *Jack Skellington* cookie jar on the counter. Autumn's current paperback is on the coffee table. A soft throw blanket draped over the back of the couch. Shifting my clothes in the closet and dresser to make room for Autumn. Her scent thick in the air no matter which room I enter.

"Did you want to do anything today? Go anywhere?"

Autumn shakes her head. "Just want to take it easy. With everyone coming over to hang out tomorrow, we should kick back today. Maybe go grocery shopping."

I hook my hands under her shoulders and drag her up my body. A half smile kicks up her cheek before she leans in and kisses me. She drops her hands to my chest and supports herself as we press our foreheads together and breathe each other in.

Having Autumn and Clementine here every day has been incredible. Not everyone pictures themselves cohabitating, but falling asleep and waking up next to Autumn every day feels natural. Right. How it always should have been.

"Might be a good idea to plan what to make for tomorrow," I suggest.

With the hearing on Monday, we thought it would be nice to have everyone over again tomorrow. A chance to hang with our friends and mentally escape the anxiety of the potential outcome.

As far as the case goes, things have been quiet. Too quiet. Almost eerie. Leo had thrown so much drama at us in the beginning, it was easy to assume his theatrics would continue. But since the note on my Jeep, there hasn't been a peep. Part of me hopes Leo has learned his surprise appearances, verbal threats, and shady notes won't rattle us the way he expects. But I am not naïve enough to believe he doesn't have other tricks up his sleeve. Men like Leo don't show up out of nowhere, make a scene, then drop off the face of the earth.

I stare up at my girl and check for any signs of worry. Look for tension in her jaw or the occasional twitch in her eye. Don't need her bottling up anything when it comes to Leo and this case. But as I study the smooth lines of her skin and fiery swirl of her cognac irises, I see nothing off-putting. All I see is happiness and warmth and love.

"Maybe we should do a themed cookout," she states with enthusiasm.

"Did you have something in mind? It is a party for you, after all."

A few days ago, Clementine came to me when Autumn stepped away to use the bathroom. She talked in hushed tones and asked what I was getting Autumn for her birthday. I asked what day her birthday was because it had been top secret. Clementine eagerly shared everything. Not only was Autumn a leap day baby, but she also rarely celebrated her birthday.

That changes this year.

So, when the idea of having everyone together again came up, I suggested we do it as a birthday/we're-going-to-win-the-case party. The shocked expression on Autumn's face when she realized I had top intel on her birthday was priceless. She may not have enjoyed celebrating her birthday before, but I promise to make each and every one of her future birthday's memorable.

"Since it should be warmer tomorrow, let's do something tropical."

Winter in Florida lasts two months, if we are lucky. And this year is no exception. Winter may not officially be over, but the sun warms the air a little more each day.

"Tropical sounds perfect. Do you want to decorate? Or only make tropical foods?"

"Definitely food. Not so much of the decor. I'd rather spend the money elsewhere."

An idea sparks. "Let's figure out the food and drinks, then stop and pick up tiki torches. They're tropical and we can use them year-round."

"Deal."

We lounge out back a little longer before heading in and planning the menu for tomorrow. Once the shopping list is made, we shop early on so we can relax the remainder of the day. We purchase several tiki torches at the home improvement store to strategically place around the yard. Then leave the grocery store with four armfuls of bags.

The back half of the day is spent lounging on the couch with movies and books and cuddles. Lazy weekends had never really been my thing, but they are growing on me fast. Who knew just being around the right person made everything perfect?

After dinner and more movie time, we shuffle off to our rooms and call it a night.

Once Autumn and I wear each other out between the sheets, I tug her against my chest and easily fall asleep.

Bam! Bam! Bam!

I startle awake and glance at the clock. Four in the morning. Autumn shoots up and holds the sheet to her chest. "What was that?"

Bam! Bam! Bam!

Spartan runs out of Clementine's room and barks in the living room. Is someone breaking in?

I jump out of bed and throw on pants. "Stay here," I tell Autumn. Bolting to the living room, I peer through the blinds and scan the porch and yard. But I don't see anyone. The motion light kicked on and illuminates most of the yard. I scan every inch thoroughly, stopping when I see Autumn's car.

"What the fuck?"

Autumn peeks her head out of the bedroom but doesn't step out. "What is it? Is someone out there?"

I walk back toward the hall and point toward Clementine's room. "Go lie with her," I tell Spartan. He jogs past me and runs into her room, jumping back on her bed. When I reach the bedroom, I search for a hoodie and my phone. I step into Autumn and frame her face in my hands. "Please stay inside while I check your car. Looks like someone busted your windshield."

Her chin wobbles as her eyes glaze over. "Please be careful."

I lean down and kiss her. "Always. Stay inside." She nods, following me to the living room and sitting on the couch.

Walking toward the front door, I grab the baseball bat I stash in the corner. I stare out the peephole before opening the door and stepping out. Everything is quiet as usual. With each step I take, I scan my surroundings again. The motion light flips on as I step into the sensory field. My eyes dart left and right. Ears zero in on the slightest sound. The closer I get to Autumn's car, the more the hair on the back of my neck rises.

"Fuck," I mutter as I get within feet of her car.

The windshield isn't just busted. In all honesty, it looks as if someone pummeled it with a sledgehammer. The glass isn't just webbed. It is thoroughly destroyed. Hammered so many times the glass is caving in. Bashed to the point that the glass is as clear as a blizzard.

I grab my phone from my back pocket and open the camera, taking several pictures. Pocketing my phone, I reach for the note under the wiper blade. Walking to the end of the drive, I glance up and down the street and see nothing out of the ordinary.

I unfold the paper and growl.

I warned you.

Throwing my hands up, I shake my head. "Too chickenshit to come at me? Not man enough to discuss this face to face? Breaking shit and leaving notes doesn't scare me. And you're no man. Just a fucking coward." I want to scream and pound my chest, but I maintain my composure before heading back inside.

In the house, Autumn runs up to me. Eyes scanning me head to toe. "What happened?"

I explain what happened to her car and the new note. She covers her mouth and shakes her head. "Come here," I tell her, opening my arms. I hold her a moment before bracing her at arm's length. "Need to call Dad in a bit, so we can tow your car to the shop. Should also update the police report with the incident."

"Why?" Autumn whispers. "Why do this? What does smashing my windshield gain?"

I take a deep breath and circle my thumbs over her shoulders. "Probably trying to rile us up."

Does this piss me off? You better believe it. Will I cave to this juvenile behavior and the cowardice threats? Not a chance in hell. There is too much at risk to allow my emotions to take over. No, I need to remain levelheaded. To be the real man in this scenario.

After checking the locks on the doors, I guide us to the couch and lie down. "Let's rest a little longer. Then we'll get up and take care of this."

I pull Autumn against my chest and hold her. Soon, her breathing levels out and I close my eyes, drifting off.

～

"Miss me already?" Dad says when he answers his phone.

"Ha ha, old man. Actually, wanted to ask a favor."

"What's up?"

I take a deep breath. "Someone smashed in Autumn's windshield last night. I need it towed to the shop, but I'm not comfortable leaving them alone at the house."

"What the hell?" When Dad starts cursing, you know a nerve has been struck.

I relay the alarming wake up in the early morning and explain the condition of the glass and the note left behind. He mumbles unintelligible words into the phone. Dad and I are similar creatures and right about now, he's working hard to keep his temper in check. Autumn may not be his daughter, Clementine not his grand-daughter, but he protects and stands up for them just the same.

Dad agrees I shouldn't leave and tells me he will head down to the garage and drive the flatbed over.

"Really appreciate it, Dad. Thank you."

"We're family, Jonas. Wouldn't have it any other way."

After breakfast, we hang on the couch until Dad shows up. We chat while he loads the car on the flatbed. He tells me he knows where we can get a windshield to replace Autumn's and not to worry. Before he drives off, he promises to secure her car in the body bay of the garage. Thankfully, we have security cameras around the shop. If anything happens while we aren't there, we have "eyes" on the place.

When Dad drives off, I head back inside and sidle up to Autumn on the couch. "All taken care of." She tucks her lips between her teeth and nods slowly. I bring my thumb and forefinger to her chin and lift her gaze to mine. "Hey, there isn't much else we can do right now. So, as best we can, let's try to enjoy the day and our time with everyone later. Okay?"

She blinks back the tears fighting to escape. "Okay," she croaks out.

I press a chaste kiss to her lips. "This will all be over tomorrow. Let's focus on that and celebrating you."

We spend a little longer on the couch before hopping into action. We have a long list of things to do before everyone arrives—food, cleanup, setup—and divvy up the list so no one is overwhelmed. For obvious reasons, we give the simpler tasks to Clementine. But she will also help Autumn with a few recipes.

In no time, the house is clean and the kitchen counters are littered with bowls and platters of food. Going with the tropical theme, everything we have on the menu contains either fruit or Polynesian flavors. Autumn also messaged Cora before we went shopping yesterday and asked what to buy, so she didn't have to bring separate food.

Our friends slowly arrive at the house. No one asks where Autumn's car is, and we don't bring up the topic. Instead, we spend hours with our favorite people. Our family. We smile and laugh and enjoy ourselves.

Gavin, Rez, and Micah man the grill with me. Cora, Shelly, Penny, and Tatyana lounge on the outdoor couch with Autumn. Rex, Erin, Iliana, and Trevor chat near the cooler and banquet table of snacks. And Clementine plays tag with Ashton and Spartan in the yard.

I love how we have all easily blended together. Four months ago, I never would have pegged this as my life. In love. A backyard packed with people who care about me as much as I do them. None of those people my kin. Each and every one of them there for me in a heartbeat.

Couldn't ask for a better life.

After we devour dinner, Clementine lights the candles on Autumn's pineapple upside-down cake and everyone sings "Happy Birthday". Cake is eaten and gifts are handed over. Autumn blooms under the attention and I vow to make each of her birthdays going forward better than the previous. She had no expectations of being showered with gifts, but doesn't turn a single one down.

One by one, our guests give us hugs and say good night. Penny, Cora, and Gavin hang around long enough to help us clean up. After the last farewells are given, we tuck Clementine in and get ready for bed.

"Thank you for today," Autumn says as she peels away her clothes.

I step into her and wrap my arms around her. "My pleasure, scarlet." I kiss the tip of her nose. "Next year will be even better."

She holds my gaze a moment. "As long as I have you, every year will be perfect." Her gaze drops to my lips as she licks hers. "Now, I'm ready for my favorite present," she whispers.

"Oh, yeah?" She nods. "And what's that?"

"You." She peels my shirt over my head and pushes me down onto the bed.

As she crawls up my body and presses her skin to mine, I wish her a happy birthday and lose myself to her.

I scoop cheesy scrambled eggs onto a plate and add a slice of buttered toast. Setting it on the breakfast bar for Clementine, I pour her a glass of orange juice.

Clementine swings her dangling feet as she eats her breakfast. To her, today is just a typical Monday. Breakfast before school. Getting dressed and gathering her backpack of school supplies.

But today is far from a typical Monday. Quite the opposite, actually. Today, my daughter's future is in the hands of a judge. A judge I have never met and know nothing about. A judge who reads over a stack of papers and listens to our attorneys as they plead our case. And there is nothing I can do except try to remain calm. On the outside, at least.

Jonas strolls into the kitchen in jeans and a T-shirt. Last night, we decided to dress as we normally would in the morning. We didn't want Clementine to go to school asking why we were dressed up or with worry in her heart. So, for now, we go about the morning as if nothing is different.

"'Morning, scarlet." Jonas steps up behind me, wraps his arms around my waist and kisses my temple.

"'Morning. Hungry?"

He nods. "Little bit."

I portion out the last of the eggs and make us each some toast. After we finish eating, we gear up and drive Clementine to school. She bops and sings in the back seat, and I can't help but tear up a little. But I resist the urge to cry and swallow the wad of emotion lodged in my throat.

Just before we reach the drop-off point in the car circle, I spin around in my seat. "Hey, pumpkin. Hope you have a good day at school. Are you doing any fun projects?" Jonas rubs small circles on my thigh, trying to soothe me as I engage with Clementine.

I don't want to consider this my last opportunity with my daughter, but what if it is? What if the judge sides with Leo and I am ordered to hand custody over to him before the end of the day? Doesn't seem logical, but I have also never been in a situation like this. I have never had to think about the possibility of losing my child to someone who never cared until eight weeks ago.

"We're making aliens in art class today," she says with exuberance.

"How cool. Do you know what you want your alien to look like?"

Until we reach the drop-off, Clementine goes into animated detail on how she plans to create her alien. When it's time to say goodbye, I choke back my words and hug her harder than normal.

"Have a good day, pumpkin. See you later."

"Bye, Mama. Bye, Mr. Jonas. See you after school." She hops out of the Jeep and walks past the gate into the school.

I stare after her until she heads into the building. As soon as she vanishes, I lose it. Tears spill down my cheeks and I sob at the plausibility of not doing this every day. Of not dropping my daughter off at school. Of not hugging her whenever I please. Or being able to enjoy the little moments. The animated conversations.

Watching a movie with her every night. Witnessing her evolve from a girl into a young woman.

"Know it's not easy, but try to stay optimistic. Keep telling the universe you *will* get to keep her. Put it out there."

And I do. I pray to whoever listens and ask them to let today end well. To let Clementine stay with me, where she is loved and happy and healthy. To let today be the last day I hear from or speak to Leo again.

We get back to the house and rush to get ready. Jonas changes into gray dress slacks and a black button-down. Considering I see him in jeans and a T-shirt most days, I look forward to peeling his clothes off later.

"Quit looking at me like that," he states.

"Like what?" I play coy.

"Like you want to rip my clothes off." He chuckles when I shrug and my favorite dimple makes an appearance. "We'll have time for that later. When we're celebrating."

"Celebrating," I mumble. "Yes."

I finish getting ready. Apply a light coat of makeup and pin the top half of my hair back while letting the rest hang in loose waves. I lint brush my knee-length black and red dress, shifting the skirt a little to make sure the small pleats at the base sit over my knees.

"You look beautiful," Jonas says from the doorway. "We should get going."

We head out the door and drive toward downtown. The traffic is light heading toward the beach this time of day. Most residents are heading out, and it's still early for the snowbirds to drive to the beach.

By the time Jonas turns on Court Street, my palms are clammy. As he pulls into the parking lot, locates a space to park, and feeds the meter, my nails dig into my skin. My heart beats out of my chest as Jonas opens my door and holds his hand out.

"I've got you. Don't worry about what's going on around us."

He guides us into the courthouse and we go through security. Past the screening area, I spot Theresa and wave. Once we catch up to her, she shakes Jonas's hand before pulling me into a hug.

"Today is a big day. I know you're nervous, but I need for you to compartmentalize it as much as possible. Show your strength. Wear it on your sleeve. Do not bow or bend or show vulnerability. It won't matter to the judge, but if his defense sees it, they'll use it as ammunition."

I take a deep breath and shake my arms at my sides. "Okay. I can do this."

Theresa turns to Jonas then. "Glad to see you here, Jonas. Autumn will need your support here today, but do me one favor." Jonas's brows shoot up in question. "While in or near the courtroom, do not speak for Autumn. Although you may have good intentions, she needs to display her strength and not be outshone." Then she bounces her eyes between the both of us. "And both of you, try not to engage in any unsavory behavior. Don't speak to Leo or his attorney. Better to err on the side of caution."

Once we both agree, Theresa walks us through the courthouse and leads us to the courtroom where the case will be decided.

As we approach, Jonas speaks up. "Theresa, there was also another incident." Jonas looks to me briefly. "Autumn's windshield was smashed and a note was left."

Jonas pulls his phone from his pocket and shows Theresa shots of Betsy and the note.

"Were the police notified?"

"Yes," he responds, stowing his phone.

"Perfect. Hopefully we don't need it, but the evidence ways in our favor."

We sit on a bench just outside the room and hold each other's hands. No words are exchanged as I lean into Jonas. He draws small circles on my skin and soothes the anxiety ripping through my bloodstream.

Theresa clears her throat and we both look up in time to spot Leo and an older man at his side. I release Jonas's hand and sit up straighter. For the next however long, I shove every insecure thought about myself and losing Clementine in a closet in my mind. Leo's attorney steps up and shakes hands with Theresa. I suppose most attorneys in the area know each other and are cordial, even when they are on opposing sides.

Leo stares at me and Jonas. A wicked gleam on his face. He doesn't say a word, just stands beside his attorney with his hands shoved in his overpriced suit pockets.

The door to the courtroom opens and a man in security attire steps out. "You may come in now. Judge Walton will be ready to proceed momentarily."

Leo's attorney heads for the door, Leo on his heels. Before Theresa moves to enter, an older couple steps in line to go inside.

The moment I get a good look at them, I stop breathing. *What the actual fuck?*

Every muscle in my body turns to stone. I clutch Jonas's arm to stabilize myself. My throat runs dry and my mouth feels tacky. I blink a few times, wondering if my mind is playing tricks. But they are still there.

And when they sidle up to Leo, his wicked gleam grows tenfold. They enter the courtroom, and I hold us outside a moment longer.

"What the fuck," I whisper.

"Who are they?" Theresa questions.

"My parents. They kicked me out after learning I was pregnant and that Leo and I were no longer together."

"Why would they be here?" I shake my head at Theresa. "Either way, shove aside whatever you're feeling. Remember what I said earlier?" I nod. "Okay. Take a deep breath. Loosen your grip on Jonas. And let's go in there and win this."

I inhale deeply, over and over. When I loosen my grip on Jonas, I shake out my hands. With a few minutes left, we stroll into the courtroom and I keep my eyes forward, away from Leo and my parents.

A moment after we sit and Theresa takes out a thick binder, Judge Walton walks out. We rise from our chairs and stand.

"Be seated," she says. Judge Walton scans the documents in front of her. "Today's case is a petition of custody for Clementine Arianna Rooker." She glances at Leo and his attorney, then us. "Ms. Rooker. If I'm reading the documentation correctly, you have had sole custody of Clementine since birth?"

I glance at Theresa and she nods. "Yes, Your Honor."

Judge Walton nods then looks to Leo. "Mr. Parker. It is my understanding you have not formally met your daughter. Please tell me why."

Part of me jumps for joy when Judge Walton puts Leo on the spot. Although, no doubt he has been schooled in his responses.

"Your Honor, I was a young man when I learned I would become a father. I made a juvenile decision and walked away. I am here today to correct said decision."

Judge Walton hums and shuffles through the documents in front of her. She pins Leo with her gaze again. "Mr. Parker, your daughter is seven and a half years old. Why are you suddenly interested in her well-being? Why are you filing for sole custody when you have never interacted with her?"

Leo swallows. Beneath the table, I catch his leg bouncing. I give a mental victory fist pump at his nervousness.

Since this all started, these are the exact questions I have asked. No normal person files for sole custody when they have never made attempts to be in a child's life. When they have never shown signs of caring or wanting to get to know the child.

"Your Honor, there aren't many decisions in my life I regret as much as abandoning my daughter." His knee bounces faster. "I would like to make amends. Provide her with whatever her heart desires. Make sure she wants for nothing." He fidgets with the hem of his jacket under the table. "I want to get to know her."

Judge Walton purses her lips and doesn't look away from Leo. "I see." I don't miss how Judge Walton's eyes shift back to my parents before coming my way. "Ms. Rooker. Would you be open to shared custody with Mr. Parker?"

Theresa glances at me before speaking up. "Your Honor, when the initial suit began, Ms. Rooker agreed to allow joint custody so long as she maintained majority. She also wanted to include Clementine's opinion in the matter, seeing as she has never met her father and may be frightened to be left unattended with a stranger. Ms. Rooker stated she would allow supervised visitation with Mr. Parker and his family until Clementine felt comfortable being alone with them."

Judge Walton faces Leo. "Mr. Parker, did you refuse these terms?"

Sweat beads on Leo's temple and I beam inside. This is not going according to his plan. *See, money doesn't always work in your favor.*

"I did, Your Honor."

"Why?" Judge Walton asks, bluntly. "Why do you feel your daughter needs to be fully removed from her mother's custody? Has Ms. Rooker done something untoward?"

"No, Your Honor. I just..." Leo shifts his face enough to side-glance my parents. And that glance answers every question I have asked since the day he stood in front of my apartment. It isn't Leo who wants Clementine. It's my damn parents. Again, what the actual fuck?

"Mr. Parker. May I ask your relationship to the man and woman behind you?"

Leo fists his suit jacket. The bead of sweat rolls down his temple and drips from the angle of his jaw. I am dying to hear his answer. "This is Burton and Kathryn Rooker. Autumn's parents."

"Ah, I see. And why are Ms. Rooker's parents sitting behind you and not her?"

This just keeps getting better and better. If I asked these questions, Leo would give me an angry rebuttal and storm off like an adolescent. But he can't be a loose cannon with Judge Walton.

"I'd like to rescind my petition for custody," Leo belts out. I gasp at the same time my parents turn beet red and sneer. "My choice to file for sole custody was irrational and hasty. My apologies to everyone."

"Well, this makes my day run a bit smoother," Judge Walton states. "But, you're not off the hook yet, Mr. Parker. We will not discuss the details today, but your attorney will be receiving documentation from my office regarding missed child support."

Leo hangs his head. "Yes, Your Honor."

Judge Walton looks to me. "Ms. Rooker. I hear by award you sole custody of Clementine Arianna Rooker." She lifts her gavel and claps it to the base. "This hearing is adjourned."

We all stand as Judge Walton exits the courtroom. As soon as she enters her chamber, I spin around and hug Jonas.

"See, scarlet. Nothing to worry about." He hugs me tight to his chest. "It was great to watch him sweat, though."

I laugh. "It was, wasn't it."

Autumn stands tall beside me, and I have never been prouder to have her on my arm.

While we wait for Leo, his attorney, and Autumn's parents to leave, Theresa talks softly about next steps. Paperwork that will follow in regards to back child support and any future support. Autumn disputes the notion, stating she doesn't want a dime of the money. But Theresa comes back with a better solution—a future savings for Clementine. Whether for college or a first car or when she decides to move out.

Leo and his attorney, as well as Autumn's parents, start for the door, but Leo pauses before exiting.

"Autumn, I apologize for all this." He rocks back on his heels. "And I want to forego any visitation. With me and my family. Sorry to have put you through all this. I will pay your attorney's fees."

Well, well, well. Mr. Hotshot is just full of surprises today. Either way, I am glad he had a change of heart. Not sure what provoked it, but maybe his morality kicked in. Thank god it did before the judge made a decision.

Autumn nods and gives a gentle smile. "Thank you."

The four of them leave the courtroom. Autumn's parents still appeared perturbed by the outcome, but I really don't care. We hang back for a few minutes and allow them to get a head start on leaving.

"See, nothing to worry about," I say, squeezing Autumn to my side. "I knew everything would swing in our favor."

Autumn peers up at me with a sparkle in her intoxicating eyes. "Oh, did you now?"

I nod. "Yep."

After a few minutes, we exit the courtroom. Before parting ways with Theresa, she tells Autumn she will reach out to her as soon as she receives the paperwork. Should be straightforward and only need signatures.

We walk down the steps outside the courthouse, hand in hand, smiles plastered on our faces. "We should definitely celebrate," I suggest. "A nice dinner, or maybe a special dessert. Something."

"I..." Autumn stops short and I follow her line of sight. To my Jeep. Where her parents stand, arms tight across their chests.

Not sure what their game is, but I kept an eye on them the entire time in the courtroom. They sat behind Leo, hands folded in their laps, expressions blank. Mostly.

As soon as Autumn told me who they were, something didn't sit right with me. Why the hell would they show up to a custody hearing for Clementine? One—Autumn hasn't spoken to or seen them in almost as long as Leo. So, it's not as if they heard the news from her. Two—they sat behind *Leo*. Her parents sat behind *him* in silent support.

Why?

Not as if he and Autumn had been dating for several years and her parents developed a loving relationship with him. From what Autumn said, she and Leo had been together less than a year. During their time together, not much of it revolved around time spent with either of their families.

And then it clicks into place. The puzzle pieces lock together and form the bigger picture. I see it now. When their faces turned bright red in the courtroom as Leo forfeited. The way Autumn's father gnashed his teeth as the judge announced Autumn the sole custodial parent of Clementine. Their balled fists as they rose from the bench. The disgust in their eyes as they left the courtroom.

They did this. They went to Leo and orchestrated this whole mess.

Her father steps closer. "She doesn't belong with you," he seethes.

Pissed, I step protectively in front of Autumn and point a finger at him. "You need to back the fuck up."

"What are you going to do, boy." He steps closer. "You gonna hit me? Go right ahead. Plenty of cops around here to haul you to jail."

"Actually, I won't hit you. That's what you want. To see me hauled off in cuffs."

Autumn's mother comes to her father's side with a sneer on her face. "That's what you deserve, lowlife."

Behind me, Autumn's body tenses. Her nails dig into my biceps. Before I can stop her, she steps around. "No," she shouts. "You don't get to come here and act high and mighty. Not after sending your daughter to live on the streets. Not after you shielded yourselves behind a man who abandoned his child. Who the hell do you think you are?"

Her father steps within feet of Autumn and I shove him back. "Don't test me."

He throws his head back and laughs. "You don't scare me, boy." Then he faces Autumn. "You don't deserve her. What kind of mother works in a tattoo parlor and dates a mechanic? Don't you realize the damage you're doing to that girl? She won't live up to her potential."

"Think you can do better, *father*?" Autumn breathes heavily. "Because, in your eyes, I didn't turn out so great."

Her remark meant to make him falter has me wondering if she sees herself this way. As a failure. But I don't dwell on it now. There isn't time. Because he steps closer. Too close.

"How dare you speak to me with such petulance. Your mother and I raised you with good morals and faith. You best respect me, girl."

"Respect you?" Autumn inches closer to him. I remain on her heels. "Respect is earned, not handed over. Clergy collars don't make you righteous, *father*. Nor do they mean you *deserve* respect more than someone else."

"I warned you," he sneers. *I warned you.* The note on Autumn's car yesterday. Moments ago, he said *she doesn't belong with you.*

Holy shit. Holy. Shit.

"It was you," I mutter.

Autumn faces me, brows pinched. "What?"

I meet her eyes. "The notes, your windshield. It wasn't Leo." I point at her father. "You did this." His smug smile all the response I need.

But before I react, Autumn's mother storms forward and backhands her. Autumn falls to the ground and everything around me goes red. I won't hit a woman, but I sure as shit won't stand for anyone hitting Autumn.

I reach out and grab her wrist. "Get your filthy hands off me," she screams. But I refuse to loosen my grip.

Her father steps forward and I glare at him. "Don't test me. I won't hit her, but I will gladly knock you out."

I glance around the lot, scanning for a police vehicle. Spot one in the distance, an officer sitting behind the wheel, and wave my arm high. The police cruiser veers our way and stops a few car lengths back. After talking into the radio on her shoulder, the officer steps out of the car and approaches us.

"What seems to be the problem?"

I lift Autumn's mother's arm. "This woman just assaulted my girlfriend. She, and this man, approached us in the lot after our hearing in the courthouse."

The female officer steps closer to Autumn, who hasn't stood up yet, and squats in front of her. "Are you alright, ma'am?" Autumn nods and the officer extends a hand to help her up. "Tell me what happened here." Her question directed at Autumn.

Autumn explains the reason we came to the courthouse today. How she was shocked to see her parents with her ex. Then, she gives a small backstory regarding her parents before explaining what happened as we approached the Jeep.

Before the officer begins questioning Autumn's parents, I interject about the harassment and police report she filed. I add how Autumn's father basically confessed to the notes and damage after I put the pieces together.

"You can't prove shit, lowlife," her father hisses.

Autumn steps up to her father. Gets in his face. Emboldened with the officer at her back. "Did you do this? Did you write those notes and trash my car? Try to take my daughter away from me by using her birth father as a scapegoat?"

His lip curls. Eyes narrow. He leans in, inches from her face. "You don't deserve to be her mother. Gallivanting around like a whore. Living a trashy life. No sign of God in your life. Worthless." He inches back and spits at her feet. "You're no daughter of mine."

The officer steps around Autumn, grabs his hands and yanks them behind his back. She reads him his rights and steers him to the back seat of her car. All the while, Autumn's mother thrashes in my grip.

"Who do you think you are?" she hollers at the officer. "How dare you arrest a man of the cloth. You'll burn in hell for this." She shifts her gaze to Autumn. "As will you. You disgust me. At least your sister knows what it means to be a good Christian woman. At least I don't regret her coming from my womb."

I tighten my grip on her wrist. "Best if you stop speaking now. Before you dig yourself in a deeper hole."

Autumn sidles up to me, takes my free hand and shakes her head. "No, it's okay. Let her say whatever she wants." Autumn turns her attention on her mother. "I've always known who you are, mother. Always known I wouldn't live up to your expectations. As a child, it hurt when I never made you happy or proud. As a woman…" she sighs, "I don't care. There has never been a day in my life where I felt your love. Ever. Growing up under your scrutiny made me feel small and meaningless. The day I left… that was the day I woke up. Came to life. I may have lived in a shelter for a short time, but even those people cared for me more than you ever did." Autumn wraps her hand around my waist. "And finding Jonas, discovering true love, has wiped away every ounce of hurt you and father inflicted upon me."

Caught up in her proclamation, I miss the slight shift as Autumn's mother swings her free hand forward. A crack ripples in the air as her hand connects with Autumn's face.

"You ungrateful little witch," her mother hisses.

The officer jogs over from the cruiser, yanks Autumn's mother's wrists behind her back, and cuffs her. As she walks her to the cruiser, she prattles off Miranda rights.

I face Autumn, framing her cheeks in my hands. "Are you okay?"

Her eyes glaze over as she stares up at me. "Yes. No. I don't know."

On the verge of tears, I hug her to my chest and turn her face away from the police cruiser. "Got you, scarlet." She fists the back of my shirt, trembling against my frame. "Shh, shh, shh. I got you." I sway her slowly in my arms.

As her grip loosens on my shirt, the officer approaches us. "Ma'am, I need to know if you'd like to press assault charges."

Autumn peeks up at me, seeking guidance. I want to tell her yes. Want to tell her she should not allow them to get away with everything they have done. But I don't. Instead, I give her a soft smile that says the choice is hers. I will never rob her of her choices. And this decision, although it weighs heavily, is one she should make on her own.

She swallows and meets the officer's gaze. "Yes." Her frame relaxes in my arms. "I want to press charges."

The officer takes out a business card from her breast pocket and writes on it before handing it to Autumn. "The case number is on the card. As soon as possible, we need you to come to the station and give a formal statement." Autumn nods. "If anything else occurs, call the number on the card." The officer smiles, the corners of her eyes crinkling. "Sorry this happened to you. Try to enjoy the rest of your day."

Turning on her heel, she walks to the cruiser, gets in, and drives off.

Autumn sighs and I steer her toward the Jeep. "C'mon. I know exactly where to go."

What the hell just happened?

Jonas helps me up into the Jeep. I buckle my seat belt and stare out the windshield, the world around me a clouded haze.

Today has been a roller-coaster ride from hell. And it isn't noon yet.

When my parents appeared outside the courtroom, confusion set in. The last time we spoke was the day they banished me from their lives. *"No daughter of mine will have a child out of wedlock."* Those were my father's final words to me. Literally disowning me with my mother at his side. She hadn't even flinched at his words. If anything, she appeared relieved I was leaving.

What kind of people do that?

Jonas gets in the Jeep but doesn't start it. We sit in silence as the last thirty minutes process. Their cruel words. Bringing a hand to my cheek, I rub against the sting beneath the surface. I zone out and scan memories over the last seven and a half years. Plucking out every oddity I couldn't explain. Wondering if my parents had been preying on me—preying on my daughter—all this time.

"How are you?" Jonas asks, breaking the silence. He reaches across the console and weaves our fingers.

I twist in my seat and face him, leaning against the headrest. "Freaked out. Puzzled. Hurt." I shake my head. "Relieved. Glad this is all over."

He brings my hand to his lips and kisses my knuckles. "Sorry you had to deal with all this in the first place."

"Not your fault."

"No, but no one deserves to deal with what just happened."

We stare at each other, his thermal pools a swirl of emotions. Sadness. Worry. Happiness. Hope. I grab hold of the last two and hug them to my heart. I fear the first two will linger if I don't tell him more about what happened with my parents. And the way I was raised.

"Hate to say it," I croak, my throat like sandpaper. "But I expected nothing less."

Jonas juts his bottom lip out, the corners of his eyes turning down. I lift my free hand and trace his lower lip from corner to corner.

"Growing up in the Rooker house was not like being around your family."

"You don't need to explain, Autumn."

I nod. "That's one of the things I love about you, ya know. How you don't hold expectations over my head." He smiles as I stroke my thumb over his cheek. "But I need to get this out."

"Okay. Just don't feel obliged."

I close my eyes and take a deep breath. Jonas turns into my palm and kisses the center. His touch buzzes under my skin and shoots a current straight to my heart. When my eyes open and lock on his, peace washes over me. Even with the pain of the past thrown in my face minutes ago, Jonas settles every anxiety-ridden memory.

Swallowing, I take one last deep breath and dive in headfirst. "When you're only exposed to one way to live for the first thirteen years of your life, it's difficult to believe another way exists. As a little girl, I looked up to my parents. Did as I was told. Took the beatings when I disobeyed. Listened to the constant verbal beat-downs. How did I know being treated as such was wrong? I had nothing to compare it to. Father enrolled me in the church's private school at age three. It wasn't a bad place. The teachers were wonderful, as were my classmates. With my father giving sermons several times a week at the church, everyone looked up to him. Saw him as a role model. Even me."

I close my eyes a moment and collect myself. Jonas tightens his grip on my hand, showing silent support.

"Even when he hit me. I was taught to believe disobedience equals punishment. Punishment in the Rooker household equals a hole-laden wooden paddle against your bare butt. Obviously, I avoided this as much as possible. But, sometimes, I received punishment simply because father had a bad day."

I tuck my lips between my teeth. Jonas caresses my cheek with his knuckles. "Sorry this happened to you, Autumn." His voice soft and sad.

"Wasn't until I went to public high school that I learned how different my life was. Compared to my new friends, I was sorely lacking. Yes, I had intelligence. But only from textbooks. And even then, my education had been tweaked around scrip-ture. Wasn't necessarily a bad thing, but it secluded me. Put me in a box with the teens labeled as weirdos or freaks by the popular students. I didn't let it bog me down, but I wished to make at least one friend who didn't look at me like I traveled through time from the 1950s in my handmade dresses."

Jonas laughs and my brows shoot up in question. "You still dress like someone from another era. Just look sexy as hell now."

I join in his laughter. "Touché." He makes a fair point. "Anyway… the longer I spent in public school, the more I opened up. Not just verbally, but in the way I expressed myself. Clothing, makeup, hairstyle. My parents never spent a dime on any of it, though. I had to earn it working at the grocery store near the house." Taking a deep breath, I lick my lips. "I remember the first day I wore makeup and my mother called me a whore. The first time I wore clothes that showed my curves and she backhanded me so hard I had a bruise on my cheek for a week. Every time I painted over it with concealer, I cried."

Jonas stares at me, glassy-eyed. "Wish I would've found you sooner." I love the way Jonas wants to heal all of my scars. Wants to replace every action that has blemished my life.

"Me too. But if you had, I may not be who I am today. And I love who I am. Especially with you."

He leans across the console and kisses me. So tender. So sweet.

"Esther—my sister—never received punishments. For whatever reason, she did no wrong. She was the daughter my parents always wanted. Obedient, quiet, subservient. When my parents threw me out, she stood by their side with disgust on her face. My parents had learned to keep her in private school after seeing how it changed me. Last time I spoke with her was about a year ago. Although she still feels my parents were doing what they thought was best, she is slowly being exposed to the world. Hopefully, in the future, we'll be in a better place. I'd love for Clementine to meet her cousins. And I pray one day to get to know her again."

"You will," Jonas states with confidence.

I exhale and release it all. My mother and her twisted version of love. My father and his rigid outlook on life. I breathe in fresh air and expel every ounce of the hurt they inflicted upon me.

"Thank you." Jonas scrunches his brows. "For letting me get that off my chest. For allowing me to shed weight I didn't know I still held on to."

He strokes his thumb over my cheek. "You're welcome." Leaning in, he kisses my forehead. "Can I take you somewhere?"

"Yes."

He kisses my lips. "Nowhere fancy. But after the day's events, I think it's the perfect place to be."

Jonas starts the Jeep and drives away from downtown. Billie Eilish croons through the speakers as the city zips past us. Every minute of the last two hours flashes in my mind. The worry and anxiety, joy and fright. Then I relax. Melt into the seat and close my eyes as realization hits.

This is over. And Clementine won't be going anywhere. Relief washes over me and I bask in it. Let it heal me and steal all the pieces of my past that threaten my well-being.

Before long, Jonas parks in front of his parents' house. I glance over at him and tilt my head.

"Only Mom is here. She wanted me to call as soon as the hearing ended. Since I didn't have the chance, thought this might be better."

For whatever reason, my nerves skyrocket. The few times Clementine and I have been over for family dinner night, his parents—the entire family—have been lovely. Treated me like I belonged. Hugged me like their own daughters.

So why are my palms sweaty?

We go inside the house and Jonas calls out for his mom. I clamp onto his arm, mirroring a timid child. His mom steps out of the hall, her smile bright, wide, and welcoming.

"Hey, you two." She pulls Jonas in for a hug, then me. She holds me at arm's length, eyes searching mine. "How'd it go?"

Jonas guides us to the living room and we all sit. Over the next hour, we share the craziness of the morning. Along with the good news. More than once, Jonas's mom tugs me into her arms and just holds me. The second time she does, I cry on her shoulder. She holds me close, strokes my back softly, and tells me to let it all out.

Irene Thompson may not be my birth mother, but she is the most maternal person in my life. And she embraces me as her own. For that, I have never been more grateful.

When I finish spilling my heart, she drags us to the kitchen and we make lunch together. The simple sandwiches taste better than any meal I ate in my youth. We sit at the dining table and enjoy each other's company.

As it nears time to pick Clementine up from school, we exchange hugs and goodbyes.

"Hope to see you all on Wednesday."

I curl into Jonas's side. "We'll be here," I answer for us.

"See you then. Give that little girl a hug for me."

We say one last goodbye before leaving. Jonas drives us through the city and in the direction of Clementine's school. And the entire time, I ogle him.

How did I get so lucky? How did I land a guy as sweet and caring and desirable as Jonas? A man who doesn't just love me, but also my little girl. A man who goes above and beyond to make us happy. Who doesn't hesitate when it comes to our hearts and our happiness. Who will drop everything to be there for us.

I don't know what I did to deserve Jonas, but I will never take him or us for granted.

"What're you thinking about so hard over there?"

"How lucky I am," I answer without hesitation.

He reaches for my hand and brings it to his lips. "Think you're mistaken." When I continue to stare at his profile, unspeaking, he fills in the blank. "I am definitely the lucky one."

Clementine darts across the house, Spartan hot on her heels as they search for Lex. Giggles echo from the pile of blankets on the other side of the couch as Clementine keeps calling his name. When she finally lifts the blankets away, they both run off laughing.

I help Jasmine and Jillian make dinner while Autumn sets the table with Mom. They chat while placing plates and silverware and napkins on the table. But their conversation is too quiet for me to hear.

"Really good to see you smiling so much," Jasmine says, bringing my attention back to the kitchen.

"Thanks, I guess."

How can I not smile when Autumn and Clementine are near? They bring a joy into my life I never imagined possible.

Yet, it seems as if Autumn still has hesitations about living together.

Almost a month has passed since I gifted her a key to my house. Since I set up a room for Clementine. And yet, I still don't have her in my bed every night.

Is it wrong for me to expect such things? Yes, I suppose so. Considering we have only been together roughly four months, asking Autumn to uproot her and Clementine's life for my own selfish needs would be a dick move.

Doesn't mean I don't want to, though.

Anyone else in my shoes would be grateful to have what I do. Autumn and Clementine stay at the house four or five nights a week. Practically full time. And on the nights they don't stay, I sleep in my bed alone.

Since the case closed with Leo, and since learning Autumn's parents were behind the damage to her car and the notes, there doesn't seem to be a need for extra eyes.

And it sucks.

Don't get me wrong. I am beyond grateful she and Clementine are safe. In fact, they are more than safe. Safer than before the trial began.

When Leo and Autumn's attorneys spoke after the hearing, something unexpected and surprising happened. Not only did Leo pay back child support, interest, and Autumn's attorney fees; he also signed away his parental rights. Theresa had to explain it to Autumn several times. We also learned Autumn's father threatened to throw Leo into a shitstorm with local media about his abandoned child. Leo is by no means a celebrity, but when you own a massive hotel chain, news spreads quickly in the community. The news may have ruined the life he'd built.

Basically, Leo told his attorney he didn't want a similar occurrence to happen to Autumn or Clementine in the future. He didn't want someone to try and use his paternity to hurt either one of them. He never had ill intent and honestly didn't realize what he was getting himself into. I don't know how much of that I believe.

Either way, at least Autumn sleeps better at night knowing no one can take her daughter from her.

"Is the roast ready?" Jillian asks as she finishes smashing the potatoes.

I open the oven and jab the pot roast with a thermometer. After the needle hits the temperature Mom deems as the perfect roast, I grab the potholders and take it out. "Ready."

We carry the food dishes to the table then holler for everyone to come eat. Dad, Anton, and the kids rush to the table. Once we are in our usual seats, Mom tells everyone how grateful she is to have them at the table again. Then everyone fills their plates.

Dad encourages Lex to be mischievous while Clementine giggles. He nonchalantly picks up a green bean with his finger and pretends like he will throw it at Mom. A minute later, Lex tosses a green bean and Jasmine snaps at Dad to not goad him. I don't remember Dad being such an instigator when we were kids. No matter, he loves making the little ones laugh.

Although it's only March, Jillian rambles on to Mom about the fall fashion line the store will receive soon. Turtlenecks and scarves and gloves. Wool jackets and thermal-lined pants. Honestly, fall and winter attire in Florida is a strange concept. The actual fall season feels like a mild summer. And winter resembles what northerners experience as fall. Most clothing stores in Florida sell swimsuits year-round. No joke, we could get away with wearing fall attire in the winter without discomfort.

Beside me, Autumn focuses her attention on Jillian. Every now and again, Jillian pipes up and asks what she wears during different seasons with her rockabilly style. Genuinely intrigued by Autumn's fashion. How she wears it with ease, although not many local stores carry her style of clothes.

I lean back in my chair, eat my dinner, and absorb the ease with which Autumn talks with my family. Autumn and Clementine both. As if they have been sitting at this table and sharing meals with the Thompsons for years. Watching them blend in without effort has my heart stuttering before it takes off in a sprint.

With each passing day, our relationship grows stronger. Our bond more inseparable. We gravitate toward each other like the moon does the earth. As if finally where we are meant to be. In synergy. Two halves of one soul coming back together.

In the same breath, I miss her. On the nights she and Clementine don't sleep under the same roof as me. When Autumn doesn't lie next to me in bed. I miss her weight on my chest and her breath on my skin. Miss her soft snores and the twitch of her fingers when she dreams.

Do I wish the two of them lived with me full time? Hell yes. Do I question why they aren't? Also, yes.

The last thing I want to do is pressure Autumn. Especially after the debacle with Leo and her parents.

But I also can't stand not knowing if she wants to take the next step. If she wants to move in together. Or if she wants to keep things as they are.

Is it too soon to live together? This question has popped into my head more times than I care to count. Perhaps timing keeps her hesitant. Four months isn't long in the grand scheme. Some couples live apart for years before moving in together. But some move in within weeks.

"What do you think, Jonas?" Mom asks, and I have no idea what I missed.

"Sorry, was zoned out a minute. What'd you ask?"

"If you wanted to join us for Easter. Nothing fancy. Egg hunt, sugary treats, and dinner."

I glance over at Autumn to see her watching me with a shy smile. "Sounds like fun, Mom. Just tell us when to be here."

She claps and rubs her hands together. "Wonderful."

Autumn curls her hand around my bicep and leans into my side, resting her head on my shoulder. I kiss her forehead then press my cheek to her hair. Taking a deep breath, I close my eyes and absorb every ounce of love she radiates.

Move in with me.

Beside me, Autumn stiffens. Minus Clementine and Lex, the entire room goes silent. *Shit.* "Did I just say that out loud?" I whisper, although everyone hears.

Autumn sits up straighter and faces me. She tucks her lips between her teeth, eyes darting between mine. "You did," she croaks.

Dad sparks random conversation with Mom, thank god. Soon, everyone else chats among themselves again and pretends to ignore us.

I lean in closer to her, in the hopes of shielding our conversation somewhat. "Wasn't trying to put you on the spot. Sorry. The idea has crossed my mind before. And I'd love you both to be with me every night. But I didn't realize it came out of my mouth until you froze."

Passion mixes with fear and swirls like wildfire in her intoxicating irises. She clamps down on her lips harder and I have to fight the urge to graze my thumb over her chin, just beneath her lips. Beneath the table, her knee begins to bounce. Body stiff, her eyes dart toward everyone in her periphery.

"Can we discuss this later?" she whisper-squeaks. "In private."

I nod. "Of course. Like I said, it was a slip of the tongue."

Clamping down on her lips one last time, she releases them and spins in her chair to face everyone else again. She picks up her fork and pushes food around her plate, but doesn't eat much else. And for the next hour, she resumes prior conversations as if the subject never came up.

Just before eight, we exchange hugs with everyone and head out. Before heading over tonight, Autumn agreed to stay at the house. As she sits silently in the passenger seat, I pray she doesn't regret the decision.

I reach across the console and take her hand in mine. She weaves her fingers with mine and I breathe a little easier. *Thank goodness.* Not sure how I would handle it if Autumn shirked away from me.

After I park the Jeep in front of the house and we wander inside, Clementine gets ready for bed while I let Spartan outside. The nightly routine goes much the same as usual. Autumn and I give Clementine kisses and hugs good night and ruffle Spartan's fur before we turn off the light and close the door halfway.

In our room, blanketed in darkness, I reach for Autumn and pull her into me. Kiss her forehead, between her brows, the tip of her nose, her lips. Her body goes lax, melts into my touch, my lips. She fists my shirt then releases the cotton, sliding her palms up my chest to my neck, lacing her fingers at the base of my skull.

Apple lingers on her tongue from dessert and mixes with the taste of her. Her cherry vanilla aroma billows around me. From shoulder to hip, she eliminates any measure of space between us. I hum against her lips, her tongue, as she threads her fingers through my hair and tugs at the strands.

With my slipup tonight, I worried—still worry—she would pull away. I have no intention of taking back what I said because I meant it. Just didn't mean to say it aloud. Yet. So much has happened since we started seeing each other, the last thing

I want is for Autumn to believe I'm pressuring her into something she isn't ready for. Although, in my eyes, she is more ready than she realizes.

We take our time stripping off clothes and falling in to the bed. Tonight, our kisses and touches and whispered moans weigh heavier in the shadows. Our bodies move slower, with more intention and adoration. This isn't just sex. Not just a physical need for release or routine activity. And when we climax, the energy around us radiates heart and heat and traces of forever.

My front to her back, arms holding her snug against my skin, we start to drift off. The last thought floating in my mind is how we never brought up the conversation from dinner again. Either of us. And I wonder if that is a good thing or bad.

Before Jonas and I started dating, I rarely went out. Not that I didn't want to. Penny tried several times to drag me out of the apartment to let loose. Clementine had always been more important. My sole focus.

Now with the custody case closed, I sleep better and breathe easier. Leo signing away his parental rights was the most selfless and unexpected act. Burton and Kathryn Rooker now have assault charges on file and are undoubtedly being ridiculed in their community with a restraining order on record. I have never been a vindictive person, but I do believe in karma. And several years' worth has unleashed upon them.

"Sure you're good watching her tonight?"

Penny tilts her head. "You act as if I've never had girls' night with Clementine before." A palm rests over her heart as her eyes go wide. "You wound me."

I throw my eyeliner at her. "Such a drama queen."

"Be glad your makeup's done, otherwise I'd be holding this hostage until you groveled for forgiveness."

After applying my lipstick, I spin around and latch on to her neck. "You love me." Penny shoves me as laughter spills from both of us. "Say it. Say you love me."

"Will you get off me if I do?"

I peer up at the ceiling and pucker my lips, feigning contemplation. "Hmm… only if you mean it," I tease.

Penny surprises me and throws her arms around my waist, hoisting me off the floor. "Love you, Auti," she coos, delivering air kisses near my face and hair—careful not to mess up either.

With my feet firmly planted on the ground again, I blow her a kiss. "You're the best." Penny being Penny, she curtsies then saunters off to the living room.

In front of the full-length mirror in the bedroom, I do one last scan, hair to heels. The black and white plaid-print strapless crop top sits high enough to cover the girls, but shows two fingers of skin above my waistline. Charcoal slacks hug my skin from navel to ankle. A simple pair of black heels shine at my feet. My signature scarlet lips for an added pop and hair in a ponytail.

Jonas steps in the room and closes the door. He sizes me up, licking his lips. "Not sure if we'll make it out tonight."

I push out my lower lip and bat my lashes. "But I got all dressed up."

"Fuck, scarlet. Don't pout. I might mess up your makeup." He comes up behind me, staring at me in the mirror over my shoulder, arms slithering around my waist, hips flush against my low back. "Sure I can't convince you to stay in?" Jonas kisses beneath my ear and I roll my eyes closed.

"Our friends are waiting for us," I rebut huskily.

He kisses farther down my neck, hands roaming my abdomen. "They'll understand."

God, I want him to keep going. Explore my skin with his lips and tongue. Taste me. Heat ravages my skin as he kisses along the curve of my neck. "Jonas…"

"Yeah, scarlet."

"I want to." Spinning in his arms, I lock on to his otherworldly eyes. "But after we go out."

My favorite dimple appears as his lips kick up at the corners. His lips hover over my ear. "Hours of torture." He groans then releases me.

"It'll be worth it."

Before I change my mind about going out, I rush us out of the room. Jonas chuckles, his hand on my hip. Hugs and good nights are exchanged with Penny and Clementine. We buckle up in the Jeep and drive toward Tampa.

We crack the windows enough to let the cool night air sweep inside the cab. Salt and sand and earth perfume the breeze. Brilliant shades of tangerine and magenta dust the horizon as the sun dips below the water. "Level of Concern" by Twenty One Pilots plays on the radio as Jonas draws circles on my thigh with his thumb.

My eyes drift closed, amplifying every sense but sight. The whorl of Jonas's calloused thumb swirls on my thigh and stirs heat low in my belly. Hints of sunscreen mixed with Jonas's scent float in the Jeep cabin, and I take a deep breath. A brisk gust whips across my cheek and tampers the heat slowly building from his touch. And as the song on the radio fades from one to the next, I picture dancing with Jonas tonight, sweat dripping off our bodies.

Tonight celebrates a first, of sorts. Not the first occasion going out without Clementine. Jonas and I have gone on several dates. Gone out to hang with our friends and have fun—which is where we are headed now.

But tonight is different.

Because when we all go our separate ways tonight, Jonas and I will go home to his house. Alone. Without Clementine.

Part of me screams inside and waggles a motherly finger in my face, berating me for not being under the same roof as my daughter when I go to sleep. Another part of me hoots and hollers and jumps on the bar top whirling a towel over her head. She praises me, tells me *it's about damn time*, teases I won't get any sleep tonight.

"Should be there in five," Jonas states as he exits the highway.

I shoot a text to Cora and let her know our ETA. She replies and indicates where they parked. A few more turns and Jonas parks the Jeep one row back from Gavin's Range Rover. We stroll to the Rover hand in hand and meet up with everyone. After hugs and quick hellos, we enter the club.

Although I never experienced the clubbing stage of my late teens/early twenties, I suddenly *feel* years younger. A rush of excitement fuels me as we walk through Roar. Bass and occasional treble pour from the speakers and rattle my bones. Sporadic flashes of colored lights illuminate the dark club while dim lights softly brighten the bars. Sweetness and salt filter through my nose as we pass people bumping and grinding on the dance floor. Jonas guides me through the club with his hands on my hips, provoking the urge to dance.

Gavin maneuvers the group toward a table near the bar. As we circle around, Micah waves then signals he will be over in a minute.

Jonas stands flush to my back, not a breath of space between us. His hands clasp at my belly as his fingers tickle the sliver of visible flesh near my navel. Light caresses fan the flame already heating my skin. Lips lightly nibble at my ear as I roll my eyes back and press my butt against his thighs.

"Mmm... definitely dancing tonight," he muses, breathy on my ear.

I tip my head back, rest it on his shoulder, and meet his gaze. His lips lower to mine and break away far too soon. When I display my best pouty face, Jonas shakes his head and chuckles.

Micah joins us at the table, exchanging hugs and bro back slaps. Although he works tonight, he promises to hang during breaks. He goes around the table and jots our drink orders on a napkin.

After he scratches the last drink down, Micah steps between two people at the bar and hollers. "Peyton." A woman midway down the bar, blonde hair loosely pulled back in a ponytail glances up. Close to our age. She's tall—closer to Shelly's height than the rest of us. Her eyes scan the bar to find who called out. When her eyes land on Micah, she grinds her jaw. He tosses the napkin on the bar and slaps it. "Drink order," he yells.

She drifts down the bar to stop in front of him. From my vantage point, I can't hear the exchange. But hostility rolls off the two of them. Or is that sexual tension? He says something else to her and she shakes her head while grabbing a glass. When he spins around, she aims her middle finger in his direction.

I laugh and Jonas peers down at me. "What's so funny?"

He leans in close and I cup my mouth to his ear. "Little love-hate relationship between Micah and the woman behind the bar." Jonas looks to the woman in question and nods. "Not sure if they're dating or have dated, but there's definite tension."

Micah delivers the drinks to the table then darts behind the bar to help. We sip our drinks and catch up on life. Before long, everyone drifts out to the dance floor while Jonas and I hang back at the table.

Jonas faces me, snakes his arms around my waist, and hauls me closer to him. "Want to dance when they wear out?" Lacing my fingers behind his neck, I nod.

His gaze holds mine for a beat before dropping to my lips. Without preamble, he kisses me breathless. The flashing lights and thumping music fade away. Wet heat traces the seam of my lips and I open up. With hundreds of people nearby, Jonas kisses me wild.

Our lips break apart, but he peppers kisses along my jaw. When he reaches my ear, he sucks the lobe between his lips and growls. "Autumn." My moan in response vibrates my chest. "Move in with me."

I fist his shirt and bite near the collar at the base of his throat. He growls again, fueling the flame in me. "God, I want to."

Jonas leans back and I immediately miss his weight on my nipples. Finger under my chin, he tilts my head back. "Then say yes."

Music blares from every corner and hidden speakers in the ceiling. Sweaty bodies gyrate on the dance floor and near the tables. Upbeat energy bounces off every surface. And yet, it all disappears as I study how the blue marries gold in Jonas's irises.

This is the second time Jonas has proposed Clementine and I move in with him. The first was a slip of the tongue at his parent's a few nights ago. After I told him I wanted to discuss it in private, rehashing the subject hasn't happened. Until now.

Will Jonas be upset if I tell him I decided the very same night? That as he drifted to sleep, I imagined—not for the first time—what living together would be like. Waking up next to him every morning and falling asleep in his arms. I wanted to rouse him from sleep and tell him yes. But so many people say making rash decisions isn't smart. So, I simmered on it.

With each passing minute, hour, day, the desire to say yes expanded in my chest. Consumed me. Begged to be let out.

I lift up on my tiptoes and press a kiss to his lips. "Yes," I whisper, breathy.

Leaning back, his eyes dart between mine. "Yes?"

I nod and, in a blink, he hoists me off the floor and spins me in circles. Glad I haven't drunk much. My feet hit the floor and he crashes his lips to mine. Tasting me. Devouring me. I fist his hair. Moan when he kneads my hips and grinds me to him.

"Get a room," Micah yells from the bar. Catcalls and wolf whistles echo around us as we peel apart.

As Jonas flips Micah off, the blonde bartender yells something at Micah I don't hear. But if the curl of her lip is any indication, she probably told him to shut up or mind his own business.

As our group trickles back to the table, we share our news. Cheers erupt as the ladies crowd around me and squeal. The guys exchange fist bumps or shoulder hug-slaps. Once the congratulations die down, we lose ourselves to the music.

Jonas threads his fingers with mine and walks backward toward the dance floor, tugging me along. His smile illuminates the dark club as he pins us chest to chest, palms flat on my low back. Our bodies grind and sway. Sweat slicks our skin and drips from our temples. Jonas drops his forehead to mine and holds my gaze.

"I love you," he mouths. His silent declaration louder than the thumping music.

"Love you, too."

He dips his chin and tastes my lips. One song bleeds into another. Then another. All the while, Jonas and I sway in the middle of the dance floor, lips locked, tongues tasting, oblivious to the world around us.

When he breaks the kiss and we come up for air, he whispers in my ear. "Let's go home, scarlet."

Better words have never been said. "Let's go home," I repeat.

For someone who cohabitated in a small apartment with another adult and a child, Autumn has more shit than imaginable.

"We may have to add another room to the house," I tease, heaving another box from the floor.

Autumn sticks her tongue out. "Ha ha. If we fit everything in here" —she waves her arm around the bedroom— "we can fit it into the house."

My house—our house—may be small, but I have upgraded majority of it over the years. Done my fair share of walks through the Ikea showroom for innovative ideas in small spaces. Learned how to make the best of unused wall space. And although my belongings don't fill all the shelves and cubbies and rods in the closet, I made the most of the space when updating it.

Which means Autumn will have plenty of space for her clothes and shoes and purses and whatever else she owns. And if the closet fills, there is plenty of room in Clementine's closet.

Back seats laid down in the Jeep, I wedge the box between two others and go back for more. Everything leaving the apartment is small enough to fit in the Jeep or Autumn's car. After talking with Penny, Autumn opted to leave the furniture in the apartment for whoever rooms here next. Better it go to use than sell it.

In the apartment, I wander to the Jenga pile of odd-sized boxes. "This the last of them?"

Autumn pops up behind the open kitchen counter and brushes a stray hair out of her face. "Just packing up the last of the kitchen items. Everything else is done."

One by one, I carry out the larger boxes, followed by several small boxes labeled *bathroom*. As eager as I am to share the same living space with Autumn and Clementine, the number of personal care items going into the bathroom intimidates the hell out of me. What do I have? Maybe less than ten hygiene/personal care items in the bathroom. By the looks of it, Autumn owns the entire beauty care department in Target.

The bathroom may need revamping. Again.

Not that I am opposed.

Once everything is crammed inside the Jeep and Bel Air, we drive back to the house and haul everything inside.

The house looks like a war zone. Boxes in every room. Piles of wadded news-paper from unwrapping fragile pieces. We pile the boxes according to room then disburse accordingly.

Clementine spends the day in her room, putting away her own belongings as Spartan supervises. Every once in a while, we hear her direct him where something goes—although he isn't capable of putting it away. Or so I thought. At one point, I peeked in her room and watched Spartan carry a stuffed animal on the bed and place it by the pillows. Huh. Only for her.

We spend all of Saturday unpacking. Only taking breaks to eat and sleep. When Sunday morning rolls around, I glance around the house with fresh eyes. It's the same space, but not. The energy vibes differently. Feels more lived in. Comfortable. A home.

While the girls are still asleep, I cook breakfast. Our first official Sunday living under the same roof. And I plan to treat my girls.

Clementine wanders from her room first. Balled fingers rubbing her eyes as she yawns big. Spartan ambles lazily beside her. Before Clementine, Spartan was this wild child. Barking and running like his ass was on fire. Now, he peers up at her, docile and at her beck and call.

"'Morning, sunshine. Did you sleep good?"

She nods. "Can I let Sparty out?"

"Sure. Just open the back door. He'll bark when he's ready to come back in."

After she lets Spartan out, she sidles up to me in the kitchen. "Whatcha making?"

"French toast, sausage, eggs, and fruit."

Spartan barks to come back inside. Clementine tends to him as I finish cooking. When I spin around to grab plates from the cupboard, Autumn stands at the opposite end of the kitchen, ogling me.

Sleepy eyes rake over my bare chest and sweats. The hunger in her eyes is a delicious assault that lights me on fire. Her tongue sweeps out and licks her lips. Chest rises and falls quicker. And I love how easily she is affected by me. Just as I am her.

Each morning, I am rewarded with her natural beauty. Although I love seeing Autumn styled to the nines—hair pinned to perfection, lips and nails scarlet red, outfit glamorous even when casual—seeing her fresh from sleep is my favorite. Tank top and pajama shorts hugging her curves. Face free of makeup. Hair frizzing in every direction. Feet and legs bare.

I saunter over to her, grip her hips to bring her flush to my chest as I kiss her. "'Morning, scarlet."

Eyes closed, a warm smile curves her lips up. "'Morning," she says, breathless. "Smells good."

"Was about to plate everything. Pull up a stool." I kiss her nose and smack her ass as she heads for the breakfast bar.

Maple, herbs, and citrus waft in the air as I deliver breakfast to my girls. As we eat, the topic of tonight's gathering comes up.

Although I have owned the house for some time, having Autumn and Clementine here makes it feel new. Our recent Sunday get-togethers with friends have been wonderful, so we opted to do a housewarming. As I see it, tonight's shindig is just another of our Sunday gatherings, just using the guise of Autumn and Clementine moving in as a reason to ask everyone over.

Once we clear our plates, I clean up the kitchen. Autumn and I sit down to write a shopping list while Clementine showers.

If there is one thing that will take time adjusting to, it's the fact I now have to share one bathroom with two additional people. Thankfully, the water heater holds enough to let us all shower without the water running cold.

Though we are slowly settling in to the idea of living together, I wonder how long we will be able to stay in this small house. Does it have everything we need? Absolutely. Will it be a struggle to live in a small space with one bathroom as

Clementine approaches her teen years? More than likely. But we will cross that bridge when we get to it.

With the list made, we gather clothes for the day while waiting for Clementine to finish.

I sit on the edge of the mattress and follow Autumn around the room with my eyes as she plucks a shirt from the hanger and tugs jeans from the dresser. She lays them beside me and returns to the dresser for bra and panties. She twirls the minimal material lace panties around her finger and saunters over to me.

I look between the sexy as hell panties and her eyes, swallowing. "Don't think I've seen those," I squawk like a hormonal teenager.

Her knees bump mine before she plants each on the bed, straddling me. I stare up at her in complete fascination as she licks her lips. "You haven't. Bought them online a few weeks back."

My hands go to her hips, knead once, twice before dipping to her ass. I cup her cheeks and drag her closer to my chest. "Can't wait to see them on you." Her plump lips tug at the corners. "And to peel them off later."

She drops her mouth to mine and kisses me with fire on her lips. "Later." Hopping off my lap, she tosses the panties to the bed and takes my hand. "Let's go shower."

There are pros and cons to having a single bathroom and shower in this house. Con—you have to wait your turn. Whether to shower, brush your teeth or use the toilet. Con—you never know how long the wait will be. Pro—more joint shower time with Autumn to "conserve" water or time. At least that is the excuse we give Clementine.

Until today, I'd never had shower sex. Movies and television make it look easy. In reality, it's awkward and slippery and complicated. Guess we will have to practice until we get it right.

Won't find either of us complaining.

~

Lifting the beer to my lips, I swallow down the hoppy brew and glance around the back patio.

Everyone being here feels almost dreamlike. Six months ago, if someone would have told me I'd be head over heels in love with someone other than my best friend, I would've laughed in their face. If they also told me the love of my life came with the cutest little girl on the planet, I would've laughed harder.

Sometimes fate surprises you. Throws a wrench in your ideal plan because it has something better in store. Seeing my friends and family together tonight proves you can't stay single-focused forever. You have to learn that people enter your life for a purpose. To show or teach you love so you recognize it when it enters your life. To tear you down so you learn how to rise and be the strongest version of yourself. And how to locate your own path.

For some, it takes a lifetime. Thankfully, I didn't have to wait so long. But I thank fate for the years I traveled down my path. Through the heartache and uncertainty. The friendship and laughter. Without them, I might not have met Autumn. I might not have been ready to meet her. Unwilling to open up or see the big picture. Feel the way my soul hums when she enters the room.

Tonight wouldn't be what it is without her.

Cora, Erin, Shelly, and Penny lounge on the outdoor couch with Autumn, laughing. Watching them whisper like school girls is a sight. Autumn snorts then smiles and I can't take my eyes off her. That woman belongs to me, and I am damn lucky.

Mom and Dad play with Clementine, Ashton, and Lex in the yard, chasing them around until they squeal with delight. Spartan is hot on Dad's heels, barking playfully. With Clementine living here now, I contemplate adding kid-friendly fun to the backyard. A swing set or trampoline or treehouse. Maybe Jasmine will bring Lex over to play more if I do.

Gavin, Rex, Anton, Micah, and Reznor are in what looks like an all too serious conversation. Anton animatedly tells them something and I am certain it is in regards to finances. Anton has always been a great guy, but as soon as someone mentions saving for the future or making significant life changes, he flips into the most passionate numbers man.

Jasmine, Jillian, Trevor, and Iliana sit opposite the couch near the fire bowl and talk softly. And, if I am not mistaken, Trevor glances a little longer than typical at Jillian, but I won't call him out on it. Trevor has been through some shit with his ex. Considering how long we have been friends, I know he wouldn't hurt my sister. Especially if he wants to keep his dick intact.

Cora rises from the couch and walks my way. Sidling up to the grill, she refills her drink then faces me.

"I'm happy for you."

After I flip the chicken, I glance at her. A smile I used to think I couldn't live without stretches across her face. The appearance brings me joy, but a form much different than it once did. So much has changed between us. It isn't often men and women remain friends. Usually, relationships or emotions meddle. At one point, that was almost the case for us. But it never felt right. Although I love Cora, my love for Autumn is a million times more powerful.

As Autumn once told me, maybe Cora came into my life so I could experience love and see it firsthand with her and Gavin. Cora was never fated to be mine, just a teacher to prep me for the future. For Autumn and Clementine.

"Thank you. Never thought this would be my life." I wave my beer bottle around. "But I'm damn glad it is."

Cora leans in and hugs me. "Knew she was out there. She was waiting for you too."

I break the hug and smile. "Yeah." I glance over to Autumn, who peeks up and smiles back. "Lucky I found her."

One year later

"I miss your face," Penny whines as she wanders into my booth.

"Just my face?"

She pops her gum and plops down on my freshly cleaned client chair. "Would you be mad if I said yes?"

"What's the matter, Rex not as pretty as me?" I tease.

A month after I moved out of the apartment with Penny, Rex and his girlfriend at the time got in a huge fight. Seeing as they were living together and her daddy paid the rent on their apartment, Rex got the boot. Thankfully, Penny hadn't found anyone to occupy the second bedroom. When Rex came into work "sobbing like a baby" as Penny so gracefully stated, she took pity on him and let him move in.

Over the last few months, I noticed a slight shift in how they act around each other. Small things.

The way he glances over to the reception desk more often than before. Her obvious avoidance of him at work—overtly intentional. And anytime we all hang out, they stay as far apart as possible.

If I didn't know any better, I may believe they are sleeping together. Either that or they fight the urge.

Penny rolls her eyes on a huff. "Definitely not. He also isn't the cleanest human on the planet. And is it too much to ask for him to put the damn toilet seat down?"

I chuckle and she narrows her gaze at me. Taking a step back, I hold my hands up in surrender. "Sorry, but you have to admit, it's kind of funny."

She pops off the seat, plants her hands on her hips, and shoots me a pointed glare. "It isn't funny, Auti." Her hot pink fingernail aimed at my chest. "And you're supposed to be on my side."

"I am on your side," I cajole. "Sorry Rex is a bad roommate. Have you talked with him about it?"

Slowly, over the last year, I have lightened my schedule at the shop. Now working four lighter shifts, Tuesday through Friday, so I have more time with Clementine and Jonas. On a typical day, Jonas works until five and Clementine attends an after school martial arts program. And if I pick her up earlier than four thirty, I regret the decision all night.

In the not too distant future, I see myself working even fewer hours. But we will play it by ear.

"You're joking, right?" She shakes her head while tapping her Mary Jane on the linoleum. "Talking to Rex about anything is a lost cause."

I tuck my lips between my teeth to stop myself from laughing and focus on finishing my cleanup. "Pen," I start with a headshake. "You need to talk with him. Even if he's a pain in the ass, you need to sit down and hash this out. It won't get better otherwise."

Tossing my gloves in the trash bin, I grab my purse from the cabinet and exit the booth with Penny on my heels. She plops down in her chair behind the reception counter on a huff.

"I hate it when you're right, Auti."

"Glad you still love me." I bend and bear-hug her. "Let me know how the talk goes. Love you."

"Yeah, yeah. Go be with your man." She shoos me away.

I hop in the Bel Air and drive to the dojo to pick up Clementine. As she gathers her belongings, Clementine brags about the instructor's praise on her kata technique. As girly as my daughter is, I never expected her to love martial arts the way she does. But it warms my heart she discovered something she is not only good at, but also loves enough to flaunt.

On the way home, I remind her we're going out for dinner. In the past year, having Jonas as a father figure and Spartan as a daily companion has been a good change for Clementine. Her sass has knocked down a notch and she interacts more with us than being glued to screens. Undeniably, my little girl has grown up so much.

As soon as I cut the engine, she darts in the house, loves on Spartan a moment, then takes off for a quick shower.

Not a foot in the door, Jonas has his arms around my waist and his lips pressed to mine. "How was your day?"

"Uneventful, unless you count Penny flipping out because Rex is a slob."

He chuckles and shakes his head. "When I went out with the guys last weekend, he went on a tirade about her nagging. Seems like some love-hate going on there."

"Agreed."

We break apart as Spartan bolts past us and we stumble into the couch edge. Jonas scolds Spartan, then frames my face in his palms. "You alright?"

I nod. "Yeah. Just stumbled a bit. The house gets smaller the bigger he and Clementine get." Nonchalantly, I hint at needing more space for the second time this week.

Jonas shrugs it off and repeats the same line he said last time. "We'll figure something out."

Once Clementine finishes getting ready, we pile into the Jeep and drive to Red Robin. Instead of bopping and singing in the back seat, Clementine prattles on about how eager she is to earn her next belt in karate. Her hands animated while she talks about the new kata she learned today. Her enthusiasm pastes smiles on our faces. He clutches my thigh a little tighter as he steers us into a parking space.

No matter how gentle or firm, I love Jonas's touch. Live for the warmth and tingle it provokes. In the last year, every touch has held more meaning. Lit me on fire further. Had me falling more and more in love with him.

After a table full of appetizers, three burgers, and a few drinks in funky cups, we decide to wander the mall to burn off the obscene number of calories we consumed.

In one of the department stores, we wander to the kid's section and stare after Clementine as she scrutinizes every item on the racks. As we steer closer to where her sizes butt up against the baby clothes, I get lost in the soft gray and subtle green onesies, sleepers, and outfits. Before I stop myself, my hand reaches out and grazes the delicate cotton.

Jonas steps up behind me, snakes his arms around my waist and whispers in my ear. "Everything okay?" His voice riddled with questions. "You've been quiet the last few days."

I drop my hand from the sleeper and spin to face him. "Yeah. Just been thinking."

His fiery hazels lock on to my goldens and study me with great intensity. "About?"

Clementine bounces over toward us with a rock band shirt in her hand. "Can we get this? Pleeeease."

I nod. "Sure, pumpkin. But that's it." As she skips away from us, I peer up at Jonas. "When we get home."

After we pay for Clementine's new "Girl bands rock!" shirt, we walk back to the Jeep. The ride home is quiet and heavy with questions. Out of the corner of my eye, Jonas peeks my way every opportunity he gets. I keep my eyes forward and my fingers curled with his.

At home, Clementine and Spartan lock themselves away in her room, leaving Jonas and I alone.

It's now or never, Autumn. Just tell him. No need to worry yourself sick. Everything will be fine.

Jonas guides me to the couch and we cuddle the moment we plop down. He strokes my hair and I close my eyes to focus solely on his touch. The heat of his skin on mine. His jagged breath as he hugs me closer to him.

"You can talk to me, scarlet. About anything," he croaks against the crown of my head.

No doubt my silence has him worried. Roles reversed, I would feel the exact same.

I tuck my lips between my teeth and take a deep breath before releasing them. "I'm late." Jonas goes still beneath me. Too still. I close my eyes and pray this won't be an issue. "And I took a pregnancy test a few days ago."

After a yearlong minute, Jonas scoots away an inch. I pinch my eyes until the corners hurt, until the warmth of his palms rest on my cheeks. Slowly, he tilts my head back until his eyes meet mine.

"Autumn..." he breathes my name as if it is his last breath. "Why didn't you tell me sooner?"

Tears sting the backs of my eyes and I question myself as to why I waited so long. Who the hell knows? I shrug and swallow the emotion swirling at the back of my throat. "Don't know. Guess I was worried how you'd react."

"Autumn, I love you. No matter what." He leans in and kisses me soft and sweet. "What did the test say?"

A tear spills down one cheek, then the other. "That you're going to be a daddy." I smile as his eyes dart between mine.

"Really?" he questions with wonderment in his voice. I nod with my eyes on his. He kisses me again, this time greedier. "I-I don't even know what to say."

I grip his forearms and study his ear-to-ear smile. "Tell me that you're happy and you want this. A baby."

"Hell yes, I'm happy. And damn right I want this." He crashes his lips to mine and makes me breathless. When he breaks the kiss, he glances around the open floor plan before coming back to me. "Guess we will need more space after all."

I trace from his temple to the angle of his jaw before cupping his cheek. "I love you, Jonas."

His thumbs stroke my cheeks a moment before he drops his palm to rest over my lower abdomen. "Love you, too." His glassy eyes meet mine. "Thank you," he whispers.

"For what?"

My favorite dimple makes an appearance. "For loving me." He presses my hand to his sternum and covers it with his own. "And for giving me something I never thought I'd have." I scrunch my brow. "A family of my own."

bonus content

one

AUTUMN

"I don't know," I mutter as we wander through the third house this week.

Searching for a new house is not as fun as I once imagined. Definitely nothing like the reality shows on HGTV. And I swear I have told our realtor a dozen times exactly what we are looking for. Yet, here we are, staring at another house that meets none of the specifications either of us mentioned.

"What don't you like about it?" she asks, dumbfounded.

And because I am six months pregnant, I don't bite my tongue. "How about it isn't what we're looking for."

"Autumn," Jonas groans.

I face him and give a *don't you side with her* look. "Well, it's not. And I refuse to look at one more house if it doesn't meet our specs. I'm tired and my feet hurt," I bark out as I rub my belly.

The realtor goes red in embarrassment. "My apologies, Autumn. Just wanted to show you several houses in your price range."

"Under normal circumstances, I might appreciate your thoughtfulness. But now is not the time to lug me all around town."

"Yes, ma'am." She cowers and scurries toward the exit. "There is one more house to see and I promise it meets your requirements."

As soon as she is out of earshot, I mumble, "It better."

Jonas chuckles at my side as he wraps an arm around my shoulder. "C'mon, scarlet. Let's go see the last house. Then we'll head home so you can relax."

We drive north for ten to fifteen minutes before winding through a quiet neighborhood. I stare out the passenger window and eye the lush landscaped front yards and pale painted two-story homes. Kids run through the grass playing tag. A woman mows the grass while a man tends to the weeds near the flowers. And when we step out of the Jeep, the subtle scent of jasmine floats up my nose and relaxes me.

The house exterior is a steely blue with white and navy trim. Colorful shrubs line the front of the house along with native grasses and a variety of small flowers.

At the base of two tall oaks, ferns form a thick diameter. A narrow walkway winds through the yard from the street to the porch. And off to the right of the main house is a two-car garage.

Unlocking the door, the realtor walks us inside. Ten feet into the house and I know we have found our new home—long as there are no issues.

We are shown the bottom floor first—living, dining, kitchen, breakfast nook, den, fourth bedroom, full bath, laundry room, garage, back patio and caged-in pool. As gorgeous as it all is, the enormity of it all overwhelms me. Then we trudge up the stairs and look at the three bedrooms and two full baths.

As I study the largest tub I have ever seen in the upstairs main bedroom, the realtor quietly leaves us to look and talk.

Jonas comes up behind me and rests his hands on my hips. "I can think of several things we could do in this tub."

I turn and play slap his bicep. "You're naughty." He laughs. "Which is one of the reasons I love you."

"What do you think, scarlet?"

Glancing around the room, I wish my growing belly didn't prevent me from jumping up and down. "It's perfect. Clementine will love it."

He bends his knees and levels with my line of sight. "Do you want to put an offer in?"

I tuck my lips between my teeth then release them. "Yes."

Two

JONAS

"Only five more minutes."

Autumn screams in the passenger seat of the Jeep while she drains all the blood from my hand with her death grip.

"I'm not going to make it," she belts out between pants.

"Yes, you are." I steer the Jeep into the parking lot of the hospital. "See, we're here. Let's get you out."

I jog around the front of the Jeep and lower Autumn from the passenger seat. Tossing the delivery backpack over my shoulder, I wrap my arm around her and guide us toward the hospital entrance at her pace.

Once we check in, a nurse brings us to a delivery room, helps Autumn change into a hospital gown, and checks her dilation.

"You're doing good, Mom. At seven centimeters. Shouldn't be much longer. I'll page the doctor and be back to check on you."

The nurse leaves the room and I try to remember everything from birthing classes over the past four months. At the moment, every single breathing exercise and soothing technique has flown the coop.

I hold Autumn's hand between mine. "How're you feeling, scarlet?"

"Argh!" Her grip on my hand intensifies tenfold. "Like I'm going to die."

"You're not going to die." I kiss her knuckles. "You're the strongest person I know. If anyone can get through this, it's you."

She grits her teeth in an attempt to smile. "I love you, but please don't hate me if I say mean things while this is happening."

"Say whatever you need to, scarlet. I'll be here, no matter what."

"Hey, Mom and Dad. I hear the little one is ready to come out and play," Dr. Heidi singsongs as she enters the room. "Let's see how you're doing, shall we?" The doctor does a brief exam and asks Autumn her pain level. After determining the contractions are a minute apart, she preps for delivery. "Dad, you should put scrubs on." I glance her way with a pinch between my brows. "Promise not to start without you."

I rush to the en suite bathroom and throw scrubs, cap, and booties on. When I reenter, the room is abuzz. Dr. Heidi barks out orders to the nurses while she sits poised between the stirrups at the foot of the hospital bed. Monitors next to Autumn's bed beep frantically and she pants on the bed.

Fuck.

I bolt to Autumn's side and grip her hand. "What's wrong?"

"My water broke and the alarms started going haywire." She pinches her eyes tightly, panting. "Dr. Heidi thinks it's rapid labor." My eyes widen as Autumn grits her teeth and numbs all the feeling in my fingers. "Basically, my body is ready to get the baby out now."

Over the next hour, Autumn bears down and pushes when the doctor tells her. Between contractions, she drops her head back and focuses on her breathing. I hold her hand and tell her to break my fingers if she needs to. The entire experience inspires me and shows me a strength I never knew a woman could possess. Leaves me absolutely awestruck.

And at seven thirty-one in the evening on January twenty-fourth, two days before my own birthday, I hear my son cry for the first time.

Seconds after I cut the cord, he is placed on Autumn's bare chest. I stare at the full head of dark hair and broad shoulders on his tiny human body. He curls his little fingers and lays his cheek above Autumn's breast. I have never seen a more beautiful sight in my life.

Swiping at the tears streaming down my cheeks, I lean in and kiss Autumn on the forehead. "He's perfect and beautiful."

Autumn smiles brighter than the sun as she caresses his cheek. "Hi there, handsome. So nice to meet you, Ryker Wade Thompson. Time to say hello to daddy."

I rip away my scrub top as the nurse scoots a chair closer to Autumn's bed. Once seated, the nurse hands Ryker to me and I place him on my chest. And in this moment, the world stands still. His little fingers toying with my chest hair as I stroke my fingers along his back.

"Hey, big man." A tear slips down my cheek. "Mommy and Daddy have been waiting forever to meet you." I kiss his tacky skin. "So glad you're finally here."

Autumn reaches her hand out for me and I take it. I peek up at her through my tear-stained vision and see the tears running down her cheeks. "I love you, scarlet. Look what we did." I smile down at our son and kiss his forehead. "Best birthday present ever."

three

AUTUMN

April 21st — the following year

"Quit messing with my hair," I bark at Penny.

"Who the hell was that hairdresser? Do they even know how to pin up hair like ours," Penny huffs out.

When I asked Penny to be my matron of honor, I never expected her to be the bridezilla type. During the whole wedding planning process, I have remained calm and collected. Penny, on the other hand, has been a basket case.

I swat at her arms as she reaches for my hair to "fix" another bobby pin. "Stop it. My hair is exactly how I want it. Can we just focus on getting me in my dress, please?"

Click. Click.

Cora has the camera at her eye as she captures my big day. Too bad she has to witness matron of honor-zilla. But I trust her instinct to take all the perfect pictures today.

With a huff, Penny stomps over to the hook where my dress hangs. Cora snapped pictures of it on the hanger earlier before capturing my hair and makeup being done.

As I step into my dress, a knock raps at the door.

"I'll get it," Cora states.

She cracks the door open and peeks out. Then she opens the door wider and lets Jonas's mom enter. The moment she sees me, she gasps and covers her mouth before fanning her eyes.

"I will not cry. Not yet, anyway." She hugs me close. "You look ravishing, Autumn. Aaron will wait outside the door with Clementine."

Blinking back tears, I nod. "Thank you, Irene. Love you."

"Love you, too, sweetie. Whenever you're ready, everyone will start on your cue."

Irene exits and closes the door behind her. A minute later, Cora leaves the room so she and Erin can get in place to take photos from every angle possible.

"Ready for this, Auti?" Penny grips my forearm and gently squeezes.

I tuck my lips between my teeth and nod. "Never been more ready."

Penny stands in front of me, rests her hands on my shoulders, and locks eyes with me. "Remember to breathe. And hang on to Aaron." I nod and blink rapidly. "You look absolutely stunning. Love you."

"Love you, too."

Penny picks up my bouquet—baby pink ranunculus, soft green succulents, and hot pink berries—and hands it to me as she takes her own smaller version. Then she sweeps out of the room in a pink dress to rival her hair color.

Throughout my life, I never envisioned having a wedding day until Jonas proposed.

We had been in the new house just shy of four months. Ryker was barely five weeks old. And Jonas got down on one knee with the most stunning rose gold morganite and diamond ring. I wanted to scream with glee but didn't so as not to disturb Ryker. When he slid the ring on my finger, I stared at the stones for so long, smiling because it looked like a sparkling flower.

I glance down at the ring on my left fourth digit and sigh. Soon, the matching bezel diamond band will rest on the same finger, closer to my heart.

A knock at the door captures my attention. "Come in."

The door cracks open and Aaron peeks inside. "Hey, sweetheart. It's time."

I exit the dressing room, hooking my arm on Aaron's proffered elbow. In front of me, Clementine smiles so big it makes my face hurt. Her dress the same bright pink as Penny's. She waves and starts sprinkling rose petals on the pavers as she marches her way along the path into the wedding garden. Ten heartbeats later, Penny follows in Clementine's wake.

Aaron lays his hand on my forearm and meets my gaze. "From the first day we met, Autumn, I had a feeling you would be more than a woman whose car I towed. And when I saw the way my son looked at you, I instantly knew you'd be in our lives a very long time." I smile up at his handsome face and pray Jonas will age as gracefully as Aaron. "Love you, sweetheart. And I'm proud to call you my daughter."

I tip my head back and bat my lashes at the sky. "Love you, too, Dad."

In my periphery, Cora snaps photo after photo of us. But I lose all focus.

"Here we go." Aaron steadies me as we march forward and head into the garden.

Cora darts in front of us and backs into the garden so she has a head-on shot of Aaron walking me down the aisle. The moment she shifts to the side and unblocks my line of sight, I gasp.

Fifty feet away, just past the rows of chairs where our friends and family sit, Jonas stands with his hands clasped in front of his waist. His charcoal suit snug on his broad shoulders and firm glutes, white dress shirt crisp, plaid pink and charcoal tie snug beneath his Adam's apple. But the most stunning part of my view is his smile and glassy eyes as he stares down the aisle at me.

Cameras click and flash all around us, but I ignore it all.

Everyone rises as Aaron and I approach. I hug him impossibly closer at the elbow as he guides me down the aisle, where I will officially become his daughter and Jonas will be my husband.

JONAS

Dear god.

I have never seen a sight more breathtaking than Autumn on my father's arm walking toward me in white lace and tulle. She looks like royalty.

With a sweetheart neckline, tulle billows down from her waist and dusts the grass as she shuffles her way toward me. A thin layer of rose embroidered lace decorates the skirt, bust, and sweeps down her arms to her wrists.

For as long as I live, I will never forget the way she looks in this moment.

My girl.

When she and Dad reach the arch, Dad gives her away and places her hand in mine. Her soft, warm skin steadies my jitters. Soothes every anxiety in my world.

But marrying Autumn doesn't make me anxious. Quite the opposite, actually. The only thing making me unsteady in this moment is that it didn't come sooner. And the minister isn't talking fast enough.

As the ordained minister reads the wedding script, I lock eyes with Autumn. Her cognac irises an intoxicating swirl of gold and cinnamon. Lips classic red. Hair pinned off her neck in whirls with a small rose gold comb encrusted with gems tucked in the back.

Just as I part my lips to whisper how gorgeous she looks, the minister pipes up and cuts me off.

"The bride and groom have prepared their own vows. Jonas…"

I reach inside my suit jacket and pluck out the paper. Unfolding it, I smile as I read the words.

"Autumn, from the first night I laid eyes on you, I knew. I couldn't look away. Didn't want to. No one gives me solace the way you do. In a matter of minutes, I was bewitched. Enchanted. Enamored. Then I fell in love. Pictured every waking moment with you in my arms. And when I learned about Clementine, I was a goner. The love you both brought into my life is incomparable. And when I didn't think I could possibly love you more, you gave me a son." We both glance over to see Ryker tugging on Mom's hair. "If not for you, my heart wouldn't be full. My life wouldn't be complete. Autumn, you make every day better than the day before, and I cannot wait to see where life takes us next. Together."

Autumn tucks her lips between her teeth and tips her head back, blinking. She levels her gaze, swallows, and releases her lips before extracting a slip of paper from her bust. After a deep breath, she glances down and reads.

"Jonas… I remember the first night I saw you in the shop. You didn't see me that night as you flipped through artist albums on the couch. But I had trouble focusing on my client—Mr. Heaven." Penny snorts behind Autumn. "Anyway. I peered up every opportunity I had. There was just something about you. Something familiar. A piece of myself, dormant inside you, that I recognized. Then we officially met, and that was the most challenging tattoo I've ever done. Because all I wanted to do was look up at *you* and get lost in your eyes. After years of being on my own, you taught me how to love again. Not only love you, but also love myself. You have brought so much joy and compassion into my world. Lifted me up and held me steady. Given me a son as handsome as you and as silly as his sister." She pauses and takes a deep breath. "And today, Clementine and I have a gift we'd love to give to you."

Clementine pops up from her chair beside Mom and sidles up to Autumn. She sticks her hand in her dress pocket and fishes out a piece of paper, handing it to me.

"What's this?"

"Open it, silly," Clementine prompts.

I unfold the paper and scan the page. *Joint Petition for Adoption by Stepparent.* My eyes fly up to meet Autumn's and glaze over immediately. Mouth floods with emotion as I work to swallow past the golf ball in my throat.

"Jonas," Clementine states my name with confidence. I drop my gaze and hold the eyes that match her mother's. "Will you be my dad?"

Every guest gasps. I try to remember how to breathe as I squat down in front of her. "Clementine, I would be honored to be your dad."

Clementine leaps into my chest and wraps her arms around my neck. "Love you, Dad." I wrap her in my arms and rise up. Tears spill down my cheeks as I hug the life out of this little girl. *My little girl.*

"By the power vested in me by the state of Florida, I now pronounce you husband and wife. And family. Jonas, you may kiss your bride."

I lean into Autumn and kiss her sweetly. Clementine briefly hugs both our necks before Mom brings Ryker up and we walk toward our forever together. As a family.

four

VALENTINE'S LOVE LETTER - LOVE BUZZ CHAPTER 20

Dearest Autumn,

Thank you. For coming into my life. For giving me a reason to smile each day. And for loving me. I can't imagine a better life than the one I have experienced with you by my side. And it is only just beginning.

I hope you don't get upset with all the gifts I give you today. And all the gifts I give Clementine.

I've never had someone to shower with gifts until you. I hope you don't think I'm going overboard. Because this is only our first gift-giving occasion. I have years to make up for—no arguing how we didn't know each other.

Having both of you in my life is the best gift you could have ever given me.

Yours always,

Jonas

Restless Night

INSOMNIAC DUET
BOOK ONE

Past…

Another day, another round of bullshit. High school… it goes one of two ways.

You are either popular—the queen bee with a swarm of followers. Every girl wants to be you. Wants your boyfriend. Dresses and talks like you. Is at your beck and call without question. And you are artificial as fuck.

Or two—my current life status—you walk around with a "kick me" sign stuck to your back. Girls point and laugh and say fucked-up shit. They write your name on bathroom stall walls with the word "trash" or "loser" or "slut" beneath it. They gather their posse and gang up on you. Start rumors and throw shit in your direction. Toss out every possible degrading word with your name to boost their own esteem and make others laugh and point.

How I landed in category two is beyond me. But here we are, another day in hell.

I exit the bus and spot them as I step off. As if they waited for me to arrive in the big tangerine beast. Just to antagonize me. To start their day with a fresh load of assholism.

Do mean bitches have nothing better to do with their lives?

"Mandy, did you hear the school slut banged the baseball team last night?"

That would be Mercedes, Queen Bitch.

"Ew." And that would be Mandy, the girl parked so far up Mercedes's ass, she no longer sees light. "But what else do sluts do?"

They laugh and start following me as I pass them without so much as a glance. As pretentious and mighty as they believe they are, one would think they have more in life to do than follow "trash" like me around campus. But whatever.

I walk through campus and head for my locker. They continue their not-so quiet artifice. And I continue to ignore them as best I can. After dealing with their bullshit for the last four months, I learned to tune them out. On occasion, anyway.

I spin the dial on my locker as they prattle on. Voices loud as they encourage others to join in on their hate fest. Only one other does. Meredith. Now my day is complete. Triple M is here and in their full glory.

While I swap my books and folders in my locker, I laugh at my own wayward thoughts. *Triple M. Damn, those are big tits. Slut tits. Who's the slut now?*

"What's so funny, loser?"

Shit. Did I laugh out loud? Oh well. No backpedaling now.

I spin around to face the blonde trio. Hair, makeup and clothes pristine and wrinkle free. Unlike me. My blonde locks currently wear a thick layer of black dye. My makeup equally dark and thick around my eyes. And my ensemble… you guessed it. Black. Let's just say the current phase of life revolves around the saying *black is life.*

Courage bubbles in my chest as my nails dig crescents into my palms. Sick and tired of these bitches, I am ready to blow my top. Go full-on banshee and punch the smiles off their cakey faces. But not now. Maybe just a dose to appease my dark heart.

Just a dose.

"You," I say with a laugh. "You're what's funny." Confidence builds and I run with it. "If you're not careful, someone might think you're in love with me. Obsessed. I mean, god, you seek me out. Follow me like a lost pet. Talk about me all day. Like you have nothing else you'd rather be doing." God, this feels good. Talking shit to her face. Calling her out in front of others. Should I kick it up a notch? Add to her embarrassment? *Do it!* "Hey, everyone," I shout and several eyes glance our way. "Mercedes is in love with me."

Her face turns stop sign red. If possible, steam would shoot from her ears. Her arms stiffen, hands fist at her sides and she literally stomps a foot. I bite my cheek to resist laughing at her charade, as it will definitely worsen the situation.

She shoves a finger in my face, centimeters from my glasses. "You'll pay for that. When you least expect it." She spins on her heel and storms down the hall with her followers up her ass.

At least she is gone for the time being. Shouldn't see her or the other two until sixth period. Thank fuck.

Classes start and end as the day ticks by uneventful. And soon, the bell rings and a sea of bodies ambles toward the cafeteria. I hoist my messenger bag up my shoulder and follow the masses.

A strange square chunk of mystery casserole, a banana and water bottle on my tray, I weave through the tables in search of an available seat. Parked in the corner, I poke at the food and remind myself—again—that I need to bring food tomorrow.

The buzz in the room quiets an octave when a group enters the cafeteria. Micah Reed and half the district-winning track team. They saunter past several tables, all eyes on them, and sit at their usual spot. Chatter resumes and people pick at their mystery lunch.

But I keep an eye on Micah through my raven locks.

The first time I paid any attention to Micah Reed was a week into the school year. Parked under a tree, I read *Wuthering Heights* for English Honors. Micah and several others on the track team jogged out of the gym in tank tops and short shorts in the school colors, with bright running shoes on their feet. I followed them as they went toward the paved oval track surrounding the school football field. Watched as they stretched and bounced on their toes before they took off running.

I dog-eared my page and observed Micah with fascination. His long, lithe frame glided over the pavement like the gazelles on nature documentaries. Blond hair a bird's nest from the breeze. Cheeks red as he huffed and circled the track.

He never saw me under that tree. No one did. No one ever sees me. And I am okay with not being seen. Okay with being the odd girl that makes others gawk. The loner who sits in the corner and keeps to herself. The quiet girl who admires a guy from a distance.

The next time I peek up, Mercedes stands beside Micah in the cafeteria. She smiles and laughs and flips her hair, all but begging for attention.

"Fake bitch," I mutter to myself.

As if she hears the words leave my lips, her eyes scan the room and land on me. She notices the one time my eyes dart between her and Micah, and I hate the action immediately. Because a slow, wicked grin plumps her cheeks.

Fuck.

She combs her fingers through Micah's short locks. He peers up at her with a *what the hell are you doing* look on his face. But what she says next wipes the look off his face.

"I had a good time the other night," she says to Micah loud enough for half the cafeteria to hear. Especially me. "Sorry I'm not as easy as the school slut, though." Her lips protrude in a fake pout, but her eyes scream pure evil.

Not that I have expressed my baby crush on Micah, but she saw it the second I let my eyes drift to him. And I royally fucked myself.

Micah shakes his head and doesn't feed into her comment. This pisses Mercedes off.

"Didn't you hear?" she asks, as if her lies are common knowledge.

"Hear what?" he says with boredom in his voice. And he doesn't meet her gaze.

"Little Miss Slut" —she points her polished dagger directly at me— "had an orgy with the baseball team."

My face lights on fire as every set of eyes in the cafeteria turns my way. *I fucking hate her. Hate. Her.*

But the way Micah looks at me flips my stomach upside down. Has the mystery casserole ready to reappear.

The first time Micah Reed notices me, really sees me, and he stares me down as if I am an easy lay. A conquest to mark on his bedpost and brag over with his jock buddies. His eyes narrow as he rises from the table. For a split second, I think he may walk off and ignore the bullshit Mercedes dishes out.

But I am dead wrong.

"Hey, pretty slut." Eyes searing my skin, Micah fists his dick through the denim and licks his lips. "The track team is always game."

The silence of moments ago vanishes as the entire cafeteria bursts into laughter. Fingers point my direction as eyes spill tears from laughing so hard.

Whooshing floods my ears as the laughter fades and the room swallows me whole. Pressure compresses my rib cage and squashes the tiny, erratic beating organ in the center. The small bites of casserole in my stomach threaten to make an appearance.

God, I want to stab something. Or someone.

And just like that, I am done.

Can't. Do. This. Anymore.

I shoot up from the table, scream at the top of my lungs and throw my tray toward Mercedes. And before I act on my irrational thoughts, I scoop up my messenger bag and run. Run from the cafeteria. Run from every person in this piece of shit school. Run from a life I didn't ask for and don't deserve.

Fuck this place. Fuck Mercedes. And fuck Micah Reed.

one

Present…

Music blares in my ears and vibrates my bones as I walk through Roar.

Hot, sweaty bodies rub against each other in time with the music. Hands grope and lips tease and hips grind. Alcohol drains from glasses faster than refills can keep up. And clothes get looser. As do inhibitions.

I weave through the crowd, brush arms with several women, and toss out my flirtatious smile. Some smile in return. Others reach out and graze an arm or my chest. And I let them. It comes with the territory when you manage a night club. Can't work in a place like Roar without being groped or hit on at least once a night.

I love and hate the attention in equal measure.

Love it because I have easy access to women. Love it because most of the women that come to Roar are hot as fuck. I have a different woman between the sheets each week. None complain when we go separate ways. And none beg for another round. They know the hookup is a one-time deal. No names, no numbers exchanged. Just sex.

Which is part of the reason I hate it. Hate my official manwhore status. A badge I wear often because of my cheating ex, Rochelle.

I hate that I let her tear me down. That she still holds power over my thoughts and life. That her actions still sway my decisions.

After walking in on her, I should be free. Free of her and the bullshit. Small things I didn't notice until after she was caught in the act. I had been her pawn. A middleman in her game to get an even younger guy. Cougar isn't an appropriate term for Rochelle. More like super cougar. Jaguar. Maybe she likes it when he calls her mommy.

A shiver rolls up my spine and I shake away all thoughts of Rochelle. I may be down to try new shit in the bedroom, but that isn't one of them.

"Hey, man," I shout as I approach Dan, one of the bouncers. "All good?"

Dan, a man twice my muscle mass, gives a thumbs-up. "Yeah, boss. Busy tonight." He scans the crowd with a straight, serious face. All business once he punches his time card, Dan is one of our best bouncers.

Outside of work, Dan is all smiles and laughter. But I appreciate his professionalism inside the Roar walls. Never know what someone will do after too much alcohol.

I pat his shoulder. "Let me know if you need anything." He nods and I move on.

Several times a night, I weave through the club. Check on each staff member. Make sure everything is on the up-and-up. And I always end each round at the bar. Where Peyton pours drinks like a bartender from *Cocktail*.

Peyton Alexander. The bane of my existence. Pure, undiluted, sexy-as-sin torture.

She glides around her end of the bar. Flirts with males and females alike. Bats her lashes and pushes up her breasts to enhance her cleavage. Licks her lips and leans in close.

I fucking hate her. Hate that she flirts with every goddamn person who sets foot in Roar. Every person but me.

Most of all, I hate that this eats at my psyche. Keeps me up at night while I fist my cock between the sheets.

I step behind the bar—where I hang when not doing rounds on the floor or managerial tasks in the office—and unleash my undesirable jealousy.

"Peyton," I shout. And I know she hears me because her spine straightens. Her fingers coil, then flatten out.

She glares past Adam, another bartender, and curls her lip a beat. "Yeah, boss," she shouts back, voice saccharine.

"Quit fucking flirting and pour drinks," I bark out. Adam cringes beside me as he pours a beer from the tap.

Peyton lifts her middle finger to her forehead and mock salutes me. "You got it, *Micky.*"

"Bitch," I mutter.

She turns her back to me and goes back to flirting. *Goddamnit.*

Like every other night I work with Peyton, I regret the day I hired her. But one of the owners interviewed and loved her before I had a say in the matter. So now, I grit my teeth, make her life miserable, and trudge forward.

Peyton actually tends the bar better than the other employees. People gravitate toward her each night. Loiter at her end of the bar and wait patiently. Buy more drinks when she tosses them a bright smile and flirts without care. And her tips are proof the crowd loves her. She earns double, if not triple, what the others do in tips.

Her only downfall… she seems to hate me to the pits of hell. The *I want to gouge out your eyes* kind of hate. And I have no idea why.

Unable to witness her endless flirting any longer, I exit the bar and distract myself with another round. Engage in idle chitchat with the staff and patrons.

On the dance floor, I pass a curvaceous blonde. Her golden locks remind me of a certain feisty bartender across the room. So, I step closer and do a little flirting of my own. One song fades into another as she grinds her ass against my dick and wraps her hands around the back of my head to keep me close.

I'm not going anywhere.

Ani and Sean, the club owners, don't mind if the staff join the scene. In fact, they encourage it so long as the partying doesn't interfere with business. Drinks are acceptable, but we don't go past tipsy. Grinding patrons on the dance floor is fair game, but we don't make anyone uncomfortable or assume it will go further. If it does go further, it happens outside these walls.

So, I dance with the woman who grabs and rubs me like she would fuck me in the middle of the room. I kiss down her neck and fist her hips. When the song transitions into the next, I step back. She spins and pouts and it is adorable as fuck.

I bring my lips to her ear. "Gotta work, sorry. Stick around till close?" She nods. "Wait for me. We can have fun after." I back away and she smiles.

The next few hours go by as per usual. Alcohol flows freely, intoxicating the patrons as much as the music. Every now and again, I look down at the other end of the bar and watch Peyton. Inconspicuously stare at her as her eyes glitter under the lights. As she bites her lower lip and half smiles. As she throws her arms in the air and dances behind the bar and several people wolf whistle.

During those hours, my dick strains against my zipper. Aches for an ounce of her attention. To have those glittery eyes shift their focus my way. Her plump lips around my cock. Her curves bouncing above me in a dark room on cool sheets.

But that will never happen.

The blonde from the dance floor wiggles her way between people at the bar. After serving a drink, I saunter her way and she smiles at my approach. I catch Peyton in my periphery and note her not-so-subtle staring at our interaction.

Good.

"Should be done soon. Still good with waiting?"

She licks her lips and I hear Peyton groan. "Yeah. Got nowhere else to be."

And just to irritate Peyton further, I pinch the blonde's chin between my thumb and finger, then crush my lips to hers. The kiss quick and angry and meaningless and all for show. I give two fucks about this woman. Actually, only one fuck.

"Hey, *Micky*," Peyton shouts. Her nickname for me makes my blood pressure rise. She says it just to piss me off. And I let it, but don't flaunt that fact.

"Yeah, bar wench," I throw back with a cocked brow.

She bristles and my insides sing. "Shouldn't you be, I don't know, managing something." Her words meant to be a stab. To throw my own words in my face when I tell her to quit flirting.

But unlike her, I take her bait and roll with it.

I point to the blonde. "That's what I'm doing." Peyton furrows her brows. "Managing my hookup." Her eyes go wide at my bluntness. The fact that I own my manwhore status shocks her. "Should try it sometime."

She glances at the blonde, then back at me. Bass rattles the air around us while I wait for her comeback. Our banter turns me on and fuels the hungry beast inside.

"Nah," she shrugs and taps her chest. "Not one-night stand material." She turns her eyes on the blonde. "I have standards when it comes to who lies in my bed." Her eyes shift back to mine. "Sluts aren't my thing."

Internally, I laugh. But I mask it and come to the blonde's defense—kind of— who shoots daggers at Peyton.

"But sluts are so much fun," I tease. The blonde turns her attention to me. Her jaw drops, but closes when I suck my lower lip in my mouth. "Don't like fun, wench?"

God, I'm hard as fuck right now.

"Oh, I love fun." Peyton saunters closer, but keeps a good five feet between us. "Never been a fan of venereal diseases, though."

I don't hold back my laughter this time. In fact, I double over and release the sexual tension between us. She may not recognize it as such, but what the hell else would it be?

The blonde mutters, "Bitch."

Peyton faces the blonde, leans on the bar and cocks a brow. She shakes her head with light laughter. "I'm the bitch?" Peyton pushes off the bar and takes a step back. "Maybe I am." She shrugs. "But I'd rather be a bitch than spread my legs for every guy who gives me attention."

Heat crawls up the blonde's neck and blooms on her cheeks. I should be worried, but this whole situation amuses me too much to care.

The blonde shifts her attention from Peyton to me. "I'll wait at a table." She points in a general direction behind her.

"Be done soon." I pinch her chin again and crush her lips. "Don't worry about her."

The blonde melts in my hand. "She's just jealous." Then she turns and wanders to an empty table.

Peyton and I return to our typical uncomfortable, disgruntled silence. I pour a few more drinks before last call gets announced. The crowd thins and the first set of overhead lights kicks on. I grab and clean drained glasses. Then wipe down the empty sections of bar top.

When the next set of lights flicker on, ninety percent of the club is vacant.

I toss my towel in the bleach mix. Closing out the registers, I take the tills and tip jars to the office. Once the tills are reset and the cash balances, I stash the cash in the safe and lock up the office.

In the club, the blonde scrolls over her phone screen while Peyton throws her a murderous glare. Peyton has yet to see me walk out, so I hang back a moment and observe. How she washes glasses with aggression. How she wipes down the bar like she needs to remove the varnish.

Interesting. Is she actually jealous? Her actions indicate a flare of jealousy.

So, I use this to my advantage.

I step out from the hall and pass the end of the bar. Peyton locks on to me as I stroll over to the blonde. Her eyes burn my skin—not with hatred, though. They burn with bitterness and maybe a hint of lust. The fire trails over my skin and I stow it away.

I will need it in an hour.

"Ready?" I ask, approaching the blonde.

She peers up from her phone and smiles. In the light, she still flaunts pretty features. Not *take my breath away* gorgeous, but pretty enough to look at while I fuck her brains out. And when I flip her on her hands and knees, I will picture a different blonde.

"Yeah." She locks her phone and stows it in her back pocket. Her eyes shoot over my shoulder and narrow before coming back. "Let's get out of here." She slides off the stool. "Mine or yours?"

"Yours," I say as I wrap an arm around her shoulders.

No one comes back to my house. Ever.

"Perfect."

We head for the exit, but I halt us a moment and glance over my shoulder. "Peyton," I bark out and she glances up from the bar with a bored expression. "Bar better not look like shit in the morning."

Her jaw muscles tighten and shift. Scarlet pricks her cheeks. "Has it ever?" she bites.

I don't answer her question and opt to bark another order. "Don't leave until everything's spotless."

The blonde and I head for the door, but I don't miss Peyton's grumbled *asshole* as we walk out. The ammunition I needed to get through the next couple of hours.

"Morning, sunshine." Reese kisses my hair as he stumbles past the breakfast bar to the Keurig.

"Morning, bum." He swats me away over his shoulder and I laugh. "Late night?"

He sets his cup under the drip, inserts a pod and presses the button. Then he twists to face me. "Surprised you didn't hear." I widen my eyes as a chuckle spills from his lips. Not that Reese's shenanigans are anything new. "You either sleep like the dead or you came in much later than me."

"Probably the latter." I lift my own mug to my lips and sip the creamy brew. "Manager Asshole was in rare form the other night."

Reese adds sugar and hazelnut creamer to the mug, then gulps his morning elixir and sighs. He stands opposite me, hip leaning on the kitchen island, brow cocked in question.

"Sounds juicy. Tell me more while I make breakfast."

Before I get in a word of protest, Reese turns his back to me and grabs pans from the cabinet. I love when he makes breakfast. Everything he cooks tastes ten times better. Even scrambled eggs. Plus, it gives me more time to sip my coffee.

"He just raked my nerves more than usual."

Reese peeks over his shoulder with a devious smile. "Most people call that flirting, sunshine. You should fuck him already."

I shudder and he laughs. "Well, I sure as shit am not flirting with Micah Reed." The idea of purposely flirting with Micah makes my skin crawl. "Nor do I want to fuck him." I ignore the shiver that rolls up my spine. "He's just as much an asshole now as he was back in high school."

Reese grabs eggs, milk and cheese from the fridge. Then a bag of hash browns and sausage patties from the freezer. He cracks half the carton of eggs, adds milk and whips them longer than I ever do. Probably the secret behind why his scrambled eggs are so damn fluffy. I just don't have the patience.

He pours the mix into the pan and adds two handfuls of cheese. In two other pans, he starts the hash browns and sausage. I stare after him in fascination. Not that I can't cook. I just prefer to make simpler foods that only take one pan. Or the microwave. Less dishes equals less cleanup.

"Still think he doesn't know who you are?" Reese sips his coffee, then tends to the pans.

Does Micah know *who* I am? All signs and interaction with him lead me to believe he has no clue.

One—the first time he laid eyes on me, I was in my all-things-black, loner-girl phase. Black hair, black clothes, black makeup. If it was black, I probably owned it.

Don't get me wrong, I still love black. But the dark shade no longer rules my life. Sometime in the last decade, yellow took precedence. I don't plaster it everywhere like I did black as a teen, but I have splashes of it here and there.

Two—Micah looks at me differently now. In high school, he jumped on the Triple M hate train without learning a thing about me. Back then, he looked at me like gum stuck to his shoe. He said shitty things because he was a popular jock and it was funny to pick on the loner girl.

But now… his eyes hold intrigue when they look my direction.

He must think I don't notice his traveling eyes or the frequency of his stares. But I don't miss a single glance. Don't miss the spark of lust in lapis-blue eyes. Or how they drag over my curves when I face away from him.

I have always noticed Micah Reed.

His angular jaw and lean frame. His slight reservation unless he wants to impress someone. Or the truth his eyes tell, but lips can't manage. I once believed Micah was a good guy. Someone who would stand up for others when they need it most. But that rule seems to only apply to family, close friends and impressionable people.

Here is my opinion. Micah Reed can suck my dick. If I had one.

"He has no idea," I answer confidently.

Reese dishes scrambled eggs on to three plates, then adds a hefty portion of hash browns and sausage. He sets the mountainous plate on the bar, then hands me a fork. "His loss, sunshine. Think he'll figure it out?"

I shrug. "If he does, it'll be too late."

He picks up the two other plates and levels me with his gaze. "You say that now, but…"

"But nothing," I say around a forkful of food.

"Alright." He starts for his bedroom. "Just prepare yourself for the day he puts two and two together. May not be anytime soon, but it'll happen."

I point my fork at him. "Go feed whoever's in your room and leave me be."

He strolls down the hall, chuckling. "Love you, sunshine."

"Yeah, yeah. Love you, too."

〜

"Is this right?"

Ms. Jenkins peers down at the yarn and hooks in my hand. Scrutinizes my crochet skills with crinkles at the corners of her eyes and lips.

She pats my hand. "Such a fast learner, dear. You'll make a hat or scarf in no time."

"Let's not get carried away. Plus, when would I wear a scarf? The one day a year it gets cold?"

She laughs, then lifts a hand to her mouth as it transitions to a strangled cough. Decades of smoking evident in the harsh, nonstop hack. If the doctor allowed it, she would still smoke today. But being attached to an oxygen tank and smoking doesn't mix well. So, she quit. Now, she almost always has a toothpick in her mouth.

"No, dear. You take a trip when it's cold up north and use it then. Thought you were smart enough to figure as much out."

Ms. Jenkins was once a world traveler. On my days at the assisted living facility, she takes me on journeys with her stories. Adventures I dream about taking one day. My bucket list grew miles longer when I learned of all the places she'd visited.

Hiking mountains and valleys and sand dunes. Camping under the stars in the middle of nowhere without a care in the world. Witnessing the aurora borealis.

Seeing the pyramids in Egypt. Visiting the Inca citadel in Machu Picchu. Wandering the hanami—aka the cherry blossom festival—in Japan.

I envy her younger, fearless years. Packing a bag and exploring the globe on a whim. One day, I want to travel the way she did. Just get up and go. When? No telling, but I made it a goal.

"Never seen snow," I admit.

"What?" She stares at me in mock horror.

I laugh and raise my right hand. "Swear." She shakes her head. "Where would you recommend? For a first timer."

"You kids." We both laugh. In her eyes, I am still a kid. Not like we bring up age, but I haven't technically been a "kid" for fourteen years. "Where's your sense of adventure?"

My sense of adventure is on the back burner. Who has time or money to travel? Most people my age work more than one job just to live. Me included. I work at Roar four nights a week. And although I earn enough from Roar to pay the bills, I still work two days a week at Gulfside Assisted Living.

The small paycheck from the ALF helps pad my savings and save for rainy days. But adding to my savings isn't the sole reason I work here.

Before Gulfside, I spent several days a week with my grandma. We chatted mostly, but other memories were also made. Baking bread and cookies and pies. Tending to her small garden in the backyard. Sipping tea and coffee on her back porch while bird-watching. Organizing old photographs and adding them to albums. Short walks in the park.

Time with Grandma Isabel warmed my heart. She was a selfless woman. Did whatever she could, within her means, to help others. Always had a shoulder to lean on and offered sound advice freely. I remember her gentle spirit, and that she didn't take shit from anyone.

When she contracted pneumonia, we all thought she would pull through. Her fighter spirit had survived much worse. But her older immune system couldn't fight off the pneumonia. Not after all the years she smoked. Her lungs gave up the fight before her spirit.

I promised her I would give back in her memory. Help others, even if that meant contributing my time or learning to crochet baby hats. Plus, it lessens the void of her loss when I visit the residents of Gulfside. When I sit with Ms. Jenkins and talk about living life to its fullest.

"It's there, I promise. Just have some other obligations to tend to first."

She sets her hooks down and narrows her eyes. "I hope those obligations don't involve a man."

This makes me laugh harder than it should. "No, ma'am."

"Good. Women don't need a man to stand tall." She looks me square in the eye. "If my Stephen was still here, he'd tell you just as much too. We loved fiercely. But he never smothered my light. He helped me shine brighter." She lays her hand on mine. "That's what a real partner does. Helps make you a better version of yourself."

One day, I pray to have a love as fierce as the one she shared with her late husband.

"Enough of that," she says. "Let's finish. Then, you can wheel me to the dining room for lunch."

Over the next hour, I crochet two rows of a baby hat. After I wheel Ms. Jenkins to the dining hall, I hug her goodbye and promise to see her tomorrow.

Exiting Gulfside, I text Aunt Leanne to tell her I am on my way. Every Monday, we meet for a late lunch after I finish my shift at Gulfside.

I have always had a close relationship with Aunt Leanne. She feels more like a second mom than an aunt. When Dad passed ten years ago, I made a point to spend more time with family. To never take time or the future for granted. You never know what will happen from one day to the next.

On Monday, I spend time with Aunt Leanne.

Two songs and a radio commercial later, I park in front of our usual café. We hop out, exchange hugs, and wander inside. After we order, we chitchat and catch up on what we have missed in the past week.

She asks about Ms. Jenkins and how my crocheting is coming along. Asks if Mom and Harold are well—although she checks in with Mom every other week. And then she broaches the subject of Roar. She always skirts around the Micah topic, but she doesn't fool me. I see her secret need to ask intrusive questions and know all the dirty details.

Aunt Leanne, bless her soul, is a gossip queen. The unflattering trait has evolved over the years, but she still knows everyone's business. After our conversations, she forms her own opinions on why Micah is an asshole. I choose to ignore those opinions.

"So…" She drags the two-letter word out to ten. "How's nightlife going? Meet anyone interesting?" I also tend to believe Aunt Leanne lives vicariously through me. She states life wasn't as interesting in her late twenties to early thirties. I beg to differ.

"Good. And yes, I meet interesting people every night I work."

I play coy. Every time she asks, I dance circles around the answer. The way her eyes narrow as I tease her makes me laugh. She never lets me off the hook, though.

She tosses her best death glare across the table, but gets disrupted when our server delivers our food. She stabs at her salad with faux aggression, then points at me with her full fork.

"Why are you avoiding the answer? Did something happen? You better tell me."

I bite into the sandwich and chew slowly to give myself more time before answering. The slower I chew, the thinner her eyes get. When the bite is soup in my mouth, I swallow and mentally prep for the onslaught of questions. Questions I don't want to answer.

"Nothing new happened. Not really." *Shit.* Why the hell did I add the last part? Might as well have handed her the gas canister while I held the match.

"Elaborate," she commands, her fork pointed my way again.

"Put that thing down. You'll take an eye out."

"Quit avoiding."

I sigh. Aunt Leanne knows bits and pieces about Micah. She remembers people bullied me in high school but doesn't know Micah was among them. All she knows of him now are the tidbits I share from time at work. His asshole tendencies, but also the way I spot him checking me out.

She has her own hypotheses on all things Micah Reed. And after today, no doubt she will add even more.

I rehash the events from two nights ago. Reiterate his order barking. Bring up the blonde and how he acted around her with me nearby. Like his goal was to make me jealous. How we went tit for tat. I give the whole rundown. And when I finish, her shit-eating grin irks my nerves.

After a moment of pause, she asks, "You want honesty?"

Yes. No. We never lie to each other, but occasionally keep opinions to ourselves. I want honesty, but don't want another person to say Micah is flirting. I have been on the receiving end of flirting many times. What Micah and I do is not flirting. Our back-and-forth exchanges are more about getting under each other's skin. And it doesn't take much effort.

I know my motivation. But what prompts Micah?

"Always." Even if I don't want to hear it.

"He likes you." She sips her drink. "More than likes you."

I shake my head. "How? This isn't elementary school. Adults don't pretend to hate someone because they have a crush on them."

"Says who?"

"Society."

She rolls her eyes and shakes her head. "So, because society says something, it makes it true. Really, Peyton?"

I hate when she gets semi-philosophical. I also hate when she makes a valid point when I thought otherwise. Ugh.

"Okay, fine. Say he acts like an asshole—"

"Peyton," she scolds me like a juvenile.

"Say he acts like a *jerk* because he likes me. Should I really pursue a relationship with someone with such childish behavior? Why not just come out and ask me on a date?" I pause to sip my water. "Not that I'd say yes."

"Oh, my dear sweet Peyton." She reaches across the table and pats my hand similar to how Ms. Jenkins does. "Because men don't always know how to use their voice. It's easier for them to act the fool than express how they feel."

I tip my head back, stare at the ceiling tiles, and let my vision blur. "Argh. This is so annoying."

"Yet another reason why I stay single. I prefer friendships. Less drama and scrutinization."

With this, she leaves the topic alone and we finish our lunch. Our conversation shifts to something that doesn't spike my blood pressure. She tells me about a new candle shipment they received at work. Practically sells me each scent. But she loves the small, independently owned shop. They sell a variety of knickknacks and stay busy near the beach.

Finished with lunch, we pay the bill, slide out of the booth and head toward our cars. We stop at the back of mine, exchange hugs and promise to see each other the same time next week. I unlock the car and toss my purse onto the passenger seat.

"Peyton?"

I spin back to face her. "Yeah?"

"Not everything is black and white. Be sure to look for the hints of gray and occasional splashes of color."

Skirting around her thoughts, Aunt Leanne just told me to consider the possibility that Micah may have feelings for me. Not the I-hate-everything-about-you feelings he so boldly displays. But perhaps the exact opposite.

Even if he does, I don't see the point. Micah may not remember me from fourteen plus years ago, but I sure as hell remember him. Remember the hurt he put me through and the web of lies he spun. The harsh words on his lips and how he painted me the fool among our peers.

Micah Reed is an asshole and a manwhore. No point seeing him as anything except that. He treats me like trash whenever possible. And dips his dick in anyone with a hole. No thanks, I will pass.

But I appease my aunt for the time being. Toss out a smile and tell her what she wants to hear. "Will do. Love you."

"Love you, too. See you next week."

Next week… Hopefully, I won't have anything new to share about Micah Reed. Not him ogling me behind the bar. Not him flaunting his promiscuity in my face. Not him barking at me to crawl under my skin. Nothing. Only him leaving me the hell alone.

three

I love days like this. Days when I kick back with my best friend and enjoy the outdoors. Hanging with Gavin equals time at the beach. The sun heats our skin while the sand sticks to it. Coconut and brine float in the air. And bodies fill every possible open space between the seagrasses and surf.

Just like old times. When life was less complicated and stressful.

I need more days like today.

Gavin said we should hit the beach. And wherever Gavin goes, so does Cora. Who called and invited Shelly—which is no big shake. Definitely like old times.

When Gavin flew back to the Bay Area last year for work, I knew shit would go down with him and Cora. With how they left things when his parents moved him to California, I expected shit to blow up. But sometimes, life works out when two people are meant to be together.

Maybe I will get lucky one day and find *the one*.

Gavin and Cora just click. They did from the very beginning. The ease of their relationship annoyed me. Hell, it still annoys me. Because I never found a parallel bond with a woman. Never shared a connection so deep, I felt lost without my other half.

My envy knows no bounds. And now that they are married, envy is too small a term for what I feel regarding their relationship. It isn't fair to begrudge my friend for finding love and happiness.

At one point, I thought Rochelle was *the one*. The woman I would ring shop for and get her name branded over my heart. The woman to make me say *I do*, invite friends over for game nights, and grow old and gray with in rockers on the porch.

Unfortunately, I saw Rochelle with blinders on.

Rochelle sought me out. Approached me. Brought up the conversation of a more serious relationship first. And I fell for each crumb she tossed at my feet. I never suspected a woman of her maturity level would treat me with such juvenile tendencies. Would stoop to such low-level actions. In my bed, no less.

All thanks to Rochelle, I now have an issue seeing women as anything other than a means to an end. Sexual gratification. A temporary fix to what ails me. A warm place to stick my dick when the loneliness peaks.

And I fucking hate it.

I don't want to see women as objects. I don't want people to look at my sister like she is good for one act and disposable otherwise. But after trusting a woman with my heart, I fear putting it out there so freely again. Fear the vulnerability of fully exposing myself. Fear another woman crushing my heart when she tires of me and moves on.

I glance at Gavin, my best friend of nearly twenty years, and notice how he eyes Cora. His observation isn't territorial. He has her heart, and she has his. No, his fixed gaze is more a fear of what he will miss if he looks away.

That is the type of love I want. Where you don't take your eyes off one another because you can't bear to miss a moment.

While Cora and Shelly swim, I opt to ask the questions I don't want the girls to razz me over.

"So," I say, and Gavin breaks contact with Cora to face me. "How's married life? Tired of each other yet?"

Gavin tips his head back and chuckles. "I will never tire of her, bro. Never." He pauses to look at his wife briefly. "But things are different than before."

Hmm, color me intrigued. "How so?"

He purses his lips and takes a deep breath. "Guess the best way to describe it is we're the same as before, but also new."

Now, I laugh. "Yeah, that explains nothing, my cryptic friend."

"Sorry." He shrugs. "When Cora and I first met, we lived in a fantasy world. Yes, we were madly in love. Although teenage love is intense and all-consuming, you're blind to what happens after high school. College, moving out, the weird phase of wanting to experience life on your own." He pauses and shakes his head. "We skipped all that. And tons of relationships don't survive those years post high school."

"So, you think you and Cora would've split after high school?"

He stares out at the water and watches Cora as she laughs with Shelly before returning his gaze. "No, I don't think so. But we wouldn't appreciate each other the way we do now. Thirteen years apart really fucked with both of us. We never forgot each other. But we remembered each other differently. I missed her, but the years of resentment I held for my parents painted the memories differently. Cora had no one to hate but me. And even then, she only hated me on the surface."

Yeah, I definitely envy my best friend. None of the girls from school were "forever" material. They all thought their shit didn't stink. They were either too consumed with themselves or had ugly personalities.

"How did that translate into how things are now?"

"Neither of us wanted a serious relationship with anyone but each other. Sure, our reunion wasn't pretty. But we had a lot of pain to hash out. And I deserved to feel every ounce of her pain. I fucked up, man. I left her when I said I never would. Instead of finding a solution, I took the easy way out." He presses his hand to her name tattooed on his chest. "Her pain is my pain, bro. Plain and simple. And I'll never intentionally cause her pain again."

God, I want to talk to Gavin about my own shitty love life. Or lack thereof. Neither of us is an expert. No one is an expert when it comes to love. But maybe he can steer me in the right direction with advice.

Great as it is to experience life and all it has to offer; variety isn't always what it is cracked up to be.

Part of me longs for the comfort that comes with being in a monogamous relationship. Getting to know someone on a deeper level. Seeing the world through their eyes. Evolving with the same person. I don't envision children or gray hair at this stage—I am not that far ahead.

But I do see the same person at my side, day after day. Waking up with the same woman in my arms. Wrapping my arms around her and hugging her close. Kissing her ear, her neck, her shoulder. Loving her—not just physically, but in all aspects of life.

At thirty-two, though, I feel like time doesn't weigh in my favor. And I have no clue how to remedy the situation.

"Can I ask you something?"

Gavin pushes his glasses down the bridge of his nose and gives an inquisitive stare. I see the line of questions form, but he won't ask them. "Always, man. What's up?"

"If you and Cora hadn't reconnected, do you think you would've made a life with someone else?"

Without hesitation, he answers, "No. I tried relationships in California. Never stuck. I compared every woman to Cora. Which only made me want her more." He looks out at the water. "She's all I've ever wanted. Everyone else just filled time and provided a temporary distraction."

I nod. "There's someone…"

Without looking, I know his eyes are on me. "The blonde behind the bar?"

My eyes snap to him. "How?" It's the only word my lips form. Because how the hell does he know I meant Peyton? Have I mentioned her to him?

As of recent, my head has been a fucking mess. Whatever.

"The sexual tension between you two can be felt miles away. The bickering and constant eye contact. I only caught a glimpse, but sure as shit felt it. What's her story?"

Fuck, I wish I knew her story. The not knowing is half the problem. Peyton is elusive. An unsolved crime with a six-inch-thick file folder of stats. Only they are written in a foreign language.

"Wish I knew, bro." I shake my head. "For whatever reason, she's hated me since day one. And I did nothing to offend her."

Gavin laughs at this. Laughs so hard he bends at the waist as tears stream down his cheeks. *Dickhead.* I give him his moment to laugh at my expense. Let him get it out of his system.

"Gonna tell me what's so fucking funny?" I prompt.

"Mr. Hot Shit can't get a girl." He laughs again, but it doesn't linger as long. "You have always been a *lady's man*. You always got the girl with your smile and a one-liner. Insert new girl, one you actually *want*, and she won't give you the time of day. She actually throws shit back in your face." He winces. "Hate to say it, brother. Sounds like karma is working her mojo on you."

Ugh. Why the hell did I ask? Should have known Gavin would give me shit.

But I hate to admit… he has a point.

Over the last sixteen-plus years, I have been an asshole. Not just with women, but in general. I always saw myself higher and mightier than the guy next to me. Is this my punishment? To look, to want, to dream about, but not to touch. To never have the chance to show I can be a good guy.

I have no clue how to come back from that. How to make up for all the shit in my past. For all the one-night stands. For picturing one woman while I stared down at another. For wanting to belt out another woman's name when I orgasm.

Yeah, I am a goddamn prick. Is redemption even possible at this point? Or should I just give up and leave things how they are? Would be easier.

"Quit thinking so fucking hard over there." I peer over at Gavin, who drills holes in my temple. "You like her, man?"

"Yeah, but I don't know if it's because she fights me at every turn, or if it's actual attraction."

"Forbidden fruit always tastes better," he admits.

"Truth."

"But there's something to be said about having a favorite fruit. The one that never lets you down. Always tastes the same and makes you happy."

I chuckle. "This fruit analogy is getting dirty, bro."

He smacks my chest. "Shut up and listen a minute." I swat his hand away and feign pain. "You need to sit down and really think about this. Think about her. Whip out pen and paper. Write down what you're attracted to, the parts that make you want more. Then make a list of all the things that make you insane."

I stare at him, incredulous. "Gavin. Brother. Are you seriously telling me to make a pro/con list of this woman?"

He shrugs as if it is that simple. "More or less. You got any better solutions?"

If I had a better solution, would I be asking for help? After Rochelle, women are a haze of mixed signals and lost translations. The more time passed, the less I tried figuring it all out.

Keeping things short and sweet makes life a hell of a lot easier. It also keeps me from getting my heart broken again.

"No, obviously I don't."

I stare out at the horizon and let my focus relax. Can I do this? Write a pros and cons list on Peyton? The idea of writing down what I love and loathe about this woman makes me itchy. But what other option is there?

Any time Peyton is near, I gravitate toward her. Something about her is so familiar and bewitching. But I can't figure out how to scratch the surface. Get past the anger she harbors. Anger I don't quite understand. Anger she unleashed when Ani and Sean left the room and we were alone for the first time.

That rage stems from somewhere deep. A niggling voice in the back of my head tells me I am the root cause of it all. But how?

I met Peyton only a year ago. Right? I search my memory bank; search the long list of women I have been with over the years. But no hits pop up on my radar. Peyton is definitely someone I would remember.

But the boulder beneath my diaphragm begs to differ. And I have no clue where to go from here.

I park in the employee lot behind Roar and survey the other parked cars. Most everyone is already here. Including Micah.

Great.

I really should talk to Ani about switching some of my days. Micah and Gina, the other manager, draft the staff schedule, but I would love at least one shift without Micah in the picture. A reprieve from his constant stares and assholism. If I talk to Ani, though, she will blather until my ears bleed and probe me harder than an alien abduction.

So, that is a no go.

Guess I just suck it up like a good cookie. Doesn't mean I should make his life easy, though.

Walking through the back door, I stash my purse in the employee lounge, clock in, then head to the bar. No sign of Micah yet. Good. If I'm lucky, he is in the storage room or doing paperwork in the office.

Without the worry of bumping into Micah, I get to work on my prep. I cut citrus and fill the bar condiment boxes. Stash the extras in the fridge beneath the counter. Next, I replenish the napkin stacks, drink umbrellas, and straws. Finally, I double-check the glassware is clean, wipe the counters down again, and scan the liquor bottles and keg levels.

Recently, Wednesday and Thursday nights have grown in popularity. After work gatherings hosted by local businesses or special events with larger parties keep the drinks flowing and the music booming. Fewer bodies and chatter, but still a busy night. My favorite weekday perk; the bar also closes hours earlier. And the tips are still great. Different populous, different mindset, different tipping standards. Of course, Friday and Saturday always bring in the masses and flood the tip jar. But I love the weekday vibe.

Tonight—and any other Wednesday without scheduled events—is Woman Crush Wednesday. Cliché, I know. Basically, it's ladies' night with an updated name. On ladies' night, we serve fruity drinks at half price.

Half price drinks equals lots of ladies soothing their workday with colorful, alcoholic beverages. Lots of ladies drinking and de-stressing equals hefty tips. Works in my favor.

The overhead lights flip off and the colorful lights come on. Music pumps out of the speakers. Not the same music we play on the weekend, but still upbeat and catchy. Moments later, Micah appears from the back and unlocks the front door.

He seems different today.

I shake off the thought as a flock of women storm the bar. Time to whip up some magic.

Five thousand nine hundred and a bazillion fruity drinks later and I am officially beat. One more hour until the door locks. Hallelujah. Then, I can clean up, drive home, and sleep until noon.

Micah joins me and Adam behind the bar. He fills drink orders, cleans glasses and restocks the napkins and fruit. He moves behind the bar as if this is his job, not managing the rest of us. Oddly, he doesn't look my way. Not once. Considering we never go one shift without snapping at each other, I question what parallel universe we landed in. Because silent-and-closed-off Micah is just… weird.

Maybe something happened with his family or a close friend. I peek down the bar, give him a brief once-over, and hope he doesn't notice.

He doesn't look sad or angry. No downturned lips or eyes. No slumped shoulders and hunched back. He just looks… blah. Meh. Like his emotions took a hiatus.

Does it make me a dick if I want to stir the pot? Provoke him a little for my own pleasure. Probably. But work isn't the same if Micah and I aren't going at it like alley cats. And his boring side makes the night drag out.

"Hey, *Micky*," I shout over the music. His spine stiffens and I know I hit the mark. Sweet relief.

He rolls his eyes and turns to face me. "What is it?"

His words have no punch to them. Although I hear the annoyance in his tone, the usual sting is missing. Part of me wants to drop it. Give up and call it a wash. But the feisty side of me says *hell no*. I like feisty me more.

"Your cat die or something? You get your period today? Take a break, I got this handled."

The muscles in his jaw tighten as he grinds his teeth. Inch by inch, his face stains red. His nostrils flare. But he takes slow, measured breaths and lets his frustration or anger with me pass.

Challenge accepted.

"Best watch what you say to me. Seeing as I'm your boss."

Ooh, he wants to play the boss card now. Game on. "Actually, you aren't technically my boss. Ani and Sean are my bosses. You just do everyone else's job plus paperwork and count money."

This pisses him off. The red resurfaces, and he turns his back to me briefly.

What's the matter? Does little Micah not know how to keep his feelings in check? Poor little baby.

He faces me again and steps forward until we are a foot apart. This close, I see the heat from his cheeks has trailed down his neck and onto his upper chest. Smell the woodsy amber scent of his cologne. Hear how hard he grinds his molars and resists speaking, the words dangling on the tip of his tongue.

But I want to coax every word from his lips. Want to hear the hatred and anger. The desire and lust.

I am no idiot. Micah Reed may hide parts of himself from others, but I have known him a long time. Longer than he has known me. For years, I watched Micah from a distance. Saw who he was when everyone was looking. But I also saw who he was when he thought no one was nearby.

Micah is an asshole and a manwhore. Nothing changes that truth. History cannot be erased. It is what it is.

But he is also a big brother and protector. A loner, when his posse isn't around. Although he humiliated me in high school, I still crushed on him. Still followed him when no one paid attention. Still got a glimpse of the guy behind the facade.

My stalker ways faded when Micah graduated and I still had a year left. Senior year was the best year of high school. No more Triple M and no more Micah Reed. The lack of harassment was a nice reprieve. But I hated that I missed seeing Micah every day. I hated that I wondered what he was doing out in the world.

"Maybe you should read the employee handbook again, *wench*." There he is, even if his tone still feels squishier than normal.

"Is this the Micah Rules Roar handbook? Because Ani never gave me a manual to do my job. She knows me better than that."

The few women left at the bar side-eye each other and throw smirks at our back-and-forth. *That will be ten dollars for your evening entertainment, ladies.*

If steam could waft from his scalp, it would be now.

"What is your problem?" he blurts out. He throws a cleaning towel in the sink and steps closer. So close his breath tickles my cheek. The sensation triggers a tingle at the base of my spine. "Why is it your mission to piss me off?" His hissed words only loud enough for me to hear.

Beside us, the women at the bar ooh and ahh. But I don't focus on them. I can't. Not with Micah close enough to press his lips to my skin. To my lips or my neck.

A light sheen of sweat slicks my skin. I resist the urge to step back. To let him win. I got this. Micah Reed doesn't hold power over me. Not anymore.

"I love how easy it is," I tell him. "And because I need to."

He cocks a brow at this. "You need to?"

Too close. He is still way too close. I need to step back. Need clean, cool air. Need to see something other than his supple round lips and beard stubble. Stubble that probably feels so good between—

Shut. Up. Peyton. Do not go there. Do not think of Micah Reed and sex simultaneously. Just. No.

"Someone needs to put you in your place," I croak out. Great. Nothing like sounding less confident when I need to come across bolder.

"And where exactly is my place, Peyton?"

He called me Peyton. Not bar wench or wench. Peyton. That doesn't happen often. It never happens when we stand this close to each other. Hell, we never stand this close. Ever.

"You don't know?" I tease.

His head shakes subtly. "Enlighten me."

The angry part of me wants to yell, "In the pits of hell." But I don't need to scare off the small number of people that visit on Wednesday nights.

I don't want to lie to him, but throwing down my whole hand makes me vulnerable. Micah Reed doesn't own those rights. He doesn't get to choose when I open myself up. Only I get to decide. Me.

So, I take the easy way out. Toss out a statement that still applies, but doesn't reach the heart of the matter. That he hurt me. He may not remember, but one day he will. And he needs to feel what I felt when it all hits him.

"With all the other assholes and manwhores." I step back and smirk. "No doubt there's a special place in hell for all of you. Don't you think?" I take another step back and twirl the length of my hair.

He winces. I expect him to lash out. To step back into my space and give as good as I deliver. But he doesn't.

Instead, he takes a step back. Then another. And without another word, he retreats and heads for the office.

The women at the bar watch his retreat, then snicker among themselves. I cash them out and they leave me a heftier than normal tip. Does bickering with Micah in front of customers equal better tips? If so, I need to turn that shit all the way up.

Once all the customers leave, I start my nightly cleaning routine. Micah has yet to return from wherever he went. He may not help clean up, but he needs to run sales numbers and take the tills to the office. Which means avoiding me until we leave is impossible.

The tables have been cleared of glasses and wiped down. The condiment boxes refilled and stowed in the fridge. Glasses cleaned and napkins restocked. When I start cleaning the floor, Micah reappears.

Not irritated. Not angry. But maybe a little defeated.

Did I cross the line? Was I too harsh? Banter and frustration are nothing new with Micah. But tonight feels different. Micah *seems* different. And I have no idea why.

Do I cave and apologize? No. Nope. Not happening. If I apologize, he wins. Not that the constant tension and barking at each other is a game. For me, it is all too real.

I have been on the receiving end of his shit and the people he associates—associated—with. I know what it is like to go home and cry until I pass out. Know what it is like to just want friends, not even a boyfriend, and have that squashed like a bug.

Micah Reed may not be the sole reason for my pain, but he holds a significant piece of the pie.

"Why?" I startle at his voice. His proximity. When did he step so close?

I swallow down the sudden lump in my throat. "Why what?" I choke out.

"Why do you hate me so much? Give me a real answer. Not some bullshit reason."

He wants the truth? How convenient. How fortunate.

Well guess what, Micah Reed? You need to work for the truth.

I face him head-on and shake my head. My gaze locks with his and all the words on my tongue swirl like alphabet soup.

Have I seen his eyes this close before? Seen how they shimmer under the brighter light. Earlier, I thought his eyes were lapis blue; a rich, dark blue. Now, with his proximity, I really see the resemblance. And the hints of gold. Like stars in the night sky.

Focus, Peyton. Now is not the time to get lost. Especially in his addictive irises.

"Always want things the easy way, huh?"

His brows pinch at the middle. His eyes dart between mine and try to read all the words left unsaid. But I don't wear my emotions on my sleeve. Not anymore. Now, I cover them in armor.

"I don't know what that means."

Of course, he doesn't. Why would he? Instead of sitting down and thinking, he just wants the answer handed to him. Sorry, Micah. No such luck.

"It means, if you want the answer, you'll have to work for it. Dig deep. Real deep. The answers are there. You're just looking in the wrong places."

Before he asks me another question, I back away and head for the storage room. I fetch the dustpan, but don't leave immediately. Instead, I grab hold of the shelf, bend at the waist, and heave for air.

Did I really do that? Did I tell Micah to go hunt for the truth? To search his past —our past—to find answers?

Damnit.

This isn't how it is supposed to go. I should keep up the back-and-forth quips. Not hand over the key to everything.

What if he unlocks the door? What if he remembers me from years ago? Remembers who I am, what he did and the cruel words he said. Will he look at me with fresh hate? Pity me, perhaps? Stir the pot and try to shove me down? Again.

No. Hell no.

You know… I hope he unlocks our history. Hope he remembers who I am and all the shitty things he did. Maybe, if I'm lucky, he will man up and apologize. Grovel. Beg for my forgiveness.

That would be a sight.

But I see the flip side of the coin. If it all comes crashing back, I picture him playing it off or acting ignorant to save face. Because that is who he is. Micah Reed. Asshole extraordinaire.

Holy. Fucking. Hell.

Hot water sprays down my spine, but the temperature isn't what heats my skin. The scalding spray is the excuse my mind created so I could bury the guilt. The guilt that ensues as I grip my thick, angry cock in my palm and tug with too much aggression. Stroke and squeeze with eyes pinched tightly as I slap my free hand on the tile.

No matter how long I stroke myself, no matter how firm or soft my technique, satisfaction never comes.

My cock doesn't want my hand. What it needs is a feisty blonde who I can silence with my dick.

Fuck.

I finish jacking off, feeling no relief in the end, then wash up double time.

Peyton wants me to think. She wants me to dig deep to find the answers. Well, I did plenty of that last night while I had lain awake in bed, staring at a cobweb on the ceiling for hours. I scavenged the corners of my mind and came up blank. Not a goddamn explanation. Hell, a hint would be helpful at this point.

The way she spoke… as if I *know* her. Or I did, once upon a time.

But I would remember Peyton. Her sexy as hell curves. Champagne locks and addictive eyes. Her unparalleled spunk and vicious banter. No chance I would forget any of those qualities.

Question is, if I *did* know her, was she not who she is now? Quite possible. If so, then yeah, I have no idea who Peyton is—or was—and rewinding time, week by week, is the only way to find answers.

That takes a lot of time and effort. Neither of which I will expend today.

Today, I suit up and prepare for battle. Give Peyton a taste of what she is missing. Give her a taste of what I have to offer.

"Game on, hellcat."

Stepping out of the shower, I towel off. I add product to my hair and comb my fingers through to give it that just-fucked look. The look women seem to ogle and beg to touch. Sliding open the closet, I yank a navy button-down and charcoal slacks off the hangers. After I zip up my pants and latch the last button, I add a splash of cologne, then slip on socks and dress shoes.

One last glance in the mirror—because looks need to kill tonight—and I smile at my reflection.

Before leaving for work, I cook a quick dinner, packaging half of it to eat during break later.

The drive from Clearwater to Tampa isn't clogged this time of day. Driving over the causeway allows me time to clear my head and take in the scenery. Sunny, blue skies with the occasional cotton-puff clouds. Salty breeze off the Bay. The occasional boom of music as I pass beachgoers. And the obvious jubilance of people as they enjoy the weather. The energy here invigorates me.

I park behind Roar forty minutes later. No one else has arrived yet. I don't expect to bump into staff for at least another hour.

In the office, I go through my normal routine before the crew trickles in. Reset the register tills. Count and verify the cash from the previous night. Log the sales numbers. Prepare the bank deposit for Ani or Sean. And do a once-over of the interior while the space is empty.

Ani enters the office just as I seal the deposit bag. "Hey, Micah."

I peer up from the computer and lean back in the chair. "Ani," I say with a nod. "How are you?"

Since tension has been slowly building between Peyton and me, I hesitate on what's safe conversation with Ani. Peyton and Ani have an obvious relationship outside of Roar, but I'm not sure what it entails. Ani hired Peyton without input from Sean, Gina, or me. One thing I have learned working for Ani and Sean, if Ani makes such a snap decision, she has her reasons. Which she keeps to herself.

"Good, good. Sean and I have been drumming up new ideas for the slower nights. If you have suggestions, shoot us an email. Business hasn't been bad, but I'd love it to be better."

Slow nights tend to be Monday through Thursday for Roar. Typical with most bars, clubs, and restaurants. When we changed Wednesday to ladies' night—aka Woman Crush Wednesday, Roar style—our profits doubled the first month. Tonight, Roar does Throw Back Thursday. Hours of '80s and '90s music and half-priced beer on tap. This draws more of a male crowd. Thursday sales… they tripled the first month.

Monday and Tuesday are my days off unless Gina goes on vacation. Monday and Tuesday at Roar are worse than sweaty balls stuck to your thigh. I suspect those are the days Ani wants to improve. Can't say I blame her.

"Sure thing. I'll think on it and shoot you guys an email later tonight or tomorrow."

Ani takes the deposit bag from the desk and stows it in her duffel-sized purse. "How're things otherwise? Any staff issues I need to be aware of?"

A layer of sweat builds in my armpits. Is she searching? Either that or I am reading into her words too much. *Paranoid much, Reed?* Bound to happen when you have a one-track mind.

"Not off the top of my head," I tell her. "We may need to hire more staff if you're plotting new ideas."

She taps a finger to her lip. "Good point. Let's see what we come up with and we'll go from there." Ani starts for the door. *Thank god.* I never sweat in front of my boss, but today is an exception. Just as I breathe again, she spins to face me. "Hope you and Peyton are getting along."

Whiplash. Where did that come from? And why the hell is it important?

Tread lightly, Reed. "We get on fine."

She nods as her eyes look away from me, thoughtful. "So, she's doing well?"

Why does this conversation make my stomach twist? I don't recall past conversations where Ani seemed so invested in my compatibility with Peyton.

"Yeah. The crowd loves her. Hasn't messed up orders. People are genuinely happy to see her." I want to ask Ani why all the questions, but I remain tight lipped. No need to open another door.

"Glad to hear." She turns away from me and twists the doorknob. "Have a great night, Micah." Then Ani disappears, leaving me in a state of nauseated confusion, like I just exited the county fair roller coaster.

What was that all about?

Yes, Ani and Sean vet employees to make sure everyone meets specific criteria. Hardworking, ambitious, friendly, ethical. But they also aim to hire people who will fit in with our little family. Ani asking questions about Peyton is… odd. Especially since she hired her without anyone's input.

So, why the questions?

Who the hell knows. I also don't have time to ponder her reasons. Staff will be here soon and shit needs to get done before the doors open.

I finish reports and place supply orders. After I wrap up calls to businesses interested in hosting at Roar, I exit the office. The main floor smells of lemon bleach and artificial pine. The usually dark or dimly lit room is *shield your eyes* bright as the janitorial staff deep cleans every surface.

"Hey, Ma," I say and smile at the woman older than my mother. "How are you?"

Linda stops cleaning to wrap me in a hug. Hugs from Linda are like toasty blankets while watching windy beach sunsets. All you want to do is hold on and keep her close. No doubt her kids and grandchildren love her hugs too. Roar dubbed Linda and Norm—her husband and co-cleaner—Ma and Pop of our little family. They have worked here since the beginning and always lend an ear or strong opinion.

Linda releases me and holds me at arm's length. "Looking sharp today." I don't miss the twinkle in her eye. "Hot date after work?" She waggles her brows.

I laugh and shake my head. "If I'm a good boy," I tell her and smirk.

A hand slaps my chest. "Need to find you a nice girl. One that'll make ya want more from life."

What if I don't want a *nice* girl? What if I want a fiery, rip-the-clothes-from-my-body girl? One that begs me to spank her and cries when I don't. One that loves when I grip her throat. How about one of those girls?

"If you find her" —I pat Linda's shoulder— "be sure to send her my way."

Linda looks past me and smiles. "Will do, honey." The gleam in her eye doesn't go unnoticed. But she gets back to work before I question it.

When I spin to see what caught Linda's attention, I spot Peyton. Hope it was sheer coincidence she was here when Linda stared this way, all googly eyed.

Behind the bar, Peyton has her back to the main floor and I steal the moment to check her out.

A sleeveless black shirt hugs her like a second skin. Hair up in a high ponytail with soft curls sweeping her upper back. I lick my lips as my eyes trail the sun-kissed skin along her neck and arms. The way she glides from one end of the bar to the other, reaches high and bends low… I adjust myself and take a deep breath.

She spins to prep the front side of the bar, peers up, and rolls her eyes when she catches me looking. Funny enough, my dick gets harder. Like it loves this side of her. The spirited fighter banging their gloves together in the corner of the ring. Always ready to go.

Well, guess what? Me, too, hellcat.

I stroll toward the bar, crank my neck left, then right, and prepare to have a little fun with Peyton. She pretends not to watch, but fails. Time and again, I witnessed her scurry down the bar to someone with their hand up, just in the cusp of her periphery. So, her subtle *I don't see you* bullshit won't work. Not with me.

As I approach, she keeps her eyes downcast on the limes. She cuts them with such slow precision, I picture her screaming inside her own head. The thought makes me want to laugh, but I bite back the urge. Her stubborn determination to ignore me provokes me further.

Peyton and me... there is no love. Maybe shades of like, but definitely no love. The fire between us stirs a tolerate-hate relationship. And I live for the whirling pleasure in my chest each time I antagonize her.

"Cut those limes any smaller and they'll just be peels."

Her hand freezes mid-slice as she lifts her gaze. Eyes narrow as they meet mine; a slight snarl on her lip. "How about you let me do my job and you" —she waves the knife inches from my face— "go do whatever it is you do."

I prop my forearms on the bar and lean in, the knife dangerously close to my eye. But I don't flinch or back down. "This *is* what I do."

"What? Annoy the hell out of people." She lowers the knife and massacres the limes more. "'Cause it's working," she mumbles.

The corner of my lips kick up as I bite the inside of my cheek to not laugh. "No, wench. My job is to make sure you do yours." She rolls her eyes. "Probably why Ani was asking about you today."

That gets her attention.

She sets the knife on the cutting board and peers up at me as curiosity tugs at her brow. "She asked about me?" Her voice squeaks at the end. Wonder why Ani asking about her makes her nervous?

"Mmhm. Standard stuff. How you're doing in your role. If the customers like you. If there's been any issues." I cock a brow. "And if you get along with the staff. Me included."

She swallows and her tension piques my interest.

"What did you tell her?" She tucks fallen strands of hair behind her ears, then shoves her hands in her back pockets.

I want to toy with her. Drag out the silence to inflame her uneasiness. After all the times she gave me shit, after all the times she threw daggers at me, I want her to feel a hint of discomfort before I answer.

This is me and Peyton. We go head-to-head. Give as good as we get. Purposely piss each other off and bask in the other's misery. Dangle bait and tempt the beast. I love and hate the way we bicker like juveniles. Her enthusiasm and irritation— which I'm not certain is real—fuel me on.

Do my snappy retorts give her ammunition too?

Her hands slip from her pockets, ball into fists, and rest on her hips. *Tap, tap, tap.* A foot taps the floor in sync with her head bobs. Lips pursed, eyes narrowed, Peyton is at the end of her lit fuse. And I love the surge of power it delivers.

She opens her mouth to speak, but I hold up a hand and stop her. A huff from her lips makes mine tip up.

"That you're a pain in my ass," I say with my best poker face.

Her jaw drop is priceless. "What the fuck, Micah?" *Micah, not Micky.* She scans the club as if Ani will jump out and berate her.

I let her panic to the count of ten, then put her out of her misery. "Peyton, calm down." Her dilated pupils land on me and suck me into a black hole. "I didn't actually say that to her. I may be a dick, but I would never do that without coaching you first."

Left, then right, her shoulders loosen. Her chest deflates faster than a balloon. And her eyes smooth out at the corners as her lips lose the paleness of tension.

"Why are you such an asshole?"

With a shrug, I say, "Natural talent, I suppose."

"Don't know why I believe a word that comes out of your mouth. Been nothing but bullshit since day one."

Since day one? What the hell is she talking about?

The day Ani introduced Peyton to the staff, I was all smiles. How could I not be? A gorgeous new woman to distract me while I worked. Ani must have thought the world of her to hire her on the spot. On her first night at Roar, as Ani introduced her to everyone, Peyton's eyes lit up, she smiled and said a kind *hello* to everyone. Except me. When Ani introduced me, Peyton remained straight faced and gave a lackluster wave. No verbal greeting. No smile or kindness.

Initially, I thought her disrespectful. But after a year, her behavior seems rooted in something incomprehensible. The worst part… she won't fucking tell me what about me bothers her.

"Since day one?" Peyton throws me a smug half smile. "Funny. The only hostility I recall on that first day was all you. Which I still don't get, but whatever." Before she counters me, I turn on my heel and go back to the office. "Don't need this bullshit," I mumble on the way.

The next hour, I scour mindless ideas online for Ani and Sean for the slower business days. Most of it is a crapshoot. Man Crush Monday would be a lame addition, but I won't veto it until something better pops up. Monday and Tuesday just aren't days most people want to go out. Attracting them won't be easy. But I have confidence that between the four of us—Ani, Sean, me, and Gina—we will find something better.

A knock at the door distracts the numbness of scrolling search engine results. "Come in."

The door swings open and Peyton fills the frame. Earlier, I didn't glimpse her fully behind the bar. But now, I see her crown to heel. The skintight black V-neck flashes her ample cleavage. Pants equally skintight hug her curvy hips and show off her muscular legs. Pulled altogether with heeled boots.

I fight the desire to lick my lips or adjust myself in her presence. That would give her the upper hand. Give her something to wave in my face and tease me with endlessly. Strong women are a turn-on. But the foreplay is so much better.

Clack, clack, clack. Her heels clap the concrete floor as she steps closer to the desk. Inches away, she stops, leans forward and plants her palms close enough to touch.

Don't look at her tits. Don't look at her tits.

I swallow as subtly as possible. "Something I can help you with?"

A slow grin lifts the corners of her mouth. Like she knows I struggle with her proximity. "Mmhm." But she doesn't elaborate. It pisses me off and makes me hard at the same time.

"Well…"

"You don't know?" My brows cinch together. "Guess you aren't all-knowing." *Poker face. Keep your poker face.* "Ted needs you," she says after a minute of silence.

Ted needs me? She came in here, went all temptress on me, for that?

Ted, another bouncer, works Monday to Thursday, so he isn't bored at home. All in all, Ted is a nice guy. But if he *needs to talk* to me about another one of his fishing trips, I may keel over and die a slow, boring death. I get it, the man is lonely. Just because we have the same genitalia, doesn't mean I like and do all the same activities. Sometimes, men want to swim or read, go bowling or play putt-putt. Organized and unorganized, sports aren't my jam.

"Did he say what for?"

Her eyes drift down the column of buttons on my shirt as she shakes her head. When her eyes meet mine, I detect a hint of mischief in their violet hue. "Nope." She pops the P.

The chair stutters back as I stand. And fuck my life as my eyes drop and zero in on her cleavage. *Damnit all to hell.*

I check my watch at note we have ten minutes until open. "Come on." With a hand, I gesture toward the door. "Get back to the bar and I'll go see what Ted needs."

Peyton saunters down the hall in front of me as I lock the office. A rumble rises in my chest as I witness the sway of her hips after getting an eyeful of her cleavage. Mix it with her fierce attitude and I want to fuck someone against the wall, here and now.

As I head toward Ted, Peyton goes behind the bar. When I reach him, he seems bewildered at my showing up.

"Need something, boss?"

At least some of the staff respect my position. "Peyton said you needed me for something."

Ted looks past me at what I assume is Peyton. Eyes back on me, he shakes his head. "No, I'm good. But since you're here..."

For the next nine minutes, Ted talks my ear off about his day. Fishing near the causeway. His buddies that he wants to introduce me to—he swears we will be buds in no time. All the fish they caught today. He offers to bring me some of the smoked fish tomorrow night after he cooks them. I humbly accept his generosity. May not like to bait hooked poles and catch fish, but I do eat them.

When the doors unlock, I walk behind the bar and prepare to help Peyton and Adam. After the initial rush, I sidle up next to her and smile at her sharp intake of breath.

"That was cute."

She side-eyes me. "Don't know what you're talking about." Her game face is strong tonight.

I point toward the main door. "Telling me Ted needed something. Cute."

She gives a one-shoulder shrug. "Thought that's what he said. Maybe he didn't say, 'I need Micah'. Maybe it was, 'I feed us dinner'. As in the fish he caught." Her nonchalance irritates and turns me on.

So, I turn the tables on her.

I step closer to her. Slip into her personal bubble. Invade her space. She shoots me a look of warning, but I ignore it. Instead, I push on. Breathe in her minty coconut scent and step within inches of her.

"You can admit it."

She turns to face me, her nose a breath from grazing mine, eyes narrowed. "I'll play along." A pause. "Admit what?"

My chest expands and contracts as quick as hers. Neither of us steps away. Both of us equally stubborn and unwilling to own it.

I inch impossibly closer. Kissing her would be easy. So fucking easy. "That you wanted me out here. That you wanted my attention."

Eyes locked in a silent battle of wills, now is the first time I spot small gray flecks in her vivid violet irises. Like a dusting of stars in a nebula. The contrast commands my attention. Invites me in like an old witch in the woods with cookies. I don't want to look away. Can't look away.

Then, in my periphery, her tongue darts out and wets her lips. Without second thought, my eyes drop to bear witness. Soon as her tongue disappears, her lips kick up in a wicked curve.

"Hmm…" My eyes meet hers again. "Maybe I did. Maybe not." Her shoulders lift, then drop. "Even if I did, I'd never admit it." Without shame, her eyes drop to the bulge in my pants. Her smile in response makes me sweat. "But you admit it without a word spoken."

Before I bite back, she turns on her heel and goes to the end of the bar. Where customers stand idle and tap the bar top to the beat of the music. *When the hell did the door open?*

Passing Adam, I bolt to the bathroom with a limp in my step. In the privacy of a stall, I undo my pants, whip out my dick, and jerk myself to relieve the ache.

Argh!

Why the hell does this woman rake my nerves so much? *Thrust, pump.* What spurs her on? What did I do to her? *Thrust, pump, pump.* And why can't I stop thinking about her? *Pump, thrust, pump.*

I groan as my load splashes into the bowl. And then the bathroom door swings open. I freeze and don't make a sound. Well, any other sound than my semen splashing in the toilet. At least it sounds like normal bathroom business.

After I clean myself up, I straighten my shirt and pants, then exit the stall. I open my mouth to extend a friendly greeting to whoever came in. But I slam my mouth shut before a single word leaves my lips.

"You alright?"

My arm flies up, my forefinger pointing to the door. "What are you doing in here?" I belt out. "Get out!"

Peyton crosses her arms under her breasts, pushing them up in the process. I hate that I don't want to look away, but force my eyes to hers.

Her face shifts from professional poker player to pouty schoolgirl in point five seconds. And *fuck* if it doesn't wake my body back up.

"Is poor baby Micah okay?" she asks in a mocking baby voice while looking down at my crotch.

Gah! Why is she so frustratingly sexy? I should be irritated with her. The way she taunts and teases me. The way she shamelessly checks me out, yet acts as if I turn her off.

But I see the way her nipples pebble beneath her top. The way she steps closer and her breath comes in quicker bursts. Deny all she wants, but Peyton craves me too. And as bad as I ache to give it to her, I refuse. I refuse to be the one who caves first. Who gives in to the obvious chemistry and tension between us. Nope, my feet will stay firmly planted in place.

"Maybe you should come closer and inspect him yourself?" I cock my brow in challenge.

For a beat, she just stares at me wide eyed. The cogs in her mind spin over and over as she searches for a snappy response. A laugh bubbles up my chest and I bite my cheek to stave off my amusement.

When the pieces click into place in her mind, she grinds her teeth. "A little much, don't you think? Ani might not like hearing management is sexually harassing employees."

Banter with Peyton is similar to walking through a minefield. Always on alert, mindful of where you step and ears focused for any little sound. And now it would appear I stepped on a land mine. Can I defuse the situation?

"You're joking, right?" I shake my head and chuckle.

She slaps her hands to her hips and narrows her eyes. "Do I look like I'm joking?"

Time to test the water. "Go on, call her. I'd love to hear what you tell her." Her knuckles whiten as her shirt stretches at her hips. *"Hey Ani, I lipped off to Micah. Then followed him into the men's room and asked him about his dick. But then he made a sexually suggestive comment to me and my feelings got hurt,"* I whine out in an attempt to mock her. Her face grows redder by the second. "I'll stand next to the phone when you call. That way I can explain the real situation when you're done bitching."

Head tipped back, Peyton screams at the ceiling. Splotchy redness coats her throat and chest. I stand frozen in place, unsure what to do.

"You're such an asshole." She pauses, her eyes sweep down and up my body, then her lip curls. "Never thought I'd be this disgusted by you. Guess things never change, do they?" Then she storms out of the bathroom and leaves me stunned.

What the fuck was that?

Jesus, this woman frustrates the hell out of me. If someone threw hundreds of mixed signals into a blender and pressed liquefy, that might come close to what swirls in my head right now. Maybe.

I wash my hands and do a quick appearance check in the mirror while drying them. If Peyton wants to play hardball... game on. After all the bullshit surrounding my breakup with Rochelle, I refuse to bow or break for another woman. Ever.

Hours of '80s and '90s music drone on. At least the deejay plays enough variety we don't hear the same song until three or four weeks later. I go about the night as per usual. Helping behind the bar. Schmoozing the customers. Sparking conversations with pretty blondes. For the most part, the slower days draw an older crowd. Monday through Thursday has more of the thirty-plus crowd. The weekend is more the twentysomethings. I enjoy both.

Two hours in and I can't stop talking with a woman at the bar. Intelligent, gorgeous, and flirty as hell. From what I learned thus far, she works in corporate accounting and recently broke up with her boyfriend.

"He was too clingy," she says with an eye roll. "I'm forty, for crying out loud. Not fourteen."

My type of woman. "Some men don't understand the need for independence. I get it, though."

We chat and flirt and make plans for when the bar closes. Her maturity turns me on and is a nice change from the childish, younger women. I love a woman who knows what she wants and goes after it. A woman who stands tall and proud and self-sufficient. All qualities I deem sexy.

Down the bar, Peyton does her best to not look my way. She flirts and laughs and talks with several men. And as focused as I am on the woman in front of me, my eyes and ears drift to the other end of the bar every other minute.

Don't let her dominate your thoughts, Reed. No woman owns you.

The crowd thins as the evening comes to a close. I follow my usual routine and start cleaning and closing out the registers. When all but the blonde leave, I speed up the closing process.

"In a hurry for disease transmission," Peyton barks, loud enough for the blonde to hear. I clench my jaw and ignore her. But she doesn't give up. "Baby Micah feeling better? Know he had issues earlier."

Done. So fucking done.

I stomp over to her and immediately step into her space. "What's the matter, hellcat? Jealous?" Note, this is the first time I call her hellcat to her face. Usually, I reserve that nickname for when it's just me, my fist, and my cock.

She scoffs. "Please. Jealous?" A finger jabs her sternum. "Why would I be jealous?" I don't miss the slight crack in her voice.

I take a step back and wave a hand up and down my body. "Because you hate how much you want me. You hate that you love when I piss you off."

"Cut the music," Peyton calls out as she slashes her fingers in front of her throat. The music dies a second later. "You think I *want* you? After all the bullshit you've put me through." Word by word, her voice escalates. "News flash, asshole. The world doesn't revolve around you." Her eyes zero in on the blonde, who looks slightly alarmed. "You're aware he fucks two plus different women a week, right? Might want to save yourself now."

The blonde slaps me with her glare. Before I offer an answer, she shoulders her purse and walks toward the door.

Every cell in my body explodes with rage. She doesn't want me? But she doesn't want me with anyone else either? Did someone pick me up by the ankles, flip me upside down, and shake me? Because I have no clue what the fuck is going on.

Back in her space, I jab my finger in her face. "What's your problem, Peyton?"

"You," she screams. "You are my fucking problem."

My feet stumble back two steps. "Why?" I want to yell, but my traitorous voice is feeble and small.

"Because you ruin everything you touch." She pauses and shakes her head with glassy eyes. "Because you ruin lives and don't care enough to remember."

I narrow my eyes and *really* look at her. "What... I don't know what you're talking about."

She huffs and shoves past me. Feet pounding against the concrete floor as she heads toward the back. I follow with no clue what is happening. She retrieves her purse from the locker and shoulders it.

Before I ask where she is going, she knocks her shoulder with mine and exits.

"I hate you," she screams.

What the actual fuck just happened?

six
PEYTON

"Asshole," I scream as I slam the car door and bang my fists against the steering wheel. "Why? Why do I let him get to me like this?"

Question of the century. Too bad no one answers it.

I start the car, but don't leave right away. My eyes drift shut and I work to recenter myself. After a few deep breaths, my blood pressure lowers and my body sags with slight relief.

Every now and again, I question my sanity. Question why I keep working at Roar when Micah drives me mad. Question why I put up with his shit four days a week. Then I remind myself of the endgame. The discussion Ani and I had about the future. A future I refuse to let Micah Reed steal from me.

Digging through my purse, I locate my phone and send Ani a quick text.

Heads-up. I left before close.

Anything I should be concerned about?

Oh, ya know. Micah just being Micah.

He said you were getting along. Want me to talk to him?

No and no. But I'll let you know if I change my mind.

Hey! Do me a favor. Think up ideas for Mondays and Tuesdays for the bar and text them to me.

On it. Miss your face.

After my phone connects to the car audio, I crank the music, roll down the windows, and drive home. The loud lyrics, thumping bass, and wind on my cheeks slowly wipe away the anger Micah brought to the surface. And before long, my mood is ten times better as I park next to Reese's car.

Every light in the apartment appears to be on as I unlock the door and walk in. I pray Reese doesn't have a houseguest tonight. Not that I mind the company. My silent plea is answered when the door swings open and I spy Reese on the couch with a platter of tacos.

His eyes land on me as his lips freeze around the taco. "Home early," he mumbles.

Reese is exactly what I need. A soothing presence with the occasional laugh. An ear to listen as I gripe about life and words to give advice as I navigate what to do next.

"Any more of those?" I point to the taco.

He takes a bite and chews a few times. "In the kitchen."

I toss my purse on the floor, dash to the kitchen, and inhale the taco-scented deliciousness. I stuff the tacos full, add refried beans and cheese to the plate, then park myself next to Reese on the couch.

"Whatcha watching?"

The Haunting of Bly Manor. Want me to start it over? Started it just before you walked in."

I shake my head. "Just tell me what I missed."

The next hour passes with the slow demolition of tacos as we can't look away from the screen. When the episode ends, I hope Reese wants to watch the next. But he presses pause and stares at me without a word. The air thickens and I have the sudden urge to cower. To shrink in the corner like a scolded child.

"You gonna tell me? Or do I have to pull it out of you?"

This is what happens when someone has known you as long as we have. Almost twenty years of friendship equals knowing someone better than you know yourself. And Reese reads every emotion I have better than anyone.

"Another day at the office, dear," I joke and he rolls his eyes. "Micah was in rare form tonight. And…" I pause, tip my head back and stare at the imperfections in the ceiling. "And I blew up." I level my head and meet his gaze. "I left work early. Ani knows, so at least I'm covered there."

Reese collects our plates and wanders to the kitchen without a word. Water splashes against plates and pans and utensils. Then the dishwasher kicks on. A moment later, Reese walks back in with two pints of ice cream and spoons. A man after my own heart.

Neither of us speaks as we dig into the creamy confections. Mint chocolate chip for me and cookies 'n cream for Reese. If one thing remains the same, it's our favorite ice cream flavors. Sure, we eat other flavors. But why not just enjoy the one you love?

"Sorry you have to deal with him," Reese says around his spoon.

I nod, swallow my bite, and twist to face him on the couch. "The worst part of it all… he doesn't remember."

Reese goes wide eyed. "Any of it? How is that even possible?"

My shoulders lift to my ears. "Your guess is as good as mine. I get how people forget from early childhood. But teen years are different. You make conscious decisions then. You *choose* to be nice or cruel."

"True. Maybe something happened to his brain." Reese laughs and I can't help but join in.

"No doubt." I sigh, stare down at the ice cream as I scrape the spoon over the surface. "I may not look the exact same, but how does he not know who I am?" The handful of times he's been in my face recently, how does he not *see* me? The goth chick he teased and bullied for three years.

The screen saver on the television flickers off and we continue eating our ice cream. Just as I scoop a heaping spoonful, Reese steals my pint and takes it back to the kitchen. "Hey!" I protest around the melting minty cream.

He returns to the living room, plops down on the couch and grabs hold of my biceps. "I have an idea." His warm, tawny-brown eyes sparkle as his lips kick up in a devilish smile.

"Don't know what you have in mind, but I'm suddenly scared."

The deep chortle I have come to love echoes from Reese's chest. "No need to be scared, sunshine. You'll like it."

"Says you. Bad enough I have to deal with Micah's annoying ass at work. I don't need anyone else adding to the problem or baiting him."

Reese gasps as he slaps a hand to his chest. "When have I ever made things worse?" He cocks a brow. When I don't answer, he continues. "Exactly, I haven't. Trust me, please."

Do I want to put Micah in his place? Hell yes, I do. But I also don't want to cringe every time I walk inside Roar. I love my actual job. Reese stirring the pot could cause future problems.

"Fine," I say with heavy exaggeration. "What do you have in mind?"

For the next thirty minutes, Reese spills his plan. During the first minutes, I wince. A lot. My forehead sore and tense from pinching. A slight headache forms beneath my brows. And my eyes beg to close for the night. Like a good friend, though, I sit and listen to every word.

"Sound like a plan?"

Actually, his plan does sound fun. Reese was never on the receiving end of Micah's bullshit, but he heard all the gossip. In high school, rumors and artifice pass faster than STDs. Although none of the shit was said about him, it impacted him as if it was his name and "slut" written on the walls. Ironic how the tide shifts.

"Yeah." I lean over and hug him hard. "Thanks for always being here for me. You're the best friend a girl could have."

We rise from the couch and head for our respective rooms. "Don't go getting all soft on me now. Need you in tough-bitch mode tomorrow night."

I salute him. "Yes, sir." His laugh is the last thing I hear before he shoves me in my room and shuts the door. "Good night," I yell into the darkness.

"Go to sleep, sunshine," he says before his door clicks shut.

～

The energy inside Roar buzzes more than usual. But the buzz is nothing compared to the adrenaline in my veins. Not sure if it's the crowd or the fact Reese will be here soon.

The spring break crowds fizzled out over the last two weeks. Now we get a slight lull until late May. The lighter traffic is a nice reprieve. Just means I have to work harder for the extra tips.

For the most part, Micah has distanced himself from me tonight. But it won't last long. When nine o'clock hits, the crowd always triples. Should really talk to Ani about getting an additional bartender for Friday and Saturday, even if just for a few hours.

Beer flows freely from the taps. Colorful fruity drinks get adorned with pierced cherries and citrus on plastic swords. And cash tips fill the jars behind the bar.

Just as I deliver a drink, I spy Reese at the end of the bar. I thank the man who tips me and move down the line to Reese.

I lift the flap at the end of the bar and step out to hug Reese. His arms wrap around me like the summer sun and I sigh, relieved he's here. Since the summer between seventh and eighth grade, Reese has always been my person. The one I could go to with anything and everything. We don't hide the truth from each other. And our shared truths are full spectrum. Nothing left out.

"Glad you made it," I mutter against his chest.

"I'd never let—"

"Peyton," Micah barks and I stiffen. I keep my eyes on Reese and steady my urge to scream. "You planning to work tonight? Or make out with the customers?"

Several sets of eyes home in on me and my face heats. *Fucking asshole.*

"You go," Reese says. "The night is still young." A sinister smile stretches his lips and tips up the corners of his eyes.

I spin around, step behind the bar, and bark back at Micah. "What? You the only one allowed to get handsy with customers?" I hold my hands up in surrender and push out my lips. "Sorry, *Micky.* Didn't know the rules were lopsided."

"Just get to fucking work," he bites out, then storms to the opposite end of the bar.

Over the next hour, I make and pour countless drinks. A rainbow of colors flash and dance over exposed skin and gyrating bodies. Bass vibrates my bones and treble sings in my bloodstream. I get in my groove, dancing behind the bar as I fill orders. Every fifteen minutes, I chat and fake flirt with Reese. It reminds me of when we turned twenty-one and we would use each other to fend off undesirable hookups.

When a club favorite song comes on, half of the Roar crowd loses it and heads for the dance floor. With the bar quieter a minute, I hang out at the end with Reese.

"You bored yet?" I tease.

He throws his head back and laughs harder than necessary. All part of the game. "Nah, sunshine. Been scoping out the eye candy. Eye fucking a few."

I shake my head and chuckle. "And how will this" —I gesture between the two of us— "work if you leave with someone else?"

Reese leans across the bar and curls a finger at me. I lift up on the bar and meet him in the middle, our lips a breath apart.

Reese and I, we will never be anything other than best friends. We tried more once and it felt wrong. So, we went back to how we have always been. Besties.

But that is not to say we won't kiss on the lips for extenuating circumstances. Circumstances such as this. A kiss between us is just that—a kiss. Nothing sexual, just two sets of lips pressing together. Like acting, and only when necessary.

"He can't keep his eyes off you," he says, only loud enough for me to hear. "And if I want to hook up tonight, I'll just tell whoever that I'm here to help make some dipshit jealous for my friend. Don't worry about me."

Reese closes the space between us and kisses me. He and I both know it is all for show. And I think we put on one hell of a show.

Question is, does Micah fall for the facade? If so, does it piss him off? That's the question I need answered.

seven

MICAH

Who the fuck is this guy? Who is this motherfucker with his lips on Peyton?

And why does seeing her kiss another guy make my vision red?

I grip the bar, knuckles white as pain shoots up my forearm. A spear lances me in the chest. Spreads fire through my middle. But I take hold of the pain and squeeze it tight in my palm. Shape it into a weapon. Hot and heavy swirls of green in my fist.

Call me a hypocrite, I don't give a fuck. But Peyton won't be sucking face with some prick. Not in front of me, anyway. Yes, I own my whorish ways. Yes, society doesn't degrade manwhores the same as women. Only so much I can do about that. And yes, my inner supreme asshole is about to make an appearance.

Whether it is jealousy or the fact she won't cave to my advances or that I can't figure out why she hates me so much, the charade has gone on long enough. Doesn't matter if I have flirted with the same woman all night. I won't condone Peyton and some fuckboy.

"Peyton," I yell down the bar. She continues to kiss mister tall, dark and possessive, ignoring me. But I am not having it. "Peyton," I yell louder. "Time to quit playing with your fuck toy and do your job."

Several sets of eyes land on me and I bite my inside cheek. Adam sidles up to my right. "Boss, might want to go over and talk to her," he suggests with a quiet hiss. Adam means well and I don't want to dole my skewed emotions out on him.

I shoulder slap him in thanks and nod. "Sorry for the outburst." Kaylynn, working the far end of the bar, forces a smile my way. Scrubbing a hand over my face, I give her a sad smile and mouth *sorry*.

My eyes shoot down to the end where Peyton lingers. Thank god she no longer has her tongue shoved down some guy's throat. Though, every other second, she makes eyes at him. Smiles so big I swear her face may split in two. Has she smiled this much before? Can't think of a time when she glowed like this.

Has she smiled at *me* before? I sift through night after night. Replay shift after shift. Not a single night flashes through my mind where Peyton smiled. Not at me, anyway.

Sure, she smiles and laughs and teases other men in the bar. But never once has she done that with me as the recipient. With me, she spits vitriol and abhorrence and repulsion.

More than once, Peyton has suggested I dig deep for answers. Indicated we share history during some point in our lives. I have yet to peg down when we met or when I knew her. It has me second-guessing her and the possibility she has me confused with someone else.

The spear beneath my ribs thrusts deeper. Tightens as it twists and digs. Burns as I consider the prospect of what I may have done to Peyton in the past. Something wretched enough to warrant her immediate hate.

But how can I apologize for missing moments? How can I redeem myself when I don't know what I have done?

I stop three stools down from Peyton and fill a drink order. Then I swallow my pride. Something I haven't done in years.

"Peyton…" I say, loud enough to be heard, but softer than usual.

Eyes focused on the drink she pours, she ignores my call. But I don't budge. After she serves and thanks the customer, she spins to face me and plants her hands on her hips.

"What, Micah? What is it you need that can't wait?" She waves a hand down the bar. "You have eyes. And I have work to do."

Why can we never have civil conversations? Just now, I planned to apologize. But her bitterness dissolves the apology on my tongue like acid.

"You're right. Wanted to offer an olive branch, but nah." Her eyes widen and I wonder if she regrets not hearing what I had to say. Oh well. "Get back to work. And quit fucking around."

I turn my back to her. "The day you apologize, the day you offer me kindness…" My feet are tree roots anchored to the earth below. I don't look back, but can't move until she finishes speaking. "That day will mark history." Now I peer over my shoulder and furrow my brow. "The day Micah Reed says something nice about me. That's a day I'll never forget."

What am I missing? Wish I fucking knew. Unfortunately, now is not the time to relive the last thirty-two years of my life.

Peyton goes back to work and I exit the bar to do rounds in the club.

I walk the perimeter of Roar. Check in with the servers and bouncers as per usual. Hang out by the door with Ted and catch up on his life. He and his wife recently welcomed their second child. When there is a lull in the line, he takes his phone from his pocket and shows me pictures.

"Here she is," Ted all but squeals with delight. "Baby Rose."

Image after image, he scrolls through with a heart-stopping smile. Pictures of a pink bundle in a bassinet. Pictures of their three-year-old son, Theo, holding his baby sister with pure awe on his face. Ted with baby Rose. His wife cradling her. And so many family photos.

Ted stares down at the screen as if nothing but those three people exist. And part of me wonders what that feeling is like. Aside from Shelly, my parents and extended family are all I know. But familial love doesn't compare to love that smacks you in the chest and doesn't let go. Love so powerful, you lose all sense of morality. You don't know which way is up or down—and it doesn't matter.

Once upon a time, I loved Rochelle. The sentiment never passed either of our lips—thank god—but the emotion settled comfortably in my chest. My thoughts sparsely drifted to the image of wedding bells, but I wanted more with her than a notarized document bonding us. I wanted to experience life and the world beside her. Unfortunate for me, she just wanted a younger fuckboy.

"She's beautiful, Ted." I lay a hand on his shoulder and squeeze. "You did good. Congrats to you and yours."

I continue my leisure rounds and park myself in a corner. One song after another plays as I people watch. When I glance across the club and spot Peyton laughing with the guy again, I groan.

What irritates me most with Peyton is the not knowing. The invisible truth that hangs in the atmosphere between us. That she won't help me find the missing puzzle piece and snap it in place.

People dislike each other all the time. But her anger with me is rooted deep. Stuck in place and unwilling to budge.

I push off the wall and weave through the crowd. Before I make it to the bar, a hand wraps around my arm and stops me. I turn to see a slightly younger, pretty brunette. Her smile lifts some of my weighted thoughts.

"Want to dance?" she shouts as her other hand grabs the opposite arm.

The distraction she could provide has me agreeing without hesitation. Music swims around us as she swings her hips left and right. Ass pressed against my groin, hands over her head. I grab her hips and tug her impossibly closer. Close my eyes. Get lost in the rhythm, her body plastered to mine. Her head tips to the side and I press my lips to the spot beneath her ear.

Fingers comb through the back of my hair and fist the strands. With a slight shift, she lifts her lips to mine. My hands glide across her body, fingers splayed on her belly. A moan rumbles from her mouth and vibrates my chest.

In the middle of the dance floor, I mouth fuck this woman. Taste sweet strawberries on her tongue. Inhale the floral scent on her skin. Graze her heated skin as she spins to face me and I slide a hand up her back until I fist the hair at her nape.

I love and loathe everything about this woman.

No doubt, she is beautiful. I love her bravery and extroversion. How she takes what she wants and doesn't shy away from it. How she owns who she is and flaunts her charm. Her boldness turns me on more than anything.

But... she isn't my type.

It is no secret, I love blondes. Don't get me wrong, there is room for every woman in my world. But the women I find most attractive all look the same. They all look like Peyton.

Fuck my life for realizing this while I kiss another woman.

I break the kiss and hate myself for my wayward thoughts. "I have to work." She tilts her head with narrowed eyes. "Club manager."

She pushes out her lower lip and makes weepy eyes. Damn, she is cute. I resist the urge to lean in and suck her lip.

"We were having so much fun," she says.

Yes, we were. "And we can have more fun later, if you want. But it'll have to wait until after close."

Leaning in, she presses a chaste kiss to my lips. "I'm good with that."

I take a step back and run my hands down her arms until I reach her hands. Another step back. "Catch me later. Either behind the bar or wandering the club."

She winks and I walk off. The brunette may not be my first choice, but I will never turn down a beautiful woman who pursues me.

As I near the bar, I spot Peyton talking with the guy again. All smiles and laughter. It pisses me the hell off. Time to cut the rope. She may know him, but I don't give a fuck.

When Peyton sees me, her spine stiffens and she steps away from the guy. Perfect.

I insert myself between the guy and the customer at the bar beside him. "Hey, man." Slowly, he faces me. "You know Peyton?"

The smug bastard smirks. "Yeah, we go way back." He doesn't elaborate and I grind my molars.

"*Great*," I mumble with a layer of cynicism. "Then I'm sure she's told you how busy this place gets." He cocks a brow, but doesn't respond otherwise. "And that she needs to focus on paying customers."

He lifts a tumbler of Jack to his lips and sips it. "Yep. Last I checked, I paid for this drink. So…"

Who the hell is this guy? My fingers curl into fists at my sides. In and out, I breathe deep and remind myself of where I am and the position I hold. The last thing I need is to lose my shit over a woman who mind-fucks me four days a week. The last thing I need is to lose my job over defending said woman who royally hates me.

"So… as one of the managers, I ask you to not hoard my staff when she has a job to do."

He glances down the bar where Peyton pours and blends drinks faster than Adam and Kaylynn combined. "Seems like she has everything under control, boss man." He sips his drink behind a smug grin.

Don't know who this fucker is, but he grates my last nerve each time his lips part. "Yes, unless she's over here talking with you. So, do me a favor, *friend*. Let her do what she's getting paid to do. Her job."

I push off the bar and turn to walk away. But his words stop me. "Oh, I'll let her do her job. Now… and later tonight." I grind my molars, but don't face him. "Cheers, boss man."

For the next hour, I occupy my mind with paperwork in the office. Yes, coming in here is a pussy move. But if I didn't step away and calm down, things would get ugly. Real quick. If I dive headfirst into a different task, the distraction will help extinguish the fire in my blood.

Calm and collected, I head back out to the club. I make my rounds and settle in behind the bar between Adam and Kaylynn. One song blends into another and the drinks flow easily. Peyton and I keep our distance, but she never leaves my sight. Neither does her *friend* at the end of the bar.

As closing time nears, the crowd thins. The brunette from the dance floor sips a strawberry daiquiri twenty feet from the bar. Adam and Kaylynn start the bar closing cleanup while Peyton preps to leave. Friday and Saturday nights, the three of them rotate who stays past close. And tonight, Peyton leaves early.

Finished with her tasks, she lifts the bar flap and heads down the hall to get her things. Before I walk after her, she reappears and loops her arms with *him*. I stare after them as they head for the exit.

My eyes still on them, everything turns red when *he* peers over his shoulder, meets my gaze and winks with a smug smirk on his lips.

And then, they vanish. A chill blankets me as I question if Peyton actually does know him. Or did she just leave with a strange man? A man who seemed all too eager.

The protector in me wants to run outside and chase after them. To tell Peyton not to leave with some random guy who claims to know her. But I don't. Can't. Instead, I stay put and finish my routine tasks.

When I leave, it is with a brunette on my arm. A woman I don't want to spend time with, but will, in order to distract myself from the woman I want but can't have.

Best night at work. Ever.

Reese and I walk out of Roar in a fit of laughter and clenching our stomachs. Every minute behind the bar with Micah tonight was nothing short of perfection. I bit my tongue so often it went numb. He fired round after round at me, but I restrained more than normal to get a rise out of him.

Each time I seemed unaffected by his words, his jaw flexed and face reddened. His response was quite intriguing.

Micah spends more time barking versus biting. Spends more time whoring himself around the club than caring about me or the staff. Tonight was different. Micah flashed a new side of himself. An anomalistic side.

The possessive, semi-protective side of Micah Reed made an appearance. And it has me seeing him in a new light. A light similar to the early days, before he jumped on the Triple M train and ruined my teen life.

Reese and I reach my car and I unlock it. "Food?" he asks as he unhooks my arm from his.

"Definitely."

We agree to meet at our favorite twenty-four-hour diner near home. Once I crank the engine, Reese jogs over to his car and gets in. Within minutes, we drive over the bridge, crossing the Bay and wind through Clearwater.

The diner is busy as always. Bright lights shine down on worn booths and paper placemats with crossword puzzles, word searches, and hangman. A coffee mug full of crayons sits next to a napkin dispenser, salt and pepper shakers, sweetener packets, and a half-used bottle of ketchup on the table. Fresh brewed coffee scents the air with a hint of bacon grease and toasted bread. Mumbled chatter, the clinking of cutlery, and the cook calling finished orders echo throughout the dining area. The hostess, an older woman with a messy updo and a pencil behind her ear, hands us laminated menus.

"Andy will be over in a minute." Then she resumes her position near the front door, rolling cutlery in paper napkins.

Don't know why either of us reads over the menu, we always order the same thing. But we read the long list of greasy goodness anyway. When Andy arrives, Reese orders the western omelet with home fries and I get the two pancake breakfast with an egg, crispy bacon and hash browns. Decaf coffee for both of us. Andy takes our menus and waltzes off with exaggerated enthusiasm.

"He has it bad for you," Reese says after the coffee carafe and mugs are left at the table.

I fill my mug and ignore the fact Reese refers to Micah. Grab a packet of raw sugar from the caddy, shake it, tear it open and add it to the coffee. Peel back the lid on two creamer pods and dump them in the mug. Stir with more noise than necessary, all while staring at the decaffeinated beverage and not Reese.

I lift the mug to my lips and blow on the surface. "What makes you think that?" The coffee sears my tongue but tastes like heaven.

Reese fixes his coffee how he likes, then stares at me as if to say, *"You're joking, right?"* He doesn't, though. "Let's count them off, shall we?"

I roll my eyes so hard it causes ocular muscle pain. With a wave of my hand, I say, "If it makes you happy, enlighten me."

For a moment, he leaves me hanging. Sips his coffee and holds my gaze with a hint of mischief. I white knuckle my mug and this makes him laugh.

"Fine," he huffs out. "One, the man can't keep his eyes off you. Literally. Every time I looked his way, his eyes were on you or us."

"That doesn't mean anything." Micah stares at anything with boobs.

"Maybe not to you, but guys don't look—not like he was—unless there is definite interest." I shake my head and gesture for him to continue. "Two, the way he tries to steer you from men. It's quite telling. Possessive."

"You mean when he barks orders? That's just because he's an asshole."

Reese sets his mug down and shakes with laughter. "No, my dear, sweet best friend. He barks at you, and only you, when you give other men attention. It's his way of making you stop and telling the guy to back off."

Why can't men just be straightforward? Although I would still despise Micah, maybe the intensity of said hatred would be less if he were honest. Honesty says a lot about character. And when it comes to Micah, honesty may tip the scales in his favor. Slightly.

"Whatever you say. Still think it's because he's an asshole."

Reese reaches across the table and lays his hand over mine. "Not denying that. But you should accept the fact he has a thing for you. Even if it makes your skin crawl, it doesn't make it less true."

I open my mouth to argue, but the server interrupts as he sets plates between us. My mouth waters and stomach grumbles. All thoughts of work and Micah and his possible infatuation with me go out the window as I dig in.

I stab the last bit of pancake, swipe it through the last of the yolk and bacon grease, then shove it in my mouth. *So freaking good.* Tonight, I will sleep solid. I swallow down the last of my coffee and we settle the bill.

"See you back home," I tell Reese as we each get in our cars.

The drive home takes less than ten minutes. And some of the conversation with Reese at the diner rolls back in. I don't know how to feel about any of it, so I shove it away for another time.

Reese parks in his space as I hop out of my car. Thankfully, neither of us has to be up early. Late nights/early mornings aren't new to either of us, but Reese aims to be in bed—not sleeping—before midnight. I regularly tease him about his *old man status.*

Inside, we hug and go opposite directions at the end of the hall.

"Night, sunshine."

"Night, Reese. Thanks again for tonight."

He bops me on the nose. "That's what best guy friends are for."

I go about my nighttime routine and soon switch my bedside lamp off. As the light fades to darkness, my mind flips on and runs ramped up.

Reese's words from the diner repeat in my head. *The man can't keep his eyes off you. Literally.*

Does Micah look at me *that* often? Not possible. Reese only noticed Micah looking because he was keeping an eye out for such things.

"The way he tries to steer you from men. It's quite telling. Possessive."

Is Micah really trying to keep me away from other men? Does he actually believe he has a claim on me? Ha! Not a fat chance in hell, Micah Reed.

What I don't understand is why Micah would feel possessive. On day one at Roar, I radiated nothing but abhorrence when we were introduced. He felt it, too. Mom always said hate is a strong word. I use the term sparingly and only associate it with a handful of people. Since age fourteen, I have hated Micah Reed. He was cold and callous and hurt others to make himself look good.

Question is… is it time to grow up? Is it time to let go of teenage pain and trauma? Is it time to give someone I have loathed more than a decade a fresh start?

Maybe.

I don't want to live life with hate in my heart. Don't want to be someone who focuses solely on all the negative aspects. If I let go of the past so easily, does it make me weak?

Part of me says yes. By giving in, all the hurtful words, constant teasing and bullying… it feels as if I accept them. That Micah and those bitches all get a free pass. I may be the bigger person by extending forgiveness, but I don't want to be a doormat.

The other part of me says no and states, in order to grow and evolve into a better version of myself, I must make peace with my past. To make peace, I have to battle my inner demons. The voices of doubt that tell me to build a wall around my heart, to keep people like teenage Micah Reed out. People who know nothing about me, yet hand out opinions like Halloween candy. People who know nothing about my life, yet they mock and judge and lie about me.

I am not that girl anymore. That fragile teenage girl who only wanted to be accepted for who she was. Now, I stand tall. Strong—physically and mentally.

Perhaps it is time to expand my strength to emotionally as well. Perhaps it is time to be the bigger person and give Micah Reed a chance. A chance he probably doesn't deserve, but maybe needs.

Tomorrow, I will offer up his second chance. How he handles it is up to him.

~

"You planning on handing out heart attacks tonight?"

I glance over my shoulder in the body-length mirror at Reese in my doorway. His eyes rake over the length of my body before he whistles. The reaction is exactly what I hoped for, and I laugh.

"One. Maybe." I spin to face him. "Think it'll work?"

In three long strides, Reese stops in front of me and grips my shoulders. "Yes. And if not, someone might need to visit an optometrist." He shakes his head. "Damn, sunshine. You don't play fair. Best have 911 on speed dial."

I step out of his touch and go to my dresser. Add a few spritzes of perfume to my wrists and at the base of my skull. Snap on my favorite leather bracelets. Swipe one last coat of clear gloss on my lips. I have never been the type to wear a lot of makeup, but I do like to accentuate the features I love about myself. So, my eyes and lips always get attention. Even if minimal.

After I fetch my four-inch-heel boots from the closet, I plop on the bed and finish getting ready.

Not sleeping the first three hours I had lain in bed last night, I devised a plan for work tonight. Let's just say I will test Reese's theory about Micah. And in order to do that, I have to be on my best behavior. I have to be the first one to hold up the surrender flag.

But there is no reason to not look like the smoking-hot temptress I am. Mom always said use what life has given you. She probably meant talent and skill, but I reserve the right to believe she silently included beauty too.

I shoulder my purse and head for the front door. Reese follows in my wake. "Never said I played fair. Do you blame me?"

The corners of his mouth droop slightly. "No, of course not. But it wouldn't be right if I didn't give you some shit before you left."

"True." I turn and hug him. "Thanks for everything."

His arms tighten around my middle. "What'd I do?"

I loosen my grip and kiss his cheek. "Nothing. Just being you. And that's exactly what I need. So, thank you. You really are the bestest best friend."

As the words leave my lips, Reese slaps my ass. Hard. "Get out of here, sunshine."

I rub my butt and jab a finger in his chest. "Damn, that stings."

"Good. Now go." He shoos me out the door. "And you better tell me everything in the morning."

Pivoting slightly, I lift a hand to my forehead in mock salute. "Yes, sir. I'll have my report on your desk at oh-three-hundred hours."

He shakes his head. "You're such a weirdo. Love you."

"Love you, too" I blow him a kiss before he shuts the door.

Now, on to the most challenging night at work. Hope my claws don't come out.

nine

Have I stepped into another dimension? Either that or I am seeing shit. I rub my eyes and blink a few times.

No fucking clue.

Glass bottles clang against loud music as they get tossed in bins. Sweat mixed with perfume and alcohol floats through the air. Colored lights dance down from the ceiling and bounce over exposed skin and gyrating bodies.

Roar is in full swing, as busy as any other Saturday night, yet I don't see or hear any of it.

Because Peyton fucking Alexander just smiled. At me. Smiled.

Has hell frozen over and I missed the memo?

"Can you hand me that jigger?" Her dainty finger points to the steel measuring device less than six inches from my hand. But I don't move. She waves a hand in front of my spaced-out eyes, a bright as sunshine smile on her face. "Hello? Earth to Micah. The jigger."

I shake my bewilderment away and hand it over. "Sorry."

She doesn't bitch or scowl. Nope. She simply laughs it off. "No worries. Thank you."

For a moment, I scan down the bar and throughout the club. Looking for something else out of place. A camera, maybe. Or people watching us as this whole turn of events takes place. I wait for the shoe to drop. For everyone to burst out laughing at my expense.

But everything looks… normal.

Then a knife stabs me between the shoulder blades as realization hits. A thought I don't *want* taking up residence in my mind, but would make sense, if true. Because, let's face it, Peyton is an attractive woman. An attractive woman who left here with a guy last night. A guy I have never seen at Roar but swears he's known her years.

Is Peyton happy because she hooked up with him?

My stomach churns and I turn my back on the bar. I grab the back counter and take shallow breaths with my eyes closed. Swallow down the bitterness on my tongue, the thick lump in my throat.

No woman, aside from family, has bent me out of shape. Has riled me up or tossed me to the wayside. But for some unknown reason, Peyton does. She spirals in like a tornado, tears my world up, then leaves me dazed in the aftermath.

Her combative side is one I enjoy, though. The unpredictability and sarcasm and tough as nails exterior. Where others may see her as a bitch, I see her as fierce. And damn if that doesn't make me want her more.

But this…

A hand rests on my shoulder and I glance to see the owner. Of course. Peyton.

"You okay?" Her violet irises scan my eyes, my cheeks, my lips with an edge of concern. "You look kind of pale." She hasn't taken her hand off me yet and I don't know if I should enjoy it or freak out.

"I'm fine," I croak out, then clear my throat. "Just need some water. Probably something from dinner." The lie rolls off my tongue with too much ease.

"Go sit in the back a minute. We'll be fine." Then her hand slides down between my shoulder blades and rubs small, gentle circles. I close my eyes and relish the touch until she removes her hand.

When I no longer feel the heat of her body near mine, I turn and exit the bar. I rush to the office, plop down in the chair, plant my elbows on the desk and my head in my hands. I take slow and steady breaths. In through my nose, out through my mouth.

What is going on? And why does this change in Peyton put me on edge?

Since the beginning, she has been nothing short of hostile toward me. Is it weird that her wrath is something I look forward to? After a year of working together, her malevolence is all I know.

Over the next hour, I occupy my mind with the staff schedule. Stare at the empty boxes on the spreadsheet and will them to fill in. Then I remember Ani asked for fresh ideas for the slower days. I switch my focus and zone out as I search the web.

A soft knock, followed by the office door opening, snaps me out of my incessant scrolling. Page after page and I still haven't found worthwhile ideas to spruce up Mondays and Tuesdays.

I look up to see Peyton smiling near the door. As heart stopping as her smile is, seeing it so much in one night has me dizzy.

"Getting a little crazy out there. Might want to do your rounds and help Adam and Kaylynn after."

Any other night, she would bark at me for slacking off. She would have stormed in here without knocking, stepped up to the desk, slammed her hands down, and bitched at me for not doing my job. But not tonight. Tonight, she offers suggestions and uses polite tones.

"Yeah, sure. Thanks for letting me know."

"No problem." And then she leaves and closes the door behind her. Quietly.

I make my way back out into the club and do my rounds. After I touch base with the last staff member on the floor, I weave through the crowded dance floor.

Working anywhere with high capacity, you have to be okay with random people touching, bumping, or engaging with you. It comes with the territory, no matter which role you hold.

But as people dance beside me, rub up against me, reach out for and grope me, my tolerance level vanishes.

The world shrinks and blurs. People appear out of nowhere and steal my air. The music booms louder and thumps harder. Sweat breaks out across my skin and my breath won't come quick enough. My pulse whooshes behind my ears. The room spins and I wobble on my feet. I stumble out of the crowd and stagger sideways until I hit a wall. My stomach churns as I drop to the floor, shirt drenched.

And then she is there. Peyton. In my face. Holding my cheeks and yelling. But I don't hear her. She shakes me gently and yells again. This time, the faint tones of her voice break through the white noise.

"Put your head between your legs, Micah." My brow tugs together at her words. "It'll help you from passing out."

Oh. I nod and do as she says. Head between my knees, I close my eyes and breathe steadily. A chill hits my neck, but I don't move. It feels good. Settles the pang in my chest and stops the constant flow of sweat. Fingers comb through my hair and a wave of comfort washes over me.

I want to lift my head and see if Peyton is still here. If she is the one nursing and consoling me. Providing me with this unfamiliar comfort. Comfort I don't want to end.

"Micah?" Her voice is soft next to my ear. "Slowly sit up straight. You need some water."

I do as she says and she hands me a glass of cold water. One sip at a time, I drink the cool liquid. She watches me like a mother would a sick child. I love and hate that I worried her, but am glad I didn't collapse.

"What did you eat for dinner? Maybe you got food poisoning."

Here comes my inner asshole. Yes, I lied to her earlier. Said maybe it was something from dinner. Which isn't possible. Because I haven't eaten. Not since yesterday.

"Uh, I may have fibbed about dinner earlier." Her brows creep down. "More like I haven't eaten since yesterday."

"Oh, Jesus." She shakes her head, rises from her haunches and offers her hand. "Come on."

"What? Where are you—"

"You need to eat something. Before you actually *do* pass out."

I wince but recover. "I have snacks in the office. Maybe we can grab something to eat after work. Together." The word vomit leaves my mouth before I stop it. No way to retract or turn back now.

Hour-long seconds drag out. Peyton stares at me with a novel of confusion written on her face. Confusion morphs into something akin to struggle. I hate that she has to put so much effort into the decision. And I have half a mind to rescind.

"Sure. How about Teddy's?" she proposes.

Teddy's is a modernized version of homestyle. Open twenty-four hours, they let you order anything from the menu any time of day. Best part, it is less than a mile from Roar.

"Sounds perfect."

She proffers her hand to help me stand and I take it without hesitation. Once upright, I hold steady a moment and get my bearings. Less dizzy, I put one foot in front of the other and inch my way down the hall toward the office.

"Eat something," she hollers down the hall as I open the door.

"On it, boss."

This grants me a smile just before she walks off. I swear I have seen more smiles from Peyton tonight than I have in the last year. Combined with the lack of food in my system, the constant smiles fuck with my head. And body.

On the tattered couch in the office, I lie back and eat one of the emergency packages of peanut butter crackers. When I reach the bottom of the package, the room looks less like a house of distorted mirrors and my hands tremble less. My stomach grumbles, suggesting the crackers better be the appetizer.

I close my eyes and throw an arm over them. The music from the club vibrates the walls and lulls me to sleep. A hand shakes my shoulder and whispers my name. I ignore the dream until it happens again, a little louder.

"Huh?" I lift my arm a bit and spot Peyton's chin and lips.

"Time to wake up, sleepyhead." Slowly, I sit up and she inches back. "If you're too tired, we can skip food."

I shake my head. "No, I'm good. Just give me a minute." Now is when I notice the silence. The lack of music or blended chatter. "What time is it?"

"Almost three."

Well, damn. Definitely needed the sleep, but I didn't mean to sleep the last three and a half hours. With tomorrow off, the additional sleep shouldn't throw my schedule off much.

"You ready to go?" I ask as I stand and stretch.

"Whenever you are." She points to the desk. "Brought the tills in."

"Thanks."

After I stow the money and lock the vault, we leave through the back. We head for our individual cars and I wait for her to put hers in drive before I take off.

In the seven minutes it takes us to drive from Roar to Teddy's, I question every reason why Peyton agreed to eat with me after work. Was it out of sympathy? Did she feel bad because I almost fainted in the club? The Peyton I have known the last year would have left me on the floor and hollered at someone else to call 911 while she stood behind the bar and watched.

But something is different about her. And, for the life of me, I have no clue what.

We step inside Teddy's and are promptly seated at a booth in the corner. Peyton smiles ear to ear as she scans the menu. Meanwhile, I stare at the laminated page and let my eyes lose focus.

I just don't get it. After all this time, why be nice now? What does she stand to gain? Is this a game?

Or has she turned over a new leaf?

My hope leans toward the latter. Because if this is just a game, the end may be severe.

Ten

PEYTON

Why am I here? Why did I agree to come here with him?

Obviously, I am an idiot. That's why.

I have been to Teddy's enough times to know what I want to eat. The best breakfast sandwich this side of the Bay. Egg, sausage, hash brown patty, and cheese slapped between two pancakes.

So. Freaking. Good.

But I dart my eyes over the menu as if I need time to figure it out. Meanwhile, I spot Micah in my periphery. Staring at me like a stoner. He doesn't open his mouth to speak, doesn't flinch or move his eyes to read the menu. He just stares straight ahead as if he's broken.

The wicked part of me wants to reach across the table and slap his cheek to wake him up. Instead, I sit here like a friend would and fake read the menu. I scan the egg breakfast plates so many times I have the entire section memorized. So, I move on to the sides.

Just as I read cheese grits for the fifth time, our server arrives with a pen pressed to her green guest check pad. From across the table, Micah eyes me with a silent request to order first. I bite my cheek to stop myself from laughing.

After I order my sandwich and juice, Micah orders enough food for two and a coffee. Wasn't kidding when he said he hadn't eaten since yesterday.

"So…" It feels awkward just sitting here. But I have no clue what to talk about with him. Not like we have ever been friendly.

"So…" he repeats, but continues. "Sorry about earlier."

About to tell him he doesn't need to apologize, I get interrupted when the server drops off our drinks.

"Just don't do it again."

A corner of his mouth kicks up as he stares down at his mug and dumps several packets of sugar in the brew. "Didn't mean to. Nice to know you were concerned." He picks up his spoon, stirs the overly sweet caffeine and lifts his eyes to mine. "Nice to know you wouldn't leave me to die."

I roll my eyes with a headshake. "Things may not be great between us, but I'd never wish death on anyone. I'm a firm believer in karma."

"Lucky me," he teases.

We both go silent a moment. My hands sit firmly between my butt and the booth while Micah has his clasped in front of him on the table. He fumbles with his lower lip like he wants to ask me something, but doesn't know how. His reluctance and uncertainty douse my blood with a thrill. Funny yet odd, I have never been this excited by someone feeling out of sorts.

He takes a sip of his coffee, then slowly sets the mug on the table, eyes fixed on the steam. "If you don't mind my asking…" His eyes lift to meet mine. The gold hints shimmer in the brighter light and it throws me off balance for a breath. "Why do you hate me so much?"

I stare back at him with pursed lips. It would be so easy to just tell Micah my reasons. To spill my truth and help him remember the past instead of learning the answers on his own. But I won't. After years of having to rebuild my confidence and strength, I vowed to never let anyone walk all over me again. Especially the man sitting across from me.

"The answer to that would take more time than we have tonight. And I'd have to answer that when *I'm* ready. Hope you figure it out before then."

He drops his hands to his sides and leans back into the booth. "See, that's what I don't get." I lift my brows in question. "More than once, you've insinuated we knew each other. Before you worked at Roar."

I lean back and match his position. Stare at him and study every line and twitch of his face. Look for indications of deception in his brow line, eyes, or lips. But all I see is honesty and perplexity.

"You really have no idea, do you?"

He leans forward and wraps his hands back around the mug. "No. So, will you please tell me?"

"Not tonight," I whisper before picking up my juice to drink. "Let's talk about something else. Anything else."

Anger still eats away at me for all the pain and embarrassment Micah and half the high school student body created. Yes, it happened several years ago. Yes, a therapist once told me I would never get past it if I don't let go. But damn, letting go of such cruelty inflicted on me is difficult. If only he remembered. If only he apologized.

Maybe then I could move past the imprisoned emotions. God, it would be nice to free those demons.

"What do you do when you're not at work?"

He wants to know about my life outside the bar. Learn more personal details. The question is vague enough to leave it open for any response. I doubt he wants to hear about my grocery trips and spring cleaning. He wants dirty details. Like if I have romantic interests with anyone. Especially after seeing me with Reese last night.

But he needs to work harder to earn that information.

"Mondays and Tuesdays, I work at an assisted living facility."

His head jerks back in surprise. "You do?" I tuck my lips and nod. "What do you do there?"

Does he really want to know? Or is this just some jab at polite conversation?

Micah Reed finding anything I do interesting seems far-fetched. But he also doesn't remember who I am. Not the younger me, anyway. Would he still be keen on knowing me if he did remember? A voice in the back of my head screams *no, you dumbass!* A different voice chimes in with *what if he has changed?*

Is it possible he has matured? That he actually cares about what women have to offer, other than what lies between their legs. I suppose all things are possible.

"Mostly crafts and games. I entertain and give them someone to talk to. Many don't have family in the area and they get lonely. Friendships within the ALF help, but it isn't the same."

"Wow." His lapis blue eyes hold mine and sparkle with amazement. "She's beautiful and kindhearted."

I don't know how to respond to his sentiment. The compliment throws me off balance and makes me question what I have thought of him over the years. I may have started out the night with a charade, but it has opened my eyes slightly. It has shown me a side of Micah Reed I didn't know existed. A softer side with gentle words.

"Well, my family would murder me in my sleep if I weren't. So…" I shrug, drop my gaze to the table and toy with the corner of the napkin.

He laughs. "Mine, too."

This grabs my attention. Makes me want to shake his shoulders and yell, "Well, they obviously don't know everything about you." But making a scene will open up a fat can of drama I don't want, so I keep my thoughts to myself.

Before the air around us shifts to awkward, uncomfortable silence, the server steps up to the table with our food. Soon as my plate hits the table, I reach for my sandwich and chow down. The server drops one large and three small plates in front of Micah. He dives fork first into the biscuits and gravy before the server asks if we want drink refills. We both give a thumbs-up.

Odd to think, but it feels like tonight has been pivotal between me and Micah. Like we have reached the center of our book and the story is shifting. Flowing more smoothly. The tension has eased slightly and made room for something else. What that something is, I have no clue. Not sure if I want to know.

The server returns with a fresh glass of juice and refills Micah's coffee. After he steps away, Micah spears a sausage link on his plate, then points it at me.

"Don't think just because food arrived we're done talking." Why not? I want to ask, but bite my tongue. "What do you do for fun?"

I would be an idiot to ignore his obvious attraction for me, now that I'm paying closer attention. Can't exactly say Micah is hard on the eyes, either. Before he opened his mouth my freshman year, my black heart swooned over him. Hard. Then he crushed it with his words. Over and over again.

Now, though, he seems different. A bit more mature, if I discount our never-ending banter and his predilection for a new female every night of the week.

Are women what he does for fun? Fucks 'em and leaves 'em? I don't picture him playing basketball with the guys or having a movie night with piles of junk food.

"What I do for fun would probably seem lame or old ladyish to you."

He eats the last of the sausage off his fork. "Humor me."

Micah Reed wants to know what I do for fun. Alright.

"Fun for me is curling up on the couch with a good book or movie. Maybe bingeing on my favorite ice cream and greasy takeout with a friend." I sip my juice. "Working where we do, I don't care about going out to party. What about you?" He tilts his head. "What is it you do for fun?"

Micah cuts into his French toast, dips the chunk in syrup, then brings it to his lips. For some idiotic reason, I follow the entire process with my eyes and salivate when he opens his mouth to eat it. I pray I don't look like all the other women who fawn over him.

Last thing I need is him getting the wrong idea.

But he watches me with obvious interest. Watches as I bring my own food to my lips and distract myself from whatever it is that is happening. Is this some weird version of food porn? People who get off watching other people eat. A sexual fetish. Like *"Hey girl, eat the toast next. Does it have butter? You like it all buttered up, don't you?"*

And now I have that stuck in my head. Fuck my life. Guess my dreams will be bizarre as hell tonight.

"A little bit of this. A little bit of that," he says after a sip of coffee that makes his face scrunch. He grabs two packets of sugar and adds them to the cup.

"Vague much?" I point to the coffee he now stirs. "I like sweet stuff, but I think you have sugar issues."

He waves me off. "Nah." Another sip and his eyes blissfully close. "And maybe I like to be mysterious." His brows waggle.

"Or… you don't want people to see the real you."

Across the table, he pushes scrambled eggs around his plate with a fork as a child would. Finding ways to avoid eye contact. Doing menial things to distract from the conversation at hand. Doing everything and anything to not own the truth.

"I let someone see the *real me*, as you call it."

What? That's it? Finally going to open up, then shut it down just as fast. Why am I not surprised?

"And?"

His brows pinch at the center as he forces out a breath. "And… she fucked a guy ten years my junior while she thought I was working. Except, I left work early that day. Thought it'd be nice to surprise her. When I walked in on them fucking, it was definitely a surprise."

The teenage girl inside me wants to jump up, poke my finger in his chest and yell, *"Ha! That's what you get."* Maturity clears her throat and wags her finger. Damn maturity.

"Sorry that happened to you," I tell him instead. "Can't say I know what that feels like."

"I don't picture guys stepping out on you," he mumbles, but I hear it clear as day.

True. No guy I dated has cheated on me. Two of my three serious relationships ended somewhat tragically. I believe all things happen for a reason, but I wish they could have happened differently. Death should never ever be the reason you lose love.

"So mysterious, Micah. Tell me what you do for fun." I work to pass the somber mood.

"Relentless, aren't you?"

I shrug. "A trait I've gotten good at over the years."

He plucks a grape from his plate and pops it in his mouth. "Hang with buddies, I guess. Friends of mine get together on Sundays and we just bullshit and catch up. When the weather's great, we hang at the beach. And the occasional gathering with the fam."

"Sounds nice. I lost some family and would give anything to spend time with them again."

Just like that, I bring us right back into sad territory. Not that my life is sad. I make the most of what I have. Spend time with Mom, Harold, and Trina—my step-father and stepsister—when able. I see my aunt Leanne more often, though. She reminds me so much of Dad.

The server steps up to the table and surveys our empty plates. After stacking the plates on his arm, he lays the check facedown on the table. "They'll cash you out up front." Then he walks off.

I go for the check, but Micah beats me to it. "It was my idea to come here. I'll pay."

The notion unsettles me. Only because it makes tonight seem more like a *date* and not two coworkers grabbing a bite to eat after work. And this was not a date.

"That's nice of you, but I don't mind paying for myself."

He scoots to the edge of the booth and rises. "Look, you're independent. I get it. But it's okay to let people buy you a meal every now and then." He starts for the register near the door. "It's the least I can do after my episode earlier."

I don't want to fight with him. Not after we have spent the last hours cordial. "Fine." I cave. "But only if I get to tip the server."

"Deal."

While Micah pays, I toss a stack of bills on the table. I wave to the server and head for the exit, Micah on my heels. Feels like his eyes are on my ass, but I don't check.

He walks me to my car. The air thicker as we approach and I dig the fob from my purse with shaky hands. My throat drier than burned toast as I swallow. My teeth clack together as I press the unlock button.

This isn't a date. And we aren't technically friends. So why the hell am I so fidgety?

Tonight ends with us both getting in our cars and driving away. Alone.

There will be no affectionate exchanges. No kisses or promises to talk later. No "I had a nice time." or "Let's do this again."

None. Of. The. Above.

Yet, this still feels like the end of a date as Micah opens my car door. As he looks into my eyes, equally as confused.

He steps closer, his arm lifting up. Is he going to hug me? No. Nope. Not happening.

I move to get in the car and he drops his arm. "Glad you got some food in you. Don't do that again."

His eyes drop to his feet, then meet mine again. "Yeah, sure," he says as he closes my door and I roll down the window. "Drive safe."

"You, too." The corners of his lips curve up slightly. "Night, Micah."

He steps back. "Night."

I leave Teddy's and make it home in record time. That is the beauty of driving the highway in the middle of the night.

After I brush my teeth and dress in pajamas, I snuggle under the blanket and shut my heavy eyes. My body relaxes one limb at a time. On the verge of sleep, I hear a fire truck siren nearby and it jolts me awake. Once it passes, I wiggle in place and try to settle my alert brain.

But my brain and I are obviously not on the same wavelength. Nope. Now, my brain wants to do a minute-by-minute replay of the whole evening. What it was like to have a cordial evening with my archnemesis. To smile and laugh and share a healthy conversation. To feel something, if only for a moment, other than hate for this man.

Good thing I don't work tomorrow. It's going to be a long night of overanalyzing.

Stupid brain.

eleven

I park behind Gavin's Range Rover, two houses down from Jonas and Autumn's place. Our Sunday get-togethers are the best tradition started with our group. Friends, family, and food—three of my favorite F's. My other favorite F wouldn't be appropriate in a group setting. Not my kink.

Feet from the front door, hickory hits my nose as rock music vibrates in my eardrums. I knock and Autumn yells from the other side. "It's open."

I twist the knob and step inside. In the open floor plan, I spy Autumn as she bustles around the kitchen. Takes buns out of packages, dumps cold sides into bowls, grabs condiments and toppings from the fridge. Her pace makes me dizzy.

I set down a bag with beer, tortilla chips, and salsa. "Anything you need help with?" Mom taught me and Shelly to always offer assistance, especially when we are guests. Long as Autumn doesn't need help cooking, I will pitch in.

My cooking skills are a running joke in the Reed family. When we were growing up, Mom wanted to make sure we were all—me, Shelly, and Dad—self-sufficient in the kitchen. That we knew how to make basic meals in case she wasn't able to. Let's just say I flunked from day one when I made gummy pasta with burned tomato sauce. Not my finest hour.

Can I cook now? If following microwave directions counts, then yes. If ordering takeout or dining out counts, then yes again. Basic breakfast foods and I are friends. But it works best for everyone if I stay away from stoves and ovens. Besides, every now and again, Mom stops by because she is "in the area"—she lives a solid twenty minutes from my house—and brings me a casserole dish of my childhood favorites.

Or nights like tonight. Everyone leaves with a container of leftovers. Autumn demands it. No matter what, I never starve or burn down the house.

"Could you dump the snack foods into the big bowls?" She points to a stack of large bowls at the end of the counter.

"On it."

Maybe Shelly told her not to let me near anything that requires heating. If so, I need to thank her later.

As I dump cheese puffs into a bowl, Jonas comes in from the backyard with Clementine on his heels. She is the cutest little girl ever. A spitting image of her mom, but with additional sass and a major bond with Spartan, Jonas's husky.

"Hey, man. Didn't realize you were here." He steps up to me and we backslap hug. "Gavin and Cora are out back with your sister and Erin."

"What? They left Autumn in here to do everything. Shelly is definitely getting a ration of shit."

Autumn shoves a large spoon in the coleslaw and spins to face me. "No, leave them be. I forced them outside."

"But you asked me to help?" I deadpan.

She shrugs. "I like to rotate through my helpers. What can I say?"

A knock at the door has Spartan running to the window and peeking through the blinds. His tail wags just as Jonas opens the door to Penny, Rex, Reznor,

Tatyana, and Ashton. Everyone files in and exchanges hugs. The house is abuzz with chatter. Smiles and laughter float around the room easily.

But right now, I feel the odd man out.

Although I'm not the only person without a significant other here, it feels… wrong at my age to be so alone. The moment my thoughts veer down this path, Shelly comes out of nowhere and bumps my shoulder with hers.

"Hey, big brother. What's new?" I wrap my arms around her and lift her from the floor. She squeals and smacks my back. "Put me down, dumbass."

I set her back on her feet and she swats my chest. Hard. "Ow! What was that for?"

"Did you really need to pick me up?"

"Are you my sister?" She rolls her eyes. "Nothing too exciting."

She grabs my hand and leads me out the door to the backyard. "Too crowded in there." She plops down on the lounger and brings me with her. "Life may not be exciting, but surely there must be something you've done since we last spoke."

Gavin and Cora take a seat across from us. Hickory clouds billow from the smoker, thin out with the mild breeze, and scent the air. A Bluetooth speaker shuffle plays rock music near the house. The late April temperature's mild enough to not make you sweat outside this time of day.

Three sets of eyes on me feel like a packed concert crowd.

"Work is much the same. Maybe less chaotic."

"The blonde?" Gavin pipes up and I want to slap him.

"Yep." I grit my teeth.

"What blonde?" Shelly asks Gavin.

Great. Here goes the attention I do not want or need.

"The bartender he banters with. You remember her from our last outing?" Shelly rests a finger on her lips, deep in thought. Gavin trudges forward and I want to smack him upside the head. "The one getting Micah all hot and bothered."

Shelly taps her lips and looks to the heavens. "Must've been otherwise distracted. Tell me more, big brother. What's her name?"

If I don't open up now, Shelly will be on my ass all night. Annoying the hell out of me.

But what is there to say about Peyton? We work together. She drives me absolutely mad, in the best ways. Her body is stellar, and I bet she isn't all fire and claws. Although, I like those aspects of her.

Hanging out with my sister and friends and talking about a woman I work with seems… wrong. Inappropriate. It feels like hair salon gossip. But if I keep my mouth shut, she will spend the next few hours in my face. Then she will pay a visit to Roar. Ogle my every move as Peyton and I work behind the bar. That is the last thing I need.

"You are a pain in my ass," I say.

She sticks out her tongue. "And you wouldn't want me any other way."

I inhale a deep, methodical breath and speak on the exhale. "Her name is Peyton." Shelly jerks back as her brows pinch together. "What?"

"Peyton?" she asks and I nod. "Has to be a weird coincidence."

"What are you talking about?"

"In high school, there was a girl. Peyton. She was a year ahead of Cora—and me, if we'd gone to the same school. Anyway, I remember Cora saying she was super nice, but half the school bullied her. I heard all of the horror stories second-hand, but…"

A fist wraps around my stomach, squeezes and twists. Bile rises up, up, up in my throat.

No. No, no, no.

"Do you remember her last name?" I croak out.

Five seconds feels like five hours as Shelly looks to Cora, then back to me, tilts her head and stares. Written all over her face is *you seriously don't remember* and *how did you not recognize her.* I bite the inside of my cheek until tangy iron hits my tongue.

"Alexander," Cora answers.

I bolt up from my seat and dash around the corner of the house to vomit in the yard. But seeing as I haven't eaten in hours, making room for the feast here, I spend more time dry heaving than actually expelling stomach contents.

A gentle hand rests on my shoulder. Soft floral, citrus, and earthy notes hit my nose. Shelly. As only a sister would, she rubs small circles on my back and remains silent. When I stand up, she hands me a napkin and bottled water.

Without a word, she guides us back to where we sat. The moment I return, I expect everyone's eyes on me. But my friends don't embarrass me with daunting stares and endless questions. When I stepped off, and Shelly followed, they sparked new conversations.

Now that I have returned, though…

"So, I assume you don't remember her from school?" Shelly asks for clarification.

I shake my head before taking a sip of the water. The cool liquid soothes the residual burn in my throat. "No. How do I not remember? People don't change *that* dramatically from high school to early thirties. Do they?"

Shelly turns her attention to Gavin. "You said she's blonde?" Gavin nods as he lifts a beer to his lips. Shelly faces me again. "That's it."

Dear, sister. Please elaborate for the rest of us who cannot hear your thoughts. Sincerely, brother. "What's it?"

"Sorry." Shelly smiles, then taps her temple. "Cora, correct me if I'm wrong. In high school, Peyton wasn't blonde. She was a goth chick. Black hair, black clothes, black everything. It's why…"

The way she trails off sends a chill up my spine. I flashback to high school, some of the best and worst years of my youth. Frame by frame, I search old memories. Try to see Peyton with dark hair and clothes. But I didn't pay attention to girls like Peyton. At least not the type of girl she was then. My preferred type has always remained the same.

Looking through four years of memories will take longer than tonight. Maybe Cora and Shelly will do me a solid and jog my memory with more specifics.

"I hate it when you leave me hanging, Shell." She winces. "Just lay it out. I'm a man. It's why what?"

Shelly finds every means to procrastinate. One small sip of water after another. She eyes Cora, who shrugs and flaunts the *might as well* face. Argh! Any second, I am going to lose it if someone doesn't speak up.

"It's why she was bullied," Shelly says. That wasn't so hard now, was it? "By you."

Wait, what? "Come again." I glance around to my closest friends. The ones I spent time with during those years. And they all nod at me.

When the hell did I bully Peyton? Pain scrapes my throat as I swallow. I chug half the water as I think harder. When the hell did I bully anyone? My hand fists my hair, tugging at the strands until pain shoots down my neck.

"It happened the year before we started high school," Cora chimes in. "Think she was a year behind you. But the rumors ran wild during my freshman year too. Girls wrote on bathroom tiles with Sharpie, *Peyton Alexander is a slut*. Never stayed on the tile long, but was up again within a day or two. Guys whispered, *Micah Reed called her a slut*, and with your popularity status, people believed. From what I heard, you called her names in the cafeteria in front of half the school."

The nightmare of that day rolls in like an evening thunderstorm—angry and violent. My friends and their lighthearted chatter disappear. A second-by-second replay of the day flashes through my memory.

Mercedes and her bitch friends were annoying the hell out of me that day. Coach had been pressing me to push harder on the track. And Mercedes found me at the perfect moment to verbally bash some unknown girl. Peyton.

All Mercedes ever wanted was to be seen and heard. My popularity on the track team attracted her. But there was nothing about her I deemed attractive. She was a bitch. Through and through.

That day, she pranced over to me and I wouldn't give her the time of day. So she riled me up. Told me the girl in the corner had been eye fucking me for days. Then she told me the girl had slept with half the baseball team and was slut-shaming the guys. In my hazing thoughts, I thought *this bitch isn't messing with any jocks at this school.*

So, I shut her down. Or at least that is what I thought I was doing.

Obviously, I had no moral compass. Instead of opening my mouth, I should have left well enough alone. I should have known Mercedes was a conniving bitch. But I was too wrapped up in myself. Worried some girl would try to ruin what was already toeing the line.

Leaning forward, I rest my elbows on my knees and my face in my hands. "Jesus," I mumble into my palms. "What was I thinking?"

Shelly rubs a hand up and down my back. The motion meant to soothe me. But hatred runs rampant inside me like a viral contagion. "Think of this as a second chance. A way to right your wrong."

"No wonder she hates me. I was so self-absorbed, I gave no fucks about her feelings. Or how my words messed up her life."

"Yes, you screwed up big time." I peek up at my sister and she shrugs. "If Mom and Dad knew, they'd be pissed. All those years of teaching us to put other's thoughts and feelings before our own."

I comb my fingers through my hair and sit up, eyes on Shelly. Her eyes, just as blue and sparkly as mine, stare back at me with deep sympathy.

"How do I fix this, Shell?"

She takes my hands in hers and holds my gaze. "First, you apologize. Apologize like you never have before. And mean it." I nod and she continues. "Second, you beg for her forgiveness. Grovel if necessary. After what you did to her. After how she was treated during those pivotal years, she may not forgive you. That's her call. You can't just ask for forgiveness, either. Show her you want it."

"How do I do that?"

"Be the man I know you to be. The man Mom and Dad raised. Simple gestures and kind words. They go much further than most expect."

I take mental notes of the sound advice only a sister can provide. "I will."

"And lastly, don't do anything to hurt her. Ever again." I nod and she pokes my chest with a finger. "I mean it, Micah. You already hurt her once. Who knows what would happen if you did again."

When I don't respond, Shelly turns toward Cora and chats about the next bowling or karaoke night. Everyone around me carries on various conversations. Me? I stay in my own head and sort through the onslaught of memories and advice.

Little by little, I devise how I will fix this. Fix what I broke all those years ago. Fix the hatred Peyton harbors.

Because I like her too much to let her hate me any longer.

twelve

PEYTON

After a full crank of the handle, the black-and-white ball rolls down the shoot. I pick it up, twirl it in my fingers, then peer up at the crowd of hopeful eyes.

"B4."

Whack, whack, whack. The slap of bingo markers fills the room, followed with the occasional groan or *yes* with a fist pump.

Ms. Jenkins looks up from her ten-card spread, gives me a thumbs-up and a wink. The woman to her left, Ms. Roberts, darts narrowed eyes to me, then Ms. Jenkins. They exchange words as I crank the handle for the next ball to drop. Ms. Jenkins waves a hand at her, then shakes her head.

"G53," I call the next number, then crank the handle again as the bingo markers create music. "I25."

"Bingo!" Mr. Calhoun croaks from three tables back. He lifts his winning card and waves it above his head. One of the nurses takes the card from him and brings it to me to verify his win. Once I confirm Mr. Calhoun's win, several people ball up their cards and grumble.

Metal chair legs screech against the linoleum in stilted beats as several players inch back and rise from their seats. Ms. Jenkins lets her reading glasses hang around her neck as she stuffs her lucky bingo markers in the seat of her walker. She wheels to the front table where I clean up the bingo cage and master board.

"Sticking around for lunch?" She tugs her pink cardigan closer to her midline.

"Wouldn't miss it. I'll meet you there."

I stare after Ms. Jenkins as she leaves the game room and notice her gait stutters more. Since I started at Gulfside, I have never not noticed her slow pace. But the hobble is new. Seeing her wear herself out to leave the room pinches my heart.

Once I have the game components boxed and stored, I walk over to one of the nurses still in the room.

"Hey, Jim."

"How are you, Peyton?"

I give him a weak smile. "Same old, same old." I shrug. "Hey, is Ms. Jenkins okay? She seems more frail today."

His eyes divert to the door then back to me, lips slightly downturned. The pinch from a moment ago intensifies and I press my palm heel to my chest.

"Last night, she pressed her panic button. When the nurse got to her room, they found her on the floor. She says it was a slip when she walked from the bathroom to her bed. But the nurse thinks she may have fallen out of the bed."

A hand slaps over my mouth. "Oh no!"

"Although she argued, they took her to X-ray. No broken bones. Just bruises—on her hip, arm, and ego."

Ms. Jenkins is a sweetheart. Willing to help anyone in need. Talk your ear off for hours and listen with equal skill. Teach you how to crochet or knit as if she invented the craft. Most importantly, she gives the best hugs. So full of warmth that has nothing to do with temperature. She may be up there in age, but she still has so much love to give.

"Just glad she is okay."

Not sure what I would do or how I would feel if I lost Ms. Jenkins. Seeing her smile and being wrapped in her arms each week provides me with so much love and happiness. A solace I once shared with my grandmother, Isabel. A peacefulness that shattered three years ago when she passed away.

I didn't start working at Gulfside to replace what I lost with my grandmother. But being here with Ms. Jenkins each week helps sew the fissures of my heart. The fault lines that opened when Nana passed. The ones that barely started to heal from losing Dad seven years earlier.

I shoot Aunt Leanne a quick text and tell her I'm eating at Gulfside today. She responds and says we will catch up next week.

Down the corridor from the game room, I hook a left and enter the dining hall. The beige painted walls hold several pictures from over the years. Of staff and residents. Special events and holidays and birthdays. Alongside the photographs are paintings and drawings from current and past residents. Plus, framed posters with beautiful scenery and positive sentiments. Long wooden tables are spread throughout the room, with four chairs on the long sides and one on each end. Each table decorated with a centerpiece for the season. Residents can walk to the counter and get food, cafeteria style. Or they can sit at the tables and have the staff bring food to them.

The setup is pleasant and welcoming and provides a level of independence and community.

At eleven fifteen, the lunch crowd has already packed the room. I shuffle to the end of the line and grab a plastic tray. After I select a sandwich, fruit and water, I pay and find Ms. Jenkins at her usual table.

We catch up for a bit while she enjoys her tomato soup and grilled cheese, and I have my turkey sandwich. She tells me how upset Ms. Roberts was during bingo. Swearing I only called numbers on Ms. Jenkins's cards. Which is laughable.

As lunch fills our bellies, I contemplate how to ask about her fall. Last thing I want to do is upset or embarrass her. But I need to know if she really is okay. Since the day we met, Ms. Jenkins has been nothing but forthcoming and honest with me. It is one of the reasons I love her so much. No beating around the bush.

"So…" She sets her spoon down and grants me her attention. "Jim tells me you had a fall."

Anyone who says eighty-seven-year-old women can't roll their eyes or show indignation needs to meet Ms. Jenkins. Her skills could trample teenagers, which is quite telling.

"He needs to mind his tongue."

I rest a hand on hers. "He only told me because I noticed your limp and I asked about it."

Her other hand pats, then covers mine with a layer of reassurance. "Don't you worry about me. A little fall won't keep me down."

Therein lies the problem. I do worry. If the last decade of my life has taught me anything, it is that time with people you love should never be taken for granted. Losing too many loved ones matured me in many ways. It also inhibited me in others.

People I love? I love them fiercely and let them know often. And I have learned to let smaller fights go when it comes to loved ones.

But losing them also hardened my heart. Made letting new people in that much harder. I loved hard in a few committed relationships, but life just kept throwing me one curveball after another. So, I threw in the towel. My heart couldn't take the endless cycle of pain anymore.

Now, I don't allow myself to travel down the road to love again. Not saying it will never happen. But when heartache knocks on your door over and over again, you find every possible way to not let it in. Turning my heart to ice has been the only method to work.

I appease Ms. Jenkins, but only because she is stubborn and will shut me down if I keep talking about it. "Alright. But if I hear this happens again, you're not allowed to argue about me caring."

"It won't, so the point is moot."

That's it. End of conversation. When Ms. Jenkins puts her foot down, it is best to just bite your tongue and let it go. Although, I plan to check in with the nurses more frequently and have them reach out if something else happens. I may only work here more as mental support, but I adore Ms. Jenkins—and several other residents at Gulfside. They're like a second family.

We finish our lunch in relative silence. After I take our trays to the bin, I help Ms. Jenkins to her feet and we wander from the dining hall, through the community room and exit the double doors that lead outside. I walk at her pace and never give her the impression she needs to hurry.

Today, Ms. Jenkins selects the wooden bench between two old oak trees. The canopy shades the seat, but allows the occasional sunrays to highlight your skin. Birds chirp from the branches as squirrels run from tree to tree in a game of tag. A gentle breeze tames the too warm spring temperatures—not that either of us mind the heat. Hints of jasmine and rose drift in the wind from the flower garden to our left and I let the perfume fill my lungs.

The facility also has a fruit and vegetable garden. Residents with green thumbs are welcome to tend to the plants but aren't required to keep them maintained. The facility has a groundskeeper that checks the plants weekly and tends to any needing attention.

As per usual, we sit the first few minutes in silence. Both of us soaking up the warmth and breathing easier.

"Peyton." Ms. Jenkins rests a hand on my forearm and brushes her thumb over the skin. Her touch is gentle. Soft. Kind. A reminder of my nana. "You worry about me too much." Her words are tender and quiet. "I have lived a full life. And as you get older, things change. Your perception of life, what matters… it all changes."

Why is she telling me this? Has a new health issue come up that I don't know about? I don't like that she talks about herself as if she doesn't have much time left. It unnerves me. Makes my stomach twist in knots. Robs me of breath.

With a slow twist of her body, she faces me head-on. The crinkles near the corners of her eyes and mouth turn up. "I love that you come to see me. That you want to spend time with a cuckoo old bat. But sweetheart, you need to live life too. You're so young. Have so many years ahead of you. Don't waste them visiting me."

I shake my head, unwilling to absorb her words or give them life. "No. You don't get to say that." The backs of my eyes sting. "Coming to see you matters to me."

"Why, Peyton? Not that I don't enjoy our time together. But why does seeing me matter?"

Because you make me smile. Because I love hearing your stories similar to those my nana told. Love how I experience a simpler happiness with you. And how life doesn't feel as messy and complicated when I get to talk with someone wiser.

"Seeing you makes me happy." My thoughts summarized in that singular line. It doesn't matter why. Spending time with this woman makes me happy. Provides some peace.

She pats my forearm, then leaves her hand to rest there. "Okay, Peyton."

The next half hour ticks by with the sun on our shins. We don't speak again until I walk her inside and leave for the day. She gives me a hug and says she will see me tomorrow. As I drive home, pain radiates beneath my rib cage. Pulsing and pounding and unrelenting.

Why did it feel like Ms. Jenkins was saying goodbye?

Reese laughs as Mom regales us with one of the weddings she catered over the weekend.

"Over the years, I have seen every kind of wedding. Or so I thought. But having livestock in the crowd and pictures… definitely new."

"Cows?" Reese asks and Mom nods. "Pigs and chickens?"

"Yep. The whole shebang. Cows, pigs, chickens, goats, horses. Ducks, too."

"Why?" Reese voices the question we all want answered.

Mom shrugs. "Said she grew up on a farm out west. She moved to Florida two years back to be with her now-husband." My brows lift. "They met through a dating app," she clarifies. "When the couple started planning the wedding, she got the groom's approval for a country theme. But I don't think even he knew how country she meant."

Wow. Just wow.

After being less than cheerful once I left Gulfside, Mom's story definitely lifts my spirits. Not one hundred percent. But some is better than none.

Reese and I attempt to help her make dinner, as we have every other time we visit, and she shoos us away. Suppose that's what you get when your mother cooks and bakes and caters for a living.

Sweet T's isn't a big operation. Mom caters four to five events a week. Most of them office events or weddings with less than a hundred people. She appeals to the masses and is willing to explore all food and baking options with her clients. With two full-time employees working alongside her, they are a booming small business.

I may be biased, but her quiche, almond cake with layered fruit and whipped cream frosting, and macaroons are pure heaven. Being the daughter of a woman who loves the kitchen is never a bad thing. Unless you are concerned about your figure. Which I am not.

"Tracy, you have to take me to the next wedding," Reese tells Mom. "I need these stories firsthand."

She waves a hand at him. "They're not all this outlandish."

"Maybe not, but I love weddings. Don't you, Peyton?" Reese flashes me with sparkling irises.

What the hell is he talking about? Reese and I have never discussed anything wedding related unless chatting with Mom. And never once have I mentioned a love for weddings. Hell, I barely hold on to boyfriends.

"Not so much," I respond with narrowed laser eyes.

Mom adds roasted root vegetables to a serving bowl and the lemon-rosemary chicken to a platter. Without request, Reese takes them to the large cedar table in the dining room. Mom preps the last of the salad as I add a sliced baguette to a basket.

"You two sit. Be back in a sec."

Mom wanders down the hall and disappears from view. Off to get my stepfather, his daughter, and her girlfriend. Who never seem to participate in family time until absolutely necessary.

Don't get me wrong, Harold is a great guy. He loves my mom fiercely, which she needs and deserves after what happened with Dad. His job is safe and nine-to-five typical in the print shop he owns, Designs of the Times. But he is otherwise aloof. At least when I am here. Mom says Harold is simplistic and introverted. When it's just the two of them, he is more outspoken and affectionate.

As for my stepsister, Trina, she just does her own thing. Five years my senior, Trina Williamson struts around like she knows all. I long since gave up offering support or opinions. Since Mom and Harold first started dating three years ago, we have always been cordial with one another. But it isn't difficult to read her body language and determine she would rather not spend time with me or Mom.

As adult children, yes, it is weird to have our parents find new love. Especially when we both had parents we loved. Harold's first wife, Trina's mother, and he divorced when she was thirty. They had been married thirty-one years. But in the last year of their marriage, the misses went through a late midlife crisis. She wanted freedom and independence. With no way to recoup his marriage, Harold agreed to let the love of his life go.

Three years later, he met Mom.

She had a booth set up at the local Saturday market. So did Harold. Before the influx of traffic, Harold stopped at her booth and sampled some of her food. They kept in touch after that day. Harold initially said it was for business, but later told Mom he couldn't stop thinking about her.

Their story of finding love again melts my heart. Mom dealt with major depression after losing Dad. It is one thing to grow apart in a relationship. But when the person you love dies in a tragic, fatal accident, there is no easy way to overcome the pain. Harold helped steer Mom from the darkness. For that, I am eternally in debt to him.

"Hey, guys." Speak of the man. "Sorry I didn't come out sooner. Was finishing up with a new client."

If he can print it, Harold does it. Business cards, fliers, bookmarks, car wraps, trinkets, and more. Harold started his business decades ago. Once a one-man operation, Designs of the Times has boomed over the last five years. Partly because Harold had nothing but time when he and his ex-wife separated. But also because Mom encouraged and supported him wholeheartedly.

"No worries. We were just catching up with Mom," I tell him.

Trina and her girlfriend, Sierra, walk in. No *hello* or *how's it going* or even eye contact. None of us dislike each other, but Trina isn't fond of her father remarrying.

She and Mom get on fine. But Trina loves her own mother and has admitted as much to her father when she thought no one else was listening. Not that she wasn't especially quiet about it.

So, Trina tolerates me and Mom. Her problem, not mine.

After everyone fills their plates, idle chitchat circulates the table. Harold tells us about the new client he and Trina just acquired. Yes, Trina works with her father. It isn't odd they work together, but it surprises me she doesn't want more distance from her parent.

Reese mentions the influx of people at the restaurant and rec center. Mom blathers on about her upcoming week and the next wedding she will cater. Reese immediately jumps in and asks to attend and Mom shakes her head with a laugh.

Then the table goes silent. Too silent.

I glance up from my fork and knife, ready to bring the bite of chicken to my lips, but stop when I notice all eyes are on me.

"What?"

Mom gives a small smile. "I asked what was new with you. Anyone new in your life?"

Oh, lord. Here we go.

Since Mom and Harold fell in love, she has been adamant about finding someone for me. I love my mother's natural determination and desire for me to have the best in life. But her meddling in my love life is *not* something I want to deal with.

I spear the chicken harder than necessary and shove it between my lips. Chewing the bite until it turns soupy won't take long, but at least it gives me a moment to mentally prepare. Because this conversation won't finish with my answer.

"No, Mom."

She sips her wine, then sticks out her lower lip. "Aw, Peyton." I hate when she does that. Makes it sound like my choice to be alone is horrible. "Sweetheart, I know things ended on a sad note with James, but don't let that darken your heart."

James. My last boyfriend. The first guy I had truly loved since Chad—my first everything. James said he would always be there for me, through thick and thin. But when Nana passed, and I mourned, he didn't know how to be there for me during the darker days. Said he didn't know how to make me smile or love me anymore. He went to two joint therapy sessions with me, but couldn't seem to grasp why I didn't easily snap out of my sadness.

Bless his heart for trying, but we drifted apart after a year and a half together. Deep down, we still had love for each other. We just weren't meant to be more than what we had.

And we were okay with that. Although we broke up two years ago, we still catch up from time to time. His current girlfriend understands our friendship and has zero jealousy when we talk. She is a true woman.

"Mom, James and I are still friends. Nothing about us *darkens* me or my heart."

"I just hate to see you so alone."

Why won't she let this go? I don't want to hurt her feelings, but the continual conversations about relationships make me feel as if she thinks life isn't worthy if you don't have someone at your side.

I take a deep breath and prepare for the calm storm that is Tracy Williamson.

"What if I want to be alone? Have you considered that?"

"Why would you want to be alone?" Her voice shakes slightly.

I stab at the lettuce and cucumber in my bowl. I don't want to fight, not with Mom. But she needs to understand that not every person *needs* another person to have happiness. It is possible to be happy and be single.

"Mom, there's nothing wrong with being single. I come and go as I please. I don't have to worry about upsetting someone if I don't come home immediately from work. I get time to feel comfortable in my own skin, without the pressure of pleasing someone else. The list goes on and on." She goes to speak and I hold up a hand to cut her off. "And before you say something like *what about love...* Mom, I've had love. Twice. One I lost and can never get back. And the other, well, it morphed into a different love. I have come to terms with both of those. But for now, I want time for me. If I get lucky enough to find love again, I will accept it with grace. I won't go hunting for it, though. When it's meant to be..."

"I just feel like you're missing out," Mom mumbles to her plate.

Mom is the second person to indicate as much to me today. Although Ms. Jenkins didn't necessarily mean love, she thought I was missing out on life by hanging out with elderly folks.

Everyone at the table falls silent. Not that Trina or Sierra have said much anyway. I didn't raise my voice at Mom, but this is the first time I have really laid it all out in front of others. Reese knows how I feel. He teases me about dating every once in a while, but he gets that I'm enjoying me time. Mom, on the other hand, doesn't seem to get why I want independence. Maybe because she loved belonging to someone. It made her whole.

But I want the ability to feel whole *without* someone. Once I achieve that, being with another person is a bonus.

The rest of dinner goes by with quieter, blander conversation. After we help Mom clean up, Reese and I exchange hugs with Mom and Harold and say our goodbyes.

Back at home, Reese and I change into comfy clothes and he tells me to grab my Caboodles box of nail polish. The very same Caboodles I have had since high school. Once upon a time, it held only black polish, black mascara, black eyeliner, and shades of black shadow. Now, a rainbow of polish rests inside. Nothing else.

Reese plops down on the sofa with two bottles of beer and chips. After he tears the bag open and pops the top from the beers, he grabs my feet and starts rubbing them.

"Did Mama T upset you tonight?"

I shake my head and moan as he massages the ball of my foot. "No. Just wish she'd let me live life how I want."

"She means well."

"Yeah, I know. Her persistence frustrates me, I guess. It's like she doesn't understand that women don't *have* to be in a relationship to be happy."

"True." Reese switches to my other foot. "But all she knows is her own experiences. It's hard to speak of what you don't know or understand."

"I get that." Grabbing my bottle from the table, I take a sip. "But after countless conversations, you'd think she'd understand *my* stance on the matter. I love that she wants me to be happy. But she doesn't get that romantic relationships don't always equal happiness."

Reese grabs his beer from the table and extends it toward mine to clink necks. "Cheers to that." We both drink, then set our bottles down. "So… you went out with Micah the other night."

"Not now."

When I agreed to eat at Teddy's with Micah, I texted Reese. All I got in return was a slew of emojis and obnoxious GIFs.

"Fine. But we will talk about it. I don't care what does or doesn't come of it, we will discuss Micah Reed."

"Fine," I agree with a huff. "For now, will you just paint my toenails."

"Only if you do mine." Reese drops his feet in my lap and wiggles his toes. "I'm feeling the sky blue." I grab said blue from the Caboodles along with the bottle for my toes. I toss it at Reese and he looks at the color. "Really?"

"Yep."

"You got it."

For the next hour, we decorate each other's toes. Reese's in a bright baby blue. Mine in a rich, bold red. The color I reserve for when I want something. Thing is, I don't exactly know what I want. Mom's and Ms. Jenkins's words continue to ring through my head.

Is it true? Am I missing out?

thirteen

MICAH

Peyton hasn't been the same since last Saturday. Can't pinpoint what is different, but something just seems *off*.

Wednesday and yesterday, we only spoke when absolutely necessary. Every time I peeked in her direction, she appeared lost. Somewhere besides Roar. Eyes staring off in the distance, but without focus. She chatted with patrons in the bar, but her conversations lacked their typical zeal. Her harrowing smiles seemed forced.

Between the early morning hours of Sunday, when we parted ways at Teddy's, and early Wednesday evening, something shifted in Peyton's world.

But my life and perspective had shifted too.

After the conversation at Jonas and Autumn's Sunday night, I didn't sleep for shit. Didn't get much sleep the two days following, either.

What I had done to Peyton all those years ago weighed heavily on my mind and heart. Made me twitchy and restless, night after night. I had lain awake in bed for hours and replayed all the horrible words I'd said to and about her. Each night, I counted the bubbles in the popcorn ceiling to distract myself or fall asleep from boredom. But it neither distracted nor induced boredom. To my amazement and pitifulness, the highest I counted was 412. The only reason I stopped… the wind kicked up outside, swept the tree branch near my window and the dancing shadow caught my attention.

Exhaustion is no comparison to how I feel. My cement-pillar legs drag with each step forward. My lead-beam arms and robotic hands move only because my mind wills them to. Thank goodness my lungs and heart do their job without directive.

Did our conversation Saturday upset her? Dredge up old memories?

I grit my teeth and hang my head, ashamed at the person I was to her years ago. Had my parents known how I behaved back then—especially to a girl—they would have had me booted from the track team and on house arrest for months.

The question now is… how do I fix this? How do I make up for the asshole juvenile I once was? Will she forgive me and my deplorable behavior? Or will she forever harbor hatred for me in her heart?

When a crowd favorite booms through the speakers, the horde of bodies shifts from the bar to the dance floor.

I inch closer to Peyton, her eyes downcast, and focused on the glass she has cleaned three times. I knock her shoulder and she lifts her gaze and blinks.

"Everything alright? Seems like you're somewhere else tonight."

She smiles, but it doesn't reach her eyes. "Yes. No. I don't know."

"Want to talk about it?"

One shoulder shrugs as she sets the glass down. "Not now. Another time, maybe."

Seeing Peyton like this stirs the memories I recalled this past week. Although I was a royal prick to her, I did see her around school. I honestly don't recall any feelings for her—positive or negative. Back then, Peyton was just a random girl. Day after day, week after week, month after month, she remained the same. Decked head to toe in black. Baggy pants and a hoodie with the hood up. A black-and-white, checker-print backpack hooked on both shoulders. A folder, textbook, and mass market-sized book clutched close to her chest. Head up, but eyes on the ground.

Yes, Mercedes and her twat gang of besties got me to call Peyton a slut. But when I caught sight of her during my senior year, I wondered why those girls had it out for her. Were they jealous of her individuality? Did they envy she had male friends without having to put out? Was it her curves that had them calling her names and spreading lies? Or were they just bitches who refused to like people not similar to them?

Not that it matters now, but I think it was all of the above. Plus, Peyton wasn't a follower. Still isn't. She does her own thing, in her own time.

Before she walks off, I wrap a hand around her forearm. Her eyes drop and stare at her arm a beat before she lifts her gaze. "Meet me at Teddy's after work," I say with an added softness in my voice. Hoping she doesn't hear it as a demand.

Her eyes dart between mine. Brows twitch imperceptibly. Glassiness highlights the gray flecks in her vibrant violet irises. She licks, then tucks her lips between her teeth.

Not sure why, but she looks on the verge of tears.

The chambers of my heart contract and expand faster. An ache climbs from beneath my ribs and up my throat, lodging itself at my Adam's apple and swelling. I swallow and it does nothing to taper the sensation. To quell the emotion stuck firmly in place.

The overwhelming urge to hug her weighs my limbs. To haul her into me and press her close to my chest. Wrap my arms around her waist, squeeze tight and slide a hand up her spine to her neck. To feel her breath and heat on my skin.

"I'll think about it," she says hoarsely.

I drop my hand and she drifts to the end of the bar. A smile dons her face, but the gesture is all for show. The feisty and vivacious woman that lights up the bar four nights a week is nowhere to be found. In her place is a woman with a difficult past and wounded heart.

Hopefully tonight, she will let me heal part of her wound.

Neck deep in logging invoices, I press the heels of my palms to my eyes. This is what happens when I lose focus. Shit piles up. Work doesn't get done and mounts up day by day.

Invoices don't necessarily take long to input. But my mind has been elsewhere this week. Focused on a woman I hope joins me later at the diner.

"Only a dozen more to go. Just get it done, Reed."

The stack thins as I key stats into the spreadsheet. Three invoices from the bottom, a knock at the door startles me out of my zone. Then it swings open. I finish keying in the line, then look up to see who entered.

Peyton stands just inside the door, the fingers of one hand picking at the nails on the other.

"What's up?" I swivel in the chair to face her head-on.

"Three things." I lift my brows. "Yes, I'll meet you at Teddy's later." A corner of my mouth kicks up, but falls flat as she winces. "Dan has an issue with someone's ID at the door. And Ted is trying to break up a fight near the bar."

"Shit." I bolt from my chair and race out the door with Peyton on my heels. "Let Dan know I'll be at the door as soon as I'm done with Ted."

"On it."

The moment I round the end of the hall, chaos smacks me in the face. A crowd encircles Ted and two men. A woman hovers behind one of the men and I assume she is the reason the two men are throwing punches.

When I approach, Ted spots me with wide eyes. He has one man pinned in his grip, but the other won't calm down. I step between the two and get in the free man's face.

"Back the fuck up," I yell.

His bloodshot, glassy eyes wobble as he stares me down. He holds his ground; well, rocks a little. "Asshole touched my wife."

I step into him but don't make contact. Yet. "I said, back the fuck up."

The man peers over my shoulder with narrowed eyes. Jaw muscles taut. Shoulders to his ears. He jabs his finger in the direction of the other man. "I ever see your face again, you best run." He meets my gaze, takes a step back and nods. "I mean no disrespect. But no one touches my woman without permission or repercussions."

I lift both my hands to either side of my face. "I get it, man. But take the fight outside. Can't be having that shit in here." I peer over my shoulder at Ted and lift my chin. He escorts the other man to the door and I turn back to face the couple. "You're welcome to stay. But no fights."

He extends a hand and we shake before I walk to the door to resolve issue two. Thankfully, this resolves much faster. Fake or forged IDs get spotted easily with all the UV lighting. The hardest part is convincing the person we know it is tampered with. The old days of laminated or non-hologram licenses are long gone. Fakes are easier to spot and confiscate.

"Your fakes may work at other bars and clubs, but not this one. Have a good night." I take the ID, grab the scissors we keep at the podium near the door, and cut the ID into jagged pieces. Then walk off as the punk curses me out.

Back in the office, I collapse in the chair behind the desk and run my fingers through my hair. I love my job, but sometimes it sucks.

I love the fast pace and upbeat energy that bleeds from the walls and floats in the air. The thump of the bass and pitch of the treble. The bright lights and dark corners. The smiles and bright eyes and exhilaration. I love it all. Hell, I even love the desk work. Filling orders and spreadsheets. Writing schedules and implementing procedures. Inventory is a beast, but I do it with a smile on my face.

But every once in a while, my job comes with a pile of bullshit.

The occasional bar fight over women or spilled drinks. Fake IDs and dealing with underage people trying to enter. Idiots harassing the staff or touching them inappropriately. Dealing with people who can't settle their tab.

Each instance is never pretty, but most resolve without bloodshed or police.

I focus back on the computer and the last of the invoices. *Almost done.* Just finish the last of the desk work and wrap the night up behind the bar. Get the brunt of the work done, then round out the work night with Peyton nearby.

With a deep breath, I pick up where I left off. Line by line, I input the last of the invoices and save the spreadsheet to the cloud. Once everything is filed away and I straighten up the desk, I roll back the chair and exit the office.

Smile on my face, an extra bounce in my step, I walk down the hall and out to the bar. Peyton glows like the sun. Her bright smile hasn't quite returned, but I hope to make it shine again later.

Peyton agreed to meet me at Teddy's. And tonight, I will man up and apologize for every time I hurt her in our formative years. I pray she accepts and allows me to make it up to her. However she deems worthy.

Peyton saying yes gives me hope. I hold on to that hope with every ounce of strength I own. Because hope is all I have right now.

fourteen

I really wanted to say no to Micah when he asked me to Teddy's after work. But the severity in his eyes wouldn't let the word slip between my lips. When I said I would think about it, I hoped my resolve would strengthen. That the word *no* would fall from my tongue with greater ease.

Alas, it did not.

Which leads to now. Me, parking my SUV and getting out to join Micah inside the bustling diner up the street.

We step inside and the hostess seats us right away. More than half the tables are occupied. Conversation and laughter erupt from all corners and the spaces between. The hostess seats us near a back corner. The two tables near us empty.

"Thanks for agreeing to meet me here again."

I nod and scan the menu. Although I always order the same thing, I feel a change of pace might be nice. Just as the server steps up and deposits water glasses on the table, I decide on the two egg breakfast with crispy bacon, home fries, and a biscuit. Micah orders the same as last time and we both ask for coffee.

The server takes our menus and wanders off to check on another table before going to the kitchen.

"So, why'd you ask me here?"

Micah fiddles with the edge of the paper placemat and avoids my gaze. His reluctance to speak or make eye contact has me curious and a little on edge. Since last weekend, Micah has been… different. Quieter. Hesitant whenever he gets within twenty feet.

This side of Micah piques my interest. What makes a man like Micah Reed soft?

"First and foremost," —he finally meets my eyes— "I want to apologize."

Is this *the apology*? An apology fifteen years overdue, but necessary. Is Micah Reed about to apologize for being one of the most epic assholes?

Slow down, Peyton. Best not to assume and get my hopes up. For all I know, the apology may have something to do with Roar.

"For?" I clutch the hem of my shirt beneath the table until my knuckles burn and nails bite my skin through the fabric.

His lips tilt up a fraction at the corners. The smile loaded with sympathy and regret.

This is it, isn't it? *The* moment. Would it be wrong to take out my phone, open the camera, switch it to video, and record this moment for posterity? Would he tell me to not act so childish? Tell me to take the moment seriously?

When you wait for a moment such as this for more than a decade, wanting to document it isn't strange. After living with self-doubt and being taunted for years, wanting to replay the moment one of the instigators apologizes is *not* wrong.

"I think you know what for." He tilts his head and holds my gaze with watery eyes.

"Humor me."

He yanks his hand from the paper placemat that now misses bits of the lower right corner. His hands drop to his sides. And by the way he shifts, I wonder if he now sits on his hands.

"Peyton, I was young and stupid. What I did to you… What those girls provoked me to do to you…" He drags his lips between his teeth and looks to the side for the count of three before meeting my gaze. His eyes red and veiny. "I'm sorry for the things I said to you and about you in high school. They weren't true. It was all a ruse to make a jealous, egotistical *girl* feel better about herself. It was wrong of me to say and I am truly sorry."

Frozen is the only rational term to explain my physical and mental state. Frozen.

Micah Reed just apologized. To me. Of his own volition. He admitted his words and actions were wrong and cruel and hateful. The bidding of a girl—a bully—who would do whatever it took to make those not in her circle feel worthless. But he owned the role he played in it all.

Nervous energy zips through my limbs and begs for me to jump off the seat. To garner the attention of everyone in the diner. To scream at the top of my lungs, *"Micah Reed apologized."* The words *I'm sorry* left his lips and hit my ears.

Weight lifts from my shoulders. My teenage self sags with a sigh in my mind. His apology doesn't wash away all the hurtful words and unkind acts he and his group of friends enacted. But his apology heals some of the old wounds that marred my heart long ago.

I hold his gaze as I stretch out my fingers. His normally bold blue eyes are dull and damp. Lips firmly tucked between his teeth as he fights his body's inclination to cry.

This apology is real. From the heart. Sincere and honest. Exactly what I waited all this time to hear.

"Thank you."

He sucks in a breath, then turns his head to the side. A hand meets the cheek not facing me and swipes. Then a tear rolls down the other cheek and I drop my eyes to the table. Grab my napkin-rolled silverware and unravel it. Toy with the tacky napkin band. Organize my silverware on the placemat—fork on the left, knife on the right, spoon at the top.

I give him this moment. Let him soak it up. Give him a chance to process the reality of what happened years ago, bask in the ownership he just took, and the apology only he could deliver. Couldn't have been easy. Owning the atrocities of your past never should be.

Once he collects himself, though, I have questions.

The server stops at the table, grabs each of our empty mugs in turn, and fills them with coffee. Then sets a thermal carafe on the table and walks off.

Micah tears open several packets of sugar and dumps them in his mug while I add one and some creamer. Our spoons clink the mugs in tandem with each other. Like synchronized swimmers, we both lift our mugs, blow on the steamy caffeine and sip the nectar of the gods. Although, I still don't understand how he tastes the coffee with that much sugar.

He sets his mug in the center of the placemat but doesn't remove his hands. Eyes on his thumbs as he paints them along the rim. Then he meets my gaze. His addictive lapis-blue eyes still a bit dull, but more beautiful. Raw. Real.

I swallow and try to quell the flurry rising and expanding in my chest.

"Now it makes sense."

"What?" I choke out.

"The instant hatred you had for me. It makes sense. I would've acted the same."

Arms at my sides, I lean forward and press my chest against the table, eyes locked with his. "How did you not know?"

"Who you were?" I nod and lean back. He lifts a shoulder, then drops it. "Guess I just forgot. Does that make me more of an asshole? Probably. But it's the truth. With the exception of track and my closest friends, high school is just a blur."

Wish it was a blur for me. Wish there was some way to make all the horrible memories and name calling and stunts vanish. Hypnotherapy. A magic pill. Years of speaking with a therapist helped, but it never made the memories disappear.

But all things happen for a reason.

If it weren't for those girls bullying me and the guys following their lead, I wouldn't be who I am now. Without their hurtful words and acts, I may not have thick skin. I may not be as bold and outspoken. Who knows… I could have ended up as some doormat.

There are no pros to bullying. No justifiable reasons to be hateful. But I found strength and courage and ferocity because of my high school experience. Yes, there were definitely some low points, but I had Mom and Dad to help me keep my head high. To not let me drown in the trenches. And for that, I am a new woman.

"One day, I hope it disappears for me too."

His back stiffens and eyes go wide. "I didn't mean it like that," he rushes out.

"Yeah, I know." He sags against the seat. "What I mean is, I hope enough time passes that I don't let those memories own me anymore." I lift the mug to my lips and sip. "What made you remember?"

"Shelly." I scrunch my brows and tilt my head. "My sister," he clarifies. "She was two years behind me, one behind you. She went to a different school, but her best friend, and mine, attended ours. And friends talk."

"Ah."

"Shelly, my friends, and I get together often. Gavin, my best friend, asked how work with *the blonde* was." I perk up at this. "They were in Roar a while back and noticed us barking at each other." He laughs and I join.

"Our bickering is an art form."

"Indeed. Anyway, I guess neither Cora nor Shelly had paid attention or were focused on the dance floor that night. They never saw your face. But when I said your first name the other night, they probed me for answers."

"That must've hurt." I smirk at him.

"Ha ha." He turns up the corner of his mouth and makes a goofy face. "Then, they took me on a trip down memory lane." His eyes drift to the table, then back up. "If it makes you feel better, it made me sick. Literally."

"It doesn't. But I'm glad you weren't okay with it. Says a lot."

"Peyton, I—"

The server interrupts Micah to set plates on the table. Once the buffet is spread out, the server double-checks the carafe, then leaves.

"Peyton, I may not be the best guy out there. I have done plenty of stupid and horrible shit. Shit I'm not proud of. Haven't we all. But adult me is disgusted by teenage me."

I break the egg yolk, spear some home fries and dunk them. Micah stares, fascination glittering his eyes as I bring the yolky potatoes to my lips.

"What?" I mumble around my food with zero care for manners.

"That's cute."

Cute? Eating food is cute? Or is he mocking how I eat now?

I grab a strip of bacon and crunch down on it. "Define cute."

He shakes his head with a laugh. "Don't know many other people who do that." He points his fork at my runny egg. "Break the over-easy yolk to dunk their potatoes."

"And toast," I interject.

His head tips back and he laughs before leveling with me again. "And toast." Inch by inch, he leans closer. Face over the center of the table. "Like me," he whispers.

I stop chewing. Stop breathing. My body frozen and eyes unblinking as I stare straight ahead. The gold flecks in his rich-blue eyes twinkle. Is he serious? Or just yanking my chain?

"Are you making fun of me?"

A shadow passes over the line of his jaw. His smile flattens out. But that damn twinkle is still there.

"No. Definitely not." The corners of his lips curve up. "Never again," he states with reverence.

The muscles in my jaw contract as I chew the remaining bacon. "Good." I point the last of the bacon strip at him. "Wouldn't want to hurt you." Then I shove the bacon in my mouth.

"Might like that," he mumbles and sits back.

I drop my focus to the table, pick up my toast and dunk the corner of the triangle in the yolk. Peeking through my lashes, I spy a look I have never seen on Micah Reed's face. A look I never thought him capable of portraying.

Less than three feet away, eyes on his plate, fingers toying with his fork, Micah Reed blushes. At this time of night, others may pass it off as a night of partying or too much alcohol. But the only thing he's had to drink tonight is Dr Pepper and coffee.

Since our food arrived, I noticed slight variations in Micah's posture. Less rigidity. His spine not as straight and arms not as stiff. The fidgeting has also tapered off. As if he carries a new level of comfort. With me.

Other hallmarks I notice… more softness. The ridge of his cheekbone and how it accentuates his masculinity. The plumpness of his lips and the way they transform when he looks me in the eye. Firmer edges. The angle of his jaw, the light dusting of stubble, and the straight line of his nose until just the end where it bends slightly left. A gentleness. The way his lashes splay and stick beneath his eyes when on the cusp of crying.

When was the last time I saw a man cry? Saw them spill their emotions for all to see. I don't recall.

Maybe when I was seven and fell from the tree in the backyard. When Dad rushed from the deck chair, cradled me gingerly in his arms, and asked if there was pain. Was he crying then? The memory is there, but I don't see his face as clearly as I once did. Not without photographs or home movies.

We finish eating in relative silence. But a new tension builds between me and Micah. A tension I never would have imagined possible with this man. A man who currently has one leg between mine while the other skirts the outside. He has yet to touch me, but I *feel* how close he is. All it would take is the slightest move from either of us and we'd make contact. And hell… my skin flames from the near touch.

The server clears our plates and leaves the check. And just like last time, Micah snatches it first. He throws me a boyish, flirty smile and I can't help but smile in return. Once he pays and I leave a tip on the table, we walk toward my car.

Near the hatch, I stop and face him, hands fidgeting with the hem of my shirt. Why does this suddenly feel like the end of a date? This isn't a date.

Keep telling yourself that, girl.

"Peyton…" Micah stares over my shoulder, but his eyes seem out of focus. Then he blinks and brings his gaze back to mine. "Hope you believed me earlier when I apologized. I meant it. I mean it."

I nod. "Thank you, Micah. And I do."

He takes a step closer. Close enough to touch me without effort. "And I hope you can forgive me. Don't expect you to right here and now. But one day. I'd like…"

His eyes drop to my lips and I lick them. He follows the movement but doesn't speak.

"What?" Bright eyes leap to mine. "What would you like?" My voice low and rumbly.

Hundreds of words and phrases flash in his eyes. Across his face. His lips part, he takes a breath then closes them. He does this again and again. Unspoken words on the tip of his tongue. Wanting. Waiting. Hopeful.

"It's been a long time since I've smiled and laughed this much." He nibbles his bottom lip, then swallows. "And I have zero expectations of anything." He shoves his hands in his pockets. "I'd like if we can be…"

If we can be what?

Why am I sweating so much? And in the most awkward places.

"If we can be…" I parrot his words and drag them out.

"Friends." Oh. Friends. Why was part of me hoping he would say something else? Jesus, he only just apologized. He notices my shift and jumps back in. "Unless you're not okay with that."

"No," I answer, too quick and rowdy. "Yes. Sorry." He laughs as I straighten out my thoughts. "Yes, we can be friends."

"Good." He takes another step closer. His eyes all I see now. And then he wraps his arms around me and presses me to his chest. "Really am sorry, Peyton."

My arms encircle his waist as I rest my chin on his shoulder. Do friends hug like this? Opposite-sex friends. Reese and I hug all the time. But Reese is more of a brother, someone I have been close with for decades, and someone I ask for advice. Micah is definitely not in the same spectrum as Reese.

His breath hot on my neck, I close my eyes. Then the breeze cools my cheeks and neck as Micah takes a step back.

"Drive safe, hellcat." Another step back and a wink. "See you tomorrow."

I lift a hand and wave. "Tomorrow."

In the car, I press the ignition, buckle my seat belt and stare out the windshield. The radio plays, but all I hear is white noise. The lights from the dash brighten the cab, but I zone out into the dark night.

Micah drives off and waves as he goes. I mimic the movement but don't focus. Not really.

Tonight, Micah Reed apologized. More than once. Then, just minutes ago, asked for my forgiveness. Said he wants to be friends. But his flirtatious behavior and his arms around me screamed much more than friendship. Those sweet smiles and warm touches and soft tones spoke volumes. Of what happens beyond friendship.

And that nickname. Hellcat. That is new. Well, he muttered it once before, but I don't think he meant for me to hear it.

Damn, am I confused. Thrown off. Flabbergasted.

"What the hell just happened?" The question of the hour. One I have no idea how to answer.

What the hell was I thinking? Hugging Peyton had not been part of the plan. Not by a long shot. But now that I had, I wanted to hug her again. And with more frequency.

God, she was so warm in my arms. So responsive. Her minty coconut smell, potent and intoxicating and addictive.

How long had I wanted to do that? Hold her in my arms. Inhale her fragrance. Be impossibly close to her. Can't recall a day since she started at Roar where Peyton hasn't crossed my mind. Her fiery spirit wouldn't let me forget.

But I wanted more. More than the borderline friendly hug we exchanged.

What I wouldn't give to trace the tip of my nose along the bridge of hers. Taste her plump lips and impassioned tongue. Feel her soft skin under my fingers, her hot breath on my neck. Her gasp at my ear. And those brilliant violet eyes… I want them on me. Everywhere.

"Hey, big brother."

I jolt on the barstool at the high-top table as Shelly rounds it and parks across the table. Judgment billows off her as she narrows her eyes.

"Hey," I choke out, then clear my throat.

"Everything alright?"

"Yeah. Of course," I answer too quickly. "Why?"

Eyes that match mine rake over my face. Study every crease, line, and twitch. Search for clues why I jumped at her presence—something I have never done. But my poker face is strong and she gives up sooner than expected.

She huffs, sets her purse down, and laces her fingers on the table between us. This is Shelly's way of telling me we aren't leaving this table until I speak the truth. *Great.*

"Micah, I have known you my entire life." *Here we go.* I roll my eyes. "Which means I pick up on everything. *Everything.*" Her added emphasis makes me squirm in place.

I shift my gaze to the parking lot through the window. Get momentarily lost as the sunlight gleams on the row of cars. When I look back to my sister, her brows lift and lips purse.

"Can we at least order lunch first?"

"Fine."

She snatches a menu from the metal clip on the table caddy. Not that she needs to read it. This bar and grill is a regular destination for our group. More during the evenings for karaoke, drinks, and laughter. But if I have more than half the menu memorized, she has the entire thing etched in stone. She, Cora, and Jonas ate here once or twice a week before Gavin moved back. Now, it's half that—which is still more often than my attendance.

A guy sporting a black polo with the bar logo sidles up to the table. He sets glasses of ice water in front of us. "Hey, Shelly."

The flush on my sister's cheeks poses new questions. "Hey, Tom."

He glances my way. "Micah." I give a polite smile and lift my chin. "What can I get you guys?"

Shelly and I place our orders. Tom scribbles them on his small notepad, tosses a stellar smile at Shelly, then walks off.

"What was that?" I gesture over my shoulder with a thumb.

With a slight shift to the left, she peers over my shoulder, then straightens. "Tom and I have gone on a couple of dates."

"Really?" I ask with humor in my tone.

She narrows her eyes and jabs the air with a finger in my direction. "Don't try to distract me from what's going on with you." I mentally sag but show no emotion. Both her forearms rest on the table as she leans closer. "What *is* happening, Micah?"

Sometimes, I wish I hated talking with my sister. Wish we weren't as close as we are. Don't get me wrong, I love Shelly. Would walk through fire for her. But when the more intimate topics come up—my dating life and hers—we both tend to clam up. There are just certain topics and details siblings shouldn't discuss. Right?

No matter how much I dance around answering her, she won't let up. Like when we were kids and she followed me on her bike. I had told her I wanted to play with boys my age, not my little annoying sister. But she never backed down. She pedaled faster. Kept pace with me. Told me boys and girls can play together. And her refusal to play with only girls led to us bonding more each year. If two years didn't separate us, people would swear we connected like twins.

Unwrapping the straw, I jab it between the ice and take a sip of water. Desperate to swallow past the nervous clump in my throat. This is Shelly. My sister. The one person I can spill all my truths to. She may be judgmental a moment, but once she processes, that harsh criticism falls away.

"I apologized."

She tilts her head and regards me for three, two, one. A light kicks on in her thoughts as her eyes grow wide. "To Peyton?" I nod and take another drink from the glass. "How'd that go?"

"Better than expected."

When I don't expand, she lifts a brow. "Elaborate for me, big brother."

Conversations with Shelly will never be basic. Will never be brief. We come from the same parents, were raised the exact same way, and will always want more details. To understand all the ins and outs in full description.

So, I lay it all out for Shelly. Tell her how I mulled over what to say all week. How I didn't say anything unnecessary to Peyton until last night. That I asked her to Teddy's after work—which piqued her interest and created a slight detour. A detour where I tell her we had gone there once already.

When I veer back to the original topic at hand, I explain how the apology went down. How I only remembered what happened all those years ago after talking with my sister and her friend. How my behavior made me physically ill.

"Shell, she accepted my apology with such grace. Made me feel worse."

Reaching across the table, her hands wrap around mine. "If you'd actually taken the time to know Peyton years ago, you would've learned then that she's pretty great. But everything happens for a reason. Cora said she kept to herself and had a small circle of friends. And that she was always with a tall guy with dark hair." I lift a brow and Shelly reads my curiosity. "Reese, I think. Her best friend. Anyway... my point is Peyton is kind and genuine. Your reaction is normal. That's called guilt, big brother. And feeling it, owning it, admitting it is a step in the right direction."

Is Reese the guy who occupied her attention in Roar last weekend?

The eight days since I watched Peyton smile and laugh with that guy feel more like months. Never-ending, nails-on-the-chalkboard months. I had never seen her so relaxed and carefree as I did that night. The way she leaned his direction. How easily she gave him the smile I wanted from her. Her comfort with another man made my skin crawl and blood pressure rise. Made my thoughts scatter like fall leaves on a windy day.

But if they were friends… well, that changes everything.

Did he come into Roar to intentionally provoke me? Was the idea hers or his? The answer makes all the difference. If it was his, I would venture to guess he was making a statement. Flaunting how incredible Peyton is and how easy it is to *not* have her. To say *see what I have and you don't, asshole.*

But… if it was Peyton's idea. That opens a whole new door.

If she asked her friend to fake flirt with her all night to piss me off, it says I cross her mind more than inside those four walls. That thought alone has my ego high above the powdery clouds.

Best not to get ahead of myself, though. Not without answers. Shelly is right. First, I need to absorb what my apology to Peyton means and where it leads us next.

"Have I told you lately how much I love you?"

She brings a finger to her lips and taps, eyes skyward to the left. "Hmm." Tap, tap, tap. "I'm drawing a blank, big brother. Better tell me again."

"You're ridiculous." I ball up my straw wrapper and fling it at her. "But you know I love you."

Her mouth drops open as she picks up the offending paper projectile and launches it back at me. "Love you, too."

Just then, Tom reappears with burgers and fries. His eyes dart between us and he sets our plates down with too much ease. Soon as his hands are free, he shoves them in his back pockets and gives Shelly a sheepish smile.

"Anything else I can get you?" His voice shakes.

"I'm good." Shelly smiles at him, then looks to me. "Need anything, brother?" The word brother leaves her lips louder than the rest.

Does this guy think Shelly is on a date with me? By definition, this is a date. Between two siblings. Zero romanticism going on here. But the fact she needed to clarify who I was says this guy is not only insecure, but has no clue who I am to Shelly. Yes, he knew my name because I frequent the place. But his knowledge doesn't extend much further.

When his shoulders drop and eyes land on me, he appears less concerned. I may not be of romantic interest for my sister, but *who* I am should bother him. Shelly is my baby sister. Which makes me her overprotective, overbearing big brother. That should make him shake in his Nikes, not sigh in relief.

So, I pull an asshole move. Because that is what big brothers are for.

"Thought I asked for a side of barbeque." Tom's brows pinch in the middle and Shelly huffs.

Tom goes from at ease to freaked out in point five seconds. "Shoot. Sorry, man. I'll go grab that." He scurries off to the kitchen without another word.

The moment he's out of earshot, I laugh. Shelly throws a fry at my face and I dodge it. "Not funny, asshole." I laugh harder. "And you didn't ask for a side of anything. Why are you being a dick?"

I pick up the fry she hurled and toss it in my mouth. "Because that's what big brothers do."

Tom rematerializes and deposits a full dipping cup of barbeque sauce on the table. "Sorry again. Anything else?" I bite my tongue at his shortness of breath.

"We're good. Thanks, Tom," Shelly answers. The guy flashes her an award-winning smile then leaves us to our lunch.

"What's going on with you and him?"

Rather than answer me, she scoops up her burger and takes the biggest bite possible. She did this to avoid speaking for the next however many minutes, but I pick at my fries and wait for her to finish chewing. Once she swallows down the last of it, she takes a sip of water and pretends I'm not waiting on her answer.

"Shell?"

She shakes her head. "Ugh. Why can't you just move past this?"

"Because I'm your brother. Why do you want me to?" If that guy so much as laid a hand on her without permission, I will kick his ass.

"No reason." She sighs and hangs her head. "Tom is nice. Like I said, we've been on a couple dates." Picking up a fry from her plate, she swirls it in the ketchup over and over.

"But…" I drawl out the word. "Has he… done something you're uncomfortable with?"

Twin eyes bolt to mine. Her head shakes furiously. "No. No, Micah." She drops the fry and wipes her hands with the napkin. "He's actually been sweet. Never makes me feel pressured."

"Good. 'Cause I'd kick his ass."

"I don't know. It's just…" She trails off and I give her a moment to collect her thoughts. "Have you talked to Mom in the last week?"

I search my memory for the last time I spoke with either of our parents. Last I remember was a few weeks back. "No. Why?"

"Well, she called me a couple nights ago. Said she'd call you, too. Anyway, she wants to start regular family dinners. Like scheduled dinners once a month or every two weeks. I don't remember the specifics."

"Okay… is that a bad thing?"

Shelly speaks with and sees Mom and Dad more often than I do. But I don't see anything wrong with spending more time with them. Maybe I am missing something.

"Normally, I'd say no. But Mom started dropping hints."

"Dropping hints?"

"*Shelly, your father and I aren't getting any younger.*" She mocks our mother's voice. "*Would love to have more Reeds to love.*"

"What?" Not sure if Mom is insinuating what I think she is, but I sure as hell hope not.

"Yep." She pops the *p*. "Mom basically told me she wants grandbabies. Seeing as neither of us is in a relationship" —her eyes dart across the bar to where I assume Tom stands— "that's not happening anytime soon."

"Are you not in a relationship with Tom?" I whisper-ask, unsure of his presence.

A huff leaves her lips. "He's nice. Treats me well. And I can tell he wants more." She looks over my shoulder again. "But I don't."

"Then you need to end it. Don't drag it out. It'll just make it worse."

"Yeah, I know." She stares down at her plate and shoves a fry in her mouth. "After that talk with Mom, it got me thinking." She peers up and winces. "Please don't be weirded out."

I place a hand over my heart. "Promise I won't be."

Shelly takes a deep breath, places her palms flat on the table, and looks me in the eye. Her lips twitch every other second as her eyes dart between mine. I have never seen her like this. Concerned about sharing her feelings.

"Micah, I haven't…" She takes another deep breath as I wait patiently for her to finish in her own time. "I haven't been with… anyone."

Setting down my burger, I tilt my head and study her expression. The way she bites her lip to stop the occasional twitch. How her eyes dance around the room every few seconds to be sure no one eavesdrops on our conversation. And how she keeps stretching out her fingers, then balls them again. Her actions have me on edge.

Is she still a virgin? Not that I ever want to imagine my baby sister with any man, but how? How is it possible my thirty-year-old sister is still a virgin?

"Ever?"

She shakes her head. "Hasn't felt right."

Before this conversation, there's no question I classified myself as a whore. Now… is there such a thing as a mega-whore?

Shelly has had zero sex. None. I, on the other hand, have lost track of how many women I have bedded. Hell, it's only the beginning of May and I have gone home with more than a dozen women this year.

"Not sure what to say, Shell. But don't let Mom's need for grandchildren pressure you into something you don't want." I toss a quick thumb over my shoulder. "If you don't want to be with him, cut it off. When the right guy comes along, you'll know it. You'll feel it. And if you don't want kids, there is nothing wrong with that. That's your choice to make. Happy, romantic relationships don't always equal marriage and children."

"Do you want kids?"

Do I? At some point, when things were good between me and Rochelle, I considered the idea. But Rochelle was past the safe age of bearing children and I dismissed it. Would I give it more thought now? Couldn't be sure. With the right person, anything is possible. But I don't dream of picket fences and children's laughter. Not like some people do.

I shrug. "Not sure. Haven't put much thought into it."

"I don't think I do." She shoves another fry in her mouth.

Reaching across the table, I take her hand. We hold each other's gaze a beat. "Then do what makes you happy, little sis."

We finish lunch and pay. Shelly waves bye to Tom and we go separate ways in the lot after a hug and promise to see each other Sunday. On the way home, I replay our lunch together. My confession and Shelly's. And the fact our mother is practically guilting us to fulfill her own desires. Something I will chat about with Mom soon. Need to nip that in the bud.

Difficult enough to find a partner you love and trust. Going balls to the wall with commitment plus family is a whole other realm. One I am not ready for.

~

Sean texted when I got home from lunch with Shelly and asked everyone to come in early for a staff meeting. No details, just a *be here an hour early*. So, here I am. In the office. Waiting to hear what is going on.

Peyton shuffles past the office. I jump up from the chair, jog out, and call her name. She stops and assaults me with a smile. *Damn.*

"Hey," she says.

"Hey, yourself. Sorry you had to come in early."

Her shoulders bounce up a beat as she gives me a lopsided smile. "No worries. It happens every now and again."

We take a seat at the same table after greeting a few others. Ani and Sean walk in soon thereafter and the room goes quiet. Too quiet. My knee bounces beneath the table and I mentally yell at myself to stop.

"Thanks, everyone, for coming in early," Ani announces, with Sean at her side. "Wanted to touch base with everyone. Maybe start having staff meetings similar to this once a quarter, so we're all abreast of how things are going." Unscrewing the cap, Ani drinks from a bottled water then continues. "Foot traffic and sales have been on the rise since last quarter. And we're looking into ways to keep the momentum going."

Shit. I was supposed to search ideas for the slower nights and send them to Ani. A task I started but never finished. That is priority number one as of now.

"That being said," Ani continues. "Sean and I will be looking at staff changes." Several sets of eyes go wide. "Sorry, let me clarify. We will be adding more staff. So, if you know anyone in need of a job who would be a great addition to the family, pass along the news."

For the next fifteen minutes, Ani carries on with sales numbers and I tune her out. I see the sales numbers for Roar on a nightly basis. Business has been on the rise. Not sure if the themed nights are a hit or if the new apartment complex blocks away has brought more foot traffic. Either way, the influx in business is a good thing.

Out of the corner of my eye, I spy how attentive Peyton is of Ani. How she hangs on her every word. Glued to sales totals from the fourth and first quarters. Giving a nod when Ani mentions the uptick in patron count. Or a subtle smile when Ani looks her way.

Peyton seems more invested than a typical bartender. While most of the staff zones out, she zeros in. This minor detail makes me question Peyton and Ani's relationship, and what her attentiveness means.

What am I missing here?

sixteen

"Let's end this quarter with a bang," Ani cheers as she wraps up the meeting. Then she claps her hands and everyone parts like the perfect comb over.

Those who aren't working tonight share hugs or goodbyes before heading out the back. The rest of us shuffle off to our designated areas to prep for another busy night. Just as I remove fruit from storage to slice and add to the condiment trays, Ani sidles up to me.

"Before you get bogged down, let's chat."

I nod, set the fruit down, and wipe my hands clean. Ani leads me around the bar and toward the hall. As we pass Micah and Sean, I don't miss the way Micah follows us with his eyes. *Great*, something else I will need to handle. Micah's curiosity.

In the office, Ani closes and locks the door. She ambles to the couch, lowers herself onto the worn leather and gestures for me to do the same. Without hesitation, I join her.

"Been a little bit since we last chatted. How are you?"

I sink into the cool leather more, rotate to face her, and tuck a foot under my bottom. "Oh, you know. Much the same."

"And Micah?"

My head teeters left, then right. "That has improved. Surprisingly."

Ani rubs her hands together in front of her mouth. "Do tell."

I wouldn't say Ani and I go way back. But we have known each other coming up on seven years. We met three years after my father died. At the time, my mother still suffered severe depression and was having trouble making ends meet. I still lived at home when Dad passed and refused to let my mother live alone. So, I stayed, stepped up and got another job when one wouldn't cut it.

That is how Ani and I met.

During the day, I scanned groceries at the local supermarket. The job was dull and monotonous, but it paid a decent wage and provided benefits. I met plenty of interesting and odd people, drummed up conversations about random items they purchased and smiled until my cheeks burned.

Ani came through my checkout line with a barrage of alcohol. Red and white wine, tequila, whiskey, vodka. You name it, she placed it on the belt. Along with soda and fruity concoctions. Beep after beep, I stared down at each bottle and assumed this woman was throwing one hell of a party. I'd asked, *"Where's the party. I'd love to tag along."*

It had been a joke. Something to make my customer laugh. A way to spark conversation. But Ani jumped on board and invited me to her place. At the time, she and Sean were engaged. The wedding a couple months out. They'd met late in life. Both established in running their own business. Both ambitious. They also fell instantly and madly in love.

In their lavish home, we partied and laughed and I made them the grossest mixed drinks ever. We laughed harder. Ani said she and Sean were thinking of buying a bar and that I should work for her. She'd train me, of course. The job sounded fun at the time, but I was worried about leaving Mom home alone.

So, I got a second job at a fast-food place on my days off from the supermarket. Ani and I still kept in touch. Text messages. Random girly days at the salon. The occasional trip to the beach.

As time moved on, Mom got better. She also met Harold. Once I knew she was happy, I moved on too. Moved out of my childhood home and rented an apartment with Reese. It felt amazing to finally be on my own. To be my own woman.

Time after time, Ani begged me to come work for her. Told me all the lavish details when she and Sean bought the club in Tampa five years ago. It wasn't in the best part of town, but it wasn't horrendous either. And the neighborhood was cleaning up. The club was always busy and they saw larger profits each year.

When she begged me again, just over a year ago, I caved. I had never seen her so giddy.

My first night working, the first time I laid eyes on Micah since high school, I spilled our shared history with Ani. From day one, she has known it all.

"He apologized."

Her jaw drops as she smacks the air between us. "Shut up. Are you serious right now?"

"Wouldn't joke about it."

"How did that come about?" I recount the story as she sits back and stares at me in awe. "Who knew? Don't get me wrong, I was hopeful things would get better soon."

"Me, too. I've about had it with his constant antagonizing bullshit."

She reaches across the space and pats my forearm a minute. "You know I love catching up, but we should talk business too. For at least one minute."

I roll my eyes. "Always such a party pooper," I tease.

"Never," she gasps. "I'll address that later. Did you come up with any ideas for Mondays and Tuesdays?"

"Yes." I inch closer and share a list of ideas that may drum up more business for the slower nights.

Ani leans an arm against the back of the couch. A hand at her chin and forefinger over her lip. Her attention focuses solely on me while I talk animatedly. Ani is my friend first and boss second. Which may be one of the reasons she values my opinion more. Years ago, she met *me*. Got to know and bonded with me before business was added in the mix. When she asks my opinion, it isn't only a business transaction. She *wants* and values my input.

Ideas fly from my lips. Charity bingo nights. Karaoke. Bar Olympics. Trivia nights. Plenty of bars do these things. Some nearby, others across the Bay. But we have the space to accommodate more bodies. Yes, we may need to invest in more tables, chairs and equipment. But the profit some of those nights would bring to Roar is endless.

Most bars offer food. Roar does not. But I toss out the idea of offering small options. Food that doesn't require a kitchen. Either that or connect with local businesses and have them serve or cater food. They pay a fee to set up and split their profits between them, Roar and the charity if we chose to offer bingo.

Of course, drinks would be offered. Maybe special drinks for different nights at a different price point. Again, splitting profit with charity.

When I finish, Ani claps her hands and presses them to her lips. "I love this, Peyton. Thank you. When I'm back at my computer, I'll mull over what days will work best for each. Make some calls and create a marketing plan." She reaches forward and takes both my hands in hers. "Still on board with—"

A knock at the door cuts her off and I nod in answer. "Yes," I say as the door handle clicks, but doesn't open.

Ani rises from the couch. Her heels clap against the concrete as she nears the door. Lock disengaged, she twists the knob and opens the door. From my seat on the couch, I spot half of Micah past Ani's petite stature.

Once, twice, thrice, his eyes dart between me and Ani. Brows pinched and eyes narrowed. Countless questions written on the lines of his face. Questions he will surely ask once Ani leaves. Questions I need to avoid answering until Ani gives me the go-ahead.

Hello, awkward party of one. Especially since Micah and I are trying to heal our past.

"Hey, Ani. Just wanted to let Peyton know I did most of her prep, but there's some left before open." Dark-blue eyes glimmer at me across the room.

With a shake of her wrist, Ani glances down at her diamond-encrusted rose gold watch that cost more than my monthly rent. "Shit, Peyton. Sorry. Didn't mean to keep you so long."

I have never been envious or bitter toward Ani and Sean and their obvious wealth. Simple things make me smile. Not to say I haven't wondered what it would be like to live a lavish lifestyle. Would my purchase habits change? I'd like to believe the change would be subtle. That I would maintain my same style, just purchase better quality items.

I rise from my spot on the couch and walk to the door. I rest a hand on Ani's shoulder and turn my attention to Micah. "No worries. I'll head out."

Squeezing between Ani and Micah, I head down the hall and out to the bar. A moment later, Micah strolls out with Ani on his heels. She looks my way and winks. Micah doesn't miss the interaction. His brow twitches before he joins Sean and Ani. They chat another minute before Ani shoulders her purse and hooks herself on Sean's arm.

She guides him over to the bar and they both say goodbye before leaving through the back door.

Micah's eyes burn my profile, but I don't spare a glance in his direction. Now is not the time to answer all his questions. Ani and I agreed not to share what's coming until she and Sean are ready.

I finish prepping the bar. Cut the last of the fruit, fill condiment bins and stash the extras in the fridge beneath the bar. All the while, Micah leans his hip against the counter and watches me like a predator.

Neither of us says a word. A battle of wills. But my will is stronger. And he will cave long before me.

"Whatever," he grumbles and pushes off the counter. He stomps across the club and checks in with everyone working tonight before unlocking the doors.

The doors open and the masses flood the bar within minutes. Worries of Micah giving me the death stare for the next seven hours vanish. One after another, I focus on the crowd. On pouring shots of whiskey and tequila. Filling mugs from the keg taps. Mixing fruity froufrou drinks and blending daiquiris. Spreading smiles and jokes and laughter.

At some point, I sense Micah behind the bar. I keep my eyes on the task at hand, but catch him out of the corner of my eye. He slings drinks on pace with me. Muscles stretch his black button-down taut while he works. Forearms and biceps flex as he shakes and pours martinis. Jaw more defined by the light layer of stubble and his occasional smile. And every once in a while, he dances to the music while working.

I hate and love how I notice him now.

Before our first night at Teddy's, I was aware of Micah. Knew where he was—to avoid him. Didn't seek him out, but stayed attune to his whereabouts. Of when he walked the floor or stepped behind the bar.

Now, I am much more cognizant.

Years ago, I saw Micah with rose-colored glasses. Dreamed of a boy my mind construed as appealing. Soft hair, long muscular legs, strong arms, and stare-at-them-all-day eyes.

Although he still acts immature, Micah is very much a man. A man my eyes refuse to shift away from. A man I notice now more than I care to admit aloud.

The way his slacks hug his long, thick, muscular legs and rest low on his hips. How his broad chest tugs at his shirt when he stretches or reaches certain directions. The flex of his forearms that makes me bite my lower lip. Far too often, my eyes trail up the exposed skin of his neck. From the hollow of his throat, up over his Adam's apple, to the sharp line of his jaw. From there, his lips garner my attention. Pink and plump and soft looking.

Fingers snap in front of my face. I blink and look to my right.

"Sorry, what?"

Two striking blue irises search my face. "I called your name three times."

"You did?" Someone needs to slap me from my damn daydreams.

"Yeah." He steps closer. Close enough for me to smell his sweet, woodsy amber cologne. Close enough for me to identify the gold flecks in his eyes like stars in the night sky. "Everything okay?" His eyes dart between mine, on the hunt for answers.

I don't trust my voice or my words right now. So, eyes locked on his, I nod. In my periphery, his hand twitches at his side. Balls into a loose fist, then flattens out. Inches forward, then lands back at his side.

He licks, then captures his lower lip before setting it free. "You sure?" He inches closer. So very close. My breasts centimeters from grazing his chest.

Heat slicks my skin. My pulse hammers in my ears as my breath comes in short, shallow bursts. He licks his lips again and my eyes drop to witness the action. I swallow and mentally whimper. My tongue eager to taste him.

"Yep," I choke out, then clear my throat. "Everything's fine." My voice cracks on the last word like a pubescent boy. *Great.* 'Cause that will convince him.

"If Ani gave you a hard time earlier" —he jerks his thumb toward the office— "I'll speak with her."

I shake my head. "Not necessary. We were just catching up."

His brows pinch. "Catching up?"

"Mmhm. Girl talk."

Micah steps back and goose bumps prickle my skin. He squints but relaxes his eyes just as quick. Then he throws me a smile. Not the one that makes me want a second helping. But the one painted in hard lines and artifice and bullshit. Before I say another word, he shifts his gaze elsewhere and walks off.

Tempting as it is to rake my eyes over Micah's broad shoulders and ample ass, now is not the time. Instead, I focus on the actual retreat. On the tension in his shoulders. The hand rubbing at the back of his neck. The rush in his stride and flat expression on his face when I glimpse his profile once more.

He weaves between the tables and heads for the outskirts of the room. At the wall, he glances back to the bar and sees me staring after him. He crosses his arms and widens his stance. His body stiffens. Lips form a flat, tight line. Then he simply shakes his head.

One, two, three breaths. His eyes hold mine captive. My thoughts a prisoner to him. Until he breaks contact, mouths what looks like *whatever,* and gets lost in the crowd.

Just as things were on the upswing with Micah, I ripped it to shreds. "Whatever," I mumble to myself. Soon, it all changes anyway. Best to keep things as they have been. With Micah at a distance.

seventeen

MICAH

Fourteen days have passed since the meeting at Roar. Fourteen days since I knocked on the office door and waited for Ani to unlock it. Fourteen long-as-hell days since I asked Peyton what she and Ani were discussing in the office. And nearly just as long since she gave me some bullshit answer.

An answer I have done my best to ignore and move past. An answer my gut tells me isn't all lies. But it isn't all truth either.

Peyton and I, since the night before the meeting, aren't the same people. As individuals or within feet of each other.

For more than a year, Peyton was at my throat. A lioness out for blood. Claws extended and ready to attack. She did her best to ignore my advances, but I never backed down. Never cowered under her snarl.

Now, she teases me. Eggs me on with her smart mouth and mischievous smile. Has switched from calling me Micky—*thank god*—to starlight. Which isn't any better, but sounds less creepy.

And I have taken the liberty of calling her hellcat—a name I reserved for when I was alone with my fist and thoughts—more openly.

But fourteen days ago, some other force in the universe shifted. Made Peyton look at and talk with me in a way unlike our previous interactions. Yes, she still has that feisty edge I live for. But now, it has softer edges. And not knowing if Ani is the reason behind the change irks me.

At the end of the bar, Peyton delivers two beers and two fingers of whiskey in a tumbler. A man with dark hair and a protruding belly hands her a bill, flashes a toothy smile, then walks off with the drinks. The moment he disappears, she spins and catches my eyes on her.

In one, two, three strides, Peyton stands less than five feet away. "You looking at my ass, starlight?"

The corner of my mouth curves up and I waggle my brows. "What's it to you, hellcat?"

She steps closer. So close her breasts brush the starched cotton of my button-down. "Maybe I don't want your eyes on my ass."

"No?" She slowly shakes her head. "Then where *do* you want them?"

A millimeter at a time, her lips form a wicked smile. "Get more creative."

I press us impossibly closer. Her breasts flatten against my pecs. One of my legs between hers. Lips a breath apart. *Fuck.* In one move, my lips would crush hers. But damn if the foreplay doesn't turn me on.

"Creative, huh?"

She hums and the vibrations ripple through my chest, my abdomen, my balls. "Yes, creative." Her breath hot and damp on my lips.

Jesus fuck.

I lick my lips—almost lick hers—then unwillingly inch back. "I'll work on that."

She turns to the register, rings up the drinks, cashes the tab out and puts the excess in the tip jar. "Good. Creativity is the spice of life." She winks, then sashays down the bar alley to the next waiting customer.

Screwed. One word and the definition of my current existence. But I wouldn't want it any other way.

The rest of the night goes much the same. We work and tease and laugh. She provokes and bats her lashes with a wicked smile on her lips. Bets me she mixes and serves better drinks. Draws attention from the crowd as she challenges me to a face-off. My hesitation widens her smile and she pushes harder.

"What's the matter?" She leans in, her breath hot on my ear. Her sweet scent in my nose. "Afraid to lose?"

I lean away, lock on to her radiant violet irises and shake my head. "What do I get when I win?"

"Ooh, confident." Her eyes drop to my lips and I stop breathing. "Who says you'll win?"

"Can't deny facts." I lick my lips and her eyes follow the movement. Her breathing hiccups once. But once is more than enough.

"We'll see." She spins to face the crowd. "Ladies and gentlemen," she shouts with hands in the air. "Can I have your attention?" Everyone within earshot faces the bar and falls quiet. "Boss man and I are having a little showdown." The crowd hoots and hollers and whistles. "He says his drinks are better than mine," she yells. Men boo at this and she laughs. "So, I challenged him to a duel of sorts. Who wants to be the judge?"

Cheers erupt from the crowd and three people slap a twenty on the bar top.

I sidle up to her, my hand brushing hers. "Three people, three different drinks."

"Agreed."

Over the next few minutes, we decide on rules for the challenge. One—the customer selects their preferred drink. But it cannot be premade or from the tap. Two—they don't watch us make or serve the drinks. They will be blindfolded. Three—they will blind taste test the drinks and choose the winner before removing the blindfold and meeting the maker. Four—best two out of three wins.

The three people shuffle up to the bar and take a seat as the crowd steps back. Becky and Jake—two of the servers—step up between them. After the rules are explained, makeshift blindfolds made from Roar tank tops are put in place.

Contestant one requests a mojito. Peyton and I dive for shakers and get to work.

I pinch a cluster of mint leaves from the bin, toss them in the shaker and muddle them with a pestle. Then I measure rum and lime juice before pouring it in. I glance over and spot Peyton adding fresh lime and crushing it with the mint. *Fuck.* Should have used fresh. No going back now.

Simple syrup and ice go in next. I cap the shaker and make a show of blending the ingredients. Several shakes later, I swap the cap for the strainer and pour the drink in a glass, adding a splash of soda water. I place the drink on the bar and Becky helps the first contestant find the glass.

As I rinse the shaker, I peer over at Peyton. She pours her drink, unstrained into a glass, adds soda water and garnishes it with sugar crystals and a mint leaf. Good thing these people aren't basing the winner off of appearances, because mine is nowhere near as fancy as Peyton's liquid art.

The man sips mine. Swishes it around in his mouth. Lets it sit on his tongue a moment. Then swallows. He asks for water, takes a sip, then moves to Peyton's drink. Follows the same taste test routine. And then, silence. After seconds that mirror hours, he raises an arm for the drink he preferred.

Peyton. "Damn it," I mutter under my breath.

The crowd roars as the man removes his blindfold. While we move on to the next contestant, the man throws Peyton a wink and sips his mojitos.

Contestant two orders Sex on the Beach. I bite my cheek to restrain the dirty joke on the tip of my tongue.

We both grab high ball glasses and get to work. This go-around Peyton measures with a jigger. And I don't measure at all. I have made Sex on the Beach thousands of times over the years. Enough to know how much to add without measuring. Enough trial and error to know women suck it down and request another.

Cranberry and orange juice, vodka and peach schnapps, a small scoop of ice and an orange slice and cherry to garnish. Peyton and I add straws and stir at the same time and deposit the drinks in front of the woman. Jake guides her to the glasses and she tastes each one.

Without hesitation, her hand flies up and declares me the winner. Like a child, I stick my tongue out at Peyton and she mocks me in return.

We step over to the last contestant. A lumberjack of a man—inches taller than me, thick beard and more muscle than necessary. His appearance intimidates me. Thankfully, this is all about the drinks.

"White Russian," he announces after Becky taps his shoulder.

A simple drink. Also a drink that is easy to fuck up if not measured correctly. Of course, the drink with fewer ingredients makes me sweat the most.

While Peyton grabs the vodka and coffee liqueur, I fetch the cream from the fridge. I measure out the vodka while she measures the liqueur. Then we swap. I let her add the cream to hers first, then pour it in mine as she hands over her drink.

Cream swirls like storm clouds as it blends with the alcohol. The man stirs the drink, then lifts it to his lips and tastes. Every person within ten feet of the show-down remains deathly quiet. He sets the glass down and repeats the process with mine. His poker face as hard and unforgiving as stone. Then he tastes them both again.

Dampness coats my skin and stains the armpits of my shirt. My palms clench and unclench as if the muscles glitch. My foot bounces and knee taps the cabinet beneath the bar.

Why the hell does the outcome have me on the edge of a cliff?

I peek over at Peyton and see her biting her lower lip. Watch her pick at the bottom hem of her shirt. When she notices me checking her out, she throws me a half smile.

Her apprehension is cute as fuck.

The bar erupts in cheers and I shift my eyes back to lumberjack man. Who has a hand in the air. The hand that says I just fucking won.

"Hell yes!" I shout as Peyton pushes her lower lip out to pout. And fuck if I don't want to suck on her lip.

"What's my punishment?" she asks as we clean up and business returns to normal.

My bicep grazes hers as we clean glasses and I freeze. Heat starts as a low simmer at my elbow and burns hotter as it nears my chest. A peek down at her still hands tells me she feels it, too.

"Have to think on it," I rasp out. "I'll let you know before we leave." Once everything from the *Micah makes the best drinks* contest is cleaned up, I dry my hands. "Going to do paperwork," I tell her, then walk on uneven legs to the office.

Behind the closed door, I adjust myself and groan as I sit. The worn, stiff chair does me no favors as I shift to find a more comfortable position. Damn, I was on edge. Her pouty lips and punishment inquiry… my dick grew ridiculously painful beneath the zipper.

I close my eyes and her face pops up behind my lids. The occasional flyaway lock of blonde hair on her cheek. How her violet irises glow when she gets excited and the gray flecks enhance the darker rim. Her not too thin, not too thick button nose. And her perfect fucking lips. So pink and fleshy and suckable.

My eyes fly open as I curse and adjust myself. Again.

I wiggle the mouse to wake the computer and open the invoice spreadsheet. Dragging the wire basket across the desk, I get to work plugging numbers and updating inventory. Spreadsheets… a surefire way to kill arousal.

Peyton enters the office as I pick up the last invoice. "Last call," she informs me.

My eyes dart to the upper right of the screen and note the time. Almost two in the morning. "Well, shit."

She laughs. "Time flies when you're having fun."

I wave an invoice in the air. "Were you a math nerd?" Only numbers people get excited over this kind of stuff. Not that I failed math, but when they added letters with the numbers to equations, I questioned everything.

"Wouldn't say *nerd*. But me and numbers are good friends."

She spins and starts for the hall. "Peyton."

"Yeah?" She eyes me over her shoulder.

"Hang out with me tomorrow."

"Sorry, what?" She backtracks and faces me again.

"Call it your punishment. Hang out with me." A wince stretches her lips. "My friends will be there. And my sister."

"Uh…" Her eyes dart around the room a moment then land on mine. "That sounds…"

"Fun?"

"Actually, I was going to say awkward."

I raise my right hand, then lay it over my heart. "Swear it won't be."

"Says the man who knows everyone attending."

"Cora remembers you. And by proxy, Shelly."

"No, they remember high school Peyton. The loner girl who preferred dark spaces and hidden alcoves."

"Don't you still?" I tease.

"Shut the hell up." I laugh. "Micah, we've hung out a couple times. Yes, things are less shitty between us now." I wipe away a nonexistent tear and she flips me the middle finger. *You wish.* "But I don't think we've reached the 'let's hang out with other people together' phase of our friendship yet."

"At least you admit our friendship." She rolls her eyes. "C'mon. Please?" I exaggerate my plea and aim for my best sad-puppy expression.

A groan rumbles in her chest and spills from her lips. "You are so annoying."

"Before the contest, you agreed to winner's choice," I remind her with a smirk.

"True. But I didn't think it would be you forcing me to hang out with you and a group of people I don't know." I give her a look that says, *really?* She narrows her eyes as she tries—and fails—to give me her most menacing expression. "What?"

"Don't you pretty much do that every night we work?"

Once again, she presents me with her middle finger. "It's different and you know it."

"Please, Peyton," I say, softer this time. "Promise not to make it weird."

Peyton hangs her head. She stares at the floor and taps her thigh with her fingers. When she lifts her head, the look in her eyes stops my heart. Veiny damp eyes stare back. Her chin wobbles as she clamps down on her lower lip.

The chair legs scrape the concrete floor as I bolt up and dash over to her. I halt in front of her, desperate to frame her face in my hands and soothe her. But I don't know if she will shirk my touch. Only one way to find out.

One at a time, and with slow precision, I bring my hands to her face. She doesn't shy away from my touch and that small action has my heart galloping in wide-open pastures.

"Hey." I tip her head little by little until our eyes meet. "It'll be okay."

"You can't know that."

"I'll make sure of it," I vow.

"I-I just can't…" She swallows and gathers her thoughts. One deep breath, then another. "I just can't go through that again." She holds my gaze. "How people were all those years ago."

"You won't. I promise." Fuck, I want to kiss her. Seal my words with our joined lips.

She nods. "Okay. But if shit goes south" —she gestures between us— "this is done."

"Then nothing will go wrong." She takes another deep breath and I reluctantly release her. "Give me your number and I'll text you the address and time."

This snaps her back to reality. "You want my phone number?"

"Yes," I drawl out. "To text you the info. And in case you get lost, you have my number."

That sounded like a legit reason to ask Peyton for her number. Right? Not that I couldn't get it from the employee contact list. But I'm not that much of a dick.

"Fine," she huffs out. I hand her my phone and she texts herself from my phone. When she hands it back to me, I read the screen.

Starlight 😏

"Couldn't resist?"

"Nope." She starts for the door again. "Need to go finish up. See you tomorrow."

Sunday. "Tomorrow," I parrot.

∼

"You did what?" Shelly shouts in my ear. I yank the phone away and rub my ear.

"Shell," I drag out her name with a groan. "It's too early to yell."

"I don't care," she yells louder. Thank fuck the phone is still a good six inches from my face. "When you text your sister that you invited Peyton Alexander to our Sunday night get-together, what did you think would happen?"

"Maybe that you'd text me back with shouty capitals. You know I work until three in the morning. Cut me some slack."

She laughs some twisted, maniacal sound. "You want *me* to cut *you* some slack?"

"Please." I bring the phone closer, hopeful she got all the yelling out of her system.

"Micah…" she huffs and I picture her eyes rolling. "What possessed you to invite her?"

A question worth asking since Peyton and I don't have stellar history. But we decided to be adults. I extended my long overdue apology for labeling and shunning her during high school. For intentionally getting under her skin at work. For every single pain she endured with the ripple effect of my words.

More than anything, I hold immense gratitude for Peyton.

Peyton didn't have to accept my apology. But she did. She didn't have to agree to Teddy's the first or second time. But she did. She rose above and acted more mature than most. We aren't children anymore, but plenty of people our age refuse to grow up. Thankfully, that doesn't apply to us.

"Shell, please don't make this weird."

"It is weird. You don't agree?"

"I don't," I say with an air of confidence. "Was I an asshole to her more often than not? Yes. But we talked it out. Laid everything on the table. I apologized, Shell. And she has slowly let me in. We're friends." Although, I hope to one day be more than friends with Peyton. After wrapping my arms around her, after inhaling her sweet scent up close, I want so much more.

For now, though, I plan to keep that secret locked up tight.

"I just… how?"

"It's not something I question. She's willing to give me another chance. Willing to be friends. And if it doesn't work out, then it ends." I refuse to fuck up with Peyton again. Refuse to not have her in my world.

"It's still weird."

"Only if you make it that way." I take a deep breath, then rest my forearm over my eyes. "Both of us are trying. Can you do the same? Maybe let Cora and Gavin know too. They're the only other people in our circle that know her."

The line goes quiet. Too quiet. I lift my arm and pull the phone away to see if the call dropped. Nope. Just my sister in her head. And for someone who preaches love and fate and all that cosmic mumbo jumbo, she fights my friendship with Peyton hard.

But I give her a moment. To gather her thoughts and formulate her words. To swallow down reality and move forward with a smile on her cute face.

"Fine," she huffs out. "I'll talk to Cora and Gavin. But I make no promises on how they'll behave."

"You're my favorite sister."

"I'm your only sister, dumbass."

"Which is why you're my favorite." She growls on the other end. "Love you, Shell."

"Guess I love you, too."

The call disconnects and I toss my phone on the comforter. I roll over, bury my face in the pillow and groan.

When I asked Peyton to hang out tonight, I didn't realize I would have so much prep work. To tame my sister and spread the word to the other two people who knew Peyton. To ask them to be cordial and *normal*. But I should have expected it.

Bringing new people into our circle is a big deal. And not something we do often. But the invitation has already been delivered and accepted. Now, I need to do my part. I need to make sure tonight feels like every other Sunday. Just friends hanging out and enjoying life.

'Cause that is all Peyton is… my friend.

I fling a shirt across the room and Reese laughs. "Not helping," I say as I poke my head out of the closet.

Reese lays across my bed, feet dangling off the side, and holds up the most recent flying article between his thumb and forefinger. Then proceeds to twirl it like a lasso. Definitely not helping.

"I have never seen you so nervous about hanging out with a *friend*?"

I storm out of the closet, stomp across the lush carpet and stop in front of him. Hands on my hips, I pin him with what feels like my *shut up* glare. And what does he do? He laughs harder.

I snatch the shirt from his hand. "And I've never seen you be such a jerk. But here we are."

"Ouch." He sits up and presses a hand to his heart. "You wound me."

"No." I smack his bicep and a hiss leaves his lips. "But now I have."

He rubs the red palm print on his arm and inspects it far too long. "That really hurt."

"Then I hope you never get into any physical altercations." I riffle through the shirts on the bed in the hopes one will stand up and say *pick me*. But shirts don't stand up. Nor do they speak. "Will you please help me?" I give Reese my best pouty lips and sad eyes.

"Peyton…" He rests a hand on my shoulder. "We aren't teenagers anymore. This is not a date. Quit thinking you need to look perfect. He said it's a group of friends hanging out. Right?" My eyes on his, I nod. "Just be comfortable. Throw on your favorite jeans and graphic tee. Pick a hoodie to take, just in case."

"Ugh." I fall face-first into the mountain of shirts. Inhale the lavender detergent and dryer sheet scent as I take a deep breath. The smell does little to calm me. "Why did I agree to this?" My voice garbled by the cotton.

A warm hand rubs up and down my back. Slow and steady and rhythmic.

Reese has always had the touch. A way to soothe me without effort. If he felt like less of a sibling, our relationship could have been much different. But I love Reese how he is and who he is in my life. He has been my foundation for years. The friend who walked home with me in middle school. Who shared corny jokes and never held anything back. The friend who took my hand in high school, came to my defense and never let me down. Who let me cry in his arms while he stroked my hair and reassured me everything would work out.

Even now, while he razzes me, it isn't meant to be serious. More like an icebreaker. A joke to lessen the anxiety wreaking havoc in my veins.

"Because you're a glutton for punishment," he muses. I lift my head and give my best death stare. "Joking." He lifts his hands in defense. Then his expression turns more serious. "Honestly, you always try to see the best in people. Even those who have wronged you." He shrugs and toys with the shirt in his hands. "You talking and hanging out with Micah, that's you giving him another shot. A chance to make amends."

I hate when Reese is right. When he turns somewhat philosophical on me.

Makes me see the truth behind my actions. They aren't bad truths. But speaking them aloud can be jarring.

I wiggle into a sitting position and lift my eyes to his. "Guess you make a valid point." He opens his mouth and I slap my palm over his lips. "Don't you dare."

"Wha—?" he mumbles against my skin.

"Say I told you so." I pull my hand away.

"I wasn't—"

"And don't lie." My finger jabs his direction, inches from his face.

Reese's booming laughter echoes off the walls. "Fine, I was. Can't help myself."

My palms slap against his chest, then shove him back. "Always such a pain in my ass."

"You love me." He winks.

I sit back on my haunches and stare at the mess on my bed. "And if you love me, you'll just tell me what to wear. Isn't that what besties are for?"

"Like a fifth of the time." He sticks his tongue out and makes a face at me. "But sure, I'll help." Searching the hurricane of cotton on my bed, he plucks a shirt from the pile. "Wear this with your black boyfriend jeans and all-black Chucks."

The shirt lands on my head and shields my eyes. "Hey." Reese just laughs. The bed shifts as I tug the shirt off. I jump up and follow him to the door. "Thank you." His eyes soften. "I know this isn't a date, but I've never felt this nervous about hanging out with people. And you always make me feel better. So, thank you."

Reese lifts a hand, clutches my hair and gives a slight tug. "You're welcome. That's what friends are for." He flashes his sweet smile. The one that only appears on rare occasions. "If he hurts you, though…"

"He'll answer to you," I finish.

"Damn straight."

∿

Reese all but shoved me out the front door and latched the security chain so I would leave.

Once I was dressed, he suggested I leave my hair down and put on minimal makeup. That was how I spent most of my days not at the club anyway. But when it actually came time to leave, I had second thoughts. Argued all the reasons I should stay home, slip on pajamas and eat pizza while watching Netflix. Reese wasn't having it.

Nervous as I am, him shoving me out the door was a good thing. Sometimes, I need that push. And he knows when to deliver.

The music quiets in the car as the Australian male Siri voice chimes in and tells me to turn left in a quarter mile. Something about that voice makes cell phone navigation much more pleasant. I turn onto the street and the voice takes over the speakers again, telling me my destination is a hundred feet on the left.

But I don't need to guess which house it is. Nope. Because there is only one house on the street with an overflowing driveway, cars in the yard and cars on the street.

Spectacular.

Two houses down, I park my SUV on the curb. Micah's gray pickup is in the driveway, which can only mean he has been here quite some time. I tap my phone screen and check the time. Only ten minutes after he told me to arrive. Would have been here sooner if I hadn't stopped up the street for bottled water.

One last deep breath. I grab my hoodie off the passenger seat, exit the car, and shove the fob in my pocket. Unlocking my phone, I type out a quick text to Reese.

Why am I here? There's like 10 cars.

Exaggerate much

Since I can't smack him, I send him a picture of all the cars.

Sorry Stay an hour at least.

Fine

Phone tucked in my back pocket, I trudge for the house. A black Bel Air sits next to an off-roading Jeep in the driveway. "Black Dog" by Led Zeppelin belts out as I step closer to the door. Just as I lift my hand to knock, a dog barks from inside the house.

I step back and glance at the window. A husky has his snout shoved between the blinds as he rattles the slats. He barks again before someone shushes him.

The door swings open and I feel like I stepped back several decades. A petite brunette smiles at me as she wrangles the dog. Her hair swept up in a ponytail. A bandanna knotted in a headband atop her head. Denim hugs her legs and a graphic tee depicting hot rods is tied above her navel.

Not only is she pretty, she also makes me feel welcome when I know only one person here.

"Hi." She extends her free hand and I shake it. "Please, come in. I'm Autumn. And this" —she points to the husky currently licking a little girl's face— "is Spartan and Clementine."

"Peyton," I say and step inside. "Thank you."

"Hope you're hungry." Her red-painted lips curve up farther. "Sometimes we get carried away at the store."

My stomach grumbles at the mention of food, but I'm thankful she doesn't hear. Don't think I can eat right away. "Smells wonderful. Thanks for having me."

"The more, the merrier. Follow me." She starts for another door. "Everyone's out back." My feet stick to the floor and I swallow. Autumn peers over her shoulder, then comes back to my side. She wraps a tattooed arm around my shoulders. "No need to be nervous. Everyone here is family. If anyone fucks with you, they'll answer to me."

I may have only just met this woman, but I like her already. "Appreciate it."

"If you want, when we get outside, I'll introduce you to everyone."

I sag under her arm. "That'd be great."

The door opens and Spartan bolts out with Clementine on his heels. "Sparty, wait." She chases after him and disappears into the yard.

"Simple Man" by Lynyrd Skynyrd starts playing through a speaker off to the side. Two steps down, we land on a paver patio. Hickory and oak drift in the air from a smoker. Tables span the side of the house with paper goods, drinks, and food filling every inch.

Autumn takes my hand without hesitation and tugs me toward the smoker. And several men. None of them Micah. But I feel his eyes on me.

Here we go.

"Jonas," she calls out and a man spins to face us. Roughly the same height as me, he has messy brown hair that's long on top, but buzzed short everywhere else. He sports a Black Sabbath shirt, loose jeans and bare feet. And the way he smiles at Autumn makes me feel as if I'm interrupting their privacy.

"Yes, scarlet." I look to Autumn and she mouths *nickname.*

"This is Peyton. Peyton, this is my boyfriend, Jonas."

He steps closer and extends a hand. "Nice to meet you, Peyton." We shake and it feels more welcoming than awkward. "Burgers, brats, and chicken should be done soon. Help yourself to whatever." He gestures to the buffet.

Tonight will be an abundance of handshakes and *thank yous.* But I don't mind. From the overall vibe, everyone here seems nice.

Next to the grill with Jonas, I meet Reznor, Rex, and Trevor. Reznor and Rex work at the same tattoo shop as Autumn. Both decorated in tattoos and have a few visible piercings. Reznor seems the quieter of the two, only talking when he has something to say. Trevor is introduced as Jonas's best friend. They have known each other since girls were gross, as Jonas puts it.

"Alright, let's go meet some other faces," Autumn suggests.

Maybe it's the fact I meet new people and have random conversations weekly that has kept me from freaking out so far. The panic I felt before arriving has cooled and now simmers in the background. Autumn, being a gracious hostess, might have something to do with it. Whatever the reason, I'm grateful the urge to puke has tapered off.

The next cluster of people are more of Autumn's tattoo family. Penny—who has bubblegum-pink hair and pops chewing gum more often than not—jumps up and hugs me.

"Pen, don't scare the girl. Jesus," Autumn scolds.

Penny steps back and smiles. "Sorry." She glances at Autumn. "If the guys didn't scare her, no one will." *Pop.*

"Let's not test it."

Then, Autumn introduces Tatyana and Ashton—Reznor's girlfriend and son— and Iliana. We exchange greetings and chat a moment. Penny pops her gum twenty times in less than ten minutes. She speaks with animated hands and doesn't care what anyone thinks. I love her automatically.

Autumn wraps up our conversation with them and prepares to shift us to the last group outside. Where Micah sits with three other people and talks. Where he has kept an eye on me since the moment I stepped outside.

I may not have looked directly at Micah, but I have known exactly where he is from the moment Autumn led me out back. Felt his eyes roam my untamed hair, my face, my body. Heard the occasional falter in his words as he spoke with friends. Caught him staring out of the corner of my eye as I interacted in his world.

"Hey, guys," Autumn says as we approach. "Cora, Gavin, Shelly, this is Peyton."

Familiar names. My eyes dart between their faces as I shove my hands in my back pockets.

The woman next to Micah bears the same eyes and blonde locks, and I assume this is his sister, Shelly. Makeup paints her eyes and face with perfect lines and strokes. And she wears pink as if she would own no other color, but it doesn't look bad on her. Micah mentioned her the night he apologized to me at Teddy's, but she seems otherwise familiar.

Across from Micah and Shelly is a woman and man who I presume to be Cora and Gavin. Both have black hair—hers cut to her shoulders and his almost just as long, but only on the top of his head. Gavin has his arm around Cora in a way that says they are a couple. A swift glance at her left hand tells me they're married. And god, do they make a beautiful couple.

Shelly pops up from her seat and steps up to me. I expect another handshake and generic greeting. Instead, she surprises me. Her arms wrap around me and squeeze tight. "If he hurts you, I'll kick his ass," she whispers, then steps back and holds me at arm's length. Her eyes don't leave mine until I nod. "You may not remember me. We went to different high schools, but I saw you near the track when I'd stop by to watch Micah run." I stiffen. "We were a year behind you." Shelly points to Cora and Gavin.

Cora rises from the lounger and offers her hand. "Nice to formally meet you, Peyton." Gavin follows suit and shakes my hand.

Just as I open my mouth to return the sentiment, Autumn hollers after Spartan —who just stole food off the table—then excuses herself.

Awkward, party of one?

"Shell, scoot over," Micah says. For a split second, I silently beg her to move closer to Micah and leave me the open end of the seat. But my plea goes unanswered as Shelly slides farther from Micah. He pats the cushion. "Come sit."

I shuffle between Shelly's legs and the unlit fire bowl to sit on the lounger. When my butt hits the seat, I lay my hoodie over my lap and tuck my hands underneath, where I fumble with the threads without prying eyes.

"How's your Sunday been?" Micah asks.

All eyes land on me, and I remind myself to inhale every other second. Cora and Gavin look at me with kindness as they curl into each other. Shelly practically bounces next to me. Everyone appears genuinely interested in my answer.

I can do this. Have nonwork conversations with Micah and get to know these people.

"Somewhat boring. Reese and I hung out."

Micah's whole frame goes rigid at the mention of Reese. Is that jealousy I detect? Interesting. May have to keep that tidbit in my arsenal.

"Reese Triggs?" Cora jumps in.

I peer up at her and smile. "Yeah. You know him?"

"Just remember him from high school. Nice guy."

"The best," I say, with dreamy eyes.

"You two still attached at the hip?"

"When we're home. We both work odd hours, but try to have at least one day off together."

The lounger shifts beside me and I turn to see if Micah is getting up. He isn't. Instead, he inches forward, leans closer with his eyes on me, rests his elbows on his knees and clasps his hands. "You live with him?" The growl behind his words doesn't go unnoticed by anyone.

I bite my cheek to resist smiling. His jealousy flashes like a neon sign in a porn shop window. It's amusing and annoying at the same time.

"Yep." I pop the *p*. "For years. Did I not mention that?" Not that I *need* to mention anything to Micah. We are just friends. My inner circle—not that I have much of one—and romantic life aren't his business.

"Can't say I remember you telling me," he says with too much bite for my liking.

"Well, he does. He also happens to be my best friend. If that's a problem for you…" I lift my brows in question.

"It's fine," he mumbles.

Beside me, Shelly shakes with silent laughter. And for a beat, I wonder if she and Cora tag-teamed to rile up her brother on purpose. If that's the case, we will be friends in no time.

Ready to jump on the 'terrorize Micah' train, I open my mouth to add gasoline to the fire. But Jonas cuts me off as he yells the burgers, brats, and chicken are ready.

The vultures flock to the buffet, but Micah and I stay seated a moment longer.

His vibe has gone from antsy to excited to irritated in minutes. Not sure what he expected when he invited me here, but I won't sit around and be the reason he pouts. He either needs to accept who I am and how I live or leave me be. I refuse to change who I am for another person. Especially Micah Reed.

I bump his shoulder. "You good?"

He rotates his head, but doesn't face me fully. Licks his lips. Eyes on the fire bowl a moment before his gaze meets mine. In those bold blue depths, I see more than expected. Curiosity and confusion. Regret and fear. But most of all, desire.

The ground wobbles. My heart beats faster, harder. My breath all but forgotten.

It's no secret I thought Micah lusted after me. Hell, as much as I despised him, his eyes continued to visit my dreams. By now, I had memorized the constellation the gold flecks formed in his eyes.

But that was all fantasy. All in my head. Right?

Apparently not.

"Sorry for my reaction. It was juvenile," he admits.

"Yes, it was. I forgive you." The blue in his irises brightens. "Don't do it again." His brows pinch above his nose. "Act jealous."

"Peyton, I—"

I hold up a hand and stop him. "I will let you finish as long as you don't say you're not jealous." My arm presses against his as I lean closer. Our lips inches apart. "Do not lie to me," I whisper.

The chatter and music around us fades away. All I see are his twinkling blue eyes, guiding me like the North Star. All I feel is the heat of his body and breath on my skin, on my lips. If either of us pressed forward, our lips would meet. Soft and hot and ready.

"Peyton, I was jealous. Am jealous," he confesses, only loud enough for my ears. His pupils dilate. Breath comes in bursts. He licks his lips and I *feel* his tongue ghost the edge of my lower lip.

I close my eyes but don't dare move. "Why?" The single word loaded with several questions. Why are you jealous? Why me? Why does it matter?

Micah remains tight-lipped until I open my eyes. And when I do, I swallow at the intensity staring back. The swirl of fire and hunger in his eyes.

"Thought it was rather obvious," he declares, voice gruff.

"Humor me," I whisper.

The corner of his mouth kicks up. "Peyton, how can I not be jealous of any man who sleeps under the same roof as you?"

"I live in an apartment. Sure there's more."

"Smart-ass." I smile. "Seriously, though. If I haven't made it obvious enough, I kind of have a thing for you."

"Kind of have a thing?"

He rolls his eyes and shakes his head until our noses bump. "No, not kind of. I *have* a thing for you."

The attraction between me and Micah has been plain as day for weeks. Not sure if his feelings go beyond then, but that's the first time I really paid attention. Neither of us can deny the spark. The ever-expanding ache between us.

But we have history.

Yes, I accepted Micah's apology. Forgiving him, on the other hand, may take more time. It's easy to let the words leave my lips. *I forgive you.* Feeling them, though, is a completely different wall to scale.

"Micah…" I inch back from him. Drag in a deep breath and hold it for five, four, three, two. "I… I don't know how to respond to that."

In my periphery, I follow his hand as it moves from his space to mine. And then he rests it on my thigh. Not too high, but somewhere in the middle, at the edge of the hoodie. Warmth radiates through the denim and heats my skin. I forget, for the umpteenth time, how to breathe.

"Don't need to. Just wanted you to know." He gives my thigh a slight squeeze, then rises from the lounger. I already miss the scent of his cologne in my nose. "C'mon." He holds out his hand. "Let's grab some food."

I take his hand and we shuffle over to the table. We fill our plates with too much food and each grab a bottle of beer. Once we resume our seats, conversations shift to lighter topics. Autumn regales us with stories of outlandish tattoos. Jonas shares his mechanic wet dreams about working on a 1965 Shelby Mustang. We all hem and haw, but don't appreciate it the same as he does. Gavin and Cora talk about upcoming photo shoots—she photographing a wedding and he's modeling a new line of exercise gear.

I listen as they all carry on. In comparison, my life seems boring. Yes, I meet people from all walks of life in Roar. But I interact with them for maybe a few minutes. It's pure coincidence if I pour all their drinks for the night.

Sometimes, though, boring isn't so bad.

When everyone cleans their plates, Reznor, Tatyana, and Ashton say their good-byes. With a little one to tend to, they still have plenty to do once they get home. Penny, Rex, Trevor, and Iliana leave next. As each person leaves, I get hugs instead of handshakes.

I take my phone from my pocket and check the time. Almost nine.

Micah taps my foot with his. When I look up, he tips his head toward my phone. "Hot date?"

With a shake of my head, I tell him, "No. Just don't want to be out too late. I'm at the ALF tomorrow."

"Finish your drink first?" He poses it as a question. Leaves me the opportunity to choose.

I lift the beer and swirl the contents. Two, maybe three, sips left. "Yeah."

For the next fifteen minutes, the ladies chat with me. Ask what it is like working at Roar. If I deal with a bunch of pervs. I joke and tell them the only perv in Roar is Micah. Everyone but Shelly laughs. She merely slaps him.

When my bottle empties, I toss it in the trash, gather my hoodie and start my goodbyes. Shelly gives me a more exuberant hug than the one I received upon arrival. She also reminds me she will kick her brother's ass if he hurts me. Cora and Gavin hug me next. Their embrace warm and friendly. Autumn and Jonas are next in line. After hugs are exchanged, Autumn says she hopes to see me again.

As weirded out as I was before I arrived tonight, leaving feels more nerve-racking. Like I am leaving behind family. Such a strange sensation, burning in my chest.

Micah trades hugs with everyone after me. "I'll walk you out."

"You don't have to."

"I know. But I'm heading out too. Plus, it's late and I hear there are some crazy old men in this neighborhood."

I laugh with a shake of my head. "Whatever. Let's go."

The front door clicks behind us as we step onto the porch. And suddenly, every sense amplifies.

I shiver as Micah's cologne gets caught on the breeze and drifts up my nose. Cicadas sing alongside the occasional whoosh of a car driving on the cross street a hundred feet away. I jump when the motion light kicks on and beams down on the driveway. Then heat flushes my skin when Micah rests his palm on my lower back.

Breathe, Peyton.

Thirty-seven steps later, we reach my car. I reach into my pocket and press the fob to unlock the door. But I don't open it. Instead, I stand there, frozen, staring at Micah like I'm broken.

"Thanks for inviting me," I finally squawk out then clear my throat. "I had a nice time."

Micah takes a step closer. The toe of his shoe inches from mine. "Glad you came. I had a great time, too."

Before the words good night leave my lips, he steps forward and snakes his arms around my waist. And then I feel him toe to top. Pressure and heat and... desire. I drag my fingers up his arms, lace them behind his head and close my eyes as I breathe him in.

His lips hover near my ear. Breath ebbing and flowing and heating my skin. If he kissed me right now, I wouldn't stop him. Don't think I could. Not with how good he feels flush against my front.

A hand trails up my spine and halts at the base of my skull as his fingers comb through my loose strands. "I love this. Wish you wore your hair down more often. But know why you don't."

My head swirls with want versus need. An internal battle of whether I should take a step back or press my lips to the spot beneath his ear. In the end, my rational side waves a flag in attention and I ease back.

"Thanks again," I whisper, inches from his lips. "Talk to you later."

He licks his lips and nods. Which is the perfect time for me to go. Before I launch myself at him and kiss the hell out of his soft lips. Then question my sanity.

I open the car door and slip inside. "Let me know you got home safe." He closes the door then taps the roof and walks to his truck with steady steps.

My eyes drift low in the side mirror and zero in on his ass. His jeans hang low and loose, but the definition of his glutes more than noticeable. When he reaches his truck, he unlocks the door but doesn't open it. No, he peeks over his shoulder at me. Well, my car.

The motion light on Jonas and Autumn's house kicks on and creates a halo around his frame. His face unreadable. But his body language begs for more. Tells me way more than his unspoken words.

My heart pounds, pounds, pounds in my chest until he gets in his truck, cranks the ignition and drives off. My knuckles burn and whiten as I fist the steering wheel and watch his taillights in the rearview. Then he turns and disappears into the night.

I gasp and relieve the fire in my lungs. Take a few deep, methodical breaths and cool the burn in my chest. Once my heart slows, I put the car in gear and drive home with one question swirling like a cyclone in my head.

What the hell is happening between me and Micah Reed?

nineteen

Peyton sits parked on the street as I turn and she disappears from view. Why hasn't she left yet? Did I freak her out? I half expected her to bolt the second she got behind the wheel. But her headlights hadn't even come on before I turned the corner.

I jolt when my phone rings through the truck's audio. Shelly's name flashes on the screen and I tap the answer button on the steering wheel. Had I forgotten something?

"Hey, Shell."

"Don't hurt her."

Jesus. Hadn't been gone ten minutes and am already on her shit list. Suppose that's how it is between siblings. Always keeping each other in check. Or trying to, at least. "I won't."

"I'm serious, Micah." Micah, not big brother. Serious is an understatement. "I saw you."

She saw me? "What does that mean, Shelly? You saw me."

A huff of irritation rustles through the phone line and I picture her rolling her eyes. She doesn't say anything as my knuckles stretch and pale against the steering wheel. My thumb hovers over the disconnect button, but I pull it back. Shelly may annoy me at times, but she would have to commit genocide for me to ignore her.

"Outside." She blows out a breath as I sort through my thoughts, but come up with nothing of substance.

"Be more specific. We were all outside tonight."

"Why is this so difficult?"

The question is meant to be rhetorical, but I answer anyway. "Because you won't spit out what you want to say."

"Argh," she groans. "Fine. You want me to just come out with it?"

"Would make this call a little less one sided."

"Outside. At her car. I saw you… holding her."

I pinch the bridge of my nose and thank the traffic gods for a red light. Irritation spreads like the molten searing of a branding iron. Scalding at the epicenter, but distributing the sting in an effort to temper the pain.

"Were you spying on me?" I bark into the truck cab.

"No," she counters with a fevered pitch. "Not intentionally. I was a couple minutes behind you. When I stepped out the door and saw your truck, I was confused. So, I looked for you—from the porch—and saw you at Peyton's car."

Can't remember the last time I felt stabby toward Shelly. Compared to friends who had siblings, Shelly and I had a great relationship. Sure, we didn't always see eye to eye, but no one does. When she admitted to seeing us, I assumed she followed us outside all ninja-like. Seeing us by accident… I can't be mad at her.

"Sorry I snapped at you."

"You're forgiven, big brother. Still doesn't change things. Don't hurt her."

Bless my sister and her need to look out for others. Any other time, I would deem the trait admirable. Mom and Dad did their damnedest to raise us as respectable and responsible. *"Lead by example."* Those three words spoken by Mom or Dad at least once a week during our childhood. With the exception to high school and my whore habits post-Rochelle, I have done my best to uphold said qualities. To be an example.

But we all get tested from time to time.

"I love how protective you are, Shell. And I have no intention of hurting Peyton."

On the other end of the line, a beep echoes, followed by a soft thump and electronic dings. After a beat, she speaks up and sounds farther from the phone speaker.

"You may not intentionally. But your life has been a hot mess for a short while. Don't let that bleed into her life." Hot mess doesn't remotely describe the path my life has taken since Rochelle fucked me over. Literally.

The day I walked in on Rochelle and the young stallion she mounted, in the bed we shared no less, I lost my shit. I have never been physically violent toward women, but furniture and picture frames and inanimate objects were fair game. I'd flung them across the room. My fists so tight, blood spilled from the crescents in my palms. Holes littered the hallway drywall—a smarter alternative than jail after beating the guy's ass.

The worst part of it all… she wasn't sorry. Rochelle had zero regrets bringing another man—who looked barely old enough to be a man—to the bed we shared and fucking him. Not a single ounce of remorse. How had I become so blasé about who she was and her predatory ways?

Because I was a fool.

We hadn't been living together full time—thank fuck. But once I kicked her to the curb, threw all her shit outside, along with the mattress, I made a pact with myself. To never let a woman so close to my heart again. To never let a woman take the reins and steer me down an unknown path.

Not bedding the same woman night after night helped solidify my pact. But these last few weeks, Peyton has me second-guessing said agreement.

"Swear I won't hurt her. Not intentionally."

"Good to hear." The relief in her voice filled the truck cabin. "Will I see you at Mom and Dad's party?"

Ah, yes. The parents' thirty-fifth wedding anniversary. Our parents don't always insist on our appearance, but if we missed this occasion, we wouldn't hear the end of it.

"Wouldn't miss it."

"Cool." A car horn honks in the background. "Well, I'm on my way home. Talk to you later."

"'Kay. Love you, Shell."

"Love you, too, big brother. Night."

The call disconnects as I turn into my driveway. I cut the lights and engine, then stare at the tan-painted single-car garage door. Let my eyes lose focus as I watch tree limb shadows dance over the house. House, not home. The only way it would ever feel like a home is if I wasn't alone.

In my mind's eye, I pictured what having a home would be like. How two people blended their lives together and became one. Similar to Gavin and Cora. On so many levels, I envy my best friend. Not that his and Cora's journey was an easy one. Life ripped them apart. Obstacles stood in their way. But they persevered. Because they wanted each other more than anything else.

I would kill for that type of love. Love that bulldozes walls and eviscerates loneliness. Love that pulls you in, wraps its arms around you, and never lets go. That crushes all insecurities and makes you feel safe in your vulnerability. That is the love I want.

But after the bullshit with Rochelle, letting another woman near my heart scares the shit out of me.

Without realizing it, Peyton has unintentionally wiggled her way in. Staked a claim on my heart. And fuck… here I am, handing it over. No resistance. No second-guessing. Just willingly plucking the scarred organ from my chest and presenting it to her, in the hopes she will know how to handle it.

Fuck.

I exit the truck, check the mailbox—then remember the mail doesn't run today when I see the box empty—before I amble inside. I flip the kitchen light on, empty my pockets, and grab a beer from the fridge. I pop the cap, chuck it in the trash and take a long pull from the bottle. After flipping the light off, I snatch my phone from the counter and wander down the hall to my bedroom, bottle at my lips.

Plopping down on the mattress, I don't bother with the light. It isn't long before I polish off the beer, strip my clothes, set the phone on the charger, and slip under the covers.

Alone in bed, the silence is deafening. I close my eyes and images of Peyton flash behind my lids like an old movie reel. In the last two weeks, I had seen her smile more often than not. And her smile is magnificent. Like sunshine after the rain. Blinding, yet you can't seem to look away. Marry that smile with her radiant violet eyes and golden hair, she rendered me speechless more often than not.

When had Peyton become such a fixture in my head? In every waking—and sleeping—thought I had?

For more than a year, we were at each other's throats. The constant back and forth. Her yelling at me and vice versa. She did it out of disgust and a hatred for her high school bully. I did it because I loved to work her up, to ruffle her mane. Can't speak for Peyton, but for me, taunting her is the best version of foreplay. A lead-up to where we are now.

Unfortunately, I have no clue where we go from here.

Do I really want another relationship? Dates and intimacy and late nights filled with laughter. Shared time and small tokens of appreciation. A voice buried deep in my psyche screams, *"Yes, idiot. We want all those things."* But another voice—one closer to the battlefield, one more recent—speaks up and reminds me of what I went through last time I traveled down that road. *"You'll just end up here again. Hurt and alone."*

My eyes snap open and stare up at the ceiling I am all too familiar with. "No," I whisper into the darkness. "Peyton and Rochelle are nothing alike." Peyton would never hurt someone she cared about. Not after all the bullshit she has dealt with.

Question is, does Peyton care about me? On any level?

Without a second thought, I blindly reach for my phone on the nightstand. I squint at the screen and open up the messaging app. Before I stop myself, I tap on the text history with Peyton and type out a message. Seeing as she works at the ALF tomorrow, she probably won't answer. But this can't wait.

Is this too much?

I stare at the blue bubble on the screen. The word delivered beneath it. Then I lock my phone, toss it on the bed and press the heels of my palms to my eyes. "I'm a goddamn fool."

The words are barely out of my mouth when the phone vibrates the bed. I pat the blanket until I locate the phone and see a text alert. From Peyton.

Is what too much?

How do I translate my thoughts into simple terms? My brain knows the words, but my fingers forget how to type them. My lips forget how to say them. But I do my best to spell it out.

Me. Us. Hugging earlier.

I hit send and close my eyes. The text is ridiculous. It explains nothing and probably confuses her further. Why does my brain turn to mush whenever Peyton Alexander is in the mix?

The hug threw me off. But I won't lie and say I didn't like it.

Peyton Alexander just admitted to liking my arms around her. My body pressed to hers. My lips near her skin.

I liked it too. More than expected.

Oh yeah. How much more?

Is she flirting? Or does my bewildered brain have me misconstruing her message? It's late and she is probably in bed, half asleep.

Enough that I still feel your heat on my skin.

Fuck. I slip a hand beneath the blanket and grip my hardening cock. Eyes on the screen, I take a deep breath as the dots dance inside the little gray bubble.

Where do you feel it?

Fucking hell. Is this seriously happening? In five simple words, Peyton has me virtually on my knees, begging for relief. Without hesitation, I would worship her like no other.

You really want to know?

Humor me.

I laugh into the darkness. Those two words. We toss them back and forth to lighten the moment. But those two words weigh heavily each time they are said.

> Fisted in my hand.

And just like that, my innocent inquiry has flipped to sexting. Well, suggestive sexting. Will my response freak her out?

> And how does that feel?

This woman will be the death of me. Via text messages or her smart mouth. Either will do, though.

> Nowhere near enough.

> Sometimes, not enough makes the end result that much sweeter.

> What end result would that be?

I will not put words in her mouth. Other things, perhaps, but not words. With our history, Peyton needs her voice. Needs to use it to guide me. To guide us. I won't mislead her, but I also want the same in return.

> My crystal ball says that still remains to be seen.

> Hmm. Think your crystal ball may need to be cleaned.

> Really?

> Yep. I offer up my ball cleaning services to you.

Oh lord. I really need to think before I type and hit send. And I'm not drunk. Maybe a little buzzed, but not drunk.

> I bet you do.

> Sorry. Was that too much?

> I'm a big girl, starlight. I handle balls just fine.

And now my vision fills with images of Peyton and the ways she could *handle my balls.* I am so fucking screwed.

> You really are a hellcat.

> You wouldn't want me any other way.

There are several ways I wouldn't mind having Peyton Alexander. But it is too early to put those out in the open. Even with both of us braver behind our screens.

> True. Question… why do you call me starlight?

Her new nickname for me is quirky and cute, but it also feels childish. God, I hope it isn't something so inane.

> Really want to know?

> Humor me.

Seconds drag on for minutes as the dancing gray bubble pops up and disappears again and again. Either she is typing a novel or she deletes her words and starts over. The wait is gruesome.

> Because of your eyes.

Not a novel. And definitely not what I expected.

My eyes? What about my eyes made her come up with starlight? I picture Shelly's twin irises. The rich blue with lighter hints. But nothing makes me think of starlight.

> What about my eyes?

> Hidden in the blue, you have these little gold sparks. Like stars.

Like stars. I read those two words over and over. Sift them through the confines of my mind. Interpret the fact she has studied my eyes hard enough to notice small gold flecks. *Like stars.* That every time she uses the nickname, it has more meaning than other pet names people share. That she sees deeper than surface level. *Like stars.*

> I never noticed.

The screen dims after no response for a couple minutes. I tap the screen and it brightens. Then I note how late it is. Seeing as she has to be up earlier in the morning, it wouldn't surprise me if she fell asleep.

> Night, hellcat. Sweet dreams.

I lay my phone back on the charger and stare up at the ceiling. After texting Peyton, staring at the slight texture above the bed seems less interesting. Worth less of my time. So, I close my eyes and let my imagination wander.

Images of Peyton from earlier in the evening pop up from my memory. Of her relaxed attire and loose strands. Of her easygoing smile and breath an inch from my lips. How at ease she was around my friends, my family. And how perfect she felt flush against my chest, my hips. Most of all, I recall the way her brilliant eyes studied mine.

Like stars.

Small waves crash along the shore. Salt licks my skin. Cocoa butter and the distinct smell of seaweed float through the air. Seagrasses ruffle in the wind between the parking lot and white sand. The sun bright and high in the cloudless blue sky.

I peek up from my romance thriller as Ani exits the water and treks back to our spot in the sand. For a woman in her late forties, Ani is smoking hot. I have never been sexually attracted to women, but will openly admit when they steal my attention. Ani works hard for everything in her life—physically, emotionally, and financially—and it shows.

Our friendship is one of the greatest gifts, and I thank my lucky stars she entered my checkout line years ago.

Ani has given me so much. More than I ever expected. She provided me with opportunities I wouldn't have easily come by without her. But she is also a great friend. Without a doubt, one of my best friends—after Reese, of course.

Over the years, my tally of female friends has remained small. One—I don't have time for petty nonsense. Drama happens, but I don't need women who provoke and promote drama in my circle. Two—I enjoy the more laid-back nature of guy friends. Plus, guy friends give better hugs when you need them.

But Ani is the exception in my circle. Her drive and no-bullshit attitude make her admirable. She busts her ass for what she wants and ignores everyone who tells her she can't have something or accomplish her goals. As a woman who wants more from life, I hold Ani in high esteem. With her guidance, I have the opportunity to become a better version of myself too.

Women empowering women tops crushing them beneath your heel any day of the week.

Ani flops down on the lounger next to me, slides her sunglasses into place, and sips her water. "The water feels amazing today. We need more beach dates."

I bookmark my page and set the book in my bag. "Agreed." I stare out at the water and how the sun shimmers along the surface like stars. In a blink, my thoughts drift to Micah and his starry-night-sky eyes.

Two weeks have passed since I hung out with him and his friends. Since he wrapped me in his arms and touched me more like a lover than a friend or coworker. Since he texted me from his bed and our conversation went from concerned to heated to confessional.

And since that night, Micah Reed has texted me daily.

Random and not-so random messages. Texts asking how my day was at Gulfside. A barrage of questions in an obvious attempt to learn every fine detail of who I am.

"Favorite style of music?"

"Favorite movie snack?"

"Last show you binge watched."

"Place you want to visit, but haven't."

A different question hit my messages every day. Even days when we would see each other at work. Some I answered within minutes. Others I left unanswered for hours. Not because I didn't have an answer, but because there is something thrilling about delayed gratification.

"You ready for tonight?"

Tonight… I have been ready and waiting for this day for ages. The day I become more than just a woman behind the bar. The day I take the next step.

"Yes. Already adjusted my schedule at Gulfside."

"I love that you'll still be there one day. They're lucky to have you."

When Ani called me last weekend and said things were moving forward at Roar, I spoke with human resources at Gulfside. And Ms. Jenkins. HR accepted the change without complication. They understood the younger staff wouldn't stick to the same routine. But they were excited when we stayed. Ms. Jenkins, on the other hand, was a bit peeved. Not that I would only be at Gulfside one day a week, but that I'd still show up.

The woman loved me as much as Nana did. Wanted to see me thrive in the world. Wanted me to not be "one of those people that works more than lives." I promised her this change would help me do that. But I still need Gulfside. Need the solace it provides when life is hectic. Need the conversations and interactions with Ms. Jenkins that parallel to those I shared with Nana. Moments I miss more than anything.

"The feeling is mutual." I take a deep breath and lose focus as I stare out at the water. Then twist to face Ani. "How's this going down?"

Her legs sweep over the edge of the lounger as she looks my way. A hand pushes her sunglasses into her hair. Eyes survey my face. "Are you nervous?"

Am I nervous? I scrutinize my own feelings. The expanding flutter beneath my diaphragm. The one that sparked to life when Ani called last weekend. But it was the same sensation when I agreed to work for her. Delight. Exhilaration. Having the chance to be more.

But I also can't ignore the lump in my throat. The one I woke with this morning when realization kicked in. When I stared at the text notification on my phone.

"Morning, hellcat."

It wasn't necessarily the text that had my body in slight hysterics. Micah started texting me that same message following the night I hung out with him and his friends. And I love seeing it each morning.

Today, though, his message sent a wave of panic. Has me second-guessing what happens next. Not about the overall change at Roar, but how Micah will react with the announcement. Will he be pissed? Or will he praise me? For some stupid, girlish reason, his reaction matters. Suppose that's what happens when you get closer with someone.

"Yes," I answer honestly. "What if this pisses people off?"

"And by people, you mean Micah." Ani poses it more as a statement than question.

I huff out the irritation I have with myself. Irritation over the fact that I am worried what a guy thinks. "Not just him." Half-truth. "But also Gina and the others who have been there longer."

Ani reaches for my hand and clasps it between hers. "This is happening because I want it to. It isn't just about you. The move is also smart for business. Sean and I always mull over business decisions before putting them into action. Hard and heavy. This decision wasn't made because we're friends or on a whim. I believe in you and what you have to offer. And that's why I'm doing this."

My breath comes easier. "Thank you. Didn't know I needed to hear that."

"You're welcome." She drops my hand, then shifts to lie back on her lounger. "How do you think he'll take it?"

She doesn't have to say Micah's name for me to know who she's talking about. "Wish I knew. Things have changed between us. But I don't know him well enough to answer."

"Well, don't let it worry you. He's a grown man. If he can't handle it, that's his problem. Not yours."

Every rational part of me knows Ani is right. That if Micah gets upset with tonight's announcement, it is on him. But part of me still feels as if I am betraying him. Betraying the friendship—or whatever the hell -ship—we formed. Things between us get better with each passing day. I don't want all that to go down the shitter.

I only hope he takes the news with a managerial mindset and does not let it bruise his ego.

❧

You can do this, Peyton.

I stare at the back of Roar from the comfort of my car. The aged brick more red than brown today. A fresh coat of paint over the club name adds an extra pop. Large string lights near the roofline already lit, although the sun doesn't set for another two hours.

Parked two spaces to my right is Ani and Sean's Tesla. Another space down is Micah's truck. Both vehicles empty of passengers. Seeing both adds a new layer of nausea.

Get out of the car. Go inside.

"Ugh." I grip my hands at ten and two on the steering wheel and rest my forehead at twelve. "Why is this eating at me?" What I wouldn't give for a couple saltines right now.

Leaning back, I press my head into the rest and drop my hands. I take a few steadying breaths. *In through the nose. Out through the mouth.* When my pulse settles and the compulsion to vomit wanes, I step out of the car, shoulder my purse and head for the employee entrance.

On any other day, if I were to walk in Roar two hours before open, it would be quiet. A radio may be on, quiet in the background. But otherwise, the space would be still. Peaceful. The calm before the storm.

But today is a new day. And new days come with music at normal levels and the chatter of several close people. I stroll past the office, skipping the time clock or stashing my purse. When I enter the main area of the club, the space seems smaller. Claustrophobic. Restrictive. The walls inching closer to the tables.

All eyes shift my way as I step out from the hall. Smiles and waves and greetings I don't hear beyond the white noise in my ears. I pinch the front of my shirt, pull it off my chest, then push it back rapidly, over and over.

Is it hot in here?

Ani pats Sean on the shoulder, then strolls over to me. "Peyton?" I hold her gaze. "You okay?"

I nod. "Just need some water."

She shuffles me over to a stool and forces me to sit. "I'll grab you some. Sit tight."

Ani waltzes over to the bar as Micah takes her place at my side. Brows drawn together, he bends at the knees so we are eye to eye. For one, two, three breaths, he doesn't speak. Then he reaches for my hand. His warm touch a partial balm to my anxiety.

"You look like you've seen a ghost." He lifts a hand and lightly brushes my cheek with his knuckles. "If you need to go, they'll understand."

My eyes dart between his and memorize each gold fleck against their inky sky backdrop. Certain I may not see them this close again, I etch them into my mind to recall when I am alone.

"I'm fine," I choke out as Ani approaches with water. "Just have a lot on my mind."

Ani sets the glass on the table and winks before going back to Sean. She whispers in his ear—a signal the meeting is about to start. My stomach churns and I sip the water in the hopes it will settle.

"Want to talk—" Micah starts, but is cut off when Ani speaks up. He shifts to stand beside me. Hand on the back of my chair. Thumb absently drawing small circles between my spine and shoulder blade.

"Thank you all for coming in early or on your day off." Ani and Sean flash bright white smiles to everyone. "We called this meeting to update you on new changes with Roar." A mix of excitement and concern mar some of the faces in our group. Others remain impassive.

I grip the edges of the seat until pain shoots up my forearm. The next words out of Ani's mouth will be the ones I have waited to hear for far too long. Words that will change *everything*. I relish and fear the change. But I won't let anyone snuff out what I worked hard to achieve.

Not even Micah.

"First announcement… Roar has a new manager on staff." Micah freezes beside me and Gina, two tables over, looks ready to puke. *Right there with ya, girl.* "Everyone, please join me in congratulating Peyton on her promotion."

Applause and cheers erupt and echo throughout the room. But one clap stands out more than the rest. The one less than a foot from me. Slow and exaggerated and far from congratulatory. Each time his hands smack together, I twitch in my seat. Jump at the vibration of anger each strike sends my way.

This is exactly what I expected would happen. That Micah would go off the emotional deep end. Instead of smiles and hugs and overall happiness for what I achieved and earned, I had a feeling the opposite would happen. My assumptions weren't wrong.

Without hurry, I peek to the right. Prepare myself for the sight that will undoubtedly make the pain beneath my rib cage worse. But no amount of preparation will ease the anger and hurt I see on Micah's face.

His nostrils flare. Eyes cold and distant as he meets mine. A measured headshake full of disbelief. And then he breaks contact. Not just his eyes, but also the hand he'd had on the back of my chair. With each harsh breath I take, he takes a step away.

Asshole.

Fuck him. If me achieving success pisses him off, he can crawl in a hole and weep like a toddler. Alone. I will not lower myself so he feels better about himself. Fuck. That.

I sit up straighter, pick up my water, and sip it as Ani continues.

"Gina, we'll be switching you to Tuesday through Friday. Micah, your days will remain the same. Starting next week, Peyton will work Monday through Thursday. We will also add three new bartenders, two servers and another doorman." Light chatter kicks up, then dies down when Ani continues. "They will be arriving for introductions in a half hour. I wanted to give the original Roar team this moment before they joined us."

Micah leans forward, his breath hot on my ear. "Can we talk later?" he growls.

I purse my lips and meet his gaze as he rights himself. "Sure." My mouth stretches into a tight, forced smile before I face Ani again.

Over the next fifteen minutes, Ani shares the changes coming to Monday through Thursday. All the ideas I tossed out at her plus drink specials for each night. She drones on about contacts who are eager to partake in charity bingo night and companies who want to host trivia night for their employees. With each new idea that leaves her lips, Micah grows more frustrated and tense.

More than a month ago, Ani asked Micah for ideas to boost the slower nights. Asked for his input because of his role in the company. She'd also asked Gina, who suggested board game night, speed dating, and painting parties. Some of which Ani plans to incorporate once or twice a month. But Micah never responded. Never gave a single suggestion.

Maybe it had something to do with me and the distraction I provided. Or maybe his head was elsewhere. Distracted with other things I was unaware of. Either way, he didn't hold up his end of the bargain. And now, he has to deal with what Ani and Sean decided. Without him.

The new employees arrive and introductions are made. Josiah, Caleb, and Mable will join Adam and Kaylynn behind the bar. Charity and Dylan will be new additions to the tables with Becky and Jake. And Julio will work with Dan and Ted. The new cliques chat among themselves and get to know each other. All of the new additions will be working with us tonight, so management will get more time with them.

Before long, Ani announces everyone needs to start prepping for open. She shoots me a worried look, but I wave her off. Micah may be upset, but that is his burden to carry. Not mine. As the meeting carried on, this sank in more and more. That I should not be wrung tight because Micah cannot handle life and the positive things happening in mine. If he can't step off his pedestal one minute and allow others to shine with him, I don't need him in my life. Period.

So, I let it go. Enjoy the bliss of promotion and all the possibilities in my future. And later, I will celebrate with a drink and the people who cheer me on. Life is too short. I don't have the time or patience for someone not in my corner.

Fuck Micah Reed and his piss-poor attitude.

No way this happened overnight. No way Peyton did not see this coming before today. Yet, she never said a goddamn word. Not once. None of our conversations hinted this colossal change was coming.

Manager.

Peyton just got promoted to manager after working at Roar for one year. One fucking year.

How hard had I slung bottles before Sean and Ani considered me management material? The first time Sean broached the subject had been three and a half years in. *"We need to see more professionalism,"* he'd said. *"You have what it takes, but need you to step it up. Show us you want it."* Those days, Sean and Ani spent more time at Roar than not.

But they rarely set foot inside nowadays. Not unless they were meeting with me or Gina or an event happened during the day. Yes, they kept tabs on their business. But they were less involved with the actual day-to-day functionality. They left that up to management and staff, only stopping by if things were amiss.

So how did Ani know Peyton was management material? Without working side by side with her a single night, Ani had no idea how Peyton worked inside these walls. And I hadn't received any calls, texts or emails asking my opinion on Peyton's work ethic. Only the occasional generic inquiry when Ani stopped by to grab bank deposits or paperwork for the accountant.

The only reasonable explanation is Peyton and Ani's friendship. But I had to know. I need answers from the source. Peyton.

As the meeting came to a close, Peyton stood from her stool and took a step toward the bar. The color had returned to her cheeks. Her skin less clammy and gray. Eyes more alert and chin held higher.

Before she stepped out of reach, I took her elbow. She jerked to a stop as her eyes flashed to mine. Lips are a brutal flat line. A crease between her brows. If she had claws, I'd be shredded to bits by now.

"Can we talk?" My voice low as my eyes dart toward the hall, to the office.

She drops her gaze to my hand, then brings it back to my face. The ferocity in her stare makes me drop my hand and take a step back.

"Please," I add in a softer tone.

Am I angry? Absolutely. But not for the reasons Peyton presumes.

"Fine. But make it quick. I need to do prep."

Behind the bar, Adam and Kaylynn get to work with Josiah, Caleb, and Mable. Without being asked, they went into instructor mode. Showing their new coworkers how Roar operates. By the time Peyton and I finish our talk, the bar prep will be done with time to spare.

Without another word, I storm toward the office. The *tip-tap, tip-tap* of Peyton's heeled boots clacks loud in my wake. I step into the office and move off to the side. Once she steps in, I slam the door and lock it.

"What the hell, Micah?" Her tone is fire and rage and trembles slightly.

Feet away, I huff out a laugh. "You're angry at me? Seriously? Seems a bit backward."

Her nostrils flare as her chest expands and contracts in rapid succession. The muscles of her jaw flex and tighten. Fists balled at her sides. "How so?"

"Shit like this doesn't just happen overnight, Peyton." I wave a hand in the air. "This type of change gets planned. Weeks and months ahead of time."

"Your point?"

I take a step in her direction. "You think I'm mad at you? Mad about the promotion?"

She waves a hand in the air, up and down the length of my body. "Body language speaks volumes. As soon as it was announced, you retreated from me."

I had pulled away from her. Stopped touching her. Stepped out of her bubble. Only because I felt betrayed. Betrayed by my bosses. And betrayed by Peyton, a woman I thought I had a connection with. I needed to hear everything without distraction. Needed to absorb the words being spoken. And I couldn't do that with Peyton so close.

I take another step in her direction. "I'm not mad at *you*. More like the situation."

"Not a fan of me being on the same level," she bites out.

A smaller step. Her body close enough for me to touch. "That's not it either," I say with a shake of my head.

"Then what is it, Micah?" She cocks a brow. "Humor me."

The corner of my mouth twitches, then relaxes. "Do you know how long I've worked here? How long it took me to step into a management role?" She doesn't answer or react. "Longer than you. I busted my ass for three-plus years before it was even a possibility. And even then, it came with stipulations."

Peyton's shoulders lift, then drop. Her lips puckered and eyes unyielding.

"Not to sound petulant, but it feels like I had to bust my ass for something that landed in your lap."

Her spine stiffens, the action inching her closer. "You think I haven't paid my dues, Micah? You think Ani just handed me this? Goes to show, you don't know shit." She spins to face the door. "This conversation is done."

Before she takes a step, I grip her elbow and twirl her back around. "No. Uh-uh. Not done yet."

Peyton steps into me. The tip of her nose a millimeter from mine. "What else is there to say?"

My hand drops from her elbow and lands on her hip. Her lips part just enough for me to notice. I rest my other hand on the opposite hip. Her breasts brush my chest as her breath coats my lips. Her violet irises sparkle and don't deviate from my pinned stare.

"Why did you hide the news? All the texts and times we've talked, you never mentioned it. Why?"

She exhales and I briefly close my eyes. *God, I want to taste her lips, her skin.*

"Nothing was set in stone. Ani and I talked about it here and there, but she never gave a timeline. Until last weekend. As in four days ago."

I fist her hips, but not enough to bruise them. "Still could've told me." The words practically inaudible.

"Micah..." My name rolls off her tongue and lights a fire beneath my sternum. "I wasn't trying to hurt—"

My lips crash to hers. Hot and aggressive and hungry. For one, two, three beats of my pulse, she doesn't kiss me back. I start to back away as defeat and mortification form a dark cloud overhead.

Until she fists my shirt and hauls me closer. Fuses our lips together again and licks the seam of mine. I part my lips and she dives in. We lick and taste and wage war with our tongues. Peyton tastes of sweet cream and something distinctly her.

A groan builds in my chest, rises up my throat and spills from my lips. I snake my arms around her waist and draw her impossibly closer. Her hands trail up my chest, my neck, my face until her fingers fist my hair.

An inferno blazes around us as I walk her backward. Her back hits the wall, the bulge behind my zipper pressing hard against the junction of her thighs. I run a hand down the side of her leg, then hoist it up to hook my hip.

My hips circle once, twice, and she moans against my lips. Sucks them between hers. Dives back in and siphons my tongue like a succubus. Devours me whole. My dick on the cusp of tearing my slacks.

Bam, bam, bam.

"Peyton? Everything okay?" Ani jiggles the door handle.

Our lips break apart on a gasp and I inch back. But only enough for her to speak.

Chest heaving, she looks up and licks her lips. "Fine," she pants out. "Be out in a minute."

Ani jiggles the handle again. "I heard yelling. Don't piss me off, Micah."

I huff out a laugh. "Everything's fine." I lock on to my new favorite color. Violet. "Wouldn't be in my best interest to piss you off."

Another shake of the handle. Relentless. "If you're not out in five minutes, we'll be having a different conversation soon. An unpleasant one." Not a second later, her heels clack against the concrete and grow quieter with each step.

Without hesitation, I kiss Peyton again. This time, the kiss is less rushed. More tender. Engrossing. And all too soon, with much reluctance, I break the kiss and take a step back.

"We should get back out there," I say, and drop a chaste kiss on her lips.

"Yeah. Okay." She steps into me, hands framing my face, and returns the kiss. "Let's go." Another kiss.

Fuck. If I don't put five to ten feet between us, we will never leave this room. Not that I *want* to, but we need to. We have a job to do and a boss outside this room that will bite my head off if neither of us make an appearance soon.

Peyton steps over to the small mirror beside the door, flattens some of the kinks in her hair and adds a swipe of gloss to her lips from a tube in her pocket. Her eyes meet mine in the mirror as the brightest smile stretches her lips wide. She spins around, then steps into my space. Without a word, she runs her palms up my chest, my neck, then combs her fingers through my hair. And fuck me, I don't want her to stop.

Her hands drop to my collar and straighten the folds. Eyes locked on my lips as she swallows. When her hands fall, her eyes lift to mine again. "Time to work, starlight." She drops one last kiss on my lips before turning on her heel, unlocking the door, and strutting out of the office.

My tongue sweeps over my lips, her coconut gloss sweet on my tastebuds. Tonight may be the most challenging yet, but the test is worth the prize.

~

This has to be the slowest Wednesday in humankind. Slow-est.

Monday to Thursday has never brought in crowds like the weekend, but I don't remember them being this slow in months. With kids out of school, the start of summer usually has mothers stopping by for half-priced cocktails. For whatever reason, tonight is dead.

The new staff left more than an hour ago. They sliced enough citrus to fill the condiment bins for the next three nights. Fifteen minutes ago, I told Kaylynn she could head out for the night as well. Seeing as Roar is only open another hour, Ani wouldn't be too pleased if unnecessary staff stood around with nothing to do.

"Cosmo, please," a brunette says as she parks herself on a barstool.

"Coming up." I get to work on her drink and make light conversation with her. Generic topics such as the weather and asking if she has kids.

I pour the drink, place it on a napkin in front of her, and slide my hands back to my side of the bar. She plucks a bill from her purse and goes to hand it to me. When I reach for it, she takes hold of my hand and keeps it prisoner.

"If you're not busy after—"

"Micah," Peyton barks from the other end of the bar. I glance her way and smile. "How's the rash?"

Dear god, woman.

I sincerely hope Peyton has no concerns about me picking up other women. Not when I kissed the hell out of her three hours ago. But the way she marks her territory without it being obvious to outsiders has me biting my cheek.

"Better since the cream."

The woman quickly removes her hand. "Never mind." She hops off the stool. "Have a good night." And then she waltzes over to a table of women, whispers something to them and they all look my way with wide eyes.

I wipe down the bar top and head toward Peyton. She restocks the disposables —one less thing to do tomorrow before open.

"Did you enjoy that?" I ask when I reach her.

She bats her lashes excessively. "Whatever do you mean?"

"Cute."

"What's cute?"

I love how she plays coy. Goes toe to toe with me or lips off. But this new possessive side… I think I love this side the most. The spunk and bite and territorialism. The unspoken claim only I hear when she fends off other women. Her silent, *"He. Is. Mine."*

Fuck. The ownership makes my dick swell.

One year ago—hell, two months ago—I would never have imagined this raw hunger I harbor for Peyton. Or vice versa. But damn, do I love the energy vibrating through my body. The extra bounce in my step. The constant compulsion to smile. The rapid beat of my heart and expansion of my lungs.

Never imagined I would feel like this again. That I would want more than friendship or meaningless sex with a woman. That I would want to caress and taste a woman more than once.

But Peyton… she changes everything.

"Hang out with me tonight."

"At Teddy's?" I ask, unsure what his definition of hanging out entails.

Micah shakes his head. "We can get food, but that's not what I mean."

I seriously hope after one kiss—a really fucking great kiss—Micah doesn't think I will sleep with him. No doubt the man holds me captive with his looks alone. But I am not like one of the floozies he has taken home time and time again.

Never once have I given up the goods easily. I make men work for more. Make them woo me and prove their loyalty. One and done is not my style. Never has been, never will be. And Micah Reed will not change this.

"What *do* you mean?"

A small step brings him close enough to touch. His eyes drop to my shoulder as he reaches up and toys with the end of my ponytail. "Come back to my place." I wince. "Or yours. The place doesn't matter. I'll order pizza and we can watch a movie."

From point A to B in no time. For a short time, he had me fooled. Had me believing he could be more than a douchebag. The occasional brush of his skin on my arm. Confessions in softer tones. The way his eyes searched mine—deeper, harder. Guess I read the signs wrong. Read him wrong.

"Um." I stall a moment to find the right words to let him down. "Not sure what you thought would happen tonight after that." I point toward the office. "But I don't hook up."

Bright, wide eyes fly up and take me captive. "Peyton, that's not what I meant. Wasn't my intention to suggest—"

"Then tell me your exact intention."

He takes another step closer. A knee comes between mine and knocks them apart. Heat licks my skin—could be his, but I know it comes from within. With each erratic breath I take, he inches closer. Close enough to taste, but I fight the urge. Remind myself we are at work. And kissing Micah behind the bar is not a good idea.

"Pizza, a movie and you sitting on the couch. Believe it or not, I can behave. May take a bit of effort, but it's possible."

No sex. Possibly no making out. Sounds like a solid plan. Although kissing Micah again, away from prying eyes, is definitely on the to-do list. Not that I plan to share this news. For now.

Dinner and a movie and couch time with the man I just kissed. The first man I kissed in more than a year. And damn, what a kiss it was. One for the record books.

If I agree, will either of us keep our hands—and lips—to ourselves? Better yet, which of us will cave first?

"Okay, I'll hang out. But the moment you start sneaking bases, I'm out."

Micah tips his head back and laughs. The rumble loud and deep and unrestrained. Has he ever laughed like this around me? Not to my recollection. But I love the way it shakes his frame. The way his throat reddens and his Adam's apple bobs.

"Noted." He fetches the broom and starts sweeping behind the bar. "Let me know where you want pizza from? I'll order when we leave and pick it up on the way."

"You got it, starlight."

Over the next half hour, we do all the end-of-night tasks. Jake leaves once he wipes down the tables and stools, then cashes out. After Micah takes the tills to the office, we do one last sweep of the club and shut everything down.

On the way to our cars, I tell him where to order my ham, pineapple, garlic and onion pizza from. He makes a face but doesn't insert his opinion. Smart man.

"Mine or yours?" he asks.

My mouth goes dry. I work to hide my sudden need to excessively swallow. "Yours," I choke out.

The hint of a smile twitches at the corner of his mouth. "I'll text you my address, in case we get separated. See you in a bit." Then, as if second nature, he presses a chaste kiss to my lips before going to his truck.

His truck starts up, but he doesn't leave the lot until I drive off. For most of the drive from Tampa to Clearwater, we ride in line with each other or side by side. I feel like a fool with this painful smile stretching my face most of the ride. But no one sees or judges it. So, I leave it in place as the wind whips my hair and the radio plays loud rock tunes.

When I hit the first red light after crossing the Bay, I plug Micah's address into the map app and connect it to the car audio. After I turn off the main road, I scope out the area. This stretch of town is slightly unfamiliar. The map tells me to take the next right.

My brows pinch in the middle. *I cross this exact street almost daily. A couple miles down the road.*

A left turn, then another right. "Your destination is on the right," the navigation announces.

I park on the street and stare out the window at a quaint house. The streetlight one house down illuminates the yard more than the dual lamps on either side of the garage. From the front, the khaki and rich green house appears small. But the extended roofline past the tall wood fence indicates otherwise.

A tall oak, with a trunk too round to hug, occupies a hefty section of the yard to the left of his driveway. Thick branches with lush foliage extend over the house, driveway, and street. On the right of the driveway, white flowers highlight two mature crepe myrtles.

A short distance from the left of the garage, three small steps lead up to a screened-in porch. Soft white light brightens the lanai enough to see a wood bench swing at the end, pair of Adirondack chairs and small table.

As I lean forward and squint to see the flowering shrubs along the porch front, headlights flash in my rearview mirror. I lift a hand to shield the light and drop it as Micah's truck turns into the driveway.

I open the car door and Micah jogs over before I step out. "The street isn't busy, but it's probably best to park behind me."

"'Kay."

In the thirty seconds it takes me to start the car and park in his driveway, my body sprints into panic mode. Sweaty pits, clammy hands, stomach in knots. The whole shebang.

Before I exit the car, I remind myself Micah and I have already hung out. Eaten after work a couple times. I joined him and his friends at a get-together. Hell, I kissed the man like no other only hours ago.

So why the sudden freak-out?

Because we have never been truly alone.

Dining out came with the steady flow of patrons and restaurant staff. Hanging out with his friends... well, that explains itself. And earlier tonight, when we couldn't keep our mouths off each other, people stood less than twenty feet from us —the office walls and door our only form of privacy.

But inside the four walls of Micah's home, it would only be me and him. No one to stop at our table to interrupt conversations. No one to jiggle door handles and inhibit us from touching. Or kissing.

Micah strolls over and opens my door, two pizza boxes balanced in his other hand. "C'mon." He jerks his head toward the house. "Let's get inside and eat."

He shuts the door and I press the fob's lock button. I follow his sure steps on slate pavers. Slow down as we approach the screened porch. Stop breathing as he opens the front door and gestures me inside. He flips a switch beside the door and warm light filters through the space.

"Make yourself at home." He sets the pizzas down on the coffee table and starts unbuttoning his shirt. "Be back in a sec." He disappears down a short hallway.

I step farther into the room, the scent of Micah's cologne and lemon float in the air as my eyes scan every square inch. The house isn't small but feels big for one person. Has Micah always lived alone?

Light oak planks the open floor plan. The exterior wall to the right has more windows than concrete or drywall. During the day, I picture the living and dining area bright and warm and serene.

An earthy-brown couch with a chaise faces the front wall of the house. A natural-edge, wood coffee table with wide iron legs sits within reach, a television mounted feet from the front door. Warm light spills from a lamp between the television and wall of windows, and a second lamp near the corner of the couch.

Across the room, near the windows, is a dining table—the same natural edge as the coffee table—with two chairs on either side. Large round bulbs hang at uneven lengths from thick black cords. In the dark, I bet they glow like stars. Like Micah's eyes. Beyond the table, a large, sepia-tone world map is pinned to a corkboard. A collage of photographs surrounds the map and I step closer to view them.

I reach out and stroke a finger over a younger version of Micah. One I remember from years back. When life was simple and not so simple. In the photo, he has an arm around Shelly and who I assume is their mother. All three of them smiling without a care in the world.

"That was in the Smoky Mountains."

I jump and slap a hand over my chest. "What are you, part secret agent?" He laughs with a shake of his head. "Don't sneak up like that."

"Didn't mean to." Another chuckle leaves his lips. He presses his front to my back as his arms snake around my waist. "Just saw you here and didn't want to disturb you." Warm, soft lips press against the skin beneath my ear. "I like seeing you in my space."

I wiggle out of his arms and twist to face him. "And how many other women have you delivered that exact line to?" The question is meant to be a joke, considering all the women that have left Roar on Micah's arm.

But guilt swirls like a waterspout beneath my diaphragm as his face pales. *Shit.*

"The women I left the club with… they never set foot in this house." His eyes close as he inhales deep. On the exhale, his eyes reopen. "The last woman to step foot in this house brought another man." Dark, starry irises swallow me whole. "You being here… let's just say it's a big step."

Wow. Just wow.

Way to make an ass of yourself, Peyton.

"I didn't—" I fumble over my words. Unsure how to pedal back and fix my mistake. "Sorry."

A hand brushes mine before our fingers intertwine. "Let's eat." He nods toward the couch.

We plop down on the sofa and I open the pizza boxes as Micah scans a list of movies on the television. When I look up, he selects *Pulp Fiction*, presses pause and sets the remote on the table.

"Want a drink?" He rises from the couch and ambles toward the small, yet spacious kitchen. Whoever designed the kitchen knew how to make the most out of the limited space.

I follow Micah with my eyes. Take in his relaxed demeanor and attire. Drop my gaze down his backside and swallow. Something about gray sweats and a snug cotton tee…

He fetches a pitcher from the fridge and sets it on the small island while getting glasses. The island sits askew in the open space, three barstools on the side facing the living and dining area. The overall vibe of the kitchen is a blend of dark wood cabinets, stainless steel appliances, and light granite counters. A large window over the sink faces the backyard. For someone who doesn't cook, his kitchen is dreamy. I would cook in it.

Wait. What?

Why does being here—in Micah's space, his home—feel so natural? So comfortable? Why does it conjure thoughts of us wrapped up in each other? Laughter and flour handprints and water fights with the sink sprayer.

"Water, please," I croak out and turn to face the television.

Snap out of it, Peyton.

When half of my pizza—and all of Micah's—vanishes, I set the box on the table and pat my belly. Micah scoots over until our arms bump, and then he rests a hand on my thigh. The contact is simple and non-suggestive. Yet it warms me more than the summer evening.

I rest my head on his shoulder and do my best to focus on the movie. Which works out… until Micah kisses my hair. Then does it again. And again.

His hand on my thigh takes on a new weight. Feels heavier and hotter.

Before I overthink what happens next, I lift my head and rotate to lock on this softer side of Micah. I hold his gaze for three breaths before dropping my eyes to his lips. I lean closer, slowly eradicate the space between us, and kiss him.

A low frequency hum purrs in my bloodstream when our lips collide. The kiss is soft and chaste at first. A slow buildup to the fiery kiss we shared earlier, but equally soul stirring.

Our tongues stroke with languid movements. Hands and fingers explore uncharted terrain but don't cross the line. A hand slips under the back of my top and guides me back to lie on the couch. One of his legs wedges between mine. His weight above me is welcome and constant and perfect. The planes and lines and musculature of his frame mold to mine as the kiss picks up tempo.

My hands trail up his chest, his neck, and fist his hair. He moans and rocks his hips forward, grinding his thick erection against the junction of my thighs. Lust clouds every rational thought, and I do it again. He breaks the kiss with a gasp. Teeth nip along my jaw, my ear, the column of my neck, the base of my throat. Then he licks leisurely up, tasting me, until our lips crash together.

We kiss like horny teenagers. His erection rock hard between my thighs. My panties drenched and clit throbbing. But neither of us leads the moment beyond heavy kissing and light petting. Micah staying true to his word—that nothing further would happen tonight—makes my heart happy and body frustrated.

As if my thoughts were broadcasted aloud, he breaks the kiss and gasps. "You'll be the death of me."

Before I get a word in, he shifts us both so we lie on our sides and face the television. His front to my back. His hips lined up with mine, I'm acutely aware his erection hasn't calmed whatsoever. And I love that he doesn't hide his body's reaction.

He reaches for a throw pillow and tucks it beneath our heads. His hand on my hip dips as his fingers trail the faint line of exposed skin between my shirt and pants. Fingers skirt beneath the shirt hem and splay over my belly. Although his hand doesn't move, the tips of his fingers paint small circles near my navel. I feel every whirl and loop and stroke, at the point of origin and throughout my body.

I close my eyes. Forget about the movie. Forget about everything except the tingles rippling over my skin from his touch. How can something so simple feel so damn good?

Then he licks up my neck from the curve of my shoulder and I moan. Press my ass against him. Lose myself in the intoxication of it all when his free hand clutches my throat. Squeezes enough that I see his starry irises behind closed lids.

"You have it wrong," I choke out.

He licks and nips his way to my ear. Sucks my lobe between his teeth. "What's that?"

I lift a hand over his at my throat and hold it there. "You'll be the death of me first."

Bzzt. Bzzt.

Peyton twitches in my arms, then relaxes. Her chest rises and falls in a steady, rhythmic tempo. I nestle more into her neck and curl my arm tighter around her midsection. Hold her closer as I drift back to sleep.

Bzzt. Bzzt.

I shake half awake. Peyton groans, twists in my arms, snuggles closer to my chest and burrows her face near the base of my throat. My leg drapes hers as our lower limbs tangle. I draw her impossibly closer. Kiss her hair. Cradle her against the length of my torso. Her warm breath at the hollow of my throat soothes and settles me back to sleep.

Bzzt. Bzzt.

Peyton grumbles against my chest and I tighten my hold on her.

Bzzt. Bzzt.

"Who is that?" I complain, my words like sandpaper.

Peyton shifts in my arms and I open my eyes. I look down at her as she peers up. Inch down to press my lips to hers. Her phone buzzes on the coffee table again. For the umpteenth time.

She stretches an arm behind her and slaps the table until it lands on her phone. When the screen lights, she bolts upright. "Oh, shit."

If I wasn't awake a minute ago, I am now. "What's wrong?" I scrub a hand down my face and blink several times to shake off the sleep.

"It's after eight." I stare at her and patiently wait for the reason why this is a bad thing. That was the best sleep I have gotten in weeks. No sense in complaining. "In the morning. As in, I stayed the night at your house."

"This is a bad thing?"

Unlocking her phone, she opens her text messages and starts typing. "No. Yes. No."

My hand draws lazy circles on her lower back. "Take a minute to wake up. I'm sure everything is fine."

She drops the phone in her lap, then gives me her profile. Stares at the ceiling as her weight presses into my side. "It is. But Reese is freaking out because I didn't come home or let him know I was staying out."

I wiggle to the cushion edge and rise from the couch. Head toward the kitchen for water before I say something irrational about their close relationship. The water staves off an inkling of my jealousy. So, I drink more.

Last thing I need to do after sleeping with Peyton in my arms all night is to piss her off. My unjustifiable green monster needs to sit the fuck down and chill the fuck out. I have no right to be jealous over a friendship she's had for decades.

Peyton saunters into the kitchen, steps up behind me, and wraps her arms around my waist. Her arms crisscross over my chest as she presses her palms flat to my pecs. God, I love the feel of her body against mine. No awkwardness or mismatched placement. She fits every angle and curve as if meant to be there.

"He's not mad because I stayed out," she whispers along the curve of my neck.

"Just wanted to make sure I wasn't lying in a hospital. We usually text or leave notes when staying out late. He was worried. That's all."

My rational brain processes this and shakes a finger. *Don't be a dick. They are just friends.*

I rotate my head and drop an innocent kiss on her lips. "Glad you have someone who worries. Sorry."

"No need to be sorry." Her arms form parallel lines on my stomach and constrict. "All this between us..." Warm lips trail up my neck and my eyes roll shut. Fuck, every touch Peyton gives feels amazing. "Is new. For me and you."

I twist in her grip and wind my arms around her. Drop my lips to hers, but don't deepen the kiss. When we break apart, I tuck loose tendrils of her hair behind her ear. Study her freshly woken features—hair in a messy topknot, pillow crease lines on her cheek, brows a bit shifty, eyes bright but not yet alert.

If I woke up next to her each morning, it would be a great life.

I kiss the tip of her nose. "Gonna go brush my teeth." Her eyes widen as a hand covers her mouth. As if she just thought about her own morning breath. "Probably have extra toothbrushes in the bathroom." She lifts a brow. "From the dentist goody bags." I kiss her forehead, wrap her hand in mine, and lead her to the bathroom.

After we get the bathroom to ourselves a moment, I dig out a spare toothbrush. We hover near the sink, squeeze paste from the tube, and brush simultaneously. And it's so bizarre. How scrubbing our teeth together is the most normal my life has felt in a long time.

"Confession," I say as we enter the main space of the house. "Although I fail at cooking most foods, breakfast is not one of them. So, you're in luck." She laughs as I guide her to the barstools. "Have a seat, hellcat. I'll whip us up something. Promise it'll be edible."

Peyton parks herself at the breakfast bar, props her elbows on the counter, and rests her chin in her hands. Her violet eyes sparkle as they follow my every move. And damn, I love how good it feels to have her eyes rake over my backside. To survey my body without shame. Heat my skin and drive me wild.

From the fridge, I collect eggs, milk, cheese, and butter. Sausage links from the freezer and the loaf of bread on the island. I set a pan on the stove, crank the heat to medium-low and add some oil. Next, I crack eggs in the bowl, add milk and whip them together. All the while, Peyton watches me in mesmerized silence.

Domesticity has never been something I pictured in my life. Mom and Dad have it down to a science. A natural flow whenever they are together. Synergy. Anyone in their presence sees it, feels it. Obviously it exists, but I never considered I'd have the same simplicity in my own life. Not even with Rochelle.

But as Peyton's eyes follow me around the kitchen, watch me season and mix and flip, my mind considers new possibilities.

I drop bread in the toaster, then add shredded cheese to scrambled eggs as the sausage finishes. After I grab plates from the cabinet, I fish a butter knife from the drawer. The toaster clicks and the bread pops up. I butter, then cut the slices in half and add them to the plates. Followed by the eggs and sausage.

"Your breakfast, m'lady." I deposit a plate in front of Peyton and hand her a fork. "Coffee, milk or juice?"

"Coffee, please."

I brew us both a cup from the Keurig, then join her at the breakfast bar. We eat in relative silence. Her knee bops mine a few times until she leaves it there. Until our plates empty, we find some way to keep physical contact. Knee or foot or elbow. The contact has my chest fluttery and limbs tingly.

"Really should head home," Peyton says as she sips the last of her coffee.

She slides down from the stool, ambles to the couch, and puts her shoes on. Usually going separate ways from a woman gives me relief. But as Peyton collects her purse and phone, an ache builds beneath my sternum.

"Would it upset you if I said I don't want you to leave?"

A soft smile tugs at the corners of her mouth. "Quite the opposite. But I need to shower, put on fresh clothes, and do errands before work."

I follow her to the door, but neither of us moves to open it. "Know it wasn't intentional, but I'm glad you stayed." Inching closer, I plant my hands on either side of her and box her in. "Haven't slept like that in a long time."

Her palms flatten on my pecs. "Oh, yeah. And how's that?"

My head lowers, lips an inch from hers. "Solid. Restful." I drop my lips to hers and taste the coffee on her lips. "All because you were in my arms."

Pink paints her cheeks as she swallows. Her reaction sends a rush throughout my body. "Me, too," she admits with an unfamiliar level of softness.

I dip down and take her mouth again. She fists my shirt and I drop my hands to her hips, heaving our bodies closer together. Her lips part and our tongues duel. Hands trail up my chest and dive into my hair, clenching the strands and tugging. A growl rises in my chest and spills into her as she deepens the kiss. Mouth fucks me near my front door.

Then she breaks the kiss, pins me in place with her vibrant irises, and inches back. "Really should go." Her breathy words lack oomph.

I drop a kiss on her lips. Then another. "Okay. I'll walk you out." After a quick adjustment, I unlock the door, take Peyton's hand, and lead her out the door.

The car beeps when she presses the fob, but she doesn't get in immediately. We exchange a few more chaste kisses before she opens the door and slips behind the wheel. The engine starts up and she rolls down the window.

"Best unintentional sleepover," she says, leaning out the window. I bend and kiss her one last time. "See you tonight."

"Tonight." I tap the roof of her SUV. She rolls up the window and backs out of the driveway. Within seconds, her car vanishes from sight.

I trudge my way to the front door and stumble inside. Flopping down on the couch, I rest my head on the pillow we shared not long ago. Inhale her lingering coconut and mint scent on the throw pillow. And bask in the simplicity and tranquility I felt—still feel—with Peyton in my space. In my arms. In my world.

Lost fucking cause. Might as well etch it on my skin now.

I straight up pouted when Peyton arrived at Roar fifteen minutes prior to open. With all the extra prep done yesterday and Kaylynn showing Mable and Caleb more tonight, Peyton didn't need to rush. Which means I got zero alone time with her beforehand.

And now, I stomp around the club with a permanent frown and childish demeanor.

"Someone's not having a good day," Peyton teases when I step behind the bar.

I bump our shoulders together. "Hmm. Wonder why?"

The corner of her mouth kicks up in a playful half smile. "Maybe someone needs a nap or caffeine." Her tone pouty and mocking. Makes me want to bite her lip.

"Or…" I drawl the two-letter word out as an idea sparks. "Maybe I need to take someone in the office." Her violet eyes go wide. "To show you how the invoices need to be cataloged, of course."

Her frame sags a hair, but her eyes don't leave mine. Unspoken questions on whether or not sneaking off to the office is a good idea. The fact I won't see Peyton every night at Roar is the perfect reason. Although, we are most definitely seeing each other outside these walls again. Often.

I approach Kaylynn as she explains the non-serving aspects of the job to Mable and Caleb. Both listen with rapt attention. "Hey." Kaylynn shifts her gaze and pauses her instruction. "You all good out here if I teach Peyton management tasks in the office?"

Kaylynn scans the club. Still early, the place doesn't have much activity. The Thursday crowd usually picks up in an hour. "Yeah, boss. I'll come get you if it's busy."

Peyton hesitates until I round the corner of the hall. Her heels clap on the floor in quick succession as she catches up. Not a breath after the office door closes, and the lock flips, I smash her against the wall. Kiss her hard and rough. Grind my stiffening cock to the junction of her thighs. Moan as her taste hits my tongue.

We kiss like brutal beasts ready to shred the other's clothes. Fingers fist my hair and yank hard. I bend at the knees and rub my pulsating cock over the seam of her pants. A sweet whimper exits her lips and I swallow it down.

All we have done is kiss and dry fuck. If she gets this turned on and desperate with our clothes on, she will no doubt ravage me when we are skin to skin.

Presumptuous of me to assume Peyton and I will have sex, I know. Although I plan to take my time with Peyton, not jump the gun and ruin the foundation we are building, our relationship will go next level. And beyond.

I break the kiss, take a step back, and smash my palm to my dick. "Fuck, hellcat."

She bends at the waist, drops her hands to her knees and gasps. "Back at ya, starlight."

It takes a hot minute, but once our breathing levels out, I guide us to the desk. "We really should do some work. Can't drag you in here constantly and leave you still not knowing what to do." I chuckle.

Peyton drags a chair from the guest side of the desk and parks it next to the one reserved for the manager on duty. For the next hour, I slip on my leader mask and focus on the task at hand. Peyton hangs on every word as I go over payroll, inventory, invoices, and scheduling. Watches my every move as I key figures into the spreadsheets. Asks questions to clarify how often we do full inventory and handle the cash each night. In my unbiased opinion, Peyton learns and catches on quickly. Which is great for two reasons.

One—I don't have to repeat myself. Not that I wouldn't have if necessary. And two—I get more alone time with her while I show her the ropes. It's a win-win.

Everything has fallen into place. Work. Life. Both feel more on track than any other time in the past. For once, I am headed in the right direction.

Can't remember the last time life flowed so smoothly. Had this level of comfort. Streamlined without effort. Maybe with Chad?

Chad Lark—the first guy I dated, post high school. Guys in high school weren't worth my time, effort, or energy. But Chad was different. Mature and kind and gentle—although he knew how and when to be rough and harsh. In our two years together, we were inseparable. A team. He was the marrying type and I would have said yes.

Unfortunately, Chad never got to ask.

One morning, Chad didn't wake up. The coroner said a natural defect caused the chambers of his heart to not contract as normally. He died peacefully in his sleep. He was twenty-two. We had started planning for the future. Hinted at taking the next step. Neither of us aware that his heart had a sooner expiration date.

They say you never forget your first love. The sentiment is true. I will never forget Chad.

Sadly, I have dealt with enough heartache to last multiple lifetimes. One can only hope I have met my quota.

Life is on an upswing. Work is taking steps along a positive path. I busted my ass—contrary to what Micah believes—to get here. Learned so much about the business and have done my fair share of hands-on. Ani groomed me little by little over the span of our friendship. Long before the announcement of my promotion, she pegged me as her go-to person. Someone she trusted. Someone she wanted to help run her business. I was more than thrilled to be chosen by her. Ani will always be more than my boss. She's the sister I never had growing up.

Outside of work… well, that seems to be pretty damn good too.

In a matter of months, I went from loathing Micah Reed to fantasizing over our next kiss. The way his lips devour, the way he puts every ounce of passion into each kiss… my body quivers. Trembles and whimpers, imagining the idea of more. Of his bare chest against my breasts. Of his hands and fingers tracing lines and peaks and valleys as he maps my body. Of his lips on my breasts, my abdomen, and between my thighs.

"Hey." Micah sidles up to me behind the bar. "Everything alright? You're flush." Starry eyes survey every exposed inch of my skin.

I pour a glass of water and drink it. "Fine. Just got warm."

When the glass empties, Micah inches closer and brings a hand to my cheek. "Sure you're alright?" I knock his hand away and he has a light bulb moment. Leaning closer, his lips and hot breath brush my ear. "Were you thinking about me just now? About us?"

I breathe in short, quick bursts. My breasts rise and fall and graze his pecs. Heat blooms from my chest, paints my skin, my neck, my cheeks. Fingers trail up the side of my thigh, stop at my hip bone and squeeze.

Part of me worries what our interaction looks like from an outsider's perspective. Are we the center of attention? Can people not look away? Not that Roar has brought in a crowd tonight.

The other part of me doesn't give a damn and aches to drag him closer. Smash my lips to his. Kiss him like he is my last meal. Ignore the audience and take what I want.

"Yes," I answer, breathy. No sense in skirting around the truth.

"What were you thinking about?" His tongue licks the shell of my ear. My eyes roll shut as my bones turn to putty. "Tell me, Peyton."

Jesus fuck. Now is not the time for this conversation. Roar—among employees and patrons—is not the place to have this conversation. But with each passing second, my will to steer this talk in another direction becomes more difficult.

I hook fingers in his front pockets. Eager to pull him to me, but keep him rooted in place. "Was thinking about last night." I lick my lips. "Kissing you."

"Kissing me then?" He nips my earlobe. "Or kissing me now?"

"Both," I admit, softly. "How I want your hands on my skin."

His chest vibrates as a growl tears up his throat. A hand fists my hip. "Come over again tonight."

It isn't a question. More like a directive. I hate the way I love his subdued demand.

"We aren't having sex," I whisper, in the hopes no one hears this not-safe-for-work conversation.

The hand on my hips tightens and releases. "There're other ways to enjoy each other without sex. Figured you'd know that, hellcat." He inches away. "Come over."

The lights and '80s music flood back in as cool air smacks my face. My eyes scan the club, behind the bar, but no one pays us any attention. At least not now.

"Yeah, okay."

A bright, toothy smile lights up Micah's face. I love this smile. "Perfect." He smacks my ass. "Now, get back to work."

The rest of the night goes as slow as last night. Weekdays during the summer can be hit or miss for places like Roar. Hence why Ani wanted fresh ideas. New attractants to draw in the same crowd and maybe new people. With Ani, her market research, and how she wants things perfect from the get-go, the new changes will be great for business.

As the night wears on, the crowd thins and Micah lets the staff leave early, one by one. With thirty minutes until the door locks, Kaylynn and I start stocking and cleanup while Micah serves.

Sweeping the floor behind the bar, I peer down at the opposite end as a blonde woman steps up. In a blazing-red dress that leaves nothing to the imagination, she smiles at Micah and leans toward him. A shiver rolls down my spine as he returns the smile. Although it's forced, I recognize the familiarity between them.

He says something and grabs a shaker, ready to mix her a drink. But she shakes her head. With each stroke of the broom, I inch my way down the bar and closer to them. Micah's face reddens as he works his jaw, then says something else. Their conversation too quiet for me to hear yet. So, I sweep down the line faster.

"I just want to talk," she complains as I pretend not to hear.

Still far enough away, Micah might not realize I hear the exchange.

"Before we hooked up, I told you there'd be nothing else. What's there to talk about?"

Not that I didn't know Micah was a manwhore. But hearing him verbally duke it out with some desperate floozy is insane. Another reason to resist temptation and not have sex with Micah yet.

"I really don't want to do this here," she shoots back with a huff.

"No one's stopping you from leaving." Micah waves a hand in the air.

I step closer after sweeping the same square footage for too long. Micah has to know I am within earshot now.

"Why are you being such an asshole?" she shouts.

Now is when I opt to turn around. Time for me to get acquainted with my managerial role. We don't get a ton of bullshit in Roar, but every now and again, we have to deal with the belligerent and physically violent.

"Ma'am." Her eyes snap to mine and she stiffens. "Not sure what the problem is, but you need to calm down or leave. Your choice."

She crosses her arms and forces up her breasts. "I'm not leaving until I talk with him."

"And I already said, not happening," Micah states as I sidle up to him and form a stronghold.

"Fine," she huffs out. "Don't want to go somewhere private? We'll do it right here." My brow pinches at the middle, and Micah rolls his eyes. "I'm pregnant, asshole. And you're going to be a daddy."

A Love So Bright

INSOMNIAC DUET
BOOK TWO

one

MICAH

"I'm pregnant, asshole. And you're going to be a daddy," the blonde—whose name I don't remember—shouts.

My feet stumble backward until I bump the back counter. The earth quakes beneath my feet. And no matter how deep I inhale, air refuses to fill my lungs. I shake my head, refusing to believe a word this woman says.

A loud clang rings out and I snap my head to the left. Peyton stands frozen in place, the broom handle on the ground. Her eyes wide and mouth agape.

Shit. Fuck.

Peyton doesn't move, doesn't breathe. Her eyes locked on the woman spewing lies on the opposite side of the bar. All the color has drained from Peyton's face. Her hands tremble at her sides. Any moment, she may explode with fury. Question is, will that fury be directed at me?

I need to fix this. Now.

"Sorry to break the news to you, but I always wrap up. Go trap some other random guy you hooked up with." I fold my arms over my chest, widen my stance, and hold my ground. Appearing more confident than I feel.

The woman throws her head back and laughs. Laughs. Like she has secret intel. "Condoms aren't always a hundred-percent effective."

She didn't own or discount sleeping around. Note to self. "You don't look pregnant." I wave a hand toward her skintight, come-fuck-me dress. "You on the prowl for another man to trap?" She grinds her jaw as her face reddens. "Until you have legal proof of what you're claiming, you need to leave."

The woman slams her palms on the bar and shrieks. A few people linger as Roar prepares to close, but their eyes don't deviate from the madness. I don't move or react to her obvious attempt at baiting me. And it seems to bother her more.

Oh. Fucking. Well.

Yes, it's true, I have slept with a shit ton of women. Maybe two or three different women per week over the last year plus. The title manwhore was earned—not that I am proud. But I swear to whatever deity listens, I never went without a condom. Ever. And each one that got tossed in the trash was intact. If it wasn't, the woman would have known then and there, and other preventive measures would have commenced.

Which is why I refuse to believe this woman. No doubt she slept with some schmuck she can't pin down. Next easiest resolution, nail it on a guy you can find.

Sorry, bitch. Not happening.

After minutes of not caving, she grunts, pushes away from the bar and heads for the door. But not before calling over her shoulder. "You'll see me again. Count on it." Then she disappears.

Thank fuck.

For the first time in what seems like hours, I breathe. I turn to face Peyton and notice she hasn't moved. At all. Is she breathing?

Shit.

"Hey," I say and lift my hands to frame her face. She doesn't respond. Her eyes vacant and off in the distance. "Peyton?" I step in front of her, crowd her, so she will look me in the eye, and stroke my thumbs over her cheeks. "Peyton, look at me."

I stop breathing. My eyes refuse to deviate from hers. Then, she blinks several times as if waking from a deep sleep. Her usual fiery violet irises are duller as they refocus. My thumbs continue to stroke her cheeks as she starts to shake her head. When her chin wobbles, my pulse jolts.

"I need to go," she mutters.

"What?"

"Micah..." Her eyes glaze over as she tucks her lips between her teeth. "I... I need to go."

Go? What does she mean she needs to go? Go where?

Maybe she needs to sit down and breathe a minute. Shake off the crazy bitch that flew in and stormed out. If I were her, I would need time to process what just went down.

"Why don't you go sit in the office. I'll finish up out here. Then we can head out."

Glassy violet irises whip to my starry blues. "No, Micah." Her breathing picks up. Lungs heaving as if they can't pull in enough oxygen. "I need to go *home*. Knew this was a bad idea."

She starts to step away from me, but I catch her elbow. "Peyton." Her name is a plea for mercy on my tongue. "Please, just come back to my place. We can talk about this." I point toward the door. "There is no possible way that woman is pregnant by me. Or any woman, for that matter."

Realization of how loud this conversation is has my eyes sweeping the club. I breathe easier when I see everyone has left. Well, the patrons are gone. The remaining staff has scattered to give us privacy.

"How can you be so sure? I'm no rocket scientist, Micah, but even I know the tiniest pinprick can lead to pregnancy."

Jesus fucking Christ.

Why is she on this other woman's side? Is it the whole "women band together" thing? Because in this situation, that is complete and utter bullshit. Not when one of the women is shady as fuck.

If Peyton walks away from me now, I have a feeling I won't stand a chance in the future. Again. No matter what, we can't go separate ways tonight. Not with this fake ass shit lingering in the air. Not without talking this through and seeing reason.

"Peyton." Her name is a whisper on my tongue as I step back into her space. "This whole situation is a clusterfuck. But I know, without a shadow of doubt, there is no possible way that woman is pregnant with *my* child. Not a chance. So, please..." I fully invade her space. Bring my lips to her ear. Feel her tremble beneath me as I rest my hands on her arms. "Please, don't do this. Don't walk away. Don't shut me out. Not without giving me a chance. Not without giving *us* a chance."

For day-long seconds, she remains a statue in my arms. Stoic and silent. Her hot breath on my neck the only reminder this is real. That this isn't an epic nightmare— at least not the type to vanish when you open your eyes. This nightmare is manageable. It would be more manageable if Peyton took my side. If she believed the truth. *My truth.*

Do pregnancies happen when condoms are worn? All the time.

But I am no damn fool. Maybe off my rocker at times, but not a fool. The guy in the contraceptive aisle inspecting the condom boxes with hardcore scrutiny… yep, that would be Micah Reed. The guy who opens the box when he gets home and examines every wrapper for any cuts, tears or holes. That would also be me. Condoms don't go in my wallet unless I am one-hundred-percent sure they are tamper-free. Hell, I even buy the ones with spermicide.

Don't care what the woman said, her baby—if she is actually pregnant—doesn't share my DNA.

Peyton fights an internal battle. Her fingers ball into fists, then relax, over and over. Much as I don't want her to walk away from me tonight, she gets to make the decision to stay or go. What is happening between us is fresh, new. Wouldn't surprise me if she took a step back and told me to fuck off. That she didn't sign up for this.

But I really want her to step up and fight. Stick with me as we navigate our feelings. Then, give in to those emotions. Allow me to give in to mine.

For far too long, Peyton has consumed my thoughts. I suspected the moment I had a chance with her, I would shred her clothes and relish my name on her tongue.

The moment my lips crashed down on hers, though… it was as if my synapses fired right for the first time. Pieces fell into place and life started to make sense. And if I felt all that after one kiss, I fantasize what life may be like after I taste more than her lips. More serious and intense. Addictive and engrossing. I won't be able to stay away from her.

Which is why *I'm* not ready to have sex with Peyton.

Hands brush the sides of my torso and snake around my waist to connect at my lower back. I inhale deeply for the first time in minutes. Let the cool air fill my lungs and settle my anxiety. Allow my body to relax and melt with hers.

"I'll come back to your place under one condition," she whispers in my ear. "We talk. That's it. Tonight will not be a rerun of last night."

I nod. This, I accept… with one slight variation. "Can we at least grab food?" I lean back, sweep wayward strands of hair from her face, and brush my knuckles down her cheek. "Microwave meals from the store or order delivery. Don't care which. But we should eat."

"That's fine." She looks to the broom on the ground. "We should finish up and close."

I don't want to free her from my hold, but we will never leave otherwise. So I loosen my grip and step back. I drop a kiss on her forehead, take a deep breath and nod.

We get back to work and finish our nightly tasks. Twenty minutes fly by faster than expected and it isn't long before we say good night to the staff walking out the door with us. I tell Peyton I will order Chinese and pick it up on the way to the house. After she gives me her order, she hops in her car and drives out of the lot.

As her taillights disappear, an odd sensation slithers up my spine, spreads through my limbs and I shiver head to toe. The sensation eats me alive like a microbial plague. Makes me second-guess Peyton's reason to come over tonight. Acid rises in my throat and I swallow to stanch it from exiting my lips.

It's all in your head, man. Don't make something out of nothing.

After several deep breaths, I call the Chinese joint near my house. I order more than either of us will eat, but plan to have leftovers for another meal or two. Once the order is placed, I take one last deep breath, death grip the steering wheel, and drive off.

When I hit the bridge, I pray the salty air whipping my face and filling my lungs will untwist this knife in my gut. Will loosen the knot gradually getting tighter with each mile my truck eats up. Will vanquish the overall bad feeling swallowing me whole.

No matter how many breaths I take, no matter how I steer my thoughts, the pang beneath my diaphragm doesn't fade. If anything, the knife twists deeper. Grinds my bones and digs into the marrow.

Please, let this be my imagination running wild. Don't let the beginning of what we have go to shit. Not over this.

I repeat this again and again. A dictum to reign over what will come of tonight. A precept to dictate the future, regardless of the irrationality steering my thoughts. Because if you repeat something enough times, if you put the energy out into the universe, it becomes truth. Not like prophecy. More like guidance down the path of my choosing.

The red-dress woman made an attempt to derail my life, my future, tonight. Tried to trap me with a pregnancy scare. But she won't rattle me so easily. She won't cuff me at the ankle and drag me beside her. Not without hard proof. And until that day arrives, I will live my life. On my terms.

Who knows what my future holds. If Peyton is a part of said future, I will be forever indebted to her and whatever celestial being grants me the opportunity. An opportunity to right the wrongs I have committed. An opportunity to see where our connection leads.

"Thank you," I mutter into the wind. "Whoever is looking out for me, thank you."

I won't let you down.

Two

Why the hell am I here? Why did I agree to this?

Agreeing to meet Micah at his house after what just happened is not a good idea. Especially with my mind all over the place. I don't know which way is up or whose truth to believe. Anger and frustration and anguish claw me up one side and down the other. My guardian angel has one hand on her hip while she wags a finger from the other in my face. The words *I told you so* on the tip of her tongue.

I want to heed her advice and drive off before Micah gets home. Save my heart from another walk down Shitty Life Lane. Yet, here I am. Waiting. A glutton for punishment.

I press the heel of my palm to my breastbone and rub. Do my best to sooth the ache and simmer the heightened sting. One by one, my heart leaks every ounce of hope and joy and possibility I had for Micah. Spills it at my feet. And I simply watch it puddle before it seeps into the earth.

Fuck.

When it comes to me, Micah Reed breeds misfortune.

As a young woman, I pined for him. Watched him from afar on the track. Peeked his direction whenever he was near. Even after he crushed my soul with his words, even after he made a mockery of me in front of half the school, I still yearned for his affection. For his attention. For any fondness he would bestow upon me.

Then, I grew up.

The memory of him always sat in the shadows of my mind, but I moved on. Found people who knew my worth. Knew I wasn't just some loner girl with a crazy obsession for all things black. Knew I had more to give. And those people surrounded me with smiles and laughter and love. They lifted me up and brought me back to life. Showed me real friendship and what it meant to care for others. I owe them more than I will ever be able to give.

So why the hell am I here?

Why did I willingly choose to walk into the lion's den? Why am I setting myself up for more pain? More pain inflicted by Micah Reed.

"Because I'm a fucking idiot," I whisper into the dark cab of my SUV.

Unlike last night, Micah's house holds no interest. I don't stare at the shrubs and flowering plants along the front and try to guess what they are. I don't stare at the wood fence and wonder what setup he has beyond the wall of windows. I don't have the energy to care. Not tonight. Not after the wake-up call from Little Miss Red Dress.

Not focusing on anything in particular, I stare toward the end of the street. Let my eyes glaze over as they land on the yellow diamond sign that reads *no outlet*. Space out and let my mind blank as I wait.

Before long, Micah's headlights beam around the corner and blind me in the rearview mirror. Once he parks in the driveway, I move my car to park behind him. He hops out of his truck with two hefty bags of food and waits for me to join him.

Here we go.

The thirteen steps from his driveway to the front door feel like miles. Neither of us says a word as he unlocks the door, flips the light on and gestures me toward the couch. He sets the bags on the table, kisses the top of my head and wanders down the hall to what I presume is his bedroom.

Twenty-one breaths later, he settles on the couch, his leg brushing mine. Silence dominates the room like a deprivation chamber. And with each passing tick of the clock, a new pin gets pushed into the voodoo doll made to inflict me with pain.

Cursed. That's what this is. My life curse. If not, I am all ears for some other logical explanation. Some magical reason as to why I can't seem to hold on to... love, happiness, anything worthwhile.

I don't *love* Micah. It is way too soon to feel such a powerful emotion. But I do like him. More than I imagined possible after all the hurt he caused.

But every person I get romantically close to... the relationship always goes south. Every. Single. Time.

Am I destined to be a loner hag? A cat lady minus the cats. Always just me, myself and I as my hair turns gray and wrinkles define my face more than my expression.

As a little girl, I don't remember a time when I played dress-up, pretended to marry the boy up the street, and have babies in our perfect house with the perfect yard. I never fantasized about a prince sweeping me off my feet and rescuing me from tragedy. I didn't dream of a happily ever after and forever love. It just wasn't who I was.

But as years passed, my perspective on life shifted. I see things in a different light and with occasional filters. I wonder what would happen if I took a leap, tried something new, explored all the possibilities.

I don't want to spend my life alone. But I also don't want the heartache that comes with giving your all to another person.

And with Micah's history, heartache has an open-ended invitation.

Carton by carton, he pulls the food from bags. Sets a small container of shrimp egg foo young, rice and gravy in front of me on the coffee table. Places a fork and chopsticks on top.

"Hungry?" I choke out as Micah removes another four cartons and a container of soup.

He gives a timid smile. "I like leftovers. Makes my life easier."

Life probably won't be so easy for the next however many months. I want to say this to him. Want to tell him just because he says the baby—real or not—isn't his, doesn't make it true. Only science will prove one way or the other. And as crazy as the woman was in Roar, I don't picture her backing down. She will return, with a smug smile on her face. She will be a constant smack in the face, a constant reminder of who Micah was before.

I open the cartons and poke at the food. Eat a few small bites. Taste the egg, shrimp and vegetable pancakes, but don't savor them. Not like I usually do. When I peek at Micah from the corner of my eye, he appears to be in the same predicament. Half an egg roll eaten, some missing lo mein noodles, and a few slurps of egg drop soup gone.

"Micah..." He sets the egg roll down on the wrapper, wipes his hands clean, then meets my gaze. His eyes are veiny and damp. The starry flecks less visible in his dark-sky irises. "We have to talk about this."

Have to, versus want to, are two different animals.

I don't *want* to talk about the possibility of some random woman being pregnant from the guy I just started spending time with. We just sorted out our differences. He apologized and I mentally forgave him sometime over the last two weeks. Things between us were headed in a good direction. And now we *need* to talk about this.

We need to talk about the *what-ifs*.

"Yeah, we do." He huffs and sags into the couch. "For the record, though, this sucks."

This does suck. Hairy, sweaty, nasty balls.

He sits back up, plants his elbows on his knees, then leans forward and hangs his head. His broad shoulders stretch the cotton of his shirt. Put the definition of his muscles and stress on display. I swallow at the sight. My fingers itch to reach out. To trace the lines of tension in his neck and upper back and soothe his suffering. I lift a hand, then hesitate. Resist temptation. Drop my hand, curl my fingers into fists at my sides and force them to stay put.

Micah may need comfort right now, but so do I. This situation may not be directly impacting me, but it impacts me nonetheless.

"What if she is pregnant?" I pose the first of many questions.

He sits straighter. "She might be." He twists to face me and our knees knock. "But I won't believe anything without proof."

This I understand. If I were in his shoes, I would want hard evidence too. To be present as the tests are performed. Receive my own letter of proof when the results become available. Micah may have slept with his fair share of the female population, but I believe him when he says he practiced safety measures.

"What if tests prove the baby is yours?" I wince as the words leave my lips.

My reaction may give the vibe I don't care for children. Couldn't be further from the truth. I love their chubby cheeks and chunky legs. Love their expressions and laughter when you make faces or speak in different tones. Love how soft they are and how good they smell. Their innocence and untainted view of the world. Babies and young children are just happy.

But the idea of potentially dating someone while another woman carries his child… not sure I have the strength to handle it.

Micah reaches for my hand and I let him take it. He cocoons it in both of his. I focus on the warmth of his touch. The way his thumbs draw small circles over the top of my hand. And how he stares at our joined hands as if scared they will disappear if he looks away.

"Don't think it will." He lifts his red eyes. "But if the baby is mine, I'll take responsibility." I jerk my hand back, but Micah doesn't release me from his grip. "That doesn't mean anything changes between us, Peyton."

I love and hate that he won't let me go. That he refuses to surrender to outside forces. That he plans to fight for what he wants, but will still do the right thing in the end if need be.

The Micah in front of me isn't the same from my teenage years. Teenage Micah was more selfish and did whatever benefited his life the most. Adult Micah still has some of these same tendencies, but knows when to step up and be a man. When to do the right thing, but not let anyone rob him of life and the prospect of love.

"I want to believe you. God, Micah, I really do. But you can't deny a baby would flip your world upside down."

"Not denying it. But life is what we make it. If this woman *is* pregnant with *my* child, I will do my part. Doing my part does *not* equal being in a relationship with her." Fingers brush the underside of my chin and lift. Our eyes lock. Neither of us breathes. "If I haven't made it obvious yet, I want a relationship with *you*."

You know what they say about assuming… and I am definitely not going to assume with Micah Reed. Not when it comes to matters of the heart. Not when he has the ability to squash me like a bug and walk away unscathed.

His fingers drop away from my chin. Then his knuckles brush along my cheek. I sigh, and my entire frame caves forward. There will always be a piece of me that is weak for Micah. A part always ready to crumple to his demands, his will. This doesn't necessarily make me weak as a woman. Just weak when it comes to making informative, clear-minded decisions regarding him.

And I cannot afford to be weak.

"Let's eat," I suggest. My appetite may not have returned, but I hate food waste.

Micah flips on the television, but neither of us pays attention as our food slowly disappears. Dinner tonight is riddled with silence and anxiety and stress over what the future holds. Not only *my* future with Micah but also his if he becomes a father. Like it or not, fatherhood will change his life more than he realizes.

When I can't eat another bite, I close up the containers and put them in one of the bags. "I should go."

I need time alone to process this evening's news. And maybe some best-friend time to mull it over. When too close to a situation, it's always better to talk with someone not in the thick of it. Someone you trust and will listen to when they give advice.

"Sorry," Micah mumbles as we rise from the couch.

"For what?"

"Fucking this up. Seems to be my specialty." He laughs without humor as I lead us to the door. "But I'll make it better. I swear."

I don't doubt his proclamation. Micah is the type to go after what he wants. If what he wants happens to be yours truly, it will happen. Doesn't mean I won't make him work for it, though.

Before I get out the door, before I stop him from stepping closer, Micah crushes my lips with a smoldering kiss. And for one, two, three vicious beats of my pulse, I remain stone cold. Frigid as he tries to coax a kiss in return. The softness of his lips, the warmth of his arms circling my waist, and the sweet woodsy scent of his cologne… the triple whammy makes me surrender. I fist his shirt and haul him closer. Kiss him as if this may be the last time—because who knows what tomorrow will bring.

My body says to never let go. But my mind tells me to stop, take a step back, and leave. To get out of here before my feet refuse to go. Difficult as it is, I break the kiss. I unclench my fingers and turn my back to Micah.

"I should go," I mutter and twist the knob.

From the door to the car, the only noise to fill the silence is the clack of my heels and the soft thumps of Micah's bare feet hitting the ground. No buzzing insects. No wind gusts to rustle the leaves. No chatty neighbors or rumbling car engines.

Nothing but undiluted silence. An awkward, unbearable silence until I unlock the car.

I start the car and roll down the window. "Thanks for dinner."

He reaches forward, his knuckles brush down my cheek. "Sorry it wasn't as great as last night."

God, this is so weird. Why does this have to be so fucking weird? "I better go."

With a solemn nod, he takes one, two steps back. "Drive safe. See you tomorrow."

I roll up my window, back out of the driveway, and watch as Micah disappears in my rearview mirror. The moment he vanishes, a fist tightens around my heart as the floodgates open and spill down my cheeks. I drive the short distance home in a mental and visual blur. The minute I walk through the front door and Reese takes one look at me, two warm arms engulf me.

This annihilates the dam wall on my emotions. My frame shakes as I drench Reese's shirt. He hugs me impossibly tighter, rubs a gentle hand up and down my spine, and shushes me as we rock in place. My purse hits the floor with a thump, and my keys clang when they land next. At some point, without me realizing, Reese walks us to the couch and sets me in his lap.

After hour-long minutes, the tears form dry salt lines to my chin. Snot clogs my nose and stains Reese's shirt. My throat withered; eyes puffy and achy. My heart an ashy mold waiting for the breeze to blow it to dust.

Reese holds me close while his one hand continues its journey up and down my spine. Every other stroke up, he stops to tuck a strand of hair behind my ear or run his fingers through the strands.

"Talk to me, sunshine," he whispers, his breath warm and comforting at my temple.

I inch back and stare into kind brown eyes. Eyes full of love and sincerity. More times than I can count, Reese has held my hand. Been my stronghold or lifted me up. Been there for me without judgment or conditions. No matter what bullshit life throws at either of us, our friendship never crumbles. As if fate knew I needed someone to love me in every way except romantically.

Reese is my person, and I am his. Day or night, through thick and thin, we are there for each other.

I spill every unsettling second about tonight. About the woman and how Micah reacted to the whole situation. How the entire scenario felt like a dull knife pushing into my rib cage. How the knife twisted each time Micah denied the possibility. And how the knife gutted me when Micah wanted to go about things as if the woman never stepped foot in Roar.

"My sweet Peyton." Reese hugs me close again. "I understand your pain and frustration with all this." He releases me and leans back to look into my eyes. "But if I were in his shoes, I'd be equally defensive. Especially if I took every precaution."

"Are you seriously taking his side?" I whine and narrow my eyes.

Warmth wraps my hand as Reese takes it in his. "This isn't about sides, sunshine. First of all, you'll always be number one. Always. Second, stop and really think about it. Put yourself in his position. If someone approached you and told you something equally life changing, wouldn't you question it?" I teeter my head left and right. "The answer is yes. We've known each other too many years to say otherwise."

He has me there. For obvious reasons, I can't put myself in Micah's shoes. Me impregnating someone is impossible. But if someone accused me of something heinous that I felt was inconceivable, I would deny it without evidence too.

"This is one of a long list of reasons why I need you. You know me. You explain it from different views until I have more than one perspective." I huff out a deep breath and my shoulders cave inward. "Not that it resolves how I feel, but thank you."

Reese pats my hand. "Don't drive yourself crazy thinking about it. But don't let it go without giving it genuine thought. It's a big deal, but not the end of the world. No sense in worrying over something that may not hold merit."

I rise from his lap and he stands too. "Thanks for always being here. Don't know what I'd do without you." I wrap my arms around his neck and hug him hard.

His arms circle my waist and hug with equal strength. "Live a boring life, I'm sure." I drop a hand and poke his ribs. "Argh! It was a joke. Geez."

"Ha ha," I deadpan. I pick up my purse and keys from the floor and start for the hall. "Going to try and get some sleep. Night."

"Sleep tight, sunshine. I'll make us French toast in the morning."

I press a hand to my heart. "With extra powdered sugar?"

"Always."

After changing into a knee-length nightshirt, I slip under the covers and close my eyes. Sleep doesn't take me quickly, like usual. Instead, my brain clicks on and evaluates every possible outcome to several scenarios. An hour of mental torment passes, and I have no viable answers. I can't.

Because I don't know Micah well enough to know what he would do. Nor what the truth is when it comes to the red-dress woman.

So, I do my best to let it go. Let go of an outcome I have no control of. Let go of a future I can't predict. Let go of the what-ifs and fabricated scenarios my mind created.

～

"You look like shit."

Nothing like bluntness when you need softer edges. "Thanks, Aunt Leanne. I love you, too," I say with a dash of sarcasm as I slide into the booth across from her.

Monday has always been our day. Lunch after I leave Gulfside. An hour or two of girl time as we catch up on life. My weekly dose of Dad's side of the family. But with the new change in my work schedule and last night's bullshit, I need to see her today.

"Don't get your panties in a bunch. All I meant is you seem exhausted."

Exhaustion is a good word to explain how I feel. My limbs are heavier than Corinthian pillars. Eyes swollen, veiny and dry. My mind spends so much time in the fog, I'd swear we lived near the San Francisco Bay rather than Tampa Bay. And my heart… well, my heart currently teeters on barbed wire. Sleep was a joke last night; or should I say this morning. I may have slept three hours max as I tried my damnedest to let go. Easier said than done.

"Yeah, yesterday was rough. Glad you could meet up."

Aunt Leanne reaches across the table and covers my hand with hers. "Me, too. Now let's get some food and talk."

We study the menu and pick out lunch as the server approaches the table. Once we place our orders, I sip my water while Aunt Leanne lifts a brow and waits for me to spill every detail.

In so many ways, Aunt Leanne reminds me of Dad. Her bluntness and no-nonsense attitude. But also, her never-ending patience and practical mind. Whenever life feels off-kilter, Aunt Leanne uses her saintlike restraint and listens to every word. Just like Dad did. She lets me spill all the crazy details, then sits quietly for a bit and lets my words marinate. Figures out which parts are most important and starts there first.

"Remember the guy at work I told you about?"

She studies my eyes a beat. "Mmhm."

"Well, a couple nights ago, we kissed. And not your basic peck. More the hot and heavy kind."

Just like Dad and Aunt Leanne, I don't beat around the bush either. Some conversations are tougher to have, but they spill out sooner or later.

"Why do I get the feeling this kiss was great then, but isn't now?"

I take a deep breath and hold it to the count of five. "Because last night at work, some woman came in and claimed to be pregnant with his baby."

Aunt Leanne chokes on her sip of water. *Jesus, Peyton. Could you not have waited until she swallowed first?* I jump up from my seat and smack her back over her lungs. She waves me away as the coughing slows.

"Damn, girl. Trying to kill me?"

I purse my lips and raise my brows. "Hope you're being sarcastic, 'cause that's not remotely funny."

"Sorry." She coughs one last time, then takes another sip of water. "Of all the scenarios I expected, that was definitely not one of them. Took me by surprise, is all."

"Just be glad you didn't witness it firsthand."

The corners of her mouth turn down as her lower lip juts out slightly. Some may confuse the look with pity, but I recognize the fraction of heartbreak she has for me in this moment. With all the painful tragedies of my past, adding another to the list sucks.

"It probably hurts, but tell me everything. From start to finish."

So, until our lunch arrives, I regale her with the events of the last forty-eight hours. Tell her the good news with work, Micah's reaction, and mine in turn. The kiss in the office and later at his house. I share how happy and weightless it felt to be around him, and the potential of what the future holds.

Then, I go into the bomb drop. How worked up this woman was about Micah not accepting her word. I share how the woman looked ready to party, and take another random man to her bed. And then, how I went back to Micah's house to talk. Our awkward silence and kiss before I said good night. How I felt empty and broken the moment I drove away.

Our plates slide in front of us and I snag a fry from my plate to munch on. As per usual, Aunt Leanne goes quiet after my story. She eats her BLT and I eat my fish sandwich. I pick at my fries and she eats her pineapple coleslaw. When our plates are empty, Aunt Leanne pushes hers aside and clasps her hands on the table.

"I assume you asked me here today because you want advice."

Mimicking her movement, I push my plate aside and lean forward. "That and to see if you think I'm overreacting. Is it weird for me to presume she's telling the truth? To think Micah should act differently?"

Taking my hands in hers, she rubs back and forth. "No reaction is wrong, Peyton. We all see and hear and feel and react to things in our own way. Just because it's different than someone else's reaction doesn't make it right or wrong. Your reaction is your own."

"I hate that instinct has me leaning away from him instead of standing closer."

She releases my hands, but doesn't stray far. "Sweetheart, you two have history. One that has messed with you for years. I'd find it odd if you *didn't* feel the way you do." My brows shoot to my hairline. "Just because you played tonsil hockey with the man, it doesn't erase history."

"Tonsil hockey? Seriously?" Feels like I'm a kid again.

Laughter floats in the air as tears spill down Aunt Leanne's face. "Would you rather I say sucking face? Or swapping spit? Canoodling, perhaps?" I drop my head in my hands. "Doesn't matter what you call it, you've had your tongue down the man's throat."

Jesus. Heat surges up my chest to my neck and face. No doubt my cheeks look more like pomegranate skin. I lift my gaze enough to see no one is paying us any attention. Thank god. Then sip my water in the hopes it will cool down the heat of embarrassment.

"Where were we?" I ask once I drain the water glass.

"Having good weeks with a person doesn't erase the bad years in your memory. You may enjoy his company now, but you still have barriers in place. Protection measures, in case he messes up again. By the sounds of it, you've already got the razor wire in place and the gate closing around your heart."

The waiter stops at the table to check on us and clear our plates. A thirty-second break in our conversation. Enough time to ponder what to say next. The moment he walks off, Aunt Leanne perches her chin on her hands and waits with eager eyes.

"If you were me, what would you do?"

"Obviously, I never experienced *your* pain years ago. But if I were in your shoes, I'd give myself a little time. Nowadays, everyone feels decisions have to be made immediately. That no one should have to wait. In some situations, this may be true. But in others, time is what you need. Especially when it's personal."

"So, I should give it time?" Time to sink in? Or time apart? This is so damn confusing.

This is why relationships are a pain in the ass. Don't get me wrong, I love sharing a connection with someone. Love not wanting to be apart from them. But drama and uncertainty are not qualities I want to embrace in a relationship.

"Give yourself time to really grasp the situation. Look at it from your perspective. Then, look at it from his. Write down your feelings on each. Imagine how you'd feel if someone threw news like this in your face and expected you to halt your life and cater to them. Let yourself *feel* what it'd be like to be in that scenario. Then make a decision from there."

Wise beyond her years, just like her brother had been. This is the reason—

among several others—why I ask Aunt Leanne all the hard questions. Why I bring up the life-changing stuff with her. Not that Mom wouldn't give sage advice. Mom's advice just happens to slant toward whatever is easiest. And easy isn't always the best choice.

"Thank you. You always know how to make me see situations with fresh eyes."

"Glad to help." She pats my hand and scoots out of the booth. "Now let's get out of here. You need to nap before work."

I chuckle at her vague way of telling me I look like shit again. But I wouldn't want this woman any other way. There are few people in this world whose opinions matter to me. Aunt Leanne gives it to me like it is, straight and to the point, and I appreciate it each and every time.

We hug near my car. "See you Monday?" she asks.

"Yeah. My schedule changed, but lunch is still good. Maybe an hour earlier?"

She kisses my cheek. "Sounds good. Keep me posted until then. Love you."

"Love you, too."

I hop in my car and press the ignition. For a moment, I stare out the windshield and lose focus. *"Look at it from your perspective. Then, look at it from his."* Call it my homework assignment, but I need to sit down and really evaluate us and both sides of the coin.

No matter what happens in the end, no matter what I choose, I trust my intuition won't lead me down the wrong path. Not again.

three

The longer Peyton is silent, the more I wither at the seams.

Yesterday, she walked in the back door of Roar, set her belongings in a locker, threw me a half-assed smile, and got to work. I had sent her a text in the morning—like I had for weeks—and got no response. All night, she slung drinks behind the bar and laughed with patrons. But the moment she glanced my way, an impossible wall erected between us.

I hate walls. But she needs space. I get it.

Does space equal zero interaction? No standard greeting or cordial exchanges. Fuck if I know. But her avoidance is the slowest, most torturous death. Like getting thrown on the rack, limbs bound at the wrists and ankles, torso stabilized, and, inch by inch, my starfished body gets stretched to its limit.

"Hey, boss," Ted says as I approach the front. "You good?"

Irritates me to no end that people read my emotions without a word. It isn't my nature to flaunt my feelings. Yet, I don't shut down or dodge them. But having my heart on my sleeve—at work, no less—is an open invitation for questions. Questions I have no desire to answer.

"Yeah, man. Just got a lot on my mind is all." The two seconds I pause to take a breath, Ted opens his mouth to speak. But I beat him to it. "Things good here?" I point toward the door.

He nods, then prattles on about the few people who tried to get in without paying cover or were underage. His voice hangs in the atmosphere, but I don't absorb a word. Not when I spot Peyton across the club, smiling and laughing with two guys.

How many days had passed since she smiled at me with gaiety? Two. Two decades-long days. And I hated every single, solitary second of those two days.

Ted stops talking and I have enough sense to notice. I pat his shoulder, force a smile, and leave him to stroll the perimeter of Roar with Peyton in my periphery. Her champagne locks secured in a high ponytail, I recall the silky gloss of the strands. Her laughter floats across the club as flashes of her under me as I tickled her ribs invade my vision.

Fuck.

When was the last time I focused so much attention on one woman? Let her occupy my every waking and sleeping thought.

Sadly, the answer to that question comes too quick. Rochelle.

Rochelle Cook was the only woman I let consume me. In every way possible. She lured me in and sank her perfectly manicured claws into my heart until every drop of blood dried at her feet. I hadn't realized it at the time, but my entire life revolved around her and her needs.

Until the day she drove her five-inch heel through my heart and left me a fraction of a man.

Is the same happening? Am I setting myself up to suffer all over again? Maybe, but I don't think Peyton has a malicious bone in her body. I don't picture her hurting me on purpose.

As I step behind the bar, I approach Peyton like a scared animal. I plant each foot forward with care. Keep my frame relaxed and expression neutral.

The extended silence between us has run me ragged. Sleep has been shit. Two nights ago—when she sat in my living room and occupied my space—was the last time I ate. And the constant nausea has my throat raw.

I sidle up to her but leave inches between our arms. "Need help?"

She peers from the corner of her eye, then tucks her lips between her teeth. Just when I think she may say yes, she shakes her head. "I'm good. Thanks, though."

I don't want to walk away. Can't force my feet to move. "Ready for Monday? We can do one last walk through." At this point, I am throwing darts in the dark and hoping something sticks.

"No. Ani went over most of it with me." Of course she did.

"Well, if you need anything, I'm here."

Ugh. This fucking sucks.

I exit the bar without hurry. Send voiceless wishes to the universe Peyton will stop me as I head for the office. But my wishes go unanswered as I enter the hall and turn into the office. I drop into the chair, plant my elbows on the desk, and drop my head in my hands.

Only two days have passed, yet I don't know how much more of this I can take. Peyton's silence is a life sentence on death row. Years in solitary confinement with my arms in a straitjacket and soiled floors beneath my feet.

I swallow down my personal agony and bury myself in work. Distract myself with every possible task. Stay in the office until closing time and wallow in my new personal hell.

When Peyton and I go our separate ways at the end of the night, I say nothing. Not good night or goodbye. No "talk to you later" or "good luck on Monday." Nothing.

The worst part… she does the same. And after she drives out of the lot, I open my car door and spew the empty contents in my stomach across the concrete. No relief comes. Just the same emptiness I have felt since Thursday night.

I need to fix this. Fix us.

〜

"What's up with you?" Gavin knocks me in the shoulder with his. "You've been scary quiet."

I am not in the mood to deal with questions or criticism. Life is shitty enough, no need to add another helping to the heaping pile. "Nothing," I grumble.

"Bullshit." I tilt my head to face Gavin and narrow my eyes. "We've known each other almost twenty years. Your lame, short answers don't fly with me, bro. You don't spill, I'll spew some bullshit to Shelly to make you talk."

Jesus fuck. Can a man not get one goddamn night without diving headfirst into the dark? All I want is one night. One. One night where Peyton doesn't own every other minute in my head. Is one night too much to ask?

Seems as if tonight will *not* be that night.

"Please don't."

"Then you better start talking."

This whole situation has repeated so many times in my head, new trails have been worn into my brain. Bone tired doesn't touch the fatigue in my muscles or the weariness in my bones. Each day moves in a blur as I go with the motions.

I flip into robot mode and reiterate the last week with Gavin. The good and bad. Moments I never wanted to end and the minutes that have yet to end. My best friend listens without interruption. Nods and winces and pinches his brows at all the appropriate times. Then he turns introspective as he processes it all.

"First things first. I'm on the same page as you." I scrunch my eyes. "Shit happens with condoms, but I wouldn't believe anything without proof. Sucks to think like that, but there's some crazy bitches in the world."

"Thank you." I take the first deep breath in days. "For days, I've felt like *I* was the asshole for being skeptical. Don't know how else to explain it other than saying *I just know*."

"Know what?" Shelly says as she steps into view and plops down on the lounger across from us.

Great. Obviously, we weren't *alone* in Jonas and Autumn's backyard. But I hoped Gavin and I would be able to finish this conversation without other ears or opinions in the mix. Looks like that isn't happening.

"Nothing," I mumble.

"Uh-uh." Shelly wags her finger in the air. "You don't get to be in some serious secret conversation with Gavin and not me. I'm your sister."

"Shell…" I hang my head. The second I tell her everything, she will rip me a new asshole. Guaranteed.

"What did you do, Micah?" Irritation laces her tone.

I lift my head and lock on to her familiar irises as mine glass over. Saliva floods my mouth as a boulder expands in my throat. I open my mouth, but nothing comes out. Gavin slaps my back when I don't say anything, then fills in the blanks for Shelly and the others lingering nearby.

"Told you not to hurt her." Her words are a growl on her lips.

"Yeah, I remember. Not like I predict the future. And this… do you think I did this on purpose?"

"Of course not. But how did you not see this coming? You've probably banged over a hundred women in the last year. Did you expect *nothing* would happen except sex?" She crosses her arms over her chest and shakes her head. "If you say yes, you're dumber than I thought."

"Ouch, Shell. Tell me how you really feel."

"Maybe you need a reality slap, big brother."

"Well, consider me slapped. Punched is more like it, though. I know I fucked up. That's nothing new." I close my eyes, inhale deeply, then reopen them. "Now that we've discussed my shitty life, maybe you can help me fix it. Because…" I tip my head back and blink rapidly. Swallow, again and again. When I drop my eyes to meet Shelly's, hers glaze over too. "I don't know how. I fucked up and have been lost since."

Shelly hops up and comes to sit beside me. Her hands take mine and squeeze painfully tight. "Sorry I yelled." A tear rolls down her cheek, but she doesn't wipe it away. "But I knew messing things up with Peyton would be bad. Not just for her, but you too. You flaunt a hard exterior, but I know you, big brother."

Only around Shelly and close friends will I admit to being a softy. Not that there is anything wrong with not being a burly man twenty-four seven. That just isn't me. Hell, majority of the population walk around with phony fronts. Always splashing the best of the best. Do I want a good life with nice things? Sure. Who doesn't? But I don't give anyone a false sense of who I am. Have I made shitty decisions since Rochelle fucked me over? Definitely. Any self-respecting person would have lost their shit the same as me. Not everyone would fuck their feelings away, though.

"Shell, tell me what to do. She won't talk to me. She doesn't answer my texts. I'm trying to give her space. But if I give too much, will she walk away?"

I don't mean for Shelly to answer the last part, but she will. It's in her nature. In both of ours.

"Hate to say it, big brother, but you need to give her time." I drop my head in my hands and groan. Her hand finds my back and rubs the length of my spine. "In this instance, time sucks. But she needs to be able to form her own thoughts without you interfering. If you give it time, I'm sure she'll speak up sooner rather than later."

"This fucking sucks," I grumble against my palms.

"Yes, it does. What about this other woman?"

I straighten my spine, meet Shelly's gaze, and shake my head. "Told her to leave and not return without proof."

"How would she prove it's yours without DNA?"

"I meant that she's actually pregnant and can take a paternity test with me present." I close my eyes for three breaths. "Shell, I know my life has been out of control. That I have made such horrible choices. But I would never put myself in a situation like this. I have no plans to father children. At least not without being committed to someone and we both decide we want that."

She leans back and looks to the sky in deep thought. Her particular brand of silence is one I can handle because I know she's mulling over ideas.

Please let her have some solution to this.

Fatherhood may not be something I have given much thought, but if a paternity test proves—without a doubt—this woman is carrying my child, I will step up. I may not be ready to parent, but it doesn't mean I won't do my part. You do the deed, you take responsibility. Period.

"I have no absolute answers for you," she says with a pout, pushing out her lower lip. "But I'd suggest you quit fucking around, try not to worry over it until you have to, and just have patience." My eyes shut as I drop my head back to rest on the lounger. "Sorry, big brother. Not much else you can do at this point."

"Thanks, Shell," I whisper into the night.

She means well, I know this. But, fuck. I hoped she would say something—anything—that would lift me up. That would flip on the light bulb in my brain because I can't quite reach the cord. Her advice is solid. Just not what I want to hear.

What I really want is to text Peyton. To grovel and beg for her to talk to me. For her to tell me she needs time to herself, but she will be there in the end. Just some words to let me know all is not lost.

Because right now, all I feel is lost. I have never felt so alone and in the dark as I do now. Like I have no way out. Like each breath may be my last.

And I have no one to blame except myself.

I have never hated silence and distance. Not until now.

When one day bleeds into the next, when your mind never shuts off, gauging reality is a feat. And reality has been one gigantic blur since the woman in the red dress walked into Roar. Since I pretty much shut Micah out.

In the two weeks since she walked up to the bar and dropped the ticking time bomb, I have noticed a significant change in Micah. Not just physically, but also in his demeanor. With my new schedule, we see each other less. Which makes the changes that much more dramatic.

Across the club, I spot the purple crescent moons beneath his eyes. Notice the looseness of his shirt on his shoulders and chest, and the bagginess of his dress slacks. Every smile he flashes to the employees or guests is forced and brief. And he hasn't looked my direction in days. Too many days.

Seeing Micah like this, slowly sinking without a life preserver, wrings my insides to no end.

Is it the woman who has him gaunt and a shell of himself? Does the idea of becoming a parent scare him this much?

Our in-depth conversations prior to this never revolved around serious topics, such as marriage and children. Sure, we have both been in serious relationships and the idea of next steps may have crossed our minds. But obviously, ideas are where it ended since we are single and childless.

Or am I the reason for his frail frame and sullen disposition? Has my standoffish attitude and silence whittled him to this state? My eyes trail over his caved frame and dulled irises. Study his timid, forced smiles and the minimal energy he exerts with everyone—staff and patrons alike.

Micah and I share a horrid history, but we were headed in a new direction. To a positive place. A place full of second chances and possibilities, genuine affection and his lips on mine.

What if he hurts me? *What if he doesn't and this turns out to be what you've been waiting for?* The voice in my head has me backpedaling for the hundredth time in days. Has me seeing both sides of the coin. The same voice keeps me from making a sound decision. Because that voice belongs to my heart and it continues to argue with my brain.

"Making my rounds," I tell Mable as I exit the bar. Mable has been doing exceptional. Slaying Monday and Tuesday with me and working Wednesday with more hands on deck.

I wander through Roar, doing my best to steer away from the karaoke stage setup in the middle of the dance floor. Out of the corner of my eye, Micah stays opposite me and heads for the hall. He lengthens his stride and his feet tread quicker. Before I fully turn my head to see him, he darts inside the office and closes the door.

Finishing my circuit around the club, I check in with the staff and patrons, then head to the office. Being away from Micah has given me time to think. More than enough time. At this rate, I am surprised my brain hasn't swollen or some form of self-combustion hasn't occurred with all my thinking.

But I am done thinking. Done seeing him suffer. Done asking myself questions I don't have answers to. Questions neither of us have answers to. Now, all that's left is us, suffering. And I hate it.

Although unnecessary, I knock on the door before turning the handle and entering. One, two, three steps into the room, Micah finally lifts his head from his hands. His starry eyes are puffy and lackluster and rip my heart to shreds. The dark marks beneath his lashes are more noticeable this close up. A vise squeezes my middle and holds me captive at what he has dealt with. Alone.

"Hey," I choke out and close the door without taking my eyes off his.

He licks, then tucks his lips between his teeth. His head tilts slightly off-kilter as he breaks eye contact and stares down at the desk. "Hey," he says almost inaudibly.

I flip the lock on the door, then walk across the room. Wood scrapes concrete as I drag the guest chair around to park it beside Micah. He remains frozen as I sink into the chair and stare at his profile. Aside from the horrendous singing outside the room, silence consumes the space.

It eats me alive.

"Micah…" His breath stutters and, without second thought, I reach for his hand. "Please. Look at me."

Soft blond lashes dust his skin as his lids close. I give his hand a gentle squeeze and wait him out. Give him whatever time he needs. Life has changed so much— for us both—in the last two weeks.

Waiting, I focus on my breath. Count each inhale, each exhale. Concentrate on the warmth of his hand. The occasional callous where his fingers meet his palm. How his fingers twitch—just the slightest bit—every other heartbeat. And when his breathing calms, mine does too.

As if in slow motion, he tilts his head my direction. The muted-gold flecks over his dark-blue irises remind me of dying stars in distant galaxies. Their light fading and swallowing the darkness around them. Seeing them this close, seeing him this close, is a punch to the solar plexus.

Life-altering information was hurtled at him and I abandoned ship for my own selfish needs. I harbor no guilt for wanting to keep my heart safe. But I do foster guilt for not supporting him or lending an ear or shoulder. Especially when he needed me most.

"Sorry," I say, although the five-letter word doesn't feel adequate.

He laughs without humor. "Why are you sorry?"

My free hand comes to his cheek. Thumb brushes the arch of his cheekbone. Fingers comb through his hair. His eyes close as he leans into my touch. And the pang beneath my breastbone wanes slightly.

"Of all the times for me to go tight lipped, it's when you need my voice most. So, I'm sorry. For ignoring you and not being there when you probably needed me most."

He shakes his head and I drop my hand. His legs swing around and weave between mine as he scoots closer. "I did need you. But you needed space to think too." Fingers brush over my temple, down the angle of my jaw and to my chin. "Not gonna lie. Your silence, your distance, it sucked. But I respect it."

"Thank you."

His fingers continue to trace the ridges and valleys of my face. I close my eyes and bask in the trail of tingles his touch leaves behind.

"Missed you."

"Me, too." My eyes meet his with a list of questions, but I start off with a simple one first. "When's the last time you ate?" I probably sound like a nagging partner, but I don't care.

His momentary silence speaks volumes. "Haven't had much of an appetite. Been snacking here and there."

This jacks my guilt up to level ten. "Please eat." I grip his biceps. "You've lost weight." Not in a healthy way either.

"I'll try." His thumb swipes slow over my bottom lip, his eyes following the movement. "Maybe we could hang after work. Make sure I eat." Doubt and hope lace his voice as he lifts his eyes to mine.

My first thought is to tell him yes. The last two weeks have been shitty. For both of us. But I don't want to give the impression that this is an easy fix. A supposed pregnancy won't just disappear. Not for weeks or months. But I also want to support him… and more.

"Can I think on it?" His gaze drops as he nods. "Let you know soon." I rise from the chair and bend to kiss his hair. "You do paperwork. I've got the floor."

After depositing the chair back in its place, I head for the door. Just as I reach for the knob, Micah's voice stops me. "Peyton?" The rough scrape of his voice fiercely hugs my heart.

I pinch my eyes for two breaths before peering at him over my shoulder. "Yeah?"

"Thank you." My brows scrunch. "Even if you don't say yes, this" —he gestures at the now vacant space beside him— "I needed it."

"Sorry it took me so long." I unlock the door and twist the knob. "Talk to you in a bit." And then I walk out.

Karaoke Night is in full swing. Beer pours from the taps and fruity cocktails fill fancy glasses. Laughter and cheers and the occasional perfectly tuned voice belts out over the sound system. Since we made the changes and Ani has advertised the hell out of Monday through Thursday events, the bar has seen an uptick in guests and income.

After another circuit around the club, I help Mable and Kaylynn behind the bar. The next two hours bring interesting versions of Miley Cyrus's "Wrecking Ball" and Alanis Morissette's "You Oughta Know." The one to grab everyone's attention was the middle-aged woman dancing provocatively while singing Madonna's "Like A Virgin."

Yeah… I will never unsee that.

The crowd starts to thin as the evening wears on. Most people need to get home for decent sleep before work tomorrow. Mable and Kaylynn start cleaning up behind the bar and I help clean tables on the main floor. With the majority of the work done, I leave Charity to finish up while I check on Micah.

After a light knock, I enter the office. Micah sits studiously behind the desk, entering invoices. It takes him a minute to look up from the screen. But when he does, he rewards me with a smile I haven't seen in weeks.

Damn, I missed that smile.

"Almost done?" I ask.

"One more after this. Everything good on the floor?"

"Mmhm. Should be able to close on time."

The urge to laugh at our avoidance of whether or not we will meet after work takes center stage. I bite the inside of my cheek and resist.

"About after…" Micah, on the other hand, comes right out with it.

"I'll come over." Feet away, I catch the stars in his irises as they glimmer. Just from my agreement. Who knew Micah Reed's soft spot was the girl he picked on as a teenager? Certainly not me. "But only if food is involved."

"Bossy," he teases. That he jokes at all is a step in the right direction. "Think I like you bossy."

Well, that shifted quick. If the erratic thump beneath my sternum is any indication, I rather enjoy his response. I miss our banter. The constant teasing. And the way his eyes eat me alive.

I shrug a shoulder. "What can I say… I like taking charge."

"Hmm. You in charge sounds… fun." He licks his lower lip. "I'll order food as we leave and have it delivered."

Narrowing my eyes, I point a finger. "No weird shit."

"Says the woman who eats pineapple on her pizza."

"What's wrong with pineapple on pizza?"

"It's a fruit," he says as if that concludes the debate.

"Technically, tomatoes are fruit too. And you smear that shit all over the crust. So…" My lips pucker and brows lift. Let's hear your response now, fruit boy.

"Fine, I concede." I give him a snide smile and he sticks out his tongue. "And I promise nothing weird."

"Good." I start for the door and stop just as I step through. "I'll finish up out here. Then we can close up."

Before he answers, I head down the hall and back into the club. Most people have left and the few that linger appear to be finishing their drinks. Karaoke is being packed up as tables get shifted for tomorrow night's Bar Olympics.

The last of the stragglers leave and I lock the door. Mable, Charity, and Kaylynn wrap up the last of their closing duties and wish me good night as they head out the back together. The overhead and bar lights go black as I flip off switches. My heels clap down the hall as I head to the office.

Behind the desk, Micah scrolls on his cell phone and doesn't see me straight away. I lean against the doorframe and, for a moment, take him in.

The last two weeks have been rough, for him more so than me. Guilt still eats at me for ignoring him so long. But then I recall Reese and Aunt Leanne telling me to do what felt best for my well-being. If I wasn't strong enough to handle the situation, there was no way I could deal with it and stand strong beside Micah. I needed to work through some things in my own head. Decide whether or not it was possible for me to take this on. To date and stand beside a man who may or may not become a father to someone else's unborn child.

In the end, I changed my viewpoint. Looked at the entire scenario as an outsider.

Nowadays, people have children outside of wedlock all the time. Most of those people aren't in committed relationships. Some try a relationship for the sake of the child, but end up parting ways. Sometimes, what is best for the child isn't always the parents together. Especially if love doesn't exist between them. A forced relationship only adds more stress—for the parents and child.

This realization changed everything. Just wish it didn't take me so long to figure it out.

"Ready?"

Micah looks up from his phone. A soft, lopsided smile dons his face, and my heart rate spikes. God, I missed his smiles.

"Yep." He nods, taps the screen, then locks his phone. "Just ordered food. Should arrive about the same time as us." His voice is still scratchy, but less melancholy than hours ago.

I shuffle into the office and dig my purse from the desk drawer. "Perfect. 'Cause I'm starving."

Rising from the desk, Micah turns off the computer monitor. I flip off the light as we walk out. The trek to our cars is short, but filled with silence. A comfortable silence that has been missing between us for too many days.

"Drive safe." He leans in and I stop breathing as he presses his lips to my forehead. "See you at the house."

"'Kay." It's the only word I manage to get past my lips as he ambles to his truck. My heart squeezes a little tighter and I take it as a sign.

This may be the best thing—a relationship with Micah—to happen to me. Or I purchased my own one-way ticket to hell. Hopefully, it isn't the latter.

five

I scoop up the bag from the porch and punch in the front-door code. Peyton, less than a foot behind me, has my heart beating with purpose for the first time in weeks.

She's here. We are talking again.

Within hours, my life feels less daunting. All the craziness weighing me down—the possibility of fatherhood and an unhinged ex-bedmate—is pounds lighter now. Because Peyton is here. Her presence alone gives me a boost I didn't know I needed. Our relationship—the weird place between friendship and next level—may never be what it was pre–bomb drop, but Peyton approaching me tonight was a step in a favorable direction.

Over the last thirteen days, I had my doubts. Questioned whether she would speak to me again. With each passing day of silence and her obvious avoidance, I closed off more and more. Every time my phone alerted me to a text, excitement soared in my veins. Only to fizzle out a second later when I didn't see her name on the screen.

Work was worse. Ten times worse. Because of her promotion and the schedule changes, we spent less time in the same space. Her not stuck behind the bar all night changed things, too. Before her promotion, she stayed in one place all night. I could count on her proximity by stepping behind the bar. Could easily keep my eyes on her. But now, she is as mobile as me and almost impossible to pin down.

Until tonight.

Tonight, Peyton opened up to me again. Took initiative. Gave us another shot. And I won't waste the opportunity. Won't do anything to fuck this, us, up again.

We settle on the couch and I take containers out of the bag and set them on the table. "Hope you're good with Italian."

"Let me just get this out of the way." Shit. Does she have food allergies? I mean, she eats pizza. Practically devours it. Figured Italian was a safe bet. "I haven't met a food I *don't* like. Not yet, anyway."

Thank fuck.

"Good to know for future reference."

I open boxes to reveal cheese ravioli, meat lasagna, salad, and garlic knots. I hand her a paper plate and a package of plastic cutlery from the bag. We portion a little of everything onto our plates before scooting back on the couch, cross-legged, and digging in. Well, I eat a bit slower since my appetite was absent for too many days. Last thing I need is to run to the bathroom and embarrass myself at the throne.

"Still working at the ALF?" I ask to spark some form of conversation. Although the quiet has been mostly comfortable with Peyton, I miss talking with her. More than expected.

"Mmhm," she mumbles around a bite of food. "Only on Sunday for a few hours, though." The corners of her mouth turn down slightly.

I love that Peyton is doing well for herself, but hate that her promotion has taken away something she enjoys. I may not know the entire backstory or understand her reasons, but working at the facility brings her joy. Spending time and chatting with a group of elders makes her smile. That is what matters.

"Sorry you don't get to visit as often."

"Thanks." The corners of her mouth tip up in a halfhearted smile. "Knew being there less would be a side effect to the promotion. Ms. Jenkins is happy with the change."

"Ms. Jenkins?"

"An older woman I visit with regularly. She's always telling me to move on and quit visiting the old folks. I tell her it makes me happy to see her."

"Does it?"

"Does it what?"

"Make you happy?"

Without an ounce of hesitation, she answers. "Yes. It's probably weird, but it reminds me of when I spent time with my Nana. She passed a few years back. I visited with her often. We talked for hours about my life and hers. She'd ask about my goals and how I'd accomplish them. I traveled the globe with her stories of adventure. On lazier days, we played cards or sewed cross stitch. Life with Nana was simple and peaceful and full of love. Every memory of or with her squeezes my heart." She places a hand over her heart and pats. In a blink, her eyes glass over and I see and feel every ounce of love Peyton had for this woman.

Her spending time at the facility makes more sense now. And I am more in awe of the woman beside me.

"Your Nana sounds like a wonderful woman."

"She was," she says with a sniffle.

"Sorry." Peyton scrunches her brow as she wipes under her eyes. "For upsetting you."

Peyton waves me off. "I love talking about her and reliving those memories. Please don't apologize."

"I'm sorry for two weeks ago. For what went down. I'm sorry it happened and you had the stress on your shoulders, too. I would never want that for you and it wasn't—isn't—fair."

"Not like you knew it would happen," she states.

"True. Still sorry. This whole ordeal shouldn't be yours to take on. Not the stress or concern. None of it. And I get why you needed time to sort through it all and how you felt."

Peyton jabs at her lasagna, her eyes darting left and right, then left again. When serious matters come up, I love that Peyton doesn't word vomit her feelings. She digests them and sorts through them before speaking her mind. She carefully crafts her words before opening her mouth. Because once out in the open, words can't be taken back.

"I didn't mean for it to take so long," she mumbles before lifting her gaze to mine.

A zing flares in my chest. My heart does a little dance, knowing she didn't want to be apart as long as we were. But the jubilation is quickly replaced with a pinch. I hate the melancholy in her voice, the slump in her shoulders, and the downturn of her lips.

Between the two of us, only I should be riddled with guilt. Not Peyton.

My knee grazes hers and I delight in the connection. "I know. But we all do things in our own way and time. Please, just don't shut me out again. I'll beg, if necessary. If you need space or time for yourself, just tell me. But check in from time to time."

Her eyes glaze over as she nibbles her lower lip. *Damn, I want my lips on hers.* Unhurried, she nods and frees her imprisoned lip.

"I will."

Unable to resist, I reach forward and brush the wetness off her cheek. "Please, don't cry." I lick the lone, salty tear from my finger. "Things were good between us. Then, my past barreled in and threw us in reverse." Closing my eyes, I inhale deeply, then meet the violet irises I have missed dearly. "And I'll understand if you want nothing more than friendship. For however long. I don't like the idea, but understand and respect it, if that's what you need."

Peyton stabs the middle of her lasagna with the plastic fork, then sets the plate on the table. Her fingers fidget in her lap. Her eyes downcast, watching the movement.

Why did I do this? Every good person or situation to enter my life... one way or another, I always fuck it up.

The few long-term relationships I had, Rochelle was the only person I envisioned a future with. A life beyond dinners, nights on the town, and sex. I had never fantasized about children or gray hairs. Just years—decades—spent loving each other.

The two women prior to Rochelle... the first wanted more when I wasn't ready. The second—we just grew apart. Both women were lovely, but never made me weak in the knees.

Early in my relationship with Rochelle, I felt that spark moment. The one where your heart flutters every time you think of the person. When your skin breaks out in a sweat seeing them. When your world wobbles a little because she is near. At the time, I thought fate was telling me she was the one.

Obviously, I was a gullible guy wearing rose-colored glasses.

Rochelle was my first real love. The woman who opened my eyes and heart to things I never knew. She was also my first heartbreak. The pain of her betrayal had nothing to do with the sex. It was more about my naivete and how someone I trusted completely stabbed me in the back.

I never wanted to experience pain like that again. Which led to my nighttime escapades. It was a way to vent my frustrations and fulfill my primal needs. Without getting attached. My philosophy—if I didn't form attachments, I would never suffer heartbreak again. Great philosophy for my mind. My heart didn't get the memo.

What I felt for Rochelle—during the best parts of our relationship—is nothing in comparison to what I feel for Peyton.

With Rochelle, my heart did this odd flutter. Nothing more.

With Peyton, my heart charges forward like an Olympian sprinter. Pound, pound, pounding in my chest. A fanatical swirl of energy sparks to life beneath my diaphragm. A passion that feels bigger than either of us. Powerful. Life altering. And more often than not, I forget how to breathe. Forget how to speak or function. My world doesn't just wobble with Peyton, it flips on its axis.

She may need us to dial it back a notch before jumping in the deep end. If so, I will understand and heed her wishes. I will tone down my feelings. A little. At least the emotions I put on display. The idea terrifies me, but I will do whatever it takes and keep my promises.

"Not that we titled our relationship weeks ago, but let's just call it friends," she says, voice shaky. An audible exhale leaves my lips as I sag deeper into the couch. "Until I mentally wrap myself around everything."

I should be grateful for any form of Peyton in my life. Not pouting like a petulant child. Hopefully, the shadow over my heart isn't flaunted on my sleeve.

"Long as I have you in some way, I'll call it a win. Thank you."

Friendship may not be what I want with Peyton, but time without her is out of the question. So, I take it and plan to do everything within my power to set things right. To show her I am not that guy anymore. That I am someone worth having as more than a friend. Not just a lover, but also a true companion. Someone she can rely and depend on. Someone she deserves and wants in her life.

We finish eating dinner and watch an episode of *Supernatural* on Netflix. With each passing minute, she inches closer to my side of the couch. Midway through the episode, she curls her legs under her butt and leans into my side. Head on my shoulder and hands clasping my bicep. Her breath warming the cotton of my T-shirt. Legs brushing my thigh.

If this is her definition of friendship, I take it tenfold.

When we evolve beyond friends again—because let's face facts, we will—I look forward to more cuddle time with Peyton. And what happens beyond first base.

Each time Peyton puts her lips on mine, she kisses me as if it will be the last time. Kisses me as if it's her dying wish. Full of heat and passion and frenzy. I only imagine what it will be like when I kiss her elsewhere. When I taste the saltiness of her skin and arousal on my tongue. When I watch her come undone with my mouth alone. Or when she learns about my… accessories.

A wicked smile threatens and I bite my cheek. *Shift your focus, Reed.* Now is not the time to sport a hard-on.

All too soon, the episode ends. If it were up to me, I would let it roll right into the next. Keep Peyton curled up on my left. The last thing I want is for Peyton to leave. But bidding her good night is inevitable. For now.

"I should head home," she says and lifts her head from my shoulder.

Inch by inch, I trace a hand from her ankle to knee. When I reach the top, she shivers and the energy at my center swirls to life.

"Yeah. Okay." Although, what I want to say is *"no, don't go."*

Baby steps, again. Baby steps.

She starts picking up the trash from dinner, but I shoo her away. She puts her shoes on and I internally laugh at the pace. Slow. As. Fuck. Seems I am not the only one who doesn't want her to leave. My heart does a backflip.

Rising from the couch, we amble to the door. Those ten steps go far too quickly. Maybe it is time to rearrange furniture. Make the walk to the door twice as long. Who cares if it messes with the open space and feng shui. If it equals a few more seconds with Peyton, I am more than game.

"Thanks for dinner." Her violet irises closer to indigo when our gazes lock. She licks her lips and swallows. "Was nice being here again. Spending time together."

Unable to resist, I lift a hand and reach for the loose strands at her shoulder. She sucks in a breath. Her body freezes on the spot. I stare at the tendrils. How the indoor light accentuates her champagne locks differently than the morning sun. Study the natural wave that stands out enough to be noticeable.

I'd love to see her in a dress. Nothing fancy. Perhaps a sundress. Yellow, like daffodils. Hair down her back with more wave. Her bright smile across the table from me as we enjoy dinner by the water.

"Couldn't agree more," I say, voice scratchy.

Without warning, Peyton leans in and presses her lips to mine. The kiss innocent. Nothing more than a peck on the lips. But I don't dare move. Not to breathe. And certainly not to deepen it.

This kiss may be much tamer than previous ones we shared, but it is the most intimate yet. This kiss speaks volumes. Tells me she forgives me for my past discretions. Says she doesn't quite know how to do the friendship thing either. At least not with me.

Of all our kisses, this one is my favorite. This one, I will tuck away and keep safe.

Our lips break apart and she takes my hands in hers. "See you tomorrow." She spins and opens the door.

It takes a beat for me to notice Peyton is out the door and halfway to her car. I jog outside, down the steps, and catch up to her a second later. Her headlights flash before she opens the door and hops in. Once the engine purrs softly, she rolls down the window.

I want to kiss her again, but tell myself to stand down. Until she is ready for more than friendship, Peyton should initiate intimacy going forward. I won't ruin us. Not again.

"Drive safe." I tap the roof and reluctantly step back. "Tomorrow."

After a gentle smile and finger wave, she backs out and drives away. Watching her drive off sucks. But I was lucky to have had her here at all.

I press my fingers to my lips and smile. Until I see her again, the tingle her kiss left behind will remain on my lips.

Was last night a mistake?

I asked myself the same question for the umpteenth time since leaving Micah's house. The question distracted me the entire drive home. Cars and landmarks had passed in a blur. I vaguely remember saying good night to Reese as I zombie-walked to my bedroom. But the question kept me wide eyed in bed more hours than desirable. Woke me after maybe five hours of fitful sleep.

And now, as I lie in the comfort of my bed and stare at the ceiling, the question still haunts every synapses.

Was going to Micah's house and kissing him a mistake?

Over the last two weeks, I watched Micah morph into a shell of himself. Watched him turn into someone unrecognizable. More sullen. Frail. Lackluster. Each day, his posture slumped farther forward. The shadows under his eyes grew darker, more purple. And he refused to make eye contact with anyone longer than necessary.

Going to Micah's after work felt like the right thing to do when he asked. Agreeing to a friendship with him did too.

Then I blurred the lines less than an hour later. What a disaster I am.

I don't regret kissing Micah. Not one bit. I am, however, pissed at myself for sending mixed messages. If I say I want friendship, I shouldn't kiss him. Friends don't kiss. Well, not the way I kiss Micah.

"Damn it," I huff out as I slap a pillow over my face. Too bad smothering myself won't fix the situation. Too bad I don't know how to separate what I *should* do from what I actually feel.

Friendship with Micah is important and a major component of our relationship. Having a foundation—learning more about our backstories, what makes us tick, our individual mannerisms—matters. Doesn't need to be life altering facts. Small pieces build up. Like whether or not he picks his nose. Does he prefer the toilet paper over or under? Cats or dogs? Animal preference says a lot about a person. No matter, I don't want to enter a serious relationship without a history between us; even if the history is short.

Micah and I definitely have history. A path we navigated together and worked to improve. Then a tree snapped and fell over the path. Blocked us from moving forward. While Micah stood in front of the tree and tried to move it, I retreated. Stepped back into the brush and tucked myself away. Stayed hidden until comfortable enough to step into the light again. Now, we are back at the start. Trying to get around the tree and learning how to be a team again.

Starting over isn't easy. Not when you want to skip steps.

Hours had passed and I still feel the softness of Micah's lips on my lips. The scrape of his stubble along my chin. His taste on my tongue. It is too much and not enough.

A shiver rolls up my spine. A thin sheen of sweat blankets my skin. Heat blooms at the base of my tailbone and pools between my thighs.

"Ugh." I groan at how fast my thoughts went from point A to B. How I went from telling myself I need a friendship with Micah first to fantasizing about him. Am I a lost cause or what?

Peeling my arm away, I squint at the morning sunshine brightening the room. Sleep will have to wait. I throw back the covers and drop my arms in a huff.

Shower time.

Staying in bed any longer is not an option. My wayward thoughts are the last thing I need.

I make quick work of washing my hair and body. Then throw on lounge pants and a tank top. In the kitchen, I spy a folded paper on the counter. Unfolding it, I chuckle at Reese's scratchy script.

Morning Sunshine,

Stop laughing at my handwriting. Anyway... leftover breakfast casserole in the fridge.

Xo

I amble over to the fridge and retrieve the casserole dish. Scooping out enough for two, I plop the egg, sausage, and potato concoction on a plate, put it in the microwave, and press the two-minute button. I pour a tall glass of orange juice and toast a slice of bread while I wait. Settling at the breakfast bar, I eat and scroll through new emails, deleting the junk and scanning the keepers. Then I clear the other notifications. Same stuff, new day in social media land. No surprise.

After cleaning the dishes, I stretch out on the couch and distract myself with a few episodes of *Supernatural*. As the intro credits come to an end, my mind wanders to Micah. Until I suggested it, he had never seen the show. This seemed absurd. The show has fifteen seasons for crying out loud. As for me, I have rewatched the show. Not difficult when it is my "I don't have anything to do, so I'll watch TV" show. But Micah doesn't need to be privy to this information.

When the episode ends, I turn off the television and rise from the couch. "Lazy time is over," I mumble as I enter my room.

Since the promotion, I dress slightly less provocative for work. My tops are still a bit snug with a dash of cleavage. But my bottoms are less second skin and more loose skinny dress pants. After wearing snug, curve flaunting pants for so long, dressing in looser attire has been an adjustment. The pants are growing on me more each day.

I twist left, then right as I check myself out in the full-length mirror. The yellow top has wide straps on the shoulders, forms a *V* at the start of my cleavage, flows over my breasts and hangs loose a few inches below the waistline of my black pants. The more I stare in the mirror, the more I evaluate myself. And the more I tell myself I look like a sunflower.

"Why is this so difficult?" I tug at the shirt hem. Contemplate switching out the top for a different color. "Ugh." I give up and stick with the yellow.

In the bathroom, I add enough makeup to be noticeable but not take an hour to apply. Brush my hair and opt to leave it down for once. Since I no longer dart like a madwoman behind the bar for nine-plus hours a night, I worry less about my hair in my face or drinks. Plus, not having my hair strangled in an elastic band all night is a nice change.

With my hair styled into soft waves, I exit the bathroom and slip on a pair of heeled boots. Grab my purse and phone, then head for the kitchen. I whip together a quick lunch, eat, then pack some snacks in my purse for later. One last trip to the bathroom, I lint brush my pants and swipe gloss over my lips before tucking the tube in my purse.

The sun beams down as I drive toward Tampa. Temperatures are too hot to ride with the windows down on the way to work. But I look forward to the salty wind in my hair on the drive home.

It isn't long before I park behind Roar, next to Micah's truck. How long has he been here?

I check the time on the dash—thirty minutes early. Either he arrived early to set up the rest of the Bar Olympics or in the hopes we would have more time alone. I have no qualms about spending time alone with Micah. But I am, on the other hand, still kicking myself for blurring the lines last night.

"Get it over with already," I coach myself as I exit the car.

Soft music echoes in the hall as I step through the employee door. I squint at the overhead lights as I reach the main floor. Scrunch my nose at the artificial lemon-scented cleaner in the air. I don't mind most cleaning product scents, but whoever decided this one was lemon is sorely mistaken.

I take a deep breath and enter the office. My brave face falls when I discover it is empty. I release my held breath and stow my purse in the desk drawer. Then I set off in search of Micah.

I exit the office, the click of my heels loud on the concrete. *Clap. Clap. Clap.* The sound thunderous compared to the music in the main room. The hall shrinks and my footsteps slow. At the end of the hall, I stop and scan every square foot of the club. It takes seconds to spot Micah.

Micah is across the room with his back aimed this way. He shuffles tables around and sets up the various games and events. Leaning on the wall, I observe him a moment. Take him in while his attention is elsewhere. Study the flex of his arms. Rake my eyes down his broad shoulders, defined back, and firm glutes. Call me piggish, but I want to enjoy this blip in time. To ogle the man without him giving me a ration of shit for doing so.

Then, I take a breath. Sooner than desirable, I shut the moment down and snap back to reality. Time to work.

"Hey," I say as I waltz in his direction.

He spins around, eyes me head to toe, and flashes me with the best smile. A smile I haven't seen in weeks. And I can't help but return it. Micah licks his bottom lip and I swallow.

"About finished with setup. If you want to lay out the beer pong cups." Micah points to a nearby banquet table.

I lay out the cups and set the balls in a bowl at each end. We don't fill the cups until people start playing. And the cups are changed out between each player rotation. Health code and all.

It isn't long before Roar fills with countless bodies. The deejay now takes requests on Thursday nights and plays upbeat music between those songs. Bar Olympics night—along with the other new themed days—has only been going for two weeks and already brings in a decent crowd. Roar easily makes double profits on Thursday nights since we changed it up. Adding fresh ideas was a smart business move for Ani and Sean. Each night continues to bring in new faces.

On the nights Micah and I both work, we trade off who gets paperwork duty. It eases me into my new role, but gives us the chance to not stare at a computer monitor and rows of numbers all night. The monotony of filling in spreadsheets, filing paperwork, writing schedules, and updating payroll doesn't bog me down. At times, I enjoy the simplicity and repetition. But hours later, my eyes grow weary. My mind a bit sluggish.

I tap Micah on the shoulder and he turns, giving me his starry gaze. A brilliant smile plumps his cheeks and brightens the room. And once again, I question whether or not kissing him last night was smart. Too late now. Turning back time only exists in fiction. Now, I just put one foot in front of the other and trek forward.

"I'm doing rounds, then going in the office."

Micah steps forward, stopping inches from me, close enough to touch without effort. And I forget how to breathe.

Son of a bitch. Breathe, Peyton. Deep breath in. Then exhale.

I inhale a deep breath, doing my damnedest to keep the action undetectable, and shuffle back an inch. But it's too late. The scent of his sweet cologne hits my nose and the room goes foggy. I beg my legs to move, my feet to carry me away from him, but nothing happens. My legs grow heavy and bury themselves deep in the earth like tree roots.

I am so screwed.

Perspiration slicks my skin and I send a silent prayer to the air conditioning gods, pleading for the cool air to kick on. Micah locks me in place with his magnetic eyes; the gold flecks sparkling with more intensity. I want to look away. I want to flee to the office and use the brick walls and industrial metal door as a barricade.

But I can't. Breaking eye contact feels impossible. A fool's errand.

Neither of us says a word, but I need space. And air. Air that doesn't smell of Micah and desire. I clear my throat and he blinks as if I woke him.

"I'm going to..." I circle my finger in the air and step around him.

One, two, three steps and I take a breath. A burst of cool air hits me, clears some of the Micah-induced fog, and allows me to think clearly. I take another breath and drop my shoulder, thinking I'm home free. Then a hand grips my bicep.

Without looking, I know whose hand is secured around my arm. Every sensory organ in my body alerts me to Micah's proximity. Even through the hate-filled years, I was aware of all things Micah Reed. Always.

I peek over my shoulder and flash my best work smile. "What's up?"

A tingle ripples from his touch down to my fingers and up my shoulder, neck, and chest. I conjure up any and every thought to distract me from the sensation. Public bathrooms, cottage cheese, scooping the litter box as a kid. And it works... until his grip loosens and his fingers traipse down my bicep, my forearm, my wrist. Then he steps into me again. Invades every molecule of air within breathing distance.

Damn it. Damn it. Damn it.

Why must this be so difficult? Why am I torturing myself? For what?

It would be so easy. To take his hand in mine. Lace our fingers together and curl them tight. To feel the callouses on his warm skin as he strokes my thumb with the pad of his. To get lost in euphoria as sparks travel from my fingertips, my forearm, up and across my chest, to coil around my heart.

Believe me, I want to hold his hand. Want him so close, all I see and feel and breathe is him.

Should I, though? Let him invade me completely. Should I jump back in without reservation? My subconscious screams to slow down and use the time to learn more about Micah and the years we didn't know each other. Meanwhile, my heart beats erratically and begs me to cave. To give in to my desires; come what may.

Argh!

"Thank you," he says and steps closer.

My skin buzzes under his touch. God, I want to feel him everywhere. "For what?" I rasp, then swallow.

Get ahold of yourself, Peyton.

"Last night." A finger draws small circles over my pulse and I fight the urge to close my eyes. If he picks up on my galloping heart rate, he doesn't let on. "It may not have meant much to some, but it meant the world to me."

I will myself to respond. Tell my brain to part my lips and let the words flow freely. But nothing happens. My lips go on lockdown as I stare foolishly at Micah. When I manage to string words together, I sound like a bumbling idiot.

"Yeah. Sure. No problem."

What the hell is wrong with me?

Since when do I get tongue-tied around men? Around Micah? This isn't high school. A boy isn't asking me to a damn dance. I am an extroverted, grown-ass woman who doesn't take shit from anyone. My step has never faltered. Neither have my words.

Until recently.

One more circle on my wrist and Micah releases me. My skin prickles where we were joined. I want to wrap a hand or glove or bandage around the area. Trap the sensation so it will stay put. But I fight the urge.

"You look beautiful." The soft edges of his voice warm and soothe the wild organ beneath my breastbone. "See you in a bit," he says, then turns back to the bar and helps a waiting customer.

I shake off the daze that is Micah Reed and exit the bar alley.

Once I check in with the staff, I enter the office and lock the door. If I were the only manager on duty, the door would remain unlocked. But with us both here tonight, locking isn't an issue. Plus, I need solitude.

After catching up with the paperwork, I busy myself with straightening the office. Organizing drawers and tidying shelves. Rearranging the folder icons on the computer desktop and shifting furniture in the room. I do any possible thing to avoid exiting the office.

It sounds cruel—ignoring Micah—but I don't know what else to do. Last night, we agreed to friendship. But shortly thereafter, I kissed Micah. Jumped right over the friendship line. Possible presumptions were made. Thoughts strayed—at least mine did.

For now, I need this—us—to slow down. I need time to marinate in the idea of more with Micah. Again. Need time to consider how I might feel if Red Dress *is* pregnant.

I won't ghost him again. But with the weight of the situation hanging overhead, it only seems fair for me to be a little selfish. Right?

~

I scrunch up my nose and swat the air. Dust or a bug or hair tickles the tip of my nose. Pinching my eyes tighter, I rub the heel of my palm over my nose. As I drift back to sleep, whatever it is tickles my nose a third time. Bolting up in my bed, I flail my arms.

"Ow!" Reese belts out as I make contact with him.

My eyes fly open and I squint at the too-bright sunlight coming through the blinds. Reese sits on the edge of my bed, rubbing his arm.

"What are you doing in here?" I groan out and fall back on the mattress.

"Well, I was trying to wake you up. Thought we could have breakfast out before my shift at the rec center."

I sit back up and stare at his faux wound. "Maybe you should wake me like a normal person. Nudge my shoulder. Call out my name." I purse my lips and lift a brow. "Not tickle my face and wait to get hit."

"Where's the fun in that?"

Throwing the covers off, I scoot out of bed and point to the door. "If you want to go out, I need to get dressed. Which means you need to exit, mister."

"Grumpy, sunshine."

"Yeah, yeah."

When the bedroom door clicks shut, I slump forward, press the heels of my hands to my eyes, and sigh. I love my best friend. Wouldn't want anyone else as a roommate. But sometimes, he really knows how to get under my skin. And laugh at my expense.

Fumbling through my dresser and closet, I go for easy and comfortable. It's early and I give no fucks about my appearance. Not after Reese woke me via tickle torture. Once my jeans are zipped, I drag a brush through my mane to tame the scary, then twist it up in a topknot. I slip on my black Vans, grab my phone and keys, and meet Reese in the kitchen.

Reese and I agree to take separate cars so he can go straight to work after. We meet up at a local breakfast and brunch restaurant not far from the apartment. Thankfully, since most morning people have gone to work and it's the middle of the week, the place isn't jam-packed.

We get seated and order coffee while we peruse the menu. The server returns with a carafe and fills our mugs. Reese orders as if eating for two while I get biscuits and gravy with a side of hash browns and fruit.

With our orders scribbled down, the server takes our menus and wanders off. Silence stretches over the table as we fix our coffee how we like and take the first sip. No good conversation happens before this moment. At least not with me. I have no shame in admitting this.

"You sleep better?" Reese asks as he toys with the empty stevia packet.

I take another sip of coffee, then nod. "Yeah. Like a rock, actually."

"What changed?"

"Good question. Maybe it's all the office cleaning and rearranging I did last night to avoid Micah." I shrug a shoulder.

Reese's jaw tics as he glances out the window next to our table. "Thought things were better between you two," he growls, then meets my gaze.

"They are," I say in a rush. "It's just…" I pluck the creamers from the bowl and stack them into a pyramid to buy myself time.

"Just spit it out, Peyton."

"I may have confused him." After I stack the last creamer, I knock them down and start again.

"How so?"

The more I ponder this over, the more I question if I am overthinking the whole situation. Am I the only one focused on the fact I kissed Micah? Am I the only paranoid one reading too much into the moment? Probably. And also not surprising.

I stop stacking the creamers to look up at Reese, the corners of his mouth slightly upturned. His eyes bright as they stare back, as if he knows something I don't. *Feel free to share with the class, Mr. Triggs.*

"I told Micah I wanted to be friends again. Give things between us time, then go from there."

"Okay," he drawls out the word.

"I told him this two nights ago. And then I kissed him. More than once." I drop my head in my hands and groan. "Wasn't hot and heavy. But still…"

"Hey." Reese reaches across the table and jostles my arm. "Look at me." This feels like a parenting moment, one of those annoying times you get told what you did right and wrong. I don't want to look up, but I do. Reese lays his hand on the table, palm up, and I place mine on top. The warmth and slight curl of our fingers is a comfort I have only ever gotten from Reese. "You didn't do anything wrong. Can't help what you feel."

"Ugh. This sucks." He squeezes my hand. "I need things to slow down. Me kissing him counteracts the whole purpose."

"Why?"

"Why, what?"

"Why do you need things to slow down?"

My brows pinch at the middle as my head jerks back. "Are you serious?" Reese nods with the most somber expression on his face. "Did you forget what happened two weeks ago?"

"No. But I don't think Micah should be punished for something out of his hands and which may be false. Without proof, it's all hearsay."

Since when did my friend jump off the Peyton wagon and on the Micah train? Not cool.

"So, I'm supposed to forget it ever happened? Act as if his world is hunky dory and may not flip upside down in months? Seems idiotic, if you ask me."

Reese shifts his gaze out the window and loses focus. A few breaths pass and he gives my hand a light squeeze as his eyes drift back across the table. "What if all this stress you're taking on is for nothing? What if the woman isn't pregnant? And if she is, what if it isn't his? Then you put yourself through all this for nothing."

Does he not think I have considered this? God, I have thought over every possible scenario. Problem is, I have no clue which way to go or how to feel until the truth comes to light. I want to believe this outcome—that Micah has nothing to do with this woman's pregnancy. But I should also be mentally prepared for the possibility of it becoming a reality. And I need Reese to see both sides of the coin.

"What if she is and it is his? If I don't prepare myself for that, how will I cope? How will I know if I can have a relationship—in any capacity—with him? If I don't consider the possibilities of what our future may look like, how will I know?"

"Sunshine…" He sandwiches my hand between both of his as the most endearing expression touches his face. "There's no way to know what the future holds. But you impact it." I tilt my head and narrow my eyes. "If you constantly focus on the potential negative outcome, that's all you'll see and think." I open my mouth to rebut and he holds a hand up. "I'm not saying to discount the possibility. What I am saying is you shouldn't focus all your energy on the bad. If you like him, really like him, do what feels right *for you*. If that means time apart, so be it. But if it means time together, don't second-guess it." He leans down and kisses my hand. "Life is too short to miss out on the good. You of all people should understand this."

This is why I love and hate conversations with Reese. He tells me like it is and doesn't sugarcoat a damn word. And that last part… god, that hits home. Hard.

Far too often, I questioned if I'd ever find and hold on to love. Whether familial or romantic. Because the universe has thrown a lot of shitty cards for my hand. And it's difficult to believe anything else.

Reese releases my hand, sits back in his seat, and gives me time to process. To mull over what it is I want with Micah. To decide what steps I should take next. A decision only I can make.

Before I get too deep in thought, the server steps up to the table and delivers plate after plate. I unwrap my silverware, lean over my plate and inhale, and sag at the hearty scent of sausage gravy and fresh biscuits. Forks clink the ceramic plates as we eat in companionable silence. The entire time, I dissect everything Reese said. Take it apart, one word at a time, then restring it together to see if it makes better sense.

As his words cycle through my head for the hundredth, two questions pop up. Questions I need answers to, but fear what they will be.

Am I wrong to keep Micah at a distance? Or am I sheltering my heart so I don't lose someone else? Sadly, only I have the answers. If only I knew where they were hidden.

seven

Why did I agree to this? Why did I let Shelly talk me into coming here?

Naturally, Shelly is running late. Which is why I am still in my truck, with the engine and lights off, waiting for her arrival. Because I refuse to walk into the lioness's den without her. Okay, I may be exaggerating a bit. But after what Shelly said the other day, I can't muster the energy to enter my childhood home without her as a buffer.

So, while I wait, I stare at the only home my parents have owned. Picture perfect. I love everything about this house. All that it stands for and the love that resides in each square foot of the property. It irks me I haven't quite reached this comfortable stage as a homeowner yet. It's a marathon, not a sprint. Mom and Dad have worked their asses off for what they own. Have spent countless hours on every little detail, inside and out, to make their home shine. I remind myself of this each time I upgrade a room in the house or update the backyard and patio. All good things come with time. And patience.

Including love.

I stare at the two-story, natural brick home. The pristine white trim, decorative shutters and modern double front doors with large stainless fittings. Grass cut three inches tall. Hedges manicured and colorful flowers blooming along the front and down the walkway. Twin maple trees taller than the house rooted on either side of the long drive leading to the three-car garage. The house surrounded by an acre of land, an iron-and-brick fence and a gate.

The house wasn't always this gorgeous. All the hours and labor my parents have put in are an inspiration. It energizes me to take on the next project in my own home. Baby steps eventually lead to full strides.

Shelly pulls up and I breathe easier. We exit our vehicles and converge to walk to the house as a unit. We both love our parents, had a happy and healthy upbringing, but have zero excitement about tonight's dinner.

"You ready for this?" she asks.

"Not in the slightest. You?"

"No. Last thing I need is a reminder of my singledom. Or my lack of offspring."

Same. Although, if I play my hand right, I plan to not be single much longer. No comment on the offspring. But Mom and Dad won't be privy to either bit of news. Not yet. No need to have them barrage me with questions I can't answer. Nor do I want them to nag or ask to meet Peyton. Our relationship hasn't crossed that bridge yet.

Shelly opens the front door and leads the way. We toe off our shoes and set them on the rack past the foyer. Less than ten feet inside, the scent of pork, citrus, garlic and herbs wafts in the air. Soft jazz notes echo throughout the house. Mom says something about opening wine and I assume she talks to Dad.

We round the corner and spot our parents canoodling at the stove with their backs to us. Before we disturb the moment, I take it all in. How after thirty-five years of marriage—and seven years unmarried—they still hang on each other and kiss like teenagers. Dad has his arms locked around Mom's waist, her back to his front, as he whispers in her ear and she swats the air near him as she giggles. My heart swells seeing them so in love. The simple touches and secret conversations give me hope I will one day have a similar happiness.

"Hope we're not interrupting," Shelly pipes up as Dad kisses Mom's cheek.

They spin around, smile wide, and stop what they are doing to come hug us.

"How's my baby?" Mom asks as she wraps her arms around my neck. I circle my arms around her waist, lift her off the ground, and squeeze her.

"Good, Mom. Miss you."

When I set her down, she takes a step back and frames my face with her hands, eyes soft as she regards me. The lines on my forehead, the arch of my brow, the light in my eyes, the scruff on my jaw. "Miss you, too. Both of you." She peers over at Shelly, then swaps places with Dad.

"How's work been?" Dad asks as he hauls me to his chest and knocks the wind from my lungs.

"Good," I say once he releases me. "The owners have made some changes and it's been great for business."

"Like what?" Dad guides us farther into the kitchen, where he and Mom resume cooking.

I prattle off the new changes—leaving out all things Peyton-related. When I finish, Shelly looks at me like she did the one time I stole her clothes and towel from the bathroom forever ago.

"What?" I ask, scared of her answer.

"Why am I just learning about Karaoke Night?" Her brows shoot up and eyes widen.

Damn it. How the hell did I forget that my sister, Cora, and Jonas are karaoke buffs? Probably because I haven't hung out during the week with them in a while. After learning this new information, though, I bet I will see them Wednesday nights. Often.

I love my sister—and my friends—but seeing her at work feels a bit much. Maybe I am overanalyzing, but I like having time and a place that is just mine. Kind of.

"Uh…" Dad stands far enough behind Shelly she doesn't notice his *yikes* face. "Because I don't talk about work with you," I answer in staccato.

She rolls her eyes, then slaps a hand over her sternum. "Wound me, why don't you. If karaoke doesn't make you think of me, I feel like we need to bond more."

Oh, Jesus.

"Throwing it on a little thick there, Shell."

"What do you expect? My feelings are crushed." She play weeps and Dad bites his fist to resist laughing.

"Oh, please." I laugh and Dad joins in. "Work on your weeping skills, little sis."

"Alright, you two," Mom intercepts with hands on her hips. "Time to plate up and eat."

We line up beside the counter near the stove, grab a plate, and pile on the food. Mojo pork tenderloin, oven-roasted red potatoes, steamed green beans and home-made rolls. Needless to say, I put too much on my plate.

Mom and Dad lead busy work lives, but always make time for what matters.

Family. Mom still works forty hours a week as a corporate marketing manager. She has the ability to retire in a few years without worrying, but she won't. That's what happens when you love what you do. Dad owns an insurance company that handles mostly vehicles, vessels and property. For a short time, he dipped his toes in the health and life side, but it became too taxing. Dad hit retirement age earlier this year, but said he plans to run the business a few more years before selling.

Both my parents have done so much in their career lives. They started at the bottom, put in their time, learned more about what they love, and worked hard for their career dreams. As a child, Dad often said, "Micah, you should never expect your dreams to be handed over. You have to put in the effort. Bust your butt until you get what you want. If you don't earn it, you won't respect it."

And I guess that applies to anything you want in life. Not just your career.

We sit in the same chairs we have since I was a child. Mom to my right, Dad on the left, and Shelly across from me. Dad fills glasses with sauvignon blanc while Mom lights the two candles in the table centerpiece. Nothing fancy. Just the norm.

Quiet consumes the first few minutes around the table as we taste the meal. I sample a little of each before the silence is broken.

"Excellent as always, Nicole."

"Agreed," I follow after Dad. "Really wish I had your cooking skills, Mom."

Mom eyes Dad across the table as her cheeks pink. "Thank you." Eyes that mirror mine shift my direction after breaking contact with Dad. "And you, too." She cuts and pierces a piece of pork loin. "We can try cooking lessons again. If you want."

One trait I love about Mom… she never gives up. I may burn or undercook every dish I attempt, but Mom still holds on to hope. I love how she feels I am not a lost cause.

"Maybe." I reach over and rub her forearm. "Might be best to start with recipes written for kids, though."

The entire table erupts in laughter. Years have passed since I cared whether or not I got teased in the cooking department. Can't be good at everything. May as well own it.

"I'd love that, Micah. Let me dig up some recipes and we'll plan a day to get together."

"Sounds great, Mom."

So far, tonight has gone smooth. Shelly had me frazzled for days. Worried about conversations over relationships and grandchildren. But the night has been normal. Good food, smiles and laughter. Everything I love about my parents and where we grew up. Couldn't be more perfect.

"Shelly," Dad starts and she turns to face him. "Still seeing that nice young man from the Italian market?"

And… I jinxed us.

Thank goodness she swallowed her bite before he finished speaking. Her eyes flit to mine and beg for help. But I have nothing. The second I come to her defense, Mom will jump on me with a similar question. Then we will both sweat under the spotlight. Better to let her go first, then I will follow. Cruel, yes. But that's what older siblings do.

Shelly stabs a potato with pent-up aggression. "No, Dad. We went on one date and I felt really uncomfortable." I widen my eyes at her and she shrugs. "He didn't *do* anything wrong. Just a vibe."

Dad takes her hand and consoles her. "Never be upset for turning down someone who makes you uneasy. I will always be in your corner. You mean the world to us, Shelly Bear."

"Same," I say. Speaking up and agreeing with Dad is right. I will always be there for my sister and family. In a heartbeat. And they will do the same.

The seriousness of the moment fades and we all breathe easier. Then, Mom shifts her attention toward me and whips out her inquisition claws. *Damn it.*

"What about you, Micah? Is there a special lady in your life we should know about?"

Why? Why did I agree to this? And why are our parents pestering us about our romance lives? Well, lack of romance.

What spurred this on? Dad had his annual birthday checkup with Doctor Harris not long ago. Hopefully, it all went well and this isn't Mom and Dad's way of saying they don't have much time left. I don't enjoy their nosiness, but I would take it over bad health any day of the week.

"No, Mom. Can't seem to nail down the right one." Which is not a lie. Mom just won't hear my words how I mean them.

We all quiet and go back to eating. I chew the pork and potatoes way longer than necessary. Keep my mouth busy in case one of my parents decides to pry further. I pray the relationship talk will stay where it is. In the past. And once again, I should quit thinking. It's as if Mom or Dad have a sixth sense, as if they hear my every thought or pick up on the exact vibe of my mood.

"With the massive population in the area and technology, I figured my kids would've married by now," Mom mutters before biting her roll.

Why didn't I put a contingency plan in place? Should have asked Gavin to text or call. He does owe me a favor, after all. Or have Cora do the same with Shelly. Both of us came here knowing our parents were on a mission. To marry us off and make us baby factories. Not really, but that is how it feels under the current spotlight.

Part of me wants to counter Mom's comment. But if I open my mouth, it will fuel the fire. So, I bite my tongue. My sister, on the other hand, didn't get the memo to keep her mouth shut.

"You'd think with the massive population and all the dating apps, there wouldn't be thousands of creepy guys in the area." Shelly shrugs, then stabs the pork loin on her plate with pent-up anger. *Shit.* "But most only want one thing. And it isn't commitment." She shovels the bite in her mouth and doesn't look up.

My blood boils that Shelly feels the need to defend herself like this. Especially to our parents. Are they aware of her lack of sexual experience? Doubtful. If they were, there is no way they'd be so eager to push her into the arms of a random guy. All for some picture-perfect idea they have in their heads.

"Surely, they're not all bad."

That's it. Conversation over. "Mom!" I bark out. Her fork freezes halfway to her mouth. "Drop it."

"Micah, don't speak to your mother with that tone."

My eyes dart to Dad. "Don't mean to be cruel. But this conversation... it's uncomfortable. For both of us."

"Sorry, sweetheart." Mom rubs Shelly's forearm. "Just don't want either of you to miss out on the opportunity to have a family of your own."

I turn back to Mom, softening my tone as I speak. "I get it. But have you given thought as to *why* we aren't with someone? Sure, I could stay with a random hookup—"

"Micah," Dad grumbles.

"No, Dad. Hear me out." I set my fork down, wipe my mouth, and fold my arms across my chest. "Is it so wrong for Shelly to be picky? Shouldn't she wait for the guy—or girl—that makes her happy? She has her own reasons for being single." Shelly's eyes widen. "Which are none of our business unless she wants to share."

"Okay, we're sorry," Dad says with sincerity. "Hope you understand this conversation came from a place of love." He and Mom look at each other, then us.

"We do," I answer. "And as soon as either of us wants to introduce someone, we will. So, please, can we not bring this up again?"

Mom scoots potatoes around her plate, her eyes following the motion. Dad does the same with the last of his green beans. *Jesus.* They act like pouty children. I love my parents, always, but this is ridiculous.

Chair legs scrape the wood floor as I rise and grab my plate and head for the kitchen. I scrape the last of my food into the trash, rinse the plate and put it in the dishwasher. I drag my fingers through my hair and tug.

Shelly prepped me for what was coming tonight, but I had no idea it would set me off. Not like this. I don't typically lash out at my parents. Tonight, though, feels different. The weight, the pressure… an expectation I have never dealt with from them fists my heart in painful ways.

And I don't know how to handle it.

"Micah?" Mom calls out, her voice soft as she approaches.

"In the kitchen."

She rounds the corner, sets her plate on the counter, walks straight to me and wraps her arms around my waist. My arms wrap around her waist as I haul her closer and rest my cheek on her head.

"Sorry," she mumbles against my chest.

I rub a hand up and down her back. "It's fine, Mom. Just please, respect our choices. And privacy. We'll tell you when the time comes. Promise."

She drops her arms and steps back. "Okay." Matching eyes hold mine as a gentle smile curves up her lips. "Just want you both happy."

Shelly and Dad shuffle into the kitchen and clean their plates. The thorny topic gets dropped and we dish out dessert—mixed berries and chocolate cake with fresh whipped cream. Shelly and I hang out a while longer once our plates empty. Fortunately, everyone but me has to be up in the morning. So, the evening ends early.

Hugs are exchanged on the front porch as Shelly and I step out to leave. Mom says she will reach out to us both for the next get-together.

On the way to our cars, Shelly mutters, "Thanks for the save earlier."

I bump her shoulder with my arm. "Always, little sis. They mean well, but their persistence frustrated me."

"Yeah, I picked up on that." She chuckles as we reach her car and she opens the door. "Remind me to never pester you."

"Whatever." I play shove her in the car. "Drive safe. Love you."

She blows me a kiss. "Love you, too, big brother. Talk to you later."

~

I drain the last of my beer. The *Peaky Blinders* episode ends and I shut off the television. Silence engulfs me as I turn off lights, close blinds and curtains, and check the door locks.

The short distance to my bedroom is a mile long tonight. My usual solace with solitude has taken a back seat.

I strip my clothes, toss them in the hamper, pull back the bedding and slip under the covers. For a moment, I lie in the dark with an arm tossed over my eyes. Take a few breaths as all the relationship talk filters back in from earlier tonight.

My parents mean well, but don't grasp the example they set for us. Shelly and I will never just settle. Not for some random person who we check *some* boxes off with. No, whoever we choose will have to check off all the boxes. Will have to fill all the cracks and seal old wounds. Make us see the world with new eyes. Make us *feel*.

We aren't emotionless people, but Shelly and I don't give away love freely. And letting someone new get close is a feat. Years ago, I let people in easier. Loved more openly with family, friends, and romantic interests. Then Rochelle fucked me over and my trust in the opposite sex fizzled. At least when it came to love.

Until Peyton.

I slap a hand in the direction of the nightstand and locate my phone. Tapping the screen, the background lights up. A picture of me and Shelly smiles back at me from my birthday this year. I unlock the phone, open the message app, and tap on Peyton's name.

Too many days have passed since we texted back and forth. As of recent, the texts have been one sided. From me. She needs time, I get it. But I reject the idea of leaving her alone altogether. Out of sight and all that.

Before the idea dies, I type out a message to her and hit send.

> Awkward dinner with the parents tonight 🙂 You'd think that'd end when you're an adult.

I lock the screen, lay the phone on my stomach and stare at the wall. The shadows from the oak tree and streetlight dance over the cream-painted wall opposite my bed. Leaves flutter on the branches and I try to create other shapes out of their combined shadows.

I jolt when my phone vibrates. Fumble as it slides off my chest and hits the sheet. Scramble until I locate and unlock it.

> Probably wasn't intentional.

For a moment, I stare at the screen and forget to breathe. *She answered.* That has to mean something. Right? Probably best to not read into it too much. Not yet, anyway.

> Nah. They want us happy, but approached it all wrong.

What happened?

I scoot closer to the headboard, toss the second pillow on the one under my head, and inch upright.

Asked if either of us is dating. They're worried we'll miss out.

What'd you say?

Her response makes me smile. I may read into it more than intended, but it seems she wants to know if I told my parents I was dating someone.

That when either of us wants them to meet someone, they will. It got a little heated. Which isn't normal.

Sorry you had a crazy night.

Thanks. Better now.

Is that so?

I read the last text with her voice in my head, imagining her hands on her hips and brow perked up. *Fuck.* How I miss this side of her. The snark and banter and sass. The side that has me crawling like a bumbling fool.

Damn straight.

And why is that?

Hmm Maybe because a certain someone is awake.

Do you have a pet?

God, she makes me laugh. Lifts away the heavy and provides incomparable comfort.

No. Do you?

No, but I want a cat.

Good to know.

Are you allergic?

No. But it's always good to know the competition.

For the next hour, we text back and forth. Talk about randomness. Some with substance, but not much. By the time we say good night, a peculiar bouncy sensation ping-pongs beneath my rib cage. I press the heel of my palm to my sternum, take a deep breath, hold it until my lungs burn and relish in the bliss Peyton delivers.

I have no clue what this is between us. But I plan to do whatever it takes to keep it. To keep her. Who knows... maybe in the not-too-distant future, I will have dinner with my parents and tell them about Peyton. Introduce her to them. One day...

How do so many people know this much random shit?

When I first suggested Trivia Night to Ani, I figured it would revolve around movies, television and basic geography. Questions like "what is the capital of Arkansas?" or "name the show with a woman who performed magic with a twitch of her nose." or "who crushed on Penny first in *The Big Bang Theory*?"

What we got instead was some serious nerd action. Super. Nerd. Action. And it's kind of hot. I never pictured myself interested in highly intelligent men—the nerds of my youth were… odd—but I have a newfound appreciation for them. The women too.

"What's the diameter of Earth?" the trivialist asks.

Bzz.

"It's 7,917.5 miles," Mr. Rolled Sleeves answers.

"Name the largest sea on Earth."

Bzz.

"Philippine Sea," Mr. Tall and Lanky states.

"List three Wonders of the Ancient World."

Bzz.

"Great Pyramid of Giza, Hanging Gardens of Babylon, Lighthouse of Alexandria," Ms. Hot Librarian says as she straightens her spine and pushes glasses up her nose.

Gina sidles up to me and fans herself with a coaster. "Damn."

Tipping my head back, I laugh. "You and me both, girl. Never saw this day coming." She lifts a brow. "When intelligence ranks in the top three traits to tick off." At this, Gina laughs with a shake of her head.

"Speaking of guys…"

Over the last six weeks, since my promotion, Gina and I have bonded. We aren't to the point where we hang outside Roar. But it has been nice forming this new relationship. Having another woman to shoot the shit with. Someone I can vent with or tell dirty details to.

She hadn't been blind to the chemistry between me and Micah. Neither has most of the staff. My stomach constricted when she let me in on this non-secret. Guess I had been willfully blind to the staff and everyone else setting foot in Roar. Now, I notice every little detail. Pay attention to the way they watch us on the nights we work together. Pray our interactions don't disrupt work.

Because things between Micah and I could definitely disrupt.

"Yes?"

Pulling down on the tap, Gina fills a pint glass and hands it to a shorter man with shaggy brown hair. He scurries back to his chair, sips the beer, and holds his hand over his buzzer. This crowd stirs the best belly laughter and intriguing inquisition. Trivia Night was one of the best ideas, hands down.

Hands on her hips, mouth in a firm, straight line, Gina shakes her head. "Don't play coy."

I put on my best poker face while I laugh internally. *But it's fun.* "Well" —I wipe the bar— "you didn't ask a question."

A sharp sting bites my skin after Gina whacks my bicep with a bar towel. "Smart-ass." Rubbing away the sting, I shrug. "How's things with starlight?"

Gina has no idea why I call Micah starlight. One night, she overheard us talking and my casual use of the nickname. Since then, she throws it out on occasion when we chat. I have no intention of telling her the meaning behind the name. All that would do is add another twenty questions to her mile-long list. For now, she believes it's just me teasing him. I have no intention of changing her opinion.

"Good."

With Gina, I give vague answers. One—it drives her crazy. Two—I don't feel the need to divulge my entire life. Our friendship fairly new, I choose to keep some parts of my life private. Only one friend gets all the dirty details. Reese. Our bond wasn't always what it is today, but we have been tight for years.

"Good?" she deadpans.

"Yeah. Good."

"Remind me to never ask you for detailed opinions in the future."

I laugh and mix drinks for an order Charity drops at the bar. "You got it." Setting the Jack and Coke, Cosmo and IPA on the tray, Charity flashes her award-winning smile, then walks off to deliver the drinks. "Things have been good," I say once Charity is out of earshot.

The staff may be aware Micah and I are friends—or more than friends, no definitions have been laid out. I don't make a point to ask their opinion. What Micah and I have should not interfere with Roar. All workplaces are different—some lenient on personal relationships outside work, others not so much. Seeing as Ani is a friend and I tell her quite a bit, she is cool with whatever Micah and I have, so long as it doesn't interrupt business.

For the most part, we maintain our managerial persona when on the floor. Sporadic flirting and banter are good for business. What we do away from the crowd is a different story.

Things with Micah haven't veered back to steamy kisses and hands under shirts. Yet. But we seem to be speed walking the same path that led us there before. Part of me jumps at the idea of kissing Micah again. Ready to feel his soft, warm lips pressed to mine. Taste his hunger on my tongue. Thinking about it makes my mouth water and thighs clench.

My phone vibrates in my back pocket and I snap out of my wayward thoughts. Slipping it from my pocket, I glance down at the notification and snort. Micah's ears must have been ringing.

"What's funny?"

"Micah." I shake the phone in my hand. "Like he knew we were talking about him."

"Creepy." Gina wanders down the bar, chats with customers not playing trivia, and leaves me to read the text in privacy.

Come over tonight 🙏

In the last month, Micah and I have hung out after work more. Gone to Teddy's on occasion, but spent more time in his living room with take-out boxes and episodes of *Supernatural.* Last week, he introduced me to *Peaky Blinders.* Although he watched three of the seasons, he swears starting over is fine.

> I don't know. These trivia guys are kind of hot.

> You want to play twenty questions, hellcat?

I bite my lower lip and fight the grin begging to come out. I spin to face the wall of liquor bottles and hide the heat on my cheeks. Don't know what it is, but the nickname he gave me makes me hot, bothered and goofy.

> Depends...

> On?

> Mood. Food. Booze.

Why did I press send? It isn't only my brain that forgets how to properly function around Micah Reed. Obviously, my fingers have a mind of their own as well. *Swell.*

> Really?

> Yep.

> Best get your ass here after you say good night to the trivia BOYS.

I laugh out loud and Gina shoots me a *that good, huh?* With a shake of my head, I wave her off and resume texting.

> They are definitely MEN. Who knew nerds this good-looking existed?

Now, this is fun. Something about banter with Micah makes my chest lighter. Tugs at the corners of my lips. Makes my heart stutter. My breathing stammer. I dish it out and he gives it right back. It's who we are, only the context has morphed over the last two months.

> You want nerdy?

> I mean...

> Be here after work

The urge to drag this out further tempts me, but I cut the conversation short. If I head into the office, paperwork will occupy me long enough for the night to end soon.

> I like it when you're bossy Later.

I stow my phone in my pocket and ignore the final buzz. Passing Gina, I signal toward the office and she nods. Behind the closed door, I slump down in the desk chair and eye the stack of work. Most of it is menial, but necessary. Never expected to be a number cruncher. Someone who sits behind a desk and fills in spreadsheets. But here I am, squeezing the armrests on the chair while tucking myself closer.

And I love it.

nine

I read the last text I sent for the tenth time.

You haven't seen bossy yet 😏

She hasn't opened the text, but she will once work wraps up.

My connection with Peyton over the last month has been this force. Gradual yet powerful. Strong yet gentle.

After the night we agreed to give friendship another try—let's not forget the kiss, I sure as hell won't—our relationship has bloomed. Neither of us has titled the relationship beyond friendship. Yet. But the chaste kisses from week one have morphed into longer kisses and frequent caresses. No suck-your-soul kisses or groping of parts, but my crystal ball indicates we are headed that direction.

I order pizza online and schedule it to be delivered around the time she typically arrives. Then I surf through movie options. Usually, we watch an episode or two of my show or hers. But after her snarky comments earlier, a change of plans seems in order.

After I choose the movie, I peel off my shirt on the way to the bathroom. Ditching the last of my clothes, I crank the shower and step under the hot spray. I wash up in record time, towel off, and sort through my wardrobe for the perfect attire.

I wander from the bedroom into the kitchen and dig out the candle lighter and jar candles. Next time I see Shelly, I must thank her for the obscene number of candles she gifted me over the years. Most of them have been decorative dust collectors for years strategically placed in the main space of the house.

Tonight, though, they will be put to good use.

After I light enough candles to heat the house, I stow the lighter, then grab a bottle of wine from the fridge. I pop the cork, set the bottle on the counter, and let it breathe.

Mood. *Check.*

Booze. *Check.*

And any minute… the doorbell chimes. "Food."

I open the door and am greeted by a smiley young man that hands me two large boxes and a bag. The moment he exits the porch, Peyton parks in the driveway. She cuts the ignition, hops out, and practically skips to the front door.

Fuck, she's adorable.

"Hey," Peyton singsongs as she openly ogles me. "Look at—" She freezes as she takes in the main room of the house. "What's this?" Spinning around, a crease forms between her brows.

"Mood, booze" —I set the pizza, salad and garlic bread on the counter— "and food."

"And this?" Peyton lays her palms beneath my collarbones, then, inch by inch, drags her hands down my abdomen. Her thumbs brushing the column of buttons.

"Going for the nerdy look." She lifts a brow. "Didn't find the fake glasses before you arrived."

Her arms sweep around my waist and rest on my lower back. "You don't need them."

Hands on her hips, I secure Peyton in my grip. If I leaned forward an inch, her lips would be under mine. But anticipation is everything. And I love the push and pull between us.

I lean in and she gasps. Instead of kissing her, I brush my cheek along hers and stop at her ear. "Time to eat," I whisper, then nip her lobe. Her body shudders beneath me and the corner of my mouth twitches. My fingers drift along the inside of her forearm and lace with her fingers. "C'mon."

I guide her to the couch, park her in the spot I dubbed hers and go back to grab the food, wine and glasses. Everything on the coffee table, I sort the boxes while she pours the wine. I turn on the television and hit play on the movie as we dig in.

"Really?" Peyton asks on a laugh-squeal as the intro of *The Princess Bride* pops on the screen.

"What? It's a classic."

"Never pegged you as someone to watch *The Princess Bride*. That's all."

"Well…" I cock a brow at her. "I'm full of surprises."

The movie starts and we settle back on the couch, cross-legged, with salad and pizza in our laps. For a bit, we focus on the movie and dinner. Several years have passed since I last watched this movie and I forgot its greatness.

Around the time when Iñigo talks with Westley about the six-fingered man, Peyton leans forward to set her box on the table. Her knee brushes mine in the process. And when she sits back with her wine, her leg presses and remains butted to my thigh. The motion natural, leisure. As if it wouldn't be any other way.

And I no longer want to hold back. No longer want to resist the one person I want. Her.

I set my box on the table, reach for her glass and put it down. "Hey," she contests.

But before she gets another word in, I lean back, twist in place, frame her face in my hands and bring my lips to hers. She freezes for one, two… then her lips move with mine, soft and sweet at first as her hands snake behind my neck. It isn't long before her lips part and she sucks on my lower lip. She tastes of tangy grapes and herbs and something distinctly Peyton.

My hands drop from her face to her hips as a growl rips from my throat. Her fingers trail into my hair and fist the strands.

Fuck. She will unman me on this couch.

As the thought takes residence, she shifts and slowly lays back, bringing me down with her. I hover inches above her, my arms framing her face and weight pinned between her thighs. Our lips and tongues dance in sync as we give in to the desires we stowed for too long. Her back bows off the cushion and her breasts press to my pecs as she rubs my dick with her pelvic bone.

God, she is fucking perfect.

My hand skims down her shoulder, along the curve of her breast, and she pushes into my touch. I continue my venture down her torso, graze her abdomen, and slip my fingers under the edge of her top. The heat from her skin ripples up my arm and undulates across my chest. Jolts my heart. Expands my lungs. Gives me life.

A hand trails down my back to my elbow. Her fingers drift down my forearm to my wrist and rest on my hand. I am ready for her to stop me, us, from taking this moment any further. Our mouths continue their assault, my hand still on her skin. What I don't expect is what happens next. Peyton guides my hand up her body. Skin to skin, my fingers float over her abdomen, her stomach, her lacy bra cup.

A moan spills from her lips and I swallow every thrum. The resonance vibrates against my palm. Drives me wild. Urges me further.

I shove her top up, tug it over her head, and toss it to the floor. Dropping down, I kiss the spot beneath her ear while I unhook her bra from behind. Peeling the lacy fabric off, I take in her bare breasts for three jagged breaths. Not too big nor too small. Dark-pink areolae with pert nipples in the center. "Perfection."

My mouth crashes down on her lips with another vicious kiss. My hand palms her breast while I twist the nipple between my thumb and forefinger. She rocks her pelvis and rubs my cock with flawless precision. I snake a hand around the back of her neck, comb my fingers through her hair, fist the strands and yank her head back.

Her gasp breaks the kiss and I trail my lips down the front of her throat, past the hollow and between her breasts. Lick my way left, suck the stiff bud between my lips, add a little teeth.

"Micah," she breathes out. "Fuck."

"You like that?" I ask and circle her nipple with my tongue.

"God, yes."

I pay equal attention to her right nipple. Peyton claws at my scalp, tugs my hair, mewls as I lick my way down, down, down her abdomen. When I reach the hemline of her pants, I lift my gaze to meet hers and ask permission.

"Yes," she says, breathy.

My lips drop back to her belly, kiss her sweet flesh, lick her navel. I unbutton her pants and tug down the zipper. I sit up, scoot back and drag the fabric down her thighs, her calves, then drop them on the floor. As badly as I want to rip her panties off, I leave them in place. For now.

"So fucking perfect."

I lift her leg, drop her ankle on my shoulder and kiss the lower inside of her calf. Drag my fingers up the length of her leg as I lick a trail up the inside of her knee, her thigh. Mid-thigh, I suck the skin there. One hand at her hip. The other trails up her belly to her breast and pinches the nipple.

Peyton claws at my shirt. Tears at the buttons. Rips the fabric apart and sends buttons skittering across the room.

"I want your skin on mine."

Hooking her leg on my hip, I wrench the shirt off and toss it behind me. Drop my weight over her, crush my lips to hers, smash her breasts with my chest, and grind the bulge in my pants against her apex.

My hand snakes around her backside, my fingers trailing up her spine. Peyton lined up with my body… damn, this woman was built with me in mind. The lines of her neck and swell of her breasts. The planes of her abdomen and angles of her hip bones. How her lips move in synergy with mine. Her tongue dances the same familiar tune with mine.

Peyton and me, we are perfection.

I clutch the back of her neck, break the kiss, and make the trek back down her body. Taste the saltiness of her skin as I trail down her breastbone, her abdomen. Inhale her coconut mint scent with each new area of skin my lips touch. Trace the soft flesh along the outside of her thigh with my fingers as I drop low, low, lower.

Peppering kisses on her lower abdomen, I peer up at her and lick along the low hemline of her panties. She fists my hair and shoves me lower.

"Something you want?" I mumble over the thin strip of fabric separating her skin from my lips.

"Teasing time is over."

I blow gently over the apex of her thighs and she trembles. "Is it, though?"

She props herself up on an elbow, clutches my chin and tips my eyes to hers. Her violet irises glow with hunger and I swallow. For a beat, her eyes drop to my lips as she licks hers.

"Taste me," she moans out before dropping her hand and shoving my face between her legs.

Jesus fucking Christ.

Until both of us are bone tired, I do exactly that. Taste her. Give her one orgasm after another. Torture her in the best possible ways. And when she offers to return the favor, I decline. At least for tonight.

Peyton needs to know I want more than one thing from her. That I want more than casual sex with her. That I want the whole package. Her smart mouth and brilliant mind. Her shapely body and sutured heart. All of it. The only way I know to show her this is to deprive myself of the one thing I am synonymous with—sex.

It may not be the perfect answer to show her I care. But it is the only way I know. For now.

And she doesn't seem to mind. Not one bit.

Ten

Last night feels like a dream. A really fucking good dream. One of those dreams you never want to wake from, but inevitably do. The ones you can't revisit, no matter how quickly you fall back asleep.

Being known as a town whore isn't always the best title for anyone—man or woman. But the experience Micah has gained from said relations… let's just say no one will hear me complain. Not once.

The man weaves witchcraft with his tongue. Spins gold with the tip. Just the tip. And could make my shower singing voice Grammy-worthy in just one night. That is pure talent.

My experience with men—as far as number of partners—is minuscule in comparison to Micah. The few relationships I had were long term, the shortest a year and a half. Each man had his own talents or mannerisms I loved—a specific maneuver, the way he touched my cheek, how he looked at me like no one was in the room. Each of them sweet in their own way. Each of them someone I cared for deeply at the time.

But none of them shared similarities with Micah. Which strikes me as odd. Looking back at my past relationships, all the men shared identical physical features and comparable ways of thinking. All of them were the complete opposite of Micah. Part of me wonders if it was my brain's way of sheltering me from the past. Steering me away from men like the one I crushed on, but crushed me in a different way.

Compared to the men of my past, Micah Reed is wild. Untamed. Unrestrained. With the words that leave his lips and the tricks he performs with his tongue.

But Micah has also displayed a tender side; a side he keeps hidden from those not in his inner circle. This is the side of Micah that holds my gaze as if nothing exists but me and him and the moment shared between us. This side remembers my food preferences and what shows I watch and the spot to kiss that makes me melt. The playful side that spurs me on for fun, makes me laugh and puts a smile on my face.

Micah Reed is a true anomaly. A mysterious man with countless layers to unfold. A man who puts on a decent front, but harbors much more within himself. With what happened with his ex, I get not allowing your heart to be vulnerable. But at some point, if he wants more out of life, he will need to expose himself emotionally more than ever. Especially if he wants our relationship to evolve.

"Hellcat!"

I snap my head up from the glass I cleaned for the last however many minutes. Surprised I haven't scrubbed the bar logo off in the process. Glancing down the bar, I spy Micah looking my way with a cocked brow.

Great. I will never hear the end of this.

After I set the glass down, I spin to face him. "Yes?" I draw out the one-worded question.

"Been calling you the last five minutes. Need a break?"

Five minutes? No fucking way have I been washing the same glass, spaced out, for five minutes. I narrow my eyes. He is messing with me, right?

Rather than holler down the bar, especially with every set of female eyes in the club on us, I walk the short distance and aim for a quieter conversation. Well, as quiet as a conversation can be with karaoke playing in the background.

"One," I say when I reach him. "You have *not* been calling my name that long." He opens his mouth to interrupt, but I hold up a hand. He snaps his mouth shut and flashes me a lopsided smile. "Two, what makes you think I need a break? We've only been open an hour."

The other corner of his mouth curves up and presents me with the most wicked grin to don his lips. A grin that trickles a thrill in my veins and dampens my panties. A mischievous smile that hints at secrets only we share and heats my skin from crown to root.

He shrugs, then tilts his head. "You look a little tired. Like you were up past your bedtime."

Smart-ass.

I step closer. His starry eyes playful as his tongue darts out to lick his lips. Taking another step in his direction, I inhale his cologne and refuse to exhale until necessary. The scent dances in my nasal cavities, swirls in my lungs, then takes up residence in my memory. It has me begging for more of him. Another taste of his lips, his tongue. But I won't tell him that. Not here. Not yet.

"I'm a big girl, starlight." I toss a smirk his way. "And I go to bed when I'm ready." My tongue sweeps over my lips and I bite and hold the lower for one, two, three breaths before releasing. Micah shifts his weight from right to left as I lean in, my lips less than an inch from his ear. "Maybe you should've offered me yours."

Micah sucks in a sharp breath, then releases it. Heat paints my skin as his breathing spikes. I startle when fingers tug at the hem of my shirt. Claw at my hip bone. Neither of us takes a step back. The bar may be packed with women wanting fruity cocktails and countless people hoping to make it big on stage, but they all vanish.

Right now, all I hear, all I see, all I feel is Micah.

Memories of last night play on a repetitive loop. The gentle and hungry ways his fingers caressed my skin. How he worshiped me with his lips. And how he took my body to places I never knew existed.

Yes, I have orgasmed with other partners—and myself. But what happened last night... that was not just oral and orgasms. Something else simmered beneath the surface. As if a dormant piece of me woke up and opened her eyes for the first time.

And I can't get enough.

"Best be careful what you ask for, hellcat." He kisses beneath my ear and a shiver rolls up my spine. "I make good on my promises. Do you?"

Before I open my mouth to respond, a female voice grabs both our attention. "Well, don't you two look nonproductive at work."

We simultaneously inch back, but stay within reach. A twin pair of starry eyes stare at us. When I broaden my view, six other sets of eyes leer at us. Their expressions range from *way to go* to *that's interesting*. No matter how they regard me or us, I don't want to be seen like the other women Micah has been with. Easy and replaceable.

Thankfully, none of them look at me in this manner. Perhaps because they never met any of the women Micah bedded. Works in my favor.

"What's up, Shell?"

She rolls her eyes and points to the makeshift stage as if the answer is obvious. "Karaoke, big brother. It may be out of our way, but we're here for it. Plus, we get to see you."

Although I have hung out with everyone opposite us, I remain quiet. Not that I feel uncomfortable in their presence or sparking conversation. My personal relationship with each of them is still new. With new people, I tend to be more reserved and less of an open book. Talkative, but not open.

Cora and Autumn smile, the corners of their eyes lifting with the gesture. Cora nudges Shelly. "Let's grab a table." Then Cora returns her attention to me. "You guys able to sit with us for a song or two? Or does it get super busy?"

I open my mouth to tell her we have other stuff to do, but Micah beats me to the punch.

"Sure." He glances my way. "Give us a few to wrap up paperwork in the office."

Shelly nods at her brother, but I see the *sure you have paperwork to do* glint in her eye. Because in what universe does it take two of us to plug numbers into spreadsheets for an average-sized nightclub/bar? Simple answer—it doesn't.

Do I correct him? Nope. Because after our conversation moments ago, I am dying to have his lips on mine again. Dying to taste and tangle tongues with him.

"Sure thing, big brother."

The group wanders to two vacant tall tops and scoots them closer together. Jake greets them and takes their drink order. Before Jake brings over the order, Micah starts popping off beer lids and mixing drinks. He knows his friends—family—well.

"Why don't you head back to the office," he suggests. "I'll be there in a few."

"Micah…" I start with a laugh. "Do they honestly believe we both need to do paperwork? It takes one of us a couple hours, at most, to get through it."

He stops shaking the drink, sets it down and steps into my personal space. "They have no clue what our job entails. Even if they did, I wouldn't give a fuck." Another step in my direction and we are toe to toe. Heat radiates off him and is like a match to my libido. "Go. I'll be there soon."

I drop the towel I picked up at some point and start for the office. As I pass the group, I give a courteous wave and smile. Seven return my way. When I reach the hall and step out of sight, my stride kicks into high gear. Once in the office, I shut the door but leave it unlocked.

With no idea when Micah will waltz in or what he had in mind, I plop down in the desk chair and get to work. Whether or not it is his intention for us to actually work, invoices and orders still need to get done.

Thirty minutes later, I input the third invoice and set it in the "to be filed" pile. As I pick up the next, the office door swings open and Micah strides in. He studies me behind the desk, licks his lips, and locks the door.

Dear lord, someone help me with this man.

"Almost done," I croak out as he saunters across the room.

"Good. Means we have more time."

"More—"

Before I finish the question, he spins the chair so I face him, bends down and smashes my lips with his. Stunned, it takes me two swipes of his lips over mine before I react. Then I fist his shirt and haul him closer. The chair slides back, smacks into the wall, and we laugh.

Micah loops his hands under my arms and stands me up. He brings his lips back to mine, snakes his arms around my waist, and walks us toward the couch. Carefully, he lowers himself to sit on the couch, then hauls me forward so I straddle him.

Fingers grip my hips, my ass as I rock against him. Lips and tongues and teeth assault each other, hungry. Starved. Downright famished. He breaks the kiss and licks his way down the column of my throat. A hand palms my breast, pinches my nipple between the material.

Fire and ache and titillation course through my veins, awaken every nerve ending, and scorch every square inch of my skin. If we were anywhere else, I would rip off my shirt then his. Press our bare flesh together and taste him.

But we aren't somewhere else. And I will *not* take this next level at work. At least that is what I tell myself.

"Micah." His name jagged and breathy on my tongue as I grind against his erection. "We have to…" God, this feels so fucking good. "We need to…" He nips at the skin along my collarbone and my eyes roll back. "Stop," I pant out. "We need to stop."

He licks from the thick strap of my top to the hollow of my throat. I rock against his hips and moan in his ear.

"You want this to stop, hellcat? You're gonna need to stop doing that," he mumbles into the crook of my neck.

Did I say I *wanted* this to stop? The word *want* never left my lips. No. Because I *want* this to continue. More than anything. But we *need* to stop. Not that she has in quite a while, but Ani—or Sean—could waltz into Roar at any moment. Last thing either of us needs is to have just-fucked hair and rumpled clothes.

I inch back and lock eyes with Micah. The starry gold flecks in his dark irises smolder. Burn hot and beg for more as he continues to fist my hips.

"Never said want," I say, my voice gruff and wobbly.

His brows pinch above his nose. "Huh?"

"You said if I *wanted* this to stop… I never said want. Need is what I said. That we need to stop."

He drops his forehead to my shoulder and groans. "Why do you have to be right?" And I love how his whiny and muffled words vibrate my skin, my chest. I comb my fingers through his hair, scrape his scalp with my nails. The pads of his fingers dig into my hips as a groan rumbles up his throat. "Better stop doing that or we won't stop."

Huffing out a breath, I lean away and force myself off his lap. I offer my hand once upright. "Come on, starlight. If you want to hang with your friends, we need to get some actual work done."

Micah takes my hand, rises from the couch and adjusts himself. "I'll finish with the invoices if you'll work on ordering."

"Deal," I tell him.

When we keep our hands to ourselves, work actually gets accomplished. Over the next hour, we wrap up the invoices, file them away, and input a supply order. Everything done and back in its rightful place, we head for the door.

But before I unlock it, Micah whips me around and pins me to the door. He clutches my chin between his thumb and forefinger. Eyes locked on mine. Lips a breath away.

"Kiss me. Before we leave this room and have to force ourselves to maintain a distance, kiss me."

This side of Micah is so new. His urgency to have me. To taste me. Feel me. Possess me. It calls out to my baser instincts. Wakes me up and revitalizes parts I didn't know were asleep.

As for his steady demand for me to kiss him…

With his grip still on my chin, I lean closer. But rather than give him the kiss he craves, I lick up the stubble on his chin, over his lips and stop at the top of his philtrum. He reacts with unfathomable speed.

Micah wraps his fingers around my wrists and pins them over my head. Presses his hips to mine and locks me in place—not that I planned on moving. Slides a foot between mine and kicks my feet out. Then leans in and traces the tip of his nose up the column of my throat, stopping just below my ear.

"Tsk, tsk, hellcat. Really should be mindful of your actions. You wanted me on my best behavior, but that… you just handed over your one-way ticket. There's no going back."

My chest heaves, nipples taut and chafing the material of my bra and shirt. With the taste of him on my tongue, his scent invading my nose, his body pressed to mine… fuck, I am tempted to provoke the beast. Within him and me.

"One-way ticket?" I wheeze out.

He gyrates his hips, his erection unyielding as it rubs my clit through my pants and his.

"Mmhm." A hand trails down my arm, the side of my torso and lands on my hip. His tongue darts out and licks the spot beneath my ear. And I don't fight the shiver that rolls through my body. "Best hold on, hellcat."

Before I ask what he means, he drops to his knees in front of me. Deft fingers make quick work of the button and zipper on my pants. Two breaths later, my pants are at my ankles as he traces his nose along the fabric of my panties. Inhaling deeply, his palms slide up my thighs, grasp the thin straps of my underwear and wiggle them down, down, down.

We shouldn't be doing this. Not at work.

Then his tongue drags leisurely over my lower lips and I forget everything. The office, the fact half my clothes are missing, the club and people outside this room. All of it… gone.

Micah shimmies a foot out of my clothes, spreads my legs wider, hikes one over his shoulder and devours me like his last meal. One of my hands fists his hair while the other clutches the door handle. I grind myself on his mouth, moan as he slips a finger inside me, then another, and revel in the abrasiveness of his stubble against my sensitive skin.

The back of my head smacks the door as I tug his hair. Grind harder. Faster. Unladylike moans crawl up my throat and spill from my lips. His fingers pick up speed as he sucks my clit between his lips. My legs tremble and breaths come in short bursts. I slam my eyes shut as the room spins.

Then Micah performs sorcery in a one-two combo with his tongue and fingers. Stars light the back of my lids. Shock waves surge through my body as the orgasm pulses over and over. My legs give out and he grabs my hips to keep me upright.

Again and again, he licks up my seam. Feasts on every drop of my orgasm as I quiver atop him. Slowly rises to his feet then slams his mouth down on mine.

The taste of me on his tongue does libidinous things to my body. I fist his shirt and drag our bodies flush. Suck his tongue like I plan to his dick when given the opportunity.

"You taste like fucking nirvana and sin," he groans against my lips.

"Wait until you experience it too."

"Fuck," he whisper-hisses. "How the hell can I leave the room now?"

I laugh, haul his lips back to mine, and kiss him with unrestrained aggression. As his hands glide from my hip up my abdomen, I break the kiss and shove him back a step.

"We should stop." I say the words, but they hold no umph. Because right now, all I want to do is shed his clothes and drop to my knees. Worship him in ways I never have, in ways he has never known.

Who knew Micah Reed would turn me into a craved vixen? Certainly not me. But here we are.

He palms his cock as I reach for my panties and slip them back on, followed by my pants. Zipper up and button in place, I walk over to the small mirror in the office and work to make my hair resemble what it did prior to Micah entering the office. In the end, I twist it in a topknot and say fuck it.

After I swipe a fresh coat of gloss on my lips, I spin to face Micah. "You know we can't walk out of here at the same time."

He lifts a brow as the corner of his mouth kicks up. "Why?"

"One—I look freshly fucked." This garners a bigger smile from him. "Two—it would just be odd. We're never both in here together this long in the first place. To walk out of here at the same time would definitely bring unwanted attention our way."

"Who says it's unwanted?"

"Me," I say on a sigh. "Micah, the last thing we need is the staff thinking we're acting inappropriately. And that they can do the same." I shake my head before dropping my gaze to the floor. "I've worked hard to get here. If anyone even remotely believes I slept with my boss to get promoted…"

"Hey." Micah steps up to me, pinches my chin between his thumb and forefinger, and lifts until our eyes lock. "That is not what's happening here." The edge to his words sharp enough to sever any doubt.

"You and I know that." I point toward the main part of the club. "They don't, though." My eyes glaze over. "Please, can we just go back out there? You first and I'll follow in a few."

"Under one condition." He steps closer and we stand toe to toe.

"What?"

"I don't want to hide this. Us." He trails a single fingertip from the hollow of my throat to the v of my shirt. "Working here isn't the same as a corporate job. Rules are different. More flexible. Besides, I think Ani knows about us and she doesn't seem bothered by it."

Considering Ani and I have been friends for years, she definitely knows more about Micah than he realizes. Nothing outlandish. I do keep some things private.

But I shared our history with her. And where our relationship resides now—minus the intimate details. Gossip over such personal aspects of my life will never happen. No matter how close I am with someone. In my opinion, certain things should stay between the two people involved.

"She knows."

He shifts to hold my gaze easier. "Yeah? And she's cool with us?"

My entire frame sags. "Yes," I mumble.

"What's that?"

"You're such a pain in the ass." I straighten my spine and roll my eyes. "Yes, she knows about us. Kind of. Not the nitty-gritty, but that we've been hanging out."

"And?" My brows inch up as I look away. "She's fine with it, isn't she?"

Micah Reed lives to drive me insane. I just know it. Of course, Ani is fine with Micah and me being together. As long as our relationship doesn't interfere with work or cause future problems, Ani has no issue with us being together. In any capacity.

"Mmhm." I nod.

"Then why are you so worked up?"

He doesn't get it. Either that or he doesn't comprehend how other people may perceive the situation. Anyone with eyes would have seen me and Micah close prior to the official promotion. It wouldn't matter that the job had been offered to me months back. Some people may still assume I slept my way up the ladder.

And that... is not acceptable.

"Have you ever been a woman?" I ask the question knowing I will get a smart-ass answer. But I hold up a hand before he gets a word out. "No, you haven't. So, you don't understand what it's like. To have to bust your ass ten times harder for the same opportunity. To work extra just to show you're worthy of the same pay. It isn't our fault we were born with different parts between our legs and on our chest, but our part of the world was founded by men. And most of society doesn't see men and women as equals." I close my eyes, take a deep breath, and reopen them. "So, please... do this for me. Straighten your clothes and hair, walk out of here, and pretend like we were working back here and nothing else."

Warm hands engulf mine as Micah erases any remaining space between us. He lifts my hands and deposits them on his shoulders, then snakes his around my waist.

"Sorry," he whispers, inches from my lips. "I have no intention of flaunting what you and I do behind closed doors. But Peyton?" I meet his starry night eyes. "I won't hide our relationship. Not saying I plan to walk up to everyone and tell them. But this..." He presses his lips to mine briefly. "You aren't some dirty secret or sidepiece. For you, I'll walk out of here alone. But make no mistake, if someone asks about our relationship status, I won't lie. We haven't defined us, but there is an us."

He kisses me once more, steps back and walks out the door. No tension or awkwardness lingers. Just Micah giving me the space I need while fulfilling my request. When the door shuts after him, I take a deep breath and collect myself—physically and mentally. Organize my thoughts on what happened over the last thirty minutes and stash them for later conversation, when we are alone.

I take one last glance in the mirror, brush my hands down my outfit, and head for the door. Each step away from the office weighs heavily. But the moment I hit the main club floor, spot Shelly and Cora on the karaoke stage making asses of themselves to Wreckx-N-Effect's "Rump Shaker," I breathe easier.

No eyes dart my direction. No whispers or pointed fingers. Everything is just… normal.

After checking in with the staff, I join Micah at the table with Gavin, Trevor, Erin, Jonas, and Autumn. Cora and Shelly still dominate the karaoke machine while the crowd cheers them on. For a moment, I sit beside Micah and enjoy myself. Enjoy the laughter of the people nearby. Enjoy the ease at being with this group of people and with Micah.

Cora and Shelly skip off the stage when the song ends, park on their stools, and sip their drinks. A fifty-something woman picks up the mic and preps for her song to start. When the intro of the song spills from the club speakers, everyone at the table goes wide eyed. Cora and Shelly set their drinks down and spin to face the woman on stage who breathes heavily into the mic with the intro of "My Humps" by Black Eyed Peas.

"Thought Karaoke Nights at our hangout were great, but this…" Cora points to the stage. "This is gold."

Micah leans in and kisses my temple. "You good?"

My eyes do another scan of the club, the staff, the group at the table. No one bats an eyelash my way. No one curls their lip or rolls an eye. Life continues to exist around us as if this is normal. As if *we* are normal. And I have never loved the feeling more.

"Yeah."

"Peyton!" My gaze darts to Shelly, who all but bounces on her stool. "Hang out with us on Sunday."

I scan the two tables, take in the other sets of eyes peering my way. Cora leans into Gavin as they both give me a content smile. Jonas wraps his arm around Autumn's shoulders before they both nod. Trevor and Erin smile my way before she rejoins a conversation with Cora and he looks back at his phone.

How many years did I want this form of acceptance? To have my own people. Yes, I have Reese and love everything he brings to my life. But I always felt like something was missing. I always wanted more. Like dreaming of the big family you never had but wished you did.

Is that what this is? An opportunity at my own family. Maybe.

"I'll be there."

Beneath the table, Micah rests a hand on my thigh and squeezes. Our eyes lock and something new passes between us. An unnamed emotion. A flicker. The start of something more.

The start of us.

eleven

MICAH

"That's a lot of meat."

I peer over my shoulder at Shelly and laugh. Did she really leave that comment wide open? My sweet baby sister. Naive and not in the same breath.

"That's what she said."

Shelly slaps my bicep. "Shut up, asshole. Seriously, though. Who's going to eat it all?" She points to the grill where Jonas flips burgers, brats, chicken, and ribs.

It is a lot of food, but Sunday always involves this much or close to it. Our Sunday get-togethers have slowly evolved into a massive gathering and tend to last several hours. The food gets eaten. If not, Autumn packs it up and ships it out with us as we leave. Which is a win for me since my kitchen skills still suck.

"Considering close to twenty people will be here, it won't go to waste. Why're you freaking out? You're never this antsy."

Shelly isn't the quietest person among us, but also not the most exuberant. That award goes to Penny. But I know my sister. Her fretting over the amount of food is… weird. Then again, she has her moments. I find it best not to question the change unless instinct tells me otherwise.

Her hands plop down on her hips. "I'm *not* freaking out." Then she storms into the house where Cora and Autumn work on side dishes.

"Dude, what's up with your sister?" Gavin asks as he grabs a beer from the cooler.

Sipping from my own bottle, I shrug. "Who knows. Probably something or someone irritating her and I'm her scapegoat today." If she continues with the theatrics, I will pull her aside later and ask more probing questions.

Gavin, Jonas, and I shoot the shit while the ladies are inside. Still early, only the six of us here, we catch up on monotonous stuff. Work, homelife, day to day boring stuff.

Gavin tells us about an upcoming photo shoot for sportswear. No travel is involved, which makes him and Cora both happy. Before coming back to Florida, Gavin traveled extensively for work. But once he and Cora reunited, they don't leave each other's side often. Can't say I blame them after spending so much time apart.

Jonas says his dad continues to hint at working less. His dad working less at the garage equals him slowly taking over the business. He always knew the day would come, but the fact it is happening has him slightly on edge.

I share how busy work has been since the changes made in early June. It sucks not seeing Peyton at work four nights a week, but we would never get things done if we worked every shift together. But with each passing week, we spend more and more time together outside of work. And I want more.

As if my thoughts summon her, Peyton walks out the back door and down the steps. Arm hooked with Shelly's, they laugh at something I wasn't privy to hear. No doubt, Shelly told her an embarrassing story of my younger days. I expect nothing less.

"Hey," I say as she approaches and unhooks from Shelly. "Glad you made it." I kiss her temple and wrap an arm around her waist. "Drink?"

"Please. And did you think I wouldn't show?" she asks with a chuckle.

With reluctance, I drop my hand from her waist, set my beer down, fetch one from the cooler for her, pop the top and hand it over. "I never want to assume anything when it comes to you." I guide us over to the loungers and sit. "How was Gulfside?"

Her face falls as her frame caves. "Good. I miss being there as often."

Peyton went from working two weekday shifts at the assisted living facility to one. Then, two weeks ago, she cut it back to every other Sunday. Roar doesn't interfere with her days at the facility, but the extra hours at the club and spending time with me have stretched her thin.

Wrapping an arm around her, I stroke up and down her spine. "Sure they miss you too."

Before either of us get another word out, cacophony erupts as Penny, Rex, Reznor, Tatyana, and Ashton walk outside. Clementine steals Ashton from his mom and they run into the yard with Spartan hot on their heels and laughter in the air. Greetings and hugs are exchanged before new conversations start.

Three rock ballads later, everyone has a plate in their hands and is piling it high with a little of everything. I tease Peyton at the excessive amount of food on her plate, even though I don't give a fuck. I simply love our banter. She tosses me the middle finger, then shoves a coleslaw-covered brat between her lips.

Fuck me.

I groan and bunch the cotton of my shirt near my zipper in an effort to disguise my stiffening cock. Sensing my hopefully not obvious discomfort, Peyton brings her lips to my ear. "Need help?"

Of all the things I expected her to say, that was not one of them. A tease, yes. Offering assistance with my *dilemma*, no. I choke on the heaping forkful of potato salad I shoveled in my mouth seconds ago.

Peyton sets her plate and mine on the table, lifts my hands over my head, then slaps my back. My face turns red—not only from inhaling food but also embarrassment—as tears spill down my cheeks. The cough doesn't quit and almost has me laughing.

Rising from the lounger, Peyton takes my hand and hauls me inside. "Be right back," she tells everyone as we head for the house.

Inside, she steers us into the bathroom, shuts the door and locks it.

"What are you…" My cough, lighter this time, cuts me off. Before I finish the question, Peyton reaches forward and grabs me. More specifically, my cock.

"Offering to help." She bats her lashes and strokes me through my shorts.

I grind against her and growl. "No chance in hell I'm letting you get me off in this tiny-ass bathroom."

Her grip tightens. "Why not?" she asks, breath hot on my neck.

"The first time I get off with you will be after hours of foreplay." *Holy hell.* If she doesn't stop, my shorts will flaunt evidence of our bathroom escapade in no time.

"Foreplay, huh?" she purrs in my ear and my eyes roll back.

I grip her hand and stop her teasing. "Yes." Unwillingly, my fingers peel hers away. "Lucky for you, we have hours ahead of us."

She lifts a brow. "You speak as if *tonight*, here, is foreplay."

I bring her hand to my lips and kiss each knuckle in turn. "She gets it," I whisper. "Hope you're ready, hellcat."

Dropping her hand, I adjust myself then waltz out of the bathroom with an ear-to-ear smile. Not until I reach the door do I hear Peyton rushing to follow me out.

When we return to our seats on the patio, half the group looks our way. We weren't gone long, but definitely longer than necessary. I don't give a fuck, let them think of all the possible things we didn't do that we could have.

After no one says a word for too long, I tap my throat. "Potato got stuck." I shrug, pick up my plate, and act as if nothing happened.

Peyton, on the other hand, has rosy cheeks. *Way to put our bathroom rendezvous on display.* I love it.

The next ten minutes pass uneventful. Beer, food, music and good conversation occupy the group. Peyton turns her attention to Penny and Autumn as they talk about weird tattoo placement. Penny recants the story of some guy who had the word *sweet* tattooed on his right ass cheek.

As Peyton goes to respond, I set my hand on her thigh and slowly trail it toward her midline. She sucks in a breath and doesn't say a word. Penny drones on about Mr. Sweet Cheek, not realizing I cut Peyton off.

Peyton doesn't move. Doesn't shift her attention. She keeps her eyes forward and pretends to listen, nodding at the appropriate times.

Inch by inch, my fingers dance over her skin. Slide over the exposed flesh and toy with the frayed hemline of her denim shorts. The action hidden from observation by the empty plate in her hands. The tip of my pinkie slips under the denim and she shifts her weight. The outside of her thigh presses firmly against mine as her thighs part imperceptibly to anyone looking. But I feel the change. Her breath hitches and skin pinks.

Much as I love the reaction, I remove my hand and bring my lips to her ear. "Dessert?"

She huffs out a laugh. "Yes." The huskiness in her voice pauses my rise from the lounger. I take my plate and hers, deposit them in the bin, and load up a single plate with sweets.

Most of the night at Jonas and Autumn's continues much the same. Me toying with Peyton while she tries to carry on as if I don't affect her. A brush of the arm. Graze of the thigh. Breath near her neck. Hand on her lower back. With each touch, I pick up on her twitches and startled moves. Subtle enough no one speaks up. Obvious enough, I detect every single one.

Then I switch gears. Drape an arm over her shoulders and draw circles on her skin with my fingertips. Drop my lips every few minutes to her hair, her temple, the angle of her jaw and leave chaste kisses. Toy with the ends of her hair or the hemline of her top.

Reznor announces their departure. While hugs get exchanged, I lean closer and whisper in Peyton's ear. "Want to go?" My thumb strokes her shoulder. "To my place."

Twisting enough to face me, Peyton's eyes dart between mine. Two dazzling violet irises glitter in the dim light of the tiki torches. The way she regards me, the way she searches for answers to questions left unspoken, brings doubt to the surface. With Peyton, I never want to presume. She may have forgiven me for past discretions, but that doesn't mean she has forgotten.

Her tongue darts out and licks her lips, slow and calculated. The corner of her mouth kicks up when my eyes drop and follow the action. After a beat, I bring my eyes back to hers. Study the intent behind her stare since she has yet to answer.

Reznor and Tatyana step up to the lounger, ready to bid us good night. But I want Peyton's answer before they do.

"Promise to behave," I whisper, hoping it will provoke a response.

At this, she cocks a brow. "What if I don't want you to?"

Hello, hellcat.

"Then maybe I won't." I nudge my head toward the door. "Shall we."

She tips her head left and right as if pondering the idea. As Reznor all but begs for a goodbye hug, she answers, "Yes."

One word is all it takes and my mind goes through all the steps we need to take to leave like civilized people. We rise from the lounger, say good night to Reznor and Tatyana. Then we go through the process with everyone else. I do my best to act casual. Behave as if there is no rush. When, in fact, my feet won't move fast enough and the hugs seem to never end.

Finally, we escape out the front door and I walk Peyton to her car. "See you in a few." She nods.

I hop into my truck and crank the engine. As I throw the truck in reverse, I coach myself to not speed on the way home. Traffic violations will only add misery to the evening. But damn, am I eager to have Peyton all to myself. Eager to see how this night ends. Because once she is in my bed, there is no going back.

twelve

PEYTON

A few blocks from Micah's house, I text Reese while at a stoplight.

Might not be home tonight. FYI

I expect details.

I don't respond. Last thing I need is an endless back-and-forth exchange with Reese before possibly taking my relationship with Micah next level. Reese is the brother I never had. And who talks with their brother before making out—or more —with someone. Certainly not me.

Micah parks in the driveway and I pull in behind him. Turning off the head-lights, I cut the engine, stare out the windshield, and take a deep breath.

"This is Micah," I mumble to myself as I watch him exit his truck. "The man you've been kissing for weeks. The man who's gone down on you." He steps closer to my car and I take another deep breath. "Don't go acting shy now."

One last deep inhale through my nose, then I open the door on the exhale. I lock the car before he takes my hand and guides us inside. Neither of us says a word, but the silence is pleasant. Tranquil and a little energizing.

With each button he presses to unlock the door, my pulse thumps a faster rhythm. A thin layer of moisture slicks my palms and I pray to whoever hears my call to not let Micah notice.

As we step into the house, I expect him to maul me. To slam me against the door and crush my mouth with his. Pin my hands over my head and grind his erection against the junction of my thighs. Moan my name and bite my lip.

But none of this happens.

We step inside and he guides us to the couch. Gives me a chaste kiss on the lips, lets go of my hand and goes to the fridge for water. After a sip, he offers me one. I take it in the hopes it will cool off my immeasurable fever and wake my rational side.

Does he sense my low-level anxiety over what might happen? God, how embar-rassing. I feel like a trembling virgin. Who knows why? My virginity flew out the window more than a decade ago. And I haven't exactly been celibate—although, it has been a while.

When he turns the television on and starts an episode of *Supernatural*, I start to second-guess every thought from tonight. We kick off our shoes and settle into the couch. When he tugs me closer to him, I stop thinking and sag into the warmth of his frame. After fifteen minutes, my anxiety vanishes and I curl into his side and rest my head on his shoulder.

Three-quarters through the episode, Micah kisses the top of my head. The gesture sweet as his lips linger for a beat. I tip my chin up to return the kiss. The act natural and innocent.

Until the kiss evolves. Grows from chaste pecks to the delicacy of tasting lips. Slow and gentle mixed with heat and the occasional scrape of his stubble.

A hand cups my cheek. Fingers weave through the hair at the base of my skull as he draws me closer and keeps me in place. A match strikes beneath my breast-bone when his tongue traces the seam of my lips. The chambers of my heart pound, pound, pound against my rib cage as I gasp and his tongue slips in and tangles with mine.

And then everything explodes. Detonates like a ticking time bomb.

I fist his shirt, throw a leg over his lap, and straddle him. Rock my hips and rub against the thick bulge beneath his zipper. Tangle his tongue with mine before I suck it like a popsicle.

He clamps down on my hips hard enough to bruise me for days. Adds more pressure where I stroke him through our clothes. Sits up straighter, trails a hand up my spine until he reaches the base of my skull, wraps my hair around his fist and jerks my head back.

The motion stings my scalp as I gasp for air. He sucks and bites his way down the column of my throat. Kneads my hip with his other hand. Paints his tongue along my collarbone. My hands glide up his chest, snake around his neck, take hold of his hair and yank. Hard.

His lips break from my skin in a hiss. *"Fuck."*

Before I voice a comeback, he scoops under my ass and stands. His lips back on mine as we move through the house. Greed and hunger taste so fucking sweet on his tongue.

And then I am airborne. But not long.

In the dark room, I land on a cloud. Micah crawls up the bed and reinstates our kiss. His hands at the bottom hem of my shirt inch up my body—slow, too slow— as they tug the material away. Lips and teeth and tongue imprint my skin as he unclasps my bra. The skimpy fabric gets tossed aside and replaced with his mouth.

I thread my fingers through his hair as I arch my back and press my breasts into his hungry mouth. He grips my wrists, breaks my hold on him, and pins my hands to the mattress. Clamps down on my nipple before popping it from his lips and paying equal attention to the other.

"Micah," I whisper-moan into the darkness.

He releases my nipple and hovers above me. Stars burn white hot in his dark irises as he holds my gaze. The intensity in his irises slicks my skin, and I swallow.

"Keep your hands here," he commands in a thick baritone. I nod and he shakes his head. "No, Peyton. In here, you need to use words."

"Yes," I whisper. "Won't move my hands."

"That's my hellcat."

He drops his lips back to mine, kisses me one, two, three times before sucking my lower lip between his. Then his lips leave mine and kiss a trail of fire up the line of my jaw. Nibble on my earlobe as my eyes roll back. Suck the tender skin beneath my ear as I grind my clit against his erection.

As his lips move down my neck, he releases my wrists. Skims the tips of his fingers along my forearms, my triceps as he kisses his way down. Fever flares over my body as he tattoos my skin with his tongue. Marks me as his with his teeth. Bruises my flesh with his mouth.

His hands squeeze my breasts, graze the sides of my abdomen, then land on the button of my shorts.

And then he freezes.

I lift my head and glance down my midline. I lock eyes with him as he watches me, studies me, questions me. As he silently asks for permission. As he waits for consent.

"Micah?"

"Yes, hellcat," he purrs, his breath hot on my skin.

"Take my clothes off."

He cocks a brow and tilts his head. "Anything else?"

I love and loathe how he wants me to say the words aloud. I am not a shy lover, but Micah and I haven't traveled this road yet. And I get his need to hear me verbalize what I want.

Sitting up—which causes him to do the same—I come face-to-face with him. Inches separate our lips. My bare breasts a breath from brushing his cotton shirt. I hold his gaze. Read the carnality in his eyes. It adds fuel to the roaring fire beneath my skin. Possesses me. Makes me ravenous.

Without moving my hands, I lean forward, bite his lower lip then growl as I release it. A breath between us, I whisper-hiss, "Fuck me."

Unexpectedly, his eyes widen a beat. A growl rips from his chest and spills from his lips. Then his hand wraps around my throat and constricts as he shoves me back to the mattress. My oxygen is cut off enough to make me dizzy, but not knock me out and I roll my eyes before closing them.

The button on my shorts pops open seconds before he bites the fabric and separates the zipper teeth. Cool air stings my lungs when he removes his hand from my throat. The mattress shifts before his hands scoop my ass cheeks and he shimmies my shorts and panties down my thighs.

Completely bare on his comforter, he stands at the foot of the bed, palms his cock, and licks his lower lip. My hands itch to reach down, not to cover myself, but to touch myself too. But I resist the urge and let him visually devour me.

Micah traces his fingers up my shins, then slides them back down to my ankles, takes hold and yanks my ass to the edge of the bed before dropping to his knees. He hooks my left leg over his shoulder, followed by my right. Lips press to the inside of my thigh. Teeth nip their way up, up, up my thigh, tongue tasting me along the way.

When he reaches the apex of my thighs, he licks everywhere but where I want him. Teases me with slight touches. Tortures me with occasional bites. Makes me moan as he marks my flesh on the upper part of my inner thigh.

Then he licks my lips, bottom to clit, and hums his appreciation. "Fuck, I love how sweet you taste." Before rational thought forms from his words, his mouth is on me. Lapping and sucking, tasting and devouring. He adds a finger, rubs that sweet spot inside me. Flicks his tongue over my clit again and again before inserting a second finger.

I fist the comforter as my back bows off the mattress. Thighs clamp the angle of his jaw. Ankles hook behind his head and force him into me as I rock against his mouth. Against the scrape of his stubble. Against the perfect strokes of his tongue and drive of his fingers.

Heat builds between my legs, curls up my spine, blooms across my chest, up my neck, over my cheeks. Consumes me in every possible way as Micah picks up speed. Curls his digits and pumps faster. Sucks my clit between his lips and performs voodoo on my body.

In the past, I had never been a vocal lover. Never moaned or screamed or cried out a name in pleasure. But with Micah, I whimper. Mewl for more. Beg him not to stop. Moan his name like it pains me not to.

He makes me wanton. Carnal. Hungry for only him.

And the way he looks at me now—eager to consume every part of me—sets me off. Has me fisting the comforter and cursing at the ceiling. Tremors rock me head to toe. Blind me in the darkness. Steal my breath and stall my heart.

"So fucking sweet," he says on a moan as he licks the orgasm from my skin.

As the shaking settles, I shift to my hands and knees. Crawl to where he stands at the foot of the bed, shorts tented by his erection. He grins down at me lasciviously.

"Whatcha going to do, hellcat?" He cups my cheek and tips my chin up so we are eye to eye.

I lick my lips, rock back on my haunches, and reach out to drag him closer. Still fully dressed, I slip my hands under his shirt, force it up and off him. Before the cotton hits the floor, my fingers unbutton his shorts, then slide down the zipper. A low thump sounds in the room as his shorts drop to the floor.

Eyes locked on his, I lean forward and drag my tongue from his navel to his nipple. "Taking what's mine," I state.

"Fuck," he whisper-hisses. He fists my throat, locks me in place, and crashes his lips to mine.

But it is my turn.

I slide a hand up his abdomen, over his pec, and land on his throat. When my fingers tighten, as my nails bite his skin, he releases my neck. Moans in my mouth.

I crawl backward on the mattress and he follows. He plants his knees on the mattress and I shift our positions. Drop my hand to his chest, shove him down and straddle him. Grinding myself against him and soak his boxer briefs.

His eyes roll back briefly as he grips my hips. "Confession."

I wiggle my way down his body and reach for the band of his boxer briefs. "This isn't church, Micah. But feel free to worship me."

I yank his briefs down and off, then toss them aside. I rake my gaze over him and stop when I reach his cock. *Sweet fucking Jesus.* The size makes me stutter mentally, but that isn't what has me praying for mercy. No, what makes me swallow and crawl closer are the three barbells.

When my eyes flash to his, a smirk kicks up the corner of his mouth. He tucks an arm under his head and fists his cock with the free hand. "As I started to say—"

"You're building a ladder," I interrupt and tilt my head. "Lucky for you, I'm into construction."

As he opens his mouth with what I bet is a witty comment, I bend down and lick the length of him.

"Dear god," he hisses out as he fists the comforter. A hand comes to the back of my neck and tightens as he hauls me up his body.

"Wasn't done," I mumble against his lips.

He flips me over. "Don't care." With a rock of his hips, he rubs the piercings over my clit. My eyes roll back as I dig my nails into his obliques. "Fuck." Another hiss from his lips. "I need to be inside you."

"What's taking so long then?" I lick along his jawline, then bite the angle of his jaw.

Fingers comb through my hair, fist the locks and yank to the side. He nips and peppers kisses over my cheek, my jaw, my throat until he reaches my ear.

"I need to *feel* you, Peyton." He lifts enough for our gazes to meet. "I'm clean. Got tested weeks ago. Haven't been with anyone in months."

"I'm on the pill."

Although more than a year passed since my last boyfriend, I continued birth control. The other benefits were a perk, but I also continued taking them in case someone else came along. Figured no harm, no foul.

In this instance, my indifference paid off.

"Thank fuck."

My hair still in his grip, Micah rocks his hips again and teases my lips and clit with the barbells. I carve new crescent moons into his flesh and bite down at the curve of his neck.

Holy Christ. He hasn't put it in yet and I am ready to claw my name on his back. "Micah." His name a moan on my lips.

"Patience, hellcat." He lowers his lips to mine. "I want to take my time with you. Savor you. Own you."

Dear baby Jesus. Not sure what I did to deserve this delicious torture, but thank you.

Micah continues to take his time. He worships every inch of my body. Focuses on places I never knew I wanted a lover to pay attention to. Places that spark cosmic pleasure. After my body convulses a second time, he finally shows me what sex with ladders is all about.

Needless to say, I will never look at a ladder and not blush. Micah may have slutted around town more than a year, but I reap the benefits in the end. Because no chance in hell anyone else in the future will enjoy the Micah Reed adventure. Not on my watch. Not after I felt him bare and engraved my name in his flesh with my nails.

It's quite possible I had an out-of-body experience when my third orgasm hit. Or I blacked out. To be honest, the likelihood of both happening is conceivable. I won't discount the chances.

What I do know with certainty… Micah more or less just staked his claim. Marked me as his. Not only on my flesh, but also on my soul.

Micah Reed has no idea what it means to be mine. But from this moment forward, I plan to show him.

thirteen

How long can I get away with watching her like this? With thin lines of sunlight highlighting her hair and skin. With soft blonde lashes fanned out just above her cheekbones. And champagne wavy locks spilled over my pillow.

I don't dare move or breathe too heavily. Don't reach out to brush to wayward strands out of her face and tuck them behind her ear. Don't trace my fingertips over her skin and write secret messages only I can decipher.

That would disturb this moment. And this is solely mine.

Instead, I bask in the sight of her. Her fair skin and peaceful expression as she sleeps. The soft snores from her lips as she dreams, hopefully, of me or us. Relish the memories from last night. Every line and curve of her body under my hands. How she reacted to my touch—the bow of her back, quiver of her muscles, moan of my name. How we exhausted ourselves, yet it was nowhere near enough.

In the early morning hours, we collapsed in a pile of loose limbs and sated souls.

For more than a year, I have yearned for Peyton. Watched her from the sidelines while I took my frustrations out on nameless and faceless women. Taunted her so I had her attention. Because every second she paid me attention, she gave it to no one else. Even if the attention was negative, I wanted it all to myself. Her irritation and poutiness was, is, such a turn-on. In the beginning, I craved something strictly carnal with Peyton. To blow off steam and get her out of my system. Fulfill a need clawing at my insides.

But now… my need for her is so much more. An unquenched hunger. A deep, primal demand. A vital component of my existence. She floods my veins and occupies my marrow. Spins an endless web beneath my sternum that encases my heart and refuses to relinquish its hold.

It steals my breath and awards me life simultaneously.

My fingers twitch beneath the sheet. Itch to feel the warmth of her skin again. But softer this time. Delicately trace the arch of her brow, the bridge of her nose, the swell of her lips. Twirl her soft hair around my finger and toy with the strands in the sunlight. Kiss her until her our lips or tongues tire, whichever happens first.

Her nose twitches, followed by her lips. A gentle pinch of her lashes as she slowly stirs awake. I train my eyes on every tweak her face and body make as she leaves the land of dreams.

Damn, she's gorgeous.

Lucky doesn't begin to describe how I feel as her violet eyes flutter open and lock with my blues. Countless breaths pass and neither of us says a word. She tucks a hand beneath her cheek as a soft smile brightens her face. Waking up with Peyton in my bed, her angelic features the first thing I see in the morning, is the best way to start the day.

"Morning," I whisper and reach for the fallen hairs on her cheek. Her eyes close at my touch. When they reopen, gray flecks dance against the violet backdrop and render me breathless.

"Good morning." Her voice raspy and soft and sexy as hell. Another trait to add to the long list of characteristics I like about her.

Morning breath be damned, I want to kiss her. Feel her beneath and above me in the early morning hour. Well, early for us.

I quit resisting my need for her and eliminate the space between us. Press my lips to hers, light and tender. Skim a hand down the side of her breast, her waist and stop when I reach her hip. The subdued kiss turns hungry as she throws her leg over my hip. Rocks herself against my cock as her fingers comb my hair and fists the locks.

Within seconds, she has me on my back and straddles my waist. Long champagne locks curtain us as the kiss turns ravenous and she coats my erection with her arousal. On the next circuit up, she shifts so the tip of my cock presses between her lips.

Up and down and up and down. She teases the head of my cock over and over. As I open my mouth to tell her to quit being a tease, she pushes back and fills herself to the hilt.

"Dear god, woman." I fist her hips and keep her in place. "You give religion new meaning."

She sits up, tosses the hair from her face and plants her palms on my chest. "Won't stop you from worshiping me," she says with a rock of her hips. Her hooded eyes look down and pull me into her orbit. "Welcome to heaven."

Peyton rides me like the goddess she is. Head thrown back, tits pushed out, lips parted as her whimpers mingle with the slapping of our bodies. Nails bite my skin to mark me as hers. Marks I will gladly own and flaunt whenever possible.

When her moans and whimpers escalate in pitch, I tighten a hand on her hip and wrap the other around her throat. Piston harder into her sweet, tight pussy. Groan when her walls tighten around me and her claws dig deeper. Revel in the blotchy flush that decorates her breasts, her neck, her cheeks.

And the moment she can no longer hold herself upright, I flip her on her back, hook her legs over my shoulders and drive into her. Skin slapping and grunts echo off the walls as I grip her shoulders and pound her pussy. The violet of her eyes a thin rim around her glassy dilated gaze.

A hand claws its way up my chest and wraps around my throat. Her grip slight as she tugs me down to her lips. Kisses me until her body climbs, climbs, climbs back toward that delicious peak and she gasps for breath.

My pace kicks into fifth gear as I all but slam her body into the headboard. Slide one hand from her shoulder to her throat as I beat her clit with my pelvic bone.

Slap. Slap. Slap.

Her pussy slowly tightens around my cock. Sweet, stuttered cries of pleasure spill from her lips. Nails dig so deep, I swear she pierces my flesh. And it all just adds to the intensity of the moment. Wakes the beast inside me.

Tingling manifests in my balls. Liquid fire slithers up my spine, then winds its way back down. Converges low in my abdomen. Immense pressure and the need to come makes me dizzy, breathless, a slave to the act.

But I hold off. Wait until Peyton gets there first. Wait until her body convulses and milks me.

Hand still on her throat, I lean down and lick her chin, her lips, her cheek. "Let go, hellcat."

I crush my lips to hers. Slam my hips forward and adjust my angle to hit her sweet spot better. Annihilate her clit with my pelvis. Her nails dig deeper. Our bodies slick and hot and on the brink.

Then her walls fist my cock with ferocity. A lyrical staccato of moans echoes in my ears as she trembles beneath me. My next thrust forward ends in a detonation of euphoria as my balls draw up and I release inside Peyton.

For a split second, I feel invincible. On top of the world. Atop the tallest mountain peak, howling at the moon. An incomparable high. A high that dissipates much quicker than Peyton's; her eyes rolled and back arched as her body continues to grind and writhe.

When both our bodies settle, I lower her legs and massage her hips. Then I kiss the fuck out of her. Aggressive at first, then almost submissive and more emotional. She tangles her legs with mine. Wraps me in a full-body embrace. Lightly runs her nails up my back and into my hair.

This single moment more intimate than any other. And it is in this exact moment a warmth builds beneath my sternum. Expands and contracts, conforms and comforts. Takes me prisoner and sets me free.

Much as I want to keep her in my bed all day and night, I can't. Much as I want to kiss her for hours and never release her, I can't. Although early, she needs to start her day before work. And I have to learn how to not be selfish and hoard her from the world.

"C'mon." I break the kiss, slowly sit back on my haunches and offer my hand. "Let's shower. Then I'll make you breakfast."

Peyton takes my hand, scoots off the bed, and holds on to me as her noodle legs give out on the way to the bathroom. She walks all wobbly like a newborn giraffe and I bite back laughter as I crank the shower and we step under the spray.

After soaping each other up for longer than necessary, we rinse and towel off. I hand her a pair of my sweats and a T-shirt, and don the same.

I admit I never thought a woman would look sexy in my clothes, but fuck me running because I never want to see Peyton in anything *but* my clothes. None of it snug on her frame or exposing skin other than arms and above the collar. *Just damn.*

Reaching out, I fist the shirt near her belly and tug her until our bodies are flush. Drop my lips to hers, clutch the back of her neck and kiss the hell out of her. Then cut the kiss short before I get carried away.

"Really need to leave the bedroom and feed you," I mutter, my lips still on hers.

Slender arms wrap around my waist and pin me to her. "Probably right. Although, I'd rather stay exactly where we are."

"Ugh," I huff out, grab her hand, and stumble out of the bedroom. "C'mon. Time to eat."

Peyton plops down on a stool at the breakfast bar as I get to work in the kitchen. I pull out all the ingredients for French toast, bacon, and sliced fruit. Within minutes, the scent of maple and cinnamon fill the room as I flip the bacon one last time and add the final pieces of French toast to the pan. When the last piece turns golden brown, I plate it, add fresh fruit and bacon on the side, and top the French toast with powdered sugar and whipped cream.

"A girl could get used to this," Peyton states as I set a plate in front of her and hit the brew button on the Keurig.

"Is that so?" I set down our coffees, park on the stool beside her and kiss her temple. "Good to know."

Breakfast with Peyton gives life a new definition of comfortable. With her, I am more at home than I have been in years. I don't second-guess myself or wonder what comes next. There are no absurd expectations or the need to be someone I am not.

With Peyton, I get to be myself. Not the guy who put up a front and bedded any willing woman because he felt empty and sad. I haven't been me in so long, haven't felt comfortable in my own skin with anyone else, and I love how she has guided the old me back into the light.

All too soon, our plates empty and Peyton prepares to head home before work. I don't let her change back into her clothes—the idea of her out in the world in my tee and sweats is a major turn-on.

"Talk to you later."

"Damn right you will," I say as I frame her face and kiss her one last time. "Have a good night at work, hellcat."

Peyton gets in her car, backs out, and drives off. I walk back into the house, go back to my room, and plop down on the bed. Hints of her coconut mint scent hit my nose and I close my eyes.

It may be too soon—what the hell do I know—but I more than like Peyton. But because I have been burned, I still fear the word that comes with the next level of emotion. So, I ignore the anxiety-inducing four-letter word and just think of her. The woman with golden hair and violet eyes. The woman who has bewitched me in every way possible.

∼

Poorly sang rock music pierces my eardrums in an attempt to ruin yet another classic. As great of an idea as karaoke was for Roar, I may have to suggest some songs stay off the list of options. Peyton, on the other hand, snort-laughs her ass off next to Shelly and Cora. The sound equal parts disturbing and adorable as fuck.

My hand on Peyton's thigh under the table gives a gentle squeeze. Turning to face me, her laughter pauses a beat as my favorite smile lights her face. A smile that screams happiness and affection and gratitude. This single glance spreads heat through my chest. Gives me a sense of weightlessness. Fulfills me in an unfamiliar way, but one I don't want to end.

"You seem all too happy these people are trashing classic songs," I tease.

Peyton play smacks my bicep and shakes her head. "Not happy. Plus, I can forget their rendition, if I choose to. But c'mon." She waves a hand toward the stage. "You can't tell me this isn't hilarious to watch."

I narrow my eyes at her, then shift my gaze to the makeshift karaoke stage inside Roar. Karaoke always seems to bring in the oddest mix of people. Every age group and a wide array of music. Current and classic and everything in between. The man with the mic to his lips right now, he slaughters "Ramble On" by Led Zeppelin. Every muscle inside me cringes, but I suppose it is for entertainment.

"Whatever." I shrug. "Gonna go work in the office." I lean closer, so only she hears my next statement. "Join me in a bit."

"Yes." She inches back. "I'll hang here a bit longer, do rounds then be there."

Pressing a kiss to her temple, I rise from the chair and excuse myself. "See you guys later."

I don't rush to the office. My stride is a hair slower than usual as I nod and smile to patrons on the way. I make my way inside the office, shut the door, and drop down in the chair behind the desk. Get to work and don't fret over when Peyton will join me. Although most have inferred we are a couple, we don't need people believing either of us slacks off on the job.

In the middle of ordering, the door opens and in walks Peyton. Hair half up in a messy bun with the rest trailing down her back. Black dress slacks snug on her thighs, her sculpted ass partially visible under the tail of her mint-green top. A top that allows me an occasional view of her cleavage.

"How's it coming along in here?" Peyton asks as she saunters over.

"About done." I spin the chair to face her, lean back and tilt my head as I bite my bottom lip. "Things good out there?" I avert my gaze to the door momentarily with a nod.

"Mmhm." She braces herself on the chair arms, slips a leg between mine and closes the space between us.

When our lips meet, I sit up straighter. Snake my arms around her waist. Awkwardly lower her to my lap; the two of us a fumbling mess of limbs. She shifts her leg and scoots forward as I do the same. My hands slip up the back of her shirt and press her impossibly closer.

It would be so easy to strip her bare and take her on the desk. Swipe my arm across the oak and send paperwork flying. Fling pens to the floor and bend her over. Slap her ass and take her from behind. Press her cheek to the grain and tug the loose strands of her hair as I pummel her over and over.

God, would it be easy. Which is why I won't go through with it.

Much as I would love to fuck Peyton every waking minute of the day, we need rules. Rules that include behaving—minus the occasional kiss—at work. If rules aren't set, we will spend every Wednesday and Thursday in this office doing R-rated acts. Ani may be Peyton's friend, but she would not be too pleased to pay us to make out or fuck like horny teens on the clock.

I break the kiss and lean back into the chair. "We should work." The jut of her lower lip and batting lashes is adorable as hell. And damn, it begs me to break every rule put in place. "I'd much rather kiss you all night, but—and I can't believe I'm the one saying this—we should behave."

She leans back, a smirk on her lips and a knowing look in her eyes. "Who knew?"

My brows bunch together. "What?"

"That Micah Reed would choose to be the responsible one." She rises from my lap, gives me a chaste kiss and adjusts her top as she starts for the door. Twisting the knob, she stops and looks over her shoulder. "I like it." The corners of her mouth kick up. "A lot." Then she waltzes out the door and leaves me to finish the office work. Alone.

For a solid five minutes, I stare at the door. Not in the hopes she will walk through again. The opposite, actually. Because Peyton Alexander is nothing like I expected. She is next level. A commanding force, but also a woman who will submit when asked. An exquisite creature who captivates me at every turn. She keeps me on my toes and surprises me with each step forward we take. She has me dreaming of possibilities.

Of next steps and the years to come. With her.

fourteen

Arriving at Roar early, I park beside Micah's truck with a wide-stretched smile on my face. Neither of us gets here early to do anything untoward. But the free time with no eyes on us is nice.

Before heading inside, I walk the short distance to the mailbox cluster for the plaza, unlock the club's postal box, and retrieve the mail. Thick stack of envelopes in hand, I hike my purse higher on my shoulder and enter through the employee door. Low-volume rock music plays from the speakers in the main room and floats down the hall. I drop the stack of mail and my purse on the desk and stroll out to the main area of the club.

Micah sets up the Bar Olympics, unaware of my presence. As I have on several occasions, I hang back at the edge of the hallway and watch him. Stare at his broad shoulders, thick arms, and dexterous fingers. Fingers that have clenched my throat and pinched my nipples. I swallow and drop my gaze to his trim waist and sculpted ass, snug in his slacks. An ass I have dug my nails into more than once. I lick my lips as he moves around with ease and an air of masculinity.

Oblivious to company, Micah is his true self. More laid back and effortless. Relaxed. No front or phony disposition. No flashy smiles or smart remarks. He is just… him.

And I love seeing this side of him. Love seeing him more himself. Quiet and focused and determined. It is a side not many get to see. Not even his family. I consider myself lucky I get the privilege.

"Gonna keep fawning over me?" he says, barely over the music, with his back to me.

Pushing off the wall, I walk in his direction. "What can I say? I was enjoying myself." When I reach him, he sets the red plastic cups down and grabs hold of my hip. "How long have you been here?"

I rest my forearms on his shoulders and toy with his hair. "Not long. You?"

"Maybe thirty minutes." He presses one, two, three chaste kisses to my lips.

Doing my best to behave, I don't push for more. I will save that for after hours. "Need help?"

He kisses the tip of my nose, then steps back. "Sure."

After the Olympics are set up, we both head to the office. Olympics night has become such a hit in the last few weeks, it ends up being an all-hands-on-deck-while-open event. Micah and I help out on the floor and behind the bar to keep the night flowing as smoothly as possible.

Micah shakes the mouse to wake up the computer as I start opening the mail. A few invoices and payments later, I come across an envelope addressed to Micah. There is a return address, but no company name.

"Here." I hold the envelope out in his direction. "This is addressed to you."

His forehead scrunches as his brows pull together. He takes the envelope and stares at the return address as if waiting for it to tell him the sender's name. After a moment, he flips it over and tears at the flap. Takes out a folded piece of paper and flattens it out. He scans the paper but doesn't move otherwise.

From where I stand, the words are unreadable. The typed letter appears brief with a printed logo on the top left.

Unable to bear the silence any longer, I speak up. "What is it?"

When he lifts his head and his starry eyes meet mine, I stop breathing. He looks as if he has seen a ghost. Skin gray, eyes dull, lips slightly parted. Frozen in fear.

Nausea rolls in my belly. Has me taking slow breaths and swallowing to settle the sensation. But until he answers, I know the feeling won't vanish.

"Micah?" I walk around the desk and touch his shoulder.

He holds up the letter for me to take. "It's from a clinic." I glance down at the paper. "To take a paternity test." Glassy eyes stare up at me in shock. His jaw shifts left to right, again and again. "Tomorrow."

Oh shit.

How long has it been since the woman in the red dress set foot in Roar and claimed Micah fathered the baby in her belly? More than a month. Hell, closer to two months have passed. Her silence hadn't made me forget her. But I had hoped she would take her accusation train somewhere else.

Who knows… maybe Micah was the easiest guy to pin down because she knew his workplace. Her other rendezvous may have been with random guys in clubs. And if no names were exchanged, she would have no way to find the *actual* father. Unfortunately for Micah, his job made him an easy target in this situation.

I take the paper from his hands and read it line by line.

Mr. Micah Reed:

This letter serves to notify you of a scheduled paternity test requested by Ms. Janine Vallons and her attorney, Kristin Montgomery, Esq.

The test will be performed at Life and Wellness Health Facility, Friday, August 5th at 12:00 p.m.

Please bring one form of government-issued identification and arrive at least thirty minutes prior to the appointment time listed to fill out paperwork.

Regards,
Life and Wellness Health Facility

"How the hell is it acceptable to give a person less than twenty-four hours' notice?" I bark out.

Micah keeps his eyes trained on the desk and doesn't say a word. I swipe the envelope up and look at the date stamp from the post office. Postmarked on Tuesday. Even if it arrived yesterday, the short notice is unprofessional and mind-boggling—especially by mail. I would love to give this facility a piece of my mind. But without knowing if it was them or the attorney acting through them, it would be uncouth of me to do so.

Frozen in place, Micah has yet to look up, react, or speak in regard to the situation. He needs time to process it all, but seeing him like this forms an empty pit in my stomach. But now is not the time to focus on how I feel. Now, I need to pour all my energy into Micah. Help him—us—get past this momentary road block.

Because we will get past it.

I comb my fingers through his hair—slow and gentle. Over and over, without a word spoken. Little by little, he leans into my touch. Closes his eyes, then slowly spins the chair until he faces me. Places a hand on my hip, then the other, and pulls me into him. Rests his forehead on my belly and draws in ragged breaths.

"Don't ask me how, but I *know* this baby isn't mine. But taking a test, having some lab run my DNA against an unborn baby's sample, terrifies me more than anything." His voice trembles as he hugs me closer.

Fingers still in his hair, I continue to comb through his locks and soothe him—and me—the best I can. "I believe you. This letter… anyone receiving this would be nervous as hell. But we'll get through this."

Slowly, he leans back and lifts his eyes until they hold mine prisoner. Red veins crowd the whites of his eyes. The usual sparkle in his irises is absent. "Will you go with me?" Tears well his eyes as he digs his fingers into my hips and awaits my answer.

Seems such a simple question to answer. A short word in response. Weeks ago, my first response would have probably been no. Or that I needed to think it over and get back to him. Not that there is much time, but the me from weeks ago would have made him wait. Possibly until hours before the appointment.

Now, Micah and I are different people. Apart and together. The dynamic of our relationship has changed. Leveled up. It holds power and strength and heart. Isn't solely based on attraction, but something more powerful. Hidden beneath the surface. Deeper. More profound. Something only he and I see and feel and grasp.

I frame his face with my hands. Brush my thumbs over the slight stubble on his cheeks. Hold his starry, constellation gaze. "Yes." I bend and press a kiss to his lips. "I'll go with you."

"Thank you," he whispers, then turns into my hand and kisses the center of my palm.

"Anytime." I press another kiss to his forehead. "Do you want to stay back here tonight? Or be on the floor?"

Unsure how his mood will be around others, I give Micah the option to choose. I would want the choice if our roles were reversed.

"If I stay in here, I'll drive myself mad."

"'Kay." I comb my fingers through his hair again. "Let's wrap things up in here and then we can both spend tonight on the floor. Sound good?"

"Perfect." He gives my hips one last squeeze, drops his hands and swivels back to face the desk. "And Peyton?"

"Yeah?"

"Thank you." I tilt my head at him. "For not running. For agreeing to go with me to the clinic."

I give him a small half smile. "You're welcome." I hold his eyes a beat longer. "Now, get to work, starlight."

"Yes, ma'am, hellcat."

fifteen
MICAH

Fuck.

Can't hold the goddamn pen to save my life. But I will be damned if *Janine* sees my hand—or any other part of me—shake. Hell. No.

I stare down at the stack of papers trapped under the metal prong on the clipboard and lose focus. Zone out as the reality of what is happening hits harder. Black printed letters swirl in a sea of white and yellow and green sheets of paper. The letters jumble and spell new words. Words I refuse to believe until they are proven true.

I am not the father of this child. I am not the father of this child.

In thirty minutes, I have to let some unknown doctor or nurse stick an oversized cotton swab into my mouth and swipe it over the inside of my cheek. Take a sample of my DNA, seal it in a tube, and process it in some random lab to tell me whether or not I fathered an unborn baby.

I lift a loose fist to my lips, close my eyes, take a deep, shaky breath, and fight the bile creeping up my throat.

Then, the sensation subsides. Warmth radiates in my chest and settles every anxiety-ridden thought. I open my eyes and spy Peyton's hand on my thigh. Her thumb stroking back and forth, back and forth. The small motion and weight of her hand is exactly what I need. An elixir.

She leans in, her breath hot on my ear and soothing for my soul. "Want me to fill it out?"

Peyton doesn't ask because I appear incompetent. She asks because this is one of the most stressful circumstances in my adult life. Although I try to mask my difficulties, she sees the slight tremor in my limbs. The occasional bounce in my knee. Hears the slight hiccup in my breathing. Notices the fact I haven't brought pen to paper and filled out the documents yet.

And this amazing woman—one I am damn lucky to call mine—offers to help. Offers to be my strength when I fear I cannot be.

"No, I got it." I take a slow, deep breath. "Just don't move your hand. Please."

Once I finish the paperwork, which was way more involved than the basic questions a general practitioner asks, I hand it back to the man behind the reception counter and he returns my identification. Janine has yet to make an appearance, but I assume since she set all this up, she completed paperwork ahead of time.

Somewhere nearby, a clock second hand ticks softly behind the generic doctor waiting room music. A muted television plays a home renovation show. Disinfectant mixes with artificial rose air freshener and creates an unpleasant smell. And every five seconds, the man behind reception gives me a sad half smile.

The walls inch closer and my breath comes in short bursts. My nails bite the skin at the center of my palms and form deep crescent moons. I blink a few times as the room seems to bend and flex around me. The need to vomit and pass out hit me simultaneously as I break out in a cold sweat.

Can't say I remember being claustrophobic at any point in my life, but I feel trapped inside myself. Incapable of doing anything, of speaking up, of running away. Is that what claustrophobia feels like? Being a prisoner in your own skin?

"You okay?" Peyton whisper-asks.

I subtly shake my head. "Not so much."

She studies my face a beat. "Shit. You're pale. Don't move." She bolts from the chair and steps into the bathroom off the waiting area. Before the count of ten, she sits beside me and presses a cool, damp paper towel to the back of my neck. "Deep breaths," she whispers. "Close your eyes. I'm here. I got you."

I do as she suggests and close my eyes. Focus on my breathing and her hand at the back of my neck as the other draws small, lazy circles on my thigh. And it helps. Settles my heart rate and breathing. Calms my crazed thoughts of *what if*.

And Peyton is the key. The epicenter of tranquility. If not for her, I would be passed out on the floor.

"Thank you," I say and lay a hand over hers. "Wouldn't be able to get through this without you."

She kisses my temple. "Glad you have me."

"Me too."

"Mr. Reed?" a shorter woman asks as she steps into the waiting area with a file folder clutched to her chest.

"Yes," I choke out. "That's me."

She gives a bright smile, one I am sure she reserves for clients. "If you'll come with me."

Looking at Peyton, I ask, "Can she come back too?"

"Yes." She nods to reaffirm. "She may join us."

We rise from our chairs and head for the door. Just as we reach it, the front door to the clinic office opens and in walks Janine. The first thing I notice is how *large* her belly is. Like way too big to be only roughly three months pregnant, but not quite third trimester pregnant.

But I don't have time to think on it as the woman in the white coat escorts us farther into the lab.

The first thing I notice as we walk down a corridor is how sterile this place looks and feels. Not that doctor offices don't typically appear neat and hygienic, but this place is next level. Bare white walls—no generic health posters in cheap frames or doctorate degrees. Shiny light-gray linoleum floors that reflect the fluorescent lighting and squeak if you stub your shoe sole. And the antiseptic smell... the stinging smell ten times worse back here than the waiting room.

White coat lady leads us into a small room off the hall and directs me to sit on the exam table. Peyton sits in a chair off to the side and remains quiet as the woman explains the process.

"Mr. Reed, the procedure to collect your DNA sample is simple and painless." She points to a paper-lined tray on a rolling cart where sealed tubes and packaged cotton swabs wait to be used. "This tube is labeled with a barcode matching that in our file." She opens my file, then holds up the tube and shows me the matching barcodes. "This is to protect your sample once it goes to processing. Your name will not appear on anything, which keeps the test confidential. After processing, your DNA sample is then destroyed." She sets the tube back on the tray and closes the file. Then points to the sealed cotton swab. "The sterile swab will be used to catch saliva and cells from your cheek. Then it is placed in the tube and a new seal is placed on the sample. Do you have any questions before I collect the sample?"

The test seems pretty straightforward and noninvasive. I expected needles and hair plucking and skin scraping until I searched the web last night. When I learned a ball of cotton on a long stick would be rubbed along the inside of my cheek, I questioned the testing system. Seems too easy. To swipe someone's cheek to learn their internal fingerprint.

"How long will the results take?" I ask.

This is the biggest question of all. First and foremost—gut instinct told me from the start, this baby isn't mine. Second—seeing the size of Janine's belly when she walked into the clinic, instinct went into hyperdrive. The sooner I have the results, the sooner this clinic confirms what I know deep in my soul, the sooner this whole debacle will be over.

And although I swear the outcome will swing in my favor, it doesn't stop the constant, violent buzz from the hornet's nest inside my rib cage.

"Test results typically come back in two to five days, depending on how busy the lab is. With the pregnancy at nineteen weeks, the sample from the mother is easier to attain. As soon as the results are available, we send them to the email address you listed as well as a physical copy via postal mail. Any other questions?"

I shake my head. "No, ma'am." But I do stash the pregnancy time frame away for further thought.

"Very good."

The tech or nurse or doctor—whatever she is—walks over to the small sink and sets the file on the counter before washing her hands. She resumes her position in front of me and goes through a routine she probably does dozens of times per day.

She picks up glove one and works her hand into it. Sweat pricks my forehead and temples.

Repeats the process for glove two. A drop of sweat rolls down my temple and lodges itself in the stubble I have yet to shave.

She breaks the seal on the tube and sets the stopper on the tray. I swallow in an effort to rid the lump in my throat.

Next, she peels open the cotton swab package and removes the largest Q-Tip I have ever seen. My pulse whooshes loud and fast and hard in my ears.

"Open your mouth as wide as possible, please," she instructs.

I follow her instructions and avert my gaze to the ceiling. Bad enough I have to do this, but to witness the process… no thanks. Seconds that mirror centuries pass as the cotton wad scrapes and swirls and gathers from my cheek. My fingers curl into fists as my breathing escalates. I work to focus on anything except the fibrous material collecting my cells.

"All done," the woman states. My eyes open and I watch as she places the swab in the tube, replaces the stopper, peels a red strip off a paper and seals it around the tube and stopper. "This sticker assures your sample is not contaminated before processing. If the sample gets opened, this sticker separates and lets the technician know the sample has been opened and compromised."

She peels the gloves away, tosses them in the red biohazardous waste bin and washes her hands again. She dries her hands with paper towels, tosses them in the bin, collects my patient file and sample, then guides us to the door.

"One last stop before you leave," she states. "If you'll follow me."

We continue down the corridor and stop another twenty feet down beside a smoky sliding window. She knocks on the window and a moment later, it slides open.

"Afternoon, Becca," a man says with a smile.

"Hey, Frank. Sample drop off."

My eyes remain locked on the long tube as she hands it over to the man. He takes it and tosses me a cordial smile. Before another word is spoken, the tube disappears from view and the window shuts.

"You're all set. Let me walk you out to the front." The woman steps in front and leads us to the waiting area door.

Peyton laces her fingers with mine and gives them a squeeze. I glance her way, take in her subtle smile and gentle eyes. How she studies me, reads the words I don't speak aloud. I soak up her quiet strength and tenacious affection. An affection I never expected to receive, but will cherish every day I have it.

No one occupies the waiting room when we step out. The receptionist confirms my email and mailing address and phone number one last time before we leave. He reiterates how and when I will receive the results. Then we leave.

"Hungry?" Peyton asks as she drives us out of the lot.

"Yes and no. Probably should eat."

"I'll find somewhere closer to the house."

For a beat, a small sliver of my brain focuses on how Peyton said *the* house and not *your* house. Call my thought process juvenile, I don't give a fuck, but small differences like that do crazy things to my heart.

Unfortunately, all happy thoughts leave my head as I recycle what just happened at the clinic. Hundreds of what-if questions cycle through my mind. Questions that have no resolute answer until the results hit my inbox. Of course, I can speculate where all this will lead, but without answers, it isn't worth expending the energy or torturing myself.

Then, I recall something else. *"With the pregnancy at nineteen weeks, the sample from the mother is easier to attain."* Nineteen weeks. Nineteen. Weeks. What is that in months? Just shy of five, and half the normal gestation period of human pregnancy.

Five months seems like too long.

Two months have passed since she came into Roar with her announcement. Call me crazy, or ignorant, but don't most women have some sign or symptom of pregnancy within a month or so? If she is nineteen weeks, that means she was roughly eleven weeks along when she spoke up. Which makes no sense whatsoever.

I think back to months ago. Run through the faces of women I went to bed with and when. A not-so-simple task since I slept with dozens of women in the months leading up to me and Peyton. The moment sparks flew between us, the moment I thought it possible to have more with Peyton, I refused to be with another woman.

When I finally recall Janine's face, my eyes go wide. She was literally one of the last few women I slept with before cutting myself off. At the end of April.

"This baby isn't mine," I say over the radio.

Peyton pats my thigh before leaving her hand there. "I hope that's true, but we won't know until the results are back."

I turn in the passenger seat to face her and all but slice my throat with the seat belt. After I adjust the belt, I continue my thought. My voice stronger, louder, bolder this time. "No. I mean, there is no possible way this baby is mine."

Peyton takes her eyes off the road a split second to narrow them at me. "How can you be so sure?"

I lay my hand over hers and take a cleansing breath. "The person who took my sample, she said Janine is nineteen weeks."

"Yeah, so?"

"Since the letter yesterday, I've been in my head a lot. One thing I remembered…" I pause for a beat and take a deep breath. "…is when I was with her. Yes, I have been with a lot of women, but I don't forget a face. Ever. And I've been thinking about it, really thinking about it, since that woman said nineteen weeks."

I stare out the driver's side window. Take in the Bay as the sun glistens on the water. Stare after the seagulls as they fight over scraps from an unlidded trash bin. For the first time in less than twenty-four hours, a sense of relief washes over me.

"And? Don't leave me hanging."

"I was with her near the end of April. Fourteen, maybe fifteen weeks ago. Tops. Just before I stopped hooking up."

"You mean, before there was potential for us."

"Yes." I wrap her hand with my own. "Even if the chances were slim, I didn't want to fuck up the opportunity." I lift her hand and kiss her knuckles. "So, without a doubt, I *know* this baby isn't mine."

"Why do you think she came to you then?"

I shrug. "Was probably the easiest person to find. She knew where I worked. If she hooked up with random strangers in clubs or bars, chances are she has no way to find them. Not unless they exchanged numbers or hooked up at the other person's house."

"Are you sure you're remembering the correct person at the correct time?" She peers over from the driver's seat, a smirk on her lips. "You do have a thing for blondes. No doubt they all blend together." Her tone is teasing, but I get her meaning.

With my free hand, I reach over, pinch a strand of her champagne locks between my fingers, and give a slight tug. "Blondes have more fun. I should know, I am one."

"Ha ha." She makes a silly face, but I only catch her profile.

I twirl her hair around a finger and simply watch her as she drives. Can't recall a time in my life where a woman has made me so introspective. Has made me really dig deep and see past the mundane. Has made me want more from life—not because that is what I should do, but because I want more with her.

"Or maybe I wanted one specific blonde and the others were mental distractions."

We reach a red light and she faces me. "What?" She appears genuinely confused by my admission.

"Peyton, it's no secret I pined for you from the beginning. Even the days when you verbally bit my head off, I still wanted you." Laughter vibrates my chest. "For so long, I never knew why you despised me from the get-go. At first, I thought it was your form of banter. But soon realized it wasn't. I didn't want to give up, though."

The light turns green and she faces the road again. We remain quiet the rest of the drive until Peyton parks at a delicatessen near the house. The restaurant somewhat busy considering the time of day.

Unbuckling her belt, she twists to face me fully. I mimic the action, and for a moment, we just sit and stare at each other. Her violet irises hidden behind dark lenses as she holds my gaze. With some, I would shake off their nonstop gaze. But with Peyton, I want her eyes on me as often as possible. Want the attention she gives and the radiance it generates just beneath my sternum and to the left.

"Glad you didn't," she says.

Glad I didn't what? I scrunch my brow. "What?"

"Give up. I'm glad you didn't."

For three breaths, I sit immobile. Then I lean across the console, wrap my hand around the back of her neck, pull her close, and kiss the hell out of her. We make out like teenagers in the parking lot for several minutes. I don't know who breaks the kiss, but I press my forehead to hers when it ends.

"Me too, hellcat. Me too."

sixteen

Rolling over, I curl into Micah's side. Breathe in the scent of him; a faint hint of his cologne mixed with a scent distinct to Micah. Bask in his warmth and comfort, and snuggle his frame. He curls an arm around my waist, hugs me impossibly closer, and eliminates all space between us. Then he kisses the top of my head and I sigh and kiss his shoulder.

"Morning." His raspy tone wakes up more than my mind.

Throwing a leg over his hips, I roll to straddle him and press my breasts into his chest. "Morning."

Since Sunday evening, after hanging out at Autumn and Jonas's place, I have spent every night in Micah's bed. Woken up the next morning with our limbs twisted in new pretzel shapes. Been pummeled by or ridden on his dick after we say good morning. Dug my nails into his skin and bruised it with my lips.

And each morning after we come, I want him again. In the shower. On the couch or kitchen counter or dining table. Against the glass wall facing the backyard. Out back on the veranda. Wherever I can have him. His head between my legs or me on my knees in front of him or both our mouths on each other.

Micah Reed makes me insatiable. A wanton creature. For him, and only him.

How many times per day is considered abnormal? Is too much sex unhealthy? I would think not, but I am no sex therapist. All I know is I have never felt so damn good in my life.

I bury my nails in his pecs. Mark my ownership of him next to the previous marks, now fading. Rock my hips harder as he holds on to them and jerks up into me over and over. The delicious rhythm drives me higher and higher. I tip my head back, hair tickling my tailbone as I close my eyes and gasp at the ceiling. He rams into me as I slam down on him.

Familiar, delicious heat builds low in my abdomen. Spirals up, up, up until it hits between my breasts and disperses like wildfire. Fire crawls up my chest, my neck, my face. My eyes roll back in my head. Panted high-pitch whimpers and throaty grunts ricochet off the walls. The animalistic scent of sex drifts through the air. My body starts to constrict Micah's cock. He clamps down on my nipples—hard—and tugs with a twist.

I sink my nails deeper and shatter around him. My body exhausted yet eager for more. He flips me on my back and pistons hard and fast. The headboard smacks the wall as skin slaps skin. He bruises my thighs with his fingers. Slides a hand up my abdomen, my breast and stops at my throat. His thumb, third and fourth fingers clamp down, making me dizzy and euphoric.

Slap. Slap. Slap.

Stars fill my vision, my breaths come in short bursts, and my body constricts his once more. Micah growls into my neck, crushes my pelvis with his, and releases inside me.

His arms buckle and he gives me his full weight. And I welcome it. Wrap my legs around his waist and arms around his chest. Bear-hug him to my chest and breathe in the scent of our sweat and orgasms. Trace my fingers up his spine and over his scalp.

"Never want to wake up without you," he mumbles into the crook of my neck.

I freeze at his words. Not because they frighten me or make me want to bolt. Quite the opposite, actually. A lightness I have never experienced with anyone slips into my bloodstream. Consumes me. Fashions a new energy in the chambers of my heart and pumps it through my veins. Warms me in ways I never thought possible.

My limbs relax and I comb my fingers through his hair. "Me either."

He kisses up my neck, sucks the sensitive spot beneath my ear, then kisses his way to my lips. "C'mon." He pushes up and scoots off the bed. "Let's shower, then eat." Standing at the foot of the bed, he grabs my ankles and yanks me down. Me and the bedding plummet to the floor and I erupt in a fit of laughter.

When I gain control, I sit eye level with his cock. His not-so-soft cock. I lift my gaze to his and lick my lips.

"Hellcat…" he says in warning. "Shower." I push out my lower lip and aim for my saddest puppy eyes. He growls. "Now." He offers his hand and I take it.

"Fine," I say on a huff, then stomp off to the bathroom.

Little does he know, I have tricks up my invisible sleeve.

By the time we step out of the shower, our skin is wrinkly and legs wobbly. But damn, do I feel like a queen. Micah definitely makes a great devotee and king.

We move around the kitchen like an old married couple. He whips up eggs, sausage, home fries, and toast while I cut fruit and brew coffee. His task seems more daunting, but it works for us. In no time, we plate up food and sit at the bar to eat.

We push food around our plate more than eat it. Forks scraping the ceramic, occasional chewing, and coffee slurps are the only sounds in the room. Breakfast came out perfect… we just don't have the oomph to enjoy it.

Today is day five. Five treacherous, unbearable days have passed.

And although I haven't seen him on his phone this morning, Micah has probably checked his email several times. Which means nothing has arrived yet. If it had, whatever the result, I would be the first to know—after him, of course.

We finish breakfast in amicable silence, then plop down on the couch and watch a movie until it is time to dress for work. Arms wrapped around each other, we cuddle on the couch and do our best to not pick at our nails or tap our fingers with unreleased nervous energy.

But every now and then, Micah's knee bounces or his breathing picks up. He tries to not let it show, but I notice. I just keep it to myself.

The movie ends and we amble to the bedroom to dress for work. We move slower than usual, but it isn't long before we head for the door. Since I have stayed with Micah the past few nights, we decide to take one car to work on the days we both go in. Why waste the gas?

In this very moment, driving together works out in our favor.

His phone alerts him to an incoming email as we slip into my SUV. He opens the message after buckling his belt. All I can do is stare and wait while he reads the screen.

How can five seconds feel like five years? My heart beats out of my chest as I wait for some reaction from him. The downturn of his lips. A smile worthy of conquering the world. Anything.

Finally, he breaks the silence.

"Hell yeah!" he screams in the confines of the car. "Woo!" His whole body vibrates as the biggest smile I have ever seen brightens his face.

This has to be good news for him. Please let it be good news.

"Not a match?" I ask, just to be certain.

"There is zero probability that the donor tested has any familial relationship," he reads from the email, then faces me. "Zero. Zilch. Nada. I knew it! I fucking knew it!"

Thank goodness I hadn't backed us out of the driveway yet. Micah bounces around like a kid high on too much Halloween candy. No way in hell I would be able to focus on the road with his excitement. Not to mention my own.

Relief I never knew possible hits me like a summer downpour. *Zero probability. No familial relationship.* The sudden weightlessness exhilarates and consoles me. *Jesus.* I didn't realize how badly I needed to hear those words.

Not that I wouldn't have stood by Micah's side if the opposite result was delivered. But this… happy and relaxed are a microscopic percentage of the elation I feel right now.

I unbuckle my belt, claw across the console for him, haul him to me and hug the hell out of him.

"Deep down, I knew it too. Glad the results finally came and were what we thought and hoped they would be."

Strong arms hold me close. "Just glad this is over and we can put it behind us now."

"Me too."

Micah leans back enough to look me in the eye. "We should go, but…" He waggles his brows, his radiant smile still firmly in place. "We are definitely celebrating later."

"Celebrating, huh? And what exactly did you have in mind?"

He shrugs. "Hadn't gotten that far yet. Still have plenty of time to figure that part out."

After I buckle my belt again, I back out of the driveway and head toward Tampa. Micah cranks up the music and sings obnoxiously with the songs on the radio. From the corner of my eye, I watch him every chance I get.

I love his new ease and cheery disposition. The endless smile highlighting his sharp jaw. The additional sparkle in his starry eyes. The happy-go-lucky attitude emanating from him.

I am beyond glad this whole fiasco with the red-dress woman will soon become a distant memory. One we will have no problem erasing.

Now… it is time to build new memories. Better ones to replace all the bad. And I am eager to get started.

seventeen

MICAH

All stress left my body after reading that email. An email I plan to print and stash in the miscellaneous file for years to come. Not that I think Janine will try to pull something in the future. More as a reminder of my idiotic past choices and how they could have ruined what continues to bloom between me and Peyton.

Nothing will ruin what I have with Peyton.

My face hurts from the smile that won't fade. But I will take the pain and smile twice as hard. Brighten the world with my pearly teeth and endless exuberance. This pain is the best pain. And later tonight, I don't care what we do, but we sure as fuck will celebrate.

Peyton pulls into a space behind Roar. Soon as she throws the car in park, I whip off my belt, frame her face with my hands, and kiss the hell out of her. Kiss her until we both gasp for breath. She whimpers as the kiss breaks and it only makes my smile stretch wider.

I love how I leave her wanting more. Love how difficult it will be to resist temptation all night. Most of all, I love how it leads into the best seven-plus hours of foreplay. By the time we get home, her need for me will be ravenous. Even then, I may drag it out a bit longer.

"You head in. I'll get the mail," I say, then smack her ass.

"Best watch yourself, Reed." The way my last name rolls off my tongue does crazy things to my body.

"Yeah? Why's that, hellcat?"

"You're not the only one who likes to play games." Her lips kick up in a devious half smile, and then she winks. "See you inside." She disappears inside Roar and leaves me standing in the lot, bedazzled and horny.

After fetching the mail, I head inside. Peyton has parked herself behind the desk and works on all the monotonous tasks. So, I head out to the main part of the club and prep for Karaoke Night.

Time flies faster than usual and soon the rest of the staff arrives, does their prep work, and we unlock the doors for the evening. Drinks get mixed and poured. Horrible renditions of songs I love get belted out. And my favorite group of people walks through the front door.

Although karaoke had never been a favorite pastime, I love that I see Shelly and my friends more than once a week now. Love that I have a chance to sit with them and catch up more often. With my odd work hours, it hasn't always been easy to hang out.

Before long, Shelly and Cora skip off the stage after their third song. Everyone finishes their drinks, exchanges hugs, and says they will see us Sunday.

Last call is announced and the Wednesday crowd starts to thin. A few patrons linger to slam one more glass before calling it a night. The staff shuffles around the club and rushes to complete their end-of-night duties. Minutes later, the front doors lock and we clean up faster than any previous night. One by one, the staff clocks out and heads home. In less than thirty minutes, Peyton and I do the same.

"Food from the diner near the house?" I toss out.

"Sounds good. Maybe we can grab dessert too."

It is on the tip of my tongue to tell her *she* is the only dessert I want. But I resist the urge and think of what I may do with said dessert. "Yeah, sure."

I place an order online for burgers, fries, milkshakes, and half a peanut butter pie from the diner near the house. We drive across the Bay with the windows down and the music loud. Salty air licks our skin and whips our hair. Our fingers laced over the center console and thumbs brushing the other's hand.

This right here… this is perfect.

Some of the simplest things in life are the most notable. Like a lover's hand in your own. Listening to them sing with the radio as you drive down the highway. The glimmer in their eye when they give you a side-glance and smile. Those small details are ones I deem most precious. I hug them close to my heart and don't take them for granted.

Lost in thoughts of us, I miss the moment Peyton pulls into the diner parking lot. Miss her pull into a space and put the car in park. But I don't miss her laugh when she looks over at me with raised brows and wide eyes.

"You want me to get the food?"

I break contact with her and stare out the windshield. Bright neon lights spell out *open* in red as the smell of fryer grease hits my nose.

"Oh. No, I got it," I fumble over my words as I unbuckle and exit the car.

In and out of the diner in less than a minute, we head back to the house with growling stomachs. Peyton parks behind my truck and I scoop up the bags. We amble to the front door, hand in hand, without a worry in the world.

We drop down on the couch and I take the food out of the bag, depositing take-out boxes on the table. She moves beside me as she has every night for weeks. And then it hits me. A new version of contentment. The ease at which Peyton and I have fallen into this new routine. Eating dinner on the couch with our legs crossed and knees bumping. Watching movies and television shows together as she curls into my side. Kissing and groping until we land in the sheets and sweat and moan our way toward ecstasy.

And I hope to do this every night and day with her in the future. Enjoy the simple moments. Like a shared meal or making breakfast together. Merge our lives. Become something bigger than who we are individually. Discover a new way to exist together. Find a happiness no one can dull. A happiness brighter than any star in the galaxy.

I finish my burger, set my empty take-out box on the table beside hers, hit pause on the show, then pull her onto my lap and hug her close. Peyton combs her fingers through my hair as I tip my head back and close my eyes. Being like this with her—vulnerable and more myself than ever—is the most freeing moment in my life.

Yes, I want to tear her clothes off and taste every inch of her right now. But the intimacy in this moment—her fingers lazy in my hair, eyes heating my skin, her coconut mint scent in the air, breath inches from my lips—I want it just as bad.

Intimacy without sex is somewhat new in my life. And I never knew how amazing it could be.

Her weight shifts and the heat of her breath hits my lips a beat before our lips connect. The kiss light at first. A tender graze of soft warmth. Her fingers stop in my hair and lightly tug on the strands as the kiss takes a gradual turn. From sweet and subtle to exploratory and eager to desperate and ravenous.

My hands at her knees inch up her thighs without hurry. The inclination to map her body, memorize every peak and path and adventure it takes me on, overwhelms me. To learn every perfection and imperfection and love them equally. To chart her freckles and name them like constellations. Discover each scar and kiss away any pain they cause.

Sex with Peyton is indescribable. Unlike any experience I had with another person. It isn't just the physicality. Being with Peyton... yes, what we share is raw and primal, deep and carnal. But it is also impeccable and disorienting, covetous and euphoric. Our bond makes me weak in the knees. Light-headed and unsteady.

With Peyton, I don't just picture the physical endgame when we have sex. I envision where it will lead us years from now. Sharing the same bed, day in and out. Not just for sex. I picture her limbs tangled with mine. Breath steady on my chest and palm over my heart. Hair splayed on my shoulder and the pillow. Breasts and hips snug to my side.

"Take me to bed," she whispers against my lips, then kisses me softly.

I snake my arms around her waist. "Hold on tight."

Peyton laces her fingers behind my neck. Scooting to the couch edge, I rise and walk us to the bedroom, her ankles locked at my lower back. Every step forward, she kisses my lips, my chin, the line of my jaw. Nips the lobe of my ear. Sucks the spot just above the pulse in my neck.

Every step forward is a match to the fuse only Peyton lights. One she sparks with her heady touch and reverent kisses. Fire and vibrancy and undiluted need spills from my veins. Every nerve ending wakes and begs for more. And deep in my marrow, my soul connects with hers.

The sensation engulfs me. Swallows me whole with no promise to let go.

And I never want it to let go.

I lay her on the bed. Kiss her as if she may crumble at my touch. Unhook her feet and peel away her clothes. Then my own.

Skin to skin, the world around us disappears. For the next several hours, we connect like never before. Slow and sentimental, as if we have been lovers for a lifetime and not weeks. Every touch is special and new and incomparable to any previous connection we shared.

And when we curl into each other, breathless and sweaty and sated, an imaginary bulb lights in my head.

For the first time, I made love to a woman. Linked myself to her. Connected with her on the most intimate level. Bonded beyond the physical. Something I have never done. At this realization, a sense of wholeness engulfs me. Aligns all the little pieces that never fit right with anyone else.

Peyton does this. Straightens all the jagged edges and fixes all the broken parts. Without effort, Peyton makes me whole. Better. A man.

I squeeze her closer to my side, kiss the crown of her head and resist saying the three small words on the tip of my tongue. Words I have never said to any woman. Words I won't be able to resist saying much longer.

Question is... will Peyton reciprocate? Or has my love for her blinded me?

Hoots and hollers mingle with the cacophony of hundreds having conversations. Ping-Pong balls and red plastic cups slap tables. Quarters bounce to the floor. Stacked, precut two-by-fours, grow taller with each move and threaten to teeter.

Bar Olympics night is in full swing. Body odor and upbeat music fill the air. People stand on the sidelines and cheer on the players.

Smaller tables host card games or tic-tac-toe with shots. Bowls of peanuts and pretzels on every other table. While most people here play, several just drink and enjoy watching the festivities. Games aren't tracked via Roar, but most of the regulars make note of who leads who in the different games.

In the last two weeks, Ani and Sean hired more staff for Thursday, Friday, and Saturday. Roar has definitely had an uptick in patronage and sales since the changes took place. At first, the newer crowd was easily handled with the current crew. But not long after, it stressed out the former staff. Now, everyone smiles and goes about business as Ani and Sean envisioned—giving time to the customers and engaging with them so they will return. A win-win.

"One more hour," Micah says as he presses flush to my back, squeezes my hips, and kisses the spot beneath my ear.

"Mmm. Did you have something in mind for when said hour ends? Cause we still have to clean up."

His chest vibrates as a groan spills from his lips. "Several things we shouldn't do here." He kisses my neck and steps back as I spin to face him. "Let's get an early jump on cleaning, so we aren't stuck here all night. Then…" He pauses and stares as if he has something to say but isn't sure. "Maybe we can stay at your place tonight."

Stay at my place? Micah has a quiet, cozy house with no roommate. Why on earth would he want to stay in my tiny two-bedroom apartment with my best friend slash roommate? Not sure why, but it strikes me as odd.

"Something wrong at your house?"

He shakes his head. "No. Thought it'd be nice to experience your bed for once."

He wants to *experience* my bed? What does that mean? My imagination wanders in a blink and I picture Micah jumping on my bed like a child. Compared to his king-size bed, my full will be quite the *experience*. As in, snug and sweltering and a fight for covers.

But, whatever. If Micah wants to *experience* my bed, then that is what we will do.

"Sure thing. We'll pick up food on the way. Haven't grocery shopped since I've been staying at your place."

His lips press to my forehead a second before he smacks my ass. "Now, get to work, hellcat. Don't want to be here all night."

Micah saunters off as Kaylynn approaches with a blinding smile. An all-too-eager smile with dozens of questions. Questions I will *not* answer at work.

Kaylynn and I have been acquaintances from day one. But that is it. We never did anything outside these walls. Not because neither of us wanted to; it never came up. And now, I am her boss. Although we still behave somewhat the same around each other, there are boundaries we shouldn't cross. Boundaries *I* crossed before my promotion. But Ani was aware the entire time.

"Hey, girl," Kaylynn says as she sidles up beside me. "So, you and Micah, huh?"

"Mmhm," I mumble, loud enough for her to hear. Grabbing the clipboard beneath the bar top, I inventory what bottles and beers need to be brought from the storage room.

Less than a foot away, Kaylynn vibrates with curiosity. She has never been one to gossip, but I have never been one to spill my private life to people I don't know well. Yes, we have worked together for more than a year. But... I don't really *know* Kaylynn.

Is she single? Married? Divorced? Straight or bi or lesbian? Does she have children or pets? They are all basic questions, but I don't know the answer to any of them. To be honest, I have no intention of asking either. Unless it is generic conversation and not one where we take mental notes of what shampoo we use and what happens behind closed doors.

Because that is where the conversation seems to be headed.

"How long? And how... is it?"

Micah and I have been hanging out for weeks. Hell, two months plus have passed since the first night I went to his house. But it wasn't until this past weekend, a few days after he made love to me for the first time, that we slapped a title on our relationship. That we dubbed each other boyfriend and girlfriend. Granted, we had been in the role already, we just hadn't given it a name.

But with the direction of our relationship, we figured, why not? In all ways, we fulfilled the role. Why not give the title to everyone who asked?

"For a while. Things are great."

The second half of my response left intentionally vague. She didn't outright ask anything specific. All aspects of our relationship are great, so the answer isn't false.

As she opens her mouth to ask another question, a customer steps up to the bar and distracts her. I take the opportunity to walk off under the guise of restocking the bar.

Down the hall, I unlock and enter the storage room across from the office. On the opposite side of the hall, the office and employee lounge divide the space. The storage room, though, takes up the whole length and is roughly twice as deep.

Everything is organized by type, brand, and what sells faster. Beer fills more than half the space with kegs and cased bottles stacked high. Liquor sits on industrial shelves in rows. Paper goods, glassware and miscellaneous shelf-stable goods fill the remainder of the room.

I grab the items jotted down and set them on a rolling cart we keep for larger restocks. Exiting storage, I lock up and push the cart slower than necessary. Not because it has an overabundance of glass or weighs a lot. More because I want to creep out and locate Kaylynn before she does me.

Peering around the corner, I spot her wiping down the bar. With her back to me. As I round the corner, cart in tow, she reaches for the broom and gets to work on the floors.

Thank god.

Kaylynn is nice. Probably had no ill-meaning behind her inquisition. But I hate being in the position to say *no, I don't want to share my life with you.* Especially with someone who I have somewhat known a little more than a year.

Micah locks the door after the last person leaves. One pro Monday through Thursday… we close early. Much as I love the energy in those late-night hours on Friday and Saturday, I don't miss the exhaustion it brings. Yes, I miss the upbeat tempo and bass vibrating my bones. But not much else. If Micah and I still worked Friday and Saturday together, it wouldn't be like the other days. We would both be too busy to stop and say hello, much less wave across the packed club.

Kaylynn finishes the last of her cleanup as Micah and I stash the Bar Olympics tables in the storage room. We wave her off and do one last sweep of the bar and club before leaving.

I shoulder my purse while Micah shuts off the lights. We walk out, hop in my car and drive toward home.

"Stop by the house so I can grab some clothes."

"Sure. What sounds good to eat?"

At the mention of food, Micah quiets for a moment. His focus out the passenger window with his chin resting on a loose fist. From my vantage point, he appears too serious to be weighing food options.

On our side of the Bay, less than a mile from the house, he speaks up. His voice more reserved than usual.

"Sorry. Was just thinking."

"About?"

"This Sunday is family dinner night."

"Okay." I drag out the second syllable.

"And…" He tucks his lips between his teeth, swallows, then meets my gaze. "Mom wants me to bring you." My eyes widen briefly. "But please don't feel pressured to come if you don't want to," he adds quickly.

Have we reached this point in our relationship? Hell, less than a week has passed since we officially declared ourselves a couple. Does official status equal meeting the parents?

A thin layer of sweat blankets me and makes my clothes cling to my skin. White noise blocks my hearing as my heart pounds harder with each beat. My knuckles whiten as I fist the steering wheel.

Thank god we reach his house without me running a light or rear-ending someone.

I don't *think* it is his parents that have my nerves bouncing like live wires. But the step of meeting family is *huge*. It screams the legitimacy of our relationship. That I am no fluke. That Micah plans to have me around for weeks and months, and possibly years, to come.

Don't get me wrong, I love that he feels this way toward me. That I am not a random woman in his bed. He pictures more for us in the future. He *wants* there to be a future.

Me from a year ago—hell, four months ago—would laugh at the idea of a steady, solid relationship with Micah Reed.

Me today… she smiles painfully big.

Meeting the parents is a big deal, but we have overcome so much in the last three months. If I found a way to forgive Micah for his past discretions, I can swallow my nerves and join his family for dinner.

I pull into his driveway, throw the car in park, and shut off the engine. Since he said his parents wanted me to join family dinner, Micah has sat deathly quiet with his eyes on my profile. And I am grateful he allowed me a moment to digest the request without interruption.

"Dinner on Sunday would be nice," I say as I twist to face him.

His bright smile I love makes an appearance as he leans forward and kisses me. "Are you sure?" I nod. "Okay. We'll talk more about it later. For now, I want to grab clothes, my toothbrush, then some food." He plants a chaste kiss on my lips, then exits the car.

Once he has everything, we drive off and stop at the Chinese restaurant near my place. It is one of the few places that has late hours. One massive bag of noodles, rice, veggies, and meat later, I drive to my apartment.

As I park in front of the building, it dawns on me I didn't warn Reese. Not that an actual warning is necessary. More like I don't want us walking in the door and interrupting anything. Seeing as I haven't been at the apartment much in the last week or two, Reese has probably had his boyfriend over more. And neither of them understands quiet, if you catch my drift.

Like someone on the prowl, I creep up to the door, slowly insert my key and twist even slower. Micah looks at me as if I have lost my mind. I don't care, though. Twisting the knob, I tiptoe inside and listen for any sounds of fornication.

Micah chuckles behind me. "Will you just go." He taps my ass. "No one will jump out and grab us."

I slap the air behind me, straighten my spine, and step out of the way for Micah to enter. "Sorry. Just wanted to make sure the couch wasn't occupied."

Leading Micah to the kitchen, he sets down the food and his overnight bag. His brows pinch together at the same time his lips pucker. "Does that usually happen? Your roommate having sex on the couch."

His ears must have been ringing because, as Micah finishes speaking, Reese strolls into the kitchen. With no shirt on. And sweat dripping down his abdomen.

"Who's having sex on the couch?" he asks and my cheeks heat.

"No one. Working out?" I ask and pray that was what he was doing.

"Sure." He smiles, then chuckles. "All done now, though." His eyes land on the bag of food. "Did you happen to get *me* dinner? I did just burn a shit ton of calories."

I slap his bicep. "Ew! Shut up. And yes, I got you orange chicken."

Reese hugs me against his sweaty chest. "You're the best." I shove him off with a laugh and he steps toward Micah with his hand extended. "We haven't been formally introduced. Reese."

Micah takes his hand and they shake. "Micah, but I'm sure you already know all about me." This time, they both laugh.

"Wouldn't say I know *all*, but quite a bit."

A moment of awkward silence passes and I beg for someone, anyone, to swoop in and make it end. Thankfully, Reese says he needs to wash up. He also asks if I mind his guest joining us. Of course, I agree and tease him about working out again.

We plate up food and get comfortable on the couch. After we select the next episode of *Peaky Blinders*, Reese and his new beau, Trent, join us.

The next hour is more normal than I imagined it would be. We all laugh and gasp at the same parts as we eat dinner. When the episode ends, we clean up, say our good nights and go to our rooms.

It isn't until we step foot in my room and I watch Micah's expression morph that I laugh. My room isn't girly or dirty or cluttered. But the bed is small. Way smaller than his. Literally half the size. In his defense, I didn't really warn him because I thought it would be fun.

"Great for cuddling," I say, his eyes still zoned in on the bed. "Best way to get closer. Don't you think?"

He laughs with a shake of his head. "I can think of other ways to get closer."

"Oh, really?"

"Mmhm. Come here." He curls his finger in a come-hither motion. "Let's see exactly how close we can get."

For the first time in however many years, I love how small this bed is. And I love how Micah knows the ways to use it to his advantage. Every night and day with him is brighter than the previous. Every one a new experience.

And I never want them to end.

nineteen

MICAH

Weekends at Roar don't hold the same level of energy and exhilaration since Peyton switched days.

Yes, the club is packed with bustling bodies. Loud music spills from the speakers and the air reeks of sweat and hops. Flashes of blue and yellow and red lights hit gyrating bodies and casual bystanders. Everything *looks* the same as it always has.

The missing factor, though, is Peyton. Her heart-stopping smile and infectious laughter. How people hung out at the bar more often because she chatted with them. Funny to say, but I also miss watching her flirt with customers.

Yeah, I have that level of confidence in Peyton and our relationship. Her flirtatious nature exists only between us and with the customers inside these walls. With the customers, it is more about retention and tips. She may not collect tips anymore, but she wants the other staff members to get paid well too.

I finish pouring a round of beers, then tell Caleb I will be back after rounds. He, Adam, and Kaylynn handle the bar while Charity and Jake bus and serve tables. I check in with both of them first. Ask if either need help or if they've had any customer issues.

Then I weave my way toward the front to check in with Ted and Julio. Ask about current occupancy and if there is anything I need to know about. Thankfully, we don't get too many people who cause a ruckus. The occasional belligerent person goes berserk and tries to cause problems. But our team is a solid unit and we don't put up with shit.

"Let me know if anything comes up," I tell them and wander the club's perimeter.

A few weeks back, Sean and Ani invested in wireless communication for the busier nights. Walkies with wired earpieces. Makes me feel like a sleuth or retail security guard. On countless occasions, I respond with "over and out" or "roger that." At this point, it is a running joke to see how goofy we all act over the walkies.

I spend the next ten minutes against the wall opposite the bar. Mindlessly scrolling through social media, I look up every now and then to check the crowd. Bored with my phone, I pocket it and wind my way toward the office. Saturday is one of two days Roar only has one manager on staff. The other night being Monday, when Peyton manages Charity Bingo night solo.

Feet from the office door, I jolt as my walkie crackles in my ear. "Hey, Micah?" Caleb speaks a little too loudly into the mic. Probably to be heard over the music.

I press the button on the corded earpiece. "What's up, Caleb?"

"There's a woman at the bar asking for you."

The first person I picture is Peyton, but I dismiss the idea as quick as it appears. One, she wouldn't come here on her night off unless something was going on. Not only that, but Caleb would refer to Peyton by name. And why would she come to the bar for me. Simple; she wouldn't. Peyton would have texted or come in through the back. She has the means to find me without asking Caleb.

The next person that comes to mind is Janine. Which freaks me the fuck out. There would be no reason for Janine to come into Roar, much less ask for me. Everything with her and the whole pregnancy situation got resolved a week and a half ago. No valid reason would bring Janine here. I expect to never see or hear from her again.

So, who the hell is here? What woman would come here asking for me?

A shiver rolls up my spine at the idea of some other woman claiming some other bullshit.

Nope. Not happening, universe. No more bullshit. You hear me?

"Did she give her name?" I ask, undecided if I want to peer around the end of the hall and look.

"No. When I offered to get you, she paled."

How fucking weird. A woman comes to the bar and specifically asks for me. But when Caleb says he will get me, she freaks. Why? What purpose does that serve?

"Is she still at the bar?" I walk closer to the open end of the hall and stop a foot short.

"No." He pauses, but still has the button pressed. "She's walking toward the door. White dress, brown hair."

From the end of the hall, I scan the crowd between the bar and door, looking for said woman. When I spy the head of brown hair and white dress, my blood turns to lava.

"What the fuck?" I whisper-growl to myself.

Weaving through the crowd is a brunette with a frame I will never forget. Not because she is drop-dead gorgeous. But because the last time I saw her, she was stark naked, riding another man's cock. One never forgets a moment like that.

Rochelle fucking Cook.

The simple fact she stepped foot in Roar has me nauseous. More than a year has passed since I caught her cheating—moaning another man's name in my bed without care—and ended our relationship. Needless to say, I replaced the bed the next day. No way in hell was I touching or sleeping in a bed someone else fucked my supposed girlfriend in.

My entire relationship with Rochelle wasn't bad. The beginning was absolute fire. We laughed and enjoyed each other's company. Went places and had fun together. But… each month of the twelve we were together became less fire and more monotonous. I didn't see it at first; blinded by infatuation and what I thought was love. Once the relationship ended, I saw everything with new perspective.

And through the grapevine, I learned Rochelle had been unfaithful more than once. Each occurrence was a knife to the chest. Hence, my unwillingness to invest myself with anyone else.

Until Peyton.

Peyton is the light I need in life. Sunshine on the darkest, shittiest day. She gives me hope and promise for the life I never knew I wanted until her. Not necessarily picket fences and immaculate gardens and two-point-five kids. But a life filled with laughter and joy, wonder and intimacy. A life of adventure and challenge and thousands of memories.

"Thanks, Caleb. If you need anything else, I'll be in the office."

"Everything alright?"

I turn on my heel and stroll down the hall and into the office. Closing the door, I flip the lock into place. "Yep. All good." Peachy fucking keen.

~

Be there in ten.

PEYTON

Perfect timing. Pizza just arrived.

On more than one occasion, the word *love* has come to mind when talking with or thinking of Peyton. Oddly enough, it doesn't freak me out. Not like it did past me and guys in my inner circle.

Love is an anomaly. Every life form on the planet experiences love in some capacity. For a parent, friend, family member, or partner. Each type different from the previous. But one difference happens among humans versus all others.

Humans often resist what they feel. Especially when it comes to love. Time and again, they fear voicing emotion for someone. Fear the outcome it may bring. The possibility of rejection weighs heavier than acceptance.

Why?

When did humans start to fear the key to our existence? When did loving someone become something to dread? Wish I had the answers. Right now—as my heart pounds a vicious rhythm and dizziness whirls beneath my diaphragm—answers would be handy.

I park my truck across and a few spaces over from Peyton. Cutting the engine, I stare a moment at her bedroom window. Watch her silhouette haloed by the soft lamplight in her room. Her form, her profile, soft and angelic. Watch as she combs her fingers through her hair and secures it with a hair tie. The move makes me want to run my fingers through her silky, wavy locks.

The times I have been on the cusp of dropping the infamous *L* word, I force myself to resist.

I resist because I don't know if Peyton is ready to hear the word. I resist because I don't want to ruin what we have if my emotional decree isn't reciprocated. Granted, my worries may be all for nothing. But no use in voicing how I feel until the time is right.

And the time hasn't arrived. Not yet.

Exiting the truck, I grab my overnight bag and stroll across the lot to her door. Seconds after I knock, the door swings open and her bright smile greets me. Renders me speechless, breathless. Has me swallowing past the knot in my throat as my heart rattles in my rib cage.

And just like that, all coherent thought goes out the window. That four-letter word scoots a little closer to the tip of my tongue.

"Hey," I croak out, then swallow. Stepping into her, I tug at the hem of her shirt, bring her closer and press my lips to hers. "You look cute." I skim the side of her nose with the tip of mine.

"Cute, huh?" Peyton glances down at the oversized band tee and baggy sweats. *My band tee and sweats.* Fuck, I love her in my clothes. "Do I get to say you look cute when you wear them?"

I tip my head back and laugh. "Sure. If it makes you happy, I don't give a fuck." Then I pull her in, kiss her harder, and close the door behind me.

The night goes much the same as normal. We eat dinner, snuggle on the couch watching an episode of her show choice or mine, then we fall into bed but don't sleep for hours. Everything else in the world slips away.

And that four-letter word begs to be spoken as she wraps her limbs around me and falls into a deep sleep. This right here... life couldn't be more perfect.

Rolling over, cool sheets greet me along with the morning sun brightening my lids. With a groan, I pat the bed in search of Micah's warm body and come up empty. Slowly peeling my eyes open, the room comes into focus.

Why are the blinds not shut all the way? I never forget to crank them closed before bed. But I answer my own question as flashes of Micah's lips and hands and weight on me replay in my memory. His body hovering as he slowly moved in and out of me, eyes always connected.

As of recent, sex with Micah has been different. Better. More… just more.

Some nights feel like a fight to the death. Me ripping off his clothes, or vice versa. Lips smashed together and tongues at war as we try to fulfill our hunger, our insatiable *need* for one another. Growls and screams of pain and pleasure and everything in between.

But… there are also nights filled with tenderness.

A subtle touch of fingertips. Kisses so soft, I question whether his lips met my lips or skin at all. I know they did, though. The prickling tingle they leave in their wake grows, grows, grows until heat licks my skin from the inside out. Spreads slow and steady until it consumes every inch and I combust internally. Our bodies rock and glide in sync without hurry. Unearth a bond, a force we never knew existed but can't live without.

Now that I have Micah in my life, I don't picture a day without him. Nor do I plan to.

Laughter echoes down the hall and through my door. Laughter from the man missing from my bed. And laughter from the man who sleeps across the hall.

I toss the covers aside and slip on the sweats and shirt I wore last night. Combing fingers through my tangled hair, I pull it back, twist and secure it with a hair tie. After a quick trip to the bathroom to freshen up, I wander down the hall as quietly as possible. Tiptoe to the edge and hope neither of them spot me right away.

Peering around the corner, I catch sight of Micah and Reese. Both in the kitchen, backs to me, and cooking. Not sure who cooks what, but the scent of biscuits, peppers and onions, bacon, and eggs hits me with the first full breath I take.

My stomach rumbles so loud, I am surprised neither of them hear. I press the heel of my hand to my stomach. *Just another minute.*

Micah and Reese carry on a conversation as they cook breakfast. They speak loud enough for me to hear their voices, but soft enough the words are gibberish. No doubt, I have been the subject of their conversation at some point, if not now. And that is okay.

Seeing them like this—talking like old friends, sharing a laugh, existing in the same space—creates this ever-expanding warmth beneath my breastbone. A merriment of my past and future—not that I am getting ahead of myself. I do see Micah in my future for years to come, though.

Unable to deal with my stomach trying to eat itself any longer, I step into the open living space that connects with the dining area and kitchen. Neither Micah nor Reese hear me, so I sit at the breakfast bar until one does.

"You seriously can't cook anything other than breakfast?" Reese asks Micah.

"Don't judge me," Micah retorts on a laugh. "Mom tried. Just didn't stick."

"Trust me, you want to learn." As the words roll off his tongue, Reese reaches for his coffee and spots me. "Morning, sunshine. How long you been eavesdropping?"

Micah peeks over his shoulder and gifts me with my favorite smile of his. He doesn't care if I heard every word.

I stick my tongue out at Reese. "Only long enough for you to learn Micah can't cook. He does make kick-ass breakfasts, though."

"Thanks, hellcat." He winks.

Jutting my chin toward the stove. "Speaking of breakfast. What're we having?"

"Southwest omelets, bacon, and biscuits," Micah answers.

Before I voice my opinion, my stomach groans and responds loud enough both guys laugh. "Shut up." I flip them both the middle finger. "Is it almost ready? I need to get dressed soon."

As if they have worked in kitchens together their entire life, they plate up my food. Micah places the omelet on the plate, then Reese adds three strips of bacon and a biscuit. Micah sets the plate in front of me and hands me a fork. Reese fetches the butter and honey while Micah pops a mug under the Keurig drip and presses the large button.

If they aren't careful, a girl could get used to this. Two guys tending to her. But I keep the thought to myself.

One—Reese and I will only ever be friends. I know that. He knows that. But Micah may still misconstrue the statement if said aloud.

Two—I honestly don't think I would ever be able to mentally handle more than one person in my life. My romantic life, that is. If I were into one-night stands or casual, no-strings-attached relationships, I might consider the idea. But I'm not. So, the point is moot.

Halfway through my breakfast, Micah plops down beside me and starts eating his own. Considering I eat slower than the average person, we will probably finish at the same time. Mine and Micah's plates are almost empty when Reese sits on the third stool.

"You seeing Ms. J today?" Reese asks around a mouthful of omelet.

"Yeah." My fork clatters against my plate. "I hate not being there as often. Seeing her every other Sunday feels wrong. Like I've abandoned her." I pick at my biscuit and eat it bit by bit. "Hope she's better today."

"Me too, sunshine." He swallows his bite. "Having lunch with Aunt Leanne after?"

"Yes." Spending time with Aunt Leanne is one of the week's highlights. "She wants to take me to some new deli. If she says it's good, I'll love it."

Micah bumps my knee with his. "Busy day."

"I love it, though." Busy doesn't cover it, but I love seeing people who make me happy. Hopefully, I will add Micah's family to the list when we have dinner with them tonight.

When I clear my plate, Micah takes both ours to the sink, rinses them off, and places them in the dishwasher.

"He's domesticated," Reese announces with a shit-eating grin. "Does he have a clone?"

I chuckle and scoot off my stool. "Just a sister. But I don't think she's looking for love."

"Boo. Well, let me know if you find his doppelgänger in the world."

"What happened to Trent?" Last I knew, he and his beau were still together. Which is a record for Reese. Long-term relationships aren't high priority for him—not that I judge how he lives his life.

Reese drops his head between his shoulders. "He wanted to take a break while on his work trip. Said he didn't want me to feel tied down." Reese lifts his head and meets my gaze. "But I like it when he ties me down."

"I almost felt bad for you," I say as I slap his arm. "Ass."

"No, seriously. I like him. Enough to make roots. But that's a story for another day and when he returns." Reese slaps my ass. "Now, go get ready for Ms. J. I want my crochet beanie before winter."

In the bathroom, I crank the shower and strip out of my clothes. As the sweats slide down my thighs, Micah steps up behind me, grabs my hips, and peppers kisses along my shoulder.

"Don't have much time," I moan out as he nips the skin below my ear.

"A quickie." *Kiss. Lick. Suck.* "Then I'll wash you."

Will I learn how to say no to this man again? Don't see it happening. And the notion doesn't bother me one bit.

～

Ms. Jenkins has lost weight. A lot of weight. And her skin doesn't seem to bolster the same radiance I usually see. It appears more translucent and wilted. Will she crumble if I touch her?

Seeing her like this—slowly fading—stirs up unpleasant memories. Memories that brought me to work at Gulfside in the first place.

Naturally, death is a part of life. Is unavoidable and happens to every species. Doesn't mean I have to like it. Doesn't mean I need to be okay accepting it.

"How've you been? Feel like I never see you anymore."

Ms. Jenkins stares at the crochet hook and yarn in my hands. "Your cap looks great. Who's the lucky recipient?"

Why didn't she answer my question? She never avoids answers. In fact, she usually tells me what is on her mind without hesitation. Gives me her two cents and a few quarters to boot.

So, why the evasion now?

I set down the beanie project in my lap and lay a hand on hers. Her hand is so cold. Too cold. And her skin feels as if it could peel away any minute. The need to wrap her in a thick blanket and hug her close overwhelms me immediately. Something about this entire situation is off and I don't like her obvious avoidance.

"Tell me what's wrong. Please," I say an octave above a whisper.

Ms. Jenkins sets down her own project—a baby blanket—and faces me as best she can. "You're such a sweet girl, Peyton." A cool hand cups my cheek as she gives me a soft smile. "I'm just an old lady. And my time is almost up. That's how life works."

For a minute, I stare into her warm brown eyes and digest what she said. Yes, eighty-seven is old. But I have known several people to live well into their nineties. Does she think she won't? Why would she think that?

"Last I saw you, everything seemed good. What's changed?"

Her thumb brushes slowly over my cheekbone. "Not sure. I just feel a change inside me. It isn't painful. More like my body is preparing for the inevitable."

A tear rolls down my cheek. "I don't want you to go."

The corner of her mouth lifts as she wipes away the tear. "I know. But when it's time, it's time. We can't fight what is meant to be. But we can use what time we have left wisely. Pass on pieces of ourselves so we live on in others." She looks down at the crocheted beanie in my lap. "Life has more meaning when we share and enjoy it with someone. That is my wish for you."

"Your wish?"

"Yes, sweet Peyton. Live your life. Seek adventure. Learn new things. Don't live your life in fear. Share yourself with others, so you too can live on through them when your time comes."

I don't want to leave here today. Ms. Jenkins says to live without fear. But how can I do that when I fear what will happen when I walk out the front door today? Why does today feel like *goodbye* and not *see you next time*?

"Why are you saying all this?" I ask through fresh tears.

She lifts her other hand to frame my face. "You know why."

"What if I want to be selfish and keep you?"

Her thumbs wipe at my tears. "As much as you want to, you won't be. It's my time. And Stephen is waiting for me. I won't be alone."

Oh god. Right here, in the middle of the community room at Gulfside, I am about to lose my shit. Weep and wail like a child. Throw a fit because this isn't fair. Life isn't fair.

And yes, it is petty of me to want her to stay when she seems ready to go. But I am so tired of loss. Downright exhausted at feeling it time and time again. Ms. Jenkins may not be my family by blood, but she is my family nonetheless. Not seeing and hugging and chatting with her will rip me apart. Not hearing her stories or crocheting beanies or sitting in the sun with her will gut me.

She drops her hands from my cheeks after one last swipe at my tears. "I have lived a long, happy, and fulfilling life, Peyton. Today will be the last day you cry about me. Understood?"

"How can you ask that of me?"

"How can I not?" She tucks loose strands behind my ear. "Last thing I want is people mopey. Remember all the wonderful moments. The ones that make you smile and laugh. Those are the ones that matter most. Not some morbid ritual where people think only of loss and not all the joy that person brought to others. Remember the joy, Peyton. Then go out and live your life. Experience love and the world. Hopefully, both at the same time. And when you remember me, I want you to think about our talks and crocheting and strolls outside. You hear me?"

I nod and wipe under each eye. "Yes, ma'am."

"Now, let's finish this cap and blanket."

The rest of my time at Gulfside is spent learning all the final touches on my project as well as hers. And when I walk out the front door, I do so with a heavy, full heart. I pray today isn't the last time I see Ms. Jenkins, but know the possibility is there. Not that I will ever be okay with losing someone I care about, but at least we had today. At least, I got to say goodbye.

~

"So, you're meeting the parents tonight, huh?" Aunt Leanne asks before she shoves the club sandwich between her lips.

"Yeah. From what Micah's said, they sound like nice people."

"Then why do you look nauseous?"

Because I am. Because today has a lot happening and my body is on the fritz with how to handle it all.

"Ms. Jenkins pretty much told me she's dying today." It isn't the sole reason for why I feel—and probably look—like garbage. But it is a major player in the game.

Aunt Leanne sets down her sandwich. "Oh, Peyton. I'm so sorry." She moves to my side of the table and hugs me a moment before returning to her seat. "Do you think she meant it? Or is she just losing it?"

This crossed my mind more than once as I finished my shift at Gulfside. The possibility something triggered her to say what she said. A friend in the facility passing. A family member passing. Death changes people's perspectives. It has certainly changed mine.

"Don't know. Part of me *feels* she won't be there in two weeks. But I pray she is." I sip my drink and the cool liquid does nothing to settle the unease in my chest. "She said some pretty profound things today. Things people say when they aren't sure another chance will happen."

Aunt Leanne reaches across the table and takes my hand. "I'm glad you had today with her."

"Me too."

She gives my hand a gentle squeeze, then releases it. "Now, what can I do to make tonight less stressful?"

I shake my head and laugh. "Wish I knew. Not like I've never met the parents in previous relationships."

"So, why the jitters?"

The answer crawls its way to the tip of my tongue. Ready to escape, but I restrain it a little longer. Right here, right now, with Aunt Leanne, isn't the time to confess.

"Because everything is different with Micah." And that little fact excites and frightens me equally.

Lifting a hand, I knock on Peyton's front door.

On the other side, a thump sounds. Followed by Peyton saying "shit" and Reese laughing at whatever happened. The lock disengages a second before the door flies open.

"Hi," Peyton huffs out. "I'm not ready."

I step in and shut the door. "No worries, I'm early." I check her head to toe and bite back laughter. "You okay?"

Reese laughs again and Peyton rolls her eyes. "Fine. Just bumped the wall trying to put my shoe on."

Peyton wanders down the hall to her room and I follow in her wake. Inside, I close the door and sit on the bed. For a moment, I track her rapid-fire movement as she plucks clothes from the closet and dresser, then stuffs them in the bag she brings to the house.

Tonight, she put on a golden maxi dress and black flats that peek out when she walks. Her hair is down in thick, soft waves and stops an inch or two below her mid-back. A light layer of gloss makes her lips shimmer. And with each pass in front of me, I inhale my favorite scent—Peyton's coconut mint.

She stops within reach and looks around the room. "Got that and that," she mumbles to herself. She carries on, ticking things off on her fingers.

I lift my hands and grab her hips. "Hey," I say and tip my head back to see her better. She stops and meets my gaze. "Something wrong?"

"No. Just making sure I have everything. I think I have everything. What if I forget something?" The words spill from her lips faster than her movement around the room.

I rise from the bed and pull her into me. Releasing a hip, I bring the hand to her cheek and caress it with my thumb. "Are you nervous about tonight? About meeting my parents?" Her eyes widen just enough for me to know the answer is yes. "You have nothing to worry about. Mom can be a little much at times, but Dad levels her out. Plus, if she says anything *I* don't find appropriate, I'll open my mouth. She gets excited."

"What if they don't like me?"

What a ridiculous question. Who would not like Peyton? Petty bitches of the past, but no one else.

"What if they love you?" I counter, biting my tongue so I don't add *"like I do."*

She huffs and a few strands close to her lips fly up and tickle my face. But I don't brush them away. Instead, I relish all the contacts and connections we share. Leaning in, I press a chaste kiss to her lips and come away with glossy coconut on mine.

"C'mon. If you forgot anything, we'll figure it out." I take her hand in mine and weave our fingers together. With my free hand, I shoulder her overnight bag. "Ready?"

After a deep breath, she nods. "Yeah. Let me grab my purse."

We say good night to Reese, hop in the truck and toss her bag in the back cab seating. Peyton picks a music playlist from my phone as I steer us onto the highway. The drive is spent with our fingers weaving in and out of each other's and rock music quietly vibrating from the speakers.

Less than thirty minutes later, I park next to Shelly's Beetle in Mom and Dad's driveway. Surprisingly, Shelly isn't in her car waiting like prior dinner nights. Maybe—hopefully—she tames Mom a bit before we step inside.

Inhaling deeply, I open my door then walk around to open Peyton's. With her hand in mine, we stroll to the front door in silence. Peyton may be nervous to meet my parents, but I am nervous too. I am nervous Mom may be too eccentric or Dad too dull. Shelly may be a little extra tonight, too, but I doubt it.

After Mom's declaration of wanting us to find happiness with another person, Shelly and I remain tight lipped when possible. Arranged marriages aren't really a thing around here anymore, but I wouldn't put it past Mom to try.

"Ready?" I ask as my hand hovers over the knob.

Peyton nods. "Ready as I'll ever be."

I twist the knob and the door flies open with Shelly on the other side. "You guys making out?"

Please don't let this be a precursor for the entire evening. "No, Shelly, we were not making out. This isn't high school. I act like an adult when necessary."

"Whatever." She rolls her eyes at me, then gives Peyton a big smile and hug. "Glad you're here. Maybe Mom will be less… maybe she'll just be less."

Peyton's eyes widen as she death grips my hand. I stroke the top of her hand with my thumb in reassurance. "It'll be fine. Quit freaking her out, Shell."

"Sorry," she says with a wince.

Inside the house, we follow Shelly toward the kitchen. Hints of garlic and cheese and bread float in the air. Mom asked if Peyton had food allergies, but didn't tell me what was on the menu tonight. By the smell, I'd guess lasagna. Guess we will find out soon enough.

We round the corner and Mom stops whatever conversation she and Dad are having. She looks from me to Peyton, to our hands and back up to me. The warmest, gentlest smile lights her face as she walks toward us.

"Hey, honey. Glad you made it." She gives me a longer than normal hug. "And you must be Peyton," she says. "I'm Nicole. It's wonderful to meet you." Without permission, Mom hugs Peyton.

I stare at the embrace with shock and embarrassment heating my cheeks. Mom *never* hugs strangers. Ever. Peyton and I are in a relationship, but she has never hugged any of my past girlfriends the first time they met.

"Mom, let's not scare her. Okay?"

Mom detaches her octopus tentacles from Peyton and takes a step back. "Oh, I'm sorry, dear. Don't know what came over me."

The oven timer goes off and rescues us from another round of awkwardness. "Be back in a minute," I announce. "I'm going to show Peyton around the house."

"Dinner will be on the table in a couple minutes," Mom replies.

Hand in hand, I lead Peyton through the house and away from my overzealous mother. I point and prattle off each room. "Dining and living room. Mom's home office, formerly Shelly's bedroom. Dad's home office, formerly my bedroom. Bathroom. Parents' bedroom." Then I lead her into the last room on the right and close the door. "Guest room."

The room is minimal, with white walls and smoky blue accents. A queen bed with gray-blue bedding, a white bed frame, and a mountain of throw pillows. A small, four-drawer white dresser and matching bedside table. Gray-blue curtains against white wooden blinds. The white-framed pictures on the wall of blue marine life or beachy images.

Not sure how my mother managed to replicate the same color for the entire room, but she did. On occasion, I wonder if she hired someone and gave them a color swatch. Wouldn't surprise me.

"Doing okay?" I ask as I step into Peyton and hug her close. "Mom has been a little much recently. Not sure what provoked the change, but I hope it fades. Soon."

Light laughter spills from her lips. "It's fine. All mothers probably go through this stage. Wanting to see their children happy as adults." Peyton breaks the hug, walks around the room and stops in front of one of the frames. "I won't try to guess how my mom will be when you meet her. Generally, she's pretty laid back. But I've also seen her at her best and worst."

I step up behind her and wrap my arms around her front. "If she asks weird questions, you don't have to answer. Shell and I are used to deflecting when necessary. You can use a code word, if she makes you uncomfortable." I chuckle but mean every word. Mom isn't *bad*, she just gets intense. Especially if you don't know her.

Peyton rests her hands over mine. "It'll be fine. No matter who we are, parents are always strange to us or people close to us."

"Still think you should have a code word," I mumble into her hair.

"Fine," she says with a laugh. "How about sushi?"

"Sushi?"

"Mmhm."

"How the hell would you work that into conversation?"

She shrugs. "Maybe I won't have to. But if I do, I'll figure it out."

"Alright, sushi. Let's go before they think we're fucking on the bed."

"What?" Peyton's face pales as her eyes go wide.

"Joking, hellcat. C'mon."

We join everyone in the dining room and sit at the table. Each place setting has a small salad and dipping oil for bread. Bread baskets sit at either end of the table—because we love bread. Mom brings out a large casserole dish and sets it at the heart of the table.

"Baked ziti, made with creamy pesto instead of marinara," she announces with a glowing smile.

Peyton shifts in her seat and stares at me with a slack jaw. "Your mom makes dishes like this and all you can cook is breakfast?"

Across from us, Shelly snort-laughs and tries to cover it with a cough.

"Shut it, Shell."

Mom joins in on Shelly's laughter for a second, then stops when she sees my face. "Sorry, Micah. It is funny." Mom shifts her gaze to Peyton. "I've tried to teach Micah for years and it doesn't stick. But I refuse to give up. One day, he'll surprise me, or you, and make something else."

Once all the food is on the table, everyone settles and starts on their salad. Easy conversation flows around the table. Thankfully, Mom hasn't said anything off-putting the entire time.

Every time she glances over to Peyton's and my side of the table, though, I see the sparkle in her eye. The barely noticeable uptick at the corners of her mouth and eyes. And when Peyton speaks, Mom listens. She lets her say every word, then comments back as if she and Peyton have chatted hundreds of times.

By the end of the evening, we leave with full bellies, a heaping container of leftovers, and warm hugs.

"That wasn't so bad," I say once we are on the road.

"Your mom is nice. She loves you both and just wants the best for you and Shelly."

"Yeah, she does. Glad she didn't make you uncomfortable." I lace my fingers with hers, lift them to my lips, and kiss her knuckles.

A couple songs and commercials on the radio later, I park in the driveway and we walk into the house. I lock the dead bolt and drop her overnight bag to the floor. She opens her mouth to ask something, but I cut her off with my lips to hers.

I frame her face in my hands and kiss the hell out of her. Her hands snake around my waist and fist the back hem of my jeans. We stumble toward the bedroom, our lips never apart. When her legs bump the mattress, I kiss along her jaw, down her neck, along her shoulder.

Grabbing the back collar of my shirt, I yank it off and toss it on the floor. I reach out, trace my fingertips along the dress seam at her breasts. Her eyes drift shut as a shiver rolls through her body.

But I don't want her to shut out the world. Not tonight. Not now.

I trail my fingers up the column of her throat to her chin and tip it up slightly. "Open your eyes, Peyton." Violet irises meet my blues and hum with anticipation. The gray flecks sparkle with delight. I lean in, my lips a whisper over hers as I hold her gaze. "I love you, Peyton."

The sentiment flows with such ease. My whole body comes alive. A blazing buzz spreads like an electrical current, zapping and sparking and jolting anew. Breath fills me with life as my heart learns a new rhythm.

"I love you, too." Peyton closes the space between us and kisses me as if we have found ourselves. Here, in this moment. Together.

We peel away our clothes and rediscover each other. Learn who we are with our proclamations in the open. Make love to each other until we are bone tired and in a pile of tangled limbs. And in the early morning hours, I hug her close to my side and whisper I love you in her ear as we drift off to sleep.

Happy, sated, and head over heels in love.

"Stop!" I shout between giggles.

"Stop what?" Micah digs his fingertips into the side of my rib cage for the umpteenth time.

"Tickling me." I pry at his fingers in the hopes of getting free. But he has a death grip on my waist. "We need…" *Tickle.* "To get ready…" *Tickle.* "For work." *Laugh.* "Oh, god." I clamp my thighs together and clench my internal muscles. "Seriously, Micah. Stop. I'm going to pee."

He digs in harder and laughs. "Liar."

"No, seriously." If I don't make it to the bathroom now, this won't be pretty. I tug him in that direction and hope he picks up on how severe the situation is. "My bladder is about to let go."

He drops his hands. *Thank fuck.* I bolt to the toilet, drop my pants and call it a win that I made it in time.

Micah walks in and winces as I finish up. "Sorry. Didn't mean for that to happen."

"Yeah, yeah. But remember this…" I point a finger at him. "If I say I have to pee, I'm not joking." I stare at his pouty lip while I wash up. For a split second, I consider apologizing. But I let it go.

"Sorry, hellcat." He pulls me in for a hug. I hesitate on returning the hug, wondering if he will tickle me again. When he doesn't, I wrap my arms around his middle and lean into him.

Cool air hits my skin as he brushes hair off my shoulder. Before a shiver passes, warm lips kiss the width of my shoulder, along the curve of my neck and up to that spot beneath my ear. Hands roam the landscape of my body—gentle and rough, caressing and kneading.

One hand slides up my spine, dives into my hair, fists the locks and tugs back. The brightest constellation stares down at me and I lick my lips. Clench my thighs for a different reason.

Micah reads me like an open book. Sees the need in my eyes. Feels my taut nipples on his chest and subtle grind of my hips.

He lowers his lips, stopping a breath above mine. "We don't have time," he says with a smirk on his lips.

"Please," I moan. At this rate, I am willing to be late or speed to work, if necessary. Not like we aren't always early.

Micah tightens his grip on my hair and licks the seam of my lips. "Gonna be quick and dirty. You good with that?"

"You know I am."

Then, he releases my hair, spins me around to face the bed, yanks my pants and underwear down, and forces me to bend at the waist. With a clunk, his pants and briefs hit the floor. He draws circles on my skin just above my ass crack.

As I open my mouth to tell him to quit teasing me, his finger glides between my cheeks. He pauses at the tight hole and presses slightly. "One day, I'll claim this too." The rumble in his tone and the promise in his words make me push into his touch. "Not now, hellcat," he growls out. "But soon."

His finger slips lower, separates my lips and toys with my clit. I fist the comforter and grind against his touch.

"So wet and eager." *Whack.* His free hand slaps my ass. "I love when you're starved for me."

His finger vanishes, but is quickly replaced with the tip of his cock. He rubs the head between my lips—up and down, over and over. Teasing and taunting.

Then he slams forward and fills me. "Jesus fuck," I belt out as I claw the bedding.

"Hold on, hellcat. Quick and dirty time."

Micah slides a hand up my spine, circles around the front of my throat, and tightens his grip. With the other hand on my hip, he holds me in place as his cock pistons between my thighs. Balls slapping my clit. My moans and his bouncing off the walls while pheromones and arousal fog the air.

When the pitch of my cries escalates, he shifts the hand on my hip to my nipple and tweaks the tight bud. His hand around my throat constricts and I go into sensation overload. Heat spirals up my spine, spreads across my chest and up my neck as my walls tighten around his cock. He twists my nipple harder. Slams into me with more aggression. Tips me over the edge and jumps after me.

"God, I love when you come," he growls in my ear and releases my neck. "Fucking spectacular."

"Thanks," I say on a laugh. "I'll take it as a compliment."

~

We walk in the back of Roar—still early—with loony smiles on our faces. Good thing the staff doesn't arrive when we do. It would be ridiculously difficult to hide our euphoria.

Micah and I decide to split tasks to make the evening easier. He will set up for Karaoke Night while I work on scheduling and payroll. Recently, we started dealing with invoices and ordering on Tuesdays and Fridays. Days when we don't work together, but still have another manager on duty. It frees up our joint work nights more and gets us off the floor most of the night when everyone else has it handled.

It isn't long before the staff arrives and Roar opens. The bar lines with patrons ordering drinks. A line forms near the makeshift stage as people add their name to the karaoke roster. Tables fill with people and conversations. And it isn't long before the first singer steps on stage and blesses us with their song selection and voice.

Pouring a beer from the tap, I look up and spot the group walking in. I finish pouring and serve the customer before pressing the button on my headset.

"Starlight."

"Hellcat."

"Everyone's here."

"Be out in a sec." As the walkie cuts out, Micah rounds the corner with bottles from the storage room in his hands.

We both help with drink orders until the line is manageable for Mable and Josiah. Then we exit the bar alley and join our friends at the table.

Great songs spill from the speakers as squawky voices belt out lyrics. Our friends drink beer and discuss which songs they will sing when their turn comes. Micah and I sit back, join in the conversation, laugh and enjoy the evening and our surroundings.

Shelly tugs Cora toward the stage as both my and Micah's walkies crackle in our ears. "Boss man," Ted calls out. "Someone I admitted in asked if you're working tonight."

I meet Micah's gaze with a scrunched brow. He shrugs. "Did you catch their name?"

"No, sorry. But she's wearing a red dress and has brown hair."

Closing my eyes, I take a deep breath and search for my inner zen. Never would I suspect Micah of adultery. So, my mind doesn't go in that direction when I hear a woman is asking for him. Instead, my mind travels to the long list of women he was with over the years and prays another one isn't coming at him with some outlandish accusation.

Micah spins to face me head-on. "Please don't freak out."

"Not the best way to start a conversation," I say.

He nods. "Saturday, I was headed to the office after rounds to catch up on paperwork. Caleb informed me over the walkie that a woman asked for me. By the time he brought it up, she was headed for the exit. I only caught the back of her, but knew who it was."

"Who?"

An angry nest of hornets buzzes in my belly and sends venom through my veins. I am sick and tired of all these women. Do they not understand the concept of one-night stands? From what Micah told me, he made it abundantly clear to all of them.

"Rochelle," he says, loud enough for only me to hear.

Rochelle? As in his ex-girlfriend? As in the woman who fucked another man in his bed and crushed his heart? If Rochelle is here, this isn't some pregnancy situation. This is next level. And I have had it with the bullshit.

I lock eyes with Micah. See fear as his eyes dart between mine and sweat slicks his brow. Feel anxiety roll off him as he clenches my hands and waits for me to say something. Anything.

"Ted?"

"Yes, Miss Peyton?"

"Please be on standby to escort someone from the premises."

Micah's eyes widen. "What're you doing?"

"Handling this; after we figure out what she wants."

Out of nowhere, Shelly stops singing mid-song. Cora slaps Shelly's arm. "Too drunk to sing already?" Cora teases. But when I look to Shelly, her eyes are laser-focused behind me.

One-way ticket to party town coming up.

"There you are," a brunette says as she stops in front of Micah, in front of us.

Dressed in an overpriced dress and heels, Rochelle has the audacity to rest her hand on Micah's shoulder as she steps into his space. Micah shirks from her touch and inches back.

"First, don't touch me. Second, what are you doing here, Rochelle?"

The woman smiles as if Micah didn't just say to back the fuck up nicely. I ball my fingers into fists and keep them pinned at my sides. I will let Micah be the nice one. But if this bitch doesn't catch on soon…

"Wanted to see you. I miss you."

"Are you fucking kidding me right now?" Micah says louder than before, and eyes dart our way. "You miss me? What, did your fuckboy leave you?"

Rochelle jerks her head back as if slapped. "No need to be ugly. To answer your question, no, he didn't break up with me. I broke it off with him. He was too immature. And like I said, I miss you."

She reaches forward and is inches from touching Micah when I rise from my stool. "Do not touch him."

"Who are you?" she asks with a snarl. "His flavor of the day?"

I step closer, invading her space, and use the few inches I have on her to get in her face. She doesn't back down but looks a little gray in the face. For a moment, I don't say anything. I simply stare down at her. When she swallows, I know I have her.

"Actually, it doesn't matter who I am. What matters is he isn't yours. Hasn't been for quite some time. You don't deserve him. Hell, you don't deserve anyone."

"You don't know me," she bites back. "How dare you—"

"How dare I what? Not be a frigid bitch. Not treat someone like trash." I hold my hands in front of me, palms up, and wave my fingers. "Let's hear it. And it better be good." Rochelle looks past me to Micah. "No." I push her back. "You don't get to look at him."

"I don't know who you think you are, but if you touch me again, I'll call the police."

I tip my head back and laugh. "And I'll laugh as they issue you a trespassing notice because you're harassing an employee." I force her back as I step farther into her. "You can go peacefully or not. The choice is yours."

"You don't know who you're messing with," she bites out. "He's only good for sex. So, you can have him."

A fuse lights in my veins. Burns slow and hot as the flame gets closer to the ticking bomb beneath my rib cage. My breathing kicks up a degree as my cheeks flush. And before I give serious thought to my actions, I take a step back, grab her shoulders, rear back, and drive my knee between her legs. Hard.

Rochelle crumples to the floor and wails in pain as she grabs herself. "Bitch!"

"Right back atcha," I say with a half smile, then press the button on my walkie. "Ted?"

"On my way, Miss Peyton."

No doubt Ted heard and witnessed the entire altercation. And if anyone asked who was in the wrong here, several would say I asked the woman to leave. Did I need to get physical? No, but she wasn't backing down or following Micah's or my request to leave. Her presence was—is—unwanted, and she refused to give in. If I hadn't taken it next level, she would probably continue to harass us.

Ted helps Rochelle off the floor. Soon as she is upright, she goes on a tirade. "You'll be sorry, little girl."

"Actually" —Shelly steps up to Rochelle— "no she won't. Several of us just witnessed the whole thing. You put your hands on the manager without permission. Were asked to leave by another manager and refused. Then you threatened her. She was protecting herself."

Well, damn. Shelly is a viper. Not someone you mess with or want on your bad side. Noted. The fact she stepped up—whether for Micah, me, or us both—has my spine straighter and head higher. No doubt Shelly knows Rochelle and has some inkling of what she did to Micah. She would go to bat for him any day of the week. But for her to reinforce me, that says a lot about us—me and Shelly—and the small bond forming.

Rochelle turns her pathetic eyes in my direction. "You'll get bored of him, just like I did. Then, you'll wish I relieved you of him."

I shake my head. "Love that you're telling me why you fucked around on him, yet here you are." I look her up and down. "Begging for another chance. I feel sorry for you and your pitiful life. He's moved on. Found happiness. Found someone who loves him as much as he loves her. And you lost out. If you step foot on this property or come near me or Micah again, you'll see how much of a bitch I *can* be."

Ted guides Rochelle toward the doors as the crowd claps and cheers. I don't look away until Rochelle is out the door. And for the first time in who knows how long, I breathe.

Until Micah swoops in, cups my cheeks, and kisses the hell out of me in front of everyone. Wolf whistles and hollers to *get a room* come at us from every direction. The kiss is far from innocent as his hands roam my body. To be honest, I don't give a fuck. Because one fact is certain in this moment.

Micah Reed belongs to me. And he sure as hell is letting everyone know I belong to him. Wouldn't want it any other way.

Laughter mixes with rock music as Peyton and I sit on a lounger in Jonas and Autumn's backyard. Our typical Sunday get-together underway.

Gavin and Jonas man the grill; flipping burgers, brats, and mojo-marinated chicken quarters while chatting. Autumn, Cora, and Shelly load one of the banquet tables with buns, side salads, fruit, and condiments. Penny and Rex go back and forth over something frivolous—socks in the living room. Reznor and Tatyana watch their son, Ashton, play with Clementine and Spartan. Iliana, Trevor, and Jillian—Jonas's younger sister—sit on the lounger across from us and chat about an upcoming baseball game.

Life feels pretty fucking amazing right now.

A year ago, I would not have pictured my life like this. With Peyton at my side, holding my hand and laughing at jokes told by my closest friends. A year ago, I had no smiles to give. Felt empty inside. Did all I could to fill the void. But nothing worked.

Now, I know the reason.

Fate has never been something I put much thought in. Especially when my relationship with Rochelle ended how it did. But now I give fate some credit. Give in to the notion that two people are meant to find each other and live their best life together.

Several years ago, fate brought Peyton and I together. I wasn't ready, though. She'd had her eye on me back then, but who is to say where our relationship would have gone had we gotten together.

I look toward the grill, watch how Cora latches on to every word Gavin says with hearts in her eyes. Watch how he kisses her forehead, then whispers something in her ear and causes her cheeks to flush.

Could that have been me and Peyton? There is no definite answer. Although Gavin and Cora are madly in love, shit beyond their control tore them apart early on. Fate found a way to bring them back together. If Peyton and I had been different in high school, would we have drifted apart? Or would we still be together? If our lives were different back then, I don't think we would be who we are now. Nor would we feel the same.

And that is not something I care to dwell on. The what-ifs.

What I *do* know is that I have never been happier. And I owe it all to the hellcat at my side.

I lean in and press my lips to her temple. "I love you."

Peyton stops whatever she was saying to Shelly and faces me. "Love you, too." Then she presses her lips to mine. I break the kiss all too soon, not wanting our friends to give us shit.

Gavin and Jonas announce the meat is off the grill—which is our version of a dinner bell. Everyone evacuates their seats, grabs plates, and piles them high. Minutes later, the only sound outside is the music, occasional crunch of food, and Spartan's whimper for scraps.

Off to the side, Cora asks Shelly about work and I shift my attention.

"Is the shop staying busy? Whenever I ask Mom, she says yes. But she thinks five customers in one day is busy," Cora says with a laugh.

Shelly swallows her bite and takes a sip from her beer. "It's gotten busier in the last few months. Not sure why. We've done a little more marketing, but not much. Whatever the reason, the uptick is great."

"Mom jokingly said maybe she'll retire sooner."

Shelly pales, which I find interesting. It is no secret that Shelly will take over the florist shop when Cora's mom retires. She plans to buy the business over time and make minor changes. But I don't think the plan was for her to own the shop for three to five more years. As a planner, if something changes the overall picture, Shelly freaks out.

Shelly laughs without humor. "Hope she's joking. Not quite ready to fill her shoes yet."

Cora waves her off. "I'm sure she is. Anyway… on to less stressful topics. Have you talked to the hottie painting the shop mural?"

"What *hottie*?" I ask, shooting daggers at my little sister.

She rolls her eyes, then stabs a chunk of potato salad and stuffs it in her mouth. It's an obvious attempt to avoid the subject, so I just sit and wait and stare like the annoying older brother I am. Until she caves. And because I know my sister well, she will cave. Soon.

"Argh!" Like clockwork. "He's just some guy painting a mural on the outside of the shop. No big deal."

"Cora seems to think it's big enough a deal to bring him up," I say.

Shelly narrows her eyes at Cora. "And we will talk about *that* later." She shifts her gaze back to me. "Seriously, though. He's just some artist Elizabeth hired. Nothing else."

I stare at my sister a moment. Try to read between the lines. Zero in on the fine details she leaves out. But for some reason, she has sealed herself off. Has put on her best poker face and enforced the most neutral body language. That alone tells me there is definitely more to this. Tells me she doesn't just look at this guy as *just some artist Elizabeth hired.* She looks at him with newly formed interest.

For now, I won't push her on it. Won't make her uncomfortable and embarrass her in front of friends. But I will get more answers. Soon.

"If you say so. Just don't let Mom find out about said *no big deal* or you'll never hear the end of it."

For a beat, her body sags. The only reason I don't miss it is because I know my sister. Know that finding *the one* is a big deal to her. As an avid romance reader, she is big on the fated-lovers concept. Believes everyone will get their happily ever after.

For years, she harped on most of us about destiny and love written in the stars. Now that someone pops up on her radar, she keeps secrets. Doesn't let anyone pry as she has in the past.

Maybe I need to stop by the floral shop and buy Peyton flowers next week. Find out more about this artist.

The rest of the night flows with great conversation, an intense game of *Never Have I Ever* and belly-aching laughter. Everyone says their goodbyes and goes separate ways until next week.

After the short ride home, I park in the driveway and we walk hand in hand to the door and inside. The door clicks shut and I wrap Peyton in my arms. Kiss her as if I will never get the chance again.

"What was that for?" she asks when we come up for air.

"For everything."

"Everything?"

I nod. "For the longest time, life, and the world, was a restless night. Since you, life is colorful. More brilliant."

"Bright," she adds.

"Bright," I repeat, then kiss her. "And I can't imagine life any better. Or a love any brighter."

One year later

Micah steps up behind me and wraps me in his arms. "Almost ready?" His starry-sky irises meet mine in the mirror and, for a moment, we breathe in sync with each other.

Although Micah and I have become practically inseparable the last year, we took things slower than most couples. With our pasts, Micah and I decided there was no need to rush things.

We spent every available minute of the day together and every night in each other's arms. Yet, we waited until two months ago to move in together. The wait had nothing to do with my rent at the apartment or that we wanted occasional solitude. More like we wanted to ease into this step. Ease into sharing space full time with a new person. Ease into cohabitation.

"Yeah. One more minute."

Micah kisses my bare shoulder. "I'll wait in the living room."

He exits and leaves me to finish getting ready. I do one last once-over to make sure nothing is out of place. After a quick swipe of gloss, I tuck the tube in my purse and join Micah in the living room.

"Ready when you are," I say and offer my elbow to him.

He takes my arm and guides us out the door and to the car. We wind our way out of the neighborhood, then Micah drives us south to an undisclosed location for dinner. He hasn't told me the reason why I needed to dress up, but I suspect it has something to do with us celebrating our "official" one-year anniversary. Yes, we casually dated for weeks leading up to August tenth, but we didn't want to label our relationship.

Then a switch flipped. Since that moment, we let the world know there is an us.

Miles of highway pass before Micah exits and drives along the city streets. I have no clue where he is taking me, but I do know we are in Tampa. Two more right turns, then a left and Micah drives the car into a parking lot. No name appears on the rustic brick building, just a logo of a setting sun.

"What is this place?" I ask, staring out the window.

"You'll see. I only know about it through connections at Roar."

I spin in my seat to face him as we pull up to a valet in a white dress shirt, black slacks, and a black tie. "Micah, this place looks really expensive."

"If it was too much, I wouldn't have brought us." He says that, but I am not buying a word of it.

The valet opens our doors and helps us out. Micah steps around the front of the car, takes my arm, and escorts me inside. The moment we step through the double oak doors, I stop breathing.

This place is expensive. Ridiculously expensive.

My heels clack on antique hardwood as we walk down a long corridor. The interior walls the same brick as the exterior. Soft white light glows from candelabra chandeliers above. Photographs from different eras sit in thick black frames on the left wall—some sepia-toned, others black and white. Tall windows with half-moons on top line the right wall and look out into an enclosed atrium with bonsai, bamboo, stones, and a waterfall pond. From my vantage point, the garden appears to be surrounded by windows, including the rooftop.

We reach a podium where a man and woman wait with warm smiles. "Good evening, sir, miss," the man says. "May I have the name for your reservation?"

"Reed-Alexander," Micah answers.

Why did he put the reservation under both our last names?

There is no time to ponder the answer as the host gathers menus and asks us to follow. He leads us through the restaurant and, as suspected, the entire dining area encompasses the atrium. We are seated at a cloth-covered square table for two. The host lights a single taper candle at the heart of the table, bids us a good evening and steps away.

For a moment, I scan the dining area in slight shock. This place isn't some random place to eat dinner. It is literal fine dining.

Beside the candle is a small vase with a single yellow rose and a sprig of baby's breath. On a spotless white plate in front of me is an intricately folded cloth napkin. More silverware than I use in a day sits on three sides of the plate. A small plate off to the right and two empty wineglasses also fill my place setting.

Not far from where we sit, a wine cellar with a glass front contains several hundred bottles. Chandeliers from the entry—but larger—hang from thick oak beams in the tall ceiling.

"Micah," I whisper across the table. "This place is *too* expensive." I haven't looked at the menu yet, but dinner here feels like hundreds for the two of us.

Micah lays his hand on the table, palm up, and waits for me to take it. Without hesitation, I join our hands. A year has passed and I still feel a jolt when we connect. If anything, the jolt gets stronger with time.

"And as I said before, I wouldn't have brought us if it was too much." He leans in, lifts my hand, and kisses my knuckles in turn. "Let's enjoy the evening. Okay?"

Inhaling a deep breath, I nod. "Yeah. Okay."

Before I pick up the menu, a woman approaches the table in black slacks, a white button-down with a black tie, a black apron tied at the waist that extends below her knees, and a black towel on her forearm.

"Good evening. Welcome to Dusk. Is this your first time dining with us?"

Micah responds with yes and the woman goes into a small story on how the restaurant came to be. Then, she explains the menu. That this is a five-course meal. The menu is a guide for us to choose one of three options for each course. We can choose the same or different. The main course is paired with wine and dessert has beverage options. The dishes are spaced out to give us time to eat and not feel full as each course ends. Once explained, she fills the glasses on the table with water and excuses herself to give us a moment to decide.

I pick up the handheld menu and stare down at the printed card. The options seem simple, but the idea of choosing just one makes me sweat.

"Hey." I peek past the candle to Micah. "It's just dinner." I nod and take a deep breath. "How about we pick different items so we can try more than one."

"Yeah. Sounds good."

When the server returns, we place our full course of options. Micah went with sausage-stuffed roasted cherry tomatoes, spicy tuna tartar, caprese salad, filet mignon, and the chocolate box. I chose the champagne shrimp on endive, caramelized onion and pear tartlets, fig and goat cheese salad, miso-glazed salmon, and berries and cream cake. The server takes our menus and states the hors d'oeuvres will be out shortly before leaving the table.

The moment we are alone, Micah reaches for my hand and I gladly give it.

"This place is more upscale than anywhere else we eat, I know." I lift my brows and pucker my lips, which makes him laugh. "But… today deserves more."

I know what today is, but does he? Not that men should be singled out for forgetting dates, but most men aren't the best at remembering birthdays, anniversaries, or special occasions. At least not the ones from my past.

"It does?" I ask with faux curiosity.

His lips kick up in a half smile. "Don't play the oblivious card with me. You know what today is." My eyes go up and to the right as I shrug. Micah shakes his head and chuckles softly. "As I was saying, today deserves more. Which is why I brought us here." He squeezes my hand. "I never want to take you or our time together for granted. And I plan to celebrate every momentous occasion we share. You're just going to have to deal with it."

I laugh. "Is that an order?"

He tilts his head and half shrugs. "Maybe." He pauses and takes a deep breath. "I love you, Peyton. More than I have loved anyone. And every now and then, I want to spoil you. Take you to nice places and eat fancy meals together. Hope you're okay with that."

More than okay. The longer our relationship is, the more I know the real Micah. See his sensitive and caring side. His protective and defensive side. The man who will yank my hair and choke me one minute and kiss me tenderly as we make love the next.

I love all the facets of Micah Reed. And I love that there are still more to discover.

"Guess I'm okay with it," I tease.

Our time at Dusk passes with small dishes, sampling each other's food, laughter and our hands connected across the table. After we finish dessert and coffee, Micah pays the bill without giving me the slightest notion of cost. Arm in arm, we casually stroll out of the restaurant, wait for the valet to bring the car up, then hop in and drive home.

"Did you have a nice time?" Micah asks as he lifts my hand to his lips and kisses my fingers.

"Yes. The restaurant was wonderful. Thank you." I lean over the console and kiss his cheek.

"You're welcome. And so you know, the night isn't over."

"Good to know." Anniversary sex sounds like a great way to end the evening.

Before long, Micah parks in the driveway and we stroll up the walkway to the house. Not much has changed with the house since I moved in. A few minor details —more flowers in the yard, additional accent pieces inside, picture frames of us and family and friends. I didn't have much furniture of my own and sold it since the house was furnished.

Micah enters the code to unlock the door and steps inside, me on his heels. On the ride home, when Micah said the night wasn't over, I expected him to tear my clothes off when we got home.

But Micah is full of surprises tonight. And the sight before me is beyond expectation.

The entire open floor plan glows. Lit candles rest on every possible surface. As does a plethora of flowers. Every type of yellow flower sits in vases with greenery and baby's breath. I step farther into the room as my eyes dart from one candle and vase to the next.

"When did you? How?" I spin around to find Micah right behind me.

"Shelly."

I turn back to the room and take it all in. Who knew Micah Reed was such a romantic? Over the last year, he has softened around the edges—only on occasion in the bedroom—and I love seeing this side of him.

"This is…"

I whirl around to tell him how romantic this is, but he is no longer eye level. All the air leaves my lungs as I drop my gaze to meet his. Micah, down on one knee, stares up at me as if I hold all of life's secrets.

A hand flies to my mouth as my vision glazes over. "What are you doing?" I choke out.

His soft chuckle floats through the air. "Being romantic. Now, shh." He presses an index finger to his lips for a beat, then reaches for my free hand. My *left* hand.

"Peyton, it's no secret our relationship didn't start in the best light. In all honesty, I was the biggest asshole." We both laugh. "Through all the banter and harsh words, you still called out to me in a way I couldn't ignore. So, I kept up with my persistence. Once I realized who you were and what I'd done all those years ago, I thought there'd be no chance for me." He rubs circles with his thumb over the top of my hand. "But you gave me a chance. You forgave me."

I blink and the first tear rolls down my cheek. Eyes locked on his, I drop my hand from my mouth and nod.

"Slowly, you went from this woman at work I had the hots for to the woman I don't want to live without." I gasp. "Peyton, I don't picture a single day in my future without you. Nor do I want to." He reaches into the pocket of his slacks and takes out a small black box. He flips the lid open and turns the box in his hand. Nestled in the velvet is a platinum band bridal set—the engagement ring with a yellow cathedral round diamond and the wedding band with small white diamonds that hug the engagement stone.

"Oh my god," I whisper in disbelief.

"Peyton Isabel Alexander, I want to spend every day of forever with you. Will you marry me?"

Tears cascade down my cheeks and blur Micah and the room. But my eyes don't leave his. Not for a second. Not as every ounce of love this man holds spills from his heart through his lips.

Micah just asked me to marry him. Never in my life did I imagine this day, this moment.

"Yes," I whisper. "Yes, I'll marry you."

A new smile lights Micah's expression. A love so bright it blinds me. He plucks the engagement ring from the box, lifts my left hand to his lips, kisses my ring finger, then slides the ring into place. Rising from the floor, he wraps his arms around my waist, lifts me off the floor and kisses the hell out of me.

"Thank you," he says when the kiss breaks.

I scrunch my brow. "For what?"

"For you. For saying yes. And for wanting forever with me."

I plant a chaste kiss on his lips. "I love you, Micah Reed."

"And I love you. Future Mrs. Peyton Reed."

He kisses me slow and soft as he walks us to the bedroom. And then, Micah shows me every way he loves me. Now and forever.

bonus content

MICAH

When I asked Peyton to marry me, I had no clue what I was getting myself into.

Leading up to the proposal, I pictured her in a beautiful white gown. Half her hair pinned up with wavy champagne locks trailing down her back. I imagined bright bouquets, hundreds of people in pews with tears in their eyes, cameras flashing, and frankincense in the air.

What I didn't expect was this…

To be standing in the middle of Roar on a Sunday. The club magically overhauled since the door locked less than twenty-four hours ago. The decor is simple yet perfect. Ani and Sean hired an event company to come in and glam up the place for Peyton's and my big day.

Originally, the idea of saying I do to Peyton in the middle of Roar was weird. But Peyton explained it in the simplest of terms.

"This is where we got our second chance. If it weren't for this place, who knows if we would've met again."

I was sold in an instant.

White gauzy fabric hangs from the open ceiling in long torrents, creating strategically placed sheer walls. Countless strands of white fairy lights dangle from metal beams in the ceiling—the only light in the entire space—and float above the small gathering. Twenty collapsible white chairs decorated with the same gauzy fabric sit feet from where I stand. A large copper arch at my back with green vines and the occasional lavender, yellow and white rose tucked between the foliage.

The day after the proposal, I asked Peyton what type of wedding she envisioned for us. How long she wanted to wait for the big day. If she wanted to save for a while and go all out. I expected her to buy one of those wedding organizer books or hire a planner. To purchase bridal magazines and clip pictures of her ideal dress, the perfect bouquet, the dream location, and the ultimate honeymoon.

Did she do a single one of them? Nope.

"I want something simple. We could just elope."

Her words were a shock to the system. Threw me off guard. Peyton never presented herself as someone who wants elaborate or upscale. Not that she doesn't like the finer things. She has just found a way to love the smaller, simpler things in life.

But when you sit down to plan your own wedding, people surprise you. Peyton did; just not in the way I expected.

I convinced her to not elope. Told her our families would never let us live it down. She agreed, thank goodness. But she had one condition—that we not wait.

"What's the point in waiting?"

Which brings us to now. Less than two months after I got down on one knee and asked Peyton to be mine forever. October second.

Soft classical music plays from the speakers overhead. The air smells like I just walked into Shelly's florist shop. Clementine comes into view between the gauzy walls. In a dandelion-yellow sundress, she ambles down the aisle with the biggest smile on her face and sprinkles yellow rose petals on the ground. When she reaches the row where Jonas and Autumn sit, she takes the empty chair between them.

She whisper-asks Autumn, "Did I do good?"

Autumn nods and kisses her daughter's hair.

The music shifts into another classical tune; an unfamiliar song with a sweet, whimsical sound. It starts slow and soft, builds into a stronger harmony, and weaves a web around my heart.

Absolutely perfect.

Two breaths pass before I catch movement on the other side of the gauzy walls. And then I see her.

Peyton comes into view. Reese hooked on her elbow as she walks in my direction. With each step she takes, I remind myself to breathe. To unlock my knees. To carve every second of this moment into my memory.

She has never looked so beautiful.

In a sleeveless ivory gown, intricate lace decorates the bust. Tiny yellow jewels sparkle in the material with each step she takes toward me. In the light of day, I bet she would shine brighter than the sun. The chiffon skirt flows to the floor and glides as if she walks on clouds. Her hair is piled high in an artsy bun with occasional tendrils framing her face. A simple bouquet in her hand with lavender, yellow and white roses and artfully arranged greenery.

When she reaches me and unhooks her arm from Reese's, my heart slips into fifth gear.

This is it. Today, Peyton will tell the world she is mine forever. And I will do the same.

PEYTON

I will not cry. I will not cry.

I chant the words in my head over and over, trying to make them true. But the sting behind my eyes has other plans in store.

The minister drones on with the well-practiced ceremony. I don't hear any of her words, though. Because every sensory response I own is homed in on the man holding my hands.

Micah Reed.

If a fortune-teller would have told me two years ago, I would marry the man formerly known as my high school antagonist, I would have laughed in their face. I would have demanded my money back and never returned.

But in this moment, as I stare into my favorite starry-sky eyes, I believe all things are possible. Especially redemption.

The minister stops talking and I startle in place. *Time to pay attention, Peyton.*

Micah glances down at my hands a beat before meeting my gaze again. "Fluffy words aren't my strong suit, so bear with me." I laugh, and everyone joins in. "Peyton, I loved you before I truly understood what the word meant. Our beginning started in the darkest of days. And I count my lucky stars each day I wake up next to you. Because you make each day brighter than the last. You make me a better man. A better version of myself. All because you love me too." A devious smile tips up the corners of his mouth. "And I can't wait to call you Mrs. Reed every day of forever."

I laugh through my blurry vision as Micah slips the wedding band on my fourth finger, brings it to his lips, and kisses the band.

"Peyton," the minister chimes in. "When you're ready."

I sniffle and blink a few times. I take a deep breath and swallow.

"Micah Reed…" I chuckle under my breath. "You surprise me at every turn. Who knew my high school crush would one day be my husband." Gasps float through the room as I watch Micah's eyes glaze over. Not everyone knows our history, but enough do. So, to say he was my crush probably shocks them. "The day I walked through these doors and saw you for the first time in years, I never pictured us here." I squeeze his hands harder. "But I wouldn't change a single step of our journey. Because each step we took led us to where we are today. Madly in love. And I can't wait for you to call me Mrs. Reed in the presence of others" —I cock a brow— "and other names when we're alone."

Laughter bursts from Micah's chest as a tear rolls down his cheek. When his eyes meet mine again, I slip a simple platinum band on his ring finger. "I love you, Micah Reed. Today, tomorrow, forever."

The minister prattles on with the final words of the ceremony. But the second she says, "Micah, you may kiss your bride," the room vanishes.

Under the starry lights inside the place that brought Micah and me back together, we kiss as if no one else is in the room. Kiss as if this is the first and last time, wrapped in one. And when the kiss breaks, I stare into my favorite constellation.

"I love you, starlight."

"I love you more, hellcat." He kisses the tip of my nose. "Forever."

Reese

one

REESE

So damn tired of being lonely.

Never thought I'd see this day, yet here it is, slapping me in the face. Hard. Reminding me that I played the field far too long and took people for granted. Nagging me that it is time to grow up and settle down.

Too bad the man I want to settle with isn't here.

Once again, Trent is gone. Away on business. Flying across the US to oversee the next construction site in his business empire. A mirror image of the one in Tampa, just thousands of miles away.

I should be happy for him. Should congratulate him on the feats he has accomplished. Should be his biggest cheerleader as he nears the top of the wealthiest-people list in the Bay Area. He worked hard to get where he is and I should applaud his diligence.

Instead, I sit in my dark living room, surrounded by filth, pouting. Berating myself and my decisions.

Trent left three days ago for California. Told me he would be gone five days. As with every previous trip, he basically broke things off. Gave me permission to hook up with other people, guilt-free.

And I hate it. Hate his easy dismissal of me, of us. Hate that every time he does this, it feels like a knife to the chest. An effortless rejection that slashes and scars and fucking hurts for days. Makes me feel disposable and worthless.

"We don't need to do this." I wave my hands between us. *"Break up every time you go out of town."*

He rubs the back of his neck, averts his gaze, and sighs. "Reese, I don't want you to feel obligated or tied to me when I'm not here." His eyes close as he takes a deep breath. "And I'm gone more often than not." Dark-green irises meet mine, a silent plea in them begging me to understand. To accept and drop the argument. "It isn't fair to you. Don't limit yourself because I can't be here."

Irritation heats my skin as I consider his words. Play them over and over and let them sink in. Is it me who is limited *or him? Maybe he does this every time because* he *doesn't want to feel guilty for any acts he commits when he goes out of town.*

"You sure it's me you're worried about?" I ask before I lose the nerve.

His brows pinch together, his eyes narrowing. "Not sure I follow."

"If I complain about us breaking up every *trip you take, I don't think it's me who feels limited." Without outright saying it, I insinuate he is the one who doesn't want limitations. He doesn't want to be obligated or tied down. Because maybe his trips have more side adventures than I realize.*

"Say what you mean, Reese," he bites out. "We're grown men. No sense in skirting around how we feel." His face reddens as he works his jaw.

Braving a step forward, I swallow past the lump in my throat. Ignore the pang in my gut and building sweat on my brow. Take a deep breath and straighten my spine as I open my mouth to speak my truth.

"Are you sleeping with other people? While you're gone, I mean."

God, now that it is out in the open, I feel foolish. Immature and needy. Like a damn jealous nag.

Minutes pass as Trent simply stares. His face is void of expression. No hurt or shame or anger. No disbelief or confusion or humor. He's just... blank.

And damn if it doesn't throw my head into more of a tailspin.

On the verge of walking away, I study him for one last deep breath. Scrutinize his impassive expression. Stab. *With a shake of my head, I step back, pivot, and start my retreat.* I don't need this bullshit. I don't deserve this bullshit.

On the second step, a hand wraps around my bicep.

"Wait," Trent whispers. "Please."

I halt my retreat but don't spin to face him. Not yet.

"Are you?" I ask again.

His hand falls away, but the heat of him remains. A constant reminder Trent is more *than anyone that came before him. Trent is who I want. Who I need. If only my affections were reciprocated. If only luck were on my side.*

"No, Reese," he answers, sadness softening his voice. "I don't have sex with or date others while I'm gone."

I spin around at a dizzying speed. Drag a hand through my hair. Open my mouth to speak, then snap it shut as my mind races. Sucking in a deep breath, I close my eyes, count to three, and pray for clarity. As my eyes open, Trent runs a hand over his mouth and jaw.

"Then why?" The two-word question laced with incredulity. "Why all the dramatics when you leave? I... help me understand."

He steps into me, invades every ounce of my personal space, and frames my face with his hands. I gasp from the simple yet intimate touch. Because all I want to do is kiss him. Kiss him and make all this nonsense end. Kiss him and tell him with my lips I want no one except him.

But I don't move.

"How long have we been together now?" His question is rhetorical, so I don't answer. "Close to a year. Unless I discount my time away." He inches closer, his breath warm on my lips. "I hate leaving you. Hate that I'm gone a week or two at a time, and you're just here, waiting for me to return." On a deep inhale, he shakes his head. "It isn't fair to you. To sit and wait. To wish I was here. So, I give you a pass. Give you the freedom to do as you please, without guilt."

"But you're wrong," I whisper with my eyes on his lips. "You say the words, but there is no pass. Not really. Because the moment you return, we're right back where we left off."

He inches back and pinches the bridge of his nose. "This will get old, Reese."

"For who?" I rear back and meet his gaze as his hands clap his sides. "Because it sounds like you're fishing for excuses now."

Trent steps back, and I shiver at the chilled look on his face. "I don't need to make excuses, Reese," he bites out with more volume. He checks his watch and huffs out a breath. "And I don't have time to argue." He turns away and walks toward the bedroom.

"So that's it?" I ask, following in his wake. "You don't have time, so the conversation is done?"

He pops up the handle on his carry-on suitcase and wheels it out of the room. "No, of course not. But I have a flight to catch. I can't spend the next several hours debating this."

"When?"

He pockets his wallet, keys, and phone. "When, what?"

"When will we finish this conversation? Because it needs to happen."

He checks his watch again, and I want to scream. It has been maybe a minute since he last looked.

"When I'm back," he states, unlocking and opening the front door.

"Which is…"

"Five days."

Five days. I can hold off for five days. It isn't the longest he's been away. "Fine. Have a safe trip. See you when you're back."

Without another word, Trent leaves. The immediate silence is deafening. The sharp pain in my chest is excruciating. And with each new breath, I wilt from his absence. With every heartbeat, I shrink in on myself.

It's only five days. He'll be back in no time and we'll talk.

Five days.

Three days have come and gone without a word from Trent. On most of his trips, I get texts or picture updates. Small check-ins that let me know he thinks of me, that he cares.

This time around, nothing. Complete radio silence. And I hate it with every cell in my body. Hate the rift that suddenly exists between us. Hate that our relationship was left on a sour note. More than anything, I hate the feeling beneath my diaphragm. The one that begs me to reach out and initiate contact, but I fear it will do more damage than good.

His silence has taken its toll. Made me question if staying with him is really what I want or deserve. With each passing second, the gray cloud following me in his absence grows darker. Thicker. Angrier. Miserable.

I need to do something to fix this, fix us. Help us find balance in our off-kilter lives. Help us find a middle ground. A place where we can be together and not feel at odds.

Trent leads a busy life, but his workload is a lame excuse for us to not move forward. Countless couples with hectic schedules have meaningful, happy relationships. If he didn't care, he would let me go. And he hasn't. Not completely.

Deep in my bones, I know we will make this work. He just needs proof. Needs to be shown that if we both want this, us, we will overcome every obstacle thrown our way. Together.

Whatever it takes.

Because, dammit, I don't want a day without him.

Two

TRENT

Hands gripping the armrests, I jolt forward as the plane touches down in Tampa. No matter how many times I've flown, I still hate landings.

The pilot steers the plane toward the gate then slows to a stop. Clinks echo in the cabin as passengers unbuckle their seat belts, rise and fumble for their carry-ons. Everyone except me. Although I want off the plane, I am in no rush. Not with what awaits once I deplane.

"I fucked up," I mumble.

For the first time, I despise my job. Despise the guilt over being busy nonstop, something I once enjoyed. Most of all, I despise the ache in my chest every time I walk away from Reese. The hurt I cause him.

Before him, there was never a dull ache beneath my breastbone. Never a doubt about what I wanted from life. Never an impulse to give up everything to spend time with someone.

Now, my need for him is inescapable. A living, breathing life force. Something I won't exist without. I love and hate the hold he has on my heart. This unrelenting fist wrapped around the small organ in my chest. Reese gives me a new sense of purpose. New reasons to smile. But being with him also makes me irrational and unsteady and skeptical.

How the hell can our relationship move past sex and the occasional dinner together? How can we survive as a couple when I am often absent?

As the plane empties, I rise from my seat and stretch my limbs. Fishing my carry-on from the overhead compartment, I extend the handle and inch toward the exit. With each step forward, my stomach twists in a new knot. With each step forward, my breaths turn more jagged.

Only one person will ease this ache. Only one person will soothe the uncertainty. And damn, do I regret the last words we exchanged. Words that punched me in the gut. Words bearing resemblance to the end.

Please, whoever is listening, I beg you, don't let this be the end.

~

I should have called or texted him.

Mentally, I berate myself as I park next to Reese's car. We haven't spoken in five days, yet I assume it is perfectly acceptable to show up on his doorstep unannounced. Assume he wants to see me after how we left things.

Idiot.

What if he isn't alone? What if he actually took my words to heart and spent time with someone else? In the heat of the moment, I said something I didn't mean. Told him he had a free pass when I left. All but handed him a permission slip to be promiscuous.

What if, in a moment of anger or to spite me, he followed through? What if he *slept* with someone else?

Bile rises in my throat at the thought, but I shove it down. "No," I whisper to myself. "He wouldn't." Not after he fought so hard to keep what we have.

Leaving the suitcase in the car, I put one foot in front of the other and follow the path to Reese's front door. Sweat slicks my brow and temples as my heart pound, pound, pounds a vicious rhythm in my chest. Each step feels a mile long until I reach the door. My pulse kicks into fifth gear, the whooshing behind my ears all I hear.

Fuck. I am going to puke.

Bracing a hand on the wall, I close my eyes and take a deep breath. Then another. When the ground feels more stable beneath my feet, I open my eyes.

Everything will be fine. Once we talk, it will all be okay.

Knuckles meet metal as I knock on the door. My other hand drums my thigh as I wait for Reese to open the door. *Tap, tap, tap. Tap, tap, tap.* The concept of time vanishes as I wait for him to answer. Wait to see him, speak with him, touch him. When he doesn't answer, I knock again, this time with more gusto.

On the other side of the door, I hear a groan. *Or was that a moan?*

My heart drops. A fresh dose of acid trickles up and burns my throat.

Before I can bolt, the door swings open and I stop breathing.

Devilishly sexy, Reese stands shirtless in the doorway with his dark, curly locks rumpled. His skin slightly red and damp. Breath ragged and pulse pounding hard enough to see the vein throb in his neck.

Fuck, fuck, fuck. Too late. I am too damn late. We fought and I dismissed him. And now, he is done with me, with us. He took my words to heart and moved on.

Fuck.

I open my mouth to speak, but can't find my voice. Can't breathe. Can't think. Bending at the waist, I grip my knees and try to suck in a breath. Try to ease the sudden panic taking hold. My lungs burn as the world spins and I close my eyes.

"Shit." The word echoes in my ears as warm arms snake around my middle. "Breathe, T. Nice and slow. I got you."

I do as Reese says. One breath at a time, cool air fills my lungs. One breath at a time, my wobbly world stabilizes. With a stronger foothold, I inch back to my full height and open my eyes. Take in the room. Register during my momentary haze, Reese guiding us into his apartment.

Is he alone? God, please let him be alone.

"I… uh…" Scanning the apartment, I spot several take-out containers and beer bottles on the coffee table. The room dimly lit from the barely cracked blinds. "Sorry," I mutter.

Reese turns away from me and ambles into the kitchen without a word. I press my thumb and finger to my temples before finger-combing my hair as I take in the space again.

The apartment is a disaster. Reese isn't the tidiest human on the planet, but I have never seen his space in such disarray. Chinese food cartons, pizza boxes, ice cream containers. *Hope those are empty.* Beer bottles and energy drink cans. Mugs and paper plates and plastic utensils. Clothes on the table and couch and trailing down the hall. Envelopes and grocery store adverts on the floor.

I wrinkle my nose. *What the hell is that smell?* Like a mix of curdled milk and body odor and something else.

Blech.

"Sorry for what?" Reese asks as he exits the kitchen and hands me a bottle of water.

"Thanks." I take a long pull from the bottle before twisting the cap back in place. "Where do I begin?" I laugh without humor, and Reese stares at me with the blankest expression. I take in his sweat-slicked skin and can't hold back what I say next. "Are you alone?"

His eyes drop to his chest and he scowls. "Not that you deserve an answer, but yes. Was just trying to get out of my head. Thought maybe time on the treadmill would help."

Stupid, stupid, stupid.

Just because I created this fracture in our relationship doesn't mean Reese deepened the crack. If anything, he wanted to stitch us back together. Make us whole. And I refused him the time to do so.

"I fucked up," I blurt out. "And I shouldn't have left the way I did. It was wrong. *I* was wrong."

Reese nods but doesn't say a word. Not in agreement or to refute. And I deserve every bit of his silence. Every ounce of his torment.

"Can we please talk?" I ask, my tone pleading.

Again, he nods, then walks toward the living room. He shoves shirts and socks aside on the couch but makes no move to clear the trash on the table. Parking on the far end of the couch, he angles himself in my direction before crossing his arms over his chest. I take a seat, not quite at the other end of the couch, but also not the middle.

He needs space.

"I fucked up," I repeat. Feels as if I will reiterate this for weeks to come. "Relationships aren't my strong suit, obviously. Between my office hours and the constant travel, I've never had time for anyone. Never had someone I needed to make time for." I shake my head, eyes downcast as my fingers peel away the water bottle label. "But I want to make time for you." My brows pinch then relax as I look up and hold his stare. His tawny irises unwavering as they watch every word form on my lips. "It's just..." I close my eyes and search for what to say, but nothing seems sufficient.

"It's just what?"

My eyes open to meet his as I hear the slight change in his tone. Concern, maybe?

"How?" I lean forward, set the bottle on the floor, drop my elbows to my knees and put my face in my hands. My fingers lightly bruise the skin of my forehead before diving into my hair and tugging the strands. "How do I balance everything?" I straighten and give one last tug of my hair before holding my hands out. "How is it fair if I can't be what you need? If I can't be *here* when you need?"

The room falls silent once more as my words float through the air. As they sink in and take root.

This is why I never give myself over to someone fully. It isn't that I don't *want* to commit to someone. It's my lack of free time that keeps me from taking the next step.

Not being present... no one wants a nonexistent partner. Absence steals the possibility of healthy, long-term connections. So why put in the effort? Why hurt ourselves?

"Do I get a say?" he asks, voice gruff and pained. "Do I get a choice?" His voice a touch louder now as he shifts in his seat. "Yeah, when all this started"—he gestures between us—"I didn't expect it to be more than one night. Maybe two." Looking away from me, he works his jaw. "But here we are."

His eyes meet mine and I *feel* his ache. See his hurt in his glassy stare. And fuck... it burns like a hot branding iron to the heart.

"Here we are," I parrot on a whisper. I swallow past the dryness in my throat. Swallow past the nerves fizzling beneath the surface. "Of course, you get a say." I hang my head and stare at the stitch lines of the couch fabric. "But I don't want you to resent me," I admit, voice almost inaudible. "Ever."

The couch cushion wobbles slightly as Reese inches closer. Comfort I have no right to feel blankets me as he lays a hand on my knee. His thumb draws small circles and I bask in that simple touch. Delight in the fire that stirs just beneath the surface. Revel in the man that makes me feel more alive now than any day before he entered my life.

And god… I don't deserve him. Don't deserve his affection or forgiveness. But here he is, gifting me both.

Because Reese Triggs is a good man. A man worthy of much more than I give him. Oh, how I want to deserve him. How I want to be worthy of his heart.

"Our relationship may not fit some preconceived mold, but I don't care."

I lift my gaze to his. See the sincerity of his words in the set of his features. Feel the conviction of his words vibrating off him. And I do my best to soak it all in. Let his truth settle in my bones. Let it fill my lungs and pump my heart. I allow myself to believe him.

Because I want nothing more.

To be with Reese.

To *love* him.

For him to love me in return.

"Okay." I roll my lips between my teeth. "But how will this work?" My eyes drop to his lips and damn, I want to kiss him. Want to wrap him in my arms and ravage him breathless. But before I lose complete focus, I snap my eyes back to his. Concentrate on our conversation and think of how to make this work with him. "I work insane hours. Fly across the country for days at a time." With a soft shake of my head, I sigh. "How is that acceptable? You'd only have me for small slivers of time."

Every time I leave Reese, a new splinter etches my heart. It isn't only him suffering, but I don't dare act selfish in this moment. Don't compare my misery to his. They aren't the same.

When I started Centro Collective, I never imagined it growing to what it is today. A large-scale operation. Booming. Thriving. Fulfilling an undiscovered need.

Before I spoke full sentences, Dad had been shaping me to take over Callahan Financial and Associates. His father passed the business to him and he wanted to do the same. Pass a legacy torch. For years, I'd been convinced no other career path was suitable. No other career would bring me joy. Callahan Financial was endgame.

Until I saw a need.

Fresh out of college, I'd been working for my father's investment firm for six months. I'd had an appointment with a client that requested we meet outside the office. It was a first, but I agreed without hesitation. The man was a major player. Someone I needed to keep on my roster. Someone Callahan Financial wanted to keep happy.

So I drove more than an hour to meet him. We sat at a secluded table in the back of a coffee shop. And as we'd gone over investments, I'd surveyed the room. Taken in how many other people were talking business with a cup of coffee or tea and a bite to eat. Questioned why there wasn't a better place for meetings.

That day, my vision of Centro Collective was born. A place where people can meet with privacy. A place where professionals without storefronts can rent space to work from when necessary.

From the start, it has blown up. Taken on a life of its own. Morphed into more than I imagined possible.

Some of my travel is to curate items for the buildings. Other trips are to oversee new Centro Collective structures coming to life. What started as an idea has slowly turned into an empire. Being the head of it all is a thrill. Earning the title "Top-Tier Entrepreneur of the Bay Area" was a bonus.

But what have I sacrificed for said power?

"I'll take what I can get," Reese says, snapping me back into focus.

"Why?"

I don't mean to question him, but I need to know. Why is he so willing to take small percentages when someone else can give him one hundred percent? The notion seems ludicrous.

He lifts his hands and cups my jaw in both. Strokes his thumbs over my cheeks. Steals my breath as his penetrating gaze locks with mine. Then, ever so slowly, he leans forward to kiss my lips.

"Because I'm in love with you."

three

REESE

Did I say I'm in love with him? Out loud?

Shit.

Before I wrap my head around my confession, he frames my face, hauls me forward and crushes my lips with his. My stiff muscles loosen as his lips dance over mine. My pulse thunders beneath my sternum for a new reason. Every dark and panicked thought to cross my mind in his absence is replaced with warmth and light and love. Every worry I harbored about my feelings not being reciprocated evaporates.

He hasn't said the words back, but this kiss… Trent Callahan loves me too.

I groan when he breaks the kiss. A breathy chuckle leaves his lips as he drops his forehead to mine, our labored breaths floating between us.

Soft thumbs stroke the stubble on my cheeks. Slow and rhythmic. Hypnotic and gentle. On instinct, I melt into his touch. His affection. Him.

God, I missed him. Terribly.

"Never want to fight again," I mutter, reaching for his shirt and fisting the fabric in my hands.

"Me either." A chaste kiss presses my lips. "And I…"

I stop breathing as I wait for him to finish his thought. As I wait for him to tell me he feels the same. That he is in love with me too.

But with his hesitation, the room turns deathly silent. A chill sweeps over my skin as the weight of his silence suffocates me. Pulls me under and refuses to let go.

Inching back, I break the physical connection. Put several inches between us and take a deep breath.

I am a goddamn fool. He doesn't love me. Not in the way I want him to. How can he?

Rising from the couch, I step around the coffee table and aim my feet toward the hall.

Less than twenty steps and I will be in my room. Less than twenty steps and I will escape this awkward, one-sided love confession.

But I don't make it far. On my third step, Trent bolts from the couch and darts around the other side of the table, blocking my path.

"Please don't walk away." His eyes widen with panic. His chest rising and falling faster with each breath.

I want to cave to his wishes. Want to stand here with him, be here with him, love him, but fuck... it hurts. It hurts to expose yourself to someone, spill your heart at their feet, and not get an inkling in return. Yes, he kissed me as if he were confessing his love. But he hasn't *said* anything.

Should I expect him to say he loves me too? Absolutely not, and I didn't assume he would. I shouldn't need to hear the words, but I want them. Something, *anything*, to let me know he wants more than the occasional hookup and slumber party with cuddles would be a comfort.

"I don't know what else to do."

"Give me a minute." He holds up a finger. "Please. I have more to say and, for the first time in my life, I can't seem to articulate a damn word." He laughs without humor, a slight shake of his head. "Please, Reese." His glassy eyes plead more than his words. "All I ask is you give me a moment. Let me try to get what I'm feeling out."

I step into him, my gaze locked on his evergreen irises. "Yeah. Okay."

We move back to the couch and I send a silent petition to the universe. *Please, don't let this man crush my heart.*

∼

After hours of conversation and confessions, a new tranquility blankets my heart.

The first thirty minutes, Trent expressed his concerns over our relationship moving forward. Difficult as it was to remain tight lipped and not counter his justification to stay casual, I kept my thoughts to myself and gave him the floor.

With his chaotic schedule, Trent harbors a world of guilt for not being able to devote more time to me or our relationship. When he said his piece, I jumped in headfirst and squashed his reasons immediately. I explained how I knew what I was getting into as our relationship evolved. He argued and I opposed. When I told him his passion and drive and tenacity were reasons why I loved him, he cut off the debate.

And then words I didn't expect from him so soon came tumbling out.

"I love you, Reese. And it scares me to no end."

The next hour was spent exploring why he feared loving me. More than anything, his apprehension stems from his inability to be present enough. His inability to provide me with what I need emotionally.

"I don't want you to wake up one day and resent me for not being what you hoped for or needed."

Our conversation ended long ago, but we haven't made a move to leave the couch. His head on my shoulder, our arms hooked at the elbow, his sweet, woodsy scent is a balm for my soul. I close my eyes and breathe him in as the room grows darker from the setting sun.

For the first time since he walked out the door five days ago, the world feels more stable. As if my knees won't buckle. As if I won't crumble each time I wake up alone.

"I'm in this for the long haul," I whisper into the fading light of day.

He nods subtly, giving me more of his weight. "Just bear with me. That's all I ask."

Twisting, I press a kiss to his crown. Hug him closer to my side. Bask in the revelations of the day. "Wish granted."

four

TRENT

The hardest thing I have done is ask for help. It isn't a matter of pride. More my penchant for perfection.

But the Monday following my return from California, help is exactly what I started scavenging for.

I walked into the office and dove headfirst into work. Financials and emails and travel plans hadn't been at the top of my list as per usual. Instead, I made several calls to friends in my network. Calls I never thought I would make, but I knew it was time.

If I wanted a future with Reese, I needed to take this step. So I did.

Glancing at the time on my laptop, I wrap up an email to Centro Collective's local event coordinator. Bernadette has spent the last month preparing for our seventh-anniversary party. Each year, the festivities grow more grandiose. Decadent food, lavish drinks, live music, and memories our guests will share for years to come. Tickets to the event sell out in hours. The celebration ranked by several media outlets as *one party you don't want to miss.*

As I click send on the email, my phone intercom buzzes. "Mr. Callahan?"

"Yes, Dale?"

"Ms. Prescott is here for your two o'clock, sir."

"Please bring her back. Thank you, Dale."

The intercom disconnects and I take a deep breath. Work to calm the jitters beneath my diaphragm. Wipe my damp palms on my slacks. *When was the last time I was this nervous?*

You'd think it would have been when I realized my relationship with Reese was turning more serious. When we shifted from casual hookups to… more. But I never got jittery when it came to Reese and how I cared for him. For some inexplicable reason, I never broke a sweat at Reese and the possibility of a serious future together. Our relationship discovered a stronger foothold as of recent, but I never doubted how he felt. Now and again, I worried if we would last. Worried if my career would rip us apart. But each time I was hit with uncertainty, I quashed it. I never let the restlessness take hold.

Unlike now.

Maybe because Centro Collective is, for lack of a better term, my child. And what parent easily finds an adequate and respectable *stepparent* for their baby? Isn't that what this meeting is—an interview to find the right *co-parent* for my *child*?

Knocking sounds as Dale raps his knuckles on the doorframe. "Ready, sir?" I bite my tongue not to laugh at Dale calling me sir.

As CEO of Centro Collective—nationally known as Callahan Industries Inc—I have heard the rumors. That I am a stuffed shirt and drill sergeant to my employees. Of course, the people that spread such fallacies have never worked for or with me or stepped foot in any of my buildings. They are also the same people that call me a daddy's boy. That whisper how I didn't work for what I have, that my father must be a silent partner or major financial contributor.

None of the rumors are true. Those who have stood by me since the beginning know the truth. Dale is one of those people, and he most definitely does not call me sir unless a new face is around.

"Yes, Dale. Thank you."

As he steps aside to let her enter, I fetch the folder from my credenza with Beverly Prescott's résumé. Hers is one of many I sifted through the past two days. A résumé detailed with prestigious business names and experience in all aspects of the companies. She'd climbed the ladder and had the accolades to prove it.

Pushing back, I rise from the chair, step around the desk, and offer my hand. "Ms. Prescott, I'm Trent Callahan. Pleasure to meet you." I gesture toward the love seat, chairs, and coffee table where I prefer to conduct in-person meetings. "Have a seat."

As we settle in, a wave of repose hits me without warning. Something about this woman puts me at ease. Perhaps it is her maternal vibe. Or the fact she has worked in businesses similar to mine for more than twenty years. Whatever it is, my anxiety from minutes ago evaporates.

This is what I need. This is how I better my relationship with Reese. By taking back my time.

I pluck the pen from inside my suit jacket and open the folder with her résumé. "Tell me a little about yourself, Ms. Prescott."

∼

TRENT

Celebration is in order.

REESE

I won't say no. What are we celebrating?

For the first time since starting Centro Collective, I leave work on time. Well, on time for me. While most people work eight-hour days, I typically work ten to twelve, if not more. And weekends… what are those?

But after a lengthy interview and chat with Beverly Prescott, I made her an offer. What I didn't expect was for her to accept the offer before exiting my office. Not a minute after her departure, I called human resources, and Beth Anne pulled up the necessary paperwork.

In a blink, I'd hired an assistant. Well, Beverly would be more than an assistant —more like my counterpart, my right-hand woman. Not only would she take on the bulk of the paperwork I disliked, but she would also share some of the travel load. Similar to a COO, but with less overall company control. Beverly will help ensure Centro Collective runs without hiccups. Yes, I would have my hands in all things while she acclimates, but knowing I would no longer be attached at the hip to my job is a breath of fresh air.

I hired my interviewee.

Definitely calls for drinks and dinner.

Let me take you out. A proper date.

Dots dance in the little gray bubble then disappear. This happens again and again as I wait for his response. I bite the inside of my bottom lip as his message comes through.

Like flowers and candles and a romantic table for two?

My lips curve up in a smile. In two weeks, Reese and I will celebrate one year together. Though our relationship has felt on and off during the past twelve months, neither of us stepped out. During the weeks apart, when I "broke up" with Reese, we had the opportunity to be unfaithful. We remained loyal.

But I have never taken him on a date. A *real* date. Sure, we have attended events at Centro Collective together. Occasionally had drinks with his friends or grabbed a quick bite at a restaurant. I wouldn't classify those as dates, though. Not romantic dates.

Now that I will have more personal time, I plan to court and date the hell out of Reese Triggs.

Possibly. Be ready in an hour. I'll pick you up.

I love it when you're bossy 😌

Don't I know it.

Tapping the phone icon, I call a friend and cash in on a favor. Less than five minutes later, I pocket my phone, grab my keys, exit the office and lock up for the day.

As I slip behind the wheel of my car, happiness stings my cheeks. A delight I gladly accept, so long as Reese is the reason. So long as he is at my side.

five

REESE

I toss my phone on the bed and dart to the bathroom.

One hour. That man only gave me one hour to get ready. Who does that? Trent Callahan, of course.

Cranking the hot water in the shower, I strip and dash under the spray. Wet my hair and lather it with shampoo. Rinse, then repeat the same steps with the conditioner. I load the loofah with body wash and do a thorough scrub down. As the last of the suds swirl down the drain, I shut off the water and step out to towel off.

After some quick manscaping, I head for the closet in search of clothes.

Trent gave no clues as to where he plans to take me for dinner. Knowing him, though, it won't be the mom-and-pop Italian joint up the street. No, Trent Callahan will wine and dine me tonight.

I pluck black slacks and a charcoal button-down from hangers. After slipping them on, I head back to the bathroom to add product to my curls and splash on the cologne that makes Trent ravenous. With one final look in the mirror, I exit the bathroom, grab socks and shoes, and head for the living room.

Days ago, the apartment was unrecognizable. Literal garbage and sweat-drenched clothes blanketed every surface. The smell was wretched, but I'd somehow become immune in my wallowing. And since no one else has set foot in here since Peyton moved out, I had zero concerns over the appearance or funk.

Until Trent and I talked and mended things.

The next day, I'd woken up hours before my shift at the rec center. Filled trash bags with days' worth of debris. Loaded the washer with a mountain of laundry. When I got home from the rec center, I continued my cleaning frenzy until it was time for my shift at the restaurant. I sprayed and wiped every table and countertop. Dusted and vacuumed and mopped. Sanitized the hell out of every room. Tossed the wet clothes in the dryer. And before I left for job two, I felt ten times better. The embarrassment over my living space dwindled.

Trent and I spent most of the weekend together. When we weren't cuddled on the couch, strolling along the beach surf or in bed, making up for lost time, we were at work. He at the Collective and me at the restaurant or home cleaning.

Parking on the couch, I get to work on my socks and shoes. A knock echoes through the apartment. Rising from the couch, I stumble as I wiggle my foot into the second shoe on the way to the door.

"Damnit," I mutter as I almost face-plant on the floor.

Righting myself, I walk a little slower to the door. *Like a nervous preteen all over again.* I disengage the lock, twist the handle, and open the door. At the sight of Trent, my skin heats as a massive smile stretches my face.

The man bought me flowers. Fucking. Flowers.

Swoon.

"Hi," I choke out then clear my throat. I open the door wider and step back. "Come in."

One step, then another, Trent leans forward and presses his lips to mine. "Hey." The three-letter word comes out raspy. He holds up the colossal bundle of red roses in brown paper. "Should put these in something before we go."

Can't believe he bought me flowers.

I had been joking when I texted him about flowers and candles. Should have known better.

Rummaging through the kitchen cabinets, I find an old vase buried in the back of one. Peyton must have forgotten it when she packed.

I fill the vase halfway with water and bring it to the counter where Trent unties the bouquet. After sprinkling in the flower food packet, he shoves the whole bouquet in the water. He fluffs out a few stems then smiles, obviously proud of himself.

"I love them," I admit quietly.

He turns to face me and takes a step closer. Inches apart, his warm, minty breath paints my lips. He lifts a hand and cups my cheek. "I love you." His eyes close for a beat. "God… never thought I'd say that to anyone other than family."

Leaning forward, I close the space between us and press my lips to his. The kiss is sweet and tender for one, two, three breaths. And then the energy between us shifts. Grows hungry. Wild. His tongue swipes my bottom lip before he sucks it between both of his. My hands go to his hips and haul him forward, my fingers bruising his flesh beneath the wool. Our tongues tangle and taste and beg for more.

And all too soon, he breaks the kiss. A groan rumbles in my chest and he chuckles at my obvious objection.

"We'll have time for more later." He drops a chaste kiss to my lips then inches away. "Don't want to miss our reservation."

"I'd rather stay in and have you for dinner," I tease.

"Another night." He takes my hand in his and walks backward toward the door. "I've never truly dated. Let me date the hell out of you. Dinners and movies and romantic walks under the full moon. Let me court you, love you." The last two words come out a touch softer.

As we reach the table in the foyer, I pocket my keys, wallet, and phone. I give a slight nod as we step out into the warm evening air. "Alright. Show me what you got, Callahan."

～

From the beginning, before Trent and I got to the *let's share more about ourselves* phase, I knew he was affluent. Not because he told me as much or I was up to date on who was wealthy in the area.

Trent radiates prestige. In the way he carries himself, in his choice of attire and how he speaks. Hell, the man owns an influential business and travels at least once a month for work.

But I have never taken stock in *how* wealthy Trent is. His money isn't why I love him.

In this place, a restaurant with napkins that probably cost more than my attire, I shrink inside myself. Crumple under judgmental eyes. Grow nauseous as I read the prices on the menu. *I don't belong here.* The words bounce around in my skull as I scan the restaurant for the third time.

Dim lighting from opulent chandeliers overhead. A single, lit white candle and red rose in a narrow, cylindrical vase at the heart of each black cloth-covered table. Each place setting with more plates and cutlery than I use in two meals. A wine menu as long as the book I recently read… with no prices listed.

Perspiration dampens my temples, my forehead, the back of my neck. The words on the menu go blurry as I stare at the price of the appetizers. *That is more than I make in an hour. Jesus.* Covertly, I glance over my menu and across the table to Trent, who appears completely unfazed by the dainty menu items and prices that could fill a cart of groceries.

"Anything catch your eye?" Trent asks as he lays his menu off to the side.

I swallow down the desire to scold him for bringing me here, to a place I don't belong. Voicing such opinions will only serve to upset us both. The last thing I want is to spark another argument. If I want to be with Trent, I need to change my perception of his lifestyle. Trent is more than a beautiful face and brilliant mind. He also wields power.

Awkward as it may be to adjust to this reality, this side of him, in order for us to have a future, I need to be willing to bend and flex with him. Dine at the ritzy restaurants and wear the nice clothes as I lock arms with him at events. It won't be an everyday occurrence, but it will happen often enough to be considered normal.

Pushing past my natural inclination to veto every item due to the price tag, I inhale deeply and say, "Can't decide if I want fish or steak."

"Had my eye on the New York Strip. Get the fish and we can share."

I nod, picking up my water and downing half the glass. "Sounds like a plan."

The server returns and takes our respective orders, not writing anything down. Trent adds the artisanal cheese appetizer to the order as well as a bottle of cabernet sauvignon.

Dark-green irises lock me in place the moment the server steps away. His fingers twist the stem of the water glass back and forth, back and forth, as his head tips slightly to the side. Wordlessly, he regards me for a beat. Studies me as my brows twitch on occasion and I bite the inside of my cheek. His scrutiny doesn't add to my anxiety or make me uncomfortable. If anything, it has me curious about how much he sees when his eyes take me in.

"You're uneasy," he states. Since he didn't pose it as a question, I don't respond. One corner of his mouth kicks up. "But not with me."

I shake my head. As I open my mouth to tell him he is partially correct, the server returns to the table with the wine and two glasses. Setting the glasses down, he uncorks the bottle, pours a small amount into one glass, and offers it to Trent.

Mesmerized, I watch as Trent swirls the wine in the glass before bringing it to his nose and inhaling deeply. He shifts the rim of the glass to his lips, tips back, and takes a small sip. Two breaths pass before he swallows and nods. The server fills both glasses, places the bottle on the table, then disappears.

Needing something to settle my nerves, I scoop up the glass and guzzle half the contents. Trent doesn't say a word, but I see the smirk on his lips behind his own glass.

"Uneasy isn't the right word," I finally say. "More like overwhelmed. This"—I gesture around the room with my chin—"is a lot to take in."

He gives a slight nod. "At times, it is for me too." His eyes latch on mine as he grants me his devilishly handsome half smile. "Believe it or not, this isn't my scene most of the time. Sure, I know a thing or two about quality and what I like, but most of that stems from my upbringing." Leaning forward, he braces his elbows on the table and clasps his fingers in front of his mouth. "My scene is more like where we met."

Flashes of that night, almost a year ago, play in my memory. The gay nightclub in Tampa. Too many drinks. Dancing and sweating and gyrating against him for hours. His lips on mine in the middle of the dance floor. The drive back to my place. Lips and tongues and teeth on skin. The way he moaned my name and fisted my hair.

Damn, that was a great night.

"We should go there again," I say, heat crawling up my neck and cheeks.

"Mmm, I agree." He sips his wine. "Another night, though. We already have plans tonight."

"We do?"

"Yes."

Over the next hour, I focus on Trent and push away the luxury bleeding from the walls. He tells me about the woman he hired today and how that will alleviate a hefty amount of his workload and travel. I tell him about the sixtysomething that wouldn't stop flirting at the rec center pool today. We talk and laugh and enjoy our first legit date.

When the server delivers the bill, I sip my water and think about anything other than money. Minutes later, we are in the car and on the road.

We drive a few miles down Gulf Boulevard before Trent flips the blinker and turns onto a cobblestone driveway. Before I can ask where we are, he rolls down his window and punches in a code to access the gated drive. I stop breathing as the car stops in front of a million-dollar house. The sheer size of it swallows me whole.

This is his *house.* I swallow. Try to remember how to breathe. *This man is worth more at thirty-six than I will earn in my lifetime.*

I don't deserve him. And he deserves much more than the likes of me.

Six

TRENT

Bringing him here without warning was foolish. I see it in the glazed-over look in his eyes.

Fuck. What was I thinking?

My hand hovers over the keypad to unlock the front door. "We can leave," I blurt out as my hand falls to my side. "If this is too much."

He reaches for and takes my hand, giving it a squeeze. "No." His eyes shift from me to the front door. "It's just… a lot, and all in one night." Soft laughter leaves his lips. "It's been almost a year and I'm just now seeing this side of you. I knew it existed." He shrugs. "Guess I compartmentalized it all."

Makes sense. It hadn't been my intention to wait this long to bring Reese to my home. Between my work schedule and wanting time with him, it had been easier to stay at his place. But it was time for that to change.

In the past, I'd never brought men home. My father taught me at a young age to be leery of outsiders. *"Learn who they really are before they step foot in your home."* I'd thought he was paranoid… until one of his newer employees got caught stuffing Mom's jewelry in his pocket. One occurrence was all it took for Dad to never host parties at the house again.

Reese has never given me reason to mistrust him—not in life or love—which is why I feel safe opening my home to him. But I didn't consider how he would take in the magnitude of my life. It is no secret to him that I have money. Tonight just happens to be the first time I *flaunt* said money.

"Promise me something."

He narrows his eyes for a breath. "Okay," he drawls out the word.

"If you want to leave, at any time, you'll tell me."

Leaning forward, he presses a gentle kiss to my lips. I don't miss the slight tremble in his touch. "Promise."

Entering the code, I unlock the front door and walk us inside. I disengage the alarm and flip on the light in the foyer. Much as I want to show off my house and give Reese a tour, I don't want to add fuel to the *too much in one night* fire.

His fingers threaded with mine, I steer us toward the kitchen. As we step into the room, lights under the cabinets come to life and glow softly in the darkness. Beside me, Reese stiffens, but I continue forward.

"Nightcap?" I ask as I twist to face him.

He nods. "Yeah, sure."

Releasing my hold on him, I go to the bar area of the kitchen, turn over two tumblers, and pour bourbon into the glasses. He watches my every move until I hand him a drink, his eyes dropping to the glass as he brings it to his lips. I wait for his reaction as he sips the sweet, earthy liquor.

His Adam's apple bobs. "Smooth," he whispers.

I down the contents of my glass then set both of ours on the counter. "It is."

In the next breath, I take his hand and walk us through the house. A slow trek up the stairs, down the north hall and into the bedroom suite. The moment we pass the threshold, my skin buzzes and body hums.

No one has felt this right.

"Take off my clothes, Reese." I drop his hand, spin to face him, and walk backward into the room. "Stake your claim. On me. In my home. In my bed."

His apprehension from moments ago morphs into fire. He toes off his shoes and kicks them aside but makes no move to strip his own clothes. Like a hunter stalking prey, he saunters in my direction.

Hypnotized by his gaze, I swallow when his tongue darts out to lick his lips. A hand reaches for my belt, unlatching the buckle and whipping it from the loops. Dexterous fingers tug at the base of my dress shirt, pulling the tails from my slacks before popping each button and shoving the material down my arms.

Inches from my skin, his breath is hot and hungry as he slowly strips me bare. But he doesn't touch my exposed flesh. Not yet. Our labored breaths echo in the room as my slacks puddle at my feet. I kick them to the side and pant as I wait for what Reese will do next.

Before I conjure the countless ways he might take me, he drops to his knees and stares up at me as if I am a god. His hands take my hips, knead my flesh for two breaths, then slowly peel my briefs down.

I cup his cheek as my cock stands proudly before him. "Take what's yours, Reese. What will always be yours."

Eyes on mine, his calloused fingers trail up my thighs and around my hips until they dig into the muscles of my ass and haul me forward. And before I can take a breath, the heat of his mouth wraps around my length.

Fuck.

~

The scent of sex mixed with Reese's cologne fills my nose as I wake. Darkness blankets the room and I don't know if it's because the sun hasn't risen or the curtains block it out.

Either way, I don't care. Reese is in my arms, his back to my front, and there is nowhere else I want to be.

My eyes drift closed as I inhale the smell of him. Let it soothe my soul and give me life. Reese has always done that, provided comfort and brightened my world. Since day one, he wrapped me up and never let go. Not that I would want him to.

Without thinking, I kiss the back of his neck. Tighten my hold on him.

A groan rumbles in his chest before he rubs his ass against my now-thickening erection. "Naptime over?" He laces his fingers with mine and rocks against me once more. "Mmm. Definitely over."

Before I get a word in, he guides my hand down his chest, his abdomen, to the junction of his thighs, where his cock is hot and thick and waiting. I kiss the back of his neck again, this time with tongue and teeth, as I wrap my fingers around his cock.

"So fucking perfect," I growl in his ear.

Reaching behind, he palms the back of my head and holds me to him. I pump his cock in slow, measured strokes with a slight pinch when I reach the tip. Just how he loves it. His other hand fists the sheet as I stroke myself between his ass cheeks.

His cock thickens further in my hand, and I know he is close. I rock my hips faster while keeping the same pace with his cock. A deep, guttural moan fills the air and I bite down where his shoulder and neck meet. He comes on the next stroke up, and I follow, our orgasms painting the sheets and our flesh.

And before either of us comes down from our high, I blurt out, "Move in with me."

Reese freezes, and the air turns to ice.

Fuck.

seven

REESE

Heat of the moment or legitimate question?

After a year together, Trent asking me to move in isn't outrageous. But midorgasm…

Did he actually mean to ask?

Not giving a damn about the sheets or the mess, I roll over until we are face to face. *I need to see him.* Though the room is dark, my eyes immediately find his. Hope glints in his eyes while fear tugs at his brows.

"Are you serious?" I ask, keeping my voice as level as possible. "Or was that a slip?"

His hand comes to my cheek as he leans in and kisses my lips. "I didn't mean for it to come out like that, or during sex, but yes…" The soft skin of his thumb caresses my stubble. "I love you, Reese. I want to be with you. Share my life with you. Exist in the same space." His eyes dart between mine. "Move in with me," he whispers.

I digest his words. As much as I would love to scream *yes*, this should be something I give more consideration.

"It's not a no, but can I think on it?"

I don't miss the slight flinch in his expression, but it is probably because he isn't used to waiting for answers. "Yes. Of course." He glances at the clock on the side table. "It's early. Let's shower and have breakfast before I drive you home."

And just like that, it feels as if the topic never came up. *Ugh.*

We shower in silence and without any attempts at teasing or tasting. Although he says to leave them, I strip the sheets while he heads downstairs to make breakfast. *I just need a minute to think.*

As I tug the linens free, I give the idea of living with Trent merit. Of living in this monstrosity of a house. Transitioning from minuscule to immeasurable. Taking this step with him is huge. Just as momentous as us exchanging I love yous.

Can I do this? Coexist with him in this world every day?

By the time I reach the bottom floor, Trent has scrambled eggs, bacon, and buttered toast on plates. Silence clouds around us as we eat and get ready to leave. A silence more deafening than the loudest sound. I hate everything about this silence. It is a punishment. A punishment I don't deserve.

As we pull out of the driveway, I swallow past every ounce of fear. Reaching over the console, I take his hand and thread our fingers. Stare at our joined hands. "You know I love you, right?"

"Why do I not like the start of this conversation?" he asks, emotion thick in his voice.

I risk a glance at his profile and see him swallow. "I love you. I'm *in* love with you."

His eyes leave the road for a split second and flash in my direction. "I love you too." Warm fingers reinforce their hold on my hand.

"I want to say yes."

We reach a red light and he twists to regard me. "Then say yes." A horn honks and he groans before facing forward to drive.

I swallow past the truth lump thickening in my throat. "What if living together isn't what we expect? You're busy running an empire and I work two jobs to make ends meet." He opens his mouth to cut in and I hold up a hand. "And before you tell me I don't need to work, not happening."

Steering the car into the apartment complex, he remains quiet as he parks beside my car. He cuts the engine but doesn't make a move otherwise. He simply stares out the windshield. Several breaths pass before he shrugs and turns to meet my panicky gaze.

"I'm pretty optimistic. In most things. And this, us"—he gestures between us—"I am damn confident will work out."

"Damn confident, huh?" He nods and I continue. "So what happens when I complain about your hours and not giving me what I need?"

His lips kick up into that devilish smile I can't resist. The smile that lured me in. "Then I work less or take you with me on trips. As far as giving you what you need…" He leans over the console and crooks his finger. Leaning in, I leave a breath between us. "Reese Triggs, I will *always* give you what you need." With that, he crushes my lips with his.

When the kiss breaks, I feel dizzy. Not just from his lips on mine but also because I am about to change everything. I am about to leap. Change us forever.

"Then I say yes," I whisper.

As long as Trent is by my side, as long as he loves me, the answer will always be yes.

eight

TRENT

Too much is happening all at once. Major changes at work with the addition of Beverly Prescott. Even bigger changes in my personal life as Reese slowly packs up his apartment and prepares to move into my house. I welcome change, but to have two major life events simultaneously… my ribs constrict and shorten my breaths.

In the past month, Beverly Prescott has learned a lot about Callahan Industries. More than any other person. With the exception of me, naturally.

Each morning, her heels clap the polished concrete floor as she enters her office. The office next to mine. She stows her purse and swanky tote, brews a cup of coffee in her aqua-colored Keurig, then walks into my office with the cinnamon roll-scented beverage, pen and paper. On Mondays, we discuss the week's schedule and any changes. What meetings I will attend and the ones on her roster. Trips out of state and which of us will go. And that is just Monday.

Tuesday through Friday is… exhausting.

For someone with a stellar résumé and jaw-dropping accolades, Beverly Prescott needs a lot of assistance and attention. Time was something she was to grant me, not take away.

Overall, the addition of her position has been good. Hiccups were something I expected, as well as the unease of bringing in an unfamiliar face and sharing my role. Any person in my shoes would be uncomfortable handing over a key to the kingdom. I built this company from the ground up. Have invested millions of dollars and countless hours. Letting go, even just a little, is difficult.

New employee and expected hiccups aside, something is *off*.

Relinquishing smaller tasks has been easier. Ms. Prescott is now a major point of contact within the company. She checks in with construction managers at the sites being built then reports back with details. Anything requiring an executive decision still comes to my desk. It is too soon to allow her that level of power. She also reaches out to the general managers at each location. Discusses day-to-day business and concerns. Offers solutions to drive revenue.

Also on her list of responsibilities is data collection from each Centro Collective location. She enters the details into spreadsheets for weekly review by yours truly. Eventually, the task will involve cross-checking the data with sums on invoices and statements.

The majority of the jobs I've doled out are monotonous. Figures and number crunching, paperwork and general tasks most would handle without assistance. Basic administrative work I'd expect someone with a lesser skill set to accomplish effortlessly.

Giving up bigger components of the job has been stressful. Allowing her to fly in my stead to different locales and touch base with each Centro Collective crew in person—which has only happened once to Orlando. Talking with the managers and staff and being an integral part of the company I spent years establishing.

I get that not many CEOs visit every branch of their company. I get that they don't immerse themselves in the day-to-day tasks that can be delegated to someone else. But I am not like every other business owner.

Being involved, in some fashion, with every facet of my business is vital. This company is my name, my lifeblood, my future. How will I recognize problems within the company walls if I am clueless about the standard operation?

I don't *need* to do it all, but relinquishing parts of my job twists a knife in my gut.

"Morning, Mr. Callahan," Beverly singsongs as she waltzes into my office with her confection-scented beverage. A smile on her pink-painted lips as she reaches the chair. She sets her coffee and notepad on the table then takes a seat.

"Good morning, Ms. Prescott."

Unlike everyone else in the office, I still address Beverly Prescott formally. Those not in my inner circle would call me an asshole for still using formalities with her, but I don't care what others think. Not when it comes to *my* business. Informal titles are earned with time and trust and evidence you will stay long term.

One month is nowhere near enough time for any staff member to earn my trust or easygoing persona. If the queasiness over the past week is any indication, trust will be a challenge with this woman.

Trust your intuition. It hasn't failed you yet.

Can't quite put my finger on it, but something is not aboveboard with Beverly Prescott. Her sunny disposition and penchant for long hours seem too... perfect. Now and then, I question the sincerity of her smile and high-pitched greetings. I analyze her eagerness to stay late at the office, later than everyone else. More than anything, it is the random questions she asks out of nowhere. Questions that dig a little too deep into Callahan Industries. And questions too personal for someone speaking with her new boss.

I collect the tablet from my desk and meet her at the circle of seats. "What updates do you have for me?"

She flips through a few pages of her notepad and I grind my jaw to keep from huffing in frustration. I drum my fingers as I wait for her to locate her current notes. The longer she fumbles, the more my blood heats.

"Raul from the Chicago store—"

"Location," I cut her off, the word blade sharp as it leaves my lips.

"Yes, Mr. Callahan." She clears her throat, takes a sip of her coffee, then continues. "Raul from the Chicago location says all the spaces have been rented and there is now a waiting list for openings."

Expansion of specific Centro Collective locations has been brewing for several months. Waiting lists equal demand. And demand means it is time to move forward with add-ons.

"What else?" I tap on the notes app on my tablet and type *speak with Raul.*

She shuffles through the scribbled pages of her notepad again and I growl internally. Scanning the next page, she stops. "Nothing else to report this week." A white, toothy smile spreads wide on her face.

"Nothing?" I deadpan as I set down my tablet.

She shakes her head, her smile falling as she takes in my clenched jaw and obvious irritation.

"Ms. Prescott, what job am I paying you to do?" I bite out. I don't ask the question to get an actual answer. So when she opens her mouth to speak, I hold up my hand. "I know what you are being paid to do." My lips purse as I cross my arms over my chest. "Hell, I created the job. Wrote the damn job description myself."

"I-I—"

"Dale is my personal assistant, Ms. Prescott. I don't need another. What I *do* need is someone to pick up the excess. Someone to act in my stead when I cannot attend a meeting or travel or spend all night in the office. I need someone competent and not just pretty on paper." With each word, my voice escalates. Takes on an acerbic edge. "Someone organized, that can multitask and answer a damn question in regard to my business without fumbling."

Her glassy eyes widen as she fidgets in her chair; my blunt nature not something she is accustomed to. Until now, I have coddled her. Let her dysfunctionality slide.

But the time for games is over. I hired her because she was the best of all the candidates. Her résumé was gold. Speech articulate and professional. Appearance sharp and polished. She walked into the interview and delivered everything I was looking for. She wowed me with promises. Held her own.

That Beverly was a ruse. And if there is one thing I despise, it is dishonesty.

I will not be played the fool.

I rise from the chair, walk back to my desk, and rest my hands on the surface. After two breaths, I meet her gaze. "You have two weeks to prove you can do the job as described, Ms. Prescott." I straighten my spine and square my shoulders. "If I deem you incapable of the role, I have no choice but to let you go." I sit in my desk chair and wake my computer up. "You can go," I dismiss her without looking in her direction.

In my periphery, she gathers her belongings, hugs them to her chest, and shuffles out of the office. When the soft click of the office door closing sounds, I deflate in my seat.

"Fuck," I whisper, dropping my head in my hands.

When something appears too good to be true, it most likely is. And fuck my life, because Beverly Prescott came across as the perfect person to be my right hand.

Now, I am not so sure. Now, I have more work to do.

nine

REESE

"Sorry, Reese. If it were up to me, I wouldn't fire anyone." Jake props his hands on his hips and looks to the side. He purses his lips and huffs out a breath. "Not that it'll make you feel better, but it looks like the owner is selling or declaring bankruptcy. Better to get out now."

Is there a great way to lose your job? No, never.

Hell, I could be a server at one of the thousands of restaurants in the Bay Area. Could make bank at plenty of the flashy places on the water or in the ritzy hotels. Stockpile my savings and pay off my car loan a year earlier. But I chose to stay at this family-owned, twenty-four-hour diner because I love the people—customers and coworkers. They are family. People who share their life stories with me and vice versa.

Being fired… I'm gutted. Like my family got ripped away.

I clap Jake on the shoulder and plaster on an artificial smile. "Just doing your job, man. Really hope they don't sell. Would be a shame to lose what they worked so hard to build."

"Agreed." He reaches for and takes my hand. "Been a pleasure working with you, Reese. We'll mail the final pay stub."

I drop his hand and take one last look around the open storeroom. Large cans of vegetables and fruits and crushed tomatoes line the bottom shelves. Rice and dried beans and pasta on the shelves above. As my eyes climb, my vision blurs. *I hate this.*

"Actually, will you call me and hold it? With the move, I don't want it lost in the mail."

He cups the back of his neck and squeezes. "Shit, how did I forget that was coming up? You ready?"

With a shake of my head, I chuckle. "Is anyone ever ready to move?" I untie my apron and toss it in the bin. "Everything but necessities are packed. The heavy lifting happens this weekend."

Discomfiture rolls over me like an incoming tide, a sense I no longer belong here, and I hate how much I want to bolt for the door. Run from a place I've always felt welcome, at home. Jake says it isn't personal, that several others will suffer the same fate, but damn, it stings. Like a parent slapping you across the face, then crying because they hurt you.

Nausea hits out of nowhere. Sweat slicks the back of my neck. I take a deep breath, beg the bile to stay down, then swallow. *I need out of here.*

I take a step toward the back door, lift a hand and wave. "See you in a couple weeks."

A sad smile dons his face. *Slap.* "Yeah. See you."

I exit through the back, unlock my car, and slip behind the wheel. I crank the engine and air conditioning, my knuckles pale as I grip the steering wheel. A thump ricochets in my head as it smacks the wheel between my hands.

Concerned as I was about moving in with Trent, thank goodness I am. Better to have decided because we want to live together rather than out of necessity.

Without the restaurant job, I'd be royally fucked living in the apartment on my own. Thank goodness I had the sense to stash money away when Peyton and I were roomies. Little by little, I padded my savings account. Put enough away to pay bills for a few months in case anything went south.

Losing my job sucks, but it came at a time when I don't have to worry as much.

I straighten in my seat and suck in a deep breath. Stare at the faded blue paint on the restaurant wall. Say one last goodbye, then throw the car in reverse, back out, and aim the car toward home. Well, what will be my home for a few more days.

"One week," I mutter to myself. "Then go out and find a new damn job."

I set down my chopsticks and rub my stomach. "Damn, I needed that."

Trent laughs as he lifts a brown bottle to his lips. "You and me both."

Reaching across the table, I take his hand. Bat my lashes and smile. "Tell me about your day, dear."

He snorts. "Please, don't call me *dear*. Sounds like something Nana L would say."

"Nana L?"

"Lucille, my father's mom. Sweetest person you'll ever meet. The type of grand-mother that squeezes cheeks then gives sloppy kisses on said cheeks." A softness settles over Trent's features. An unspoken fondness for his grandmother. Someone I hope to meet, along with the rest of his family, in the future.

I have never met *the parents* with anyone. Not having a serious relationship before Trent, I never went through any of the "normal" phases of a relationship. No schmoozing over dinner at a nice restaurant. No heavy topics of discussion. Defi-nitely no cohabitation. And never the chance to meet relatives.

Until now, meeting extended family held no appeal. Until Trent, sex was all I wanted from someone.

"I look forward to meeting her," I say. "But seriously, how was your day?" Can't be worse than mine.

"Beverly Prescott is walking a fine line." He takes a long pull from his beer and sighs. "Had such high hopes for her." He peels the label back on his bottle. "She wowed me with her résumé. Intrigued me during her interview. But now... I didn't expect her to be so lacking."

Rising from my seat, I tug Trent's hand and walk us to the couch.

In two days, all the large furniture will be picked up by a local charity that helps low-income households—singles and families alike—that desperately need furnish-ings but can't afford the steep prices in retail stores. The dining room table with four chairs will be sold for fifty dollars. The couch for twenty. Households add their name to a waiting list after financial proof of hardship. They check off what they need and get notified when an item becomes available.

If I knew the people firsthand, I'd gift them the furniture for free. But I under-stand the need or desire for anonymity. People don't want to be judged—not that I would judge them—and prefer to keep their financial woes as private as possible.

"Lacking in what way?"

Trent tips his head, resting it on the back of the couch. He rocks his head left, then right, then stops when he hits center. "With her supposed level of experience and expertise, I shouldn't have to hold her hand"—he tilts his head to look at me—"every damn day. Figuratively, but still."

I wince. "You raved over her credentials. From everything you shared, she sounded perfect for the job. Sorry things aren't what they seemed."

He lifts a hand from his lap and traces the design on my graphic tee. "Me too." His hand falls to my thigh and clamps the muscle. "Please tell me your day was better."

I purse my lips and slowly shake my head. "Define better."

Lifting his head, he twists in his seat to face me, his hand taking mine. "What happened?"

"The restaurant isn't doing well financially." I shrug and drop my gaze to our joined hands, my thumb stroking his soft skin. "And I was let go."

The words are barely out when Trent pinches my chin between his thumb and forefinger, lifting until I meet his gaze. I expect to see excitement or relief or some awkward version of happiness that I no longer work at what Trent may deem an unnecessary job. But none of those emotions color his expression.

Instead, an edge of sadness turns down the corners of his mouth. Softens his evergreen irises. Has him leaning closer.

It makes me love him that much more.

"That fucking sucks."

"Yeah. It does." I twist and kiss his palm. "But I still have the rec center. And after the move, I'll start looking for something else."

Trent opens his mouth. Words try to shape his lips but fail.

I don't want to fight. Not tonight. Not after things have been going smoothly the past month. Arguments, or the thought of one, make me nauseous. Make me want to curl in on myself. Healthy debate? Cool. I have no issue expressing my point of view in a calm manner and listening to someone do the same, followed by finding middle ground. But spewing hurtful words at loud volumes with grotesque expressions… no one forgets those moments.

Right now, I need my boyfriend to hold me. To tell me it will all work out. That I will find a job I love more than the previous. To encourage and cheer me on.

As if he hears my thoughts, he tugs me into his side, wraps an arm around my shoulders, and kisses my temple. I drop my head to his shoulder and snake an arm around his waist. My eyes fall shut as his thumb paints small circles on my bicep.

"Do you want another hospitality job?" he whisper-asks.

I give a halfhearted shrug. "It's what I know, so probably."

A hum vibrates his throat before he rests his head on mine. "Crazy ideas are crowding my thoughts."

I open my eyes as my fingertip traces the rim of the button on his dress shirt, one lazy circle after another. "Crazy how?"

Trent goes momentarily silent. His thumb continues to stroke my arm, rhythmic and gentle. Without interruption, I grant him time to declutter his thoughts. Organize them before he speaks up.

And while he thinks, I relax and focus on all things him. The clean, crisp scent of his starched button-down mixed with the sweet bergamot cedar smell of his cologne. The warmth of his skin through the fabric of his shirt. The rise and fall of his chest with each steady breath. The buzz along my skin as his hand drifts over my shoulder, up the back of my neck, and into my curls.

"Would you be open to trying something new?" he asks as his fingers massage my scalp with soft strokes.

I haven't put thought into looking at jobs outside of hospitality. When you've worked in the same industry your entire adult life, you gravitate toward what you know. On the beach, especially near Trent's house—our house—hourly pay and tips are the best in the county. Like all industries, hospitality folks talk. We meet in bars and chat about the good, bad, and disturbing. With any job, working in restaurants has its ups and downs. But the only way I see myself not serving tables is if the perfect opportunity strikes.

And I have no clue what said opportunity looks like.

"Depends on what it is. I wouldn't discount anything without knowing more."

Beside me, Trent grows oddly quiet again. Deepening the pressure, his fingers continue massaging my scalp and I hum at his soft but firm touch. *God, I love his hands on me.* Every brush of his skin on mine. Every dig or scratch or graze ignites undeniable heat. Makes me want him more. Makes me love him more.

His fingers drift to my neck, soft, lazy strokes lighting a fire under my skin.

"Would you work with me?" he whisper-asks.

My breath catches in my throat. My forehead tightening as my brows tug in and down. *Work with Trent?*

The idea doesn't repulse me, but I also know nothing about his job or business. Or what he would ask me to do if I said yes. Sitting at a desk all day, answering the phone and being an errand boy holds no appeal.

And isn't it a big relationship no-no to work with your significant other? I am by no means the morality police, but working with someone you are romantically involved with seems unethical. A one-way street to breakup town.

"Uh…"

I sit straighter and twist to face him. Read his expression and gauge if this is a serious proposal. Dark-green irises lock me in place. The corners of his mouth tip up, the action almost hidden by the scruff lining his jaw. Then I scan the line of his body, make note of his relaxed posture and widespread legs. His free hand rests on his thigh.

Has Trent ever looked this comfortable in his own skin? It isn't often we just get to be like this. Chill. Laid back. Between work schedules and the recent decision to move in together, downtime is a rarity.

"Maybe?" My answer comes out as a question. I need more details before giving a definitive answer.

His warm breath paints my lips as he chuckles. His hand is back in my hair, sweeping the curls from my face before his fingers trail my jawline. He leans in, presses a chaste kiss to my lips, and makes me melt.

"God, I love you."

Smiling wide, I fist his shirt and pull him in for a deeper kiss. "Love you too, T."

Seriousness replaces the soft lines of his expression. "I'll probably fire Beverly." His entire body deflates with a sigh. "I told her two weeks, and I will give her as much, but I don't think she's cut out for the job." Fingers dive into his hair and pull once before his palm slaps his thigh. "Ugh. I really hate being the boss sometimes," he teases.

"Liar." I wink at him.

He rolls his eyes. "At times like this, it sucks." The pad of his thumb strokes my cheek. Slow and steady. Back and forth. "Even if she shows major improvement, I don't think I'll keep her for the role. It's not worth the risk. Tomorrow, I'll check with human resources and see what other openings we have. Maybe we have something more her style in a different department."

At this, all the pieces lock in place. Trent doesn't just want me to work for his company, he wants me to be his second-in-command. The person who takes work off his plate so he has more time outside the office.

Again, I question how great this idea is.

Won't we get sick of each other? Argue and complain more?

Last thing I want is to become one of those couples that can't stand the sight of each other but continue forward in the hopes it will get better. That isn't love. That is coasting along.

But what if the complete opposite happens? What if we love working together? What if this experience opens up doors for us both? What if this job is something *I* love?

I initially thought it might be a desk job. Grunt work and mind-numbing boredom. But Trent wouldn't stick me in a job I'd tire of easily. He'd load up my schedule and surrender tasks he trusts in my hands.

"And you want me to take her place?" I ask, needing clarification before I get ahead of myself.

Subtly, he nods. "Yeah." His thumb drifts to my chin before brushing over my lips, his eyes following the action. "First off, you're brilliant. I know you love serving and lifeguard duty. If you want to do that, I'll understand. But I'm not oblivious to how organized you are. Even on your worst days, you know where everything is." He shrugs. "Learning paperwork and the scope of the job are basics. You'd have it down in days."

Inching back, I hold up a hand. Cock my head and narrow my eyes. "Listen to you. Talking like I said yes already."

"You will."

"And what if I don't?"

"You will."

Laughter spills from my lips. "Cocky much?"

The corner of his mouth kicks up. "Not cocky. Certain. There's a difference." He fists the collar of my T-shirt and tugs me to him. "One week. Think about it."

I lick my lips, swallow, and groan. "I fucking love it when you're bossy."

He crushes my mouth with his. Parts my lips with his tongue and fucks my mouth with his until we are both gasping for air.

Rising from the couch, he takes my hand and hauls me from the cushion. He laces our fingers, taking one step, then another. "Let's go to bed and you can show me how much you love my bossiness."

"Yes, sir, boss man."

Brow cocked, he smirks. "Yep. You most definitely will accept the job." He leads us down the hall and into my mostly bare bedroom. Spinning around, he unbuttons his shirt. "Now… fuck me like you mean it."

Ten

TRENT

Today is it. The last straw. The end of the line. And she is fucking late.

Not just a little late, as in she hit traffic or every red light on the way. A stickler for punctuality, I forgive circumstances beyond someone's control. But her tardiness is her own doing. The woman lives five miles from the office, traffic isn't a major issue of concern.

I shake my wrist and glance down at my watch. "Thirty-five fucking minutes," I grumble under my breath.

Several unsavory facts about Ms. Beverly Prescott have come to light in the past week. Facts that cannot be ignored.

I'd granted her two weeks. Two weeks to prove she could handle the job. Two weeks to demonstrate I didn't waste valuable resources, time, and money on someone incompetent.

A week and a half have passed, and I am done. Beyond done.

When we started the hiring process for this role, human resources did blanket checks of each applicant. Arrest records with a focus on felonies. Generic calls to the former employers listed on each résumé. Standard calls to listed references. During this process, no red flags popped up in regard to Beverly Prescott.

Once I voiced concerns to human resources—Beverly's blatant inability to perform the job and her overexuberance to be at the top—they made more calls. Reaching out to fellow human resources friends in the area and digging deeper. Like all lines of work, people working in the same circles talk. Beth Anne, the human resources director for Callahan Industries Inc., made calls and had lunch dates with industry friends in the area.

According to the human resources reps from the businesses on Beverly Prescott's résumé, she was a wolf in sheep's clothing. They had never been able to point the finger directly at her—she'd covered her tracks well—but financial records weren't matching the bank accounts. It started weeks after each new job. Beverly Prescott had funneled money from each business into untraceable accounts.

It started small at first. Pennies at a time out of large accounts she oversaw. She'd manipulated the books for years. Tweaked spreadsheets and "lost" bank statements. No one was able to point a finger directly at Beverly. No trails led solely to her. So no charges were pressed. She was fired and security precautions were taken.

And in her absence, the problem disappeared and the companies recovered.

When I asked Beth Anne about calls made to previous employers and references, she said receptionists or assistants handled the former employment calls. They answer basic questions and could be none the wiser to Beverly's indiscretions. When it comes to personal references, those are easier to manipulate. Anyone could be on the other end, ready to boast and highlight Beverly's false work ethic. Indisputably, Beverly's references are partners in her fraud scheme.

Unfortunately for Beverly Prescott, I don't fuck around. People who know me say I am cutthroat when it comes to business. I won't deny that truth.

When I started Callahan Industries, I wasn't in business to make friends. I was in business to fulfill opportunities, meet needs, and build a future. I didn't reach this point in my career with kind words and a lack of authority. Callahan Industries is what it is today because I spearheaded this company with an iron fist. I inserted myself in every part of the process. I approved each project and oversaw every penny spent. This company is more than dollar signs, it is my blood, sweat, and frustrations. It is a dream I worked my ass off to achieve. It holds the key to my future and livelihood.

And no one will smile to my face and rob me behind my back. No one. Especially a conniving twit like Beverly Prescott.

Winded, Beverly bounds into the office formerly deemed hers. "Oh." She slaps a hand to her chest. "So sorry I'm late, Mr. Callahan." She shrugs her purse higher and hugs it closer to her chest. Her eyes avert and spot the box on the desk. "Is everything alright?"

Arriving at the office before the sun rose or anyone clocked in, I plucked an empty storage box from the file room and started packing Beverly's belongings. Beth Anne collected the company laptop from the office a little more than an hour ago, taking it to technology security to be scrubbed for malware and searched for all past activity since given to Beverly.

I take a deep breath and audibly exhale as I push off the edge of the desk. "Ms.

Prescott, it has come to our attention that you were dishonest during the hiring process."

"I don't know—"

Holding up a hand, I silence her. I don't need more of her lies. "It'd be best if you don't speak."

Swiping the box off the desk, I hold it out for her to take. Her eyes pinch for a split second as she eyes the box. The muscles in her jaw flex as her nostrils flare long enough for me to take notice. And then she straightens her spine and squares her shoulders. The corners of her mouth tip up in an unrepentant, false smile as she steps forward and takes the box.

"Please follow me."

I exit the office, stand in the hall, brush my hands down my suit jacket, and wait for her to follow. Head held high, she steps out of the office and distances herself. I close the door behind her and check the newly changed lock has engaged.

Without a word, I lead her down one hall, then another, before we reach human resources. I open the door, step aside, and gesture for her to enter. Sneer firmly in place, she passes me and walks into the office. Beth Anne and Radford—the head of technology security for Callahan Industries Inc—stand poised in reception. I fight the chill that rolls over my skin as Beverly regards the present company.

"This is where we part ways, Ms. Prescott. Beth Anne will collect your keys and badge then answer any questions regarding your termination. All personal items are in the box," I state, pointing to the box in her hands. "All company property has been accounted for and you may leave when Beth Anne finishes speaking with you."

I shift my gaze to Beth Anne, give a tight smile and nod, then spin on my heel to leave.

Instantaneous relief relaxes my muscles as I walk back to my office.

If not for my meticulousness and apprehension, Beverly Prescott might have masterminded more schemes before anyone at Callahan Industries took notice. She had the tools and access to cause irrevocable damage. To steal millions and tear apart my business from the inside.

I mentally clap my hands in prayer and send a silent thank you to my father. In my years at Callahan Financial, I'd heard the whispers and break room gossip. Paranoid and ludicrous were words people used to describe Michael Callahan and his obsessive need to keep an eye on all aspects of his business. I saw it more as a defensive measure. Had he not instilled the same strong virtues in me, my business might have gone down the shitter.

"Bless your paranoia, Father," I mutter as I enter my office and shut the door.

Pushing the events of the morning out of my head, I sift through my list of contacts. Type out an email detailing Beverly's departure from the company. Send it to every person she may have spoken with during her time with Callahan Industries. Inform them she is no longer a point of contact or privy to company information.

By lunchtime, it feels weeks later. But the moment a soft knock sounds on my office door, the stress of the day fades to the background.

Reese.

"Come in," I say as I straighten the scattered papers on my desk and close my laptop.

The door swings open and in walks Reese, a brown bag in his hand and my favorite smile on his lips. In black slacks and a lavender button-down with the top button undone, he is sharp and delectable. *And mine.*

He closes the door, crosses the room, and sets the bag on the corner of the desk. Stepping around the desk, he swivels my chair until I face him, plants his hands on the arms, and drops his mouth to mine.

The kiss is gentle, a light caress, but powerful in its own right. A breath before I part my lips to deepen the kiss, he inches back and winks.

"No office shenanigans, boss man. Don't want to get in trouble before I officially work here."

I push out my bottom lip and give my best *hmm* whimper. "Suppose you're right." Straightening in my chair, I point to the bag. "What's on the menu?"

Reese walks around the desk, snaps up the bag, and heads for the small table and chairs in my office. He removes boxes from the bag, followed by drinks and cutlery. "Bowls from the new Greek restaurant around the corner."

Shoving away from my desk, I rise and meet him at the table, taking the seat next to him. "Hope the hype is real because I'm starving."

All conversation ceases as we dig into our lunch. Garlic and lemon and a hint of fish perfume the air. Sharp and subtle flavors dance on my tongue with each bite. And I don't know which of us moans the loudest as we eat, but I have a mind to laugh and shush Reese at the same time.

"Are you nervous?" I ask before the next bite.

He chews the rest of his bite of chicken souvlaki, takes a sip of water, and pats his lips dry with a napkin. "Yes, and no." Setting the napkin in his lap, he sets his hands on the table, palms down. "You wouldn't put me in a position to fail"—his eyes meet mine—"but I have no clue what I'm doing. And you're putting a lot of faith in me." His eyes fall to the table and study the grain with too much care.

I rest a hand over his. Caress his tanned skin with my thumb. "I would never ask you to do something I didn't think you were capable of." I duck my head until our eyes connect. "And this… not only can you do it, but you'll blow me away in the process." Bringing a hand to his chin, I tip his head back until our gazes are level. *Equals.* "The best part… I'll be by your side the entire time. I get to watch the man I love become my co-mogul."

A snort-laugh shakes his frame as the corners of his eyes crinkle and tip up. "Co-mogul, huh?"

"Damn straight." I lean in and press a chaste kiss to his lips. Lighten the moment as realization slowly creases his forehead. As Reese puts two and two together. As the gravity of his role sinks in. It's a lot to take in, but I have every confidence in him. "Reese, I believe in you. More than anyone else. And it is an honor to have you by my side."

His tawny-brown eyes glaze over as they bounce between my greens. I lift a hand and cup his cheek. Stroke the thin layer of stubble lining his jaw. Study his features as he processes what I've told him. The subtle twitch of his brows and slow blinks of his eyes. The bob of his Adam's apple before his tongue darts out to wet his lips. But those small nuances are insignificant when compared to the stiffness of his shoulders. As if what I've said is unbelievable. As if my faith in him is incomprehensible.

But I do believe in him. I do have faith in him and what we will accomplish together.

Reese has given me something no other man has. True, endless affection. A reason to wake up each morning, to breathe. Because of him, I am confident of my worth. Because of him, I am more than my career. And because of him, I have love. His love.

He has shown me what it means to *live*, what it means to *love*, and I will never take him or us for granted.

eleven

REESE

Squirming in the passenger seat, all I want is to strip off my clothes, crack open a beer, and think of anything other than work.

Days into my new gig at Callahan Industries and I am ready to crawl out of my skin. It isn't Trent or the actual job—I love both. What has me constantly fidgeting is the clothes and how claustrophobic they make me feel. The starched stiffness of my shirt as it chafes my neck and throat. The annoying loose thread in my slacks that tickles the inside of my thigh every time I move, yet I can't seem to find it when I tug my pants down. The tightness of my dress shoes and cramping of my toes as the day progresses.

I've kept my aversion to the dress code to myself, not wanting to come across as bitchy or ungrateful. That and, if I complain, he will call his tailor and surrender my measurements. Within a week, I'd have new suits, dress shirts, and shoes in the closet next to his.

Like all occupations, this job has pros and cons.

Initially, I worried seeing Trent all day, every day, would not bode well for our relationship. We would grow sick of the sight of each other and the lack of alone time. I'd love the deep timbre of his voice less as he barked orders or whispered in my ear. I'd regret taking the job after moving in together and having no division of personal and business schedules. And our sex life would plummet.

But those concerns vanished by the end of day two.

The day Beverly was fired, I received keys, a photo badge, passwords, and a long, detailed description of what my job entailed. Human resources went through formalities to cover their ass, but they know who I am. Not just my name, but who I am tied to—who I belong to—as do the rest of the staff.

When I walk through the door, the staff throw smiles in my direction. Lift a hand and greet me immediately.

"Hello, Mr. Triggs."

"Good day, Mr. Triggs."

I don't have their names memorized—yet—but they sure as hell know my name. Weird as it is, their immediate respect is a shot of adrenaline in my veins. It makes me feel taller, mightier. Has me squaring my shoulders and straightening my spine. Each greeting puts a smile on my face and boosts my day.

In most large corporations, my relationship with the boss would nix my chances for the position. Fraternization would be screamed to anyone who'd listen. People who've busted their asses for years might bitch I had an unfair advantage. I'd agonize over curled lips and whispered gossip as I walked to my office.

Those concerns melted away on day one.

There has only been one drawback to the job. The damn clothes.

Every job before this, I wore loose attire. My days at the restaurant consisted of T-shirts and jeans with an apron tied low around my waist and broken-in sneakers on my feet. At the rec center, I rocked red board shorts and a whistle around my neck, my flip-flops at the base of the umbrella-shaded lifeguard stand. The low-key ensemble at both jobs fit my laid-back personality. Made my job feel less like work.

My new work wardrobe is the polar opposite.

Shirt buttoned to the base of my throat and snug on my Adam's apple. A tie beneath the collar that I reach up and adjust no less than twenty times a day. Slacks that pinch my waist, squeeze my ass and hug my thighs. The fact I haven't ripped the crotch seam yet is a damn miracle. The dress socks... I like them. I bought several pairs with fun quotes and images. Too bad the socks don't stop the shoes from rubbing blisters on my pinkie toes and heels.

"Your silence has me worried," Trent says from the driver's seat.

I blink out of my inner ramblings and twist in the seat to see him better. His hand on my thigh tightens and I lay a hand over his, tracing the length of his finger with my thumb.

"Do I need to wear ties at the office?"

After a quick glance in my direction, his eyes return to the road. He tucks his lips between his teeth, biting back a smile and possibly laughter. Then he shrugs. "Don't think it's an actual requirement for the job." A chuckle leaves his lips. "Do you not want to wear ties?" he asks, his tone playful.

I take his teasing tone and go with it. "In the bedroom? Sure. Anywhere else? Not so much."

A smirk highlights his profile. "Noted." He lifts my hand to his lips and kisses the back before setting it back on my thigh. "Any other requests?"

Not sure if this is a test or if he genuinely wants to know. Either way, I don't care. Trent won't be bothered by my not wanting to wear constrictive clothes. Hell, maybe voicing my opinion will open up new doors.

"The dressy clothes make me itchy. Figuratively and, on occasion, literally." I stare out the windshield and look at the sea of brake lights along the causeway. The mad rush of people heading home from one side of the bay to the other. As the sun sinks closer to the water and paints the sky pink and orange, I take a deep breath. "It's an adjustment and I'm trying."

"The job comes with a certain appearance."

"Yeah," I say on an exhale.

His hand squeezes my thigh. "That said, what would you rather wear? Needs to model the professionalism we uphold at CII, but I'm willing to be flexible."

His willingness to bend the rules speaks volumes and reiterates how much this man loves me. In the past year, I have learned a lot about Trent and his business. The one thing I know with certainty... he doesn't fuck around, and he holds every employee to a strict standard. No exceptions.

Until now.

My cheeks sting as a smile dons my expression. "I'll think on it this weekend."

"Good." His hand trails up my thigh, stopping just before the bulge beneath my zipper. "Speaking of the weekend, we should celebrate."

"Yeah?"

"Definitely." His fingers skirt the thickening bulge in my pants. "We haven't been to the club in months."

With Trent's busy schedule, Peyton moving out, me moving into Trent's house, and just general life responsibilities, we haven't spent much time out. A night at the club sounds like the perfect way to celebrate. The two of us, in our element. Drinks and dancing and groping for hours. And if the night ends like our previous club nights, we will be sweating for a different reason before we crash.

"A night at the club sounds perfect."

Twelve

TRENT

The thump, thump, thump of bass vibrates my bones as we walk into Scandalous. Streams of colorful lights glow on damp skin. Earthy hops and the sweet smell of cocktails mix with sweat and sin. Lips are on lips and skin while hands tug hips closer and grind. People line the bar, crowd the tables, and flood the dance floor. Some sip fruity drinks and catch up. Others skip the drinks and search for someone to leave with later.

Electricity buzzes through the air and has the hairs on the back of my neck standing up on end.

My fingers lace with Reese's as we weave through the throng of people. I look over my shoulder and take in his bright, toothy smile as it glows under the blacklights. Returning the gesture with a smile of my own.

This right here… I have missed this part of us. Though the nightlife scene isn't an essential part of who we are, it is the root of us. Where we met. How we came together. It doesn't define us, but it is a crucial component. A piece we shouldn't ignore or forget.

Leaning into Reese, my lips ghost the shell of his ear. "God, it feels good to be here."

His fingers unthread from mine before he reaches for my shirt at my hip and tugs me closer. "Yeah, it does." His tongue darts out and swipes his bottom lip. "Should come more often."

The tips of my fingers trail up his cotton-covered chest until my palm rests over his heart. Fingers curling into a fist, I drag him forward and crush my lips to his. Shove my tongue in his mouth and taste him openly without shame.

He clutches my hips. Bruises my flesh through the denim of my jeans. Hooks his fingers in the belt loops. Keeps my hips pinned to his as our tongues taste and tangle and devour. Reese gives as good as he gets without hesitation. And in this dimly lit club, where we feel more ourselves out in the open, we let go. Give over to our primal nature. In here, we don't worry about who will see. Don't worry about what they will think or say or do.

In this place, we are *us*. Trent and Reese. Two people in love.

I break the kiss and drop my forehead to his. Work to steady my breathing. "Fuck, I love you."

He draws me back in and kisses me chastely. "Will never tire of hearing those words." Another kiss. "Love you too."

"Drink then dance?"

He nods, takes my hand, and winds us through the crowd toward the bar.

∿

We stumble through the front door, mouths glued together. Blindly, I reach for the alarm panel, set it to home arm mode, and guide us up the stairs to the bedroom. My fingers tug at the bottom hem of Reese's shirt and yank up. The kiss breaks long enough to tear his shirt away and toss it aside.

At the second-floor landing, Reese jerks my shirt from my jeans and shoves the cotton up my chest. In one swift move, the shirt is off and flying across the room. His hands trail down the planes of my chest, the pads of his fingers grazing the ripples of my abdomen. I part my lips and suck in a stuttered breath.

"What do you want, T?"

I discerned, after our second night together, Reese loves to be dominated in the bedroom. The first time I told him to get on his knees and pull my cock out, his eyes darkened. When I told him how I wanted my cock sucked, how I wanted him to choke on my thick length, he licked his lips and did exactly as instructed. And the first time I said *good boy*… power surged in my veins as he swelled with pride. Fuck, the exchange was heady. Addictive. Insatiable.

I clamp his jaw with my fingers, tip his head slightly to the side, and ghost my lips over his chin. Breathe him in for one, two, three beats before my tongue darts out. Taste his skin. Feel the burn of his stubble against my tongue as I lick up and over his lips to the top of his philtrum.

A raspy growl consumes the air. Vibrating his chest and mine before I shove him away and walk backward.

"Hands and knees."

His eyes light up.

"Be a good boy and crawl." I point to the floor at my feet.

Without hesitation, his knees hit the carpet. Tawny eyes on my greens, his palms smack the floor next. My eyes drag over the curves of his bare spine, swallowing when I hit the dip at his lower back. The dimples above the waistband of his jeans. The proud protrusion of his ass in the air.

Eyes trained on mine, he inches across the room until he reaches my feet. Silent, he holds my gaze as he waits for the next directive. His fingers claw at the floor. Tongue darting out to moisten his eager lips. Rib cage expanding and contracting with every labored breath he takes.

My cock swells painfully seeing him like this—eager, wanton, starved—for me. The power exchange between us… nothing compares to the high it delivers. Reese at my feet, willing to do what I demand without argument, is intoxicating. Exhilarating. Liberating. The ability to be myself with him, to temporarily relinquish my rigid CEO persona, is freeing and euphoric.

Hooded eyes on his, I cup his jaw and drag my thumb over his stubbled cheek.

The perfect blend of smooth and abrasive. The perfect juxtaposition when his soft lips and hot mouth consume every inch of my body.

"Unfasten my pants," I command as my hand falls away.

He inches closer and rocks back to sit on his heels. Lips a breath from the fly of my jeans, his tongue darts out and sucks in his lower lip, pinning it between his teeth. Fingers trail up the backs of my calves, loop around to the front of my legs at the knees, and spread wide as they crawl up my thighs.

Foreplay is the headiest game with Reese.

He craves my authoritarian persona in private. Subliminally begs for my imperious nature. And when I yield, undeniable gratitude shimmers in his eyes. When I subjugate him in the bedroom, make him feel small when he is anything but, he rewards my body with his. Though I command him with words, Reese retains all the power. Has the ability to deny me, to say no, to walk away.

But he doesn't. He won't. He loves the trade-off as much as I do.

He flattens his palm over the bulge beneath my zipper. Wraps his fingers around my denim-covered shaft and grinds the heel of his palm along the base of my cock. Tawny irises command my attention and demand I don't move. My jaw slackens as he strokes my length. My breaths quicken as he increases the pressure, as he teases my tip through the denim. His touch has me throbbing, aching, desperate.

My fingers comb through his locks and curl into a fist. "Take. Them. Off," I demand with a growl. "Now."

The corner of his mouth kicks up in a smirk. "Yes, *sir*."

I tip my head back. "*Fuck*," I heave out.

Since I suggested Reese work with me at Callahan Industries, he has taken it upon himself to call me sir. At first, he'd said it in passing with a cheeky smile on his face. I'd rolled my eyes each time the word left his lips.

Until he said it in the bedroom.

And fuck, hearing the single word leave his lips before he took me in his hand, his mouth, his body…

Fire and electricity simmer beneath my skin. Heating me top to toe. Amplifying every touch he delivers as he unfastens the button and drags the zipper down the teeth of my jeans. As he peels the material down my thighs, followed by my briefs, I grip his chin and tip his head back. Swallow at the inferno burning behind his dark-honey irises.

My jeans and briefs hit the floor with a soft thump. Eyes locked on Reese, I step out and kick them aside. Lift a hand to his hair and toy with his curls. Trace my knuckle from his temple to his chin. Take his chin between my thumb and forefinger, stroking his stubble-lined jaw over and over. In my periphery, his chest expands and contracts faster. His lips part. Eyes drunk on lust and need. I drag the pad of my thumb over the soft cushion of his lips.

"Be a good boy and put my cock in your mouth," I order, desire dripping off every word.

His hooded eyes darken as his fingers wrap around my length. With slow strokes, his grip on me tightens as he moves up and down my shaft. His tongue darts out, licks his top lip, followed by his bottom. Hot and wet, he drags his tongue up the underside of my cock from root to tip. He hums in appreciation then wraps his lips around my tip and takes me to the back of his throat.

"Oh, fuck," I whisper-growl. I fist the curls at his crown and keep his rhythm steady. "Such a good fucking boy."

He moans the moment the words leave my lips, the vibration reverberating in my balls. One hand moves up and down my shaft with his mouth. The other hand finds my balls and massages. With each stroke and fondle, he edges me closer to orgasm. Skirts me closer to a high only he provides.

And then he changes pace. Slows down. Drops his hands seconds before my cock pops free from his mouth.

By the time my brain registers the shift, Reese is kissing his way up my body. Lips and tongue and teeth grazing my lower abdomen, my belly, my pecs. His short nails dragging up the sides of my torso, digging into my flesh and making their mark as he rises from the floor.

He clutches the back of my neck and crushes my lips with his. Tasting. Taking. Devouring. A moan spills from my lips and he swallows it down. Deepens the kiss and backs me up until I hit the mattress. He breaks the kiss and shoves me down on the bed. I fist my cock as his eyes coast up the length of my body. Cock a brow as his gaze lingers on my erection for one, two, three strokes before lifting to my line of sight.

"See something you want?"

"Mmm."

I jerk my chin at him. "Strip." On the next stroke up, I pinch the tip of my cock. "Then, be a good fucking boy and get on this bed." Another slow stroke. "And fuck me."

The corner of his mouth quirks up for a split second before he brings his hands to his chest. Runs them down the bare flesh of his abdomen and undoes the button and fly. Too damn slow for his own good, Reese shoves his jeans down. Beneath the denim, he is bare and hard as steel.

I moan out my appreciation, my need, my absolute desperation for him as he fists his cock.

One knee hits the mattress, then the other. He towers over me near the foot of the bed and I tighten the grip on my cock. Tug faster as his eyes drop to my throbbing erection. Then slower when he doesn't move closer. I like to watch—him jerking off, him watching me jerk off, both—but that isn't what I want right now.

Right now, I want him to spread me wide, pin my legs to the mattress, and fuck me with urgency. Like we haven't touched each other in weeks. Haven't kissed or tasted or moaned the other's name in months.

When my hand falls away, his eyes drift up my body until they meet my gaze. Brows pinched together, he tilts his head in silent question.

I bend my legs at the knee and widen them in invitation. Hold his stare and mouth, "Fuck. Me." I curl my finger in a come-hither motion, then mouth, "Now."

The corners of his mouth curve up as a mischievous smile plumps his cheeks. A playful glint twinkles in his eyes. With a single glance, I glimpse his dirty, lascivious thoughts. Then he blanks his expression and rakes his eyes down my body. Thrill ignites my bloodstream as fire licks every inch of my skin.

His palms slap the backs of my thighs before he shoves me up the bed. My head tunnels through the pillows, stopping before I smack the headboard. I watch his every move as he crawls up the bed and stops shorter than expected. Soft hands with the occasional callous trail up the backs of my thighs and force my knees closer to the mattress. Rapt, I refuse to look away as he lowers his head.

Realization dawns and I open my mouth to protest. Tell him I don't want my cock in his mouth. Not yet. But the words never leave my lips.

His tongue darts out and licks the puckered hole of my ass. Fingers dig into my thighs as he pins me harder to the mattress. A growl vibrates his mouth on my skin as his jaw relaxes and he devours me. I moan as he swirls his tongue in dizzying circles. Blindly, I reach for his hair, tugging hard once it's in my fist. He toys and teases and drives me wild.

Jagged breaths echo in the room. Sweat slicks my skin as fire snakes down my spine. Slamming my eyes shut, I roll my hips and give myself over to him. Give him the upper hand. He circles my hole once, twice, and then drags his tongue up, painting my balls, the length of my erection, and the tip of my cock in his saliva.

Unintelligible curses slip from my lips as I yank his curls.

Fingers wrapped around my cock, he buries his face beneath my balls. Eats my ass as if it's his last meal. Makes me moan, growl, fist the bedding as I beg for more. Hands on my thighs above my ass, he inches back and hovers, gently blowing where his mouth devoured me ruthlessly. My balls tighten and I groan.

Thwack.

His palm swats my ass, and I jolt from the contact. With gentle strokes, he soothes the spot his hand struck. Then he slaps me again. My skin heats, tingles, begs for more. Precum coats the tip of my cock and I reach down to smear it over the head.

Releasing my legs, Reese stretches toward the nightstand and opens the drawer. Then he is back between my legs, a bottle of lube in his hand. It falls to the mattress as he drops to all fours, cages me in, and crushes my lips with his. He parts my lips with his tongue and devours my taste, my moans, my love for him.

Breaking the kiss, he licks and nips the line of my jaw, the column of my throat, and the hollow between my collarbones. He drifts lower. Sucks my nipples between his lips, biting the budded peaks until a hiss leaves my lips. Drags his mouth and tongue over the ridges of my abdomen, nails digging into my sides as his teeth mar my flesh.

Reese is equal parts gentle and brutal as a lover. He stirs up the most complex emotions in my head, my heart, my soul. Each soft caress leaves fire in its wake. Every bite of his nails, of his teeth, zaps me with an explosive current. But when his lips taste me… every molecule in my makeup comes to life. Gravitates toward him. Vibrates with need. Begs for another hit.

His lips abandon my skin, and I immediately miss the feel of him. He rocks back on his heels. Grabs the bottle of lube, pops the lid, and squirts liquid in his palm. He snaps the lid closed and tosses the bottle aside. Coating the length of his erection, my eyes fall to his hand as he strokes himself. Jaw slack, lust clouding his vision as he watches me watch him.

And then he drags his lube-coated fingers over the seam of my ass. The pad of his thumb circles my tight hole, over and over. On the third circuit, he adds pressure. Slowly pushes in as I drag in a sharp breath. In and out. In and out. His thumb teases the tight hole before coming away.

Reese scoots closer and I push up on my elbows. He lines up the thick head of his cock with my ass. I stop breathing as I wait for him to thrust forward.

But he doesn't.

My eyes dart to his in question, and what I see knocks the last ounce of air from my lungs. I fall back to the mattress and lift a hand to his face. Cup his cheek for three strokes of my thumb and then let go.

Inch by painstakingly slow inch, he lowers himself until his breath paints my lips. His mouth drops to mine, and he kisses me with a slow, gentle force. Strong arms bracket my face, his fingers toying with the short strands of my hair. He sedates me with his lips and the unspoken message they speak.

He kisses a lazy trail to my ear and sucks the lobe between his lips. "Love you so fucking much, T," he whispers, a breath before his hips rock forward and his cock fills me fully.

I band an arm around his waist and trail my free hand up his spine. My fingers dive into his curls and guide him back to my mouth. Gazes locked and lips ghosting his, I reply with equal tenderness. "Not like I love you."

And then we get lost in each other for hours.

thirteen

REESE

What the hell?

The past few weeks have been a major adjustment. New jobs are always a challenge. New jobs in an unfamiliar line of work are exhausting. But every day I sit at my desk at Callahan Industries, I feel more at ease in my role. More confident with my responsibilities.

Overseeing finances sits at the top of my daily to-do list. Someone else logs the figures into spreadsheets from bank statements and invoices. My job is to review, compare, and monitor the numbers for accuracy. A tedious task, it isn't for the faint of heart. The more I stare at the figures, the more they swirl together.

But this is different. My eyes aren't buggy.

Something is off. *Way off.*

Pushing away from the desk, I rise to my feet, scoop up the laptop, and exit my office. In three strides, I knock on Trent's open door, step inside, and close the door behind me. The jovial smile on his lips falls away when he sees the concern on my face.

"What's wrong?"

Taking the seat across from him at his desk, I set the laptop down and spin it so we both have a view of the screen. I highlight a figure on the spreadsheet and shake my head.

"This number should be much higher."

We stare at the income from the San Francisco branch of Callahan Industries, a location that opened its doors last year. Through last week's report, the site had steady earnings with a slight increase each week. Reviewing the recent figures, there is a noticeable dip in revenue on the spreadsheet. Karina, a long-term, trusted employee in the finance department, populates this particular log with figures from the bank accounts. She doesn't cross-reference them with invoices and payments, that duty belongs to Tracy.

It isn't in my job description to study itemized finances, but this weird vibe had me digging deeper today.

Trent turns the laptop to face him fully and drags it closer before tilting the screen. I stand and drag a chair around the desk to sit beside him. The arm of my chair grazes the arm of his as we lean in to study the screen.

His eyes dart back and forth as he reviews and compares the numbers on the spreadsheet before toggling to the detailed list of invoices I have up on another document. With each new line he reads, his face turns a deeper shade of red.

"What the fuck?" he mutters with a growl.

His hand freezes over the keys as his eyes lose focus. Anger charges the air in the room. Trent stiffens, his shoulders and spine rigid. A feral look flashes in his eyes as he stares at the screen. At the audible grind of his molars, Trent is a force to be reckoned with.

I lay a hand on his forearm and he startles in place. "Tell me what to do, T."

His breathing spikes, his unbridled rage evident in each exhale. I keep my hand on his forearm. Let it be an anchor to ground him as he cools off. One by one, his breaths grow quieter, less intense. He twists in his chair and looks me square in the eyes.

Anger dilates his pupils, setting his lips in a firm, flat line, flaring his nostrils. He isn't angry with me. Trent is angry at the situation, at whoever is responsible.

"Dig," he says in a stern tone. "As deep as you can. And don't say a word to anyone." His eyes narrow for a split second. "*No one.*"

To anyone else, his harsh words would be taken as a personal jab, a slap in the face. But I don't take them as such. His words, his tone, his fury, are aimed at the thief. The person that fucked with his empire. The person he trusted and who broke their loyalty. The person that stole from him.

And now, with the exception of me, his trust in others is gone. Until we get answers, he trusts no one outside this room. Not without time, discovery, and a shitload of vetting.

I nod and stand, moving the chair back to the other side of the desk. Closing the lid on the laptop, I swipe it up from the desk and head for the door. If I thought Trent had worked endless hours before, both of us were in for a surprise. Until this is resolved, our jobs will be our life.

"Reese." My name on his lips stops me at the door.

I spin to face him. "Yeah?"

"Thank you."

The corner of my mouth lifts in a sympathetic half smile. "No need to thank me, T. Just glad I found it now and not down the road."

He tips his head to the side and his neck cracks. "Me too." He takes a deep breath. "This is top priority until it's sorted out. The other shit on your agenda, we'll get through them together at the end of each day."

"Understood."

I twist the handle and open the door. As I step through, he calls my name again.

"Love you, Triggs."

I wink at him. "Love you, Callahan."

I take a deep breath as I step into the hall. *This is bad.* Had I not found it, it could have been a hell of a lot worse.

∼

Jesus fucking Christ.

The deeper I dig, the longer this rabbit hole goes.

Elbows on the table, I drop my head in my hands and fist my hair. Close my eyes and visualize the end of this nightmare coming sooner rather than later. Suck in a ragged breath and try to ease the stress from my stiff muscles.

In the past seventy-two hours, I have journeyed down a long and well-disguised path of deceit. Though the brunt of the losses started when Beverly Prescott took her position at Callahan Industries, it isn't solely her who is responsible. Two others have joined the mix. Two people that have worked for Trent for more than three years.

Neal from payroll has pilfered small amounts from every hourly employee's paycheck for the last year and a half. Company-wide, there are nearly five hundred hourly paid employees. From the cleaning crew to secretaries to hospitality staff and more. Each pay period, this man has stolen anywhere from one dollar—in the beginning—to fifteen dollars from every hourly paid person. He adds the deduction to their stub—the name varies from insurance costs, retirement funds, tip fees or bonus taxes, depending on the employee—to make the missing money appear legitimate. And through all the evidence I've unearthed, not many have questioned the missing funds. The few that have, Neal has issued them an additional check—money from Callahan Industries and not the pot where he has filtered the money—to reimburse the loss. Then, he stopped skimming from their checks.

Altogether, Neal has embezzled close to seventy-five thousand dollars. And I am nowhere near done looking at everything he has had his hands in.

The other person slowly building a rap sheet is Tracy from finance. Her list of crimes isn't as steep as Neal's but has climbed steadily in the past few months.

Responsible for matching billing itemization to the bank account spreadsheets, Tracy has fudged numbers to her advantage. A minor adjustment to the deposit amounts on the spreadsheet. The addition of a few small company purchases here and there. Like Neal, Tracy has access to the company "checkbook" and credit card and has purchased items online or deposited money in her personal account under the guise of work expenses. Several online purchases were traced to the company's local Amazon account. I accessed and retrieved the order history, then stared slack-jawed at the screen as I scrolled pages of purchases. Books, purses, graphic T-shirts, mugs. The list was endless and her boundaries were nil.

To date, Tracy has stolen more than fifty thousand dollars' worth of merchandise and cash. Her trail was not as intricately masked as Neal's, which makes her crimes much easier to slap with fines and jail time.

Trent plops down in the chair next to me and sets a tumbler with two fingers of bourbon on the table. Two may not be enough when I divulge the latest news.

"Give me details."

I rock my head in my hands and tug my hair before releasing it to sit straight. Tilting my head, I meet Trent's gaze. Worry lines crease the corners of his eyes and wrinkle his brow. Light-purple half-moons paint the skin beneath his lower lashes. Over the past three days, he has aged a decade from the stress of the situation.

Lifting the tumbler to my lips, I swallow half the contents before setting the glass back down.

"Neal in payroll and Tracy in finance. Between the two of them, almost a hundred and twenty-five thousand in the last twenty months."

"*Fuck, fuck, fuck.*"

My thoughts exactly. "Not that you didn't know this, but you need an attorney. Someone that has your absolute trust. Because this"—I wave a hand toward my laptop—"is not petty theft."

Trent brings his own glass to his lips and downs every drop before slamming the tumbler on the table. His entire frame vibrates with rage. A rage incomparable to what I feel. Anger, frustration and exhaustion have been constant as I've dug for answers. But my indignation is child's play next to Trent's fury.

"You think they're in cahoots?"

I shrug and speak honestly. "Not sure. I need someone with better tech skills for that. Someone who can look at digital trails through coding. Not necessarily a hacker, but someone with an equivalent skill set." I down the last of my bourbon. "Got any computer gurus you trust implicitly?"

Dragging a hand over his face, Trent groans as he pinches the bridge of his nose. Humorless laughter spills from his lips as he drops his hand with a thud to the table. "I trusted the two fuckers stealing from me." He drags in a jagged breath and meets my gaze with uncertain eyes. "How the hell am I to know if I can trust anyone else in the company? How the hell can I ask someone to look into this from within?" Wood creaks as he grips the edge of the table. "It's probably isolated, but this puts a major fracture in my trust in anyone." He lays a hand on my thigh. "With the exception of you, of course."

"Never thought otherwise." I lace our fingers together. "Maybe we bring Radford in for a meeting. Play it off as making sure tech security is in place after what happened with Prescott. Let him do most of the talking. We analyze his answers, his body language and overall vibe." I shrug. "Then, we go from there." I give his fingers a squeeze. "If we need to hire someone outside the company, then that's what we do. But we shouldn't wait much longer, and we need to be discreet. They can't know we suspect anything. Shit will tank quickly if they suspect we're onto them."

He runs a hand through his hair. Grips the back of his neck and sighs heavily. "This is beyond fucked up."

"Agreed."

"After all the bullshit my father dealt with in business, I swore I'd never be in his shoes. I vetted people with a fine-tooth comb. Dug up every ding on their record and made decisions based on evidence." Wood scrapes wood as Trent pushes back on his chair and rises. "How did I not see this? People start shit like this early on and leave trails."

"True." I scoot away from the table, stand, and stretch my limbs. "But maybe these people worked for smaller companies before you. Maybe they got away with more because no one looked over their shoulder or checked their work. And before anyone caught on to what they'd done, they jumped ship. Found a shinier prize to target." I wince, hating that Trent and his company are the shinier prize.

"Let's take a break tonight." He wraps my hand with his and leads me to the kitchen. "Help me make dinner. Food and wine and nonwork conversation." Pleading evergreen irises hold mine. "Please."

Dinner and drinks won't make this nightmare end, but we need some semblance of normalcy. Something to steal the limelight for an hour or two. Something less stressful and more intimate. A night off.

I sidle up to Trent at the open fridge as he grabs butcher-wrapped salmon steak, carrots and broccoli before closing the door. He hands me the vegetables. "Cut these to roast with the potatoes and garlic in the basket." He points to the produce basket on the counter. "I'll ready the fish."

As I rinse the produce, he pours heavy-handed glasses of chardonnay. We move in tandem in the kitchen, and before long, our meal is plated. We park on the couch with dinner, flip on the television, and get lost in fictional cinematic bliss.

And when bedtime arrives, we ignore the dirty dishes and take the stairs two at a time. Strip each other bare at the foot of the bed and lose ourselves in one another for hours.

Our heads hit the pillow, my back to his front, our limbs tangled and eyes heavy. Soft snores float through the room as Trent's frame relaxes. I drift off to the rhythmic sound of his snores and rise and fall of his chest.

Just before sleep takes me, another thought hits… *Everything will work itself out.* Not sure how, but I feel resolution in my bones. *Everything happens for a reason.* And damn if I am not determined to find answers.

fourteen
TRENT

Reese sits with me at the table in my office. His fingers fly across the laptop keys as he digs further for evidence of misappropriation. This whole Neal and Tracy situation has me livid. On the cusp of inflicting violence. If not for Reese, my knuckles would be bloody and my wrists in cuffs. He has been my sounding board through this bullshit.

Enraged with each development, I endeavor to not dwell on the unchangeable. The past can't be erased. What's done is done.

Now, my attention is centered on reparations and preventing further damage.

Step one in the process… speak with Radford. Inconspicuously interrogate him and determine whether or not I trust him. If deemed trustworthy, we proceed with step two—putting our hands in the slime-infested embezzlement waters to find secrets and answers.

Please, I beg you, let it be an isolated issue.

"Should be here any minute," Reese mumbles as he adds more to the long list of crimes committed by Neal and Tracy.

Taking the handkerchief from my pocket, I wipe my brow then stow the cloth. I clench and straighten my fingers over and over. Shoving away from the table, I rise from the chair and go to the mini-fridge hidden beneath the coffee bar.

"Drink?"

Reese stops typing and peeks over his shoulder. "Coffee, please."

I place a mug under the drip, insert a pod of Reese's favorite dark roast, and press the brew button. While coffee fills the mug, I grab a bottle of orange juice and the cream from the fridge. I tear open and empty a couple packets of stevia. Add cream until the coffee swirls from black to light brown. As I set the mug in front of Reese, a knock sounds at the door.

"Come in," I call out as I take my seat. Radford steps through the door with an apprehensive smile on his face. "Close the door, please."

His smile falls, and he swallows before shutting the door. One foot in front of the other, he makes his way to the conference table. Almost undetectable, his brows twitch and eyes narrow in evident confusion.

"Everything alright, Mr. Callahan?" His eyes shift to Reese—who hasn't looked up or acknowledged Radford—then focus on me once more.

"Please, Radford, take a seat."

I study his every move as he pulls out a chair, skirts around the seat, and finally sits. His hands drop to his lap, hidden by the wood table. He leans back and relaxes his shoulders. Appears at ease. But I don't miss the indecision and distress radiating off him.

It isn't every day your boss calls you into his office without warning, then tells you to close the door.

In my younger years, anytime I got called in to speak with the boss—whether it was my father at Callahan Financial or the manager from the small retail job I worked for two years as a teen—it was always an unsettling feeling. Like wanting to shit your pants and throw up at the same time.

"Want anything to drink?" I offer.

A squishy *V* forms between his brows a beat before he swallows. "Uh... water," he croaks out.

I grab a bottle of water from the fridge, set it in front of him, and return to my seat.

"Radford, I'd like to start this meeting off with two things. One—everything we're about to discuss needs to remain between the three of us. Not even your family hears a peep. No exceptions. Period."

He nods, twists off the bottle cap, takes a long pull of water, then secures the lid.

"Two—you aren't in trouble."

His body visibly sags in the chair.

"But"—I hold up a finger—"I am having trust issues with staff right now."

For a beat, I remain silent. Let him digest what little I've said. Study his physical response to my statement. The way he cradles the water bottle. The minor tilt of his head as he tries to decipher who or what has me on edge.

What I don't see are nervous tics. Sweat on his brow or temples. Fidgety fingers or a shaky frame from leg bounces beneath the table. Constant nose twitches or blinking eyes.

His eyes haven't left mine—except to glance at Reese—since entering the room. Still, I plan to tread lightly. Radford may not have given me reason to mistrust him, but this is a delicate situation.

Uncapping my juice, I take a sip and then set it on a coaster. I toy with the lid and watch it spin on the table for one, two, three revolutions before it falls flat on the table.

"It has come to our attention"—my eyes lift to meet his—"some employees have been deceptive in their role at Callahan Industries."

Reese stops typing on his laptop and finally looks at Radford, whose eyes have widened exponentially.

"Not sure what to say, Mr. Callahan."

"Not much you can say, Radford. But we do have a request."

"Okay."

I gesture to Reese. "Mr. Triggs."

In my periphery, I witness the slight change in Reese's posture. Hear the almost inaudible hitch in his breath. I make a mental note of his reaction and stow it away to address in the future. If we weren't here to discuss egregious news about the business, I'd ask Radford to come back in thirty minutes.

"Thank you, Mr. Callahan," Reese states, his tone meant to be serious, but I pick up on the faint lilt. He nods infinitesimally, shifts his gaze to Radford, and dons a mask of solemnity. "Callahan Industries has suffered at the hands of thieves. I've spent the past three and a half days investigating and have hit the point where help is required."

Radford sits straighter in his chair, inches closer to the table, rests his forearms on the wood and leans in. "And you believe I may be able to help?"

Reese nods. "Exactly. Before we get into the nitty-gritty, we need to again express how crucial it is for you to keep this under wraps." Reese picks up the manilla folder on his right and sets it between us, opening the folder and removing the NDA I had Vincent, my attorney, draft this morning. "This is a nondisclosure agreement. Please read it over, but it states all matters regarding this situation are to remain one-hundred-percent confidential. Tasks can only be done on Callahan Industries–approved technology, in the office, and only during business hours. For this project, any overtime you accrue has been preapproved—within a reasonable limit, of course."

Reese slides the document across the table, then laces his fingers and rests his forearms on the table. Radford thumbs through the pages, his eyes widening as the gravity of the situation sinks in. Several minutes of silence pass as he reads each line. When he reaches the end, he straightens the pages, looks across the table, purses his lips, and nods.

"Do you have a pen?" he asks.

From my suit jacket, I pluck a pen from the inside pocket, twist it, and offer it to Radford. He signs on the line, lays the pen on top, and pushes the document toward us. I flip to the back page and sign, then give it to Reese to do the same.

With legalities out of the way, we dive headfirst into this nightmare.

Over the next hour, we spell out our discoveries. Reese forwards the detailed log of findings to Radford's email. We outline a plan of attack and schedule regular check-ins via phone, video or in person. Since tech support isn't often needed on a regular basis, we limit in-person meetings and agree to conduct them during times with fewer staff present.

Maintaining appearances, we end the meeting and agreed to say Reese was having laptop issues, if anyone were to ask. Radford leaves my office exactly how he came, with nothing in his hands.

He opens the door and peers over his shoulder. "If you have any other issues with the laptop, Mr. Triggs, please reach out." The facade up firmly in place for prying ears.

"Appreciate the assistance," Reese replies before the door closes.

Reese spins in his chair to face me head-on. "Thoughts?"

"Antsy, as I am bringing in another person, it's necessary." My tongue darts out and wets my lips. "My eyes were on him every second. I trust my gut and our decision to work with him."

"Me too." Reese sips his now cold coffee. "My typing while you talked didn't distract him. And the energy in the room… I got no bad vibes."

"Me either."

Reese rests a hand on my knee. "We'll get this sorted out. Promise." He gives my knee a gentle squeeze. "Until then, we keep a vigilant eye on things. Don't say anything we wouldn't normally. More importantly, we go about business as usual."

Playing ignorant with staff irritates me almost as much as the problem. But Reese is right. To catch the thieves, we let them believe everyone is clueless about their crimes.

"Well, don't forget business as usual also includes our trip next week."

When Reese and I started dating, work trips lost their excitement. Before our relationship, trips were adventurous. Business consumed the majority of my time but exploring the city was never not an option. I love Tampa, love the bustling life of big cities, but no two are identical. Bumper-to-bumper traffic is the same everywhere, but the attitude of commuters changes the drive. Skyscrapers shine differently in the sun when surrounded by water or trees or mountains. The biggest surprise is how unique life is in each place. While some make you claustrophobic, others make you feel at home.

And I look forward to time with Reese outside of our small city bubble.

My favorite smile brightens Reese's expression. "Can't wait to see the world with you, sir."

He rises from his chair, plants his hands on my armrests, and drops his lips to mine. The kiss is soft, sweet and ends way too soon.

"Mmm. Something about the taste of coffee on your lips does things to me."

Swiping up his laptop from the table, he starts for the door. "Consider it foreplay." He winks. "Meet for lunch?"

"Absolutely. I'll have Dale order food. One o'clock?"

"Perfect, *sir*." He cocks a brow then disappears out the door.

Prior to suggesting Reese work for Callahan Industries, I questioned mixing personal and business. My father said mingling the two was the perfect equation for failure. Only one would survive. Until Reese, I agreed with him.

Then life changes. Your view of people sharpens. Your perception of what matter shifts. The world evolves, as does business, and you must choose whether or not to move forward or remain stagnant.

Would it be bad for business if Reese and I split? God, yes. My devastation would bleed into my workload. Would render me defunct. Broken. Which is why I tread lightly with the offer.

Reese and I have been in a committed relationship for more than a year. Though I *broke up* with him before every trip, neither of us was unfaithful. I'd thought my frequent trips would strain our relationship—on occasion, it did—but we never let go. Considering we'd never put down roots before our relationship, our commitment to each other speaks volumes.

Hiring my boyfriend to be my second-in-command was risky. But damn, it was the best decision I've made.

Reese isn't some random guy. He isn't a fling. Dare I think it, let alone say it aloud… Reese Triggs is my match. The man that settles the crazy in my hectic life. The man that makes the world more stable under my feet.

He is the best decision I made. Saying yes. Keeping him. Loving him.

Without Reese, I am a man without direction. Without him, I am a shell of myself.

"Damn, did I luck out," I mutter to myself.

And with each breath I take, I will prove myself worthy of Reese's heart.

Salty air fills my lungs as a light breeze from San Francisco Bay sweeps hair across my cheek. The early fall sun warms my face while the crisp, cool air has me tugging at my long sleeves. I drag in a deep breath, count to three, and sigh on the exhale. My stomach growls as the breeze wafts scents from local restaurants and cafés. Fresh baked bread and cheese from the pizzeria, the nuttiness of brewed coffee from the café, and the sweet pungency of smoked salmon.

At the end of Pier 39, my eyes scan the bay.

To the left, the iconic Golden Gate Bridge begs to be seen with its rusty-red paint, high towers, and lengthy suspension cables. Trent promises we will cross the bridge and get a better view of it and the city from a less populous lookout point before we leave. Either way, it steals my breath to see it in person.

Straight ahead, the island of Alcatraz stares back with ominous eyes and cursed walls. Another tourist adventure on our to-do list while here. Thrill hums through my veins at the idea of walking the corridors and seeing where legendary criminals spent their final years. It is said the island is haunted… if you believe such things.

And off to the right is the San Francisco-Oakland Bay Bridge. Though it doesn't bear bright colors like the Golden Gate, the bridge is massive and begs to be seen.

Trent tightens his hold around my waist as he rests his chin on my shoulder. His body molds to mine as a soft sigh leaves his lips. My fingers weave with his before I turn my head to kiss him.

Though we don't hide our relationship publicly back home, being this intimate out in the open doesn't happen often in Florida. We live in an area where the majority accept same-sex couples. It isn't often we get prolonged stares or curled lips, but it happens.

Here, in the heart of San Francisco, I have never felt more comfortable in my own skin and sharing intimacy with my boyfriend in public.

This city is… liberating.

"Hungry?" Trent asks when he breaks the kiss.

"Starved." In more ways than one.

He takes a step back, reaches for my hand, and laces our fingers together before guiding us through the throng of people. The walkway between the shops isn't so crowded we can't walk side by side, but residents and tourists alike pack the promenade.

Trent steers us toward the Italian seafood restaurant on the pier, and soon, we are seated at a cloth-covered table with a view of the water. As my eyes roam the tables, my frame relaxes into the chair. With the white linens, goblet water glasses, and folded cloth napkins between more forks and spoons than I typically use in one meal, the restaurant gives the appearance of fine dining. But the more my eyes wander, the more this place boasts the aura of casual. Most people wear jeans and T-shirts with sneakers rather than button-downs, slacks, and dresses.

Compared to the few pricier places Trent has taken me back home, this place feels more us. Elegant, yet relaxed. Less stuffy and more *we welcome everyone*.

We order a bottle of pinot noir, an appetizer to share, and our meals before the server gathers our menus and heads for the server alley between the kitchen and dining room.

My eyes drift out the window and across the water, watching the boats as they move through various parts of the bay. This city is nothing short of busy, but it is a different kind of busy from home. Everything here feels alive and fresh and receptive. Vivacious energy lives in the air. Begs for you to feel it, absorb it, experience it.

I love home. But I can't deny loving here too.

My lips curve up as Trent's fingers cascade lightly over the top of my hand. Eyes shifting from the window to him, my breath catches in my throat. My heart jumps a gear and pound, pound, pounds in the confines of my rib cage. Trent could be in tattered clothes and in desperate need of a shower and he would still be beautiful. But right now, in this place where we can be ourselves so freely, this laid-back look, this dreamy, lovestruck look, renders me speechless, breathless, jittery.

"Love you, Reese," he says just over the background noise of the dining room. He weaves our fingers, his thumb stroking the base of mine as his green eyes soften. "More than I thought possible."

This garners the biggest, dopiest smile from my lips.

I never intended to fall in love with this man, but fall I did. Hard and fast. Without effort. Without question. Without a chance of survival if he chose to leave one day.

But as I hold the dark-green depths of his eyes in this very moment, I know every single day of my future will include him—us.

"Love you too, Trent." I lift his hand to my lips and kiss his knuckles in turn. "So much it makes me breathless."

The server sidles up to the table seconds after my proclamation. After showing us the bottle, she pops the cork, fills two glasses halfway, then sets the bottle to the side and walks off. The remainder of dinner goes by in a blur of mouthwatering dishes, more wine, and endless smiles and laughter.

I love this city, and by the end of dinner, it is blatantly obvious Trent loves it here too.

After dinner, we indulge in the best tiramisu to hit my taste buds. The moans this single piece of dessert elicits should be criminal. Once I've made a fool of myself over the chocolate espresso sweet course, Trent settles the check.

With his hand on my lower back, my skin heating from the small public display of ownership, Trent guides us out of the restaurant. His hand doesn't leave its spot, his fingers painting soft strokes as we move through the thinning crowd. The warmth from his touch intensifies with each brush of his fingers. My breath stutters as his fingers leisurely purposely inch up the fabric of my shirt. Graze the bare flesh beneath.

"Coffee?"

I suck in a breath and turn to look at him, the spot between my brows tight. "Huh?"

The corners of his mouth curve up in a suggestive, cocky smile. "Before we head back to the hotel, do you want a coffee?"

Caffeine probably isn't the best idea this late in the evening. Then again, my body is all out of whack from the three-hour time difference, so it won't hurt. Plus, with the way Trent is touching me, teasing me, waking every live wire in my body, I don't see us sleeping anytime soon.

"Coffee sounds perfect."

Trent orders a *normal* coffee—café Americano—while I opt for the Biscoff latte. If the caffeine doesn't keep me up, surely it will be the sugar from this and dessert.

We sip our drinks as we stroll the waterfront hand in hand. Rose and lavender and sherbet-orange paint the darkening blue sky; the Golden Gate Bridge and mountains a spectacular addition to the sunset I'd never see back home. Several pedestrians pause on the sidewalk to snap pictures of the skyline. When we reach a less crowded spot, I jerk to a stop.

"What is it?" Trent asks, ridges marring his brow.

I drop his hand and fish my phone from my pocket. "Tourist time," I answer, holding up my phone and wiggling it.

Near the edge of the sidewalk, where it meets the sand, I open the camera on my phone and flip it to selfie mode. Trent takes my drink and his and sets them down. He bands his arm around my waist and tugs me close. The action makes me smile instantly, and I take the first photo. My finger taps the button, again and again, capturing our smiles, our laughter, my lips on his, and more.

At some point, I stop taking pictures and shove my phone in my pocket. His hands land on my hips and mine clutch his cheeks. Without a care in the world, we kiss in the biggest public display.

In this city, we are just two people in love. In this city, no one shames us for who we are.

At the end of the week, we have to leave. Part of me wants to stay, though. Part of me says this is where I belong. Where we belong.

Chest heaving, Trent breaks the kiss and drops his forehead to mine. "Let's go."

With a subtle nod, I lean back and lace my fingers with his. He fetches my drink and hands it over before picking up his own. Then, he all but drags me a few blocks to the hotel.

The moment we step into the suite, our drinks are forgotten.

We strip each other bare as we stumble toward the bedroom. With lips and tongues and teeth, we worship and devour and love one another. I moan his name as he plunges into my ass. Fist the sheets with my face pressed into the mattress. And before he comes inside me, before I paint the sheet with cum, he pulls out and flips me on my back. Pushes himself inside me once more. Drops his weight over me, into me, and strokes ever so slowly as he drops his lips to mine.

He kisses me drunk. Makes love to my mouth, my body, and my heart with each measured stroke of his tongue and cock. Strong forearms bracket my head while I reach up to frame his face with my hands. His fingers toy with the length of my hair as he deepens the kiss. As he consumes me. Marks my soul as only his to touch, forever.

And it is with that thought, I orgasm. Paint our chests with my undiluted love for him, for us, for everything we will be.

"Oh, fuck, Reese." He crushes my lips with his. Rocks his hips faster. Plunges into me harder. Curls his fingers in my hair and tugs until fire stings my scalp. "Fuck, I love you."

And before I respond in kind, the heat of his orgasm floods my body. Has me clutching his ass and holding him in place. He drops his mouth to where my shoulder and neck meet, his teeth clamping down as the last of him spills into me.

He collapses on my chest, lungs heaving as he kisses the skin along my collarbone. My legs circle his hips, hook at the ankles and pin him in place. And for a beat, we lie there.

My fingers comb through his hair with the barest of touch. "I love you, T."

Pushing up onto his elbows, his green irises glow as they look down. "Love you more."

sixteen

TRENT

My gut twists for the umpteenth time this morning and I press a loose fist to my stomach. I have no idea what kicked this into motion, but something is… *wrong*.

"Not hungry?" Reese asks, eyeing my barely touched breakfast as he finishes his.

The tines of my fork push the scrambled eggs around the plate. I should eat more, it angers me to waste food, but every time I load the fork and consider taking a bite, my stomach cramps.

Did the seafood from dinner not sit well with me? Can't be that. I would have felt the effects shortly after. Maybe I drank too much wine. A drink with dinner or after a rough day is normal, but mixed with the trip and work chaos, it might have been too much last night.

My stomach wrings again, and I mentally admonish the organ. *Stop it.*

Blaming this feeling on bad food or too much alcohol doesn't fit. No, this… this is something else. Something just out of reach. Something instinctual waving its hand and begging for attention. But what?

Reese and I are good. More than good. Since we landed in San Francisco, our relationship has only gotten stronger, better, more intense. This trip, this place, has brought us closer together. Connected us on a new level.

The twinge in my gut does a nauseating flip and I slap a hand over my mouth. Beneath my palm, my skin feels cool, clammy. "Something isn't right," I mutter through my hand.

Reese's fork clangs on his plate. He pushes back on his chair and is at my side in two strides.

"Are you going to be sick? Do you need help to the bathroom?"

I shake my head but wonder if throwing up will help whatever is causing the problem. "I don't think so." My words a borderline question. Closing my eyes, I take a breath and think of anything other than the cramp in my midsection. As the room comes back into view, I feel incrementally better. Picking up a slice of toast, I take a small bite and say, "Maybe some water. Please."

Reese darts from the two-seater table, enters the suite's small kitchen and fetches a bottle of water from the fridge. He returns to my side seconds later, twisting off the cap and shoving the bottle in my hand.

I swallow down one sip, then another. Little by little, my stomach relaxes. Recapping the bottle, I sigh. "Thank you. Not sure what happened, but it appears to have settled."

"Should we cancel the meeting?"

I focus on my body for a minute. Do a mental scan head to toe. Stretch my limbs, my fingers, and toes. Feel the expansion and contraction of my chest with each inhalation. Implore my stomach to remain calm.

"No," I say with a shake of my head. "I'm better." Reese narrows his eyes. "Swear," I vow.

His tawny eyes soften before he rests a hand on my shoulder. "Fine." His fingers give a gentle squeeze. "But if you start feeling sick again, the meeting is done. Period."

I smirk. "Yes, sir."

After I finish the last of my toast, we tidy up our dishes. Reese slips on a sharp gray button-down and I watch, mesmerized, as he fastens each button. I button my own shirt and slip a tie around my neck. Loop it into a knot and slide it to the base of my throat. Reese licks his lips in appreciation and I cock a brow in return. I don my suit jacket while Reese drapes a blazer over his arm.

A few steps in his direction, I press my lips to his. Give him a kiss that ends far too soon.

And then my hand is on his lower back as I guide us out of the room.

~

Dazed, I blink a few times. "Sorry, Catarina. What?"

Across the table, Catarina winces and shrinks in her chair. "I, uh…" Her eyes dart to Reese, then hesitantly return to my gaze. "I updated your assistant," she says in a staccato. "She said there'd been a breach, and she needed the account log-on information for our location. She said she'd reset it and provide the new details soon."

My elbows thump on the conference room table. I drop my head in my hands and smash the heels of my palms to my closed eyes. Curl my fingers in my hair and growl out my frustration.

One vertebra at a time, I straighten my spine and drop my hands to the table. Inhale deeply to cool the fire dancing in my veins. Do my damnedest to not scream at one of my most valuable employees. "Did you not think to call anyone and verify her before giving out confidential information?" My fingers curl and flex. "An email went out weeks ago that a woman working closely with me was termi-nated." I grind my molars and take another deep breath. "Did you not read the email?"

She twiddles a pen between her fingers. "Patrick has been reading and relaying my emails." Her fingers drop the pen when she sees me eyeing her nervous tell. "He said a woman was let go, but didn't say who she was or what level of authority she'd had." Her eyes fall shut as she pinches the bridge of her nose. "*Shit*," she mutters. "Shit, shit, shit." She opens her eyes and meets my stony gaze. "I'll understand if you fire me. I am one hundred percent at fault. I was just trying to delegate—"

I hold up my hand to stop her. "Catarina, you aren't fired."

Her entire frame sighs.

"But there will be severe consequences. Something we'll discuss another time. For now, we need to put out this fire." I twist in my seat to face Reese. "Call Radford and update him. Then call Dale and do the same. He'll know who to relay news to." Before leaving Tampa, I opened up to Dale about the office mishaps. Gave him the basics and asked him to keep an eye out for suspicious activity while Reese and I were out of town. I needed someone else in our corner. Someone who'd report to me, Reese, Radford, and Beth Anne if anything popped up.

"On it," Reese says as he rises from his chair and steps away from the table.

Once Reese is out of earshot, I sit in silence, my gaze laser focused on Catarina.

It took years for me to understand, but my father always said silence is the best way to learn the most from a person. *"Remain silent and let their body language and lips do all the talking."* And every single time, it works. Big or small, all details come to light as I sit in wait.

Brows pulled tight at the middle, teeth nibbling on the corner of her bottom lip, Catarina's gaze refuses to look anywhere but at me. The tip of her finger taps the table at a pace too fast to count. Her lips part to speak, but she snaps them shut. Then she repeats the action. Twice.

Catarina and I have always shared a comfortable business relationship. As I conducted interviews for upper management for the San Francisco location, she had been the one person I felt the most right about. She is personable, innovative, perceptive, and sharp as hell—in business and life. When she walks in a room, heads turn and conversations quiet. It isn't her beauty that commands attention—though, she is stunning. It is her presence, her aura, her energy that screams for you to take notice.

She is a force to be reckoned with and won't go down without a fight.

Except now.

Today is the first time I have seen her appear so defeated. Spine curled and shoulders caved forward. Fidgeting worse than a child lying to a parent. Red rims her glassy eyes. A slight wobble to her chin.

She doesn't need to say she is sorry. I hear her apology in every unspoken word. See it in the slump of her spine and in the threat of her tears.

"Trent, I—"

I hold up my hand again. "Some people need to hear the words, need apologies verbalized." Leaning forward, I reach across the table and rest my hand over hers to settle the nervous tap of her fingers. I give her what I hope is a soft smile. "Without saying it, I know you're upset and remorseful." Pulling back, I recline into my chair. "Not going to lie. This is a mess. A big fucking mess." I purse my lips. "But it will get fixed. And the people responsible will be handled."

Her face pales. "What about me? What about Patrick?"

"When I have a day or two to mull this over, I'll write up the formal disciplinary action. Some permissions will be temporarily withheld. Controls you once headed will be monitored for a period. Salary increases and bonuses will be on pause until said period ends. As for Patrick, his penalties will be less severe. But you delegated duties, and he didn't properly relay critical information. That isn't just on you, but him too."

At the fallen look on her face, I sigh.

"Cat, you are one of the few people I hold in high esteem within the company. But I can't play favorites right now. Had this been anyone else, depending on the severity of the situation, I'd have done the same or worse."

"You're right." She nods. "I just hate that I put the company in jeopardy in the first place."

"Actually"—I hold up a finger—"it was me who did that. I hired the woman responsible and gave her too much access too soon." My hands drag up my face and into my hair. "Was trying to lighten my load. Not work as much. Be there for Reese. Have a life."

Her brows shoot up as she points toward the door. "Reese? The guy with you?"

Often, I forget not everyone is aware of my relationship with Reese. I once thought it a good thing—less gossip in the workplace—but now, I just don't care what people think or feel. First off, it is my damn business. Second, Reese has been stellar at the job. He knows what I want, isn't afraid to go after it, and knows that maintaining a happy work life equals a superior homelife.

I nod. "Reese and I have been together more than a year. We had our challenges with my travels and crazy hours, but that has leveled out since I brought him into the fold."

"No unsavory arguments because you see too much of each other?"

I chuckle with a shake of my head. "I worried about that too, but no. We're pretty good about switching business on and off when necessary."

"Good to see you happy," she says as Reese steps back inside.

"Radford has set everything in motion. Dale is making the appropriate calls in the office and to the banks. He'll call or text with updates as they come in."

I hold his confident stare for a beat then smile. "Thank you." Pushing back from the table, I rise and gather my belongings. "Cat, let's have dinner tonight. Bring Shayla." I stow my phone in my suit jacket. "Let me get some work done and then we can meet around seven."

She stands and gathers her laptop, pad, and pen. "That'd be nice. How about The Stinking Rose?"

"The garlic place?" I ask and she nods. I look to Reese and he shrugs. "See you there at seven."

In no hurry, we all trek toward the door. I take in Catarina's posture—still a touch fallen, but not as prominent as earlier.

Her actions were foolish but not done with malice. This much, I believe. Though she will have a major ding in her file and trust to make up with me, I know this slip is a huge learning moment for her. She won't make any such mistake again.

This morning, my stomach twisted in unease. Some instinctual part of me knew something was off. That issues would pop up in the aftermath of Beverly Prescott. Now that we have learned what that something is, the wringing has unraveled a bit. It is a disaster but a manageable one.

Beverly may have slipped through the cracks with her flashy résumé, fabricated resources, and bright smile. But with her weaselly ways and assumption I wouldn't be so hands-on after hiring her, she got cozy too soon. Lucky for me, and thanks to my father, I had paranoia on my side.

I cut her out early. Shut her down before real damage could be done. Not that what she'd done hadn't tampered with Callahan Industries; her actions definitely made a sizable dent. But thanks to Reese, the problem was caught early. Authorities will handle Beverly Prescott and the banks will work hard to get the money back in the rightful accounts.

All things happen for a reason, they say. On occasion, I follow the falling dominoes to figure out what good comes from the bad. The trail confuses and amazes me. Had I not been with Reese, I would have never hired Beverly Prescott, and this whole mess wouldn't exist. But this catastrophe did take place. And Beverly Prescott wasn't the only person involved. This disaster would've still existed, regardless.

I *am* with Reese. Now, he isn't just my boyfriend and lover. He is my partner in every sense of the word. Him by my side—in life and business—makes me a better person, whole, in every way.

Reese is the good.

seventeen

REESE

Good thing we are appointment-free for days. Days are what it will take for the garlic to leave my system. For it to not be a natural cologne or flavor I taste every time I eat.

But damn, was it worth every bite.

Trent asked Catarina and Shayla to join us for dinner. Though she was less frazzled by the end of our meeting yesterday, she still wore exhaustion like a second skin at dinner. But as the evening progressed and we threw back drink after drink, her stress became less evident. By the end of dinner, conversation flowed easier than the alcohol and smiles highlighted our moods.

Who knew eating garlic-impregnated meat would reduce tension? Let's not forget the garlic ice cream, which freaked me out. But when the sweet and savory confection hit my tongue, I moaned.

San Francisco is not a place I will soon forget. From the scenic landscape to the buzzing energy to the expansive diversity. We will return, and I look forward to the day.

"Want to view the bridge from the lookout today?" Trent asks.

He tugs a black T-shirt over his head, the cotton snug against his muscular chest. The lean muscles of his biceps and forearms pop against the dark material. Stonewash denim hugs his hips, his sculpted ass, his thighs. His black hair product-free and finger-combed. A day's worth of scruff lines his sharp jawline. And when I meet his dazzling green eyes, I spy his cocked brow and the smirk lifting the corner of his mouth.

"Keep looking at me like that and we aren't leaving this suite."

I bite my lower lip and fight a smile. "Would that be so bad?"

In two quick strides, Trent stands between my denim-clad thighs. He grips my chin with his thumb and forefinger, tips my head back, and lowers himself until we are a breath apart.

"No, it wouldn't." He sucks my bottom lip between his. "But we should explore. Enjoy our time here." He releases my chin and steps back. "I want to see the city with you." He walks over to the closet and plucks his jacket from the hanger. "Visit the places I've missed out on because of meetings and schedules." Arms in the sleeves, he shrugs the jacket on and adjusts the collar. "And..." Rich-green irises meet my tawny browns, a hint of secrecy in his stare. "I may have something planned."

Rising from the bed, I pad to the dresser, grab socks, then head to the closet for my sneakers. Shoes secure on my feet, I fetch my hoodie and tug it over my head as I walk past Trent out of the room.

"Fine," I say with dramatic flair. "But you need to feed me first." My stomach grumbles at the mention of food.

Hot on my heels, Trent wraps his arms around my waist and pulls my back flush to his front. He kisses a path up the side of my neck and I moan in response. On the next step, he sucks my earlobe between his lips and nibbles the soft flesh. My eyes roll closed as we stumble toward the door.

"Thought you wanted to go out," I say, voice low and throaty.

"I do." He releases my ear then peppers my neck in open-mouthed kisses. "But fuck if you aren't adorable when you're grouchy and demanding." Teeth mar the skin where my neck and shoulder meet, and then he steps back. "Couldn't help myself."

"Grouchy, huh?" I spin around to face him.

A smirk kicks up the corner of his mouth. "Don't forget demanding, too."

"Yeah, yeah," I tease. Fisting the lapels of his jacket, I haul him forward and kiss the hell out of him. When the kiss breaks, I rest my forehead on his and hold his gaze. "Feed. Me."

He laughs with a shake of his head. "As you wish."

Lacing his fingers with mine, he yanks me out the door and toward the elevator. As we enter the car, I curl into his side. Bask in his warmth. Inhale his crisp, fresh scent. Revel in the love I share with this striking, fiercely loyal man.

With a ding, the doors slide open, and we enter the lobby. I slip on sunglasses as we exit the hotel and step onto the sidewalk. And on my next breath, I take in the man on my arm. Not his looks. Him.

Without Trent, I wouldn't be on the opposite side of the country, ready to explore. I wouldn't have this incredible life, one that gives me opportunity and purpose. I wouldn't know love. Real love. Love that eclipses everything.

Our relationship was rocky in the past. On unsteady ground every time Trent left me for work. I feared the long distance and time apart would end our love story. Turns out, neither of us was willing to let go.

Each day I wake up next to Trent, I thank the gods for him. Each time he says he loves me, I pray I never know a day without him.

eighteen

TRENT

Sweat slicks my skin as I squirm in my jacket. With slow movements, I fan the leather lapel and pray Reese doesn't notice. Unfortunately, the crisp fall air doesn't hit my skin and is of no help for my anxiety-induced perspiration.

I have never been this nervous in my life. Not once.

Purchasing million-dollar properties—done with the flick of a wrist as I signed my name on the dotted line. Flying across the country and striking deals most would walk away from—done with confidence and the shake of a hand. Entertaining prospective clients and convincing them Callahan Industries is the place to be—done hundreds of times without breaking a sweat. The jitters I experienced interviewing Beverly Prescott are incomparable—although now I see them for what they were. A warning.

Still, none of them measure up. This... what I am about to do... I might throw up.

We step up to the rail and stare at the pristine view of the Golden Gate Bridge. The rusty-red bridge pops against the cloudless blue sky and I can't help but think how perfect the backdrop is for today. Every other time I visited San Francisco, clouds blanketed the bridge and fog horns howled in the distance. The most I'd seen of the bridge before today was the lanes while driving across or the peaks as I approached.

Call me superstitious, but getting this view today is a sign. A silent message from the universe telling me what I am about to do is the right move.

Please let it be the right move.

"We need pictures," Reese says, snapping me out of my introspection. He pulls his phone from his pocket and opens up the camera app. Handing it over, he says, "Take a few in case I blink."

I take several pictures of him before we trade places and he does the same. He sidles up to me, leans in close, and holds the phone up to take selfies of us. As Reese pockets his phone, I spot a couple not far from us taking pictures too.

"Be right back," I tell Reese. I approach the couple and offer to take a photo of them. As I hand back the phone, I ask, "Would you mind reciprocating?" I point over my shoulder toward Reese. "Except I'd like a video."

The woman narrows her eyes and stares for a beat before realization hits.

Yep.

"But can you make it look like you're taking pictures?"

Thrill has her bouncing in place. "Absolutely."

We walk back to where Reese waits and I hand her my phone before stepping up next to him by the rail. "I asked if they'd take pictures of us."

My favorite smile lights up his face as he wraps an arm around my shoulders. "Much better than a selfie."

Reese turns to face the woman with my phone, his smile brighter than the sun as wind whips his hair. I take a deep breath, dig in my pocket for the diamond-lined black band, and drop to one knee. The woman with my phone gasps and time stands still as Reese twists to face me.

I'd planned this day for weeks. Rehearsed my speech whenever Reese was out of earshot. Pictured this moment and his reaction countless times.

But every word I planned to say vanishes as I look up. Tears rim his addictive brown eyes. His Adam's apple bobs as he waits for what happens next. His knuckles bleach as he holds the rail tighter.

"Reese," I choke out, then swallow past the lump in my throat. "I memorized an epic speech for this moment. But as I kneel before you, I can't remember a damn word." I laugh without humor as I toy with the ring in my palm. "I've never known love like yours. Never thought it was possible to be loved by someone like you." Pinching the ring between my fingers, I hold it up. Offer him the most valuable token of my love. "What I do know is that I never want a day without you. I want you today, tomorrow, and every day that follows." Sucking in a sharp breath, I count to three and exhale. "Reese Triggs, will you do me the greatest honor and be my husband?"

In the periphery, the woman with my phone sniffles. I ignore her. Ignore everything except Reese, who is way too silent.

A new layer of perspiration layers my skin as I wait for Reese to answer, to react, to give some indication he heard my question. Hour-long seconds pass as he remains tight lipped. With each deafening second, I grow more concerned. Worry that his answer will be a resounding *no*. Nausea builds beneath my diaphragm. Bile creeps up my throat.

This moment may end us if his answer is no. This moment may be our final memory if he doesn't want to spend forever with me.

Before I chance a trip down heartbreak avenue, Reese drops to his knees in front of me. Frames my face with his hands. Stares deep into my eyes and swallows. And when the corners of his mouth tip up just the slightest bit, every dark thought and concern for our future floats away.

"Yes," he whispers. "A thousand times, yes."

He hauls me closer and crushes my lips with his. Kisses me without restraint. His hands fall away from my face, slip beneath my jacket, and band around my middle. Fisting the cotton of my shirt, he hugs me breathless. Says yes to my proposal again and again with his hands and lips on mine.

Reluctantly, I break the kiss. Remind myself we are in public and a random stranger is documenting this entire moment with my phone. But I'm not ready to leave the moment. Not yet. I drop my forehead to his. Lift a hand to his hair and toy with the curls. Give him a chaste kiss, followed by another.

"Love you," I whisper. "So damn much."

His lips curve into a soft smile. "Love you the most, future husband."

nineteen

REESE

I lift my hands in surrender and stare wide eyed at the computer screen. "What the hell?"

The clicking of keys silences as Trent looks up and across the table. His brows pinch in obvious confusion as he regards my frantic state. "What's wrong?"

I drop my gaze back to the screen and watch in horror as pop-ups appear, one after another in rapid succession, flooding the screen. The cursor flies across the screen, but my hands are far from the touchpad. *Someone hacked my computer.* Someone is invading my files and doing who knows what. Stealing files. Downloading viruses or malware or Trojan horses. Whatever the hell is happening, it isn't good.

With the barest of touches, I spin the laptop and share my screen with Trent. "Something or someone is in my computer. Right now."

His eyes widen in shock. Then his phone is in his hand. He taps the screen three times before bringing it to his ear. An unfamiliar seriousness consumes his expression and stiffens his posture. The humorless CEO, that is who this is.

"Radford," he says, voice razor sharp. "I need you in my office. Now." Before Radford gets a word in, Trent disconnects the call. He points to the screen. "What were you doing just before that started?"

I take a deep breath and think past the panic. Close my eyes for one, two, three seconds, then focus my attention on Trent. "I opened the share drive and clicked Karina's folder. When I accessed the invoice spreadsheet, everything went crazy."

A knock sounds at the door before it swings open and Radford steps inside, closing it behind him. "Mr. Callahan." He nods to Trent, then repeats the gesture in my direction. "Mr. Triggs."

Trent's stern expression returns. "Radford, we have a problem." He twists the laptop in his direction as he approaches the table. "This occurred when Reese opened a file in the share drive."

"Shit," he mutters.

Pulling out a chair, he settles at the table with us. His fingers fly over the track-pad, tapping it every other second. Then his fingers are on the keyboard, striking the keys in rapid succession. He inches closer to the screen, narrows his eyes, and doesn't breathe. None of us do as he works.

And then he straightens in his chair. Sucks in a deep breath, his eyes finding ours on the exhale.

"I've locked down the computer and disconnected it from the internet and server. Not sure how extensive the damage is, but this is bad," he says with a wince. He pushes away from the table and rises from the chair. "I need to grab a few things from my office. Not that it needs to be said, but don't touch the computer."

"Thank you, Radford," Trent says.

He exits the office, the quiet click of the door closing is deafening. The moment he is gone, Trent rests his elbows on the table and drops his head in his hands. His fingertips dig into his skin at a bruising level. With each inhale, I detect the jagged edge of his breathing. The worry over what this all means.

This invasion isn't minor. It was calculated. A plan laid out by a desperate and disgruntled woman. A woman wounded by her past and hell-bent on making others pay. A woman intelligent enough to cover her tracks after years of experience. The more we unearthed about Beverly Prescott, the less hope we had of her arrest.

Since our return from San Francisco last week, I learned Beverly's legal last name is Westcott and not Prescott. The last names were close. Close enough that calls verifying employment history were mishandled and the possible mishearing of the name was swept under the rug.

When I discovered that gem, I wondered how many other names Beverly used. Turns out, the more we dug—Callahan Industries, the attorney's office, and law enforcement—the more dirt we found.

Via facial recognition, we stumbled upon several arrests. All minor offenses that allowed her to go free in less than a year. A hundred dollars missing from the register, inventory counts off, numbers matching on paper but not adding up when the money counts were completed.

Her face matched each offense but not her name. Sally Graham. Danielle Roberts. Elenore Crowley. Those names were tied to jobs that paid under the table. Employers that didn't run her social security number or ask many questions. Employers that didn't take action until the losses started to pile up. Having Beverly arrested, the businesses were penalized for not following proper tax laws. I assume it was worth it for them in the end.

But that was only the beginning for Beverly.

When she'd gained enough felonious insight and stepped up her game, she started using her given first name. She recruited help. But there is one thing she didn't learn from her history of crime.

Don't fuck with Trent Callahan. Ever.

Reaching across the table, I tug a hand from his face. "May not seem like it, but everything will work out."

He lifts his gaze as his hand squeezes mine. A humorless laugh leaves his lips. "I'm losing confidence." His free hand scrubs down his face. "God, I want to believe. I want to trust that we'll find her and she'll go to prison long enough to never bother us again."

I lay my other hand on the table, palm up. He rests his hand in mine and I grip it tightly. Send him every ounce of strength and positivity. *We will get past this. And when we do, we'll be stronger than before.*

"Put your intentions out there. Say it with conviction. Mean it." I lift his hand as I lean forward and press my lips to his skin. "We will get through this."

His eyes lock with mine as he digs deep for strength. I tighten my grip on his hands. Telling him with this simple touch I am his rock. His anchor. The person to hold and lift him up when times get rough. The person he can trust and lean on. Always.

And with each breath he takes, I witness the return of his power. His spine straightens. His shoulders square. The reluctance in his expression melts away. The muscles of his jaw flex. His gaze hardens.

After one last squeeze of his hands, I release him. "There you are." I wink. "My formidable fiancé."

He shoves back on his chair and stands in one quick, fluid movement. In the next breath, he is at my side, gripping my chin, tipping my head back. His mouth crashes down on mine. Mint mixed with desire sweeps over my tongue. As a moan spills from my mouth into his, he releases me and returns to his seat.

"Thank you," he says, swiping a thumb over his bottom lip.

My brows shoot up. "Uh… shouldn't I be thanking you?" I lick my lips and smile when I taste him there.

Light laughter floats through the air just as Radford returns. "Later." He winks in my direction, then gives his full attention to the head of tech security. "Let's hit this bitch where it hurts."

Radford eyes Trent, then me, purses his lips, and nods. "She won't make it out unscathed. Not this time."

Trent slaps him on the back. "Exactly what I needed to hear."

And then we spend several hours hunched over the computer, on the hunt for the grenade pin that started this entire war.

Twenty
TRENT

Two days, three hours, and twenty-one minutes. That is how long it took to find the root of what Beverly Prescott—or whatever the hell her name is—set in motion.

Not only did we pinpoint the spyware she planted in our company server, we also picked up the location of her last log-on. With one phone call, she was in handcuffs and booked in the county jail hours later, awaiting further prosecution. My attorney warned she may not serve more than five years, but I had every confidence. Vincent started building a case against Beverly the minute I explained what she'd done. Although she committed significant and disastrous cybercrimes against Callahan Industries, the judicial system may look at the acts as less than worrisome.

She put on a stellar front during her interview. No doubt she will give the show of her life in front of a judge.

With her behind bars, we are in damage correction mode. After more than a week, Radford and a few trusted others in security have cleaned up Beverly's destruction. Reports were filed with the bank and monies are being returned to the proper accounts. Each time we dig into Beverly's past, we encounter new evidence to present against her. And each time she is questioned by law enforcement, she turns more loose lipped.

Not wanting to take the fall on her own and hoping for a lesser sentence, her attorney advised she come forth with names of those in cahoots with her. When Beverly proclaimed Neal and Tracy were in on the scheme, I punched a wall.

Then I got to work.

Tracy and Neal were arrested on the same day as Beverly's confession. We'd been monitoring them since Reese unearthed their misappropriations. Since their activities hadn't picked up steam, I'd focused on Beverly first with the intent of dealing with them after.

But shit hit the fan fast.

When Beverly's confession hit my desk, fresh background checks were run on every employee under the Callahan Industries umbrella. No stone was left unturned; I wanted all the dirt, even the small deeds. If I lost several employees in the process, so be it.

But no one would fuck me over again.

Vincent says not to get my hopes up for more than five years and heavy fines. But after research of my own, when it is just me and Reese, I voice the penalties I want this woman and her minions to incur. Twenty-plus years in federal prison. Thousands of dollars in fines. A ding so profound on her record, no one will hire her. If she gets out. And with the support of former employers she swindled, my wishes may come true.

"It's too early to be thinking so loudly," Reese grumbles into the crook of my neck.

I rub a hand down his back and hug him closer. His hand slides up my abdomen, the diamonds in his engagement band glinting as they catch a sliver of morning sunlight. And damn, it is the sexiest sight.

Turning onto my side, I tangle my limbs with his and kiss his shoulder. "Sorry. Promise, I'm done." Short nails scratch up my back and I moan in his ear, my cock hardening against his hip. I take his ass in a bruising grip. "Mmm," I moan out. "Cock before breakfast. Perfect way to start the day."

And then I am on my back, arms pinned above my head as Reese takes my mouth with his. The kiss is punishing, hungry, addictive. He rocks his bare erection along my thick length—up and down, up and down—while sucking my tongue as if it were my cock.

Releasing my hands, he kisses his way down my body. Lips and tongue and teeth taste the lines of my collarbones, the stiff peaks of my nipples, the thin happy trail leading to where I want him most. As if he hears my thoughts, he licks the crown of my cock. Swirls his tongue around the swollen tip. Over and over. Teasing and tasting the drip of precum.

Fisting his hair, I lift his gaze to mine. "Be a good fucking boy and suck my cock." I raise my hips and jab his mouth with my dick. He flashes me a smirk, parts his lips, and takes me to the back of his throat. My back bows off the bed as he delivers a vicious rhythm. "Such a good..." *Slurp.* "Fucking..." *Scrape.* "Boy," I growl.

He pinches a nipple with one hand and fondles my balls with the other. His head bobs as he sucks me off with steady strokes. Releasing my nipple, he wraps a hand around the base of my shaft and kneads my cock for one, two, three strokes.

Then his soaked fingers are on my ass. Petting. Playing. Prodding the tight hole.

I groan. "No one likes a tease, Triggs."

Cold air slaps my wet cock as Reese releases me. I look at him in confusion and he snickers. Then he is on all fours and crawling up my body. He straddles my neck and shoves his erection between my lips. "Get me wet and I'll reward you."

I take his cock in my hand, part my lips, and lick the underside of him, root to tip. He clamps down on his bottom lip a second before I swallow him down. His tip hits the back of my throat and I gag. Relaxing my jaw and adjusting my position, I devour every inch of him with ease. Hand in my hair, he fucks my mouth without restraint.

As he swells further in my mouth, he pulls out, shimmies down my body and takes my mouth with his.

"Not yet," he whispers, more to himself than me.

He sits back on his haunches as I bring my knees toward my chest and out. Fingers dance over my cock in lazy, soft strokes. Then he cups my balls. Lifts and massages them. With his free hand, he spits in his palm then coats his dick.

The tip of his cock nudges my entrance, and I press into him. Encourage him to rock his hips forward. To take me, fill me, fuck me. When his crown breaches the rim, we moan simultaneously. Inch by glorious inch, he charges forward and stretches me to perfection. Saltiness filters through the air as our sweat-slicked bodies slap. His forearms bracket my head as his fingers fist my hair. Breath hot on my neck, his moans of pleasure consume my hearing and vibrate my chest.

"So close," he grunts in my ear.

I take his ass with both my hands and rock him harder. "Pump me full of cum, Triggs."

His hold on my hair tightens. "Got to stop… calling me… Triggs." He rocks his hips faster, his cock swelling as I process his words. "Callahan," he moans in my ear. Slowing his strokes, he lifts enough to meet my gaze. "Reese Callahan." And then he fills me with his cum.

I fist my cock and stroke. "Say it again," I demand.

"Reese Callahan."

"Fuck, that's the hottest thing to leave your lips."

Then his hand is around mine, both of us stroking my cock. Bringing me higher. Lifting me to the precipice. He whispers his future name one more time and I growl as hot cum spurts over my chest. My hand flies to his throat, my fingers digging into his flesh as I yank his mouth to mine in a bruising kiss.

Moans vibrate his chest, his throat, his lips as I swallow the taste of him. The kiss transitions from feral hunger to soft licks. A beat passes before he breaks the kiss, pushes up on his forearms, and stares at me like it's unimaginable that this is real. That this is our life.

"You're really going to take my last name?"

I never assumed Reese would change his name when we married. Taking someone's name is an outdated tradition. Although I prefer to dominate Reese in the bedroom, the thought of actually *owning* him is unnatural. He is his own person as much as I am my own person. Yes, he owns my heart, but it was my choice to hand it over.

When it comes to Reese, I never question his loyalty. I never question his love. But with this one thing, I will question him. Confirm he made this choice for himself and not because he thinks it is what I want. So long as I have him, I don't care what last name he bears.

He traces my jawline with his knuckles. "Yes. Is that okay?" Lines mar his forehead as his brows draw inward.

I smooth the worry lines in his expression with my finger. "Absolutely. As long as it's what you want."

Warm lips press to mine in a brief kiss. "It's what I want." He seals his vow with another kiss, this one slow and heated and heartfelt.

A whirl of thrill stirs in my belly. Heat blankets me from foot to crown as I hold his gaze. *Reese Callahan.* Goose bumps spread the length of my limbs as I shiver beneath him. *Damn, I love the sound of his name blended with mine.*

"Then it's yours for the taking."

epilogue
REESE

February—one and a half years later

The sticky air blankets my skin as I step into the early afternoon sun. I shield my eyes and inhale the salty Atlantic air as I scan the beach. Not in search of Trent—he's locked himself away while he dresses for the ceremony. No, I am on the hunt for Peyton.

As if she hears my thoughts, she peeks over her shoulder and waves.

I trek across the sugar-fine sand barefoot and wrap her in my arms when I reach her. "Hey, sunshine." A squeal of laughter echoes in my ear as I spin her around. I set her back on her feet and extend a hand to Micah.

He takes it and pulls me into a shoulder-slapping hug. "Congrats, man."

"Thanks," I say as we break apart.

The three of us huddle together, one of Peyton's arms locked with mine and the other with her husband's. And it is exactly what I need. Familiar contact with someone close.

To say I am nervous would be an understatement. But marrying Trent isn't what has my stomach in knots. Life with him has been blissful. What has me on the cusp of puking is keeping him happy. Giving him what he needs. Staying his person through thick and thin.

Relationships are hard work. It doesn't take degrees or high IQs to figure that out.

The start of our relationship was rocky. Some days, I woke up wondering, *Is today the day he leaves and doesn't come back?* But he always came back. It was rough, but once we spilled our truths and shared our desires, our love life found its natural rhythm. After a couple blips, our nonromantic life leveled out as well.

Thank fuck.

"Doing okay?" Peyton asks as she hugs me closer to her side.

I scan the growing crowd. Many of them friends and family. And then there is the occasional familiar face from Callahan Industries. Dale and his husband. Radford and his girlfriend. Catarina and Shayla from the San Francisco office. Raul and Clint from the Chicago office. And there will be more to come.

Nodding, I bend and kiss her cheek. "Just ready to get this over with," I say with a laugh.

Peyton looks to Micah and a bright smile lights up her face. Then her eyes meet mine. "The minutes leading up to the ceremony feel endless. But before you know it, you'll be declared mister and mister Callahan. The stuff in the middle is kind of a blur." She leans into the huddle and drops her voice. "Thank god for pictures and videos."

"I'll second that," Micah states.

I open my mouth to voice it isn't the actual ceremony that has me jittery. But before I get a word out, the ordained minister interrupts us.

"Reese, time to get in position."

I throw her a smile. "Thank you, Frannie." Unhooking my arm from Peyton, I hug her and Micah again. "Go find your seats. See you both soon."

While they head for the chairs in the sand, I walk toward the house Trent and I rented for two weeks. On the first floor, I step inside the open Florida room and duck out of sight from the stairwell to the right. Any minute, Trent will walk down those stairs from our honeymoon suite and walk across the sand. And I will be twenty paces behind him.

For weeks after the proposal, we mulled over when and where to get married. Trent said we could travel to any location—in the States or internationally. Amazing as it would be to get married in another country and see the world, I didn't want the people closest to us to miss the day. Hosting two ceremonies was out of the question.

Work was the only reason we waited so long. That and the trial.

Days after Neal and Tracy were behind bars, Vincent asked the courts for a trial. He'd said, *"Trials don't always happen with cases such as this, but we want her locked up for good. And her lackeys."* With a few clicks of a mouse and swishes of a pen, we had a court date. Eight months out, but we had a hearing date. And in those eight months, we unearthed every wretched and despicable thing Beverly, Neal, and Tracy did.

In May last year, we endured a week in the courtroom. Days of testimony and boxes of evidence were heard and seen. And on the final day, the judge read the verdict and slapped the gavel on the sound block.

Guilty.

Not only was Beverly Westcott guilty of embezzlement in the first degree with Callahan Industries, she was also convicted for the other companies she pilfered. Altogether, she received seven embezzlement charges. Her penalty... fifteen years in federal prison for each count and ten-thousand dollars in fines for each count plus the monies stolen from each business.

Beverly would never see the outside world again.

As for Tracy and Neal, their penalties were less steep but still harsh. Ten years behind bars with no chance for parole and ten-thousand dollars in fines plus the monies they stole from Callahan Industries.

It'd been a relief to put the nightmare behind us and move forward with our lives.

Once we had a date set for the wedding, everything flowed together seamlessly. Trent found this gorgeous house in the Keys. He paid for travel, board, and food for all our guests—our closest friends and family sharing this house with us for a week. We decided on casual attire for the big day—white linen, bare feet, and nothing else. The only people we needed to coordinate dates with were the caterer and officiant. We opted for no flowers or fancy getups.

All that matters today is us.

Soft slaps carry on the breeze as Trent pads down the steps. I peek around the wall of my nook and see the back of him as he walks next to the swimming pool toward the private beach. When he reaches the far side of the pool, I step out and follow.

With each step forward, every worry I harbored over keeping this magnificent man happy evaporates with the tide. In our time together, we have overcome every obstacle thrown our way. And each time, we came out better than before. Stronger.

Challenges keep us on our toes, but love glues us together and never lets go.

Trent Callahan isn't some snobby mogul living at the top of an ivory tower. Trent Callahan is mine. My number one. The love of my life. My rock. And this is our beginning.

I walk through the sand down the makeshift aisle between white chairs. There is no wedding party, only us and Frannie at the front of the crowd.

"Hey," he whispers before a wide smile plumps his cheeks.

"Hi." I can't help but mirror his jubilance.

We take each other's hands and lock gazes as Frannie speaks. Every now and then, I listen in. Hear the words *love* and *devotion* and *forever*. And in this moment, nothing except us matters. Us and the here and now.

"Trent, whenever you'd like to start."

He gives my hands a light squeeze, then releases them and pulls a slip of paper from his pocket. Unfolding the paper, he swallows and studies the vows he wrote.

"There's a distinct line in my life. It divides the time before and after I met you." He takes a deep breath and meets my gaze. "Reese, you brought wonder and delight into my life. You revived me in a way I didn't know I needed. And after one night with you, I wanted more. I'd never wanted more until you." He inches closer, drops the paper, and takes my hands. "You give me purpose and drive and love. You make me want to be better." His forehead drops to mine. "You're it for me, and I am damn lucky to have found you."

Tears sting the backs of my eyes as I stare into his and fight the urge to kiss him. I suck in a sharp breath, hold it, and bask in the burn as my lungs beg for oxygen. On a shaky exhale, wetness coats the slope of my nose. The small tear falls, landing on our joined hands, and Trent tightens his hold.

"Love you," he says, a breath above a whisper.

Unable to resist, I drop a quick peck to his lips then straighten to my full height. Neither of us releases our hold on the other. Our eyes still firmly locked in place.

"Reese," Frannie says. "Whenever you're ready."

For weeks, I pondered over what to say in my vows. Weddings and public proclamations of love are unfamiliar territory. Though we don't hide our relationship from the world, we also don't put it on display. Boring as it is, we are just... normal.

Peyton and Micah's wedding is all I had to reference when I pulled out pen and paper. I'd even gone so far as to look up *how to write wedding vows* online. Every time I picked up the pen and pressed the tip to paper, nothing happened. Minutes passed and the blue lines on the page blurred. The blankness of the page mocked me and made me question if I could really do this. Get married.

After throwing the pen across the room, I called Peyton. Begged for lunch or dinner to catch up. I didn't want to admit over the phone or through text that I was having trouble spilling my heart on paper. No, I'd needed face-to-face conversation. I'd needed to match her expression to the tone of her voice. I'd needed a boost of confidence and one of my best friends to tell me this anxiety over words was normal.

Over pizza, I'd confessed my fears. Over ice cream, she'd reassured me it would all flow naturally.

"Just speak from your heart. As long as you do that, nothing else matters."

After she'd said those words, I'd come up with a solution.

Instead of writing and rehearsing my vows, I chose to improvise in the moment. Let's just hope I don't ramble or make an ass of myself.

"Love was something I never thought I'd have." I hug his hands harder. "Someone to call my own. Someone to make me look at the world with new eyes. And then you appeared." Fresh tears prick my eyes as I sniffle. "You took my hand and whisked me away. I may have loved you on that first night." Trent trembles in my hold and I give him a soft smile. "From the beginning, it's been one adventure after another. Some tested us and our bond. Some made us prove we really wanted this, wanted each other, over everything else. And at the end of the day, our love always won." I release one of his hands and cup his cheek. "I never have and never will love anyone the way I love you, Trent Callahan. You give me strength and passion and constant inspiration. Because of you, I am a better man. Because of you, I stepped out of my comfort zone." A tear streaks his cheek and I swipe it with my thumb. "And because of you, I know love. Real love."

Before Frannie announces us husband and husband, my lips are on his. On a private beach in the Keys, I marry my best friend, my person. As cheers erupt around us, I smile against his lips. Melt into his touch. And sigh… because he is officially mine forever.

Blank Canvas

ARTIST DUET
BOOK ONE

prologue
DEVLYN

Four Years Ago

"We should break up."

I rear my head back as if Kelsey slapped me. Did I hear her correctly?

The crowd continues to cheer and dance as high-volume music plays around us. A tassel smacks my cheek as another graduate from our senior class squeezes through the throng of bodies.

Leaning in, I speak next to Kelsey's ear. "Sorry, didn't hear you over the noise." At least I don't think I heard her. "What'd you say?"

Kelsey takes my hand and guides us through hundreds of our classmates and their families. Her hand in mine feels different, colder, less comforting. Nothing like the girl I've known the past three years. The abrupt change has me queasy and unsettled.

Once we reach the outskirts, she stops and spins to face me. The downturn of her lips is an instant red flag. A warning sign telling me I didn't mishear what she said a moment ago. But I refuse to believe it. Not until I hear the words clearly from her lips and the reason why.

"Devlyn, I'm sorry." Her bottom lip juts out as her eyes droop at the corners.

She's sorry? You have got to be kidding me. Her *sorry* appears a little too forced, a little too practiced.

Kelsey and I have been practically inseparable since Andrew Bishop's "We survived freshman year" party three years ago. It wasn't an instant love connection, but she carried herself unlike other high school girls. More mature and less catty. She had this air about her; a strength I gravitated toward. Plus, she made me laugh. A lot.

We had hung out all summer. By the time sophomore year started, Kelsey Martin was officially my girlfriend. Not a single day passed where I doubted our relationship or its backbone. We were solid. Practically attached at the hip. In love.

Or so I thought.

"You're sorry?" The words leave my lips harsher than intended, but I don't regret the severity of my tone. Not when the girl who has owned my heart for three years says she wants to break up. I glance off to the side, too stunned to see anything. When I return my gaze, every soft line of her face—the ones I drew from memory with pencil and charcoal—blur into a blob of unpleasant colors. "Doesn't seem like you're sorry," I choke out.

A hand grazes my forearm and I yank it from her grip. Her head falls forward as she sniffles. "Please don't hate me." Sadness laces her voice and makes me question reality. Makes me question the reason behind this sudden change.

"How did you expect me to feel?" I shiver, cross my arms over my chest and hug myself. "Did you expect me to be okay with this?" I close my eyes, take a deep breath, and open them on the exhale. "You gave no indications. We see each other every day and you've never said or shown you're unhappy."

"I'm not," she says quickly.

Our eyes meet and I shake my head. "Then why?" I want to touch her. Want to reach out, wrap my arms around her, and mold her to my frame.

But I won't. Never again. Doing so only muddles the water more.

She stares off toward the crowd, laughs without humor then meets my doubtful eyes. "Graduation day," she murmurs. "Today should be one of the happiest days of our non-adult lives." I nod but keep my lips sealed. Right now, I don't trust my voice or the words I might spew. "Last night, as I got everything ready for today, it blindsided me."

My brows pinch at the middle. "What did?"

Kelsey waves a hand toward the massive gathering, as if I should automatically know the storm of thoughts brewing in her head. "This!" She points to random people, then waves a hand at the room. "Graduation. The end. And not just the end of high school, but the start of what follows."

This isn't hot off the press news. Most of our senior year was spent in assemblies discussing what would happen this year and what it all meant. Most of junior and senior year was packed with college discussions and plans for after high school. Kelsey and I had discussed all this at length with each other. Us taking different paths after high school wasn't anything new. And we talked, on more than one occasion, about our relationship post high school.

Our conversations never revolved around breaking up. Of course our relationship would be different, but we planned to stick it out.

Yes, hundreds of miles would separate us—Kelsey starts Florida State in the fall while I start at Ringling. Less than a day's drive away, our plan was to spend as many weekends and breaks together as possible. We had it all mapped out.

Or so I thought. Obviously, unbeknownst to me, those plans flew out the window.

"And?" I drag out the single-word question. "We talked about this."

She shakes her head, not wanting to hear what I have to say. "No, Dev. We talked about our fantasy life, post high school." Her eyes close a beat, then meet mine. Another shiver racks my body at the coldness in her eyes, the stiffness in her posture. "Reality check, we aren't kids anymore. Even if we met in the middle, seeing each other on off days would be exhausting. Both of us will get behind in our studies. It's just too hard."

She averts her eyes to the senior class twenty feet from us. Her spine straightens as she wipes all emotion from her face. Bile rises in my throat as I take in this new side of her. A side I have never seen. A side that makes me sick to my stomach.

How long has this part of her existed? How long has splitting up been on her mind? I refuse to ask because I fear learning the truth. That she has considered the idea of breaking up for much longer than a day or two.

"Breaking up is for the best," she says without looking my way. "We should get to experience college and this new phase of our lives. Make new friends. See the world… without fear of hurting each other."

All I hear is… *I want to have fun and be open to new experiences without being tied down. Better to break up now than cheat on my boyfriend and feel guilty.*

I won't throw the words in her face, but I am no fool. Well, maybe I *am* a fool. A heartbroken idiot who believed the girl he loved would want to be with him for years to come. A naive guy who thought his girl cared for him as much as he did her.

What the fuck is wrong with me?

What boy believes he found his soul mate at fifteen? Trusting boys with mold-able hearts, that is who.

Kelsey continues on her tirade of why our breakup is for the best, but I don't hear a word she says. Her voice is white noise in my ears. The words scrambled and vacant and pointless. When I don't respond to something she said, she pats my shoulder, mouths something else, then walks off.

Week-long seconds pass as I stand in the same place and stare at the fuzzy basketball championship banners over the collapsed bleachers. A warm hand settles on my shoulder, a perfume I have known since childhood fills my nose. My mom says something beside me, her voice saccharine and insincere yet firm. A woman not to be crossed. I have no clue what she said, but I nod.

I exit the gymnasium with my parents, thankful when Dad's arm hooks around my shoulders, and walk to the car. Our drive to the restaurant is a blur. Graduation dinner goes by in a haze of disbelief. With each passing minute, a black vignette clouds my periphery. Blankets my vision. The thumping organ in my rib cage beats with less enthusiasm. And it doesn't take long before the pericardium around my heart shrinks. Withers. Splinters into thousands of jagged pieces and stabs the vital organ it holds.

With each new wave of darkness, I make a new vow.

I will never let anyone in again. Never let someone close enough to ruin me with such severity. And never will I give another my heart. The agony in the fallout isn't worth the risk. No one is worth this endless heartache.

Then, I give in. Let pain and darkness swallow me into the abyss. Let my world go numb.

one

SHELLY

I love pink. Much of my wardrobe consists of various shades of the hue. But seeing this much—balloons, streamers, cake, clothes, drinks—has me nauseous.

Another round of oohs and awes fills the room as Cora opens another gift and holds up an infant-sized black dress with tiny pink hearts. Then she pulls out a pair of black Mary Jane's, small enough to fit in her palm, and her eyes glaze over.

The smile on my face is genuine. The joy in my heart is real.

I am happy for my best friend and her husband, Gavin. They deserve nothing *but* happiness and love after the journey their relationship has endured. I never pictured them as parents, but since finding out Cora was pregnant, they smile more than ever before.

Truly, I am happy for them.

The last two and a half years have been a whirlwind. For everyone in our circle. Everyone except me.

My best friend since forever—the woman we are here to celebrate joining motherhood soon—reunited with the love of her life. Gavin. Their reunion tipped the first domino.

Watching Cora and Gavin come back together and fall in love all over again, was magical. Like something from one of the romance novels on my bookshelf. I sat front and center with popcorn in hand. Consoled my friend when she needed someone to listen and give advice. Offered my shoulder when she needed to cry. But deep down, anyone who knew them before knew their relationship would stand the test of time. After more than a decade apart, their love was timeless. Genuine. The real deal.

"Oomph." Cora sets down the gift bag, shifts on the couch, and rubs her growing belly.

Elizabeth, more affectionately called Mom by more than just Cora, rises from her seat in the living room and wanders down the hall. Not a minute later, she strolls back in with an office chair lumbar pillow and offers it to Cora.

"Might make you more comfortable."

"Thanks, Mom." She tucks the cushion behind her, leans back, and sighs. "She has been so active the last week. I swear she's rearranging my organs in there." Cora laughs and we all join in.

My eyes drift around the room. Take in the small group of women gathered to celebrate the impending arrival of Cora and Gavin's bundle of joy. So much love resides in our close-knit circle, and I am blessed to have these women in my life. Women who will drop whatever they are doing to help one another. Friendship and family like ours cannot be bought. It brews over time and strengthens with each passing day.

Cora continues to rub her belly, then sucks in a breath. "She kicked." A pained smile lights up her face as her gaze shifts from one person to the next, until she reaches me, her best friend. Cora is the one person I know better than anyone else walking the earth, and vice versa. "Come here, Auntie Shell. Check out Miss Clara's latest dance moves. Something tells me she'll be our karaoke choreographer one day."

I laugh and shake my head as I cross the room and plop down beside Cora. "I have a feeling this little girl will change us all." Looking over at Autumn, whose belly has just started to round as well, I smile. "Just as Clementine did."

I lay my hand on Cora's belly and she guides me to where baby Clara kicks. The second her little foot punts my hand, tears pool in my eyes. Feeling this sweet girl stretch her limbs warms my heart. She will be loved and spoiled, not by just her parents, but by us all. Especially me.

Cora sucks in a breath and looks to me for confirmation. "Did you feel that?" I nod but don't answer, too scared my voice will be sandpaper. "Girl is one tough cookie. She'll exit the womb kicking her legs."

Elizabeth and Autumn laugh. Of the small group of women in attendance, only two have experienced pregnancy and childbirth. Elizabeth, of course, and Autumn. Gavin's mom didn't fly out for the shower but will be in town a while once Clara joins the world. Erin, Penny, Peyton, and I sit in silent awe. Motherhood has never been big on my radar, but I don't discount the idea. If the right person came into my life and our relationship became serious enough to travel down that path, the possibility of motherhood would be given merit.

But motherhood, let alone love, is such a distant reality in my life. Not intentionally. I love the idea of finding the one and falling in love. I love knowing, one day, I will have someone special at my side.

If anyone listens to my inner ramblings, go ahead and send him my way. Please.

"Can't wait to meet her," I say, then look to Autumn. "And your new addition too."

Little Clara settles and ·Cora resumes opening gifts. We play strange baby shower games for hours. Tasting jars of baby food while blindfolded and trying to guess the flavor—which is disgusting, in case you were unaware. Guessing the number of candies in a baby bottle. Speed changing diapers on dolls while someone covers our eyes. Each game is equally fun and weird, and the laughter never lets up.

Once the games are done, we scope out the massive buffet of food.

Peyton—my soon-to-be sister-in-law—told her mom about the baby shower and Tracy insisted on catering the day. No complaints here. I file into line near the end, pick up a pink paper plate with "It's a girl!" swirled in the center, and pile food onto my plate.

Being that it is Cora's day, Tracy got a list of her favorite foods and things she steered away from while pregnant. Needless to say, much of the buffet has Asian flavors. A variety of vegetable sushi, rice noodle dishes, and spring rolls. But there are also macaroni and cheese balls, lettuce wraps, muffin-sized fruit tarts, and large trays with fresh vegetables, fruit, cheese, crackers, and dips.

Tracy is awesome in the kitchen and made enough to feed three times the people present. She also made two dozen chocolate cupcakes with white-and-pink frosting. No doubt we will all leave with tons of leftovers. Again, no complaints.

With Micah and Peyton's wedding only three weeks away, I am eager to see what Tracy makes for her only daughter's reception.

Another nail in my love life coffin… my brother is getting married. To the woman who crushed on him in high school. Who also happens to be the woman he bullied in high school. The entirety of their relationship leaves me baffled.

When Micah and Peyton started hanging out as acquaintances-slash-friends, I never expected it to go anywhere. Their history was a hot mess. Not only had my big brother been her high school bully, Micah had been burned by his one and only serious relationship. And Peyton was far from interested in finding love after past losses. As a romantic couple, they were wobbly and jagged. Destined to fall apart.

But they found a way to grow beyond the horrible parts of their past. Developed an irrefutable friendship. Then slowly, they fell in love. Their love story was rocky, but neither of them gave up. What they felt for each other superseded every obstacle thrown their way.

Is there anyone in my life I *don't* envy? *Someone send help. Please.*

All I want is to find *the one.* Have a boundless love that captivates me from the start. A love that makes you forget anything and anyone else exists. A love that consumes every molecule of air you breathe. That owns every beat of your heart. A love you would crumble without.

That's not asking for too much, right? Wanting someone to look at me like I am the reason they breathe isn't asking too much. Wanting someone to take hold of my hand and never let go isn't asking too much. Not from where I stand. My friends have that type of love. It's only fair I have it too.

Sure, my notion of love and romance and happily ever afters are skewed by the countless romance novels I read. So what? There is nothing wrong with a woman knowing what she wants. There is nothing wrong with setting emotional expectations. There is nothing wrong with wanting immeasurable love.

Could I have dated half the county by now? Sure. Plenty of men have flirted and let me know they were interested. And who knows, maybe I would have found *the one* had I put myself out there more. Of the men I flirted with and casually dated, my *the-one* alarm never rang. Not once was there a whirl in my belly. No instinctual voice to tell me *give this one a chance.*

Does this make me pathetic? Not in my eyes. Does this make me a sad excuse? Depends who you ask. But I would rather be single than exist in an unhappy relationship. I'd rather be single and sad than tied to a person and dismal. Period.

Most of the men I dated were nice. Gentleman. Never pushy or angry I didn't give it up—which shocked me more than expected. The men in my everyday life—family and friends—are mixed bags in this department. That is, until they got hit by Cupid's arrow and settled down. My brother was the worst of them all, but only because of how things went down with his ex. Can't say I blame him.

Out of the inner circle, the original group—Cora, Micah, Jonas, Erin, and me—I never expected to be one of the last standing solo. The woman who preaches love and fate is one of the last to find it herself.

Erin has been dating on and off, but stays too focused on work for a relationship to stick. Leading a solo life doesn't bother her. At least she gets out there and makes an effort, which is more than I can say for myself.

"You okay?" Cora parks in the chair next to me and wraps an arm around my shoulders. "You're quiet all of a sudden. Which is not you."

I twist in my seat and smile at my best friend. Neither of our lives has been perfect. The years she and Gavin were apart were harsh and painful—for her and those of us who cared for either or both of them. All the nights I spent hugging my best friend and shushing her cries were tough. At the time, I didn't understand her heartache. How losing Gavin caused her to cry for days and weeks and months. Couldn't comprehend how her soul ripped in two at the loss of him.

And I still can't.

Not because I have a cold heart or am numb to emotion. Simply put, I have yet to experience an all-encompassing love. A love that owns every piece of you. I also don't know what it feels like to lose something so profound. To have your heart torn in two.

Instead of moping at her baby shower—one of the most joyous moments in her life—I should be giddy. The excited aunt showering my most loyal and lovable friend with pink frilly outfits and pacifiers and boxes of diapers. I should be hyping the party, not bringing it down.

Unfortunately, the small cynical part of me refuses to relinquish my selfishness. Refuses to spread false joy.

I take her hand in mine and meet her sincere, bright gaze. "I'll be okay. Just in a funk."

"Say no more." A very pregnant Cora hobbles out of her chair and tugs me upright. Before I admonish her, she hugs me tight to her body—a challenge in and of itself. My arms wind around her frame as I bite the inside of my cheek to halt the threatening tears. "I love you, Shell," she whispers in my ear. "No matter what, you can always come to me with whatever. You know that, right?"

Biting my cheek harder, I nod. "Yeah," I choke out. "I know."

She leans back enough to look me in the eye. Swipes my hair from my cheek. Studies my glassy irises. Tips up the corners of her lips slightly. "Whenever you want to talk, I'm here. Always. Doesn't matter what time or what it's about, I'm here."

I nod again. "Okay." I swipe beneath my eyes and sniffle. "But not today. Today is about you and"—I rub her belly—"Miss Clara."

Cora narrows her eyes for a split second, then drops her gaze to her swollen belly and rubs large circles. "Can't wait for us all to meet her, Shell. Pregnancy has been the most astonishing and uncomfortable experience." We laugh. "But I wouldn't trade a second of it." Cora lifts her gaze and locks me in place. "One day, you'll know too."

"Yeah, okay," I scoff. "Procreation requires a deposit, if you catch my drift. And no one's stopped by the bank."

Cora snort-laughs and braces herself on my shoulder as a hand holds her belly. "Oh my god, Shell. Finances have never sounded so dirty." She laughs harder, then stops abruptly. "Shit. I gotta pee."

I giggle to myself as my best friend waddles down the hallway as fast as her feet and belly will allow. What an interesting sight.

The rest of the shower goes by with more food, baby talk, and laughter. I smile and laugh at all the right times. I am happy for my friend. Happy that the stars in her life have finally aligned. Happy she and Gavin reconnected and rediscovered their love.

In many ways, their love story gives me hope. Tells me all things are possible.

Now, I need to *believe* it.

If romance novels have taught me anything, it is that love happens when you least expect it. Not all love is explosive. Not all love hits hard and fast. But... love happens for us all. In one way or another. I just need to practice patience while I wait for mine to show.

No matter how long it takes.

Bars are not my scene. The noise and unruly behavior make my skin crawl. Hundreds of desperate people vying for attention. Countless others drowning their sorrows and problems with a temporary numbing agent. The occasional few just here for food and a laugh with friends.

Like me.

I wouldn't be sitting at this high top if not for the guy across the table. Chet Yarborough. The man who got me through some rough days at Ringling. Days I avoid thinking of at all costs. Chet graduated with his Bachelor of Fine Arts spring of last year and moved to New York a month later to pursue his career. Since arriving in the Big Apple, his name has splashed the artist headlines a few times. In our world, having your name in the headlines is a big deal—no matter how big or small the media outlet.

When Chet called last week and said he would be in town, I jumped on the chance to hang with him. Even if that means sitting in a bar and shirking away from swaying bodies. It isn't often I leave the house or my studio. Not without a reason. Some might call me a hermit. I don't really care. There is no point in wasting gas or time or money if my leaving serves no purpose.

Chet dunks an onion ring in an odd but tasty barbecue-ranch sauce. Before it reaches his lips, he asks, "How've things been? Tell me what's new."

Before I get the chance to avoid and spin the question back to him, he shoves the onion ring in his mouth. If I say nothing, the empty time while he chews will be awkward. Not that I care about uncomfortable situations—life is full of discomfiture. I just go with the flow.

But Chet is the opposite. A rarity among our kind. The extraverted artist. The guy who paints and sculpts and draws for others more than himself. A people pleaser artist with a chatty disposition.

"Not much, man. Graduation was a few months back. Still doing my own thing—side projects, special requests, and whatnot—like before. Staying busy. What about you? How's New York?"

He finishes chewing and washes it down with a swig of beer. "New York is its own world. Bustling and alive and nothing like Florida. Like all places, it has its ups and downs, but I love the energy. It inspires me in ways I never expected."

New York is arguably one of the best places for the arts, in all forms. I never picture myself in places like New York or San Francisco, Los Angeles, or Miami. They are fantastic cities, hands down. Artist friendly and more welcoming than most. But the constant crowds, people in my space and nonstop business make me queasy. Bad enough I already live in one of the most populous areas of Florida. No need to up the ante and suffocate myself.

"That's great, man. I hope to move away too. But somewhere less crowded. Somewhere I can sit outside with an easel, a blank canvas and my brushes, and get lost without interruption."

Chet nods and then stares off into the crowd. Zoning out and getting lost in the idea. "Sounds nice," he mutters.

More than nice, actually.

Before either of us gets in another word, a man's voice booms from the far wall. "Good evening, ladies and gents. Welcome to another night of glory and excellent renditions. Also known as karaoke night."

The night went from a three out of ten to a five with this announcement. I don't necessarily love karaoke, but at least it may simmer down the crowd nearby. Have fewer people in my personal bubble for the rest of our time here.

A server arrives at our table, offers refills, and asks if we need anything else. With Chet more than happy to talk all night, I order something more substantial than an appetizer. She scribbles down my turkey burger and fries, our drink refills, and Chet's buffalo wings on a small notepad, then wanders back to the bar.

An older man steps up onto the karaoke stage and the crowd roars to life with wolf whistles and rapturous applause. Obviously, he is karaoke famous in this place. A local favorite.

I study the man as he takes the stage. Old enough to easily be my grandfather, the man sports attire of someone half his age or younger. His vibrance captivates and holds your attention. For a beat, I picture him in a swirl of blues and reds and whites on canvas. The wrinkled lines of his face a testimony of a life well lived.

Across the dining area, a voice screams above all the rest and steals the spotlight momentarily. "We love you, Karaoke Grandpa."

The old man blows kisses to the masses. "I love you too, sugar."

I scan the sea of excited bargoers in search of the woman who called out to him. Not sure why, but I need to put a face to the voice. I crane my neck and survey hundreds of men and women, looking for the one face excited to see this man grace the stage and microphone.

And then I land on her.

Familiar and not in the same breath. Sun-kissed golden skin. Dark, twinkling irises fanned by long lashes and accentuated with bold brows. Thrill on her naturally pouty lips and at the corners of her eyes. A slim yet prominent nose. Thick, dark-blonde waves swing from her ponytail; the occasional stubborn lock grazes her cheek, but she doesn't swipe it away.

Where do I know her from?

I dig through my mental archive and search for her face. Run the contours of her cheekbones and lips and nose against my mental database. Scour all the places I frequent and the jobs I have done. And it doesn't take long before I get a hit. Before her familiarity becomes crystal clear.

Last year. The mural I painted outside Petal and Vine Florist before fall semester. The woman more vibrant and spectacular than all the blooming buds in the shop. The woman I spent hours sneaking glances at, only to get small snippets of her profile or the way her hair glowed in the sunlight. The woman whose name I never learned because our paths barely crossed.

No matter how many peeps I got of her partial profile, I wanted more.

I had never spent so much time on such a simple project. Never purposely dragged out my art to spend more time in someone's presence. I may not know her name, but the fading memory of her had been a muse for much of my art this past year.

How odd I didn't recognize her right away. Must be the lighting or this place; both so very different from the flower shop.

Fingers snap in front of my face and I jerk back. My eyes snap to Chet and his shit-eating grin. I don't crumble under his scrutiny. Nor do I feel shame or guilt. Instead, I stare back with a look that asks why he got all snappy.

"Who is she?"

I shrug. "Don't know." Not a lie. We never shared a conversation. Far as I know, she has no clue who I am either. "Looks like someone I've met but can't place." Half-truth. But that is all I plan to give Chet. Last thing I need is a long list of intrusive questions I have no answers to.

He glances over his shoulder at her profile; too long for my liking. I bite my tongue, stow the possessiveness simmering in my veins, and wait for him to break his stare. Thank goodness, for his sake, I don't wait long.

"You should talk to her." I raise my brows at his suggestion. He shakes his head and laughs. "I have no intention of hooking up with anyone while I'm home. Not my style. You, on the other hand, will be around. And she has obviously caught your eye."

You have no idea.

I pick up my water and sip it to avoid responding for a moment. Before I set the cup down, the server comes to the rescue. She deposits red plastic baskets lined with red-and-white-checkered paper beneath our food. Soon as she steps away, I pluck my burger from the basket and take a monstrous bite.

The entire time we eat, neither of us says a word. I pretend to listen and focus on the crowd favorites. Chet appears to enjoy the entertainment.

While he does, I sneak the occasional glance at my anonymous muse. Take in her smile. The brightness with a hint of shadow. A touch of shade not all eyes would detect.

But I see them all. The light, the dark, the spectrum in between.

There is something beautiful about capturing all the facets of another person. Without words, without touch. Just what the naked eye sees. Translated through the mind of another. An unspoken truth sketched in graphite, scrawled in charcoal or stroked in oils.

Nothing speaks louder than the voice of art. A transcription of one's mind interpreted differently by another.

Five karaoke performances later, I eat the last of my fries. The server deposits our bills on the table and we pay. Chet has long since moved on from provoking me to talk to the woman. Hallelujah.

"How long are you in town?" I ask as we step into the balmy, late-September air.

"Few more days. If my folks don't shackle me to the house, maybe we can hang again before I go."

Neither of us is an idiot. Chet will spend half his time with his parents and the other half catching up with other friends, but I nod anyway.

"Sounds great, man. Let me know."

One backslapping bro hug later, we go our separate ways. I hop into my car, exit the lot, and speed down the road. My fingers twitch with the need to be in my studio. To bring the golden-haired beauty to life on paper or canvas.

Her image had faded in my mind's eye. Not much, but enough. Tonight, though... I did all I could to memorize every angle of her supple skin and flushed cheeks. The way her locks escaped from the elastic and framed her face. How her cheeks rippled near the corners of her lips as she pushed them upward. The subtle arch of each brow as it highlighted her already ethereal appearance.

I park in the driveway, jump out, and stop myself from running inside. Not that I care what the neighbors think. Surely, they already find me peculiar. They wouldn't be wrong, but I own my awkward nature. All artists are quirky in their own way.

I kick my shoes off at the door, weave through the house, and take the stairs two at a time. The closer I get to my studio, the stronger my pulse pounds. Scents of the earth filter through my nose—the fibrous sixty-pound sketch paper, the metallic tinge of graphite, the pungent, piney odor of turpentine. I inhale deeply as I step through the studio. Breathe in the smells so familiar and comforting.

Snatching a sketchbook from the long table along the wall, I go to the drafting table, sit down on the stool, and pick up my pencils on the side table. With ease, I sift through the sketchpad to the first blank page and run my palm down the endless possibilities.

Closing my eyes, I see her again. Beauty. Charm. Abundance. Sharp and soft angles. And a hint of melancholy.

That small dash of despair calls out to me. Begs me to bring it to life and set it free. Spill the hurt onto paper and release it from her soul.

I press the tip of the pencil to the paper and begin. In a matter of minutes, I already have the rough contours of her heart-shaped face and jaw definition. Hunching over the table, I shift the pad this way and that, over and over. I zone out. Let the art pull me in. Possess me and flow through my fingertips. With each line drawn, each stroke of a softer or harder lead, each brush of the pad of my finger to shade, I breathe easier.

It isn't purely about bringing her to life with my fingers and a set of tools. It is about connection. A connection so foreign, yet so intimate. A connection I crave, yet don't know how to manifest.

This woman wakes up the lost pieces of my soul. Stirs the biochemistry in my brain and paints it with color. Draws me into her orbit and locks me in with her gravity.

The scary part?

I want to stay there. In her bubble. In the one place I don't have to imagine the twinkle in her dark, mysterious eyes. Or the subtle pout of her bottom lip. Or the sadness that emphasizes her stellar smile.

I want to stay in her bubble and never leave. Exist in her space and breathe her air. Stand at her side and lace my fingers with hers.

But I won't. I can't.

Being in anyone's bubble isn't in the stars.

Not for me. Not ever.

three

No place I'd rather be than right here.

Petal and Vine wasn't always my dream job, but I consider myself lucky to have this place. In a world full of craziness and uncertainty, standing in the middle of this florist shop gives me purpose and eases the stress in my life. Working here started off as an accident, but I don't regret a day I walk through these doors.

Early junior year of high school, my aspirations lie in interior design. For homes and businesses alike. As far back as I recall, I had an eye for design and flow and symmetry. Oftentimes, I rearranged my bedroom when the air felt stagnant. Rearranged my clothes in the dresser and closet. Hung posters and photos in new places. In change, I discovered new life. Energy invisible to the naked eye, yet it made the hairs on my arm vibrate with intention.

On a Friday girls' night, years ago at Cora's house, her mom interrupted our hundredth *Lord of the Rings* marathon. I didn't mind, though. That girl and that movie—cue eye roll. Anyway… Elizabeth asked if we would help her at the shop the next day. She had a huge wedding order to fulfill and her employee called out sick. Like the good daughter and daughter's friend, we obliged.

That was the day I learned to love all things floral related. It wasn't only the natural perfume that woke me up, but also the way I could create something beautiful. How something so small and simple could bring a smile to someone's face. Improve someone's day with a gift. A single bloom or three dozen.

Working at Petal and Vine has been a long journey. I have worked here half my life. Literally. This career, this life, has gifted me so much over the years. Stress. Tears. Days when I wanted to throw in the towel. But also joy. Courage. Strength.

Most of all, opportunity.

In little more than a year, my name will appear as the owner of Petal and Vine. In a year, I will own a business. Elizabeth and I have gone over all the fine print little by little, so neither of us is overwhelmed by the transition. But this step is huge—for us both—and thrilling.

"Got another online order," Elizabeth says as she steps up to the arrangement table.

I wiggle a dahlia between a fern stem and baby's breath, then look at Elizabeth across the table. Without question, Cora is a younger, spitting image of her mother. Working with Elizabeth has been like working side by side with my best friend. With my family. Within the walls of Petal and Vine, it feels like home. Warm and comfortable and welcoming. Over the years, Elizabeth has transitioned from mother figure to boss to coworker to friend. But she instantly snaps back into mom mode when any of us needs that side of her. I count my lucky stars to have such a wonderful woman in my life.

No offense to my own mother. Nicole Reed is a lovely woman. Strong and brilliant and thoughtful. I wouldn't be who I am today without her. She and Dad raised my brother and me in a loving environment. Taught us to go after our dreams and never give up.

But as of recent, Mom has been a bit overbearing. Intrusive and suffocating. The incessant probing started before Micah and Peyton became official. Questions about relationships and love. And babies. God, has it been agonizing. No one would ever accuse me of being anti-baby, but the pressure Mom puts on us for grandchildren has me double-locking the chastity belt.

Which is why it is a blessing to have two mother figures in my life. Elizabeth balances out the crazy Mom puts on my shoulders. Gives me another person to express what has me bogged down when I feel Mom may go off the rails.

"Great!" I survey the full vases in the cooler behind her. All orders waiting to be delivered or picked up today and tomorrow. "Business has been picking up steam. Not sure if it's the ads or word of mouth. Whatever it is, I'm here for it." Majority of our orders are online, but we have regular foot traffic as well.

I get back to work on the current arrangement and Elizabeth starts the online order. Setting it in the cooler when I finish, I stare at the abundance of lavender, yellow, and white rose bouquets, boutonnieres, table arrangements, and more. All for one momentous occasion.

Tomorrow, my brother is getting married. Never thought I would see the day. With his track record, I sure as hell thought I'd marry before him. But life had other plans and I am so happy for him. Thrilled he found love.

Micah and Peyton have come a long way since high school. A year and a half ago, when I'd learned Micah had started hanging out with Peyton, Cora and I jogged his memory of who she was and what he'd done to her. I had never seen my brother so petrified in his life. Horrified by the ghosts of his past. Ghosts he created. He did anything and everything to right his wrongs, stepped up and became a better man, and Peyton forgave all his past transgressions.

Every time I see the two of them together, their dopey, lovesick eyes, I know love can overcome every obstacle. And if *they* can defeat history with love, all things are possible.

Which means I, too, will find love one day. I only hope it happens before a full head of gray hair and a dozen cats.

"Is everything set for the wedding tomorrow?" I ask, although I know the answer. We finished the last of the arrangements before close yesterday. But the stress of my brother's impending nuptials makes me ask anyway. Last thing I want is to forget an arrangement and throw the whole day off.

Elizabeth steps up to my side, places a hand on my shoulder, and strokes her thumb back and forth. "Yes. Never thought I'd see this day."

I turn to face her. "What do you mean?"

She shakes her head and laughs. "I remember all the stories Cora shared. *Shelly's brother is gross. He's always staring at girls and licking his lips,*" she says in a mocking tone.

I tip my head back and laugh.

Cora and I have been friends since elementary school. It wasn't odd for our families to hang out together on weekends to appease us. Which also meant my annoying brother was around. Two years wasn't a major age difference, but it was enough to steer me away from him before entering middle school. Rumors of my brother kissing most of the girls in middle school before my first year there spread faster than STDs. It was nothing compared to the year before he and Peyton became an item. I have no intention of walking down that dirty alley again.

"He was gross." I laugh harder and Elizabeth joins in. "But I'm glad he and

Peyton found each other. It was questionable for a bit, but they came out stronger on the other side. She makes him a better man."

Elizabeth pats my shoulder. "Agreed." She goes back to the table and continues the online order.

Rounding the table, I clean up my mess and put the pruning tools back in place. I start for the small office in the back corner of the store when Elizabeth speaks up.

"Oh, I almost forgot." I turn around and give her my full attention. "Patty from my book club asked about floral arrangement classes. What do you think?"

Petal and Vine has had more business in the last two years than the previous five years combined. We aren't hurting for business or income. But as a small business owner, it is always wise to have other sources of revenue. Anything could happen to taper off orders. Supply shortages, economic changes, clients unhappy with the ownership transition. The last one seems less than likely considering we hide nothing from our clients, especially those that have been loyal from the beginning.

"Classes are a wonderful idea. Floral arrangement, buying for the seasons, how to maintain planted and trimmed flowers. The possibilities are endless."

"Excellent. The ladies will be thrilled." A smile brightens Elizabeth's face.

"I'll do some research, come up with a list of classes to offer and when, price them reasonably yet still be competitive with the market."

A list forms in my mind of all the options we could offer. Different skill levels. Showing attendees how to artfully decorate their space with one bundle of flowers. Ways to use flowers for special occasions such as birthdays, anniversaries, holidays, and gatherings.

I smile and spin to face the office. I don't make it three steps before Elizabeth stops me again.

"Also…" I pivot on my back foot and meet her gaze. "Remember when we had the mural done last year?"

What an odd question, but I roll with it. "Yes, of course." I don't add anything else, unsure what to say.

"I spoke with the artist last week. He'll be by in a couple weeks to do some touch-ups on the mural and add a thicker layer of sealant. To help prevent fading from the elements."

Oh. My. God. Ohmygod.

A thin layer of perspiration blankets my skin. At the rate it seeps from my pores, I will undoubtedly look like I walked in the rain without an umbrella in no time. My heart does this bizarre somersault in my rib cage before bounding into fifth gear. Then my stomach flip-flops beneath my diaphragm.

Is it hot in here?

Will Elizabeth be weirded out if I stand in the walk-in cooler for the next half hour? Probably not. We go in there so frequently, she won't bat an eye. But if she sees me without a jacket, she will ask questions.

"And since he'll be here," she continues as if I am not having an existential crisis, "I asked him to paint a mural on the west wall inside the shop." Her gaze shifts to the wall she references. "When the morning sun hits it, it'll feel like we're in a meadow."

Elizabeth's eyes light up as she envisions said meadow-like mural. Meanwhile, I seem to have forgotten how my lungs operate. *Inhale through the nose, hold it, exhale through the mouth.* Is it too much to ask my heart to settle? *Jesus.*

The Artist—that is what I call him since he never introduced himself and I was too chickenshit to ask his name—consumed too much of my free time last year. Not to mention my dreams for months after. Elizabeth hired him to paint the mural on the outer east wall. The entire time he was here—twenty days to be exact—I made up every possible reason to step near the small east window panes, just to sneak a peek at him. When I ordered lunch, I asked if he wanted anything… just to hear his voice.

We didn't exchange many words in those twenty days, we barely looked at one another, but there was just something about him. Not a physical feature, per se— although, he was easy on the eyes. But he had this zeal. A vibrancy that radiated off him. Anytime my eyes landed on him, anytime I stood within ten feet of him, my brain shut down. My motor skills went on vacation. Every outgoing function I possessed hid in the shadows.

I don't know what it is about *the artist,* but he feels familiar. Not in the sense that I had seen him at the grocery store every Wednesday after work. No, his familiarity resonates deeper. Rooted in layers of past lives. Memories of a time lived lifetimes before this one.

And now, he will be here again. Adding more to the flowery garden scene on the outside of our building. Creating an indoor meadow for all to admire, for me to admire, every day.

"Sounds lovely." I clear my now dry throat. "Can't wait to see the outcome. It'll be beautiful, I'm sure."

Before Elizabeth reads too much into my suddenly scratchy voice, I turn on my heel and pick up the pace as I head for the office. Once inside, I close the door behind me, lean against the grain, close my eyes, and take deep breaths.

Get it together, Reed. He's just a guy. I repeat the words until they turn into Scrabble squares in my head. *He's just a guy.*

Out of nowhere, a new voice whispers in my mental ear. *Keep telling yourself that. He isn't just some guy, and you know it. Why else would you be freaking out?*

"Ugh!"

I stomp over to the desk, wake the computer up, and sort through emails to distract myself. It works… for a little while. But it isn't long before my mind drifts back to the man with floppy brown-and-golden hair. To the way his body moved with the art. How *he* was as much the art as the brushes and paint and strokes.

A year has passed since he was here. A year since I have seen him in person. Yet, the image of him is quite predominant when I close my eyes. Tall and lean, his jeans and T-shirts loose on his frame. His quiet demeanor as he focused on the art. The soft timbre of his voice faded long ago, but just the thought of hearing it again forms a bubble of anticipation beneath my breastbone.

I drop my head in my hands and sigh. "God, I'm hopeless," I mumble into the empty office.

Hopeless or not, *the artist* will be here in two weeks. Time to prepare myself to not look the fool. On the outside, at least. The mess brewing inside me will undoubtedly magnify between now and his arrival.

Where are you, inner zen master? Because I definitely need to locate my inner calm. Stat.

Get out of the car. It's just a job.

The same nine words cycle my mind for the sixth time. Yet I remain glued to the driver's seat. My grip tightens on the steering wheel as I stare at the flower shop through a trellis of jasmine, beyond the three-foot wooden fence. One breath. Then another. My fingers loosen and I unbuckle the seat belt.

Get out of the car. It's just a job.

I open the car door and get hit with more than a dozen floral fragrances. The exterior of Petal and Vine is unlike any other florist shop in the area. Similar to a small business outdoor nursery, except the plants outside are for visual appeal, not purchase. The shop has an old-world feel. An impression of simpler times and forgotten contentment.

Walking under the jasmine-woven lattice, my sneakers crunch the gravel as I come to a halt. Clusters of flowers greet me with their version of good morning. Butterscotch yellow and boysenberry purple. Blush and fuchsia pinks. Apricot and tiger orange. Sage and rosemary green and several shades between. Bushes and vines decorate the earth and the store with foreign strategy. The gravel path weaves between the plants for visitors to see and smell and touch. Bright and subtle. Sweet and pungent. Smooth and prickly. The occasional bench or chair along the way, parked beneath tall crepe myrtle and oak trees, so one can enjoy more time with the blossoms.

Past the blooms and slithering greenery is the shop. The exposed cinder block on the east wall is slathered in layers of paint. An image of another garden beyond this one. Cobblestone frames the cinder block and gives the feeling you are stepping through realms, into the place where only flowers and plants exist. The color hasn't faded much, but the paint isn't as bold as it was last year. To the right of the cobblestone, two tall windows with wide black borders frame glass-paneled French doors. Black lacquered wood rests above the windows and doors with *Petal and Vine* written in white script.

It's just a job.

Taking a deep breath, I start for the doors. Brush my fingers over soft rose petals and wispy grass shrubs along the way. Turn the knob and step inside, a blast of cool air hitting my skin. The shop is the equivalent of a three-bedroom, single-story home, minus several walls. Dried lavender hangs in twined bundles from the ceiling. Before I take in more of the shop, a voice calls out.

"Devlyn." Elizabeth steps around a rack of flower bins, wipes her hands on an apron at her waist and offers one to shake. "Good to see you again."

"You as well, Ms. Davies."

A smile lights up her face as a hand rests over her heart. "Please, call me Elizabeth." She drops her hand, but her smile remains. "We have gotten several compliments on the mural. Thank you for coming out to touch it up and give the inside a little face-lift."

I tuck my hands in my pockets and rock back on my heels. "My pleasure. I'll add a better sealant to the exterior this time. Should preserve the color for years to come."

"Elizabeth," a voice calls from farther back. My blood fizzles in my veins. A whirl forms beneath my sternum. *It's her. My otherworldly muse.* "Is the delivery truck here?" Her words fade as she enters the main floor and spots me with Elizabeth.

Her feet jerk to a stop as she goes rigid next to Elizabeth. Her twinkling eyes capture mine and I get the first *real* glimpse. Twilight-blue irises hold me prisoner for three breaths. During each inhale, I notice something new.

One… her eyes literally twinkle.

Two… the gold flecks resemble constellations.

Three… she is *my* constellation. *My Andromeda.*

She shakes her head and addresses me with a smile she no doubt grants everyone. But this is not the smile I want. Or the smile I need.

"Didn't mean to interrupt."

She goes to step away, but only takes two steps before Elizabeth speaks up. "Shelly, this is Devlyn, the artist who painted the mural."

The glimmer in her eyes arrests me. As if she wished on a star to learn my name. And today, her wish came true. Guess you could say mine did as well.

Shelly.

I scan through the random wealth of knowledge I stowed over the years and remember, in some beliefs, Shelly means "meadow." How fitting. In a blink, the meadow I plan to paint inside the shop has new meaning. A new purpose. A life all its own. I won't paint the meadow solely for the shop, but more so for her. A place of beauty, but not more beautiful than her. Scenery to let her imagination wander. To let her escape.

Blush tints her cheeks and she swallows.

Another random fact about the name Shelly… it means one of purity in Hebrew. Although Shelly has youthful features, the way she carries herself indicates maturity. Most women with her level of maturity don't blush. The fact she does is intriguing.

"My apologies." She offers her hand. "It's nice to meet you formally, Devlyn."

I slip my hand from my pocket and place it in hers. Soft skin with the occasional nick from a thorn and callous from the floral shears. But otherwise, smooth and warm and perfect against my own.

"Nice to meet you as well."

I don't want to free her hand, but know holding it captive makes for an unpleasant first encounter. So, like a gentleman, I slip my hand from hers and stuff it back in my pocket. I do my best to ignore the tingle still on my palm. The lingering warmth where our fingers touched and hands clasped.

It's just a job. Just stop. Getting romantically involved is a bad idea. Always.

"At the end of next year," Elizabeth starts, snapping my attention back to her, "Shelly will take over Petal and Vine." A smile lifts the corners of Elizabeth's lips and eyes. Thin lines accent her cheeks and temples; years of wisdom and joy evident in those creases. Pride and delight and maternal love echo from her aura as she beams at Shelly. Within minutes, I learn Shelly is more than just an employee or coworker. She isn't just someone buying out a business. Shelly is family, even if not by blood.

"Congratulations," I say. And I mean the sentiment. Owning a business is no simple feat. "Elizabeth picked a wonderful woman to carry on her legacy."

Whack.

I need more than a mental slap.

What the hell am I saying?

First, I don't know Shelly. Not really. Sure, I caught a glimpse or two of her last year while painting the outside mural. Caught her from the corner of my eye, checking me out through the shop windows. Seeing her two weeks ago at the bar doesn't count.

Second, I barely know Elizabeth. I stumbled upon the job last year after my mother stopped by the shop to have an arrangement delivered to a grieving friend. She'd instantly fallen in love with the *cute flower shop.* Bragged about it for weeks, months. She also bragged to Elizabeth about her son who made everything more beautiful with a paintbrush. Not long after, I received a call and was asked to spruce up the outside of Petal and Vine.

I love my mother. Assume her intentions are honest and come from a place of deep affection for her only son. That is what I have told myself over the years. I have yet to convince myself it's true. Much as I appreciate her effort, she needs to stop meddling. Give me the opportunity to spread my wings. Find my way on my own. Let me be my own person. Without her.

As a child, her words and actions seemed harmless. I always thought of her as a role model, a strong woman with sheer determination. She didn't get to where she is today by standing quietly on the sidelines.

But as an adult, my lens of perception has changed. With age comes wisdom. With wisdom comes enlightenment. And with my developed awareness comes perspective and uncertainty.

I love my mother, but as more time passes, I learn with each word she speaks and act she commits, it is only to benefit her. To put her in the limelight. To make people fawn over her. To elevate her onto the shiny, stage-lit pedestal. She brags about her son because, in return, she gets praise for raising such a wonderful and talented young man. She glows under that praise and slowly transitions those conversations to focus solely on her.

In this one instance—tossing my name out to a prospective client—I make an exception.

Because, Shelly.

But god, I pray her meddling stops, and soon.

Another dose of crimson paints Shelly's cheeks and heats my blood. I memorize the color. Stash it away for the next time I have a brush in my hand and canvas beneath the bristles.

"Thank you. That's very kind of you." Her eyes pull me into her orbit and hold me steady. Her chest rises and falls in my periphery, over and over. Then she blinks and breaks the spell she cast. "I'll be in the back." She shifts her gaze to Elizabeth. "Let me know when the truck arrives."

"Will do."

Before another word is said, Shelly spins around and vanishes behind a wall of flowers. The second she disappears, I miss her presence, her energy, her aura. All things eidetic memory cannot replicate. At least the image of her is carved into my memory.

I blink a few times, shake myself back into reality, and look over at a smiling Elizabeth. Her smile speaks volumes, whereas her voice remains silent. The eye of an artist picks up on these small idiosyncrasies and uses them to convey deeper meaning in their work. As for now, I ignore the hidden message in her smile.

"Show me where you were thinking of placing the indoor mural," I say to steer the moment back to business.

In a blink, Elizabeth transitions into proud businesswoman and owner. She guides me to a wall opposite the entrance. Several tin pails, large and small, occupy the floor space. Eucalyptus stems, wheat sprigs, grassy bundles, lush greenery, cattails, and more fill the taller baskets on the floor. On a short shelf behind them, shorter pails are filled with lavender, sprigged red berries, oblong fiery flowers, blue thistle, baby's breath, fern stems, and wispy twigs with pink flowers that remind me of weeping willows and cherry blossoms. Off to the left, white and blush roses grow on a wooden ladder.

Visions of the meadow pop into my head. Various greens, hints of gold and brown, small splashes of violet and honey and berry, and subtle touches of white and indigo. With a slight shift of the pails, the illusion of a natural slate path in the mural will give patrons a feel of stepping into the meadow while shopping.

"It isn't much to work with…"

I hold up a hand and shake my head. "No, it's perfect." Beside me, Elizabeth beams. "Do you mind if I shift things around? Obviously while I paint, but also for when the mural is finished."

"Not at all. I trust your vision."

Hearing those words never gets old. When a client trusts you to bring the art to life, it is the ultimate gift.

"Thank you." I give her a sincere smile. "Also, a suggestion." Her brows lift as she holds my gaze. "When I finish the touchups outside, you may want to invest in a small awning. Nothing extravagant. But something that will shade the mural from the midday sun. It'll add years to the painting after I add the extra seal."

"I will look into them immediately. Thank you for the tip."

Elizabeth guides me back to the shop's office. I don't miss the opportunity to smile at Shelly as I pass. Her cheeks pinken again, then plump as she returns the smile. I don't know what it is specifically about this woman, but she steals my attention when we exist in the same space. Her aura controls the room and says *look at me*, and I cannot help but oblige.

But I shouldn't be caught looking at her like some creeper. So I shift my gaze and focus on the task at hand.

Elizabeth and I look over our schedules and coordinate—not as if my schedule is packed, but no one needs to be privy to such information. Minutes later, we both mark our calendars for the project to start in a few days. I give her a guesstimate of how long the entire project will take, mentally stretching the time frame longer than necessary.

Because, Shelly.

We walk out of the office and Elizabeth pats my shoulder. "Thank you again for doing this. Your art will add an elegant touch to the shop and make everyone's visit more pleasant."

I stop us near the table where Shelly studiously works on an arrangement, desperately trying not to make eye contact. But I need one last walk under the stars before I leave.

"If you don't mind, I'd like to bring you ladies drinks on the mornings I work. A token of my gratitude for the additional work."

Elizabeth waves off the idea. "Not necessary." Shelly peeks through the sunset-colored petals with a small smile on her face. I let her hypnotize me for three wobbly heartbeats.

"True, but I'd like to anyway. So, what is your beverage of choice?"

"Relentless," Elizabeth mumbles, and I laugh. "If you insist, coffee. No cream or sugar." She pats my shoulder again. "You're too sweet, Devlyn."

Shelly steps aside and out of the arrangement's protection. And for two breaths, we don't speak. I don't know what it is, but this woman crosses my wires. Makes me forget how to function on a day-to-day level. For whatever reason, it doesn't bother me in the way it would with anyone else.

"What about you?" I ask, desperate for more than just her eyes.

She swallows, then wipes her hands on her apron. "I'm more of a tea drinker." She clears her throat. "Not sure where you'll be going, but I'll take any type of tea drink. With oat milk, if it comes with milk. If it doesn't, no milk is okay too." She purses her lips and attempts to hide a huff. Obviously upset with her slight rambling after being silent so long.

But I like her rambling. I like everything about Shelly. Even how different she is near me than she was when I saw her with friends not long ago. I like her shy side, but hope I get to know her outgoing side as well.

"Tea it is." I tip up one corner of my mouth, lightly tap the table between us, and take a step back. "I will see you ladies on Thursday."

Elizabeth gives an enthusiastic goodbye. But it is the quiet farewell from Shelly I hear the loudest.

I have zero intention of involving myself in any type of romantic relationship. With Shelly or anyone else. But non-romantic relationships aren't off the table. And I would very much like some type of relationship with Shelly. The fair-haired beauty with stars in her eyes.

five

Lavender London Fog. That is the name of the tea Devlyn brought me today. The last four days at the shop, he has brought me something different. Hot teas. Cold teas. Tea lattes. Some florally, others earthy.

And I love each one of them.

Elizabeth smiles like a schoolgirl when Devlyn hands over her coffee and deposits a brown bag with fresh baked goods each morning. The bakery items are unique and different each day. Today, he brought two lemon-frosted lavender scones with a side of honey butter. Yesterday, it was brown butter pear galettes.

With his arrival each morning, my cheeks sting and neck heats. No doubt he sees the flustery embarrassment on my skin. But he doesn't say a word. Just smiles and says good morning.

I have never been so enamored with someone. Enough to blush like an adolescent.

And it is so freaking odd.

Shy is not my typical style. Sure, I quiet down on the first two or three dates with a guy, but I am not *quiet*. Not like this. Not as if I fear fumbling over my words or saying the wrong thing.

And let's get one thing straight, I am most definitely not dating Devlyn. Not that I wouldn't want to.

Devlyn is attractive with his sun-streaked, floppy brown hair, sharp, square jawline, and reserved nature that has me wanting to know more. To ask countless frivolous and meaningful questions. Without effort, Devlyn easily garners my attention. Lures me in. Holds me captive with unrestrained interest.

If Devlyn asked me out, my brain would conjure a hundred ways to word vomit yes in a heartbeat.

Someone stop my internal rambling. Jesus.

Devlyn is a nice guy. Quiet in ways different from my sudden shyness. His muted words and subtle smiles seem more his true nature. His way of processing the world around him without breaking it apart with meaningless words. In less than a week, I feel a sense of comfort from his taciturn nature. Like a warm hug you never want to end. This bewilders me in inexplicable ways. Drives my curiosity further. Makes me want to share more hushed moments in his presence.

When Devlyn exists in the same space as me, I see and think and process the world differently. Give myself a moment to *really* take in my surroundings. The bow of flower petals. The jagged edges of leaves. The soft brush of dried bunny tails. The potent scent of clove and cinnamon for the upcoming holidays. Each strikes me with new perspective. They aren't just plants in a shop to sell, but also a part of something more. Something bigger.

I sip the tea and sigh. "This is wonderful. Thank you."

Devlyn gives me his boyish smile, one that makes me, without hesitation, smile in return.

"My pleasure. Glad you're enjoying it."

Then he walks through the front room and out the door.

My brow furrows as confusion runs rampant. Not from what he said, but how I feel. The way I miss his presence the second he disappears. Such an off sensation. Is it weird that I enjoy the jittery calm only he delivers? Probably.

I sigh and sip my tea.

The touch-ups Devlyn has done to the outside mural have been minimal thus far. During my occasional work near the window, I have seen him add touches of fresh paint where the colors have dulled the past year. Blues and reds, but nothing extensive.

For the last four days, I fabricated reasons to be near the windows. Like I am right now. Stealing every opportunity to sneak a glance at the wall he paints. To daydream as I watch his arms flex and his head tilt as he works the brush over the concrete.

Watching Devlyn work is art in and of itself. The way his hair flops over his temple with each tilt of his head. The way he studies the wall with the end of a paintbrush pressed to his chin. How he zones out and becomes one with the art. How he only adds paint where he deems necessary.

Devlyn fascinates me in ways I never thought possible. Not solely how he views art, but also his physical presence.

I gawk at him way longer than appropriate. But no one stops me because no one is around to witness my lewd behavior. Hell, Elizabeth would probably encourage me. Tell me to spark a conversation with him. Push me to do more than spy on him through the window.

But she is in the office with a stack of bills and invoices.

So, I sip my tea, swirl the lightly sweet, floral flavors on my tongue, admire the man outside, and pretend to tend to the flowers at the front of the store. Flowers that need no organization whatsoever.

When lunchtime approaches, Devlyn steps inside. Perspiration glistens his brow, his temples, the line of his jaw, his philtrum, and I forget how to use words in the correct order. At least I stop myself from speaking early enough. No need to embarrass myself further. My hot cheeks have already done more than enough.

"I'm ordering lunch," he says before dabbing his mouth on the sleeve of his shirt. "Would you like anything?"

The leftover spaghetti I stowed in the fridge calls out. Tells me I should save my money and not waste food. Whispers that I should gracefully decline his offer. Especially since I need to save every penny with the shop purchase next year.

"I… uh…" I fumble for the answer. *No, thank you* sits on the tip of my tongue, yet the muscle won't curl properly to say the words. *Dammit.*

"It's my treat," he adds, a half smile pushing up the corner of his perfect lips and tempting me further.

My cheeks heat and I tuck my lips between my teeth. The action does nothing except make my embarrassment more evident.

Way to go, Shelly. He probably thinks you're batshit.

Get it together. Jesus. Take a deep breath, thank him and carry on.

"You don't have to buy lunch. I brought leftovers." I point toward the back, where our office-slash-break room resides.

Many moons ago, the shop was a house. But when the streets widened and the neighborhood became more commercial than residential, some of the houses turned into small businesses. At first, it was odd seeing houses turn into real estate agencies and restaurants and veterinary offices, but it didn't take long to become normal.

When Elizabeth purchased the building, it still had many of the interior walls. The previous owner ran a beauty salon. Hair, nails, facials. They may have had a massage room too. Completely understandable why the previous owner wanted the separate rooms.

Elizabeth had a vision when this place became hers. To have it as open and airy as a field. To make the atmosphere inviting. For the business to not look like an old home, but a unique storefront. Slowly but surely, she brought her vision to life. Watching the changes, small as they were, happen over the years has been wonderful. And I am so fortunate to have such an amazing business to step into when it changes hands.

The only original walls Elizabeth left intact were ones for a bedroom, bathroom, and the short hall leading to the garage. Now, the bedroom is the office-slash-break room—the bathroom en suite—and the garage is set up for storage and cooler space. All other walls were removed. Beams were erected to stabilize the ceiling wherever necessary. But now, over two thousand square feet are an open, usable storefront.

"Will they last another day?" I scrunch my brow, confused. *What were we talking about?* "Your leftovers," he clarifies, deepening that small half smile.

Right. *Dumbass.* "Oh, yeah. Probably. It's just spaghetti."

"Then eat it tomorrow. Let me get you lunch today."

Three. Freaking. Letters. Say yes. You know you want to eat lunch with him. Not just to sneak closer looks, but maybe to strike up a conversation. One where you use your words. In order. And not too quickly.

Say it!

"Uh, yeah. Yes. Lunch would be nice. Thank you."

He retrieves his phone from his back pocket, unlocks it, and scrolls. All the while, I simply stare at him. Watch as he hunches over the phone, the thumb of one hand scrolling while a finger of the other hand presses his lips. *Oh, to be that finger.* His head pops up and heat hits my cheeks at being caught.

He simply smiles.

"Sandwiches or sushi?" I laugh a little too hard and he leans closer. His scent hits my nose and I stop laughing. Remind myself to breathe, slow and steady breaths. *God, he smells good.* "Maybe over lunch, you can tell me why that's so funny."

Suddenly, lunch feels like a date. But I don't know Devlyn. Not really. Not that I knew the guys I dated either. So I brush off the notion and think of it as two friends eating a meal together. Like I would with Gavin or Jonas or one of the guys from the tattoo shop.

"Sandwiches. And yes, I'll let you in on the joke."

Devlyn picks a delicatessen two miles up the street and we both choose sandwiches. He asks what Elizabeth likes and I give him her typical order.

See, Shelly. Just friends. He's buying Elizabeth food too.

He places the order for delivery, then says the food will arrive in a half hour.

The next thirty minutes take hours to pass.

Devlyn goes outside to clear some of his supplies from foot traffic. Me… I wander the store and pretend to straighten the already clean and organized shelves and flower buckets… while watching Devlyn… through the windows.

Am I a lost cause or what?

I force myself away from the windows and head for the office. While we wait for lunch to arrive, I clean the small card table we eat at in the break room. Spray it down with all-purpose cleaner and wipe with a little too much gusto. After I straighten the napkins in the holder and resituate the salt and pepper shakers, I exit the room.

Elizabeth busies herself with bouquets and table settings for an upcoming Halloween wedding. Seeing the bride's vision come to life has been impressive. Dark red and vibrant orange roses mixed with black calla lilies and black wispy spirals. As usual, Elizabeth places each stem in the perfect place. Her arrangements are always immaculate. Perfection.

My goal is to one day create bouquets and arrangements as coveted as hers.

I step up to the tall banquet-length table we use to arrange. Classical music plays in the background, loud enough to hear, but not so loud it hinders conversation. Elizabeth is in the zone as she shifts and adds stems. I don't want to mess with her chi, but I don't want her to miss lunch either. We generally don't eat at the same time, but I always give her the option to go first.

"Hey," I say softly. She peers up from the flowers, gives a small smile, then returns to the piece in front of her. "Devlyn insisted on buying us lunch. Got you cheddar and turkey on rye. Should be here any minute."

"He's so sweet. You eat first." She snips the end of a rose and feeds it into the vase. "I still have a bit to go until this one is finished and I don't want to leave it half done."

"Are you sure?"

She leans back from the flowers, twists the vase left then right, scrutinizes the arrangement from every angle, then returns to her original position. Although I have learned a wealth of knowledge from Elizabeth over the years, seeing flowers the way she does isn't a skill you learn. It simply exists. Elizabeth has an uncanny eye for arranging. A true gift.

"Yes." She lifts her gaze. "By the time you finish up, I should be done with this one."

I nod and watch her work.

In the beginning, I followed her every move for hours. Observed the way she selected flowers. The precision in which she clipped the stem. How she started an arrangement or bouquet, then brought it to life as she added one flowering stem after another.

In some regards, watching Elizabeth with flowers was similar to watching Devlyn with paint and a brush. Both mesmerized me with how they viewed the piece and how their fingers seemed to move without instruction. It isn't a job to them. Put simply, it is an extension of them. Their creativity brought to life.

Devlyn steps up to the table with a large brown sack in his hand. "Lunch arrived."

"You two enjoy. Just set mine in the fridge and I'll get it soon." She slides a black calla lily into place then looks at Devlyn. "Thank you for lunch. Was kind of you."

"You're welcome."

Without a word, I lead the way to the break room. Take a seat near the wall and am surprised when Devlyn slides the chair out to my left instead of across the table.

Is it normal for friends to sit so close?

Don't put the cart before the horse. Is Devlyn my friend?

He digs through the bag, oblivious to my internal inquisition, and pulls out three sandwiches, individual bags of potato chips, small paper cups of fresh fruit, and bottled waters. He picks up Elizabeth's sandwich and sets it in the fridge, along with her fruit and water.

Brown butcher paper crinkles in the otherwise silent room as we unwrap our lunch. I use the paper as a placemat and dump out my chips. Then pop the lid off the fruit cup and water, ready to dive in.

The first few minutes of lunch pass in silence as we satiate our stomachs. Covertly, I side-eye Devlyn as he eats. Watch the muscles of his jaw work as he chews. Lick my lips when he swallows.

Do you believe what you eat says something about your personality? If so, what does the Cuban without mustard or pickles say about Devlyn? While on the topic, what does the roasted veggie with brie and orange marmalade say about me?

Most of my guy friends eat anything you put in front of them. Does that mean they are more open? Can't be sure. I mean, I am kind of picky with food—eating familiar dishes to avoid change. Is that a personality trait that extends into the rest of my life? Is that why I am picky with men? Not that men are the same as sand-wiches, or food of any kind.

"How long have you worked here?" Devlyn asks, startling me back to reality.

I swallow my bite then sip my water, praying I don't have a piece of spinach stuck between my teeth. "Sixteen years next month. It's the only job I've had, but I love it. Wouldn't change it for anything."

"Wow." He pauses and stares at the pressed meat and cheese in his hand. "You don't look old enough to have worked here so long." He bites his bottom lip and I don't hide my blatant stare. His bottom lip looks tastier than my sandwich. "If you don't want to answer, I'll understand..." He swallows and my eyes refuse to look up from his throat. "How old are you?"

Some women lose all sense of reason when someone asks their age. Me? I don't care. Age is just a number. Age happens to us all. No sense in dwelling on some-thing that happens regardless of how you feel about it. I say, never be ashamed of all you endured in your lifetime. Scars from years past can be painful, but they also remind us how far we have come. What we endured to get here. Own yourself— age and body, scars and wrinkles.

My gaze drifts up his throat and finally lands on his eyes. "Thirty-two. You?"

He tilts his head to the side and studies the contours of my face. On cue, my cheeks heat. His stare doesn't unnerve me. It is more like he *sees* me. Sees the parts no one else does. It intrigues me more than unsettles.

"Twenty-two."

A myriad of emotions swirl through my chest at hearing his age. Devlyn is *young*. Much younger than I suspected. A voice in the far corner of my mind says he is *too* young. Ten years is a big difference. Maybe not when the younger person is in their thirties, or older, but that isn't the case.

Should I be uneasy with my attraction to Devlyn? Hell, when I graduated high school, when I stepped into the adult world, he was finishing third grade. It feels...

strange, wrong, to find him physically appealing. To watch him through the window as he works because of some newfound mental addiction. To think desirous thoughts about him and what his lips would feel like pressed to mine.

It feels wrong. Yet, it doesn't.

We are both adults. Yes, I have a decade on him. Yes, people might stare longer than usual or say off-putting statements. But societal standards are absurd. Invisible lines drawn to make others feel guilt or shame for loving someone or something that others deem controversial. In general, I am not the type to buck the system. But when it comes to pivotal topics, I am front and center.

Is age difference one of those topics? Potentially.

No one I know has been in this particular situation. The opinions of others have never bothered me in the past, but this feels different.

"Does that bother you?" he asks, jolting me from introspection.

I meet his gaze. Stare at his translucent green irises, so similar to stained glass. For the first time, I study their depths close up. See beyond the man. Deeper. Through the window, getting a glimpse of his soul. Without a doubt, his soul has lived more than one lifetime.

"No," I answer just above a whisper. I sip my water then speak with more confidence. "No, it doesn't bother me. You?"

He shakes his head. "Nah. Age is a number, tossed out every year by someone who wanted to mark time. I don't let it rule how I live."

Such a profound statement from someone barely in adulthood. Quite philosophical.

The room quiets and we go back to our lunch. I do my best to not blatantly stare at Devlyn. Every few breaths, though, I glance to my left. The more I get to know Devlyn, the more fascinated I become.

"So," I start, wanting more conversation in our limited lunchtime. "When are you starting the interior piece?" I stab a tangerine segment and study the piece of fruit longer than necessary.

"Tomorrow."

I perk up at the news. Granted, he was only touching up the exterior, but I assumed the exterior would take another week.

"Oh," I squeak out. Heat blooms over my cheeks at my juvenile response. "Thought you'd be outside longer."

Eyes on his water bottle, a hint of a smile glints his face then disappears just as quickly. "No. After lunch, I'm applying the sealant. Then it's finished." He pops a potato chip in his mouth then meets my wide eyes. A confident yet laid-back vibe rolls off him.

I like the feeling more than I should.

Then a sudden burst of panic infiltrates my bloodstream. With Devlyn inside the shop eight-plus hours a day, for the next week or longer, will I be the creepy voyeur lady? Yep, that sounds like me. The woman who stays in his periphery at all times, gawking. The woman trying to put the Devlyn puzzle together. The woman asking endless questions to learn everything about him.

Ugh! Please don't let him find me as disturbing as I do.

"That's great. Guess I expected the touch-ups to take longer."

I finish my fruit cup and stare down at the brown butcher paper, wondering if my embarrassment will swallow me into the pits of hell.

Devlyn strikes me as the intuitive type. Aren't most artists? That said, there is no possible way he doesn't pick up on my attraction toward him. Or my occasional self-consciousness, which is most peculiar. Ask any of my friends if I am shy, laughter would fill the room. Every one of them would say I don't have a timid bone in my body.

Until Devlyn, that statement held truth.

"Some colors fade easier in the elements. I touched them up. The sealant will help, and Elizabeth is adding an awning."

Why does it sadden me there won't be a reason for Devlyn to return in a year or two? Unless I figure out some other project for him.

"That's great." Is that the only response I am capable of speaking? My words lack enthusiasm, which makes him smile. I really like his smile. It isn't artificial or something he hands out to everyone.

He crumples up his sandwich paper and deposits it in the bin with his other lunch trash. All too soon, conversation time ends. Rather than feel down, I inwardly smile at seeing him inside for the next week. Fingers and toes crossed it will be longer.

Devlyn keeps to himself for the most part, and I don't mind. The trait adds to his allure. Gives me ambition to learn more about him through conversation. Devlyn may be quiet on the outside, but something tells me the inside is the polar opposite. Eclectic and mysterious and affectionate. Perhaps a little loud and overzealous.

Maybe, just maybe, I will find out.

Six

DEVLYN

The past ten days at Petal and Vine, constantly inhabiting the same space as Shelly, reminds me of *The Mulberry Tree* painting by Van Gogh. Subtle hints of color illuminating vitality and brilliance. A hidden fire, out in the open, waiting for the right kindling to set it ablaze.

Oh, how I want to be her kindling.

But after years of solitude and single-minded focus, I feel so out of my element in personal conversation. Sharing pieces of myself with someone, especially an attractive woman.

It isn't the actual conversation I find challenging; I speak with strangers often.

Conversations related to business flow with ease. Someone purchases or praises my art online or in the community, my introversion takes a back seat. The typical interaction at exhibitions, some might say I don't shut up. Shoptalk doesn't make me uneasy.

But talking about something other than art—my pieces or someone else's—isn't something I do often.

While Chet was in town, even our conversations were clipped. Not that we didn't have anything noteworthy to share, we just understand each other. Understand the inner workings of the creative brain. That we don't necessarily voice everything we think or feel or perceive. Instead, we digest it in our head and translate it via art. Some on a sketchpad, others on canvas, and many with another medium.

Oddly enough, I enjoy conversations with Shelly. Conversations about something other than work or art. With each passing day, she opens up more. As do I. Like the petals of a morning glory. Slow and steady, then all at once.

Since walking through the doors of Petal and Vine, I have learned a lot about Shelly.

Her preference for pink is unrivaled. Pink isn't the only color she wears, but it is somewhere on her person each day. Whether it be accents in the attire or the elastic securing her ponytail.

She prefers tea lattes over tea with a splash of milk, but won't disclose this. There was no disguising the twinkle in her twilight eyes when I handed over the extra spicy chai tea latte. Never had I seen someone so excited for a drink.

Which is why I bought her the same drink today.

"Enjoy the rest of your day," Shelly says to an older man leaving with a bundle of flowers in paper and twine. The bell over the door jingles, the man waving goodbye as he exits. My eyes are glued to the door when I feel Shelly sidle up to my right. "Looks dreamy." Her voice soft and fantastical.

I twist and take in her profile, her gaze lost in the meadow on the wall. *Her meadow.* The one I painted with her in mind.

Whimsical weeping willow branches in the foreground. Tall grasses a pale green and golden brown. Wild purple flowers and sunset-colored echinacea buds. Common daisies and bold-blue cornflowers. And a small cobblestone path that starts at the floor and trails a few feet into the meadow before disappearing.

"Good. Was the impression I wanted to give."

She stares at the meadow. Studies the intricate lines and detailed strokes. Meanwhile, I revel in the contours of her profile. The minor slope of her forehead and prominent arch of her brow. The subtle angle of her nose, slight flare of her nostrils, and dip of her philtrum. The plumpness of her lips, the bottom fuller than the top. And the strong yet soft line of her jaw and chin.

Shelly is real-life art. An artist's model. A muse. A goddess.

I shake my head. Shake away the fantasy of something more.

It's just a job. Nothing more. Never anything more.

Shelly snaps her gaze away from the meadow and meets my stare. The usual sparkle in her twilight eyes is muted, duller, less dazzling. I want to ask her the cause of her sudden mood shift. What brought on her melancholy?

But I don't, fearing I already know the answer.

After I leave Petal and Vine tonight, I won't return. Not for work, anyway. And this fact displeases her.

A twinge expands in my solar plexus. Reminds me not seeing Shelly every day will be difficult for me as well. Something I am not used to... missing another person.

What alternative is there?

I don't want this to be it. The end. The last day I see her. But I don't want to give her the wrong impression. Don't want to lead her on and spread false hope. It wouldn't do either of us any good. Still... this can't be it.

"Would you want to hang out sometime?" The words leave my lips in a rush. Then I mentally smack myself as they replay. *What the hell are you doing?* But it is too late. The offer has already been extended. Perhaps I should amend it. "As friends," I clarify.

Her eyes dart between mine, searching for unspoken clues.

Good question. If you find answers, let me know.

"Uh..." Her teeth nibble at her bottom lip. In the periphery, her fingers tug at her waist apron. "Sure, I guess. Sounds nice."

God, how does she make apprehension look adorable? Her hesitation makes my heart beat faster and breath come in bursts. Spreads warmth in my veins and stirs me to life. Gives me an inkling of hope for something more. Something I swore off years ago.

But it shouldn't give me hope. It can't.

Shelly is a friend. Only a friend. Plenty of men and women have strictly platonic friendships, and so can we.

Keep telling yourself that. Maybe if you repeat it enough, you'll believe it.

"Before I leave, we should exchange numbers," I say, then add with too much enthusiasm, "To coordinate." *Take a fucking pill already. Jeez.* "What do you think about lunch and a museum?"

Seriously, this feels like more than friendship. Asking her to lunch and the museum sounds more like a *date*. But what do I know? I haven't had many female friends since high school. That is what happens when you keep to yourself. So what do adult, opposite-sex friends do?

The museum sounds like a safe atmosphere to visit with a friend. Lots of people. Plenty of distractions.

At least it isn't my house, on my couch, with the bedroom in close proximity. Or worse, my studio. Although my desire to be intimate with a woman is minuscule, I fear the temptation of having Shelly in my space. Near my bed. Near my creations. Her scent in the air and on fabrics. The image of her permanently etched in each room she enters. God, it would make my home my own personal torture chamber.

"I haven't been to a museum since I was a kid. I'd love that."

Her smile is worth every questionable thought. Worth the agony of where we go —as friends—from here. If a day at the museum excites her, I wonder what other places will?

"Great." I almost slip and add *it's a date.*

For a moment, we stand there, unsure what to do next. The corner of her mouth twitches, and I drop my gaze. Before temptation gets the better of me, I face forward and start cleaning up my mess. This snaps Shelly into action and she goes back to her workspace and cleans up the table. As I gather the last of my brushes, she fills the low-stocked flower pails with more blooms and tidies up the shop.

When she locks the front door and flips the welcome sign to closed, I wilt like a thirsty flower. She does a few last-minute tasks and then we exit through the back door.

After I stow my supplies in the back of my SUV, we stand unmoving, unspeaking, between our cars. I barely know Shelly, but today feels like goodbye. Like letting go of someone important. And I don't like the pang beneath my diaphragm. The ever-increasing twinge between my ribs.

"Talk to you later," I say as I reach for the door handle. "Drive safe."

"You too. Talk to you later."

We get in our cars and I wait for her to leave first. When her car is out of sight, I drop my head on the steering wheel and close my eyes. Take a deep breath. Then another as I wrap my fists around the wheel.

"What *are* you doing?"

Of course, I don't answer myself. What the hell would I say? I have no legitimate answer. Wish I had an idea of what happens next. Wish someone would give me advice on where I go from here. I don't need step-by-step instructions, but a look in the crystal ball wouldn't hurt.

If I keep the boundaries clear, keep us both on the same page, everything should be fine.

Shelly and I are friends.

Only friends.

⁓

I stare at my phone screen, waiting for a response like a needy teenager. Like a boy desperate for attention or affection or both. No matter how hard I stare, no matter how long I keep the screen awake, a response doesn't come.

And I hate how much this bothers me. I hate how I can't look away or put the phone down.

Three hours have passed since we left Petal and Vine. Three hours is both too long and not long enough.

I wanted to wait longer to text her to set up our "friend date." I hate the word *date.* But what else do I call it? Casual meetup? Get together? An engagement or rendezvous? None sound right. Especially the word *date.*

I hate myself.

Hate the inner workings of my mind and how I overanalyze every little detail. Hate that she hasn't answered me, and it has only been ten minutes since I sent the message. Hate how I have worked myself up over something I deem friendship.

Have I ever been so frantic to hear from a *friend*? No. No, I have not.

Rising from the couch, I lock my phone, stow it in my pocket, and head up the stairs to my studio. If anything distracts me, it is a pencil or charcoal or brush in my hand.

As I reach the landing, I laugh at myself. A little too hard. Why? Because I plan to use my art as a means to escape the thought of Shelly. But as soon as I fill in the blank canvas or heavy stock paper, it will be her I see. Best if I own and accept facts… there is no escape. Not when it comes to Shelly.

I am sick. Sick in the head and a glutton for punishment. My own worst adversary.

Sitting on the stool at my drafting table, I flip to a new piece of stock. Grab my charcoals and blending tools. Turn on the repeat playlist I listen to in the studio. Then, I hunch over the paper and let my fingers and mind roam freely.

I smudge a lock of hair near the corner of her eye and angle of her jaw when my phone chimes. Jolting at the sound, I sit up and set down the blending stump. Staring down at the table, I know the profile of the woman on paper is the person who just texted.

It is no secret I keep to myself. Not that I don't have friends or socialize with people. I simply prefer solitude. Family and friends know this about me, and only reach out when something noteworthy happens. Texts and calls are never just a *hey man, how's it going?*

So, when I pick up the phone, I know exactly who texted. The woman I messaged over an hour ago with a date, time and place for us to meet for our non-date.

> Sunday works. I haven't been to the Black Cat Tavern yet.

> Perfect. Meet you there at 12:30.

Meeting Shelly at the restaurant versus picking her up and riding together sends a clear message. *This is not a date. We are just friends.* Opposite-sex friends who enjoy each other's company. That is all. Period.

In college, I had female friends. We shared meals and philosophical conversations all the time. So I know friendship with Shelly is possible. I can do this.

If I tell myself this enough times, perhaps I will believe it into existence.

> I'll be the cute one in pink. See you then.

Her comment is meant to be funny or endearing. But of course, my mind veers down every other path. Searches for every hidden meaning in her words. Focuses on the way she refers to herself as cute. Pictures of different pink tops or attire she has worn in the short time I have known her.

And I hate that my mind does this. Sends me down a road I should not travel.

Why? Why do I torture myself? Overthink and scrutinize every word someone says. Look for a double meaning that, more than likely, isn't there. Look for reasons to reschedule or cancel. Or worst of all, look for clues that say this is a *good* thing. That a friendship with Shelly is exactly what I need. To feel alive again and get past the shadow masking my heart.

Since the day Kelsey put my heart through the shredder, I refuse to believe romantic happiness is an option. The heartache she inflicted still haunts me. It sets the tone for every interaction I have with a woman. Causes me to doubt the intention of every woman. Causes me to question my own feelings. Destructive as it is, what Kelsey did changed the way I perceive romantic relationships. The harsh way she ended our relationship, the way she threw our love in the trash, it made me turn my back on love and trust.

It irritates me she still has this power. Over me and the way I live life. Over my happiness and future. Over my heart and the love I could give another.

My mother and her frigid, heartless temperament toward me didn't help matters.

Maybe Shelly is the key. The one person to unlock this darkness that has consumed me for far too long. The sunshine after the storm. The light at the end of a very long, dark tunnel. Hope. *My hope.*

My relationship with Shelly doesn't have to be romantic to be fulfilling. Romantic ideals cloud what matters most. Connection. Trust. Loyalty. All components of a solid friendship.

Repeat the word friendship enough times and you might spur it into existence. Eat, sleep, rinse, repeat.

"Play it by ear," I mumble as I stare down at her charcoal profile. "Maybe Shelly is exactly what you need."

More than I realize.

seven

I scream and all but evacuate my skin as Gavin laughs inches from my trembling frame. "Jerk!" I slap his cloaked form and he laughs harder.

"Your expression was priceless."

"What? My *I almost pissed myself* face? How sweet of you."

He lifts the terrifying mask from his face and juts out his lower lip. Not fair. Just because he is my brother's best friend and my best friend's husband, it doesn't mean he gets a free pass. He needs to learn his lesson. And grovel a bit.

"I'm sorry, Shell." His pout becomes more prominent, but I really want him to work for it. So I purse my lips and narrow my eyes, then firmly plant my hands on my hips. "Really, I'm sorry." The corners of his eyes downturn, a telltale sign his apology is genuine.

Relaxing my stance, I nod. "Apology accepted." I jab a finger in his chest. "But don't do it again."

Cora waddles toward us, one hand on her rotund belly and the other carrying a bottle of water. She surveys the situation, then gives Gavin a stern yet affectionate look. "What did you do?"

He holds his hands up in surrender. "Nothing. Just some Halloween fun. I swear."

"Mm-hmm," she mumbles. "And your version of fun versus mine and Shelly's is totally different. Please, don't give my friend a heart attack. Or I might have to hurt you." Gavin gives Cora a look that says *oh, really*. She arches a brow. "Don't press your luck, mister. I may be ready to pop any day, but I'll still go to bat."

For a second time, and for Cora's benefit, Gavin apologizes. "Sorry, Shell. Just trying to liven up this party. If Micah didn't have to work, I'd have someone else to joke with."

My dear, sweet, sometimes pain-in-the-ass brother. Over the last year and a half, he has become a new man. A better man. Mature and caring and respectful. But put him in the same room with Gavin—best buds more than half their lives—and all levelheadedness disappears. I love my brother. Love Gavin like a second brother. And like any sibling does, they both get under my skin from time to time. I always forgive them, but it's fun to watch them squirm first.

"Yeah, yeah." I narrow my eyes and give him my best death glare. "Next time, I may not be so forgiving." Lies.

Panic fills Gavin's eyes. Beside him and a step back, Cora clamps her lips impossibly tight to not laugh. Cora knows me better than anyone. Which is how she knows I am messing with him. Knows I am giving him shit, just like he did to me moments ago. She loves it as much as I do, if not more. My cheeks sting as I fight the urge to laugh. My faux seriousness on the verge of crumbling any second.

Thankfully, it doesn't have to.

"Promise, Shell." Surprising me, he hauls me in for a hug. Forces the air from my lungs. "Won't do it again." He releases me and holds me at arm's length. I pat his shoulder in acceptance. "Let's eat."

"I vote yes to food," Cora answers and I agree.

Gavin wraps his arm around Cora and kisses her temple as we wander toward the spooky-themed buffet.

Tonight is similar to our Sunday night get-togethers. Tons of food. Music in the background. Good conversation between friends. Not everyone is here, but most of the group has gathered. Tonight's festivities will end with cobweb cleanup and candy inventory instead of leftover burgers and talks of seeing each other in a week. With Sunday around the corner, we will gather again in no time.

Halloween is different this year. Still fun, but more adult than previous years.

With Cora pregnant—very pregnant—her costume of choice is more about comfort than fun this year. Black maternity leggings and a top that says *The goblin stole my candy* with a cute, animated goblin baby on her belly.

Autumn is also pregnant. Although her belly is less round, her outfit is practical as well. She and Jonas will welcome their new bundle of joy a little more than two months after Cora and Gavin. They decided not to learn the gender ahead of time and, every once in a while, I hear their whispered exchanges of baby names. Some male, some female, and a handful of gender neutral. Watching both couples share openly affectionate moments and fawn over their upcoming additions warms and jump-starts my heart. Has me wistful as I think back to missed opportunities. Has me questioning when my life steered down this path. The lonely path.

I sound envious. To say I am not, would be a half-truth.

So much has changed in such a short period of time. For everyone. Everyone but me.

My friends and family seem to have their lives figured out. On track. Moving forward. Marriage, cohabitating, starting a family, buying a home. They have it all figured out.

Me… I feel stuck. Stuck in singledom. Stuck in place. The next phase of my life in my sights, but just out of reach. And I hate how immovable life feels. In a continuous loop with no forward motion.

As with our Sunday get-togethers, tonight's shindig is at Jonas and Autumn's place. Their new house. Their gorgeous, *we are definitely adulting*, new house.

The house isn't grandiose, but it is a big step up from the small two-bedroom they lived in previously. Now, they have two stories and double the bedrooms, which they will need once their new addition arrives. Clementine, Autumn's first-born, has been the sweetest helper since learning she will be a big sister. Doing extra chores, talking to Autumn's belly, getting drinks or snacks or blankets for her mom.

Her sass makes an occasional appearance, but she makes up for it with pampering later.

Tonight, Clementine plays hostess. Tidying up the buffet table, greeting everyone, offering drinks. Jonas and Autumn rave over Clementine helping with the decorations too. Hanging fake cobwebs with plastic spiders. Carving ghoulish faces into pumpkins and toasting the seeds. Stabbing fake tombstones in the front yard and stringing tattered sheets to large oak tree limbs. And instead of the usual rock music we listen to, haunted house music plays from the front porch.

"Aren't you trick-or-treating?" I ask Clementine as we fill our plates with finger foods. Some actually look like fingers.

"Yes." She munches on a deviled egg that looks oddly like an eyeball. "Mr. Jonas is taking me out soon. I'm super excited, Miss Shelly." She bounces on her toes. "One of the kids from my new school said our neighborhood gives out *whole* candy bars. Like the big ones you get at the store." Her eyes widen and jaw drops.

Oh, to be young again. To have simple things—like regular-sized candy bars given on Halloween—bring you joy.

"That's amazing!"

"I know, right?"

"When I was your age, we would trick-or-treat around our neighborhood, then go to my friends' neighborhood. If it was a weekend, we went to as many houses as possible. Some years, we had candy for months."

"Wow." Clementine peers up, awe in her expression. "Maybe Mr. Jonas will do that for me next year, after my baby brother or sister is born."

"Maybe. Just make sure you ask days before. You have to make a plan."

Clementine salutes me. "Yes, ma'am." Spartan appears out of nowhere and sniffs along the edge of the table. "No, Sparty. Mama said you can't eat the people's food. It upsets your tummy. Come on." She steps away from the table and Spartan follows without another word. "Later, Miss Shelly."

"Later, cutie Clementine."

I load more food onto my plate and head for the living room. Plopping down on the couch between Cora and Autumn, I scoop up spinach artichoke dip that came from a carved pumpkin mouth. Listen to my friends discuss pregnancy and pending motherhood. Sit in silence and wonder if I will experience more than solitude one day. If I will experience the pangs and joys of pregnancy and motherhood.

Part of me still envies their lives. The natural progression. Attaining happiness and love.

My inner romantic reminds me I will walk the path too, when the time is right. To just be patient. Quit looking at every guy I meet as a potential love interest. Let nature run its course. Things will pan out on their own. Bloom when the time is right. That I just need to stay confident and calm.

My time will come. I want to believe this. Need to believe this. But some days, convincing myself is more of a challenge than not.

Jonas hooks Spartan on his leash before he and Clementine kiss Autumn goodbye.

"Don't pick up anything heavy while we're gone, Mama," Clementine says with a stern expression. I swear that girl will make others bow to her one day. Once Autumn agrees, Clementine skips out the door, telling Spartan they are going to get the best candy stash ever.

"Is it wrong to be happy I don't have to do the trick-or-treating this year?" Autumn laughs and Cora and I join her.

"I'm just waiting for all the Halloween candy to go on sale tomorrow, so I can buy my own stash," I admit. "That's the only trick-or-treating I'll do." We laugh again.

"Get me some," Micah says, entering the room with Peyton at his side and surprising us.

"Thought you were working, big brother."

He kisses me on the forehead. "I was. We got out early. The owners decided to give management an early night." He waves a hand around the room. "So, here I am. Ready to indulge in mountains of sugary, ghoulish treats and torture people I love." I narrow my eyes at him and he sticks out his tongue.

"Help yourself. There's food and drinks in the kitchen and dining room," Autumn says.

Peyton gives us hugs, then she and Micah wander toward the buffet hand in hand.

I stare after my brother and his wife of less than a month, and smile. More than anyone else in our circle, they give me the most hope. If they were able to forgive and let go of the horrid history they share, overcome crazy obstacles thrown at them, find love and a happily ever after together, how can I not believe in a happy ending for myself?

Autumn rises from her seat next to me and dashes for the hall, grumbling about the constant need to pee as she walks off. Not a second later, Micah plops down and knocks my arm with his.

"What's up?" I ask.

"You look better."

I cock a brow at him. "Thanks, big brother. You really know the way to a woman's heart."

He rolls his eyes. "Ugh, you know what I mean. You're smiling more since I last saw you." He sets his plate on the coffee table then wraps his arm around my shoulders. "No offense, but you look happy. What changed?"

Everything. Nothing.

My life is pretty much the same. Work eight to ten hours a day, five to six days a week—depends on time of year, orders, events, and staff. Each day, I go home to my empty apartment, eat something simple or order delivery, and watch an episode or two of my current television drama. On occasion, I sneak in a romance movie on Hallmark or Passionflix.

Oh yeah… I also have a new friend. A new male friend.

Is that what Devlyn is? My *friend*? That is not a question even *I* can answer. Devlyn feels like more than a friend, yet not a romantic interest. At least, that is what I tell myself. Over the past two weeks, I have gotten to know a fraction of what makes the man. But Devlyn is still a mystery, and I feel a bit like Nancy Drew trying to figure him out.

"Work's been good. Tonight's been fun with everyone." I bite the end of a dough-wrapped mummy dog. "Just so happy for Cora and Autumn."

Micah narrows his gaze; his twin eyes study mine in search of falsehoods. But nothing I said was a lie, so…

He lays a hand on my shoulder, his thumb stroking back and forth as his eyes resume their normal shape. "You know you can talk to me about anything, right?" I nod but don't say a word. "Just need to know everything is okay. That *you're* okay. I need you, Shell."

I don't miss the undertone in his words. Fear. Worry. Love. The backs of my eyes sting. An expanding ball of emotion forms in my throat. A tsunami of love builds in my chest. Micah isn't emotionally detached, but he also doesn't freely share how he feels. For him to openly express such things, it hits harder than expected.

I never lie to my brother. Not about the important stuff, anyway.

As of now, there isn't much to share with him about Devlyn. When something notable happens, he will be one of the first to know. After Cora.

Now, though, Devlyn and I are friends. Nothing more.

"I need you too, big brother." Twisting in my seat, I snake my arms around his torso and hug him hard. "Love you."

"Love you, too." He feigns a cough and I shake my head. "Sorry. Trouble breathing." He smacks his chest over his lungs.

In the affection department, Micah and I have been opposites for years. Since he and Payton became serious, he leans more toward the mushy category and I don't think he knows how to handle it. So I give him a free pass. Let him fake his cough rather than own his emotion. But I love how Peyton has made him a better person. Caring and soft and more sensitive.

The night carries on like our Sunday get-togethers, with added special treats and a mountain of candy. With each new conversation, bout of laughter, and hug given, I am thankful to have this tremendous group of people in my life. People I love and who love me in return.

Perhaps one day, I will have someone special at my side. Someone new to our inner circle.

One day.

∼

Fifteen minutes early. Better than being late, I suppose.

I park in the lot for the Black Cat Tavern, but don't shut off the car. It may be the beginning of November, but the cool weather won't hit this part of Florida for at least another four to six weeks. So, I scroll through social media and clear notifications while the air conditioner blows my hair and dries out my skin. I click the heart reaction on a few Halloween photos friends posted. Comment on those same posts with praise for costumes or treats or candy hauls.

Then I look out the windshield and spot Devlyn's black SUV. A BMW as mysterious as the artist himself. *How does he afford such an expensive car?* Maybe artist incomes are better than I realized. Murals on flower shop walls don't pay for cars like his. With his talent, he probably commissions work often, sells pieces online, and isn't hurting for paychecks. Or women.

I shake my head at the errant thought.

Devlyn is a good-looking guy, no sense in denying it. Beautiful in an unconventional way. Some may disagree due to his lack of thick muscles, but I see beyond the outer layer. Sure, I can lie to myself until blue in the face, but doing so is pointless.

I enjoy looking at him. Being in the same space as him. Talking with him.

Our conversations, even the most mundane, are my favorite. Less than twenty words might be shared between us and the conversation feels profound. Those brief, meaningful conversations are one of his most attractive features. One of many.

I cut the engine, stow my phone in my purse, and step out. Before I close the car door, he spots me across the lot. He stops walking and locks on to me with his sunglasses-covered eyes. As if my mere presence is a beacon. And that notion does strange things to my head and heart. Makes me dizzy. Has my stomach in knots and my pulse jumping hurdles. Makes my knees weak.

My reaction to him gives me pause. Has me unsure how to proceed after such an emotional response. On unsteady feet, for sure.

Devlyn has given me no indication he likes me more than a friend. All the kind gestures—drinks, lunch, conversations—weren't only bestowed upon me. Elizabeth was included in those treats, although she may argue that he included her to disguise his true intentions. That said, he also hasn't given any signs to state the opposite either. When he suggested we hang out, spend time together, just the two of us, he emphasized the word friend. A little too much. Like he needed to stress the word before I agreed. Still not sure if the emphasis is for my benefit or his.

I try not to give it much landscape in my head.

His stride resumes, picks ups steam, and he reaches me five breaths later. "Hey," he says. "Sorry you had to wait."

I shake my head, then swallow past the dryness in my throat. "No need to apologize. I haven't been here long. Didn't want to be late. So I occupied myself with the black hole that is social media." Cue rambling Shelly. God, he must think me an idiot. I sure as hell would. The babbling woman who blushes more than any person her age.

I bite the inside of my cheek to stop myself from blurting more nonsense, and I swear he notices. A half smile flashes on his lips and has me biting a little harder.

"Hungry?" I nod, not trusting myself to speak without blathering, and he gestures toward the restaurant. "Let's eat."

We step into the restaurant and I silently thank whoever manages the air conditioning in here. You would think it was the peak of summer at the rate I am sweating. The host seats us, hands over menus and indicates the server will be with us in a moment, then walks off.

Devlyn and I lift the menus like shields and I almost laugh at our identical behavior.

Is he as nervous as I am?

Devlyn is always cool and collected. A perfect example of chill. Him on edge is unimaginable. Impossible. Preposterous.

We place our order, and now the only thing we have to shield or distract us is two glasses of water. And I should try to pace my drinking. Take small sips and not too many. Repeated trips to the bathroom will do nothing but kick my anxiety into overdrive and embarrass me to no end.

"How was your Halloween?" he asks as I study the ice cubes in my water.

I peer up and spot genuine interest on his face. His gentle smile and pale-green eyes calm me a fraction. "Good. Hung out with friends, had spooky-looking food, handed out candy. You?"

He plays with his straw, but his eyes don't deviate from mine. His stare isn't intense or uncomfortable. If anything, eye contact with Devlyn feels automatic. Natural. Effortless. As does his company. And this poses question after unanswered question. Because I get the sense he doesn't want anything more than this. Lunches and trips to museums and whatever else it is non-romantic, platonic friends do. Together… but not.

I think back to all the times I'd hung out with Jonas before he and Autumn were together. Our friendship came naturally. Our connection more like siblings or cousins. Things have always been straightforward and comfortable with Jonas. The definition of our relationship always clear and never tricky or confounding.

Not like with Devlyn.

Don't think I will ever regard Devlyn with that same brotherly mindset. The idea is ludicrous.

"Quiet. Not a lot of kids live in my neighborhood. So I get a small bag of candy and make sure it's something I'll eat eventually." He laughs and I follow suit.

"I hand out candy if I'm home, but it's minimal too. But don't be fooled, the day after, I'm the lady raiding the shelves. For myself and the shop."

"Hmm. Too bad I didn't start the mural later. Bet you have good taste." My eyes widen a fraction. "In candy choice," he adds.

I love how he feels the need to clarify. As if I didn't know he meant the candy.

Lunch arrives and silence settles over the table. I dig into spring greens piled high with turkey-craisin salad, feta, veggies, and sweet dressing.

Every now and then, I peek up from my food to find Devlyn staring. Not the creepy type of staring that makes my skin crawl. But the type that makes my chest and neck and cheeks hot. The type that makes my throat dry and causes me to swallow over and over.

The server returns as we finish our lunch. Her eyes dart in my direction, a big smile on her face. "One check?" she asks.

My brows pinch together as to why she asks *me* this. Not that I am the type to assume the guy always pays or that Devlyn will pay for my lunch. But something in the way she looks at me while she asks has me thinking there is an underlying assumption. One I am not privy to.

"I'll take the bill," Devlyn speaks up.

The server shifts her focus to Devlyn as her cheeks pinken and eyes widen. "Oh. God." She closes her eyes a beat and shakes her head. "I am so sorry. I just assumed he was…" Her eyes come back to me, her blush darkening. *What am I missing here?* "Your son or little brother."

What. The. Fuck?

I stop breathing. Stop every motor function I control.

She thought he was my son? She thought Devlyn was my son?

Jesus. How old do I look?

Yes, Devlyn looks young. Maybe a year or two younger than his actual age. But there is no possible way we look that far apart in age. That I look sixteen-plus years older than him. Do I?

How many people over the years have told me I look young for my age? How many have asked what skin regimen I use because of my youthful appearance? Far too many to count. So, how is it this woman thinks I am Devlyn's *mother*?

Soon as Devlyn hands her a card with the check, she bolts from the table. No doubt she is as mortified as I am. Just for different reasons. Bet this curbs any future assumptions she'd voice aloud.

"Hey," Devlyn says from his seat across the table.

I want to look up. Want to stop staring at the same drop of condensation on the water glass. Want to unhear that my lunch partner, the guy I have an undeniable crush on, looks young enough to be my *son*. Or that I look old enough to be his *mother*.

My stomach flips and I close my eyes. Take a few deep breaths and beg the contents to stay down.

Calmer, I open my eyes and look up. Meet his gaze and try to read the unspoken thoughts in his expression. But the server returns, hands Devlyn the check presenter, apologizes again, and wishes us a good day before she dashes away.

Exiting the restaurant is a blur. I barely hear or register Devlyn telling us we can walk to the museum. I just follow alongside him, trusting he won't let me stray or bump into anyone.

Most opinions don't hit me like this. Don't render me speechless. Don't muddle my thoughts so thoroughly.

But her assumption is a slap in the face. A punch to the gut. It makes me question myself. Makes me question if hanging out with Devlyn, as friends or something more, is a good idea.

I want this—us—to be a good idea. I want it to be more.

Ten years may divide us, but I have never felt closer to another person. Does that make this—us—wrong? If only I had the answer.

I hate this. Hate that something so trivial bothers her this deeply.

Yes, there is a ten-year age difference between us. Yes, I look younger than my actual age. But damn, I sure as hell don't look young enough to be Shelly's child. And Shelly sure as shit doesn't look old enough to parent a grown-ass adult.

What bothers me most is how deeply the woman's preconceived idea sticks. How Shelly has let it sink its claws in, make roots, and sour her mood. And the mood for the day.

More than anything, I hate how much I care. How my mind won't let the matter go. And how much I want to storm back into the restaurant and complain. Question the server's ability to see clearly or think before opening her mouth. My heart isn't cold. Cruelty isn't how I approach situations. And dammit, I shouldn't care this much.

I *can't* care this much.

Things between me and Shelly should stay casual. For her sake and mine. Shelly is my friend. *Just a friend.*

Friend or not, I damn sure won't let anyone drag her down or make her feel less than. Intentional or accidental.

Distress turns her aura stormy gray, and I don't like the shift in her energy. I much prefer the raspberry red I often see around her. The passion and strength and love. Qualities that magnetize me to her.

I bump her arm with mine as we walk past storefronts. "Hey." She doesn't lift her gaze. Doesn't answer. Just keeps her eyes ahead and semi-downcast, still in a daze. So, I bump her again. "Hey," I repeat, a touch louder.

She snaps out of her momentary fog and grants me her full attention. A nameless emotion burns white hot inside me as I stare back at the dulled color in her irises. Eyes that would no doubt shimmer in the sun. Radiate and add a new layer of appeal. An appeal I work hard to shut down.

Just a friend.

"Sorry," she says just above a whisper. "That was just…" Shelly leaves the rest unsaid. Leaves me mentally bereft.

Nope. Not having it.

I reach for her elbow, steer her away from other people on the sidewalk, and stop us under a store awning. "Was just what?"

I shouldn't care this much. Shouldn't worry about a statement from someone neither of us will see again. But it isn't so much what the woman said that bothers me. It is the fact Shelly is so thrown off by the misunderstanding.

"Does it not upset or frustrate you? What she said." She points down the street toward the restaurant.

Please don't let her think I am dismissing her feelings. "Actually, no." Her forehead scrunches in confusion, disbelief, hurt. I hurry to explain my reasoning. "Shelly, if I let other people's opinions rule my life, I would be disappointed or depressed or irritated more often than not. I'd rather spend my energy on what makes me happy." I glance down the sidewalk, let my eyes lose focus. "The last time I let someone's words consume me, it almost cost me my life." Blinking, I turn back to her. "And I won't do that again."

Her dazzling twilight irises glass over. Breathtaking and tragic at the same time. The idea of Shelly in pain—whether physical, mental, or emotional—bothers me on an unhealthy level. But seeing her exposed and vulnerable, seeing her look at me with hundreds of questions in her eyes, has my soul begging for more. More of her heart. And me giving her more of mine.

I should not want either.

I cannot want either.

She lifts a hand and sets it on my forearm, giving a light squeeze. "I'll do my best to let it go."

A strand of her hair catches the wind and grazes her cheek. And god, do I want to tuck it back into place. Brush my knuckles over the apple of her cheek and reassure her. Tell her everything will be alright.

But I leave my hand at my side. Refrain from speaking such reassurances. Don't move an inch. Because friends don't touch each other that way. Not the way I want to touch her.

"Good," I choke out, then clear my throat. "Shall we?" I offer her my elbow and smooth out my expression. Act as if we didn't just share emotional intimacy.

She loops her arm with mine and straightens her spine. "We shall."

We walk two more blocks, our steps leisurely as we take in the city. Most of Downtown St. Petersburg is plastered in art. Paintings by local artists on the sides of buildings. Sculptures in front of local businesses. Even some of the older structures are art without effort.

Soon, I steer us toward the Morean Arts Center, where the local Chihuly Collection is on display. Although sculpture and glasswork are not my specialty, I appreciate the love and labor and artists who construct such astounding masterpieces.

"Oh, wow." An air of awe occupies Shelly's expression. "I haven't been here, but I've heard wonderful reviews about the exhibit."

"Well, then I'm glad we came."

Gone is her morose mood from the restaurant. Now delight and anticipation set her aura on fire. Excitement and a hint of passion. The shift soothes something deep inside. Something I won't question or spend time trying to figure out. Not now.

After we go through check-in, a curator in the museum explains the rules while inside. As with most museums, there is no touching. Unlike most museums, you have permission to take photos.

Without hurry, we go through each room. Read the placards and learn about Dale Chihuly and his glasswork. Stare at the blown glass that defies logic or gravity. His pieces are pure imagination brought into existence. His gift to the human eye. Globes in various sizes. Bowls resembling ocean waves. Spirals and pillars and tentacles.

With each room we enter, each new piece we see, I study not only the displays but also Shelly. Really study her. How she reads about each display thoroughly. How she steps back and looks at the display from afar. Then steps closer and takes in the intricate details. The fine lines and layers of color woven into each piece. The unprecedented design and craftsmanship.

She sees each piece as more than just *pretty* or *neat*. She finds inspiration in the work. Looks at it from one angle then another. I would swear she *feels* the art. Immerses herself in the mind of the man who created each piece and display.

When we walk beneath the *Persian Ceiling,* I swallow past the dryness in my throat. Breathe deep and work to calm the ever-expanding organ beneath my sternum. The one that should *not* be beating so profusely. Yet, I can't stop what happens naturally.

Not when it comes to Shelly.

Under the lights and strategically placed glass pieces in the *Persian Ceiling* is a rainbow of color. The space is a sea of stained glass and wonder. The sight of Shelly beneath the art, reds and blues and yellows splashing her cheekbones and neck and jaw, stuns me. Renders me speechless. Bonds me to the floor where I stand. Robs me of breath and reason and practicality.

And I do nothing to stop or fast forward the moment. I can't. Not when I see her like this. Not when it makes me eager to dip a brush in pigment and paint her in this new light. A spectrum in a world of gray. A myth brought into existence.

"I found one," she whisper-shouts.

I snap out of my Shelly-induced stupor and step closer to her. "Found what?" With my fantasizing, I have no idea what it is we are looking for.

"A cherub."

Ah, yes. Chihuly and his affinity for the childlike angel. "That you did."

While Shelly scans the ceiling to locate more, I remain a step back and watch her. Watch her fascination, her excitement, her eagerness to find the next special piece in the art. I don't need to search for cherubs. My eyes on her is all I need in this magical place.

Once we leave the *Persian Ceiling,* the rest of the museum tour speeds by. Wraps up far quicker than I would like. In the gift shop, we each buy a small token to remember the museum and our visit. Not that I need a token to remind me of today, or any day with Shelly.

We step out into the warm November air and pause. After getting swept up in the whimsical world of Chihuly, we both need a minute to reset ourselves. Find our footing back in the real world.

A voice in my head tells me to ask Shelly to dinner later. Well, only a couple hours from now. The words are on the tip of my tongue. Ready to spill out and be heard by someone other than myself.

As I open my mouth to ask, another voice speaks up. Reminds me of the last time I gave too much of myself to another. Reminds me of the heartache and pain and dark, dark days that followed when she ripped me apart. When she left me to waste away. When she abandoned me without care.

And the fear from that singular moment is why I bite my tongue. Why I seal my lips and close off my heart. Because if I ever let anyone that close again, if I allow myself to be truly vulnerable, it sets me up for loss. For anguish. For the darkness.

I can't go back to the darkness. Not again. Never again. Who would pull me out?

"Ready to head back?" I mutter. This time, I don't offer my arm. Don't add pep to my voice. Don't glance in her direction.

And she picks up on the sudden mood shift.

Shelly wraps her arms around her middle and looks in the direction of where our cars are parked. "Sure."

No doubt, she probably wishes we didn't have to walk back together. Not after my abrupt coldness.

But shutting her out like this is the only way. The best way. All I know. She may not be grateful now, but she will eventually thank me. When she moves on and finds someone worthy of her smile and warmth and heart. Someone who won't love only the idea of her.

All too soon, we arrive back in the lot. The lukewarm goodbye we exchange is pathetic. Friends give better farewells than this. Usually a *see you soon* gets said at some point. But not with us. Not today. And I hate that I did this. Put a damper on our *friendship*. Ruined a perfect day.

But it has to be this way.

Not a complete asshole, I wait until her car starts before walking to my own. Behind the protection of tinted windows, I stare, stare, stare at Shelly's red Beetle. Watch for any sign of dismay; a look of disgust toward my car. But nothing comes. So I wait impatiently for her to drive away. And maybe flip me off. But she sits idle a moment, and I wonder if something is wrong with her car.

I narrow my eyes and look through her windshield. With the blinding sun, it is difficult to see her. See what she is doing. If she needs help.

Maybe she is waiting for me to leave. Wants me gone before she drives away. Just as I give the thought merit, her car rolls forward and exits the lot. No slow down to smile or wave. She just… leaves.

My knuckles pale as I grip the steering wheel tighter. I close my eyes, bang my forehead on the leather, and berate myself. Mentally slap myself upside the head.

"Did you really need to do that? Did you really need to fuck up something good?" I ask myself aloud.

Yes, I did. Because although I keep telling myself Shelly is just a friend, my thoughts continue to step over the invisible boundary. The boundary dividing friends and lovers. A boundary I dare not cross. A path I refuse to travel down. Not again.

If Shelly and I don't cross the boundary, if we remain strictly friends, neither of us will get hurt. Defining the line today was for the best. For me and her and our friendship.

Did I need to be so cold when defining said line? No. But I don't know how else to set the tone for our relationship. Our friendship. And the definition of us definitely needs to be precise. Black and white. No gray. No color.

Lifting my head from the wheel, I take a deep breath and attempt to clear my cluttered thoughts. I put the car in gear, exit the lot, and drive home in a fog. I speed down the road faster than responsible. Faster than safe. And in no time, with no memory of the trip, I park in the driveway. Amble out of the car. Unlock the front door. Kick off my shoes. Wander through the house and take the stairs two at a time. Step into my studio.

And breathe.

I close my eyes and inhale. Find comfort in my safe space. In my solitude. In my art.

Then I pick up a blank canvas, park it on the easel, sit on my stool, and paint. A woman in full spectrum with wonder and delight and amazement in her twilight eyes. A woman, no matter how hard I try, I can't erase from my mind. A woman I will apologize to sooner rather than later.

Because there is not a chance in hell I won't be seeing her again.

Even if it hurts.

Even if it breaks me.

Even if I should walk away.

nine

"Ouch!" I bring my thumb to my lips and suck on it.

When was the last time a thorn stabbed me? Years ago. Probably not since the first or second year I worked at Petal and Vine.

Yet, here I am. Getting stabbed by flowers with a vendetta. Really, they have no discord with me. But picturing a flower with revenge in its veins gives me a reason to laugh. Imagining every thorn prick brings the flower joy is the only humorous way to deal with the sting.

Why do some of the smallest wounds hurt the most? Thorn pricks, paper cuts, the slip of a needle tip while you sew.

I step back from the arrangement table and study the full vase of blooms. Contemplate adding more filler or flowers. Maybe a little of both. Anything to keep my hands and mind busy. To distract me from what I have been waiting to hear. What we all are waiting to hear.

Baby Clara is on her way.

Any second, Cora will go into labor. Baby Clara will make her debut. Everyone in our circle is on edge, eager and ready.

Elizabeth and I decided not to take on any major orders in the two-week window of her due date. Which happens to be tomorrow.

Our part-time employee, Francine, is on standby. She typically works two days a week, less than sixteen hours, to help out when either Elizabeth or I am alone, or we have major events to work on. She will work more hours if either of us is under the weather, but prefers the lesser hours. Plus, she told Elizabeth early on, her minimal time here each week gives her a sense of purpose.

Our delivery drivers, Joe and Melanie, won't be affected much. They come and go with orders, but keep an eye open for delivery and store updates.

With the impending arrival of her first grandchild, Elizabeth has busied herself more than usual. And driven me a bit crazy, to be honest. For the last twenty minutes, she has swept the same section of the shop repeatedly; not a speck of dirt to be seen.

But I don't blame her.

If I were in her shoes, I would be jittery too. On edge. And I am, but my anxiety is nothing compared to that of a parent waiting to become a grandparent.

Any minute now, my niece will enter the world. We may not be genetically related, but Cora is one hundred percent my sister. Always.

The arrival of baby Clara will change all our lives. In a good way. I never thought it possible, but her birth will bring us all closer together. Bond us in a way we never imagined. Start a new phase of our lives and expand our friendships.

"You okay?" Elizabeth points to my hand.

"Yeah. Just zoned out and the thorn attacked." I narrow my eyes at the thorny flower in question.

Elizabeth laughs. "They get you when you least expect it."

I go back to the arrangement, one of several premade bouquets we have available. Elizabeth and I wanted an abundance of grab-and-go flowers in the case so Francine won't be overwhelmed in our absence.

Elizabeth switches from sweeping to dusting, mumbling to the flowers as she moves through the shop.

I insert the next stem into the vase, then twist the arrangement left and right to see where I need to put the final flowers. My gaze drifts toward the front of the store. Toward the beautiful meadow painted on the wall. The wispy grass and abundant wildflowers. And I zone out again. Imagine myself in a magical place like the one Devlyn created.

A little more than a week ago, Devlyn and I shared the best and worst day. Between the age mentioned by the server and his aloof behavior after the museum, I considered throwing in the towel on our friendship. Everything about us is new. So breaking ties with Devlyn wouldn't be the same as losing a friend I'd had most of my life.

At least, this is what I've told myself every day I'd considered texting him.

Then Devlyn took me by surprise. The next day, he reached out.

When the notification popped up on my phone, I expected to see a text with *it's been fun* somewhere in the bubble. Those words were nowhere to be found. What I saw instead was an apology. A real apology. More than the basic *I'm sorry*. His message read… *I didn't mean to be such an ass. It's a long story. But I'd love another chance at friends. Please.*

I have never been the type to hold on to anger toward another person. Not unless they did something major. Something unforgivable. Ninety-nine percent of the time, I forgive easily and let the past roll off my shoulders.

With Devlyn, though… the man needs to figure out what he wants.

He dishes out the word *friends* more than an all-you-can-eat buffet. Not sure if the constant reminder is for me or him. Either way, it leads me to believe two things without hard evidence.

One—he fears anything beyond friendship with a woman. The thought hurts my heart on so many levels and stirs up a list of questions as to why. Two—part of him wants more than that with me. More than friendship.

More than once, I've wanted to ask who broke his heart. Who made him so anti-love. To love someone is human nature. His vehemence to avoid love has to stem from past hurt, past pain. Putting him on the spot, coming out and asking him who did this to him, won't yield answers. And with our friendship so new, so on the edge of tipping one way or the other, asking would only push him away.

In his own time, and however he processes things, Devlyn needs to work through his emotions. I simply ask him not to rake me over the coals in the process.

Since his apology, we text or talk daily. No philosophical or life-altering chats. Just normal day-to-day stuff. Conversations similar to those I have with any other friend. Chats about work, strange clients, weird conversations we overheard at the grocery store, great jokes someone shared. And like all new friendships, we learn each other's quirks and boundaries.

Another change since the apology… we hang out a lot. Like every other day. For my own sanity, I compare time with Devlyn to hanging with Jonas or Gavin. We meet up at restaurants, eat pizza or Chinese or sandwiches. Talk, laugh, and ask questions. Nothing too deep, though.

My cheeks have stung more over the past few days than any previous time. Devlyn makes me smile. Often. More often than a friend.

Our late-night phone calls—Devlyn is anti-text whenever possible—aren't like the calls Cora and I shared as kids. The kind where you stay on the phone all night, trying to find something, anything, to talk about. Conversations between Devlyn and I hold more definition, more purpose.

Last night, we talked about college. How my experience compared to his. The way he spoke about art school and the people—professors and student body— enthralled me. His experience sounded otherworldly. In a sense, I suppose living and breathing art is a different way of life.

I shared my time at college, which was boring in comparison. How I originally studied interior design, then switched gears to get my bachelor's in finance and business. Working at Petal and Vine fulfilled my creative heart. Learning how to successfully own a business was more important for my future.

Time and conversations with Devlyn are a nice change of pace. A change I didn't see coming, but enjoy more than expected.

I take the finished vase of flowers to the open-air cooler, then return to the table and clean up. As I brush stem bits off the table into the bin, Elizabeth appears out of nowhere.

"It's time!"

My eyes widen. "*Time*, time?" She nods and I drop the can to the floor. "Okay. Shit." I fumble with my apron strands. "Grab our purses. I'll flip the sign and lock the door."

A minute later, we dash across the lot. I tell Elizabeth I will call Francine on the way. We hop into our cars and speed toward the hospital. Most of the drive is a blur of bumper-to-bumper cars, red lights, and finger taps on the steering wheel.

Cora consumes my every thought until we reach the hospital.

Is she in pain? When did her labor start? Is she all deep, practiced breaths and cool as a cucumber? Or is she detaching Gavin's hand from his limb and screaming at the hospital staff? Will she be in labor ten more hours or two?

I park a few spaces down from Elizabeth, jump out and press the lock button on the fob, then jog to catch up. She presses the button for the elevator car more times than an impatient child. I don't say anything to stave off her anxiety. Instead, I lay a hand on her upper back and draw small circles. Soothe her as best I can while she worries over missing this monumental moment.

The doors whoosh open and we dart inside the elevator. Elizabeth smashes the button once, twice, then takes a step back as the doors close. Seconds later, the elevator doors open to the labor and delivery floor. Elizabeth runs to the nurses' station while I go to the waiting area, where I spot Jonas, Autumn, and Erin.

"Any news?" I ask when I reach everyone.

"Gavin came out to update us a few minutes ago. She's eight centimeters dilated. Shouldn't be much longer," Jonas shares.

Admittedly, I know nothing about pregnancy or having babies or motherhood, except for the basics and what I have heard recently. This whole centimeters-dilated thing is jibber-jabber. A foreign language only parents and parents-to-be know. I want to ask how many centimeters she has to be dilated before she has the baby. Babies are big, so it has to be a lot. Right?

Autumn chuckles at my deer-in-headlights look. "Shelly, ask me anything."

Autumn must have a sixth sense. Probably hears my inner monologue and confusion. In another couple of months, our friends will gather here again. For Autumn and Jonas and their new arrival. Probably best to ask now.

"The centimeters thing…" I pause and Autumn nods for me to continue. "What's the magic number? Like twenty?" Sounds legit.

Autumn laughs, then grabs her belly and stops. "Don't make me laugh. I'll pee." My eyes widen. Do I ever want to be pregnant? The big belly, the whole squeezing a watermelon from your body thing, the fear of peeing your pants. The more I think about it, the more I don't think I want to be. "Ten. Ten is the magic number. She's almost there. Which means it won't be long. Within the hour, most likely."

Oh. Well, that is good news. But how the hell does such a big baby come out… No. I don't want or need to know. I zoned out during that part in health class for a reason. The entire concept is just too painful.

"I'll get us drinks," I offer. "Any takers?"

With everyone's drink order, I head downstairs in search of the hospital cafeteria. It isn't long before I pop two coffees, two hot cocoas, and a pile of creamers, sweeteners, and stir sticks in a cup carrier. When I step off the elevator in labor and delivery, Jonas is pacing with a larger-than-life smile on his face.

I rush over to him and Autumn, noticing Elizabeth's absence, and set down the drinks. "Is she here? Did I miss the excitement?"

Jonas shakes his head. "No, but she's pushing now. Elizabeth went in the room while you were gone."

For the next thirty-seven minutes, Autumn, Erin, and I sit in uncomfortable chairs while Jonas continues to pace. Autumn and I sip hot cocoa while Erin drinks coffee and Jonas takes the occasional sip. I continue to watch my friend. Watch as he wears a new pattern into the shiny, bleach-scented linoleum. Watch as he picks at the edges of his nail bed with other nails. Listen to the scuff of his boots and occasional huff from his lungs.

No doubt, he is envisioning the day he and Autumn return to this floor. What it will be like when his girlfriend gives birth. How his family will be as they wait in this very room. What their smiles will look like when they meet their new grand-baby or niece/nephew.

I rise from my chair and step into his space. He pauses his trek and meets my eyes with his antsy ones. "You okay?"

He nods. "Yeah. Just trying to absorb it all. It'll be different when Autumn's on the hospital bed and I'm in the delivery room." He takes a deep breath. "I'm just trying to not freak out."

Hooking my arm with his, I steer him toward the chairs. "Sit." He obeys. "There is nothing to worry about. We've gotten happy and healthy news about their baby and yours." Autumn laces her fingers with his. No doubt, she has dealt with his anxiety more than either will admit. "And I can't wait to meet my next niece or nephew." The three of us laugh.

"Who would've guessed?" Jonas's question is rhetorical, but I answer anyway.

"What?"

"That we'd all be here. Less than three years ago, we hung out at the bar every week. Listened to horrible, but hilarious karaoke. None of us were where we are today. In relationships. Having children."

Erin glimpses my way and I spy the subtle, quick wince. I want to say, *"I feel you, girl."* But I keep my lips shut. Jonas rambles because his nerves are shot and his thoughts are scattered. Although Erin and I are definitely not the same women we were three years ago, neither of us is in a romantic relationship or expecting a child. His comment isn't meant to offend, so I don't take it as such.

"We're adulting," I tease. "You guys"—I point down the hall, then between Autumn and Jonas—"are just adulting hard core."

Erin laughs and we follow suit. Then Autumn stands up with an *oh-shit* look on her face.

"Where's the bathroom?"

Jonas is at her side immediately. "I'll walk you." I love how sweet my friend is. How attentive he is with Autumn. Jonas has always been such a good man. And it makes my heart happy he and Autumn found each other.

For years, I worried about him. Long before Gavin returned to Florida, I watched Jonas pine for Cora. And Cora almost gave in to the idea of a romantic relationship with him. Almost. But Jonas was the bigger person. He put aside his feelings for her and encouraged her to follow her heart.

Karma, in return, brought Jonas and Autumn together. And I honestly believe everything went according to plan.

Sometimes you have to deal with pain and heartache before you get your happily ever after. Which is what I keep telling myself. One day, I will get my happy ending too.

Elizabeth dashes into the waiting room with the biggest smile on her face. Peter —a.k.a. Mr. Davies—appears out of thin air. *Has he been here the entire time and I ignored him?* His smile is as big as Elizabeth's and I have my answer. Obviously, he arrived before us and was in the room.

"She's here!" Elizabeth says louder than ever before. "Seven pounds, eight ounces. And she is perfect." She steeples her fingers in front of her lips. Her smile locked in place. A smile that will never fade.

"When can we see them?" Erin asks.

"In about fifteen minutes. They're getting cleaned up and settled," Peter states.

By the time Jonas and Autumn return, we are allowed to see Cora, Gavin, and Clara. We wander down the hall and, one by one, enter the room.

The hospital room is unlike any I have seen. So spacious and welcoming. Cora lies in a hospital bed that looks more comfortable than most regular beds. A rocking chair and stool take up the corner by the draped window. A small sofa and table sit opposite the bed. And tucked in the corner near the door is a collapsible bed. The room has everything for the new family.

A small, clear bassinet sits parked next to Cora's bed, empty. I step farther into the room and locate my best friend. And she is positively glowing. Baby Clara rests peacefully in her arms, snug to her chest, fast asleep. Cora stares down at her in what can only be described as pure amazement. Gavin watches them both with similar awe in his eye.

And I want to cry. Shed a million tears for my friends and this newfound joy in their lives.

Cora peers up and sees me near the foot of the bed. "Hey," she whispers.

"Hi."

"Does Auntie Shelly want to hold her niece?"

I nod because I can't seem to find my words.

Elizabeth appears at my side then guides me to the rocking chair. Gavin scoops up Clara so gently, I mentally gasp at how different he is as a father. Such a beautiful sight. He sets Clara in my arms and reminds me to support the back of her head. And we just rock.

Clara doesn't wake. Her eyelids flutter now and again. Her lips twitch just as often. She makes the sweetest little sounds. And she smells amazing. All I do is stare at her and whisper how lucky she is to have such a wonderful mommy and daddy. That she is loved by so many. And when she gets older, I will do all the fun stuff with her.

"Do you want a picture?"

I peer up to see Jonas waving his phone in the air. "Please."

He snaps several pictures and then Clara goes to the next set of arms as I evacuate the chair. Jonas sends me the pictures and I ooh and awe over them. Then, I send a photo to Devlyn.

> My best friend just had her baby. Isn't she precious?

The small bubble pops up and dances a beat.

> Two beauties in one masterpiece.

I stare down at the screen. Read his response. Then read it again. And again. Question if I misunderstand the message. But no matter how many times I read it, I decipher it the exact same way. Each time I read it, I hear Devlyn's voice telling me I am beautiful. That I am a masterpiece.

And it confuses me. *Devlyn confuses me.*

One minute, he says the sweetest things. Compliments me like a lover and not a friend. Leans in closer, hooks my arm with his, watches me from a distance. He inserts himself in my life in ways unlike any other friend.

Perhaps he doesn't know I notice his eyes on me more often than not. That I don't feel the weight of his stare on my profile. The slight shift in his posture or held breath. But I notice every glance. Feel the way his eyes scorch my skin. I see it all. Feel it all.

Then, abruptly, he gives me the cold shoulder. Skirts around a past he hasn't gotten over. A past that keeps him from moving forward. When it comes to love and trust and his heart on the line, anyway.

So… I remain his friend. Act as I do with Jonas or Gavin or any of the guys in the tattoo family, and maybe sometimes with my brother. Try not to say anything flirty or dreamy or lovey. Do my damnedest to remain neutral.

But when he says stuff like this, when he tells me I am beautiful, I don't know what to think or feel or say. Do opposite-sex friends compliment each other's appearances? Sure. But Devlyn isn't like any guy friend I've had. When Devlyn tells me I am beautiful, the sentiment is layered with complexity and hidden meaning. So hidden, I don't think he even knows what is underneath.

Gah! Devlyn is a frustrating man.

Since I sent the picture of me with baby Clara, since I provoked the conversation, talking baby-related stuff wouldn't be awkward. Would it?

Thanks. I've never given thought to having kids. You?

Not so much. Even if I did, I'd want to be in a long-term
relationship first. Don't see that happening anytime soon.

This man is like a damn seesaw. A mood swing waiting to happen. I press a loose fist to my stomach as nausea begs for relief. His text is another reminder. A reminder I don't need, but receive almost daily. A reminder that feels like a constant slap to the face.

Friends. Devlyn and I are only friends.

His random sweet words, charming smile, and desire to spend time together throw me off balance. Make me question my sanity and perspective. Make me ask myself if I am interpreting his words through a romanticized lens. Because I have no clue.

God, he makes me dizzy.

Well, they're asking us to go. Talk to you later.

Later.

No one asked us to leave yet, but probably will soon. Cora and Gavin must be exhausted. No doubt baby Clara is as well.

The conversation with Devlyn needed to end, though. We haven't known each other long, but part of me *knows* him. And every once in a while, I want to smack some sense into him. Tell him to wake up and see what is right in front of him. Ask him what I can do to help heal his heart.

But I don't. I won't.

As always, I keep my eyes forward, mouth shut, and just go with the flow. And I pray one day it will all work in my favor. That I will find the love I have been looking for. Without mixed signals and crossed wires.

If that person happens to be Devlyn, I would be surprised.

If that person happens to be Devlyn, I would show him what being loved is really like.

Ten

DEVLYN

Did I fuck up?

For days, Shelly has been in a funk. Absent is the timid yet passionate woman I met more than a month ago. In her place is a more lackluster woman. She gives no indication I am to blame, but the pang in my gut says otherwise.

I want to ask what happened. What has her more hesitant and quiet? What has her avoiding eye contact?

But I don't say a word. I won't.

Asking questions leads us down a path of uncertainty. A path where I ask the questions, but won't answer hers. A path that muddles the lines of friendship, once again. And as much as I'd love to wipe the friendship line from existence, my heart trembles at the idea.

I am not a cold person. Not empty or devoid of emotion. Not intentionally. I do *feel* things, emotions. Love and happiness. Hurt and sadness. Joy and pain. The good and the bad. I feel it all.

Years back, prescribed by my dear mother, I visited a therapist regularly. My mother had it in her head that I was empty inside. Soulless. The irony isn't lost on me, but maybe she assumed this because I didn't express myself in a way that made *her* happy.

With each therapy session, my mother sat in the room—something abnormal on all accounts, but she insisted upon it. With each session, I opened up more. Expressed what I dealt with in school and how it made me feel. Mother wasn't keen on my responses. Perhaps they didn't suit *her* needs. She told the therapist she'd done her own research and was convinced she knew what was *wrong* with me.

Thanks to my mother, in one session, the therapist teetered on the idea of me having anhedonia—the inability to feel pleasure.

What a crock of shit—the doctor and the prognosis.

For years, all I felt was the good, the wonderment, and the delight in the world. There had never been a dark cloud in my sky. Sometimes, I experienced the pleasure a little too much.

And perhaps, that is the problem.

I feel *too* much.

But isn't feeling too much part of being a creative? A fault in the genetic makeup of an artist, any artist. We feel *everything*. Which is why we create. Why we draw or paint, journal or write, sculpt or build, play instruments or sing. So we have a way to release the pent-up emotion, a way to express what consumes our mind and soul. So we don't lose our minds. Mostly.

Shelly and I walk along the park trail. I stay just a hair back so I have my favorite view of her profile. The one I stare after too much, yet not enough. Sunlight filters through the trees and dances over her prominent cheekbones, her toffee-blonde ponytail, the column of her throat. The play of light heats my skin more than hers. I lick my lips, swallow, then avert my eyes forward.

Don't go there, Templar.

"Hey." I bump her arm with mine. Her gaze shifts from the path, but only for a second. "Everything okay?" A shiver shakes her frame, but she tries to disguise the action by tucking a nonexistent stray hair from her cheek. A cold front swept through yesterday. The air a touch crisper today, but not cold. The sun warms us as we walk through the park. A hoodie on me, as well as her. "We can head back if you're cold."

She stops walking and I follow suit. In the front pocket of her hoodie, her hands squirm. Too fidgety to be from the temperature.

Is she nervous? Why would she be nervous?

Before I open my mouth to suggest we turn back, she speaks up.

"I'm not cold. And…"

She lifts her eyes to the trees. Her twilight irises twinkle in the sunlight as she thinks of what to say next. Moments such as this, I wish for telepathy. The ability to hear her thoughts. Hear them unfiltered straight from the source. To know what confounds her so deeply.

Then, I nix the idea. Because with the thoughts I want to hear comes the sentiments she keeps to herself. The ones I want to hear, want to reciprocate, but refuse to accept or return.

"Sorry," she says after a long pause.

"Why are you apologizing?"

She lowers her gaze and I come eye to eye with Andromeda. Immerse myself in her starry eyes. Swallow past the expanding lump in my throat. Berate myself for leaving my sunglasses in the car because, right now, I feel completely vulnerable. Exposed. Nude in a crowded room. I love and despise the feeling. I crave and evade the eddy beneath my diaphragm. Beg for more while wanting to bury myself deep in the earth.

"Sometimes, it's hard being your friend."

My brows tighten. What does she mean?

Yes, I have been wishy-washy. Been open and interested one minute, then cold and reserved the next. I know this. But the stony mask is my shield. How I protect myself. How I protect her.

"Not sure what you mean." I truly haven't the slightest idea. And guessing will only dig a deeper hole.

Her steps resume and lead along the path again. Without hesitation, I follow her. "You confuse me."

"How?"

"I've had guy friends all my life. When you have an older brother, it just happens." I nod and hum, although siblings are foreign territory. "And none of them have been like you."

Is this a compliment or an issue? Her tone gives nothing away.

"Thanks," I say on a wince.

She laughs and knocks my arm with hers. I take it as a good sign. "Don't be a weirdo."

Laughter bubbles in my throat. "It's who I am." I shrug as if my awkwardness is common knowledge.

"What I mean is, none of my guy friends really connect with me." I stop breathing for one, two, three strides. "We have stuff in common," she continues as if her declaration is no big deal. "But they never seemed to get me. Not like you do."

I do get her. With Shelly, everything clicks into place.

At one point, everything clicked with Kelsey too. Or so I thought. Then, she pummeled me with her proclamation and I lost sight of all perspective. Doubted every gut instinct I felt. Because how did I not see that coming? How did I not know my girlfriend of three years, who seemed happy and in love with me, wanted to break up?

Is this where things are headed with Shelly? Down the path of promises and hearts on display. Souls exposed and futures on the line. Not sure I can walk down that path again. Not after where it led me last time.

Shelly is not Kelsey. Shelly has years of wisdom and heart guiding her. But if I let her all the way in and lose her, the end would be pure devastation. For us both.

"Not sure what to say."

Part of me wants to nix our friendship. Call it quits before it becomes something more, deeper, unbreakable. Before either of us navigates this irreversible path.

I should walk away now, say goodbye as we go our separate ways. But abandoning Shelly is impossible. Just the idea of walking away steals my breath. Forms a fault line in my heart. Has me mentally bending at the waist and retching.

I hate the piece of me that needs her. Needs her aura and light. Craves her smile and warmth. Begs for her timid conversation and unrelenting attention.

I also love how much I need her.

She spins around, walks backward, and grants me the smile I see every time I close my eyes. "You don't need to say anything. I just wanted to tell you." She spins back and walks beside me again.

The next quarter mile of our walk around the lake is blanketed in silence. Our pace leisure. Her arms swing at her sides as she glances up at the trees. I shove my hands in my hoodie pockets to avoid reaching for hers. Wouldn't be surprised if my body did it involuntarily. Not with the level of gravity Shelly harbors.

Her behavior the last few days wiggles its way to the surface. The uncomfortable, tense silence. Her stiff posture and dejected body language. I work to force the memory away but fail miserably.

"Can I ask something?"

"Yes."

Deep breaths. It's just a question and I am probably overreacting. Still, my stomach twists and flips. "Did something happen?"

"Not sure I understand?" Her gaze falls from the trees and heats my cheek, my jaw, my neck.

"The other day, you texted about your friend having her baby. You seemed really happy. Since then, not so much. Did something happen?"

A chill blankets my skin the second she looks away. Shelly stays quiet for several paces, and I wonder if the question was too personal or somehow upset her.

We happen upon an empty bench by the lake. She ambles off the path and goes straight for the bench without a word. I stay a few feet back until we both sit. Out of the corner of my eye, I watch how intently she focuses on the lake. Watch as she searches for a way to tell me what occupied her mind. What had a gray cloud floating over her.

"This is going to sound stupid." Her eyes scan the bank of the lake as she works her jaw back and forth.

When she doesn't continue, I bump her shoulder with my arm. "Nothing you say is stupid."

She laughs without humor. "Just wait." I grant her the time she needs. Don't interrupt while she compiles the words in her mind. And then she spills her secrets. "I read too much into your response after I texted you that day."

"When your friend had her baby?"

"Mm-hmm."

What did I say? Think, think, think.

I go back a few days in my memory bank. Remember the picture she sent of her with the baby. Recall the way I stroked her cheek in the image before I replied. Then, I hang my head. Mentally slap myself for the responses I sent her. I'd let my mind wander and didn't think before typing either text. *Shit.* No wonder she has been distant. If our roles were reversed, I would be too.

I complimented her. Told her she was beautiful. Which is true, but could be taken out of context. Considering I define the friendship line every time we see each other, my words undoubtedly confused the hell out of her. Then I drove the nail deeper and told her I wouldn't have children without full commitment. Followed by my disinterest in serious relationships. With two texts, I went from one extreme to the other. Said something wonderful, then followed it up with distance and heartless words.

God, I am a fucking idiot. And a goddamn mess.

"It wasn't my intention to upset you."

"I know."

"Seems I can't help myself when it comes to you."

She twists on the bench, props a leg up on the seat, her knee grazing my thigh as she faces me head-on. "Like that." She jabs my arm with a finger. "You sound as if you can't stay away from me. But one false move on my part and you go cold. Feels like I can't win."

Unfortunately, she is right. No sense in denying it. No matter how many times I remind myself Shelly and I are only friends, the voice in my head, the one I stomp down often, laughs and calls me a fool for believing such hypocrisy. The number of hours I think of Shelly… I am a moron if I believe we will remain strictly friends.

But I keep that to myself.

"Sorry," I say, hypnotized by her sparkly blues. "I'm too selfish for my own good. And yours."

She opens her mouth, ready to respond, but my phone rings and cuts her off. Her lips form a tight line before she smiles and twists to face the lake.

Immediately, I hate the lack of eye contact. Hate that she shifted away.

I pull my phone from my back pocket—the number not in my contacts—and answer. "Hello?"

"Good afternoon. May I speak with Devlyn Templar, please?"

"This is he."

The woman on the other end goes into a well-rehearsed spiel. For a moment, I zone out. Don't listen to a word she says. Until I hear her say, "We'd like to feature some of your work in the exhibition. I realize it's last minute. My apologies. Another artist gave us your information and, after seeing your pieces online, we'd love to showcase your work with other local artists."

"You've piqued my interest. When is the exhibition again?"

"Saturday. In a few days. If the notice is too short, I understand."

"Count me in."

"Wonderful," she says with jubilance. "Can I send details to the email listed on your website?"

"Yes, that'd be perfect."

"Thank you, Mr. Templar. We'll see you on Saturday."

I disconnect the call and stow the phone in my pocket. Last-minute calls for exhibitions are few and far between, but they happen. When the email hits, I will read up on the exhibition. Whether or not there is a set theme. Either way, I know which pieces I will show.

And I would like if Shelly saw them.

"Do you have plans Saturday?"

She studies the lake without a word. Takes a deep breath. Tightens her grip on the edge of the bench seat. Then meets my gaze. Left then right, left then right. Her eyes dart between mine. Seeking, hunting, searching for clues or answers to a question she has yet to speak aloud. Feels as if I know the question, but I refuse to give it a voice. I won't jeopardize time with her. I need every second she grants me.

Clamping down on her lips, she shrugs. "I work a few hours in the morning. Other than that, no. Why?"

Inviting Shelly to the exhibition with me sounds like a date. A legit date. Unlike the *friend non-dates* we share more often than not, there is no avoiding implications with this. No matter which way I spin it, asking her will suggest we are more than friends. Call me cruel or self-centered or destructive, I don't care. I want Shelly there. At my side. On my arm. To see my art on display. To decipher what she sees and feels. To watch her gravitate toward each piece. To decipher how she sees what I see.

Our friendship is still in the infantile stage, yet she consumes much of my day.

I ache for and detest how she rattles my heart. How she makes my breaths uneven. How she spins a tornado in my head. Each day, I wake up with Shelly as my first thought. It gives me life and scares me to death.

"Was just invited to display some of my work at an exhibition." I pause for two breaths. "And I'd love it if you came."

Shit. Should not have used the word *love.* Maybe she will bypass it or think of it in the general sense and nothing more. Hopefully.

"I'd like that, thank you." Her toothy smile is infectious. As is the way it lights up her eyes. Like a visual hug.

God, I want to conquer my demons, my insecurities. For me. For her. For us.

Shelly is the first woman to truly monopolize my every thought. The amount of time I spent thinking of Kelsey years back is child's play compared to the hours and days I think of Shelly. Often, I chastise my obsession with Shelly. Tell myself it isn't healthy to spend every waking—and non-waking—minute with one person invading my thoughts.

Art is how I cope with this obsession. How I release the emotions growing, building, expanding exponentially inside. The emotions I don't expose to anyone— at least not verbally.

Will Shelly pick up on the underlying emotion I don't—can't—voice when she sees my art?

Part of me hopes she sees it all. Part of me begs her to solve the big mystery. To put an end to my constant indecision. The other part of me pukes at the possibility.

"The curator is sending me the details. I'll share more when I get the email. Most exhibitions are casual. The food is hit or miss. Might be a good idea to eat before or after, depending on the showtime."

Yep, definitely making this sound more and more like an official date. While I didn't outright suggest dinner together, it won't shock me if she interprets it as an invitation. I won't deny her if she does. I will never deny Shelly.

Keep telling yourself it's her *you're not denying. You know it's* you.

"Okay." She looks back out at the lake, her smile still firmly in place. "We should head back. I smell rain."

We look up simultaneously. Looming overhead is a cluster of gray clouds, slowly drifting in from the coast and stealing the blue sky.

Rising from the bench, I wait for Shelly to lead. Her eyes scan the lake one last time as she takes a deep breath. On the way back, the rustle of leaves and clap of our shoes on the path chase away the silence. Our pace faster with the impending storm.

Peeking at her profile, I will her to speak. Will her to tell me what is on her mind.

Does she think Saturday is a date? Or just two friends hanging out, one supporting the other, while possibly sharing a meal together? Not like we haven't shared several meals or spent time together. Regardless, the list of questions grows longer with each step forward.

But I don't ask a single one. I won't ask.

Because more than anything, I fear her answer. Fear she believes Saturday is a legit date. Fear I will have to cut ties with her because being emotionally vulnerable scares the hell out of me. Fear that I feel more for her than I am willing to admit to anyone, including myself.

I care for Shelly. More than a *friend* cares for another *friend*. And no matter how hard I try to define our relationship, the lines are blurring. From where I stand, they blur more each day.

The biggest question of all… do I let those lines disappear completely? Or do I draw them sharper in the sand?

God… how I want that line to disappear.

eleven

We reach the parking lot as the first drops of rainfall.

I dig the fob out of my pocket and unlock the car. Feet away, I slow my pace. Ready to turn on my heel and tell Devlyn I will talk to him later. Before I get the chance, his fingers lightly brush my lower bicep. Curl into a firm yet gentle grip above my elbow. Stop me in my tracks.

Heat radiates from the spot where his hand touches me through the hoodie. Briefly, I close my eyes and take a deep breath. On the exhale, I open my eyes and slowly spin to face him.

"Shelly…" His voice is soft, scratchy, hesitant. His pale-green irises a touch darker and loaded with unspoken emotion.

I lick my lips and his eyes drop to follow the action. "Yeah?"

His eyes flick north as he swallows. Drizzly rain kisses our skin, yet neither of us attempts to escape it. And it is in this moment that I see it. The emotion he works so hard to keep hidden. The feelings simmering in his veins that he refuses to give control.

Since Devlyn and I fell into friendship, I questioned how he really felt. Not that I need more than he gives, but it oftentimes feels as if he holds back. Restrains himself from temptation. Resists what he truly wants. What we both want.

I have no idea what it is Devlyn wants—for himself, from me—but I wish he wouldn't fight his heart.

He scratches the back of his neck. His brows pinch together for a split second before he smooths his expression. "Come back to my place?" Of all the things to come from Devlyn's mouth, that was *not* what I expected to hear. "The weather and that call"—he tosses a thumb over his shoulder—"cut our time here."

This right here, this exact moment, is why my brain is a scrambled mess. We have hung out several times, but not a single occasion has been at my place or his. Probably his method of keeping our *friendship* in check. If we don't step into each other's personal space, the wall between friends and lovers stays upright. Solid. Permanent.

Not to be presumptuous, but him asking me to come over… did a few bricks from his highly erected wall just tumble?

"Uh…" I drop my stare to the hoodie strings near the hollow of his throat, swallow, then lift my gaze to his. "Yeah. Sure."

For someone so adamant about keeping us indefinitely in the friend zone, it seems as if Devlyn handed me an exclusive, *I never give these to anyone* invitation to the next step. I don't want to feed my inner romantic—the one currently singing and doing backflips—and think more into what all this means. But ignoring this gesture is asinine and ignorant.

"I'll text you my address. Give me an hour to clean up the house?" His fingers finally unravel from my arm and I miss the warmth of him immediately.

I nod. "Sounds good." If this was any of my other guy friends, we'd plan food or movies or games. "Need me to bring anything?" A small crease forms between his brows. "Takeout or a movie?"

He steps back, inching closer to his car and farther from me. "Nah. We'll figure it out."

Who is this guy?

Everything with Devlyn has always been on the straight and narrow. No room for deviation. Sure, the occasional misunderstanding occurs, but he is quick to put us back on the path he finds most comfortable.

In the span of an hour, the space around us feels bigger. Expansive. Ever growing. Like a new side of him has emerged. One he kept locked away. Hidden. Safe. And I am not sure how to feel about the change. Should I welcome it with open arms? Or should I remain rooted and hesitant, arms hugging my chest? I'd rather it be the former, but mentally prepare myself for the latter.

"Okay." I open the driver's side door. "See you soon."

Devlyn throws me a half smile. "See you." Then he is in his car and driving out of the lot.

Minutes go by in a haze. I start the car but sit idle in the lot. The oak tree near my front bumper blurs into a blob of brown and green. The music on the radio fades into a low hum. Rain smacks the windshield in fatter drops, mottling my vision more as I get lost in thought.

What does this all mean?

Spending more time with Devlyn—in his home, no less—has my mind in a spiral. I don't want to overthink the invitation—to his house or the exhibition. Overthinking is the enemy of happiness. But I need some form of clarity before taking another step.

What if this is just an extension of what Devlyn deems friendship? What if it's not?

Devlyn is a great guy. Different than anyone I have met. More reserved, but it suits him. Occasionally cold, but I think him acting distant is a front to protect his heart from whatever—whoever—hurt him. Most of all, he has this complex, sensational energy. A magnetic field that pulls you in and holds you captive.

I don't want to set myself up for heartache, but I don't want to ignore the shift between us.

My phone dings with an incoming text, snapping me from my introspection. Unlocking it, I read the message with Devlyn's address. I connect my phone to the car and map his address. *Twenty minutes.* Should be enough time to get my brain in the right headspace.

"God, I hope so."

With a huff, I put the car in reverse and back out. I make a quick stop at home. Change out of my damp clothes. Eat a few pieces of chocolate. Give myself a pep talk in the bathroom mirror as I fix my ponytail. Then, I jump back in the car and drive east, toward the unknown.

~

"The destination is on the right."

I park in the driveway behind Devlyn's SUV and stare at the moody blue house. In the dark, with how far back it sits from the road, I'd easily miss it. The house a single story along the front with an additional story over the rear of what I assume was once a garage. Tall crepe myrtle trees fill the spacious front lawn—minimal foliage on the branches and bare of flowers.

Exiting the car, I shoulder my purse and walk toward the front door. Along the front of a small screened-in porch is a kaleidoscope of flowering plants. Dark-pink coneflowers and sunny bright coreopsis. Vibrant orange gerbera and purple shooting stars. Behind them, fountain grasses butt against the porch and fill in the space.

Before reaching the door, I already have a new perspective of Devlyn. One I never expected. Comprised of a large house and an even larger yard. Of plants to tend to and patio furniture on the porch. It all feels… odd. But in a good way.

I lift my hand and tap my knuckles on the door. Clattering echoes on the other side of the door, followed by a *dammit*. A soft chuckle spills from my lips as I shake my head.

Then the door whips open and I remind myself to breathe.

Devlyn finger-combs his hair a beat before gesturing to the space at his back. "Come in."

I duck my chin as a rush of heat blooms across my cheeks and I step over the threshold. Entering Devlyn's space is taking a step into the inner workings of his mind. Sure, he didn't construct the house, place the walls or windows, but his touch is everywhere.

The entry is a formal sitting room. Rustic wood floors as far as the eye can see. A simple yet sleek pale-gray sofa against the right wall, several throw pillows in various colors consume most of the sitting space, a khaki throw blanket draped over an arm. A white rug with eccentric black lines parked beneath an ashy oak coffee table. On the table is a thick book of artwork, a black three-wick candle and a small vase of common daisies. Two white lattice-woven chairs with frames matching the table sit on the opposite side of the table, facing the sofa.

Moody paintings on canvas hang on the gray wall above the sofa. The images purposely staggered, but all part of the same portrait. A woman walking in the distance, trees and flowers and tall grass in her surroundings. The image reminds me of the meadow Devlyn painted in the shop, only the observer stands farther back.

"You have a beautiful home."

Devlyn shuts the door, sidles up to me, and shoves his hands in his pockets. "Thanks. My mother insisted I get more square footage than a single person needs." He shrugs. "She isn't a woman easily ignored."

I chuckle under my breath. "Yeah, I get that. I love my mom, but sometimes she can be a little too persistent."

"Can I get you a drink?"

"Water, please." I set my purse on one of the chairs and follow him to the kitchen just past the sitting room.

A framed pass-through-slash-bar connects the kitchen and sitting room. Rather than use the bar for eating, Devlyn has another vase of flowers. This one shallow and wide and filled with magnolia buds. The fragrance a gradual scent in the air.

The kitchen is U-shaped with white cabinets, black marble countertop, dark-gray marble backsplash, and stainless steel appliances. A small window over the sink at the end looks out on what I assume is the backyard. A small basket of fruit sits on the counter in one corner, a coffee-and-tea station in the other.

Devlyn pours water from a pitcher in the fridge then hands me a glass before filling his own.

Being in Devlyn's space, without the possibility of interruption, without outside means of distraction, feels claustrophobic and bizarre. Time alone with Devlyn isn't what has me worried. More often than not, our time together is spent alone.

But this is different.

There is no one to interfere. No servers or patrons or park-goers. No visual deviations such as menus or trees or walkways. And that realization adds a layer of sweat to my skin. Makes my breaths come in short bursts. Makes my pulse whoosh louder in my ears.

Devlyn sips his water, oblivious to my inner freak-out, and steps past me. "Come on." He glances over his shoulder. "I'll give you a tour."

To say I am overwhelmed by the time we finish the tour would be an understatement. This house is *huge*.

Five bedrooms—although he showed three, the other two I assume are his bedroom and the studio upstairs—three bathrooms, living and dining room, laundry area, and the backyard. The backyard is as spacious as the front, but inhabited by a large jasmine-covered pergola over canyon stone pavers with short, fine grass between each. A slate-tiled table is parked under the canopy with eight chairs. An oak tree with a trunk too wide to hug halfway shades the yard on the left, a bench swing hanging from a thick limb. Several crepe myrtles appear strategically placed in the yard to add color, shade, and beauty.

We step back inside and I down the last of my water.

The sheer size of Devlyn's home, how he has attained a level of adulthood I have yet to, sends my head into a tailspin of questions. Has me asking where I went wrong. He has acquired so much at twenty-two and I am barely able to add to my savings each month at thirty-two.

He bumps my shoulder with his bicep. "You okay?"

Am I? Yes. No. I have no freaking clue. "Yeah." I lift my glass, then remember I have no water to quench the drought in my throat.

Devlyn takes a step and twists to face me head-on. He lifts a hand and presses the tip of his index finger between my brows. "If this spot gets any tighter, it'll never relax," he says, dropping his hand. I sigh and close my eyes. "Relax, Shelly." His voice barely above a whisper. "It's just me. Us."

I open my eyes and meet his. There, I see something familiar yet foreign. The man in front of me is Devlyn. Complex and quiet and mysterious. Only now, a darker shade of green rims his pale irises as he holds me captive. Steals my breath and has my brain foggy.

Did a switch flip in his brain?

My voice refuses to work. Even if it did, I wouldn't know what to say. This is yet another moment where Devlyn confounds me. Says things I easily misconstrue.

So, I simply nod in response. He rewards my bewilderment with a subtle half smile.

"Let's order food. Was thinking Asian." His smile grows. "Maybe you'll also share the story I never heard over lunch at the shop?" My eyes narrow as I think back. "Why you laughed when I asked sandwiches or sushi."

"Ah." I nod with a smile. The day comes back in a flash of colors. I was so nervous to eat lunch with Devlyn that I completely forgot. "Yeah, I'll share over dinner."

Devlyn pulls up the website for a Japanese restaurant nearby. He hands me his phone, a pad of paper, and a pen. "Write down what you want."

I arch a brow. "Before I do, you should know… I order a lot. More than a lot."

With a shake of his head, he laughs. "Doesn't matter. Leftovers always taste better."

"True." I point a finger at him.

A mile-long list later, Devlyn calls in the order. He guides us to the living room —a room he probably spends more time in, if I read the vibe accurately.

The walls throughout the house are painted the same midgray tone. Except this room. The living room is a darker gray. Cavernous with floor-to-ceiling black curtains blocking out any light from outside. Oak beams have been added to the ceiling and down the length of one wall. An oak-and-black-steel-framed bookshelf consumes the wall behind the L-shaped couch. The shelving unit decorated with small, green plants in black pots, stacked books, an eclectic wire-framed lamp with an Edison bulb, and several other statuesque knickknacks.

The L-shaped gray couch has pillowy cushions, an array of monochrome throw pillows, and a gray-and-black blanket draped over the back near the chaise. Two wooden block tables sit in the center of the room, wheels on the base, candles in the center, a drawer on one side, bolts and antique hinges and leather straps at the joints. A light tweed rug blankets the floor. Across from the couch is a black-painted brick fireplace, unburned logs on the grate, the mantel matching the oak beams. Above the fireplace, mounted to the wall, is the largest television I have seen in a home.

Devlyn doesn't strike me as someone to sit in front of the television for hours on end. But who the hell knows. We still have so much to learn about each other. Maybe Devlyn is a closet binge-watcher. Up all hours of the night, glued to endless episodes on Netflix.

Devlyn digs through the table drawer, turns on the television, then hands me the remote. "How about you find us something to watch and I'll go get us fresh drinks." I take the remote, his fingers grazing mine in the process. Heat sizzles my fingers, my forearm, my blood. No doubt my cheeks are crimson. He swallows and slowly retracts his hand. "Any requests? Water, hot tea, beer, cola."

"A beer would be great. Thanks."

The moment Devlyn exits the room, I drag in a deep breath.

Jesus, Reed. Get a hold of yourself.

Alcohol isn't something I partake in often, but maybe a beer will help settle my anxiety. While Devlyn fetches drinks, I surf Netflix. Would help if I knew what Devlyn likes and dislikes watching. I have no die-hard preferences and will give any show or movie a shot. With how creative Devlyn is, I assume the same of him.

After scrolling past far too many romantic movies, I scan the Netflix original series list and stumble upon *Dark*. Reznor, from the tattoo shop, raved about the show during one of our Sunday night gatherings.

Watching a mystery with Devlyn sounds a hell of a lot safer than anything else. *Dark* it is.

"You find something?" Devlyn asks as he walks back in and hands me a brown bottle.

Glancing down at the label, I laugh. "Interesting." His brows lift. "You just happen to have Japanese beer in the fridge. Like you planned this."

Devlyn sips his own beer as his eyes dart up in an unspoken answer. I laugh internally as I lift the bottle to my lips. The smooth, rich malt rolls over my tongue and cools my throat on the way down.

He probably planned this on his way home and stopped at the store. Don't overthink it.

"So… what are we watching?"

Oh. Right. "Since I wasn't sure of your taste, I picked something a friend recommended. *Dark.* Have you watched it?"

He shakes his head and twists to see the show synopsis on the screen. Sipping his beer, he nods. "Sounds interesting."

Next up on the list of awkward events… where do we sit on the couch?

The plush corner couch easily seats six with wiggle room. If this were my couch, I'd sit centered with the television. Which is probably where Devlyn sits when in here. I don't want to take his seat.

Should I sit in the corner spot? It's probably the most comfortable. But would I come off as distant if I sat there and Devlyn sat two seats away? Maybe I sit one off from the center. Then I appear close, but not to the point of crowding him.

Why the hell is it so damn hard to figure where to sit? Why am I overthinking couch space and seating arrangements?

Because you're in Devlyn's home. In a dark room with minimal lighting. About to have the most intimate moment between the two of you.

Ugh!

It may only be dinner and a show, but this is the *most* intimate span of time we have shared. Out in public, the looks and conversations we exchange don't feel as cozy or profound. In public, disruption is inevitable. It's easier to take a step back, to shy away from his stares when I can pretend something has caught my attention.

Here, in his home, all that disappears. The security blanket of distractions vanishes.

Devlyn takes a seat exactly where I knew he would, sets his beer on a coaster on the table, then pats the seat next to him.

Seriously, who is this guy?

"I won't bite." A smirk tips up the corner of his mouth as he fails to hide a light chuckle. "Promise."

What if I want him to bite?

Shut. Up. Shelly.

Tossing throw pillows to the side, I sit in the space beside him. Our arms inches apart, his heat hits my skin. His scent—a blend of graphite and pine and earth—hits my nose. Head forward, I close my eyes, take a deep breath, and remind myself to breathe. To not fidget. To act *normal.*

When my eyes open, I spot Devlyn in the periphery. His gaze heating my cheek more than any flush ever would.

Is it wrong to love his intensity? How deeply he studies every curve and line, dip and shadow of my profile?

I rotate my head until he comes into view. I sip my beer then pick at the label. Lick my lips. Swallow when his stare falls to watch the action. Break the spell when I lean forward and set my bottle on the table, next to his.

"Should we start the show?" I point to the screen. "Or wait for the food to arrive?"

Devlyn extracts his phone from his pocket and checks the time. "Fifteen-ish minutes until food. Let's start."

As I press play on the remote, Devlyn turns off the lamp. The room goes dark. Darker than dark. The inches between my arm and his vanishes. His heat may as well smother every inch of me on this couch, in this room.

An Albert Einstein quote fills the screen in German, subtitles listed below. A second later, ominous music follows and a man's voice floods the room. And it is all I need as a distraction. The deep timbre demands my attention. The words beckon me to listen, to pay attention.

I thank whatever instinct told me to choose this show. Because I need the diversion. Need something to grab my attention more than Devlyn.

An eerie sound fills the air from a cave on the screen just as the doorbell rings. I all but jump out of my skin. Devlyn… laughs.

"Not scared, are you?" I shake my head and he laughs again. Rising from the couch, he exits the room. "Be right back."

As my heart settles back to its normal rhythm, Devlyn strolls back into the room with two brown bags, sets them down, and rolls the two tables together. As I empty the bags, Devlyn tosses pillows on the floor between the couch and table. When I eye him, he simply says, "Makes it easier to share."

Devlyn stares at the containers in front of me as if waiting for a sign to pop up with descriptions for each. I point to each dish and tell him what they are.

"Seaweed salad, veggie tempura, bulgogi."

"Bul-what?"

"Bulgogi. Uh… essentially, it's Korean BBQ. And so good." I point to my last dish. "Yaki udon. Noodle soup with veggies and shrimp."

He glances at all the food I ordered, then looks to his salmon teriyaki, rice, miso soup, side salad, steamed veggies, and noodles. His eyes dart back and forth a few times before he looks up.

"Will you eat all that?" His voice is absent of judgment but loaded with curiosity.

I shake my head. "Definitely not. I just love all the flavors and have a hard time deciding."

A smile kicks up the corners of his lips. "Will you tell me the story behind why you laughed at sandwiches or sushi at the shop that first day I ordered lunch?"

"Only if you promise to try everything."

He tips his head side to side in contemplation. "Deal."

We dig into food. The screensaver replaces the pause point of the show, and I dive into the story.

"My best friend, Cora, loves every type of Asian food. We've known each other since elementary school and she wasn't always this way. I remember when I stayed the night at her house. She begged her mom, Elizabeth—"

"Elizabeth from the shop?"

I nod. "Yep. That's a story for another day." There I go being presumptuous. "But she always begged her mom to cook us Kid Cuisine TV dinners. She always wanted the one with chicken nuggets, macaroni and cheese, corn, and chocolate pudding. That's how it was until early high school. She loved those damn things." I laugh. "Then, one day, out of nowhere, she didn't. She wanted lo mein and egg foo young. Teriyaki and phở. Sushi and katsudon. When I asked her what sparked her sudden interest, she said her dad received a stack of gift certificates for restaurants near the beach. A few of them were to Asian restaurants. Went downhill from there."

Devlyn's lips plump as he mulls it over. Longer than a friend would, I stare at his lips. Unfortunately for me, I don't look up until he clears his throat.

Cue my virginal blush.

Someone save me from a lifetime of humiliation. I beg you.

"So, me asking sandwiches or sushi was funny because you've probably had sushi with your friend thousands of times." I nod. "Makes sense." He takes a sip of beer. "What's *your* favorite food?"

"Way to put a lady on the spot." I chuckle while dipping a piece of fried squash in the tentsuyu. "I don't know. I like variety. Picking one thing seems impossible." Tipping my head back, I stare at the ceiling. "If I had to pick *one* food, it'd probably be bread. Any kind except white sandwich bread. And fresh out of the oven." I hum, and out of the corner of my eye, Devlyn shifts his position.

What was that?

"Bread, huh?" I nod. "I'll have to remember that."

"I'll have to remember that." Why? And what does that mean?

Devlyn picks up the remote and presses play, ending the story. Our conversation may be over, but we both wear ridiculous smiles on our faces.

When our bellies are full, Devlyn puts the leftovers in the fridge. We relocate to the couch, seemingly closer than before, and watch more episodes of *Dark*. I do everything within my power to focus on the show and not how close we sit.

Inevitably, I lose the battle and it isn't long before I lay my head on Devlyn's shoulder and press my weight into him. Never more comfortable than in this moment.

Twelve

DEVLYN

A pinch in my neck stirs me from sleep, but I don't dare move. Not when my senses spark to life and a scent I know all too well drifts through my nose. Jasmine, orange blossoms, and patchouli. Such a unique combination. Each note detectable on its own, but addictive when combined.

Shelly.

I crack an eye open, take in her blonde locks, then inhale deeply.

Face buried at the base of my throat; Shelly's body curls into mine. Our legs a tangled mess. Her arms sandwiched between us, palms pressed to my chest. One of my arms supports her head while the other drapes her waist.

I close my eyes and absorb the moment, the connection, the gravity we can't escape.

Oddly, in this blip of time, fear doesn't grab me by the ankles and pull me under. In fact, fear is nowhere to be found. No fear, but anxiety bubbles just below the surface. That will never not exist when close to Shelly—physically and otherwise.

Thinking back to last night, Shelly sank into me more with each passing minute. Our bellies full after we gorged on the living room buffet. The second she laid her head on my shoulder, I closed my eyes and fought the voice of doubt in my head. The voice I heard often when it came to Shelly.

I don't want to fight what I feel for her. I also don't want to hurt again.

Question is, how do I balance what I feel for her and the self-doubt eating at my heart?

Shaking away my thoughts, I focus on the here and now. Focus on the sleeping woman in my arms. Opening my eyes to see her in a new way, a new light, close up and unrestrained. Expression soft, hair disheveled, lips slightly parted.

God, it feels good to hold her. *Really* hold her. How many times have I pictured this moment? Well, not this *exact* moment, but a similar one. One where I wrap my arms around her frame and haul her snug to mine. One where her touch provides me comfort and not unease. One where I sweep my knuckles softly over the line of her jaw, her cheekbone, her chin just before I lean in and brush my lips with hers.

Too many times. Not enough times.

A mumble leaves her lips. Something unintelligible. By her tone, I assume it was endearing or sweet, but can't be certain. She mumbles again, a soft *please* against my skin. The heat of her breath, mixed with the weight of her plea, sends goose bumps across my skin.

Then she moves… and I freeze.

Her legs weave more with mine like vines climbing a trellis. One arm wraps around my torso and hugs me while the other fists my shirt. Her nose burrows into the bend where my shoulder and neck meet. And then she sighs. Melts into me more. Holds me physically captive. Arrests my heart. Consumes my soul.

I love and hate it equally.

I love how easy it is to love Shelly. To fall into her in ways I never did with Kelsey. To look forward to her smile and voice and presence. To feel the radiance bounding off her aura and spilling into mine. I love how her dark, starry eyes suck me in and send me soaring. Shelly makes me dream of possibilities, of the future, of a life with her.

In the same breath, I hate how easily I give in to my emotions with her. How easily I am willing to tear away the barrier guarding my heart, the one that has kept me sane and safe and whole for the last four years. The armor that shielded me from making irrational decisions based on what my heart wanted versus what my brain knew.

But Shelly isn't Kelsey.

Shelly is vibrant and charismatic, brilliant and vivacious. When she walks in a room, she brings light and laughter and love with her. More than any of that, she is wise. Wise beyond her years. Mature. She would never just drop someone because she wanted to explore life freely.

We haven't discussed our pasts—not in-depth—but her rosy cheeks every time I toss out a compliment give her away. Tell me her experience with men isn't as vast as other women her age. She is selective with who sees her heart. If that's true, it only adds to her allure.

"Stupid thorn," she mumbles against my skin.

I bite my cheek to not laugh. For a little longer, I want this side of her. To see her in the faint, dim light creeping in from the edge of the curtain. To watch her while she sleeps. While I can look at her features without restraint, without fear of being caught. Her toffee locks with hints of sunshine. Matching lashes fanned beneath her lower lid to the apple of her cheek. The three small freckles lateral to her right eye. The soft line of her jaw and curve of her chin. And lips so soft and full and kissable.

Licking my lips, I picture what it would be like to kiss Shelly. To give in to the urge, the desire, the need to feel her lips pressed to mine.

I close my eyes and let the fantasy take over. Allow myself to daydream about how warm and supple and perfect her kiss would feel. How demanding she'd be. How demanding I'd be in return. What her moan would sound like when I drag her bottom lip between mine. What she'd taste like when she finally bloomed like a flower and let me in.

Her fingers on my lower back curl slightly, tug at my cotton shirt, and I stop breathing. My eyes fly open and I think of anything except kissing Shelly. Because fuck my life, I'm hard.

Sure, if she wakes now, I can pretend to do the same and play it off as morning wood. This is most definitely *not* morning wood.

What is the one thing that automatically sends my mood south? Is an instant buzzkill?

My mother. Mom, Mom, Mom.

And thank god it works. Just as my erection softens, Shelly opens her eyes. She groans and leans back. A smile slowly plumps her cheeks.

Without a doubt, this is my favorite view of Shelly. Soft and unkempt and not a worry marring her beautiful face. Perfect.

Then the corners of her mouth sag. Her brows wrinkle at the middle. Pupils go wide as realization dawns. That she is wrapped around me tighter than a koala. That she is on my couch, in my house, and we fell asleep.

Before I open my mouth to say everything is okay, she bolts upright.

"Oh my god!" She looks around the room so quick it makes me dizzy. "Oh my god," she whispers and slaps a hand over her eyes.

I sit up beside her, rest my palm between her shoulder blades, and rub small, slow circles. "Shelly, it's okay. We fell asleep."

She drops her hand. "Shit. What time is it?"

Crawling across the room, I fetch my phone from the table and tap the screen. "Five thirty-eight."

A groan spills from her lips. "I need to go. The shop. I have to go home and shower and change and eat and—"

"Shelly"—I add more pressure to my touch—"it's okay. You have time. Breathe."

And she does. She inhales through her nose and out through her mouth. Then does it again.

"Better?"

She nods.

"Before you go, let me at least make you breakfast."

"I don't—"

"Please. Promise I'll be quick." Her brows twitch. "I'll even pack it to go if you want."

"Sure. Okay. But only if it's quick."

"Pinkie promise."

She gives me her beautiful smile. Warmth floods the center of my chest, my heart thumping in a new pattern. And after I rise off the couch, before my brain can stop me, I bend at the waist and press my lips to her crown.

Neither of us moves. My pulse shifts again. Beats more erratically. Fear jolts my nerves as a dose of cortisol enters my bloodstream.

I took it too far. Shit. Shit, shit, shit.

Then she reaches for my hand, lifts her eyes, and shows me her rosy cheeks. "Thank you," she whispers. "I'm just going to use the bathroom."

"Right. Yeah." I step back, give her room to pass. "I'll be in the kitchen."

By the time she walks into the kitchen, I have cheesy scrambled eggs and buttered toast ready. Immediately, I want to make her a better breakfast. One that isn't rushed and we can enjoy together. But I am getting way ahead of myself.

She tugs on her shoes and shoulders her purse. I hand her the container and a fork as we awkwardly head for the door. And because I am not ready for goodbye, I follow her out to her car.

After unlocking the car, she sets her purse and the container inside then spins to face me, the door partially between us.

I won't lie… I hate it. The barrier and the fact she has to go.

"Thank you, again. For dinner and a show. It was wonderful."

"We should do it again. I do have leftovers." I lift a brow. She opens her mouth to answer, but I hold up a hand and cut her off. "Think about it."

She rolls her eyes and chuckles. "Fine," she says on a huff. "But I really do need to go."

I want to kiss her. Right here. Right now. I want to lean forward, cradle her cheeks in my palms, and kiss her.

But I won't. Now is not the time.

Soon, though.

"Then I won't keep you any longer." I reach out, take her hand, and give it a quick squeeze. "Drive safe. I'll send you the exhibition details later."

She drops into the driver's seat. "See you."

"See you."

I close her car door and take a few steps back. Watch her back out of the driveway and wave as she pulls away. The moment she is out of sight, I pivot and jog back to the house. Weave to the stairwell off the dining room and take the stairs two at a time.

The moment I step into my studio, the moment graphite and Turpenoid and canvas hits my nose, I sag with a heavy exhale. Then I snap into action. Bolt into the closet and grab a fresh canvas. Set it on my easel then grab my brushes and paints.

In seconds, I get lost. Lost in the image of her face this morning while she snuggled my chest. Lost in the contours of her face. In the sunshine highlights in her hair. In the fullness of her lips.

Not for the first time, I transfer my memories of Shelly into art. Stroke the bristles over canvas and create the outline of her heart-shaped face. Well, half of it.

Barely a fraction into the piece, I see it all so clearly in my head. Half her profile —plump full lips, rosy cheekbone, twilight iris with a touch of gold, and her slightly arched brow, framed by her golden hair. Behind her, pink blossoms. Primrose and meadowsweet.

This is the moment—*the moment*—when it truly hits me. The moment I can no longer deny what I feel, even if it scares the hell out of me.

What I feel for Shelly isn't love. No, it is way too soon for such a deep emotion. But I like her. *Really like her.* A lot. More than I should.

I admit this, but only to myself. Our relationship is too new for verbal confessions. But I feel it all the same. In the turbulent beat of my heart. In the shortness of my breath. In the thick of my marrow.

Question is, where do I go from here?

It is too soon to put my heart on the line. To cut myself open and hand her my heart. Every instinct inside me says to trust Shelly, that she won't hurt me. But once upon a time, the same instinct existed in regard to Kelsey. I'd thought we were inseparable. Endgame. And then she crushed me. Broke me in half and left me without a care in the world.

I refuse to let that happen again. To be blindsided and thrown away.

Shelly is not Kelsey. She won't hurt you. Not on purpose.

As I paint the rich blue of her iris on the canvas, I inhale deeply. "I really hope that's true."

Surviving the breakup with Kelsey was painful and life-altering. If Shelly and I went separate ways—no matter the cause—not only would it be painful, it would be downright devastation. A crippling debilitation. Losing Shelly would be a darkness I'd never overcome. A shadowed life I'd never be able to escape. Losing Shelly... I would give up. On everything.

Shelly isn't just endgame... she is so much more.

A dangerous thought slips into the foreground. One that scares the hell out of me, but I cannot deny.

From the moment I laid eyes on her, with every re-creation of her image, I say without a shadow of doubt... Shelly is the one.

And recognizing this simple fact terrifies me more than anything.

thirteen

I have never sweated so profusely in my life. And it's sixty degrees outside.

Devlyn picked me up for the art exhibition minutes ago. When he sent me the event details, I offered to drive myself, in case he needed to be there earlier. He insisted on arriving at my door almost two hours before the event and chauffeuring me to the exhibition.

It only took one deep breath for me to cave. To give in to his persistence. Let him take control of the evening.

Devlyn in control is one of the reasons my pores are mini waterfalls.

Please don't let me have sweat stains under my pits. I mentally put my hands in prayer position. *Please.*

The drive to Sarasota—the gallery near the college Devlyn attended—isn't far, but it's not right around the corner. The distance and the fact I don't know my way around Sarasota is another reason I let Devlyn drive.

The event starts at four and runs until six. Then, we have dinner reservations at a restaurant near the gallery. Dinner. Reservations. As in a premeditated meal at a nice establishment.

God, this feels like a date. An expensive date.

With Devlyn, it is hard to know. My new rule with him is to never assume. Assumptions get me nowhere. After movie night the other day, and falling asleep on his couch, he seems different. More open. Closer. But assuming we are anything but friends may shut him down.

So, unless he mutters the word *date*, I will keep repeating… This. Is. Not. A. Date.

On the way, Devlyn talks more about his time at college. I lean in closer and listen with rapt attention. His willingness to share has me on the edge of my seat. Although our friendship has shifted, taken on a new persona, I don't often get this side of Devlyn. The more personal side. A deeper look into his past. Small glimpses into his life, into the way he sees the world. I soak up each new story he shares and pray it won't be the last.

My college years centered around lectures and term papers and parties. Devlyn's focused on honing his current craft, finding love in new mediums, and immersing himself in everything art related. Polar opposite lives; his ten times more fascinating.

We hit the peak of the Skyway Bridge and I stare at the bright-yellow stay cables. Blink at the strobe effect they cause as we pass at highway speed. As with all bridges, this one has history. It wasn't always this mammoth bridge supported by massive cement pillars. The old metal bridge… it had a tragic ending. It was before my time, but I remember the stories my family shared anytime we drove over the new bridge and the local history lessons taught in school.

Are Devlyn and I headed that direction? Tragedy. Not like Romeo and Juliet's tragedy. Love that deep makes me uneasy, but not fully. With tragedy, I mean more like an ending where neither of us comes out happy.

Please, don't let that be our trajectory. A one-way road of devastation.

After the other night, after waking up in his arms, I'd like to think not. But presuming anything with Devlyn is dangerous and foolhardy. A nonrefundable ticket to heartache.

I try to forget the cold shoulder moments. The instances he shut down and said the word friends for the thousandth time. Instead, I focus on the days he has shown me tenderness. Spoken sentiments friends don't exchange. Stared at my lips or neck or body with more interest than a friend.

Would it shock me if he said I read too much into any of it? No. I may be outgoing and perceptive with friends and family, but when it comes to romance, all that awareness goes out the window. It's difficult to not read between the lines with rose-colored glasses. Especially when he looks at me as if I am his world, as if I am his next breath. To say it confuses me is an understatement.

"Almost there," he says, interrupting my inner tirade.

"Are you excited?"

A smile brightens his face—the one I love more than I should—and I have my answer. "Yes and no."

When he doesn't expand on his answer, I mentally reach across the console and shake him. "Care to elaborate?"

I love Devlyn's mysterious nature. His solemnity and zen. He sees the world like no one I've known. Sees it in black and white, but also brilliant colors. Finds the beauty in all people and places and life. Depicts emotion as if it walks among us. Adds zeal to everything he touches with the flick of a brush.

And I breathe it all in.

He guides us off the interstate and my eyes zero in on the city. Most of the Bay Area cities have similar vibes and one uniquely their own. Yes, it is another coastal city with beaches and nightlife and shops, but it feels different here. More alive. Maybe because this place is new to me. Or maybe because the history of the city is different. Either way, I love the vibe.

"Seeing my work in a gallery never gets old. I don't create to have it on display, but people seeing my art opens up doors. The opportunity to sell more pieces or create custom originals."

Like most artists, Devlyn creates because the need is ingrained in him. A deep-seated urge to spill his emotions without speaking. To express himself without becoming one-hundred-percent vulnerable.

"Sounds more yes than no."

"True." He purses his lips a beat. "The downfall of these events is being in the spotlight. People asking about your personal life. Criticizing your work. Putting their two cents in. I don't necessarily mind criticism from peers or people I look up to. They give me new perspective. Help me improve who I am as an artist. It's the snooty folks who think, because they have art hanging in their house, they know what *good* art looks like."

I reach across the console and touch his bicep. "Ignore them."

Briefly, he glances down at my hand on him. I pull it back and drop it to my lap before I spot the slight uptick of his lips. "I do my best. Isn't always easy." I don't miss his brief glance at my hand again, and I wonder if he enjoyed the small physical connection.

Since the other morning, Devlyn and I haven't touched. Friends don't share intimate touch. And until I know how movie night and the morning after makes him feel, I am doing my damnedest to stay on my side of the friendship line. Keep our physical contact to arm bumps and the occasional hooked elbows. We don't hug hello or goodbye like I do with my other friends or family. No teasing slaps on the arm or ruffling of hair. And we both know why.

To form a stronger connection—to touch easily, without second thought—our friendship would morph into more. Evolve beyond pizza lunches and walks in the park. Move beyond movie night with takeout and awkward mornings the next day. Blossom into something neither Devlyn nor I am prepared for, if I am honest with myself.

We haven't talked much about our pasts, but I know someone hurt Devlyn. I see it in the way he fights his feelings. The hidden stares followed by cold shoulders. The invitation to spend time together accompanied by the reminder of that ugly line drawn in the sand.

Hurt bruises my heart that a past relationship shook him so deeply, he refuses to let it happen again. Refuses to let love in. By choice, he shelters his heart—well, he attempts to shelter it. I do and don't understand, mainly because the subject has never come up. So, I grant him all the time he needs. Let this—us—be whatever it is while it exists. Let Devlyn set the pace. Allow him to set the tone and shape our relationship.

But I see the small cracks in his exterior. Notice how his stares last longer. Hear the undercurrent of desire and longing in his voice. Feel his warmth and impulsive need for physical contact when we exist in the same space. All of which weighs more heavily since my limbs tangled with his and he didn't let go.

Is going at Devlyn's pace fair? Not when I don't know where his head is at.

But I like Devlyn, more than he'd deem comfortable. I enjoy our time together. The brief chats as well as the lengthy conversations. The fleeting lunches and hours strolling in the park. If we remain only friends, I consider myself lucky to have him. If we become more… loving Devlyn would be sublime.

When it comes to this complex man, I set no expectations.

He parks the car, exits, and jogs around to my open door. I open my mouth to ask what he is doing, but when my eyes meet his, I zip my lips and smile at the gesture. His chivalry may be unexpected, but I refuse to depreciate the moment. Not with the way my heart flip-flops in my chest.

This is not a date.

We walk into the gallery, elbows hooked, and are bombarded. The event doesn't open to the general public for another thirty minutes. All the people flocking to Devlyn's side are peers and professors and fellow local artists. People who have seen or heard of his work. His fan club.

Although Devlyn doesn't care for the spotlight, he smiles and laughs and boasts about other artists whose work is *better*. Watching him here, now, I get another new side of him. He isn't necessarily more outgoing, just more himself. More comfortable in his own skin around those who share the same passion.

I love this side of him.

After a few minutes, he introduces me to the group. He doesn't introduce me as his girlfriend, but he also doesn't introduce me as a friend either. Just Shelly. A low hum whirls beneath my diaphragm. A new layer of perspiration dampens my skin. I work to not let the moment go to my head. Much. Easier said than done.

"Want a drink before the doors open?" he asks.

"Please." Lord knows I need something to temper the heat in my veins.

Drinks in hand, Devlyn guides us to the start of the exhibition. Tonight, there are seven local artists on display, including Devlyn.

Offering his elbow, my favorite smile of his makes an appearance. "Shall we?"

A fresh wave of heat blankets my skin as I hook my arm with his. I swallow past the thick swell of emotion in my throat and nod. "Yeah," I say, voice hoarse and low. Clearing my throat, I try again. "Yes."

The first showcase is Tomas Suarez. His medium of choice is watercolor and, as I gaze at each canvas, I am already at a loss for words. I never knew watercolor could be so bold. So evocative. Pops of bright blue and fuchsia. Subtle greens and soft yellow. Powerful yet subdued. Tomas paints landscapes, and this one reminds me of the meadow Devlyn painted in the shop—*my meadow*—but with softer lines. As if out of focus. We study his other pieces, digest their beauty, then move on to the next artist.

Kanesha Winston. Her three-dimensional art on canvas has me utterly fascinated. Oil paintings with book pages or paper-mache or origami added, then painted to blend in. I have never seen anything like it. The art is literally in my face, screaming to be seen. Begging me to reach out and run my fingers over it. Shifting left and right, I look at each piece from a different angle, a different perspective. See it come to life in its own way.

Akira Yamamoto and Leonard Denver are the two sculptors on display. The clay artist has softer appeal. A profile bust of a man in mourning. An ancient warrior mask. A mosaic of a woman in a garden. Each beautiful and mesmerizing in their own right. The metal pieces have harsher lines and are made of scraps. A hummingbird on a flower. A bionic cat. And my favorite—the softest of the metal pieces—is the embracing couple. Two human forms from the waist up, holding each other. One of them shiny and without imperfections. The other a mix of chain mail and luster with minor cracks.

Devlyn and I stare at this piece the longest. As if it represents us. Soft and rough. Smooth and harsh. Solid and broken. When I peek at him from the corner of my eye, I want to ask what he is thinking and feeling as he stares at the piece. If he sees the uncanny resemblance of us in the art. The strength and instability.

For now, I keep the thought to myself.

The last two artists before we reach Devlyn's work are Justine Thomas and Harrison Beaufort. Their charcoal pieces are remarkable. The art world is still so new to me, but it blows my mind how people create such beauty with paper and charcoal.

One piece, dubbed *Blue Woman*, is easily life size. Drawn on a six-by-three-foot paper scroll, the *Blue Woman* hides behind messy strands and a large sweater. Without question, the term blue depicts her mood. And I don't know why, but I *feel* her pain, her despair. So much it has me on the cusp of tears.

As if he senses my mood shift, Devlyn leans into me more. Gives me more heat and weight. Soothes the sting with his natural balm. Dropping his chin, his breath heats the skin of my earlobe and just beneath. "On to the most embarrassing moment of the night," Devlyn says, and I shiver.

He rests his free hand on my forearm and gives it a slight squeeze. For a split second, I stare down as if imagining things. The lingering sensation of his breath on my skin. The warmth of his hand on my arm. It isn't weird or uncomfortable, but it is different. New.

Without second thought, I lay my hand over his. Allow his warmth to blanket my skin and seep into my veins. Let my heart pound viciously, my lungs inhale erratically, and my nerve endings light on fire.

This feels more like holding hands. Forming an entirely new bond. A connection miles past the friendship line. Because friends don't hold hands. Not unless they are drunk or exhausted or injured. And I am none of the above.

"Don't be embarrassed," I say, voice unsteady as I peer up at him. Eyes on mine, he swallows and nods.

I tighten my hold on our connection, close my eyes for two breaths and savor how perfect this feels. Then I let him lead the way.

Ten steps and several rapid heartbeats later, we stand in front of a collage of pencil drawings. Two on larger pieces of stock, five on smaller pieces and surrounding the two larger.

I step closer to the images and Devlyn steps with me, not relinquishing my arm. My eyes graze over the first smaller drawing. Fingers, the top of a hand, a wrist and forearm, the start of a bicep. The limb feminine, soft, shaded, intimate. I swallow as heat blooms in my cheeks. A sudden sense of voyeurism hits the center of my chest. As if I am invading an intimate moment.

Taking a deep breath, I shift my gaze to the next small piece. The supple curve of a shoulder and border of the throat. Extra shading to emphasize the collarbone and subtle dip of the hollow spot at the base of the throat.

Jesus. Is it hot in here?

How does he make simple body parts, parts we see on people every day, so striking? Something you can't not take pause to stare at, to absorb, to get lost in. Something that makes your pulse race and your breath catch.

The next is the profile of a neck and jaw. I assume the muse for all the pieces is the same due to the feminine depiction. I want to ask Devlyn who she is. If she is the person who has him scared to move forward. To open himself to another.

But I don't ask. I fear his answer. Fear whoever this woman is, he will never move past her.

The last two smaller pieces depict a shadowed profile of her face and a pair of eyes. The eyes tug at something inside me, beg me to open my mouth and ask questions. Dark irises with the occasional shimmer resembling stars.

My eyes narrow as I step closer. Study the irises more critically. The occasional shimmer in the darkness makes me think of my sister-in-law, Peyton. How she calls my brother starlight. Because of his eyes. The same eyes that match my own.

And suddenly, I can't breathe.

My heart rattles in my rib cage. Bangs in the hopes of escape. And I do my best to settle the irrational thoughts and emotions surging inside. I don't *know* this is me, and should not assume as much. For all I know, these drawings are years old. Depictions of the woman that broke his heart. Someone he once loved, but who is no longer in his life. Someone other than me.

I try to collect myself. Calm my racing heart. Normalize my breathing. Not stiffen my arm looped in his. Focus on the rest of the images—the two larger ones I have yet to see. All while not letting on the path my mind has taken.

When I shift my gaze, when I take in the last two pieces, I stop breathing all over again.

Confused. I am so damn confused.

One is the back of a woman. Light wavy strands down her back. The edge of her profile on display as she looks off to the side. The second… it is the same woman. In a meadow. A meadow strikingly similar to the one painted inside Petal and Vine.

I don't know what to think. What to say. How to feel. How to function.

Devlyn leans into me, his breath warm on my ear as his body presses into mine. I might have a heart attack in the middle of this gallery. "What do you think?" he whisper-asks.

What do I think? What a loaded question.

My eyes roam the drawings as I ponder how to answer his simple yet complex question. A question so heavy, I'm not sure if there is a right answer. Right or wrong, I think Devlyn feels much deeper for me than he realizes. Either that or he refuses to accept how he feels.

"I… uh…" I close my eyes and swallow. How do I act myself, act as if everything is still the same, after seeing these? How do I go on pretending we are just friends? Because this—these drawings—screams more than friendship. This is passion and longing and heartache. Beauty and fantasy and hunger. These aren't just depictions of an elegant woman, they are intimacy and affection and hope. A desperate cry for more. Of what, I can't be sure.

No doubt they took weeks to draw. Weeks. Our friendship was only weeks old.

What rattles me most is that Devlyn *chose* this collection to display tonight. Purposely selected these drawings for hundreds to see. Is all but silently telling everyone we are more than friends. That I don't just occupy his thoughts, but also his heart.

Friends don't draw provocative, intimate angles of another friend's body. Friends don't focus on eyes and lips and freckles. Friends don't invite friends to see how much they think and feel and desire the other. Lovers do.

And in this moment, it feels as if Devlyn has always thought of me as more than a friend. Whether he wants to admit it or not.

"They're beautiful," I say after a long pause.

His breath wafts my hair and I close my eyes. "Couldn't agree more."

When it comes to this man, this beautifully broken, soft-spoken, timid man… I am screwed. No matter where we go from here, no matter if we remain friends or take the next step, I am, without a doubt, screwed. After all I have seen tonight, my heart no longer wants to fight what it feels. The only problem with that… Devlyn might not be ready to reciprocate. His walls may be slowly crumbling, but I doubt they will ever fully fall. Not anytime soon.

Devlyn may not be ready to confess his heart, but I am willing to push his boundaries. Willing to cross the line with him. For him. No matter the outcome, at least he will know where I stand.

Best buckle up and enjoy the journey. While it lasts.

fourteen

DEVLYN

I must be having an out-of-body experience. It's the only logical explanation as to why I have practically erased the line between me and Shelly.

As often as I tell myself we are just friends, that we will *only* be friends, my actions and thoughts and feelings toward Shelly supersede that of a friend. I am a walking contradiction. Saying and doing things more like a lover than a friend. The subtle touches that come off as normal, but are far from it. The whispered words close to her ear as I inhale her intoxicating scent. The constant need to be closer to her, to feel her warmth and weight.

Worst of all, I don't stop myself.

I no longer *want* to stop myself.

"Am I underdressed?" Shelly asks as we pull up to the restaurant.

I stare out the windshield at the glass-front brick structure. The restaurant gives off fine dining vibes, but is quite casual. Online reviews raved over the food, atmosphere, and service. I studied the menu long enough to learn it had decent variety. So I set a reservation.

"You look great. The website didn't mention dress, so I wouldn't worry."

She laughs under her breath. "Easy for you."

And I wonder what she means. Why would it be easy for me and not her? If anything, Shelly outshines everyone. Me? I'm the scrawny, quirky guy at her side. The person everyone will look past to glimpse her.

I park the car then jog to the passenger door to help her out. Not that she needs help. Shelly is a strong woman. Capable of standing tall on her own.

But having her at my side and on my arm tonight was a new, unfamiliar high. Something I never expected. Something I want more of. Her warm hand wrapped around my bicep, her eyes on my art. Nothing has ever felt so right and perfect and exhilarating.

Am I walking a dangerous line? Yes. I have never been on a slope this slippery. Do I care? At the moment, no. I'd tread the steepest incline for her.

When was the last time I felt a connection like this? When was the last time someone *wanted* me? It had been too long. Scary as it is, I crave Shelly. More than my next breath.

Instead of fearing what may happen, I offer my arm once more. Lock onto my favorite constellation and wait for her acceptance. And she does not disappoint. I don't think it's possible for Shelly to ever disappoint. At least not me. She hooks her arm with mine, wraps her dainty fingers near my elbow, the digits giving a gentle squeeze. I live for that squeeze. For any near or intentional touch she bestows. Each has my breath more erratic. Each little reassurance says she enjoys being on my arm.

I am so fucked. *We* are so fucked. In the best way.

We step into the restaurant and I give the hostess my name. She escorts us through the restaurant, toward a table in the back near another set of large windows that looks out onto the Gulf. Shelly takes her seat, then I take mine across from her. As much as I would love to sit closer, to be within easy reach of her hand or knee, I love this unobstructed view. To see half her face aglow from the setting sun and the other half from a candle at the heart of the table.

There are a million and one ways to take in Shelly. To catalog her features in a new light. To discover a new angle of her delicate profile. A new light to absorb the beauty of this woman. Taking the time to learn them all has my body abuzz. Shoots thrill through my limbs and to the center of my chest.

I want to view all million and one.

"Devlyn." My name is soft and worrisome on her tongue. I snap out of my Shelly-induced daydream, lower my menu and lock onto her wide eyes. She curves the menu to the side of her face to shield our conversation from other tables. The gesture is cute. "Did you look at the prices on the menu?"

I give her a half smile. "Didn't cross my mind."

Her eyes go impossibly wider. "You may want to."

To appease her, I stare down at the menu. See a thirty-dollar chicken dish and don't think twice. Not that I eat at places with price points like this on the regular, but it wouldn't be the first time. Not with all the fancy dinners and fundraiser events I attended with my parents as a child.

Mom always has to have the best. Be the best.

Cue mental eye roll.

Since living on my own, most nights I cook at home or get takeout from small, local places. Nothing pricey or lavish. I tend to not dine out often since crowds aren't my thing.

Tonight is an exception. Tonight is a special occasion. My art in a gallery—without the help or influence of my mother—warrants celebration. And there is no other person I would rather share an overpriced, intimate meal with than Shelly.

"It's fine, Shelly. Tonight is a special occasion and I'd like to indulge. Order what you'd like and don't worry about the cost."

She shifts the menu so it hides her eyes. After a few deep breaths, she nods and scans the menu again. Thank goodness she doesn't fight me on this. On the price of a meal. Yes, the cost of dinner here is more than I typically spend. But tonight is worth every cent. *She* is worth every cent and much more.

The server comes to the table, tells us the chef specials for the evening, takes our drink order and gives us another moment to decide. Before either of us sets our menu down, the server returns with two glasses of red wine and takes our order.

Shelly stares out the window at the fire-tinged horizon. Studies the skyline, sips her wine, and sighs. I don't hide my stare. Don't hide my eyes as they trace the arch of her brow, slope of her nose, and plump lines of her lips. I drink her in more than ever. Get drunk on her and not the wine. Love how at ease she is in this moment, at a table with me, sharing a meal after an evening on my arm.

Our easy connection has me dizzy. The comfort she gives has me wobbly in my chair.

The entire night—the drive, the gallery, dinner—is more than I expected. With Shelly, I set zero expectations. But she shocks me at every turn, with what she says and the feelings she stirs up from deep, hidden places.

The more time Shelly and I spend together, the more I want to open myself to her. Give her pieces of myself I have given no one. Not even Kelsey.

Over the last two months, Shelly has wiggled her way in. Not with her wit or charm or beauty—although, I love these traits too—but with her magnetic energy and gravitational pull.

In our minimal conversations, we communicate more with silence and body language than most do with words. Our quiet chats reflect my introversion more than her natural disposition. Shelly lights up a room with her exuberance. Being the center of attention has never been my cup of tea, but I want to test the waters. Dip my toes in, ask the questions on the tip of my tongue, and learn more about Shelly Reed.

And share more about myself.

"Do you visit the beach much? When it's warmer, obviously."

She inhales deeply then shifts her gaze from the setting sun to me. "Not as much as I did years ago. This adulting business is bullshit."

I laugh, far louder than I should, but it can't be helped. Thinking back, I can't recall many occasions when a curse slipped between Shelly's lips. Not that I pictured Shelly as a complete saint.

"Couldn't agree more. Whoever came up with the idea you had to pay to live, to exist… I'd like to have a word with them."

Now, it's her turn to laugh. Head slightly back, hand over her heart, lips and eyes tipped up at the corners. I love how effervescent the sound is. Like carbonation and sunshine. A gust of wind on a still day. Her laughter is one more thing to like about the woman sitting across the table.

"What about you?" she asks. "Do you visit the beach much?"

"I actually enjoy the beach when it's cooler. Not the water, but bundled in a blanket on the sand with my sketchpad. A unique creativity sparks when I'm out in the elements. It challenges me in a fresh way. Changes how I interpret what I see and feel on paper, or canvas later. It also depends on my mood."

She nods then sips her wine. Before either of us gets in another question, the server returns with the appetizer—ricotta-stuffed figs with a balsamic reduction. I gesture for Shelly to taste one first.

"What's your favorite color?" The question is generic. One I probably know the answer to, based on her wardrobe, but I ask anyway.

"Pink." Correct. Shelly may not be decked out in pink daily, but she incorporates the color in her life. Polish, hair accessories, jewelry, lip gloss, pins. I see each touch, each shade and variation.

"Favorite foods? Aside from bread." We both laugh under our breaths.

"That's a little more difficult." She taps her lips with a finger and my eyes magnetize to the action. "Household staples… I *love* cashew butter. Too much for my own good. Slap it on crusty bread"—her frame wilts slightly as a dreamy look fills her eyes—"and I'm in heaven." Her exaggeration of the word love makes me chuckle under my breath. "Prepared foods, especially ones I don't cook"—we both laugh—"bulgogi. There's more, but those rank highest."

Flashes of the other night, of Shelly in my house, eating dinner with me in front of the television, pop in my head. Followed by waking up with her wrapped in my arms. I want another night with Shelly. I want another morning with her snuggled against my frame.

"Still can't believe I'd never eaten it before the other night."

"Right? I'll make it your favorite too." She winks and the corner of my mouth instantly lifts.

With simple ease, we slip into a more intimate space. One I learn to love more each time it happens. One that doesn't put me in panic mode. Doesn't have me fleeing the scene like I committed homicide. I never want to be scared at the ease flowing through my veins, at the comfort I feel being with Shelly. Ever.

After years of letting heartbreak rule my heart, I decide it's finally time to push all the negativity aside and bask in this woman. Indulge in the way she makes me feel. Give over to my heart and ignore the hushed voices of warning in the back of my head.

The more we talk, the more I let loose. Shelly pumps life into my veins. Makes me laugh more and lean in closer. Makes me smile so much my cheeks sting. She is the light I have missed all these years. A light I never want extinguished.

When our meals arrive, we eat and talk and enjoy the evening. Worry evades me and I give merit to the idea of Shelly being more than a friend. For a minute. Only a minute.

Four and a half years have passed since I relished the company of a woman. Let it swallow me whole and never let go. When Kelsey ditched me for frat boys and the *college experience,* I shut down. Closed myself off from emotion and intimacy and anything that would hurt me further. I became numb. To everything.

With Shelly, I never want to let go. Never want to spend a day without seeing her or speaking with her or knowing her. Is this healthy? Probably not. No form of addiction is. But Shelly… her brand of drug is exactly what I need. What I never knew I needed.

As our plates empty, the server comes with a tray of desserts. Shelly ogles them with wide eyes and her lips trapped between her teeth. Much as I'd like to trap her lips with my own, now is not the time. Instead, I agree on her choice of dessert, a thick slice of chocolate ganache cake with fresh whipped cream and berries, to share.

All I will say about dessert… I have a new love for chocolate cake that has nothing to do with the taste and everything to do with watching Shelly eat it.

Oh, how I wish to be that cake. Sweet and warm on her tongue. Eliciting the most provocative sounds.

After I settle the bill, we walk to the car, arms hooked at the elbow. The drive to Shelly's apartment is a blur of quiet music, good conversation, and our arms a breath apart. Hushed as we are together, our talks flow with more ease now. As if we have known each other for years and not months. And I want more.

More of her. More time. More of whatever she will let me have. More *us.*

I park in the guest spot near her building and walk her to the door. The cool November night grows hot and thick and edgy. There has always been this unspoken familiarity between us. An energy that brings us closer. Since day one, I fought the sensation with every molecule I control. Little by little, I've slowly let it take over.

"Would you like to come in for coffee or tea?"

At her question, that stupid voice in the back of my head speaks up. Tells me to say no. Tells me to get in the car and drive home. To leave and not take another step toward her front door.

I hate this voice. Hate that it still creeps in and tries to sway my life in one direction or another. Tries to keep me from moving forward and moving on. Eerie as it is, I hate this voice even more because it suddenly sounds like my mother. Full of acid and judgment.

Tonight has been perfect. More than perfect. If I leave now, will it end perfect? Or will I wake up in a cloud of regret? Miserable from not doing what *I* want versus listening to the *no one will ever love you* voice in my head.

I am not ready for tonight to end. The more I have Shelly in my world, the more I want to exist in her bubble. Breathe her in. Share my life. Make her mine.

A new voice storms forward and tramples the doubt. The voice of selfishness. Soft and lovable and coaxing. She whispers, *"Go inside. Spend more time with her."* And without a second thought, the selfish part wins.

"I'd like that."

A timid smile pushes up her flush cheeks. Shelly unlocks the door and steps aside to let me in. The apartment is small but quaint. Enough for one person. Cozy enough to entertain guests. The vibe and appearance simple, but very much Shelly.

Ivory walls with occasional family photos and framed print art. Soft-pink sheer curtains accent standard blinds. A beige sofa with throw pillows to add a pop of color and a knitted blanket slung over the back. An ivory-shaded lamp on a side table farthest from the door. A rectangular, cherrywood table sits between the couch and a small entertainment center with a television, DVD player, and streaming device. Fuchsia and taffy and blush flowering buds in a vase on the table.

"Make yourself at home," she says as she hangs her purse on a hook behind the door. "Coffee or tea?"

"Tea. Please."

"I'll be back in a moment."

Shelly walks to the left, past a small dining space, and into a kitchen big enough for just her. The dining has a small, round table with two chairs. Another vase, this one smaller, with the same array of flowers rests at the heart. A chandelier fixture that doesn't match Shelly's style, and probably what comes standard with the apartment, hangs above the table. The kitchen, from my position in the living room, has stainless steel appliances, oak cabinets, and dark countertops. The kitchen appears to be the darkest part of the entire space.

I sit on the sofa, run my fingertips over the fabric, the throw pillow and blanket. Soft. But not as soft as Shelly. So much of her is woven into this small place. Although it isn't vast, it casts a warm energy. An energy I recognize any time Shelly and I exist in the same space.

While I wait, I breathe it all in. Fill my lungs with her floral and patchouli scent. Fill my heart with her kindness and radiance. After tonight, everything will be different. Everything. Yes, inviting her into my home was huge. Sitting beside her in my living room was heart stopping. Falling asleep curled up beside her was unreal. Waking up with her wrapped in my arms was life altering. But tonight… it feels… more.

"Hope you like chamomile."

I open my eyes as she rounds the couch and hands me a mug. "Chamomile is perfect." Because I need something to calm the buzz swirling in my head and beneath my diaphragm. Going from zero to one hundred may be exhilarating in a car, but with my heart…

We sip our tea and sit in silence a moment. A silence vastly different than any other we have shared. Why? Because it's in her home. Her most sacred space. And for the first time in minutes, I realize just how close we are. That her knee brushes my lower thigh. Her lips a mere foot away.

She sets her mug on the table and I mirror the action. Was I this nervous when she came to my house? No, not to this degree. Sure, I was hyperaware of Shelly the second she set foot in my home, but her presence soothed me otherwise. Maybe it's the size of the space. How, in her apartment, I feel like I am on top of her.

"Do you want to watch something? A movie," she clarifies.

Without checking the time, I know it's late. Easily after ten. A movie would keep me well past midnight. Much as I want to entertain the idea, I probably shouldn't press my luck. The temptation is real, though.

"No, I—"

She cuts me off. Frames my face with her hands and brings her mouth to mine. Then everything goes dark as my eyes roll back. Dark and warm and euphoric.

Her lips move against mine in gentle strokes. Sweet and soft and pink. On the second wave, my lips move with hers. Perform a dance they haven't in years. I tilt my head to the side, change the angle of the kiss, and she shifts too. My hands reach for her, land on the curve of her hips. Glide up either side of her rib cage, skirt the length of her collarbones until I trail up her neck and take her face in my palms.

I need to taste her. See if she is as sweet as I have imagined.

Parting my lips, I lick the seam of hers. Like the blooming petals of a flower, she opens up and invites me in. Lets me sweep my tongue over hers. Tangle it with hers. Taste her.

And I am done.

Lost with no desire to be found.

Lost in her warmth. In the electricity. Her earthy-floral scent. Her sweet and succulent taste. Lost in the high that hits my bloodstream with my lips on hers. Obliterated by the volatile rhythm she teaches my heart.

I kiss her as if I never will again. As if she is my last supper and I am a starved fool.

You are a fool.

A ping sounds in my brain. A system override. A tripwire. An alarm telling me to abort. To stop kissing Shelly because we can never be anything more than friends. Because emotional attachment beyond friendship only leads to heartache. To pain and suffering. To an inevitable end. Because one day, she will decide she no longer wants me. No longer needs me. Doesn't want me at her side to touch her or hold her or give her whatever she needs.

She will throw me away.

Just like Kelsey did.

I break the kiss and scoot away from her. Eyes downcast, I shake my head and hold up a hand. "No." I shake my head again. "No, I can't. We can't. I can't do this." Finally, I meet her gaze and see the tears already rimming her eyes. "I'm sorry."

Fuck.

I hate myself. Hate that kissing a woman I want, a woman who wants me, a woman I *trust*, ends in catastrophe. More than anything, I hate that my brain is wired this way. Ready to ruin everything good.

It's bullshit, but I already lit the fuse.

I need time to think. Time to figure out how to fix the messed-up shit in my head. Time to make myself worthy of Shelly. She deserves better than this. Better than me.

Rising from the couch, I look everywhere but at her. Mutter my apologies over and over as I slowly make my way to the door.

I need to get out of here. Away from her. Before I lose the strength to go.

"I shouldn't have… I'm sorry, Devlyn. You don't have to go. Please, I'm sorry." She is off the couch, taking slow, deliberate steps in my direction. Approaching me like a scared, wounded animal.

She can't touch me. If she touches me, I will cave. Lose all willpower and give in to her pleas. And I can't. Not yet. Not now. Not until I unscramble my warped brain. Otherwise, I will just make it worse. Hurt her worse.

I meet her eyes again. Take one last look at her glassy, veiny, twilight irises. "I can't," I whisper. "I wish I could, but I just…" Two more steps and I grab the knob. Twist and take another step, this one outside. "I'm so sorry."

And then, I leave. Dash to the car, start the engine, and drive home in a fog. In my pocket, my phone vibrates over and over. Without fishing it out, I know who it is. Know that Shelly is texting or calling. And I want to answer her. Want to tell her how I feel. Want to confess how much I care for her. Explain what just happened. Why I reacted the way I did.

Just as I closed her door, I saw the first bout of tears glide down her cheeks. And now, it will be all I see when I think of her. Her pain and misery and regret. And I deserve that to be my reminder. I deserve to only see her suffering. Her pain is my punishment.

I reach a red light and pull out my phone. Thirteen text messages, all from Shelly and all various forms of an apology.

"I'm sorry too. You don't know how much." I look at the screen and shake my head. "God, I wish it was that easy. I wish I could give you more. But I can't. Not yet."

And then I power off my phone, stow it in my pocket, and finish the drive home.

Tonight started out as one the best nights in a long time. Correction, tonight was *the* best night of my life—the second being Shelly in my house, in my space. Leave it up to me to ruin it. To ruin her. To ruin us.

I fucking hate myself. But dammit, I will do whatever it takes to fix myself and make things right between us. Because Shelly… I *need* her.

fifteen

Have you ever felt like your life has been one major clusterfuck of an amusement park ride? The more time passes, the more I feel this all too deeply. And it just fucking hurts. A bone-deep ache that won't go away.

Night after night, I stare at the romance books on my shelves. Scan their worn spines and tattered covers. Books I have read over and over. Others waiting for me to pick them up. And I just can't do it. I refuse to let myself get swept up in some happy fairy tale where everyone ends up with their happily ever after. Meanwhile, I'm over here plucking the occasional gray hair, developing wrinkles at the corners of my eyes, and contemplating if I should buy one cat or ten.

Not like I don't want to experience those "all the feels" moments in my own life. For my heart to rip apart the cage holding it captive. For my lungs to burn when I forget to breathe. For my skin to heat and dampen with just his eyes on me, his body near mine. To feel each and every one of those don't-ever-let-me-go moments.

God, do I want them. *Really* want them. I thought I had them—some of them— for a blip of time. A very small blip. But I was wrong.

And now… I am exhausted. Utterly spent. Out of gusto.

So tired of faking happy twenty-four seven. Tired of contributing one hundred percent to everything and getting shit on constantly. Tired of being paired with the other single friend in our circle, Erin, because we don't have someone on our arm.

During get-togethers—like Autumn's baby shower today—they seat Erin and me together. Why? Because we have singledom in common. Because we haven't found someone to sweep us off our feet. Because we are lepers when it comes to love. At least, that is what it feels like.

Gah! I want to fist my hair, scream at the top of my lungs, and rip the strands from my scalp. I want it to hurt more than the unyielding pain beneath my breast-bone. Physical pain, I can handle. Gut-wrenching emotional pain…

Autumn unwraps and opens a box wrapped in black-and-white baby farm animals. Since she and Jonas don't know the sex of the baby yet, everything has been neutral. Light and soft tones. Khaki, gray, cream. No pink or blue, yellow or green. The gifts, the cake, the decor. All of it is just… neutral. Plain. Simple.

My life is plain. Neutral. But not simple.

I wish it were simple. That I didn't spend most of my time each day trying to fix what I broke. To mend fences with Devlyn. Unfortunately, some things can't be fixed. Not when only one person does the work and two are required.

God, I miss him.

I took our friendship for granted. Got swept up in the moment. In his earthy, artsy scent. The way his smile only popped up on occasion and not for just anyone. I only ever saw him smile at me and Elizabeth. And the smile he gave me was not the same he gave her. And I miss the contrast between his dark, floppy hair and pale-green eyes.

His eyes still linger. When I close mine, I see them with such clarity. Staring back at me. Haunting me. Crushing me. Which is why sleep has been shit recently. Distracting yourself while you dream is a bit difficult.

Why did I have to mess things up? Why did I kiss him?

No, I am not the only one to blame for all of this. I felt it. The way he gravitated toward me any chance he got. The subtle, unspoken hints of something more than *friendship*. Always wanting more time together. That night and morning at his house…

"Shh, shh, shh," Cora shushes as baby Clara starts fussing. "Someone's hungry." After a few wiggly moves, Clara latches onto Cora's breast and suckles.

Everyone in the room watches in awe. Everyone but me.

I love my best friend and niece fiercely. Would do anything for either of them. But watching them share this intimate bonding moment makes the backs of my eyes sting. Forms a lump in my throat. Makes the ache in my chest more pronounced.

Rising from the couch, I wander out of the room and mumble, "Be right back."

I step into the bathroom, shut the door and lock it, then slide down the back until my butt hits the cold tile. Silently, I weep into my sweater sleeves. Cry long enough to get it out, but short enough to not let my face puff up. Then I get up, take a deep breath, use the toilet, and rinse my face with cool water.

Minutes mimic days as I stare at my reflection. As I question my life, my past, my way of thinking. Question what the hell is wrong with me. Question why two weeks and hundreds of text messages and phone calls from me to Devlyn go unanswered.

Why? What have I done to warrant this level of extreme solitude? What karmic rule did I break to receive this overflowing spoonful of loneliness?

I love people. Family, friends, strangers. I do right by others. Help out whenever possible. Give back to those less fortunate in the community. Always contribute if possible. I care for others. Am loyal without question.

But it never seems enough, and I don't know why.

Someone, please tell me why.

Hell, the fact that I haven't given up my *virtue* should count for something. Give me bonus points in someone's book. Not that being a thirty-two-year-old virgin was a goal, but here I am…

Why won't he talk to me?

My hands hurt from wiping them so long with the towel. I hang the cloth back on the bar, give myself one last glance in the mirror, take a deep breath, then turn for the door.

Back in the living room, the crowd has thinned. Guilt seeps into my veins and rattles me.

How long was I in the bathroom? I didn't get to say goodbye.

After a deep breath, I sit in the same spot on the couch and try to pick up on what I missed. Which proves difficult because no one says a word. When I survey the room, all eyes are on me.

Great. Just fucking great.

"Shell, what's wrong?" Cora asks, her tone treading lightly.

Much as I don't want to dump my lackluster life onto my friends, I refuse to lie. Especially to Cora. She leaned on me countless times in the past. To deny her the truth would make me a hypocrite and a horrible best friend.

If only the truth didn't throb painfully in my chest.

Eyes on my lap, I tuck my hands and fingers in the sweater sleeves. Hide them from view, so no one sees me pick at my cuticles. The room goes quiet, too quiet, but the stares I feel burning my skin scream deafening tones. And I just want the silent questions and eye-piercing volume to stop.

"Remember the guy at the shop last year?" I don't need to elaborate. Cora knows who I mean. It's not often I talk shop… or guys.

"*The artist* who did the mural?" Cora questions.

"Yeah."

"Sort of. I remember Mom talking about him. Only saw him briefly during a visit. I remember him being there, but not *him*." She rises from her chair and sets Clara—who fell asleep while I was in the bathroom—in her carrier. Then she parks next to me on the couch. "Is he the reason you're down?"

This is so weird, awkward. Maybe because guys don't stick around past date number two. Maybe because I have never had a long-term romantic relationship. Not that Devlyn and I are—were—long term or romantic anything. But he is the first person I connected with on a profound level.

Then I ruined everything with a stupid kiss.

What a great kiss it was, though.

"Yes and no," I say with a shrug. "He was back at the shop, touching up the outside mural and painting a new one inside." I drag in a deep breath and exhale loudly. "He was there daily for weeks and we talked. A lot. When he finished, we started hanging out. About a month and a half. Nothing serious. Guy friend stuff."

I pause and close my eyes. Fill my lungs with fresh air and swallow past the lump forming in my throat. I peel my eyes back open, but keep them on my lap and trudge forward.

"A couple weeks ago, I kissed him. He was into it. Really into it." I lift my gaze to Cora and see the wince already building on her face. All it does is amplify the pain in my chest. A pain that just won't quit. I press the heel of my palm to my breastbone and get no relief. "Then, he freaked. Couldn't leave fast enough. And I haven't heard from him since."

The spear pushes straight through my heart and lets every drop of life puddle at my feet. When did I become this woman? An emotional wreckage pile. The woman who lets the idea of a guy rule her life.

Cora scoots closer as Autumn presses her weight to the opposite side. A hand swipes my cheek. Wipes away the tears I hadn't realized were leaking from my eyes. Which makes me cry harder. Then, I am swathed tighter than a newborn. Surrounded by arms and warmth. Friendship and love. Family.

And I let it all go. Cry as if my ducts hadn't been used in years. Weep as if I lost the love of a lifetime. And I don't stop until my eyes are puffy and cheeks are hot.

"What did I miss?"

Cora, Autumn, Peyton, and Penny lean back. A whoosh of cool air smacks my face as Elizabeth steps closer. When she wasn't in the room when I returned, I assumed she left. Guess she was in the kitchen or off doing something with Clementine.

"Nothing, Mom," Cora says. "Shelly's just been a little down. So, we were giving her some love."

Elizabeth regards her daughter, then me. She may see me more times a week than Cora, but I haven't mentioned anything to her. Just kept my head low and hands busy at work. But I see the questions in her eyes now. See her motherly armor slip into place.

"Devlyn?"

All she asks is his name. She doesn't need to elaborate. The woman isn't oblivious. Although she appeared to not notice my interaction with Devlyn at the store, she didn't miss a thing. Maybe it is her motherly intuition. Or perhaps, it is the wisdom that only comes with time and life experience. Either way, she knows. And it eases the pain a little.

At least it's Elizabeth and not my own mother. Mom's mission to see me married with children is *not* what I need right now.

I nod. "Yeah."

"Oh, sweetheart." Without hesitation, she steps closer, takes my hand, hoists me up from the couch, and gives me the best mama bear hug. A fresh batch of tears spill down my cheeks. Dampens my shirt and hers. It only makes her hug me harder. Tighter. Longer. "I got you," she says as she softly strokes between my shoulder blades. "Get it all out."

And I do. For the longest time, Elizabeth embraces me with a fierceness only mothers possess. She strokes my hair and shushes my cries. Whispers reassurances and motherly love in my ear. When my ducts run dry, we pull apart and she holds me at arm's length. Gives me a gentle smile that soothes the pain. A little.

Elizabeth and I take a seat among the others. Heat crawls up my neck to my cheeks as guilt swirls in my veins for stealing the spotlight during Autumn's baby shower. For making my personal problems more of a focus than Autumn's impending delivery.

"Sorry," I mutter, then abandon my spot on the couch to refill my glass of water. When I return, I *feel* more than see everyone's stare on my face.

"What are you apologizing for?" Autumn asks.

I park on the couch, sip my water then set it on the table, but keep my eyes trained on the glass as I lean back. This isn't my day. No one is here to celebrate me or a child I am bringing into the world. And it feels ten kinds of wrong to steal the spotlight from Autumn.

"Nothing. Can we talk about something else, please?"

"Nuh-uh," Cora says with a shake of her finger. "You've been up and down a lot recently. Then, you cry your eyes out for almost an hour. Baby talk can wait a few. Am I right?" Cora looks to Autumn, who nods.

"I'd like to talk about something other than pregnancy and babies, thank you very much," Autumn states as she purses her lips. She rests a hand on my forearm, the touch soothing yet serious. "You matter, too, Shell."

I peer down at Autumn's hand before meeting her dark-amber eyes. All I see is love when I look at her. Not an ounce of anger or frustration or jealousy that her baby shower has turned into some form of a Shelly Reed soap opera. A fresh sting bites the backs of my eyes and I tip my head back, blink a few times and swallow past the lump in my throat.

How did I get this lucky? To be surrounded by such wonderful women who support me regardless of what is happening in their own lives.

"Thank you." I sniffle. "Still don't want to be the center of attention." I laugh without humor.

"Well, then, you best get it all out now. Tell us everything weighing you down."

"Might need something stronger than water."

Autumn rises from the couch and waddles toward the kitchen. "I've been saving this ginger beer for a special occasion, but…"

Laughter fills the room, even from me, as she returns with brown bottles of ginger beer. She pops the lid off one and hands it over. I take the first sip and go into a coughing fit.

"Jesus." I cough into my elbow. "Is that just liquid ginger?"

She shrugs. "Don't know, but I love it and so does the little one." She rubs her belly.

Over the next hour, I spill my heart out to my friends and family. Tell them about every day or evening Devlyn and I spent together. Our minimal conversations and how I never knew so little could mean so much. How he always looked at me more than a male friend looks at a female friend. How he went out of his way to do nice things for me. That he always wanted more time together. And was the one that pushed us in the direction we ended up in.

"He never wanted to get me those drinks in the morning," Elizabeth chimes in. "But he did so it wouldn't look like he was showing his affections toward you."

I narrow my eyes at her. "What makes you say that?"

"Just because I've been married most of my adult life, doesn't mean I am blind to flirting and gestures."

I shake my head in disbelief. "No, he was just being nice."

"Keep telling yourself that, if it helps you sleep. But that young man sees you, sweetheart. Not just the woman on the outside, but what's here, too." She presses a hand to her heart. "He just doesn't know how to express that verbally."

Elizabeth has a point. Devlyn hasn't opened up much since I have known him. Not that I expect his entire life story after knowing me a minute. Those six-plus weeks were the best. Each week, I got a fresh glimpse at Devlyn. A new side to him. Some days, he was so deep in thought while he painted, I could've screamed and he wouldn't have flinched. Other days, we were so in tune. The slightest look my direction and it heated my skin.

The night at his house… the next morning… those memories strike the hardest. Hurt the most. Everything about that memory feels like a lead-up to the kiss.

He wanted me there. In his home. In his space. Alone with him. Inches away in the dark. Snug to his body as we slept. He made me breakfast. Didn't want me to leave. At the car, I saw it… he wanted to kiss me too.

But maybe Elizabeth is on to something.

"Yeah, you're probably right." I sigh and stare down at the fumbling fingers in my lap. "What do I do now? He doesn't answer my calls or texts." Tipping my head back, I stare at the ceiling and huff. "I hate how bereft I feel."

Cora wraps an arm around my shoulders and tugs me into her. "Wish I had the right answer. The one to put a smile on your face. But everyone operates differently. Especially Devlyn, from what you've told us." She gives my shoulder a squeeze and I peer up at my best and longest friend. "You either need to give him patience or…" Her eyes dart between mine for two breaths. "Let him go." My shoulders drop and Cora's lips turn down at the corners. "You don't want to, I'm sure. But you need to do what's best for you."

The backs of my eyes sting for the umpteenth time today. "Why does this have to be so hard?" I garble out.

Autumn embraces me from the other side. "Because you obviously have feelings for him. Beyond friendship." A palm rubs up and down my back. "Jonas and I went back and forth so many times because I wanted to do what was best for Clementine. Little did I know, what I was doing wasn't best. But I had to learn that in my own time." Autumn leans her head on my shoulder. "What's meant to be will play out. But don't stop living because he won't own his feelings."

I nod, absorbing Autumn and Cora's words. Letting them sink deep and fill me with the strength I need to get past this. More than ever, I am grateful for the wonderful women in my circle. All my family, none by blood. Lucky is an understatement. I take their love and support and harness it as armor. Feel their courage pass to me as I wipe the tears from my cheeks.

"Thank you," I say as I glance at each of them in turn. "Thank you for always being there."

Cora squeezes me a bit tighter. "Wouldn't have it any other way." Her arm drops from my shoulder as she gives me a smile. "Now, let's talk about something else. Since none of the guys are here, let's talk shit about them and laugh when they get here later."

Everyone laughs, including Elizabeth, and I love how the mood in the room became ten times lighter. And for the next few hours, life is normal. Happy. Loaded with jokes. When the guys show, we make plans for another get-together. Karaoke or bowling. Something in addition to our Sunday gatherings.

I leave Jonas and Autumn's house with less weight on my shoulders and a warmer heart. Now more than ever, I need to spend time with people who make me whole. Who bring me joy.

Which is why what I am about to do is more important than anything else. I have to do this if I want to move on. If I want out of this dark place.

Parking the car in my designated spot, I cut the engine and stare at my front door. My apartment has been occupied with the energy of that night. *The night.* The night when I kissed Devlyn, and he reciprocated long enough to give me hope. Only to squash it just as quickly.

Tonight, I am detoxifying my space. Lighting sage, opening the windows and letting all the negative vibes out. Time to make it mine again. To make it a place I love.

Exiting the car, I walk to the front door with a straighter spine. I insert the key, turn the knob, and step inside. Plopping down on the couch, I fish my phone from my purse and pull up the text history between me and Devlyn. After two deep breaths, I tap out the most difficult seven letters of my life, then hit send.

A tear splatters on the screen and the word *goodbye* blurs... just like my life. But I am taking my life back. After this final cry.

sixteen

DEVLYN

My phone lights up on the table, the message icon on the notification. Without leaning for a closer look, I already know the text is from Shelly. Over the last two weeks, she has texted and called more times than I care to admit. Although I haven't responded to a single call, voice mail or text from Shelly, I listen to and look at each one. She is none the wiser since I disabled my read message receipts.

Yep, I have become *that* guy. The biggest asshole in the Bay Area.

And I detest the person I have become. Hate that I hurt her. Hate that I led her on then flipped.

I opened myself up to her, let her in the slightest bit, gave her a glimpse of who I want to be, that I want *her*. Then I smashed it all with a foolish mistake.

Kissing Shelly was *not* the mistake. Losing my shit and walking out the door was the mistake. Not responding to her daily texts and calls was—is—a mistake. Sitting on this couch instead of driving to her apartment and apologizing in person is a big. Fucking. Mistake.

Now I fear it's too late to repair the damage.

Fuck. I hope it isn't, but I feel stuck. Unsure what to do to fix myself or how to make things between us right.

Memories of the kiss drift back in—not that they ever leave. Shelly's lips pressed to mine, so soft and warm and inviting, knocked the air from my lungs. The memory of it still does, each and every time. As does the searing pain at my epicenter. The pain that never leaves. The pain I deserve, not Shelly.

If I were the only one suffering, I would willingly take a dagger to the heart. Let it twist over and over.

But Shelly is suffering too.

Her pain spills across the screen with each word she types. Is evident in the crack of her voice when I play back her messages. Hearing—*feeling*—her pain is ten times worse.

Ignoring the nature documentary in the background, I pick up the phone, take a deep breath, and open the message.

Goodbye

Goodbye? What the hell does that mean?

I stare at the screen until I lose focus. Until my eyes glaze over and my thoughts swirl into a vicious hurricane. One after another, I take a deep breath. Try to settle the erratic line of my thinking. Sending a text with only *goodbye* in the message could translate a hundred ways.

Goodbye, I no longer want to speak to you.

Goodbye, I never want to see you again.

Goodbye, we were obviously never friends.

Goodbye, you're an asshole.

Or the one I don't want to think, but can't ignore.

Goodbye world.

I shake my head at the last one. Shake off the dark direction my thoughts took. Shelly and I may not have shared everything, we may not have fully exposed our pasts, but I don't picture her harming herself. Not with her sunny disposition. Not with the brilliant smile she flashes the world. Not with the long line of people who love her. She would never hurt herself. Right?

Fuck.

Why can't I be a better person? Why can't I step up and own what I feel? Tell this woman, this phenomenal woman, how I feel about *her*. Tell her she invades every waking moment of my life. That the kiss we shared is all I think about. That I still feel her lips on mine when I close my eyes. Still see her starry eyes. Still picture her in my home, in my arms, nestled against my chest. That I still smell her in the couch fabric and haven't slept in my own bed since that night.

Why haven't I told her any of this? Why haven't I acted?

Because I am a fucking coward. A chickenshit. A pathetic excuse. Rather than opening up and letting her in, I cower in the corner and shut out the world.

Any chance I had at a friendship with Shelly in the future has flown out the window. Because Shelly just cut ties with one word. In a text message, no less, because I won't speak to her. I shut her out and she locked the door for good. Threw the key in the landfill.

A red, hot dagger pierces between my ribs. I smash the heel of my palm to my sternum and curl my fingers into a fist. I drop the phone to the floor, drop my head to my knees, and rock in place on the couch. Fist my hair and tug until the pain steals my vision. Gasp for the breaths that refuse to fill my lungs.

"Aaaah!" I scream until my vocal cords strain. Then I scream again. Louder. Not giving a damn what the neighbors hear or think. I bolt up from the couch, scoop my phone from the floor, and throw it at the wall. I grab the next thing in reach, then the next, and throw them across the room.

Pain and anger are poison in my veins. Seeping slow and steady into my bloodstream, the marrow of my bones, every atom and cell. Turning everything black. Dark. A shadow of its former self. And I let it. Allow it to consume me. Swallow me into a never-ending abyss. I deserve nothing less.

I dash up the stairs, taking them two at a time. Enter my studio and scan the room. Study the countless drawings and paintings along the walls, on the floors, on my desk and easel. Each and every one of them inspired by the same person. The woman I wouldn't open up to because of past insecurities I refuse to face.

"Fucking idiot," I scream into the room. "Dumb. Fucking. Idiot."

Stepping farther into the room, I stand inches from the canvas on the easel. Stare at the stormy, dark-blue backdrop, the strategic gold splatters, the fine, faint white lines forming a half face. My Andromeda.

No, not yours. Shelly was never yours. She never will be.

I fist my hair and scream at the canvas. Scream at the pain I inflicted on Shelly and myself. Scream until my vocal cords shrivel and my lungs exhaust themselves. Then, I take the canvas in my hands. Grip the wood frame until it bites my skin. Rotate it in my hands, lift my foot from the ground, and crack the frame over my knee. The canvas doesn't tear, which only serves to fuel the flames of my anger.

Stomping to my tools, I dump them on the floor, drop down on my knees, and dig for the spackle knife. The wooden handle grazes my fingertips and I grip it until my knuckles whiten. I lay the floppy canvas on the ground, hold the edge with one hand, raise the blade in the other, and freeze.

The room blurs. My lungs quiver. The hand harnessing the blade trembles.

I don't want to do this.

Goodbye.

But I have to.

Goodbye.

Have to erase every piece of her.

Goodbye.

Have to let the idea of her go.

Goodbye.

I brought this upon myself. Opened us both up to heartache. Heartache Shelly doesn't deserve. But I do.

Goodbye.

Tipping my head back, I close my eyes and let the salty tears spill down my cheeks, my temples. "Give me her pain," I croak out. "Give me her sorrow, her heartache, her anguish. I deserve it. Not her."

I drop my head to the floor, grip the tattered canvas in my hands, and crowd it around my face. Again and again, my heart spasms. I accept the pain. Absorb every strike without complaint. Beg for more if it means Shelly feels none.

With each new hit, I rise to my feet. Take my pencils, my brushes, my oils and throw them across the room. I rip the drawings from the wall. Tear them down the middle twice and toss them in the air like confetti. I swipe my arm over the shelves and spill everything to the floor. Punch my fist through one painting after another until my fist meets drywall. My foot connects with the trash bin and scatters debris in a wide radius.

I stop and stare around the studio. Stare down at my fist and watch in fascination as a thick layer of crimson drips from my fingertips. Gaze at the chaos, the shredded sketches, the demolished canvases, the splattered paint. The sight should throw me off balance. Should have me in hysterics. Eager to put everything back in its rightful place.

Instead, I laugh. A delirious, maniacal sound spilling from my throat. I bend at the waist and grip my knees. The hysterical laughter transitions into an unsteady wheeze. I take in the disaster that is my studio and a fresh wave of panic hits. Punches me in the gut and knocks the air from my lungs.

"Damnit."

I drop to my hands and knees. Grab the tattered drawings on the floor and try to match them up. Try to salvage them and make them whole again. I put all the pieces in a pile. Then create another pile of the decimated paintings. Frantic hands sift through the first pile, trying to match the images and edges like a puzzle. When none of the pieces fit, I move to the next pile. Try to right my wrong.

But I am too late. Just like with Shelly.

Goodbye.

I fucked up and now I am paying the price. "Stupid, selfish idiot. Why did you do this? Why are you ruining every good thing in your life?"

Crawling across the floor, I grab a blank canvas from the stack. Rise to my feet and pad over to my easel. Gingerly set it on the stand. My eyes dart between the debris and the blank canvas, an idea developing.

Much as I should eliminate all reminders of Shelly from my life—most of which are locked in my memories—I simply can't. So, this is my punishment. To live with mental photographs and videos of her. To paint or sketch her likeness until my digits and limbs no longer work. To torture myself, day after day, because I deserve nothing less. I deserve pain and anguish—mine and hers.

I sift through the catastrophe on the floor, locate some brushes and a handful of paints, and then I start anew. Use bits of the drawings I shredded and add them to the new project. To twist the knife deeper in my chest, of course I recreate Shelly. If this is the only way I can have her, so be it.

Parked on my stool, I paint the canvas a blue so rich, it appears black. Using the scraps, I adhere them to the damp canvas. Create a mosaic of sorts. I rummage through the room and look for other bits I can add to the canvas, tools to add other forms of texture and dimension. Before returning to the stool, I turn on music. Play something other than the typical classical music I listen to in this room. Tonight, I need something to match my mood. Beats and lyrics filled with irritation or fury. Music with grit and rage. Songs to scream and thrash and smash objects to without concerning the neighbors. In the short time I have lived here, they have adapted to the weird guy in the neighborhood.

Loud, violent rock music spills from the speaker. The growly vocals against the fast tempo crowd the room. The hairs on my arms stand on end. The bass vibrates my bones. And the noise steals all potential space for thought.

This… this is what I need.

To not think. To get lost in something. Anything. To forget about what I lost and the pain I caused us both. This may not be the cure, but it will help the time pass easier. Help ease the pain, if only the slightest.

Goodbye.

The seven-letter word will be one I never hear or say in the same context again. I hate it had to be said in the first place. I never wanted to say goodbye to Shelly. Part of me hoped, after enough time passed, we would find our way back to each other. As friends.

Yes, I want to be more than Shelly's friend. No sense in denying the truth now. If I felt the cosmos collide when we kissed, she felt the intensity ten times stronger. I am not emotionless. I simply feel on a different scale. A scale tipped closer toward numb. Void. But not completely.

"Goodbye." The word singes my throat and burns my lips. Leaves a rancid taste on my tongue.

I swipe up a piece of a charcoal drawing. Home in on the thick black lines. Without question, this is Shelly's brow. An arch I memorized weeks ago, when the sun shone on the lateral edge. I brush the tip of my finger over the line. Swallow the pooling saliva in my mouth. Blink and look away for two breaths. Bite the inside of my cheek until a metallic tang hits my tongue.

"Wish we could've been more. Wish I was strong enough to be who you want. Who you *need*." I close my eyes and shake my head. "You're always in here, you know." I tap my temple. "That'll have to be enough, for now." A half-hearted laugh spills from my lips. "Maybe one day, I'll get my shit together. Maybe one day, I'll be strong enough, good enough, for you."

No! No, no, no, no, no.

Get your shit together, Templar. Now. And make this right. Quit wallowing in self-pity and fix this.

My eyes drift around the studio, take in the disaster once more, then land on the fresh canvas. "I fucked this up," I say to the canvas as if it is Shelly. "Now… I need to make it right. Hopefully, you'll forgive me. Hopefully, I'm not too late."

Because this pain… I won't survive it. Not for long.

seventeen

SHELLY

Sleep evades me as I lie in bed and stare up at the hints of moonlight slipping through the blinds. And for the hundredth time since I sent the *goodbye* text hours ago, nausea rolls in my belly.

If letting go of Devlyn was the right thing to do, why am I sick to my stomach?

The urge to rip my phone from the charger and type out a new message hits me like a freight train. I want to delete the message. Rescind it. Pretend like the thought never crossed my mind.

In its place, I want to send my longest apology. An extensive plea for him to forgive me for crossing the line. To beg him to take me back as his friend. Something. Anything.

God, I am such a fool.

How many times did Devlyn tell me he could only be my friend? So many times, I hate the word more than moist. Did I listen and respect his boundaries? No, but with good reason.

There is no possible way I read him wrong. Right? In our last week together, he threw one hint after another. Showed me his interest with small gestures and sentiments. His romantic interest. By no means can I professionally read people, but I picked up every hint and smile and longer-than-normal stare he sent my way. Honestly, I thought it was his way of telling me he wanted more without using words.

Obviously, I am an idiot. And supremely horrible at body language and gauging others.

"Ugh," I huff out, throwing the comforter and sheet from my body. I sit up and stare at the clock on my bedside table. The dull-blue numbers stare back and mock me—3:21. "Fuck you," I whisper to no one as I rise from the mattress.

Maybe a steaming mug of chamomile will settle my mind enough to allow sleep. Even if only a few hours, some sleep is better than none.

The electric kettle comes to a boil just as I hear something outside. Flipping the switch to off, I abandon the kettle and tiptoe to the window near the door. Slowly, I inch back the curtain and part a slat of the blinds to peek out. A gasp leaves my lips.

Why is Devlyn on my porch?

Hands shoved in his hoodie, he paces back and forth in front of the door. Every other direction change, he stops and looks at the door. In the artificial light, I watch the lines of his forehead scrunch and flatten then repeat. It's obvious he wants to knock on my door, but refrains from following through.

After watching him pace the same ten feet several times, I close my eyes, drop my hand from the blinds, and take a step back. Part of me wants to ignore Devlyn outside my door. Ignore him and hold firmly to the goodbye I sent earlier. He hurt me when he left here without explanation. He hurt me when he ignored my obsessive texts and calls.

Until I sent the one that hurt him.

Much as I want to ignore the upset man on my porch, I also want to fling the door open and give him a chance. Allow him the opportunity to explain why he flipped. Let him grovel and beg for forgiveness. Not that it would take much for me to forgive Devlyn. My feelings for him would override any stint of torture my mind wanted to inflict.

My fingers wrap around the door handle as my lungs take one last deep breath. *Give him a chance.* After I unbolt the lock, I twist the knob and swing the door wide.

Devlyn stops his trek past my door, his back to me goes rigid. Then his head drops, shoulders cave, and his entire frame deflates. Neither of us speaks, but the tension between us is a living, breathing entity. Harsh energy radiates off him and spills over me, causing a shiver. Devlyn is angry, but it isn't directed at me. Perhaps that is why he hasn't faced me yet.

Minutes pass before he lifts his head. Measured and hesitant, he spins around and meets my waiting gaze.

Translucent-green irises hold my blues. He takes a step in my direction, eyes darting between mine, silently asking why. Then with another step, he stands inches away. It's now that I notice the red veins hugging his irises. The puffiness around his eyes. The dampness on his lashes. The permanent valley between his brows.

"No," he whispers, his eyes holding me prisoner.

My brows bend in the middle. "No?"

He shakes his head slowly. Steps impossibly closer. Slips his hand around mine and holds it like I am his lifeline. "No goodbye."

I open my mouth to rebut him. To tell him I won't be the recipient of mind games. That I won't always wait in the wings while he melts down and abandons people who care about him—including me. That I won't let him break my heart because he is too scared to feel or own what he wants.

But I say none of those things. Don't even get the chance.

Devlyn lifts his free hand and cups my cheek. Captures my eyes with his as our breaths turn ragged. Then, ever so slowly, he leans forward and presses his lips to mine. I freeze at the initial connection but melt when he lightly sucks my bottom lip between his.

Warmth spreads through me as our lips dance together. His hand abandons my cheek as his fingers weave through my hair. I fist his hoodie, walk backward and drag him inside. The door shuts behind us and I assume he kicked it. He lifts our joined hands between us, between our hearts, and trails kisses along my jaw, my ear, my neck.

"So sorry," he mutters between kisses. "Such an ass." At this, I chuckle. His lips break free of my skin, eyes meeting mine. "I want to explain. Please, let me explain."

I drop my forehead to his and sigh heavily. His thumb on my hand draws lazy circles while the fingers of his other hand massage my scalp. The hurt side of me wants to pull away and drag out the agony. Make him feel an iota of what I felt after he ran off. But the sensible side shakes her head and tells me to hear him out. Let him talk. Let him share the pieces he keeps hidden from everyone else.

Sensibility wins.

Nodding, I pull back. "Okay." I drop my hand from his hoodie. "I was making tea. Would you like some?"

He presses his lips to my forehead. "Thank you." Why does this kiss feel more intimate? "I'd love some tea."

I head for the kitchen while Devlyn takes a seat on the couch. Filling two mugs with hot water from the kettle, I deposit chamomile in both and let them steep as I watch Devlyn.

His head falls back on the sofa. Eyes closed, he looks as exhausted as I feel. The last two weeks have obviously tormented us both, yet neither of us did anything to rectify the situation. Well, not until I sent the most recent text message. That was all it took to truly rattle Devlyn to the bone. To wake him up from whatever dream— or nightmare—he'd abandoned me for.

Whoever hurt him in the past… I have never been a violent person, but I want to strangle them. Then maybe thank them. Devlyn wouldn't be who he is now without them, but I hate that he was hurt.

Setting the mugs on the table, I take a seat beside him on the couch. He rolls his head my direction and opens his eyes. And for a minute, we sit in suspended animation. I read his every movement, every unspoken word scrawled in the worry lines of his face. See his apology in the redness of his eyes, in the defeat of his posture.

I want to comfort him. Tell him I forgive him. Let him know we will be okay.

But I won't say a word. Not until he gives me more. Explains what made him panic.

He extends his arm closest to me. Lays it palm up on his thigh. An open invitation for me to take his hand. To twine our fingers. To connect us physically while he exposes himself emotionally.

Without hesitation, I take his hand. His eyes drift shut as a heavy breath stutters from his lungs. A sad smile on his lips.

"Sorry will never be enough," he says as his eyes open and capture mine. His thumb glides up and down in gentle, measured strokes over my skin. "But it's a start." He sits taller. Scoots an inch closer. "And I promise to make it up to you. Every day of forever, if necessary."

Forever. The word holds a heavier weight than imaginable. And I want to let it pin me down. Blanket me in comfort.

He brings the mug to his lips and takes a sip before setting it back down. His gaze fixes on our joined hands. The fingertips of his free hand lightly dance over the top of my hand. Draw invisible lines permanently etched in my soul.

"When I think back, the reason I'm so closed off seems childish. Immature. The result of a young love lost. Something millions have dealt with, but overcome with little struggle."

He shakes his head, again and again, as if he can't believe he let someone from his youth disrupt his life with such severity.

Bringing my free hand to his cheek, I brush my knuckles over the line of his jaw. "Devlyn," I say in a hushed tone. He leans into my touch, but keeps his head down. "Your feelings are valid. Justifiable." He tips his head to the side. "Just because you were young, it doesn't mean what you felt was inconsequential. It was real. It mattered. *You matter.*"

At this, he lifts his head. Glassy eyes meet mine, unbelieving. Full of questions. I cup his cheek and stroke the stubble with my thumb. He closes his eyes and leans into my touch again, parallel tears painting lines down his cheeks.

"I don't deserve you," he whispers into the darkened space. "Your heart. Your…" His eyes pinch tighter. His head gently rocks in my palm as he swallows. "Your love."

I sweep my fingers beneath his chin and lift. "Look at me," I whisper a breath from his lips. His eyes pop open, dart between mine, flash me with worry and fear. My stare doesn't deviate from his as I lick my lips. "Devlyn, you deserve so much more. And I'll spend every day of forever proving it to you." I use his words from earlier to tell him I am in this with him.

To seal my promise, I lean in and press my lips to his. The kiss chaste, but equally potent.

I may not have long-term relationship experience, I may not be the person people go to when they need relationship advice, but I will do whatever it takes to help Devlyn heal. To show him that what we have is not the same as his past. That what he felt then and what he feels now are similar and yet completely different.

Everyone has experienced young love—whether it be a crush, deep infatuation, or heartfelt love. The only difference between the love we feel in our youth versus what inhabits us in adulthood—wisdom. And wisdom only comes with time and experience.

I may not have long-term relationship experience, but I have dated my fair share of men. From sweethearts to assholes, I have dated them all. But none of them *felt right*. None of them made me feel alive. None of them made my palms sweat or my knees weak. And none of them made me want more than a simple meal a time or two.

None except for the man next to me.

Devlyn may be young, he may be inexperienced at life and love and hardship, but he has an old soul. He sees the world through a unique filter. And I should be so lucky as to sit at his side and let him see me. Let him love me.

"I'm here. Always," I say, then kiss his lips again.

eighteen

DEVLYN

The next couple of hours on Shelly's couch are filled with me telling her about Kelsey. From the start of our relationship to its abrupt end. And the entire time, Shelly sits beside me, her hand encased in mine, in silent support.

How am I worthy of this woman?

"Thank you for telling me," she whispers, eyes closed as she rests her head on my shoulder.

I kiss her forehead. "Thank you for listening." I tighten my hold around her waist and inhale her sweet and earthy floral scent. "Should get some sleep," I mumble as my eyes drift shut.

Shelly curls into my side, fists my hoodie above my heart and snuggles into my neck. "You too."

I startle awake, Shelly nestled in my arms. Without waking her, I dig my phone from my pocket and check the time. Quarter to seven. Must have drifted off. Thank goodness it's Sunday and Shelly doesn't work today. Neither of us is mentally capable of much right now.

Shifting on the couch, I scoop an arm beneath her knees and haul her into my lap. She groans slightly and I bite the inside of my cheek to resist laughing. Rising from the couch, I walk down the small hall and step into her bedroom. A space that suddenly feels more intimate than a place to rest.

With the curtains drawn and a small amount of light peeking through the blinds, it's difficult to make out the intricacies of her space. But the energy radiates Shelly the farther I step inside.

Sidling up to her bed, I lower her onto the side I assume she sleeps on since the covers are pulled back. The moment I set her down and remove my arms from around her, she reaches for me.

"Stay," she says in her groggy state.

The single word weighs heavy on my mind the more it sets in. I am in no condition to drive, but I don't want to invade her privacy.

Bending over, I kiss her cheek. "I'll be on the couch," I whisper in her ear.

Her head moves side to side in slow motion. "Don't be silly." She yanks at the covers on the opposite side of the bed then pats the sheet. "Lie with me." When I don't move for a beat, her eyes crack open. "Please," she adds and gives my hand a gentle squeeze.

Sleeping. You're just sleeping.

"Okay," I acquiesce.

Once she frees my hand, I move to the other side of the bed and sit. I toe off my shoes then ditch my hoodie and shirt. Something as simple as removing clothes has never felt this rousing. Heady. Potent. Although I hear the soft cadence of Shelly's breathing as she drifts off to sleep, every nerve ending in me is wide awake. Ready to feel and consume every physical touch shared.

Considering we slept on my couch weeks ago, I shouldn't be this antsy. Shouldn't feel this on edge.

But Shelly isn't just anyone. And as much as I wanted to keep things between us black and white, Shelly showed me how vivid and glorious and breathtaking life can be when you fill it with color.

We have spilled our pasts. Exposed our hearts. And now… we move forward.

I slip beneath the covers and turn on my side to face her. The moment I stop moving, she shifts from her side of the bed. Scoots impossibly close and curls into me, face to face, like the night on my couch. I wrap her in my arms and snuggle her closer. Breathe in her scent and tangle my legs with hers.

Not a minute later, her body relaxes completely. Her breathing slows and quiets. Her palms on my chest lax and leg between mine slack.

With one last kiss on her forehead, I let go of every worry and drift off to sleep with the most incredible woman in my arms.

~

The rest of Sunday is spent on Shelly's couch with takeout and more episodes of *Dark*. With Shelly curled into my side, I have never felt more comfortable in my own skin or life. By no means is my life perfect, but she makes each day better than the previous.

Shelly tells me about the upcoming classes she and Elizabeth will offer at Petal and Vine in the new year. Nothing elaborate, maybe five to ten people, and only once a month.

"Do you have plans for the holidays?" she asks around a mouthful of fried ravioli.

I shake my head with a laugh. "Not yet, but I'm sure my mother will text the day before and demand my presence." I aim for it to sound like a joke, but with the way Shelly stares at me in the periphery, I must not have succeeded.

I love my mother. I do. But sometimes—okay, a lot of the time—she can be a bit much.

As a child, I never paid attention to her insistence. Never put much thought into her need for perfection. Honestly, at the time, I admired her desire for everything to be in its place or exactly how she wanted it. Friends would come over and describe her as a neat freak or controlling. I shrugged it off and said she just didn't like dysfunction or disorganization.

Now, as an adult, I see her differently. Especially after college and living on my own, making new friends and meeting their parents, I have a new perspective.

My mother isn't just a perfectionist. She isn't your classic control freak. There is more to it. I picked up on it the first month home after college graduation. She invited colleagues from the museum to dinner. Hours before their arrival, she walked into my bedroom, went straight to my closet, plucked clothes I only wore for dressy occasions from the hangers and handed them to me with a sour look on her face.

"We have dinner guests this evening," she'd said. "You will wear this and be downstairs no later than five thirty. You will be well-groomed and behave like a proper young man. Do not speak unless spoken to. Do not say anything untoward or questionable. They are not coming to hear your opinions. They are coming to talk about the museum and what I'm doing."

That night, I saw my mother in a whole new light. She'd spoken to me like a disobedient child. As if I never used manners. As if I didn't grasp common courtesy. At first, I played it off as nerves. Gave her the benefit of the doubt. These people must have been important. Probably on the fence about donating funds or art to the museum and this dinner might seal the deal.

But as I dressed that night and combed my hair, one piece of her tirade stuck out. Playing on repeat and unnerving me in a way unlike any previous occasion.

What I'm doing.

Since that night, I paid closer attention to our conversations. The more I listened, really listened, the more I heard it. The constant me, me, me. Anytime Mom called to "catch up," she led the conversation. Talked about everything driving her crazy, followed by the incompetence of everyone around her. Anyone not doting on her or lifting her up or making her life easier was unworthy in her eyes, and she voiced as much during our one-sided conversations.

As it stands, I ignore most of her calls. Let them go to voice mail. Listen to them when I am mentally prepared. Call her back when I have the energy but cut her off after thirty minutes. My mother isn't just an energy vampire. She is something entirely different. And after hours of research, I gathered my mother is a narcissist. Or something along those lines, since she hasn't been professionally diagnosed. Unfortunate for me and everyone who encounters my mother, we will never live up to her standards. And my father—sweet man that he is—is her enabler.

"My mom can be a bit much too," Shelly states. "Before my brother Micah started dating his now wife a little more than a year ago, Mom wanted to start having these regular family dinners." She sips her wine. "At first, we both thought it was no big deal. Just our parents missing us."

"Why do I sense a but coming on?"

Shelly laughs without humor. "They did miss us. But Mom also wanted to pester us about our love lives, or lack thereof."

"Ouch."

"Yeah." Her lips kick up in a meh half smile. "Nothing like sitting down for dinner and your mother asking if you've been dating or plan to give her grandchildren before she dies." Shelly rolls her eyes then twists in her seat. "What if I don't want kids?"

"Then that's your choice."

She spears another ravioli and eats the edges off before stuffing the rest in her mouth. "Have you ever thought about it? Having kids, I mean."

If any other person would have thrown this question at me, I'd probably fly off the handle. But with Shelly, I know this is her curiosity. Us still getting to know each other.

For a split second, I remember the texts I sent when her friend had a baby. What a damn fool I was.

"Honestly, I haven't given it much thought. Like I said that day when you texted from the hospital, I'd have to be in a serious relationship before the idea ever crossed my mind. And since I avoided relationships—until you—there was no sense in thinking such things."

Shelly nods. "I get that. The guys I dated before, none lasted past date two." The look on her face says there is more, but she doesn't add anything else. She shrugs and pokes at her dinner.

"Why does it feel like you want to say more?" Her cheeks stain pink, a color I haven't seen on her in weeks. There is more. "You don't have to tell me if you don't want to."

Her lips tip up at the corners. "I appreciate you saying that." She takes a deep breath and exhales slowly. "But I'm going to say it anyway."

She grabs her wineglass and downs the remaining half glass. *Whoa.* "Shelly, you don't—"

"I'm a virgin," she blurts then smothers herself with a throw pillow.

Wait, what?

No way I heard her right.

By the way she is actively trying to cut off her oxygen, I'd say I heard her perfectly fine.

How is that even possible? I mentally roll my eyes. Okay, I *know* how it's possible. But how in the hell does someone as stunning and magnificent as Shelly reach her early thirties and not lose her virginity? Not that I have loads of experience, considering Kelsey is the only sexual partner I've had.

I reach for the pillow and pull it away from her face. She resists me at first but finally lets me take it.

"Shelly…" I encase her hands in mine. "You have nothing to be ashamed of or embarrassed about." She tucks her lips between her teeth and rocks her jaw side to side. "If anything, the trait makes you more attractive. Not because of some male need to claim you. It says more about your character. Defines you as particular, selective. That you associate the act with love and not physicality. That you don't just hand your heart or body over to anyone who shows interest."

She releases her lips and looks up. "No one ever felt right. Not before."

"Not before." I will not overanalyze Shelly's words. Will not read into them and conjure up my own fantasies. But I also won't leave here tonight until I ask what she means.

"Not before?"

Her cheeks turn crimson, but she doesn't try to hide it. "I make no assumptions." I narrow my eyes in question. "About you or me or us."

I nod. "Neither do I."

"And…" Her hands fidget in mine. "With you, things lean that way." I tilt my head and beg her to elaborate. To shape her thoughts into words. "They feel… right."

I free her hands and bring mine to her cheeks. Before she gets another word in, I pull her to me and press my lips to hers. Kiss her gentle and slow. When a moan spills from her lips and down my throat, I deepen the kiss. Wrap my arm around her waist and drag her onto my lap. Fist the hair at the nape of her neck and hug her body flush to mine.

The kiss lasts forever and not long enough before I break it. Before both of us gasp for air.

It is in this moment that realization hits. This very blip in time that I finally believe. In paths and fate. That everything happens for a reason. The struggles of our past align us for the beauty of our future.

Kelsey may have been my first love. The teenage girl I pictured with me for eternity. Although she broke my heart, although she threw my life into a tornado, I wouldn't be in this very moment if none of it happened. I wouldn't have Shelly or this constant swell beneath my sternum. I wouldn't appreciate and reciprocate the emotion spilling from my heart without first experiencing the cracks and aches.

If I bump into Kelsey one day, I will thank her. If it weren't for her need for freedom, I wouldn't have stumbled upon the woman in my arms. If it weren't for her selfishness, I wouldn't have fallen in love. Real love.

Yep, I said it. In love. Although, I may just keep that to myself a little longer.

Lights twinkle from every direction. Red and green, blue and white. Rainbows and blinking and solid strands. Some wrapped around tree trunks and limbs. Others clinging to bushes and rooflines. Animals on lawns with robotic animation. Blow up snow people—because actual snow doesn't happen here—and cartoon characters on the grass and rooftops.

Each year, the amount of holiday decorations people add to their homes is mind blowing. Every Christmas, I ooh and ahh over the displays. Drive slowly down my parents' street to glimpse each setup. Note the new additions from the previous year. Hem and haw over my inability to put up exterior lights, with the exception of my small porch. Complain how I wish I had a blow-up reindeer or Santa to put outside.

I love Christmas. Well, I love all holidays. They all have their own kind of magic. Christmas just happens to be the one I go the most bonkers over.

But this year is a bit different.

This year, the lights twinkle brighter. Candy canes have a little more zip in the peppermint. Balsam firs smell fresher and more piney than any previous year. And the slight chill in the air puts a smile on my face.

During the holidays, I add a minimal amount of decorations to my tiny apartment. A small artificial evergreen. Citrus and clove-scented candles as well as balsam fir. Strands of white fairy lights. Garland made of evergreens and cranberries. An evergreen wreath on the door with blue thistle, white berries, eucalyptus, holly berries, and lightly wrapped gray ribbon. Festive bouquets on the coffee and dining tables as well as the kitchen and bathroom counter. Festive towels hanging from the oven door.

If I had the space, my home would be a holiday mecca.

Every year, I purchase gifts weeks before the holiday. Lug the bin out from under my bed and riffle through rolls of festive paper and ribbons and bows. Play cheery Yuletide music and sip hot cocoa as I write jolly messages in cards. Decorate the tree and light candles.

For years, this has been my ritual. Not down to an exact science, but pretty damn close. This year, everything changed.

A month ago, things with Devlyn went haywire. Out of nowhere, I kissed him and he kissed me back. Then, he panicked and disappeared for two weeks… until I sent a text that scared him more. The night he paced outside my apartment, I had no expectations of what would happen when I opened the door. I definitely didn't expect our relationship to manifest into what it is now.

Devlyn has shifted himself out of the friend category and sits firmly in the boyfriend category. And over the last few weeks, we have been solidifying that new status. Spending every free moment together. Kissing… constantly. And losing track of time.

Which is why, two days ago, I was frantic. One of those berserk people in Target searching empty shelves for the perfect gift. I scored a few small gifts but caved and bought gift cards for the rest. Gift cards are not my style. They feel so impersonal. But I'd rather give a gift card than nothing at all.

"Hallelujah," I whisper as I park next to Peyton's car in my parents' driveway.

I love my parents. Really, I do. From time to time, though, Mom gets a little pushy. Not in the way Devlyn described his mother. Mom has a big heart and means well, she just gets a bit overwhelming here and there. The only thing Nicole Reed wants is for her children to have a happy life. Unfortunately, her version of a happy life includes the perfect spouse, the perfect house, and babies.

I have none of the above.

With the newness of my and Devlyn's relationship, I don't assume to have any of the three in the near future. At this point in the game, I go with the flow. Marriage and picket fences and offspring don't necessarily equal a happy life. Happiness comes from a deeper place. One I have barely started to discover but am eager to explore.

From the moment I witnessed it on screen and read it in romance novels, there has only been one thing that matters when it comes to the future. Love. Deep, hungry, *I can't go a day without seeing you* love. One that steals the air from your lungs, whisks you off your feet and has your heart banging out of your chest.

Above everything else, I want that type of love. If the other things follow in love's wake, so be it. But without love, the other three don't matter.

Walking under the row of icicle lights, I step onto the porch and pause in front of the door. A fresh evergreen wreath with red berries hangs on a hook. My hand hovers over the knob as I inhale the earthy pine scent and let it relax me. "It's Christmas. Mom won't nag me. Not today," I mumble. I nod as if to reassure myself, then twist the knob and step inside.

Three things hit me at once. Deep, booming laughter, mouthwatering baked cheese, and the clanging of pans.

I toe off my shoes in the foyer, set my purse and bags down, and tiptoe toward the kitchen. Peering around the corner, I spy my dad and Peyton seated at the breakfast bar. Tears roll down Dad's cheeks as he presses a loose fist to his mouth. Peyton clamps down on her lips, her cheeks and neck blotchy, as she tries not to laugh.

Across from them, in the heart of the kitchen, are Mom and Micah. My dear, sweet, occasional pain in the ass brother is decked out in Mom's *I love to rub meat* apron. Mom is at his side, coaching him as he sautés carrots in one pan and stirs gravy in another. Sweat beads his forehead and temple. His tongue peeking out between his lips as he shifts his weight left then right.

To most, this sight would be endearing. A son helping his mother cook Christmas dinner. Lovable as the moment is, Dad's tumultuous laughter when I walked in the house now makes sense. Because Micah in the kitchen is equal parts frightening and hilarious. I love my brother, but his ability to cook is null. Mom refuses to give up on him, though. Has him over or goes to his house once a week and shows him something new. Before Peyton, Micah burned water. Now, he successfully cooks five full meals without supervision. This is the first holiday meal he has cooked, and I am proud of him.

"Look at you," I say as I enter the kitchen. "Keep this up and you'll be cooking all the holiday meals."

He shoots me with wide eyes and a slight shake of his head. "Ha ha. Best not push your luck."

Stepping around Micah, I hug Mom and kiss her cheek. Dad and Peyton slide off their stools and pull me in for hugs next. Since Micah is too focused on not burning dinner, I wrap my arms around him and squeeze until he taps my arm.

"You're doing great, big brother," I whisper so only he hears. "Proud of you."

He sets the spoon on the rest, spins around, and hugs me properly. "Thanks, Shell." He kisses my crown then releases me. "Means a lot."

The stove timer buzzes and he goes back to work. I fill a glass with sparkling cranberry-apple cider—a Reed family tradition—then join Dad and Peyton. Micah and Mom put the final touches on dinner while we all catch up. Mom declares dinner is ready and we all file into a line with plates in hand.

I pile my plate high with herb and citrus roasted duck, potato gratin, baked macaroni and cheese, sautéed carrots, cranberry-orange relish, balsamic Brussel sprouts, and a homemade roll. The next ten minutes pass in silence as we savor the meal.

"Starlight, this is the best yet." Peyton beams at Micah. "You might have to cook some of this again. Soon."

My brother glows from her compliment. And as if they were alone, he takes her elbow, tugs her closer, and kisses her. Not a sweet peck on the cheek. Nope, this is my brother we are talking about. He kisses his wife as if his parents and sister are nowhere in sight. When the kiss breaks, Peyton's cheeks pink.

I doubt her flush is darker than mine.

Public displays of affection don't bother or embarrass me. I adore seeing people so happy and in love. It reminds me true love exists. The heat on my cheeks comes more from picturing myself in a similar situation. Caring for someone—Devlyn, perhaps—so deeply, I can't not kiss them. Regardless of who is around.

The last month plays like a movie in my head.

The night I took Devlyn's face in my hands and kissed him. What it felt like when he kissed me back. The splendor in that first kiss. How perfect the moment was. All the romance novels I'd read finally made sense. The rapid pulse and shortness of breath. It all made sense because I felt them too.

Until Devlyn pulled away. Until I saw the fear on his face. The dread. The regret. I now know why, I understand it, but it still hurts.

Fast forward two weeks later. The text. His appearance at my front door in the middle of the night. Hours of apologies and shared history and heartache spilled between us. In less than twenty-four hours, Devlyn and I had become somewhat inseparable. And over the last three weeks, our need to be with each other has magnified.

Now, we just need the balls to share our relationship with everyone else. We aren't intentionally hiding our relationship, are we? Maybe. I don't know.

A sharp sting on my shin snaps my eyes across the table. Micah winces, his silent apology for kicking my leg. "You okay?" he mouths.

I nod, subtly.

"Liar," he mouths before taking a bite.

Great.

It isn't a lie. I just haven't figured out how to tell him the truth. I have a boyfriend.

God, I feel his brotherly wrath and see his macho chest slaps already. Someone preemptively saves me from my brother.

We decide to save dessert for after gifts.

For the last five years, my parents have told us no gifts. Micah and I refuse to give them nothing. So, we coordinate. We both buy them a card and gift certificate for their favorite restaurant. The first year, they smiled and accepted the gift. Since then, they invite us out for dinner and take us to the restaurant. The first time they did this, Micah and I argued with them and tried to pay our part of the bill. We were unsuccessful. Now, we pick somewhere everyone likes and add more to the gift price, so we are still paying for ourselves.

Mom and Dad graciously thank us for the cards and gift certificates. Micah surprises Peyton with a photo album full of pictures of their first year and a half together. Since falling for Peyton, my brother has become such a romantic. He isn't all goo-goo eyes and flowers every week, but he is more affectionate than I have ever seen him. Hand-holding, whispering in her ear, subtle touches on her cheek, neck or shoulder. And the occasional flower delivery from Petal and Vine.

I envy what they share so openly. Fingers crossed, one day in the near future, that will be me. Giggly and doe eyed and curled into Devlyn's side while we spend time with loved ones.

"Here, Shelly," Mom says as she hands me a gift.

I take the large, thin rectangular package. As I peel back the paper, I wonder if my parents framed our family photo from last Christmas. Wouldn't be abnormal. With each passing year, my parents get more sentimental. Valuing time together and photographs over anything else.

I discard the paper and flip the frame over, prepared to plaster on my fake enthusiasm for an oversized family photo I won't hang. Instead, my jaw drops and my heart stammers.

"Wha-What is this?" I mumble as the backs of my eyes sting.

"Isn't it beautiful?" Mom asks as she leans into Dad. "A friend at work gave me the link to a local artist's website. She wouldn't shut up about his work. So, I went on and found this. The moment I saw it, I knew I had to get it. Like it was drawn for you."

Not for me, I want to tell her. *This* is *me*.

Framed in light oak is an up-close view of a woman's face. From just above the brow to the edge of the top lip, from the bridge of the nose to the lateral edge of the eye. The piece is in pencil with no color. Impeccable detail over every inch. A constellation mapped out in her eye.

The only pieces I have seen of Devlyn's are what he painted at the shop and those from the gallery—which were also me. Perhaps that is why he didn't let me into his studio while touring his house. Would it freak me out? Are there more images of my likeness in his studio? On his website? Something tells me there is a lot more where this came from.

"Let me see," Peyton says.

I close my eyes briefly and swallow. The second Peyton takes in the image, she lifts a hand to her mouth and gasps. Micah may not pick up on the connection as quickly as Peyton. He doesn't stare at his eyes like she does. Plus, Peyton was at the baby shower when I spilled my heart out about Devlyn.

"It's…" She pauses and bites her bottom lip a moment. "It's stunning."

I restrain the tears begging to roll down my cheeks. Last thing I need is for Mom to think I don't appreciate the gift. I do love it. More than any other gift I received.

Mom gifting this to me feels like another sign. A broadcast alert that my relationship with Devlyn is bigger than either of us realizes. How big exactly? I have no clue.

"It is," I garble out then clear my throat and look to my smiling parents. "Thank you, Mom, Dad."

Dessert goes by in a blur of apple pie and light chatter. The melodies and baritones of voices echo in my ears, but I miss everything said. My eyes continue to drift to the drawing in the oak frame.

When did Devlyn draw it? How long would it take to draw something with this level of detail? Days, maybe weeks. Plus, listing it online, processing the sale, shipping. Did he draw this shortly after coming back to the shop? Are there more drawings or paintings of me in his studio?

I shake my head to dispel the endless questions I have no way of answering. Instead, I zero back in on my family. Listen to Mom prattle on over the new client her firm attained. Listen to Dad tell tales of strange client stories as they buy an insurance policy. And listen to my brother and Peyton as they regale all the wonderful parts of married life.

Scooping apples, crust, and fresh whipped cream on my fork, I smile and respond and laugh at the appropriate times. Inside, I scream for the night to be over already. I pray to walk out the front door any second, so I can call the one person with the answers. And to ask Devlyn for a tour of his studio.

~

I'd rather go to Devlyn's house than Jonas and Autumn's. Less than forty-eight hours have passed since we were together, and every opportunity to see or speak with each other gets squashed by someone else. Not that I don't want to spend time with loved ones, but I want time with Devlyn too. So I plaster on my best smile and trudge through each moment. Take deep breaths, remind myself to be grateful and that I will see Devlyn soon.

Our call when I left my parents' house was short lived due to his mother pestering him in the background. Plus, if I don't show at Friendsmas, my phone will blow up with unmerry threats and promises to come get me.

Over the last few hours, I've stared at the drawing gifted to me from my parents. Art with such precision and detail had to take Devlyn a while to draw. Weeks, possibly a month or more, to finish. The more I study it, the more intimate it feels. Like Devlyn spills his secrets through his art. The biggest secret of all… how he feels about me.

Artists don't paint or draw the same person over and over or with such delicacy without a reason. What is Devlyn's reason? When did I become his muse? Although it feels as if a lifetime has passed since October, our relationship beyond the friends stage is still so young. It's difficult to imagine him creating such a piece months ago. Is this—his art—it can't be… *love.*

Dizziness consumes me with the possibilities.

My heart has her hands in the air, hips swaying, as she screams *yes* at the top of her lungs. My head, on the other hand, has calculators and spreadsheets and pro/con lists out. A scale on the desk, weighing emotions versus life. And I hate that my brain steals this moment of joy.

With the purchase of Petal and Vine a year out, my focus has been prepping for the business handoff. Getting all my financial ducks in a row. Albeit a good one, Devlyn has been a distraction. The type of distraction I haven't had to deal with in the past. The type of distraction I need to learn how to balance in my life.

Hopping up from the couch, I take a few cleansing breaths. Close my eyes and hum with my inner zen master. Tell myself I am strong, I am capable, and I can accomplish anything I put my mind to. When I open my eyes, relief filters in.

I got this.

After a bite to eat and a shower, I dress in my comfiest jeans and long-sleeve V-neck pink sweater. I blow out my hair and dab on a light coat of natural makeup. Satisfied with my appearance, I slip on my matching pink Vans then grab my purse and gifts.

I arrive at Jonas and Autumn's just after five. Several cars are parked out front, but not everyone is here yet. Unbuckling, I exit the car and scramble to the passenger side. Snag the gifts from the seat and head for the door with full arms.

When we all asked to bring something for the food, Jonas and Autumn insisted we leave it to them. So, aside from gifting them a small houseplant and matching fuzzy socks for everyone, I got them a gift card for the grocery store. Seeing as they pay for the majority of our gatherings, this is my way of contributing. I told Cora my idea and she agreed to buy them one too.

Spartan greets me at the door with paws to the chest and attempts to lick my face. Jonas apologizes profusely and I laugh.

"For some reason, he's a little extra today. Probably because we spoiled him yesterday," he says as he hugs me around the gifts. "Let me take that off your hands." Jonas takes the gifts and parks them under the tree. He points a finger at Spartan. "Leave it."

Spartan grumbles then trots off in search of Clementine, who lets him get away with more.

"How was Christmas?" I ask.

He leads me to the kitchen where everyone lingers around the island. "Good. Spoiled my girls more than ever." The brightest smile lights his face. "How was dinner with the parents?"

"Good. Mom was less invasive than usual." I keep the news of the artwork gift to myself. Sidling up to Cora, I hug her side. "Hey, you. Merry Christmas."

She twists to face me head-on and hugs me tight. "Merry Christmas."

Her hug lingers longer than normal and I wonder if everything is okay. She releases me, but the soft sadness on her lips tells me she wanted to hold on longer. "What's wrong?" I ask.

The lines of her forehead deepen for a beat. Had I blinked, I would have missed it. Her eyes dart over my shoulder then back to mine. She either looked to my brother or Peyton. My guess... Peyton. And judging by her extended hug and careful attitude, she knows about Mom's gift last night.

Really don't want to talk about Devlyn with everyone here.

At the baby shower, I told every woman here that I was letting Devlyn go. Although I did when I sent the text, things are different now. And on Friendsmas, I get to bring them up to speed. No doubt the guys will overhear and jump in on the conversation.

SOS. This gal needs help.

"If you need to talk, I'm here."

Closing my eyes, I let out a huff. It's now or never. If I don't speak up and tell her Devlyn and I are no longer on the outs, Cora will be hurt I kept it secret. We share everything—even the painful stuff. For the longest time, I was her shoulder to cry on. Now, she wants to be mine. It would be wrong of me to let her believe I needed one.

"Thanks, but…" I throw her a look, one we have shared over the years. *There's more. Just wait a minute.* She nods subtly.

Once I give everyone a hug, I fill a plate with holiday-themed snack foods and a glass with wine. I sit in the end seat at the dining table and munch while I wait. Cranberry-peach glazed meatballs, cheesy-herb pull-apart bread, ham and Swiss pinwheels, four-cheese sausage quiche, and rosemary-garlic hasselback potatoes. There is plenty more I didn't grab, but I will save them for later.

The chairs closest to me drag against the floor and fill a moment later. Without looking, I know it is the ladies, each of them with a plate and drink of their own.

"Sorry," Cora mumbles, and I look up.

"No need. Never apologize for being thoughtful." I bring the glass to my lips and take a sip. "Things have changed since the shower."

"Changed how?" Cora asks before stuffing her mouth full of green beans and potato.

Looking around the room, I see everyone else chatting or otherwise occupied. After a deep breath, I explain what happened after I sent the infamous text to Devlyn. How twisted up I felt inside. How I couldn't sleep. And the fact that Devlyn was on my porch in the middle of the night. At this, Cora and Autumn gasp.

Then, without spilling the intricate details of Devlyn's past, I tell them about our talk. How Devlyn confided in me and explained why he shut down. The more I shared, the more my friends got dreamy eyed.

Did I tell them about the kiss? Of course, but more from a *it made me melt* point of view. They don't need all the dirty details.

I share how much time Devlyn and I have spent together these last three weeks. How wonderful it has been to get to know each other better. And for some reason, as the words leave my lips, my stomach twists in knots. Somehow, this moment reminds me of high school. How others teased me for not having a boyfriend. How hungry I was for the inside scoop on all the things boys, but never asked in fear of embarrassment. The girl of my youth rejoices that she is finally experiencing those moments. That she gets to brag to her friends. But the woman I am now wants to zip her lips and keep Devlyn to herself.

Cora rises from her chair and hugs the air from my lungs. "So glad you're happy. It's about damn time."

Couldn't agree more.

"When do we get to meet him?" Autumn chimes in just as Jonas sidles up to her and says it's time for gifts.

Halle-freaking-lujah!

The gift exchange goes down with much enthusiasm. Spartan and Clementine play with the packages and wrapping paper. Jonas and Autumn frown at the number of grocery gift cards we all gifted. Between everyone, they accumulated over three hundred dollars. Plants and ugly sweaters, gag gifts and graphic tees. Smiles and laughter abound in this more relaxed holiday celebration.

As I look around the room and take in this wonderful group of people that are the best family I know, my heart wobbles a little. So much has changed over the years, but we are still together. Through thick and thin. Our lives full and bountiful.

My only wish… for Devlyn to be here too.

Then I ask myself if he'd want to be here. Would he want to sit with this colossal group of people and share a piece of himself? Would he want to insert himself in my life, with my family? Devlyn belongs here. With me. With us. He may be timid and quirky, but I easily picture him fitting in with us all. I easily picture everyone loving him as much as I do.

It may be too soon, and I may have read too many romance novels, but I think I am in love with Devlyn. But how will I know if he is in love with me?

Holidays and birthdays have never been big on my to-do list. Growing up, my mother turned every occasion into a lavish party. No matter the event, she was the center of attention—even when the party wasn't for her. Over time, I grew to despise celebrations. Avoided as many invites as possible.

Until now. Until today.

Spending New Year's Eve with Shelly sounds like the perfect way to kick off a new year. Considering I have never watched the ball drop or made a list of resolutions, I look forward to doing both with her.

Petal and Vine closes early today and doesn't reopen until January second. I get a full, uninterrupted day and a half with her, and I have never been this damn nervous in my life.

Last night, after she spent an hour in the kitchen making the most amazing pasta carbonara and garlic bread, I asked her to come to my place for New Year's. Without hesitation, she said yes. Then, as I fisted my napkin beneath the table, I asked her to stay the night.

Considering we have spent the night together a few times now, asking her shouldn't flip my stomach upside down. But the previous times we slept in the same space were different. The first was accidental. The second, we were both exhausted. But the third, and most recent, didn't happen from falling asleep on the couch or pure exhaustion. Shelly said she was tired, took my hand, and walked me to her room. The action felt so normal. A natural progression in our relationship.

That said, we haven't broached anything beyond spooning or kissing in bed. No bare flesh or fondling through clothes. To some, our relationship may appear clean or innocent, but the truth is we are both waiting for the right moment. That unspoken word to say we are ready for more, for the next step.

Me asking Shelly to stay over—preplanning a sleepover—carries the heaviest weight yet. Pushes us to the next level of seriousness in our relationship. A step I think we're ready for, but I don't want her to think I have assumptions about what will or won't happen.

My goal in asking her to stay isn't about sex. Not that my thoughts haven't drifted to the fantasy of what it'd be like to connect with Shelly in such a powerful way. More than any other reason, I asked Shelly to stay because I hate when she leaves. I love her in my space and in my arms. Her in both at the start of a new year… I can't think of anything more right.

Parking at the grocery store, where everyone and their mother is shopping for last-minute party goods, I head inside, grab a cart, and wind through the aisles. The plan for tonight is to cook instead of order takeout. A chef I am not, but I have some meals down to a science.

After I load the cart with ingredients for tonight, essentials, dessert, and movie snacks, I head for the checkout. Four brown bags and way too much money later, I pack the groceries in the back of the car and leave. Traffic is heavier than usual with people driving to parties or beachside hotels for the fireworks.

I make it home before Shelly arrives and put everything away except the ingredients for dinner. As I toss the chicken breasts in a resealable bag with marinade, there is a soft knock at the door.

She's here.

With a simple knock, I grow dizzy. My steps wobbly as I walk to the front door. Breath stuttering as I unbolt the lock and twist the handle. Heart hammering as I open the door and see my favorite smile. Skin dampening as I take in the larger than normal bag on her shoulder.

This is really happening. Shelly is here and staying the night. In my house. In my bed.

I swallow past the nervous lump in my throat. "Hey." Stepping back, I make room for her to enter then close the door.

"Hey," she says, voice softer than usual. "Where can I…" Her question trails off as she lifts the bag from her shoulder.

Taking the bag from her, she toes off her shoes before I slip my hand in hers and start for the bedroom.

When I gave Shelly a tour of the house on her first visit, there were two rooms I intentionally left out. The studio and my bedroom. The studio because I didn't want her to panic at how often she inspired my recent work. And my bedroom because I didn't want to insinuate something or make her more uncomfortable on her first visit. After all, we were just friends then. At least, that is what I told myself a thousand times a day.

The notion of *just friends* never really stuck.

I lead her into the bedroom and set her bag on the bed. As best I can, I hide the tremor in my limbs. With our romantic relationship still in the early stages, the last thing I want to do is give Shelly the wrong impression. That I only have one goal in mind. Sex. And although I want to experience everything with her, sex is not what drives me to be with her.

But I am a man.

More times than I care to admit, I've fantasized what it would be like to have Shelly beneath me. Aura a blazing red as my mouth devoured hers. Skin damp with sweat, her nails in my back. Heels digging into my ass as I rock my hips forward. My name whispered from her lips as we reached euphoria.

Needless to say, my soap supply has depleted much quicker since meeting Shelly.

But I won't pressure Shelly into anything she isn't ready for. This woman… she is worth waiting a lifetime for. I want every other part of her too, not just the physical. Her heart. Her trust. Her soul.

"Your room is not what I expected," she whispers into the dimly lit space.

I twist to face her. Take in her inquisitive eyes as they roam the space. "No?"

She shakes her head. "Don't laugh." Heat pinks her cheeks. "I expected to see more color. Paintings on the wall and sculptures on the dresser."

I bite the inside of my cheek and fight the smile on my lips. "Not laughing. Promise." I let my smile loose. "However, I do find it cute that you'd think my room would be vibrant."

Shelly shrugs. "You're a hard man to read sometimes."

Every now and then, I felt the same about her—that she was difficult to read. Simple things that made Shelly happy were easy to see—her love for minimalism and simplicity, her food and drink preferences, the way she regarded flowers as she placed them in paper or vases.

What I wanted to learn were the things that made this beautiful woman tick. Where to touch her with fingertips and lips that would make her back bow and lungs gasp. The sights that captivated her, so I could take her to each one and memorize the way her smile lit up the sky. What quenched her soul, so I could gift it to her more often than not.

I lace my fingers with hers. "You haven't seen it yet, but my studio is kind of chaotic. Organized chaos, if you will. Which is why my bedroom is the complete opposite." I stare around at the bare pewter-painted walls. Scan the pale oak dresser free of clutter. Glance at the two nightstands in the same pale oak; soft light glows from selenite lamps on both. Then I take in the king bed with cream bedding, four pillows and nothing more. "After spending all day in a kaleidoscope of color or deep in thought, I need a blank slate. A way to reset myself."

"Never thought of it like that, but it makes sense."

Walking toward the door, I lead us back out to the main part of the house. "C'mon. You can help me make dinner." Back in the kitchen, I set Shelly up to chop and assemble salad ingredients while I work on root vegetables for roasting.

By no means am I a pro in the kitchen, but I watched too many shows on Food Network in college and some of the easier meals stuck. Bless my dorm mates. At the time, I hated how often I heard about mincing garlic and dicing carrots. They used it as background noise while working on projects. And after weeks of it, I grew to love the channel too. Not just for the distractions I desperately needed, but also the skills it taught me.

We work in silence and it's as comfortable as every other moment with Shelly. Every now and again, I glance her way and watch her work. Her precision with a knife reminds me of how intricately she assembles a vase of flowers. Arranging is her version of art, and it is so damn mesmerizing.

Once the chicken and vegetables are in the oven, I clean up. Shelly finishes the salad then pours the ingredients for a vinaigrette into a mason jar and shakes. While waiting for the food in the oven to finish, we head to the living room and set up the table and television.

When the timer buzzes, I remove dinner from the oven. After plating the chicken and vegetables, I carry the plates and salad bowls to the living room and we park ourselves on cushions on the floor. Food and wine and episodes of *Dark* on the screen. It all feels so natural and sublime and effortless.

When our plates and bowls are empty, I take them to the kitchen and leave them for later. On my return, I bring the wine bottle and two slices of black forest cake I snagged from the grocery store bakery.

"This looks so good," Shelly says as she twists the plate left and right to inspect the slice enough for two.

"Wasn't sure what you liked, but these looked too good to pass up."

She twists in her seat and gives me the smile I love too much. "Good choice."

We devour the cake in no time then move up to the couch and I flip off the light. Shelly curls into my side as we continue another episode. When this episode ends, the plan is to flip over to the broadcast of the ball drop.

The closer it gets to midnight, the louder the neighborhood gets with fireworks and party cheers. And the more my stomach wrings with nervous energy. A sensation that has become more familiar in recent weeks. A ball of chaotic energy just beneath my diaphragm that, if I tried to translate it on canvas, would look like a maddening swirl of blue and red and yellow. Bright and vibrant and begging for attention.

Shelly's breath heats the skin of my neck as the room goes black at the end of the episode. Much as I want to relish in the feel of her so close, I pick up the remote and switch the television to the channel broadcasting the festivities.

With less than a half hour to midnight, the crowd in Times Square is so boisterous I feel their excitement. For the first time, celebrating a holiday feels significant. All because of the woman in my arms.

"Hey," I whisper, unsure if Shelly is still awake. All I get is a low *hmm* in return. "I'm going to clean up in the kitchen. Need anything?"

Shelly uncurls herself from my side and I immediately miss her warmth and touch. She lifts a hand to cover her mouth as she yawns. "No. Might go splash my face so I don't fall asleep early."

With a light chuckle, I press my lips to her forehead. "Take your time."

While Shelly heads for the bathroom, I clean up in the kitchen. It doesn't take long to rinse the dishes, put them in the dishwasher and start the load. With a glance at the clock on the stove, I note it is seven minutes to midnight. Uncorking another bottle of wine, I wander back to the living room and stop when I reach the threshold.

In the corner of the couch, Shelly is curled up with the throw blanket, eyes closed and chest rising and falling at a slow rhythm. I take in the sight of her, inhale deeply, and tiptoe toward the couch. Setting the bottle on the table, I gingerly sit next to her, hoping not to disturb her from sleep. But the moment my weight shifts the cushion, her eyes pop open.

"Did I miss it?" she asks, voice thick with exhaustion as she scoots up to a seat.

"No. A few minutes to go." I tuck a stray lock of hair behind her ear. "But we can head to bed."

She sits straighter and shakes her head. "It's almost time. No backing out now." Shelly drops her head to my shoulder. "Sorry I dozed off."

I weave my fingers with hers and rest my head on her crown. "Don't apologize. It's been a long day."

On the television, the crowd grows restless as midnight draws closer. The clock in the corner of the screen drops under the minute marker. I pour enough wine into our glasses to toast the new year and hand Shelly hers. Thousands of crystals and lights change color on the screen as the final ten seconds count down.

Cheers and fireworks erupt outside the moment midnight strikes. Shelly and I clink glasses and take a swig of wine as we stare at the countless people on the screen kissing. With each new camera shot, a new couple flashes their smiling faces together in a lip lock.

Is this what couples do on New Year's to celebrate? I wouldn't know. But without a second thought, I take Shelly's glass from her hand and set it on the table with mine.

"What are you—"

I frame her face in my palms and crash my lips to hers. Startled by the sudden gesture, she doesn't kiss me back immediately. When I pull her bottom lip between mine, though, she melts into me, fists the bottom hem of my shirt and returns the kiss with heat and intensity.

Time and noise vanish as our lips dance and tongues tangle. Color dances behind my eyes as I taste the wine on her tongue and breathe in her sweet, earthy scent. When her nails graze my abdomen beneath my shirt, I drag in a sharp breath and inch back from her.

Her eyes flash open and lock on mine, worry etched in the lines of her forehead. "Sorry, I—"

I press a finger to her lips and shake my head. "Don't apologize." I wrap her hand in mine, rise from the couch and tug for her to follow. She untangles herself from the blanket and scoots off the couch. I guide her out of the living room, shutting off the television as we pass, and walk us to the bedroom.

It takes less than a minute to reach the bedroom, but my heart bangs in my rib cage the entire time. The moment we cross the threshold, Shelly grips my hand tighter. When we reach the foot of the bed, I stop and turn to face her.

Damn, she steals the air from my lungs.

Reaching up, I wrap a lock of her hair around my finger. "Hey," I whisper in the dimly lit space. Her eyes lift and rob me of my next breath. "If all you want to do is sleep, we sleep." I press my lips to her forehead. "More than anything, I just want you here with me. Okay?"

Her fingers curl in the cotton of my shirt again and drag me closer. Lips inches apart, she whispers, "Okay." Then she eliminates the remaining space between us, presses her lips to mine and picks up right where we left off in the living room.

My hands fall to her hips and hold her flush to my frame, the bulge in my pants undeniable. Her hands draw parallel lines up my torso, snake around my neck and skate up the base of my skull. Every impulse in my hormonal makeup fights the urge to strip her bare and mark her as mine. Fights the urge to be less than a gentleman and tender boyfriend.

Of the few times I had sex in the past, I never once was aggressive. Never once had the *impulse* to rip clothes and imprint skin with nails and teeth.

Right now, with Shelly flush against my erection and her lips ravaging me as if the opportunity won't come again, fighting my base instincts proves more difficult. I *want* to claw at her skin with nails and teeth. Taste every inch of her on my tongue. Inhale the perfume at her neck and the pheromones between her legs. Watch her body react as I tease her flesh with fingers and licks. Listen to her soft cries and throaty moans as I give her pleasure and drive her to ecstasy.

Her fingers tug at my hair, lips skirt along my jaw and teeth nip at my ear. My jaw falls slack as a gravelly moan escapes.

God, I want her. Desperately.

But physical intimacy with Shelly isn't just about what I want. She has to guide us along the path she wants us to take. Say when she wants more. Tell me when to stop. Because at this rate, I won't stop. Ever.

I drag my hands up the sides of her torso, beneath her shirt, along the warm curves of her body. At the base of her bra, I clutch her rib cage and drop my lips to her ear. "Shelly." My voice husky and foreign. "Tell me what you want." The tips of my fingers curl in slightly and dig at flesh and bone. My tongue darts out and I lick the shell of her ear. "Tell me."

She frees my hair, slides her palms down my chest and fists my shirt. I inch back and lock our gazes. Her eyes shine as they look up. All I see is every star in the night sky, burning hot and bright and intense. I lick my lips then swallow, on edge while waiting for her response.

Her lips part as she pushes up on her toes. "I want *you*, Devlyn." Her eyes drop and trail the length of my body before they slowly make their way back up. "*All* of you."

My eyes drift shut as her words sink in. My grip on her tightens as I stroke beneath the base of her bra with my thumbs. I drag in a deep breath then drop my forehead to hers. "Are you sure?" The question a soft stutter on my lips. Subtly, she nods and my body sighs. I press my lips to hers and kiss her softly. "I want that too."

twenty-one

SHELLY

Heat blooms low in my belly at his whispered words on my lips. His next kiss is softer, more tender as his fingers knead my skin. Trace lines between my ribs. Unclasp the closure at the back of my bra. Free my breasts beneath my top.

I break my lips from his. Gasp as his hands roam the length of my spine without interruption. Slide my palms lower to his waist and dip them below his shirt. Close my eyes as my fingers trail over the ridges and valleys of his abdomen.

I may not have had sex, but I am not virginal in all things. My experience is minuscule, but I have gotten to second base with a few guys. Of course, they got a little too handsy when the kiss deepened, going from light, over-the-clothes petting to trying to strip me bare. Needless to say, I cut things off and never saw them again. If someone won't respect voiced boundaries, who knows what else they'd push past.

Right now, this moment, is different.

Tonight is the first time I want to explore and be explored beyond impassioned kisses and hands fondling parts through clothes. Tonight, I want to be more than the woman Devlyn can't take his eyes off of. More than the woman he holds in his arms. I want to be the woman he can't get enough of. The woman he never lets go of.

His kiss travels from my lips to the line of my jaw. Every press of his lips to my skin, along my jaw, down the column of my throat sends a ripple of heat and leaves an unfamiliar, but desirable tingle in its wake. Each kiss sears me, brands me, marks me in a new way. And I love every single one. Yearn for the next kiss he gives.

With a gentle tug, Devlyn inches up my top and bra, peels them away and drops them to the floor. My breath comes in short bursts as goose bumps blanket my exposed flesh. On instinct, I cross my arms over my chest. Hide my bare breasts as my line of sight drops to Devlyn's still clothed body.

He paints his fingers along my jaw then tips my chin up. Warm affection greets me in his gentle green eyes. "Please don't be embarrassed. Not with me." His lips press mine and vanish too soon. "You ravish me, Shelly." *Kiss.* "Rob me of sight and sound and thought." *Kiss.* "Inspire me more than anyone or anything." *Kiss.* "And as hard as I fought against this—against being yours, against you being mine…" *Kiss.* "Subconsciously, I knew we'd always be more than friends." *Kiss.* "So much more."

Fire licks my skin as my arms fall away. Devlyn steps closer, cups my cheeks in his palms, and kisses me slow and deep. As his tongue tastes mine, I take the hem of his shirt in my fists and slowly push the fabric up and over his head. The moment his chest is bare, he molds my body to his. Snakes an arm around my rib cage. Digs his fingers in my hair. Tilts my head and devours every whimper bubbling in my throat.

It's too much and not enough.

Devlyn drops his hands to my hips and guides me until my legs bump the mattress. I trace his hip bones with needy fingers. Move to the dip on either side of his spine just above his waistband. Journey up his back and memorize the corded muscles beneath my touch.

The kiss breaks as I drop to the bed. Eyes locked, I press my hands into the fluffy comforter and inch back on the bed. Beneath my breastbone, my heart rattles my rib cage while my lungs beg for air. Devlyn leans forward, his hands on either side of me on the bed as he kisses the curve of my neck.

"Beautiful," he whispers, breath hot on my skin.

His lips travel to the hollow of my throat, kissing me once, twice, three times before drifting lower. An arm comes around my waist, his palm in the middle of my spine, and then he leans into me more. Guides me to lie on the mattress. Shifts me up the bed and near the pillows. Crawls up my body and cages me in.

Then his lips drive me wild again.

My eyes drift closed as each sensation stirs new life in my veins. I fist his hair as he paints my skin with his lips. Kiss by kiss, his mouth deviates from my midline. Leaves a trail of tingles as he moves toward my left breast. A rush of adrenaline spikes my bloodstream as my heavy breaths fill the room. My fingers in his hair curl tighter.

"Breathe, Shelly." He inches up the bed and pins me with his gaze. One breath at a time, my breathing settles. His greens dart between my blues a moment before he swallows. "Didn't think it was possible, but I'm more lost in your starry eyes." Eyes wide open, he presses a heady kiss to my lips. "My Andromeda."

Caught off guard by the reference—or perhaps, nickname—I tilt my head and study him a beat. A smile kicks up the corners of my lips. "Ruler of man, huh?"

Devlyn shrugs as his own smile appears. "Ruler of man. The only constellation I see when I look in your eyes." His face grows more serious. "Ruler of my heart."

"Devlyn…"

He captures my lips with his and rocks his hips against mine. "It's true," he says, cupping my cheek. "And I admit it without shame."

Heat radiates from the center of my chest as I lift off the mattress and kiss him. Trailing my fingers down his abdomen, I pause at his jeans. Trace the tip of my finger along the hemline, hip to hip. Relish in the shiver of his body and stutter in his breath at my touch.

Then I unbutton his jeans. Drag the slider down the teeth. Separate the fly and expose his cotton-covered bulge. Palm his thick erection, go wide eyed at the length and freeze.

Devlyn rears back enough to catch my gaze. "What's the matter?"

I shake my head. Embarrassment heating my cheeks as I bite back my words.

"If you want to stop…"

"No." My headshake grows panicky. "I want this. You. Us."

He presses a chaste kiss to my lips. "Please tell me what's wrong."

My pulse quickens for an entirely new reason. "It's just…" Devlyn doesn't push me to speak. Hovering above me, he gives me a moment to formulate the words to explain my suddenly tense muscles and obvious anxiety. I rotate my head slightly, enough to lose eye contact. "Nerves. It's just nerves." I swallow and close my eyes. "Then I… felt how big you are and I freaked out," I mutter in a rush.

The room goes quiet. Too quiet. Silence with Devlyn has always been comfortable. Soothing. A balm I never knew I needed. But now, his silence feels like a bomb ready to detonate. An explosion of disappointment and concern. Something I have never felt with anyone.

"Look at me, Shelly." I take a deep breath and roll my lips between my teeth. "Please." His voice barely audible.

On another deep breath, I open my eyes. He takes my chin in his fingers and brings me back to his line of sight. And what I see in his eyes is the complete opposite of what I expected.

Warmth and hope and something akin to love. I swallow and pray he doesn't hear the action.

"All of this is new for you." His knuckles graze my cheek. "Hell, it's practically new for me." I furrow my brow and a subtle smile pushes up his cheeks. "I may not be a virgin, but my experience is minuscule." He kisses the tip of my nose. "Is it weird that I kind of love how uncoordinated we'll be together?"

Out of nowhere, I laugh. And then Devlyn laughs.

"Seriously, Shelly. You have nothing to fear or be embarrassed about with me. Ever." His finger twirls in my hair. "I love that I get to be your first. Not because your virginity is a trophy or something to conquer. But because it means no one mattered before me. Even with my broken parts and odd view of the world, you chose me over everyone else."

"Wasn't really a choice," I say softly.

"Couldn't agree more." He lightly traces a finger along my jaw to my chin, his eyes following the movement. "So if you want to stop, I'll understand. I won't be upset. Promise."

I shake my head. "I don't want to stop."

He stares at my lips, hungry. "You're sure?"

"Yes."

"Thank God."

His lips crash on mine, kissing me like a starved man. With deft fingers, he unbuttons my jeans and parts the zipper. Tugs the snug denim at my hips and drags the material down my thighs, my calves, then tosses them on the floor. Crawling up my body, he stops when his eyes land on my panties and I internally berate myself.

I had no expectations of staying the night at Devlyn's house. Okay, that's a lie. I assumed we would probably fool around. Maybe grope each other under our clothes. Which is why it never crossed my mind to wear my prettier underwear. The baby-pink lacy thong and matching bra.

Instead, I wore the cotton thong with a hole near the hip and a fading floral print from too many washes. What bra had I even been wearing? The dingy white one. *Ugh. Kill me now.* I mentally slap my forehead.

I peer down at Devlyn as he hovers a place no one else has been. The longer he remains frozen, the more embarrassment claws at my insides.

Then his eyes track up my body until we connect. A subtle half smile kicks up his lips. "You know, I love these." I want to roll my eyes, but then he traces his fingertip above the waistband and I forget all thought. "That you didn't *dress* for the occasion." His finger dips below the elastic and brushes the thin strip of curls. "That I see you how you are naturally and not what you think I want to see."

His hands land on my hips. Fingers hook beneath the elastic. Slowly, ever so slowly, he peels the cotton down, down, down; eyes locked on mine the entire time.

When my panties join my jeans on the floor, he is back at my center. Breath hot on my skin. Thumbs drawing circles on my hips. Hovering. Waiting. Panting between my spread legs. I don't dare move. Don't dare say a word. I simply wait for his next move while reminding myself to breathe.

Devlyn runs the tip of his nose up my center and inhales deeply. Strengthens his grip on my hips. Kneads my flesh with his fingers. Breathes heavily over my mound for one, two, three breaths. Then his mouth meets my lower lips. A gentle, wet kiss. Followed by another. And another. Then his tongue darts out and flattens against my seam as he slowly licks up my center.

"Oh god," I moan out as I fist the comforter.

He groans at the junction of my thighs then releases my hips from his touch. In a swift move, he sweeps his arms under my legs and rests my thighs on his shoulders. His hands cup my butt and tug me closer. Bringing my center to his mouth. And then his tongue licks up my lips again. Tastes me with unmatched hunger. Flicks at the small bundle of nerves.

I squirm beneath him. Moan without restraint. Curl my fingers in his hair and tug when he hits *the spot* that has me begging for more. Grind against his mouth without shame as he inserts one finger then another and slowly pumps in and out of my core. Fist the comforter until my knuckles sting as fire and power and ecstasy swirl low in my belly and spill out of me in the form of euphoria.

Blinding light illuminates behind my closed eyes as I float in the heavens. And before my feet hit earth again, the mattress dips as Devlyn crawls up my body. His lips kiss a slow trail up my midline, stray left to suck my aching breast and pert nipple between his lips, followed by the right. Releasing my breast, he kisses and licks along my collarbone. Nips at the length of my shoulder, the curve of my neck, the column of my throat before sucking my earlobe between his teeth.

"Please tell me you're sure," he whispers in my ear then rubs his bare length along my center.

When did he remove the last of his clothes? Most likely when I was in a trance, blissed out by what he had done to my body.

"Yes, I'm sure." I lift my hips and rock against him. I don't miss the audible shake in his next breath. Or the way his fingers bruise my hip.

"Need to get a condom." Devlyn shifts his weight off me and reaches for one of the nightstand drawers. He fumbles with the box, still wrapped, and glances back with a wince. "Sorry."

I giggle under my breath. "The fact that you have to unwrap the box is more than okay." To some, this would kill the mood. Waiting while their partner fumbles with the cellophane and breaks into the box. But me? I find the action sexy. Yes, Devlyn said he hadn't been with anyone in years—not that his sexual history changes how I see him—but watching his dexterous fingers maul the box of condoms while he pins his lips between his teeth… I have a front-row seat to his inexperience. A fact that calms my jittery nerves a little more.

"Halle-freaking-lujah," he mutters as he takes a square from the box. I want to giggle again, but stop myself the moment our eyes connect.

In a microsecond, the seriousness of what is about to happen hits me full force. A fresh wave of anxiety blooms in my chest, kicks my heart into fifth gear, has my lungs begging for oxygen. Everything moves in slow motion as Devlyn tears the wrapper open, removes the condom, fumbles with it slightly then rolls it down his thick length.

Holy shit!

I shouldn't have looked. Shouldn't have watched. Shouldn't have stared at the size of him. Because my anxiety amplifies tenfold. My skin feels tight on my body. A hand wraps around my heart and squeezes, tighter and tighter. And for the life of me, I can't remember how to breathe. My sight blurs as my ears fill with white noise.

What was I thinking? I thought I was ready. Thought I could go through with this. But right now, it feels like death is swallowing me whole. Death by embarrassment. Death by panic attack because this thirty-two-year-old woman is scared to have sex for the first time.

What was I thinking?

And then he is there. Devlyn. Body pressed to mine and face a breath away. Still blurry, but slowly coming into focus as he strokes my cheek. His lips move, but his words hit my ears in a garbled mess. Then he kisses me—my lips, my cheek, the spot beneath my ear.

"Breathe," he says, soft and slow. Another kiss heats the skin beneath my ear. "I've got you." He shifts to meet my gaze. "Just breathe."

Then I take the deepest breath of my life as Devlyn rocks his hips forward.

twenty-two

DEVLYN

I never want to let her go.

Forehead pressed to hers, I tighten my hold on Shelly. Our heavy breaths mingle in the air and further dampen our skin. Still inside her, I shift us onto our sides and band my arms around her more securely. Hold her impossibly closer and kiss her forehead, the tip of her nose, her cheek, her lips.

My fingers comb through her hair as our breathing settles and the room grows still. I close my eyes and bask in the hormonal high my body is on. Relish the heat and sensation of Shelly in my arms, bare and natural and uninhibited. Cherish the subtle touches she gives as her fingers paint small circles on my lower back.

"That was…"

"Incredible," I finish for her.

"Incredible," she repeats wistfully.

Sex—making love—with Shelly was more than incredible. Once I calmed her, once the sharp sting of my invasion faded, we fumbled with our rhythm. But it didn't take long for the lack of coordination to fall away. In its place, we figured out the perfect tempo. Learned when to rock our hips at the perfect time. Discovered which position or angle made each other moan. And then she let go.

Watching Shelly come undone beneath me is a sight I will never forget. A sight I will mentally revisit time and again. The moment her orgasm peaked, it was like watching the most beautiful flower open its petals and come to life. A magical sight to behold. Her skin blotched in various shades of pink and red. Shades I will only associate with her.

But making love was more than just a physical act with Shelly.

When her starry blues locked on mine as we let go, an inferno of emotion burned beneath my sternum. The shimmering stars in her eyes sucked me deeper. The connection we shared from the start tightened its grip around my heart. And it was in that singular moment, in that infinite blip of time, I knew I would never spend a day without Shelly in my life.

Is it too soon to confess such bold statements aloud?

Minute by minute, I grow more flaccid inside Shelly. Much as I don't want to break the physical connection, remaining like this isn't ideal. So I reluctantly withdraw from her. Press a kiss to her forehead and excuse myself to dispose of the condom.

When I crawl under the sheets, Shelly is softly snoring on my pillow. I don't wake or move her. Instead, I adjust myself to mold my body to her frame, wrap my arms around her waist, and whisper good night against the skin beneath her ear.

~

I wake to cold sheets where Shelly fell asleep in my arms only hours ago. The smell of bacon and fresh bread float through the house and my stomach grumbles in response. I press a palm to my stomach to quelch the feisty organ.

Arms above my head, I stretch the sleep from my muscles. As I scoot toward the edge of the bed, I pick up Shelly's scent on the pillow. I roll over, press my nose to the space she abandoned not long ago and inhale the scent distinctly Shelly—sweet and floral and earthy. Fisting the pillow, I smother myself with her perfume.

How will I ever sleep without her in my bed again?

Now is not the time for such questions or answers. I may want Shelly in my bed —not strictly for sex—every night going forward, but that doesn't mean she is ready for the same level of commitment. Last thing I need to do is scare her off. Doesn't mean I won't skirt the subject and put out feelers.

Out of bed, I dig a pair of sweatpants from the dresser, step into them, and presumptuously grab a condom from the nightstand and pocket it before wandering to the kitchen. At the end of the hall, the kitchen comes into view and I freeze. My breath catches in my throat as I take in the view.

Screwed. I am so screwed when it comes to this woman. Without a doubt, my heart is hers.

With her back to me, I survey the scene unannounced. Shelly has her toffee-blonde locks securely piled on her head; a few stragglers tickle the nape of her neck. She wears the shirt I wore last night, and only the shirt. Her bare legs go on for miles. I swallow and try to temper the thoughts causing my sweats to tent.

Moving away from the cutting board, she spots me in her periphery. A hand slaps her chest as she gasps. "Holy shit." I amble into the kitchen as she catches her breath. "You practically gave me a heart attack," she says, smacking my bare chest as I snake my arms around her waist.

I kiss her lips. "Sorry." *Am I, though?* "Actually, I'm not sorry. I rather enjoyed watching you a minute."

My favorite smile lights up her face. "Yeah, you do have a thing for watching me."

So she has noticed the way I can't look away from her. How *long* has she noticed?

"Is that so?"

"Mm-hmm." Her finger draws circles on my pec. "Don't think I didn't notice you at the shop. Or in the museum. Or the park." She licks her lips. "And every other time before we decided to be more than friends."

Part of me is embarrassed she noticed every time I studied her face longer than normal. No wonder she was confused. My words constantly told her one thing while my actions said the complete opposite. The other part of me is delighted that she read the signs the way she did. That she didn't shove me away, that she gave me room to breathe. To figure out how to move forward with her. To clear some of my past demons and make room for her light.

The back of my knuckles brush along her cheekbone. I kiss her forehead, the tip of her nose, her lips. Press my forehead to hers. "Glad I didn't scare you off." Another kiss to her lips; this one deeper, potent, ravaging.

"Never." Out of nowhere, she straightens her spine. "Shit," she hisses and breaks free of my arms. She bolts to the stove, fiddles with the knob, and stirs what I assume are eggs. "Oh, thank goodness."

I step up behind her and peer over her shoulder. "All good?" My lips drop to her neck.

"Yeah." She melts into my touch. "Breakfast will be done in a few, if you want to set up a place to eat."

I kiss her neck again. "On it."

The dining room rarely gets used, but today I want to sit with Shelly and share a meal at the table. Add touches of her to yet another room in the house. Maybe after breakfast, if I gather up enough nerve, I will walk her up the stairs and show her my studio. The only space she has yet to see, for good reason. Weeks ago, the sight of my studio—her face and likeness on several pieces of canvas and stock—may have sent Shelly running for the hills. Now, she may accept my obsession with more grace.

Shelly walks into the dining room with two loaded plates, sets them down, and turns back for the kitchen. Before I get the chance to ask if she needs help, she returns with two mugs of tea.

"This looks wonderful." I scan the plate of cheesy southwestern scrambled eggs, bacon, tangerine segments, and toast with sliced avocado. "Thank you for making breakfast."

Heat pinks her cheeks as she shrugs. "No big deal. Just wanted to do something nice for you." With both hands, she brings the mug to her lips and sips her tea. "Plus, I might be in love with your kitchen."

It is on the tip of my tongue to invite her to use my kitchen every day of the week. But jumping on that bandwagon prematurely probably isn't the best idea. Still, I open my mouth and abbreviate the idea.

"You're welcome to use it whenever you like."

Her eyes drop to her plate. *Shit.* Stepped over the line anyway. *Dammit.* But then I catch the corners of her mouth as they tip up. That small action steals every worry I felt seconds ago and fills me with jubilation.

I devour each bite, and it isn't long before I pat my stomach and push my plate away. "So good. If you're not careful, you'll cook all the meals."

Shelly rolls her eyes. "Ha ha." She sips her tea then sets her mug down. "Aside from the occasional *when will you get married and give me grandchildren* moments, my mom is pretty great. She's no kitchen guru but made sure we knew basics before moving out. Her lessons stuck with me, but not so much with my brother."

"So what you're saying is the kitchen is his archnemesis."

She laughs. "Once upon a time, yes. But since meeting his now wife, he's putting in the time and effort to learn."

We sit in silence for a beat, both of us letting our full bellies settle while we sip tea. And I can't help but think how much I love this. Sitting here, across the table from Shelly, eating breakfast, sipping tea, having casual conversation, enjoying each other's company. I also can't stop thinking about how I want this with her more often than not.

"I want to show you something," I say, eyes on hers.

"Okay. Just give me a minute to clean up."

"No." My chair legs scrape the wood floor as I rise to my feet. "Leave it. We'll clean up after."

I offer my hand and she takes it, standing from her seat. "O-okay."

With a deep breath, I walk to the left and up the staircase. There is only one room when you reach the top. My studio. And I am about to expose the biggest piece of myself to her. Something I have never done with another soul.

twenty-three

Slowly, we ascend the stairs. With each step up, Devlyn's breathing quickens. His grip on my hand tightens. This isn't just his studio he is leading me up to. This *is* Devlyn. The inner workings of his mind. Him expressing all the things he can't find a voice for.

We reach the landing and the massive space comes into view. There is no door to separate the studio from the stairwell. The only door to this room is at the other end of the stairs. To the right, a large window brightens the space naturally. A second smaller window sits on the opposite wall higher up. A skylight in the center of the ceiling.

My eyes dart in every direction as I absorb the chaos that is Devlyn's studio.

A closet with an open barn door is packed with canvases in various sizes. Some painted, others blank. One wall of the closet is lined with shelves. Implements and brushes, cleaning supplies and rags, pencils and more sit on the shelves—many of them unopened.

A bathroom with a stall shower, toilet, and double sink with a black countertop is brightened by a small window. Hand towels hang from the bar. A bottle of mineral oil and bar of soap sit between the sinks. The faint splatter of paint from washed hands in one of the bowls.

The main room of the studio has a drafting table at one end, a cart and shelves beside it. In the heart of the room is a large table covered in used rags, large coffee cans with brushes sticking out, various-sized glass jars with dripped paint on the glass, and an abundance of paint tubes in different states of use.

Canvases lean against walls and each other. Drawings lie scattered on the floor and pinned to the walls. Some in color, others monochrome. But there appears to be a theme with several of them. A theme that doesn't shock me after seeing Devlyn's work at the exhibition or the piece my parents gifted me for Christmas.

Me. I am the theme.

Considering our romantic relationship is fairly new, this should bother me. Shouldn't it? Some women might think an artist's obsession with one person—their muse—is awkward or disturbing. But as I scan the room and take in all the various ways Devlyn has reconstructed my image, a warmth builds in my chest.

Devlyn may have difficulty expressing himself with words, but the art in this room says more than any words ever will. *Devlyn is in love with me. Madly.*

"Wow," I breathe out.

I haven't met his gaze since we entered the room, but his eyes sear my profile. His silence begs for me to expand on my single-word response. To tell him if I love it or never plan to return.

"Is it weird that I love seeing myself in so many different ways?" I ask this to lighten the tension rolling off him. And it works.

A soft chuckle leaves his lips, growing louder with each breath, and soon I join in. As our laughter fades, he gives my hand a squeeze.

"Does it freak you out?" He waves his hand around the room. "Seeing all this. Seeing how much you inspire me."

Turning to face him, I bring my body flush with his and lock my fingers behind his neck. His hands automatically find my hips. "Nope." I press my lips to his. "Maybe because of the images at the exhibition." Another kiss. "Or maybe because my parents bought one of your pieces and gifted it to me for Christmas."

Devlyn jerks his head back. "Really?"

I nod. "Mm-hmm."

"Was it the iris drawing?" I nod again. "Funny enough, I thought maybe it was someone related to you. But I'd never heard you mention a George."

"Ah. That would be my dad. Mom uses his cards to shop online."

"Gotcha." Devlyn brings his lips back to mine. "Seriously, though… you're not bothered by all this?"

I shake my head. "Is it weird that my face might be on someone's wall? Sure." I glance around the studio for a beat. "But I love that you can't get me out of your head."

His hands drop beneath the hemline and dip under the cotton of my shirt, inching up the material. One arm bands around my waist while his other hand traces up my spine.

"I don't sell paintings or drawings where the image is noticeably you. Those, I keep." Leaning in, he devours my lips. When the kiss breaks, fire and passion brew in his eyes. "Can I paint you?"

Confused by the question, considering he has painted me countless times, I narrow my eyes. "Um, yes."

The corner of his mouth kicks up and my stomach does somersaults. Before realization dawns on me, Devlyn is peeling the shirt over my head. Pushing my panties to the floor. Exposing me completely with a wicked grin on his face.

"Uh, Devlyn." The urge to slap an arm over my breasts and lady bits is strong. "I don't know if I'm okay with you putting my nude body on canvas."

His smile widens. "Good thing that's not what I'm doing." He takes my hand and walks me over to a metal stool, the seat splattered in every shade of the rainbow and more. "Sit here."

I park myself on the stool, shiver as the cool metal meets my skin, hide my breasts behind my forearms, and cross my legs. My heart pounds in my chest while Devlyn roams the studio, picks up a tube of blue paint, then pink, then yellow. I lose focus as he continues, oblivious to my mini panic attack.

I may not be the shyest woman in the room most days, but the idea of having my naked body on display—even if it never leaves this room—has me in crisis mode.

"Breathe," Devlyn says in my ear. His hands come up from behind and take hold of my biceps. He kisses along my shoulder, the curve of my neck, up my throat. "Trust me." His words hot and soft on my skin.

My entire frame sags as he peels my arms away and lets them fall to my sides. Stepping around the stool, he parts my legs and positions himself between them. With a finger under my chin, he tips my head back and presses his lips to mine. The kiss starts off slow and gentle with light pecks. But with each kiss, it grows more intense. Impassioned and hungry.

We roam each other's bodies with our hands. A moan spilling from my lips as a growl builds in his chest.

Something slick coats my skin when he palms my breast. I tear my lips away and look down. A hand-sized streak of magenta paint smears my skin. Adds a pop of contrast to my pale, bare flesh. And that is when it clicks.

"Can I paint you?"

Did Devlyn mean he wanted to put paint on my actual body? Not paint my likeness on canvas? By the questioning look in his glass-green eyes right now, I would say yes.

Off to the right, I stare at the tray of paints squeezed out. Dipping two fingers in the dark green, I swirl the paint onto my skin. Then I bring them to Devlyn's chest, look him square in the eyes, and streak his skin with the pigment.

Hunger and need darken Devlyn's green irises. Before I make a joke about him asking for it, he strips off his sweats. Kicks them aside. Grabs the paint tray from the table then wraps an arm around my waist and sits us both on the floor.

Time evades us with each laugh, moan and fondle as we paint each other. Our paint-coated fingers roam and clutch and bruise. Our mouths crash together while our lips and tongues taste. After the majority of our bodies are paint slicked, Devlyn pulls a condom from the pocket of his sweats, rolls it on, and eases his thick erection between my legs. I fist his hair as he clutches the nape of my neck. My legs wrap around his waist as his hips rock at a steady, delicious tempo. The paint on our skin swirls in a kaleidoscope of colors and it isn't long before my orgasm vibrates every nerve ending in my body. Then Devlyn is right behind me, jaw slack and body trembling in ecstasy.

Minutes pass and we don't move. Our breaths calm as Devlyn props himself up on his forearms, then kisses me deeply.

"Thank you for christening my studio. Work will never be dull again."

I slap his arm and laugh. "Painting me will never be dull."

The same hunger from earlier ignites his eyes. "If by painting you, you mean this"—he glances between our bodies—"damn right. Given the chance, I'd paint you every day."

Heat crawls up my neck to my cheeks, but the paint disguises most of it. "I'd like you to paint me every day. But only if I get to do the same."

Devlyn drops his lips to mine as his hips start to rock. I am about to mention something about the condom needing to be replaced when I hear a noise from downstairs.

Breaking the kiss, I ask, "Did you hear that?"

"Hear what?" He kisses my stained skin.

"Devlyn?" a woman calls from downstairs. "You home?"

Above me, Devlyn freezes and goes wide eyed. "Shit." His eyes slam shut. "Shit, shit, shit."

A new dose of panic floods my veins. "What's wrong? Who is that?"

"Devlyn? Are you upstairs?" The woman sounds closer than she did a moment ago.

Devlyn pulls out quickly and I wince. "Sorry." He fumbles for his sweats, my shirt, and panties. "Here." He hands me the garments with a pained look. "Give me a minute, Mother," he shouts. "I'll be right down."

Oh. My. God. Oh my god!

Devlyn's mom is here. Downstairs. Right now. There is no possible way for either of us to skirt past her without her seeing us. And with the paint covering both our bodies, literally, it won't be difficult to surmise what we were doing.

Kill. Me. Now.

He removes the condom, tosses it in the trash, then steps into his sweats. I slip the shirt over my head and pull on my panties. As I straighten, he steps into me, frames my face with his hands, and presses a gentle kiss to my lips.

"Wait here a minute. I'll see if I can get her to leave."

I tuck my lips between my teeth and nod. "'Kay."

"Be right back."

Devlyn dashes down the stairs, paint smeared over ninety percent of his body, and greets his mother. I move closer to the landing and try to listen in on their conversation without being seen.

"What in the world, Devlyn?" Her tone blade sharp. "Why are you covered in paint?"

"Hello to you too, Mother."

"Don't be smart with me." Her shoes clap the floor and grow quieter as they move away.

Hesitantly, I go down a few stairs and listen for further movement.

"What brought you by?" Devlyn doesn't hide the curtness from his words. The sharp tone so different from what I am used to hearing from him.

Devlyn has told me about his parents, but not in in-depth detail. From what I do know, she sounds like a lot to handle. And by the way she speaks with Devlyn now, I don't disagree with that opinion.

"Well," she huffs out. "I came over to ask you to lunch, but with the state of your appearance, that isn't happening." Her shoes clap the floor again. This time, they grow louder and I panic. "Your father and I have planned a post-New Year's party at the house for next Saturday. It's more than enough—"

She stops speaking the moment my foot slips on the top stair and I fall on my butt.

"Shit," I whisper as I scurry up into the studio. There is nowhere to go, nowhere to hide. So, I dash over to the table and sit on the stool. At least I can hide my bare legs.

Clap, clap, clap.

With each step she takes up the stairs, my heart shrivels a little more. When she reaches the landing, looks around the room, and spots me, a snarl displays on her face. Albeit brief, I still catch it.

The woman eyes me with disgust as Devlyn darts past her and comes to my side.

"Devlyn, who is this girl?"

Girl?

"Mother." Devlyn wraps an arm around my waist then kisses my temple. "This is Shelly." His eyes home back in on her. "My girlfriend." She grinds her jaw. "Shelly, this is my mother, Karen Templar."

If the tension were any thicker in the room, we would all suffocate.

Without a word, she turns on her heel and stomps down the stairs like a pouty juvenile. When she reaches the bottom floor, she shouts up the stairwell. "Devlyn, a word downstairs. Now."

He doesn't answer her. He doesn't move from my side. Instead, he frames my face and holds my stare. "We'll talk when she leaves. But please, don't let her bother you." He kisses my lips, my nose, my forehead. "Let me get rid of her, then we can talk."

Speechless, I nod.

Devlyn darts down the stairs and I stay put on the stool. From my seat, I hoped to not hear what his mother would say next. Sadly, I hear every seething, ugly word.

"That girl will ruin your career. She will tarnish the Templar name. I bet she only wants your money. Have you gotten a good look at her?"

All the ugly words twirl in my head like a cyclone gone astray. One by one, her words cripple me. Douse me in fear and hurt. Steal the happiness from my soul.

Then Devlyn pipes up. "Enough, Mother!" he booms. "Enough."

"Don't you dare—"

"No, Mother, it's my turn to speak. That *woman* upstairs is brilliant and wonderful and kind. More than I could ever ask for or deserve. Without hesitation, she gives me her heart. More than you ever have."

"I've heard enough."

"No, you haven't. Because you never listen." Her shoes clap the floor and get quieter. "She matters to me. A lot. And if you can't respect her or my feelings, I suggest you don't stop by unannounced. Ever."

My heart races in my chest. Tears well in my eyes. Not that no one has ever stood up for me, but this is different. This is someone I love putting me first. Over their family.

"How dare you speak to me with such disregard."

"How dare I? *How dare I?*" Devlyn laughs without humor. "I'm done, Mother. Done. Don't call or email. Don't reach out at all. I'll be changing the code to the door as soon as you leave."

"You can't just get rid of your mother, Devlyn. It doesn't work that way." The house goes eerily quiet a beat. "When that girl trashes your life, when you have nowhere left to turn, you'll beg for my forgiveness."

Dear god. What the hell is wrong with this woman? She obviously thinks of herself as holier than thou, while everyone at her feet is shit.

"Get out!" he screams. "Get out now!"

"How dare—"

"Now!"

A moment later, the door slams. Then Devlyn screams at the top of his lungs.

Immediately, I want to run down the stairs and go to him. Comfort him. See if he needs anything, even if it is time alone. But I also don't want to crowd him. Make him think he doesn't have the space or time to process what happened on his own. Be a nag or pest when what he needs is solitude and quiet.

I don't want him to think I'm like *her*.

Sliding off the stool, I tiptoe to the landing, then down the stairs. The house is quiet. Too quiet. When I reach the bottom floor, I peek around the doorway. No sign of Devlyn. I pad across the room, look left into the living room then right into the dining room. Still no Devlyn. I round the corner, walk past the kitchen, and step into the formal sitting room at the entrance of the house.

There, on the floor, near the front door, Devlyn is curled in on himself, back to the ceiling. Slowly, I pad across the room, come to his side and crouch down. I don't say a word. Instead, I gently rest a hand on his back. He startles at my touch. A breath passes between us and then he twists, wraps his arms around my waist, and clings to me as if I am the air he breathes.

His frame shakes as he sobs into my lap. I bend over him, blanket him with touch, and kiss along his spine. "I got you." I hug him tighter. "No matter what."

He grips me impossibly tighter, his fingers bruising my flesh. But I don't care. "I need you, Shelly. Always."

"You have me."

Wiggling free, he sits up and frames my face. "Promise?"

I lift my hand and stick out my pinkie. "Promise."

He hooks our pinkies then drags me onto his lap. "Never letting you go," he says before smashing my lips with his.

Good. Because there is nowhere else I want to be.

Life has never been this exhausting.

When I cut ties with my mother two weeks ago, it felt like she sucked part of my soul out. Knowing her, she probably did.

Although life feels less weighted with her absence, my body is still recovering from our screaming match. Not just my physical self, but my mental and emotional self too. Dumping toxic people from your life, especially family, isn't as simple as saying goodbye. You don't just get to wave a hand and be done with it. Because, as expected, my mother has continuously tried to keep in contact. At this point, I am ready to block her. Put a ten-foot cinder block wall around my home and shut out the possibility of her knocking on my door again.

Thank goodness I have Shelly. The only light in my life. The sole reason I wake up each morning and roll out of bed. In the last two weeks, we haven't spent a night without each other. A couple of times, she has hung out with her friends after work. As soon as they all went separate ways, Shelly came to me.

"Ready?" she asks as she exits the bathroom.

With each night she stays in my home, she adds more pieces of herself. Occasionally, we stay at her apartment, but more often than not, she walks through my door. Cooks in my kitchen. Curls into me on my sofa. Eats meals at my table. Spoons with me in my bed.

And I don't want it any other way. Well, I would rather call them *ours* instead of mine, but that is a conversation for a different day.

"Yeah, I'm ready."

Tonight is a big deal. Tonight, I am meeting her friends at their weekly Sunday gathering. But not just her friends, I also get to meet her brother and sister-in-law. The whole situation has me sweaty and itchy.

From what little Shelly has told me about her brother, he sounds pretty protective of her. I mean, I get it. Shelly means everything to me, so I am pretty protective of her too. In a different way. But since Shelly asked me to join her at the Sunday night gathering, I haven't been able to shake the jitters from my limbs.

As if she senses my unease, Shelly wedges herself between my legs at the edge of the bed. Bringing a hand to my cheek, she wipes away any discomfort with the soft brush of her thumb.

"I know crowds aren't your thing, but I promise this is a low-key gathering. Just friends hanging out and catching up." I nod as my arms band around her waist and haul her closer. "It's usually a little odd when someone new comes, like when Micah brought Peyton the first time, but I promise everyone will resume normal conversation in no time."

Being the odd man out has never been something that bothered me. Throughout my middle and high school years, I had been the subject of bullies. People who thought I was weird because I didn't dress the same or socialize the same or join all the clicks. So, instead of getting to know me, they said hurtful things, threw food at me in the cafeteria, or rigged my locker. After a while, it simply became a part of who I was and I accepted it.

When Kelsey came along, I often questioned if she was truly interested or if befriending, then eventually dating me was a prank. It took months for me to believe she cared. When she ended our relationship, the questions came back again. Nothing but heartache came from our breakup, so I brushed the idea under the rug where it belonged.

"As long as you're there, it doesn't matter how strange everyone acts." I hug her to me, bury my nose in the hollow of her throat and inhale. "Meeting new people is always uncomfortable. But these people matter to you, so I want to know them too."

I hold on to Shelly for three breaths, then let her lead me from the bedroom. After we stop in the kitchen to grab the Crock-Pot of sweet-and-spicy meatballs, we get in my car and drive toward the party. On the drive over, Shelly gives me small tidbits about everyone who will be in attendance. When she starts talking about the seventh person, my mind goes numb.

She said a lot of people would be there, but I didn't think it'd be more than a dozen. Jesus.

My heart runs rampant as the whooshing of my pulse fills my ear. I take a deep breath. Then another. And just like she always has, Shelly settles the craziness inside. She grips my hand a little tighter. Rubs her thumb in small circles over my skin. Tells me everything will be okay, that she won't leave my side. Reminds me that everyone at the party is cool and fun and can't wait for us to arrive.

I steer the car into the neighborhood and take in the homes on the street. Most are two-story and look to be built in the last twenty to thirty years. Simple yet clean and elegant. Yards with tall trees and manicured landscapes. Flower beds and wind chimes and welcome signs. Strategically placed lights to illuminate sturdy magnolias and clustered palms.

I park on the street two houses down and take the Crock-Pot from Shelly when we exit the car. She laces her fingers with mine and guides us toward the house. "They'll love you," she says softly, kissing my cheek.

Not bothering to knock or ring the doorbell, Shelly twists the knob and walks us inside. Just as the door closes, a husky gallops around the corner with a little girl hot on its heels.

"Sparty!" she shouts over the music and chatter. "No, sir." The girl's bossy tone says she is not to be messed with. Before the dog collides with our legs, it screeches to a halt like a speed skater on ice.

Not releasing my hand, Shelly squats down and the dog steps up to lick her face. "Hey, Spartan. This is Devlyn."

Woof, woof, woof. He cocks his head while looking up and assessing me.

Shelly rises and ruffles the fur on his head. "Be a good boy."

The little girl reaches us and wraps her arms around Shelly's midsection. "Hi, Miss Shelly. Sorry if Sparty was a jerk."

With a laugh, Shelly says, "He's just being himself. Clementine, this is my boyfriend, Devlyn." Shelly wraps her free hand around my bicep and molds herself to my side. "Devlyn, this is Clementine, Autumn's daughter."

Autumn. She and Jonas own this house. They also are expecting a baby any day now.

I untwine my fingers from Shelly and offer Clementine my hand. "It's nice to meet you, Clementine." The girl looks at my hand as her forehead bunches into crooked lines.

About to ask Shelly if I did something wrong, Clementine wraps her arms around me as if we have been friends all her life. "Nice to meet you, Mr. Devlyn."

Shelly leans into my ear. "She's a hugger." I chuckle and return Clementine's brief hug.

Minus the unexpected hug, everyone else greets me with the same enthusiasm as we walk deeper into the house. One by one, I put faces to the names of people Shelly told me about. Some of them are how I pictured them in my mind's eye, others the complete opposite. When Shelly introduces me to her brother, Micah, and sister-in-law, Peyton, I half expect to get the big brother lecture. But Micah surprises us both with a brief hug and big smile.

As the night wears on, I learn why Shelly is so bonded with these people. Her people. Every person here has been kind and wonderful and accepting of me. They smile my way and spark up conversation as if we have been friends just as long as anyone else here. They ask about my work and I ask about theirs. The easiest conversations are with Rex and Reznor from the tattoo shop. They show me pictures of pieces they have done and I show them my art too.

And before the night ends, I feel as if I am just as much their family as everyone else in the room. It stirs new meaning to the term family in my life. Studying the face of each person, I home in on the connection they share that is nothing like what I have ever known as family. Love. Consideration. Tenderness. Friendship.

When it is time to say good night, every hug and promise to see them again is heartfelt and genuine. Nervous as I was before we arrived, every person here made me feel as if I belonged. As if I were their family.

We load into the car and I drive us home. Our fingers laced together and resting in her lap.

"Did you have a nice time?"

I lift her hand to my lips and kiss her knuckles. "I did. Thought I'd be more overwhelmed, but everyone was very welcoming."

She leans across the console and rests her head on my bicep. "See. I knew there was nothing to worry about."

The drive home is quick with less traffic on the roads. When I turn onto my street and spot the white SUV not far in the distance, I bring the car to a halt. Even from half a block away, I know who is parked in front of my house. The woman who just won't give up.

Shelly straightens in her seat. "What's wrong?" When I don't answer, she follows my line of sight. "Is that?"

"My mother?" My knuckles whiten on the steering wheel. "Yep."

"Turn around."

"What?" I twist in my seat to look at Shelly.

"Turn around and go to my apartment. She doesn't know where I live." Shelly lifts a hand to my cheek. "I don't want her to ruin our night."

I pull into the closest driveway, back out, and exit the neighborhood the way we came. The entire drive to Shelly's place, I mull over why my mother is so damn persistent with keeping me in her life if I am such a bother. The only answer I come up with is that she needs someone to step on so she can feel higher and mightier. So she has more people at her feet to kiss them.

In the last two weeks, so much has changed. Once you step out of the shadow of someone else's light, you see the world differently. Once that person no longer has the ability to squash you under their thumb, they come back with more persistence.

After hours of online research since I pushed her away, I concluded my mother is most definitely a narcissist. To what degree? I don't know, nor do I have the time or energy to figure it out. But the further I fell down the dark online hole, the deeper it sank into my bones. The more I realized that people like her will never be happy unless they have someone to belittle or trample.

I don't want to be that person for her. I can't be.

So if I want to break the cycle, if I want to have a healthy life and relationship with Shelly, I have to cut her off. Cut all direct ties. No matter the cost. No matter who I lose in the process. Because from what I've learned, if I don't make a clean break, my mother will slowly and intentionally ruin everything I love. Everything I hold close to my heart. As long as she comes out feeling mighty in the end, she won't care who she crushes along the way.

And I refuse to let her rob me of happiness.

Everyone is on edge.

Any day now, Autumn is due to deliver. Jonas started paternity leave days ago, in case Autumn went into labor early. Clementine hasn't allowed Autumn to do a thing on her own except use the bathroom. Even then, she hovers close by.

Although Autumn and Jonas aren't her children, Elizabeth is geared up for the next baby in our group to arrive. We won't be closing Petal and Vine like we did when Cora went into labor, but she is prepped and ready to let me leave the shop and deliver bundles of flowers.

More than ever, Devlyn is holed up in his studio. When I arrive at his house after work, more often than not, he is upstairs. Music echoes throughout the house while he works on commissioned pieces. I don't go up uninvited, not because he doesn't want me up there, but because I assume he needs the time to himself.

Since the unannounced visit from his mother and then seeing her car out front days later, Devlyn has turned inward slightly. He doesn't shut me out, but is selective with what he shares. His reservation doesn't hurt—I have always known Devlyn's reticent nature—but it has me ready to go into protection mode. Not to protect me, but to safeguard him and his heart.

Art is how Devlyn processes life. How he expresses himself and unleashes what inhabits his thoughts. The good and the ugly. Whichever consumes him, he needs the time to get it out without guilt or interruption or influence.

Most nights, once I start cooking, he comes down. His warm arms band around my waist as he kisses my shoulder, as I melt into his frame and sigh. I love our new routine. Love how easily both of us have fallen into this way of life, without effort or hardship.

"Still no word?" Elizabeth asks as I fill the loose stems at the front of the shop.

I pull my phone from my pocket, tap the screen and find no new messages. "Nope." Just as I pocket my phone, it pings with a text.

GROUP TEXT - JONAS

It's time!

I spin my phone around and show the message to Elizabeth. The biggest smile plumps her cheeks as she brings her hands to prayer at her lips. Then my phone blows up.

PENNY

On my way!

REZNOR

We'll head over when the shop closes.

GAVIN

Holy shit, man! Congrats!

CORA

As soon as we drop off Clara, we'll be there.

REX

Congrats, bro! Can't wait to meet the newest family
member.

MICAH

Peyton and I will swing by in the morning. Congrats, man!

ERIN

Ahhh! Turning around now!

My fingers race over the keyboard in response.

Aunt Shelly is on the way! Can't wait to meet him or her.

Then, I flip to my text history with Devlyn and type a quick message.

Autumn's in labor. Headed to the hospital.

The small gray bubble dances at the bottom left of the screen a moment before
Devlyn's response appears.

Just left the park. Be there in a few and we can go
together.

Since the incident with his mother, Devlyn spends most of his days at the park
and evenings in the studio. Not sure if he draws or paints while at the park, but he
appears calmer on the days he visits. As if he needs to sit on our bench while working. As if he needs the energy and serenity of the trees and air and wildlife. As if he
needs to be in the same space we shared so many times before.

I fear the reason he leaves the house is on the off chance his mother will stop by
unannounced, attempting to stir up more toxic drama. The thought rakes my
nerves. No one should fear being home, in their personal space.

On the days a shadow glints Devlyn's gaze, he chauffeurs me to the shop. I
don't question his heart or motives. Small as it may seem, I grant him this minute
assurance, this form of armor. A way he can shield me from hurt, from his mother.

Yeah, that's perfect.

Shouldn't be long.

I fill a few more bins before ditching my shop apron and shouldering my purse.
Elizabeth gives me a hug and tells me to send tons of pictures. I bolt out the back
door with a small bouquet and hop in Devlyn's SUV, then we are off.

We arrive at the hospital and park in the visitor's lot. After weaving through the
main lobby, we step inside the elevator and ascend to labor and delivery. The car
comes to a stop and the doors whoosh open. The air hits my face as we step out and

my stomach rolls a little at the scent of lemon-scented bleach. I take a deep breath, hold it to the count of ten then release it.

"Hey." Devlyn gives my hand a squeeze. "You okay?"

"Yeah," I say with a nod. "Never been a fan of bleach and it smelled especially strong when the elevator opened."

"Huh."

We steer into the waiting area for the floor, and I look to Devlyn. "What?"

He shrugs. "I barely smelled it is all. Maybe it's because of the cleaning agents I use for my brushes. My nose is desensitized to the strong stuff."

The subject gets dropped when Penny, Cora, and Gavin approach. Cora wraps her arms around me and squeals a little too loudly in my ear. Gavin smiles brightly and says hello to Devlyn.

"How is everyone? Do we know if she's delivered yet?" I ask Cora, wanting to hold my next niece or nephew sooner rather than later.

"Jonas's mom came out just before you got here. They were going to have Autumn start pushing any minute."

I clap my fingers excitedly and smile so hard my cheeks sting. We settle into the chairs and place bets on if it is a boy or girl. It's three to two for a boy when Erin strolls in and evens the score. Before we get into a face-off about why each of our opinions is fact, Jonas's mom, Irene, walks out with a megawatt smile. The room goes quiet as we all rise and step closer.

"It's a boy!"

The room erupts in cheers. Irene tells us she will come get us once we are allowed to see Autumn, Jonas, and the baby. She disappears down the hall and it isn't long before she returns and invites us back to meet our newest family member.

One by one, we file into the hospital suite. The first thing I notice is how radiant Jonas is. Without question, he will be the best father. That man has the biggest heart and I have never seen it so full.

Like our last trip to the hospital when Cora had Clara, baby Ryker gets passed around for everyone to hold and coo. When I sit with him in the rocking chair, I tell him how lucky he is to have such wonderful parents and the best big sister in the world. And also the world's best aunt.

Baby Ryker has Autumn's dark hair and Jonas's hazel eyes. One thing is certain, this boy will break hearts over the years. Jonas and Autumn may have their hands full with Clementine, but Ryker will be right behind her.

I pass Ryker to Penny and squeeze between Devlyn and Cora.

"Guess you're next," Cora says with a laugh.

It's a joke. I know it is a joke. But I freeze. Not because I fear pregnancy or motherhood or permanency. I freeze because my romantic relationship with Devlyn is little more than a month old. Cora said the words in the moment because she recently had a baby. She'd probably say the same to Peyton if she and Micah hadn't openly told everyone they have no plans to have kids.

But there is another reason I freeze. Another reason my mind tailspins.

When was my last period? Think, Reed. THINK.

I search my mental calendar for my last period. It was before Christmas. A week before. Maybe two. I need my planner. Where the hell is my planner? *Oh god. Oh. God. No. No, no, no, no, no.* This cannot be happening. There is no possible chance I am… pregnant.

"Shelly?" Devlyn's lips are at my ear. "What's wrong? You're shaking. And you look… gray."

Oh god. I think I'm going to be sick. As the thought crosses my mind, my stomach rolls.

I drop Devlyn's hand, slap mine to my mouth, and dash out of the room. In the hall, a nurse smiles then frowns. A hand to the mouth is obviously the universal sign for "I'm going to puke" because the nurse rests a hand on my back and rushes me down the hall to the restrooms.

Bolting into the bathroom, I run for the stall, slam the door and lock it, then drop to my knees and expel the contents of my stomach. When my body finally relaxes, I ease up from the floor, flush the toilet, and step out of the stall. Erin stands next to the sink with concern marring her expression.

"Shell, are you okay? Jesus. You scared us all."

I turn on the faucet, splash my face with cold water and rinse out my mouth. "Yeah. Must've eaten something bad at lunch." The lie rolls off my tongue with too much ease.

She gives me a hug. "Long as you're okay." She releases me and hands me a wad of paper towels. "Devlyn's outside." She points to the door.

"Thanks. Will you tell him I'll be out in a minute?"

With a nod, she says, "No problem. Sure you're okay if I leave?"

I smile at my friend. "Promise I'm good." After another hug, she exits the bathroom.

Staring at myself in the mirror, I brace my hands on the sink and take several deep breaths. For the next minute, I have a heart-to-heart with myself.

I didn't eat anything bad in the last few hours—lunch was more than five hours ago. But the nausea could be from a number of things. The chemical smell of the hospital mixed with the adrenaline rush of being here plus not having much in my system. That has to be it.

"There's no way I'm pregnant," I whisper to my reflection. "We used protection. Every time."

But what do I know about condom usage? Other than the sex ed classes in school—more than fifteen years ago—I haven't had much experience or education in the department. Sure, I know they aren't one-hundred-percent effective, but Devlyn would have said something if the condom broke.

Regardless, I need to exit the bathroom before Devlyn panics and waltzes in. After one last deep breath, I push off the sink and head for the door. Soon as I step out, Devlyn is inches from me, his hands framing my face, eyes studying every detail.

"Are you okay?" he asks, voice low and shaky.

Tears sting the backs of my eyes because I have no clue. For all I know, I could have a virus. It is the time of year for that. I shrug. "Yes. I think." He hugs me to him and I fist the back of his shirt.

A moment later, the same nurse who guided me to the bathroom steps up. "Sorry to intrude, sweetheart. Just wanted to check on you." Her smile is bright and warm.

"Might be a bug," I tell her.

"Why don't you come with me and we can have you checked out? Shouldn't take but a few minutes, if you'd like."

Might as well since I'm here. *Will they also test to see if I'm pregnant?* "Thank you. I appreciate the help."

She walks us to the elevator then takes us to another floor, this one more clinical and cold. Coughs and sneezes and grumbles echo from every direction. The bleach scent is ten times worse and I force myself to breathe through my mouth rather than my nose.

"Hey, Suzanne," a man says from behind the desk. "How can I help?"

"Paul, this young lady…" The nurse looks my direction.

"Shelly," I say.

"Shelly wasn't feeling well upstairs. Would you please run a virus panel?"

He smiles at Nurse Suzanne and nods. "Sure thing." Then he looks in my direction. "I'll just need identification, Shelly, and some forms filled out."

I dig through my purse and hand over my identification. He hands me a clipboard and points to a group of chairs along the wall. While I fill out basic personal and health information, Devlyn wraps an arm around my shoulders and rubs small circles on my skin.

As I sign my name on the consent to treat line, Paul calls me to the counter and says he is ready. He escorts us to a small room with white walls and generic framed art across from the patient chair.

"We'll do a cheek swab and draw blood." He glances at his watch. "Results won't be available for another twelve or so hours. Will you still be in the hospital?"

I shake my head. "No. We're visiting a friend who had a baby."

He nods as he wraps and ties the tourniquet around my distal bicep. "Make a fist." He jiggles his gloved fingers over the veins at my elbow. "Nice veins." His smile makes me want to smile, but I can't muster the strength. "I'd recommend you don't return to see your friend until we know what this is. Don't want to expose the newborn."

Just before the needle pricks my skin, I look up at Devlyn. He lets me squeeze his hand while I breathe erratically.

"Almost done," he mouths.

The phlebotomist unties the elastic on my arms before easing the needle from my vein and bandaging me up. Next, he removes a long Q-Tip from a sealed tube, asks me to open my mouth and runs the cotton over the inside of my cheek. He places it back in the tube, seals it with a new sticker, then sets it next to the blood vials.

"All set," he says, peeling his gloves away and washing his hands. "Take your time getting up."

Back at the desk, he returns my identification and verifies my telephone number. "We'll give you a call in the morning. Is there a time that works better for you?"

"Any time is good. Thank you, Paul."

"You're welcome. Go home and get some rest. We'll talk in the morning."

And with that, Devlyn and I amble out of the hospital. Devlyn thinking I may have some sort of cold and me considering the possibility of being pregnant.

Devlyn just went through so much with his mother. I don't know if he is in the right headspace to discuss the likelihood of something other than the common cold. During the drive home, I keep the details of my late period to myself. More than pregnancy causes cycle disruption. Stress, diet, a change in sleep habits, physical exertion. No need to ratchet up his anxiety too.

It isn't long before Devlyn parks in his driveway, guides me inside, and tends to me like the most adoring boyfriend. He cooks and feeds me, helps me with a bath, then curls up behind me under the covers.

As my eyes grow heavy, he kisses my shoulder then whispers, "Love you, Shelly."

I tighten his grip around my belly, tears stinging the backs of my eyes. "I love you too."

We startle awake to Shelly's phone ringing on the nightstand.

"Hello," she answers, voice thick with sleep. "This is Shelly Reed." She goes quiet while the person on the other end speaks. I toy with her hair and wait for her to tell me the news. "Yes, I heard you. Thank you for the update."

Shelly ends the call and stares at the ceiling with glassy eyes. Something twists in my gut. Something that says this isn't just a cold. Maybe it's something much worse. Cancer. Something with her heart. My mind races with various ailments I have heard of. Diseases that appear like common colds but are much worse.

I hate how quiet she is. I hate how scared she looks. More than anything, I hate that she won't look me in the eye. As if I won't like what she has to say.

Unable to deal with the silence any longer, I brush my knuckles over her cheek and swallow down my nerves. "You're scaring me," I mumble. A tear rolls down her temple. "Please talk to me, Shelly."

"I don't understand," she whispers to the ceiling. "How?"

"How what?" God, I want to shake the information from her brain and soothe away her fears.

Finally, she turns to meet my gaze. "I'm scared." Another tear spills and I am ready to crawl out of my skin.

"I can't help unless you tell me what's wrong."

"Please don't hate me."

This has me confused. Why would I hate Shelly for being sick? "No matter what it is, we'll get through this." I drop my lips to hers to seal the vow. "I love you, Shelly."

She closes her eyes, takes a deep breath, then opens them. "I don't have a viral infection."

Well, that is good news. I breathe easy for only a moment. Wait? Does that mean it is something worse? My mind automatically goes back to cancer or some inherited immune disorder her family doesn't know about.

"I don't know how, but I'm pregnant."

I inch back from her and take in her wince. "What?" My voice comes out louder than I intend it to.

"Oh god."

She pulls away from me, slides out of bed on the opposite side, and fumbles for her clothes. Meanwhile, I can't move. My body weighted with a ton of bricks. My limbs in a state of paralysis.

How?

Before I get another word in, before I get off the bed, she darts for the bathroom with her purse and starts opening cabinets and drawers. As she dashes out and heads for the closet, I finally snap out of my haze and dress.

"What are you doing?" She yanks shirts from hangers and shoves them in her bag. She attempts to push past me, but I grab her elbow. "Shelly, talk to me. Where are you going?"

"You're freaking out." She sniffles and wipes her cheeks with the back of her hand. "I see it in your eyes."

"Well, I'm in shock." I take a deep breath and speak as calmly as possible. "Please, don't go."

"Did you not hear what I said?" She hangs her head. "I'm pregnant." Her sobs grow louder and I pull her into my arms. She fights it at first, but caves. Then hollow laughter spills from her lips.

"Why are you laughing?" Nothing about this situation is funny. If anything, her laugh has the hairs on the back of my neck standing straight.

She leans back and looks me in the eye. "I heard your mother say I'd ruin your life. Never thought she'd be right."

My eyes go wide and I freeze for the second time in minutes. *Why would Shelly say something like that? Why would she believe a word that comes out of my mother's mouth?*

Shelly slips from my arms. The air around me grows thick and heavy and encapsulates me. Pulls me into a fog. My pulse soars in my ears and drowns out every noise in the house. Until I hear the front door slam. I shake my head and snap back to reality. Run for the door, burst outside and chase after her car as it backs out of the driveway.

"Shelly, no!" I scream after her, desperate for her to come back. For her to park in the driveway, get out of the car, and come back in the house so we can talk about this.

But she doesn't stop. She just keeps driving. Away from me. Away from us. Away from love. With our baby in her belly.

You promised me. You promised that you'd stay.

My knees buckle, and I fall to the pavement. Sharp pain radiates through my legs, and I accept every treacherous stab as I curl into a ball. In the middle of my driveway. For all to see.

A chill that has nothing to do with the January temperature blankets me head to toe. Seeps into my bones as numbness begins to wash over me. A numbness I know all too well.

Shelly, please don't go. Please. You promised you'd never leave. Please… I need you.

Abstract Passion

ARTIST DUET
BOOK TWO

one

A block from Devlyn's house, I pull over and throw the car in park. Tears spill from my eyes in a violent torrent of pain and confusion. Every muscle in me aches with agony.

I'm pregnant. No. No, no, no. What the hell am I going to do? What the hell am I doing?

I stare out the windshield with blurred vision and try to collect myself. Try to slow the tears and quiet my irrational mind. Try to stop the convulsive sobs crawling up my throat and spilling from my lips. I close my eyes and shut out the chaos whirling in my head. Eviscerate the words like *ruin* and *over.*

Swiping at my eyes, I wipe away the tears and look in the rearview mirror. Stare down the street behind me as a new version of panic squeezes my heart. As new found alarm constricts my airway.

Devlyn.

"What have I done?" I whisper in the cab of my car.

Understandably, he went into shock with the news. So did I. Where he went completely still and utterly speechless, I went into full-on hysteria. My brain short-circuited and I made irrational decisions in the heat of the moment, undoubtedly hurting him.

What have I done?

I steer the Beetle into the next driveway, back out then drive back to Devlyn's house. The small neighborhood block feels miles long as I roll closer and closer. Two houses away, I swipe my cheeks dry and take a deep breath. When I pull into the driveway, I am definitely not prepared for what I see next. Devlyn curled into a tight ball, knees crushed to his chest, and head tucked as he rocks back and forth.

I press the heel of my palm to my chest as the pain beneath my breastbone kicks up to level ten.

Cutting the engine, I bolt from the car and run to his side. Drop down in front of him and gingerly lay a hand on his head. Lightly comb my fingers through his hair and hover over his bundled frame. "Devlyn," I whisper. His tempo and erratic rocking don't pause, so I try again and with more volume. "Devlyn."

He startles on the second call of his name. The constant shaking of his body stops. His head lifts and I am stabbed in the heart by the pain in his puffy, red eyes. The way he regards me, rakes his eyes over the lines of my face, it's as if he is unsure I am real or a figment of his imagination.

I add more weight to my touch on his head and in his hair. Slide my hand slowly down the side of his face. Wiggle my fingers in his hair and scratch them along his scalp. When my palm cups his cheek, he leans his weight into my hand. Closes his eyes. Inhales deeply and holds the breath in his lungs for three of my breaths.

When his eyes reopen, he scrambles forward and wraps me in his arms. "You can't go," he mumbles in my ear, voice strained and raw. "I need you." He hugs me tighter to his chest and kisses my neck. Takes another deep breath and sighs heavily. "Please stay."

My arms squeeze him impossibly tighter as my fingers roam his hair and my lips kiss his shoulder. "Let's go back inside." I lean back and frame his face in my hands. Hold his turbulent gaze as tears blur my vision. "I'm sorry. I wasn't thinking rationally." My lips press to his, again and again. "So, so sorry."

On unsteady legs, we rise from the pavement and wander back into the house. Devlyn's hand firmly holds mine as we wind our way to the living room and sit on the couch. He inches closer until it's difficult to tell where I end and he begins.

"Do you want a drink? Maybe some tea or water or juice," he suggests, tone antsy.

A fresh layer of guilt washes over me. I hate that my first instinct was to run away. To abandon Devlyn. What kind of person does that? *You were scared and so was he. And you both process fear differently.* Internally, I hang my head and berate myself.

"Some tea would be nice," I whisper, and he nods. Then he is off the couch and dashing to the kitchen.

While Devlyn prepares us drinks, I mull over what to say when he reenters the room. I feel the need to apologize until I lose my voice. My actions were spontaneous and foolish, but my head was—is—a scrambled mess. And when I said the words aloud—*I'm pregnant*—Devlyn froze, then thawed, only to freeze again. I went from panicked to unreasonably hysterical in a heartbeat.

So I bolted.

But I can't run away from this, from us. Devlyn or our unborn child. It may be unplanned, it may throw both of our worlds completely off-balance, but that doesn't change anything.

I lay a hand over my still flat belly, close my eyes and take a deep breath. Tell myself it will be okay. That it will all work out. That everything happens when it is meant to.

When my eyes open, I consider how to broach the conversation again. This time with calmer heads and less anxiety. Hopefully.

I am—we are—pregnant and we will be parents before the end of the year. A baby… Devlyn and I are going to have a baby. Another human to love and nurture.

Mentally, I laugh at myself. Leave it to us—the fumbling virgin and almost virgin—to mess up condom usage.

Regardless, it is done. Neither of us can change the past. All we can do now is prepare for the future. But what does that future look like?

Devlyn wanders back into the living room with a mug in each hand. He sets them both on the table, drops next to me on the couch, and wraps me in his arms again. Eliminates every ounce of space between us with a fierce hug. Holds me like he fears I will bolt for the door once more.

And I hate that I did this. Inflicted him with this level of fear. Fractured the trust he has in me. Created doubt that I will stay.

I want to stay. For as long as he will have me, I want to stay.

"Sorry I freaked out. Sorry I didn't say anything right away." He tugs me into his lap and shifts his hold. Shakes his head as he burrows into my chest. "Sorry I froze."

I lay my cheek on his head, close my eyes and comb my fingers through his dark locks. "This isn't all you, so don't you dare try to take all the blame." My arms circle his shoulders and head. Cradle him in my hold. "I'm just as guilty. I shouldn't have packed my bags and jumped in the car." My lips press to his hair. "But I wasn't thinking. Not clearly."

Nose buried in my hair, Devlyn inhales deeply. On the exhale, he leans back and frames my face in his hands. "This is scary, for both of us, but I know we'll get through it." He lowers my lips to his and kisses me with newfound tenderness. "I love you, Shelly."

Tears sting the backs of my eyes. An emotional ball grows thick in my throat. I lift my hands to his cheeks, cup either side of his jaw, and stroke his cheekbones with my thumbs. "I love you, too," I choke out.

Time creeps by, our tea cools on the table, but neither of us move. For now, I simply want to breathe him in. Want to let all the madness from earlier fall away. Want to feel his arms and warmth blanket me in love. Want to give the news of us becoming parents a moment to seep in.

Pregnant. Me. The woman that plans all the big moments in her life. The woman that makes five-year plans and intends to stick to them. I am pregnant. *We* are pregnant. This was definitely not in the five-year plan. Finding love was in the plan, but not becoming a mother.

My mind drifts to the piece of paper pinned to the wall in my apartment bedroom. My current five-year plan. The biggest thing on the list... purchasing Petal and Vine from Elizabeth.

Oh, god.

I close my eyes and sink deep inside myself. Try to steady my rapid-fire pulse with steady breaths. Clear the worrisome thoughts invading my head.

Elizabeth won't be upset about the pregnancy. Knowing her, she will rejoice at having another baby to spoil. Be excited that her own grandchild will soon have a playmate. But her happiness won't erase the guilt holding me hostage daily as I delay her retirement. Something she has looked forward to for the past two years.

Will I still be able to purchase Petal and Vine when the time comes? Will I be able to run a business with a newborn in my arms or on my hip? It's silly to think such things. Plenty of women and families manage this all the time. But maybe they planned ahead. Had all their ducks in a row before the pregnancy test came back positive.

Then my thoughts drift to Autumn and Clementine. Autumn's first pregnancy was a surprise. In a matter of months, she wasn't just a pregnant mother with an absentee father, she'd also been kicked out of her home. Abandoned in every way imaginable. Her family had been that cruel.

But she kept going. Never gave up. Moved forward and persevered. Found a place to live and got a job she loved. Thrived when some might fall. And if she can overcome such heavy obstacles—struggles much worse than the possible ones I will face—then I can do this. *We* can do this.

"You're so quiet," Devlyn whispers against my skin.

I shift off his lap, pick up my mug and sip the now cool tea, then take his hand. "Just thinking."

"About?"

Everything. "How much this will change our future."

He nods, then tucks a strand of hair behind my ear. "True." Glass-green irises lock on my blues while his thumb leisurely strokes my cheek. "But I know we'll make it work."

"How?"

For a beat, his eyes drop to my lips before meeting mine again. "I just know." He shrugs. "With you, I believe anything is possible." I raise my brows in question. "Shelly, I have been through hell. In more ways than one." He takes my hand in his, pulls it to his lap and strokes my skin. Slow and steady. His eyes on the movement. "The first round was young love gone astray. Although it sent me in a downward spiral, I'm grateful it happened. Without that loss, I wouldn't appreciate and love you the way I do."

"And the other?"

He sucks in a deep breath and speaks on the exhale. "That hell is still ongoing."

"Your mom?"

He nods. "Yeah. Not sure what to do about her." He shrugs and looks off in the distance. "Things with her… it's been brewing a long time." His chest expands as he takes a deep breath. "I don't want my past with her to affect our relationship or the baby." He trails the pad of his thumb over my knuckles. "Maybe I should talk to someone again. Get advice from a professional or someone who's been in a similar situation."

I squeeze his hand and he brings his attention back to me. "If that's what you want, what you need, I'll support you." I huff out a laugh. "Heck, maybe I should talk to someone." His eyes narrow. "About pregnancy. Motherhood. How to keep moving forward without feeling like I'm pulling everyone under."

"Shelly…"

The backs of my eyes sting and I hate how I am already so emotional. "Well, it's how I feel." I shrug. "Like I'm letting Elizabeth down." Tears well in my eyes. I take a deep breath and try to hold them at bay. "I'm supposed to buy the shop from her after this year." My jaw wobbles back and forth. "How will I be able to do that now? How will I run a business with a baby?"

"Hey," he says, voice barely above a whisper. "We'll figure it out. All of it." He chuckles and I look up. "Maybe I'll need to learn how to run a florist shop too." I furrow my brows. "So you're not doing it alone." He presses a chaste kiss to my lips. "Because you aren't alone, Shelly." Another kiss. "Ever."

"Aren't we just a hot mess," I say on a laugh.

"Wouldn't want to be in a hot mess with anyone else." Devlyn rises from the couch and extends his hand. "Come. Let's go make something for breakfast." His eyes drop to my belly. "Need to feed you two."

And in a blink, life returns to a seminormal state. We bring our mugs to the kitchen and add a touch of hot water. I scramble eggs and cook sausage while Devlyn cuts fresh fruit and toasts bread. We move around the kitchen as if we have done this for years. Been in a relationship. Existed in the same space. Loved each other.

Speaking of space… Suppose our living situation will be one of many conversations we share in the near future. A new knot forms beneath my diaphragm. Twisty and tight.

When the time comes, when we talk about housing and what will work best, I hope we are on the same page. *Please let us be on the same page.*

Two

Pregnant. Shelly is pregnant. *We* are pregnant. In the not-too-distant future, I will be a dad. Another human will depend on me to care for them. Raise them, feed them, nurture them. Turn them into a respectable human.

Is this within my power? Can I raise a child? Am I capable of molding a mini human into a decent person?

God, I hope so. Just the mere thought of letting someone down—my own child, no less—scares me to death. Has my limbs shaking and palms sweaty.

But Shelly and I will get through this. Together.

While Shelly showers and gets ready for work, I search the internet. One tab loads results of psychologists in the area. A second tab loads results of how condoms fail. And on the third tab is what steps to follow after learning you are pregnant. To some, tabs two and three may seem asinine. To me, I just want answers.

An idiot I am not. Since high school health class had a more than lackluster curriculum on sexual education, I did my own homework. At the time, I had no expectations with where my relationship with Kelsey would go, but I wanted to be prepared either way. Searching videos on how to properly roll on a condom at sixteen was awkward. After watching various oblong fruits and vegetables get sheathed, I considered myself knowledgeable enough. Kelsey never got pregnant, so I must have done something right.

Obviously that all went out the window when I rolled on condoms with Shelly. Either that or one of a handful of other factors came into play.

According to my brief research, the list of reasons why condoms fail is short. Poor manufacturing. Stored at the wrong temperature. Used after expiration date. Torn during removal from the wrapper. Wrong size. Not enough lubricant. Using the wrong lubricant, such as oil-based. The condom was rolled on incorrectly. Not pinching the tip before rolling it on. Snuggling after and going flaccid while still inside your partner.

Of all the reasons listed, two stand out the most. Two slap me in the face, hard. Snuggling and oil-based.

"Damnit," I whisper into the bedroom.

In no way am I upset with the pregnancy or Shelly. But as I read those two common reasons, I hang my head.

One—how am I *not* going to snuggle with Shelly after we have sex? Ever. After the most physically intimate moment, I will cuddle with the woman I love. Every. Damn. Time. Going forward—well, after the baby is born—cuddling will have to be after I pull out. We have time to sort out the finer details.

Two—the body painting. Although the paint never ended up between our legs, it coated my hands and pretty much every other part of our bodies. It's quite possible, I didn't clean everything off of my hands before I put the condom on. It's quite possible, I sabotaged that moment and unintentionally put us in this situation.

"Everything okay?"

I look up from my phone to see Shelly dressed in a pink, long-sleeve V-neck, light-blue denim jeans and pink Vans. Her toffee locks hang in loose waves down her back, accented with a pink headband. Her face is free of makeup, twilight eyes sparkling as they roam my face, a slight flush on her cheeks.

Not sure how it's possible, but she is more beautiful than ever.

"Yeah," I croak out, then clear my throat. "Yes. Was just researching stuff online."

Her eyes drop to my phone, then lift back to mine. "Find anything noteworthy?"

Yes. No. I shrug. "A little. Wondering what we're supposed to do next."

In slow, measured steps, Shelly closes the distance and steps between my legs at the edge of the bed. Her fingers trail up my chest, my neck, then settle in my hair. My eyes roll back and close as I get lost in her touch. Lost in the whirlwind she stirs beneath my diaphragm. Lost in the new rhythm she sets for my pulse, my breathing.

My hands find her hips. Fingertips bearing down on her denim-clad soft skin. Without second thought, I drag her closer. Sweep the tip of my nose along the column of her throat. Inhale her earthy, sweet floral scent. Allow it to soothe me in the way nothing or no one else has.

Shelly is my solace. The sunshine after the storm. We may be headed into unfamiliar territory, but so long as I have her, everything will work out.

"My guess is we visit a doctor." I lean back and look up at her. A soft smile tips up the corners of her mouth. "I know a few people to ask."

"Are you worried?"

What a stupid fucking question.

Her fingers comb through my hair as her eyes dart between mine. "Yes and no." I tilt my head in question. "It's a definite shock, but I'm surprisingly not worried about pregnancy. What I am worried about is how we'll balance our lives once the baby comes. Between the shop and your art, I worry we won't have the time or energy to do what we love."

I give her hips a gentle squeeze. "We'll find a way."

"How can you sound so sure?"

I laugh without humor. "There isn't much in life I'm sure of, Shelly. But when it comes to you, to us, I believe anything is possible."

A weighted sigh leaves her lips before she drops her forehead to rest on mine. For a moment, we just breathe each other in. Absorb this new path life has put us on. Settle into the realization that every day going forward, our lives will be forever changed. Entwined. Connected.

"I should head to work." She lifts her head and retreats a step. "Elizabeth was already worried when I messaged and said I'd be a little late."

Although I don't want her to go, I nod because she is right. This big news, this baby, will change everything we know, but we can't stop living life. And that includes going to work. "Let me walk you out."

It has only been a few hours since learning Shelly was pregnant, but it feels as if weeks have passed. Our minds are spinning, but we need to slow them as best we can. Try to focus on the day to day. Talk to those who can help us or tell us what to expect. Follow our current routines until we need to adjust them.

This may be new to us, but it's not new. With the countless number of people in Shelly's corner, we will have more support than imaginable. Support and love.

Shelly unlocks her car and slips in behind the steering wheel. She rolls down the window and I lean in to give her a kiss. "Come over after work?"

She nods. "Yeah. May be a little later. I should make up some of my missed time at the shop. Plus, I need more clothes."

"'Kay." I press my lips to hers once more. "Drive safe. See you tonight."

Shelly backs out of the driveway and waves as she drives off. This time I don't fear whether or not she will return. Don't crumble to the ground like a piece of my heart abandoned me. Deep in my bones, I know Shelly will always return. To me, to us.

I walk back into the house, wander to the living room and plop down on the couch. Pulling my phone from my pocket, I unlock it and go to the browser tab with the list of local psychologists. One by one, I click the links and read the doctor's credentials, what their area of focus is, and the frequently asked questions. In my notes app, I jot down the names and contact information of each that sounds like they may be a fit.

Visiting a psychologist is twofold. To face and conquer the demons of my past, and to make sure I don't pass my darkness on to my child. I accept that the darkness in my veins will never go away. It is part of who I am. But learning how to properly cope when it creeps in is essential. Learning how to not let the darkness win is mandatory.

Part of that darkness stems from my upbringing. The intricate ways my mother twisted my way of thinking. The type of love she taught me that wasn't love at all. I wasn't aware of her warped mindset years ago. Didn't know I was as much her pawn as anyone else.

It should hurt... the realization of who she is and what she has done. But it doesn't hurt. That part of me, the piece reserved for Karen Templar, is just numb.

Although I accept this, I want to move past the numbness. Not let her take up residence inside me any more than she already has. I want to let her go. Permanently. Not just for my own mental health, but so I can be the best version of myself for my child.

I refuse to let my past haunt my future.

The idea of my child not knowing part of their family hurts. But my family not assuming a role in this child's life is in the best interest of me, Shelly and our baby. Optimistically, I'd like to think becoming a grandparent may change my mother. That it could flip a switch inside her and she'd become a better person.

But I won't put my child in harm's way. Ever. My mother's poison slithered into my psyche for years. Her tainted words and cold actions deformed a piece of who I am. Skewed how I interpreted connections and life and love. Contributed to a mountain of untold damage. Damage I pray is reversible. Damage I hope to heal, on some level, before our baby is born.

My biggest fear is passing on the toxicity in my blood. The defect in my genetic makeup. Because like it or not, pieces of my mother live inside me. Like it or not, darkness taints my head and heart.

But Shelly... she is the one shining light in my darkness. The light leading me back to a place of love and hope. The light I refuse to let go of or lose.

Because without her light, I fear the darkness will take over. If that happens, I won't survive.

three

SHELLY

Today feels a week long and it is only noon.

On the way to work, I called Cora and asked if she had plans today. Relief relaxed my bones when she replied with a firm *nope*. But the second she asked if everything was okay, anxiety rippled through me head to toe. I played it off. Said everything was fine. Then asked her to come to the shop for lunch and to bring Clara.

The second I set foot in Petal and Vine, Elizabeth showered me with a barrage of questions. I wanted to answer each and every one of them, but remained tight lipped. Told her I invited Cora for lunch and would answer everything then. Since then, I have felt her concerned gaze on my profile. Have seen her lips part—questions written in the soft lines of her forehead—before she snaps her mouth shut.

It's been torture.

Any minute, my best friend will walk through the front door of Petal and Vine, pushing a stroller and cooing with her angelic daughter. And then, the three of us will dig in on lunch as I spill the beans about my accidental pregnancy.

Since calling her, I've mentally rehearsed more than a dozen ways to say *I'm pregnant* without saying those two specific words. For some reason, saying more feels necessary.

I hate how I'm riddled with anxiety. About saying the words aloud. About telling my best friend and second mother news that will thrill them. Speaking the words to someone other than Devlyn makes it more real. Tangible. Legit.

Nerves aside, Cora and Elizabeth are the first two women I want to tell.

Mom will find out soon enough, but I need to be in the right headspace to share such big news with her. Hell, Mom doesn't even know about Devlyn. Doesn't know we have been in this weird friends-to-lovers relationship for months. Had she known, I would've heard an endless string of pleas from her. Daily texts asking for updates on my love life. Calls more than once a week, masked as her checking in but really searching for unspoken clues.

Ugh.

Sharing the news with Mom will be a blast—insert thick layer of sarcasm. I already hear the long list of questions on her roster.

"Why didn't you tell me you were dating someone?"

"When can I meet him?"

"You found someone and *you're pregnant?"*

"Did you find a doctor yet?"

"Can I go to your appointments?"

"How long have you known?"

"Why didn't you tell me sooner?"

"When are you moving in together?"

"Are you planning to get married?"

Of all the questions I picture my mother asking, the last is the one I fear most. Deep down, Mom only wants the best for me and Micah. But I am fully aware that, in her mind, love equals marriage and babies. If the solid relationship my parents have isn't proof enough, her reasons for starting family dinners more than a year ago is definitely hard evidence.

I love my mother. Love her big heart and desire to see everyone happy. Love that dreamy look she gives Dad. I only wish she understood happiness comes in different forms.

When Micah and Peyton announced they wouldn't start a family, Mom all but lost her shit. She didn't understand how or why they didn't want children. Because Nicole Reed doesn't look beyond her own experiences. Can't fathom anything other than her own way of life being great. With Micah and Peyton not wanting children, I pray her perspective changes.

The bell over the front door jingles. I plaster on a big smile and mentally prepare myself for the most adult conversation I've had in years. Then sag against the arrangement table when a man steps around the pails of loose flowers.

He holds up two large paper bags. "Delivery from See Ew Thai."

I step around the table, dig into the pocket of my apron, hand him a cash tip then take the bags. "Thank you."

"Have a great day, miss."

As the man exits the shop, Cora walks in with baby Clara in her beast of a stroller.

Oh god. Something else to worry over. All the gadgets and gizmos we will need for a baby.

"Auntie Shelly must have big news if she's sweet-talking Mommy with Asian food," Cora coos at Clara as she sidles up to the arrangement table. Eyes wide, Clara slaps at a toy dangling inches from her face.

"Guilty," I say, bending over the stroller and lightly pinching Clara's toes. "How's my favorite niece today? Is Mommy spoiling you rotten?"

Clara makes an unintelligible noise and we both laugh. Elizabeth exits the storage room and gives Cora a warm, welcoming hug before removing her granddaughter from the stroller.

For a moment, I watch the three of them. Revel in their smiles and sweet talk. Relish the ease of this new change in their lives. Envy how simple Cora makes motherhood look, although I've heard the struggles she experienced.

My best friend may be new to parenting, but she does it like a pro. She isn't back to working full-time, but has taken a couple of small, scenic jobs this month. Her way of easing back into the norm at her own pace. Outdoor photo shoots of places and not people. That way, she can bring Clara along and not worry.

"It's not ideal, but I'd like to have lunch with all of us. At least for a few minutes," I say as I start carrying the bags to the back. Cora and Elizabeth exchange a look of concern. "I'll set things up at the table. We should be able to hear the bell if anyone comes in."

Before either of them gets a word in, I step into the office-slash-break room and set the bags down. One by one, I pull out the food boxes and set them on the table. Get everything in place. Ready for them to stuff their mouths while I confess my pregnancy and beg for advice.

I peek my head around the doorframe and spot Cora and Elizabeth fawning over Clara. Warmth spreads in my chest at the sight.

Later this year, that will be me and Devlyn.

Tears sting the backs of my eyes, but I blink them away before they well and fall. I inhale deeply in an attempt to settle the nerves fluttering in my belly. "Ready when you are," I say.

Cora parks Clara back in the stroller before she and Elizabeth wander into the break room. I point out their places at the table on either side of mine. We take our seats and open the boxes. Elizabeth dives into her pad thai while Cora bites down on a spring roll. The moment their mouths are full, I open mine.

"I'm pregnant," I blurt out.

To no surprise, both of them go into coughing fits. Okay, so waiting until they had their mouths full was a *bad* idea. I thought it would be a great way to keep them from screaming or squealing or blurting out words I'm not prepared to hear. Obviously, the method to madness is actual madness. Oops.

After a few hard slaps to the chest and half a bottle of water later, Cora's skin looks a little less red and blotchy. Elizabeth continues to cough, but at least it's calming down.

"Sorry," I say on a wince.

Cora lays a hand on mine and shakes her head. "Don't apologize," she croaks out, then coughs to clear her throat more. "I knew something was up, but I didn't think it was that."

"But you said…" I furrow my brows. "At the hospital yesterday…" I drop my gaze to her box of garlic tofu. "You were joking…"

Why the hell can I not finish a damn thought aloud?

"Shell, it *was* a joke." She squeezes my hand and I lift my line of sight back to hers. "With Clara born only months ago, Ryker yesterday… I would've said it to Peyton, but I know she and Micah aren't planning to have kids." She shakes her head subtly. "Shell, I didn't mean anything by it." Concern mars her forehead. "Is that why you ran from the room? Why you disappeared?"

"Not just from what you said." I shake my head. "But it kind of sent me into a thought spiral. Before I knew it, I felt nauseous. So I ran for the bathroom."

The three of us sit at the table as I recant the rest of the evening and earlier this morning. My initial shocked state and Devlyn's after the call from the hospital. My moment of panic when Devlyn froze. How I thought that he didn't want to do this, that he couldn't do this. Be together. Have a baby. Any of it.

And then I tell them when the moment of realization hit. While I sat on the side of the road and cried until it struck me what I'd done. That I just got in my car and left. That I ignored Devlyn as he hollered for me to stay. Then when I turned around and drove back, how I found him in the driveway. Cold and shaking and in full crisis mode.

That was the second time I found Devlyn curled in on himself. I pray it is the last.

He looked so scared. In pain. And in that moment, I hated the spontaneous choice I'd made. Getting in my car and leaving had been irrational and juvenile. To just walk away without talking more, without listening…

I will never do that again. To him or us.

The bell rings out front and Elizabeth rises from her chair. "I'll be back." She bends and kisses my crown. "Keep talking, sweetheart."

Not a second after Elizabeth leaves the room, Cora rises from her chair, yanks me from mine, and pulls me into the tightest hug. "I don't know how you expect me to feel, Shell." She loosens her hold and inches back to look me in the eye. "But

I'm happy for you." The corners of her lips turn up as she smiles brightly. "Things may be crazy for a bit, but you will be an amazing mother."

I purse my lips as my brows shoot up. "You say that now, but this gal"—I point to myself—"is freaking out. A lot."

She drops her hold on me and we park ourselves back in the chairs. Cora spears a piece of broccoli and tofu while I stab curried chicken. For a moment, we sit in amicable silence. We eat lunch like we would any other day. Me and Cora. Two best friends spending time together.

"I freaked out too," Cora says after a few bites. "Ask Gavin. We'd been back together barely two years. Irrational as it was, I thought he might leave again." She laughs without humor. "Although we were happy—are happy—I thought an unplanned pregnancy would send him away." She shakes her head, her eyes glassy. "But it didn't, Shell. He was so happy. So damn happy. I'd never seen him light up like that. It was that look, that one moment... I knew we'd be okay." Setting her fork down, she reaches for my hand again. "And you will be too."

I tighten my hold on her hand. "How can you be so sure?" I whisper-ask.

Her smile brightens the room. "Because he chased after you. Asked you not to leave. Cried in the driveway when you left. Then he opened his arms up again when you returned. He took you into the house and you talked. You made breakfast and plans."

For the umpteenth time today, my eyes burn with the promise of tears. When I walked out Devlyn's front door in a fit of anxiety, I was one step closer to messing all of this up. Ready to throw in the towel without giving him a chance. I didn't get far, thank goodness. It's almost as if fate intervened. As if something bigger than me stopped me from making a huge mistake.

"What do I do now?"

Cora points to my lunch. "Eat." She laughs. "Take a minute to breathe and soak it all in. Yes, it's big. Huge. Life changing." She picks up her own fork and takes a bite. "But it's also incredible, Shell." She looks over at Clara sleeping in her stroller. "There's good and bad days. And yours will be different than mine." Her eyes find mine again. "But it's all worth it. My first piece of advice—the only one I'll give today—is to talk to your gynecologist. If they're an OB-GYN, you're golden. If not, they'll direct you where to go next." She sips her water. "And the rest of us will always be here. You have us. And Devlyn."

For a first-time mother of an infant, Cora is giving me a confidence boost. She and Gavin still navigate being new parents, but her calm reassurances settle some of the anxiety. Instinct told me she and Elizabeth were the right people to tell first. And who knows, I may wait until after my first official doctor's appointment to mention anything to Mom. That will give Devlyn and I time to adjust a little more before Mom shrieks in joy and asks unnerving questions.

"Thank you," I say. "Somehow, I knew you'd alleviate some of my worry."

"You never have to thank me, Shell. That's what best friends are for. You'd do the same for me in a heartbeat." It's true, I would. "So, when are you telling Mama Reed?"

I wince. "Uh, not for a bit. I want to see the doctor first. Give myself and Devlyn a little more time to process this before the big reveal." I shake my head on a laugh. "Mom doesn't even know we're dating. Doesn't know Devlyn exists. So, not only will I be saying, *'hey Mom, meet my boyfriend, Devlyn.'* I will also be saying, *'and by the way, we're pregnant. Woo!'* I close my eyes and take a deep breath. "Swear to god, if the first thing out of her mouth is wanting to know when we'll get married, I will lose my shit." I startle and look to Clara. "I mean cool. Lose my cool."

Cora laughs. "Shell, it's okay. Clara has no clue what we're saying right now. Down the road, yes, the alternate swear words will be in full force. For now, you're fine." She scoops up another bite. "And I promise not to say anything to anyone else. Not until you give the green light."

Elizabeth walks back into the room and joins us at the table. "What'd I miss?"

Over noodles, rice and veggies, I share with Elizabeth everything I did with Cora. She, too, promises not to say anything until I give the go-ahead. Then she hugs me, tighter and harder than ever. She assures me everything will be fine. She tells me not to worry about the shop, that she will be here until I am ready and able to handle the change. Of course, I cry. Because today is the day to cry until my eyes puff like clouds.

And when lunch ends, I feel lighter and more stable on my feet.

After the call this morning, it felt like someone had grabbed me by the ankles and held me upside down. Now, I feel strong enough to walk. To move forward. To handle this big change in my life with more confidence.

four
DEVLYN

"How does that make you feel?"

I love and loathe therapy. Getting in my car twice a week to drive to an office across town to talk about my feelings, about my past, about what makes my blood boil and my mind abandon reality is just… awkward and relieving and unnerving.

I thoroughly enjoy the opportunity to vent. To expel the darkness that has plagued me longer than I allowed myself to realize. To shed weight I didn't realize I carried.

What I don't like is the aftermath. The emotions stirred up during each session. Emotions I walk out the door with and sort through in the days between sessions. Emotions I must process, but don't want to expose to Shelly.

The first session after my consultation, I left the office in a mass of confusion. We'd barely scratched the surface, but my mother had been a huge topic of discussion. It *hurt* to talk about her. Not just my head, but also my heart. Because the more I talk about her, the more it registers how much she *doesn't* love me. Her definition of love is warped. Whatever makes her feel important, puts her in the spotlight, has people fawning over her… that is her version of love. For Karen Templar, love has a price tag.

How sick and twisted. And sad.

During our first session, after my need to pause and take several deep breaths, Dr. Prince had said, *"You can't move past this if you don't process it."* I have to let in the feelings I concealed for years. Unearth all the memories that once seemed loving and innocent, so I can dissect and process them with a fresh perspective.

So that is what I have been doing. Processing.

And processing hurts. Profusely.

"Afraid," I answer.

Dr. Prince tilts his head and reads my expression a moment before jotting something on the notepad in his lap. "Can you elaborate? Share why you feel afraid."

Elaborate. I don't *want* to elaborate. But I *need* to open up and expand. Spread my wings. Peel back the layers and expose my heart. Let the poison spill from my veins so I can move on, move past my fears. Move forward.

My eyes shift to the window, to the somber gray sky through the cracked wooden blinds. To the semibare branches of a tree. The day as moody as I feel. For two deep breaths, I close my eyes. Give in to my fears and let them take over. Give myself permission to voice the thoughts haunting me since learning Shelly was pregnant.

I am safe here.

"What if I become her?" I open my eyes and meet Dr. Prince's gaze. My fingers toy with the bottom of my hoodie while my leg bounces uncontrollably. "What if I do to my own child what my mother has done to me? Suppress them. Make them feel less important, less than human. Worthless. Trivial."

Dr. Prince scribbles on his notepad. "Tell me an occasion when you felt suppressed or worthless."

A fist wraps around my heart. Squeezes the pounding organ until it quivers, until it begs for relief. I rock slowly in place on the sofa. Take a deep breath. Then another.

I hate this. Digging up my demons and letting them trample over my soul. Letting them sink their claws a little deeper. Chip away at what heart I have left before I vanquish them.

I get it. The process is a necessary evil. But *fuck*… it rips me apart.

"When I was eight, my school hosted an art fair for students in third through fifth grade. We'd been working on a special project since the start of the school year. Each student drew a word from a hat and was told to create something that made them think of that word. We could draw or paint or paste magazine clippings. Whatever we had access to. Whatever called to us. My word, ironically, was love."

I clamp my lips between my teeth, take a deep breath then continue.

"Love means something different to each of us. My eight-year-old brain had difficulty processing the term. Had difficulty explaining love in the form of art. Even at that age, art was the one thing I loved most." The backs of my eyes sting. "I don't think I really knew human love. I had a warped perception of it."

Leaning forward, I swipe my bottled water from the table and take a sip. "On the night of the art fair, I was giddy for my mother to see my artwork. Far back as I can recall, she's worked in museums. Art existed in her life each day. I'd been so proud of my mixed-medium painting. The clipping of two people smiling at each other. I'd added various shades of red. Painted over the magazine page around the people." I laugh without humor. "For my age, it was remarkable. My teacher raved over the piece and instilled me with so much hope. Told me how talented I was. That I'd be an incredible artist one day. Have my work on display for the masses." I tip my head back and blink a few times before leveling my gaze. "That teacher made me feel loved. More than my own mother."

I lift my hand to my hoodie strings and fiddle with the strands. "We made our way around the room and my mother criticized each piece harshly. As if children should be perfectionists. As if children shouldn't create art unless it will win awards and sell for thousands of dollars." My vision glazes over. "She didn't even know she was degrading my piece until she finished speaking."

The only words I remember hearing that night were trash and sloppy and hideous.

"When her eyes dropped to the small paper placard and she saw my name, I'd never seen my mother so disgusted. Her lip curled as she looked down on my wilting frame. She said, *'I'm disappointed, Devlyn. I expected better from you. You know what real art looks like. I never want to see such trash again. It's embarrassing. You're a Templar. Remember that next time you pick up a brush or pencil. Don't throw my name in the garbage.'*"

The first round of tears this session spills down my cheeks. The salty drops sear my skin as they trail to my chin. I swipe them away and shift my gaze to the window again. To the gloomy sky that matches my mood. Mercurial and lusterless and meh.

"I know sharing that moment wasn't easy, Devlyn. Thank you for being brave enough to share it with me." I nod and swing my gaze back to him. "Processing years of pain will take time. But each time you choose to come here and speak with me, it's a step forward. One step closer to healing." His pen scratches against the pad of paper. "How've things been with Shelly?"

My soul sighs and breathes easier with the subject change. The heavy thoughts from a moment ago drift off. Fade to background. Make room for the light to enter. My peace. My heart.

"Great." My cheeks sting as my lips stretch into a wide smile. "We have our first appointment with the doctor today."

"That's wonderful, Devlyn. Have you and Shelly talked further about the future? What either of you want it to look like?"

At the end of my Thursday session last week, Dr. Prince gave me a *homework assignment*. To sit down with Shelly and talk about my feelings. Not just the way I feel about her, but how I feel about all the changes happening in both our lives.

He also asked me to voice my desires. What I want my future with Shelly to look like.

Three months have passed since Shelly and I officially started dating. The two months prior were a bit rocky. Unstable due to my uncertainty more than hers. But in the past five months, I have never been more in tune with someone. More certain of what I want. More confident of the path I want to walk in life, with Shelly at my side every step of the way.

What I don't know is if Shelly is ready to walk the same path.

"Yes and no." When I don't expand, Dr. Prince asks me to elaborate. Secretly, I think *elaborate* is his favorite word. "I told her I want to be involved during the pregnancy. That I want to be there for her. The things left unsaid, well… I fear she may panic if I say them aloud."

"Like what?"

My fingers toy with my hoodie strings once more. "Am I crazy for wanting to ask her to move in? Is it too soon in our relationship?" I zero in on the fraying end of the string and sigh. "I don't want her to think the only reason I'm asking is because she's carrying our baby." I drop my chin to my chest and close my eyes. "It's not the only reason."

As many notes as Dr. Prince writes during our sessions, he'll undoubtedly have a novel before the end of the year. His notes are a point of reference, a way to chart my growth. I know this. He told me this. But sometimes I wonder if he takes medication after our sessions. If my long list of issues is too much for even him. He never seems put off or out of sorts, but I still wonder how he manages to breathe after such intense talks.

"First of all, not all relationships evolve at the same pace. Some couples wait years before living together. Some want to marry beforehand. And others move in together and get married in under six months. No two relationships are the same, Devlyn. There is no rule book on when to take the next step. Whether it's sex or cohabitating or nuptials. You and Shelly have to go at the pace that feels right for you both. In order to know the pace, you have to communicate." He glances at his watch and notes we only have another five minutes. "Before our next session, I'd like you to talk more with Shelly. Voice your fears with her. As many as you feel comfortable sharing. Then ease into the conversation about where you want your future to go with her."

Expose my fears and tell Shelly I want her to move in.

Nausea rolls in my stomach. My mind screams to back down. My heart begs me to wait. To hit pause. Because the last time I was so utterly vulnerable to someone I loved, they squashed me with pointy heels.

"I'll do my best," I say with a nod, as if to assure myself.

"There's no pressure, Devlyn." He sets the pen and pad of paper on the table. "If you go to bring up the future, but the timing doesn't feel right, drop it. This isn't a race. There's no prize for reaching the finish line before others. This is about progress. About letting go of what doesn't serve you and making room for what you want in your life. It won't happen overnight. And you shouldn't expect it to."

Let go of what doesn't serve me. I never thought about anything that way, but I like how it sounds.

"Thanks, Dr. Prince."

We both rise from our seats and he walks me out. "See you in a few days, Devlyn."

I unlock the car, slip into the driver's seat and crank the engine. While the cab warms, I recall Dr. Prince's words. *"This is about progress. About letting go of what doesn't serve you and making room for what you want in your life."*

To let go of my mother and all the subliminal pain she inflicted over the years, I need to rehash the memories that hold me prisoner. The memories that diminish and suffocate. The memories that make me feel less than worthy. That makes me feel undeserving. That hinder me from moving forward, from growing.

I need to let her go so I can let Shelly in fully. Let her shine her love and light on all the dark places. Cast away the demons and shadows. Replace the hurt with affection and passion. Help me heal and grow and move forward.

And if I am lucky enough, Shelly will say yes. When I ask her to move in, she will agree with my favorite smile and a resounding yes.

five

Think I'm going to be sick.

I pause at the entrance of the doctor's office. Brace my hand on the wall. Take a deep, cleansing breath. Then another. Close my eyes and allow the cool air to settle the chaos in my stomach. After a third deep breath, the nausea subsides. A little. Enough for me to stand straighter and trudge forward.

Do all medical facilities use the same lemon-scented bleach?

Ugh. This is going to be a long, *however many months I have left* pregnancy.

At least I haven't thrown up since the day at the hospital. Puking is the worst. The. Worst. Need someone to hold your hair while you hurl into the porcelain throne? I am *not* the gal to ask. Don't care how tight we are, don't care how many years we have known each other, if you bow to the porcelain throne, I will run the other direction.

I check in at the reception desk and am handed several pages on a clipboard with a pen.

When I called to set the appointment with my regular gynecologist—who also specializes in obstetrics, lucky me—the woman on the phone told me new paperwork is necessary. Standard form updates plus new documents for the pregnancy appointments and a more thorough family history.

I'd rather fill out new paperwork than have to visit a new doctor.

Halfway down the first page, the door to the office opens and Devlyn walks in. The remaining bit of my nausea vanishes at the sight of him.

Slipping off his sunglasses, our gazes lock. A brilliant smile lights his face as he walks in my direction. Warmth embraces me in an everlasting hug. He takes the seat next to mine. Curls his fingers around my elbow, leans in and presses his lips to mine.

Damn, I will never tire of him. Not the smile he reserves only for me. Not his gaze that heats my blood. Nor the simple yet potent way he caresses my skin with his masterful hands.

Not sure if I can pinpoint what it is about Devlyn that calls to my soul, but he quiets the noise. Grants a sense of peace I didn't know existed until him. Bestows me with love I hoped was possible, but never experienced until he entered my world. And he just makes me feel… alive.

"Am I late?"

I shake my head as I work to calm my heart. "No. I got here a few minutes early to fill out paperwork." I hold up the clipboard. "Should finish before they call us back."

"Need help?"

"Maybe with health questions when I get to the family history section." He nods, then sits back and wraps an arm around my shoulders. His thumb paints small circles on my upper arm, distracting me from my task.

Devlyn is my favorite distraction.

I trudge through most of the paperwork on my own. When I reach the family history page, Devlyn chimes in with what he knows about his family. High blood pressure on his father's side. Ovarian cancer on his mother's side. For the most part, my family history is boring. Grandma Reed had diabetes, but not until later in life. Other than that, our slate is pretty clean.

"Shelly," a female voice calls out. I peer up from the clipboard to see a nurse at the doorway leading to the patient rooms. "Come on back." Devlyn and I rise from the seats and walk toward the nurse hand in hand. She steps aside to let us pass, then closes the door behind us. "Hi Shelly, I'm Ramona. Don't think we've met yet." She extends her hand to me, then Devlyn. Next, she hands me a small plastic cup with a sealed lid. "We need to collect a sample before heading back."

This part of the visit isn't new.

I take the cup from Ramona, ask Devlyn to hold my purse, then enter the restroom to the right. Once the cup is full and the lid secured, I set the sample in the pass-through box in the room, wash up and exit.

Outside the restroom, Ramona has me step on a scale, measuring my weight and height. After noting the numbers in my chart, she walks us to the patient room and closes the door behind us. Paper crinkling echoes in the room as I sit on the exam table. Devlyn parks himself in the extra seat off to the side while Ramona sits on a wheeled stool after washing her hands.

"How has your health been since your last visit, Shelly?" Ramona asks as she wraps a blood pressure cuff around my bicep.

"Good. No changes. Except the obvious," I say on a nervous laugh.

She peels the cuff away and jots numbers down in my chart. "Blood pressure looks good." Grabbing the thermometer from the counter, she holds it a couple inches from my forehead until it beeps. "Temp is normal."

Her warm gaze lifts from the stack of papers in my file and meets mine. Over the next few minutes, Ramona asks a series of questions. Most of which I am used to answering at my regular checkups. Today, though, new questions get added to the mix. Questions about sexual partners and methods of protection and what changes I have noticed in diet, sleep and mood. The questions aren't awkward or uncomfortable. Devlyn knows the answers as much as I do.

Ramona rises from the stool and tucks my chart under her arm. "Dr. Webster will be in shortly." Then she exits the room.

Wood squeaks against the linoleum as Devlyn scoots his chair closer to the exam table. He wraps my hand in his, then lifts it to his lips. "Doing okay?"

My blues lock onto his greens as a small smile plumps my cheeks. My shoulders lift in a half shrug. "Yeah. It's just a lot." I lift my free hand to cup his cheek and he leans into my touch. "But we got this."

He rotates his head and kisses the inside of my palm. "We do."

A soft knock on the door interrupts our quiet moment. Dr. Webster enters the room with a cheery smile on her face. Not a single visit to her office goes by without her beaming disposition.

Before I found Dr. Webster, I'd visited a couple other gynecologists in the area. Of the three doctors, Dr. Marianne Webster made me the most comfortable. Her office and staff were warm, inviting and relaxed yet still professional. Every time I walked through the doors, I never felt like a number or just another patient to cash in on. And that stood out the most.

"Hi, Shelly." She smiles brighter then shifts her attention to Devlyn. "And you must be Dad. I'm Dr. Webster." She extends her hand and Devlyn freezes for two breaths before taking it.

Dad. She just called him Dad. Cue the waterworks.

"Devlyn," he chokes out before clearing his throat. "Excuse me. Devlyn. It's nice to meet you."

The next thirty minutes are filled with more questions—from Dr. Webster and us—answers and too much information. Of all the details she shares, one piece sticks out the most. Roots itself deep in my memory. Imprints itself on my heart. My expected due date.

September twenty-first.

The moment Dr. Webster says the date, Devlyn squeezes my hand a little tighter and we share similar smiles.

Dr. Webster tells us the date can change from one appointment to the next, but based on dates in my paperwork, September twenty-first falls in line. Next, she goes over what to expect in the coming months. The number of appointments and what to expect during visits at specific week markers. When she will order the first ultrasound. Changes I will experience, if I haven't already, physically as well as emotionally and mentally. She discusses diet and exercise and creating healthy habits now. Vitamins and changes I should experience in the first trimester.

Information overload is an understatement, yet I feel as if I need more.

She removes a gown from the cabinet, asks me to dress down for a pelvic exam and excuses herself from the room. While I disrobe, Devlyn looks at his fumbling hands in his lap. Although we've had sex several times, his timidity as I peel off my clothes in the doctor's office comes as a surprise.

Back on the table, I reach for his hand and lace our fingers together. "Doing okay?"

He nods and gives my fingers a gentle squeeze. "Yeah. Just trying to remember everything she said." His eyes widen for a beat. "It's a lot of information."

I chuckle and he joins in. "Agreed. Lucky for us, we'll walk out with a folder full of brochures."

Leaning forward, Devlyn kisses my temple. "Love you."

I tighten my hold on him as his words wrap around my heart. "Love you, too."

Dr. Webster performs a routine pelvic exam and Pap smear since my last appointment was more than six months ago. Since I had a blood panel done at the hospital and provided a copy with my paperwork, I luckily get to bypass more needle sticks.

Just when I think Dr. Webster is going to exit the room and let me redress, she rolls a cart closer to the exam table and grabs a tube of gel.

"Seeing as you're roughly five to six weeks, I don't want to set any expectations." My brows pinch together as she holds the gel tube over my abdomen. "Going to see if we can hear a heartbeat yet."

My own pulse kicks up a notch and whooshes behind my ears. In my periphery, Devlyn rises from his seat and inches closer to the exam table. His hand seeks mine once more and clutches it tightly.

This is really happening. I'm pregnant. With Devlyn's baby. Our baby. And we may hear a heartbeat.

"Just relax," Dr. Webster says, and I take a deep breath. "This might be a little chilly."

She squeezes a dollop of gel onto my lower abdomen and I startle. Devlyn strokes his thumb over my knuckles. Back and forth. Again and again. Settling my nerves and steadying my heart.

Dr. Webster picks up a wand attached to the machine on the cart and presses it to the gel on my belly. For three breaths, the room falls completely silent. Not a peep as the goop smears my belly. And then a strange but quiet, pulsing sound filters through the air.

Whoosh. Whoosh. Whoosh.

Such a strange sound. Like the rapid push and pull of water.

I look up at Dr. Webster in question. Her beaming smile is all the answer I need. The whooshing sound…

"Is that?" My gaze shifts to Devlyn and I see the same question in his eyes.

"Your baby's heartbeat?" Dr. Webster finishes and we both nod. "It is." She moves the wand and the sound intensifies. "Definitely six to seven weeks along." Then the sound vanishes as she removes the wand. She wipes the gel from my belly and closes the front of the gown. "I'll step out and let you change. Then we'll go over what to expect at your next appointment before you leave."

After I redress, she comes back in with a large envelope filled with brochures and resources. She shares what to expect at my next appointment in a month. And before she steps away from the checkout area, she gives me a brief hug and congratulates us once more.

With my next appointment scheduled, Devlyn and I exit the office hand in hand. He walks me to my car and pauses near the driver's side door.

"Hungry?"

My stomach grumbles as I say, "Yes."

"Why don't you head to the house and I'll stop at the store. Any requests?"

I shake my head. "Surprise me."

Devlyn dips down and presses his lips to mine. "I'll be quick."

As I settle in the driver's seat, Devlyn jogs to his car. I wave to him as he drives off. And then, for a moment, I sit in the parking lot and absorb the reality of today.

Yes, I knew I was pregnant. But after hearing the heartbeat… the reality of it *really* sank in.

"I'm going to be a mom," I whisper to myself. My hands settle on my lower abdomen and cradle the still flat area. I breathe deeply and close my eyes. "Wow."

Then, my little bliss bubble pops.

Time to buck up and tell Mom. *Please… someone save me.*

Six

DEVLYN

"I'm sorry, what?"

A loud clang vibrates the air as Shelly's fork falls to her plate. Her brows pinch at the middle and eyes narrow as she regards me across the table. My heart beats a vicious rhythm while I internally cringe.

I set my fork down, take a deep breath and lift my line of sight to hers.

Remember Dr. Prince's suggestion. Talk with Shelly. Share my fears. Tell her my desires for the future.

"I'd like us to move in together," I say, my voice quieter. Smaller. Meek. My palms damp and fingers twitchy as I swipe them over my denim-clad thighs.

The room fills with eerie silence. Across the table, Shelly sits frozen in place. No shift in posture or facial expression. Her eyes still on mine, but unmoving. Unyielding. I don't sense anger—which settles my anxiety a degree or two—but, for the life of me, I can't pick up what exactly she *is* feeling. Her stillness, her voicelessness, the uneasy energy around her… it has me concerned. Off balance. Scared. Lost.

If I were in my studio upstairs, painting her in this very moment, she'd be haloed in burnt orange—a color I don't typically associate with Shelly. Not due to indignation. No, the color would represent the disorientation pulsing off her. And perhaps a hint of fear.

It's okay. I'm afraid too.

"Please say something," I say just above a whisper.

Her chest rises and falls as she inhales a deep breath. She licks her lips, traps them between her teeth a moment, then releases them on a swallow.

"Devlyn, I…" Her eyes lose focus for two breaths before she blinks a few times. "Isn't it too soon?"

I twist my hands in my lap beneath the table and ask myself the same question for the hundredth time since learning Shelly was pregnant. *How soon is too soon to live together?* Dr. Prince said there are no written guides to dictate when couples take the next step. Only we determine our time line. Our future.

My shoulders rise and fall. "It doesn't feel wrong."

Wanting Shelly in every aspect of my life has never felt so *right*. Is moving in together after dating three months a premature decision? Probably. Considering I let no one in for four years after Kelsey, this change may be deemed irrational and foolish and swift. A decision made in the heat of the moment. An open invitation to doom our relationship.

But I don't care what other people think. I only care what Shelly thinks. What she wants.

"Can I think about it?"

Every joy-filled cell in my body plummets. Wilts. Turns cold. "Yeah. Sure. Of course."

What else can I say? Shelly is her own person. Makes her own decisions. I need to let her make this decision as well. Having a baby together doesn't automatically equal cohabitation. It doesn't mean our romantic relationship will last forever.

But I want it all with her.

Taking a deep breath, I remind myself that she loves me and I love her. Her asking for time to make a decision is better than her shooting the idea down immediately. Not like I haven't mulled over the idea for days. Only fair that I let her do the same.

She could've said no and walked out the door. Give her time.

After a beat of silence, she picks up her fork and I mimic the action. We eat dinner in companionable silence for a few bites. In my periphery, she sips her water, then gingerly sets down the glass. Her fingertips swirl over condensation droplets, her eyes zeroed in on the action.

"While I consider the idea of moving in" —I lock onto her mesmerizing eyes and stop chewing— "will you think about meeting my parents?"

The bite of chicken in my mouth lodges in my throat. I smack my chest and cough violently. My face and neck and chest go hot as I attempt to dislodge the food from the wrong pipe.

"Oh god."

Shelly evacuates her chair and dashes to my side. *Whack.* Her palm smacks between my shoulder blades with force. *Whack. Whack.* I cough harder and the food clears my windpipe.

"Are you okay?"

I nod as my lungs burn and beg for air. Grabbing her hand, I bring it to my lips and kiss her between coughs. "I'm—" *Cough, cough.* "Fine." Tears spill down my cheeks as I hold up a finger, asking her to give me a moment.

Her hand rubs small circles between my shoulder blades. The gentle motion calming, soothing. And soon, my lungs settle. My throat stills. I take a sip of water. Then another.

"Better?"

I nod. "Yeah." My voice like froggy sandpaper. I swallow a bigger gulp of water. "Much."

Shelly settles back in her chair and shakes her head. "I seem to have a talent for saying things at the wrong time." I cock my head as my brows scrunch together. "When I told Cora and Elizabeth I was pregnant, they both nearly choked on their lunch." She rolls her eyes and laughs under her breath. "Really should work on *when* to say certain things."

Setting my glass down, I lay a hand on the table, palm up. She places hers atop mine and I sigh.

My skin warms and tingles at the point of contact. Our connection a live wire. Buzzing. Sparking. White hot and a constant burst of light.

The pulse never dulls. The magnitude never fades or shrinks. If anything, what I feel for Shelly, the connection we share, it continually expands. Like the birth of a new galaxy. Mighty and endless.

This… her hand in mine… this is all I need.

"It's okay. Maybe next time, ease into it." We laugh until the reason I started choking circles back. "I'd love to meet your parents, Shelly. Whenever you're ready. Wish mine were worth meeting," I say with a hint of solemnity.

Shelly squeezes my hand and my eyes dart to hers. "Me too."

We finish dinner and talk about the first of many visits to the doctor's office. After I clear the table, Shelly and I snuggle on the couch and watch television. Her head on my shoulder, it isn't long before she falls asleep and I carry her to bed.

As she sleeps in my arms, I lie in the dark and mentally paint a picture of what our life will be like. When the baby comes and the years that follow.

I see it all so clearly. As if it already exists, but I have yet to live it.

Shelly and I existing in the same space. Living together. Loving each other. I see her brilliant smile and flushed cheeks as we hold our child for the first time. How she will turn my house into a home. Paint the walls with her warmth. Add small touches of joy and hope. Introduce a level of love that only exists within her. Love I want, crave, live for each day.

The mental picture soothes my soul in an unfamiliar way. Settles the unease I have over Shelly not instantly agreeing to move in together.

And as I drift off to sleep, one thought plays on repeat. I will do whatever it takes to make the image in my head a reality.

Whatever it takes.

seven

Why does it feel like every day something major happens? Where the hell did all the simple days go? Get up, go to work, eat, sleep, rinse, repeat—plus time with friends and Devlyn.

Since the day my phone rang and the nurse from the hospital told me I was pregnant, every day is filled with some form of chaos.

Okay, not exactly chaos. But is there an actual term for the craziness scale? Lunacy level. Madness meter. Deranged degree. Psycho scale. There is probably some technical term, but I have no clue what it is.

Most of my life, I have been in the chill zone. Low key. Easy, peasy, lemon squeezy. But now… now everything is pure madness. Constantly midscale or higher.

Tonight, life is reaching the high end of the scale. And I'm not sure how much more crazy I can handle. Tonight is dinner night with the family. With my *when will you get married and have two-point-five kids* mom and my dad that looks at her as if she does no wrong.

Someone… *please* help me. Help us.

Poor Devlyn is sweaty and pale, and it's maybe sixty degrees on my parents' front porch as we hesitate to step inside. Thank god, Micah and Peyton are already here. Although neither of them know about the pregnancy, at least they have met Devlyn. Not everything will be a complete shock with them.

I lace my fingers with Devlyn's and inhale deeply as I glance up at him. "You ready for this?"

His eyes meet mine as he squeezes my fingers tighter. "Yes. No." He pinches his eyes tight for a beat. "Yes. Your parents are a million times better than mine. Guess I'm just worried about your dad or brother choking me after the news." He gives me a sheepish smile.

Pushing up on my tiptoes, I kiss his cheek. "I'll keep you safe." A promise I plan to always keep.

"Pinkie promise?" He offers me his little finger.

Without hesitation, I hook my pinkie with his. "Promise."

Devlyn has yet to divulge all the secrets of his past. Can't say I blame him. It's a lot for him to unpack, to relive. But he has shared bits and pieces, and that is enough. The strength it must take to share such truths… his bravery astounds me daily.

In twenty-two years, he has endured a lifetime of heartache. Most of which occurred in the four walls he called home. The saddest part of all, he didn't comprehend how catastrophic his homelife had been until he left for college. Until he lived in and experienced the world. Gained new peers that came from loving homes. Met friends' parents and professors that never said an untoward or demeaning statement.

Devlyn had been hurt in ways I will never fathom. I don't know and couldn't possibly understand the hardships he experienced. With all he's dealt with, I also refuse to pressure him to share. In his own time, when he feels safe doing so, he will give me those pieces of him. And until that day arrives, I will stand by his side. Be a pillar of strength when he needs someone to hold him upright. Give him time and space when his mind won't quiet. Hug him impossibly tight for hours when it all feels too much. Lend an ear and a shoulder when he chooses to spill his bottled-up pain.

Digging up demons is no easy feat. Fighting those same demons alone is your worst nightmare times a hundred.

He won't fight his demons alone. I refuse to allow it. Not now. Not ever.

As my hand reaches for the handle, Devlyn lifts his free hand to my cheek. His thumb strokes my cheekbone and I sigh, leaning into his touch. He leans in closer and I breathe him in. Inhale the earthy scent on his skin that reminds me of his studio, his drawings, the way he sees me. Then his lips are on mine. Slow and steady, soft and warm, bestowing me with unrivaled comfort and peace.

"Love you, my Andromeda," he whispers on my lips.

"Love you too." I take a deep breath. "Here we go."

I open the front door and lead us inside. As we toe off our shoes, a pungent smell hits my nose and my stomach rolls. My eyes fall shut as I inhale deeply and exhale slowly. Again and again.

Devlyn takes my elbow in his hand and brings his lips to my ear. "What's wrong?" Concern evident in his whispered tone.

I straighten and lift a hand to cover my nose and mouth. *Jesus. What the hell is for dinner?* Please do not let pregnancy ruin all the foods I love.

"Just the smell," I say as I drop my hand. "I'll be okay in a minute. I hope."

Thankfully, no one has caught wind of our entrance. We stand by the door as I take more breaths to settle my stomach. The nausea subsides for the most part. I slide my hand into Devlyn's and lace our fingers in a silent ready signal.

Now that my stomach is calmer, I zero in on the chatter and laughter spilling from the kitchen. No doubt, Mom has Micah cooking again while Dad and Peyton watch the show.

My brother has been such a trooper through it all. A year ago, he would have burned the house down making dinner for the family. But through his persistence and desire to be a better man for Peyton, he learned to navigate the kitchen like a certified chef. Mom was on standby, in case he needed help, but mostly stood there with a smile on her face. Pride in her eyes as she watched her son accomplish a task he never cared for until he met his wife.

On quiet feet, Devlyn and I round the kitchen island near Dad and Peyton. Peyton spots us first and spins on her stool, a warm and welcoming smile on her face.

"You haven't missed much of the show," she says as she slides off her stool and pulls us in for a hug.

"Good. I need these moments for posterity," I say on a laugh.

Peyton hugs Devlyn briefly before everyone catches on to our arrival. "Nice to see you again," she tells him. "No need to be nervous. Promise."

My favorite smile softens Devlyn's face as he thanks Peyton. Then Mom and Dad are footsteps away. Dad appears cool and collected. Mom, on the other hand, looks as if she is about to squeal like a tween at a boy band concert.

Please, I beg you, universe, don't let Mom scare Devlyn.

"Mom, Dad, this is Devlyn." I gesture to Devlyn, his arm snugly hooked in mine. "Devlyn, these are my parents, Nicole and George Reed."

Dad offers a warm smile and extends his hand. "Nice to meet you, Devlyn."

"You too, sir." Devlyn takes his offered hand and shakes.

Before their hands separate, Mom steps in and wraps her arms around Devlyn. My eyes widen more than Devlyn's as he looks to me for help. He doesn't *not* hug her back, but the embrace looks awkward from where I stand.

"Mom," I admonish. "Please don't frighten Devlyn."

It's a half joke. A way to lighten the mood, but also tell my mother to take her enthusiasm down a notch. She just met him for crying out loud. Yes, my mother is an exuberant woman, but I damn well know she doesn't hug strangers like this. Devlyn may not be a stranger to me, but he is to them.

She drops her arms and takes a step back. Then another. "I'm so sorry, Devlyn. Where are my manners?" Pink stains her cheeks. "Please, excuse my outburst. It's just—"

"Nicole," Dad says, resting a hand on Mom's shoulder. "Give the guy a moment to breathe."

"Yes, of course." She winces. "Sorry."

Well, well, well. The hug could have been predicted, but the embarrassment and apology, not so much. Not that Mom doesn't apologize when necessary, she does. In this circumstance, though, I expected her to wave it off like it was no big deal. To throw out some excuse as to why it'd be acceptable to embrace Devlyn so fiercely.

Hmm. How intriguing.

Stirring a pot on the stove, Micah glances over his shoulder and smiles at Devlyn. "Hey, man. Good to see you again."

Devlyn nods. "You too."

Mom resumes her spot in the kitchen near Micah while Dad and Peyton return to their stools. Devlyn pulls out the one beside Peyton and gestures for me to sit. After I do, he steps up behind me, wraps his arms around my waist, rests his chin on my crown and sighs. I rest my hands over his and give him a gentle squeeze, silently asking if he is okay. He answers by hugging my middle tighter and kissing my crown.

"What's for dinner?" I ask Peyton.

"With St. Patty's around the corner, Momma Reed thought corned beef and cabbage were a good idea. We're also having roasted carrots and potatoes."

Sautéed cabbage. That must have been what I smelled when we walked in the house.

Don't get me wrong, I love cabbage. Coleslaw, in salads, cooked. To be honest, I love most foods. But something about the cabbage scent when we walked in... it was foul. Maybe they added different seasoning to it.

It isn't long before Micah pulls the corned beef and roasted vegetables from the oven. Mom sets the serving dishes on the dining room table as Dad, Peyton, Devlyn and I rise from the stools.

The six of us sit around the table. Mom and Dad in their usual seats. Micah and I on the same side we've sat on since childhood, only now with someone special next to us.

As we fill our plates, I bypass the cabbage and pray it finds a resting place far from my seat.

"So, Devlyn," Mom starts. "What do you do for work?"

This is not an interrogation. This is my family getting to know Devlyn.

"Artwork. Oil painting, pencil drawings, charcoal. Whatever calls to me for the piece."

A flicker crosses Mom's face before her eyes widen. She stares at him for two breaths before her eyes dart between the two of us. "Oh my goodness." She sets her fork down and brings her hands to her lips in prayer. "Are you Devlyn Templar?" she asks, her tone filled with awe.

Devlyn spears a potato and nods, acting as if her local celebrity moment is no big deal. "Yes, ma'am."

Mom's eyes dart to me, then back to Devlyn. This happens three times before she finds her words again. "How long have you been dating?"

I know why she asks this question. The drawing she gifted to me for Christmas. She bought it off a local artist's website. My reaction to the piece. Peyton's reaction. The pieces are slowly clicking into place in her mind.

Please don't let her give me grief for not broadcasting my relationship sooner.

"Since early December," I answer. "But we met back in October." My gaze shifts to Devlyn as I lay my hand on his thigh beneath the table. "He did some artwork at Petal and Vine."

For a split second, Mom's face falls at the time line. It doesn't take a genius to do the math. Devlyn and I have dated nearly three months. Have known each other five. That isn't what makes her face temporarily wilt. She doesn't have to say it, but I know it's because I didn't share the news sooner.

The Reed family isn't big on secrets. We share important details about our lives on a regular basis. But just as my brother didn't come right out in the beginning and tell our parents he and Peyton were dating, I followed suit. Not to hurt my parents. More to give myself time to adjust to the change. To see where our relationship went.

After what happened in my apartment the night of Devlyn's art show, had I told my mother sooner about a potential relationship, the update of our weeks apart would've been harder. Mom would have brought Devlyn up more often than not. Asked questions I wasn't prepared to hear or answer.

And my heart would have snapped sooner.

I love my mother, but she can be a handful at times.

"Oh." Two letters. One word. That is all she says as she picks up her fork. Then she blinks a few times and swallows. Pierces the beef on her plate and cuts off a smaller piece. "And the drawing we gave you at Christmas..." She doesn't finish her question before she shoves the fork in her mouth and meets my eyes that match hers. A coincidence she probably never considered when the art was purchased.

I squeeze Devlyn's thigh as he sits quietly at my side. "That's me," I say with a little too much exuberance, then laugh under my breath. "Well, it's mostly my eye. But you know what I mean." Across the table, Micah bites back a smile at my rushed words while Peyton's eyes drop to her plate. "What're you smiling at, *starlight*?" I tease my brother with an arched brow.

"Starlight?" Dad chimes in. "What the hell does that mean?"

Peyton and I burst out laughing while Micah and Devlyn pick at their dinner and my parents sit in a cloud of confusion.

"Dad, you of all people should understand. Between Micah's nickname and the drawing with the constellation in the iris." I gesture toward Mom. "Have you not noticed how identical my and Micah's eyes are to Mom's?"

Dad stares at Mom across the length of the table for two breaths. Then a soft smile plumps his cheeks. "Her eyes always remind me of the nights we used to camp in the woods. When there wasn't a light for miles. All you could see were thousands of stars." His eyes glaze over as his memories flood in from years past. "She's always been my favorite starry night."

My heart melts as I listen to Dad speak with so much love for Mom. After more than thirty-five years, they are just as in love today as they were back in their teens. If not more. And it is a beautiful and envious thing.

Dinner continues with less intense conversation. Talk about Micah and Peyton and business at Roar. Dad mentions his time line for selling the insurance firm in the next three to five years. He has an eye on the market and wants to make sure he sells before a downshift. Mom talks about trends she has noticed in marketing and the shift on how to advertise. She mentions helping me when I take over Petal and Vine at the start of next year.

At this, Devlyn fidgets in his seat. His leg bouncing beneath my hand.

Mom and Dad clear the table and suggest we head into the living room for dessert. While they are in the kitchen, we meander to the living room and sit on the love seat.

"What's going on?" Micah whisper-shouts from his seat on the couch.

Leave it to my brother to detect the blip in my radar. He may not be the most intuitive person on the planet, but when it comes to me, he knows when something is off.

"I'll explain when Mom and Dad come back." His eyes narrow. "Micah, please," I plead with him.

Devlyn wraps his arm around my shoulder and kisses my temple. "Deep breaths," he whispers in my ear. Inhaling deeply, I rest my head on Devlyn's shoulder, eyes still on Micah.

"Please," I whisper.

Mom and Dad enter the room with a loaded tray. Small portions of peach cobbler and a scoop of vanilla ice cream. They hand out dessert and spoons, then take their seat on the couch.

It's now or never. Devlyn's here. You can do this.

I set my bowl down on the table, not a bite taken. Mom looks at me with a furrowed brow and questions on the tip of her tongue.

"Mom, Dad." My eyes shift from them to Micah and Peyton then back. "Devlyn and I have some news." Unlike the last few times I announced something important, I wait until no one has food in their mouth.

"What is it, sweetheart?" Dad asks as he sets his bowl on the table.

I *feel* Micah's intense laser focus on me, but ignore it and push forward. Taking Devlyn's hand, I intertwine our fingers and form an invisible barrier to keep us strong.

"I'm pregnant."

The room goes silent. Scary silent. No one moves. No one says a word. But four sets of eyes *stare* at us. Hard. As if searching for answers as to how and when and why.

I understand why they're in shock. Hell, we were in shock too. But I at least expected Mom to be a bit more vocal and bouncy. How long has she been harping me and Micah for grandchildren? Close to two years.

My eyes land on her face and all I see is confusion and emptiness. And it is so disconcerting.

"Someone please say something," I whisper, although it filters through as a scream.

Of all the people I expected to speak up first, it wasn't Peyton. "Congratulations." She rises from her seat, sets her bowl on the table and walks across the room. Bending at the waist, she hugs me and Devlyn in turn. "Just give them a minute," she whispers between us and I nod.

The second she lands in her seat, it is as if a switch flipped. Micah pipes up next, his eyes glassy as he searches mine. "Are you happy?"

I love that this is his only concern. After all our conversations about relationships, my virginity, and how we both felt about the future, neither of us spoke deeply on the topic of children. Before Peyton, both of us were unsure. Once he and Peyton were serious, they'd decided to forgo starting a family. I fully supported my brother and Peyton's decision. Mom was harder to convince.

Last Micah knew, though, I was a virgin. Devlyn and I had been dating, but my brother knew I wouldn't take that major step easily. So this news also tells him how deeply I care for Devlyn. That he is much more than just another guy to date. After several conversations about my love life, or lack thereof, he knew no one fit the bill. Made a big enough impact for me to want more. My brother knew I'd been waiting for the right person.

"Yeah, big brother." I twist and lock onto my favorite shade of green. Lift Devlyn's hand to my lips and kiss his fingers. "I am."

"You know I had to ask."

I face him and smile. "I know."

"Are you getting married?"

Beside me, Devlyn stiffens. Can't say I blame him. If I were in his shoes, I would too. Mentally, I was prepared for such radical questions. Mom had peppered me and Micah with them for years. But I didn't quite prepare Devlyn, and that is on me.

"Nicole!" Dad shakes his head as his eyes widen at her. "Not the time."

Thanks for the rescue, Dad.

I lean into Devlyn and wait for his frame to relax. One, two, three breaths pass before his muscles soften beneath my touch.

"Better?" I whisper and he hums. "No offense, Mom, but Devlyn and I have more important priorities to consider right now." My tone is gentle and nonconfrontational. "We're still adjusting to the news ourselves."

"Have you been to the doctor?" she asks, her eyes softening at the edges.

This we can handle. Simple conversations about the pregnancy. Without asking, my parents have to know I am not that far along. Even if Devlyn and I had gotten pregnant early in December, I'd only be a few weeks further into pregnancy. Not enough for the naked eye to notice.

For the next hour, we finish our dessert, discuss doctor's appointments, and how pregnancy was for Mom. My pregnancy may be completely different from Mom's, but knowing her experiences gives me insight on how mine may go. After all, I favor her more than Dad.

When it's time to exchange hugs and goodnights, Mom makes me promise to check in after each appointment. She also tells me to update her more often. She won't admit it outright, but the double whammy tonight—meeting Devlyn and learning about the baby—caught her off guard. Probably bruised her heart.

My intention wasn't to hurt her. I wanted to wait until the time felt right for me and Devlyn. In this one thing, I should get to be a little selfish. Devlyn too.

After an endless hug from both my parents at the same time, the four of us head for our cars. We stop between the two cars and fumble over what to say next. Surprisingly, Devlyn is the first to break the silence.

"You should both come over for dinner one night."

Micah looks at me for a split second. Questions and emotions flit his expression. Although he won't come out and ask right now, I know he wants to ask if we are living together. Months have passed since the two of us last sat down for lunch and sibling catch-up. After tonight, it wouldn't shock me if he texts and sets up a brother-sister date.

"Sounds nice." A smile brightens Micah's face as he wraps an arm around Peyton's shoulders. "Just let us know when. Shell knows our schedule."

"Wonderful."

Devlyn's shoulders round as he visibly relaxes next to me. I hate how stressful this night must have been for him. Nervousness over meeting my parents. Worry over whether or not they'd like him as a person and approve of him to date their daughter. Unriddled anxiety over sharing news about the baby.

It had to have been a lot for him. He hid the tense moments well.

We exchange hugs one last time, get in our cars and go our separate ways.

I lace my fingers with Devlyn's and hold his hand the entire drive to the house. Keep my eyes on his profile and watch him as the streetlights zip past. Breathe in his earthy scent that has quickly become my favorite comfort. And fall for this beautiful man a little harder.

It may be too soon, but my answer is yes. Yes to moving in with Devlyn. Yes to sharing a home and life with him. Yes to everything us and our future.

But first, I need a minute. A little time to sort things out. To talk with Elizabeth about the shop and new time line for the sale. Talk with the apartment complex manager, seeing as I renewed my lease six months ago. And maybe I should talk with myself. Mull over what this next step means, not just for me but also Devlyn.

I just need a minute to breathe. Because this baby... they will change everything.

eight

"Can we stop at the store?"

I lift Shelly's hand to my lips and kiss her knuckles. "Of course. What do we need?"

"Antacids and more dessert."

Chuckling, I shake my head. "Sounds like a winning combination."

I steer the car into the grocery store parking lot and park in a spot near the front. With the lot almost empty, Sunday evenings at the supermarket look to be the best time for shopping. Good to know.

We hop out of the car and walk to the door hand in hand. The automatic doors whoosh open and I pick up a handbasket from the stack. Shelly guides us to the healthcare aisle first, grabbing the largest container of Tums from the shelf and tossing them in the basket.

She shrugs. "Probably going to need them all." I wouldn't care if she threw ten bottles in the basket. If she needs them, I will buy them.

"Any dessert in particular?"

"Maybe peanut butter cups and ice cream."

We stop in the aisle loaded with candy and chips next. I stand back and observe as Shelly eyes the Snickers and Reese's and Baby Ruth bars. She taps a finger against her lips. Darts her eyes from one to the other over and over. And when she finally decides, I laugh because she puts all three in the basket with a radiant smile on her face.

The ice cream aisle carries the same level of indecision. But after I add a pint of cookie dough in the basket, she reaches into the case and fetches a tub of the nondairy Ben and Jerry's P.B. & Cookies. I sense of trend. Lots of peanuts or peanut butter.

It's cute.

She is cute.

Damn, but I got lucky with Shelly. Our relationship could have ventured so many different directions from the path it took. But it didn't and I thank my lucky stars every day.

After experiencing heartbreak, I never pictured myself in this place. Happy. Excited about life. Eager to spend each day with another person. Loving someone again. Yearning for the future.

But here I am, ready for it all. Ready to share my future with someone I love. And I have never felt better.

With our dessert loaded into the basket, Shelly and I stroll hand in hand toward the checkout. We round the end of the ice cream aisle and I skid to a stop after one step. Shelly jerks back and looks at me over her shoulder.

She tugs on my hand. "Dev?" Her fingers squeeze mine tighter. "Are you okay?" I'd answer, but my lips won't move. My tongue refuses to form words. My voice box forgets how to vibrate the proper sounds. Shelly steps into me, frames my face with her hands, and looks me square in the eyes. "Devlyn," she whispers, a breath from my lips. "You're scaring me. What's wrong?"

After a beat, I blink. Take a slow, methodical breath. Swallow past the bubbling anxiety clawing its way up my throat. Shift my gaze and lock onto Shelly's starry-blue irises. Eyes that soothe me in ways nothing else does.

"My mother is here," I whisper almost inaudibly. Shelly starts to turn her head, but I grab her elbow. Switch her focus back to mine. "Please don't turn around." A surge of fear spreads through my bones and rattles me head to toe. The need to protect Shelly from her floods my veins.

"Where is she?" Shelly whispers.

"Two aisles down." I shake almost imperceptibly. "Don't think she saw us, but can't be sure." I close my eyes for two breaths. *Why is she here? She doesn't live on this side of the bay. So why is she shopping* here? "Just please… please wait a minute. I'm sure she'll—"

My words get cut off as my mother sidles up to us. "Devlyn, what on earth?"

Hours of therapy turns to dust in my head as my mother stares down at me with black eyes. In a blink, all rational thought leaves my body. And in its place… the scared little boy living inside me emerges. I don't speak. Don't know the first response to the situation. All I know is, I don't want to be here. I don't want to exist in the same space as her. Don't want to breathe the same air as her.

I need to leave. *We* need to leave. Now.

When I don't respond, she tackles me verbally. "I have been calling and texting and stopping by the house. What is the matter with you?" While she babbles on about how my lack of contact bothers her, I take note that she has yet to acknowledge Shelly. "Your father and I have been worried sick. Your behavior has made me absolutely sick."

I tighten my hold on Shelly and nudge forward, hoping she catches my signal to leave. I take a step and Shelly falls in line beside me. Then, she is the one tugging us faster to the checkout. As if she senses my absolute need to leave. To get out of this store and away from my mother, sooner rather than later.

All the while, my mother is on our heels, berating me loud enough for the entire grocery store to hear.

"You will not walk away from me, young man."

Shelly and I dart into the express line, toss our snacks on the belt and face the cashier with pained smiles.

"Look at me when I speak to you," she demands, but I don't comply.

Per Dr. Prince's advice, I carry on and try to push past the cold demands. Ignore the words that are meant to sound sad, but are actually a ploy to crush me with her pointy, overpriced heels.

The cashier scans our groceries and bags them quickly. *Thank you.* I slip my card into the reader and press the appropriate buttons to pay the bill. As soon as the receipt is in the bag, I swipe it from the counter, take Shelly's hand and dart for the exit.

"She'll leave you. Just like the last one did. Who will be there when she abandons you?"

I freeze just before the door. Close my eyes and grind my molars. Remind myself to breathe. Remind myself that she will use whatever manipulation tactic necessary to keep me exactly where she wants me. Alone and at her mercy.

Never again.

Shelly squeezes my hand. Snaps me back to the here and now. Reminds me of why I need to make a change. Why I need to vanquish the pain and hurt and misguidance of my past. For her. For our baby. A baby my mother will never know about. Ever.

"Let's go." Shelly's thumb strokes the top of my hand. "I got you." Without a backward glance, Shelly and I exit the store. When we reach the car, she makes me sit in the passenger seat. "It's better if you don't drive right now. You need a minute."

Behind the wheel, she cranks the engine, clicks her seat belt into place and throws the car in reverse. We zip out of the lot and drive slightly over the speed limit the entire way home. If we get pulled over, I'll gladly pay the fine to avoid one more second in the same space as Karen Templar.

Shelly parks the car in the driveway. And it's not until we are in the house, door locked and alarm set, that I finally take a full breath. Finally let everything that just happened sink in. I shiver from head to toe. Shelly drops the groceries at her feet and wraps her arms around my chest. She hauls me forward until not a breath of air resides between us. Then she hugs me with unimaginable force. It isn't strength. More like warmth and love and a promise to always pick me up when I fall.

Right there, near the entrance of the kitchen, I hold on to her as if my life depends on it. I hug her and cry into the crook of her neck. Sob and shake as years of pain and hurt spill from my body, from my soul.

"Let it all out." One of her hands is in my hair, the other squeezing my middle. "I got you." She kisses my shoulder. "I always have you."

When my tears slow, I lean back and cup Shelly's cheeks with my palms. "Love you so much." I press my lips to hers. Kiss her with unimaginable tenderness. "Don't know what I'd do without you."

A soft smile dons her lips and lifts the corners of her eyes. "Good thing you'll never find out." She kisses me chastely. "I love you more."

I highly doubt that.

nine

The bell jingles over the front door of Petal and Vine. I peek up from the arrangement in front of me to see an older couple. "Good afternoon," I greet them and lift my hand to wave.

They return the greeting with bright smiles, then wander the perimeter of the store. The woman runs her aged fingertips over the dried flowers and wispy grasses. Her eyes scan the bins before she leans forward and inhales the dried lavender, followed by the eucalyptus. The man with her follows two steps behind, hands clasped behind his back, eyes on her. A small smile highlights his weathered skin as he watches her with love in his eyes.

My first thought is that may be Devlyn and me one day. Meandering a store, one of us shopping while the other observes in companionable silence. Simply happy because we exist in the same space.

Then I shake off the errant thought.

My relationship with Devlyn hasn't broached six months yet. Although things are progressing quicker than imaginable, thinking about us together with gray hair and a hobble in our step is a bit of stretch. Although I don't foresee a day without Devlyn in my life, flashing forward to our retirement years isn't ideal.

While the couple scans the flower selection near the meadow painting, I covertly—at least I hope it's covertly—watch them. Watch the way she plucks stems from the pails and lifts them to smell before deciding whether to put it back or hold on to it for purchase. Then I shift my gaze to him. Watch the way he stands just a step back and off to the side. Watch the way he studies her every move with a keen eye and slightly leans in her direction. The longer I stare, the more my heart melts at the sight.

I *do* want that. The simple happiness of existing in the same space as someone you love. To find joy in the small things, like the way they look at a flower or brush the hair from their face.

"Brought you lunch."

I jump back, slap a hand to my chest and nearly knock over the vase of flowers I'd been working on. "Holy sh—" I pivot and catch sight of Devlyn. "Jesus. Make noise or something." Planting my palms on the table, I take a deep breath and give him my sharpest side-eye. "Scared the sh— crap out of me."

He leans in and kisses my temple. "To be fair, I did call your name. Twice, actually." His gaze drifts to the older couple. "But you were preoccupied."

"You did?"

A soft smile turns up the corners of his mouth as he notices what had my attention. "I did." His eyes drift back to mine as his smile deepens. "But I see why you were distracted. They're adorable to watch."

"That they are." I twist to face him fully. "You brought me lunch?"

He holds up a white paper bag. "Yes. Sandwiches from the deli. Hope that's good."

I nod as my stomach groans in agreement. "Let me go find Elizabeth so we can take lunch."

"Already done." Devlyn leans his hip on the heavy arrangement table. "When she let me in through the back, she said to give her a minute."

The words leave his lips just as Elizabeth enters the shop from the storage room. Sidling up to me, she lays a hand on my shoulder. "Go enjoy your lunch." I start to argue about not finishing the arrangement, but she sweeps it from the table and stows it in the storage cooler. "It'll be here when you're done. Now go."

Is this how it will be throughout pregnancy? Being parented, but not, all over again. Family and friends treating me as if I am fragile. Earlier, I went to pick up a box and Elizabeth rushed to my side. Told me not to lift it. The box weighed maybe seven pounds, which is nothing. Hell, most babies weigh that much when they are born.

I wish everyone wouldn't handle me as if I am breakable. Yes, I carry precious cargo, but my body is quite capable of physical activity. And while it's still possible, I'd like to do what my body will allow.

In the pamphlets I'd read, exercise and routine fitness are encouraged during pregnancy. Obviously certain movements and higher weights are off-limits, but lifting is permissible unless otherwise instructed by the doctor.

Inhaling deeply, I move past the notion that everyone will treat me with kid gloves. I remind myself they are looking out for me and the well-being of the baby. Their actions aren't meant to offend or suggest I am incapable. They love me and want the pregnancy to progress without hiccups.

"Got you the same sandwich as last time," Devlyn says as he pulls the food from the bag.

"Sounds perfect."

We take our seats and peel back the butcher paper around the sandwiches. Take the lid off the fruit cups. Dive into our sandwiches and enjoy the first bite as the flavors hit our tongues.

Except mine doesn't taste right. Or smell right.

I swallow the bite as my nose bunches. Slowly, I lift the sandwich to my nose and sniff. An odd tang hits my nasal cavity and I push away the offending scent. Set the sandwich on the butcher paper and peel back the bread. Inspect the cheese as if it were a suspect in a murder investigation. Narrow my eyes at the offensive smell.

"What's the matter?"

"The cheese smells off."

Devlyn sets his sandwich down and picks mine up. Lifting it to his nose, he inhales the unpleasant odor, only he doesn't seem as perturbed. He sniffs it again. Then again. No wince or offensive look. No puckered nose indicating disgust. Devlyn just appears… normal.

Damnit.

Please, please, please tell me this is not a pregnancy thing. Because not being able to eat the foods I love is unacceptable. I love cheese. All the cheeses.

"Smells okay to me," Devlyn says with an edge of uncertainty in his voice. "Want mine?"

I stare at his Cuban sandwich and my stomach grumbles. They have never been my thing, but maybe because I haven't tried one in years. Plus, Devlyn takes off the mustard and pickles. A win, if you ask me.

"I'll give it a try, but only if you don't mind."

Devlyn lifts his hand to my cheek, sliding it down until he pinches my chin between his thumb and finger. "Wouldn't offer otherwise."

We switch sandwiches and I take a hesitant bite. Worried the cheese from the Cuban will offend too. But as I chew the bite, as all the flavors hit my tongue, I moan. Then I take another bite, close my eyes and savor the taste. Dare I say, I love this sandwich more than my favorite.

"Better?"

I nod with a little too much enthusiasm. "Much, thank you."

"Think it's pregnancy related?"

Setting my sandwich down, I eat some of the fruit. "Probably." I swallow a bite of strawberry. "I read in one of the brochures that diet changes are different for each expecting mother. Some women don't experience any, with the exception of eating more. Other women crave foods they hated and dislike foods they've loved." I pierce another strawberry and blueberry and point to the sandwich in Devlyn's hands. "Hope that's the only issue."

"Me too."

Most of lunch goes by in relative silence. A little more than a week has passed since the Karen incident at the grocery store. The first two days post-Karen were iffy. I kept an eye on Devlyn every minute humanly possible. Watched for signs of detachment. Held him often so he didn't shut down and curl in on himself.

But being with him twenty-four seven is impossible. Life and work continue to demand our time.

Thank goodness he had an appointment scheduled with Dr. Prince two days later.

Although I want Devlyn to share everything with me, I know he needs someone else's guidance when it comes to this piece of his past. One day, when he is in a better place with it all, he will share.

Until his appointment, Devlyn and I spent every available minute together. When I worked, he was in the studio. Loud, angry music vibrated the walls when I walked through the front door every evening. The music wasn't offensive, but more like a key to his mood. A glimpse at what I was walking into each day. And with each passing day, the music became less harsh. Less *I want to throw shit at the wall* sounding.

I want to smack Karen Templar. Dig my nails in her skin and listen to her cries. Get in her face and scream obscenities. Tell her she doesn't deserve to have someone as wonderful and extraordinary as Devlyn in her life. Make her feel an inkling of the pain she inflicted on her son.

But I won't do any of the above. Physical altercations and acts of violence wouldn't help. Not me or Devlyn or the situation as a whole.

This is Devlyn's battle. One I will help him with, whatever that looks like, but only as he needs me to. I need to be strong for him. Hold him up when his knees buckle. Tell him how much I love him. How I will be there for him always. And if he needs me to step up to the plate, if he needs me to be his voice or his shield, I will do exactly that.

The butcher paper crinkles as we finish lunch and toss our trash in the bin. We tidy up the table and meander back out to the main room of the shop. The older couple from earlier is long gone. A man lingers near the cooler of prearranged vases while a woman wanders near the loose flowers in the customer walk-in.

"See you after work?" Devlyn leans his hip on the arrangement table, his eyes wandering the lines of my profile, heating my skin.

I nod. "Yeah. After I stop by the apartment first."

He straightens, then leans into me. Presses his lips to my temple. Drops his lips to my ear. "Love you, Andromeda." He tugs the loose length of my hair. "See you in a bit."

I reach out, pinch the bottom hem of his shirt as I twist to face him, and kiss him for all to see. The kiss isn't obscene, but the gentle press of my lips to his lingers. The moment his lips leave mine, I want to dive back in for another. But I resist the urge. Remind myself there is plenty of time for that later. After work.

"Love you too. I'll text when I'm on my way."

With one last kiss, Devlyn weaves his way through the back of the shop and out the employee door. I miss him the second the door clicks shut. But his earthy scent and the tingle from his kiss remains. For now, it will have to do.

Elizabeth takes lunch while I man the shop. I wrap a mix of flowers in brown paper and tie them with twine for the woman. She pays and exits the shop.

I snag the arrangement I worked on before lunch and pick up where I left off.

As I finish up the bouquet, the man steps up to the table and asks for help. He wants to send flowers to a friend who lost a loved one. Sifting through the available options, I opt for a small bundle of lilies, add them to a vase with some greenery and give him a small card to fill out for the bouquet. After he pays and exits, the shop is quiet. Too quiet.

I start a new arrangement. Grab a fresh vase and an array of colorful flowers. Add a handful of stems, various greenery and some baby's breath. As I place it in the prearranged cooler, the bell over the door jingles. Tipping up the corners of my mouth, I pivot on my heel and open my mouth to greet the next customer.

But no words leave my lips. My whole frame stiffens and I forget how to speak.

Twenty feet from where I stand, not facing me head on, is Devlyn's mother.

What the hell?

Much as I'd love to give this woman a piece of my mind, much as I'd love to shove her out the front door and tell her to never return, my lips refuse to move. Words refuse to form on my tongue.

And before she sees me, I spin around. My feet trek across the floor and toward the break room. Elizabeth hasn't been back here but maybe ten to fifteen minutes, and I hate that I will interrupt her time. But I swear to make it up to her. Give her extra time, let her come in later on a different day. Whatever she wants.

Anything but be in the same room as Karen Templar, forced to interact with her. Not on my own. Not anytime soon.

"I need a favor," I say as I enter the room.

Elizabeth looks up from her book, finishes chewing and swallows. "What's the matter?"

I pick at the pocket of my apron. Twist my lips between my teeth. "Devlyn's mother is out front." Elizabeth's brows pinch at the middle. It isn't my place to share Devlyn's past, but I need to give Elizabeth something. Some indication as to why I refuse to be in the same room as her. "It's a sticky situation." That's putting it lightly. "Things aren't good with Devlyn and his parents, and we bumped into her the other night. It was bad."

Tucking her bookmark between the pages, Elizabeth rises from the table and wipes her mouth with a napkin. "Say no more." She sidles up to me and rests a hand on my shoulder. "Stay back here. I'll come back when she leaves."

My entire body deflates. "Thank you."

Not a minute after Elizabeth exits the room, my stomach starts to roll. *Nerves or morning sickness?* It's long past morning, but I read the nausea happens at all hours. Most women just happen to get it in the morning.

I lock myself in the bathroom, crank the cold-water knob on the faucet and soak a paper towel. Then I park myself on the lidded toilet and dab my cheeks, forehead and neck with the towel. Bend at the waist and tuck my head between my knees.

As a child, I passed out quite often. My blood sugar and iron levels were never where they were supposed to be. At an early age, I learned the signs leading up to a fainting spell. The doctors told me if I felt that same woozy feeling, felt like the world was too wobbly beneath my feet, I needed to sit in a chair or on the floor. Somewhere safe. That I should tuck my head between my knees and take slow, deep breaths. In through the nose, out through the mouth. Help the blood and oxygen flow to my head. It wasn't an immediate fix, but it helped.

After the third deep breath, I slowly sit straighter. Open my eyes. Focus my thoughts on something calming.

Nights snuggled with Devlyn on the couch. Just me, him, good food and whatever show we're currently watching. His warm arms around my waist. The stroke of his fingers on my skin.

Another deep breath and the nausea passes. "I got this," I whisper with renewed confidence.

A knock on the door startles my peace. "Shelly? Everything alright?"

I rise from the toilet and toss the paper towel in the bin. Twisting the handle, I open the door to see Elizabeth, her face etched with concern.

"All good. Felt sick for a moment, but it passed."

She rubs my back between my shoulders as I walk out. "Glad it's better. May need to keep some ginger ale and saltines on hand." A gentle smile dons her face. "Just in case."

"Not a bad idea." My eyes dart to the doorway, then back to Elizabeth. "Did she... uh..."

"She left. Didn't buy anything, actually. She wandered the shop for a few minutes, then started asking questions."

"About the shop?"

Elizabeth shakes her head. "Not one. She asked questions about Devlyn." She pauses to swallow. "And you."

Shit. I hoped she wouldn't remember my face from the shop. She'd only been in here the one time, well over a year ago. I wasn't even the one to help her.

Obviously, Karen Templar has a fantastic memory. One I'd like her to forget.

"What did she ask?"

I hate that Elizabeth is suddenly in the middle of our mess. It isn't fair to her.

"At first, she asked about the new piece on the inside wall. The meadow." *My meadow.* "Asked if Devlyn had painted it." My eyes widen. "And when he was here last." A light layer of sweat dampens my skin as the nausea starts to make a comeback. "Since I hadn't seen her in a while, I told her Devlyn painted the inside when he'd done the exterior more than a year ago."

Thank god.

The last thing I need is this woman constantly snooping around the shop. Barging in at any given moment and pestering me or waiting for Devlyn to show.

"What did she ask about me?"

An audible exhale leaves her lips as Elizabeth takes my hands in hers. In that small touch, I feel every ounce of her love and concern. "Please tell me you are safe, Shelly." Her gaze pierces mine with a fierce level of protectiveness. "If that woman is harassing you…"

"For now, everything is okay." I nod imperceptibly. "There's just been some recent events with her and Devlyn." My eyes fall to our joined hands. "Wish I could share more, but it's not my place."

"I know, sweetheart. Just promise me one thing." I lift my eyes back to hers. "If it gets too bad, if you or Devlyn are in harm's way, don't keep this secret." Her gaze drops to my belly briefly. "It's not just the two of you anymore." Her eyes dart between mine. "It's okay to ask for help. Especially with this."

"I promise," I whisper.

Elizabeth's shoulders visibly relax. "She asked if the young blonde girl still worked here. I didn't answer. Just deterred her and asked how I could help. The way she left…" She shakes her head. "I don't think she'll return."

I pray she is right. The last thing any of us needs is to be on the receiving end of Karen Templar's wrath.

"Thank you." I pull Elizabeth into a hug and hold on tight. She squeezes me until I have to tap out of the embrace. "Sorry I interrupted your lunch." I point to the table where her sandwich sits. "Take all the time you need."

Before she rebuts my courtesy, I dart from the room.

The last few hours of the day go by uneventfully. But as I compile online orders and start arrangements for deliveries, the thought of that woman in here, in *my* shop, gazing at *my* meadow, eats away at my happiness.

She may not have said one word to me, but her presence alone sucked the life from one of my happy places. And I intend to get it back.

I will not let her stomp all over me or Devlyn. Will not let her ruin the love and joy we have found together. And I downright refuse to be bullied and squashed by anyone, especially that wicked woman.

Not today. Not tomorrow. Not ever.

Ten

DEVLYN

Difficult as it is, I try not to spend most days hating my mother. Dr. Prince says I should focus on how to relieve myself of the trauma. Find new ways to dispel the pieces of my past that affect my present and possibly my future. That I should forgive my younger self for not knowing or understanding the influence my parents had on me at such a vulnerable age.

It is okay to forgive past me. It is okay to let go of things I had no control over.

Forgiving and letting go of the past opens up space for the future. Is silent permission to love without fear of repercussion. To hope for the things I want in my life. To experience happiness without apprehension.

In order to move forward, in order to work through all the parts that eat away at my soul, I have to learn to forgive. And forgiving the woman who should have loved me more than anyone, but didn't, is difficult.

I *want* her love. I *want* her approval.

Knowing I will never have either is the hardest part. But knowing I will never have either also helps.

When I argued with Dr. Prince, told him I didn't have the energy to forgive my parents, he countered my rebuff. Said forgiveness and release don't need to be done face-to-face. It's more about letting go of the piece of them that still takes up residence inside me. It's about discovering a way to dig up the painful parts, dissect each moment on its own, make peace with the hurt, and then let that piece of the past go.

Weeks ago, he'd said, "Mental and emotional trauma leaves invisible scars. Healing those scars will take time. It's not something that can be rushed. We all heal at our own pace and in our own way. Grant yourself the time your mind needs. Be open to expelling the past and making room for the future."

So, one session at a time, one relived memory at a time, I learn how to forgive and let go of my parents.

During an early session, I argued with Dr. Prince that my father was not to blame. He'd never said an unkind word. Never raised his hand in physical threat. Never belittled me in private or public. It had always been my mother who'd done those things. My mother was the villain.

After my counterstatement, Dr. Prince asked how my father acted while my mother behaved in this manner. For minutes, I stared out the window of his office. Watched the birds flutter around the tree branches and chase one another. Got lost in the fluffy white clouds as they floated in the Mayan-blue sky. Drifted away mentally with the breeze, wishing it was easier to escape the disasters of my past.

It was then that I realized what he'd meant when he said my father had also been part of the problem. Because James Templar never did a damn thing. Not to help me, anyway.

He'd coddled my mother. Admonished me for upsetting her. Told me to be on my best behavior. All with a pained look on his face.

To this day, I don't know if that pained look was because my mother was upset. Or because he suffered her wrath as well.

The more I dug into my past, the more I paid attention to the little moments over the years, the more I saw it. Although my father was a victim, it wasn't the same. He *chose* to stay. He *chose* to elevate my mother. To put her on the pedestal that slowly lifted her higher and higher with each passing day.

My father fed—feeds—my mother's narcissism. He fuels her by never telling her the words she speaks or actions she takes are harmful. And together, they buried me in hurt and confusion and emotional detachment.

"Is she still attempting contact?" Dr. Prince asks from his plush leather chair.

Three months have passed since my first session. In those three months, a lot has been brought to light. A lot has been picked apart and evaluated with a new lens. But with each session, life moves forward rather than backward. With each session, I learn how to heal.

Not long after seeing my mother in the store, when she blew up and made a scene, she stopped by Petal and Vine. She'd missed me by mere minutes. Thankfully, Shelly escaped to the back and avoided another interaction unscathed. My mother probed Elizabeth with questions, but got no answers.

Surprisingly, it has been quiet since.

No constant calls or voice mails. No text messages. No incessant emails.

Almost as if Karen Templar vanished without a trace. And that has me on edge.

"No." I shake my head as I scoot to sit straighter in my seat. "Is it weird for me to be worried by her silence?"

Dr. Prince scratches a note down on his pad of paper. "Not weird at all. Oftentimes, in situations such as yours, it's alarming to feel free after years under someone's thumb."

"I just know my mother." I laugh without humor and drop my gaze to my lap. "She never lets anything go. She always has a plan. A way to come out the *winner*, whatever that looks like in her eyes." I lift my gaze and lock on Dr. Prince's steely irises. "My mother isn't the type to throw in the towel. Walking away isn't her style."

"What do you worry about most when it comes to her silence?"

I don't hesitate. "Shelly."

"Can you be more specific?"

Weeks of silence from my mother bother me more than her deranged display at the store. Since that night, I have agonized over Shelly's safety, and the baby. After days of deep breathing and mental reflection, I can't dislodge the twisted feeling in my gut. That the worst is yet to come.

"I worry Shelly will get caught in the cross fire. That my mother will do something unpredictable and Shelly will be hurt physically. And so will the baby."

"Do you believe your mother is capable of physically harming others?"

I shake my head and laugh again. "At this point, I believe my mother is capable of just about anything. She may not wield that weapon, but she is the one responsible."

Dr. Prince sips his water, then jots more notes on his pad of paper.

God, he has to have a ream's worth of paper in my file by now. Not sure if that is good or bad. Maybe a bit of both.

At least I have an outlet for my thoughts and emotions. A safe place to get everything off my chest. A safe person to help me make sense of it all so I can grow past it.

But how does this man sleep at night after hearing such stories?

"Has Shelly responded to your request for her to move in?"

Another item on the list that has me restless.

Months have passed since I asked Shelly to move in. I haven't pressed her for an answer and she hasn't hinted one way or the other. Yes, my asking was premature in our relationship and during a sensitive time. But I meant every word. Wanting Shelly in my home, at my side more often than not, hadn't been an irrational idea. I still want us to live together. Still want a future with her.

I mean, she practically lives in my house already. With each passing week, more of Shelly's belongings find a new home in my house. Small touches of her invade each room.

Her clothes hang in the closet and fill the drawers of the dresser, adding softer tones and a splash of pink. The little bit of makeup she uses lies on the vanity in the master bathroom. Her sweet but earthy floral scent is now a permanent fixture in the bedroom. *Our bedroom.* Her favorite throw blanket, the one she had draped over the couch in her apartment, now lies over the back of my couch. *Our couch.* She even brought over the container she keeps on her kitchen counter with all her favorite teas.

Whether Shelly realizes it or not, we live together. It just isn't official.

She still pays rent on the space she doesn't frequent often. A space now filled with barely used furniture, slowly emptying cabinets and less of Shelly's personal possessions. In the past two months, she has added life to my home—*our home*—as her old apartment becomes a vacant shell.

"Not yet." I pick at my cuticles, then force myself to stop. "I want to ask again, but I don't want to upset her."

"Why do you think asking would upset her?"

Great question.

Anymore, I feel like I don't have answers to any questions. That I am just going through the motions most days. Trapping myself in the studio and mood painting. Impatiently waiting for Shelly to walk through the front door with a smile on her face and arms spread wide. To bring me further into her light.

"A lot has happened in such a short period. I often question if my intentions *are* out of impulse. I wonder if she thinks I'm only asking because she's pregnant."

"Are you?"

"Am I what?"

"Asking Shelly to move in because she's pregnant?"

Guess I shoved myself into this corner.

The baby isn't the chief reason I asked Shelly to move in. I asked because I love her. I asked because she matters more than anyone. Is the baby a secondary factor? One hundred percent, yes.

I don't doubt Shelly's ability to handle herself. She is incredible and strong and lovable. But she is not alone. Not in life or love, and definitely not when it comes to the baby. *Our baby.*

"No. With or without the pregnancy, I would've eventually asked her to live together. We just click. Can't put it into words, but there's something about her that I connect with on a base level." Long before we were together, Shelly had been my muse. When I saw her again after nearly a year, she reignited that spark inside me. "When we're together, it all just locks in place. Flows smoother."

With Shelly, life isn't a chore. I look forward to each day. To seeing her, holding her, being with her. She breathes life into my soul and elevates me in an incomprehensible way.

Dr. Prince glances down at his wrist. "Homework time," he says with a hint of laughter. The homework term has become a little joke with us. Don't know if he uses the same word with his other patients, but we laugh at it. Make it lighter and less about actual work.

"Ask Shelly again?" He nods and scribbles on the notepad. "Will do."

"Remember Devlyn, asking for what you want shouldn't be a chore. Don't treat it as such. It's normal to ask for what you want. The delivery is what makes all the difference." He rises from his seat and I follow suit. "Mull it over before you ask. Think of how you want the question to come across—out of a place of love and not need—and practice how you think that should sound. When it feels right, ask."

He makes the task sound so simple. Like taking a breath or painting what I feel. If only.

I don't fear Shelly. I don't fear the love she has for me, for us. What I *do* fear is rejection. Especially from her.

For years, I handed out rejection like Halloween candy. Hell, I rejected Shelly's and my own feelings for weeks. Shoved her away after the kiss on the exhibition night. Subjected us both to suffering so *she* wouldn't hurt *me* the way I'd been hurt before.

I'd still hurt, but at least it was my own doing. At least I was in control.

But now, I need to be brave. I need to step up and ask for what I want. I need to stow my insecurities and be a little selfish. Not just with Shelly, but also in life.

I love her. I want her. And I shouldn't feel shame in that.

She makes my life better, brighter. Wraps me in her arms and warmth and heart. Gives me more love than imaginable. Soothes the pain of the past without effort and replaces it with hope and passion and conviction. Shelly gives me purpose. A reason to wake up and keep going.

"Thanks, Doc." I extend my hand and we shake. "See you in a few days."

"Take care, Devlyn."

I exit the office and head for my car. Unlocking it, I slip behind the wheel and press the ignition. For a beat, I sit idle in the lot. Stare out the window at nothing in particular. Let my eyes lose focus and my mind drift off with the clouds.

Shelly is not Kelsey. Shelly won't reject me. She won't throw me away.

I repeat this again and again. Let the words seep into my bones. Chant them like a mantra until I believe them into existence.

The past will not repeat itself. Shelly is not *Kelsey.*

Shelly's hesitation to move in is because we have dated such a short time. But Dr. Prince says no one person determines when to take the next step in a relationship. There is no handbook for love. No guide for relationships. We set the pace. We say what comes next.

Our relationship cannot be compared to anyone else's relationship. Sure, we may have similar circumstances, but our relationship otherwise is different. Because *we* are different.

Over dinner, I will ask again. Ask Shelly to move in. I just need to find the right words. Pregnancy or not, Shelly doesn't need additional stress or pressure. But I'd like to know if she has given the idea any merit.

I won't force an answer from her lips, but I would like to know if there's a chance she will say yes.

Now… time to butter her up. Thankfully, I know the way to her heart.

eleven

I just landed in heaven.

The moment I walk through Devlyn's front door, the delicious scent of bulgogi hits my nose. Savory with a hint of spice. My mouth waters instantly. *Damn, that smells good. Thank god.*

After the cheese incident, I worried what else would turn up my nose and have me queasy. I'd cry if my favorites made me cringe. To date, cheese and cabbage are the only items on the naughty list. Everything else has been ten times better.

I toss my purse on the chair in the sitting room and toe off my shoes. Winding my way through the house, I slow my pace as I approach the living room. Rounding the corner, I spot Devlyn with his back to me. He removes boxes and tubs from a brown bag and sets them on the table. And for a moment, I stand silently in place and watch him move around the room. Watch him organize dinner and set up the room for a perfect date night in.

The bag crinkles as he flattens it. Then he spins around and spots me at the edge of the room. A small smile pushes up his cheeks and I melt at the sight.

"Didn't hear you come in." He saunters across the room, steps into my space, wraps his arms around my waist and crushes my lips with his.

Damn.

Every day should be this incredible. Every day *can* be this incredible. If I let it be.

When he breaks the kiss, I peer up at him. Stare at the darker shade of green rimming his glass-green irises. Swallow at the smolder in his gaze. At the love this man gives only to me.

Damn, I mentally repeat.

"Wasn't purposely quiet," I say. "Just saw you setting up dinner and didn't want to interrupt." I kiss the tip of his chin. "Smells so good."

He kisses the tip of my nose as he unravels his arms. "Sit. I was going for drinks." Before I offer to help, he steps around me and heads for the kitchen.

A few shifts on the floor pillow later, Devlyn walks back in with water and hot tea. Setting them on the table, he situates himself next to me between the couch and table on the floor. We tear open disposable chopsticks and break the sticks apart. And as Devlyn hits play on the remote, I dive into the bulgogi.

An unladylike moan exits my lips and Devlyn laughs.

"Good?"

"So damn good." I savor the bite. Let the umami roll over my tongue. "I'll admit, I was worried." His brows pinch at the middle. "That I wouldn't be able to enjoy it. After the whole cheese thing, I wondered what other foods would gross me out."

"And?"

I shrug. "Just the cheese." I clamp down on another piece of beef, then point my loaded chopsticks at him. "Actually, most of the dairy has made me queasy."

"At least you didn't eat or drink a lot before."

"True." I pop the beef in my mouth and close my eyes. *Thank you*, I say to the pregnancy gods. At least I still have this.

The rest of dinner goes by in quiet bliss as we watch *Dark*. This show really swirls my mind into a blur. But in a good way. Romance is my bread and butter, but this multilayered mystery is a close competitor.

When the boxes empty, we pause the show, take the trash to the kitchen, and grab dessert. Curled up on the couch, I lay my head on Devlyn's shoulder while I spoon ice cream into my mouth.

"Can I ask you something?" Devlyn asks as the end credits flit across the screen.

"You know you can." I wrap my hands around his bicep.

Three breaths pass before his voice fills the room again, so soft and quiet I almost don't hear him. "Is there a reason you haven't agreed to move in?"

Feels like a lifetime has passed since Devlyn asked me to move in with him. I'd told him I needed to think about it. He granted me the time and I have mulled it over, but I have yet to answer him. Is it too early to blame that on pregnancy brain?

I lift my head and rest my chin on his shoulder before kissing it and sitting up straighter. Glance into his glassy, soulful eyes. Eyes that question if I love him enough to want this. To be with him full time. To share the same space as him. To cohabitate.

And the uncertainty in his head and heart, that is on me. Too many days have passed since he asked. Too many days have passed without me answering. God, his mind must be in overdrive. Crazy with assumptions.

How unfair of me to make him wait, considering I decided not long after he asked. I assumed my actions made my answer evident. But Devlyn needs to hear the words. With all the hurt in his past, he needs to hear the answers. When it comes to Devlyn, I should never assume.

"It's not that I don't want to move in."

He shifts in his seat to face me more easily. Arm resting on the back of the couch, his fingers toy with the loose strands of my hair. Twirl and lightly tug. "Then what's holding you back?" His knuckles graze the angle of my jaw and I lean into his touch. Let my eyes fall shut and my body relax. "So beautiful," he whispers.

The backs of my eyes sting as I swallow down his words. God, I love this man. This beautifully broken man.

"I'm scared," I say, my eyes still closed. "I'm scared to give in." Slowly, I open my eyes. "Scared to fall harder and lose you."

His other hand cups my cheek, his thumb stroking beneath my lashes. "You'll never lose me, Shelly. Never."

"How can you be so sure?" I fist the hem of my shirt and tug it over my swelling belly. "What if having the baby puts a wedge between us? What if I move in and things become too much? Right now, everything is new and happy. But what if that changes when the baby comes?"

Leaning forward, Devlyn kisses my forehead. His lips linger for three breaths before he resumes his previous position. Warmth spreads from the spot he kissed to my heart. I take a deep breath and hold his vibrant greens.

"I don't doubt things will change when the baby comes." His fingers go back to the loose strands of my hair. "But we control how they change. Yes, the baby will throw a glitch into the life we currently know, but we have the ability to shape how we want the future."

Since Devlyn started therapy, we haven't had many serious, in-depth conversations. I don't ask how his sessions go. I don't mention his mother or parents. Not from lack of curiosity, but more because I don't want to invade that area of his privacy. I don't want to rehash possibly upsetting moments. More than anything, I want to respect his boundaries.

With unparalleled patience, I wait for him to broach the heavy subjects. Wait for him to spark those weighted conversations. Because they aren't mine to bring up. They aren't my stories to tell when ready.

The strength in his words as we talk about our future tells me therapy has been beneficial. Has given him the opportunity to look at life through a new lens. With new perspective. With a positive outlook.

"I just don't want you to grow tired of me," I huff out. "Then we're both stuck in a crazy situation." I lift my hand to his jaw and trace my finger to his chin before letting it fall away. "Don't want you to feel pressured to keep me around if something changes."

"One… not going to happen." I open my mouth to rebut and he holds up a hand to stop me. "Yes, all couples experience the bad. Moments when they don't get along. It's inevitable." He takes my hand, brings it to his lips, and kisses each knuckle in turn. "But I'll never wish you away, Shelly Reed. All of my good days involve you."

He takes a deep breath and I don't interrupt. "Shelly, you are the only shining light in my life. My life preserver. The sunshine after the rain. The one person I can count on. No matter how shitty my day has been, no matter how poorly I behave, all the bad vanishes because I have you. And I realize how unhealthy and codependent that sounds. It's something I've been working on with Dr. Prince." He closes his eyes briefly. "But I also know those deep, deep feelings are genuine. They aren't misguided sentiments from a broken boy."

He presses the heel of his palm to the center of his chest. "You are here. Rooted so deep." His eyes glaze over. "I think you were here long before either of us knew. Because damn, I feel so much for you. So damn much. At times, I question my own sanity, my own mental health. But every time I do, I come up with the same result."

"What's that?" I whisper-ask.

His eyes roll closed for one, two, three beats. "That I've never loved anyone the way I love you. At times, the depth of that loves scares the shit out of me. Because I've only truly loved one other and that ended in devastation." He shakes his head as light laughter leaves his lips. "I fought this" —he gestures between us with his hand— "for so long. Tried to keep you in the friend zone. But fate knew better and I caved." He leans in and presses a chaste kiss to my lips. "Loving you was inevitable, Shelly Reed. And I will keep you forever, if you let me."

The backs of my eyes burn as tears blur my vision and emotion clogs my throat. I don't know what to say. How to react. What to do after Devlyn just spilled his whole heart at my feet.

Every truth that left his lips wrapped itself around my heart and hugged me fiercely. I will keep those truths tucked safely in my heart for the rest of my life. His sacred, vulnerable truths. His love. Him.

Concerned as I've been, I knew weeks ago I would say yes to him. I will always say yes. Not to please Devlyn, but because he will never intentionally put me in an uncomfortable situation. He will never intentionally hurt me.

More than any other person, I know Devlyn. Know his heart. Know his softness and the pieces he keeps hidden from the rest of the world. His softness is one of my favorite parts. A part he reserves only for me.

"Yes."

His eyes narrow as they study my expression, flit over the angles of my nose and jaw, home in on my eyes and lips. "Yes?" A layer of uncertainty laces his voice.

"I'll move in," I whisper, the words floating softly from my lips to his ears.

The moment they hit, the moment they truly sink in, his whole body shifts. Lights up. Comes alive.

His hands frame my face, thumbs brush my cheeks. Inch by inch, he eviscerates the space between us. Vivid green irises hold my sparkly dark blues. His breath warm on my lips.

I fist the cotton of his shirt at the heart and tug him forward until our lips meet in the middle. Soft and warm, Devlyn kisses me with unprecedented tenderness. Once, twice, his lips sweep over mine reverently. Then his tongue paints my bottom lip and I gasp. Invite him in. Taste him on my tongue. Melt into him.

Crawling into his lap, we shift until his back presses against the cushions and I straddle his hips. His fingers curl at my waist as mine lace behind his neck. The kiss deepens as his hands shift and trail up my spine beneath my shirt. My fingers finding their way into his long, thick strands.

"Love you, Shelly." His lips kiss along my jaw, down the column of my neck, across my collarbone.

I curl my fingers in his hair, scrape my nails over his scalp. "Love you, Dev."

Over the next several hours, until the faint light of dawn filters through the windows, we love each other. With lips and fingers. Light touches and whispered words. Occasional scratches and bite marks. Skin on sweat-slicked skin. Linked and bonded through the most pivotal, base connection. The most real and raw and undeniable connection. His body and mine.

Until my heart no longer beats, until my lungs no longer fill with air, I will love this man. Will share my heart with him. Will let him hold it close to his own. Let him care for me—for us—in a way no one else ever will.

Because Devlyn isn't just a boyfriend. He isn't just the father of the baby growing in my womb. This man is my heart. This man is my soul. More than anything, this man is my life. Where I am meant to be. In his arms, every day of forever.

DEVLYN

"Put that down," I shout across the living room of Shelly's apartment. She narrows her eyes. "Please," I say a bit softer. "You shouldn't be lifting anything that heavy."

Bending at the knees, Shelly sets the box on the floor and I breathe easier. "It's not even heavy." She rests fists on her hips. "Maybe ten pounds. Knickknacks from the kitchen junk drawer and the stuff I had on the fridge." Her eyes drop to said box. "Heck, it's probably not even five pounds."

Last week, Shelly had a checkup and the doctor said all looked great with the baby. We got our first baby picture with the ultrasound. Dr. Webster said the baby is roughly the size of a sweet potato, which I thought was odd as a visual reference but it works.

She asked if we wanted to know the gender of the baby. We declined, opting for the surprise.

During that same visit, Dr. Webster noted Shelly's elevated blood pressure and ordered she take it easy. Rest as much as possible. Not strain herself or lift anything too heavy.

Packing up her apartment and moving her into the house have made this directive difficult.

Shelly spoke with her landlord at the start of the week and since she only has two months left on her lease, they agreed to let her break it. Granted, she won't get her deposit back, but the money doesn't concern me more than her well-being.

One step forward, then another, I hold her at arm's length. "This sucks, I get it. But you heard what Dr. Webster said. You need to take it easy. Pack up the boxes and I'll carry them."

Her eyes fall shut as she takes a deep breath and sighs. "Ugh. I hate this." She shakes her head. "Feels like I'm helpless. Incapable."

I wrap my arms around her waist and draw her close. Press my lips to her cheek. "You aren't and you know it. Pregnancy won't last forever. We're almost halfway there." I kiss her other cheek. "It's a big adjustment, but if it keeps you both safe, then it's what matters most."

Warm arms tighten their hold on my waist. "I know." She kisses my neck, then takes a step back. "I'll go work on filling the boxes in the bedroom."

Hours pass as Shelly and I fill boxes with clothes and books, dishes and small appliances. I carry them out, one by one, and load them in my car or hers. When not an inch of empty space is visible in either of our cars, we lock up the apartment and drive across town to the house.

We park in the driveway and I start unloading both our cars. Pile the boxes in the empty space near the sliding glass doors. Do my best to separate the box stacks by room to make the next step less stressful. When all the boxes are in the house, I help unpack, but let Shelly place her things where she'd like them.

"Is everyone getting together tomorrow?"

Weeks have passed since we last hung out with her friends. Not because we haven't wanted to; life has just been busy for us all.

"Yeah. Cora messaged earlier and asked if we'd be there."

I peel newspaper off a plate and hand it to her. "Did you answer?"

Shelly spent so much time with her friends before our relationship blossomed. Now, she sees them less often. Not because of our relationship and the pregnancy, thank goodness. I'd be upset if I were the reason. Between love and marriage and babies, everyone else's lives have changed too. Both Cora and Autumn have newborns. Cora and Gavin, as well as Micah and Peyton, are still in the honeymoon phase.

She nods. "Mm-hmm. Told her we'd bring potato salad." Her eyes find mine. "Hope that's okay."

I shrug. "Potato salad's fine. Kind of prefer macaroni salad, but it's cool."

She knocks my arm with her shoulder. "I meant me responding without checking with you, not the potato salad." A soft chuckle leaves her lips and I love hearing the gentle laughter.

Setting the dish in my hand down, I take her chin in my fingers and press a kiss to her lips. "More than okay. It'll be nice to see everyone."

Sunshine lights her face in the form of a smile and I question the last time I saw her so bright. It's been too long.

Right here, right now, I vow to make Shelly smile more often. Recent worries had stolen her smiles. Worry over herself, the baby, the move. I need to be better. Do better. Take some of that stress off her shoulders. Carry the burden and help her relax.

I flatten the empty boxes and take them to the recycling bin. Shelly and I cook dinner, then settle in front of the television to eat. When the episode ends, I carry our dishes to the kitchen and tidy up.

Back in the living room, Shelly sits curled in the corner of the couch with a book. I pad across the room, take her book, mark the page, and set it on the table. Slip my hand around hers, help her stand, then escort her up the stairs to my studio.

"What're you up to?" she asks, brow arched.

When we reach the landing, I spin around to face her and walk backward until we reach the middle of the room. I frame her face in my hands and crush my lips to hers. She fists my shirt at either hip and draws me in until no space exists between us. It is just her and me and our personal bubble of bliss.

Our tongues tangle. Hands skim arms and waists. I graze the length of her spine as she kneads the sides of my neck. Fingers fist hair and tug. The kiss morphing from gentle to hungry in seconds. And when she tips her head back and gasps, I kiss my way down her neck and drag my tongue along her collarbone.

"I want to paint you," I say against the hollow of her throat. "But not like before."

Her fingers tighten in my hair and pull my lips from her skin. "How?"

I nip at her chin. "On canvas. Just you." I tug at the bottom hem of her shirt and lift up. My fingers skim down her sternum, over the center of her bra, over her belly that is slowly swelling with our child. "No barriers."

"Devlyn, I…"

"Abstract," I answer quickly. "Or not. I leave it up to you." My palm flattens on her lower abdomen and I splay my fingers. "So beautiful." I drop to my knees, my eyes peering up at Shelly as my lips press to the skin beneath her navel. "Please."

Gentle fingers comb through my unruly hair as she holds my gaze. Neither of us says a word for several heartbeats. And then her head slowly moves up and down.

"Okay," she whispers into our bubble. "You can paint me." She takes a deep breath. "However you're inspired to."

Once again, this woman astounds. Her love and bravery and confidence. Without much negotiation, she handed over an incomparable level of trust. Laid it in my hands, certain I would keep it, and her, safe. Something I will never abuse or take for granted.

I shift a few things around in the studio, run downstairs to grab several pillows and blankets, and set up a comfortable space for her to lie. As she disrobes, I prop a blank canvas on the easel and shift its position, grab my paints and brushes, and take a seat on my stool.

Shelly lies down on the pillows and shifts until she finds a comfortable position on her side.

"If you need a break," I say, "just tell me. It's late, so I promise not to keep us up here long."

Shelly folds a pillow in half and stuffs it between her head and arm. "How long will the painting take?"

My head teeters left and right. "Several hours." I lick my lips and swallow as my eyes trail over her curves. Take in her creamy, bare skin. "If we're up here daily, a couple hours each time, maybe two weeks. Or less." I trace a finger over my upper lip. "Also depends on how I paint you. The heavier the details, the longer it'll take."

She inhales deeply and swallows on the exhale. "Okay." Then she closes her eyes and her entire frame relaxes. Not a hint of resistance or timidity dons her expression.

Damn, she is beautiful. Too beautiful.

Over the next four hours, my eyes flit between Shelly and the canvas. The bristles of my brushes dip in various shades of pigment as I take in the bow of her lips, the slope of her nose, the swell of her breasts and arch of her hip. Blending. Shaping. Contouring. One stroke at a time, I bring this incredible woman to life on canvas in an unfamiliar way.

Abstract art has never been my style. I appreciate the style, but feel odd painting it. As if I'm misrepresenting the subject. Much of my art resembles the muse. Clean lines and sharp detail. When you study the piece, you see my muse.

With this, though...

Shelly bares herself to me fully, and not just her flesh. Just out of reach, she exposes every piece of herself and grants me permission to portray her beauty and vulnerability in my artwork. Allows me the opportunity to uncover an unseen layer of her charm and magnificence. Paint her nude heart and impassioned aura.

I have no plans for anyone else to see this painting. This piece is personal. The most intimate art I will create.

But accidents happen. And although I'd never intentionally betray Shelly or her trust, I can't take the risk.

So this piece will be as complex and stunning as the woman herself.

Splashes of color in a display unlike any other. Short, blotchy strokes of my brush on the canvas. Bursts of bright pigment to offset the occasional shadows.

And when she and I see it, we will know. We will see what no one else sees. We will remember the nights and hours we spent in this studio. The way her breaths evened out as she fell asleep. The way I bit the end of my brush as I looked from her to the canvas, then smiled.

We will remember, and that is all that matters.

Her love. My love. Us.

I set my brush down and open my mouth to call it a night, but snap it shut when I see her closed eyes. Her slightly parted lips. Hear her soft snores as her chest rises and falls steadily.

On and off during the session, her eyes drifted closed, but her body never fully relaxed. Not like it is now.

Quietly, I clean up what I need to. Then I tiptoe over to where she sleeps, wrap her body in the blanket, and scoop her up into my arms. Halfway down the stairs, her eyes flutter open and she curls into my chest.

"Sorry I fell asleep," she mumbles into my neck.

I press a kiss to her forehead and hug her closer. "Sleep, my Andromeda. Sleep."

In the bedroom, I lay her on the bed, but she gets up and shuffles toward the bathroom. After a moment to herself, she tugs one of my shirts over her head and slips on a pair of boy shorts. We crawl under the covers and I press my front to her back, slipping one arm under her pillow and laying the other over her belly.

"Love you," she whispers into the darkness as she scoots closer.

I kiss her hair. "Love you."

She drifts back to sleep within seconds. For hour-long minutes, I lie awake and listen to her soft snores. Stroke my fingers over her belly, over our baby, and I send a thank you to the universe.

Thank you for bringing this brave, strong woman into my life. Thank you for gifting me with her heart. Thank you for giving me the chance to find love, real love, with her.

As long as there is breath in my lungs and blood in my veins, I will protect her, her heart and our baby. I will love them. Unconditionally and without fear. Always.

After one last kiss to her hair, I drift off to sleep. My entire world wrapped in my arms.

thirteen

Something isn't right.

I take a deep breath. Then another. And another.

My heart pounds viciously in my chest. The beat hard and heavy. An uncomfortable throb beneath my sternum.

I close my eyes and try to calm the worry flooding my thoughts. Breathe deeply and picture my heart settling.

Deep breaths. Slow and steady. In through the nose. Out through the mouth.

Minutes pass and the bang, bang, banging of my heart settles a fraction. I kick my feet out from beneath the blanket and welcome the cool air. After a few more deep breaths, my throbbing heart calms further.

Devlyn shifts behind me, his fingers tracing small lines over my belly.

"Morning," he says with a rasp I've grown to love more each time I hear it.

"Morning."

His lips trail kisses down the side of my neck and along the ridge of my shoulder. His hand glides over my belly and up my body until he palms my breast. I arch my back and fill his hand further.

Rolling onto my back, I bring my lips to his. Weave my fingers in his dark, wayward strands. My heart beats a brutal rhythm, but it's nothing like the pounding from minutes ago. This rhythm is one I know, one I feel head to toe.

I peel my shirt off and strip out of my panties as Devlyn shoves his briefs down and tosses them to the floor. His lips dance over each collarbone, my sternum and breasts, down my midline until he lands beneath my navel. For a beat, he stares at my belly and caresses it with such delicacy. He kisses the slight swell, then lifts his gaze.

Tears brim his green eyes and it steals my breath. Freezes me on the spot. Thickens an emotional ball in my throat.

"Love you, Shell."

My eyes sting as I look down at him, as I stroke his cheek with my knuckles. "Love you, Dev."

His head dips beneath the sheet as his palms trail up the sides of my torso. His tongue paints the flesh between my thighs. Flicks my clit and licks up my center. Consumes me while his fingers toy with my nipples until I writhe beneath his talented tongue.

With my orgasm on his tongue and lips, he kisses his way up my body. Positions himself in the cradle of my hips. Crashes his lips to mine and kisses me fiercely. Rocks his hips forward and fills me fully. Our shared gasps echo off the walls.

And then our eyes lock. For a beat, we simply breathe each other in. Connect in the most primal way. He kisses me once, twice, three times before sucking my bottom lip between his. The simmering fire in his green irises burns brighter. Hotter. Fire that ignites every inch of my soul. Fire that arouses and stokes my love for this man.

Our bodies move in a synchronized rhythm. An incomparable rhythm. A rhythm that is only ours.

My legs hug his waist, ankles lock at his lower back. As he thrusts forward, my heels dig into his muscled glutes and drive him deeper. Harder. With each rock of his hips, I climb back up that peak. With each stroke of his bare cock, I cry out for more.

His hand drifts down the curve of my breast, my waist, my hip, then dips between us. Slowly, his thumb paints small circles over my clit.

My jaw slackens as my breaths stutter from my lips. One delicious stroke after another, he summons my orgasm from somewhere deep. His tongue traces my lower lip. Teeth nip my chin and along my jaw. He sucks my earlobe between his lips. Kisses and nibbles down the column of my throat. Wraps his lips around the flesh at my shoulder and sucks. Bites. Ravages. Hard and fast and desperate.

And it's all too much.

A harsh growl spills from my lips as heat spreads up my chest, over my breasts and throat before hitting my cheeks. My legs shake as my body hugs Devlyn everywhere. And with one more rock of his hips, his orgasm fills me.

Sweat slicks our skin as our heavy breaths float through the room. His pulse pounds in his chest to the same beat as my own. My fingers trail up and down the sides of his spine before threading in his hair.

His lips kiss the spot on my shoulder where he sank his teeth in and imprinted my skin. One kiss at a time, he works his way to my lips. Our tongues twist and tangle and taste. Say I love you in ways our voices never will.

I will never get enough of his kisses. Never get enough of him.

He breaks the kiss and lifts slightly, bracketing me with his forearms. His fingers toy with strands of my hair as his greens lock onto my blues. One inhale after another, he breathes me in while I do the same.

I hadn't anticipated how emotional sex would be. How all-consuming the act would feel. Sure, I expected it to be more than just a physical act—hence why I waited—but I never imagined feeling so much, so deeply, all at once.

With Devlyn, sex isn't just something that happens with genitalia and lips and hands. It isn't just something we do to reach physical euphoria. We make love with our bodies and hearts and souls. Connect on a deeper, more profound level. Give in to our deepest desires and share a piece of ourselves no one else will have.

Until him, I never understood the bond Cora and Gavin shared. Couldn't grasp the devotion Jonas and Autumn felt. Was confounded by Micah and Peyton's love after such a rocky history. And although I'd read countless romance novels, the concept of sex being more than a physical act left me baffled.

But I get it now. I understand.

Sex is more than a means to an end with Devlyn. I won't deny loving the bliss of orgasm. Surely, Devlyn wouldn't either. But it's more than that.

It's the way his fingers caress my body. The way his breath heats my skin. The way he whispers in my ear and tells me he loves me. More than that, it's how his eyes lock with mine as our bodies come together. How his gaze penetrates deeper and captures my soul. Pumps the fist-sized organ in my chest and floods my veins with unconditional love.

Devlyn owns my heart, is the protector of my soul, and I wouldn't want it any other way.

I comb my fingers through his damp strands and lift off the pillow to kiss him.

"Hungry?" he asks and I nod. "Take your time getting up. I'll make breakfast." He rocks back and I immediately miss the weight of him.

He kisses my forehead, then rises from the bed and grabs a pair of sweatpants. I stare after him without shame. Push up on my elbows and ogle his body as he slips on the pants. Watch his every movement as he pads across the room. Salivate as his muscles bunch and flex with each step. Clamp my thighs together as he ruffles his hair with his fingers. Lick and bite my bottom lip as a smile kicks up the corner of his lips.

He disappears into the bathroom to clean up and brush his teeth. I fall back onto the mattress, close my eyes, and breathe in the moment. Breathe in the scent of him and sex and love.

After a beat, he reappears and presses another kiss to my forehead. "Any requests?"

Countless breakfast foods flit through my head, but one continues to circle back. "French toast, please."

"Powdered sugar?"

"Is that a serious question?"

He chuckles. "Powdered sugar it is. Bacon or sausage?"

"Bacon. Oh, and the leftover eggs from dipping the French toast, add extra cinnamon."

Walking out of the bedroom backward, he blows me a kiss. "Extra cinnamon. Check."

Pans and bowls clang outside the bedroom as I slowly slip out from under the covers. As I enter the bathroom, my pulse mimics the same turbulent beating from earlier. My heart feels bigger, heavier, almost painful. Every other beat, I gasp for air, but it doesn't fill my lungs. Not fully.

I plop down on the toilet, grip my knees, and close my eyes. Bend at the waist and drop my head. Inhale deeply and hold it until my lungs burn.

Several breaths pass before my pulse returns to normal and the pain in my chest subsides. Slowly, I sit up and open my eyes. Rub the center of my chest with the heel of my palm. The backs of my eyes sting as worry seeps in.

What is happening? Maybe this is a normal side effect of pregnancy. Should ask Cora and Autumn tonight.

After I use the toilet, brush my teeth, and untangle the bird's nest on top of my head, I tug on one of Devlyn's T-shirts and a pair of sleep pants.

The scent of maple and cinnamon and butter fills my nose as I head for the kitchen. The worry from minutes ago fades to the background. My stomach growls and I press a hand to the beast, muttering, "Almost time."

Before long, Devlyn piles two thick slices of French toast, scrambled eggs, several strips of bacon, and mixed fresh berries on plates. He dusts the French toast with powdered sugar, then fills glasses with orange juice. He delivers it all to the dining room table and waves me off when I try to help.

I pour a generous helping of real maple syrup—not that sugary brown goop—and dive in, moaning around my fork. Devlyn smiles in satisfaction as he lifts scrambled eggs to his lips.

"Maybe we should have breakfast for all the meals," he suggests.

Holding up a finger, I mumble around the bite. "I'd vote yes, but there're too many other good things to eat."

His smile widens. "True, but breakfast seems to be your favorite."

It is definitely a top contender. I point my fork at Devlyn. "Anything you make is my favorite."

A brow arches on his handsome face. "I'll have to remember that."

Why do I feel like I just walked myself into a corner? *Because you did.* Oh well, too late now.

∼

We park at Jonas and Autumn's house just before seven. Two cars other than theirs are here—Gavin's SUV and Micah's truck. I scoop up the bag on the floorboard between my feet and Devlyn reaches for it.

"No." I hold it just out of reach. "I know I shouldn't be lifting anything heavy, but this is like three pounds max. It's freaking side salads."

"Shell..." Devlyn looks out the windshield and sighs. "Just trying to help," he mumbles.

My hand rests on his forearm as I wait for his eyes to meet mine. "I know you are and I love you for that." I take his hand in mine, lift it to my lips, and kiss the top. "But I'm not helpless. I can still do some things myself. Yes, I need to be cautious. But that doesn't mean I stop living." Holding up the bag, I say, "I got this." He nods as his lips fumble between his teeth. "And if I need help, I promise to ask."

"It's just..." He breathes heavily. "I worry."

I graze his cheek with my fingertips and his eyes close briefly. "Me too. But we're doing everything according to plan." I lean in and press my lips to his. Let the warmth of his touch and breath comfort me. "For now, let's try not to worry. Let's try to not stress ourselves over the what-ifs."

For a moment, we just stare at each other. Neither of us says a word. Then subtly, he nods. "I'll try."

We amble to the door, hand in hand, and are greeted by Clementine and Spartan first. Hugs are exchanged with everyone and it isn't long before I get pulled away by Cora and Autumn. Clementine watches over Clara and Ryker while we catch up for a few.

Two songs later, the house is bustling with all of our friends.

Laughter floats through the room and outside on the back patio. Hickory and the scent of grilled meats and shish kebabbed vegetables fill the air. Old-school rock plays from speakers mounted on the back of the house while fire lights tiki torches around the yard.

Devlyn chats with some of the guys while I sit with Cora and Autumn on the lounger.

The more Devlyn and I join everyone on Sundays, the more he steps out of his shell. The more he smiles and laughs and comes alive. Opens up a little more. This family... we balance in ways genetic families don't. We provide love and advice and comfort. We avoid judgment and hurt.

I love how easily Devlyn fits in our circle. How everyone accepted him without hesitation. He needed us as much as we needed him. And damn am I lucky that I get to call him mine.

Zoning out, I stare at the fire. Think back to this morning and the vicious pounding in my chest. Take a deep breath and blink away the fog. "Can I ask you guys something?" I ask Cora and Autumn.

"Always," Cora says as Autumn answers, "Of course."

"It's a pregnancy question." I toy with the bottom hem of my shirt. "I haven't said anything to Devlyn because I don't want him to freak out. Especially if it's a normal thing."

When I don't continue, Cora lays her hand over mine in my lap. "Shell, what is it?"

"A couple times now, I've had this heavy feeling in my chest." I press my palm to my heart. "Like a strange heartbeat. It doesn't *hurt*, per se, but it makes me breathless." I look to Cora then Autumn. "Did either of you have that?"

The twist in my belly sinks deep when both of them shake their head.

Not good.

"No two pregnancies are the same," Autumn says. "Clementine was a wild child in the womb and Ryker just chilled for the most part. But I never had chest pains." She winces. "Probably a good idea to talk with your doctor."

"I'll second that," Cora adds. "Clara was a little gymnast during the last trimester, and I had the occasional bout of heartburn, but nothing like what you're describing."

Great. This is what I feared. This is why I also haven't said anything to Devlyn yet.

As it is, he doesn't want me to do anything besides relax. Which, in theory, is nice, but spending every day on the couch with my feet up isn't realistic. I have a business to run, and eventually take over. There is so much to prepare for with the baby. Classes to attend. New mother skills to learn. Labor breathing and learning how to breastfeed.

The pounding in my chest kicks in and I press the heel of my palm to my sternum as I inhale deeply.

Cora leans closer and whispers in my ear, "Is it happening now?" I nod. "What were you just thinking about? Right before it happened."

I close my eyes and pinch them tightly. Breathe through the pain in my chest. "Everything that's to come. With the pregnancy, motherhood." My eyes open and I glance up at my best friend. "The shop. How this baby changes everything I thought I knew. How it disrupts so many lives, not just mine."

Cora wraps an arm around my shoulders and pulls me into her side. Autumn scoots closer and leans her weight into my other side. On a sigh, I absorb their comfort. Let it fill the cracks of doubt. Let it ease my worry about the future and motherhood and new responsibilities.

"First of all, I felt everything you're feeling," Cora admits. "Gavin and I hadn't been back together long before we got pregnant." She shifts to look me square in the eye, her gaze never more serious. "I was scared, Shell. Scared we weren't ready. Scared I'd lose him again. Scared we wouldn't be *us* with a baby." The corners of her mouth tip up in a small, soft smile. "But my fear was for nothing. Just past pain haunting my present."

"How did you let go of the fear?"

She tips her head to the side. "It never fades. Not fully. But it lessens with each passing day. With each assurance that I'm not in this parenting gig alone." She looks across the patio. Her eyes land on Gavin, baby Clara cradled in his arms while he chats with a few of the guys. Jonas is there too, Ryker bundled in a blanket and snug against his chest. They talk and joke and laugh, all while doing the dad thing. "You aren't doing this alone, Shell."

"Not for a second," Autumn adds. "After everything with Clementine's father, I worried about Jonas's reaction to the pregnancy." She lays a hand on mine. "But then I reminded myself that Jonas is a different man. He walked through hell alongside me as I fought for Clementine, for our livelihood."

"Jonas has a heart of gold," I tell her.

Her eyes find his across the patio and his entire frame lights up. "That he does." Then she shifts in her seat to face me more. "What about Devlyn? How's his heart?"

God, what a loaded question. Not one I can answer simply. Not one I can answer fully without sharing secrets he isn't ready for the world to know.

"When it comes to me, to us, he has the biggest heart."

Cora's brows scrunch together. "Why do I feel like there's more to the story?"

Because there is. Because Devlyn has demons to face, to conquer, to let go. "There is more." I look to Cora, then to Autumn, before my eyes land on Devlyn, a brilliant, genuine smile on his lips. "But his story isn't mine to tell. All I will say is he came from a past none of us can comprehend. Not fully. But he's working on it. For me, for us, for the baby."

Cora rubs small circles on my shoulder. "It's silly, but I have to ask."

"What?"

"You're safe, right?" If I thought she looked serious minutes ago, I was dead wrong. My best friend has never been more somber than she is now. "Please tell me you are."

I take her free hand and Autumn's in both of mine. My eyes darting between the two of them. "I swear to you, I am safe. And if that ever changes—for any of us—we tell each other." They both nod. "No matter what."

"No matter what," they say in unison.

After a squeeze of my hand, Cora releases mine from her grasp. "Enough of the heavy talk." Autumn nods in agreement. "Please call your doctor in the morning." She points a finger at me and narrows her eyes like a stern mother. "And tell Devlyn. I understand you not wanting to worry him, especially if it's nothing, but he deserves to know. This is his baby too."

I love and hate that she is right. But this is why I talk with my best friends. They look at my situation from a different angle, with a fresh perspective.

"I will. Promise."

The last hour at Jonas and Autumn's house goes by a bit lighter. Devlyn curls me into his side as we sit by the fire bowl and chat with our friends. By the time we exchange hugs and goodnights, I breathe easier.

Tomorrow, I will call Dr. Webster and set an appointment. Tomorrow, I will tell Devlyn what I felt earlier. Tell him about the pain in my chest. That is what partners in committed relationships do; we share everything. No matter the outcome.

fourteen

DEVLYN

My phone rings on the drafting table, inches from where I'm sketching a new piece. A drawing requested by a new client. A portrait of the woman's grandchildren, their adorable smiles—one of which is missing a front tooth—glowing in the photo she sent.

I set my pencil down and swipe my phone off the table to see Shelly's name on the screen. I tap the green phone icon and smile as I say, "Hello."

"Hi," she replies, her voice a breath over a whisper. "Do you have a minute?"

My muscles tense up at her question. Why would she ask that? Of the two of us, my schedule is nothing but flexible. "Of course. What's wrong?"

"I, uh…" She goes quiet, but I still hear noises in the background. Then she exhales audibly. "I had to set a new doctor's appointment with Dr. Webster."

Metal scrapes wood as I rise from my stool. My vision blurs and stomach twists as my mind conjures up countless reasons why Shelly would need to see Dr. Webster sooner than her next appointment. Unable to be still, I pace the length of the room. Take a deep breath and inhale the scents of the studio. Allow the earthy smells to ground me as I grow more frantic with each breath.

"Why?"

"I, uh…"

Shelly goes quiet again. I picture her fidgeting with her apron strings as she works up the nerve to answer. Why is she so hesitant? Did something happen to her? Is the baby okay? The longer she remains silent, the longer my list of worse-case scenarios gets.

After what feels like a week, she speaks again. "I've been having pains," she says a breath above a whisper.

As I reach the landing for the stairs, instead of spinning around to pace the room again, I take the stairs two at a time. Reach the bottom floor before the next words leave my lips. "What kind of pains? Is it the baby?"

I dash to the bedroom, put the phone on speaker and strip out of my clothes. I grab a clean pair of jeans and a fresh shirt, slipping them on as she talks.

"No. I don't know. I-I don't think so." Her voice stutters. "It's in my chest, near my heart."

My hands freeze as I slip on socks. *Her heart. No. No, no, no.* I take a deep breath and beg my mind to not travel down the road of misdiagnoses. Not to think of things such as heart failure or angina or embolisms. Shelly is too young for heart problems, isn't she? *Stay calm. You can't help her if you're freaking the fuck out.*

"When is your appointment?" My voice cracks at the end.

"Today at four."

"I'll pick you up."

"Dev, no." She huffs on the other end as I pick up the phone and take it off speaker. "My car is here. I'll meet you there."

My eyes close and I clamp them tightly. Let the discomfort distract me momentarily. Tell myself to take another breath and not force my insistence upon her. We don't know what the problem is. It could be something minor. Completely normal.

I need to let her make decisions. I need to not steal her choices like my mother did for me.

Unless the doctor says otherwise.

"Okay, I'll be there." I wander out of the bedroom and into the kitchen. Stare blankly at the counters and cabinets and appliances, unsure what to do next. "Do you need anything until then?"

The clock on the stove reads just after two. I inhale deeply and twist the phone up on the exhale. Close my eyes and focus on what I *can* control. In less than two hours, I will see her. In less than two hours, we will figure out why she is having chest pains. *Shelly will be okay. The baby will be okay.*

"No, thank you," she says softly, a smile in her voice.

"Take it easy until you leave. Please." I don't care if I come across as desperate. I *am* desperate.

She chuckles. "I will. Elizabeth won't let me do anything except arrange. Not even paperwork. She says it'll stress me out too much."

Light laughter spills from my lips, although I feel anything but weightless. *Thank you, Elizabeth.* "I need to send that woman a fruit basket or something. Gift her art for her birthday."

"She won't say no."

"I love you, Shell," I say, my tone more somber. "So much."

"Love you too, Dev. See you soon."

"Soon."

The call disconnects, but I don't lower the phone from my ear. My limbs remain frozen while my mind continually whirls from the news.

I don't know what is happening with Shelly, what has her heart in literal pain, but I swear to do whatever it takes to keep her safe. To keep the baby safe. She may not like what happens next, what treatment the doctor prescribes and how fragilely I tend to her every need, but I can't lose her. I *won't* lose her. Not now, not ever.

I *need* her. More than the air I breathe, more than the life force that keeps my heart beating, I need Shelly. And nothing will take her from me.

~

With each symptom Shelly tells Dr. Webster she experienced recently, I bite down harder on the inside of my cheek and curl my fingers tighter. Taste iron on my tongue as I break the skin. Feel the sting in my palms as my nails dig deeper.

These aren't minor issues. Chest pain that occasionally gets better with deep breathing, but not always. Tingling in the chest. Problems breathing and tightness in the chest. Profuse sweating and random dizziness. The more symptoms she rattles off, the more it sounds like signs of a heart attack.

Why didn't she tell me about this? I love her pride and independence, but this is different. This is serious. This not only affects Shelly, it also affects the baby.

You know why, my mind mocks. Because I would have rushed her to the emergency room. Would have begged her to stop working. Would have strongly encouraged her to sit on the couch all day and not lift a finger. All for something her regular doctor can easily help with.

Still... Shelly not speaking up and sharing this vital information makes me question her trust in me, in us. And that hurts the most.

Dr. Webster jots notes in Shelly's file, then looks up with a soft, but serious expression. "From everything you've shared, it sounds as if you're suffering from panic attacks. This isn't abnormal for new mothers or parents." She rolls herself closer to us on the stool. "But this is your body telling you that you need to relax more. Physically and mentally." She lays a hand on Shelly's forearm. "It's okay to let go of some control right now. It's okay to let others help."

Paper crinkles as Shelly drops her head back on the exam table. "Feels like I've already given up so much."

"And you may have. Just remind yourself why you're giving up these tasks. Temporarily." She scoots the stool back and stands. "When the little one arrives, life will slowly go back to normal. Well, the new normal." Dr. Webster shifts her gaze my way. "Let Dad help out. Anything heavy or stressful, let him carry some of the weight."

Pushing up on her elbows, Shelly moves to a seated position. "What about work?" She tugs her top back in position. "I need to work." Desperation licks her tone, pleading with Dr. Webster to not take work away from her.

"You're still at the florist shop?" Shelly nods. "Work is fine." Shelly sags in relief just as Dr. Webster points a finger. "But no picking up boxes or bending at the waist. Simpler tasks only. Desk work or flower arrangements. I don't foresee many disgruntled customers."

Except maybe another visit from my mother. *Please, no. No more visits from Karen Templar.*

"I know giving up some of your freedoms isn't easy, but it's not just about you anymore."

"You're right." Shelly sighs. "It's just... how will I know what's too strenuous until I do it?"

Dr. Webster chats with us a few more minutes before escorting us to the checkout desk. She mentions how panic attacks could elevate blood pressure. And uncontrolled blood pressure may equal bed rest, something Shelly definitely does not want. Before she walks off, she reminds Shelly one last time to go slow, to take her time. She suggests pregnancy yoga and meditation and more walks at the park.

We wander out the door and head for our cars. I hate that we are leaving in separate vehicles, especially after this visit, but thankfully the drive home is short. And then I will cater to Shelly while she relaxes.

The situation isn't what either of us expected or wanted, but we have to adjust accordingly. Remind ourselves this modification in our daily routine is temporary. Remind ourselves why this change is necessary.

Sidling up to Shelly at her car, I press my lips to her forehead. "See you at home."

She nods, her eyes glazed over slightly. "At home."

As she drives away, a weight forms in my stomach. A weight I cannot shake. A weight that tells me there is more to come. And honestly, I'm not sure how much more I can handle.

The next four months are going to be the death of me.

Am I being a bit dramatic? Probably, but I don't care. I have earned the right to be a drama queen. When you have done everything on your own for decades, being told you can't sucks. Losing any semblance of your independence sucks. Feeling helpless sucks.

Not a minute passes where I regret this pregnancy. If anything, I consider myself lucky to have found Devlyn, to have fallen in love with him, to start the next phase of life with him.

But so much has changed in such a short period. In the process, part of me feels as if I have lost myself. Lost the woman I was before Devlyn and pregnancy. Lost the time I once had with friends and family.

Again, I have zero regrets about my relationship with Devlyn. I love him. More than I thought I could love another person. I don't regret the baby either. It's just… I wish our time line was different. I wish Devlyn and I would've had more time together first. To explore life and love, just the two of us, before going from zero to one-hundred in the blink of an eye.

All of it happened so quickly. Us evolving from *just friends* to boyfriend and girl-friend to living together with a baby on the way. In less than six months, we went from nothing to everything.

Much as I wanted a relationship like those in my romance novels, I didn't expect to get the whole shebang all at once. The guy, the house, the baby. Fingers crossed, I get the happily ever after too.

Two weeks ago, Dr. Webster said I'd suffered from panic attacks. The most unfathomable part of her diagnosis was that I'd never experienced anxiety prior to pregnancy. Not once. Perhaps it takes a momentous occasion to trigger anxiety or depression. Or maybe it's part of our genetic makeup and remains dormant in some until the match is struck.

Hopefully my lessened activity and new meditative regimen helps reduce the attacks. Hopefully they vanish altogether, otherwise there will be medication and the possibility of bed rest. I'd like to avoid both.

"That's stunning," Elizabeth says as she returns from lunch.

I eye the bouquet on the arrangement table, twisting the vase left then right as a smile plumps my cheeks. "Thank you."

The plethora of pink flowers is at the request of one of our regular customers. His wife adores pink—she obviously has good taste—and he ordered the arrange-ment for their twenty-fifth wedding anniversary. After a hefty payment, he gave us free rein to choose the flowers and greenery. His only request… *"It needs a lot of pink."*

"How many stems have you added?"

I lean back and look for any *empty* spots in the bouquet. "Thirty." I twist my lips in concentration. "I'd like to get a full three dozen."

Elizabeth pats my shoulder. "You will." A soft smile on her lips as she wanders off. "I'll be in the back unpacking the delivery. Holler if you need me."

"Will do."

I go back to the bouquet and zone out as I add the last remaining stems to the vase. Satisfied with the bouquet, I take it into the cooler where we stash orders waiting to be delivered. As I exit, I spot a man in the store near the meadow mural.

"Good afternoon," I greet him. "Is there anything I can help you with today?"

For two breaths, he doesn't acknowledge my presence. Doesn't speak a word. He simply stares at the painting on the wall.

Queasiness twists my stomach. Has me inching away from this stranger. My eyes fall shut as I inhale deeply and tell my body and mind to relax. Tell myself to not get worked up over nothing. He could simply be admiring the work, nothing more.

Cool and a bit more collected, my eyes open as I put on my best work smile. I open my mouth to tell the man I will leave him to browse and check back with him shortly, but he speaks up first.

"Beautiful piece," he states. The soft timbre of his voice is vaguely familiar. Though I have never met this man, something about him screams recognition. My brows pinch together as I study him from the corner of my eye.

"Um, thank you." I wipe my hands on the apron at my waist. "A local artist painted the mural for the shop."

The man shoves his hands in the pockets of his dress slacks, rocks back on his heels once, then nods. "I'm familiar with his work."

Never said the artist was a man. The queasiness in my belly builds as bile climbs up my throat.

Who is this man? And why the hell does he make me uncomfortable?

Taking a step back, then another, I separate myself from the wobbly energy he exudes. "Well, if you need—"

"Are you Shelly?"

Every instinct in me screams to not answer him. Is he some kind of stalker? It wouldn't be the first time a customer obsessed over the way I arrange flowers. Odd as it is, it has happened. To both me and Elizabeth.

"Uh…"

The man twists to face me head on and extends a hand my way. "Sorry. James Templar."

For the love of all that is holy in this world. Someone, please rescue me from the never-ending surprises.

James Templar… for a beat, I take him in. Brown locks trimmed neat and close to his scalp. Familiar angular jawline. Same height. Same build. Same glass-green irises. Without question, this man is Devlyn's father.

But why is he here?

Reluctantly, I place my hand in his and shake. "Shelly. But you already knew that somehow." I quickly withdraw my hand.

His hand goes back to his pocket and he takes a step back, granting me room to breathe. Time ticks by and neither of us says a word. And in this momentary blip of time, I acknowledge that James Templar is nothing like his wife. Quite the opposite, actually. While she demands attention, he seems content with disappearing. She is the spotlight and he is the shadow. How odd.

So why is he married to her? Why does he allow her to verbally and emotionally abuse their only child?

"Is there something you needed?" I ask, my tone as neutral as possible. Although this man has not garnered my respect, my parents would berate me for weeks if I spoke to a stranger without courtesy.

"I, uh…" He glances back to the mural before meeting my eyes once more. "It's not my place or position to do so, but I came here to apologize."

My forehead tightens as my brows drop. "Apologize?"

The only person who should apologize is Karen Templar. She has inflicted one wound after another. This man, Devlyn's father, has not slighted me. As for Devlyn… I don't know their history or how often he speaks with his dad. I honestly can't recall a time when Devlyn mentioned his father.

He swallows, then nods. "Yes. For how Devlyn's mother has behaved recently."
Seriously?

Not sure what it is, but this man driving an hour to come apologize for his wife's actions pisses me off. Try as I might, calming my rising blood pressure proves challenging. But with each throb and whoosh of my pulse, I remind myself I need to find my zen. I need to relax. If not for me, for the baby.

But I swear, as soon as this baby is born, these people will hear my wrath.
"Why?"

He tilts his head and eyes me for a beat. "Why?" he asks and I nod. "Shelly, I don't know you. Don't know anything about you, but you seem like a nice person." He smiles and it instantly makes me think of Devlyn and the identical smile he doesn't grant many or often. "For Devlyn to be so taken by you…" His eyes avert to the mural for a breath. "With his past, it must mean you matter to him. Very much."

"So, you're apologizing because Devlyn and I are together and I seem like a nice person?"

What a strange reason.

First off, he shouldn't *have* to apologize for his wife. She should apologize. Not that I'd listen after her degradation. That woman believes she is the epitome of perfection, when in truth, she wouldn't know real courtesy if it slapped her in the face.

Second, and still, why? Why is he here? What has he heard in regard to our recent interactions with his wife?

Last, and probably most importantly, why does this feel like a bandage over something that requires surgery to fix?

This whole interaction feels like one big clusterfuck of confusion. Maybe James Templar usually skirts around the truth. Maybe he is always the fixer-upper. The one that steps in after hurricane Karen wreaks havoc on whatever upsets her and rebuilds the broken structures.

I don't get it. Why he is here and what he hopes to resolve with this conversation. But if he doesn't get to the point soon, I may just ask him to leave and walk away.

On an audible exhale, he shakes his head. "Not just that." His head hangs forward, his eyes on his dress shoes. "I haven't spoken with Devlyn for months." Slowly, he lifts his head and our eyes meet. "Our relationship, mine with Devlyn, isn't the same as with his mother. Since he left for college, we talked less. That's just our personalities. But we always talked. At least every couple of weeks, if only for a few minutes over the phone." He works his jaw in a nervous jitter. His eyes crinkling at the corners slightly. "I haven't spoken with him since November. Not since the day before the art exhibition."

More than six months. Didn't he spend time with them during Christmas? Maybe his father wasn't there. Devlyn attended a holiday party his mother hosted, but perhaps it was more of a schmoozing event than actual time spent with family.

Did Devlyn cut his father off because of his mother? Because of me?

"I'm not sure what to say."

It's the truth. I have no clue what to tell this man. I don't make decisions for Devlyn. And from what he has told me about his parents, he didn't really make his own decisions until he left home. Even then, his mother still directed part of the narrative.

But I won't do that. Ever. Nor will I let his parents disrupt all the progress he has made with countless hours of therapy. Therapy no person should have to endure. Not for this.

"You don't need to say anything." He rocks back on his heels again and I realize this must be a nervous action for him. "I truly am sorry for how Devlyn's mother has behaved. Toward him and you."

"All due respect, Mr. Templar, you shouldn't be apologizing for her." I give him a tight, uncomfortable smile. "And I'm not sure if an apology will ever make up for the damage she has done."

An odd flutter erupts in my belly and, without thinking, I lay a hand on my lower abdomen. The second I do, his eyes drop and land on my hand. Immediately, I shift and tuck my hands in my back pockets.

But it is too late. The deed is done. I see it in the widening of his eyes. Hear it in his loud swallow.

His eyes lift to mine and I watch as they glass over. As recognition truly sets in. As this man realizes I am carrying his grandchild, someone he may never meet because of his wife.

"It's not your place, Shelly, but will you please ask Devlyn to call or text me?" He blinks back the tears rimming his eyes. "I won't say anything" —his eyes drift to my belly for a breath— "to his mother about..." *the baby.* I see the words in his eyes. A proclamation he won't voice, maybe to protect the baby and Devlyn.

"I will make mention, but not any promises." My eyes hold his. "Devlyn makes his own choices. If he wants to speak with you, that is his decision to make. His voice has been stolen from him for too many years. I won't do the same."

James nods as he rolls his lips between his teeth. "Thank you, Shelly." He takes a step back and removes his hands from his pockets. "For what it's worth, I hope to know you one day. From what I can tell, you're a good person. I'm happy my son has you."

Every cell in my body wants to thank this man for the kind sentiment, but I stop myself. Clamp my lips tight and refuse to grant him gratitude. Not when he has enabled his wife's cruelty toward Devlyn his entire life. Thanking this man wipes away all the harm he caused by not stepping up for his own child. Thanking this man would imply compliments and recognition diminish the pain his wife—and by proxy, him—inflicted.

I won't grant him such kindness. Not because I, too, am cruel. But because I love Devlyn. Unconditionally. I stand by him, through the hurt and happiness. Through the tears and laughter.

When it dawns on James I have nothing more to say, he nods, takes a step back, pivots away, and ambles toward the door. "Hope we meet again, Shelly." He glances one last time at my belly, gives me a pained smile, then leaves.

I wander to the door and stare out the glass to watch him drive away. He slips behind the wheel of a white BMW sedan, lifts a hand when he notices me watching, then backs out.

My hand goes to my ponytail, my fingers toying with the strands as I continue to look outside. Watching. Waiting. Praying for no more surprises. Although this one isn't half as bad as the previous surprises, it still unsettles me.

James Templar may be nothing like his wife, but he still hurt his son. Making up for all he and his wife have done will take a heck of a lot more than one conversation in Petal and Vine. It will take drastic measures. A larger-than-life change.

For Devlyn's sake, I hope he gets to keep at least one parent. Without the influence of his wife, James Templar may be a good man. A man worthy of being a grandfather to our child. A man Devlyn might look up to in the future.

sixteen

DEVLYN

"Your dad stopped by the shop today."

My fork hovers between my plate and mouth as I process what Shelly just said. Slowly, I set my fork down and swallow. Let her words sink in.

My father was in Petal and Vine today.

Why?

"Are you okay?" I don't need my father stirring up my mother's wasp nest of activity and upsetting Shelly.

"Yeah," she says on a nod. "He was kind."

This doesn't come as a surprise. My father never had a mean bone in his body. He also lost his backbone standing beside my mother.

"What did he want?"

"To meet me, and to ask me to ask you if you'd call or text him."

Shelly says the words so casually. Not an ounce of concern in her tone. Which is a tremendous relief.

My father may not be barbaric like my mother, but he disregards her words and actions as if they mean nothing. As if they harm no one. Recently, I learned his behavior was unacceptable. I learned his actions were equally as damaging as saying and doing the acts themselves.

Shelly reaches across the table and lays her hand over mine. "He was kind," she repeats. "I made him no promises. That I'd tell you or that you'd follow through." Her shimmery blues lock with my greens. "Reaching out is your choice." She gives my hand a gentle squeeze. "Also…"

My eyes dart between hers as I wait for her to finish. "Also, what?"

"I think he surmised I'm pregnant." *Shit.* "I felt this flutter and my hand automatically went to my belly."

I don't curse Shelly for inadvertently letting my father know about the baby. I curse that he may say something to my mother. Which may trigger another visit. A visit we do not need.

"Devlyn, I don't know the first thing about your father, but he seems to genuinely miss you. Or at least the conversations you shared."

James Templar is a good man that has done countless good deeds for others. He never speaks ill of anyone, ever—including my mother, which is part of the problem. He may be a good man, but he doesn't know how to be strong—for himself or others.

If he has a good heart, is it possible to fix his broken pieces? Several hours per month, I work to mend my own broken parts. Perhaps he can do the same. I like to think it is possible, but as long as he stands beside my mother, I won't take unnecessary or foolish risks.

"I'll reach out to him." I pick my fork back up and lift the bite to my mouth. "How was the rest of your day?"

Over the rest of dinner, Shelly recants her day at work. Although she dislikes all the physical adjustments she's had to make, I see the impact. In the rosy blush on her cheeks and endless vibrant smile. In her twilight irises as they twinkle and shimmer. In the radiant light of her aura as she stands in my presence.

It is all I need. Her. Her smile. The peace she provides. The love she gives.

Just Shelly.

~

Bristles stroke the canvas as I paint Shelly in various swirls of pink. A splash of fiery rose. A sweep of delicate blush. A swish of addictive taffy.

Painting this piece without her here isn't the same. This interpretation is new. Poles apart from my usual pieces. An unrealistic portrayal of the woman I have come to love so profoundly.

I see her so clearly when I close my eyes. Her curvaceous breasts and hips. The hollow of her throat and contour of her collarbones. Wisps of hair on her cheek as she lies on the pillows and blankets. The parting of her lips and glimmer in her eyes as I leer around the canvas with the brush between my teeth.

The more pigment I add, the more abstract the painting becomes. As it evolves, I fall harder for my muse. *My Andromeda.*

More often than not, my art is realistic. I paint and draw objects and people as I see them with the naked eye. Maybe tweak the color or shading or position, but not much else.

This painting is unlike every other I have created. This painting is unrestrained passion.

Every tinge of red coats the canvas. From borderline black to muted pink. Because Shelly *is* the whole spectrum. She is red and pink and every tint and shade between. She is passion and love. Soft and pure. The gentlest caress and fiercest protector. She is the light to my dark. My North Star.

In my periphery, my phone lies on the table beside my easel. Taunting me. Provoking me. My hand freezes, the brush an inch from the canvas as I stare at the annoying piece of technology.

Computers and tablets and cell phones have existed in my life as long as I can remember. They were tools in school and distractions at home. Although I appreciate the ways technology has saved lives, I hate how some innovations have robbed people of their lives.

I may have grown up in the internet era, but I wish it didn't exist.

It sucks the joy from my soul and gifts anxiety in return. The pressure to always be available. Emails and text messages and calling you wherever and whenever. While people become addicted to apps and social media, I work harder to disconnect from it all. If a website wasn't essential for business, I would let it go.

My eyes shift to the table again and the urge to throw my cell phone in the garbage skyrockets. Only because my father wants to speak, wants me to call or text him.

"Should just get it over with," I mumble as I set down the paintbrush.

From everything Shelly told me three nights ago, my father was nothing but cordial and kind while he spoke with her in Petal and Vine. She said he'd even looked a bit sad.

Dad always had a forlorn look about him, but I never asked why. Was I the reason for his sadness? We hadn't spoken in so long, but it's not as if we had profound conversations. Or is it Mom who has made him unhappy?

As years passed, and I put more distance between myself and my parents, I often wondered if Dad was happy with Mom. On any level. She had always been equally wicked and degrading toward him. Criticizing him harshly and not strictly behind closed doors.

Why did he put up with it? Did he not think himself worthy of more? It boggles me how someone could be with a person who treated them as if they didn't matter, as if everything they did wasn't good enough. Even in love, a person should only tolerate so much. How did Dad love her, or even like her, when she treated him like garbage?

But asking myself these questions will get me nowhere. The only person that can answer them is him.

I need to call him. I need to talk with him. Both I have avoided, but can't put off any longer.

Swiping my phone from the table, I rise from the stool and step away from the painting. Regardless of the direction this call takes, I don't want negative energy tainting this piece. Not Shelly.

I trek down the stairs and head for the kitchen. With Shelly at work, the house is quiet. Too quiet. Months ago, the stillness of my house, my space, was something I craved. Solace in solitude. Peace among the chaos. An abrupt shift from my busy art mind.

Now, the silence makes my skin crawl. I don't like when Shelly leaves. Although her earthy floral scent lingers and I see her touch in every room, I miss her energy. Miss her sweet voice and soft words. The way she brightens a room without effort.

Her absence is why I seclude myself in the studio all day. When she works, so do I.

I fill a glass with water and reheat leftovers for lunch. As the microwave counts down to zero, I unlock my phone, press my father's contact in the list, and stare at the screen.

He isn't as bad as her, yet he is.

A shrill beep snaps my attention from my phone. I carry lunch to the dining room table and sit in my usual seat. At the heart of the table sits a small vase of peonies. Fresh flowers are a simple touch Shelly has added to almost every room in the house.

I ignore lunch to stare at the delicate pink petals for a beat. So soft, so elegant. Quintessential and very much Shelly. Even in her absence, she is here—her warmth and heart—swathing me in strength and support and love.

Unlocking my phone again, my finger hovers the phone icon as I pick at the pasta primavera.

Now or never. Just get it over with.

Before I lose the nerve, I press the icon and lift the phone to my ear. With it being the middle of the day, Dad should be at work and nowhere near Mom. The phone rings once, twice, then he answers.

"Devlyn?"

"Hey, Dad."

Silence stretches between us, but it doesn't unnerve me, not like with Mom. Dad and I have always had this unspoken language. A side effect of our reticent nature. Neither of us feels the need to fill every second with unnecessary speech. Sometimes, the most profound things come about in silence.

"How are you?" His question not abnormal, but his tone is hesitant. Unsure. Troubled.

I stab a piece of pasta and carrot. "Good. You?"

Shelly said Dad pieced together she was pregnant, but never stated as much before leaving the shop. Until he says or asks, I won't touch the topic. Until I know where Dad's head is, I will keep all things Shelly related in the background. To protect her and the baby.

"Could be better." His heavy sigh reaches me through the phone. Tugs at the sympathetic heartstrings I have for him. "Devlyn, I…" He goes silent for a moment, but I don't interject. Don't butt into the words he wants to say, but has difficulty vocalizing. While he thinks, I eat. "I have some news." The lack of inflection in his voice gives nothing away.

"Okay," I drawl out the word.

"I asked your mother for a divorce."

The bite in my mouth goes down the wrong pipe as I go into a coughing fit. I pull the phone away from my ear, beat a fist to my sternum, and cough until the stray noodle dislodges.

When I bring the phone back to my ear, he asks, "Are you okay?" True concern laces his voice.

I cough again, then sip my water. "Fine," I croak out. "What brought this on? The divorce, I mean."

While Dad sits quiet on the other end, I drink more water. I push the food away with the intent to hear him out and not go into another choking fit. Who knows what other surprises he will hit me with.

"It's been a long time coming," he finally says, a hint of relief in his words. "When your mother and I met, life was different. *We* were different." He audibly exhales. "She changed after we said I do. I'd been so in love with her at the time that I didn't give attention to the little signs. When we found out she was pregnant, those little signs got bigger, but I blamed them on hormones. I blamed it on the worry that comes with impending parenthood." He goes silent and I picture him hanging his head. "But it wasn't that at all. As much as I wanted to leave then, I couldn't. I wouldn't abandon you and let you suffer alone."

Dad stayed married to Mom more than half his adult life… for me. Wow. Just… wow. I don't know whether to thank him or slap him.

Both of our lives could have been polar opposites of what they are today. It is quite possible neither of us would feel emotionally annihilated had he left sooner. Yes, most courts side with the mother in custody cases. But I question whether or not my mother would've wanted me without my father. Sure, she may have molded me more in her likeness had he not been around, but I can't picture her *wanting* me around. Period. Unless she had something to gain.

"Dad… why didn't you say something sooner?"

"Son, it's not your burden to bear." He takes a breath. "After the incident in the grocery store not long ago, which I cringed at when your mother told me, I knew it was time. Way past time. Since you moved out and we moved to Tampa, your mother has been on some kick. I thought it'd taper off, but it's only gotten worse."

Great. My mother losing her shit more often is not *what I need. Not what any of us* needs.

"When I asked why she'd been in the grocery store an hour from home, she struck me. Told me it was none of my business. That she was working." He audibly exhales. "But it was a lie. Her work never puts her near you. So, I started monitoring her closer. Tracking where she was and her phone activity." He laughs without humor. "Sounds creepy, but I was worried about you."

"You were?"

"Always, Devlyn. I took the brunt of your mother's attacks over the years… to protect you. As much as I could, anyway." He pauses a beat. "I learned your mother had been following you and your girlfriend. More often than I care to admit. When I called her out on it, she lost it. Said you were ruining your life." He sighs heavily and I picture him tracing his brows with his thumb and finger. "I don't want to rehash the horrible things she said, but in that moment, I no longer wanted to sit idle. No longer wanted either of us to be subject to her terror. So, I've spent weeks speaking with an attorney. A lot of things are tied to your mother's name, including parts of your life. I want both of us to come out as clean as possible when it ends."

White noise fizzles around me as I mull over this new information.

Dad is divorcing Mom.

He is leaving her.

For himself, but also for me.

Although I wish it would have happened earlier, I can't fault him for his decisions. James Templar is not brainless. For years, I questioned how he loved my mother. How he loved someone so manipulative and brutal and poisonous. But he'd hid what lay beneath the surface of his relationship with her. He buried his suffering to keep me close.

Much as I wish he'd made a change years ago, I understand his reasons for staying.

"What happens now?"

Not much of my mother is entwined in my life. Her name carried weight in the art community and opened doors for me in the past, but it no longer bears the same influence. Yes, the Templar name has significance in the area, but I tip the scales more than her now. My art speaks volumes and I no longer need the influence of Karen Templar.

The only thing I question now is my house. Mom insisted on helping out when purchasing the house after college. Seeing as I had minimal credit and was just building my savings, I didn't deny her.

When was the last time I looked at my mortgage statement? Months, perhaps. And how had the deed been titled when the sale of the house finalized? My name was on the deed, but it hadn't been the only name printed. Did half of my house belong to her? *Oh, god.* Bile rises in my throat at the idea of my safe space—the house I invited Shelly into, the place where our child will grow and learn and laugh —is possibly tainted and at risk.

Shit.

"I hear your mind spinning from here. Devlyn, everything will be fine."

"What about my house?" The words a squeaky whisper on my tongue.

If her name is on this house, I will move us out. Find us a new home, far from here. Last thing I or Shelly need is my mother's torment because her life is upside down. I won't put Shelly or the baby in harm's way. I won't allow my mother to ruin either of them the way she did me and Dad.

"Your house is yours, son."

"Isn't she—"

"No. She's not on the deed or the loan. I am, which I'll happily change, if you wish."

Thank the powers that be.

Dad and I talk another twenty minutes before he says goodbye. But before he hangs up, he asks to have dinner with me and Shelly sometime soon. That and he wants more calls or texts, even if there is nothing notable to talk about.

When the call disconnects, a tremendous weight lifts from my shoulders. Not all of it is gone, but it feels more bearable. Manageable. Less pained and more healing.

It feels like my life is finally heading in a positive direction in every way. Something I need—not just for myself, but also for Shelly and our future.

For the first time in my adult life, I breathe and it hurts less.

seventeen

I might die from this incessant heat.

Far back as I remember, I have loved living the Florida life. Sunshine year round. Blue skies with the occasional fluffy cloud or two. Countless outdoor activities. Theme parks and festivals and concerts. The beach, the sand, the warmth.

But right now, in this paralyzing summer weather, my ankles are swollen. My fingers look more like small sausages than tools to write and eat and function. Sweat slicks my skin in the most awkward places. My clothes are itchy and tight and annoying. And this new ache formed in my lower back.

I am not okay with this. Not at all.

With each passing month, my body changes more and more. I get it. Really, I do. I am cooking a human.

Some of the changes aren't so bad. Nausea—gone. Me and all the cheeses are good friends again. Hallelujah. Body swelling… unacceptable. Wasting money on maternity clothes… unacceptable. Instead, I wear Devlyn's T-shirts and loose shorts or lounge pants. Hell, I will wear a robe all day if need be. Back pain… also unacceptable.

Dr. Webster recommended pregnancy massage for the back pain. I jumped on that bandwagon immediately. She also said the swelling is perfectly normal, especially in the hotter months. She recommended less salt in my diet, more water, walking daily, and the usual rest and relaxation with my feet elevated.

I feel like an elephant. Maybe a hippo. No offense to the elephant or hippo population. But if I swell anymore, I will undoubtedly resemble Violet Beauregarde from *Willy Wonka and the Chocolate Factory* after she blows up—minus purple skin, of course.

"Why don't you relax while I start dinner," Devlyn suggests as we come in from a stroll around the neighborhood.

Tonight, Devlyn's dad is coming over for dinner. When Devlyn ran the idea past me weeks ago, my blood pressure spiked. So, he pushed it off. Told his father we needed more time.

In the last month, Devlyn has spoken with his dad at least three times a week. Gotten to know the man James really is versus the man he thought he knew. During those conversations, Devlyn found a new level of comfort with his father. A bond they should have had years ago. And when his father agreed two weeks ago to have joint therapy sessions with Devlyn, some of my own worry eased.

I want our baby to be surrounded by as much love as possible. Having at least one person from Devlyn's family present would be wonderful. Devlyn deserves love too. A love he wanted for years, but didn't realize how much he'd been deprived of until recently.

"I'd like to help," I say, toeing off my shoes.

We wander to the kitchen and Devlyn starts pulling food from the cabinets and fridge. I lean my hip against the counter and watch as he moves around the kitchen.

"Kick your feet up for a few. I'll do the tedious stuff, then come get you for the rest. Deal?"

I huff under my breath. *Really hate feeling like a useless child.* Not overexerting myself is good for me and the baby, deep down I know this. But when I am used to doing it all, sitting on my butt while others wait on me, hand and foot, makes me feel like a nuisance. Like I don't contribute in any way.

That stings the most.

Sticking out my pinkie, I wait for Devlyn to hook his with mine. Two steps in my direction, he latches our pinkies as his lips kick up in a half smile. "Promise."

Making my way to the living room, I plop down on the couch and scroll through the shows. I land on *The Vampire Diaries* and hit play. It's been a while since I binged this show.

Halfway through the episode, Devlyn wanders into the living room and parks next to me on the couch. He lays his head on my shoulder and stares at the screen. Minutes of the show carry on, neither of us speaking. And it is moments like this that calm every woe. Moments like this that make all the craziness—family and pregnancy and our fast-paced relationship—worthwhile.

For years, I wanted this. Someone to love me without effort. Someone that connected with me on an unprecedented level. Someone that will stick with me through the good and not so good.

The start of our love story may be muddled with indecision and chaos, but I wouldn't change it or us. Devlyn wouldn't be who he is today without his past, and neither would I. Our love wouldn't be what it is without it either.

"Ready to cook?" he whispers when the episode ends.

"Yes."

As if we have done it years, Devlyn and I move around the kitchen with ease as we prepare dinner. Minutes before the timer goes off for the oven, the doorbell chimes.

Here we go.

Devlyn sets the spoon on the rest. With his hand on my lower back, he kisses my temple. "Be right back."

"'Kay," I breathe out.

He pads off to answer the door and I stir the couscous with more gusto than necessary. Sweat dampens my skin as I hear the dead bolt disengage and the door open before mumbled hellos filter in.

This is it. I take a deep breath and check on the chicken in the oven. *Devlyn's father is* not *his mother. This dinner will end in smiles.*

A moment later, Devlyn reenters the kitchen with his father in tow. A loud beep fills the room as the timer on the range goes off. I turn it off, along with the burner for the couscous, top the pot with a lid and remove it from the heat.

Jitters flow through my limbs as I spin around to face Devlyn and James. Two breaths pass and my nerves settle a little as I stare at the two of them. Looking at James is like looking into the future. Devlyn is definitely his father's son. If James's appearance is any indication, Devlyn will age well.

The room is filled with awkward tension as the three of us stand there, unspeaking. After a beat, James breaks the silence. "Nice to see you again, Shelly." James offers his hand.

Devlyn's father is not his mother.

I take his hand and note how similar yet different his grip is from Devlyn's. Devlyn has soft hands with the occasional callous. His fingers are thin and long. His touch gentle yet strong. James harbors a different type of strength. One built from years of labor and life. The skin where his fingers meet his hand is rougher. Yet I still feel a gentleness in his touch.

"Nice to meet you officially," I say.

Our hands break apart and Devlyn offers his father a drink. The two men open a beer while I fill a glass with sparkling cider. While I fetch plates, Devlyn takes the chicken from the oven. We dish the meal onto plates and make our way into the dining room.

James's gaze drifts around the room as if seeing it with new eyes. *How long has it been since he has set foot in this house?* Until meeting James in Petal and Vine last month, I'd never seen him. It was always Devlyn's mother that made an appearance. And until last month, Devlyn hadn't spoken to James since late November.

I watch as his eyes take in all the new additions to the house. A short vase of flowers at the heart of the table. Art on two of the three dining room walls—Devlyn's art, of course. Large candles on either side of the vase that Devlyn lit when I wasn't looking. A soft rug beneath the table and chairs. And that is just this room.

Devlyn lived a monochromatic life filled with occasional color before we met. My life had been the opposite. Now we balance each other. Spark new life where things once faded away.

"I love the changes you've made," James says, eyes darting from me to Devlyn. "Feels more like a home."

"I'll give you an updated tour after dinner," Devlyn suggests.

Wrinkles form at the corners of James's mouth and eyes as an all too familiar smile dons his face. "I'd love that very much."

Thank goodness his genetics overpowered hers.

Dinner carries on with timid conversation. James asks Devlyn about his recent artwork and me about the flower shop. Neither of us dives in deep at first, but the more we chat, the more comfortable we all become. We have yet to discuss anything about the baby, but hiding my growing belly becomes harder with each passing day.

When our plates clear, I offer to do dishes so Devlyn can show his father around the house.

Not much of the house has changed from my moving in. Not needing the furniture, I sold all but a few smaller items. The small space between the kitchen and doors to the patio had been empty prior to me moving in. Now, my small sofa, end and coffee table, and bookshelf fill the space and look out the sliding glass doors to the backyard. The small change doesn't overwhelm the nook, but makes it a cozy place to read a book or have additional seating if and when we have guests over.

As I load the last of the dishes into the washer, Devlyn and James enter the kitchen. Both wear matching smiles and carry a new sense of ease.

Devlyn needed this. They both did. The last several months have been a challenge for us both, but more for Devlyn. So much of his life has changed. He saw a new side to his mother, one he'd been willfully blind to for years, and disconnected her from his life. In doing so, pieces of his past flooded in and knocked the air from his lungs. Everything he thought he knew as a child and young man had been blanketed with falsehoods and manipulation. Although his parents, more so his mother, had twisted his mind, he has slowly found a way to unravel all the hurt and heartache and influence.

Now he has the chance at a new life with his father. One filled with love and compassion and trust—over time. And this small token warms my heart. That he gets to keep one parent. That he doesn't feel completely abandoned.

"So," James speaks up as we walk to the sitting room. "I don't know how to broach the subject..." Devlyn and I sit on the love seat as James sits in one of the chairs across from us. "Or if I should." He picks at the knee of his slacks.

"We won't know unless you do," Devlyn states with a chuckle.

I love how light and carefree he is at my side. How warm and comfortable he is as the evening progresses. Not that Devlyn has never displayed such qualities. Just wasn't sure what his reaction would be having his father nearby after a long absence.

A soft smile pushes up the corners of James's lips. "I'd like to talk about..." He pauses, his jaw working left and right, his lips clamped between his teeth. "About the baby," he says after a moment.

It wasn't a question of *if* the subject would come up before James left, it was a question of *when*. Honestly, it surprises me it didn't come up sooner.

Devlyn wraps an arm around my shoulders, tucks me into his side, and lays his free hand on my lap. If that doesn't scream his need to protect me and the baby, not much else would in this moment.

"Okay," Devlyn says, but doesn't expand further.

Tonight is more about Devlyn reconnecting with his dad than about me getting to know James. Devlyn needs this—they both do—but his instinct to shield me from the toxicity of his past far outweighs his need to connect.

Every word and action from James this evening has been nothing short of kind and caring. Not once has he been cruel. Nor has he belittled Devlyn. The entire evening felt *normal*. And we can use all the normal we can get.

That said, this man also spent more than two decades of his life with Karen Templar—a woman I will never trust.

Tension thickens the air in the room as we all wait for what happens next. Wait for what will be said or asked. As prescribed by Dr. Webster, I do my best to not let the stress of the moment consume my thoughts.

As if he senses my semifrazzled state, Devlyn's thumb draws small circles on my shoulder. I focus my attention on his light touch. Focus on the solace it provides. Count in my head with each circuit his thumb makes.

"It will take time for us to be in a better place, I know," James says with a subtle nod. "But I want to be part of my grandchild's life. In whatever way you feel is best."

"Dad, I..." Devlyn pauses and shifts his greens to my blues. "We will need to talk about it." His eyes go back to his father. "A lot has changed. With us all." Devlyn's grip on my shoulder tightens slightly. "But more will need to change before Shelly and I consider the possibility."

Across from us, James nods as he hangs his head a little. "I can't fault either of you in this. All I ask is that you give it consideration." James looks at Devlyn for a beat before his eyes find mine. "Whatever you need of me—joint therapy sessions, time, specific actions—I will do it. Just please, don't shut me out."

I feel for this man. Truly.

James, too, has been through hell. Stuck in a loveless marriage for decades just so he knew his son was safe. To some degree, anyway.

"We will," I affirm. My eyes drop as my hand comes to my belly. "This baby will be loved like no other. I'd like them to be surrounded by as much as possible." I lift my gaze as a smile lights James's expression. "But… I don't know you. Not really." I flash him a sad smile. "Your wife made one heck of a first impression. Sorry to say, but it automatically made one for you too."

"I get it."

"All I ask for is time," I tell him. "Time for me to get to know you. And time with Devlyn." I look at the man holding me close, a small smile curving my lips. "In whichever way he needs it. If it's therapy, a night out together or space without you, you need to respect and grant it."

Devlyn hugs me closer and kisses my temple.

It isn't my intention to speak for Devlyn. In the eight months we have known each other, Devlyn isn't one to always speak his mind. Scared to hurt himself or the feelings of another, he shelters his emotions more often than not. I won't speak for him, but I will speak up for him. In his twenty-three years of life, not many have. Going forward, that will change.

"Promise, I will." James checks his watch. "I should get going."

James slips on his shoes. Devlyn and I walk him to his car and share hugs and goodbyes. A minute later, we wave him off as he backs out of the driveway and drives off.

Back in the house, we wander to the living room hand in hand and plop down on the couch. Minutes of silence pass as we curl into each other and breathe through the tail end of our night.

"Was really nice seeing him again," Devlyn whispers against my shoulder. "He's so… different."

I rest my head on his. "How so?"

Devlyn traces his fingers over my own, then up my hand and forearm before drifting back down. I close my eyes and absorb his touch. Allow it to warm my skin.

"He's always been calm. Laid back. But now…" Devlyn sits up to look me in the eye. Tenderness softens his expression. "I can't remember the last time he smiled. Like a genuine smile. And tonight, he gave so many."

That he did. James's smiles varied from brilliant to subtle, but they were pleasant all the same.

"I hope he finds happiness," I say softly.

Devlyn lays his head back on my shoulder. "Me too. Although he hasn't made the best decisions, he deserves happiness. And the opportunity to change."

I wholeheartedly agree. My only hope is, after so many years under Karen's thumb, James is capable of change.

Keeping secrets from Shelly is not my strong suit. But this secret must be kept.

Better to deal with only her wrath than the wrath of everyone else.

"Breakfast out was the best idea," she says as she wipes her mouth with a paper napkin. "And this café," —her eyes drift around the bustling restaurant— "how did I not know about this place?"

I shrug and give her a half smile. "Good ole Google found it for me, so…"

She waves me off. "Give yourself some of the credit. The thought crossed your mind. That's what matters most."

"Always finding the bright side." My smile widens.

An hour ago, we left the house under the guise of me not wanting to cook. Forty-five minutes ago, several of our friends pulled up to the house, went inside, and got to work. Decorations and food and whatever else happens at fun-filled adult birthday parties.

More than a week ago, Micah sent me a text message. He mentioned Shelly's upcoming birthday and how everyone wanted to throw her a party. He promised it wouldn't be much different from Sunday night get-togethers. The only difference will be decorations, cake and more time together.

I'd stared at the screen several minutes before responding. Too stunned because I didn't know Shelly's birth date, which is partially my fault. I hadn't offered mine three months ago. Had I asked hers, she'd have felt bad for missing mine.

I answered the message and soon learned it was a group text. My phone blew up for hours. One idea after another filled the gray bubbles. Party GIFs and a slew of emojis filled the screen. I'd been thankful it was the middle of the day and Shelly was at work. Half a day and an insane number of messages later, a plan was devised. A plan for a surprise party. At our house.

My responsibility for the day… don't mention birthdays or our friends and keep Shelly away from home until I get the all-clear message. Cora and Autumn estimated two hours for party setup.

So I planned breakfast out with Shelly. Although it is for her birthday, she thinks it's just because. When we leave the restaurant, the plan is to drive to a bookstore so we can walk around in air conditioning while she picks out a few new books.

She shrugs. "We should come here more. The eggs benedict was excellent, and I saw a dozen other things I'd like to try."

The server steps up and clears our plates from the table. She asks if there is anything else she can get us—offering the restaurant's award-winning pie before ten in the morning—and Shelly's eyes light up. With a laugh, I gesture to the pie menu.

One slice of key lime and peanut butter pie later, I settle the bill and we leave. A mile up the road, I turn into the plaza with the bookstore and park the car.

Shelly unbuckles her belt and shifts to face me in her seat. Her eyes narrow as she studies me intently.

She knows that I know it's her birthday. Shit. Either that or she suspects I know. Play it cool.

"Why are we here?" she asks, a hint of suspicion in her tone.

She doesn't know. She can't. Play. It. Cool.

"You haven't gotten a new book recently. When we drove past on the way to breakfast, I thought maybe you might like to look at what's new." I shrug, hoping to come across as nonchalant. "Plus, I wanted to look at baby books for dads."

Her eyes soften around the edges. "Okay," she acquiesces without an ounce of fight.

The part about looking for a book for new dads isn't a fib. Sure, I could talk to Jonas or Gavin about first-time fatherhood and what to expect. But I'd also like a resource on hand, just in case something comes up neither of them has dealt with yet.

We wander the bookstore with no set path. Eventually, Shelly will make her way to the romance section, but she steers us toward the baby and parenting books first. I let her lead, but plan to keep us in the store until I get a thumbs-up text.

After discovering two great parenting books, Shelly leads us to her favorite part of the store. I sit on a chair randomly set up in the aisle while she peruses the titles. My phone vibrates in my pocket and, with as much discretion as possible, I remove it to look at the notification. A text from Micah with a thumbs-up and nothing more. I pocket my phone and wait until Shelly finishes browsing.

A hundred dollars later, we walk out of the bookstore and I drive us home.

"Did you find some good ones?" I ask.

Shelly nods. "Yeah. A few I'd heard other book friends online rave about and one by an author I read regularly."

"Good. Glad you found some pleasure reads. The baby books are nice, but you need books for you too."

"Do you pleasure read?" she asks as I turn into the neighborhood.

I shrug. "Not in years."

"What did you like reading when you did?"

"Mostly mysteries and thrillers." I glance over at her. "But I'll give anything a try."

As we approach the house, I note the absence of everyone's cars. Also part of the plan. To make everything look normal. Once everything was set up, all cars were to be moved a street over. The cars may not be out front, but everyone is inside. Once the surprise happens, the cars will be driven back to the house.

I fetch the bag from the back seat after parking in the driveway. Shelly and I slip out and walk leisurely to the door. She keys in her code, then swings the door wide. From the foyer, the house looks the same. But I know the second we round the wall dividing the dining and living room from the kitchen and sitting room, a burst of surprise will echo around us.

We toe off our shoes and I set the bag of books down on the chair nearby.

"Want to binge that show you were watching the other day?" I ask, knowing it will lead us to where everyone waits.

She hooks my arm in hers. "Sounds great. Maybe I'll start one of my books after."

I lead her to the living room. Just as we breach the entrance to the space, a booming "Surprise!" fills the air. Shelly slaps a hand to her chest as everyone steps up to her and wraps her in a huge embrace. Individual hugs and happy birthday wishes are given. And when Shelly sidles up to me again, her eyes are rimmed in tears.

"Did you do this?" she whisper-asks as she takes in all of our friends.

"Not just me." Micah approaches us. "Your brother actually reached out."

"He did?" I nod and she swipes a hand over her cheeks. "Oh my god."

"Hey, sis." Micah pulls Shelly in for a hug. "Happy birthday. Hope this is okay."

She sniffles. "More than okay, big brother."

The remainder of the day goes by in good conversation, hearty laughter, great food—with cake, of course—and time well spent with people we care about. As the sun sets, we congregate outside and lounge in the back. Since Shelly moved in, we have slowly added more to the backyard. More seating and plants. A firepit and grill. A wooden fence around the perimeter for privacy. An array of colorful flowers near the swing under the large oak.

One day at a time, Shelly turns this house into a home. A place I want to share with her always. A place where our child will grow and laugh and wonder. Color with crayons and paper. Play hide-and-seek. Bring more definition to our lives.

"Have you picked a date for the baby shower yet?" Cora asks Shelly.

Shelly tucks her feet beneath her butt and leans into my side. "Not yet. Should I?"

"When are you due?"

"The date changes with every appointment." I *hear* Shelly's eyes roll and I bite my cheek to resist laughing. She isn't wrong, though. "Basically, anytime between September twenty-first and October eighth. Your guess is as good as mine."

Autumn chuckles. "Clementine's due date changed seven times. Inevitably, she arrived on the original date the doctor said." She smiles at Shelly, then me. "But they come out when they're ready." Autumn looks over at Jonas, who is chatting with Gavin and Micah. "Take advantage of your free time now. You'll wish for more after the baby is here." Autumn shifts her gaze to Cora. "Maybe we should plan the shower for her?"

"You don't have—"

Cora cuts me off. "Count me in." My best friend meets my gaze with softened eyes. "Let us do this for you, Shell." Her hands come together in prayer, inches from her lips. "Let us take this on. It'll be fun. And zero stress for you."

"We won't take no for an answer," Autumn adds.

Beside me, Shelly fidgets. But not so much anyone looking would take notice. I feel the slight tremble in her limbs, though.

I kiss her hair. "Your choice, but I think they would enjoy doing this for you."

Her frame relaxes into me more. "I swear I'm not a control freak." She laughs without humor. "But after giving up so much, it's hard to give up more."

"Wish I could relieve that burden for you. I would, if possible." I kiss her hair again. "A little more than three months. And then, once you're cleared, you can do everything and I'll sit back with the baby and relax."

"Ha ha." She shakes her head. "Fine," she huffs out like an annoyed teen. "You can plan the party." Cora and Autumn clap as giddy smiles stretch their cheeks. "But…" Shelly adds. "I want in on the plans too. I don't want it to be some big secret that I walk in on" —she waves her hand around us— "like today. If you promise to keep me in the loop, you have my permission."

"Done," Cora says at the same time Autumn says, "You got it."

Jonas comes up behind Autumn and rests his hands on her shoulders. "We should head out. Let Mom and Dad get home."

Babysitters. Another thing we should look into—although I am positive Shelly's mom will want every possible minute with the baby. With my flexible schedule, a babysitter will only be necessary when we want or need alone time.

If we are lucky, it won't just be Shelly's family and our friends who will watch the baby for an hour or two. Maybe, hopefully, my dad will be in the mix too. Only time will tell.

"Ready for the next photo session, Mom and Dad?"

I lie back on the exam table for my twenty-eight-week appointment. Inching my shirt up, I suck in a deep breath and prepare for the cold gel to hit my belly.

"Yes," Devlyn and I say simultaneously, then smile at each other.

Dr. Webster told us ultrasounds aren't done as frequently during normal pregnancies, but because of my blood pressure changes and increased anxiety, she added two more to the schedule. One today and another at week thirty-two. Either way, I get another snapshot of our little one to add to the album.

The gel hits my belly and I squeeze Devlyn's hand. He squeezes back. Then Dr. Webster presses the wand to my gel-coated skin and moves it around. Three sets of eyes fixate on the monitor as the blurry image becomes slightly sharper. Head, body, and four little limbs.

My vision blurs as tears flood my eyes. Devlyn tightens his hold on my hand. The room utterly silent except for the fluttering sound of a rapid heartbeat through the ultrasound machine.

"Spine looks good." Dr. Webster traces her finger over the screen. "Everything looks on track." She presses a button on the machine and snaps the image. Her gaze meets mine, then Devlyn's. "Still don't want to know the sex."

I shake my head and Devlyn does the same.

"Okay." Her smile widens as if she has the answer on the tip of her tongue. "Just going to take a few measurements."

She shifts the wand over my round belly and pauses when she has a better view of the baby's head. She clicks a few buttons and moves on. All too soon, she removes the wand, cleans it and my belly, then makes notes in my chart before handing over our new photo.

"Everything looks great. Keep up with your vitamins and relaxation." She sets the chart on the counter and washes her hands. "Have you been experiencing any cramps, pain, nausea, shortness of breath?"

I shake my head as I tug my shirt back into place. "No."

Drying her hands, she resumes her spot on her stool. "Cramps and tightness are normal. How's the swelling been?"

"Better." Devlyn's been a trooper, making sure we walk each night, if only to the end of the street and back.

"And the baby's been as active or more?"

I rub a hand over my belly. "Yes." I peer up at Devlyn. "Our little water aerobics instructor."

Dr. Webster laughs. "That's a new one, but cute." She offers her hand and I take it. Devlyn places one on my back and helps ease me upright. "If you notice any changes that aren't normal or just feel off, call the office. But with everything we saw today, your little water aerobics instructor looks healthy and fit and right where they should be."

At the reception desk, I double-check the next appointment date and time. We exit the office, slip into the car, and buckle our belts. Devlyn cranks the engine, then looks at me over the console.

"I have an idea, if you're up for it."

I arch a brow at him. "Will there be food?"

He looks up, left then right, before meeting my eyes. "Kind of," he says on a laugh.

"Count me in."

Maybe this wasn't such a great idea.

I love color. I love seeing a wide palette of colors. But this… this is too much.

Every shade of pink—although I have a new appreciation for the color since Shelly—and blue, green and yellow, gray and khaki. Bolds and neutrals. Onesies and jumpers. Pajamas and long shirts. Pants with snaps from heel to crotch on both legs. Lace and frill. Sports logos and popular cartoon characters. Farm animals as well as sea creatures.

The baby and children's section in Target is bigger than any other section. Well, unless you go to toys. It has every possible thing you may need for a baby. Bibs and diapers. Clothing and bedding. Strollers and bouncy seats. Training potties and bathtubs. Bottles and nipples. Who knew there were so many types of nipples? *Jesus.*

And then I laugh. Shelly looks at me with pinched brows. "What's so funny?"

"Have you ever had the urge to scream *nipples* in the baby section? Like it's a eureka moment."

Shelly snorts, then stops and presses her legs together. "Stop it." She slaps my arm. "You'll make me pee."

"We wouldn't get in trouble. If a worker said anything, I'd act like we'd been looking for them and I found them before you."

"Devlyn," she says, laughing harder. "Seriously, stop."

"Fine," I huff out. "Party pooper."

I follow Shelly up and down the aisles. We stare at hundreds of baby products and read the packages of the ones we have no clue what their purpose is. Then I remember something Cora said.

"Hey, shouldn't we start a registry for the shower?"

Shelly pulls out her phone. "Oh, yeah." She pulls up the Target app and taps a few times until she reaches the registry she set up earlier. "All we need to do is scan things and add them to our wish list."

For whatever reason, I don't feel the need to add an overabundance of items. Just necessities. Then again, this is a wish list and what the hell do I know when it comes to babies. Maybe we will need the wipes warmer and double electric breast pump. Maybe we need the video baby monitor that connects to our phone and the ultrasonic humidifier. Hell if I know.

My vision grows hazy as Shelly wanders and scans items on the shelves. Bottles and nipples. Diapers and burp cloths. Tubs and toiletries. Toys and clothes. Once she has half the baby department logged on the registry, she stows her phone in her purse and hooks my arm with hers.

"I want to buy something for the baby." She rubs a hand over her belly as her sparkly blues meet my greens. "The baby will get a ton of gifts from other people, but I want them to have something just from us. Doesn't have to be big. A small toy or their first book."

Twisting to face Shelly, I frame her face with my hands and pull her in for a kiss. Not a juicy public display, but a sweet kiss that tells her I love the idea.

"Anything in mind?" I ask.

"No. Let's wander a little more. Maybe something will stand out."

We weave through the department again, but this time with new eyes. On the hunt for the perfect first gift for our upcoming little one. Hands laced, we wander with no destination. Shelly picks up a small puppy dog toy. Black and white and red. Parts of it soft while other parts crinkle or rattle. The tag says it is perfect for sensory stimulation.

"How about this?" she asks. "It's cute and functional."

"And is gender neutral, which is good for us."

We both smile and stare down at the bright and bold puppy toy. Awe hits me square in the chest. Obviously, I *know* we are having a baby. Purchasing our first baby item… it's a whole new level of reality. It has my stomach flipping and fluttering. Adds a new dose of thrill and eagerness.

I hope the baby has Shelly's dazzling eyes and cute nose, as well as her kind heart and brilliance. More than anything, I just want our child to be healthy and happy.

Hand in hand, we wind our way out of the baby maze and make our way to the checkout. Shelly leans into me and I give her hand a light squeeze. As we round the end of the aisle near the registers, my feet stick to the floor and my legs lock in place.

Can life quit throwing curveballs?

I don't know what the hell I did, but I swear I will make up for it. Whatever *it* is.

Less than ten feet in front of us, Kelsey stands in the checkout line with a small basket in her hand. Maybe I can steer us right and she won't see me. But just as I shift us and point to a register with a shorter line, I hear my name.

"Devlyn? Is that you?"

Someone, anyone, send help.

Had she not spoken loud enough for Shelly to hear, I would have ignored her. But Shelly perked up at my name. I spin us slightly and meet the eyes of my first love. The girl who pulverized my heart five years ago. Someone I planned to never see again.

But the universe is intent on torturing me for some reason.

My hold on Shelly tightens as I say, "Hey, Kelsey."

Shelly jolts beside me. "*Kelsey,* Kelsey?" Shelly whisper-asks.

I give her hand a squeeze. A small assurance that everything will be fine. "Mm-hmm."

"How've you been?" Kelsey asks with too much excitement in her voice. "It's been what… five years?"

If my life could be summarized into one word this past year, it would be perplexing. Every sordid moment of my past has made some strange appearance. Like the universe is testing me on every level. Seeing if I am worthy and capable and strong enough to move forward. Not just on my own, but with Shelly and the baby.

Dear Universe, you can stop now. I swear, I'm good.

"Yep. Five years." I turn to look at Shelly and smile. "And life is incredible." For a moment, I lose myself in my Shelly bliss bubble. Stare at her shimmering twilight eyes and forget we are in the middle of Target and Kelsey is less than five feet away.

"Um, that's... I... that's great, Devlyn."

I kiss Shelly's temple before returning my attention to Kelsey. She shifts from foot to foot. Her eyes dart from me to Shelly and back. And for the first time in years, I don't open my mouth to try and appease someone else. Don't say anything to steer the awkward tension away from her. Because for too many years, I have always done things to make other people happy, but not myself. That time is over.

Except when it comes to Shelly. Her happiness is my happiness because she doesn't hold expectations over my head like a weapon. She loves me unconditionally.

"Well, we need to go," I say and start to turn us away.

"Was good seeing you, Devlyn."

I nod and lift a hand. "Bye, Kelsey."

Yes, I realize my response sounds cold and heartless, but I don't care. I owe that woman nothing. In another life, Kelsey meant everything to me. I would have done anything and everything for her. She took advantage of my selfless heart and broke it like I didn't matter. My curtness was me being nice, mature.

We go through the checkout and pay for the baby's first toy. Shelly and I wander to the exit, arms hooked at the elbows. If I were with any other person, I would have been bombarded with questions the second we stepped away from Kelsey.

But Shelly isn't like anyone else.

Inevitably, she will speak up. Curiosity will outweigh contemplation. But she will wait an appropriate amount of time to ask the most significant question. She won't drown me in an endless interrogation. Not Shelly. She will pick one question, just one, and ask without jealousy or guilt.

I crank the engine and let the air conditioning cool the cab before we back out. Shelly removes the toy from the bag and crinkles the floppy ears. Her eyes laser-focused on the little stuffed dog as she remains deep in thought.

I reach over the console and rest a hand on her thigh. In a flash, her eyes meet mine. And I see the question already forming on her lips.

"Are you okay?"

Of all the questions Shelly could have asked, of all the terse words she could have said, this was not what I expected. Not by a long shot.

Shelly has a big heart and a beautiful soul. The fact she is more worried about how I feel speaks volumes. She could have gone into a tizzy. Spewed words of jealousy or mistrust. Pushed away from me after dealing with yet another demon of my past.

But that isn't her style. Shelly has more class and is wise beyond her years.

"Yeah, I'm good." I shrug. "Honestly, I thought I'd feel different."

"How so?"

Months after our breakup, I often wondered what it would be like to see Kelsey again. Would it be tense and awkward or fueled by anger? Would I hate the sight of her or secretly wish to wrap her in my arms? With each passing year, the same unanswered questions lingered. Took up residence in my head.

Until Shelly.

In no time, everything I'd felt for Kelsey—the good and bad—vanished. For years, the sadness over losing one girl fueled a lot of my darker pieces. She'd blackened my young, impressionable heart.

The moment I saw Shelly, Kelsey became a ghost. I no longer saw or felt her.

While the scars of what she'd done remained, her hold on me evaporated. Kelsey had been a placeholder until Shelly's path collided with mine.

"Long before you and I met, I pictured what it'd be like seeing Kelsey again. Considering her parents live in the area, the chances were likely. I'd always seen it as this big deal. Me being excited or angry when it finally happened."

"And how was it?"

My thumb strokes over her thigh and I watch the action for a beat. "Lackluster," I say on a laugh. "No anger, but there was a hint of happiness." Shelly tenses under my touch. "But not for the reason you think." My eyes lift to hers. "I'm happy because I've moved on. I'm happy because I have you." I suck in a deep breath. "Although what she did was horrible, although it sent me to a dark place for so long, had she not done it, I wouldn't be here with you."

Tears rim her eyes and add a new luster to the gold flecks.

"I love you, Shelly Reed. You." I lift my hand and rest it on her rounding belly. "I love everything about us. What we are and what we will become."

"I love you, Devlyn Templar." A tear falls down her cheek. "And I can't wait to see where we go from here." She holds up her pointer finger. "But first… can we stop bumping into the past?" she asks on a laugh.

I join in on her laughter. "Would be nice. I'm over this trip down memory lane."

Really, there is only one demon of my past left to conquer. Once that dragon is slayed, life will be as it should—happy and peaceful and full of love.

But I have a feeling that last demon won't go quietly. Let's hope I am wrong.

This is why I haven't been here more often. This is why I haven't answered my phone every time it rings. Nicole Reed may be the death of me. Not literally, but pretty damn close.

"Why don't you want to know the sex of the baby? How are we supposed to plan? How can you decorate the nursery without knowing?"

Jesus, take the wheel. I love my mother. I love my mother. I love my mother.

"And why haven't you been answering my calls? This is one of the biggest times in your life. A time when you need as much love and support as possible." Eyes that match my own lock me in place. "Family matters, Shelly."

Deep breaths. In and out.

Tell her how you feel. Best to do it now than drag it out.

"Mom, please." I pause and take another deep breath. "First of all, I'm a grown woman. I make my own decisions. Second, Dr. Webster put me on a strict health regimen. Low to no stress." My lips flatten into a straight line for two breaths. "And you stress me out." I shrug.

I will not apologize for giving myself air and room. I will not apologize for eliminating the stressors in my life, even if it is someone I love. It may not be what she wants to hear, but this isn't just about her. Not anymore.

"Shelly, I—"

My mother speechless is new. Is it wrong of me to be proud I put her in this state? If so, oh well.

How many times did Micah and I sit at the dining room table and listen to her drone on about how she wishes we'd find love and start a family? Far too many. And now that I have done both—not that the family part was planned—she complains I don't spend enough time with her. She complains I am not doing this parenting thing the "right" way, because it is not how she did it.

And I am done. Done.

My mother has good intentions, but there is more than one way to love and parent. Her method worked for her, but it doesn't make it the best way.

"Devlyn and I decided we don't want to know the gender because it doesn't matter." I rub a hand over my belly, which seems to have grown another few inches in the last two weeks. "We want to give our child everything they need, but most importantly, we want them to feel loved. They won't care what color the bedroom walls are painted. They won't care if they're wearing dresses or sports shirts. The only ones who care are the parents."

Her brows knit together. No matter how many times Micah and I have told Mom that our version of happy is not the same as hers, it hasn't clicked. And I think it may be slowly sinking in now. A little.

"I just…" Lines crinkle her forehead. "I don't get it." Her eyes hold mine. "But I'm trying. Promise."

"Thank you."

A gentle smile softens her features. "Do you have plans for the nursery?"

I wince on a shrug. "Yes and no. We're leaving the room the same gray color.

And I liked the black and white animal theme Autumn and Jonas did, so we're going with a similar vibe. Except Devlyn is painting the animals and trees and whatnot on the walls."

"That sounds lovely."

"He's excited to start." I adjust my seat on her couch and reach for my glass of water. Each week, it gets harder to move like a nonpregnant woman. "We're waiting to buy furniture until after the shower."

Devlyn and I make zero assumptions about what will be gifted to us at the baby shower next weekend. The registry list has doubled since our trip to Target. Cora told me I could add things from the website that might not be available in the store. My fingers are calloused from the new additions and the registry is jam-packed with everything a baby, infant or toddler may need for the first two years of life.

We agreed to stash money and buy whatever necessities we don't get at the shower. Furniture being the most expensive, we saved enough for those big-ticket items.

"And you're having men at the shower too?"

Dear god, mother. Just quit with the gender nonsense.

"Yes," I say and purse my lips. "If you haven't figured it out yet, I'm a little over the whole traditional way of doing things." Mom opens her mouth, ready to cast her opinion on me, but I hold up a hand. "Devlyn and I have been through a lot. He has dealt with things you couldn't fathom. I won't make him or his father feel like outcasts because of some ridiculous, asinine tradition someone started long before I was born." I take a deep breath and settle my rising blood pressure. "Baby showers should be about celebrating new life… by everyone in that life's world. No matter what's between their legs."

"Shelly," Mom admonishes me as if I am a child.

"No," I say sternly. "No," I repeat for emphasis. "I get it. You want me and Micah to fit some mold that society created centuries ago." I shake my head. "But even when those ideals were created, people snuck around and did what felt natural and right for them." I look Mom square in the eyes. "Love isn't black and white, and neither is life. Both are full of color and wonder without borders. And I wish you'd see that."

The baby sticks a limb in my ribs and I suck in a breath.

Mom scoots closer, concern etched in the lines of her face. "Oh my goodness, Shelly. Are you alright?"

I sit on the edge of the couch, raise my arms, and take in a lungful of air and nod. "Yep." I lower a hand to rub my belly. "Just the baby giving a fist pump."

That's right. You tell grandma that Mommy is right.

With too much effort, I slowly rise from the couch. "I need to head home. Devlyn's father is coming over for dinner and I need to help prep."

Mom opens her mouth to say something, but snaps it shut.

It has been a monumental day. Nicole Reed speechless more than once is something worth noting. The shock on her face is priceless. If only Micah were here to see me standing tall. Well, as tall as a pregnant woman with a hot-air balloon belly can stand.

Mom walks me to the door and helps me with my shoes. I shoulder my purse and give her a hug.

"Love you, Mom. See you at the shower."

She nods with red-rimmed eyes. "I love you, Shelly. Your father and I wouldn't miss it for the world."

I walk to the car with a slight waddle and slowly lower myself into the driver's seat. Something else I will have to give up soon—driving. My belly is getting too big to reach the wheel and pedals comfortably. Plus, the stress of traffic is too much.

With one last look at my mother, I put the car in reverse, wave to her, and back out of the driveway feeling much lighter than when I arrived.

Today, I think it really hit her. Today, I think Mom finally realized that my life, and Micah's life, will be what we make it, not what she wants to shape it as. I don't doubt my brother still gets lectured on not having children. But maybe after today, maybe after the baby shower, Mom will learn to love how we live *our* lives. Maybe she will learn to love that we are happy like this.

Thank god we don't know the gender. I might have lost it if the house was a blue or pink vomitfest. Although Shelly has given me a new appreciation for pink, having it plastered in every nook and cranny would have been nauseating.

My eyes roam over the decorations strung up and laid out in every imaginable place. Banners and balloons. Confetti in the shape of bottles and pacifiers and diapers scattered on every available surface. *At least it's recycled paper and not plastic or glitter.* Stacks of paper plates and cups and napkins. A box of biodegradable cutlery. Food, lots and lots of food. And a cupcake tower with enough for triple the number of people attending.

I haven't seen the games yet, but I bet they are equally overwhelming.

Sitting on the couch, I watch as Cora, Autumn, and Elizabeth move around the house. They work in tandem as if able to read each others' minds and know what else needs to be done. Shelly loiters in the kitchen, picking at the trays of food and making space for the last few dishes expected as others arrive.

When Cora and Autumn set out to organize the shower, they asked if there'd been anything Shelly wasn't eating during pregnancy and what she'd been craving. The only enemy had been the cheese, but that phase passed. Now Shelly craves and loves her favorite foods more.

There is no shortage of variety on the shower menu. Had it been any other party, the crowd would question the assortment.

I wander into the kitchen, lean a hip on the counter next to Shelly and snag a chocolate-covered fruit skewer.

Excellent decision adding these to the menu.

"Nervous?" I ask before biting off a piece of pineapple.

She plucks a finger sandwich from the tray beside her—sliced banana, nut butter and chocolate peeking out from the slices. "Kind of." She takes a bite as her eyes scan the room and beyond. "I'm excited to celebrate the baby and get the room put together." She pops the last of the finger sandwich in her mouth and shifts her attention to me. "Don't really want to be fawned over, though."

My beautiful Shelly. The brightest star in the night sky, yet she doesn't want all the attention. Doesn't want all eyes on her. Soon, real soon, a lot of that attention will shift.

Shelly will always be my center, my point of gravity, the person who brings balance to my world. But it won't be long before we both learn how to love each other and love someone new.

I lift my hand and cup her cheek. Slowly stroke her soft skin with my thumb. Stare into her starry eyes as her body relaxes. She leans into my touch, shuffles closer, and wraps her arms around my neck. Buries her face in the crook of my neck and breathes deeply.

Hugs are much different now. With her belly growing bigger every day, Shelly has learned new ways to do everyday activities. I won't say it aloud, but I love painting her toenails. I love massaging her feet every night before bed. And I love the way her eyes light up with both. It relaxes her and makes her smile. It also connects us in a new way. In a way more intimate than lips and tongues and sex.

Don't get me wrong, we still make out like lusty teenagers. Our sex life has never been more incredible. The hormonal changes have not only amplified her drive, but also cemented our emotional bond. Sex during pregnancy is… hot. Like *really* hot. And although we've had to learn new positions so Shelly is comfortable, it has also added a new level of spice to the bedroom.

"Won't be too long. Think of it like the normal Sunday gathering, plus some additional people and lots of baby gifts," I say.

"You're right." Her brows knit together as she clutches her belly. Before I open my mouth to ask if she is okay, she reaches for my hand and places it on the left side of her belly. "Wait for it." She shifts my hand a little lower and presses it more firmly into her belly. A second later, something jabs my hand. "Did you feel that?" she asks, eyes shimmering as they stare into mine.

"Yeah," I say in wonderment. "Is that a kick?"

She moves my hand again. "Or an elbow. Maybe a fist pump. Possibly a knee."

We laugh a moment, then fall silent as we wait for the next jab. Another two stretch her belly before the baby settles.

One hand on her belly, I cup her cheek with the other, lean forward and kiss her. The kiss is far from sweet as I haul her closer and trace the seam of her lips with my tongue. Public displays are not typical for us. Mini make-out sessions in front of people almost never happen.

But these aren't just *any people*. Every person here is family. With kindness and embraces and inclusion, these people have shown me more love than any person with my DNA. They accept me for who I am and not what I can do for them. They care for me because I care for Shelly and vice versa. And they will never say an unkind word to either of us. Doesn't mean they won't tease us later.

Slowly letting each of them into my life has been a gift I never expected. A gift I wouldn't have without this incredible woman in my arms.

"Our little water aerobics instructor," I say, pressing my forehead to hers. "Can't wait to meet them."

"Same. Won't be long."

⌇

The party is in full swing and it isn't as overwhelming as originally expected. It's like Sunday nights mixed with a birthday party. Kind of. If an actual itinerary for this shindig exists, I'd be shocked. So far, we have mingled and eaten food. I suspect gifts and games and cake will happen soon.

"Can I have everyone's attention," Cora yells over the chatter. She sidles up to Shelly and conversations quiet as all eyes turn her way. "Thank you." She smiles, then wraps an arm around Shelly's shoulders. "Today we're here to celebrate this awesome chicky." Cora presses a kiss to Shelly's cheek. "And her and Devlyn's impending arrival."

Hoots and hollers and applause fill the room. Shelly's cheeks pinken and I stare a little too hard at her heated skin. How long has it been since a blush stained her cheeks? Far too long. I'll need to remedy that in the near future.

Cora guides Shelly to a comfortable chair at the far end of the room that was decorated to mirror a throne. Once seated, Cora places a crown on Shelly's head decorated with mini plastic babies. I open the camera app on my phone and snap a picture.

"Gifts first," Cora says. "Then we'll do some corny games. And since the guys are here, us ladies should sit back and watch as they embarrass themselves." A chuckle leaves her lips.

Another chair is moved next to Shelly's and Cora gestures for me to sit.

Small boxes and big boxes. Jumbo bags and miniature bags. One by one, gifts are handed to Shelly to unwrap. After the first gift is revealed—an overflowing box of onesies and sleep shirts and jumpers—Shelly suggests we open everything together. That the day isn't really about her, but about us and the baby.

Wrapping paper tears and crumples. Tissue paper gets tossed to the side. The black trash bag at my right gets fuller with each unwrapped gift.

With each new present, shock and awe spread from my heart to my lips, tipping them up in an impossible smile. These people, our friends and family... they are the true gift. At this point, I don't think Shelly and I will need to buy much else. Their generosity is the biggest hug around my heart.

A bassinet with sheets and blankets. A crib that converts to a toddler bed and, one day, to a twin bed frame with more sheets. Clothes for home and outside the house for the next year. Bottles and nipples and cleaning kits. Baby bathtub and toiletries and cute hooded towels. Socks and mittens. Enough diapers and wipes to last us for several months—although, I hear you need more than you think—and so much more.

They thought of everything. Not just the items Shelly and I added to our registry list.

The backs of my eyes sting at their love and support and big, big hearts. Warmth floods my veins as tightness wraps my chest.

How many years have I wanted this? Love from others without conditions. Before Shelly, I thought I'd missed out on my chance at happiness and love. That my opportunity came and went after high school.

But I was wrong.

Shelly gifted me this. All of this. Love, life, a future.

Had I not been brave enough to take the leap, I don't think either of us would be here. I fought it for so long. Discounted my worth. Dismissed that love was possible again. Suppressed my feelings in fear of getting hurt.

Then, in a blink, I grew tired of fighting what my heart wanted. Grew tired of denying myself. And little by little, I opened up to her and to myself. I let myself feel, *really feel*, for the first time in years. And it was... sensational.

Shelly is sensational.

If not for this incredible woman, I wouldn't know happiness. I wouldn't know love. Wouldn't wake each day with a smile on my face and warmth wrapped around my heart. Damn, am I lucky. And I will never take Shelly or our love for granted.

I turn and see the tears ready to spill down her cheeks. Hormones aside, she would have cried at the level of love gifted today. Wrapping her hand in mine, I give a gentle squeeze. The tears brimming her eyes make the gold flecks sparkle brilliantly against her twilight irises and we stare wordlessly at each other. *I know*, I mouth.

The road of our relationship has been bumpy. Between my initial resistance and the sporadic roadblocks, it felt like we were driving the wrong way at every turn. That something bigger than us was intervening and steering us toward a dead end.

We didn't let them win, though. We never will. Our love is too strong.

"Alright, party people. Time for the good stuff," Cora shouts.

Autumn switches the music and an upbeat tempo fills the room. Gavin, Jonas and my father grab boxes and start hauling them to the nursery. I fill my arms and follow in their wake. By the time we have all the gifts moved, Autumn, Cora, Peyton and Penny are organizing something at the dining room table. Elizabeth and Nicole laugh at the display, and nervous energy floods my veins.

I don't know much about baby showers except for food and gifts. Shelly tried to warn me about the games. *Some of them are just gross,* she'd said. Time to pull up my big boy pants and do this. Enjoy the moment and suffer through the grossness with a smile on my face.

More than an hour later, we wrap up the last of the games. *Halle-freaking-lujah.*

Changing "dirty" diapers on baby dolls. Tootsie Rolls and soft fudge will never exist in my life again. Ever. Bobbing for pacifiers sounded like fun at first. Lies. All lies. Blindfolded while tasting baby food. This one wasn't as horrendous as I expected. I blame it on the organic jarred foods that were purchased.

Those were the more outlandish games. The rest I enjoyed.

Everyone was given a piece of stock paper along with pencils and crayons and asked to draw a picture for the baby. Didn't need to be pretty. Just something to look back on years later and smile over.

Next, we were all given two index cards. On one, we were asked to write names for a girl and on the other, names for a boy. Shelly and I had briefly scoured the internet for baby names, but nothing had stuck yet. This game was the perfect way to come up with fresh ideas.

The last game—although not really a game—everyone was given a small card, blank on the inside. We were tasked with writing a note or letter to the baby. Nothing specific. Whatever was in our heart.

And when I put pen to paper and slowly wrote a letter to my unborn child, I couldn't hold back the tears. I didn't sob, but the tears came and I let them flow freely as I wrote. One drop, then another, splattered on the card, but I didn't wipe them away. I left them right where they were. Exactly where they belonged.

"We'll help clean up and get out of your hair," Gavin tells me and Shelly.

"You don't need to," Shelly offers. "We can clean up."

Cora sidles up the Gavin. "Uh, no you won't. You just sit there and watch. Tell me what leftovers you want and which we should divvy."

"Fine," Shelly grumbles.

When Dr. Webster first put Shelly on light activities only, she protested with every breath she took. But as her health became more of a risk to the baby, she conceded. Although she grumbles still, I know she doesn't mind the help.

With each passing day, the circles beneath her eyes grow a touch darker. Her belly more round and body more uncomfortable. Her willingness to give up tasks she once argued to do on her own has grown tenfold. Her grumbles are more for show now.

We wave everyone off as they leave and go back inside to a quieter yet fuller house. But not as full as it will be in the next eight to ten weeks. Before long, our house will be filled with more love than imaginable. It will be chaotic in the beginning, but beautiful chaos. The thought thrills and terrifies me equally.

My inner pessimist says it is too good to be true. My inner pessimist says nothing this wonderful ever lasts.

I do my damnedest to shove that negative beast down. To smother it with all the good. To suffocate it with love. To extinguish its existence.

Maybe it is time to up my visits with Dr. Prince. Maybe it is time I ask Shelly to come with me.

I stare at the beige walls, lightly decorated with colorful framed art prints, and wonder how many secrets have bled into the drywall.

Spilling my past or how I feel doesn't make me uncomfortable. I have nothing to hide.

Guess I wonder how a person can listen to other people's problems all day, every day, and not feel overwhelmed or ready to crawl out of their skin. How do they sleep at night after digesting all the trauma or heartache?

They are saviors. True miracle workers.

On the couch beside me, Devlyn bounces his knee uncontrollably. His fingers pick at the exposed threads in the distressed part of his jeans. Every few seconds, his eyes land on the edge of my profile.

His nervous energy is palpable, comprehensible. Although we are honest with each other, tonight, in this place, sharing himself with me is different. A new level of vulnerability for us both. Devlyn is familiar with Dr. Prince. Has shared countless secrets with him. More than likely, secrets he has yet to share with me. That fact doesn't hurt. My hope is that after today—and future sessions—Devlyn won't feel uncomfortable sharing painful parts of the past with me. That I gain a new level of trust with Devlyn. Strong enough for him to consider me his safe space in all matters.

Arm extended across the table, Dr. Prince offers me his hand. "Nice to finally meet you, Shelly." His smile is kind, warm, sincere. His expression gentle and soothing as he waits for me to take his hand.

Placing my hand in his, we shake. His grip is firm yet soft. Solid yet gentle. "You as well. Devlyn speaks highly of you."

We sit back in our seats. I rest a hand on Devlyn's leg and he takes my hand in his, lacing our fingers as his bouncing knee settles. Dr. Prince takes a sip of water, then picks up a notepad and a pen. He scribbles on the paper for a moment, his eyes occasionally peeking up at us. Observing us. Making note of Devlyn's reaction to me and mine with him.

His observation doesn't unsettle me. This is part of his job, not just to listen but to also survey. I will say his perception of us has me curious.

"How've things been since our last appointment, Devlyn?"

I turn my head slightly, enough to get a better view of him but not look at him directly. He nibbles at his lips as he mulls over his answer.

"Good." He shrugs. "The baby shower was this past weekend." He looks at me briefly and gives my hand a squeeze. "Was nice, but overwhelming."

"Overwhelming how?"

His knee starts to bounce again. I stroke my thumb in a slow rhythm over his hand and, after a beat, his leg calms. Dr. Prince jots something on the notepad then meets my eyes, smiles, and returns his attention to Devlyn.

Devlyn laughs under his breath. "Not like I didn't know the baby was coming, but after the party, it just felt more real. Y'know?" His fingers toy with mine. "Plus, we got so many gifts for the baby." Green irises meet mine for a breath. A nervous smile on his lips. "I didn't expect that much… love."

I watch as Devlyn's brows pinch together, his eyes narrowing as he drops them to stare at his lap.

In this very moment, I see so much, but one thing stands out the most. Devlyn feels undeserving of this level of love. He feels unworthy of affection from other people.

And it pisses me off.

As if sensing my irritation, Dr. Prince directs his focus my way. "Shelly, tell me what you're thinking right now."

Spotlight, party of one.

My eyes linger on Devlyn's profile a moment before I turn to look across the table. I lick my lips, swallow past the anxiety ball in my throat, and tighten my hold on Devlyn. "I hate that she did this to him."

Dr. Prince tilts his head. "His mother?" I nod. "Take a deep breath and let the anger pass. Then, when you're ready, I want you to expand on that."

I do as he suggests and take a deep breath. Then another. And another. One breath at a time, I feel my pulse settle and the pang in my chest dissipate. "When it comes to Karen Templar, I can't seem to keep my emotions at bay. I apologize."

"No need to apologize. There is no judgment here."

With one last deep breath, I continue. "Devlyn and I became friends in October. We'd met in passing a year earlier through work, but it wasn't until this past October that we spoke and interacted." I grab my water bottle, twist the lid off and take a sip. "It took time and effort for Devlyn to open himself up. To let me in. Partly due to a past relationship gone sour." I turn to lock on Devlyn's soft green eyes. "But another piece was because he'd never really been shown love. Not real love." I return my gaze to Dr. Prince and press the heel of my hand to my chest. "And that hurts on so many levels."

The backs of my eyes sting as the words leave my lips. But I bite them back. I don't know if my body is overreacting because my hormones are out of whack or if I'd feel the urge to cry normally. Right now, all my body wants is to release. Heartache. Pain. Love. All for the man at my side that holds my hand like a life preserver.

"Shelly, your feelings toward Devlyn's mother are natural and reasonable." Dr. Prince shifts his attention to Devlyn, but continues to speak to me. "I don't know how much Devlyn has told you about his mother, but we have been working through the harder parts of his past." His gentle eyes meet mine again. "It will take time, but I hope the both of you are able to heal from this. That one day, you'll be able to not give so much of your energy to someone undeserving."

For the remainder of the hour, we discuss how the healing process is going with Devlyn and his father, and what my feelings are in relation to James. With each new interaction, I grow fonder of James. He hasn't told me his entire story, but from what he has shared and what Devlyn has told me, he felt trapped for years. Not because of Devlyn, but because he didn't trust his wife to raise Devlyn without him present. He wanted to escape with Devlyn, but didn't know how to safely.

But James smiles more now. The gentleness in Devlyn is equally visible in James. Excitement vibrates off James as each day passes and we get closer to the arrival of his first grandchild.

I trust the Templar men will slowly heal and become whole again. Put the harsh years of the past behind them and move forward. Both have so much love in their hearts and it'd be a shame for them not to share it with others.

Minutes before the session ends, Dr. Prince gives us homework. Before the next appointment, which I have been asked to attend, Devlyn and I are to spend time in the nursery. Whether it is unpackaging gifts and finding them a new home or building the crib or just sitting in the room. We are to spend time in the room and just feel. Fill the room with love. Talk to the baby while in the room. Get used to the idea of having more than just the two of us in the house.

After handshakes and goodbyes, Devlyn and I leave the office. And it isn't until we are in the car and driving down the road that I feel it. A newfound level of relief. A comfort that had been missing. I didn't know it was something I needed, but now that I have it, I am grateful.

Is it weird for me to be turned on right now?

Having Shelly at my appointment was beyond therapeutic. A buzz coursed through my veins. Perspiration dampened my skin. And the pain of the past was slowly released from my bones. For the first time in years, it feels as if I can draw in a full, deep breath.

And damn, it feels spectacular.

I don't keep secrets from Shelly—well, unless you count surprise parties—but I haven't unpacked all of my past with her. Not yet. Not because I don't want to, not because I don't trust her, but more because it is a lot to take on and I have no idea where to begin.

Insert Dr. Prince.

This man has been a godsend. He doesn't look at me like I have two heads. He doesn't call me crazy or judge how I feel about my mother. No, he listens, digests, then helps me look at each point in time from a different angle. One memory at a time, he guides me down the road to resolution. Shows me how to let go of the bad and find ways to forgive the guilt I feel. Teaches me how to move forward and love myself first without fear of repercussion.

When the holidays roll around this year, I plan to get Dr. Prince something to show my appreciation. He will decline and tell me gifts are unnecessary, but I beg to differ. Without his counsel, my life would still be a mess.

I park in the driveway and dash to the passenger door to help Shelly out. Early in the pregnancy, she'd wave me off. Tell me she was capable of getting out on her own. But as her belly rounds more, she waits for my hand. Allows me to take on more of the load. Smiles or kisses my cheek when I suggest she rest.

With Shelly less than ten weeks from delivering, Elizabeth insists on her working less hours. Instead of forty to forty-five, she now works closer to twenty. In a few weeks, depending on how she feels, Shelly plans to start maternity leave. Originally, she wanted to work until her water broke. With her belly rounding faster, her ankles and fingers swelling more, plus the general discomfort of being on her feet all day, she conceded on the idea. Confessing she will likely start leave a week or two before the baby arrives. Which is right around the corner.

To say I am relieved would be an understatement.

"Should we start on our homework assignment now?" she asks, humor lacing her voice as we toe off our shoes near the door.

I remember the first homework assignment from Dr. Prince. How ridiculous it felt to have *homework*. But I followed through. Completed each task without argument. And now, I have grown to like the assignments. Grown more comfortable with the familiar activities that aid my peace.

"Yes and no."

"Yes and no?"

I nod. "Mm-hmm." I lace my fingers with hers, spin to face her, and walk us down the hall. She starts to pull us toward the nursery, but I tug us in the opposite direction. Toward the bedroom. Our bedroom.

"Want to change?" she asks as her brows knit together.

I shake my head as my legs bump the foot of the bed. I lift my free hand to her cheek and stroke her soft skin with my thumb. Leaning forward, I press my lips to hers. Brush her lips with mine slowly. Paint the seam of her lips with my tongue until they part and let me in.

In two rapid heartbeats, the kiss evolves from sweet to hungry.

Her fingers curl into fists and cling to the cotton of my shirt. She tugs me closer. Drags her hands up my torso and along my shoulders before wrapping them around my neck. The kiss turns frantic as our tongues tangle and hands grope.

I break the kiss, reach back for the collar of my shirt and yank the cotton over my head before tossing it to the floor. Shelly fumbles to tug her shirt free. "Let me," I say as I reach for the hem and slowly pull it up and off her body.

Not a breath passes before I drop to my knees. Inches from my face, her belly button pokes out. Pink and brown marks highlight her belly. Marks she isn't fond of, but I find sexy as hell. Those marks are evidence my baby—our baby—grows in her womb. Can't think of anything more beautiful.

"Gorgeous," I whisper as I lean in and press my lips to her belly. I lift one hand and rest it on her belly, then the other. Tipping my head back, my eyes trail up her midline until I reach her starry blues. "The most beautiful, remarkable, astonishing woman I know."

Pink floods her cheeks as she combs her fingers through my hair. "Make love to me," she says with fierce boldness.

The further into pregnancy Shelly is, the more challenging sex becomes. It took several nights to find the most comfortable position for her, but neither of us complained.

Her shorts and mine land in the same pile as our shirts, followed by her bra and panties. I help her onto the bed, add a second pillow beneath her head, then crawl up beside her. Plant my hands on either side of her. Feather kisses over her skin. Along her jaw and neck. The curve of her shoulder and length of her collarbone. Over one breast, sucking her nipple between my lips before trailing over to the other. Inch by inch, I kiss my way down her belly, whispering words of love—for her and our baby. Then I dip lower. Drop between her thighs and lick up her seam.

She gasps and reaches for me, clutching my hair in her fist. "So good."

Her moans fill the room while I feast on her body. Her fingers in my hair tug harder. Nails digging into my scalp as her thighs tremble and tighten around my head. On the brink of her orgasm, I insert two fingers and pump at the slow rhythm she begs for every time. With one last flick and pump, her body constricts around my fingers as a guttural moan spills from her lips.

Before she comes down from her high, I crawl up the bed and kiss her deeply. Her hands roam from my face to neck and down my upper back. Moving to her side, she shifts the second pillow to the side and rolls onto hers. I brush her blonde locks aside and kiss the back of her neck and over her spine between her shoulder blades. She lays a hand over mine on her hip, lacing our fingers and encouraging me to paint her skin with my touch.

Shelly hasn't stated as much, but I get the impression she feels less attractive as her belly grows. The dramatic changes to her body have darkened her mood some days. Stolen her sunshine. And on those days, I hold her more. Closer. Tighter. Longer.

Each day of this journey… I have loved them all. The light and dark. The highs and lows. They give me perspective. Allow me to appreciate life and love and us in unimaginable ways.

She may not enjoy the changes to her body, but I love her more because of them. Love what those changes represent. Our connection. Our love. Strength and bravery and hope. The future.

Tracing my hand along the curves and dips of her torso, she releases my fingers when I reach her breast. I palm one in my hand. Massage and pinch and tease. A moan floats through the air as she grinds her butt against my erection.

I want to be inside her, desperately, but I take my time. Tease her body with lips and fingers and insatiable hunger. Make her comfortable. Make her feel good. Make her as equally desperate for me as I am her. Let her know that I love her and her body at every stage of life.

Sex with Shelly isn't just about getting off—both of us could do that easily. Sex with Shelly is uninhibited intimacy. Deep and pure and indestructible. A physical act to show her just how much I want her, need her, can't be without her. A way to show her she is still who I want, always. That when I look at her, heat floods my veins, my heart, every cell in my body.

"Devlyn," she whisper-moans as I pinch her nipple harder. She pushes her breast into my touch. "Please," she begs as moisture coats the tip of my erection.

I release her nipple and trail my fingers down her body, over the curve of her ass, and dip down between her thighs. Two fingers trace her seam and she shivers. Up and down. Up and down. I slick my fingers in her juices before pushing them inside.

Her gasp fills the air as I slowly pump two fingers inside her, over and over. She grips my forearm, her nails biting my flesh. This pain is one I have come to love, one I look forward to feeling, receiving.

My fingers pump faster, harder as her breaths come in quick, shallow pants. She rocks her hips harder against my touch, grinding, and I know she is close. I slip my fingers out and circle her clit once, twice, three times before dipping back inside. Pin her back to my front with my other arm. Circle her clit again and close my eyes as her body catapults once more.

She rides out her high with my fingers still inside her. As her body comes down, I pull my slick fingers out and paint her orgasm on my cock. Positioning my tip at her entrance and hand on her hip, I kiss her shoulder. "Love you, Andromeda."

She brings a hand to my hair and fists the locks, pinning me to the crook of her neck. "Love you, too."

With a slow rock of my hips, I fill her fully. We moan in unison. Her grip on my hair tightens as she grinds back against me. Inch by thick inch, I pull out to the tip before plunging forward. The first few rocks of my hips are slow, methodical, premeditated. I bask in every little whimper that leaves her lips. Relish every move her body makes as she silently begs for more.

And then, we are anything but slow and steady.

In a blink, the beast inside me claws its way to the surface and growls. My hips piston faster as my touch digs and bruises her hip and breast. I strengthen my hold on her frame and pump a vicious, hungry, punishing rhythm with my cock.

Her sweet cries of pleasure fill my ears. Her sweat slicks my skin and hers. And it isn't long before her body lets go and she moans my name. I bite the curve of her neck as I come undone inside her, my hold on her never more fierce.

Nothing compares to this. Shelly in my arms. Our bodies connected in every possible way. Both of us in a state of euphoria. Our connection isn't purely sexual, but the sex is explosive.

Shelly and I were lucky. We connected as friends before becoming lovers. Formed a bond I never thought possible. Discovered love slowly and together. Constructed an unbreakable connection.

In less than a year, Shelly and I have experienced so much together. Good and bad. Had we not faced the hardships and heartache, our love may not be what it is today. In our small blip of time together, we have been through a lot. Although there was hurt, I wouldn't change any of it. Although I almost lost her, and myself, we found our way back to each other.

My arms band around her body—one above her belly, one below—and hug her closer. I pepper her skin with kisses from her neck to the edge of her shoulder. Breathe her in and bask in the taste and touch and scent of her.

"Love you so much, Shell," I whisper against the back of her neck. "So much." My hands shift and embrace her expanding belly. Our baby.

She lays her arms over mine and squeezes me to her. "Love you more, Dev."

Not possible. Not by a long shot.

A chuckle slips from her lips as her body shakes. "Should we do our homework now?"

I join her light laughter. "Yeah. In a minute. Just want to lie here a little longer." And never let go.

I wake drenched in sweat, the covers tossed from my body hours ago. The ceiling fan whirs above as the air conditioning blows cool air from the vent. Yet, I look like I just stepped out of the shower.

Looking to Devlyn's side of the bed, I find it empty. The cotton sheets cool.

Pushing up on my elbows, I peer around the darkened room, Devlyn nowhere to be found. I inch up to a sitting position, scoot to the edge of the mattress and let the cool air chill my heated skin. Easing off the bed, I peel my top over my head and toss it in the hamper before grabbing a dry shirt.

I tiptoe out of the room, the house alight with the rising sun coming in through the windows on the back of the house. Wandering down the hall, I listen for any indication as to where Devlyn might be. But I hear nothing. No clanking utensils in pans or food sizzling on the stove. No muted sounds from the television. Nothing.

Just as I consider climbing the stairs to his studio, I stop between the kitchen and living room.

In my periphery, I spy Devlyn out back on the patio. A canvas on his easel, paint palette on one hand while a brush rests in the other and paints in varying shades of pink and red on the canvas.

As if he might hear me, I tiptoe toward the sliding glass doors and loiter just out of view. But not far enough that I can't watch him while he works.

In seconds, I realize the painting on the easel is the nude of me he started before my belly was so round. The full canvas isn't visible from my vantage point, but I see the length of my legs and curve of my hip. Scattered in the image are various flowers and a winding length of green vines. Looking at the canvas, I *know* the image is me. But from an outsider's perspective, someone who isn't familiar with me or us, no one would know who the woman is in the flowers.

The sun slowly rises in the eastern sky, but the pergola covering the patio keeps some of the sunbeams out of Devlyn's line of sight. Leaning on the frame, I watch him a little longer. Absorb the serenity he bleeds as he puts paint on the canvas. Breathe deeper as I watch the muscles of his back flex as he paints a new likeness of his favorite person—his words, not mine. Rub my swollen belly as I stare at the man I love.

My stomach grumbles and I decide to leave Devlyn to his solitude while I make us breakfast.

The buzzer for the turkey bacon sounds as Devlyn pads into the kitchen and leans against the counter. Sliding on a hot mitt, I open the oven and take out the pan, setting it on a trivet.

"I would've made breakfast had I known you were up," he says as I add shredded cheese to scrambled eggs on the stovetop.

Setting the package next to him, I stir the cheesy eggs and turn off the burner.

"Didn't want to disturb you." My lips curve up slightly. "You looked so peaceful and in your element."

He fetches plates as I start toasting slices of bread. "Still too hot to be outside after the early hours. I try not to wake you when I'm up at dark thirty."

Plates piled high with cheesy eggs, turkey bacon, fresh fruit and toast, Devlyn carries them to the dining room. I park myself in the chair as he wanders back to the kitchen.

"Tea, water, juice, chocolate milk?"

On the last one, the baby gives me a swift kick to the lungs. I gasp, then settle my breath. "Junior wants chocolate milk," I say on a laugh.

"Oh yeah?"

"Yep. Soon as you said it, they kicked."

"Chocolate milk it is."

The first several bites go by in relative silence. After I down half the glass of chocolaty goodness, I point my fork over my shoulder. "How's the painting coming along?"

Devlyn finishes his bite. "Almost done." He pushes around a slice of watermelon with his fork. "Maybe a few more sessions on the stool."

Next week, I officially start maternity leave from Petal and Vine. Although I am not due for another month, minimum, standing and walking all day is becoming more difficult and uncomfortable. It isn't that I *can't* do it. More like it exhausts me to be on my feet more than an hour.

Weeks ago, Elizabeth made me sit down every so often. *"I've been there, sweetheart. You will thank me later for the stool," she'd said.* And she was right, of course. Parking my butt on the stool helped some with the swelling, but so did walking. If I was arranging flowers, my instructions were to be on that stool.

And I definitely didn't want to be in trouble with Momma Davies.

Working less hours had been a big adjustment. So was learning to give up my independence. Not that I gave it up fully. Some tasks I still manage on my own just fine. But driving and setting up the nursery are not on the "Shelly is allowed to do these alone" list.

With me home full time soon, part of me feels as if I am stealing Devlyn's time from him.

For years, he was used to his solitude. He was used to climbing those stairs and getting lost for hours or days in his art. And now, it feels as if I rob him of it all.

"Why don't you spend more time on it today," I suggest as he eats his last bite of toast.

Cocking his head to the side, he narrows his eyes. "Thought we were finishing up the nursery today. Or trying to, at least. I need to put the final touches on the mural."

I swallow down the last of my chocolate milk. "But if you want to paint more of something else, you can. I can unbox the diapers then fold the washed baby clothes and put them away."

The nursery is practically finished. Some bigger items still needed to be assembled, but the crib and bassinet are done. The baby swing and items the baby won't use right away are still in the box. They don't concern me, though I know Devlyn will assemble them sooner rather than later.

"Maybe for a little bit," he concedes.

A tension I didn't realize was in my shoulders relaxes. Parenthood is a big change for us both, but I don't want either of us to forget who we are and what we love. Devlyn should still get to spend time in his studio. Although I may need him to watch over me for a short time around the birth, I don't want him to feel trapped or bogged down.

"Good, because I want to see the finished product. Please and thank you."

Wood scrapes wood as he scoots his chair back, rises from his chair and laughs. "Yes, ma'am." He picks up my empty plate and his. "I'll get the dishes since you cooked. You do what you need to do and I'll meet you in the nursery in a bit."

I brace my hands on the chair and table and push up. Following him to the kitchen, I kiss his cheek. "Take your time."

~

I sway back and forth in the rocking chair near the window. My eyes on the tree just outside the baby's bedroom on the side of the house, watching the wind rustle the leaves as birds flit to and fro. My hand rubs small circles over my swollen belly as I talk to the baby.

"Mommy and Daddy should put a bird feeder in the tree. Maybe treats for the squirrels too. Then we can watch them while we rock in the chair together." My eyes fall to my belly. "Definitely need to add some more color. A flowering shrub, so you always have something beautiful to look at. What do you think?"

A knee or elbow or foot protrudes to the left of my navel as the baby stretches. I consider it an agreement to my idea. "Glad you think so too."

Laying my head against the back of the chair, I close my eyes and continue to sway. Minutes pass before I hear Devlyn pad into the room. He doesn't say a word, but I sense him close by.

Slowly, I open my eyes and scan the room. Just out of reach, he leans against the wall, arms crossed in front of him. His expression soft as he regards me in the rocking chair. The corners of his mouth tip up.

"Didn't mean to disturb you."

"You didn't." My eyes drop to his bare chest where random streaks of paint stain his skin. Heat floods my cheeks as the memory of us painting each other comes to the forefront. "Was just relaxing after putting things away."

In two long strides, he reaches the front of the rocker and squats down. His hands come to my knees and slowly drift up my thighs. "What were you just thinking?"

"What?"

His thumbs draw small circles on either leg. "Just now, you looked at me and blushed. What were you thinking?"

Will I ever not blush around Devlyn?

Devlyn is the only man to stir up such desirous feelings and thoughts. Enough to heat every cell in my body and pink my skin. In the beginning, I was embarrassed by my reaction. Now, I embrace the way my body responds to his proximity, his words, him.

Licking my lips, I swallow and point to his chest. "Saw the paint on you and thought about the morning when we… uh… painted each other." Heat floods my cheeks anew.

His hands trail from my thighs to my round belly, his thumbs and fingers lightly massaging the stretched skin. And damn, does that feel good. So good.

"Definitely need to do that again," he says as he leans in and presses a kiss to my belly. "Maybe before you arrive into the world, little one," he whispers to my belly. Then he lifts his gaze, his eyes a shade darker. "Maybe now."

Heat spreads throughout my body for a wholly new reason. Hunger and love rise to the surface. My relaxed state from moments ago morphs into something new, something primal. Although my body wants to rest, my mind and heart scream to get out of this chair and follow Devlyn up the stairs to his studio. To squeeze colored pigment from tubes and paint him with my own abstract passion.

"Yes," I whisper. "Now."

Not needing reassurances, Devlyn rises to his full height and offers me his hand. My warm fingers slip into his hand as I stand from the rocker. Without a word, we weave our way through the house and climb the stairs to his studio. He parks me on the stool near his easel. While he sets everything up, I stare at the painting of me he has worked diligently on.

I have no words.

The piece so different from his others. A mess of pinks and reds layer the canvas. Some spots thicker with paint and in harsh yet soft lines. My face is almost absent of detail... except for my eyes. My nose is a simple streak and change in color. My unshapely lips a deep, rich red. But my eyes... I should expect nothing less from Devlyn. They pop on the canvas. Dark blue with gold flecks, naturally. Strands of hair fan over my cheek and down my shoulder to my breast.

My eyes drift along the canvas and take in the curves of my breasts, the dark pink of my nipples. The brush strokes on my body softer. Smoother. Gentle. He painted my belly—our baby—with even more tenderness. My hand splayed beneath my navel, and his hand added in and next to mine, forming a cradle.

The backs of my eyes burn with unshed tears.

The depth of this man's heart is unparalleled. He loves me in a way no one ever has. In a way no one ever will. He brought a new gentleness into my life and I showed him what real love looks and feels like. Our love is pure and breathtaking and everything I wanted in my life.

A sudden rush of images flash before my eyes. Mental snapshots of our past. Assumed depictions of our future. And it is so odd, the clarity of those pictures. Especially those yet to come. But I see it all.

Devlyn with our little one bundled in his arms. His eyes glassy with unshed tears as he stares down at them. And the way he holds my gaze when he looks up at me in pure awe. Delight. Brilliance.

Then the images flash forward to years from now. Devlyn and I swinging our mini between us as we walk down the beach along the surf. A sweet voice begging us to swing them higher. Soft giggles and shrieks of joy.

Tears spill down my cheeks without effort as my mind comes back to the present. The beautiful painting a blurry mess of reds and pinks as I swipe my cheeks and eyes. Devlyn catches the movement out of the corner of his eye and spins to face me.

"What's wrong?" A whack fills the air as he drops the supplies from his hands and strides across the room. He cradles my face in his hands and brushes away the wetness with his thumbs. "Tell me. Please," he whispers.

I lick my lips and swallow as I point a finger at the canvas. "This is the first time I've really seen the painting. It's just..." My blues dart between his greens. "It's so beautiful." I shrug. "Guess it overwhelmed me." I shake my head on a chuckle. "Damn hormones."

Devlyn leans in, kissing each tear trail on my cheeks before pressing his lips to mine. The kiss is sweet and gentle, and ends far too soon.

"You're beautiful." His thumbs stroke my cheeks again. "The most beautiful creature I know."

"For now," I mutter as my eyes fall between us.

"Hey." One hand drifts to my chin and tips it up so I look him in the eye. "No." He shakes his head. "No, Shelly," he repeats.

One of my creeping insecurities rises to the surface. Maybe because I am overwhelmed with seeing the painting. Maybe because there isn't a lot of time of just me and Devlyn left. Whatever the reason, my secret spills from my lips with too much ease.

"When the baby comes, things will change." My vision blurs for a new reason. "They'll easily be more beautiful."

"Not possible." I open my mouth to rebut his words and he shakes his head. "Not. Possible." He presses another kiss to my lips. "Yes, we will love this baby. So much." His hand falls to my belly and rubs the outer swell. "But that won't change how I love you. Ever."

"You don't know that," I whisper-choke.

"I do." Soft, warm lips press mine. "Shelly, I will never love anyone the way I love you. Will I love our baby with unmatched affection? Absolutely. But my love for them will be new. A love neither of us will understand until it hits."

As his words sink in, as they resonate in my bones, I believe them more. The love for our child will be phenomenal. Otherworldly. Surreal. But loving them will be different than loving Devlyn.

I nod. "I love you."

His fingers twirl a strand of my hair as he drops his forehead to mine. "Love you, Shell." After another chaste kiss, Devlyn straightens to his full height. "Come." He offers his hand. "Time to paint."

The corners of my mouth tip up as I take his hand. "As you wish."

Hours pass without care as I paint every line, curve and valley on Devlyn's body. And he paints mine as if it is the most precious thing his hands have touched.

Shelly shifts on the bed for the umpteenth time. I curl into her frame, my front to her back, and try to calm her.

But she isn't sleeping.

Her hand takes mine and squeezes. Just as I open my mouth to ask if she is okay, her body tightens. Her breathing pauses a beat before she grunts softly.

"What's wrong?" I whisper-ask and kiss her shoulder.

I feel her head shake in the dark. "Can't get comfortable. And my stomach…"

When she doesn't elaborate, I prop myself up on my elbow and look at her profile. "Your stomach what?"

"It's just tight. Like painfully tight."

Without a word, I whip the covers off my body and slip out of bed. Circling the bed, I stand in front of Shelly. "Close your eyes. I'm turning on the lamp." I give her a moment, then flip the switch. We squint into the lit room until our eyes adjust. I hold out my hand. "Let's try to walk a minute. See if that helps."

She takes my hand without argument. I help her off the bed and guide her out of the bedroom. We take slow steps through the house. To the kitchen, then the living room before sliding the glass doors open and stepping outside.

Minutes pass as we wander through the yard barefoot. Shelly appears more relaxed than when we left the bed. Just as we turn to head back for the house, she stops. I take in her profile and see her brows knitted together.

Something's wrong.

Is it time?

It can't be time. The due date isn't for a few more weeks. Early October. Right?

My brain scrambles back to all the doctor's appointments, trying to recall the dozen different dates Dr. Webster told us. And then it hits. A couple months back, when the number of appointments increased and we visited every other week, then every week. At one of those appointments, Dr. Webster said the baby may come sooner. That it wasn't abnormal. But as long as Shelly was in the last four weeks, it was safe.

Is that what this is? Shelly going into labor.

We hadn't attended classes like most normal new parents. With all the mothers surrounding us—Elizabeth, Nicole, Cora, and Autumn—we'd been coached on all things birth and baby related. Shelly had found several Lamaze breathing videos online and opted to do those instead of in-person classes. They made her more comfortable and we did them on our schedule.

What did those videos say? For the life of me, I can't seem to remember a damn thing about the breathing right now.

And what about the books I'd read? They talked about what happens when labor starts. But it also stated no two labors are alike. So what good is that information?

Damnit.

"Talk to me," I tell Shelly. "Do you think it's time?"

Her free hand goes to her belly and rubs circles. Over and over. Again and again. From the expression on her face, she doesn't appear to be in pain. But maybe it isn't *pain*. Maybe she is super uncomfortable. Neither of us knows what to expect with labor, least of all me.

"It just feels tight." She looks up at me, unable to straighten to her full height. "Like my skin is being stretched." Her brows pinch at the middle. "Shit."

"What?"

"Need to pee. Now."

Quickly as possible, I guide us inside and to the bathroom. I stand outside the open door while Shelly does her business. I do my best not to stare or appear overbearing, but I worry. Maybe we should hop in the car and drive to the hospital. I glance across the bedroom to the alarm clock and note the time: 3:55.

The doctor's office doesn't open for another three and a half hours.

Do we wait? Give it time and see if it passes?

I should make her something to drink. Something soothing. A mug of hot cocoa.

Shelly flushes the toilet and washes her hands. "God, it feels like I need to pee constantly, but barely anything came out."

I take her hand and walk us toward the kitchen. "How about some tea or cocoa? Maybe it'll settle whatever this is." And while she drinks, I will search the internet and the stack of baby books for answers.

A smile tips up her lips as she curls into my side. "Cocoa would be great."

With measured steps, Shelly paces the kitchen while I heat the oat milk. I scoop two spoonfuls of her favorite cocoa mix into her favorite mug and add the warmed milk.

Guiding us out of the kitchen, I park us on her old couch in our reading area. While she sips her cocoa, I Google what labor pains feel like. Thousands of results fill the screen and overwhelm me with all the possibilities.

Some articles indicate true labor starts when the water breaks. Others say labor begins when contractions start, that sometimes the water doesn't break on its own. Either way, Shelly's water hasn't broken yet. So I move on to another article. This one talks about painful contractions and the need to push. Shelly hasn't mentioned the desire to push, just the need to pee. Again, I move forward.

The next article has me blinking, again and again.

The article states some labor starts with a general pressure, low in the belly. The mother may feel like her skin is stretched to extremes—very tight. The need to use the bathroom often may be present, without much of a release. I continue reading down the page. The more I read, the more I am convinced it is time.

But the article also points out it may be false labor. That the baby may be shifting and moving into position for the big day. The article goes on and says to time how long the sensations last and how far apart they are.

Not wanting to alarm Shelly, I speak in mellow tones and relay what I just read. Surprisingly, she appears quite calm when I finish.

"I wondered as much," she says. "Right now, it isn't so bad. Like a barely noticeable ache." Her hand paints small circles over her belly while she sips her drink. "This has helped."

"Then I guess we wait." I shrug. "If it starts back up, we time it and make note." I lay my hand over hers on her belly. Lace our fingers together and help soothe her discomfort. "Until then, maybe we just take it easy. Sit on the couch, under the blanket, and watch a movie in the dark." I kiss her cheek. "In a few hours, I'll make breakfast. Sound good?"

"Perfect."

~

I add eggs to each of our plates already filled with sausage, hash browns, and toast. Setting forks on each plate, I carry them to the living room and hand one to Shelly, who has made a makeshift table with a throw pillow on her belly.

We dive into our breakfast while a Passionflix movie plays on the television.

When Shelly added the Passionflix app to the Apple TV, I asked what the channel was all about. She'd said, *"It's all my favorite romance books coming to life."*

I have yet to read any of the countless romance books on her shelf, but perhaps I should check them out. See what all the fuss is about. The movies have been interesting and lovely, but the book is always better.

Over the last few hours, nothing new has happened. No more tightness. No urgent need for the bathroom. So, we have taken it easy. Rested in each other's arms and occasionally drifted off. Perhaps it was false labor. Books state false labor —Braxton-Hicks contractions—is one way the body prepares for the big day. Kind of like a delivery practice drill.

Whatever it is, I hope it passes until the real time occurs. Last thing we need is a scare after things have been so good.

When our plates empty, I take them to the kitchen and clean up. Just as I place the last pan into the dishwasher, Shelly wanders in. I open my mouth to tell her I was on my way back. That she could have waited and I would have gotten whatever she needs.

But I don't say a word. Not when I scan her head to toe and take all of her in.

One hand braces the edge of the kitchen counter while the other rubs back and forth in rapid strokes on her belly. Her lips trapped between her teeth as her jaw works back and forth. The space between her brows wrinkled and tight.

And I know this is it.

Earlier was a drill. Like a like tremor before an earthquake. Like the warning winds and rain before the hurricane makes landfall.

But this is no longer a drill. It's go time.

"Talk to me, Shell."

"It's like before." She closes her eyes for a breath then holds my greens captive. "But stronger. Tighter. More intense."

"Did it just start?"

She nods. "A minute after you walked out of the room."

"Okay," I say, calmer than I feel. "Let's get the hospital bag and leave."

In the bedroom, Shelly puts on a pair of pajama pants before grabbing her phone from the charger. I trade my sweats for jeans and tug a shirt over my head. I grab us each socks from the dresser. We slip on socks and shoes at the door. Shelly fetches her purse from the hook while I shoulder the hospital bag.

Slowly, we make our way to the car. A minute later, I pull out of the neighborhood and aim the car west toward the hospital. Traffic isn't too bad yet, but may pick up the longer we're on the road.

At a red light, I turn to face Shelly. Her eyes forward as she takes slow, measured breaths. Her hands massage her belly from back to front, occasionally switching positions.

"Doing okay?" I ask, feeling like a fool the moment the words hit the air. *What a stupid question.* Of course, she isn't okay. The baby is trying to evacuate the womb. No way she isn't in some kind of pain. I sure as hell would be.

"Okay," she says between breaths. "But it's becoming more intense."

Sweat licks my temples as she says the words. I did this. I put her in this position. It is me who is responsible for her pain. Me, not her.

Give her pain to me.

If only it were so simple.

The city passes in a blur of fast-driving cars and a blend of residential and commercial buildings. Now isn't the time to take in scenery. Now isn't the time to observe sights and smells and places to visit in the future.

I flip on the blinker and zip into a turn lane. Tap the steering wheel as I wait for the light to turn green. An older man strolls leisurely in the crosswalk in front of us. Bass thumps from a car nearby. Sirens wail in the distance. But all of it vanishes as the light turns green.

And Shelly's water breaks.

"Oh god," she whispers. "Oh god."

Fuck. I smash the pedal to the floorboard and whip down the road. *We're almost there.*

Pain. Excruciating, inexplicable pain. It is all I feel. All I hear. All I see. Pain... it is everywhere. Everything.

I clutch my belly and bend slightly in the seat. "Ow. Ow, ow, ow!"

The car picks up speed as Devlyn takes the next right. I fist the handle above the window and hug my belly tighter.

"Sorry," he mutters. "Just trying to get us there."

"I..." Another stab of pain tears through my belly. I suck in a deep breath, hold it and count to three, then exhale. "I know. Just be careful."

Not a minute later, Devlyn whips into the hospital parking lot. He drives to the drop-off spot near the doors, jumps out and jogs to my side of the car. Flinging my door open, he helps me step out, kisses my forehead, and tells me he will be right back. From my spot near the entrance, I watch as he finds the closest parking spot to the entrance before bolting from the vehicle and running to me, hospital bag slung over his shoulder.

From there, everything but the pain is a blur.

Arm around my waist, Devlyn holds on to me as if my knees will buckle. Which is smart, because I may give up any minute.

Elevator doors whoosh open and the familiar view of the labor and delivery floor comes into view. Today, I won't be twiddling my thumbs in a hard chair in the waiting area. For the first time, I will be in the hospital bed, cursing out people left and right as I push our baby into the world.

As we reach the nurses' station, Devlyn explains the past few hours and my water breaking in the car. As the words leave his lips, another contraction rips through my lower abdomen.

"Argh!" I bite out, bending slightly and clutching my belly.

Before the contraction ends, warm hands guide me to sit in a wheelchair. A nurse steers me down the hall like she drag races cars for pleasure. Three deep breaths later, the wheelchair is parked next to a hospital bed and I am ushered onto the mattress.

"We'll need you to change," the nurse says, offering me a sympathetic smile and a hospital gown. "Or, if you'd prefer, just strip down and slip under the sheet. If you choose to wear the gown, leave the front open." Then, she steps out of the room.

"Do you want the gown?" Devlyn pulls back the top sheet on the bed.

I shake my head. "Just want to ditch the wet clothes."

Devlyn helps with my bottoms and underwear. As I lift my shirt over my head, another contraction hits. While I clutch my belly and breathe through the pain, Devlyn wiggles off my top. He situates me on the bed and covers me with the sheet.

"What can I do?"

I hold up my hand. "Just be here."

He laces his fingers with mine, leans in and kisses my forehead. "Nowhere else I want to be."

The contraction settles and realization strikes. "We didn't call anyone." Our family and friends will lose their shit if we don't let them know I am in labor.

Devlyn releases my hand, pulls his phone from his back pocket, and taps on the screen. A moment later, he locks the device and stows it once more. From my spot on the bed, I hear the repeated vibration of responses, but Devlyn doesn't answer any of them. Instead, he takes my hand again and kisses my knuckles in turn.

It isn't long before nurses flood the room. A thick band gets strapped around my belly and the nurses adjust my position in the bed. Ice chips, water, and a cup are brought in and set up on the rolling table behind Devlyn. Dr. Webster walks in decked out in scrubs with a bright smile on her face. A nurse holds a glove open for her and she slips her hand in one, then another.

She steps closer to the foot of the bed, between my feet in the stirrups. "How you doing, Mom? Dad?" Her smile intensifies. "I hear this little cutie is ready to meet everyone?"

Devlyn remains a quiet beacon of strength at my side as I relay how I feel. The pressure from earlier, the cramping, and then the pain once my water broke in the car.

"Everything sounds on track and normal. Let's have a look and check your dilation."

Once upon a time, I reddened with embarrassment even thinking about my appointments at the lady doctor. Now, I don't care. All the people in this room are trained medical professionals. They have probably delivered hundreds, if not thousands, of babies. Nudity doesn't shock them. No doubt, they have seen it all. And in this moment, I honestly don't give a damn who sees what.

Just get this damn baby out of my body.

Dr. Webster recovers my knees and removes the gloves from her hands as she stands from the stool. Tossing the gloves in the biohazard trash bin, she turns on the faucet and washes her hands.

"Dilated to seven. Shouldn't be long now." Her glowing smile makes another appearance. "I'll be back to check on you soon. In the meantime, keep breathing and resting as much as you can." Her eyes go to Devlyn. "Dad, you're in charge of keeping her as calm as possible. Water and ice chips may help. But not too much."

All but one nurse leaves the room. He pulls things out of cabinets and sets up items on counters and trays and carts. I close my eyes and listen to the machine as it registers my heartbeat, the baby's heartbeat, and contractions. I let it soothe me as I rest against pillows softer than I imagined for the hospital.

Devlyn traces my fingers and hand with his. And right now, everything is calm and normal.

But that all vanishes a second later as another contraction stretches and pulls and rips at my abdomen. Devlyn kisses my temple and encourages me to take deep breaths. I squeeze his hand hard enough to detach it from his arm, but he doesn't complain.

When the pain eases, Devlyn offers me ice chips and pours water in a cup with a straw.

Not a minute later, another contraction hits. This one like a knife to my insides. Stabbing. Painful. Burning. Before I get the chance to voice my pain, the monitor off to the side wails loudly. Too loudly.

In an instant, the room overflows with medical personnel. One silences the machine, while Dr. Webster gloves up. Her smile from earlier gone. Her demeanor and body language more serious as she reads the numbers on the monitor.

She lifts the sheet away and exposes me fully. "Shelly, are you in pain?" She surveys between my thighs. "More than the previous contractions," she clarifies.

"Yes. What's wrong?"

She feels around my lower abdomen, near my pelvic bone, and presses hard in a few spots. "Does this hurt?" I suck in a sharp breath and nod. Her eyes drift to a nurse in light-blue scrubs and she gives a subtle nod. The nurse blurs out of sight and starts grabbing more items from cabinets and drawers. "I don't want to alarm you, but it seems as if this little one isn't getting enough oxygen. Your body isn't ready to push yet, so we need to do an emergency C-section."

Tears rim my eyes, blur my vision and spill down my cheeks. "Oh god."

"This isn't abnormal, Shelly. But we can't wait."

A nurse comes to Devlyn's side, hands him a pile of green scrubs, and tells him he needs to change before the surgery starts.

He kisses my forehead. "Be right back." And then he dashes into the en suite bathroom.

I cry harder the second he steps away. Dr. Webster continues to assure me everything will be fine, but I tune out her voice. I tune out every sound in the room. Because this just feels like another snapped tree in the road. Another major obstacle to challenge me. To challenge us.

And damn it. I am so fucking tired of this. So tired of having to fight. So tired.

Once I have the scrubs on and the booties over my shoes, I exit the bathroom. The room is abuzz, and not in a good way. When I look to Shelly, I notice her eyes are closed. My initial thought is she is relaxing between contractions.

As everyone moves rapidly around the room, a curtain is erected to hide the lower half of her body from sight. I go back to my position next to Shelly and scoop up her hand, lacing my fingers in hers. But she doesn't curl her fingers.

In fact, her arm is deadweight.

"Something's wrong," I say, but no one pays me attention. So, I repeat myself, louder this time. "Something is wrong." Dr. Webster peers around the curtain, mask covering her face. "She's limp," I choke out.

If I thought the room was chaos moments ago, I was dead wrong.

Dr. Webster shouts orders, but none of them makes sense to me. Then a nurse is at my side, taking my arm and guiding me out of the room.

"Everything will be fine, Devlyn. Just let us work and we'll be out to get you in a minute," Dr. Webster says, calmer than she lets on.

"What's wrong with her? Is Shelly okay? The baby?"

"A nurse will be out to speak with you in a moment."

And then, the door is closed.

I have no idea what is happening, but it can't be good. At all.

First the baby is in distress. Then Shelly passes out. This isn't normal. Not by a long shot. Worst of all, I have no idea what is happening on the other side of the door. No idea if I am losing Shelly. Or if we are losing the baby.

Or both.

I fall to my knees. The linoleum smacks my bones hard, but I welcome the pain. I welcome every ounce. Because it is nothing compared to what is happening to my heart.

I can't lose Shelly. Or the baby.

Losing either of them isn't an option. Not even close.

Twenty-nine

Everything is foggy. The air, my thoughts. It feels as if I am floating. Lingering. Not really here or there.

What the hell is happening?

My eyes feel puffy and weighted. Heavy. Unable to open.

My throat is swollen and scratchy. Abrasive like sandpaper. My lungs dry and burning. I will myself to swallow to moisten my throat. But nothing happens. No relief comes. I try to take a deep breath, but my lungs won't fill fully.

Again, I try to open my eyes and take in my surroundings. Open my mouth and say something. Anything. Again, I fail.

What the hell is going on?

And where is Devlyn?

I don't sense him nearby. Not the smell of his addictive, earthy scent. Not his warm, charismatic energy. Not his whispered words of reassurance or the weight of his hand in mine.

Where is he?

My brain tells my muscles to move, tells my mouth to open and my voice to work, but nothing happens. I want to scream for help. Want to ask what is wrong with me. Want to ask if the baby is okay.

But none of it happens. Nothing works.

The thick fog returns. Clouds around me and pull me down, down, down. Without effort, I drift further into the darkness.

In the darkness, life feels peaceful.

In the darkness, everything feels safe.

In the darkness, the weight of the past falls away.

And now I understand. I get it. Why Devlyn liked the darkness for so long. It's like a warm hug after a long day. A welcome home when you have been away for days or weeks.

In the darkness, there is no pain. Just relief. And I welcome the repose.

The past ten hours have aged me ten years.

Shelly lies in the hospital bed. Still. Silent. Except for the beat of her heart through the monitor. The room dimly lit by a lamp off to the side. The baby in the hospital nursery being monitored by nurses and the doctor.

And me… I stand on the edge of a cliff, head tipped back as I scream at the heavens.

This doesn't feel like another test. Another measure of my strength. No, this feels like the end. The end of a long obstacle course. One I didn't choose, but one I can't seem to escape.

Dr. Webster says Shelly will wake up soon. That her body is exhausted and needs the rest. Her vitals are perfect. It's just a matter of the anesthesia leaving her system and her mind waking up. Dr. Webster says there is no need to worry.

But worrying is all I can do. It is all I know.

With Shelly's hand sandwiched between mine, I give her a gentle squeeze. Paint lines my fingertips over each finger, each knuckle. I press my lips to the top of her hand on either side of the IV line.

"I need you to wake up, Andromeda," I whisper against her skin. The backs of my eyes sting as tears surface and well. I don't fight the tears. Don't try to shove them down. No, I let them spill. Let them paint my cheeks. Let them fall from my chin to her hand. "I need you, Shell. Forever. Please," I choke out.

I close my eyes and lay my head on her fingers. Pray to whatever force, whatever deity is willing to listen. Beg them to help her wake. Open her eyes. Squeeze my hand. Whisper my name. Something. *Anything.*

Whispering voices in the room startle me from sleep. But I don't lift my head and greet them. Without seeing, I know it is Nicole and George Reed. They have been in the room almost as much as I since Dr. Webster allowed us. More than once, they suggested I get food or a drink or take a walk down the hall. That they would be here with Shelly and let me know if anything changed.

But I refuse to leave her side. Not for a minute. Food and drinks and walks can wait.

Shelly needs me more than I need anything else right now. Leaving her isn't an option. I fear what may happen if I leave this room. One step out, one minute away, and everything could change.

"We need to do something, George," Nicole whispers to her husband. Her voice scratchy and tired. "I can't stand this. The waiting." She sniffles. "What kind of doctor tells a mother to be patient while her only daughter lies in a coma? Does the woman *have* children? Does she have an inkling of what this feels like?" With each word she speaks, her voice escalates in volume.

George shushes her. "Everything will be fine, Nicole."

"You don't know that," she rebuts with a sharp edge to her words. "You can't be positive."

He audibly exhales. "You're right, I don't know what will happen. But I choose to believe she will wake up any minute. I choose to believe everything will be okay.

Is it easy? No." At this, I twist my head and peek at the two of them on the couch in the room. George points a finger toward the bed and Shelly, but his eyes remain on his wife. "But I won't give an ounce of my energy to negative thoughts. Not when it comes to our children. Or our grandchild." He lowers his hand. "She will wake up." Rising from the couch, he stares down at Nicole for a beat. "I'm going to stretch my legs and get something for us all from the cafeteria."

Then he storms to the door and leaves without another word.

Although my mind drifts so easily into the dark, I side with Mr. Reed and silently vow to Shelly I will only think positive thoughts. I won't give in to the darkness that has come to me with such ease in the past.

Shelly will wake up. She will. She has to.

I lift my head and shift in the chair that now has a permanent mold of my body. Nicole catches the movement and swipes at her cheeks.

"Sorry if we woke you."

"Don't apologize," I tell her. "We're all on edge right now."

She rises from the couch and shoulders her purse. "I'll go update whoever is still here. Maybe walk the halls for a bit. Clear my head."

I nod. "Okay."

The door quietly clicks shut and it's just me and Shelly and silence. On a normal day, I love the silence we share. It isn't awkward or uncomfortable. Many of my favorite moments with Shelly didn't involve a single word spoken.

But this silence... I never want this type of silence again.

I kiss the back of her hand and stand from the chair. Twisting left and right, forward and backward, I stretch my stiff muscles. I lift my arms over my head and roll my neck. Shake my legs and wiggle my toes. Work my body from head to toe and get my blood flowing.

While her parents are away, I step into the en suite bathroom, leaving the door wide open, and relieve my bladder. Hands soaped up, I run them under the water and rinse away the suds. As I fetch a paper towel from the holder, my ears perk up.

The monitor beeps a different rhythm. Faster. Seemingly louder.

I drop the paper towels in the direction of the bin and dash out of the bathroom. Sidling up to the bed, I take Shelly's hand in mine and lean over her.

"Shell? Can you hear me?"

Her eyelids tighten briefly. Her fingers twitch in my hold.

Leaning in closer, I press my lips to her forehead. Then drop them to her ear and whisper, "I'm here, Shell."

Her fingers curl and wrap around my own. A low groan echoes from her throat.

Hovering inches from her face, I wait for her eyes to open. Wait for her sparkling blues to meet my faded greens. It hasn't been a full day, but I miss the hell out of those eyes.

Slowly, her lids lift. She blinks and blinks and blinks. Her tongue darts out to wet her lips and she groans. She lifts her free hand and taps her throat.

"I'll get you water." I kiss her forehead before untwining my fingers from hers. I pour water from a pitcher into a cup with a straw on the rolling table. Bringing it to her, I bend the straw and press it to her lips. "Small, slow sips."

She takes one, then another. Licks her lips. Swallows. Parts her lips in a silent request for more. After a few more sips, she releases the straw and nods. I set the cup down and take her hand in mine once more.

"How do you feel?" I whisper-ask as I brush stray hairs from her face. My knuckles graze her cheek and her eyes roll shut as she leans into my touch, a low hum in her throat.

Her eyes open and lock on mine. "Tired," she says, her voice raw. "Pain." She inhales deeply before her face morphs. Deep lines mar her forehead. The skin between her brows bunches and tightens. "Where…" Her eyes dart around the room, then circle back to mine. "The baby?"

And for the first time in what feels like forever, I smile. "She's in the nursery." My thumb strokes her cheekbone. "Healthy and perfect." I press the button on the bed and call for the nurse. "When you're ready, they'll bring her in."

Tears rim Shelly's lower lids before they spill down her cheeks. "She?" I nod and wipe the tears away. "A little girl," she whispers.

Nurse Tracy wanders into the room. "Did you—" Her eyes dart to Shelly and she smiles. "Glad to see you're awake, Ms. Reed." She steps up to the bed and looks over the monitor. "How are you feeling?"

"Tired." She swallows. "Some pain."

Nurse Tracy checks the saline bag and IV line. "That's to be expected." A soft smile lifts the corners of her lips. "Your body went through a lot today. Let's raise you up." She presses a button on the arm of the bed and the bed slowly scoots up. When Shelly is sitting up, but still leaning back slightly, she stops. "Let's adjust those pillows and get you water."

Once Shelly is a touch more comfortable and a little more hydrated, Nurse Tracy gives us each a smile, tells us she will page Dr. Webster, and then be back with our baby girl.

I sit on the edge of the bed near Shelly's legs and retrieve my phone from my back pocket. "Everyone's been on edge, waiting for you to wake up." I unlock my phone and open the group chat.

Shelly lays her hand on my thigh as her eyes roll shut for a beat. "They're probably all freaking out," she chokes out.

There is no sugarcoating the situation. When I was kicked out of the room as they performed emergency surgery, I sat in front of the door for quite some time. Eventually, I ambled down to the waiting room and spoke with everyone. The shock was evident on each family member and friend's face, but no one lost it more than Micah.

I'd never seen a man so distraught, but I knew exactly how he felt in the moment. Frightened beyond words. Terrified of what might happen. Helpless because it was out of our hands.

I won't stress Shelly with all of that right now, but I will tell her. When she has her strength back. When we are home and she has a moment to rest and feel more at ease.

"Yes, they are, but they'll feel a million times better knowing you're awake and okay now." Her hand tightens on my thigh as I type out a text.

> Shelly is awake. Waiting for the doctor to arrive. More details soon.

And as suspected before I hit send, my phone blows up with one text after another.

MICAH

Thank fuck.

CORA

Give her our love until we see her.

AUTUMN

Oh, thank goodness.

NICOLE

On our way back.

One after another, the texts keep coming. I hold up my phone and Shelly stares at the screen, a small smile forming on her lips. I ignore the messages, lock my phone, and stow it back in my pocket.

And for the next few minutes, while we have alone time, I press my forehead to hers. Breathe her in. Feel her breath on my lips. Feel the weight and heat of her fingers and hand on my leg. I press a gentle kiss to her lips. Then another. Tears blur my vision as I hold her gaze. Emotion clogs my throat.

"I love you, Shelly Reed." My lips press hers again. "And I never want a day without you."

Tears roll down her cheeks as she tips her head and kisses me with desperation. "I love you, Devlyn Templar. Always."

And until Nurse Tracy reenters the room with our baby girl, we don't move an inch. Don't take our eyes off each other.

Desirée Rose.

God, she is beautiful. The most perfect thing I have seen in my life. Her plump little cheeks. A full head of brown hair. Eyes a hint lighter than my own, although Dr. Webster says both her hair and eyes may change color. Either way, she is flawless. A little piece of me and Devlyn in the sweetest package.

I stare down at our little girl as she suckles my breast and lays her hand on my skin. Soft sounds vibrate from her lips to my skin. Devlyn sits beside me on the hospital bed, his head on my shoulder as he watches her, watches us. Every few seconds, he twists to kiss my shoulder.

"God, how is it possible to love her so much already?" he whispers.

His question resonates deep in my bones because I wonder the same. How it is possible to love someone you just met. And not just love… no, it is much more complex than that. Not something I know how to define. Incomprehensible love.

"Not sure." I tilt my head and rest it on Devlyn's. "But I feel it too."

After four days in the hospital, we finally get to go home today. Of course, we will have a caravan. Since not everyone had the opportunity to come see us in the hospital, and because my labor circumstances were not what anyone expected, we will have visitors at the house on and off for the next few days. Mom already stated she will be at the house more often than not.

For once, I don't mind. I look forward to having her help. May even ask her to stay the night once or twice. While I feel less mentally foggy, my body still needs more time to recover. Until I heal fully, I can't lift anything more than one to two pounds, including the baby. Which means, to nurse her, I have to get situated before someone hands her to me.

Dr. Webster assures me I should be better in the next two weeks, then reminds me that everyone heals at different speeds.

Desirée falls asleep with her lips wrapped around my nipple. Slowly, I lower her and Devlyn fixes my gown. Then he drapes a cloth over his shoulder, scoops her up from my arms, rests her against his chest, and bops her up and down as he lightly pats her little back.

I love every side of Devlyn. The quiet and reserved. The passionate and hungry. The gentle and sweet. But seeing this side, watching him hold our daughter, care for her with such tenderness… renders me breathless.

After a soft burp leaves her lips, he carries her to the plastic bassinet and lays her down. He tightens the blanket around her tiny frame before leaning down and kissing her forehead. He whispers something to her, his voice too soft for me to hear, and I don't ask what. It's something for just the two of them. A shared moment.

Devlyn helps me up from the bed and leads me to the bathroom. Peeling away the gown and my underwear, he helps me bathe with a small tub of warm water, a cloth and soap that smells sterile like the hospital. He dries me off and helps me into my clothes. Then he brushes my hair and secures it with a hair band. After I brush my teeth, we exit the bathroom and I slip on shoes.

Dr. Webster makes one last stop in the room and reviews our appointments over the next few weeks—for me and the baby. She gives us each a hug and walks out with us after Devlyn secures Desirée in the stroller. The moment we exit the hospital, I stop and take a deep breath.

"You okay?" Devlyn takes my hand in his.

"Yes," I say on a nod. "Just happy to leave." Out of nowhere, tears flood my eyes and stream down my face.

Devlyn steers us toward a bench, lowers us to sit, and parks the stroller in front of us. His hands cup my cheeks in an instant. His eyes lock with mine as he searches for the reason for my tears.

"I've got you." His thumbs stroke my cheeks. Scooting closer, he leans in and kisses me chastely. A breath later, he cocoons me in his arms and hugs me tight to his chest. "Always."

My fingers curl around the cotton of his shirt and ball into tight fists. "I was so scared," I admit, whispering into the crook of his neck. "It was so dark. At first, I enjoyed the peace that came with the darkness. But after a while..." I shake my head over and over. "I felt empty. Lost." I sob into the collar of his shirt. "I-I couldn't find you." My arms squeeze him impossibly tighter to my frame. "Couldn't see or hear or smell you."

"Shh, shh, shh." One arm tugs me closer. Squishes me to his chest. His other hand strokes my hair, my neck, my back in an effort to soothe the fear in my veins. "It's over now. You're here. I've got you." I don't miss his hushed sniffles and tears on my shoulder. "I was scared too. So scared," he confesses in a whisper. "Never been more scared in my life." He leans back and frames my face. His eyes red and veiny and laced with unspoken pain. "If I lost you..." His eyes fall shut as he shakes his head. I wait for him to finish, but he doesn't.

I press my lips to his. Taste his salty tears on my lips. Breathe in his faded, earthy scent as our lips part. Loosen my hold on him and take a deep breath. I trace the line of his jaw with shaky fingers. The scruff on his jawline the longest I have seen it. The dark half-moons below his eyes less prominent today, but still noticeable.

"Let's go home," I whisper.

It isn't only me that needs to escape the memories of this place over the last few days. I may need to heal physically, but Devlyn needs to heal too. Needs to know I am safe. That Desirée is safe.

And home... home is safe.

∽

Much as I want time alone with Devlyn and Desirée, I have never been more appreciative of having so many wonderful people in my life.

For the last week, Mom has been a constant presence in the house. Dad practically shoved her through the front door and dropped her bag in the foyer. It didn't really happen that way, but he didn't hang out long on the first night.

Part of me thinks Dad is as exhausted as us. Sleep hasn't been easy to come by since I went into labor. But another part of me thinks Dad just needed time to himself. Time to mull over everything that happened in the hospital. Between Mom and Dad, he is the more sensitive and reserved person. Less likely to share his feelings. And seeing me in the hospital bed, completely out of it, probably took its toll on him.

With time, he will be okay.

Aside from Mom helping me with Desirée, she has also been a saint with housework and cooking. Taking on the tasks we sometimes take for granted. Not having to wash dishes every time we eat or drink has been a relief. Not having to worry over cooking or grocery shopping or general errands has been a tremendous help.

Occasionally, Devlyn goes into his studio and works. For the most part, though, he sits with me and the baby. On the couch while a movie plays softly in the background. On the back patio, when the sun begins to set and the heat is milder. We just sit together and hold Desirée and bond more.

"How's she doing?" Mom whispers as she enters the living room.

I peer down my chest and see a sleeping Desirée. My fingers gently stroke her hair. "Fast asleep."

"Want me to put her down?"

Since I still have at least another week—hopefully not more—before I am allowed to carry her on my own, Mom has helped with putting Desirée down in her crib or bassinet while Devlyn works.

"That'd be great. Thank you."

As Mom reaches for Desirée, Devlyn pads down the stairs and enters the room. He sidles up to Mom, leans in and presses a kiss to Desirée's crown. Devlyn drops on the couch beside me as Mom walks off. But the second Mom is out of sight, the doorbell rings.

"I'll get it," Devlyn says loud enough for Mom to hear, but not loud enough to wake the baby.

Devlyn starts for the door. Scooting to the edge of the couch, I gingerly stand and follow. With our friends on a daily rotation of stopping by to check on us and the baby, Devlyn doesn't think twice before unlocking the dead bolt. He doesn't hesitate before twisting the knob. He doesn't consider, not for a second, to check the peephole or peer out through the blinds.

But I wish he would have.

The door swings open and I freeze on the opposite side of the sitting room, near the kitchen. Because standing at the door, with a wicked grin on her lips, is Karen Templar. And something about her expression twists a knife in my already tender womb.

Why won't this woman just leave us be? Why won't this woman leave Devlyn alone?

Let him be happy. Without you.

Because if she isn't happy, she has to bring everyone else down. And people like Karen Templar will never be happy. Not until the entire ship sinks.

"I hear congratulations are in order," my mother says with disgust on her tongue. "You can imagine how upset I was to have heard I am a grandmother through a gossip circle." She curls her lip as her head tilts. "Don't be rude. Invite your mother inside."

I peer over my shoulder at Shelly and give her what I hope is an apologetic smile. "Be back in a second." Her eyes widen. "I'll be okay. Just stay in the house. Please."

She nods and walks toward the hallway. Toward her mother and the nursery.

I step out the front door and close it, but don't take another step. Crossing my arms over my chest and widening my stance, I form a barricade in front of the door. A barrier. A way to shield my home from this woman and the negativity she carries like a handbag.

"What do you want, Mother?"

She straightens her spine and rests her hands on her hips. "Has that girl drained you of intelligence and manners?" She shakes her head, her lips flattening for a beat. "I came to see my grandchild," she states, talking to me like an insolent child.

I take a deep breath and prepare myself for battle. I knew this day was inevitable, but hoped I wouldn't have to fight so soon. Dr. Prince's voice rings in my head as if he were here.

"You will never be able to move forward until you deal with your past. Don't let your past set the tone for your future. Sharing genetics doesn't give someone power over you. It doesn't give them the right to harm you—physically, mentally or emotionally. It is one-hundred-percent acceptable to sever ties with relatives so you may live a happy, healthy life."

"You don't have a grandchild," I say with more strength than I feel. But I refuse to back down. I refuse to give in. I refuse to let her hurt me or Shelly or our daughter. Not now. Not any day moving forward.

She rears back as if I slapped her. Disdain oozing from her every pore as she stares me in the eye. With a shift of her weight, her head tilts the opposite direction.

"What was that? I swear I misheard you."

"You didn't mishear a word." I harden my gaze. Inhale deeply and dig for the courage and strength Shelly has given me over time. Straighten my spine and square my shoulders as I speak with a firmer voice. "*You* are not a grandparent. My child is not some trophy you can parade around to get attention." I crack my neck left then right and roll my shoulders. "And I am not your son. Not anymore. You lost that privilege."

Loud laughter rips from her lips as she tips her head back. The sound and her action remind me of every on-screen villain. Heartless and maniacal. It sends a shiver down my spine and makes me nauseous. But I refuse to give in to her. Refuse to back down. Refuse to let this vicious woman squash me with her thumb. Never again.

"You can't just get *rid* of your parents, Devlyn. It doesn't work that way."

I smirk. "Parent," I correct. "Just you."

Her lip curls as her eyes narrow. "This is your father. Feeding you bullshit stories and pegging you against me."

"No," I shout. Her eyes widen, but I don't care. I am sick and tired of this woman trying to use and abuse me for her own benefit. Sick. And. Tired. "You need to leave. Now." She opens her mouth to speak, but I cut her off. "Do not return. Ever. Stay away from me and Shelly and our family. Do not look for or follow us. No calls or texts or letters. Nothing. Not one single thing." I take a breath. "I will not be your punching bag. I will not be your scapegoat." I point a finger toward her. "And if I ever see you again or if you do anything to bother us, I will file a restraining order. I will take legal action." Taking a step toward her, I extend my finger farther. "Now get the hell off my property before I call the police."

Anger flames her cheeks and burns hot in her eyes. But I don't give a damn. I am done. More than done. And I will not subject my daughter to this woman. Not for a single second.

She storms down the walkway and gets in her car. A minute later, she drives away and I breathe deeply for the first time in minutes.

Please let this be the end of her. Please.

I walk inside and see Shelly lingering at the edge of the hallway. No doubt she heard everything. Which is good because I don't really want to repeat any of it.

In three strides, she closes the space between us, wraps me in her arms and hugs me with her fierce love.

It is in this moment that I feel a shift. Like the closing of a long and horrible chapter. Like the start of a new chapter—perhaps a new story.

The story of Shelly and Devlyn. The story of our life. The story where we both learned how to love.

Life has been peaceful. More peaceful than I imagined it could be.

Baby Desirée has been sleeping through the night more often than not. According to Mom, this is a miracle at ten weeks. Unsure if she was pulling my leg, I thumbed through several of the baby books and scoured the web. In black and white, each source verified her truth. Supposedly, most babies don't sleep through the night for several months.

Devlyn also appears to be sleeping better. Since the blowup with his mother, a new version of calm has washed over him. An incomparable tranquility he has needed for years. Before the verbal altercation with his mother, Devlyn had been pretty chill. Mostly. I'd only seen him upset or angry a few times—two of those three occasions involved his mother.

Now, Devlyn is the ultimate definition of relaxed. Zen master extraordinaire.

"Who's my little princess?" Devlyn says sweetly to Desirée as she drinks from the bottle in his hand. Swaddled in the crook of his arm, he rocks her side to side. His eyes on hers as she stares up at him and curls her little fingers in his shirt.

Each time he speaks to her, a small smile tips up the corners of her mouth and she makes a bubbly sound around the nipple. Ovary. Explosion.

When she finishes the last of the bottle, Devlyn sets it on the table before lifting her to his shoulder and gently patting her back. It isn't long before a ferocious belch echoes through the living room.

"Good push, princess." Devlyn sets Desirée in her bassinet before twisting to face me. "Want to finish shopping today?"

Last year, Christmas was a bust. Leading up to the holiday, things had been weird between me and Devlyn after our first kiss at the end of November. And until things started to mend, my mood had been sour. Christmas didn't feel merry or bright.

But this year… bring on all the holiday cheer.

For the first time in my adult life, I get to *really* decorate. Not just a measly little tree in the house with a few candles and decorative pieces. I get to pull out all the stops and decorate without limits. And Devlyn gets his first dose of Festive Shelly.

I close my eyes and picture all the merriment.

Outside lights strung along the roofline, around the windows, and on the trees. A blow-up tree for the front yard and an artificial tree for the back patio. Reindeer figurines for the lawn. I wanted the animated deer, but Devlyn mentioned the likelihood of them breaking easier. So I found a beautiful set of lifelike deer figures.

Today, since Devlyn offered, I'd like to get more holiday items for inside the house. Last time we browsed Target, I spied a whole section of holiday decor that called my name. Soft colors with a vintage feel. Classic.

"Are you trying to butter me up, Mr. Templar?" I tease.

His lips tip up on one side. "Maybe."

I'd meant it as a joke, but now I'm curious. What is up Devlyn's sleeve?

I narrow my eyes at him. "What're you up to?"

Leaning in, he presses his lips to mine and kisses me breathless. All too soon, he breaks the kiss. He rises from the couch, swipes the empty bottle from the table and takes a step away. Peering over his shoulder, he taps his temple then leaves the room.

I love this side of him. Happy and optimistic and flirty. Much as I want to pry the plans from his lips, I won't ask what he has in store. Something about the surprise has me jittery, in all the right ways.

∿

While I lock Desirée's carrier in the car seat cradle, Devlyn loads our purchases in the back of the car. Warm air floats from the vents and replaces the cooler December air. Jolly holiday music echoes from the speakers at a low volume. The sky a little more gray than blue as the sun hides behind puffy clouds.

Once he has everything stowed, Devlyn hops in the driver's seat and holds his hands in front of the vents.

A minute passes. Then another. Devlyn has yet to put a hand on the steering wheel or gear shifter. *Is he really that cold?* I note the outside temperature on the dash display. Fifty-seven. Chilly, but not cold.

"Everything okay?" I ask as he rubs his hands together.

Green eyes flick in my direction. I study the lines of his face that are a hint deeper. The corners of his lips and eyes turned up a touch. And I swear I see his eyes twinkle a second before he blinks.

"Fine. Just trying to feel my hands again." He makes a fist with each hand, then flattens them out again.

"It's not *that* cold," I tease as I reach for his hands and sandwich them between my own. Immediately, I note how warm his hands feel. Not warm. Hot. I loosen my grip on him.

A soft chuckle spills from his lips. "They *were* cold. Now I'm just trying to feel them again." He jerks his chin toward the back of the car. "My fingers went numb after store number two."

Heat crawls up my neck and floods my cheeks. While I pushed the stroller through the mall and ogled all the festive decorations, Devlyn walked beside me and carried all the bags from our purchases. We visited ten stores over the last two hours, easily. Which means Devlyn grinned and trudged through the numbing pain for more than half that.

"Why didn't you say something?"

He waves a hand. "It's no big shake."

"I could've put bags in the stroller basket or carried one."

"Shelly…" He cups my cheeks, leans in and kisses me softly. "I didn't mind." His words are calm and barely above a whisper. "I'll carry twice that to see your smile again."

My eyes dart between his and look for things left unsaid. As he stares back, all I see is his truth, out in the open.

"Okay." I press my lips to his. "Now take me home," I demand, sitting back in my seat and buckling my seat belt. "Time to decorate."

He blinds me with a bright smile before he buckles up and drives us home.

I'm going to be sick.

The blinker ticks at a deafening volume as I wait to turn into the neighborhood. *Ticktock. Ticktock.* I blink a few times in an attempt to clear the fog coming in from all sides. Swallow past the building lump in my throat. Breathe slow and steady as I tell myself everything will be okay.

It will be, won't it?

With a break in the traffic, I steer the car into the neighborhood. If I drive slow enough, I can stretch the minute and a half to two minutes without Shelly asking questions.

Everything will go according to plan.

Shelly sings to the Christmas song on the radio, a slight bop in her shoulders on every other line. I mentally soak up her joy. This time last year, we were finding our way back to each other after my freak-out. The weeks leading up to Christmas were a little less cheery as we tiptoed around our relationship.

But everything worked out. Slowly, steadily, we fell in love.

Now, I am about to stir things up.

"Eeee!" Shelly squeals as I park in the driveway.

Twisting to face her, I can't help but match the bright smile on her lips. Her happiness is my happiness. Period.

"Will we see you at all today?" I tease. "Or should I take little miss up to the studio while you decorate?"

Shelly play slaps my arm. "It won't be that bad." Her eyes veer up then left and right as her lips shift side to side. "Maybe a little. But only because I've never had so much space to decorate. Plus, I get to decorate, *really decorate*, outside for the first time."

I lean across the console and press my lips to her cheek. "Decorate whatever you want." And I mean it.

When we exit the car, she retrieves Desirée's carrier from the back seat while I fetch all the goodies from the back. With each step closer to the front door, my stomach twists in a new knot. I stay a pace or two behind Shelly so she doesn't notice the shift in my expression.

It. Will. Be. Fine.

Inside the house, Shelly goes about unbuckling Desirée and getting her a bottle. I take all the bags to the reading nook near the sliding glass doors. It's the most centralized room in the house and should make it easier for Shelly to go room to room and add splashes of holiday cheer.

I stop at the entrance of the living room and watch my girls for a beat. Desirée stares up at Shelly as she drinks her bottle. One of her little hands grips Shelly's finger while the other hand plays with the ends of her hair. I snap a mental picture of the sight and make note to bring the image to life with pencil on stock paper.

"Be right back," I say just above a whisper. Shelly tilts her head enough to flash me a soft smile.

Taking the steps two at a time, I dart up the stairs to my studio. My eyes roam the room from the landing. Nothing is out of place, not that I expected otherwise. Shelly only comes up here when we are together or I am working in the studio.

In three long strides, I reach the entrance to the closet. Tucked away behind new tubes of paint is one of the biggest gifts I will ever give Shelly. Well, besides our sweet baby girl. I pick up the smallest, heaviest gift on the planet and stow it in my pocket.

I park on the stool at the drafting table and zone out. Minutes tick by as I breathe deeply and mentally work to unravel the knots beneath my diaphragm. Calm as I can be, I rise from the stool and make my way back downstairs.

Now. Do it now.

At the base of the stairs, I peer into the living room. No sign of Shelly or Desirée. The house is quiet as I pad past the kitchen, sitting room and down the hallway toward the bedrooms. Just outside the nursery, I hear Shelly whisper to Desirée.

"Nap time, little angel. When you wake up, the house will sparkle. Lights and snow people and a beautiful tree. Blue and silver and white. It'll be the best first Christmas ever."

The door slowly opens and Shelly startles and slaps a hand to her chest when she spots me just past the frame.

"Sorry. Didn't want to disturb while you got her settled."

She drops her hand. "It's okay. Just didn't expect you there."

Without a word, I take her hand in mine and walk us down the hallway. She doesn't ask where we are going as I guide her through the house. She doesn't ask what I am doing when I park us on the couch in the living room. I wrap an arm around her shoulders and tuck her into my side. Just like every other time, she melts into my side. Becomes an extension of me, of us.

"Love you," I whisper against her hair.

"Love you too."

I kiss her crown and give her shoulder a squeeze before straightening in my seat. She tips her head back enough to peek up. To steal my every breath with her shimmering twilight eyes.

The weight in my pocket digs at my thigh.

Everything will be fine. Do it. Now.

"Shell, I…"

She sits up straighter. Her hands come to my cheeks as her eyes scan every inch of my expression. "What is it?" A crease forms between her brows as horizontal lines mar her forehead.

My eyes drift shut for one deep breath. When they open and all I see is my Andromeda, every nerve in my body calms. Every doubt in my mind gets washed away.

This is Shelly. My Shelly. My Andromeda. Goddess and ruler of my heart.

Leaning into her, I press my lips to hers. Let her warmth blanket me. Let her vibrance and zeal soothe every ounce of skepticism. Let her love consume every molecule in my body.

Reluctantly, I break the kiss. Brush the hair from her cheek and tuck it behind her ear. Hold her blues with my greens. Then, I lay my heart in her hands.

"Shelly, will you marry me?"

I'm sorry, what?

Every muscle in my body, head to toe, locks up. I stare back at Devlyn, unable to breathe or think or form words. I blink to moisten my dry eyes. Then do it more.

Marriage is not something I am opposed to, but it isn't something I foresaw in the near future. I love Devlyn, but this seems… sudden. Unlike him. Questionable. Our relationship time line has flown by, one momentous occasion after another.

Is this because of Desirée?

I don't want Devlyn to feel obligated to marry me because we have a child. That shouldn't be why he proposes. God, please don't let it be the reason he is proposing.

I love this man more than imaginable. His heart is limitless. He gives without second thought. And in the past fourteen months, I've felt and experienced so much with him. A love to rival all others. A love I never thought I'd have in my life. He has gifted me so much.

That said, I pray the reason for his proposal is love and not obligation.

"Uh…" I tap my toes on the floor. Pin my lips between my teeth as I study the seriousness in his gaze. Tightness forms between my brows as my eyes narrow.

Why does this feel so weird? Me wanting to ask him the reason why he asked me to marry him. Prepregnancy Shelly wouldn't think such preposterous things. Prepregnancy Shelly would have been in his lap already, hands on his cheeks as she kisses him senseless.

So why isn't that me now? Why am I sitting here like he asked me to solve a quantum physics equation?

With each passing second, I watch the shimmer in his green irises fade. I witness the upward turn of his lips fall into a frown of despair.

Shit.

His eyes drop at the same time as his hands. Then his head begins to shake slowly. "I shouldn't have…" He scoots an inch away. "What was I thinking?" he mutters, moving back farther. "Idiot," he whispers.

Before he retreats farther, I wrap my fingers around his wrist and stop him. "No." His eyes shoot to mine, glassy. Agony pours off him in waves. I shake my head. "Not no to the question. No, as in don't pull away."

Tears brim his eyes that have reddened in less than a minute. "It's too soon." He shakes his head. "Me asking you was impulsive. Sorry for putting you on the spot. I just thought—"

"Devlyn, stop." I inch closer to him and press my lips to his. "It's not that I don't want to marry you. And proposals always put someone on the spot," I say on a laugh. "But we've never discussed marriage and I…" I pause as I try to gather the right words.

"You can be honest with me, Shell. Always."

I lift a hand to his cheek and he leans into my touch. His eyes fall shut as he takes a deep breath. Then another. And it is in this singular moment that I have my answer without even asking the question. Not like I didn't know the answer to begin with.

How could I ever think Devlyn would propose out of obligation? Nothing about us has ever been like that. Hell, he fought our relationship so hard in the beginning. Fought the inevitable with every breath we took.

"What I was going to say was I don't want you to feel obligated to marry me because we have a child together." I half shrug and work my lips between my teeth. "Before the words formed on my tongue, the thought tasted sour. Foolish. And I'm sorry it crossed my mind." I shake my head and laugh. "I swear… little Desirée sucked all my sensibility away while in the womb."

Devlyn takes my hands in his. A glimpse of a smile appears on his lips and disappears just as fast. He stares down at our hands as his fingers caress each of mine before cradling them in his. Left then right, he rocks his head on his shoulders as he sorts through what to say next.

"Desirée is not the reason I asked," he says as his head lifts. His greens lock onto my blues and all I see is vulnerability and love and hope. "Honestly, I didn't know if I'd have the courage to ask." My brows pinch together as I wait for him to elaborate. "After the way my parents' marriage played out, I didn't want that to happen to us." His eyes widen. "Not that we are anything like them."

I nod and squeeze his hands. "Agreed."

"I've never loved anyone the way I love you, Shelly. It scares me while my heart begs for more. Before you, I avoided things that scared me. With you, though… I'll gladly walk through hell. Because I know you'll be on the other side, waiting with arms wide open."

Tears sting the backs of my eyes. Emotion clogs my throat as I try to swallow the excess saliva flooding my mouth. The urge to wrap Devlyn in my arms and hug the breath from his lungs surges in my veins.

What did I do to deserve this man?

Why did I question his reasons?

Things between us have never been simple. From the start, we toed the line. Devlyn fought the undeniable love he had for me. At that point, it may not have been *love*. Perhaps, extreme like. As for me, I only sheltered my feelings because he was reluctant. Without a doubt, I knew he felt something stronger than friendship between us.

Friends.

God… Devlyn made that word my least favorite. I hated it more than *moist*. Only because I knew, deep in my bones, he wanted more than friendship. His resistance to see us beyond more than friends didn't hurt. He had been broken. Thrown away. Used until no longer necessary. Had that happened to anyone else, their trust and willingness to love would be shattered too. Hence why I didn't blame him.

But all that changed.

The night he gave in to what he felt for me, the night he kissed me, everything changed.

At first, not for the better.

We suffered on our own for several days. And when I finally found a way to breathe again, I opted to let go. To move on. To say goodbye.

That single text led us to where we are today. Lovers. Parents. Connected in a way I never thought possible with another person.

So why did I hesitate? Why did I question the path that led us to this moment?

Devlyn proposed and I doubted his reasons for asking. It was foolish and absurd. I love him, plain and simple. I love Devlyn more than I have loved another person.

"Ask me again," I whisper.

He scoots the table away from the couch, then drops down to one knee. One hand digs in his pocket while the other takes my left hand. Tears burn the backs of my eyes once more. Clasped tightly between Devlyn's thumb and forefinger is a ring with more diamonds than my eyes can count with one glance. At the heart of the ring... an oval-shaped dark-blue stone with the occasional sparkle.

His eyes lock with mine and I stop breathing. His thumb draws small circles over my ring finger as he worries his lips between his teeth.

"Shelly Nicole Reed," he says just above a whisper. "I have loved you longer than I was willing to admit. Maybe from the first moment I saw you more than two years ago." A small smile tips up the corners of his mouth. "But there's no use in denying it another minute. Shelly, you make me whole. Make life worth living. Your light and warmth and kind heart are what I was missing. Your love and passion and gaiety. *You.*" He takes a deep breath and swallows. "Before you, I merely existed. With you, I see every color. Every facet. Every angle. Light and beauty and brilliance. With you, because of you, I know love. Real love. True love." His thumb trails my ring finger from knuckle to tip. "Will you marry me, Shelly?"

Tears spill down my cheeks in parallel lines. Though Devlyn is a blur, I refuse to wipe the tears away. I swallow past the thick ball of emotion in my throat and slowly nod.

"Yes," I croak out. Swallowing again, I repeat myself with more gusto. "Yes, Devlyn." My lips roll between my teeth. "I will marry you."

The biggest smile brightens his face. I get lost in the sight as he slides the ring into place on my finger. As he lifts my hand to his lips and kisses my ring finger. As he wiggles his way between my legs on both knees, frames my face in his hands, and kisses me senseless.

In a matter of seconds, our clothes are peeled away and we are connected in every way possible. Mentally, emotionally and physically. We make love on the couch, in the middle of the day, without a worry in the world.

It is simply him and me and a love to rival all others.

epilogue
DEVLYN

June 30th — the following year

If someone told me two years ago I would fall in love, welcome the most precious little girl into the world, and marry my best friend, I'd have laughed in their face. Because two years ago, love felt like an impossibility.

Until Shelly.

The love of my life. My fiancée. The woman who I get to call wife in… I look down at my watch. In thirteen minutes, Shelly will be my wife.

God, just thinking the word seems surreal.

Wife. Shelly will be my wife. Mine. Forever.

A knock sounds at the door. "It's Micah."

Not seeing my bride since yesterday afternoon is the only "tradition" Shelly enacted today. Last night, she stayed with Cora, Autumn, Penny and Erin at Cora and Gavin's house. All the guys crashed with me at my house. And all us parents got a night free of children, courtesy of our parents.

To say it has been odd to not have my girls close by for the past twenty-four hours would be an understatement. Though it was nice to get a night off from dad duties, sleep evaded me for hours. Wouldn't put it past one of the ladies to offer to hide the dark circles I noticed in the mirror as I buttoned my dress shirt.

I'd let them put makeup on my face or style my hair, so long as Shelly and I exchange vows this evening.

"Come in."

The door swings open and in steps my brother, Micah. It's an odd feeling to have a sibling after being alone the past twenty-four years. Odd in all the right ways.

The Saturday after I proposed, we invited her family and Dad to the house for dinner. Considering we were weeks from Christmas, they assumed it was us wanting a small gathering before the main event. They weren't wrong, but they didn't know the extent.

That night felt weeks long. My knee had never bounced so much beneath the dinner table. I'd scooted food around my plate more than a child avoiding Brussel sprouts on his plate. And when Shelly finally flashed her ring to the group and announced our engagement, I'd never sweated so profusely in my life.

Thank god for dark-colored shirts.

Nervous as I was, each member of the Reed family welcomed me with open arms. Micah pulled me in for an unexpected warm hug. Not the *slap-a-shoulder, one-armed* kind. A true, genuine, constricting hug.

"Congratulations," he'd said. *"My sister is lucky to have such a wonderful man love her. Welcome to the family."*

Not only does Shelly make me whole with her love, but so does her family. *My family.* A family I never saw coming and will never take for granted. These people—Nicole and George, Micah and Peyton—fill in all the gaps and holes my mother created years ago. These people make me feel like I belong. They give me purpose and strength.

Loving Shelly had been but the beginning. Receiving more love than I knew possible in return has been the greatest gift.

"You ready?" Micah shuts the door behind him. "Only a few minutes until showtime."

I have never been more ready for anything. "Was ready the second she said yes."

A brilliant smile lights Micah's face. His eyes shimmering with excitement.

Though Micah and Shelly shared the same eyes as their mother, the three sets sparkled in a different way. At first, seeing the three of them together was strange. I'd never seen such unique irises. But with each visit together, I began to notice the differences.

Nicole's blues were a hint lighter than her children's. The luster more noticeable when she was happy or excited.

Micah's irises were the darkest. Borderline black. And the first time I heard his wife, Peyton, call him starlight, I knew the reason why. The sparkle in his dark irises was visible, but faint in comparison to Shelly's.

I may be biased, but it is my opinion that Shelly got the prettiest version of their constellation eyes. *My Andromeda.* The blue of her irises is darker than her mother's, but lighter than her brother's eyes. A rich blue. Like royalty. A queen. A goddess. My goddess. And the golden flecks that formed my favorite constellation, I knew all the ways to make them glow. With my hands and lips and words.

It took a while to see the difference between the three sets of matching eyes, but Shelly's sparkling blues are the ones that hold my heart captive and steal my breath.

And then there is my sweet little Desirée. Eyes as ravishing as her mother's, but with a thin ring of tea green around her pupil. The addition of my eye color gives hers an almost ethereal look.

"Whenever you're ready, let's get in position," he states, coming in for a hug. "Not every day my baby sister gets married and I get a kick-ass brother." He releases me from his grip. In two lengthy strides, he reaches the door and twists the knob.

Inhaling deeply, I take one last look in the full-length mirror and exit the dressing room. My fingers brush over large leaves and grassy bushes as Micah leads us through the gardens to the north lawn. White chairs sit in lush green grass on either side of a brick aisle. Thousands of red, pink and white rose petals line either side of the aisle and add a pop of color. A color that will always be my Shelly.

Pink.

At the end of the aisle, the bricks extend left and right to accommodate the wedding party. An arch of greenery and flowers and brilliant colors showcase where the ordained minister will perform the ceremony.

Micah leads me down the brick aisle. The rows of white chairs filled with family and friends. As I pass each, I hear words of congratulations, but don't stop to chat. Because any minute, music will float through the air. Bridesmaids will walk the aisle in soft-pink dresses. And behind them, my bride will make her way toward me.

When I reach the front, I give each of the guys a hug. Dressed in sharp gray suits to match my own is Micah, Jonas, Gavin and Chet. White button-downs beneath suit jackets, accented with a black-gray-and-pink bow tie. Each congratulates me on the big day.

I open my mouth to thank them, but get cut off by the change in music.

We shuffle into position and my eyes lock on the start of the brick path where Shelly will enter. To my left, Gavin mutters, "No better feeling than watching the woman you love walk to you in a breathtaking dress." I simply nod, not daring to look away from the entrance.

In a pale-pink dress that brushes the brick as she moves, Clementine steps out from the lush gardens and into the north lawn first. In one hand, she carries a small wooden pail adorned with white and blush roses, moss, and vines that trail up the handle on either side. On the front of the pail is a white heart that reads *Here comes the bride.*

With each step she takes toward us, she reaches into the pail, grabs a fistful of blush rose petals, and tosses them along the brick path.

This is happening. Shelly and I are getting married.

When Clementine reaches the back row of chairs, the first bridesmaid comes into view. Erin. Her blush dress sweeps the ground with each step. Her hair in some fancy loose braid and secured at the nape of her neck. A small bouquet of pink and white calla lilies and roses gripped in her hands.

Three breaths pass before the next bridesmaid appears. Autumn. Her appearance the same as Erin before her, with an additional splash of color from her tattoos.

Jonas sucks in a sharp breath. "Gorgeous," he whispers. "Absolutely gorgeous."

Today is my and Shelly's day, but hearing these men, my brothers, revel over their wives... it makes my heart hammer harder beneath my rib cage. Makes my breath come in short bursts. Because in less than a minute, it will be my turn. My only prayer is that my knees don't buckle.

Seconds later, Peyton comes into view. Her eyes flit to Micah as a glowing smile lights her expression before she winks at her husband.

"Goddamn, I am a lucky man," Micah says loud enough to garner a few laughs from the crowd.

Only one more bridesmaid left. The maid of honor. Cora. The second she steps into view, Gavin leans toward her without taking a step. He doesn't say a word, but I *feel* the love radiating off him as he watches his wife. Feel the connection they share. A connection that rivals what I share with Shelly.

When all the ladies are lined up on the opposite side, the music in the garden shifts.

Without warning, my palms sweat. An electric vibration hums through my veins. I lean to the right and try to peek through the thicket of greenery blocking Shelly from view, but it is no use.

My eyes laser-focused, I catch movement through the thinnest part of the plants. An hour-long second passes as I hold my breath and wait.

Then, she steps into view. Everyone rises from their seats, but I still see her. The queen of my heart. Goddess of my soul. *My Andromeda.*

My eyes trail down the length of her body as I memorize her in this moment. Breathtaking in desert-pink tulle. Wide straps across her shoulders that come to a point at the base of her sternum. A thin band of satin around her middle. The skirt layered and in waves. Small white flowers and pearls decorate the bust and trail down half the skirt. A lush bouquet of white, blush, and dark-pink roses, pink calla lilies, baby's breath and greenery clutched tightly in her hands.

Speechless, I remind myself to breathe. My vision blurs and I blink a few times, not wanting to miss a second of this moment. George rubs a hand over her forearm as they step closer, but I don't dare shift my gaze from Shelly.

Although we have forever, no day will replace this one. The day Shelly says she will be mine in every way. Always.

~

SHELLY

My pace slows as I catch sight of Devlyn.

Damn, he's handsome.

I grip Dad's arm tighter with my bent elbow. He brushes his hand over my forearm ever so gently in silent reassurance.

"Got you, Shelly Bear." His hold on me tightens. "Promise."

The backs of my eyes sting. A thick ball of emotion rests dead center in my throat. Every nerve in my body comes alive with excitement, becomes overwhelmed with joy. I blink a few times. Tip my head back slightly. Tell the tears rimming my eyes they need to wait a little longer. I swallow. Then swallow again.

"Thanks, Daddy," I whisper.

The aisle straightens as we reach the back row of chairs and I pause for a beat. Rake my eyes over Devlyn in a smart gray suit, white dress shirt, and charcoal-and-pink bow tie. On the breast of his jacket, a dark-pink calla lily and blush rose makes up his boutonniere. His floppy brown locks, a little lighter from time in the sun, parted off-center and styled to look messy on purpose. Hands clasped at his waist, I take in the slight bounce in his stance. As if he can't contain the energy flowing through him.

Faster than imaginable, we reach Devlyn and the minister. Dad kisses my cheek and I close my eyes for one rapid heartbeat. Then he places my hand in Devlyn's and takes a seat in the front row.

"You're stunning," Devlyn whispers, his hand squeezing mine.

"Pretty handsome yourself."

I pass my bouquet to Cora, then Devlyn and I turn slightly toward the minister. The next few minutes pass by in a haze of watery eyes and white noise. The minister reads the wedding script he has undoubtedly read hundreds of times prior. Every now and again, I catch a word or two, but otherwise drown out his voice.

Instead, I focus on Devlyn.

My husband.

Technically, we are already married. Hours ago, the minister went to each of our dressing rooms and had us sign the marriage license. During and after the ceremony, many things get lost in translation or forgotten. When we hired him, he told us of the few times couples forgot to sign, too swept up in the moment.

Devlyn's fingers weave and stroke and warm my own as he holds my gaze. His green irises bright and glassy under the setting sun. A burnt-orange glow highlighting his skin.

The minister quiets. Devlyn releases one of my hands, digs in the inside breast pocket of his jacket, and retrieves a slip of paper.

His vows.

He breathes deeply and swallows before my favorite smile dons his lips. And as his lips part to speak, I block out everyone but him.

"Shelly... my Andromeda." His smile brightens infinitesimally. "A warm October day, more than two years ago, was the first time I saw you. The dazzling blonde who peeked through the windows of a flower shop. For days, I denied myself the sight of you. But it wasn't long before I caved. You'd seen me and I you, but we'd never spoken a word." He takes another breath and licks his lips. "And then I saw you again. In a bar, yelling your love for Karaoke Grandpa."

At this, the majority of the wedding party, including myself, bursts out in laughter. Several seated guests appear bewildered, but most smile or shake their head.

"Bars have never been my scene, but a friend was in town and we went out to catch up." Devlyn briefly glances over his shoulder to Chet. "Had I not seen you that night, I may not have had the urge to call Elizabeth. To insist on touching up the mural I'd painted the previous year." Devlyn looks up from his paper, a small half smile softening his expression. "You see, you'd already been my muse. The woman in the window." Subtly, he shakes his head. "I didn't know your name, but I knew *you*." He presses the heel of his palm to the center of his chest. "Here. And as much as I tried to fight it, I needed to know you more. Even if I was just a friend."

I roll my eyes and Devlyn laughs.

"Shelly, you were never just a friend. Not one second. From the very start, you've always been more. It was me who needed time to learn this." Paper still in his hand, Devlyn takes hold of my free hand once more. "Thank you for loving me. Thank you for putting up with my stubbornness early on. For giving me another chance." His eyes dart to my parents and his dad in the front row, Desirée drooling in Mom's lap. "And thank you for giving me something I never thought I'd have... a family. I love you, Shelly Nicole Reed. And I will love you every day of forever."

Over my shoulder, Cora hands me a tissue. I tip my head back and blot my eyes.

Cora and Autumn warned me about this moment. Listening to the person you love as they confess the biggest reasons for loving you. Sounds simple when said aloud, but hearing it while loved ones watch and listen... cue the messy, happy tears.

Once my tears seem to be under control, I stow the tissue in my dress and retrieve my own piece of paper. I stare down at the scribbled words and question the vows I'd written days ago. Compared to Devlyn's confession, my vows seem small.

I close my eyes and fill my lungs fully, opening my eyes on the exhale. Devlyn's thumb paints small circles on my hand. His eyes locked with my own. It is him and me and no one else in this moment.

"Devlyn... the *artist*." Behind me, Cora snorts. "If you asked my closest friend, she'd tell you, without hesitation, how I rambled on about *the artist* after you painted the first mural. She'd tell you how I talked about you for weeks. The guy I couldn't stop sneaking a peek at. God, the front of the shop had never been so pristine." At this, Elizabeth chuckles in the crowd. "That display window got so much love that week." I pause and hold his green irises for three quiet breaths. "Because I just knew… I didn't know who you were, didn't ask for your name, didn't say one word to you, but I knew."

Plucking the tissue from my dress, I blot my eyes again.

"And then you reappeared a year later. Your warm smile and addictive eyes. The way you looked at me… I couldn't breathe. Couldn't form intelligible speech, which is miraculous for anyone who knows me well." Chuckles float around us. "But more than anything, I couldn't stay away."

At this, Devlyn squeezes my hand. His silent way of reciprocating the feeling.

"Devlyn, my life was monotonous before you. I had love, but nothing compared to the love you give. I had family, but not like the family we created together." I inch closer to him and tighten my hold on his hand. "Loving you is effortless. The most natural thing I have ever done. Life and love didn't make sense before you. I'd read about love, the type that steals every thought and breath and moment, but I'd never felt it firsthand. And I wholeheartedly believe it was because I'd been waiting for you." The backs of my eyes sting as my vision blurs. "I love you, Devlyn James Templar, more than I have loved anyone. And as long as there is air in my lungs and a heartbeat in my chest, I will love you. Always."

The paper in my hand falls to the ground as I step forward, ritual be damned, and press my lips to his. Devlyn frames my face with his hands and kisses me back with equal fervor. The minister says something and cheers erupt around us. But neither of us moves to break the kiss. Lost in each other, we kiss until we are breathless.

And when we break apart, the world finally levels out. Colors are brighter, bolder, more vibrant. Life is warmer, fuller, more passionate. And love… it isn't just something I read about anymore. Love is this living, breathing force. Powerful and daring. Strong and profound. Abstract and impassioned.

Mom walks to us and hands over a wiggly Desirée. She kisses my cheek and congratulates us.

And there, in front of the most important people in my life, I feel whole. Fortunate. Loved.

bonus content

one

DEVLYN

June—Three years later

This is my life. Love and laughter and joy.

I never imagined myself in this position. With so many wonderful people in my circle. Family and friends I can't picture a day without. Nor would I want to.

Our Sunday get-togethers still happen every week. Since the first I attended with Shelly, they have become much grander. Not the party, per se, but the number of guests in attendance. When Penny's husband, Jameson, bought the tattoo shop a month after Shelly and I married, he hired more staff—artists, piercers, and front desk personnel. It was an adjustment to welcome in the new faces, but it wasn't long before they were just as much family as the rest.

Today, everyone will be here. To enjoy our regular Sunday gathering, but also to celebrate Shelly and my third wedding anniversary, Independence Day, and baby Garrett's first birthday.

I peer out the kitchen window facing the backyard. Watch Shelly and Desirée as they decorate tables with small vases full of colorful flowers. Place wicker mats at each place setting and add a plate and utensils. Add candles and poppers to the center. String holiday lights around the pillars of the pergola and check the tiki torches for fuel.

Desirée skips over to Shelly and says something. Shelly surveys the tables where she had Desirée add forks and spoons to the place settings. After a kiss to our daughter's forehead, Shelly says something else and Desirée skips off to her outdoor playset-slash-mansion.

Best. Investment. Ever.

Shelly strolls inside and sidles up to me in the kitchen. "Need help with anything?"

I twist and press my lips to hers. "No. Just cleaning up and waiting for everyone to show." Glancing back at Desirée, I watch as she climbs up the ladder, runs through the wooden fort and slides down the green slide. "Can't believe she'll be four in a few months."

Shelly rests her head on my shoulder and stares at our daughter. "Me, either." A heavy sigh leaves her lips. "Think she'll be excited?"

Today is a big day. Three celebrations everyone knows about… and one they don't, but will before long.

My head tips to the side and rests on Shelly's. "Yeah, she'll be the most excited." I lift my head and kiss Shelly's crown. "Go out back and relax for a bit. I got the rest of the cleanup."

"You sure?"

Another kiss to her head. "I'm sure."

I finish cleanup in the house while Shelly sits on a lounger out back and watches Desirée play. Just as I start the dishwasher, the doorbell rings. One by one, our friends and family arrive. Additional food items are deposited on the kitchen counters. Jonas holds up a cooler and tells us if anyone needs him, he will be at the grill.

In no time, our house booms with music, conversation and laughter.

Clementine, Clara and Ryker join Desirée in the play fortress. Soon followed by Ashton, Avery and Lex when they arrive.

Again… best investment ever.

It isn't long before Jonas removes cooked burgers, brats and chicken from the grill, putting the meatless options on a separate dish. The parents plate up food for the kids first then sit them at the kiddy tables. Clementine is the oldest of the kids, and Jonas and Autumn have offered her a spot at the grown-up table several times. She declines each time and tells them she loves sitting with her brother and cousins.

Over dinner, we regale the past week's events. School and work and all the projects in between. And when the table quiets, Shelly looks to me and nods.

It's time is what that single nod says.

Pushing my chair back, I rise and look around the table. Without a word, all conversation ceases and all eyes swing in my direction.

"Shelly and I have news." All forks hit the table. All chewing stops. And suddenly, I am more nervous than excited to share.

Sensing the shift, Shelly rises and hooks her arm in mine. "We're pregnant."

For a beat, white noise fills my ears. Then it vanishes, replaced with louder-than-life roars and hoots and hollers. Behind us, I hear Clementine say to Desirée, "You're going to be a big sister." Then she gives her a high five.

And it is moments like this that overwhelm me with gratitude.

Had I not found this incredible woman, who refused to give up on me, even with my fiercest resistance, I would not have this moment today. Surrounded by dozens of people that love me for me. That treat me as one of their own. That embraced me from the moment I stepped into their circle.

This. This is family. What it should be. People that love you regardless of what you give them in return. People that love you for what you bring into their lives without expectation. People willing to embrace you during the hard times and rejoice in the best times.

These people are family.

Food forgotten, everyone rises from their seats and takes turns hugging and congratulating us. Each embrace feels more loving than the previous. Each senti-ment more heart filled. But it isn't until Cora wraps me in her arms and whispers only loud enough for me to hear that tears sting my eyes.

"Thank you, Devlyn. For loving Shelly and coming into our lives." She tightens her hold, then releases to hold me at arm's length. "This family wouldn't be right without you."

Gavin hooks an arm around her shoulders and meets my gaze. "Damn straight."

I scan the group of smiling faces. Cora and Gavin. Jonas and Autumn. Micah and Peyton. Erin. Trevor and Jasmine. Penny and Jameson. Reznor and Tatyana. Rex and Giana. Iliana and Sage. Jasmine and Anton. Chet. Reese and Trent. Parents and kids. Others from the tattoo family. *My family.*

Shelly sidles up to me and snakes an arm around my waist. I glance down into her eyes and smile as her free hand goes to her belly.

"Love you, Mrs. Reed."

The corner of her mouth kicks up into a soft half smile. "Love you too, Mr. Reed."

Two

SHELLY

December 25th — Six months later

My grip on the kitchen counter tightens as I suck in a sharp breath.

Aside from the water bubbling in the teakettle, the house is quiet. Still dark, with the exception of the glowing Christmas tree I plugged in minutes ago in the sitting room. Another two hours will pass before the sun peeks through the windows and brightens the house. And much less will pass before Desirée wakes everyone to see what Santa left under the tree.

I flip the switch on the kettle and add hot water to the awaiting tea bag in my mug. Up and down, up and down, I yank on the bag string and watch the tea bag bob as it steeps in the water. When the liquid is a rich brown, I pluck the bag out and toss it in the garbage.

Two steps toward the fridge for the oat milk and I come to a halt. The muscles and skin around my round belly constrict. One hand goes to my belly while the other reaches for the closest stable surface. I inhale deeply once, twice, then a third time before the sensation fades.

"Is this your way of telling Mommy you want to be the best Christmas present?" I whisper-ask into the dimly lit room. I rub my rotund belly. "Let us get through presents first. That's all I ask."

After I add milk to my tea, I waddle to the small sofa in the sitting room near the tree. Wrapping myself with the throw blanket, I sip my tea and zone out as I stare at the white lights on the tree. And for a little longer, I enjoy the peace of waking early and sitting by myself in silence. Enjoy the simplicity of life in this very moment, because after today, it will be busy once more. But busy in the best way.

My hand traces a continuous loop over my belly as my eyes follow the movement. A small smile on my face. A sense of wholeness filling every part of my life.

"How long have you been up?"

I startle at Mom's hushed tone as she pads into the room from the hallway. "Not long."

"Everything okay?" She tips her head to where I rub my belly.

With a nod, I smile. "Yeah, but today might be a bigger celebration than we prepared for."

Like their big sister, baby two wants to come a little earlier than projected. Not that I mind. I'd rather have a Christmas baby than a New Year's baby. Maybe they heard all the Hallmark Christmas movies I've been watching. Maybe they heard all the fun music and their big sister singing. Or maybe, they just know Christmas is my favorite holiday.

"I'll get started on breakfast. If everyone else isn't up soon, I'll wake them."

"Thanks, Mom."

Mom shuffles off to the kitchen and flips on the soft lights lining the underside of the top cabinets. From my spot on the couch, I follow her with my eyes. She grabs all the ingredients for the breakfast casserole she made every Christmas morning when Micah and I were kids. Potatoes, crumbled maple sausage, cheese, onion, and her special blend of herbs and spices.

On Desirée's second Christmas, Mom insisted on making the casserole every Christmas morning going forward. Usually, we visit Mom and Dad after Desirée has opened all her gifts at home. Casserole had been a brunch meal.

But not this year.

With baby two due any day, Mom suggested she and Dad stay at our house and have Christmas here. Less stress and shuffling all over town. Every aching muscle and tired bone in my body agreed. Although Petal and Vine closed two days ago through New Year's Day, I'd still been working more this pregnancy.

When Elizabeth heard we were pregnant again, she offered to work whenever I needed help. Since her official retirement, one year after Desirée was born, I hired a few part-time employees. With baby two on the way, I'd been gearing them up with what extra tasks they'd take on. Elizabeth said she'd handle most of the financials and paperwork—which has been a major relief.

Maple and herbs float through the air. Mom whips eggs and oat milk in a bowl, then starts layering everything in the casserole dish. As foil crinkles over the edges of the dish, Desirée comes running down the hall with Devlyn on her heels.

Her little legs lock straight, but forward momentum, plus the socks on her feet, keeps her sliding across the wood floor. Once she skids to a stop, her little hands slap over her slack jaw. Eyes wide, she stares at the mountain of gifts under the tree.

"Santa came," she whispers in awe. Before Devlyn or I answer, she dashes to the small plate on the kitchen counter and surveys the cookie crumbs and empty Santa mug. "Mommy, Daddy, Santa ate the cookies I made him. And, and, and he drank the milk."

Devlyn and I stare after our daughter. Each year, her excitement kicks up a notch with the holidays. One day, her love for the holiday season may be stronger than my own. This year, under my and Mom's supervision, she made chocolate chip and sugar cookies. I'd never seen her so careful. Every stir and whisk and measured ingredient had been precise. She refused to mess up Santa's cookies.

"Did he see your letter?" Devlyn asks as he tugs a shirt over his head and ambles toward her.

She nods vigorously. "Oh my gosh! He wrote me back," she squeals.

Devlyn scoops Desirée off her feet and parks her on his hip. Then he picks up the letter and holds it in front of them. "What's it say, little D?" She stares at the paper, her brows pinched at the middle and lips scrunched in concentration. "Sound out the words."

After a few fumbled letters, she reads the words. "Best cookies yet. Merry Christmas, Desirée. Love, Santa."

Wiggling with excitement, Devlyn sets her on her feet. While Desirée flaunts her note from Santa to Mom, Devlyn comes to sit with me on the sofa.

He presses his lips to my forehead, the tip of my nose, then my lips. "Morning." Warmth blankets me as he lays a hand on my belly and kisses me again. "Merry Christmas. You sleep okay?"

I lay my hand over his and tip my head side to side. "Sleep wasn't too bad. But someone woke me early." I glance down at my belly. "We may get another gift today."

Devlyn's eyes go wide. "Do we need to leave?"

I shake my head. "Not yet." A half smile kicks up one corner of my mouth. "I requested they wait until after presents and breakfast," I say on a laugh. "Mom has breakfast in the oven."

"If we need to leave sooner, say the word."

Minutes later, Dad appears and the festivities begin. One by one, Desirée opens her gifts. Devlyn and I are still trying to limit her time on devices and electronics, which becomes more challenging each year, but we managed to find plenty of gifts to spark her creativity without involving electronics. Art supplies, books—coloring and reading—and puzzles. For her big present this year, she got a new bicycle equipped with training wheels. Last night, Devlyn had hidden it in the reading nook near the sliding glass doors. He'd put a note from Santa on it saying it was too big to put under the tree.

The look on Desirée's face as he wheeled it around the corner… priceless.

Halfway through breakfast, the contractions kick into third gear. No matter how much I want to enjoy Christmas morning with our little girl, I can't put off leaving for the hospital any longer. The first contraction had been hours ago. Although they continued during gift unwrapping, I kept my lips sealed and breathed through the pressure.

Now, it is past the point of breathing through it. This baby is coming. Soon.

Mom and Dad help us to the car and promise to keep Desirée occupied until we give the green light for them to come to the hospital.

Buckled up, Devlyn drives us toward the hospital. While he drives, I type out a text in the group chat.

> Merry Christmas all. FYI… I'm in labor and we're headed to the hospital.

As suspected, my phone and Devlyn's pings with message after message.

MICAH

> Merry Christmas, little sis. We'll be there soon.

CORA

> Oh. My. Gawd! A Christmas baby?! Be there ASAP.

JONAS

> Best gift ever! Merry Christmas, Shell!

ERIN

> Keep us updated! Can't wait to meet them!

AUTUMN

> Be there after we drop the kids at Jonas's parents' house.

GAVIN

> This is giving me baby fever!

CORA

> Gavin, no. Not yet. It's too soon.

PEYTON

> Auntie Peyton is ready to spoil and squeeze cheeks.

When I look up, Devlyn is turning onto the street leading to the hospital. Before another contraction flares, he parks the car and dashes to my door. The hospital is quieter than expected as we enter the nonemergency entrance. We check in with reception and are soon on the elevator to labor and delivery.

Unlike last time, we are prepared for every worst-case scenario. Since having a cesarian with Desirée, I'd have another with baby two. The procedure had been scheduled months ago for January second.

Should have known the baby didn't like the date.

Nurses guide us to a room and have us change for the procedure. Also unlike last time, Devlyn won't be whooshed from the room. This time, he gets to be on the same side of the curtain as me, holding my hand and welcoming our child into the world.

Dr. Webster comes in and reviews my vitals before discussing the process again and asking if we have any questions. If either of us had more questions after the countless we asked in her office, it'd be a Christmas miracle.

"I'll give you both a few minutes before we start." The door clicks as she leaves and the room falls silent.

Devlyn wraps my hands in his and kisses my knuckles. "Love you so much, Shell."

"Love you, too."

"Boy or girl?"

Over the last couple of months, we have played this game. Boy or girl? Once again, we didn't want to know the sex of the baby ahead of time. We made lists of names—boys, girls, and gender neutral. Each time we played the game, Devlyn would guess opposite of his previous guess the day before. I guessed girl more often than boy, only because I experienced similar body changes. And if you listen to the old wives' tales about your belly position determining the gender, baby two will be another girl.

We shall see.

The next hour flies by faster than expected. Although I experience no pain with the incision, the pressure change when the baby leaves my womb is something I won't soon forget. With each step, Dr. Webster explains what is happening. The entire process is odd and fascinating and unforgettable.

At 12:25 p.m. on December 25th—couldn't have planned that, even if I wanted to—Devlyn and I welcome our second daughter into the world.

"Violet Lily Reed," Devlyn whispers as he lays her on his chest for the first time. "Daddy and Mommy love you so much, baby girl." Devlyn lifts his glassy eyes to mine. He rests his cheek on our daughter's crown. "Best Christmas gift ever."

three

SHELLY'S & DEVLYN'S LETTERS

August 20th—Desirée's shower

How do you start a letter to your unborn child? The task seems daunting, but here we go.

Today, Mommy and I are having a party for you. All of our friends and family are here with food and presents. Can't wait for you to meet them all, and for them to meet you.

I never thought I'd be a dad, but I promise to be the best one ever.

Love you more than words, little one,
Daddy

My little water aerobics instructor... oh, how I love you. I loved you from the moment I knew you were growing in Mommy's tummy. And although we had some disagreements when it came to cheese, we found our way. I can't wait for your birthday. Can't wait to meet the mini-me that fist-pumps when I eat cheesy eggs, bulgogi and consume anything with chocolate.

I love you so much, forever and ever.

Mommy

four

SHELLY

November — Seven years later

Devlyn parks the car as I spin to face the back seat. "Best behavior, girls," I say to Desirée and Violet.

"Duh, Mom," Desirée says with an eye roll she picked up from her newest friend, Kiki.

Gah! If she's this sassy in her preteens, I'll need countless hours of meditation and yoga, and to maybe take up martial arts classes, to survive.

From her booster seat, Violet smiles big and holds up a hand. "Promise to be the bestest, Mommy." Nothing but sweet innocence in her voice.

"Thank you, girls," Devlyn says. "Now, let's go have fun." This garners another eye roll from Desirée.

Heaven help me, if she keeps this up, I will take every damn electronic away from her unless it is for schoolwork. As if he hears my thoughts, Devlyn reaches across the console and gives my hand a quick squeeze.

We exit the car, me helping Violet out while Devlyn sidles up to Desirée. If anyone can break through Desirée's recent *I know all* attitude, it is Devlyn. She is definitely a daddy's girl. Not that she doesn't love me, they just connect on another level.

Stepping up on the porch, I raise my hand to knock on Jonas and Autumn's front door, but before my knuckles rap the wood, it swings open. Ryker greets us, his dark locks floppy over his right brow as he pushes thick, black-framed glasses up the bridge of his nose.

"Hey, Mr. and Mrs. R." His eyes drift to Desirée, heat pinking his cheeks as he quickly looks away. "Desi." He licks his lips and takes a deep breath before saying, "Miss Violet." Taking a step back, he gestures to the inside of the house. "Come in, please."

We wander toward the kitchen, Violet running ahead of us. "No running inside," I call after her. Devlyn and I set totes on the counter with macaroni salad, baked beans, and homemade rolls while the kids go outside. Soon as they disappear from sight, I take a deep breath and hold it for three long seconds.

Devlyn brushes his knuckles along my jawline. "Everything okay?"

"Yeah." I look toward the back door. "Just wondering how we'll survive Storm Desirée," I say with a hint of humor.

"It's normal for girls her age to be snarky. Promise I'm working on it. But fighting peer pressure is a bitch."

I hold out my pinkie and Devlyn hooks ours together. "Thank you." Stepping into him, I snake my arms around his waist and squeeze. "Let's go join everyone."

Hand in hand, we walk out to the backyard. Halfway through our hellos, a husky with white fur runs up to us. "Siku, heel," Jonas calls in a deep voice. The dog halts in place and looks over its shoulder. Jonas jogs up. "Sit," he commands before looking to us. "Sorry about that. She's still learning."

"Is this the new pup?"

"Yep. This is Siku." Jonas rubs a hand through the dog's coat. "She's well trained, but still a puppy. Can't wait for Clementine to get here."

A few years ago, the summer between Clementine's junior and senior year of high school, Spartan passed. Needless to say, it was a tragic time for all of us, but more so for Clementine. Spartan had been her best friend for ten years. Jonas and Autumn considered getting a new dog the following year, but Clementine was against the idea.

Now that she has had time away at college, has been able to experience life more and emotionally accept what happened, Jonas and Autumn found a new pup to add to the family. Siku will never replace Spartan, but she will add her own flair.

Without a doubt, Clementine will melt when she meets her.

While the kids play or hang out away from the parents, the adults catch up. With most of our children self-sufficient or in school, we have slid back into the regular work routines pre-parenthood. It has also been nice to have the occasional bowling or karaoke night, just us parents. Like old times again, but better.

Just as Jonas announces the burgers and brats are ready, Clementine walks outside. *God, has she grown.* The sweet, spunky girl who was a mini version of Autumn has grown that much more beautiful. Still a spitting image of her mother, she has taken on a style and fire all her own.

Before she gets a chance to say hello to anyone, Siku charges through the crowd and collides with her legs. Jumping and licking and begging for attention. Aside from the normal rock music playing, the backyard goes silent. All of us waiting with bated breath for Clementine's reaction.

Tears rim her eyes as she looks down at the dog, then up at her parents. Down and up, down and up. And then she drops to her knees and hugs Siku. Dog slobber hits Clementine's cheeks and chin and forehead, and she just laughs.

Devlyn leans in, his breath warm on my ear. "Maybe we should get a dog. Might help with Queen Sassy Pants."

I chuckle. "The idea does hold merit." I shift my gaze to his. "Talk about it later?" He nods.

Once the excitement over Siku meeting Clementine settles, we fall into the same routine we do every Sunday. Food and conversation and great friendship.

Devlyn wraps an arm around my shoulders and inches me closer to his side as he talks with Micah. And for a beat, I sit there and scan the yard. Look at the faces of all the people I love so deeply.

My best friends. My family. Cora and Gavin with Clara and Garrett. Jonas and

Autumn with Clementine and Ryker. Micah and Peyton. Erin and her new beau, Grayson. Trevor and Jillian. Penny and Jameson. Reznor and Tatyana with Ashton and Avery. Rex and Giana, with their five-year-old, Franco. Iliana and Sage. Jasmine and Anton with Lex, the tallest teenager I've laid eyes on. Reese and Trent.

So much love surrounds us, and we wouldn't want it any other way.

It's been an incredible journey so far. Friendships and love. Watching the next generation grow and prosper. This life… it has been surreal. The heartbreak and tears. The laughter and jokes. The hugs and memories. Not a day goes by where I don't appreciate every moment—good and bad.

The best part of it all… we have so many years left together. And I wouldn't want to spend a day of it with anyone else.

Penny

A BAY AREA DUET
SERIES NOVELLA

One

PENNY

The door swings open, the bell ringing as Oscar steps in. Sweat beads his forehead and temples. In the thick of the July heat, sweat on anyone's brow wouldn't be odd. But I know my boss. He cranks the air conditioning as high and cold as possible March through November.

Why the hell is he sweating so much?

Popping my gum, I lean into Autumn and whisper, "Is it just me or does Oscar look nervous?"

Autumn regards Oscar as he steps farther into the shop, not making eye contact or greeting any of us. "Yeah, something is definitely off." She twists to face me. "Think he's okay?" She clamps her lips between her teeth. "It's odd he asked us all here on a Sunday."

Oscar's Tattoo Emporium has been my second home for the last twelve years. To say I know this place inside and out is an understatement. This place has seen thousands of clients. Won local awards for Best Tattoo Shop in the Bay Area for several years. Had a few artists come and go, but the core of our family has remained solid.

So when I study the man across the room, watch how his foot taps incessantly as he checks his phone every other breath, I know something isn't right.

As I open my mouth to ask Autumn what she thinks is happening, Oscar looks up and finally greets us.

"Hey, everyone." He lifts a hand in an awkward wave. "Sorry to steal part of your Sunday. This won't take long. Promise." He taps the screen of his phone, takes a deep breath, then stows it in his pocket. "I have news."

I stop breathing for one, two, three seconds.

With the nervous energy radiating off him, I have a sneaking suspicion the news is not good.

Oscar looks at each of us in turn as he works his jaw. "I'm selling the shop."

The room turns deathly quiet as we all register what he just said. When my brain connects his words with reality, I chew the gum in my mouth faster. Blow a bubble and stare at the man who hired me years ago. *He looks tired. Why haven't I noticed?*

I pop the bubble and blurt, "Why?"

All eyes dart to me, but I don't care. I need to know why my family is being sold. Well, *we* aren't being sold. Not really. Of all his recent visits, Oscar has given no hints he considered selling the shop. Either he has hidden it well or something happened with him or his family.

The corners of his eyes soften as Oscar regards me. "Penny, I'd love to run the shop until I stop breathing." His lips flatten for a beat. "But Chelle isn't doing well." *What happened to his wife?* "She just had her annual checkup and the doctor found a growth on her ovary." He runs a hand through his hair. Pain mars his face as he scans the room. "I need to be there for her and Clarissa. As much as I love this place, the chain of shops, I need to sell. So I can be home."

Before he gets another word out, Autumn and I rush across the room to wrap him in our arms. Iliana, Rex, and Reznor surround us a beat later. We just hold this man. Give him strength when he needs it most. I may not like that he has to sell the shop, but I understand his reasons.

Oscar complains we are making him hot, then laughs as we break apart. "Thanks for the support. It means a lot." He rubs his hands together. "Part two." He winces. "The new owner will be here soon."

I groan and everyone else laughs.

Some people may say I am a bit much. Extra. Special. Those people would be correct. What can I say? I own who I am. I like what I like. And, nine times out of ten, I am a creature of habit.

No doubt Oscar did his homework before selling his business. Whoever the new owner is, they are probably as great as he is. Surely, he spoke with several buyers before choosing.

But I don't want someone new. I want Oscar. He is our family too.

"If I may..." Reznor lifts his hand like this is grade school and he needs permission to speak. Oscar tips his head at Reznor. "I also have news."

We all stare and wait. When he doesn't continue, I say, "Well, spit it out."

"Tatyana and I are pregnant again." The room erupts into cheers. "And I proposed." Autumn claps her hands over her mouth. "She said yes." Louder cheers fill the room. Congratulations shared with hugs. When the room settles again, he adds, "Which is why I was going to ask for fewer hours."

What. The. Shit is happening?

In less than ten minutes, it feels like our perfect little family is going in separate directions. And I am *not* okay with this. While everyone chats with Reznor, smiles plastered across their faces, I slowly melt inside. Metaphorically fall to the floor and curl into a ball.

I should be happy for Reznor. Should be excited for him, Tatyana, and Ashton. Should be smiling and asking if he knows if he will soon have a daughter or another son.

Instead, I stand paralyzed. Unable to muster up an ounce of joy for my friend.

Everyone is moving on.

Autumn and Jonas got married almost two months ago. They live in a beautiful house. Have a family. Reznor and Tatyana will be in the same position soon too.

Iliana hasn't mentioned any life-changing events. She lives a low-key life with her girlfriend, and their relationship is still young.

And Rex... well, Rex is just Rex. Once the roommate I wanted to throttle, he has matured since he took over Autumn's room in the apartment. Do I hate that we still share a bathroom? Absolutely. But at least I don't have to ask him to pick up his boxers and socks anymore. We also set up house rules for nights when either of us has company. Overall, he has been a great roommate.

"You okay?" Autumn asks as she sidles up to me by the reception counter.

"Yes. No." I stare back at my best friend. "I don't know." Exhaling, I shake my head. "Feels like everyone but me is moving forward."

"Oh, Pen." She wraps her arms around me and squeezes tightly. "We're all moving forward, just some of our paths have shifted. Yours will too."

"I'm not so sure." She unravels from the hug. "Not like anyone is knocking on my door, Auti."

We glance across the room at the guys and Iliana as they chat. Autumn clutches my hand. "You know I felt the same way before Jonas." She meets my gaze. "When it's meant to, change will happen for you too. Everything in its own time."

No matter how many times or how many ways I have heard that everything happens for a reason, I have yet to let it sink in. To root itself in my head and morph itself into truth. I *should* believe it. Autumn is proof. Maybe I don't believe it yet because I haven't been on the receiving end. Not yet.

I chew my gum and try to let in positive vibes. *Everything happens when it's meant to.* I blow a bubble so big, it blocks my line of sight. Just as I go to pop it, the bell over the front door jingles.

Shit. New boss.

I pop the bubble, tuck the gum in my cheek and drop my gaze as I smooth my hands down my thighs. Had I known I was meeting a new boss today, I would've worn something besides denim cutoffs and a graphic tee. Not that we dress fancy here. Too late now.

A pair of black leather boots come into view as I finish chastising my own attire. Slowly, my eyes rake up a pair of denim-clad legs, a black button-up—sleeves rolled to the elbows exposing a full sleeve of tattoos on both arms—to meet the person who bought the shop from Oscar. My favorite shade of blue stares back at me and my jaw drops.

"Jameson?"

Jameson Kingsley. My brother's best friend. A guy I crushed on most of my adolescence and fantasized about occasionally in adulthood. This is my new boss.

Fuck.

Two

JAMESON

Well, well, well. If this isn't the best surprise. I cock a brow and grin at the woman before me. The same woman who was checking me out seconds ago.

"Penelope," I say as I extend my hand. More than ever, I love the way my tongue flicks when I say her name. "Good to see you."

She slips her hand in mine. Warm, soft, and absolute perfection when cradled in mine. Her skin on mine feels different than it did years ago when I'd hung out with her brother and figured out every possible way to be near her.

"Penny," she corrects. "Good to see you, too, Jameson."

Several sets of eyes watch us, but I don't give a fuck. Let them think whatever. Everyone, including Penny, is lucky I haven't pulled her into an embarrassing hug.

Another time.

"Didn't know you worked here." She arches a brow in disbelief. "Seriously. Had I known, no one else would've had a chance at this place."

"Wh-what?" she whisper-asks.

Reluctantly, I let go of her hand. "We'll talk more later."

Oscar walks me around the room and introduces me to the rest of the staff. The first thing I note is how few employees this shop has. Three artists and two receptionists. One of the artists also doubles as the store manager. With the listed shop hours, they have stretched themselves thin. I make a mental note to bring on at least one new artist, if not more, and two piercers.

When we reach Reznor, the artist who also manages the store in Oscar's absence, he relays his recent news and need for fewer hours.

"Do you still want the management role?"

His lips pucker to the side as he considers his answer. He shakes his head. "With a new baby on the way, it's probably best I forfeit the job. I won't be able to put in the hours."

I extend my hand, and we shake. "Thanks for being up front and straightforward, man. We'll work out the specifics soon. All I ask is that you stay on as manager until your replacement is ready. Shouldn't take long."

Reznor nods. "Of course."

Oscar and I move to the center of the room and spin to face the group. We explain the logistics of how the shop will transfer over the next two weeks. The legalities were handled before this meeting. All we have left to do is swap the name of the business—on signs, the website and business cards, and with vendors. Most are tedious, but will be done in a week or two.

Oscar plans to stay on during the transition to help the process flow as smoothly as possible. Talk with any longtime customers who express concerns about the change.

"My goal is to be transparent with each of you. If you have questions or concerns, let's put them on the table now. We may not have an instant solution, but we'll sort one out quickly." I scan the faces of the staff, trying my damnedest to not stay on Penny longer than suitable. When no one speaks up, I move on. "The shop needs more staff." I look over to Reznor. "With future changes coming, it's best to be prepared now. Another artist or two. Piercers. A new manager." Out of the corner of my eye, Penny pops her gum, then shakes her head. "Something you'd like to add, Penelope."

Her eyes shoot to mine and narrow. Penny doesn't hate her full name but uses it only when necessary. I use it to get under her skin… in all the right ways. I remember every time her skin pinked when I called her Penelope years ago. I also remember wondering if her skin grew flush *everywhere* when I used her full name.

I still want to know.

"Penny," she huffs out as she slaps her hands on her hips. "And I hope you don't plan to hire some schmuck off the street to be our new manager."

"Penny," the woman next to her whispers as her eyes widen.

"What, Auti?" She looks around at everyone, then pins me with her stare. "I get it. You bought the shop and things will change. Whatever. But don't bring in some rando off the street to dictate our jobs to us."

God, she is fire and sass. Honest and bold. Time has been good to her—physically and otherwise. And damn… she turns me the fuck on.

"So, Penelope." I smile as her lips form a tight line. "What do you propose?"

Her brows pinch at the middle. "Wh-what? Why are you asking me?"

Crossing my arms in front of me, I widen my stance. "You seem to have strong feelings about this. Only fair if you give suggestions."

Everyone goes silent. Autumn bites down on her lip to hide her smile. Iliana looks away to disguise the laughter she fights. And the guys… they seem highly fascinated with their shoes.

"I don't—"

"You," I say, cutting her off. Her eyes narrow in confusion. "Why don't I promote you?"

"Uh…"

I love that I render her speechless. That I solved a problem for both her and me, yet she has no comeback. No smart remarks and goofy faces. In addition, my favorite shade of pink colors her skin. The color not quite as brilliant as her hair but still as magnificent as ever.

Without thought, my eyes drop to her chest. Although covered, I picture the flesh between her breasts and collarbones just as pink.

Fuck, I need to leave.

I clap my hands. "It's settled." Turning, I extend a hand and shake with Oscar. One by one, I shake everyone else's hand and tell them we will talk more during the week.

When I reach Penny, I offer my hand and she just looks at it. Stares without a word as if my touch may burn her. Who knows… maybe it will. And god would I love it if she is just as affected by me as I am her.

Seven slow and steady breaths later, she takes my hand, but we don't shake. I lean into her and drop my lips to her ear. Breathe deeply and sigh at the same artificial melon scent she has had for years. Watermelon Bubble Yum.

"Was a pleasure seeing you, Penny." I stroke her pulse with my finger and she shivers. "A real pleasure." Against my own desires, I lean back and straighten, drop her hand, and wink. "See you soon."

three

PENNY

Why did I have to open my big mouth? Why did I put myself in this predicament? Oh, right… because I didn't want some rando in the shop dictating our lives.

Elbows on the desk, I drop my head in my hands and stare down at the new stack of job applications and résumés Jameson left me to review. Every time I pick one up, a new wave of jitters rolls in my belly. The shop hasn't brought on anyone new since Iliana, and that was months after Autumn started. This place has been solid, a unit, for so long. The idea of adding new people to the mix has me nauseous.

What if they're an asshole? What if they do shitty work? What if they don't vibe with us?

All these scenarios, plus a hundred more, run through my head. I am not completely opposed to change, but too much is happening all at once. Oscar selling the shop to Jameson last month. The shop name change—King of Hearts Ink… full of yourself much, Kingsley? The constant calls and questions when our regulars saw the changes online.

I may be tough as nails and balls to the wall, but there is only so much a gal can handle at once.

As if he hears my inner turmoil through the office walls and throughout the shop, Reznor knocks on the open office door before stepping inside. He closes the door behind him, then takes a seat in the chair on the opposite side of the desk. The room remains silent for a beat, but I feel his gaze burning a hole in my head.

"Hey, Rez," I groan out, not lifting my head to look him in the eye.

"Penny, you know I love you. Right?" His words hesitant and quiet.

Inhaling deeply, I lift my head and lean back in the chair. Cross my arms over my chest. Narrow my eyes and study his expression a moment. "Yes," I say, drawing out the single-word response.

He squirms in the chair before leaning forward to rest his elbows on his knees. "If this is…" He takes a deep breath then meets my stare. "Not suggesting you can't handle this, but if it's too much—"

"If it's too much what, Rez?" He scratches the back of his neck. "Too much work for someone like me?" I point at the wall in the general direction of the reception desk in the lobby. "I may not have dealt with half this crap at the front desk, but that doesn't mean I can't handle it."

"God, Pen, I know." He leans back in the chair and looks away. Studies the photos on the office wall of us, our tattoo family, and the bright smiles we shared year after year. His eyes meet mine, a softness in his expression. "If anyone can conquer this place, it's you. But with all the changes in such a short period, even I'd be ready to rip my hair out."

"Please don't." I unlock my arms and rest my hands in my lap. "You have nice hair." My lips slowly tip up at the corners and we both laugh.

"Seriously, though." He finger-combs his hair. "I asked for fewer hours, but I don't mind helping out. Share the load until things settle more." He points to the stack of papers on the desk. "Want help weeding out interview candidates?"

I sit up, rake my eyes over the pile and sigh. "Is it horrible that I don't want to hire anyone?" My gaze lifts to meet his. "That I don't want to disrupt what we have here?"

Leaning forward, Reznor reaches across the desk and takes my hands in his. "It's not horrible. I get it. Really, I do. But at the end of the day, we need to bring in more people." He gives my hands a squeeze then releases them. "Autumn and I both work way less now. Our lives are different. Leaving Rex to pick up the rest of the slack isn't fair." He shakes his head, then says, "He won't be mad about the extra income, but he'll burn out before long. Then, we'll be in a jam."

I groan and Reznor chuckles. Pointing a finger at him, I say, "You know I hate it when you make a valid point." I really don't hate it. More like I hate that I am too scared to say the exact same. To own the changes that need to happen. "Thank you for offering to help." I pick up the applications and tap the bottom of the stack against the desk. "Maybe I just needed to vent." He arches a brow. "But I got this. Go." I jerk my chin toward the shop. "Ink some skin."

He lingers in the chair a beat before rising to his feet. Without a word, he shuffles toward the door and through the threshold. But before he is out of sight, he turns and says, "We're a family, Pen. It's okay to lean on us."

I nod with a smile and he walks off.

Reznor checking in with me was exactly what I needed. Someone who cares showing support. Someone who has sat in this very chair and done everything—minus the interviews—I am doing now, plus work in the shop. If he can manage all the roles, so can I.

I thumb through the applications and attached résumés with renewed purpose. Take a deep breath and look at the bigger picture. Yes, I love our little family as it is. But Reznor made a good point. Not bringing in new people only punishes us. And that, I am not okay with.

~

I stand and extend my hand across the desk. "It was wonderful meeting you, Sage. We'll be in touch." Sage shakes my hand as she rises from the chair.

"Thank you. If you have any other questions, please call. Anytime."

She shoulders her purse, and I walk her out of the office to the front door. When I spin around, three sets of eyes pin me in place. I smile and give an enthusiastic thumbs-up before heading back to the office. Back to where Jameson waits to discuss the interview he sat in on.

I breeze past everyone, dart inside the office and shut the door. Much as I don't want to be in a confined space with Hotty McHotterson, I also don't want to answer everyone's questions about the interview. Not yet. Need to digest it all myself first.

"I like her," Jameson states as I take my seat.

God, he is close. Too close. Why is he sitting right there?

I peer to my left but don't fully face him. If I spin the chair, my knees will knock his legs. And physical contact with Jameson… that is a no-no.

"Do you now?"

A smile kicks up one corner of his mouth and he winks. "Not how I like you, BYP."

BYP. How many years have passed since I heard that nickname? Several. Enzo stopped using it when he graduated high school and moved out of the house. Since then, I have been Pen or Penny.

At the time, I missed the cute term of endearment. Missed my playful brother. But he'd done his best to act mature. To show my parents he could adult on his own. For years, I wanted to tell Enzo nicknames didn't make you immature. If anything, they show you care.

So what does it mean that Jameson just used my childhood nickname? The Bubble Yum Princess. BYP. Is he being playful?

God, he used to give me so much shit. Teased me about my clothes and the way I wore my hair.

In turn, I gave him a hard time. Called him out.

"Funny that you tease me. Especially considering you hang out with people who dress and act just like me."

He played it off. Every single time.

Except that one time. The time I told him his girlfriend at the time looked like an older version of me. Yeah, that shut him down real quick. I didn't see him for months. Enzo hung at Jameson's house after school or they met up elsewhere.

In my teenage brain, I didn't pay attention to what it all meant. The jokes and banter. The fact that he stopped coming to the house after that comment. Or the fact that his girlfriend at the time was an older version of me with purple hair instead of pink.

But now…

Oh. My. Fucking. God.

I swallow past the sudden dryness in my throat. "BYP, huh?"

He nods. "The one and only."

"Hmm. Can't argue with that." Without thinking, I swivel the chair. My knee brushes the outside of his thigh and, for five minute-long seconds, I don't breathe. Jameson appears to forget how as well. I blink and clear my throat. "Don't you…" Voice as hoarse as if I'd been center stage at a concert, I swallow once, then twice, and start again. "Don't you think I've outgrown such childish names?"

My knee is still pressed to the side of his thigh. Such light pressure, yet it feels monumental. The fact that neither of us backs away or shifts from the contact has me sweating in awkward places. His tongue darting out and licking his lips also doesn't help the cause.

"What do you propose I call you instead?" Challenge laces his voice as he brings his hand to his jaw and toys with his beard.

Don't stare. Don't freaking stare. But my eyes refuse to look away as he strokes his beard. *Damnit, Penny! Get a hold of yourself!*

"You're a big boy, Kingsley," I say, bolder than I feel. Against every hormonal cry in my body to keep touching him, I swivel the chair away and face forward. I despise the immediate gooseflesh on my arms and legs. Loathe the whimper that wants to crawl up my throat and exit my lips. *Get. It. Together.* "Sure you'll figure something out."

He goes quiet for a beat. Too quiet. I pick up Sage's résumé and pretend to read over it. Pretend like I have lost interest in his little game.

Until his breath is on my ear. "I may have something up my sleeve."

The urge to face him heats my skin. But I don't dare. I may not see him in my periphery, but I *feel* him. If I move the slightest bit, his lips will be a breath from mine. I close my eyes, take a deep breath and swallow.

"Bet you do," I mutter, then clear my throat. "Should we discuss Sage?"

He chuckles under his breath as his chair creaks under the shift of his weight. I should be relieved he gave me room to breathe. But my traitorous body leans an inch to the left, begging for a smidge of his personal bubble.

Stupid. Freaking. Hormones.

"Yes, Penelope. Let's discuss Sage." Then his leg bumps my chair.

Why? Of all the people to buy Oscar's shop, why did it have to be Jameson Kingsley? Ooh, I know… because the universe loves to torture me.

Well, consider me tortured.

four

PENNY

"Ugh!" I huff out. "I'm at my wits' end, Auti. There's just too much damn testosterone in my life." Next to me, Autumn laughs with a shake of her head. *She laughs.* Some best friend.

"Sorry," she says between fits of laughter. She holds up her hand. "Really, I am."

I narrow my eyes at her. "Mm-hmm. Maybe I'd believe you if you *weren't laughing at me.*"

Snagging the licorice and bucket of popcorn in her hands, I face the television and shove the snacks in my mouth. I do my damnedest to ignore her as she holds her stomach and works to halt her laughter. Focus my attention on Rory and Jess on the screen. Imagine I live in Stars Hollow and Lorelai is my neighbor and best friend. She'd be a fun person to have around.

"I'm sorry, Pen," Autumn says more seriously. "If our roles were reversed, you know you'd laugh at me too." I roll my eyes because she isn't wrong. She sets a hand on my thigh and lays her head on my shoulder. "I miss this. Sitting on the couch and watching *Gilmore Girls* on repeat while eating junk."

I lay my head on hers. "Me too. But you have it pretty damn good with Jonas and the kids."

She nods. "I do. But I miss nights like this. Girl time." She plucks a Twizzler from the bag. "We need to do this more. Just the two of us."

"Agreed."

Through the rest of the episode, we stay like this. Cuddled into each other, stuffing our faces with candy and popcorn. The next episode starts and Autumn hits pause. She excuses herself to use the bathroom and asks if I want anything while she is up. I wave her off.

I tug my phone from my back pocket and go through notifications while I wait. Swiping down on the home screen, I review and swipe away each one. *Email. Email. Target sale. Netflix show alert.* Just as I am about to swipe away the Instagram notification, I stop.

Jameson Kingsley has requested to follow you.

I blink down at the screen. Narrow my eyes as if my contacts are deceiving me. I blink again. Nope, still there. Beneath it, the next notification is for Facebook.

Jameson Kingsley sent you a friend request.

Autumn plops back down beside me, but I don't move. Don't look up at her. "Everything alright?"

After a beat, I break contact with the screen, look her in the eyes and slowly shake my head. I hold up my phone and show her the notifications.

"Could be nothing," she says. "You know him. He's our boss and part of the family now. It could be completely innocent."

I wish that were true, but it feels much more than innocent. Years may have passed since Jameson and I have been around one another, but this doesn't feel like an old friend or my new boss just connecting on social media. Every interaction with him since the moment he walked in the shop has had double meaning. To everyone else, his actions may seem harmless. An old friend of the family happy to see me again.

But they don't know Jameson Kingsley like I do. They don't see the way he looks at me with mischief in his eyes. They don't feel the hum under my skin every time he stands in the same room as me.

"What if it's not?"

The television screensaver kicks on as I ramble to Autumn about Jameson. About my childhood crush who teased me with a smirk on his face. The guy who spent almost every day in my house until I opened my mouth about his girlfriend's uncanny resemblance to yours truly. The man that has flirted with me at every possible opportunity since he bought the shop. How close he has been during each interview—staying professional while the candidate is present but dropping the facade as soon as we are alone. Most of all, I tell Autumn how his proximity has me in knots. How it jumbles my brain. How it renders me speechless.

When I finish, her lips tip up in a gentle smile. One that I would normally find endearing if it were directed elsewhere. But this sweet smile feels different somehow. Heavy. Loaded. Significant.

"What?" I ask when she doesn't say anything.

This only makes her smile grow more. I open my mouth to tell her I am leaving if she doesn't fess up, but her hand on my arm stops me with a gentle squeeze.

"It's okay to like him, Pen."

"I don't." The lie tastes bitter on my tongue.

"You do, and it's okay." I shake my head. "It is. He may be our boss, but we work in a different world than most people. There's no human resources person shaking a finger at you for inappropriate behavior. There's no one casting judgment or whining about disadvantage because you and the boss are dating."

"We aren't dating," I blurt out.

She shakes her head. "True, but it'd be okay if you were." She tucks her feet under her butt and twists to look me in the eye. "Pen, I missed out on so much because I was afraid to put myself out there. Hell, with as many times as I tried to push him away, I almost missed out on Jonas." Her eyes dart between mine. "If you like him, be open to the possibility of more."

"What if it goes to shit? I'd still have to work with him."

Autumn grips my shoulders with fierce strength. "What if it's perfect? What if it's the best decision you've ever made?" When I don't respond, the corners of her mouth slowly kick up. "Don't question it. Go with it."

"I don't want to be one of those women…" I pause and Autumn tilts her head in question. "The type who lose who they are because they're infatuated with some guy."

At this, she laughs. I try to shrug out of her touch, but she doesn't allow it. She holds on tighter.

"Penelope Jane, the day you lose yourself to a man is the day the world stops spinning." She shakes her head on another laugh. "No man will steal your light. No man will steal your throne." She grips my chin. "If anything, the right man will kneel before you. Worship the ground you walk on. Be proud to call you his."

Her words grow like vines in my mind. Take over every thought and weave through every scenario.

For the first time in my adult life, I consider the possibility of a serious relationship. Something beyond flirting and fun. Is that even possible with Jameson? His girlfriends never lasted more than a month or two when we were younger. Is he still like that? Get what he wants then hightail it out the back door.

Enzo would know, but I have zero intention of asking my brother about his best friend's relationship history. That would open the door to questions I do *not* want to answer.

"I see you spinning every worst-case scenario. You'll go up in smoke if you're not careful." Autumn laughs.

I twist and face her. "What would you do if you were in my position?"

She clamps her lips between her teeth and rocks her jaw side to side. "If what you feel is anything remotely close to how I felt when I first met Jonas, I'd take the leap. Jump in headfirst."

Take the leap. Jump in headfirst.
Can I do that? Can I give in to what I feel for Jameson?
I want to. More than I care to admit.

five
JAMESON

"You what?"
This is not the reaction I expected from Enzo. Not by a long shot.
"I bought the tattoo shop Penny works at." My hands fly up to either side of my head. "In all fairness, I didn't know she worked there until Oscar and I signed the paperwork and he invited me to meet the staff." Enzo narrows his eyes, and I can't help but see the resemblance to Penny when he does it. "Swear."
Enzo and I have been friends more years than not. We met during the awkward middle school stage when girls became something other than annoying and our voices did that embarrassing squeak.
The two of us have done some crazy shit in the past. From dressing up the school mascot statue in a naughty-nurse costume to spiking the punch at the school dance with his dad's favorite single malt. I spent several years in his bedroom, playing video games and talking about shit we never told anyone else.
Lorenzo Singleton is my best friend. Always will be.
So why I never mentioned to him the idea of purchasing a tattoo shop is beyond me. Not like he wouldn't have backed up the idea. He would have been excited. Would have told me it was a solid investment.
If I would have told him.
"Fine," he huffs out. "I believe you." The doorbell rings, and he holds up a finger as he rises from the couch. "We're not done talking about this."
"Yes, dear," I joke as he walks off. His middle finger shoots up over his shoulder.
While he answers the door, I question why I didn't say anything to him. Why I didn't share what I wanted to do with the money Dad left me when he passed. Why I didn't get my best friend's opinion on such a life-altering decision.
"Life's too short. Do what makes you happy. Take risks. Fall in love. See the world."
The last words my father spoke to me play in my head for the millionth time. When he'd said them, I'd told him to quit talking like the pneumonia would win. That he'd be better the next day and leave the hospital soon. The next day, Mom and I tiptoed into his hospital room, not wanting to wake him. Less than an hour later, the machines went haywire. The squeal of the alarm bounced off the walls and embedded itself in my memory. Nurses rushed the room, and I stopped breathing as my father gasped for his own breath. Everything in that moment blurred from existence, everything but the sound telling us his heart stopped beating.
They say my father died peacefully. That his brain and body shut down as he drowned in his own fluids. But no matter how much they tried to convince me and Mom, I never believed it.
After he passed, I tried to live by his last words. Tried to live up to the man I

had admired my entire life. I did what made me happy, what brought me joy. Tattoos happen to be one of those things.

And while I was at the tattoo convention last year, I overheard artists talking about buying their own shops. As I sat in the chair and got new ink, I asked how one would go about buying a shop. How I would find someone who wants to sell. Like anything, there was a website.

For months, I checked the site. Waited for a local shop to pop up. A little over three months ago, Oscar posted he was looking to sell. He had several shops but was willing to sell them individually. Without hesitation, I jumped. Took the risk with zero regrets.

Enzo walks back into the room with a pizza box and bag. He sets them on the coffee table and retakes his seat next to me on the couch. "Dinner is served."

He flicks on the television, opens Hulu and clicks on *American Horror Story*. We dive in, stuffing ourselves with pizza, garlic knots and beer. Halfway through the episode, my shoulders loosen up. When we both pick up our last piece and he still hasn't broached the subject of the shop again, I breathe easier.

The episode ends and I pat my belly. "Thanks for dinner, bro."

"No problem."

He gathers the trash and takes it to the kitchen. When he returns, it's with two more beers and a raised brow.

Damnit. Thought I lucked out.

"What?" I ask, feigning innocence.

"Two things." He holds up two fingers for emphasis. "One… why didn't you tell me you wanted to buy a tattoo shop? Feels like you left me stranded on a highway." His hand claps my shoulder. "You're my brother. We talk about everything."

We do talk about everything. Well, almost everything. But I have a sneaking suspicion it will all be on the table before I walk out the door tonight.

"After Dad died last year, I was in such a funk." He nods but doesn't interrupt. I go on to explain how I overheard artists at the tattoo convention. How I asked where to find shops for sale. "Early May, a local shop popped up. I looked into the owner, spoke with him on the phone and we set up a meet. It all went pretty quick." I shrug. "As to why I never told you… I don't know. Maybe because it felt like I was doing what Dad wanted me to. Taking a risk. If I would've said something, maybe you would've talked me out of it."

Enzo sips his beer and tips his head side to side. He tips the neck of the bottle in my direction. "Probably right." After another sip, he says, "But now that we've cleared that up, don't do that shit again."

I nod on a laugh. "Yes, dear."

When the room quiets again, his expression turns serious. His eyes lock on mine. "Two… what is your intention with my sister?"

I startle at the question. Every muscle inside me freezes. I open my mouth to answer but snap it shut, unsure of what to say. Do I *know* the answer?

Without question, I like Penny. More than either she or Enzo probably want to hear. Not sure when it happened, but early on, I stopped looking at her like my best friend's little sister and started seeing her as someone I wanted more with. To hold her, kiss her, call her mine.

With Penny, though, it isn't that simple. If I fucked up, Enzo would have my balls. And I really didn't want to fuck things up with her.

So, I held off. Dated other girls. Girls that reminded me of her in one way or another. The day she called me on it, I freaked out. Avoided her at all costs.

Now, though… life is different. *I* am different.

"Would you be pissed if I asked her out?"

His jaw tightens and I swear I hear his molars grind. "If you hurt her…"

"Never."

"What about her job? Last thing she needs is judgment or fear of losing her job if things go south."

I sigh and shake my head. "Do you really think so little of me?" He opens his mouth, but I speak before he does. "First off, I promoted her. The shop needs more staff, but she didn't want an outsider managing the place. So I gave her the position. Second, I would never do anything to jeopardize her job. Fuck you for thinking I would. And last, I have no clue if she'll even say yes to going out."

"She'll say yes."

I sit slack-jawed for a beat. "How can you be so sure?"

He sips his beer. A larger-than-life smile splits his face in half. "Because I know my sister."

Obviously, I am out of the loop on something. Either that or willfully blind to what is in front of me.

Green eyes, just a little different than my favorite pair, bore a hole in my head. "Let me reiterate. Make myself crystal fucking clear." He tips the bottle toward me again. "If you hurt her, in any capacity, I will fuck you up. We may be brothers, but she is my only sister. And no one fucks with her."

Message received.

"On my life, I won't hurt her."

Six

PENNY

I sag into the chair, tip my head back and sigh at the ceiling. "Hallelujah!" On the other side of the desk, Jameson laughs. My head pops back up, and I give him what feels like a menacing look. Knowing my luck, I look constipated. "Are you laughing at me, Kingsley?"

His hands fly up in surrender. "Don't shoot." He curbs his laughter. "I mean no harm." For shiggles, I throw a pen at him. "Hey! What'd that pen ever do to you?"

As he bends in the chair to find the pen, I take a moment to breathe. To let the calm settle in my bones for the first time in weeks. To feel relief flow through my bloodstream as all the major changes smooth out.

Damn it feels good to have balance again. To have things falling into place.

After more than a dozen artist, piercer and front desk interviews, Jameson and I decided who we want to offer jobs. Took hours of rehashing the interviews, but I believe they will make great additions. Deciding was more difficult than I thought it would be. Introducing new faces to a tight-knit group is a big deal. Making sure each of them fit in with us was vital.

"When do you want to call them?" I ask as Jameson sits up.

"Monday. Let's enjoy the weekend and worry about paperwork when it's over."

I peek up at the clock over his head and am shocked by the time. Almost six. Where the hell did the day go? Jameson walked in with lunch around noon and we've been holed up in here since, debating over our choices. What this room needs is a damn window. Something to show the sun as it moves east to west. Something to keep me from losing track.

Staring at the north wall, the one on the back of the building, I mumble, "Right there."

"Right where?" Jameson's eyes sear my profile. "And dare I ask what?"

I spin to face him and cock a brow. "There." I point at the wall and he looks at the collection of framed photos. "This room needs a window. Big. Small. I don't care. Just some damn sunshine."

He pinches his chin between his thumb and forefinger as he stares at the space in question. Then he strokes his beard, and I avert my gaze briefly.

Why? Why the hell does that one particular action make me gooey inside? It never has with anyone else. Ever.

"Might make things tight in here when I bring in another desk, but I'll make it work."

My eyes drop to the desk and roam the surface. A few dents and scratches mar the surface, but otherwise the desk is in great shape. Maybe he prefers more modern furniture. But newer pieces aren't made with the same craftsmanship. Being that Jameson spent so much time with my family years ago and how much my dad talked about quality woodwork, you'd think he wouldn't buy assemble-yourself furniture.

"I like this desk," I tell him. "It has character and good bones."

"Couldn't agree more."

"Then why are you replacing it?"

He stares at me for three, two, one. "I'm not," he answers hesitantly. "The other desk is for me."

What the what?

I lift a hand to my ear, insert a finger, and wiggle. "Sorry. Think I misheard you. Sounded like you said you'll have a desk in here too."

A smirk tugs at the corner of his mouth, and I want to smack it off. Cocky ass.

"Oh, you heard me correctly." He waves a hand around the fifteen-by-fifteen space. "It'll be tight, but we'll make it work."

"Why do you need a desk in here?"

He cocks his head and just stares at me for a moment. Part of me wants to bolt from the chair, stomp around the desk and shake his shoulders. Demand he answer me now. But I suppress the urge. Instead, I hold his gaze and play along with his waiting game.

"Afraid you won't get much work done with me here?"

Yes. "No."

That cocky smile makes another appearance. I love and hate it.

He shakes his head and laughs. "Shouldn't I have a place to work in my own business?"

"Oscar was almost never here."

"I'm not Oscar."

This much I know.

"How often will you be here?"

"Why does this feel like an inquisition?"

"Do you like answering questions with questions?"

He laughs harder this time. "I won't be here all the time, but I do want my hands in the business I just sank a lot of money in." Honestly, it makes sense. Owners should be hands-on if possible. "And since you're the only manager, I should be here when you need time off." He leans forward and rests his forearms on the desk. "You work hard, Pen. But you don't need to dig yourself an early grave. So, please, let me help."

Moments like this, when Jameson softens those bright-blue eyes, I lose all sense of direction. My motor skills... out the door. Every now and again, this man turns me to rubber. Has me bending to his will.

"You're right."

He cups his ear and leans closer. "Sorry, what was that?"

I throw the pen again and hit my desired target—his forehead. "Ass. You heard me."

"Ow," he says, then laughs as he rubs his forehead.

Pushing out my lower lip, I tease, "Aw. Poor baby has a boo-boo."

In a blink, the room turns utterly silent. Jameson looks across the desk, his eyes on my lips as he licks his own. And damn, if it isn't hotter than the summer sun outside. I swallow and his eyes drop to follow the action. I don't know what to think, to feel, to do. My pulse pounds, pounds, pounds in my chest. Whooshes behind my ears. And I swear to god, I might be panting.

Please don't let me be panting.

"Go on a date with me."

My brows pinch at the middle as his words slowly register. "What?"

"Go on a—"

"No, I heard you." I shake my head. Try to make sense of what he said. Because Jameson Kingsley asking me on a date... how many times did I envision this moment? I am too embarrassed to admit the answer. But I never thought it'd actually happen. Sure, Autumn and I talked about the possibility. If I'm honest, I thought I'd have to pull a Sadie Hawkins. "Why?" I finally ask.

"Really?" I nod and he bites his lower lip. "Am I not obvious enough?"

Yes, he had been obvious with his interest. But I also saw him through a different lens. One a bit rosier.

I shrug. "Maybe. Maybe not. My perception of things might be a bit misconstrued."

He licks his lips then smiles when my eyes follow the action for a split second. "Why is that?"

"Am I not obvious enough?" I throw his question back at him.

"Go on a date with me, Pen."

I don't move an inch as we stare at each other. My heart bangs against my rib cage, begging me to spit out the three-letter word. Begging me for relief. It would be so easy. Saying yes. Getting swept up in Jameson. Because I have wanted nothing more for several years.

Take the leap. Jump in headfirst.

"Yes."

"Yes?" I nod and the most brilliant smile lights his face. "Can I text you later? We'll sort out details." Again, I nod. He rises from his seat and reaches for my hand, bringing it to his lips. "Talk to you later, BYP." He winks, drops my hand, and exits the office.

"Yeah," I whisper to myself. "Talk to you later."

seven

JAMESON

Never thought she'd say yes.

Penelope Singleton. The girl—woman—that tattooed herself on my heart long before I understood what it meant. The woman that I looked for in every person I dated. The woman that always lingered in the back of my mind.

No woman holds a candle to Penelope Singleton. And she said yes. To me.

God… I was prepared to beg. Prepared to emasculate myself. Lucky for me, it never came to that. She would have loved seeing me grovel. Savored it. Referred back to it for years.

I button up my shirt and roll the cuffs to my elbows. Leave it untucked from my jeans. Swipe product through my hair and beard, then comb both. Spritz cologne on my shirt—the one Dad always used and swore it was the only reason Mom never left. Then I take one last look in the mirror.

"Lucky bastard," I tell my reflection.

Pocketing my phone and wallet, I swipe my keys from the dresser and walk out the front door. Last night, a few hours after Penny said yes, my fingers hovered the phone keyboard until the screen dimmed. Twice. I typed and deleted and repeated more times than I care to admit. The reality of setting up a date with Penny made basic bodily functions forget their purpose.

Penny makes me dizzy in all the right ways. Throws my world off its axis. Makes me feel alive. And after not existing in her orbit for so long, I pray her gravity never releases me.

I weave through the city streets and drive toward Dunedin. Much as I wanted to knock on Penny's door, thread my fingers with hers and drive us to the restaurant, I also didn't want to make our first date awkward. Because it very well could be. Although a gap of time exists between now and high school, we know each other well. Really well. My one hope is that the time apart works in our favor.

Penny may have been like a little sister in the beginning, but the ideal didn't stick for long. Enzo would have throttled me had he known.

Tonight, my sole desire is to sit across from this bewitching woman and get to know who she is now. Hear about the years of her life I missed—not that Enzo never mentioned her. And if I'm lucky, by the end of the night, she won't see me as her brother's best friend. Hopefully, she will see me as someone at her side.

I park in the lot a block from the restaurant. As I reach the sidewalk, I spot a pink old-school Cadillac convertible. Without a doubt, I know Penny owns the car. Pink and vintage are her calling card.

Twenty feet from the restaurant, I spot her and come to a halt. Head down, eyes on her phone. Victory rolls pinned in place while the length of her hair trails her spine. A red-and-white sleeveless top that looks more like a corset, ties at the nape of her neck. Tattoos on full display. Dark denim hugging her legs from hip to heel.

Goddamn.

As if she senses my presence, her eyes scan the sidewalk and land on my profile. A soft smile tips up the corners of her red lips. Eyes on me, she stows her phone and holds up a hand.

Deep breaths, King. Deep breaths.

One foot in front of the other, I close the space between us. My eyes never leaving hers. Heart pounding harder with each step forward. Blood humming in my veins as I reach her side.

"Hey," I say. "Sorry I kept you waiting."

With a shake of her head, her smile widens. "You didn't. I got here a few minutes ago."

"You look incredible." I scan her head to toe now that I have a better view. *Damn.*

She reaches up and toys with my collar. "As do you."

I gesture to the door. "Shall we?"

We step inside the restaurant and I fight the need to rest my hand on her lower back. *Too soon.* The hostess seats us in the outdoor area, hands us menus and relays the specials before leaving the table. Music plays from hidden speakers in the court-yard. Soft light glows from bulbs strung between the trees and fence enclosure. The summer breeze doing nothing to alleviate the nervous energy beneath my diaphragm.

The server sets a larger bottle of water on the table and takes our order. Penny orders a dish with squid ink pasta and seafood while I get the Korean beef tacos. Soon as the server walks off and the menus are no longer a distraction, my pulse pounds in my chest.

What the hell do we talk about?

Penny sips her water, leans back in her chair and makes me her point of focus. Setting the glass on the table, she toys with the rim as her eyes hold mine.

Damn, she makes me nervous. More than anyone.

"I realize it's summer…" Her lips shift to fight a smile. "When is it not summer here?" She laughs. "But you're sweating an awful lot. You okay?"

Swiping my glass from the table, I down half the water then mimic her posture. *Calm the hell down, King.* "On a date with Penny Singleton, what man wouldn't sweat his ass off?"

Her fingers freeze on the rim of the glass as she regards me and processes what I said. She sits up, moves the glass from between us and leans in my direction. If I follow her lead, her lips would be a breath from mine. Red and irresistible. Lips I've wanted pressed to my own. Lips I've fantasized about in more ways than one.

"Do you know why I said yes?" Her question makes me mentally stumble. I shake my head and her red lips kick up at the corners. "Either you're the master of disguise or completely oblivious."

God, I want to lean into her. Make her breath catch and pulse erratic. Make her body feel half the jitters coursing through my veins.

"Consider me in the dark."

Her tongue darts out and sweeps her lips. I fist my jeans under the table and suppress the moan in my throat. What is it about this woman that makes the world wobble beneath my feet?

"Jameson Kingsley, I'm shocked," she says, resting her palm over her heart. "I mean… I did my best to mask how I felt." She looks off in the distance, lips trapped between her teeth, jaw rocking side to side. Then soft-green irises meet mine and resume their focus. Her expression serious as her cheeks and neck flush. "But you had to have known."

I straighten in my seat, but leave little distance between us. "Known what, Penny?"

The pink tinting her cheeks darkens as she swallows. "That I had a crush on you." Her whispered words barely audible, but I hear them loud and clear.

Leaning closer, I buck up the courage and ask, "Had?"

She rolls her eyes. "Had. Have." Light laughter spills from her lips. "Tomato, tomahto."

I inch closer to her. Wipe my sweaty palms on my jeans. Lick my lips as I stare at hers. "What if I said the same?" Her brows pinch in confusion. "That I had it bad for you."

"Not sure I'd believe you," she says breathily.

Just as I open my mouth to spill every truth, the server steps up to the table with our dinner. The table falls silent as we eat our meals. Both of us mulling over this newfound information. When the server clears our plates and offers dessert, my lips want to say no while my heart refuses to deny what she wants. We split a slice of key lime pie, and it is the best damn pie I've ever eaten.

After I pay the check, we exit the restaurant and walk toward the lot. Unexpectedly, Penny laces her fingers with mine. I stop breathing. A rush of adrenaline spikes my bloodstream and has me floating with the stars.

"This okay?" she asks, squeezing my hand.

We reach her car and I drop my gaze to hers. "More than okay," I choke out. For a moment, we simply stand there, gazes locked and hands clasped. Before I lose the courage, before I let my nerves get the best of me, I ask, "Can I kiss you?"

She sucks in a breath. Her eyes dart between mine. Then, ever so slowly, she nods.

Not wanting to rush this, not with Penny, I lower my mouth to hers and sigh when we connect. Soft and warm and better than I imagined. My hand cups her jaw as I kiss her, slow and sweet. As I savor the moment. I don't push for more and break the kiss sooner than preferable.

I rest my forehead on hers. "I really like you, Penelope Singleton."

Her hand rests over my heart. "I really like you too, Jameson Kingsley."

I press a chaste kiss to her lips and reluctantly step back. "Hey, Penny?" I lift her hand to my lips and kiss her knuckles. "Wanna go steady?"

A smile plumps her cheeks as she rolls her eyes. "Under one condition." I cock a brow. "I get to be the Queen of hearts."

I step back into her and crash my lips to hers. "You always have been." Truer words have never been spoken.

eight

I spent most of Sunday chatting Autumn's ear off about my date with Jameson. The way he looked at me on the sidewalk. How he was dressed. Our confessions before the waiter interrupted. The kiss and him asking to be my boyfriend.

God, it was dreamy and surreal.

The first half hour, it irritated me not seeing her facial expressions. Autumn is always so expressive in person. She probably grinned or clamped her lips shut more often than not. But after a while, I stopped caring, and she said she was happy for me.

The rest of Sunday, I cleaned while *Gilmore Girls* played in the background. Threw out the leftovers that were slowly making new friends in the fridge. Wiped down every surface in the apartment. Vacuumed the living room, hallway and my bedroom. Washed the dirty clothes in the hamper plus my bedding. Reorganized my makeup in the bathroom.

I did everything possible to not check my phone. To look for missed texts or calls from Jameson.

Needless to say, I failed. Kind of like I am right now.

Last thing I want is to be desperate or bothersome. The clingy one who irritates him until breaking up is inevitable.

"He'll be here soon," Autumn says as she wipes down her booth and preps for her first session.

Her words hold truth, but every nerve ending under my skin is abuzz. Saturday night, Jameson asked if I wanted to go steady. It felt so 1950s. Sweet and heartfelt with a pinch of romantic. Had me swooning for hours. We texted briefly last night until he said he was with his mom. I didn't want to steal their time, so I told him I'd see him in the morning.

Now, it's morning, and he isn't here yet. Granted, he doesn't have an actual schedule, so morning could mean any time before noon. And the fact that I glance at the door every ten seconds…

What is wrong with me?

"Ugh," I huff out, more upset with my neediness than him not being here yet. "Why am I like this, Auti?"

She laughs. "Like what?"

I pin my fists to my hips and narrow my eyes at her. "A desperate lunatic." Ambling to her chair, I plop down and groan. "It hasn't been forty-eight hours and I'm checking my phone like he's a missing person and I'm waiting for a bronze alert." Autumn looks at me like I have three heads. "Well, I don't know what they call it when an adult is missing. Amber is for kids. Silver is for seniors. So I'm calling it bronze." I shrug and continue. "Why?" I drag the word out way too long with a heap of dramatic flair.

What does Autumn do? What does my best friend do? She laughs. Loud and clear and with too much gusto. *Some bestie she is.*

I slip off the chair and spin to face her, hands on my hips. "Best friends aren't supposed to give each other shit, Auti."

It takes her a moment, but she gets her laughter under control. "Is that so?"
I nod.

"Well, I remember you giving me plenty when things were new and messy with Jonas, so..." She makes a goofy face and then sticks out her tongue.

Just as I open my mouth to counter her comment, the bell over the door jingles. Plastering on my best welcoming smile, I turn on my heel to greet whoever walked in.

"Welcome to—" My throat goes dry as Jameson enters the shop, cups in carriers in both hands and a large bag tucked under his arm. "Oh, hey." I meet him halfway. "Let me help you."

I take one of the drink carriers from him, and we walk toward the reception desk. Autumn and Reznor join us and Iliana. "Not sure what everyone likes, but I brought coffee and bagels. I'll put the bagels in the back for whenever."

The shop doesn't open for another fifteen minutes, so we all dart to the break room and scarf down breakfast. A round of thanks is given to Jameson before everyone goes back to their workstations and the two of us go to the office.

Jameson follows me in and shuts the door behind him. The click of the latch hitting the strike plate is deafening. Each clunk of his boots on the hardwood is thunderous. And when he stops inches behind me and traces a finger down my forearm, I suck in a breath and freeze. My eyes fall shut as my mind drifts to the feel and taste of his lips on mine. I want to spin around. Want to know what he tastes like today.

But not here. Not in this office. Not where my actions could be misconstrued if someone waltzes in.

"Jameson," I croak. "We can't." His finger trails up to my elbow and I shake my head. "Not here."

His finger drops away and I instantly miss the blaze his touch sparks under my skin. But he doesn't leave me bereft for long. Warm lips meet the bare skin where my neck and shoulder connect. He touches me nowhere else, but I feel him every-where. My pulse pounds a rhythm so vicious, he has to feel it beneath his lips.

Then his lips are gone. He doesn't step back, doesn't say a word. Part of me wants to lock the door and say fuck it. Part of me wants to spin around, palm his cheeks and lower his mouth to mine.

How long have I wanted this man? How long have I dated other men in the hopes they would make me forget him?

But I can't do this with him here. Selfish as I want to be in this very moment, I need to set boundaries. Work... we need to have rules.

He growls and takes a step back. I inhale for the first time in far too long. My feet are concrete boulders as I put one in front of the other and step around the desk. I don't want obstacles between us, but right now, I need something there to separate lust from reality.

Dropping down in the guest chair, he drags a hand through his beard. "God, I love being here with you every day." He shakes his head. "But if I make this too difficult"—he gestures between us with his other hand—"if it feels like I'm hindering things, tell me. Please."

Is it wrong for me to be happy over the fact that he thinks *he* is the only one that would disrupt the workday by us being together? He doesn't get it. Doesn't understand the gravity of what I feel for him. It may not be love—because I can't grasp the magnitude of love, not yet—but what I feel for Jameson… it has been brewing more years than not.

Sliding open the desk drawer, I pull out a pack of gum, take a piece and offer him one. He shakes his head. I drop the package back in the drawer, unwrap the cube and pop it in my mouth. Chew to soften the sweet, rubbery confection. Distract myself momentarily while I ponder how to navigate this—work, him, us— going forward. Jameson isn't going anywhere and neither am I.

"We need ground rules," I blurt out and nod. "We need to set clear boundaries of what's acceptable and not while we're working."

He relaxes in the chair further and spreads his legs wide. Like an addict, I watch his hand as it continues to stroke his beard. *God, I love the feel of that beard on my skin.* I shake my head briefly. *Knock it off, Penny. Focus.*

"Hmm." He eyes me a beat. "As awful as that sounds, you're probably right."

"Probably?" I cock my head and he chuckles.

"Mm-hmm." He straightens in the seat and reaches across the desk. I chew my gum with a vengeance as he inches closer and closer. Just when I think he is going to touch me again, he picks up the pad of paper and pen then resumes his previous position.

I am so screwed.

He scribbles on the pad, but I can't see what it says. Beneath the desk, my Chucks drum the hardwood. My nails tap the arms of the chair. And if it wouldn't be so damn obvious, my head would bob as I wait, wait, wait for him to finish writing whatever rules he thought of.

"Alright," he says, eyes trained on the paper. "Rules. Let's do this." His eyes lift from the page and lock on mine. Ready. Waiting.

My brows knit together as I point at the paper. "Did you write one down?"

He flips the pad around so I can see his tidy handwriting. On the top of the lined page, it says, *Penelope and Jameson's rules on how to not make out while at work.*

I look at him, then back at the page. I do this over and over and over. Nothing else is written on the page. And for a moment, all I think is how it reminds me of the early years, of pillow forts and rules on what you're allowed to do while in the fort. Then, without second thought, I laugh. I laugh loud and hard and until my stomach hurts and eyes water.

When my laughter settles and eyes clear, I peer across the desk to see the biggest smile on Jameson's face. A smile that gives me life and settles all worry. I love his smile. Always have. His smile is genuine and radiant and an accessory that adds to his appeal.

"You've always had the best laugh," he says.

"I'm quite fond of yours too." I blow a bubble with my gum then pop it. "Guess we should add some actual rules."

"If we want to get work done, yeah."

Over the next half hour, we shoot ideas back and forth. I veto some of his ideas —good morning kisses as well as lunchtime kisses—and he shoots down some of mine—office door open at all times and at least three feet separating us. Instead, we end up with a short list of basic office romance rules.

1. No kissing while working. If we leave for lunch, kissing is allowed.
2. No copping a feel or "inappropriate" touching while working.
3. Flirting is allowed, but nothing that gets "out of hand."
4. Everyone can know we're dating, but we won't flaunt it at work.
5. If no one is here or we're working late/after hours, rules 1-4 are null.

Rule number five was all Jameson. I fought it like this was junior year in debate class and Kyle Preston thought he knew more about women's rights than I did. Needless to say, Kyle Preston got buried with my rebuttal. Jameson, on the other hand, he wasn't taking no for an answer. Then he smiled and stroked his beard. What did I do? I caved.

Punk ass.

"Next time I run errands, I'm buying a frame for our rules," he says. He tears the page from the pad, folds it three times, then stuffs it in his pocket. "After the new furniture comes and the dust settles in here, I'll hang them on the wall."

Is he serious? Knowing Jameson, he will put it in the most obvious spot in the room. Hang it where every person that walks in will see it. Where they will read and laugh at the childish list of rules we had to make so we keep our hands and mouths off each other while at work.

"Maybe you should blow it up on an eleven-by-fourteen canvas," I tease.

He cocks a brow. "Don't tempt me. Now…" He rubs his hands together and lays his forearms on the desk. "We have calls to make. If you want to tackle the new hires, I'll call about the furniture and window."

I sit up straighter as my eyes gauge how serious he is. Not an ounce of humor or mischief lightens his smile or posture.

"Really? You'll add a window?"

"For you, yes. But also, I prefer natural light to fluorescents. Plus, maybe the chance of someone peeping in will keep me in line." He taps the pocket he stowed the rules in. "No guarantees, though."

While I call the six new faces of King of Hearts Ink—Sage, Chance, Frankie, Gage, Kennedy, and Ophelia—Jameson calls a friend who relays a few trustworthy window companies in the area. I suggest we ask my dad who to call for office furniture. If there is one thing George Singleton is an expert at, it is quality woodwork.

By lunch, each of the new staff is scheduled to come in later to pick up paperwork. Jameson has appointments scheduled for each window company to come out and give us an estimate. He wrote down addresses for two furniture galleries that said they have what we are looking for and, after lunch, we are headed to both. Since both of us will be crammed in the space, he said it was best for us to both go. To bounce ideas off each other or explain why certain pieces may not work in the space.

I shoulder my purse as we exit the office. Waving to Autumn and the guys, I stop at the front and hand Iliana envelopes for the new hires. "In case we don't make it back in time." Each envelope is labeled since not everyone requires the same paperwork.

The bell jingles as we step into the August heat. I dig in my purse for my sunglasses and slip them on as we round the building. The second we clear the windows, Jameson slips his hand in mine.

"Hey, mister."

He slides his own sunglasses into place, then flashes me a bright smile. "What? Technically, it's lunchtime." We reach my car and he steps into me, his other hand lifting to my cheek. "And if I want to touch"—the side of his finger strokes my jaw—"or kiss"—he drops his lips to mine and kisses me chastely—"my girl, I will." His finger paints a line down my throat. "Got it?" he asks, voice gruff.

Slowly, I nod. "Mm-hmm." I lick my lips, then swallow. "Got it."

"Good." He inches back and scans the length of my car. "Let's go. I've been dying to ride in this baby."

nine

JAMESON

> Have dinner with me tonight.

PENNY

> How about you ask me nicely.

I walk up the next aisle in the office supply store. How many damn versions of staplers do they have? And pens… Jesus. I stared at the pen aisle—yes, the whole fucking aisle was pens—for a solid fifteen minutes. Gel. Ballpoint. Medium tip. Fine tip. Felt tip. Black. Blue. Every color known to exist in the spectrum. Sparkly. Shimmery. I grabbed a few boxes that looked like the ones Penny had in the office. You can never have too many pens.

> Penelope Jane, will you pretty please with sugar on top have dinner with me tonight?

> Getting warmer.

Is it weird that her taunting is hot? The way she verbally teases me, eggs me on, smirks… damn, it is the best foreplay. Has me jonesing for more. Thinking of what I will say next. What she will say next.

So. Damn. Addicting.

Is it also weird that I never enjoyed foreplay until Penny?

Most of the women I dated in the past, the desire to feel that buildup, to feel the buzz in my veins and hum beneath my diaphragm, it wasn't there. The endless need for more. The insatiable hunger. I don't blame them. They were fun and beautiful and great. They just weren't who I was looking for. They weren't Penny.

> Penny, I would be honored with your presence for dinner tonight? *gets on knees in the stapler aisle*

> Warmer 😈

An employee of the store is stocking the opposite side of the aisle with boxes of paper clips. I eye him for a minute and the best idea pops in my head. I wheel my buggy close to him.

"Excuse me, sir." He spins to face me, ready to help me find whatever office supplies I need. Little does he know, I am about to make this awkward. "This is an odd request, but can you do me the biggest, strangest favor?"

He sets the rest of the paper clips down and goes into full-on customer service mode. "Sure. What can I help you with?"

I open the camera app on my phone and hand him the phone. "Can you take a stupid picture? Of me, on my knees, on the floor." He looks at me like I might need medical attention. Perhaps I do. "It's a joke for my girlfriend."

Damn, I love the way girlfriend rolls off my tongue when Penny is said girl.

"Um…" He looks left then right. "I guess." He checks again to see if anyone else is nearby. Surely no one will fire the poor guy over this. "Just hurry."

I get down on my knees and lift my hands in a prayer position. The guy snaps a few pictures, then quickly hands me back my phone. "Thank you so much. I'll leave the best rating on the receipt survey." I read his name tag. "And add that you were extremely helpful, Don."

He nods and goes back to work, probably more than happy he doesn't have to deal with the weird guy anymore.

> Pretty, pretty please. With whipped cream and jimmies and cherries.

> *photo delivered*

> Oh. My. Gawd. You made someone take a picture of you begging in the store?!

> Maybe

> Yes, Jameson. I'll have dinner with you.

Halle-fucking-lujah!

When it comes to Penny, I am obviously not above groveling or taking strange photos in public. Her reaction is worth it. Every. Single. Time.

> See you at 6.

I send her my address and take a deep breath. Then, I frolic through the rest of the aisles like the parents in commercials for back-to-school time, tossing random shit the shop probably doesn't need in the cart. 'Cause who cares… Penny will be at my house tonight.

～

Cooking a meal has never intimidated me. In fact, most days I love standing at the stove and tossing random ingredients in a pan. Concocting new meals on a whim. Mom taught me the basics and said, "There're no rules in cooking, Jameson. Except for baking. Follow the rules when baking." Some of my favorite dishes came to life by not following recipes.

Cooking has never intimidated me… until now.

I stare in the pantry, scan the rice and quinoa and pasta. Get lost in the canned beans and bread crumbs and jarred herbs. Panic when I reach the flour and sugar and cornmeal with still no plan for dinner.

Pulling my phone from my back pocket, I unlock it, open my call history and tap on the first name. My fingers tap the counter as the phone rings in my ear once, twice.

"Hey, sweetheart," Mom answers in the tone that melts my heart. "Two calls in one day. You know how to make a lady feel special."

"Hey, Ma. I need help."

Something rustles in the background. "Everything okay, Jameson?" Concern laces her voice and I want to smack myself for not choosing my words better.

"Yeah. Sorry. Didn't mean to scare you." I take a deep breath. "Uh… I invited a woman over for dinner and it seems I suddenly forgot what to do in the kitchen."

"Do I know this woman?" Curiosity floats between her words as she speaks.

Mom does know Penny. Seeing as Enzo and I were together more often than not during our teen years, Mom had been to their house. She and Dad befriended Greta and George Singleton. We mingled at holiday parties with them. Joined them for scary movie marathons with pizza and popcorn and mounds of sugar.

Their family and ours… we were tight.

Which is probably the reason I am so damn nervous about telling her. Mom has known Penny for years. Although she may not know as much now as she once did. Mom and Greta still chatted on occasion, but I doubt conversations about "the kids" came up as often as it once did. Us kids are in our thirties now. Our mothers probably have better things to gab about than us.

"Actually, yes."

The line goes silent a moment. I open my mouth to ask if she heard me, but she cuts me off. "Are you going to tell me who?" Light laughter fills the line. "Or is this some game where I guess?"

Why, why, why am I so nervous?

Mom has always loved Penny. Thought of her like a daughter. Blathered on about how cute she was in her polka-dot dresses and black Mary Janes.

But I doubt Mom has seen her in the last several years. Not as if Penny hangs out at home while our mothers catch up. Although Penny is the same woman I knew years ago, she has changed so much. Become more herself. Bolder. Vibrant. Alluring.

"I, uh…" *Just spit it out already.* "I started seeing Penny," I say in a rush.

Once again, the line falls silent. Maybe I should have had this call over Face-Time. At least I would have some idea of what Mom is thinking versus waiting impatiently for a response.

"Hmm," she hums. *What the hell does that mean? Hmm.* Before I get the chance to ask, she continues. "Well, can't say I'm surprised."

Wait. What? "I'm sorry?" I ask as if I misunderstood her.

"You and Penelope dating, it doesn't surprise me."

"It doesn't?"

Light laughter floats through the line. "No, sweetheart. Honestly, I thought it would've happened sooner."

"Really?"

The volume of her laughter kicks up a notch. "Greta and I both thought so. I mean, the way you two looked at each other when the other wasn't paying attention... the affection you shared was blatantly obvious."

My eyes fall shut as I run a hand down my face and clutch my chin. Yes, I spent several minutes each day with my eyes on Penny when we were younger. But I didn't realize she did the same. Nor did I realize our parents witnessed the exchanges.

"Um... okay." My hand falls away as my eyes pop open. The pantry comes back into view and I remember why this awkward call is happening in the first place. I shake off my wayward thoughts and get back on track. "Back to why I called."

"You need help figuring out what to cook," she says, more as a statement than a question.

"Yes." I glance at the stove and lose focus. "I'd like to cook her something nice for dinner, but every time I look in the pantry, the ideas go out the window."

For the next ten minutes, Mom asks questions about what I have on hand. Minute by minute, she helps narrow down what to cook and what to avoid. Penny would probably be happy eating burgers and fries. One night, I will put that on the menu. Tonight though, I want to cook a nice meal. Nothing fancy. Just something she will appreciate. A dish that will make her want me to cook for her more often.

With all the ingredients on the counter, Mom and I chat another minute or two as I fetch pots and pans from the cabinet.

"No need to be nervous, Jameson. You've known Penny a long time."

I grab the olive oil and rosemary. "Maybe that's exactly *why* I am nervous." My hand reaches for the head of garlic on the counter. "What if I mess this up? This is Penny, Mom. Not some random woman." I shake my head. "I can't mess things up with her."

"Oh, sweetheart." Her voice softens on the other end. "You would never hurt her. Not on purpose." She sounds so matter of fact. "Just be yourself. You don't need to impress her with extravagant meals and flashy dates." She pauses for a beat. "The attraction is already there. For both of you. This is the time to get to know each other as adults. Learn about the parts you've missed over the years. Explore life together."

Mom always knows what to say. Knows how to reassure me when life feels wobbly.

Although a gap exists in the time we have known each other, I do know Penny. What makes her smile and laugh. What gets under her skin and makes her your worst nightmare. And what makes her soft and submissive and irresistible. More than anything, I want to make up for the missed years with her. Fill in the gaps with new memories. Unforgettable memories. Of her and me and the irrefutable connection we share.

"Thanks, Mom." I fetch the cutting board and a knife. "For everything. I should go. She'll be here in..." I check the time on the stove. "Shit, a little over an hour."

"Breathe, sweetheart. Everything will be fine. I love you."

"Love you, too."

The call disconnects, and I shove my phone in my pocket then get to work on dinner.

No need to panic. This is Penny. You know *Penny. Breathe. Everything is fine.*

God, I hope so.

Ten

PENNY

From the driver's seat, eyes wide, I stare at Jameson's house. Can this even be classified as a house? Jesus. Looks like ten people could live here. Far as I know, Jameson lives alone.

So why the ostentatious house? And where the hell did he get money for something this flashy? I may have missed several years of his life, but Enzo would have mentioned his best friend buying a million-dollar home on the beach.

With a deep breath filling my lungs, I yank on the handle and swing the car door open. Step out and smooth my dress down my thighs. Shoulder my purse, shut the door and start the trek to the larger-than-life house. The heels of my shoes clap against the sand-colored pavers as I slowly approach double oak doors.

Two steps away from reaching the front door, it swings open and my belly instantly warms as Jameson welcomes me with the biggest smile.

Over the years, I have seen this man smile countless times. Have memorized each one and earmarked my favorites. This smile is new. Like an all-consuming hug that heats your blood and warms your bones.

I love this smile. Mark it as my new favorite.

"Hey, Pen." He steps to the side and holds the door open wider. "Come in."

Stepping past him, my eyes dart around the space. Tall ceilings, polished oak, marble, and so many windows. The foyer feels bigger than the living room in my apartment. Not a speck of dust in sight. Every surface sparkles more than my Cadillac after a wax job.

It's beautiful and bright and grandiose. But it doesn't feel like Jameson. Not in the slightest.

I picture him in a home more quaint. Three bedrooms, a living room big enough to comfortably seat guests, and a kitchen with lots of counter space for gatherings. A covered patio in an expansive backyard. A palette of cream and black and an array of browns.

When I think of Jameson, warmth floods my veins.

This house… it feels cold and empty and everything Jameson is not.

He closes the door, slips his hand in mine and walks us through the living and dining rooms until we reach the kitchen. My feet skid to a halt.

"Jesus," I whisper in shock.

Beside me, Jameson laughs. "Isn't it a bit much?"

As we enter the open kitchen, I survey every surface and scrunch my brows. "Kind of a weird thing to say about your own house."

Spinning around, he takes my other hand in his, steps into me and smiles. Every part of him consumes every part of me in this moment. The rich woodsy scent of his cologne. The heat from his body as he inches closer. The strength of his hold. And the way his eyes drop to my lips, I read his message loud and clear.

I push up on my toes and bring my lips to his. Kiss him chastely—once, twice—until one of his hands drops mine, glides up the column of my throat to the nape of my neck and locks me in place. Warm and wet and inviting, the tip of his tongue strokes the seam of my lips. Begs me to let him in. I part my lips. Invite him in. Stroke his tongue with mine and revel in the groan that rumbles in his throat.

God, he tastes good. Savory and indulgent. Sweet and sinful. The type of sin made only for me.

Far too soon, he breaks the kiss. If I had my wits about me, I might be embarrassed by my panting. Might care about the heat staining my cheeks. But that ship sailed on our date night when he kissed me in public and stole every coherent thought I owned.

Jameson presses his forehead to mine, frames my face with his palms. "God, I love kissing you." I hum and he leans in for another taste, this one brief. Too brief as he straightens his spine and his hands fall away. "This isn't my house. Belongs to a friend from college. He lives in Northern California most of the year, but isn't a fan of snow."

A wave of confusion crashes against me as I look around the house. It looks more lived in than if he were just keeping an eye on it. Small pieces of him in the kitchen and living room. Framed photos of him and his parents, him and Enzo, and a few others I don't know. A stack of tattoo magazines on the coffee table beneath a paperback appears well loved. A small rosemary and basil plant on the window ledge in the kitchen. Fresh lisianthus flowers in various shades of pink and white.

The house doesn't feel like Jameson, but it feels lived in.

"Are you staying here?" I ask as he kisses my hand before relinquishing it.

"Temporarily. Drink?" He opens the fridge and reaches for a pitcher.

"Please."

Fetching glasses from the cupboard, he pours us each water with citrus and cucumber slices. *Fancy.* He hands me a glass, puts the pitcher back and moves toward the stove. My eyes follow his every step. Rake over his broad shoulders as they stretch the black cotton of his T-shirt. Down his spine to the plump curves of his...

Jameson laughs and my eyes dart north. His eyes peek at me over his shoulder. A shit-eating grin splits his face in half. In point-five seconds, my face flames.

Yes, we are officially dating. Yes, I have felt every inch of my body pressed to his. But damn, I did not want to be caught ogling him. Did not want to get caught staring at his ass while he cooks dinner. It was a private moment. One I rather enjoyed. One I will conjure in the future as I lie in bed, close my eyes and drift off.

He sets down the wooden spoon, turns off the burner, and pulls a pan out of the oven. He futzes with the foil covering the pan as I sip my water. And just when I think he won't say anything, just when I think he's moved on and will plate dinner, he pivots and saunters over to me on the opposite side of the kitchen island. Grabs one of my hips, then the other. Hauls me forward until my breasts graze his chest. He dips his head, trails his nose up the side of my neck, and inhales my skin until he reaches my ear.

Who needs oxygen? This girl, that's who.

"Penelope Jane," he purrs in my ear. "Were you checking out my butt?"

I want to laugh. Want to blow off the moment as a joke. Slap the air and play off my actions.

But there isn't a chance in hell of that happening. Not with Jameson breathing down my neck. Literally. At the rate this is going, dinner will be cold by the time we sit down to eat. Not that I care.

I bite my lower lip and shrug. "Maybe." No sense in denying it, not when he caught me in the act.

He hums against my skin, his breath hot beneath my ear, and my eyes fall shut. My hands grip the cotton of his shirt. Fist the material over his abdomen. Tug him closer until every inch of us is connected.

"Could kiss you all night," he says, voice gruff. "But I want to take my time with you, Pen." His fingers bruise my hips. "Navigate this, us, slowly." He presses his lips to the skin beneath my ear. "I've wanted this for so long." He inches back until our eyes meet. "I want to do this right."

Well, damn.

Speechless, I nod. "Me too."

A soft smile peeks through his facial hair before he kisses my forehead. I close my eyes and breathe deeply until he pulls away.

He rounds the island and moves toward the stove. Dips a finger in one pot, then sucks it clean and nods. He fetches plates from a cabinet and portions out dinner. And he does it all with such ease.

As I track his every move, the only thought in my head is… *how did I not know Jameson was a romantic?*

Has he done this for every woman he dated? Or is this domestic version of the punk I knew years ago new? I would like to think Jameson doesn't cook dinner for just anyone. That he reserves this side of himself for people close to him. People who matter. Family and loved ones.

He carries the plates to the dining room table then returns for his drink. He takes my hand and walks me to the table. Pulls out my chair and scoots it back after I am seated. Sits beside me, not across from me, probably because this table is equally as grandiose as the house. Sitting on opposite sides would put too much space between us. Something neither of us wants tonight.

"This looks and smells amazing."

"Thank you."

Over dinner, Jameson tells me about the friend, Ricardo, who owns this house. Jameson met Ricardo during his second year in college. Ricardo isn't the type to party all night and Jameson found it somewhat refreshing. When his dormmates wanted to stay up all hours and party until sunrise, Jameson hung out with Ricardo. Camped on his couch every once in a while.

While Jameson recants his college years, I give him every ounce of my attention. Listen to the stories about pranks he pulled on others and the pranks they did to him. Listen to the struggles he incurred in his last year and his fear of not graduating. More than anything, I listen to how much those years shaped the man in front of me.

Jameson is still the guy I knew years ago. Handsome and loyal and genuine. He doesn't skirt around what he wants. Doesn't leave anything to chance. Dives in headfirst.

But part of him has changed. Not in the physical sense—unless you count how thick his muscles are now. Jameson has always been kind. Gentle, even. Now, though, he seems softer around the edges. Affectionate on a level I haven't seen from him.

Perhaps it is because I never saw this side of him. The side he gives to a companion or lover.

Or perhaps something happened and changed his outlook. Took his perspective and reshaped it into something new and significant and crucial.

"So where do you live when you're not shacking up in this swanky place?"

"Been house hunting without much success. Usually I stay with Mom. How grown up of me, right?" He chuckles, then sips his water.

"How are your parents? I haven't seen them in so long." Jameson freezes and his face pales. *What did I say?* I drop my fork then clutch his face in my hands and tilt his head so our eyes meet. "What's wrong?"

Tears flood his eyes as he stares back. His teeth hold his lips prisoner as he works his jaw back and forth. He does his best to not let it show, but I feel his body quake beneath my hands. A slight shake of his head as if what I am asking is unbelievable.

"You don't know," he mutters.

My thumbs stroke his cheeks. "Don't know what?"

The first tear falls and I want to swipe it away, but don't move an inch. If what I said brought Jameson to tears, whatever happened must be bad.

"My dad." He licks his lips and swallows as the next tear slides down his cheek. "He… he…" His eyes fall shut, and I hate that this hurts him so much. That he feels the need to hide himself before he confesses his pain to me. Then his eyes pop open and hold mine. "He died." My eyes widen as I go stock-still. "Last year. From pneumonia."

"Oh my…" My throat goes dry as I digest his words. *Why did no one tell me this?* I twist to face him, wrap my arms around his neck and hug him tightly. "Jameson, I'm sorry. I-I didn't know." Curse my family for not relaying such a critical piece of information. I may not have seen Jameson or his family for years, but I still cared. And we had all been so close for so many years. "God, I'm so sorry."

Time moves, but we don't. I hold Jameson in my arms as he hugs me with unparalleled ferocity. Wetness hits my shoulders, but he doesn't sob or wail. He simply lets the tears fall. Lets another dose of his pain go and allows me to comfort him.

I hate that I didn't know. But as contradictory as it sounds, I like that I heard the news from Jameson. That he shared this life update while it is just him and me and no one to shape either of our reactions.

He loosens his hold around my waist. Kisses my shoulder before swiping a hand over his cheeks. "Sorry I took the evening from happy to sad in no time."

My hands frame his face as I lift his chin. "No, Jameson." I shake my head for emphasis. "Thank you for telling me. Sucks I didn't know, but I'm glad I found out from you." I lean in and kiss his tearstained cheeks. "How's your mom?"

As we clear the table, Jameson tells me how Lorraine Kingsley has moved on since Harold passed. The hysterics and denial. The endless stream of tears for weeks. And the wake-up call she had after watching her husband leave at such an early age. Now, she teaches senior exercise classes at the city rec center. Has found comfort with friends and peace within the new life she has been handed.

Although Harold's passing was difficult for them both, he said they both learned to not take anything in life for granted. You just never know what happens next.

Couldn't agree more.

Jameson stows the last of the dishes in the dishwasher and starts the load. Then he opens a cabinet on the island and retrieves a serving platter. A charcuterie board, but not just any charcuterie board. Nope. This one is loaded with sweets.

I stare down at the artful display of Twizzlers and M&M's, Skittles and Butterfinger bars, Mike and Ikes and Baby Ruths. Let's not forget the Nutter Butters and Vienna Fingers. It takes me a moment to process what I see. That this man made a dessert platter designed specifically with me in mind. A man who remembers my sweet tooth and need for variety.

"This is..." I peer up at him and forget to breathe for a beat. My favorite smile is back in place. *Jameson Kingsley is beyond perfect.* "This is the most incredible gift ever." I scan the display again. "Where's yours?" I tease and we both crack up.

And then, Jameson escorts me to the couch. We toss a throw blanket over our legs, eat tons of sugar and stream a random show neither of us know. When I wake up hours later, Jameson is carrying me down a hallway. I don't worry about sleeping arrangements or clothes or work in the morning. Instead, I hug him tighter. Inhale his scent. And fall back asleep in Jameson's arms.

eleven

JAMESON

Mumbled words stir me from sleep, and I hug Penny closer to my side. I may be sweating two days' worth of calories with her limbs draped over my body, but there is no way in hell I am peeling her off.

"Pick up your socks," she grumbles in her sleep.

I bite my tongue and fight off the laughter begging to spill from my chest. All the years I have known Penny, learning she talks in her sleep is a fun little surprise. A trait I plan to tease her about.

Glancing at the alarm clock, I note we need to get up in the next fifteen minutes. Penny doesn't have another set of clothes and we should both get to work at a decent time.

Managing the tattoo shop isn't quite the same as a retail store or corporate business. We don't have to punch time cards. Don't have daily conference calls. Nor do we have a true, set schedule. Yes, we have a list of tasks to do daily, weekly, monthly, etc. But there is no one to hover over us, no one to shake a finger at us for not accomplishing said tasks by a certain hour.

Owning the shop is a labor of love. The least stressful job I've had over the years. Part of that is because it came with good bones. A solid foundation because of the previous owner and close-knit team.

I got lucky with this shop. Damn lucky. In more ways than one.

Penny's hand drifts up my chest, my neck, and into my hair. I toy with the length of her strands as my eyes roll back at her touch. Even in sleep, her touch is perfection. Fire in my veins and comfort to my soul. Like coming home after a long journey alone.

I never want this moment to end. Penny tucked into my side. Breath warm on my neck. Leg draped over my hips. Fingers in my hair while her nails graze my scalp. Her fruity scent on my sheets and mumbled words in my ears.

Beneath the sheet, my free hand caresses her thigh just above the knee. My arm around her back hugs her incrementally tighter. I inhale deeply and live in the moment for three more breaths before I break the bliss bubble.

"Pen," I whisper. She groans against my neck, and I allow my slight chuckle to shake my frame. "Sweets, we need to get up."

Another groan rumbles through her, this one a little louder. "I don't wanna." Her limbs tighten their hold on me. "Did you just call me Sweets?"

I turn my head a fraction and press my lips to her forehead. "Seems fitting." Not just for her addiction to all things sugary, but also because I have been sweet on this woman for years.

Her nails scrape my scalp as her lips trail up my neck. A low growl builds in my chest as I secure my grip on her. My fingers drift higher on her thigh and up her spine. With each kiss of her lips on my skin, my heart shifts into the next gear. My pulse pounding faster, harder.

When she reaches the angle of my jaw, she bares her teeth. Grazes the skin through my beard and sinks in slightly.

In a blink, I roll her onto her back. Hover inches above her. Pin her hands on either side of her face while my hips pin hers to the mattress. Stare down at her and note the shift in her green eyes. The bolder shade in her usually pale irises.

The way she stares back has me ravenous. Makes me never want to leave this bed. Makes me want to hold her captive until we have both had our fill. Not that I think either of us will ever have our fill.

I slam my mouth down on hers. Kiss her slow and deep and hard. Kiss her fast and hungry. No kiss will make up for the countless ones I wanted to give her over the years, but that won't stop me from trying. Not only will I make up for those lost opportunities, I plan to kiss this woman every day for the rest of our lives.

I release her hands, cup her cheek with one while the other drifts lower to her hip. Her hands go to either side of my waist before trailing up the sides of my spine. Her legs wrapping around my waist. Although she is fully dressed and I have on a pair of sweats, I have never felt more naked. More exposed and open.

She tastes sweet on my tongue as her curves mold perfectly against my body. Her hungry moans flood my ears while her scent consumes the air. She is everywhere, everything. Yet, I need more of her. Want more.

But it will have to wait. Not just because we need to get up and go to work, but because I want to take my time with Penny. Savor every taste of her skin and tongue and lips. Relish every one of her curves beneath my hands. Revel in the sight of her each day I have her on my arm. Take pleasure in the fall—mine and hers.

Against every testosterone-laden cell in my body, I break the kiss. Press my forehead to hers and drop one last peck. Smile as she groans in disappointment.

"We should get up."

Her hands slip down to the waistband of my sweats, pause briefly before her fingers dance over my flesh from spine to hip. I close my eyes and stop breathing.

"We should, but…" Her breath warm on my lips.

I drop a swift kiss on her lips. Growl as she tries to hold me to her. Break the kiss and roll off her before rising from the bed. When I glance back to the bed, Penny has her bottom lip pushed out. And fuck me… there is no chance in hell of me hiding what the sight does to me, to my body.

"You're trouble, Penelope Singleton."

Moving to her hands and knees, she crawls toward me. A woman on a mission. A woman determined to make me fall at her feet. Metaphorically speaking, I fell long ago.

"Never claimed otherwise," she taunts. She reaches me, eyes locked on the apparent bulge beneath my sweats before rising up on her knees. "Don't you want to get in trouble with me?"

"God, yes." I frame her face with my hands. Kiss her madly. "But we have time. Plenty of time."

Her bottom lip pops out again, and I lean in to nip at it. "Guess you're right," she acquiesces. Her butt hits the mattress. "Fine." She dramatically drags out the word. "Let's go to work."

Dramatics still in full effect, she slides off the mattress and ambles toward the door. Before she steps out of reach, I take her hand in mine, haul her to my chest and kiss the hell out of her. I hate that she has to leave. That she has to walk out the front door, drive away from the house and go back to her apartment to dress for work.

We may be in the early stages of our romantic relationship, but that little fact doesn't halt the idea of cohabitating with Penny from popping in my head. Because damn, how incredible it would be to wake up with her every morning. To see her before the day begins, hair wild and face free of makeup.

But it's too soon.

I hate that she has to leave, but I won't scare her by asking for more. Yet.

"See you soon."

～

Every night over the last two weeks, Penny and I have slept in the same bed. More in hers than the bed I occupy at Ricardo's place. Surrounded by her belongings, her smell, being in her bed and space, feels more like home.

Our nights together haven't evolved past extreme make-out sessions and heavy petting, which I am more than okay with. I hadn't lied when I told Penny I want to go slow. That I want to take my time. In a world where too many things are rushed nowadays, the best moments and experiences come from that slow build. From the anticipation of how it will all unfold. The picture we paint in our minds on just how great it will be when it finally happens.

Day by day, Penny opens herself more. Shows me pieces of her I missed in the years we saw little of each other. Exposes her heart, one layer at a time.

And I grant her the same in return.

For years, infatuation filled my veins at the thought of Penny. But I shoved it down. Buried it deep in the recesses of my mind. Ignored my attraction for her and did everything to wipe my best friend's little sister from my wandering thoughts.

Now, though… there is no need to hide. Not how I feel or what I want.

What I want is Penny. All of her. Always.

Giggles come from the end of the hall and echo into the living room, the sound barely audible over the television. Penny groans, then leans forward, grabs the remote, and cranks the volume higher. Bounces her knee as she looks down the hall every few seconds.

Roommates have as many pitfalls as they do perks. Yeah, it's great to cut the financial burdens of living solo. It's great to have someone to chat with on days off, to build a greater relationship. To call them family. But just like family, roommates can be annoying as hell. Unhygienic and loud. Eating and drinking the last of something and not replenishing it. Or worse, leaving barely any in the container and not mentioning the need for more. Then, there is the occasional night guest. Yes, I fit into this category, but I respect the fact Penny has a roommate. I keep the volume to a minimum, pick up after myself and respect Rex's space.

Wish I could say the same about the woman he brought home for the third night this week.

"Argh," Penny groans as laughter sounds over the television again.

I tuck a lock of hair behind Penny's ear and kiss her temple. "We can head out. Go to Ricardo's for the night."

She hums. "Tempting." Her fingers toy with the hem of my shirt. Fist the cotton lightly and tug. "So tempting."

I lift a hand to her chin and tip it up until our eyes lock. "Then say yes." I drop a chaste kiss to her lips.

Before I pull back from the kiss, her hand comes to the nape of my neck and she brings my lips back to hers. The kiss is slow and sweet for one, two, three passes. Then she nips at my bottom lip. Sucks it between hers. Swallows my moan as she deepens the kiss.

She shifts beside me, her leg going over both of mine before she straddles my lap and frames my face in her hands. The television show forgotten as she hauls me impossibly closer, presses her breasts to my chest, and rocks her hips over the bulge beneath my zipper.

"Let's go, Pen," I mutter as her lips trail down my neck. I fist her hips with a bruising grip.

Her teeth nip the skin where my shoulder and neck meet. "Yes." She kisses the same spot and lifts her gaze to mine. "Let's go."

Twelve

PENNY

Pure bliss.

Jameson's hands snake around my bare waist from behind. His lips on my neck as I lean into him and drop my head on his shoulder. His chest vibrates against my spine as my fingers knead his thighs.

"Damn, you feel incredible in my arms."

My thighs clamp together at his words. At the feel of him behind me, against me, around me. I want more. *Need* more.

I spin in his arms and straddle his lap. Water splashes from the hot tub over the edge as I eliminate all space between us. As I comb my fingers through his hair and bring my lips to his. As I rock my hips over his, a thin layer of swimwear between us, and kiss the hell out of him.

For weeks, it has been like this. Fiery and greedy and obsessive. But neither of us has pushed for more. Neither of us has made the first move to eliminate barriers. To move past intense make-out sessions with full on groping through clothes.

Jameson said he wanted to take things slow. Wanted us to not rush our relationship. Much as I hated the idea two months ago, I am glad we set this pace. Glad we spent time learning the new us.

Now, though… I am ready for more. Ready for the next step.

"Jameson," I breathe out. My hand trails down his midline, his abdomen, to the hem of his board shorts. I tug at the strings and he gasps. I kiss along his jaw and stop at his ear. "I want you." My fingers deftly untie the strings of his shorts before my hand inches beneath the fabric. "I need you."

His fingers bruise my hips as a groan spills from his lips. "Fuck." The word a whisper, a plea, a cry for mercy and more.

Not a breath passes before we exit the hot tub. My legs circle his waist and my hands fist his hair. His stride confident and steady and swift as we move through the house and enter the bedroom. Then I fly through the air, a burst of thrill in my veins and laughter on my tongue. Jameson crawls up the mattress until all I see is him.

"You sure?" he asks, his face never more serious.

I bring a hand to his cheek, stroke the scruffy line of his jaw and watch as he leans into my touch. "Yes," I whisper. "Never been more sure."

His mouth claims mine in the sweetest, most heady kiss. His hands roam the curves of my hips, my breasts, my ass. Fire ignites beneath my skin as his fingers scrape and knead and caress my flesh. My heart beats a vicious rhythm against my rib cage as my breath comes faster and faster. A faint hum builds low in my abdomen, begging for more.

My back bows off the bed and Jameson unfastens my bikini top. His hand glides down my spine until it reaches my lower back and lifts my hips. He rocks into me, and our moans fill the room. I toss the material to the floor before reaching for his shorts. We fumble as I work his shorts down his thighs and he tugs at my bottoms.

And then we bare every part of ourselves to each other. Expose our flesh as well as our hearts. In this moment, I have never felt more naked in my life. Never more vulnerable and anxious. But also never more at ease and safe.

Jameson's eyes never leave mine. Not to ogle my breasts or stare where our hips connect. And damn, his eyes have never been this blue. This piercing. This compelling.

I wrap him in my arms and hug him close. Bring his lips to mine. Kiss him as our bodies connect in a new way.

The kiss breaks as Jameson reaches for the nightstand and opens the top drawer. Without looking, he searches the drawer and retrieves a condom. His lips take mine again. Kiss me senseless and express every emotion neither of us has said aloud.

He tears the wrapper open and rolls on the condom. Just when I think he will rock his hips forward, he kisses his way down my body. Kisses his way to one breast—growls when he spots the barbell—then the other. He trails kisses down my abdomen until he reaches the small patch of curls.

And then he is there. Between my thighs. Licking my most sensitive place. Tasting me in the most intimate way. Moaning as his arms wrap around my thighs, he yanks me closer than close and devours me like I am his first real meal.

I fist his hair. Grind my center against his insatiable mouth. Bow my back off the bed as my moan fills the room. He wraps my clit with his lips and sucks, hard and fast and determined. My grip tightens on his hair. Tugs until he moans and vibrates my sensitive flesh. Heat builds in my chest and crawls up my neck, my cheeks. My eyes slam shut as light flashes behind my lids.

Jameson licks up my center and moans. "Fuck, you're sweet on my tongue."

I release his hair as my pulse whooshes in my ears. Not a beat passes before Jameson crawls up my body and positions his cock at my entrance. His mouth captures mine in a slow, seductive kiss. The taste of my orgasm on his tongue adds a new dose of adrenaline to my bloodstream. Makes me high—on him, on us.

He breaks the kiss, then hovers motionless above me. My eyes open and lock with his. Lock on to the icy-blue orbs that say more than his lips ever will. In them, I see the love this man has for me. Has had for me for longer than either of us will admit aloud.

For the first time, I don't fear it. Don't fear the deep emotional connection of another. The most intimate and beautiful connection. For the first time, I want nothing more. I crave it more than my next breath, the next beat of my heart.

Knuckles lightly brush my cheekbone before Jameson rocks his hips forward and fills me fully. His jaw falls lax while his eyes roll back a beat. My hands roam his back until they reach the firm muscles of his glutes. Eyes back on mine, our bodies move in tandem. Find a rhythm new to us. I can't look away. Refuse to miss a second of his pleasure as he gives me mine.

And fuck me if this is not the most erotic moment of my life. Watching Jameson as he pants for oxygen. As his pulse throbs in his neck. As his skin grows flush and his irises morph into a darker shade of blue.

It is too much and not enough. His hot breath on my skin. Our moans vibrating the walls. The scent of our arousal in the air. Our skin slapping and fingers bruising.

The same familiar heat builds in my chest. It spreads like a forest fire, dropping low in my belly, crawling up my neck and cheeks. Building. Burning. Devouring. My moans switch to whimpers as he pistons his hips faster. As he hits that spot deep inside me again and again.

"Jameson." His name a litany on my tongue. An endless whisper in the night. My first breath of oxygen and true beat of my heart.

I let go and stop breathing for a beat. Jameson's lips crash to mine as his hips work faster. Then his hips stutter, his body jerking as he fills me with his release. As he breathes my name against my lips.

As our bodies calm and reality settles around us, Jameson presses his forehead to mine. Kisses the tip of my nose as he twirls a lock of my hair with his finger.

"I love you, Penelope Singleton."

My body goes rigid. Freezes without warning. I don't know why, but hearing the words aloud… I shut down. Although I mentally and emotionally reciprocate one hundred percent, my physical self is on a different page.

"I…" My eyes dart between his as an overwhelming tightness squeezes my chest. "I…"

Fuck.

thirteen

JAMESON

Fuck.

Did I seriously just fuck this up with Penny? Did I open my big-ass mouth and drop the L-bomb?

Fuck, fuck, fuck.

I see it in her eyes. The crippling anxiety of saying the wrong thing after I told her I loved her. It isn't a lie. But hell, it is too damn soon to declare such emotions. At least it is too early for her.

"Penny, I…"

I close my eyes, take a deep breath and pull out of her. Dropping my back on the mattress, I drape a hand over my eyes and gather my thoughts. I don't regret how I feel. More than anything, I regret speaking too soon. I regret saying something she isn't ready to hear. Because I know she feels it. The way she looks at me, I just know.

After another deep breath, I trudge forward. Best to lay all my cards on the table now. Rolling onto my side, I wait until she turns her head and looks me in the eye.

"Is it too soon to confess how I feel?" I shrug. "Probably. But it doesn't change the fact that I do love you." She swallows as her eyes dart between mine. I toy with a lock of her hair before tucking it behind her ear. "Love is scary as hell, Pen. But after losing my dad, I don't hold back like I once did. I don't bottle up what I feel. Not anymore." My finger traces the line of her jaw. "I didn't intend to say that just now." I laugh. "Actually wanted it to be in a more romantic setting. A nice dinner and night out." The corners of her lips curve up in a slight smile. This is good. "Pen, you make me feel so much here." I press the heel of my palm to my sternum. "It scares me to death, but also brings me to life."

Her hand cups my jaw, her thumb stroking my cheek as her fingers scrape through my beard. Without a word, she leans forward and presses her lips to mine. Kisses me sweeter than any time previous. I moan against her lips. Melt into her touch. Bask in the gentle intimacy of her and me and premature confessions.

She breaks the kiss, inches back and holds my gaze. Her fingers still stroking my cheek and jaw. Slowly, she starts to nod. The movement almost imperceptible, but I see it.

"Love is scary." She swallows and runs her thumb over my cheekbone. "God, is it ever." Her hand drifts higher. Her fingers combing through my hair. "And although it wasn't quite like this, I loved you a long time ago."

My brows pinch at the middle as my eyes search hers for more answers. "Then why did you freeze?"

She leans in and places a chaste kiss on my lips. "When you've loved someone as long as I have you, but neither of us has been here, in the place where confessions flow freely, it's foreign. Unfamiliar territory." One of her shoulders rises and falls. "I can't tell you how many times I dreamed of us feeling the same way. How many times I dreamed of hearing you say that you loved me." Her tongue darts out and wets her lips before she swallows. "But when you actually said the words… it stunned me."

She is not freaked out. She is not deterred by the love bomb. *Thank fuck.*

"I'd rather stun you than chase you off."

Had I scared Penny away, God… I'd have been kicking myself in the ass for years. Probably pulling out all the stops to get her back. On my knees—again—embarrassing myself with the hopes of having her in my arms once more.

But I didn't frighten her. I shocked her.

By spilling my heart prematurely, I opened the door to the possibility of something incredible. With her. Now that I have her, now that I am privy to her reciprocal affection, a form of love we have both felt for years, I want to throw another bomb in the mix. Might as well get them all out in one shot.

Whoever listens to my internal ramblings, please let her say yes.

My knuckles graze her cheek before I lean in and kiss her soft lips. When our eyes meet, her body goes lax, sighing with contentment. What I say next may add to that happiness or steal it completely. Fingers crossed it is the former.

"Pen…" I lick my lips, then swallow past the lump building in my throat. Soft fingers caress my bearded jaw. For two breaths, I close my eyes and bask in the fire it sparks in the center of my chest. When I open my eyes and find her watching me, I bite the bullet and speak my heart. "I'd like us to live together."

Her fingers stop their gentle strokes as her eyes lose focus. A comatose look washes over her face. Has she taken a breath since the words left my lips? I can't be certain. As freaked out as I thought she was by my love confession, this may be the final straw.

What the hell was I thinking?

If telling her I love her felt like it was far too soon, why the hell did I follow it up with the suggestion of living together? Because I am a goddamn idiot, that is why.

I mentally slap myself as I watch Penny slip into a silent panic attack. *Please say something.* If only I could hear the thoughts flitting through her mind. If only I knew where her head is at.

Did I fuck this up? Did I break something that was on wobbly ground only minutes ago?

"Pen?" My eyes dart between hers in search of clues, but she has them on lockdown. "Please say something. I'm losing my shit here."

Then her fingers, still on my jaw, start to move again. Small soft strokes as she blinks away the fog. Although she doesn't look as if she will throw the idea in the garbage, there is no indication she likes the notion of us cohabitating either.

"You have any other major bombs to drop today? Or this week?" Her words are light, playful even, as she asks.

The corners of my mouth tighten as the slightest smile starts to form. I shake my head. "No." I draw an X over my heart. "I swear."

"Best keep that promise, Kingsley." The moment she calls me Kingsley, every ounce of heaviness evaporates from my chest. "A girl can only handle so much at a time."

I lean in and press my lips to hers. "Sorry for my flabby lips. Can't seem to help myself with you."

"You're forgiven."

Twinkling green irises stare back at me as she continues to stroke my beard. I see her urge to answer, her need to relieve the anticipation in my veins. Knots twist beneath my diaphragm as I bite my tongue and wait for her to speak. I won't interrupt her moment. Won't pull the answer from her mind, her heart, her lips. I may speak more freely since Dad passed, but that doesn't mean everyone else does with the same level of ease.

"Yes," she whispers between us.

My eyes widen as a smile brightens her face. "Yes?" I ask, wanting to hear her answer again.

She nods. "Yes." Her voice bolder and more vibrant this time.

Without hesitation, I wrap her in my arms, roll onto my back and kiss her senseless. We laugh like giddy teenagers. Smile like lunatics. And goddamn, this is the best fucking feeling in the world. The woman I love is in my arms. The woman I love just agreed to move in together.

I am one lucky son of a bitch.

"Uh, Jameson."

I freeze at the slight seriousness in Penny's voice. "Yeah?"

"Can you take the condom off? It's all gross and weird." She chuckles. "And… we may need a new one soon."

I laugh and give her a quick squeeze before releasing her. "Anything for you, Queen of hearts." I kiss the tip of her nose. "Anything."

epilogue
PENNY

November — two years later

The doorbell rings as I slide the sweet potatoes in the oven next to the cornbread casserole.

"I got it," Jameson says as he taps my ass and exits the kitchen.

"'Kay." I wipe my hands down my apron with a huff as I look around the kitchen. "Hot mess," I mumble to myself. "But we got this."

"Pen-Pen," a squealy voice calls from the living room. "Pen-Pen." Two little feet tap the tile as Ryker dashes around the counter and smacks into my legs, his little arms wrapping around me with all their might.

"Hey, little man." I bend and scoop up my nephew. "How's my favorite guy?"

"Hey!" Jameson teases as he enters the kitchen with Autumn, Jonas, and Clementine in tow.

I lean in close to Ryker and whisper in his ear. "Don't tell uncle Jameson, but you'll always be my favorite." I wink at my husband and he shakes his head.

Ryker turns his head, cups his hands around my ear and whispers loud enough for the entire room to hear. "You're my favorite, Pen-Pen." The room fills with hushed laughter.

I set Ryker on his feet and kiss the top of his head. "I got out your coloring stuff, bud. Why don't you go make some awesome pictures for everyone."

He nods his little head with more energy than I've had all day. Clementine extends her hand to him and smiles. "C'mon, Ryker. Let's go color in the living room."

Bless Clementine and her patience with her little brother. Almost ten years stand between them, but she never acts as if he burdens her. She is the most attentive, loving big sister a sibling could ask for.

Although Jonas isn't her birth father, he treats her as if he were. And not long after Ryker was born, when Autumn and Jonas saw the edge of melancholy in Clementine, they all sat down and talked. Autumn told me that neither she nor Jonas bad-mouthed Clementine's birth father, but they didn't sugarcoat anything. That night, everything got laid out. Clementine and Autumn cried while Jonas held them both. In the end, Clementine discovered a new appreciation for her mother, the strength she held, and the loving family she now has, thanks to Jonas.

Most girls Clementine's age wouldn't enjoy coloring with their little brother. They would roll their eyes and go scroll through apps on their phones, ignoring everyone in the room for hours. But not Clementine. I rarely see her with a phone or device in her hand, and that is magical.

Autumn wraps me in her arms. "What can I help with?" With a step back, her eyes take in the kitchen and the apparent food explosion. "We brought apple and pumpkin pies."

Jonas lifts a reusable tote. "They don't need refrigeration."

"I'll show you where to set them," Jameson says. The guys amble into the attached dining room and Jameson shows Jonas the layout of the buffet setup.

"At this point, it's just cleanup."

My eyes glaze over as I take in the mess. Not a lick of counter space is clean. Flour and cornmeal. A partially used stick of butter, soft and unwrapped. Sweet potato skins and an empty marshmallow bag next to the bottle of maple syrup. Emptied cans and countless used utensils. Foil and plastic wrap and wax paper boxes. Hot mitts and trivets.

Thank goodness everyone is bringing something tonight. If I had to make any more than this, I'd never get out of the kitchen.

"We got this, Pen. Everything's in the oven?"

I nod. "Yep. Checked the turkey and ham before adding the sweet potatoes and cornbread."

Without another word, Autumn dives headfirst into cleanup mode and I follow suit. No matter how much time passes, no matter how different our lives are now, Autumn and I have always been a great team. Long-lost sisters. Best friends. Always there for each other without question.

As I start on the dishes and Autumn wipes down the counter opposite me, the doorbell rings. Again and again. Over the next fifteen minutes, our closest friends and family trickle in for Friendsgiving. Each of them delivering a warm dish, hug and smile.

Jameson connects music to the wireless speakers, the volume loud enough to hear but quiet enough to not ruin conversations. Casserole dishes, cloth-covered baskets, and large pans fill the buffet as we all congregate near the dinner table.

When Jameson and I decided to move in together, we both agreed on a new place. Aside from rooming at Ricardo's, Jameson had been living with his mom on and off. Especially since his father passed. Although he didn't mind staying in the apartment from time to time, I knew it was time to move on.

After weeks of searching for the home that fit what we wanted—a house with enough space to accommodate guests and gatherings, but small enough to feel cozy and keep us humble—we hit the jackpot. A decent kitchen, a spacious dining and living room, and an expansive backyard—these were my only requests. Jameson's only request was three bedrooms and two bathrooms. Both our wishes came true two months into the search. Within three months, we were homeowners.

I scan the room, take note of all my favorite people in the same space.

Autumn, Jonas, Clementine and Ryker at the far end of the table. Reznor, Tatyana, Ashton and Avery as they walk the buffet with whispered words. Rex and Giana, his girlfriend of one year—something none of us saw coming—huddled in the corner. Iliana and Sage—another unexpected, but good surprise—setting baskets of rolls in various spots on the tables. Cora, Gavin, Clara, and baby Garrett, the quietest baby I have ever laid eyes on. Micah and Peyton chatting with Shelly, Devlyn, and their sweet little Desirée. The rest of the King of Hearts crew—Chance, Frankie, Gage, Kennedy, and Ophelia. Jonas's friend, Trevor is arm in arm with Jillian, Jonas's baby sister. Jasmine, Anton, and little man Lex, still in his Superman costume from Halloween. And Peyton's former roommate, Reese, whispers in his husband, Trent's, ear as they fill plates with sweet potatoes and corn casserole.

At the head of the formal table, Jameson cuts the turkey while Enzo slices the ham, both lecturing the other on technique.

This right here—these people and their love—makes me whole. Seeing people I love gathered together, smiling and laughing and sharing, it gives me all the feels. The Sunday get-togethers we started almost six years ago have only grown. Some weeks, only ten of us gather. Other weeks, everyone shows up—parents included. Birthdays and holidays get extra attention, but as long as we spend time together, the occasion doesn't matter.

In a few days, we will all spend the holiday in different places. With family or just our significant others. But today is for all of us.

"Sweets." I snap my attention to my husband as he ambles closer. He takes my hands in his and presses his lips to mine. "Everything okay?"

I nod. "Yeah. Everything's perfect." My hands trail up his chest and lock behind his neck. "Love you."

Another kiss. "Love you, too." He tips his head toward the table. "Let's join everyone."

We pile our plates high with a little bit of everything before taking our seats. Laughter and good conversation fill the room as we all catch up and talk about the upcoming holidays. When the food slowly disappears, we set the kids up with a movie in the living room while the adults sit outside by the fire. It all feels so familiar, yet completely new.

Years ago, I never would have seen myself here. In this house or this life. But when this man, the handsome one with his arm around my shoulders, stepped back into my life, I knew it would be nothing like I pictured it. He isn't just my brother's best friend. He isn't just the guy I had an epic crush on as a girl. No, this man is so much more.

My soul mate. The missing piece that kept me from getting serious with anyone.

My King.

And the day he asked me to be his forever, the word yes couldn't spill from my lips fast enough. My eyes fall to my hand on his thigh. To the vintage-style ring on my left fourth finger. To the pink pear-shaped diamond that has to be at least a carat. And the countless white diamonds set in the rose gold band.

Before Jameson, I never saw myself married. I never imagined the flashy ring on my finger or the handsome man on my arm who can't kiss me enough. Our marriage may be young—only nine months now—but it feels as if I have finally come home. It finally feels like I belong.

Jameson Kingsley is more than my husband. He is the sun and the stars. The dusk and the dawn. My beginning and end. The King of my heart.

I snuggle into his side more and kiss the spot beneath his ear. "I love you, King."

He twists until our eyes lock, pins me in place for three breaths, cups my cheek, and kisses me as if no one else exists. "I love you, Queen. Forever."

Connect with Persephone
www.persephoneautumn.com

Subscribe to Persephone's Newsletter
www.persephoneautumn.com/newsletter

Join Persephone's Reader Group
Persephone's Playground

Follow Persephone Online

instagram.com/persephoneautumn
facebook.com/persephoneautumnwrites
tiktok.com/@persephoneautumn
goodreads.com/persephoneautumn
bookbub.com/authors/persephone-autumn
amazon.com/author/persephoneautumn
pinterest.com/persephoneautumn

About the Author

USA Today Bestselling Author Persephone Autumn lives in Florida with her wife and psycho cat. A proud mom with a cuckoo grandpup. An ethnic food enthusiast who has fun discovering ways to vegan-ize her favorite non-vegan foods. Most days, you'll find her with a tea latte or fruity concoction in her hand. If given the opportunity, she would intentionally get lost in nature.

For years, Persephone did some form of writing; mostly journaling or poetry. After pairing her poetry with images and posting them online, she began the journey of writing her first novel.

She mainly writes romance and poetry, but on occasion dips her toes in other works. Look for her non-romance publications under P. Autumn.